FILE COPY

PUBLISHED........1983........

R.I.B. LIBRARY

R I.B. LIBRARY

R.I.B. Library
00042632

ALISTAIR MacLEAN

ALISTAIR MacLEAN

H.M.S. Ulysses

The Guns of Navarone

Where Eagles Dare

Force Ten from Navarone

R.I.B. LIBRARY

H.M.S. Ulysses first published in Great Britain in 1955
by William Collins, Sons and Company Limited
The Guns of Navarone first published in Great Britain in 1957
by William Collins, Sons and Company Limited
Where Eagles Dare first published in Great Britain in 1967
by William Collins, Sons and Company Limited
Force Ten from Navarone first published in Great Britain in 1968
by William Collins, Sons and Company Limited

This edition first published in Great Britain 1983
by Octopus Books Limited
59 Grosvenor Street
London W1

ISBN 0 86273 114 3

H.M.S. Ulysses copyright © 1955 Alistair MacLean
The Guns of Navarone copyright © 1957 Alistair MacLean
Where Eagles Dare copyright © 1967 Cymbeline Productions Limited
Force Ten from Navarone copyright © 1968 Cymbeline Productions Limited

Printed and Bound in Great Britain by
Collins, Glasgow

CONTENTS

ALISTAIR MacLEAN

R.I.B. LIBRARY

H.M.S. Ulysses

ALISTAIR MacLEAN

R.I.B. LIBRARY

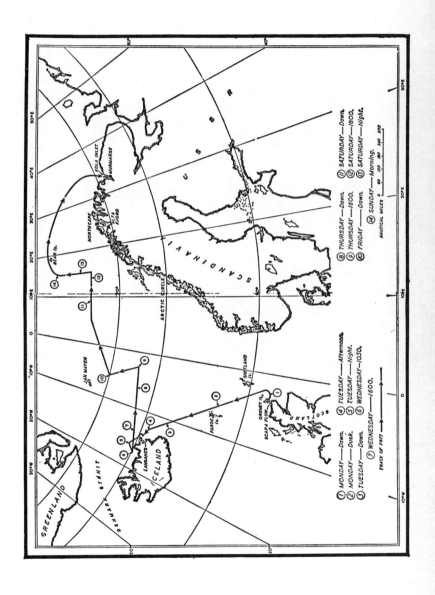

GREENLAND

DENMARK STRAIT

ICELAND

LANGANES

JAN MAYEN

FAROE Is.

SHETLAND Is.

ORKNEY Is.

SCAPA FLOW

SCOTLAND

ARCTIC CIRCLE

SCANDINAVI

NORTHCAPE

ALTA FIORD

KOLA INLET

MURMANSK

BEAR Is.

U.S.S.R.

TRACK OF FRITZ →

① MONDAY — Down.
② MONDAY — Dusk.
③ TUESDAY — Down.
④ TUESDAY — Afternoon.
⑤ TUESDAY — Night.
⑥ WEDNESDAY — 1030.
⑦ WEDNESDAY — 1600.

⑧ THURSDAY — Down.
⑨ THURSDAY — 1600.
⑩ FRIDAY — Down.
⑪ SUNDAY — Morning.
⑫ SATURDAY — Down.
⑬ SATURDAY — 1800.
⑭ SATURDAY — Night.

NAUTICAL MILES 0 40 80 120 160 240 200

I

PRELUDE: SUNDAY AFTERNOON

Slowly, deliberately, Starr crushed out the butt of his cigarette. The gesture, Captain Vallery thought, held a curious air of decision and finality. He knew what was coming next, and, just for a moment, the sharp bitterness of defeat cut through that dull ache that never left his forehead nowadays. But it was only for a moment – he was too tired really, far too tired to care.

'I'm sorry, gentlemen, genuinely sorry.' Starr smiled thinly. 'Not for the orders, I assure you – the Admiralty decision, I am personally convinced, is the only correct and justifiable one in the circumstances. But I do regret your – ah – inability to see our point of view.'

He paused, proffered his platinum cigarette case to the four men sitting with him round the table in the Rear-Admiral's day cabin. At the four mute headshakes the smile flickered again. He selected a cigarette, slid the case back into the breast pocket of his double-breasted grey suit. Then he sat back in his chair, the smile quite gone. It was not difficult to visualise, beneath that pin-stripe sleeve, the more accustomed broad band and golden stripes of Vice-Admiral Vincent Starr, Assistant Director of Naval Operations.

'When I flew north from London this morning,' he continued evenly, 'I was annoyed. I was very annoyed. I am – well, I am a fairly busy man. The First Sea Lord, I thought, was wasting my time as well as his own. When I return, I must apologise. Sir Humphrey was right. He usually is . . .'

His voice trailed off to a murmur, and the flint-wheel of his lighter rasped through the strained silence. He leaned forward on the table and went on softly.

'Let us be perfectly frank, gentlemen. I expected – I surely had a right to expect – every support and full co-operation from you in settling this unpleasant business with all speed. Unpleasant business?' He smiled wryly. 'Mincing words won't help. Mutiny, gentlemen, is the generally accepted term for it – a capital offence, I need hardly remind you. And yet what do I find?' His glance travelled slowly round the table. 'Commissioned officers in His Majesty's Navy, including a Flag-

13

Officer, sympathising with – if not actually condoning – a lower-deck mutiny!'

He's overstating it, Vallery thought dully. He's provoking us. The words, the tone, were a question, a challenge inviting reply.

There was no reply. The four men seemed apathetic, indifferent. Four men, each an individual, each secure in his own personality – yet, at that moment, so strangely alike, their faces heavy and still and deeply lined, their eyes so quiet, so tired, so very old.

'You are not convinced, gentlemen?' he went on softly. 'You find my choice of words a trifle – ah – disagreeable?' He leaned back. 'Hm . . . "mutiny." ' He savoured the word slowly, compressed his lips, looked round the table again. 'No, it doesn't sound too good, does it, gentlemen? You would call it something else again, perhaps?' He shook his head, bent forward, smoothed out a signal sheet below his fingers.

' "Returned from strike on Lofotens," ' he read out: ' "1545 – boom passed: 1610 – finished with engines: 1630 – provisions, stores lighters alongside, mixed seaman-stoker party detailed unload lubricating drums: 1650 – reported to Captain stokers refused to obey CPO Hartley, then successively Chief Stoker Hendry, Lieutenant (E.) Grierson and Commander (E.): ringleaders apparently Stokers Riley and Petersen: 1705 – refused to obey Captain: 1715 – Master at Arms and Regulating PO assaulted in performance of duties." ' He looked up. 'What duties? Trying to arrest the ringleaders?'

Vallery nodded silently.

' "1715 – seaman branch stopped work, apparently in sympathy: no violence offered: 1725 – broadcast by Captain, warned of consequences: ordered to return to work: order disobeyed: 1730 – signal to C-in-C *Duke of Cumberland*, for assistance." '

Starr lifted his head again, looked coldly across at Vallery.

'Why, incidentally, the signal to the Admiral? Surely your own marines—'

'My orders,' Tyndall interrupted bluntly. 'Turn our own marines against men they've sailed with for two and half years? Out of the question! There's no matelot – boot-neck antipathy on *this* ship, Admiral Starr: they've been through far too much together. . . . Anyway,' he added dryly, 'it's wholly possible that the marines would have refused. And don't forget that if we had used our own men, and they had quelled this – ah – mutiny, the *Ulysses* would have been finished as a fighting ship.'

Starr looked at him steadily, dropped his eyes to the signal again.

' "1830 – Marine boarding party from *Cumberland*: no resistance offered to boarding: attempted to arrest, six, eight suspected ringleaders: strong resistance by stokers and seamen, heavy fighting poop-deck, stokers' mess-deck and engineers' flat till 1900; no firearms used, but 2 dead, 6 seriously injured, 35–40 minor casualties." ' Starr finished reading, crumpled the paper in an almost savage gesture. 'You know, gentlemen, I believe you have a point after all.' The voice was heavy with irony. ' "Mutiny" is hardly the term. Fifty dead and injured: "Pitched battle" would be much nearer the mark.'

The words, the tone, the lashing bite of the voice provoked no reaction whatsoever. The four men still sat motionless, expressionless, unheeding in a vast indifference.

Admiral Starr's face hardened.

'I'm afraid you have things just a little out of focus, gentlemen. You've been up her a long time and isolation distorts perspective. Must I remind senior officers that, in wartime, individual feelings, trials and sufferings are of no moment at all? The Navy, the country – they come first, last and all the time.' He pounded the table softly, the gesture insistent in its restrained urgency. 'Good God, gentlemen,' he ground out, 'the future of the world is at stake – and you, with your selfish, your inexcusable absorption in your own petty affairs, have the colossal effrontery to endanger it!'

Commander Turner smiled sardonically to himself. A pretty speech, Vincent boy, very pretty indeed – although perhaps a thought reminiscent of Victorian melodrama: the clenched teeth act was definitely overdone. Pity he didn't stand for Parliament – he'd be a terrific asset to any Government Front Bench. Suppose the old boy's really too honest for that, he thought in vague surprise.

'The ringleaders will be caught and punished – heavily punished.' The voice was harsh now, with a bitter edge to it. 'Meantime the 14th Aircraft Carrier Squadron will rendezvous at Denmark Strait as arranged, at 1030 Wednesday instead of Tuesday – we radioed Halifax and held up the sailing. You will proceed to sea at 0600 tomorrow.' He looked across at Rear-Admiral Tyndall. 'You will please advise all ships under your command at once, Admiral.'

Tyndall – universally known throughout the Fleet as Farmer Giles – said nothing. His ruddy features, usually so cheerful and crinkling, were set and grim: his gaze, heavy-lidded and troubled, rested on Captain Vallery and he wondered just what kind of private hell that kindly and sensitive man was suffering right then. But Vallery's face, haggard with fatigue, told him nothing: that lean and withdrawn asceticism was the complete foil. Tyndall swore bitterly to himself.

'I don't really think there's more to say, gentlemen,' Starr went on smoothly. 'I won't pretend you're in for an easy trip – you know yourselves what happened to the last three major convoys – PQ 17, FR 71 and 74. I'm afraid we haven't yet found the answer to acoustic torpedoes and glider bombs. Further, our intelligence is Bremen and Kiel – and this is substantiated by recent experience in the Atlantic – report that the latest U-boat policy is to get the escorts first. . . . Maybe the weather will save you.'

You vindictive old devil, Tyndall thought dispassionately. Go on, damn you – enjoy yourself.

'At the risk of seeming rather Victorian and melodramatic' – impatiently Starr waited for Turner to stifle his sudden fit of coughing – 'we may say that the *Ulysses* is being given the opportunity of – ah – redeeming herself.' He pushed back his chair. 'After that, gentlemen, the Med. But first – FR 77 to Murmansk, come hell or high water!' His voice broke on the last word and lifted into stridency, the anger burring through the thin veneer of suavity. 'The *Ulysses* must be made to realize that the Navy will never tolerate disobedience of orders, dereliction of duty, organised revolt and sedition!'

'Rubbish!'

Starr jerked back in his chair, knuckles whitening on the arm-rest. His glance whipped round and settled on Surgeon-Commander Brooks, on the unusually vivid blue eyes so strangely hostile now under that magnificent silver mane.

Tyndall, too, saw the angry eyes. He saw, also, the deepening colour in Brooks's face, and moaned softly to himself. He knew the signs too well – old Socrates was about to blow his Irish top. Tyndall made to speak, then slumped back at a sharp gesture from Starr.

'What did you say, Commander?' The Admiral's voice was very soft and quite toneless.

'Rubbish,' repeated Brooks distinctly. 'Rubbish. That's what I said. "Let's be perfectly frank," you say. Well, sir, I'm being frank. "Dereliction of duty, organised revolt and sedition" my foot! But I suppose you have to call it something, preferably something well within your own field of experience. But God only knows by what strange association and sleight-of-hand mental transfer, you equate yesterday's trouble aboard the *Ulysses* with the only clearly-cut code of behaviour thoroughly familiar to yourself.' Brooks paused for a second: in the silence they heard the thin, high wail of a bosun's pipe – a passing ship, perhaps. 'Tell me, Admiral Starr,' he went on quietly, 'are we to drive out the devils of madness by whipping – a quaint old medieval custom – or maybe, sir, by drowning – remember the Gadarene swine? Or perhaps a month or two in cells, you think, is the best cure for tuberculosis?'

'What in heaven's name are you talking about, Brooks?' Starr demanded angrily. 'Gadarene swine, tuberculosis – what *are* you getting at, man? Go on – explain.' He drummed his fingers impatiently on the table, eyebrows arched high into his furrowed brow. 'I hope, Brooks,' he went on silkily, 'that you can justify this – ah – insolence of yours.'

'I'm quite sure that Commander Brooks intended no insolence, sir.' It was Captain Vallery speaking for the first time. 'He's only expressing—'

'Please, Captain Vallery,' Starr interrupted. 'I am quite capable of judging these things for myself, I think.' His smile was very tight. 'Well, go on, Brooks.'

Commander Brooks looked at him soberly, speculatively.

'Justify myself?' He smiled wearily. 'No, sir, I don't think I can.' The slight inflection of tone, the implications, were not lost on Starr, and he flushed slightly. 'But I'll try to explain,' continued Brooks. 'It may do some good.'

He sat in silence for a few seconds, elbow on the table, his hand running through the heavy silver hair – a favourite mannerism of his. Then he looked up abruptly.

'When were you last at sea, Admiral Starr?' he inquired.

'Last at sea?' Starr frowned heavily. 'What the devil has that got to do with you, Brooks – or with the subject under discussion?' he asked harshly.

'A very great deal,' Brooks retorted. 'Would you please answer my question, Admiral?'

'I think you know quite well, Brooks,' Starr replied evenly, 'that I've been at Naval Operations HQ in London since the outbreak of war. What are you implying, sir?'

'Nothing. Your personal integrity and courage are not open to question. We all know that. I was merely establishing a fact.' Brooks hitched himself forward in his chair.

'I'm a naval doctor, Admiral Starr – I've been a doctor for over thirty years now.' He smiled faintly. 'Maybe I'm not a very good doctor, perhaps I don't keep quite so abreast of the latest medical developments as I might, but I believe I can claim to know a great deal about human nature – this is no time for modesty – about how the mind works, about the wonderfully intricate interaction of mind and body.

' "Isolation distorts perspective" – these were your words, Admiral Starr. "Isolation" implies a cutting off, a detachment from the world, and your implication was partly true. But – and this, sir, is the point – there are more worlds than one. The Northern Seas, the Arctic, the black-out route to Russia – these are another world, a world utterly distinct from yours. It is a world, sir, of which you cannot possibly have any conception. In effect, you are completely isolated from *our* world.'

Starr grunted, whether in anger or derision it was difficult to say, and cleared his throat to speak, but Brooks went on swiftly.

'Conditions obtain there without either precedent or parallel in the history of war. The Russian Convoys, sir, are something entirely new and quite unique in the experience of mankind.'

He broke off suddenly, and gazed out through the thick glass of the scuttle at the sleet slanting heavily across the grey waters and dun hills of the Scapa anchorage. No one spoke. The Surgeon-Commander was not finished yet: a tired man takes time to marshal his thoughts.

'Mankind, of course, can and does adapt itself to new conditions.' Brooks spoke quietly, almost to himself. 'Biologically and physically, they have had to do so down the ages, in order to survive. But it takes time, gentlemen, a great deal of time. You can't compress the natural changes of twenty centuries into a couple of years: neither mind nor body can stand it. You can try, of course, and such is the fantastic resilience and toughness of man that he can tolerate it – for extremely short periods. But the limit, the saturation capacity for adaption is soon reached. Push men beyond that limit and anything can happen. I say "anything" advisedly, because we don't yet know the precise form the crack-up will take – but crack-up there always is. It may be physical, mental, spiritual – I don't know. But this I do know, Admiral Starr – the crew of the *Ulysses* has been pushed to the limit – and clear beyond.'

'Very interesting, Commander.' Starr's voice was dry, sceptical. 'Very interesting indeed – and most instructive. Unfortunately, your theory – and it's only that, of course – is quite untenable.'

18

Brooks eyed him steadily.

'That sir, is not even a matter of opinion.'

'Nonsense, man, nonsense!' Starr's face was hard in anger. 'It's a matter of fact. Your premises are completely false.' Starr leaned forward, his forefinger punctuating every word. 'This vast gulf you claim to lie between the convoys to Russia and normal operational work at sea – it just doesn't exist. Can you point out any one factor or condition present in these Northern waters which is not to be found somewhere else in the world? Can you, Commander Brooks?'

'No, sir.' Brooks was quite unruffled. 'But I can point out a frequently overlooked fact – that differences of degree and association can be much greater and have far more far-reaching effects than differences in kind. Let me explain what I mean.

'Fear can destroy a man. Let's admit it – fear is a natural thing. You get it in every theatre of war – but nowhere, I suggest, so intense, so continual as in the Arctic convoys.

'Suspense, tension can break a man – any man. I've seen it happen too often, far, far too often. And when you're keyed up to snapping point, sometimes for seventeen days on end, when you have constant daily reminders of what may happen to you in the shape of broken, sinking ships and broken, drowning bodies – well, we're men, not machines. Something has to go – and does. The Admiral will not be unaware that after the last two trips we shipped nineteen officers and men to sanatoria – mental sanatoria?'

Brooks was on his feet now, his broad, strong fingers splayed over the polished table surfaces, his eyes boring into Starr's.

'Hunger burns out a man's vitality, Admiral Starr. It saps his strength, slows his reactions, destroys the will to fight, even the will to survive. You are surprised, Admiral Starr? Hunger, you think – surely that's impossible in the well-provided ships of today? But it's not impossible, Admiral Starr. It's inevitable. You keep on sending us out when the Russian season's over, when the nights are barely longer than the days, when twenty hours out of the twenty-four are spent on watch or at action stations, and you expect us to feed well!' He smashed the flat of his hand on the table. 'How the hell can we, when the cooks spend nearly all their time in the magazines, serving the turrets, or in damage control parties? Only the baker and butcher are excused – and so we live on corned-beef sandwiches. For weeks on end! Corned-beef sandwiches!' Surgeon-Commander Brooks almost spat in disgust.

Good old Socrates, thought Turner happily, give him hell. Tyndall, too, was nodding his ponderous approval. Only Vallery was uncomfortable – not because of what Brooks was saying, but because Brooks was saying it. He, Vallery, was the captain: the coals of fire were being heaped on the wrong head.

'Fear, suspense, hunger.' Brooks's voice was very low now. 'These are the things that break a man, that destroy him as surely as fire or steel or pestilence could. These are the killers.

'But they are nothing, Admiral Starr, just nothing at all. They are only the henchmen, the outriders, you might call them, of the Three Horsemen of the Apocalypse – cold, lack of sleep, exhaustion.

'Do you know what it's like up there, between Jan Mayen and Bear Island on a February night, Admiral Starr? Of course you don't. Do you know what it's like when there's sixty degrees of frost in the Arctic – and it still doesn't freeze? Do you know what it's like when the wind, twenty degrees below zero, comes screaming off the Polar and Greenland ice-caps and slices through the thickest clothing like a scalpel? When there's five hundred tons of ice on the deck, where five minutes' direct exposure means frostbite, where the bows crash down into a trough and the spray hits you as solid ice, where even a torch battery dies out in the intense cold? Do you, Admiral Starr, do you?' Brooks flung the words at him, hammered them at him.

'And do you know what it's like to go for days on end without sleep, for weeks with only two or three hours out of the twenty-four? Do you know the sensation, Admiral Starr? That fine-drawn feeling with every nerve in your body and cell in your brain stretched taut to breaking point, pushing you over the screaming edge of madness. Do you know it, Admiral Starr? It's the most exquisite agony in the world, and you'd sell your friends, your family, your hopes of immortality for the blessed privilege of closing your eyes and just letting go.

'And then there's the tiredness, Admiral Starr, the desperate weariness that never leaves you. Partly it's the debilitating effect of the cold, partly lack of sleep, partly the result of incessantly bad weather. You know yourself how exhausting it can be to brace yourself even for a few hours on a rolling, pitching deck: our boys have been doing it for months – gales are routine on the Arctic run. I can show you a dozen, two dozen old men, not one of them a day over twenty.'

Brooks pushed back his chair and paced restlessly across the cabin. Tyndall and Turner glanced at each other, then over at

Vallery, who sat with head and shoulders bowed, eyes resting vacantly on his clasped hands on the table. For the moment, Starr might not have existed.

'It's a vicious, murderous circle,' Brooks went on quickly. He was leaning against the bulkhead now, hands deep in his pockets, gazing out sightlessly through the misted scuttle. 'The less sleep you have, the tireder you are: the more tired you become, the more you feel the cold. And so it goes on. And then, all the time, there's the hunger and the terrific tension. Everything interacts with everything else: each single factor conspires with the others to crush a man, break him physically and mentally, and lay him wide open to disease. Yes, Admiral – disease.' He smiled into Starr's face, and there was no laughter in his smile. 'Pack men together like herring in a barrel, deprive 'em of every last ounce of resistance, batten 'em below decks for days at a time, and what do you get? TB. It's inevitable.' He shrugged. 'Sure, I've only isolated a few cases so far – but I *know* that active pulmonary TB is rife in the lower deck.

'I saw the break-up coming months ago.' He lifted his shoulders wearily. 'I wanted the Fleet Surgeon several times. I wrote the Admiralty twice. They were sympathetic – and that's all. Shortage of ships, shortage of men . . .

'The last hundred days did it, sir – on top of the previous months. A hundred days of pure bloody hell and not a single hour's shore leave. In port only twice – for ammunitioning: all oil and provisions from the carriers at sea. And every day an eternity of cold and hunger and danger and suffering. In the name of God,' Brooks cried, 'we're not machines!'

He levered himself off the wall and walked over to Starr, hands still thrust deep in his pockets.

'I hate to say this in front of the Captain, but every officer in the ship – except Captain Vallery – knows that the men would have mutinied, as you call it, long ago, but for one thing – Captain Vallery. The intense personal loyalty of the crew to the Captain, the devotion almost to the other side of idolatry is something quite unique in my experience, Admiral Starr.'

Tyndall and Turner both murmured approval. Vallery still sat motionless.

'But there was a limit even to that. It had to come. And now you talk of punishing, imprisoning these men. Good God above, you might as well hang a man for having leprosy, or send him to penal servitude for developing ulcers!' Brooks shook his head in despair. 'Our crew are equally guiltless. They just couldn't

21

help it. They can't see right from wrong any more. They can't think straight. They just want a rest, they just want peace, a few days' blessed quiet. They'll give anything in the world for these things and they *can't* see beyond them. Can't you see that, Admiral Starr? Can't you? Can't you?'

For perhaps thirty seconds there was silence, complete, utter silence, in the Admiral's cabin. The high, thin whine of the wind, the swish of the hail seemed unnaturally loud. Then Starr was on his feet, his hands stretching out for his gloves: Vallery looked up, for the first time, and he knew that Brooks had failed.

'Have my barge alongside, Captain Vallery. At once, please.' Starr was detached, quite emotionless. 'Complete oiling, provisioning and ammunitioning as soon as possible. Admiral Tyndall, I wish you and your squadron a successful voyage. As for you, Commander Brooks, I quite see the point of your argument – at least, as far as you are concerned.' His lips parted in a bleak, wintry smile. 'You are quite obviously overwrought, badly in need of some leave. Your relief will be aboard before midnight. If you will come with me, Captain . . .'

He turned to the door and had taken only two steps when Vallery's voice stopped him dead, poised on one foot.

'One moment, sir, if you please.'

Starr swung round. Captain Vallery had made no move to rise. He sat still, smiling. It was a smile compounded of deference, of understanding – and of a curious inflexibility. It made Starr feel vaguely uncomfortable.

'Surgeon-Commander Brooks,' Vallery said precisely, 'is a quite exceptional officer. He is invaluable, virtually irreplaceable and the *Ulysses* needs him badly. I wish to retain his services.'

'I've made my decision, Captain,' Starr snapped. 'And it's final. You know, I think, the powers invested in me by the Admiralty for this investigation.'

'Quite, sir.' Vallery was quiet, unmoved. 'I repeat, however, that we cannot afford to lose an officer of Brooks's calibre.'

The words, the tone, were polite, respectful; but their significance was unmistakable. Brooks stepped forward, distress in his face, but before he could speak, Turner cut in smoothly, urbanely.

'I assume I wasn't invited to this conference for purely decorative purposes.' He tilted back in his chair, his eyes fixed dreamily on the deckhead. 'I feel it's time I said something. I unreservedly endorse old Brooks's remarks – every word of them.'

Starr, white-mouthed and motionless, looked at Tyndall. 'And you, Admiral?'

Tyndall looked up quizzically, all the tenseness and worry gone from his face. He looked more like a West Country Farmer Giles than ever. He supposed wryly, that his career was at stake; funny, he thought how suddenly unimportant a career could become.

'As Officer Commanding, maximum squadron efficiency is my sole concern. Some people *are* irreplaceable. Captain Vallery suggests Brooks is one of these. I agree.'

'I see, gentlemen, I see,' Starr said heavily. Two spots of colour burned high up on his cheekbones. 'The convoy has sailed from Halifax, and my hands are tied. But you make a great mistake, gentlemen, a great mistake, in pointing pistols at the head of the Admiralty. We have long memories in Whitehall. We shall – ah – discuss the matter at length on your return. Good-day, gentlemen, good-day.'

Shivering in the sudden chill, Brooks clumped down the ladder to the upper deck and turned for'ard past the galley into the Sick Bay. Johnson, the Leading Sick Bay Attendant, looked out from the dispensary.

'How are our sick and suffering, Johnson?' Brooks inquired. 'Bearing up manfully?'

Johnson surveyed the eight beds and their occupants morosely.

'Just a lot of bloody chancers, sir. Half of them are a damned sight fitter than I am. Look at Stoker Riley there – him with the broken finger and whacking great pile of *Reader's Digests*. Going through all the medical articles, he is, and roaring out for sulph., penicillin and all the latest antibiotics. Can't pronounce half of them. Thinks he's dying.'

'A grievous loss,' the Surgeon-Commander murmured. He shook his head. 'What Commander Dodson sees in him I don't know. . . . What's the latest from hospital?'

The expression drained out of Johnson's face.

'They're just off the blower, sir,' he said woodenly. 'Five minutes ago. Ordinary Seaman Ralston died at three o'clock.'

Brooks nodded heavily. Sending that broken boy to hospital had only been a gesture anyway. Just for a moment he felt tired, beaten. 'Old Socrates,' they called him, and he was beginning to feel his age these days – and a bit more besides. Maybe a good night's sleep would help, but he doubted it. He sighed.

'Don't feel too good about all this, Johnson, do you?'

'Eighteen, sir. Exactly eighteen.' Johnson's voice was low,

bitter. 'I've just been talking to Burgess – that's him in the next bed. Says Ralston steps out across the bathroom coaming, a towel over his arm. A mob rushes past, then this bloody great ape of a bootneck comes tearing up and bashes him over the skull with his rifle. Never knew what hit him, sir – and he never knew why.'

Brooks smiled faintly.

'That's what they call – ah –seditious talk, Johnson,' he said mildly.

'Sorry, sir. Suppose I shouldn't – it's just that I—'

'Never mind, Johnson. I asked for it. Can't stop anyone from thinking. Only, don't think out loud. It's – it's prejudicial to naval discipline. . . . I think your friend Riley wants you. Better get him a dictionary.'

He turned and pushed his way through the surgery curtains. A dark head – all that could be seen behind the dentist's chair – twisted round. Johnny Nicholls, Acting Surgeon Lieutenant, rose quickly to his feet, a pile or report cards dangling from his left hand.

'Hallo, sir. Have a pew.'

Brooks grinned.

'An excellent thing, Lieutenant Nicholls, truly gratifying, to meet these days a junior officer who knows his place. Thank you, thank you.'

He climbed into the chair and sank back with a groan, fiddling with the neck-rest.

'If you'll just adjust the foot-rest, my boy . . . so. Ah – thank you.' He leaned back luxuriously, eyes closed, head far back on the rest, and groaned again. 'I'm an old man, Johnny, my boy, just an ancient has-been.'

'Nonsense, sir,' Nicholls said briskly. 'Just a slight malaise. Now, if you'll let me prescribe a suitable tonic . . .'

He turned to a cupboard, fished out two tooth-glasses and a dark-green, ribbed bottle marked 'Poison.' He filled the glasses and handed one to Brooks. 'My personal recommendation. Good health, sir!'

Brooks looked at the amber liquid, then at Nicholls.

'Heathenish practices they taught you at these Scottish Universities, my boy . . . Admirable fellers, some of these old heathens. What is it this time, Johnny?'

'First-class stuff,' Nicholls grinned. 'Produce of the Island of Coll.'

The old surgeon looked at him suspiciously.

'Didn't know they had any distilleries up there.'

'They haven't. I only said it was made in Coll. . . . How did things go up top, sir?'

'Bloody awful. His nibs threatened to string us all from the yardarm. Took a special dislike to me – said I was to be booted off the ship instanter. Meant it, too.'

'You!' Nicholls's brown eyes, deep-sunk just now and red-rimmed from sleeplessness, opened wide. 'You're joking, sir, of course.'

'I'm not. But it's all right – I'm not going. Old Giles, the skipper and Turner – the crazy idiots – virtually told Starr that if I went he'd better start looking around for another Admiral, Captain and Commander as well. They shouldn't have done it, of course – but it shook old Vincent to the core. Departed in high dungeon, muttering veiled threats . . . not so veiled, either, come to think of it.'

'Damned old fool!' said Nicholls feelingly.

'He's not really, Johnny. Actually, he's a brilliant bloke. You don't become a DNO for nothing. Master strategist and tactician, Giles tells me, and he's not really as bad as we're apt to paint him; to a certain extent we can't blame old Vincent for sending us out again. Bloke's up against an insoluble problem. Limited resources at his disposal, terrific demands for ships and men in half a dozen other theatres. Impossible to meet half the claims made on him; half the time he's operating on little better than a shoe-string. But he's still an inhuman, impersonal sort of cuss – doesn't understand men.'

'And the upshot of it all?'

'Murmansk again. Sailing at 0600 tomorrow.'

'What! Again? This bunch of walking zombies?' Nicholls was openly incredulous. 'Why, they can't do that, sir! They – they just can't!'

'They're doing it anway, my boy. The *Ulysses* must – ah – redeem itself.' Brooks opened his eyes. 'Gad the very thought appals me. If there's any of that poison left, my boy . . .'

Nicholls shoved the depleted bottle back into the cupboard, and jerked a resentful thumb in the direction of the massive battleship clearly visible through the porthole, swinging round her anchor three or four cable-lengths away.

'Why always us, sir? It's always us. Why don't they send that useless floating barracks out once in a while? Swinging round that bloody great anchor, month in, month out—'

'Just the point,' Brooks interrupted solemnly. 'According to

25

the Kapok Kid, the tremendous weight of empty condensed milk cans and herring-in-tomato sauce tins accumulated on the ocean bed over the past twelve months completely defeats all attempts to weigh anchor.'

Nicholls didn't see to hear him.

'Week in, week out, months and months on end, they send the *Ulysses* out. They change the carriers, they rest the screen destroyers – but never the *Ulysses*. There's no let-up. Never, not once. But the *Duke of Cumberland* – all it's fit for is sending hulking great brutes of marines on board here to massacre sick men, crippled men, men who've done more in a week than—'

'Easy, boy, easy,' the Commander chided. 'You can't call three dead men and the bunch of wounded heroes lying outside there a massacre. The marines were only doing their job. As for the *Cumberland* – well, you've got to face it. We're the only ship in the Home Fleet equipped for carrier command.'

Nicholls drained his glass and regarded his superior officer moodily.

'There are times, sir, when I positively love the Germans.'

'You and Johnson should get together sometime,' Brooks advised. 'Old Starr would have you both clapped in irons for spreading alarm and . . . Hallo, hallo!' He straightened up in his chair and leaned forward. 'Observe the old *Duke* there, Johnny! Yards of washing going up from the flag-deck and matelots running – actually running – up to the fo'c'sle head. Unmistakable signs of activity. By Gad, this *is* uncommon surprising! What d'ye make of it, boy?'

'Probably learned that they're going on leave,' Nicholls growled. 'Nothing else could possibly make that bunch move so fast. And who are we to grudge them the just rewards for their labours? After so long, so arduous, so dangerous a spell of duty in Northern waters . . .'

The first shrill blast of a bugle killed the rest of the sentence. Instinctively, their eyes swung round on the crackling, humming loudspeaker, then on each other in sheer, shocked disbelief. And then they were on their feet, tense, expectant: the heart-stopping urgency of the bugle-call to action stations never grows dim.

'Oh, my God, no!' Brooks moaned. 'Oh, no, no! Not again! Not in Scapa Flow!'

'Oh, God, no! Not again – *not in Scapa Flow!*'

These were the words in the mouths, the minds, the hearts

of 727 exhausted, sleep-haunted, bitter men that bleak winter evening in Scapa Flow. That they thought of, and that only could they think of as the scream of the bugle stopped dead all work on decks and below decks, in engine-rooms and boiler-rooms, on ammunition lighters and fuel tenders, in the galleys and in the offices. And that only could the watch below think of – and that with an even more poignant despair – as the strident blare seared through the bliss of oblivion and brought them back, sick at heart, dazed in mind and stumbling on their feet, to the iron harshness of reality.

It was, in a strangely indefinite way, a moment of decision. It was the moment that could have broken the *Ulysses*, as a fighting ship, for ever. It was the moment that bitter, exhausted men, relaxed in the comparative safety of a land-locked anchorage, could have chosen to make the inevitable stand against authority, against that wordless, mindless compulsion and merciless insistence which was surely destroying them. If ever there was such a moment, this was it.

The moment came – and passed. It was no more than a fleeting shadow, a shadow that flitted lightly across men's minds and was gone, lost in the rush of feet pounding to action stations. Perhaps self-preservation was the reason. But that was unlikely – the *Ulysses* had long since ceased to care. Perhaps it was just naval discipline, or loyalty to the captain, or what the psychologists call conditioned reflex – you hear the scream of brakes and you immediately jump for your life. Or perhaps it was something else again.

Whatever it was, the ship – all except the port watch anchor party – was closed up in two minutes. Unanimous in their disbelief that this could be happening to them in Scapa Flow, men went to their stations silently or vociferously, according to their nature. They went reluctantly, sullenly, resentfully, despairingly. But they went.

Rear-Admiral Tyndall went also. He was not one of those who went silently. He climbed blasphemously up to the bridge, pushed his way through the port gate and clambered into his high-legged arm-chair in the for'ard port corner of the compass platform. He looked at Vallery.

'What's the flap, in heaven's name, Captain?' he demanded testily. 'Everything seems singularly peaceful to me.'

'Don't know yet, sir.' Vallery swept worried eyes over the anchorage. 'Alarm signal from C-in-C, with orders to get under way immediately.'

R.I.B. LIBRARY

'Get under way! But why, man, why?'

Vallery shook his head.

Tyndall groaned. 'It's all a conspiracy, designed to rob old men like ourselves of their afternoon sleep,' he declared.

'More likely a brainwave of Starr's to shake us up a bit,' Turner grunted.

'No.' Tyndall was decisive. 'He wouldn't try that – wouldn't dare. Besides, by his lights, he's not a vindictive man.'

Silence fell, a silence broken only by the patter of sleet and hail, and the weird haunting pinging of the Asdic. Vallery suddenly lifted his binoculars.

'Good lord, sir, look at that! The *Duke's* slipped her anchor!'

There was no doubt about it. The shackle-pin had been knocked out and the bows of the great ship were swinging slowly round as it got under way.

'What in the world—?' Tyndall broke off and scanned the sky. 'Not a plane, not a paratrooper in sight, no radar reports, no Asdic contacts, no sign of the German Grand Fleet steaming through the boom—'

'She's signalling us, sir!' It was Bentley speaking, Bentley, the Chief Yeoman of Signals. He paused and went on slowly: 'Proceed to our anchorage at once. Make fast to north buoy.'

'Ask them to confirm,' Vallery snapped. He took the fo'c'sle phone from the communication rating.

'Captain here, Number One. How is she? Up and down? Good.' He turned to the officer of the watch. 'Slow ahead both: Starboard 10.' He looked over at Tyndall's corner, brows wrinkled in question.

'Search me,' Tyndall growled. 'Could be the latest in parlour games – a sort of nautical musical chairs, you know. . . . Wait a minute, though! Look! The *Cumberland* – all her 5.25's are at maximum depression!'

Vallery's eyes met his.

'No, it can't be! Good God, do you think—?'

The blare of the Asdic loudspeaker, from the cabinet immediately abaft of the bridge, gave him his answer. The voice of Leading Asdic Operator Chrysler was clear, unhurried.

'Asdic – bridge. Asdic – bridge. Echo, Red 30. Repeat, Red 30. Strengthening. Closing.'

The captain's incredulity leapt and died in the same second.

'Alert Director Control! Red 30. All AA guns maximum depression. Underwater target. Torps' – this to Lieutenant Marshall, the Canadian Torpedo Officer – 'depth charge stations.'

He turned back to Tyndall.

'It can't be, sir – it just can't! A U-boat – I presume it is – in Scapa Flow. Impossible!'

'Prien didn't think so,' Tyndall grunted.

'Prien?'

'Kapitan-Leutnant Prien – gent who scuppered the *Royal Oak*.'

'It couldn't happen again. The new boom defences—'

'Would keep out any normal submarines,' Tyndall finished. His voice dropped to a murmur. 'Remember what we were told last month about our midget two-man subs – the chariots? The ones to be taken over to Norway by Norwegian fishing-boats operating from the Shetlands. Could be that the Germans have hit on the same idea.'

'Could be,' Vallery agreed. He nodded sardonically. 'Just look at the *Cumberland* go – straight for the boom.' He paused for a few seconds, his eyes speculative, then looked back at Tyndall. 'How do you like it, sir?'

'Like what, Captain?'

'Playing Aunt Sally at the fair.' Vallery grinned crookedly. 'Can't afford to lose umpteen million pounds worth of capital ship. So the old *Duke* hares out to sea and safety, while we moor near her anchor berth. You can bet German Naval Intelligence has the bearing of her anchorage down to a couple of inches. These midget subs carry detachable warheads and if there's going to be any fitted, they're going to be fitted to us.'

Tyndall looked at him. His face was expressionless. Asdic reports were continuous, reporting steady bearing to port and closing distances.

'Of course, of course,' the Admiral murmured. 'We're the whipping boy. Gad, it makes me feel bad!' His mouth twisted and he laughed mirthlessly. 'Me? This is the final straw for the crew. That hellish last trip, the mutiny, the marine boarding party from the *Cumberland*, action stations in harbour – and now this! Risking our necks for that – that . . .' He broke off, spluttering, swore in anger, then resumed quietly:

'What are you going to tell the men, Captain? Good God, it's fantastic! I feel like mutiny myself . . .' He stopped short, looked inquiringly past Vallery's shoulder.

The Captain turned round.

'Yes, Marshall?'

'Excuse me, sir. This – er – echo.' He jerked a thumb over

his shoulder. 'A snub, sir – possibly a pretty small one?' The transatlantic accent was very heavy.

'Likely enough, Marshall. Why?'

'Just how Ralston and I figured it, sir.' He grinned. 'We have an idea for dealing with it.'

Vallery looked out through the driving sleet, gave helm and engine orders, then turned back to the Torpedo Officer. He was coughing heavily, painfully, as he pointed to the glassed-in anchorage chart.

'If you're thinking of depth-charging our stern off in these shallow waters—'

'No, sir. Doubt whether we could get a shallow enough setting anyway. My idea – Ralston's to be correct – is that we take out the motor-boat and a few 25-lb. scuttling charges, 18-second fuses and chemical igniters. Not much of a kick from these, I know, but a miniature sub ain't likely to have helluva – er – very thick hulls. And if the crews are sitting on top of the ruddy things instead of inside – well, it's curtains for sure. It'll kipper 'em.'

Vallery smiled.

'Not bad at all, Marshall. I think you've got the answer there. What do you think, sir?'

'Worth trying, anyway,' Tyndall agreed. 'Better than waiting around like a sitting duck.'

'Go ahead then, Torps.' Vallery looked at him quizzically. 'Who are your explosives experts?'

'I figured on taking Ralston—'

'Just what I thought. You're taking nobody, laddie,' said Vallery firmly. 'Can't afford to lose my torpedo officer.'

Marshall looked pained, then shrugged resignedly.

'The Chief TGM and Ralston – he's the senior LTO. Good men both.'

'Right. Bentley – detail a man to accompany them in the boat. We'll signal Asdic bearings from here. Have him take a portable Aldis with him.' He dropped his voice. 'Marshall?'

'Sir?'

'Ralston's young brother died in hospital this afternoon.' He looked across at the Leading Torpedo Operator, a tall, blond, unsmiling figure dressed in faded blue overalls beneath his duffel. 'Does he know yet?'

The Torpedo Officer stared at Vallery, then looked round slowly at the LTO. He swore, softly, bitterly, fluently.

'Marshall!' Vallery's voice was sharp, imperative, but Marshall ignored him, his face a mask, oblivious alike to the reprimand in the Captain's voice and the lashing bite of the sleet.

'No, sir,' he stated at length, 'he doesn't know. But he did receive some news this morning. Croydon was pasted last week. His mother and three sisters live there – lived there. It was a land-mine, sir – there was nothing left.' He turned abruptly and left the bridge.

Fifteen minutes later it was all over. The starboard whaler and the motor-boat on the port side hit the water with the *Ulysses* still moving up to the mooring. The whaler, buoy-jumper aboard, made for the buoy, while the motor-boat slid off at a tangent.

Four hundred yards away from the ship, in obedience to the flickering instructions from the bridge, Ralston fished out a pair of pliers from his overalls and crimped the chemical fuse. The Gunners's Mate stared fixedly at his stop-watch. On the count of twelve the scuttling charge went over the side.

Three more, at different settings, followed it in close succession, while the motor-boat cruised in a tight circle. The first three explosions lifted the stern and jarred the entire length of the boat, viciously – and that was all. But with the fourth, a great gout of air came gushing to the surface, followed by a long stream of viscous bubbles. As the turbulence subsided, a thin slick of oil spread over a hundred square yards of sea. . . .

Men, fallen out from Action Stations, watched with expressionless faces as the motor-boat made it back to the *Ulysses* and hooked on to the falls just in time: the Hotchkiss steering-gear was badly twisted and she was taking in water fast under the counter.

The *Duke of Cumberland* was a smudge of smoke over a far headland.

Cap in hand, Ralston sat down opposite the Captain. Vallery looked at him for a long time in silence. He wondered what to say, how best to say it. He hated to have to do this.

Richard Vallery also hated war. He always had hated it and he cursed the day it had dragged him out of his comfortable retirement. At least, 'dragged' was how he put it; only Tyndall knew that he had volunteered his services to the Admiralty on 1st September, 1939, and had had them gladly accepted.

But he hated war. Not because it interfered with his life-long passion for music and literature, on both of which he was a considerable authority, not even because it was a perpetual affront

31

to his æstheticism, to his sense of rightness and fitness. He hated it because he was a deeply religious man, because it grieved him to see in mankind the wild beasts of the primeval jungle, because he thought the cross of life was already burden enough without the gratuitous infliction of the mental and physical agony of war, and, above all, because he saw war all too clearly as the wild and insensate folly it was, as a madness of the mind that settled nothing, proved nothing – except the old, old truth that God was on the side of the big battalions.

But some things he had to do, and Vallery had clearly seen that this war had to be his also. And so he had come back to the service, and had grown older as the bitter years passed, older and frailer, and more kindly and tolerant and understanding. Among Naval Captains, indeed among men, he was unique. In his charity, in his humility, Captain Richard Vallery walked alone. It was a measure of the man's greatness that this thought never occurred to him.

He sighed. All that troubled him just now was what he ought to say to Ralston. But it was Ralston who spoke first.

'It's all right, sir.' The voice was a level monotone, the face very still. 'I know. The Torpedo Officer told me.'

Vallery cleared his throat.

'Words are useless, Ralston, quite useless. Your young brother – and your family at home. All gone. I'm sorry, my boy, terribly sorry about it all.' He looked up into the expressionless face and smiled wryly. 'Or maybe you think that these are all words – you know, something formal, just a meaningless formula.'

Suddenly, surprisingly, Ralston smiled briefly.

'No, sir, I don't. I can appreciate how you feel, sir. You see, my father – well, he's a captain too. He tells me he feels the same way.'

Vallery looked at him in astonishment.

'Your father, Ralston? Did you say—'

'Yes, sir.' Vallery could have sworn to a flicker of amusement in the blue eyes, so quiet, so self-possessed, across the table. 'In the Merchant Navy, sir – a tanker captain – 16,000 tons.'

Vallery said nothing. Ralston went on quietly:

'And about Billy, sir – my young brother. It's – it's just one of these things. It's nobody's fault but mine – I asked to have him aboard here. I'm to blame, sir – only me.' His lean brown hands were round the brim of his hat, twisting it, crushing it. How much worse will it be when the shattering impact of the double

32

blow wears off, Vallery wondered, when the poor kid begins to think straight again?

'Look, my boy, I think you need a few days' rest, time to think things over.' God, Vallery thought, what an inadequate, what a futile thing to say. 'PRO is making out your travelling warrant just now.'You will start fourteen days' leave as from tonight.'

'Where is the warrant made out for, sir?' The hat was crushed now, crumpled between the hands. 'Croydon?'

'Of course. Where else—' Vallery stopped dead; the enormity of the blunder had just hit him.

'Forgive me, my boy. What a damnably stupid thing to say!'

'Don't send me away, sir,' Ralston pleaded quietly. 'I know it sounds – well, it sounds corny, self-pitying, but the truth is I've nowhere to go. I belong here – on the *Ulysses*. I can do things all the time – I'm busy – working, sleeping – I don't have to talk about things – I can do things . . .' The self-possession was only the thinnest veneer, taut and frangible, with the quiet desperation immediately below.

'I can get a chance to help pay 'em back,' Ralston hurried on. 'Like crimping these fuses today – it – well, it was a privilege. It was more than that – it was – oh, I don't know. I can't find the words, sir.'

Vallery knew. He felt sad, tired, defenceless. What could he offer this boy in place of this hate, this very human, consuming flame of revenge? Nothing, he knew, nothing that Ralston wouldn't despise, wouldn't laugh at. This was not the time for pious platitudes. He sighed again, more heavily this time.

'Of course you shall remain, Ralston. Go down to the Police Office and tell them to tear up your warrant. If I can be of any help to you at any time—'

'I understand, sir. Thank you very much. Good night, sir.'

'Good night, my boy.'

The door closed softly behind him.

—— 2 ——

MONDAY MORNING

'Close all water-tight doors and scuttles. Hands to stations for leaving harbour.' Impersonally, inexorably, the metallic voice of the broadcast system reached into every farthest corner of the ship.

And from every corner of the ship men came in answer to the call. They were cold men, shivering involuntarily in the icy north wind, sweating pungently as the heavy falling snow drifted under collars and cuffs, as numbed hands stuck to frozen ropes and metal. They were tired men, for fuelling, provisioning and ammunitioning had gone on far into the middle watch: few had had more than three hours' sleep.

And they were still angry, hostile men. Orders were obeyed, to be sure, with the mechanical efficiency of a highly-trained ship's company; but obedience was surly, acquiescence resentful, and insolence lay ever close beneath the surface. But Divisional Officers and NCOs handled the men with velvet gloves. Vallery had been emphatic about that.

Illogically enough, the highest pitch of resentment had not been caused by the *Cumberland's* prudent withdrawal. It had been produced the previous evening by the routine broadcast. 'Mail will close at 2000 tonight.' Mail! Those who weren't working non-stop round the clock were sleeping like the dead with neither the heart nor the will even to think of writing. Leading Seaman Doyle, the doyen of 'B' mess-deck and a venerable three-badger (thirteen years' undiscovered crime, as he modestly explained his good-conduct stripes) had summed up the matter succinctly: 'If my old Missus was Helen of Troy and Jane Russell rolled into one – and all you blokes wot have seen the old dear's photo know that the very idea's a shocking libel on either of them ladies – I still wouldn't send her even a bleedin' postcard. You gotta draw a line somewhere. Me, for my scratcher.' Whereupon he had dragged his hammock from the rack, slung it with millimetric accuracy beneath a hot-air louvre –seniority carries its privileges – and was asleep in two minutes. To a man, the port watch did likewise: the mail bag had gone ashore almost empty. . . .

At 0600, exactly to the minute, the *Ulysses* slipped her moorings and steamed slowly towards the boom. In the grey half-light, under leaden, lowering clouds, she slid across the anchorage like an instubstantial ghost, more often than not half-hidden from view under sudden, heavy flurries of snow.

Even in the relatively clear spells, she was difficult to locate. She lacked solidity, substance, definition of outline. She had a curious air of impermanence, of volatility. An illusion, of course, but an illusion that accorded well with a legend – for a legend the *Ulysses* had become in her own brief lifetime. She was known and cherished by merchant seamen, by the men who sailed the bitter seas of the North, from St John's to Archangel, from the Shetlands to Jan Mayen, from Greenland to far reaches of Spitzbergen, remote on the edge of the world. Where there was danger, where there was death, there you might look to find the *Ulysses*, materialising wraith-like from a fog-bank, or just miraculously, being there when the bleak twilight of an Arctic dawn brought with it only the threat, at times almost the certainty, of never seeing the next.

A ghost-ship, almost, a legend. The *Ulysses* was also a young ship, but she had grown old in the Russian Convoys and on the Arctic patrols. She had been there from the beginning, and had known no other life. At first she had operated alone, escorting single ships or groups of two or three: later, she had operated with corvettes and frigates, and now she never moved without her squadron, the 14th Escort Carrier group.

But the *Ulysses* had never really sailed alone. Death had been, still was, her constant companion. He laid his finger on a tanker, and there was the erupting hell of a high-octane detonation; on a cargo liner, and she went to the bottom with her load of war supplies, her back broken by a German torpedo; on a destroyer, and she knifed her way into the grey-black depths of the Barents Sea, her still-racing engines her own executioners; on a U-boat, and she surfaced violently to be destroyed by gunfire, or slid down gently to the bottom of the sea, the dazed, shocked crew hoping for a cracked pressure hull and merciful instant extinction, dreading the endless gasping agony of suffocation in their iron tomb on the ocean floor. Where the *Ulysses* went, there also went death. But death never touched her. She was a lucky ship. A lucky ship and a ghost ship and the Arctic was her home.

Illusion, of course, this ghostliness, but a calculated illusion. The *Ulysses* was designed specifically for one task, for one ocean, and the camouflage experts had done a marvellous job. The special Arctic camouflage, the broken, slanting diagonals of grey and white and washed-out blues merged beautifully, imperceptibly into the infinite shades of grey and white, the cold, bleak grimness of the barren northern seas.

And the camouflage was only the outward, the superficial indication of her fitness for the north.

Technically, the *Ulysses* was a light cruiser. She was the only one of her kind, a 5500-ton modification of the famous *Dido* type, a forerunner of the *Black Prince* class. Five hundred and ten feet long, narrow in her fifty-foot beam with a raked stem, square cruiser stern and long fo'c'sle deck extending well abaft the bridge – a distance of over two hundred feet, she looked and was a lean, fast and compact warship, dangerous and durable.

'Locate: engage: destroy.' These are the classic requirements of a naval ship in wartime, and to do each, and to do it with maximum speed and efficiency, the *Ulysses* was superbly equipped.

'Location, for instance. The human element, of course, was indispensable, and Vallery was far too experienced and battle-wise a captain to underestimate the value of the unceasing vigil of look-outs and signalmen. The human eye was not subject to blackout, technical hitches or mechanical breakdowns. Radio reports, too, had their place and Asdic, of course, was the only defence against submarines.

But the *Ulysses's* greatest strength in location lay elsewhere. She was the first completely equipped radar ship in the world. Night and day, the radar scanners atop the fore and main tripod masts swept ceaselessly in a 360° arc, combing the far horizons, searching, searching. Below, in the radar rooms – eight in all – and in the Fighter Direction rooms, trained eyes, alive to the slightest abnormality, never left the glowing screens. The radar's efficiency and range were alike fantastic. The makers, optimistically, as they had thought, had claimed a 40–45 mile operating range for their equipment. On the *Ulysses's* first trials after her refit for its installation, the radar had located a Condor, subsequently destroyed by a Blenheim, at a range of eight-five miles.

Engage – that was the next step. Sometimes the enemy came to you, more often you had to go after him. And then, one thing alone mattered – speed.

The *Ulysses* was tremendously fast. Quadruple screws powered by four great Parsons single-reduction geared turbines – two in the for'ard, two in the after engine-room – developed and unbelievable horse-power that many a battleship, by no means obsolete, could not match. Officially, she was rated at 33.5 knots. Off Arran, in her full-power trials, bows lifting out of the water, stern dug in like a hydroplane, vibrating in every Clyde-built rivet, and with the tortured, seething water boiling whitely ten feet above the level of the poop-deck, she had covered the measured mile at an incredible 39.2 knots – the nautical equivalent of 45 mph. And the 'Dude' – Engineer-Commander Dobson – had smiled knowingly, said he wasn't half trying and just wait till the *Abdiel* or the *Manxman* came along, and he'd show them something. But as these famous mine-laying cruisers were widely believed to be capable of 44 knots, the wardroom had merely sniffed 'Professional jealousy' and ignored him. Secretly, they were as proud of the great engines as Dobson himself.

Locate, engage – and destroy. Destruction. That was the be-all, the end-all. Lay the enemy along the sights and destroy him. The *Ulysses* was well equipped for that also.

She had four twin gun-turrets, two for'ard, two aft, 5.25 quick-firing and dual-purpose – equally effective against surface targets and aircraft. These were controlled from the Director Towers, the main one for'ard, just above and abaft of the bridge, the auxiliary aft. From these towers, all essential data about bearing, wind-speed, drift, range, own speed, enemy speed, respective angles of course were fed to the giant electronic computing tables in the Transmitting Station, the fighting heart of the ship, situated, curiously enough, in the very bowels of the *Ulysses*, deep below the water-line, and thence automatically to the turrets as two simple factors – elevation and training. The turrets, of course, could also fight independently.

These were the main armament. The remaining guns were purely AA – the batteries of multiple pom-poms, firing two-pounders in rapid succession, not particularly accurate but producing a blanket curtain sufficient to daunt any enemy pilot, and isolated clusters of twin Oerlikons, high-precision, high-velocity weapons, vicious and deadly in trained hands.

Finally, the *Ulysses* carried her depth-charges and torpedoes – 36 charges only, a negligible number compared to that carried by many corvettes and destroyers, and the maximum number that could be dropped in one pattern was six. But one depth-charge carries 450 lethal pounds of Amatol, and the *Ulysses* had destroyed two U-boats during the preceding winter. The 21-inch torpedoes, each with its 750-pound warhead of TNT, lay sleek and menacing, in the triple tubes on the main deck, one set on either side of the after funnel. These had not yet been blooded.

This, then, was the *Ulysses*. The complete, the perfect fighting machine, man's ultimate, so far, in his attempt to weld science and savagery into an instrument of destruction. The perfect fighting machine – but only so long as it was manned and serviced by a perfectly-integrating smoothly-functioning team. A ship – any ship – can never be better than its crew. And the crew of the *Ulysses* was disintegrating, breaking up: the lid was clamped on the volcano, but the rumblings never ceased.

The first signs of further trouble came within three hours of clearing harbour. As always, minesweepers swept the channel ahead of them, but, as always, Vallery left nothing to chance. It was one of the reasons why he – and the *Ulysses* – had survived thus far. At 0620 he streamed paravanes – the slender, tropedo-shaped bodies which angled out from the bows, one on either side, on special paravane wire. In theory, the wires connecting mines to their moorings on the floor of the sea were deflected away from the ship, guided out to the paravanes themselves and severed by cutters: the mines would then float to the top to be exploded or sunk by small arms.

At 0900, Vallery ordered the paravanes to be recovered. The *Ulysses* slowed down. The First Lieutenant, Lieutenant-Commander Carrington, went to the fo'c'sle to supervise operations: seamen, winch drivers, and the Subs. in charge of either side closed up to their respective stations.

Quickly the recovery booms were freed from their angled crutches, just abaft the port and starboard lights, swung out and rigged with recovery wires. Immediately, the three-ton winches on 'B' gun-deck took the strain, smoothly, powerfully; the paravanes cleared the water.

Then it happened. It was AB Ferry's fault that it happened. And it was just ill-luck that the port winch was suspect, operating on a power circuit with a defective breaker, just ill-luck that Ralston was the winch-driver, a taciturn, bitter-mouthed Ralston to whom, just then, nothing mattered a damn, least of all what he said and did. But it was Carslake's responsibility that the affair developed into what it did.

Sub-Lieutenant Carslake's presence there, on top of the Carley floats, directing the handling of the port wire, represented the culmination of a series of mistakes. A mistake on the part of his father, Rear-Admiral, Rtd., who had seen in his son a man of his own calibre, had dragged him out of Cambridge in 1939 at the advanced age of twenty-six and practically forced him into the Navy: a weakness on the part of his first CO, a corvette captain who had known his father and recommended him as a candidate for a commission: a rare error of judgment on the part of the selection board of the *King Alfred,* who had granted him his commission; and a temporary lapse on the part of the

Commander, who had assigned him to his duty, in spite of Carslake's known incompetence and inability to handle men.

He had the face of an overbred racehorse, long, lean and narrow, with prominent pale-blue eyes and protruding upper teeth. Below his scanty fair hair, his eyebrows were arched in a perpetual question mark: beneath the long, pointed nose, the supercilious curl of the upper lip formed the perfect complement to the eyebrows. His speech was a shocking caricature of the King's English: his short vowels were long, his long ones interminable: his grammar was frequently execrable. He resented the Navy, he resented his long overdue promotion to Lieutenant, he resented the way the men resented him. In brief, Sub-Lieutenant Carslake was the quintessence of the worst by-product of the English public-school system. Vain, superior, uncouth and ill-educated, he was a complete ass.

He was making an ass of himself now. Striving to maintain balance on the rafts, feet dramatically braced at a wide angle, he shouted unceasing commands at his men. CPO Hartley groaned aloud, but kept otherwise silent in the interests of discipline. And AB Ferry felt himself under no such restraints.

' 'Ark at his Lordship,' he murmured to Ralston. 'All for the Skipper's benefit.' He nodded at where Vallery was leaning over the bridge, twenty feet above Carslake's head. 'Impresses him no end, so his nibs reckons.'

'Just you forget about Carslake and keep your eyes on that wire,' Ralston advised. 'And take these damned great gloves off. One of these days—'

'Yes, yes, I know,' Ferry jeered. 'The wire's going to snag 'em and wrap me round the drum.' He fed in the hawser expertly. 'Don't you worry, chum, it's never going to happen to me.'

But it did. It happened just then. Ralston, watching the swinging paravane closely, flicked a glance inboard. He saw the broken strand inches from Ferry, saw it hook viciously into the gloved hand and drag him towards the spinning drum before Ferry had a chance to cry out.

Ralston's reaction was immediate. The foot-brake was only six inches away – but that was too far. Savagely he spun the control wheel, full ahead to full reverse in a split second. Simultaneously with Ferry's cry of pain as his forearm crushed against the lip of the drum came a muffled explosion and clouds of acrid smoke from the winch as £500 worth of electric motor burnt out in a searing flash.

Immediately the wire began to run out again, accelerating

momentarily under the dead weight of the plunging paravane. Ferry went with it. Twenty feet from the winch the wire passed through a snatch-block on the deck: if Ferry was lucky, he might lose only his hand.

He was less than four feet away when Ralston's foot stamped viciously on the brake. The racing drum screamed to a shuddering stop, the paravanes crashed down into the sea and the wire, weightless now, swung idly to the rolling of the ship.

Carslake scrambled down off the Carley, his sallow face suffused with anger. He strode up to Ralston.

'You bloody fool!' he mouthed furiously. 'You've lost us that paravane. By God, LTO, you'd better explain yourself! Who the hell gave you orders to do anything?'

Ralston's mouth tightened, but he spoke civilly enough.

'Sorry, sir. Couldn't help it – it had to be done. Ferry's arm—'

'To hell with Ferry's arm!' Carslake was almost screaming with rage. 'I'm in charge here – and I give the orders. Look! Look!' He pointed to the swinging wire. 'Your work Ralston, you – you blundering idiot! It's gone, gone, do you understand, *gone?*'

'Well, now, so it is.' The eyes were bleak, the tone provocative, as he looked back at Carslake and patted the winch. 'And don't forget this – it's gone too, and it costs a ruddy sight more than any paravane.'

'I don't want any of your damned impertinence!' Carslake shouted. His mouth was working, his voice shaking with passion. 'What you need is to have some discipline knocked into you and, by God, I'm going to see you get it, you insolent young bastard!'

Ralston flushed darkly. He took one quick step forward, his fist balled, then relaxed heavily as the powerful hands of CPO Hartley caught his swinging arm. But the damage was done now. There was nothing for it but the bridge.

Vallery listened calmly, patiently, as Carslake made his outraged report. He felt far from patient. God only knew, he thought wearily, he had more than enough to cope with already. But the unruffled professional mask of detachment gave no hint of his feelings.

'Is this true, Ralston?' he asked quietly, as Carslake finished his tirade. 'You disobeyed orders, swore at the Lieutenant and insulted him?'

'No, sir.' Ralston sounded as weary as the Captain felt. 'It's not true.' He looked at Carslake, his face expressionless, then turned back to the Captain. 'I didn't disobey orders – there

40

were none. Chief Petty Officer Hartley knows that.' He nodded at the burly impassive figure who had accompanied them to the bridge. 'I didn't swear at him. I hate to sound like a sea-lawyer, sir, but there are plenty of witnesses that Sub-Lieutenant Carslake swore at me – several times. And if I insulted him' – he smiled faintly – 'it was pure self-defence.'

'This is no place for levity, Ralston.' Vallery's voice was cold. He was puzzled – the boy baffled him. The bitterness, the brittle composure – he could understand these; but not the flickering humour. 'As it happens, I saw the entire incident. Your promptness, your resource, saved that rating's arm, possibly even his life – and against that a lost paravane and wrecked winch are nothing.' Carslake whitened at the implied rebuke. 'I'm grateful for that – thank you. As for the rest, Commander's Defaulters tomorrow morning. Carry on, Ralston.'

Ralston compressed his lips, looked at Vallery for a long moment, then saluted abruptly and left the bridge.

Carslake turned round appealingly.

'Captain, sir . . .' He stopped at the sight of Vallery's upraised hand.

'Not now, Carslake. We'll discuss it later.' He made no attempt to conceal the dislike in his voice. 'You may carry on, Lieutenant. Hartley – a word with you.'

Hartley stepped forward. Forty-four years old, CPO Hartley was the Royal Navy at its best. Very tough, very kindly and very competent, he enjoyed the admiration of all, ranging from the vast awe of the youngest Ordinary Seaman to the warm respect of the Captain himself. They had been together from the beginning.

'Well, Chief, let's have it. Between ourselves.'

'Nothing to it really, sir.' Hartley shrugged. 'Ralston did a fine job. Sub-Lieutenant Carslake lost his head. Maybe Ralston *was* a bit sassy, but he was provoked. He's only a kid, but he's a professional – and he doesn't like being pushed around by amateurs.' Hartley paused and looked up at the sky. 'Especially bungling amateurs.'

Vallery smothered a smile.

'Could that be interpreted as – er – a criticism, Chief?'

'I suppose so, sir.' He nodded forward. 'A few ruffled feathers down there, sir. Men are pretty sore about this. Shall I—?'

'Thanks, Chief. Play it down as much as possible.'

When Hartley had gone, Vallery turned to Tyndall.

'Well, you heard it, sir? Another straw in the wind.'

'A straw?' Tyndall was acid. 'Hundreds of straws. More like a bloody great cornstack. . . . Find out who was outside my door last night?'

During the middle watch, Tyndall had heard an unusual scraping noise outside the wardroom entry to his day cabin, had gone to investigate himself: in his hurry to reach the door, he'd knocked a chair over, and seconds later he had heard a clatter and the patter of running feet in the passage outside; but, when he had thrown the door open, the passage had been empty. Nothing there, nothing at all – except a file on the deck, below the case of Navy Colt .445s; the chain on the trigger guards was almost through.

Vallery shook his head.

'No idea at all, sir.' His face was heavy with worry. 'Bad, really bad.'

Tyndall shivered in an icy flurry. He grinned crookedly.

'Real Captain Teach Stuff, eh? Pistols and cutlasses and black eye-patches, storming the bridge . . .'

Vallery shook his head impatiently.

'No, not that. You know it, sir. Defiance, maybe, but – well, no more. The point is, a marine is on guard at the keyboard – just round the corner of that passage. Night and day. Bound to have seen him. He denies—'

'The rot has gone that far?' Tyndall whistled softly. 'A black day, Captain. What does our fire-eating young Captain of Marines say to that?'

'Foster? Pooh-poohs the very idea – and just about twists the ends of his moustache off. Worried to hell. So's Evans, his Colour-Sergeant.'

'So am I!' said Tyndall feelingly. He glared into space. The Officer of the Watch, who happened to be in his direct line of vision, shifted uncomfortably. 'Wonder what old Socrates thinks of it all, now? Maybe only a pill-roller, but the wisest head we've got. . . . Well, speak of the devil!'

The gate had just swung open, and a burly, unhappy-looking figure, duffel-coated, oilskinned and wearing a Russian beaverskin helmet – the total effect was of an elderly grizzly bear caught in a thunderstorm – shuffled across the duckboards of the bridge. He brought up facing the Kent screen – an inset, circular sheet of glass which revolved at high speed and offered a clear view in all weather conditions – rain, hail, snow. For half a minute he peered miserably through this and obviously didn't like what he saw.

He sniffed loudly and turned away, beating his arms against the cold.

'Ha! A deck officer on the bridge of HM Cruisers. The romance, the glamour! Ha!' He hunched his oilskinned shoulders, and looked more miserable than ever. 'No place this for a civilised man like myself. But you know how it is, gentlemen – the clarion call of duty. . . .'

Tyndall chuckled.

'Give him plenty of time, Captain. Slow starters, these medics, you know, but—'

Brooks cut in, voice and face suddenly serious.

'Some more trouble, Captain. Couldn't tell it over the phone. Don't know how much it's worth.'

'Trouble?' Vallery broke off, coughed harshly into his handkerchief. 'Sorry,' he apologised. 'Trouble? There's nothing else, old chap. Just had some ourselves.'

'That bumptious young fool, Carslake? Oh, I know all right. My spies are everywhere. Bloke's a bloody menace. . . . However, my story.

'Young Nicholls was doing some path. work late last night in the dispensary – on TB specimens. Two, three hours in there. Lights out in the bay, and the patients either didn't know or had forgotten he was there. Heard Stoker Riley – a real trouble-maker, that Riley – and the others planning a locked-door, sit-down strike in the boiler-room when they return to duty. A sit-down strike in a boiler-room. Good lord, it's fantastic! Anyway, Nicholls let it slide – pretended he hadn't heard.'

'What!' Vallery's voice was sharp, edged with anger. 'And Nicholls ignored it, didn't report it to me! Happened last night, you say. Why wasn't I told – immediately? Get Nicholls up here – now. No, never mind.' He reached out to pick up the bridge phone. 'I'll get him myself.'

Brooks laid a gauntleted hand on Vallery's arm.

'I wouldn't do that, sir. Nicholls is a smart boy – very smart indeed. He knew that if he let the men know they had been overheard, they would know that he must report it to you. And then you'd have been bound to take action – and open provocation of trouble is the last thing you want. You said so yourself in the wardroom last night.'

Vallery hesitated. 'Yes, yes, of course I said that, but – well,

Doc., this is different. It could be a focal point for spreading the idea to—'

'I told you, sir,' Brooks interrupted softly. 'Johnny Nicholls is a very smart boy. He's got a big notice, in huge red letters, outside the Sick Bay door: "Keep clear: Suspected scarlet fever infection." Kills me to watch 'em. Everybody avoids the place like the plague. Not a hope of communicating with their pals in the Stokers' Mess.'

Tyndall guffawed at him, and even Vallery smiled slightly. 'Sounds fine, Doc. Still, I should have been told last night.'

'Why should you be woken up and told every little thing in the middle of the night?' Brooks's voice was brusque. 'Sheer selfishness on my part, but what of it? When things get bad, you damn' well carry this ship on your back – and when we've all got to depend on you, we can't afford to have you anything less than as fit as possible. Agreed, Admiral?'

Tyndall nodded solemnly. 'Agreed, O Socrates. A very complicated way of saying that you wish the Captain to have a good night's sleep. But agreed.'

Brooks grinned amiably. 'Well, that's all, gentlemen. See you all at the court-martial – I hope.' He cocked a jaundiced eye over a shoulder, into the thickening snow. 'Won't the Med. be wonderful, gentlemen?' He sighed and slid effortlessly into his native Galway brogue. 'Malta in the spring. The beach at Sliema – with the white houses behind – where we picnicked, a hundred years ago. The soft winds, me darlin' boys, the *warm* winds, the blue skies and Chianti under a striped umbrella—'

'Off!' Tyndall roared. 'Get off this bridge, Brooks, or I'll—'

'I'm gone already,' said Brooks. 'A sit-down strike in the boiler-room! Ha! First thing you know, there'll be a rash of male suffragettes chaining themselves to the guard-rails!' The gate clanged shut behind him.

Vallery turned to the Admiral, his face grave.

'Looks as if you were right about that cornstack, sir.'

Tyndall grunted, non-committally.

'Maybe. Trouble is, the men have nothing to do right now except brood and curse and feel bitter about everything. Later on it'll be all right – perhaps.'

'When we get – ah – busier, you mean?'

'Mmm. When you're fighting for your life, to keep the ship afloat – well, you haven't much time for plots and pondering over the injustices of fate. Self-preservation is still the first law of nature. . . . Speaking to the men tonight, Captain?'

'Usual routine broadcast, yes. In the first dog, when we're all closed up to dusk action stations.' Vallery smiled briefly. 'Make sure that they're all awake.'

'Good. Lay it on, thick and heavy. Give 'em plenty to think about – and, if I'm any judge of Vincent Starr's hints, we're going to *have* plenty to think about this trip. It'll keep 'em occupied.'

Vallery laughed. The laugh transformed his thin sensitive face. He seemed genuinely amused.

Tyndall lifted an interrogatory eyebrow. Vallery smiled back at him.

'Just passing thoughts, sir. As Spencer Faggot would have said, things have come to a pretty pass. . . . Things are bad indeed, when only the enemy can save us.'

—— 3 ——

MONDAY AFTERNOON

All day long the wind blew steadily out of the nor'-nor'-west. A strong wind, and blowing stronger. A cold wind, a sharp wind full of little knives, it carried with it snow and ice and the strange dead smell born of the forgotten ice-caps that lie beyond the Barrier. It wasn't a gusty, blowy wind. It was a settled, steady kind of wind, and it stayed fine on the starboard bow from dawn to dusk. Slowly, stealthily, it was lifting a swell. Men like Carrington, who knew every sea and port in the world, like Vallery and Hartley, looked at it and were troubled and said nothing.

The mercury crept down and the snow lay where it fell. The tripods and yardarms were great, glistening Xmas trees, festooned with woolly stays and halliards. On the mainmast, a brown smear appeared now and then, daubed on by a wisp of smoke from the after funnel, felt rather than seen: in a moment, it would vanish. The snow lay on the deck and drifted. It softened the anchor-cables on the fo'c'sle deck into great, fluffy ropes of cotton-wool, and drifted high against the breakwater before 'A' turret. It piled up against the turrets and superstructure, swished silently into the bridge and lay there slushily underfoot. It blocked the great eyes of the Director's range-finder, it crept unseen along passages, it sifted soundlessly down hatches. It sought out the tiniest unprotected chink in metal and wood, and made the mess-decks dank and clammy and uncomfortable: it defied gravity and slid effortlessly up trouser legs, up under the skirts of coats and oilskins, up under duffel hoods, and made men thoroughly miserable. A miserable world, a wet world, but always and predominantely a white world of softness and beauty and strangely muffled sound. All day long it fell, this snow, fell steadily and persistently, and the *Ulysses* slid on silently through the swell, a ghost ship in a ghost world.

But not alone in her world. She never was, these days. She had companionship, a welcome, reassuring companionship, the company of the 14th Aircraft Squadron, a tough, experienced and battle-hardened escort group, almost as legendary now as that fabulous Force 8, which had lately moved South to take over that other suicide run, the Malta convoys.

Like the *Ulysses*, the squadron steamed NNW all day long. There were no dog-legs, no standard course alterations. Tyndall abhorred the zig-zag, and, except on actual convoy and then only in known U-boat waters, rarely used it. He believed – as many captains did – that the zig-zag was a greater potential source of danger than the enemy. He had seen the *Curaçoa*, 4200 tons of cockle-shell cruiser, swinging on a routine zig-zag, being trampled into the grey depths of the Atlantic under the mighty forefoot of the *Queen Mary*. He never spoke of it, but the memory stayed with him.

The *Ulysses* was in her usual position – the position dictated by her role of Squadron flagship – as nearly as possible in the centre of the thirteen warships.

Dead ahead steamed the cruiser *Stirling*. An old Cardiff class cruiser, she was a solid reliable ship, many years older and many knots slower than the *Ulysses*, adequately armed with five single six-inch guns, but hardly built to hammer her way through the Arctic gales: in heavy seas, her wetness was proverbial. Her primary role was squadron defence: her secondary, to take over the squadron if the flagship were crippled or sunk.

The carriers – *Defender, Invader, Wrestler* and *Blue Ranger* – were in position to port and starboard, the *Defender* and *Wrestler* slightly ahead of the *Ulysses*, the others slightly astern. It seemed *de rigeur* for these escort carriers to have names ending in -er and the fact that the Navy already had a *Wrestler* – a Force 8 destroyer (and a *Defender*, which had been sunk some time previously off Tobruk) – was blithely ignored. These were not the 35,000-ton giants of the regular fleet – ships like the *Indefatigable* and the *Illustrious* – but 15-20,000 ton auxiliary

46

carriers, irreverently known as banana boats. They were converted merchantmen, American-built: these had been fitted out at Pascagoula, Mississippi, and sailed across the Atlantic by mixed British-American crews.

They were capable of eighteen knots, a relatively high speed for a single-screw ship – the *Wrestler* had two screws – but some of them had as many as four Busch-Sulzer Diesels geared to the one shaft. Their painfully rectangular flight-decks, 450 feet in length, were built up above the open fo'c'sle – one could see right under the flight-deck for'ard of the bridge – and flew off about thirty fighters – Grummans, Sea-fires or, most often, Corsairs – or twenty light bombers. They were odd craft, awkward, ungainly and singularly unwarlike; but over the months they had done a magnificent job of providing umbrella cover against air attack, of locating and destroying enemy ships and submarines: their record of kills, above, on and below the water was impressive and frequently disbelieved by the Admiralty.

Nor was the destroyer screen calculated to inspire confidence among the naval strategists at Whitehall. It was a weird hodge-podge, and the term 'destroyer' was a purely courtesy one.

One, the *Nairn*, was a River class frigate of 1500 tons: another, the *Eager*, was a Fleet Minesweeper, and a third, the *Gannet*, better known as *Huntley and Palmer*, was a rather elderly and very tired Kingfisher corvette, supposedly restricted to coastal duties only. There was no esoteric mystery as to the origin of her nickname – a glance at her silhouette against the sunset was enough. Doubtless her designer had worked within Admiralty specifications: even so, he must have had an off day.

The *Vectra* and the *Viking* were twin-screwed, modified 'V' and 'W' destroyers, in the superannuated class now, lacking in speed and fire-power, but tough and durable. The *Baliol* was a diminutive Hunt class destroyer which had no business in the great waters of the north. The *Portpatrick*, a skeleton-lean four stacker, was one of the fifty lend-lease World War 1 destroyers from the United States. No one even dared guess at her age. An intirguing ship at any time, she became the focus of all eyes in the fleet and a source of intense interest whenever the weather broke down. Rumour had it that two of her sister ships had overturned in the Atlantic during a gale; human nature being what it is, everyone wanted a grandstand view whenever weather conditions deteriorated to an extent likely to afford early confirmation of these rumours. What the crew of the *Portpatrick* thought about it all was difficult to say.

47

These seven escorts, blurred and softened by the snow, kept their screening stations all day – the frigate and mine-sweeper ahead, the destroyers at the sides, and the corvette astern. The eighth escort, a fast, modern 'S' class destroyer, under the command of the Captain (Destroyers), Commander Orr, prowled restlessly around the fleet. Every ship commander in the squadron envied Orr his roving commission, a duty which Tyndall had assigned him in self-defence against Orr's continual pestering. But no one objected, no one grudged him his privilege: the *Sirrus* had an uncanny nose for trouble, an almost magnetic affinity for U-boats lying in ambush.

From the warmth of the *Ulysses*'s wardroom – long, incongruously comfortable, running fifty feet along the starboard side of the fo'c'sle deck – Johnny Nicholls gazed out through the troubled grey and white of the sky. Even the kindly snow, he reflected, blanketing a thousand sins, could do little for these queer craft, so angular, so graceless, so obviously out-dated.

He supposed he ought to feel bitter at My Lords of the Admiralty, with their limousines and arm-chairs and elevenses, with their big wall-maps and pretty little flags, sending out this raggle-taggle of a squadron to cope with the pick of the U-boat packs, while they sat comfortably, luxuriously at home. But the thought died at birth: it was, he knew, grotesquely unjust. The Admiralty would have given them a dozen brand-new destroyers – if they had them. Things, he knew, were pretty bad, and the demands of the Atlantic and the Mediterranean had first priority.

He supposed, too, he ought to feel cynical, ironic, at the sight of these old and worn-out ships. Strangely, he couldn't. He knew what they could do, what they had done. If he felt anything at all towards them, it was something uncommonly close to admiration – perhaps even pride. Nicholls stirred uncomfortably and turned away from the porthole. His gaze fell on the somnolent form of the Kapok Kid, flat on his back in an arm-chair, an enormous pair of fur-lined flying-boots perched above the electric fire.

The Kapok Kid, Lieutenant the Honourable Andrew Carpenter, RN, Navigator of the *Ulysses* and his best friend – he was the one to feel proud, Nicholls thought wryly. The most glorious extrovert Nicholls had ever known, the Kapok Kid was equally at home anywhere – on a dance floor or in the cockpit of a racing yacht at Cowes, at a garden party, on a tennis court or at the wheel of his big crimson Bugatti, windscreen down and the loose ends of a seven-foot scarf streaming out behind him. But appearances were never more deceptive. For the Kapok Kid, the Royal Navy was his whole life, and he lived for that alone. Behind that slightly inane façade lay, besides a first-class brain, a deeply romantic streak, an almost Elizabethan love for sea and ships which he sought, successfully, he imagined, to conceal from all his fellow-officers. It was patently obvious that no one ever thought it worth the mentioning.

Theirs was a curious friendship, Nicholls mused. An attraction of opposites, if ever there was one. For Carpenter's hail-fellow ebullience, his natural reserve and reticence were the perfect foil: over against his friend's near-idolatry of all things naval stood his own thorough-going detestation of all that the Kapok Kid so warmly admired. Perhaps because of that over-developed sense of individuality and independence, that bane of so many highland Scots, Nicholls objected strongly to the thousand and one pin-pricks of discipline, authority and bureau-cratic naval stupidity which were a constant affront to his in-telligence and self-respect. Even three years ago, when the war had snatched him from the wards of a great Glasgow hospital, his first year's internship barely completed, he had had his dark suspicions that the degree of compatibility between himself and the Senior Service would prove to be singularly low. And so it had proved. But, in spite of this antipathy – or perhaps because of it and the curse of a Calvinistic conscience – Nicholls had become a first-class officer. But it still disturbed him vaguely to discover in himself something akin to pride in the ships of his squadron.

He sighed. The loudspeaker in the corner of the wardroom had just crackled into life. From bitter experience, he knew that broadcast announcements seldom presaged anything good.

'Do you hear there? Do you hear there?' The voice was metallic, impersonal: the Kapok Kid slept on in magnificent oblivion. 'The Captain will broadcast to the ship's company at 1730 tonight. Repeat. The Captain will broadcast to the ship's company at 1730 tonight. That is all.'

Nicholls prodded the Kapok Kid with a heavy toe. 'On your feet, Vasco. Now's the time if you want a cuppa char before getting up there and navigating.' Carpenter stirred, opened a red-rimmed eye: Nicholls smiled down encouragingly. 'Besides, it's lovely up top now – sea rising, temperature falling and a

49

young blizzard blowing. Just what you were born for, Andy, boy!'

The Kapok Kid groaned his way back to consciousness, struggled to a sitting position and remained hunched forward, his straight flaxen hair falling over his hands.

'What's the matter now?' His voice was querulous, still slurred with sleep. Then he grinned faintly. 'Know where I was, Johnny?' he asked reminiscently. 'Back on the Thames, at the Grey Goose, just up from Henley. It was summer, Johnny, late in summer, warm and very still. Dressed all in green, she was—'

'Indigestion,' Nicholls cut in briskly. 'Too much easy living. . . . It's four-thirty, and the old man's speaking in an hour's time. Dusk stations at any time – we'd better eat.'

Carpenter shook his head mournfully. 'The man has no soul, no finer feelings.' He stood up and stretched himself. As always, he was dressed from head to foot in a one-piece overall of heavy, quilted kapok – the silk fibres encasing the seeds of the Japanese and Malayan silk-cotton tree: there was a great, golden 'J' embroidered on the right breast pocket: what it stood for was anyone's guess. He glanced out through the porthole and shuddered.

'Wonder what's the topic for tonight, Johnny?'

'No idea. I'm curious to see what his attitude, his tone is going to be, how he's going to handle it. The situation, to say the least, is somewhat – ah – delicate.' Nicholls grinned, but the smile didn't touch his eyes. 'Not to mention the fact that the crew don't know that they're off to Murmansk again – although they must have a pretty good idea.'

'Mmm.' The Kapok Kid nodded absently. 'Don't suppose the old man'll try to play it down – the hazards of the trip, I mean, or to excuse himself – you know, put the blame where it belongs.'

'Never.' Nicholls shook his head decisively. 'Not the skipper. Just not in his nature. Never excuses himself – and never spares himself.' He stared into the fire for a long time, then looked up quietly at the Kapok Kid. 'The skipper's a very sick man, Andy – very sick indeed.'

'What!' The Kapok Kid was genuinely startled. 'A very sick . . . Good lord, you're joking! You must be, Why—'

'I'm not,' Nicholls interrupted flatly, his voice very low. Winthrop, the padre, an intense, enthusiastic, very young man with an immense zest for life and granitic convictions on every subject under the sun, was in the far corner of the wardroom. The zest was temporarily in abeyance – he was sunk in exhausted slumber. Nicholls liked him, but preferred that he should not hear – the padre would talk. Winthrop, Nicholls had often thought, would never have made a successful priest – confessional reticence would have been impossible for him.

'Old Socrates says he's pretty far through – and he knows,' Nicholls continued. 'Old man phoned him to come to his cabin last night. Place was covered in blood ánd he was coughing his lungs up. Acute attack of hæmoptysis. Brooks has suspected it for a long time, but the Captain would never let him examine him. Brooks says a few more days of this will kill him.' He broke off, glanced briefly at Winthrop. 'I talk too much,' he said abruptly. 'Getting as bad as the old padre there. Shouldn't have told you, I suppose – violation of professional confidence and all that. All this under your hat, Andy.'

'Of course, of course.' There was a long pause. 'What you mean is, Johnny – he's dying?'

'Just that. Come on, Andy – char.'

Twenty minutes later, Nicholls made his way down to the Sick Bay. The light was beginning to fail and the *Ulysses* was pitching heavily. Brooks was in the surgery.

'Evening, sir. Dusk stations any minute now. Mind if I stay in the bay tonight?'

Brooks eyed him speculatively.

'Regulations,' he intoned, 'say that the Action Stations position of the Junior Medical Officer is aft in the Engineer's Flat. Far be it from me—'

'Please.'

'Why? Lonely, lazy or just plain tired?' The quirk of the eyebrows robbed the words of all offence.

'No. Curious. I want to observe the reactions of Stoker Riley and his – ah – confederates to the skipper's speech. Might be most instructive.'

'Sherlock Nicholls, eh? Right-o, Johnny. Phone the Damage Control Officer aft. Tell him you're tied up. Major operation, anything you like. Our gullible public and how easily fooled. Shame.'

Nicholls grinned and reached for the phone.

When the bugle blared for dusk Action Stations, Nicholls was sitting in the dispensary. The lights were out, the curtains almost drawn. He could see into every corner of the brightly lit Sick Bay. Five of the men were asleep. Two of the others

– Petersen, the giant, slow-spoken stoker, half Norwegian, half-Scots, and Burgess, the dark little cockney – were sitting up in bed, talking softly, their eyes turned towards the swarthy, heavily-built patient lying between them. Stoker Riley was holding court.

Alfred O'Hara Riley had, at a very early age indeed, decided upon a career of crime, and beset, though he subsequently was, by innumerable vicissitudes, he had clung to this resolve with an unswerving determination: directed towards almost any other sphere of activity, his resolution would have been praiseworthy, possibly even profitable. But praise and profit had passed Roley by.

Every man is what environment and heredity makes him. Riley was no exception, and Nicholls, who knew something of his upbringing, appreciated that life had never really given the big stoker a chance. Born of a drunken, illiterate mother in a filthy, overcrowded and fever-ridden Liverpool slum, he was an outcast from the beginning: allied to that, his hairy, ape-like figure, the heavy prognathous jaw, the twisted mouth, the wide flaring nose, the cunning black eyes, squinting out beneath the negligible clearance between hairline and eyebrows that so accurately reflected the mental capacity within, were all admirably adapted to what was to become his chosen vocation. Nicholls looked at him and disapproved without condemning; for a moment, he had an inkling of the tragedy of the inevitable.

Riley was never at any time a very successful criminal – his intelligence barely cleared the moron level. He dimly appreciated his limitations, and had left the higher, more subtle forms of crime severely alone. Robbery – preferably robbery with violence – what his *métier*. He had been in prison six times, the last time for two years.

His induction into the Navy was a mystery which baffled both Riley and the authorities responsible for his being there. But Riley had accepted this latest misfortune with equanimity, and gone through the bomb-shattered 'G' and 'H' blocks in the Royal Naval Barracks, Portsmouth, like a high wind through a field of corn, leaving behind him a trail of slashed suitcases and empty wallets. He had been apprehended without much difficulty, done sixty days' cells, then been drafted to the *Ulysses* as a stoker.

His career of crime aboard the *Ulysses* had been brief and painful. His first attempted robbery had been his last – a clumsy and incredibly foolish rifling of a locker in the marine sergeants' mess. He had been caught red-handed by Colour-Sergeant Evans and Sergeant MacIntosh. They had preferred no charges against him and Riley had spent the next three days in the Sick Bay. He claimed to have tripped on the rung of a ladder and fallen twenty feet to the boiler-room floor. But the actual facts of the case were common knowledge, and Turner had recommended his discharge. To everyone's astonishment, not least that of Stoker Riley, Dodson, the Engineer Commander had insisted he be given a last chance, and Riley had been reprieved.

Since that date, four months previously, he had confined his activities to stirring up trouble. Illogically but understandably, his brief encounter with the marines had swept away his apathetic tolerance of the Navy: a smouldering hatred took its place. As an agitator, he had achieved a degree of success denied him as a criminal. Admittedly, he had a fertile field for operations; but credit – if that is the word – was due also to his shrewdness, his animal craft and cunning, his hold over his crewmates. The husky, intense voice, his earnestness, his deep-set eyes, lent Riley a strangely elemental power – a power he had used to its maximum effect a few days previously when he had precipitated the mutiny which had led to the death of Ralston, the stoker, and the marine – mysteriously dead from a broken neck. Beyond any possible doubt, their deaths lay at Riley's door; equally beyond doubt, that could never be proved. Nicholls wondered what new devilment was hatching behind these lowering, corrugated brows, wondered how on earth it was that that same Riley was continually in trouble for bringing aboard the *Ulysses* and devotedly tending every stray kitten, every broken-winged bird he found.

The loudspeaker crackled, cutting through his thoughts, stilling the low voices in the Sick Bay. And not only there, but throughout the ship, in turrets and magazines, in engine-rooms and boiler-rooms, above and below deck everywhere, all conversation ceased. Then there was only the wind, the regular smash of the bows into the deepening troughs, the muffled roar of the great boiler-room intake fans and the hum of a hundred electric motors. Tension lay heavy over the ship, over 730 officers and men, tangible, almost, in its oppression.

'This is the Captain speaking. Good evening.' The voice was calm, well modulated, without a sign of strain or exhaustion. 'As you all know, it is my custom at the beginning of every voyage to inform you as soon as possible of what lies in store for you. I feel that you have a right to know, and that it is my duty. It's not always a pleasant duty – it never has been during recent months. This time, however, I'm almost glad.' He paused, and the words came, slow and measured. 'This is our last operation as a unit of the Home Fleet. In a month's time, God willing, we will be in the Med.'

Good for you, thought Nicholls. Sweeten the pill, lay it on, thick and heavy. But the Captain had other ideas.

'But first, gentlemen, the job on hand. It's the mixture as before – Murmansk again. We rendezvous at 1030 Wednesday, north of Iceland, with a convoy from Halifax. There are eighteen ships in this convoy – big and fast – all fifteen knots and above. Our third Fast Russian convoy, gentlemen – FR77, in case you want to tell your grandchildren about it,' he added dryly. 'These ships are carrying tanks, planes, aviation spirit and oil – nothing else.

'I will not attempt to minimise the dangers. You know how desperate is the state of Russia today, how terribly badly she needs these weapons and fuel. You can also be sure that the Germans know too – and that her Intelligence agents will already have reported the nature of this convoy and the date of sailing.' He broke off short, and the sound of his harsh, muffled coughing into a handkerchief echoed weirdly through the silent ship. He went on slowly. 'There are enough fighter planes and petrol in this convoy to alter the whole character of the Russian war. The Nazis will stop at nothing – I repeat, nothing – to stop this convoy from going through to Russia.

'I have never tried to mislead or deceive you. I will not now. The signs are not good. In our favour we have, firstly, our speed, and secondly – I hope – the element of surprise. We shall try to break through direct for the North Cape.

'There are four major factors against us. You will all have noticed the steady worsening of the weather. We are, I'm afraid, running into abnormal weather conditions – abnormal even for the Arctic. It may – I repeat "may" – prevent U-boat attacks: on the other hand it may mean losing some of the smaller units of our screen – we have no time to heave to or run before bad weather. FR77 is going straight through. . . . And it almost certainly means that the carriers will be unable to fly off fighter cover.'

Good God, has the skipper lost his senses, Nicholls wondered. He'll wreck any morale that's left. Not that there *is* any left. What in the world—

'Secondly,' the voice went on, calm, inexorable, 'we are taking

54

no rescue ships on this convoy. There will be no time to stop. Besides, you all know what happened to the *Stockport* and the *Zafaaran*. You're safer where you are.[1]

'Thirdly, two – possibly three – U-boat packs are known to be strung out along latitude seventy degrees and our Northern Norway agents report a heavy mustering of German bombers of all types in their area.

'Finally, we have reason to believe that the *Tirpitz* is preparing to move out.' Again he paused, for an interminable time, it seemed. It was as if he knew the tremendous shock carried in these few words, and wanted to give it time to register. 'I need not tell you what that means. The Germans may risk her to stop the convoy. The Admiralty hope they will. During the latter part of the voyage, capital units of the Home Fleet, including possibly the aircraft-carriers *Victorious* and *Furious,* and three cruisers, will parallel our course at twelve hours' steaming distance. They have been waiting a long time, and we are the bait to spring the trap....

'It is possible that things may go wrong. The best-laid plans ... or the trap may be late in springing shut. This convoy must still get through. If the carriers cannot fly off cover, the *Ulysses* must cover the withdrawal of FR77. You will know what that means. I hope this is all perfectly clear.'

There was another long bout of coughing, another long pause, and when he spoke again the tone had completely changed. He was very quiet.

'I know what I am asking of you. I know how tired, how hopeless, how sick at heart you all feel. I know – no one knows better – what you have been through, how much you need, how much you deserve a rest. Rest you shall have. The entire ship's company goes on ten days' leave from Portsmouth on the eighteenth, then for refit in Alexandria.' The words were casual, as if they carried no significance for him. 'But before that – well, I know it seems cruel, inhuman – it must seem so to you – to ask you to go through it all again, perhaps worse than you've ever gone through before. But I can't help it – no one can help it.' Every sentence, now, was punctuated by long silences: it was difficult to catch his words, so low and far away.

'No one has any right to ask you to do it, I least of all ... least of all. I know you *will* do it. I know you will not let me down.

[1] Rescue ships, whose duties were solely what their name implies, were a feature of many of the earlier convoys. The *Zafaaran* was lost in one of the war's worst convoys. The *Stockport* was torpedoed. She was lost with all hands, including all those survivors rescued from other sunken ships.

I know you will take the *Ulysses* through. Good luck. Good luck and God bless you. Good night.'

The loudspeakers clicked off, but the silence lingered on. Nobody spoke and nobody moved. Not even the eyes moved. Those who had been looking at the 'speakers still gazed on, unseeingly; or stared down at their hands; or down into the glowing butts of forbidden cigarettes, oblivious to the acrid smoke that laced exhausted eyes. It was strangely as if each man wanted to be alone, to look into his own mind, follow his thoughts out for himself, and knew that if his eyes caught another's he would no longer be alone. A strange hush, a supernatural silence, the wordless understanding that so rarely touches mankind: the veil lifts and drops again and a man can never remember what he has seen but knows that he has seen something and that nothing will ever be quite the same again. Seldom, all too seldom it comes: a sunset of surpassing loveliness, a fragment from some great symphony, the terrible stillness which falls over the huge rings of Madrid and Barcelona as the sword of the greatest of the matadors sinks inevitably home. And the Spaniards have the word for it – 'the moment of truth.'

The Sick Bay clock, unnaturally loud, ticked away one minute, maybe two. With a heavy sigh – it seemed ages since he had breathed last – Nicholls softly pulled to the sliding door behind the curtains and switched on the light. He looked round at Brooks, looked away again.

'Well, Johnny?' The voice was soft, almost bantering.

'I just don't know, sir, I don't know at all.' Nicholls shook his head. 'At first I thought he was going – well, make a hash of it. You know, scare the lights out of 'em. And good God!' he went on wonderingly, 'that's exactly what he did do. Piled it on – gales, *Tirpitz,* hordes of subs. – and yet . . .' His voice trailed off.

'And yet?' Brooks echoed mockingly. 'That's just it. Too much intelligence – that's the trouble with the young doctors today. I saw you – sitting there like a bogus psychiatrist, analysing away for all you were worth at the probable effect of the speech on the minds of the wounded warriors without, and never giving it a chance to let it register on yourself.' He paused and went on quietly.

'It was beautifully done, Johnny. No, that's the wrong word – there was nothing premeditated about it. But don't you see? As black a picture as man could paint: points out that this is just a complicated way of committing suicide: no silver lining, no promises, even Alex. thrown in as a casual afterthought. Builds 'em up, then lets 'em down. No inducements, no hope, no appeal – and yet the appeal was tremendous. . . . What was it, Johnny?'

'I don't know.' Nicholls was troubled. He lifted his head abruptly, then smiled faintly. 'Maybe there *was* no appeal. Listen.' Noiselessly, he slid the door back, flicked off the lights. The rumble of Riley's harsh voice, low and intense, was unmistakable.

'—just a lot of bloody clap-trap. Alex.? The Med.? Not on your — life, mate. You'll never see it. You'll never even see Scapa again. Captain Richard Vallery, DSO! Know what that old bastard wants, boys? Another bar to his DSO. Maybe even a VC. Well, by Christ's, he's not going to have it! Not at my expense. Not if I can — well help it. "I know you won't let me down," ' he mimicked, his voice high-pitched. 'Whining old bastard!' He paused a moment, then rushed on.

'The *Tirpitz*! Christ Almighty! The *Tirpitz*! We're going to stop it – us! This bloody toy ship! Bait, he says, bait!' His voice rose. 'I tell you, mates, nobody gives a damn about us. Direct for the North Cape! They're throwing us to the bloody wolves! And that old bastard up top—'

'Shaddap!' It was Peterson who spoke, his voice a whisper, low and fierce. His hand stretched out, and Brooks and Nicholls in the surgery winced as they heard Riley's wrist-bones crack under the tremendous pressure of the giant's hand. Often I wonder about you, Riley,' Petersen went on slowly. 'But not now, not any more. You make me sick!' He flung Riley's hand down and turned away.

Riley rubbed his wrist in agony, and turned to Burgess.

'For God's sake, what's the matter with him? What the hell . . .' He broke off abruptly. Burgess was looking at him steadily, kept looking for a long time. Slowly, deliberately, he eased himself down in bed, pulled the blankets up to his neck and turned his back on Riley.

Brooks rose quickly to his feet, closed the door and pressed the light switch.

'Act I, Scene I. Cut! Lights!' he murmured. 'See what I mean, Johnny?'

'Yes, sir.' Nicholls nodded slowly. 'At least, I think so.'

'Mind you, my boy, it won't last. At least, not at that intensity.' He grinned. 'But maybe it'll take us the length of Murmansk. You never know.'

'I hope so, sir. Thanks for the show.' Nicholls reached up for his duffel-coat. 'Well, I suppose I'd better make my way aft.'

'Off you go, then. And, oh – Johnny—'

'Sir?'

'That scarlet-fever notice-board of yours. On your way aft you might consign it to the deep. I don't think we'll be needing it any more.'

Nicholls grinned and closed the door softly behind him.

—— 4 ——

MONDAY NIGHT

Dusk action stations dragged out its interminable hour and was gone. That night, as on a hundred other nights, it was just another nagging irritation, a pointless precaution that did not even justify its existence, far less its meticulous thoroughness. Or so it seemed. For although at dawn enemy attacks were routine, at sunset they were all but unknown. It was not always so with other ships, indeed it was rarely so, but then, the *Ulysses* was a lucky ship. Everyone knew that. Even Vallery knew it, but he also knew why. Vigilance was the first article of his sailor's creed.

Soon after the Captain's broadcast, radar had reported a contact, closing. That it was an enemy plane was certain: Commander Westcliffe, Senior Air Arm Officer, had before him in the Fighter Direction Room a wall map showing the operational routes of all Coastal and Ferry Command planes, and this was a clear area. But no one paid the slightest attention to the report, other than Tyndall's order for a 45° course alteration. This was as routine as dusk Action Stations themselves. It was their old friend Charlie coming to pay his respects again.

'Charlie' – usually a four-engine Focke-Wulf Condor – was an institution on the Russian Convoys. He had become to the seamen on the Murmansk run very much what the albatros had been the previous century to sailing men, far south in the Roaring Forties: a bird of ill-omen, half feared but almost amicably accepted, and immune from destruction – though with Charlie, for a different reason. In the early days, before the advent of cam-ships and escort carriers, Charlie frequently spent the entire day, from first light to last, circling a convoy and radioing to base pin-point reports of its position.[1]

Exchanges of signals between British ships and German reconnaissance planes were not unknown, and apocryphal stories were legion. An exchange of pleasantries about the weather was almost commonplace. On several occasions Charlie had plaintively asked for his position and been given highly-detailed latitude and longitude bearings which usually placed him somewhere in the South Pacific; and, of course, a dozen ships claimed the authorship of the story wherein the convoy Commodore sent the signal, 'Please fly the other way round. You are making us dizzy,' and Charlie had courteously acknowledged and turned in his tracks.

Latterly, however, amiability had been markedly absent, and Charlie, grown circumspect with the passing of the months and the appearance of ship-borne fighters, rarely appeared except at dusk. His usual practice was to make a single circle of the convoy at a prudent distance and then disappear into the darkness.

That night was no exception. Men caught only fleeting glimpses of the Condor in the driving snow, then quickly lost it in the gathering gloom. Charlie would report the strength, nature and course of the Squadron, although Tyndall had little hope that the German Intelligence would be deceived as to their course. A naval squadron, near the sixty-second degree of latitude, just east of the Faroes, and heading NNE, wouldn't make sense to them – especially as they almost certainly knew of the departure of the convoy from Halifax. Two and two, far too obviously totted up to four.

No attempt was made to fly off Seafires – the only plane with a chance to overhaul the Condor before it disappeared into the night. To locate the carrier again in almost total darkness, even on a radio beam, was difficult: to land at night, extremely dangerous; and to land, by guess and by God, in the snow and blackness on a pitching, heaving deck, a suicidal impossibility. The least miscalculation, the slightest error of judgment and you had not only lost a plane but a drowned pilot. A ditched Seafire, with its slender, torpedo-shaped fuselage and the tremendous

[1] Cam-ships were merchant ships with specially strengthened fo'c'sles. On these were fitted fore-and-aft angled ramps from which fighter planes, such as modified Hurricanes, were catapulted for convoy defence. After breaking off action, the pilot had either to bale out or land in the sea. 'Hazardous' is rather an inadequate word to describe the duties of this handful of very gallant pilots: the chances of survival were not high.

weight of the great Rolls-Royce Merlin in its nose, was a literal death-trap. When it went down into the sea, it just kept on going.

Back on to course again, the *Ulysses* pushed blindly into the gathering storm. Hands fell out from Action Stations, and resumed normal Defence Stations – watch and watch, four on, four off. Not a killing routine, one would think: twelve hours on, twelve hours off a day – a man could stand that. And so he could, were that all. But the crew also spent three hours a day at routine Action Stations, every second morning – the forenoon watch – at work (this when they were off-watch) and God only knew how many hours at Action Stations. Beyond all this, all meals – when there were meals – were eaten in their off-duty time. A total of three to four hours' sleep a day was reckoned unusual: forty-eight hours without sleep hardly called for comment.

Step by step, fraction by menacing fraction, mercury and barograph crept down in a deadly dualism. The waves were higher now, their troughs deeper, their shoulders steeper, and the bone chilling wind lashed the snow into a blinding curtain. A bad night, a sleepless night, both above deck and below, on watch and off.

On the bridge, the First Lieutenant, the Kapok Kid, signalmen, the Searchlight LTO, look-outs and messengers peered out miserably into the white night and wondered what it would be like to be warm again. Jerseys, coats, overcoats, duffels, oilskins, scarves, balaclavas, helmets – they wore them all, completely muffled except for a narrow eye-slit in the woollen cocoon, and still they shivered. They wrapped arms and forearms round, and rested their feet on the steam pipes which circled the bridge, and froze. Pom-pom crews huddled miserably in the shelter of their multiple guns, stamped their feet, swung their arms and swore incessantly. And the lonely Oerlikon gunners, each jammed in his lonely cockpit, leaned against the built-in 'black' heaters and fought off the Oerlikon gunner's most insidious enemy – sleep.

The Starboard watch, in the mess-decks below, were little happier. There were no bunks for the crew of the *Ulysses*, only hammocks, and these were never slung except in harbour. There were good and sufficient reasons for this. Standards of hygiene on a naval warship are high, compared even to the average civilian home: the average matelot would never consider climbing into his hammock fully dressed – and no one in his senses would have dreamed of undressing on the Russian Convoys. Again, to an exhausted man, the prospect and the actual labour of slinging and then lashing a hammock were alike appalling. And the extra seconds it took to climb out of a hammock in an emergency could represent the margin between life and death, while the very existence of a slung hammock was a danger to all, in that it impeded quick movement. And finally, as on that night of a heavy head sea, there could be no more uncomfortable place than a hammock slung fore and aft.

And so the crew slept where it could, fully clothed even to duffel coats and gloves. On tables and under tables, on narrow nine-inch stools, on the floor, in hammock racks – anywhere. The most popular place on the ship was on the warm steel deck-plates in the alleyway outside the galley, at night-time a weird and spectral tunnel, lit only by a garish red light. A popular sleeping billet, made doubly so by the fact that only a screen separated it from the upper-deck, a scant ten feet away. The fear of being trapped below decks in a sinking ship was always there, always in the back of men's minds.

Even below decks, it was bitterly cold. The hot-air systems operated efficiently only on 'B' and 'C' mess-decks, and even there the temperature barely cleared freezing point. Deckheads dripped constantly and the condensation on the bulkheads sent a thousand little rivulets to pool on the corticene floor. The atmosphere was dank and airless and terribly chill – the ideal breeding ground for the TB, so feared by Surgeon-Commander Brooks. Such conditions, allied with the constant pitching of the ship and the sudden jarring vibrations which were beginning to develop every time the bows crashed down, made sleep almost impossible, at best a fitful, restless unease.

Almost to a man, the crew slept – or tried to sleep – with heads pillowed on inflated lifebelts. Blown up, bent double then tied with tape, these lifebelts made very tolerable pillows. For this purpose, and for this alone, were these lifebelts employed, although standing orders stated explicitly that lifebelts were to be worn at all times during action and in known enemy waters. These orders were completely ignored, not least of all by those Divisional Officers whose duty it was to enforce them. There was enough air trapped in the voluminous and bulky garments worn in these latitudes to keep a man afloat for at least three minutes. If he wasn't picked up in that time, he was dead anyway. It was shock that killed, the tremendous shock of a body at 96° F being suddenly plunged into a liquid temperature some 70° lower –

for in the Arctic waters, the sea temperature often falls below normal freezing point. Worse still, the sub-zero wind lanced like a thousand stilettos through the saturated clothing of a man who had been submerged in the sea, and the heart, faced with an almost instantaneous 100° change in body temperature, just stopped beating. But it was a quick death, men said, quick and kind and merciful.

At ten minutes to midnight the Commander and Marshall made their way to the bridge. Even at this late hour and in the wicked weather, the Commander was his usual self, imperturbable and cheerful, lean and piratical, a throw-back to the Elizabethan buccaneers, if ever there was one. He had an unflagging zest for life. The duffel hood, as always, lay over his shoulders, the braided peak of his cap was tilted at a magnificent angle. He groped for the handle of the bridge gate, passed through, stood for a minute accustoming his eyes to the dark, located the First Lieutenant and thumped him resoundingly on the back.

'Well, watchman, and what of the night?' he boomed cheerfully. 'Bracing, yes, decidedly so. Situation completely out of control as usual, I suppose? Where are all our chickens this lovely evening?' He peered out into the snow, scanned the horizon briefly, then gave up. 'All gone to hell and beyond, I suppose.'

'Not too bad,' Carrington grinned. An RNR officer and an ex-Merchant Navy captain in whom Vallery reposed complete confidence, Lieutenant-Commander Carrington was normally a taciturn man, grave and unsmiling. But a particular bond lay between him and Turner, the professional bond of respect which two exceptional seamen have for each other. 'We can see the carriers now and then. Anyway, Bowden and his backroom boys have 'em all pinned to an inch. At least, that's what they say.'

'Better not let old Bowden hear you say that,' Marshall advised. 'Thinks radar is the only step forward the human race has taken since the first man came down from the trees.' He shivered uncontrollably and turned his back on the driving wind. 'Anyway, I wish to God I had his job,' he added feelingly. 'This is worse than winter in Alberta!'

'Nonsense, my boy, stuff and nonsense!' the Commander roared. 'Decadent, that's the trouble with you youngsters nowadays. This is the only life for a self-respecting human being.' He sniffed the icy air appreciatively and turned to Carrington. 'Who's on with you tonight, Number One?'

A dark figure detached itself from the binnacle and approached him.

'Ah, there you are. Well, well, 'pon my soul, if it isn't our navigating officer, the Honourable Carpenter, lost as usual and dressed to kill in his natty gent's suiting. Do you know, Pilot, in that outfit you look like a cross between a deep-sea diver and that advert for Michelin tyres?'

'Ha!' said the Kapok Kid aggrievedly. 'Sniff and scoff while you may, sir.' He patted his quilted chest affectionately. 'Just wait till ye're all down there in the drink together, everybody else dragged down or frozen to death, me drifting by warm and dry and comfortable, maybe smoking the odd cigarette—'

'Enough. Be off. Course, Number One?'

'Three-twenty, sir. Fifteen knots.'

'And the Captain?'

'In the shelter.' Carrington jerked his head towards the reinforced steel circular casing at the after end of the bridge. This supported the Director Tower, the control circuits to which ran through a central shaft in the casing. A sea-bunk – a spartan, bare settee – was kept there for the Captain's use. 'Sleeping, I hope,' he added, 'but I very much doubt it. Gave orders to be called at midnight.'

'Why?' Turner demanded.

'Oh, I don't know. Routine, I suppose. Wants to see how things are.'

'Cancel the order,' Turner said briefly. 'Captain's got to learn to obey orders like anybody else – especially doctor's orders. I'll take full responsibility. Good night, Number One.'

The gate clanged shut and Marshall turned uncertainly towards the Commander.

'The Captain, sir. Oh, I know it's none of my business, but' – he hesitated – 'well, is he all right?'

Turner looked quickly around him. His voice was unusually quiet.

'If Brooks had his way, the old man would be in hospital.' He was silent for a moment, then added soberly. 'Even then, it might be too late.'

Marshall said nothing. He moved restlessly around, then went aft to the port searchlight control position. For five minutes, an intermittent rumble of voices drifted up to the Commander. He glanced up curiously on Marshall's return.

'That's Ralston, sir,' the Torpedo Officer explained. 'If he'd talk to anybody, I think he'd talk to me.'

'And does he?'

'Sure – but only what *he* wants to talk about. As for the rest, no dice. You can almost see the big notice round his neck – "Private – Keep Off." Very civil, very courteous and completely unapproachable. I don't know what the hell to do about him.'

'Leave him be,' Turner advised. 'There's nothing anyone can do.' He shook his head. 'My God, what a lousy break life's given that boy!'

Silence fell again. The snow was lifting now, but the wind still strengthening. It howled eerily through masts and rigging, blending with a wild and eldritch harmony into the haunting pinging of the Asdic. Weird sounds both, weird and elemental and foreboding, that rasped across the nerves and stirred up nameless, atavistic dreads of a thousand ages past, long buried under the press of civilisation. An unholy orchestra, and, over years, men grew to hate it with a deadly hatred.

Half-past twelve came, one o'clock, then half-past one. Turner's thought turned fondly towards coffee and cocoa. Coffee or cocoa? Cocoa, he decided, a steaming potent brew, thick with melted chocolate and sugar. He turned to Chrysler, the bridge messenger, young brother of the Leading Asdic Operator.

'WT – Bridge. WT – Bridge.' The loudspeaker above the Asdic cabinet crackled urgently, the voice hurried, insistent. Turner jumped for the hand transmitter, barked an acknowledgment.

'Signal from *Sirrus*. Echoes, port bow, 300, strong, closing. Repeat, echoes, port bow, strong, closing.'

'Echoes, WT? Did you say "echoes"?'

'Echoes, sir. I repeat, echoes.'

Even as he spoke, Turner's hand cut down on the gleaming phosphorescence of the Emergency Action Stations switch.

Of all sounds in this earth, there is none so likely to stay with a man to the end of his days as the EAS. There is no other sound even remotely like it. There is nothing noble or martial or blood-stirring about it. It is simply a whistle, pitched near the upper limit of audio-frequency, alternating, piercing, atonic, alive with a desperate urgency and sense of danger: knife-like, it sears through the most sleep-drugged brain and has a man – no matter how exhausted, how weak, how deeply sunk in oblivion – on his feet in seconds, the pulse-rate already accelerating to meet the latest unknown, the adrenalin already pumping into his blood-stream.

Inside two minutes, the *Ulysses* was closed up to Action

Stations. The Commander had moved aft to the After Director Tower, Vallery and Tyndall were on the bridge.

The *Sirrus*. two miles away to port, remained in contact for half an hour. The *Viking* was detached to help her, and, below-deck in the *Ulysses*, the peculiar, tinny clanging of depth-charging was clearly heard at irregular intervals. Finally, the *Sirrus* reported. 'No success: contact lost: trust you have not been disturbed.' Tyndall ordered the recall of the two destroyers, and the bugle blew the stand-down.

Back on the bridge, again, the Commander sent for his long overdue cocoa. Chrysler departed to the seaman's for'ard galley – the Commander would have no truck with the wishy-washy liquid concocted for the officers' mess – and returned with a steaming jug and a string of heavy mugs, their handles threaded on a bent wire. Turner watched with approval the reluctance with which the heavy, viscous liquid poured glutinously over the lip of the jug, and nodded in satisfaction after a preliminary taste. He smacked his lips and sighed contentedly.

'Excellent, young Chrysler, excellent! You have the gift. Torps., an eye on the ship, if you please. Must see where we are.'

He retired to the chart-room on the port side, just aft of the compass platform, and closed the black-out door. Relaxed in his chair, he put his mug on the chart-table and his feet beside it, drew the first deep inhalation of cigarette smoke into his lungs. Then he was on his feet, cursing: the crackle of the WT loud-speaker was unmistakable.

This time it was the *Portpatrick*. For one reason and another, her reports were generally treated with a good deal of reserve, but this time she was particularly emphatic. Commander Turner had no option; again he reached for the EAS switch.

Twenty minutes later the stand-down sounded again, but the Commander was to have no cocoa that night. Three times more during the hours of darkness all hands closed up to Action Stations, and only minutes, it seemed, after the last stand-down, the bugle went for dawn stations.

There was no dawn as we know it. There was a vague, imper-ceptible lightening in the sky, a bleak, chill greyness, as the men dragged themselves wearily back to their action stations. This, then, was war in the northern seas. No death and glory heroics, no roaring guns and spitting Oerlikons, no exaltation of the spirit, no glorious defiance of the enemy: just worn-out sleepless men, numbed with cold and sodden duffels, grey and drawn and stumbling on their feet with weakness and hunger and lack of rest, carrying with them the memories, the tensions, the cumulative physical exhaustion of a hundred such endless nights.

Vallery, as always, was on the bridge. Courteous, kind and considerate as ever, he looked ghastly. His face was haggard, the colour of putty, his bloodshot eyes deep-sunk in hollowed sockets, his lips bloodless. The severe hæmorrhage of the previous night and the sleepless night just gone had taken terrible toll of his slender strength.

In the half-light, the squadron came gradually into view. Miraculously, most of them were still in position. The frigate and minesweeper were together and far ahead of the fleet – during the night they had been understandably reluctant to have their tails tramped on by a heavy cruiser or a carrier. Tyndall appreciated this and said nothing. The *Invader* had lost position during the night, and lay outside the screen on the port quarter. She received a very testy signal indeed, and came steaming up to resume station, corkscrewing violently in the heavy cross seas.

Stand-down came at 0800. At 0810 the port watch was below, making tea, washing, queueing up at the gallery for breakfast trays, when a muffled explosion shook the *Ulysses*. Towels, soap, cups, plates and trays went flying or were left where they were: blasphemous and bitter, the men were on their way before Vallery's hand closed on the Emergency switch.

Less than half a mile away the *Invader* was slewing round in a violent half-circle, her flight-deck tilted over at a crazy angle. It was snowing heavily again now, but not heavily enough to obscure the great gouts of black oily smoke belching up for-ard of the *Invader's* bridge. Even as the crew of the *Ulysses* watched, she came to rest, wallowing dangerously in the troughs between the great waves.

'The fools, the crazy fools!' Tyndall was terribly bitter, unreasonably so; even to Vallery, he would not admit how much he was now feeling the burden, the strain of command that sparked off his now almost chronic irritability. 'This is what happens, Captain, when a ship loses station! And it's as much my fault as theirs – should have sent a destroyer to escort her back.' He peered through his binoculars, turned to Vallery. 'Make a signal please: "Estimate of damage – please inform." ' . . . That damned U-boat must have trailed her from first light, waiting for a line-up.'

Vallery said nothing. He knew how Tyndall must feel to see

one of his ships heavily damaged, maybe sinking. The *Invader* was still lying over at the same unnatural angle, the smoke rising in a steady column now. There was no sign of flames.

'Going to investigate, sir?' Vallery inquired.

Tyndall bit his lip thoughtfully and hesitated.

'Yes, I think we'd better do it ourselves. Order squadron to proceed, same speed, same course. Signal the *Baliol* and the *Nairn* to stand by the *Invader*.'

Vallery, watching the flags fluttering to the yardarm, was aware of someone at his elbow. He half-turned.

'That was no U-boat, sir.' The Kapok Kid was very sure of himself. 'She can't have been torpedoed.'

Tyndall overheard him. He swung round in his chair, glared at the unfortunate navigator.

'What the devil do you know about it, sir?' he growled. When the Admiral addressed his subordinates as 'sir,' it was time to take to the boats. The Kapok Kid flushed to the roots of his blond hair, but he stood his ground.

'Well, sir, in the first place the *Sirrus* is covering the *Invader's* port side, though well ahead, ever since your recall signal. She's been quartering that area for some time. I'm sure Commander Orr would have picked her up. Also, it's far too rough for any sub to maintain periscope depth, far less line up a firing track. And if the U-boat did fire, it wouldn't only fire one – six more likely, and, from that firing angle, the rest of the squadron must have been almost a solid wall behind the *Invader*. But no one else has been hit. . . . I did three years in the trade, sir.'

'I did ten,' Tyndall growled. 'Guesswork, Pilot, just guess-work.'

'No, sir,' Carpenter persisted. 'It's not. I can't swear to it' – he had his binoculars to his eyes – but I'm almost sure the *Invader* is going astern. Could only be because her bows – below the waterline, that is – have been damaged or blown off. Must have been a mine, sir, probably acoustic.'

'Ah, of course, of course!' Tyndall was very acid. 'Moored in 6000 feet of water, no doubt?'

'A *drifting* mine, sir,' the Kapok Kid said patiently. 'Or an old acoustic torpedo – spent German torpedoes don't always sink. Probably a mine, though.'

'Suppose you'll be telling me next what mark it is and when it was laid,' Tyndall growled. But he was impressed in spite of himself. And the *Invader* was going astern, although slowly, without enough speed to give her steerage way. She still wallowed helplessly in the great troughs.

An Aldis clacked acknowledgment to the winking light on the *Invader*. Bentley tore a sheet off a signal pad, handed it to Vallery.

' "*Invader* to Admiral," ' the Captain read. ' "Am badly holed, starboard side for'ard, very deep. Suspect drifting mine. Am investigating extent of damage. Will report soon." '

Tyndall took the signal from him and read it slowly. Then he looked over his shoulder and smiled faintly.

'You were dead right, my boy, it seems. Please accept an old curmudgeon's apologies.'

Carpenter murmured something and turned away, brick-red again with embarrassment. Tyndall grinned faintly at the Captain, then became thoughtful.

'I think we'd better talk to him personally, Captain. Barlow, isn't it? Make a signal.'

They climbed down two decks to the Fighter Direction room. Westcliffe vacated his chair for the Admiral.

'Captain Barlow?' Tyndall spoke into the hand-piece.

'Speaking.' The sound came from the loudspeaker above his head.

'Admiral here, Captain. How are things?'

'We'll manage, sir. Lost most of our bows, I'm afraid. Several casualties. Oil fires, but under control. WT doors all holding, and engineers and damage control parties are shoring up the cross-bulkheads.'

'Can you go ahead at all, Captain?'

'Could do, sir, but risky – in this, anyway.'

'Think you could make it back to base?'

'With this wind and sea behind us, yes. Still take three-four days.'

'Right-o, then.' Tyndall's voice was gruff. 'Off you go. You're no good to us without bows! Damned hard luck, Captain Barlow. My commiserations. And oh! I'm giving you the *Baliol* and *Nairn* as escorts and radioing for an ocean-going tug to come out to meet you – just in case.'

'Thank you, sir. We appreciate that. One last thing – permission to empty starboard squadron fuel tanks. We've taken a lot of water, can't get rid of it all – only way to recover our trim.'

Tyndall sighed. 'Yes, I was expecting that. Can't be helped and we can't take it off you in this weather. Good luck, Captain. Goodbye.'

'Thank you very much, sir. Goodbye.'

Twenty minutes later, the *Ulysses* was back on station in the squadron. Shortly afterwards, they saw the *Invader*, not listing quite so heavily now, head slowly round to the south-east, the little Hunt class destroyer and the frigate, one on either side, rolling wickedly as they came round with her. In another ten minutes, watchers on the *Ulysses* had lost sight of them, buried in a flurrying snow squall. Three gone and eleven left behind; but it was the eleven who now felt so strangely alone.

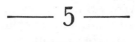

5

TUESDAY

The *Invader* and her troubles were soon forgotten. All too soon, the 14th Aircraft Carrier Squadron had enough, and more than enough, to worry about on their own account. They had their own troubles to overcome, their own enemy to face – an enemy far more elemental and far more deadly than any mine or U-boat.

Tyndall braced himself more firmly against the pitching, rolling deck and looked over at Vallery. Vallery, he thought for the tenth time that morning, looked desperately ill.

'What do you make of it, Captain? Prospects aren't altogether healthy, are they?'

'We're for it, sir. It's really piling up against us. Carrington has spent six years in the West Indies, has gone through a dozen hurricanes. Admits he's seen a barometer lower, but never one so low with the pressure still falling so fast – not in these latitudes. This is only a curtain-raiser.'

'This will do me nicely, meantime, thank you,' Tyndall said dryly. 'For a curtain-raiser, it's doing not so badly.'

It was a masterly understatement. For a curtain-raiser, it was a magnificent performance. The wind was fairly steady, about Force 9 on the Beaufort scale, and the snow had stopped. A temporary cessation only, they all knew – far ahead to the north-west the sky was a peculiarly livid colour. It was a dull glaring purple, neither increasing nor fading, faintly luminous and vaguely menacing in its uniformity and permanence. Even to men who had seen everything the Arctic skies had to offer, from pitchy darkness on a summer's noon, right through the magnificent displays of Northern Lights to that wonderfully washed-out blue that so often smiles down on the stupendous calms of the milk-white seas that lap edge of the Barrier, this was something quite unknown.

But the Admiral's reference had been to the sea. It had been building up, steadily, inexorably, all during the morning. Now, at noon, it looked uncommonly like an eighteenth-century print of a barque in a storm – serried waves of greenish-grey, straight, regular and marching uniformly along, each decoratively topped with frothing caps of white. Only here, there were 500 feet between crest and crest, and the squadron, heading almost directly into it, was taking hearty punishment.

For the little ships, already burying their bows every fifteen seconds in a creaming smother of cascading white, this was bad enough, but another, a more dangerous and insidious enemy was at work – the cold. The temperature had long sunk below freezing point, and the mercury was still shrinking down, close towards the zero mark.

The cold was now intense: ice formed in cabins and messdecks: fresh-water systems froze solid: metal contracted, hatchcovers jammed, door hinges locked in frozen immobility, the oil in the searchlight controls gummed up and made them useless. To keep a watch, especially a watch on the bridge, was torture: the first shock of that bitter wind seared the lungs, left a man fighting for breath: if he had forgotten to don gloves – first the silk gloves, then the woollen mittens, then the sheepskin gauntlets – and touched a handrail, the palms of the hands seared off, the skin burnt as by white-hot metal: on the bridge, if he forgot to duck when the bows smashed down into a trough, the flying spray, solidified in a second into hurtling slivers of ice, lanced cheek and forehead open to the bone: hands froze, the very marrow of the bones numbed, the deadly chill crept upwards from feet to calves to thighs, nose and chin turned white with frostbite and demanded immediate attention: and then, by far the worst of all, the end of the watch, the return below deck, the writhing, excruciating agony of returning circulation. But, for all this, words are useless things, pale shadows of reality. Some things lie beyond the knowledge and the experience of the majority of mankind, and here imagination finds itself in a world unknown.

But all these things were relatively trifles, personal inconveniences to be shrugged aside. The real danger lay elsewhere. It lay in the fact of ice.

There were over three hundred tons of it already on the decks of the *Ulysses,* and more forming every minute. It lay in a thick, even coat over the main deck, the fo'c'sle, the gun-decks and the bridges: it hung in long, jagged icicles from coamings and turrets and rails: it trebled the diameter of every wire, stay and halliard, and turned slender masts into monstrous trees, ungainly and improbable. It lay everywhere, a deadly menace, and much of the danger lay in the slippery surface it presented – a problem much more easily overcome on a coal-fired merchant ship with clinker and ashes from its boilers, than in the modern, oil-fired warships. On the *Ulysses,* they spread salt and sand and hoped for the best.

But the real danger of the ice lay in its weight. A ship, to use technical terms, can be either stiff or tender. If she's stiff, she has a low centre of gravity, rolls easily, but whips back quickly and is extremely stable and safe. If she's tender, with a high centre of gravity, she rolls reluctantly but comes back even more reluctantly, is unstable and unsafe. And if a ship were tender, and hundreds of tons of ice piled high on its decks, the centre of gravity rose to a dangerous height. It could rise to a fatal height. . . .

The escort carriers and the destroyers, especially the *Portpatrick,* were vulnerable, terribly so. The carriers, already unstable with the great height and weight of their reinforced flight-decks, provided a huge, smooth, flat surface to the falling snow, ideal conditions for the formation of ice. Earlier on, it had been possible to keep the flight-decks relatively clear – working parties had toiled incessantly with brooms and sledges, salt and steam hoses. But the weather had deteriorated so badly now that to send out a man on that wildly pitching, staggering flight-deck, glassy and infinitely treacherous, would be to send him to his death. The *Wrestler* and *Blue Ranger* had modified heating systems under the flight-decks – modified, because, unlike the British ships, these Mississippi carriers had planked flight-decks: in such extreme conditions, they were hopelessly inefficient.

Conditions aboard the destroyers were even worse. They had to contend not only with the ice from the packed snow, but with ice from the sea itself. As regularly as clockwork, huge clouds of spray broke over the destroyers' fo'c'sles as the bows crashed solidy, shockingly into the trough and rising shoulder of the next wave: the spray froze even as it touched the deck, even before it touched the deck, piling up the solid ice, in places over a foot thick, from the stem aft beyond the breakwater. The tremendous weight of the ice was pushing the little ships down by their heads; deeper, with each successive plunge ever deeper, they buried their noses in the sea, and each time, more and more sluggishly, more and more reluctantly, they staggered laboriously up from the depths. Like the carrier captains, the destroyer skippers could only look down from their bridges, helpless, hoping.

Two hours passed, two hours in which the temperature fell to zero, hesitated, then shrank steadily beyond it, two hours in which the barometer tumbled crazily after it. Curiously, strangely, the snow still held off, the livid sky to the north-west was as far away as ever, and the sky to the south and east had cleared completely. The squadron presented a fantastic picture now, little toy-boats of sugar-icing, dazzling white, gleaming and sparkling in the pale, winter sunshine, pitching crazily through the ever-lengthening, ever-deepening valleys of grey and green of the cold Norwegian Sea, pushing on towards that far horizon, far and weird and purply glowing, the horizon of another world. It was an incredibly lovely spectacle.

Rear-Admiral Tyndall saw nothing beautiful about it. A man who was wont to claim that he never worried, he was seriously troubled now. He was gruff, to those on the bridge, gruff to the point of discourtesy and the old geniality of the Farmer Giles of even two months ago was all but gone. Ceaselessly his gaze circled the fleet; constantly, uncomfortably, he twisted in his chair. Finally he climbed down, passed through the gate and went into the Captain's shelter.

Vallery had no light on and the shelter was in semi-darkness. He lay there on his settee, a couple of blankets thrown over him. In the half-light, his face looked ghastly, corpse-like. His right hand clutched a balled handkerchief, spotted and stained: he made no attempt to hide it. With a painful effort, and before Tyndall could stop him, he had swung his legs over the edge of the settee and pulled forward a chair. Tyndall choked off his protest, sank gracefully into the seat.

'I think your curtain's just about to go up, Dick. . . . What on earth ever induced me to become a squadron commander?'

Vallery grinned sympathetically. 'I don't particularly envy you, sir. What are you going to do now?'

'What would *you* do?' Tyndall countered dolefully.

Vallery laughed. For a moment his face was transformed, boy-ish almost, then the laugh broke down into a bout of harsh, dry

coughing. The stain spread over his handkerchief. Then he
looked up and smiled.

'The penalty for laughing at a superior officer. What would
I do? Heave to, sir. Better still, tuck my tail between my legs
and run for it.'

Tyndall shook his head.

'You never were a very convincing liar, Dick.'

Both men sat in silence for a moment, then Vallery looked up.

'How far to go, exactly, sir?'

'Young Carpenter makes it 170 miles, more or less.'

'One hundred and seventy.' Vallery looked at his watch.
'Twenty hours to go – in this weather. We *must* make it!'

Tyndall nodded heavily. 'Eighteen ships sitting out there –
nineteen, counting the sweeper from Hvalfjord – not to mention
old Starr's blood pressure ...'

He broke off as a hand rapped on the door and a head looked
in.

'Two signals, Captain, sir.'

'Just read them out, Bentley, will you?'

'First is from the *Portpatrick*: "Sprung bow-plates: making
water fast: pumps coming: fear further damage: please advise." '

Tyndall swore. Vallery said calmly: 'And the other?'

'From the *Gannet*, sir. "Breaking up." '

'Yes, yes. And the rest of the message?'

'Just that, sir. "Breaking up." '

'Ha! One of these taciturn characters,' Tyndall growled.
'Wait a minute, Chief, will you?' He sank back in his chair,
hand rasping his chin, gazing at his feet, forcing his tired mind
to think.

Vallery murmured something in a low voice, and Tyndall
looked up, his eyebrows arched.

'Troubled waters, sir. Perhaps the carriers—'

Tyndall slapped his knee. 'Two minds with but a single
thought. Bentley, make two signals. One to all screen vessels –
tell 'em to take position – astern – close astern – of the carriers.
Other to the carriers. Oil hose, one each through port and starboard loading ports, about – ah – how much would you say,
Captain?'

'Twenty gallons a minute, sir?'

'Twenty gallons it is. Understand, Chief? Right-o, get 'em off
at once. And Chief – tell the Navigator to bring his chart here.'
Bentley left, and he turned to Vallery. 'We've got to fuel later
on, and we can't do it here. Looks as if this might be the last

chance of shelter this side of Murmansk. . . . And if the next twenty-four hours are going to be as bad as Carrington forecasts, I doubt whether some of the little ships could live through it anyway. . . . Ah! Here you are, Pilot. Let's see where we are. How's the wind, by the way?'

'Force 10, sir.' Bracing himself against the wild lurching of the *Ulysses,* the Kapok Kid smoothed out the chart on the captain's bunk. 'Backing slightly.'

'North-west, would you say, Pilot?' Tyndall rubbed his hands. 'Excellent. Now, my boy, our position?'

'12.40 west. 66.15 north,' said the Kapok Kid precisely. He didn't even trouble to consult the chart. Tyndall lifted his eyebrows but made no comment.

'Course?'

'310, sir.'

'Now, if it were necessary for us to seek shelter for fuelling—'

'Course exactly 290, sir. I've pencilled it in – there. Four and a half hours' steaming, approximately.'

'How the devil—' Tyndall exploded. 'Who told you to – to—' He spluttered into a wrathful silence.

'I worked it out five minutes ago, sir. It – er – seemed inevitable. 290 would take us a few miles inside the Langanes peninsula. There should be plenty shelter there. Carpenter was grave, unsmiling.

'Seemed inevitable!' Tyndall roared. 'Would you listen to him, Captain Vallery? Inevitable! And it's only just occurred to me! Of all the . . . Get out! Take yourself and that damned comic-opera fancy dress elsewhere!'

The Kapok Kid said nothing. With an air of injured innocence he gathered up his charts and left. Tyndall's voice halted him at the door.

'Pilot!'

'Sir?' The Kapok Kid's eyes were fixed on a point above Tyndall's head.

'As soon as the screen vessels have taken up position, tell Bentley to send them the new course.'

'Yes, sir. Certainly.' He hesitated, and Tyndall chuckled. 'All right, all right,' he said resignedly. 'I'll say it again – I'm just a crusty old curmudgeon . . . and shut that damned door! We're freezing in here.'

The wind was rising more quickly now and long ribbons of white were beginning to streak the water. Wave troughs were deepening rapidly, their sides steepening, their tops blown off

74

and flattened by the wind. Gradually, but perceptibly to the ear now, the thin, lonely whining in the rigging was climbing steadily up the register. From time to time, large chunks of ice, shaken loose by the increasing vibration, broke off from the masts and stays and spattered on the deck below.

The effect of the long oil-slicks trailing behind the carriers was almost miraculous. The destroyers, curiously mottled with oil now, were still plunging astern, but the surface tension of the fuel held the water and spray from breaking aboard. Tyndall, justifiably, was feeling more than pleased with himself.

Towards half-past four in the afternoon, with shelter still a good fifteen miles away, the elation had completely worn off. There was a whole gale blowing now and Tyndall had been compelled to signal for a reduction in speed.

From deck level, the seas now were more than impressive. They were gigantic, frightening. Nicholls stood with the Kapok Kid, off watch now, on the main deck, under the port whaler, sheltering in the lee of the fo'c'sle deck. Nicholls, clinging to a davit to steady himself, and leaping back now and then to avoid a deluge of spray, looked over to where the *Defender*, the *Vultra* and *Viking* tailing behind, were pitching madly, grotesquely, under that serene blue sky. The blue sky above, the tremendous seas below. There was something almost evil, something literally spine-chilling, in that macabre contrast.

'They never told me anything about this in the Medical School,' Nicholls observed at last. 'My God, Andy,' he added in awe, 'have you ever seen anything like this?'

'Once, just once. We were caught in a typhoon off the Nicobars. I don't think it was as bad as this. And Number One says this is damn' all compared to what's coming tonight – and he knows. God, I wish I was back in Henley!'

Nicholls looked at him curiously.

'Can't say I know the First Lieutenant well. Not a very – ah – approachable customer, is he? But everyone – old Giles, the skipper, the Commander, yourself – they all talk about him with bated breath. What's so extra special about him? I respect him, mind you – everyone seems to – but dammit to hell, he's no superman.'

'Sea's beginning to break up,' the Kapok Kid murmured absently. 'Notice how every now and again we're beginning to get a wave half as big again as the others? Every seventh wave, the old sailors say. No, Johnny, he's not a superman, Just the greatest seaman you'll ever see. Holds two master's-tickets – square-rigged and steam. He was going round the Horn in Finnish barques when we were still in our prams. Commander could tell you enough stories about him to fill a book.' He paused then went on quietly:

'He really is one of the few great seamen of today. Old Blackbeard Turner is no slouch himself, but he'll tell anyone that he can't hold a candle to Jimmy. . . . I'm no hero-worshipper, Johnny. You know that. But you can say about Carrington what they used to say about Shackleton – when there's nothing left and all hope is gone, get down on your knees and pray for him. Believe me, Johnny, I'm damned glad he's here.'

Nicholls said nothing. Surprise held him silent. For the Kapok Kid, flippancy was a creed, derogation second nature: seriousness was a crime and anything that smacked of adulation bordered on blashpemy. Nicholls wondered what manner of man Carrington must be.

The cold was vicious. The wind was tearing great gouts of water off the wave-tops, driving the atomised spray at bullet speed against fo'c'sle and sides. It was impossible to breathe without turning one's back, without wrapping layers of wool round mouth and nose. Faces blue and white, shaking violently with the cold, neither suggested, neither even thought of going below. Men hypnotised, men fascinated by the tremendous seas, the towering waves, 1000, 2000 feet in length, long, sloping on the lee side, steep-walled and terrifying on the other, pushed up by a sixty knot wind and by some mighty force lying far to the north-west. In these gigantic troughs, a church steeple would be lost for ever.

Both men turned round as they heard the screen door crashing behind them. A duffel-coated figure, cursing fluently, fought to shut the heavy door against the pitching of the *Ulysses,* finally succeeded in heaving the clips home. It was Leading Seaman Doyle, and even though his beard hid three-quarters of what could be seen of his face, he still looked thoroughly disgusted with life.

Carpenter grinned at him. He and Doyle had served a commission together on the China Station. Doyle was a very privileged person.

'Well, well, the Ancient Mariner himself! How are things down below, Doyle?'

'Bloody desperate, sir!' His voice was as lugubrious as his face. 'Cold as charity, sir, and everything all over the bloody place. Cups, saucers, plates in smithereens. Half the crew—'

He broke off suddenly, eyes slowly widening in blank disbelief. He was staring out to sea between Nicholls and Carpenter.

'Well, what about half the crew? . . . What's the matter,
Doyle?'

'Christ Almighty!' Doyle's voice was slow, stunned: it was
almost a prayer. 'Oh, Christ Almighty!' The voices rose sharply
on the last two syllables.

The two officers twisted quickly round. The *Defender* was
climbing – all 500 feet of her was literally climbing – up the
lee side of a wave that staggered the imagination, whose im-
mensity completely defied immediate comprehension. Even as
they watched, before shocked minds could grasp the significance
of it all, the *Defender* reached the crest, hesitated, crazily tilted
up her stern till screw and rudder were entirely clear of the
water, then crashed down, down, down. . . .

Even at two cable-lengths' distance in that high wind, the explosive smash of the plummeting bows came like a thunder-clap.
An æon ticked by, and still the *Defender* seemed to keep on
going under, completely buried now, right back to the bridge
island, in a sea of foaming white. How long she remained like
that, arrowed down into the depths of the Arctic, no one could
afterwards say: then slowly, agonisingly, incredibly, great rivers
of water cascaded off her bows, she broke surface again. Broke
surface, to present to frankly disbelieving eyes a spectacle entirely without precedent, anywhere, at any time. The tremendous, instantaneous, upthrusting pressure of unknown thousands
of tons of water had torn the open flight-deck completely off its
mountings and bent it backwards, in a great, sweeping 'U,' almost as far as the bridge. It was a sight to make men doubt their
sanity, to leave them stupefied, to leave them speechless – all,
that is, execept the Kapok Kid. He rose magnificently to the
occasion.

'My word!' he murmured thoughtfully. 'That *is* unusual.'

Another such wave, another such shattering impact and it would
have been the end for the *Defender*. The finest ships, the stout-
est, most powerful vessels, are made only of thin, incredibly thin,
sheets of metal, and metal, twisted and tortured as was the
Defender's, could never have withstood another such impact.

But there were no more such waves, no more such impacts.
It had been a freak wave, one of these massive, inexplicable
contortions of the sea which have occurred, with blessed in-

frequency, from time immemorial, in all the great seas of the world whenever Nature wanted to show mankind, an irreverent, over-venturesome mankind, just how puny and pitifully helpless a thing mankind really is. . . . There were no more such waves and, by five o'clock, although land was still some eight to ten miles away, the squadron had moved into comparative shelter behind the tip of the Langanes peninsula.

From time to time, the captain of the *Defender*, who seemed to be enjoying himself hugely, sent reassuring messages to the Admiral. He was making a good deal of water, but he was managing nicely, thank you. He thought the latest shape in flight-decks very fashionable, and a vast improvement on the old type; straight flight-decks lacked imagination, he thought, and didn't the Admiral think so too. The vertical type, he stated, provided excellent protection against wind and weather, and would make a splendid sail with the wind in the right quarter. With his last message, to the effect that he thought that it would be rather difficult to fly off planes, a badly-worried Tyndall lost his temper and sent back such a blistering signal that all communications abruptly ceased.

Shortly before six o'clock, the squadron hove-to under the shelter of Langanes, less than two miles offshore. Langanes is low-lying, and the wind, still climbing the scale, swept over it and into the bay beyond without a break; but the sea, compared to an hour ago, was mercifully calm, although the ships still rolled heavily. At once the cruisers and the screen vessels – except the *Portpatrick* and the *Gannet* – moved alongside the carriers, took oil hoses aboard. Tyndall, reluctantly and after much heart-searching, had decided that the *Portpatrick* and *Gannet* were suspect, a potential liability: they were to escort the crippled carrier back to Scapa.

Exhaustion, an exhaustion almost physical, almost tangible, lay heavily over the mess-decks and the wardroom of the *Ulysses*. Behind lay another sleepless night, another twenty-four hours with peace unknown and rest impossible. With dull tired minds, men heard the broadcast that the *Defender,* the *Portpatrick* and the *Gannet* were to return to Scapa when the weather moderated. Six gone now, only eight left – half the carrier force gone. Little wonder that men felt sick at heart, felt as if they were being deserted, as if, in Riley's phrase, they were being thrown to the wolves.

But there was remarkably little bitterness, a puzzling lack of resentment which, perhaps, sprung only from sheer passive acceptance. Brooks was aware of it, this inaction of feeling, this unnatural extinction of response, and was lost for a reason to account for it. Perhaps, he thought, this was the nadir, the last extremity when sick men and sick minds cease altogether to function, the last slow-down of all vital processes, both human and animal. Perhaps this was just the final apathy. His intellect told him that was reasonable, more, it was inevitable. . . . And all the time some fugitive intuition, some evanescent insight, was thrusting upon him an awareness, a dim shadowy awareness of something altogether different; but his mind was too tired to grasp it.

Whatever it was, it wasn't apathy. For a brief moment that evening, a white-hot anger ran through the ship like a flame. then resentment of the injustice which had provoked it. That there had been cause for anger even Vallery admitted; but his hand had been forced.

It had all happened simply enough. During routine evening tests, it had been discovered that the fighting lights on the lower yardarm were not working. Ice was at once suspected as being the cause.

The lower yardarm, on this evening dazzling white and heavily coated with snow and ice, paralleled the deck, sixty feet above it, eighty feet above the waterline. The fighting lights were suspended below the outer tip: to work on these, a man had either to sit on the yardarm – a most uncomfortable position as the heavy steel WT transmission aerial was bolted to its upper length – or in a bosun's chair suspended from the yardarm. It was a difficult enough task at any time: tonight, it had to be done with the maximum speed, because the repairs would interrupt radio transmission – the 3000-volt steel 'Safe-to-Transmit' boards (which broke the electrical circuits) had to be withdrawn and left in the keeping of the Officer of the Watch during the repair: it had to be done – very precise, finicky work had to be done – in that sub-zero temperature: it had to be done on that slippery, glass-smooth yardarm, with the *Ulysses* rolling regularly through a thirty-degree arc: the job was more than ordinarily difficult – it was highly dangerous.

Marshall did not feel justified in detailing the duty LTO for the job, especially as that rating was a middle-aged and very much overweight reservist, long past his climbing prime. He asked for volunteers. It was inevitable that he should have picked Ralston, for that was the kind of man Ralston was.

The task took half an hour – twenty minutes to climb the

mast, edge out to the yardarm tip, fit the bosun's chair and life-line, and ten minutes for the actual repair. Long before he was finished, a hundred, two hundred tired men, robbing themselves of sleep and supper, had come on deck and huddled there in the bitter wind, watching in fascination.

Ralston swung in a great arc across the darkening sky, the gale plucking viciously at his duffel and hood. Twice, wind and wave flung him out, still in his chair, parallel to the yardarm, forcing him to wrap both arms around the yardarm and hang on for his life. On the second occasion he seemed to strike his face against the aerial for he held his head for a few seconds afterwards, as if he were dazed. It was then that he lost his gauntlets – he must have had them in his lap, while making some delicate adjustment: they dropped down together, disappeared over the side.

A few minutes later, while Vallery and Turner were standing amidships examining the damage the motor-boat had suffered in Scapa Flow, a short, stocky figure came hurriedly out of the after screen door, made for the fo'c'sle at an awkward stumbling run. He pulled up abruptly at the sight of the Captain and the Commander: they saw it was Hastings, the Master-at-Arms.

'What's the matter, Hastings?' Vallery asked curtly. He always found it difficult to conceal his dislike for the Master-at-Arms, his dislike for his harshness, his uncalled-for severity.

'Trouble on the bridge, sir,' Hastings jerked out breathlessly. Vallery could have sworn to a gleam of satisfaction in his eye. 'Don't know exactly what – could hardly hear a thing but the wind on the phone. . . . I think you'd better come, sir.'

They found only three people on the bridge: Etherton, the gunnery officer, one hand still clutching a phone, worried, un-happy: Ralston, his hands hanging loosely by his sides, the palms raw and torn, the face ghastly, the chin with the dead pallor of frostbite, the forehead masked in furrowed, frozen blood: and, lying in a corner, Sub-Lieutenant Carslake, moan-ing in agony, only the whites of his eyes showing, stupidly finger-ing his smashed mouth, the torn, bleeding gaps in his prominent upper teeth.

'Good God!' Vallery ejaculated. 'Good God above!' He stood there, his hand on the gate, trying to grasp the significance of the scene before him. Then his mouth clamped shut and he swung round on the Gunnery Officer.

'What the devil's happened here, Etherton?' he demanded harshly. 'What *is* all this? Has Carslake—'

'Ralston hit him, sir,' Etherton broke in.

'Don't be so bloody silly, Guns!' Turner grunted.

'Exactly!' Vallery's voice was impatient. 'We can see that. Why?'

'A WT messenger came up for the "Safe-to-Transmit" boards. Carslake gave them to him – about ten minutes ago, I – I think.'

'You think! Where were you, Etherton, and why did you permit it? You know very well . . .' Vallery broke off short, remembering the presence of Ralston and the MAA.

Etherton muttered something. His words were inaudible in the gale.

Vallery bent forward. 'What did you say, Etherton—'

'I was down below, sir.' Etherton was looking at the deck. 'Just – just for a moment, sir.'

'I see. You were down below.' Vallery's voice was controlled now, quiet and even; his eyes held an expression that promised ill for Etherton. He looked round at Turner. 'Is he badly hurt, Commander?'

'He'll survive,' said Turner briefly. He had Carslake on his feet now, still moaning, his hand covering his smashed mouth.

For the first time, the Captain seemed to notice Ralston. He looked at him for a few seconds – an eternity on that bitter, storm-lashed bridge – then spoke, monosyllabic, ominous, thirty years of command behind the word.

'Well?'

Ralston's face was frozen, expressionless. His eyes never left Carslake.

'Yes, sir. I did it. I hit him – the treacherous, murdering bastard!'

'Ralston!' The MAA's voice was a whiplash.

Suddenly Ralston's shoulders sagged. With an effort, he looked away from Carslake, looked wearily at Vallery.

'I'm sorry. I forgot. He's got a stripe on his arm – only ratings are bastards.' Vallery winced at the bitterness. 'But he—'

'You've got frostbite.'

'Rub your chin, man!' Turner interrupted sharply.

Slowly, mechanically, Ralston did as he was told. He used the back of his hand. Vallery winced again as he saw the palm of the hand, raw and mutilated, skin and flesh hanging in strips. The agony of that bare-handed descent from the yardarm. . . .

'He tried to murder me, sir. It was deliberate.' Ralston sounded tired.

'Do you realize what you are saying?' Vallery's voice was as icy as the wind that swept over Langanes. But he felt the first, faint chill of fear.

'He tried to murder me, sir,' Ralston repeated tonelessly. 'He returned the boards five minutes before I left the yardarm. WT must have started transmitting just as soon as I reached the mast, coming down.'

'Nonsense, Ralston. How dare you—'

'He's right, sir.' It was Etherton speaking. He was replacing the receiver carefully, his voice unhappy. 'I've just checked.'

The chill of fear settled deeper on Vallery's mind. Almost desperately he said:

'Anyone can make a mistake. Ignorance may be culpable, but—'

'Ignorance!' The weariness had vanished from Ralston as if it had never been. He took two quick steps forward. 'Ignorance! I gave him these boards, sir, when I came to the bridge. I asked for the Officer of the Watch and he said *he* was — I didn't know the Gunnery Officer was on duty, sir. When I told him that the boards were to be returned only to me, he said: "I don't want any of your damned insolence, Ralston. I know my job – you stick to yours. Just you get up there and perform your heroics." He *knew*, sir.'

Carslake burst from the Commander's supporting arm, turned and appealed wildly to the Captain. The eyes were white and staring, the whole face working.

'That's a lie, sir! It's a damned, filthy lie!' He mouthed the words, slurred them through smashed lips. 'I never said . . .'

The words crescendoed into a coughing, choking scream as Ralston's fist smashed viciously, terribly into the torn, bubbling mouth. He staggered drunkenly through the port gate, crashed into the chart house, slid down to lie on the deck, huddled and white and still. Both Turner and the MAA had at once leapt forward to pinion the LTO's arms, but he made no attempt to move.

Above and beyond the howl of the wind, the bridge seemed strangely silent. When Vallery spoke, his voice was quite ex-pressionless.

'Commander, you might phone for a couple of our marines. Have Carslake taken down to his cabin and ask Brooks to have a look at him. Master-at-Arms?'

'Sir?'

'Take this rating to the Sick Bay, let him have any necessary treatment. Then put him in cells. With an armed guard. Understand?'

'I understand, sir.' There was no mistaking the satisfaction in Hasting's voice.

Vallery, Turner and the Gunnery Officer stood in silence as Ralston and the MAA left, in silence as two burly marines carried Carslake, still senseless, off the bridge and below. Vallery moved after them, broke step at Etherton's voice behind him.

'Sir?'

Vallery did not even turn round. 'I'll see you later, Etherton.'

'No, sir. Please. This is important.'

Something in the Gunnery Officer's voice held Vallery. He turned back, impatiently.

'I'm not concerned with excusing myself, sir. There's no excuse.' The eyes were fixed steadily on Vallery. 'I was standing at the Asdic door when Ralston handed the boards to Carslake. I overheard them – every word they said.'

Vallery's face became very still. He glanced at Turner, saw that he, too, was waiting intently.

'And Ralston's version of the conversation?' In spite of himself, Vallery's voice was rough, edged with suspense.

'Completely accurate, sir.' The words were hardly audible. 'In every detail. Ralston told the exact truth.'

Vallery closed his eyes for a moment, turned slowly, heavily away. He made no protest as he felt Turner's hand under his arm, helping him down the steep ladder. Old Socrates had told him a hundred times that he carried the ship on his back. He could feel the weight of it now, the crushing burden of every last ounce of it.

Vallery was at dinner with Tyndall, in the Admiral's day cabin, when the message arrived. Sunk in private thought, he gazed down at his untouched food as Tyndall smoothed out the signal.

The Admiral cleared his throat.

'On course. On time. Sea moderate, wind freshening. Expect rendezvous as planned. Commodore 77.'

He laid the signal down. 'Good God! Seas moderate, fresh wind! Do you reckon he's in the same damned ocean as us?'

Vallery smiled faintly.

'This is it, sir.'

'This is it,' Tyndall echoed. He turned to the messenger.

'Make a signal. "You are running into severe storm.

Rendezvous unchanged. You may be delayed. Will remain at rendezvous until your arrival." That clear enough, Captain?'

'Should be, sir. Radio silence?'

'Oh, yes. Add "Radio silence. Admiral, 14th ACS." Get it off at once, will you? Then tell WT to shut down themselves.'

The door shut softly. Tyndall poured himself some coffee, looked across at Vallery.

'That boy still on your mind, Dick?'

Vallery smiled non-committally, lit a cigarette. At once he began to cough harshly.

'Sorry, sir,' he apologised. There was silence for some time, then he looked up quizzically.

'What mad ambition drove me to become a cruiser captain?' he asked sadly.

Tyndall grinned. 'I don't envy you. . . . I seem to have heard this conversation before. What are you going to do about Ralston, Dick?'

'What would *you* do, sir?' Vallery countered

'Keep him locked up till we return from Russia. On a bread-and-water diet, in irons if you like.'

Vallery smiled.

'You never were a very good liar, John.'

Tyndall laughed. '*Touché!*' He was warmed, secretly pleased. Rarely did Richard Vallery break through his self-imposed code of formality. 'A heinous offence, we all know, to clout one of HM commissioned officers, but if Etherton's story is true, my only regret is that Ralston didn't give Brooks a really large-scale job of replanning that young swine's face.'

'It's true, all right, I'm afraid,' said Vallery soberly. 'What it amounts to is that naval discipline – oh, how old Starr would love this – compels me to punish a would-be murder's victim!' He broke off in a fresh paroxysm of coughing, and Tyndall looked away: he hoped the distress wasn't showing in his face, the pity and anger he felt that Vallery – that very perfect, gentle knight, the finest gentleman and friend he had ever known – should be caughing his heart out, visibly dying on his feet, be-cause of the blind inhumanity of an SNO in London, two thou-sand miles away. 'A victim,' Vallery went on at last, 'who has already lost his mother, brother and three sisters. . . . I believe he has a father at sea somewhere.'

'And Carslake?'

'I shall see him tomorrow. I should like you to be there, sir. I will tell him that he will remain an officer of this ship till we return to Scapa, then resign his commission. . . . I don't think he'd care to appear at a court-martial, even as a witness,' he finished dryly.

'Not if he's sane, which I doubt,' Tyndall agreed. A sudden thought struck him. 'Do you think he *is* sane?' he frowned.

'Carslake,' Vallery hesitated. 'Yes, I think so, sir. At least, he was. Brooks isn't so sure. Says he didn't like the look of him tonight – something queer about him, he thinks, and in these abnormal conditions small provocations are magnified out of all proportion.' Vallery smiled briefly. 'Not that Carslake is liable to regard the twin assaults on pride and person as a small provocation.'

Tyndall nodded agreement. 'He'll bear watching. . . . Oh, damn! I wish the ship would stay still. Half my coffee on the tablecloth. Young Spicer' – he looked towards the pantry – 'will be as mad as hell. Nineteen years old and a regular tyrant. . . . I thought these would be sheltered waters, Dick?'

'So they are, compared to what's waiting for us. Listen!' He cocked his head to the howling of the wind outside. 'Let's see what the weather man has to say about it.'

He reached for the desk phone, asked for the transmitting station. After a brief conversation he replaced the receiver.

'TS says the anemometer is going crazy. Gusting up to eighty knots. Still north-west. Temperature steady at ten below.' He shivered. 'Ten below!' Then looked consideringly at Tyndall. 'Barometer almost steady at 27.8.'

'What!'

'27.8. That's what they say. It's impossible, but that's what they say.' He glanced at his wrist-watch. 'Forty-five minutes, sir. . . . This is a very complicated way of committing suicide.'

They were silent for a minute, then Tyndall spoke for both of them, answering the question in both their minds.

'We must go, Dick. We must. And by the way, our fire-eating young Captain (D), the doughty Orr, wants to accompany us in the *Sirrus.* . . . We'll let him tag along a while. He has things to learn, that young man.'

At 2020 all ships had completed oiling. Hove to, they had had the utmost difficulty in keeping position in that great wind; but they were infinitely safer than in the open sea. They were given orders to proceed when the weather moderated, the *Defender* and escorts to Scapa, the squadron to a position 100 miles ENE of rendezvous. Radio silence was to be strictly observed.

At 2030 the *Ulysses* and *Sirrus* got under way to the East. Lights winked after them, messages of good luck. Fluently, Tyndall cursed the squadron for the breach of darken-ship regulations, realized that, barring themselves there was no one on God's earth to see the signals anyway, and ordered a courteous acknowledgment.

At 2045, still two miles short of Langanes point, the *Sirrus* was plunging desperately in mountainous seas, shipping great masses of water over her entire fo'c'sle and main deck, and, in the darkness, looking far less like a destroyer than a porpoising submarine.

At 2050, at reduced speed, she was observed to be moving in close to such slight shelter as the land afforded there. At the same time, her six-inch Aldis flashed her signal: 'Screen doors stove in: "A" turret not tracking: flooding port boiler-room intake fans.' And on the *Sirrus*'s bridge Commander Orr swore in chagrin as he received the *Ulysses*'s final message: 'Lesson without words, No. 1. Rejoin squadron at once. You can't come out to play with the big boys.' But he swallowed his disappointment, signalled: 'Wilco. Just you wait till I grow up,' pulled the *Sirrus* round in a madly swinging half-circle and headed thankfully back for shelter. Aboard the flagship, it was lost to sight almost immediately.

At 2100, the *Ulysses* moved out into the Denmark Strait.

—— 6 ——

TUESDAY NIGHT

It was the worst storm of the war. Beyond all doubt, had the records been preserved for Admiralty inspection, that would have proved to be incomparably the greatest storm, the most tremendous convulsion of nature since these recordings began. Living memory aboard the *Ulysses* that night, a vast accumulation of experience in every corner of the globe, could certainly recall nothing even remotely like it, nothing that would even begin to bear comparison as a parallel or precedent.

At ten o'clock, with all doors and hatches battened shut, with all traffic prohibited on the upper deck, with all crews withdrawn from gun-turrets and magazines and all normal deck watchkeeping stopped for the first time since her commissioning, even the taciturn Carrington admitted that the Caribbean hurricanes of the autumns of '34 and '37 – when he'd run out of sea-room, been forced to heave-to in the dangerous right-hand quadrant of both these murderous cyclones – had been no worse than this. But the two ships he had taken through these – a 3000-ton tramp and a superannuated tanker on the New York asphalt run – had not been in the same class for seaworthiness as the *Ulysses*. He had little doubt as to her ability to survive. But what the First Lieutenant did not know, what nobody had any means of guessing, was that this howling gale was still only the deadly overture. Like some mindless and dreadful beast from an ancient and other world, the Polar monster crouched on its own doorstep, waiting. At 2230, the *Ulysses* crossed the Arctic Circle. The monster struck.

It struck with a feral ferocity, with an appalling savagery that smashed minds and bodies into a stunned unknowingness. Its claws were hurtling rapiers of ice that slashed across a man's face and left it welling red: it's teeth were that sub-zero wind, gusting over 120 knots, that ripped and tore through the tissue paper of Arctic clothing and sunk home to the bone: its voice was the devil's orchestra, the roar of a great wind mingled with the banshee shrieking of tortured rigging, a requiem for fiends: its weight was the crushing power of the hurricane wind that pinned a man helplessly to a bulkhead, fighting for breath, or flung him off his feet to crash in some distant corner, broken-limbed and senseless. Baulked of prey in its 500-mile sweep across the frozen wastes of the Greenland ice-cap, it goaded the cruel sea into homicidal alliance and flung itself, titanic in its energy, ravenous in its howling, upon the cockleshell that was the *Ulysses*.

The *Ulysses* should have died then. Nothing built by man could ever have hoped to survive. She should just have been pressed under to destruction, or turned turtle, or had her back broken, or disintegrated under these mighty hammer-blows of wind and sea. But she did none of these things.

How she ever survived the insensate fury of that first attack, God only knew. The great wind caught her on the bow and flung her round in a $45°$ arc and pressed her far over on her side as she fell – literally fell – forty heart-stopping feet over and down the precipitous walls of a giant trough. She crashed into the valley with a tremendous concussion that jarred every plate, every Clyde-built rivet in her hull. The vibration lasted an eternity as overstressed metal fought to re-adjust itself, as steel compressed and stretched far beyond specified breaking loads Miraculously she held, but the sands were running out. She lay far over on her starboard side, the gunwales dipping: half a mile away, towering high above the mast-top, a great wall of water was roaring down on the helpless ship.

The 'Dude' saved the day. The 'Dude,' alternatively known as 'Persil,' but officially as Engineer-Commander Dodson, immaculately clad as usual in overalls of the most dazzling white, had been at his control position in the engine-room when that tremendous gust had struck. He had no means of knowing what had happened. He had no means of knowing that the ship was not under command, that no one on the bridge had as yet recovered from that first shattering impact: he had no means of knowing that the quarter-master had been thrown unconscious into a corner of the wheel-house, that his mate, almost a child in years. was too panic-stricken to dive for the madly-spinning wheel. But he did know that the *Ulysses* was listing crazily, almost broadside on, and he suspected the cause.

His shouts on the bridge tube brought no reply. He pointed to the port controls, roared 'Slow' in the ear of the Engineer WO – then leapt quickly for the starboard wheel.

Fifteen seconds later and it would have been too late. As it was, the accelerating starboard screw brought her round just far enough to take that roaring mountain of water under her bows, to dig her stern in to the level of the depth-charge rails, till forty feet of her airborne keel lay poised above the abyss below. When she plunged down, again that same shuddering vibration enveloped the entire hull. The fo'c'sle disappeared far below the surface, the sea flowing over and past the armoured side of 'A' turret. But she was bows on again. At once the 'Dude' signalled his WO for more revolutions, cut back the starboard engine.

Below decks, everything was an unspeakable shambles. On the mess-decks, steel lockers in their scores had broken adrift, been thrown in a dozen different directions, bursting hasps, and locks, spilling their contents everywhere. Hammocks had been catapulted from their racks, smashed crockery littered the decks: tables were twisted and smashed, broken stools stuck up at crazy angles, books, papers, teapots, kettles and crockery were scattered in insane profusion. And amidst this jumbled, sliding wreckage, hundreds of shouting, cursing, frightened and exhausted men struggled to their feet, or knelt, or sat, or just lay still.

Surgeon-Commander Brooks and Lieutenant Nicholls, with

an inspired, untiring padre as good as a third doctor, were worked off their feet. The veteran Leading SBA Johnson, oddly enough, was almost useless – he was violently sick much of the time, seemed to have lost all heart: no one knew why – it was just one of these things and he had taken all he could.

Men were brought in to the Sick Bay in their dozens, in their scores, a constant trek that continued all night long as the *Ulysses* fought for her life, a trek that soon overcrowded the meagre space available and turned the wardroom into an emergency hospital. Bruises, cuts, dislocations, concussions, fractures – the exhausted doctors experienced everything that night. Serious injuries were fortunately rare, and inside three hours there were only nine bed-patients in the Sick Bay, including AB Ferry, his already mangled arm smashed in two places – a bitterly protesting Riley and his fellow-mutineers had been unceremoniously turfed out to make room for the more seriously injured.

About 2330, Nicholls was called to treat the Kapok Kid. Lurching, falling and staggering in the wildly gyrating ship, he finally found the Navigator in his cabin. He looked very unhappy. Nicholls eyed him speculatively, saw the deep, ugly gash on his forehead, the swollen ankle peeping out below the Kapok Kid's Martian survival suit. Bad enough, but hardly a borderline case, although one wouldn't have thought so from the miserable, worried expression. Nicholls grinned inwardly.

'Well, Horatio,' he said unkindly, 'what's supposed to be the matter with you? Been drinking again?'

'It's my back, Johnny,' he muttered. He turned face-down on the bunk. 'Have a look at it, will you?'

Nicholl's expression changed. He moved forward, then stopped short.

'How the hell can I,' he demanded irritably, 'when you're wearing that damned ugly suit of yours?'

'That what I mean,' said the Kapok Kid anxiously. 'I was thrown against the searchlight controls – all knobs and nasty, sharp projections. Is it torn? Is it ripped, cut in any way? Are the seams—'

'Well, for God's sake! Do you mean to tell me—?' Nicholls sank back incredulously on a locker.

The Kapok Kid looked at him hopefully.

'Does that mean it's all right?'

'Of course it's all right! If it's a blasted tailor you want, why the hell—'

89

'Enough!' The Kapok Kid swung briskly on to the side of his bunk, lifting an admonitory hand. 'There is work for you, sawbones.' He touched his bleeding forehead. 'Stitch this up and waste no time about it. A man of my calibre is urgently needed on the bridge. . . . I'm the only man on this ship who has the faintest idea where we are.'

Busy with a swab. Nicholls grinned. 'And where are we?'

'I don't know,' said the Kapok Kid frankly. 'That's what's so urgent about it. . . . But I do know where I was! Back in Henley. Did I ever tell you . . . ?'

The *Ulysses* did not die. Time and again that night, hove to with the wind fine of her starboard bow, as her bows crashed into and under the far shoulder of a trough, it seemed that she could never shake free from the great press of water. But time and again she did just that, shuddering, quivering under the fantastic strain. A thousand times before dawn officers and men blessed the genius of the Clyde ship-yard that had made her: a thousand times they cursed the blind malevolence of that great storm that put the *Ulysses* on the rack.

Perhaps 'blind' was not the right word. The storm wielded its wild hate with an almost human cunning. Shortly after the first onslaught, the wind had veered quickly, incredibly so and in defiance of all the laws, back almost to the north again. The *Ulysses* was on a lee shore, forced to keep pounding into gigantic seas.

Gigantic – and cunning also. Roaring by the *Ulysses,* a huge comber would suddenly whip round and crash on deck, smashing a boat to smithereens. Inside an hour, the barge, motor-boat and two whalers were gone, their shattered timbers swept away in the boiling cauldron. Carley rafts were broken off by the sudden hammer-blows of the same cunning waves, swept over the side and gone for ever: four of the Balsa floats went the same way.

But the most cunning attack of all was made right aft on the poop-deck. At the height of the storm a series of heavy explosions, half a dozen in as many seconds, almost lifted the stern out of the water. Panic spread like wildfire in the after mess-decks: practically every light abaft the after engine-room smashed or failed. In the darkness of the mess-decks, above the clamour, high-pitched cries of 'Torpedoed!' 'Mined!' 'She's breaking up!' galvanised exhausted, injured men, even those – more than half – in various degrees of prostration from seasickness, into frantic stampeding towards doors and hatches, only to find doors and hatches jammed solidly by the intense cold. Here and there, the automatic battery lamps had clicked on when the lighting circuits failed: glowing little pin-points, they played on isolated groups of white, contorted faces, sunken-eyed and straining, as they struggled through the yellow pools of light. Conditions were ripe for disaster when a voice, harsh, mocking, cut cleanly through the bedlam. The voice was Ralston's: he had been released before nine o'clock, on the Captain's orders: the cells were in the very forepeak of the ship, and conditions there were impossible in a head sea: even so, Hastings had freed him only with the worst possible grace.

'It's our own depth charges! Do you hear me, you bloody fools – it's our own depth charges!' It was not so much the words as the biting mockery, that stopped short the panic, halted dazed, unthinking men in their tracks. 'They're *our* depth charges, I tell you! They must have been washed over the side!'

He was right. The entire contents of a rack had broken adrift, lifted from their cradles by some freak wave, and tumbled over the side. Through some oversight, they had been left set at their shallow setting – those put on for the midget submarine in Scapa – and had gone off almost directly under the ship. The damage, it seemed, was only minor.

Up in 'A' mess-deck, right for'ard, conditions were even worse. There was more wreckage on the decks and far more seasickness – not the green-faced, slightly ludicrous malaise of the cross-channel steamer, but tearing rendering conversions, dark and heavy with blood – for the bows had been rearing and plunging, rearing and plunging, thirty, forty, fifty feet at a time for end-less, hopeless hours; but there was an even more sinister agent at work, rapidly making the mess-deck untenable.

At the for'ard end of the capstan flat, which adjoined the mess-deck, was the battery-room. In here were stored, or on charge a hundred and one different batteries, ranging from the heavy lead-acid batteries weighing over a hundred pounds to the tiny nickel-calmium cells for the emergency lighting. Here, too, were stored earthenware jars of prepared acid and big, glass carboys of undiluted sulphuric. These last were permanently stored: in heavy weather, the big batteries were lashed down.

No one knew what had happened. It seemed likely – certain, indeed – that acid spilt from the batteries by the tremendous pitching had eaten through the lashings. Then a battery must have broken loose and smashed another, and another, and

another, and then the jars and carboys until the entire floor –
fortunately of acid-resisting material – was awash to a depth of
five or six inches in sulphuric acid.

A young torpedoman, on a routine check, had opened the
door and seen the splashing sea of acid inside. Panicking, and
recalling vaguely that caustic soda, stored in quantities just outside, was a neutraliser for sulphuric, he had emptied a forty-
pound carton of it into the battery-room: he was in the Sick
Bay now, blinded. The acid fumes saturated the capstan flat,
making entry impossible without breathing equipment, and was
seeping back, slowly, insidiously, into the mess-deck: more
deadly still hundreds of gallons of salt water from sprung deck-
plates and broken capstan speaking tubes were surging crazily
around the flat: already the air was tainted with the first traces
of chlorine gas. On the deck immediately above, Hartley and
two seamen, belayed with ropes, had made a brief, hopelessly
gallant attempt to plug the gaping holes: all three, battered
into near senselessness by the great waves pounding the fo'c'sle,
were dragged off within a minute.

For the men below, it was discomfort, danger and desperate
physical illness: for the bare handful of men above, the officers
and ratings on the bridge, it was pure undiluted hell. But a hell
not of our latter-day imagining, a strictly Eastern and Biblical
conception, but the hell of our ancient North-European ancestors, of the Vikings, the Danes, the Jutes, of Beowulf and the
monster-haunted meres – the hell of eternal cold.

True, the temperature registered a mere 10° below zero –
42° of frost. Men have been known to live, even to work in the
open, at far lower temperatures. What is not so well known,
what is barely realized at all, is that when freezing point has
been passed, every extra mile per hour of wind is *equivalent*,
in terms of pure cold as it reacts on a human being, to a 1° drop
in temperature. Not once, but several times that night, before
it had finally raced itself to destruction, the anemometer had
recorded gusts of over 125 mph, wave-flattening gusts that
sundered stays and all but tore the funnels off. For minutes on
end, the shrieking, screaming wind held steady at 100 mph and
above – the total equivalent, for these numbed, paralysed
creatures on the bridge, of something well below a 100° below
zero.

Five minutes at a time was enough for any man on the bridge,
then he had to retire to the Captain's shelter. Not that manning
the bridge was more than a gesture anyway – it was impossible

to look into that terrible wind: the cold would have seared the eyeballs blind, the ice would have gouged them out. And it was impossible even to see through the Kent Clear-view windscreens. They still spun at high speed, but uselessly: the ice-laden storm, a gigantic sandblaster, had starred and abraded the plate glass until it was completely opaque.

It was not a dark night. It was possible to see above, abeam and astern. Above, patches of night-blue sky and handfuls of stars could be seen at fleeting intervals, obscured as soon as seen by the scudding, shredded cloud-wrack. Abeam and astern, the sea was an inky black, laced with boiling white. Gone now were the serried ranks of yesterday, gone, too, the decorative white-caps: here now were only massive mountains of water, broken and confused, breaking this way and that, but always tending south. Some of these moving ranges of water – by no stretch of the imagination, only by proxy, could they be called waves – were small, insignificant – in size of a suburban house: others held a million tons of water, towered seventy to eighty feet, looming terrifyingly against the horizon, big enough to drown a cathedral. . . . As the Kajok Kid remarked, the best thing to do with these waves was to look the other way. More often than not, they passed harmlessly by, plunging the *Ulysses* into the depths: rarely, they curled over and broke their tops into the bridge, soaking the unfortunate Officer of the Watch. He had then to be removed at once or he would literally have frozen solid within a minute.

So far they had survived, far beyond the expectation of any man. But, as they were blind ahead, there was always the worry of what would come next. Would the next sea be normal – for that storm, that was – or some nameless juggernaut that would push them under for ever? The suspense never lifted, a suspense doubled by the fact that when the *Ulysses* reared and crashed down, it did so soundlessly, sightlessly. They could judge its intensity only by movement and vibration: the sound of the sea, everything, was drowned in the Satanic cacophony of that howling wind in the upper works and rigging.

About two in the morning – it was just after the depth-charge explosions – some of the senior officers had staged their own private mutiny. The Captain, who had been persuaded to go below less than an hour previously, exhausted and shaking un-controllably with cold, had been wakened by the depth-charging and had returned to the bridge. He found his way barred by the

93

Commander and Commander Westcliffe, who bundled him quietly but firmly into the shelter. Turner heaved the door to, switched on the light. Vallery was more puzzled than angry.

'What – what in the world does this mean?' he demanded.

'Mutiny!' boomed Turner happily. His face was covered in blood from flying splinters of ice. 'On the High Seas, is the technical term, I believe. Isn't that so, Admiral?'

'Exactly,' the Admiral agreed. Vallery swung round, startled: Tyndall was lying in state on the bunk. 'Mind you, I've no jurisdiction over a Captain in his own ship; but I can't see a thing.' He lay back on the bunk, eyes elaborately closed in seeming exhaustion. Only Tyndall knew that he wasn't pretending.

Vallery said nothing. He stood there clutching a handrail, his face grey and haggard, his eyes blood-red and drugged with sleep. Turner felt a knife twist inside him as he looked at him. When he spoke, his voice was low and earnest, so unusual for him that he caught and held Vallery's attention.

'Sir, this is no night for a naval captain. Danger from any quarter except the sea itself just doesn't exist. Agreed?'

Vallery nodded silently.

'It's a night for a seaman, sir. With all respect, I suggest that neither of us is in the class of Carrington – he's just a different breed of man.'

'Nice of you to include yourself, Commander,' Vallery murmured. 'And quite unnecessary.'

'The first Lieutenant will remain on the bridge all night. So will Westcliffe here. So will I.'

'Me, too,' grunted Tyndall. 'But I'm going to sleep.' He looked almost as tired, as haggard as Vallery.

Turner grinned. 'Thank you, sir. Well, Captain, I'm afraid it's going to be a bit overcrowded here tonight. . . . We'll see you after breakfast.'

'But—'

'But me no buts,' Westcliffe murmured.

'Please,' Turner insisted. 'You will do us a favour.'

Vallery looked at him. 'As Captain of the *Ulysses* . . .' His voice tailed off. 'I don't know what to say.'

'I do,' said Turner briskly, his hand on Vallery's elbow. 'Let's go below.'

'Don't think I can manage by myself, eh?' Vallery smiled faintly.

'I do. But I'm taking no chances. Come along, sir.'

'All right, all right.' He sighed tiredly. 'Anything for a quiet life . . . and a night's sleep!'

Reluctantly, with a great effort, Lieutenant Nicholls dragged himself up from the mist-fogged depths of exhausted sleep. Slowly, reluctantly, he opened his eyes. The *Ulysses*, he realized, was still rolling as heavily, plunging as sickeningly as ever. The Kapok Kid, forehead swathed in bandages, the rest of his face pocked with blood, was bending over him. He looked disgustingly cheerful.

'Hark, hark, the lark, etcetera,' the Kapok Kid grinned. 'And how are we this morning?' he mimicked unctuously. The Hon. Carpenter held the medical profession in low esteem.

Nicholls focused blurred eyes on him.

'What's the matter, Andy? Anything wrong?'

'With Messrs. Carrington and Carpenter in charge,' said the Kapok Kid loftily, 'nothing could be wrong. Want to come up top, see Carrington do his stuff? He's going to turn the ship round. In this little lot, it should be worth seeing!'

'What! Dammit to hell! Have you woken me just—'

'Brother, when this ship turns, you would wake up anyway – probably on the deck with a broken neck. But as it so happens, Jimmy requires your assistance. At least, he requires one of these heavy plate-glass squares which I happen to know you have in great numbers in the dispensary. But the dispensary's locked – I tried it,' he added shamelessly.

'But what – I mean – plate glass—'

'Come and see for yourself,' the Kapok Kid invited.

It was dawn now, a wild and terrible dawn, fit epilogue for a nightmare. Strange, trailing bands of misty-white vapour swept by barely at mast-top level, but high above the sky was clear. The seas, still gigantic, were shorter now, much shorter, and even steeper: the *Ulysses* was slowed right down, with barely enough steerage way to keep her head up – and even then, taking severe punishment in the precipitous head seas. The wind had dropped to a steady fifty knots – gale force: even at that, it seared like fire in Nicholls's lungs as he stepped out on the flap-deck, blinded him with ice and cold. Hastily he wrapped scarves over his entire face, clambered up to the bridge by touch and instinct. The Kapok Kid followed with the glass. As they climbed, they heard the loudspeakers crackling some unintelligible message.

Turner and Carrington were alone on the twilit bridge,

swathed like mummies. Not even their eyes were visible – they wore goggles.

' 'Morning, Nicholls,' boomed the Commander. 'It *is* Nicholls, isn't it?' He pulled off his goggles, his back turned to the bitter wind, threw them away in disgust. 'Can't see damn' all through these bloody things . . . Ah, Number One, he's got the glass.'

Nicholls crouched in the for'ard lee of the compass platform. In a corner, the duckboards were littered with goggles, eye shields and gas-masks. He jerked his head towards them.

'What's this – a clearance sale?'

'We're turning, Doc.' It was Carrington who answered, his voice calm and precise as ever, without a trace of exhaustion. 'But we've got to see where we're going, and as the Commander says, all these damn' things there are useless – mist up immediately they're put on – it's too cold. If you'll just hold it – so – and if you would wipe it, Andy?'

Nicholls looked at the great seas. He shuddered.

'Excuse my ignorance, but why turn round at all?'

'Because it will be impossible very shortly,' Carrington answered briefly. Then he chuckled. 'This is going to make me the most unpopular man in the ship. We've just broadcast a warning. Ready, sir?'

'Stand by, engine-room: stand by, wheelhouse. Ready, Number One.'

For thirty seconds, forty-five, a whole minute, Carrington stared steadily, unblinkingly through the glass. Nicholls's hands froze. The Kapok Kid rubbed industriously. Then:

'Half-ahead, port!'

'Half-ahead, port!' Turner echoed.

'Starboard 20!'

'Starboard 20!'

Nicholls risked a glance over his shoulder. In the split second before his eyes blinded, filled with tears, he saw a huge wave bearing down on them, the bows already swinging diagonally away from it. Good God! Why hadn't Carrington waited until that was past?

The great wave flung the bows up, pushed the *Ulysses* far over to starboard, then passed under. The *Ulysses* staggered over the top, corkscrewed wickedly down the other side, her masts, great gleaming tree trunks thick and heavy with ice, swinging in a great arc as she rolled over, burying her port rails in the rising shoulder of the next sea.

'Full ahead port!'

'Full ahead port!'
'Starboard 30!'
'Starboard 30!'

The next sea, passing beneath, merely straightened the *Ulysses* up. And then, at last, Nicholls understood. Incredibly, because it had been impossible to see so far ahead, Carrington had known that two opposing wave systems were due to interlock in an area of comparative calm: how he had sensed it, no one knew, would ever know, not even Carrington himself: but he was a great seaman, and he had known. For fifteen, twenty seconds, the sea was a seething white mass of violently disturbed, conflicting waves – of the type usually found, on a small scale, in tidal races and overfalls – and the *Ulysses* curved gratefully through. And then another great sea, towering almost to bridge height, caught her on the far turn of the quarter circle. It struck the entire length·of the *Ulysses* – for the first time that night – with tremendous weight. It threw her far over on her side, the lee rails vanishing. Nicholls was flung off his feet, crashed heavily into the side of the bridge, the glass shattering. He could have sworn he heard Carrington laughing. He clawed his way back to the middle of the compass platform.

And still the great wave had not passed. It towered high above the trough into which the *Ulysses*, now heeled far over to 40°, had been so contemptuously flung, bore down remorselessly from above and sought, in a lethal silence and with an almost animistic savagery, to press her under. The inclinometer swung relentlessly over – 45°, 50°, 53°, and hung there an eternity, while men stood on the side of the ship, braced with their hands on the deck, numbed minds barely grasping the inevitable. This was the end. The *Ulysses* could never come back.

A lifetime ticked agonisingly by. Nicholls and Carpenter looked at each other, blank-faced, expressionless. Tilted at that crazy angle, the bridge was sheltered from the wind. Carrington's voice, calm, conversational, carried with amazing clarity.

'She'd go to 65° and still come back,' he said matter-of-factly. 'Hang on to your hats, gentlemen. This is going to be interesting.'

Just as he finished, the *Ulysses* shuddered, then imperceptibly, then slowly, then with vicious speed lurched back and whipped through an arc of 90°, then back again. Once more Nicholls found himself in the corner of the bridge. But the *Ulysses* was almost round.

The Kapok Kid, grinning with relief, picked himself up and tapped Carrington on the shoulder.

'Don't look now, sir, but we have lost our mainmast.'

It was a slight exaggeration, but the top fifteen feet, which had carried the after radar scanner, were undoubtedly gone. That wicked, double whip-lash, with the weight of the ice, had been too much.

'Slow ahead both! Midships!'

'Slow ahead both! Midships!'

'Steady as she goes!'

The *Ulysses* was round.

The Kapok Kid caught Nicholls's eye, nodded at the First Lieutenant.

'See what I mean, Johnny?'

'Yes.' Nicholls was very quiet. 'Yes, I see what you mean.' Then he grinned suddenly. 'Next time you make a statement, I'll just take your word for it, if you don't mind. These demonstrations of proof take too damn' much out of a person!'

Running straight before the heavy stern sea, the *Ulysses* was amazingly steady. The wind, too, was dead astern now, the bridge in magical shelter. The scudding mist overhead had thinned out, was almost gone. Far away to the south-east a dazzling white sun climbed up above a cloudless horizon. The long night was over.

An hour later, with the wind down to thirty knots, radar reported contacts to the west. After another hour, with the wind almost gone and only a heavy swell running, smoke plumes tufted above the horizon. At 1030, in position, on time, the *Ulysses* rendezvoused with the convoy from Halifax.

7

WEDNESDAY NIGHT

The convoy came steadily up from the west, rolling heavily in cross seas, a rich argosy, a magnificent prize for any German wolf-pack. Eighteen ships in this argosy, fifteen big, modern cargo ships, three 16,000-ton tankers, carrying a freight far more valuable, infinitely more vital, than any fleet of quinqueremes or galleons had ever known. Tanks, planes and petrol – what were gold and jewels, silks and the rarest of spices compared to these? £10,000,000, £20,000,000 – the total worth of that convoy was difficult to estimate: in any event, its real value was not to be measured in terms of money.

Aboard the merchant ships, crews lined the decks as the *Ulysses* steamed up between the port and centre lines. Lined the decks and looked and wondered – and thanked their Maker they had been wide of the path of that great storm. The *Ulysses,* seen from another deck, was a strange sight: broken-masted, stripped of her rafts, with her boat falls hauled taut over empty cradles, she glistened like crystal in the morning light: the great wind had blown away all snow, had abraded and rubbed and polished the ice to a satin-smooth, transparent gloss: but on either side of the bows and before the bridge were huge patches of crimson, where the hurricane sand-blaster of that long night had stripped off camouflage and base coats, exposing the red lead below.

The American escort was small – a heavy cruiser with a sea plane for spotting, two destroyers and two near-frigates of the coastguard type. Small, but sufficient: there was no need of escort carriers (although these frequently sailed with the Atlantic convoys) because the Luftwaffe could not operate so far west, and the wolf-packs, in recent months, had moved north and east of Iceland: there, they were not only nearer base – they could more easily lie astride the converging convoy routes to Murmansk.

ENE they sailed in company, freighters, American warships and the *Ulysses* until, late in the afternoon, the box like silhouette of an escort carrier bulked high against the horizon. Half an hour later, at 1600, the American escorts slowed, dropped astern and turned, winking farewell messages of good luck. Aboard the *Ulysses,* men watched them depart with mixed feelings. They knew these ships had to go, that another convoy would already be mustering off the St Lawrence. There was none of the envy, the bitterness one might expect – and had indeed been common enough only a few weeks ago – among these exhausted men who carried the brunt of the war. There was instead a careless acceptance of things as they were, a quasi-cynical bravado, often a queer, high nameless pride that hid itself beneath twisted jests and endless grumbling.

The 14th Aircraft Carrier Squadron – or what was left of it – was only two miles away now. Tyndall, coming to the bridge, swore fluently as he saw that a carrier and mine-sweeper were missing. An angry signal went out to Captain Jeffries of the

Stirling, asking why orders had been disobeyed, where the missing ships were.

An Aldis flickered back its reply. Tyndall sat grim-faced and silent as Bentley read out the signal to him. The *Wrestler's* steering gear had broken down during the night. Even behind Langanes the weather position had been severe, had worsened about midnight when the wind had veered to the north. The *Wrestler,* even with two screws, had lost almost all steering command, and, in zero visibility and an effort to maintain position, had gone too far ahead and grounded on the Vejle bank. She had grounded on the top of the tide. She had still been there, with the minesweeper *Eager* in attendance, when the squadron had sailed shortly after dawn.

Tyndall sat in silence for some minutes. He dictated a WT signal to the *Wrestler,* hesitated about breaking radio silence, countermanded the signal, and decided to go to see for himself. After all, it was only three hours' steaming distance. He signalled the *Stirling*: 'Take over squadron command: will re-join in the morning,' and ordered Vallery to take the *Ulysses* back to Langanes.

Vallery nodded unhappily, gave the necessary orders. He was worried, badly so, was trying hard not to show it. The least of his worries was himself, although he knew, but never admitted to anyone, that he was a very sick man. He thought wryly that he didn't have to admit it anyway – he was amused and touched by the elaborate casualness with which his officers sought to lighen his load, to show their concern for him.

He was worried, too, about his crew – they were in no fit state to do the lightest work, to survive that killing cold, far less sail the ship and fight her through to Russia. He was depressed, also, over the series of misfortunes that had befallen the squadron since leaving Scapa: it augured ill for the future, and he had no illusions as to what lay ahead for the crippled squadron. And always, a gnawing torment at the back of his mind, he worried about Ralston.

Ralston – that tall throwback to his Scandinavian ancestors, with his flaxen hair and still blue eyes. Ralston, whom nobody understood, with whom nobody on the ship had an intimate friendship, who went his own unsmiling, self-possessed way. Ralston, who had nothing left to fight for, except memories, who was one of the most reliable men in the *Ulysses,* extra-ordinarily decisive, competent and resourceful in any emerg-ency – and who again found himself under lock and key. And for nothing that any reasonable and just man could call fault of his own.

Under lock and key – that was what hurt. Last night, Vallery had gladly seized the excuse of bad weather to release him, had intended to forget the matter, to let sleeping dogs lie. But Hastings, the Master-At-Arms, had exceeded his duty and returned him to cells during the forenoon watch. Masters-At-Arms – disciplinary Warrant Officers, in effect – had never been particularly noted for a humane, tolerant and ultra-kindly attitude to life in general or the lower deck in particular – they couldn't afford to be. But even amongst such men, Hastings was an exception – a machine-like seemingly emotionless creature, expressionless, unbending, strict, fair according to his lights, but utterly devoid of heart and sympathy. If Hastings were not careful, Vallery mused, he might very well go the same way as Lister, until recently the highly unpopular Master-At-Arms of the *Blue Ranger*. Not, when he came to think of it, that anyone knew what had happened to Lister, except that he had been so misguided as to take a walk on the flight-deck on a dark and starless night. . . .

Vallery sighed. As he had explained to Foster, his hands were tied. Foster, the Captain of Marines, with an aggrieved and incensed Colour-Sergeant Evans standing behind him, had complained bitterly at having his marines withdrawn for guard duty, men who needed every minute of sleep they could snatch. Privately, Vallery had sympathised with Foster, but he couldn't afford to countermand his original order – not, at least, until he had held a Captain's Defaulters and placed Ralston under open arrest. . . . He sighed again, sent for Turner and asked him to break out grass lines, a manila and a five-inch wire on the poop. He suspected that they would be needed shortly, and, as it turned out, his preparations were justified.

Darkness had fallen when they moved up to the Vejle bank, but locating the *Wrestler* was easy – her identification challenge ten minutes ago had given her approximate position, and now her squat bulk loomed high before them, a knife-edged silhouette against the pale afterglow of sunset. Ominously, her flight-deck raked perceptibly towards the stern, where the *Eager* lay, apparently at anchor. The sea was almost calm here – there was only a gentle swell running.

Aboard the *Ulysses*, a hooded, pin-hole Aldis started to chatter.

'Congratulations! How are you fast?'

From the *Wrestler*, a tiny light flickered in answer. Bentley read aloud as the message came.

'Bows aft 100 feet.'

'Wonderful,' said Tyndall bitterly. 'Just wonderful! Ask him, "How is steering-gear?" '

Back came the answer: 'Diver down: transverse fracture of post: dockyard job.'

'My God!' Tyndall groaned. 'A dockyard job! That's handy. Ask him, "What steps have you taken?" '

'All fuel and water pumped aft. Kedge anchor. *Eager* towing. Full astern, 1200–1230.'

The turn of the high tide, Tyndall knew. 'Very successful, very successful indeed,' he growled. 'No, you bloody fool, don't send that. Tell him to prepare to receive towing wire, bring own towing chain aft.'

'Message understood,' Bentley read.

'Ask him, "How much excess squadron fuel have you?" '

'800 tons.'

'Get rid of it.'

Bentley read, 'Please confirm.'

'Tell him to empty the bloody stuff over the side!' Tyndall roared.

The light on the *Wrestler* flickered and died in hurt silence.

At midnight the *Eager* steamed slowly ahead of the *Ulysses*, taking up the wire that led back to the cruiser's fo'c'sle capstan: two minutes later, the *Ulysses* began to shudder as the four great engines boiled up the shallow water into a seething mud-stained cauldron. The chain from the poop-deck to the *Wrestler*'s stern was a bare fifteen fathoms in length, angling up at 30°. This would force the carrier's stern down – only a fraction, but in this situation every ounce counted – and give more positive buoyancy to the grounded bows. And much more important – for the racing screws were now aerating the water, developing only a fraction of their potential thrust – the proximity of the two ships helped the *Ulysses*'s screws reinforce the action of the *Wrestler*'s in scouring out a channel in the sand and mud beneath the carrier's keel.

Twenty minutes before high tide, easily, steadily, the *Wrestler* slid off. At once the blacksmith on the *Ulysses*'s bows knocked off the shackle securing the *Eager*'s towing wire, and the *Ulysses* pulled the carrier, her engines shut down, in a big half-circle to the east.

By one o'clock the *Wrestler* was gone, the *Eager* in attendance and ready to pass a head rope for bad weather steering. On the bridge of the *Ulysses,* Tyndall watched the carrier vanish into the night, zig-zagging as the captain tried to balance the steering on the two screws.

'No doubt they'll get the hang of it before they get to Scapa,' he growled. He felt cold, exhausted and only the way an Admiral can feel when he has lost three-quarters of his carrier force. He sighed wearily and turned to Vallery.

'When do you reckon we'll overtake the convoy?'

Vallery hesitated: not so the Kapok Kid.

'0805,' he answered readily and precisely. 'At twenty-seven knots, on the intersection course I've just pencilled out.'

'Oh, my God!' Tyndall groaned. 'That stripling again. What did I ever do to deserve him. As it happens, young man, it's imperative that we overtake before dawn.'

'Yes, sir.' The Kapok Kid was imperturbable. 'I thought so myself. On my alternative course, 33 knots, thirty minutes before dawn.'

'I thought so myself! Take him away!' Tyndall raved. 'Take him away or I'll wrap his damned dividers round . . .' He broke off, climbed stiffly out of his chair, took Vallery by the arm. 'Come on, Captain. Let's go below. What the hell's the use of a couple of ancient has-beens like us getting in the way of youth?' He passed out the gate behind the Captain, grinning tiredly to himself.

The *Ulysses* was at dawn Action Stations as the shadowy shapes of the convoy, a bare mile ahead, lifted out of the greying gloom. The great bulk of the *Blue Ranger,* on the starboard quarter of the convoy, was unmistakable. There was a moderate swell running, but not enough to be uncomfortable: the breeze was light, from the west, the temperature just below zero, the sky chill and cloudless. The time was exactly 0700.

At 0702, the *Blue Ranger* was torpedoed. The *Ulysses* was two cable-lengths away, on her starboard quarter: those on the bridge felt the physical shock of the twin explosions, heard them shattering the stillness of the dawn as they saw two searing columns of flame fingering skywards, high above the *Blue Ranger*'s bridge and well aft of it. A second later they heard a signalman shouting something unintelligible, saw him pointing forwards and downwards. It was another torpedo, running astern of the carrier, trailing its evil phosphorescent wake across the heels of the convoy, before spending itself in the darkness of the Arctic.

Vallery was shouting down the voice-pipe, pulling round the *Ulysses*, still doing upwards of twenty knots, in a madly heeling, skidding turn, to avoid collision with the slewing carrier. Three sets of Aldis lamps and the fighting lights were already stuttering out the 'Maintain Position' code signal to ships in the convoy. Marshall, on the phone, was giving the stand-by order to the depth-charge LTO: gun barrels were already depressing, peering hungrily into the treacherous sea. The signal to the *Sirrus* stopped short, unneeded: the destroyer, a half-seen blue in the darkness, was already knifing its way through the convoy, white water piled high at its bows, headed for the estimated position of the U-boat.

The *Ulysses* sheered by parallel to the burning carrier, less than 150 feet away; travelling so fast, heeling so heavily and at such close range, it was impossible to gather more than a blurred impression, a tangled, confused memory of heavy black smoke laced with roaring columns of flame, appalling in that near-darkness, of a drunkenly listing flight-deck, of Grummans and Corsairs cartwheeling grotesquely over the edge to splash icy clouds of spray in shocked faces, as the cruiser slewed away; and then the *Ulysses* was round, heading back south for the kill.

Within a minute, the signal-lamp of the *Vectra*, up front with the convoy, started winking. 'Contact, Green 70, closing: Contact, Green 70, closing.'

'Acknowledge,' Tyndall ordered briefly.

The Aldis had barely begun to clack when the *Vectra* cut through the signal.

'Contacts, repeat contacts. Green 90, Green 90. Closing. Very close. Repeat contacts, contacts.'

Tyndall cursed softly.

'Acknowledge. Investigate.' He turned to Vallery. 'Let's join him, Captain. This is it. Wolf-pack Number One – and in force. No bloody right to be here,' he added bitterly. 'So much for Admiralty Intelligence!'

The *Ulysses* was round again, heading for the *Vectra*. It should have been growing lighter now, but the *Blue Ranger*, her squadron fuel tanks on fire, a gigantic torch against the eastern horizon, had the curious effect of throwing the surrounding sea into heavy darkness. She lay almost athwart of the flagship's course for the *Vectra*, looming larger every minute.

Tyndall had his night glasses to his eyes, kept on muttering: 'The poor bastards, the poor bastards!'

The *Blue Ranger* was almost gone. She lay dead in the water, heeled far over to starboard, ammunition and petrol tanks going up in a constant series of crackling reports. Suddenly, a succession of dull, heavy explosions rumbled over the sea: the entire bridge island structure lurched crazily sideways, held, then slowly, ponderously, deliberately, the whole massive body of it toppled majestically into the glacial darkness of the sea. God only knew how many men perished with it, deep down in the Arctic, trapped in its iron walls. They were the lucky ones.

The *Vectra*, barely two miles ahead now, was pulling round south in a tight circle. Vallery saw her, altered course to intercept. He heard Bentley shouting something unintelligible from the fore corner of the compass platform. Vallery shook his head, heard him shouting again, his voice desperate with some nameless urgency, his arm pointing frantically over the windscreen, and leapt up beside him.

The sea was on fire. Flat, calm, burdened with hundreds of tons of fuel oil, it was a vast carpet of licking, twisting flames. That much, for a second, and that only, Vallery saw: then with heart-stopping shock, with physically sickening abruptness, he saw something else again: the burning sea was alive with swimming, struggling men. Not a handful, not even dozens, but literally hundreds, soundlessly screaming, agonisingly dying in the barbarous contrariety of drowning and cremation.

'Signal from *Vectra*, sir.' It was Bentley speaking, his voice abnormally matter-of-fact. ' "Depth-charging. 3, repeat 3 contacts. Request immediate assistance." '

Tyndall was at Vallery's side now. He heard Bentley, looked a long second at Vallery, following his sick, fascinated gaze into the sea ahead.

For a man in the sea, oil is an evil thing. It clogs his movements, burns his eyes, sears his lungs and tears away his stomach in uncontrollable paroxysms of retching; but oil on fire is a hellish thing, death by torture, a slow, shrieking death by drowning, by burning, by asphyxiation – for the flames devour all the life-giving oxygen on the surface of the sea. And not even in the bitter Arctic is there the merciful extinction by cold, for the insulation of an oil-soaked body stretches a dying man on the rack for eternity, carefully preserves him for the last excruciating refinement of agony. All this Vallery knew.

He knew, too, that for the *Ulysses* to stop, starkly outlined against the burning carrier, would have been suicide. And to come sharply round to starboard, even had there been time and room to clear the struggling, dying men in the sea ahead, would have wasted invaluable minutes, time and to spare for the U-boats ahead to line up firing-tracks on the convoy; and the *Ulysses*'s first responsibility was to the convoy. Again all this Vallery knew. But, at that moment, what weighed most heavily with him was common humanity. Fine off the port bow, close in to the *Blue Ranger,* the oil was heaviest, the flames fiercest, the swimmers thickest: Vallery looked back over his shoulder at the Officer of the Watch.

'Port 10!'

'Port 10, sir.'

'Midships!'

'Midships, sir.'

'Steady as she goes!'

For ten, fifteen seconds the *Ulysses* held her course, arrowing through the burning sea to the spot where some gregariously atavistic instinct for self-preservation held two hundred men knotted together in a writhing, seething mass, gasping out their lives in hideous agony. For a second a great gout of flame leapt up in the centre of the group, like a giant, incandescent magnesium flare, a flame that burnt the picture into the hearts and minds of the men on the bridge with a permanence and searing clarity that no photographic plate could ever have reproduced: men on fire, human torches beating insanely at the flames that licked, scorched and then incinerated clothes, hair and skin: men flinging themselves almost out of the water, backs arched like tautened bows, grotesque in convulsive crucifixion: men lying dead in the water, insignificant, featureless little oil-stained mounds in an oil-soaked plain: and a handful of fear-maddened men, faces inhumanly contorted, who saw the *Ulysses* and knew what was coming, as they frantically thrashed their way to a safety that offered only a few more brief seconds of unspeakable agony before they gladly died.

'Starboard 30!' Vallery's voice was low, barely a murmur, but it carried clearly through the shocked silence on the bridge.

'Starboard 30, sir.'

For the third time in ten minutes, the *Ulysses* slewed crazily round in a racing turn. Turning thus, a ship does not follow through the line of the bows cutting the water; there is a pronounced sideways or lateral motion, and the faster and sharper the turn, the more violent the broadside skidding motion, like a car on ice. The side of the *Ulysses,* still at an acute angle, caught the edge of the group on the port bow: almost on the instant, the entire length of the swinging hull smashed into the heart of the fire, into the thickest press of dying men.

For most of them, it was just extinction, swift and glad and merciful. The tremendous concussion and pressure waves crushed the life out of them, thrust them deep down into the blessed oblivion of drowning, thrust them down and sucked them back into the thrashing vortex of the four great screws. . . .

On board the *Ulysses,* men for whom death and destruction had become the stuff of existence, to be accepted with the callousness and jesting indifference that alone kept them sane – these men clenched impotent fists, mouthed meaningless, useless curses over and over again and wept heedlessly like little children. They wept as pitiful, charred faces, turned up towards the *Ulysses* and alight with joy and hope, petrified into incredulous staring horror, as realization dawned and the water closed over them; as hate-filled men screamed insane invective, both arms raised aloft, shaking fists white-knuckled through the dripping oil as the *Ulysses* trampled them under: as a couple of young boys were sucked into the mælstrom of the propellors, still giving the thumbs-up sign: as a particularly shocking case, who looked as if he had been barbecued on a spit and had no right to be alive, lifted a scorified hand to the blackened hole that had been his mouth, flung to the bridge a kiss in token of endless gatitude; and wept, oddly, most of all, at the inevitable humorist who lifted his fur cap high above his head and bowed gravely and deeply, his face into the water as he died.

Suddenly, mercifully, the sea was empty. The air was strangely still and quiet, heavy with the sickening stench of charred flesh and burning Diesel, and the *Ulysses's* stern was swinging wildly almost under the black pall overhanging the *Blue Ranger* amidships, when the shells struck her.

The shells – three 3.7s – came from the *Blue Ranger.* Certainly, no living gun-crews manned these 3.7s – the heat must have ignited the bridge fuses in the cartridge cases. The first shell exploded harmlessly against the armour-plating: the second wrecked the bosun's store, fortunately empty: the third penetrated No. 3 Low Power Room via the deck. There were nine men in there – an officer, seven ratings and Chief-Torpedo

Gunner's Mate Noyes. In that confined space, death was instantaneous.

Only seconds later a heavy rumbling explosion blew out a great hole along the waterline of the *Blue Ranger* and she fell slowly, wearily right over on her starboard side, her flight-deck vertical to the water, as if content to die now that, dying, she had lashed out at the ship that had destroyed her crew.

On the bridge, Vallery still stood on the yeoman's platform, leaning over the starred, opaque windscreen. His head hung down, his eyes were shut and he was retching desperately, the gushing blood – arterial blood – ominously bright and scarlet in the erubescent glare of the sinking carrier. Tyndall stood there helplessly beside him, not knowing what to do, his mind numbed and sick. Suddenly, he was brushed unceremoniously aside by the Surgeon-Commander, who pushed a white towel to Vallery's mouth and led him gently below. Old Brooks, everyone knew, should have been at his Action Stations position in the Sick Bay: no one dared say anything.

Carrington straightened the *Ulysses* out on course, while he waited for Turner to move up from the after Director tower to take over the bridge. In three minutes the cruiser was up with the *Vectra*, methodically quartering for a lost contact. Twice the ships regained contact, twice they dropped heavy patterns. A heavy oil slick rose to the surface: possibly a kill, probably a ruse, but in any event, neither ship could remain to investigate further. The convoy was two miles ahead now, and only the *Stirling* and *Viking* were there for its protection – a wholly inadequate cover and powerless to save the convoy from any determined attack.

It was the *Blue Ranger* that saved FR77. In these high latitudes, dawn comes slowly, interminably: even so, it was more than half-light, and the merchant ships, line ahead through that very gentle swell, lifted clear and sharp against a cloudless horizon, a U-boat Commander's dream – or would have been, had he been able to see them. But, by this time, the convoy was completely obscured from the wolf-pack lying to the south: the light westerly wind carried the heavy black smoke from the blazing carrier along the southern flank of the convoy, at sea level, the perfect smoke-screen, dense, impenetrable. Why the U-boats had departed from their almost invariable practice of launching dawn attacks from the north, so as to have their targets between themselves and the sunrise, could only be guessed. Tactical surprise, probably, but whatever the reason it was the saving of the convoy. Within an hour, the thrashing screws of the convoy had left the wolf-pack far behind – and FR 77, having slipped the pack, was far too fast to be overtaken again.

Aboard the flagship, the WT transmitter was chattering out a coded signal to London. There was little point, Tyndall had decided, in maintaining radio silence now; the enemy knew their position to a mile. Tyndall smiled grimly as he thought of the rejoicing in the German Naval High Command at the news that FR77 was without any air cover whatsoever; as a starter, they could expect Charlie within the hour.

The signal read: 'Admiral, 14 ACS: To DNC, London. Rendezvoused FR77 1030 yesterday. Weather conditions extreme. Severe damage to Carriers: *Defender*, *Wrestler* unserviceable, returning base under escort: *Blue Ranger* torpedoed 0702, sunk 0730 today: Convoy Escorts now *Ulysses*, *Stirling*, *Sirrus*, *Vectra*, *Viking*: no minesweepers – *Eager* to base, minesweeper from Hvalfjord failed rendezvous: Urgently require air support: Can you detach carrier battle squadron: Alternatively, permission return base. Please advise immediately.'

The wording of the message, Tyndall pondered, could have been improved. Especially the bit at the end – probably sounded sufficiently like a threat to infuriate old Starr, who would only see in it pusillanimous confirmation of his confirmation of his conviction of the *Ulysses*'s – and Tyndall's – unfitness for the job. . . . Besides, for almost two years now – since long before the sinking of the *Hood* by the *Bismarck* – it had been Admiralty policy not to break up the Home Fleet squadrons by detaching capital ships or carriers. Old battleships, too slow for modern inter-naval surface action – vessels such as the *Ramillies* and the *Malaya* – were used for selected Arctic convoys: with that exception, the official strategy was based on keeping the Home Fleet intact, containing the German Grand Fleet – and risking the convoys. . . . Tyndall took a last look round the convoy, sighed wearily and eased himself down to the duckboards. What the hell, he thought, let it go. If it wasted his time sending it, it would also waste old Starr's time reading it.

He clumped his way heavily down the bridge ladders, eased his bulk through the door of the Captain's cabin, hard by the FDR. Vallery, partly undressed, was lying in his bunk, between very clean, very white sheets: their knife-edged ironing crease-marks contrasted oddly with the spreading crimson stain. Vallery himself, gaunt-cheeked and cadaverous beneath dark stubble of beard, red eyes sunk deep in great hollow sockets, looked corpse-like, already dead. From one corner of his mouth blood trickled down a parchment cheek. As Tyndall shut the door, Vallery lifted a wasted hand, all ivory knuckles and blue veins, in feeble greeting.

Tyndall closed the door carefully, quietly. He took his time, time and to spare to allow the shock to drain out of his face. When he turned round, his face was composed, but he made no attempt to disguise his concern.

'Thank God for old Socrates!' he said feelingly. 'Only man in the ship who can make you see even a modicum of sense.' He parked himself on the edge of the bed. 'How do you feel, Dick?'

Vallery grinned crookedly. There was no humour in his smile.

'All depends what you mean, sir. Physically or mentally? I feel a bit worn out – not really ill, you know. Doc says he can fix me up – temporarily anyway. He's going to give me a plasma transfusion – says I've lost too much blood.'

'Plasma?'

'Plasma. Whole blood would be a better coagulant. But he thinks it may prevent – or minimise – future attacks. . . .' He paused, wiped some froth off his lips, and smiled again, as mirthlessly as before. 'It's not really a doctor and medicine I need, John – it's a padre – and forgiveness.' His voice trailed off into silence. The cabin was very quiet.

Tyndall shifted uncomfortably and cleared his throat noisily. Rarely had he been so conscious that he was, first and last, a man of action.

'Forgiveness? What on earth do you mean, Dick?' He hadn't meant to speak so loudly, so harshly.

'You know damn' well what I mean,' Vallery said mildly. He was a man who was rarely heard to swear, to use the most innocuous oath. 'You were with me on the bridge this morning.'

For perhaps two minutes neither man said a word. Then Vallery broke into a fresh paroxysm of coughing. The towel in his hand grew dark, sodden, and when he leaned back on his pillow Tyndall felt a quick stab of fear. He bent quickly over the sick man, sighed in soundless relief as he heard the quick, shallow breathing.

Vallery spoke again, his eyes still closed.

'It's not so much the men who were killed in the Low Power Room.' He seemed to be talking to himself, his voice a drifting

110

murmur. 'My fault, I suppose – I took the *Ulysses* too near the *Ranger*. Foolish to go near a sinking ship, especially if she's burning. . . . But just one of these things, just one of the risks . . . they happen. . . .' The rest was a blurred, dying whisper. Tyndall couldn't catch it.

He rose abruptly to his feet, pulling his gloves on.

'Sorry, Dick,' he apologised. 'Shouldn't have come – shouldn't have stayed so long. Old Socrates will give me hell.'

'It's the others – the boys in the water.' Vallery might never have heard him. 'I hadn't the right – I mean, perhaps some of them would . . .' Again his voice was lost for a moment, then he went on strongly: 'Captain Richard Vallery, DSO – judge, jury and executioner. Tell me, John, what am I going to say when *my* turn comes?'

Tyndall hesitated, heard the authoritative rap on the door and jerked round, his breath escaping in a long, inaudible sigh of thankfulness.

'Come in,' he called.

The door opened and Brooks walked in. He stopped short at the sight of the Admiral, turned to the white-coated assistant behind him, a figure weighed down with stands, bottles, tubing and various paraphernalia.

'Remain outside, Johnson, will you?' he asked. 'I'll call you when I want you.'

He closed the door, crossed the cabin and pulled a chair up to the Captain's bunk. Vallery's wrist between his fingers, he looked coldly across at Tyndall. Nicholls, Brooks remembered, was insistent that the Admiral was far from well. He looked tired, certainly, but more unhappy than tired. . . . The pulse was very fast, irregular.

'You've been upsetting him,' Brooks accused.

'Me? Good God, no!' Tyndall was injured. 'So help me, Doc, I never said—'

'Not guilty, Doc.' It was Vallery who spoke, his voice stronger now. 'He never said a word. *I'm* the guilty man – guilty as hell.'

Brooks looked at him for a long moment. Then he smiled, smiled in understanding and compassion.

'Forgiveness, sir. That's it, isn't it?' Tyndall started in surprise, looked at him in wonder.

Vallery opened his eyes. 'Socrates!' he murmured. 'You would know.'

'Forgiveness,' Brooks mused. 'Forgiveness. From whom – the living, the dead – or the Judge?'

Again Tyndall started. 'Have you – have you been listening outside? How can you—?'

'From all three, Doc. A tall order, I'm afraid.'

'From the dead, sir, you are quite right. There would be no forgiveness: only their blessing, for there is nothing to forgive. I'm a doctor, don't forget – I saw those boys in the water . . . you sent them home the easy way. As for the Judge – you know, "The Lord giveth, the Lord taketh away. Blessed be the name of the Lord" – the Old Testament conception of the Lord who takes away in His own time and His own way, and to hell with mercy and charity.' He smiled at Tyndall. 'Don't look so shocked, sir. I'm not being blasphemous. If that were the Judge, Captain, neither you nor I – nor the Admiral – would ever want any part of him. But you know it isn't so. . . .'

Vallery smiled faintly, propped himself up on his pillow. 'You make good medicine, Doctor. It's a pity you can't speak for the living also.'

'Oh, can't I?' Brooks smacked his hand on his thigh, guffawed in sudden recollection. 'Oh, my word, it was magnificent!' He laughed again in genuine amusement. Tyndall looked at Vallery in mock despair.

'Sorry,' Brooks apologised. 'Just fifteen minutes ago a bunch of sympathetic stokers deposited on the deck of the Sick Bay the prone and extremely unconscious form of one of their shipmates. Guess who? None other than our resident nihilist, our old friend Riley. Slight concussion and assorted facial injuries, but he should be restored to the bosom of his mess-deck by nightfall. Anyway, he insists on it – claims his kittens need him.'

Vallery looked up, amused, curious.

'Fallen down the stokehold again, I presume?'

'Exactly the question I put, sir – although it looked more as if he had fallen into a concrete mixer. "No, sir," says one of the stretcher-bearers. "He tripped over the ship's cat." "Ship's cat?" I says. "What ship's cat?" So he turns to his oppo and says: "Ain't we got a ship's cat, Nobby?" Whereupon the stoker yclept Nobby looks at him pityingly and says: "'E's got it all wrong, sir. Poor old Riley just came all over queer – took a weak turn, 'e did. I 'ope 'e ain't 'urt 'isself?" He sounded quite anxious.'

'What had happened?' Tyndall queried.

'I let it go at that. Young Nicholls took two of them aside, promised no action and had it out of them in a minute flat.

Seems that Riley saw in this morning's affair a magnificent opportunity for provoking trouble. Cursed you for an inhuman, cold-blooded murderer and, I regret to say, cast serious aspersions on your immediate ancestors – and all of this, mind you, where he thought he was safe – among his own friends. His friends half-killed him. . . . You know, sir, I envy you. . . .'

He broke off, rose abruptly to his feet.

'Now, sir, if you'll just lie down and roll up your sleeve . . . Oh, damn!'

'Come in.' It was Tyndall who answered the knock. 'Ah, for me, young Chrysler. Thank you.'

He looked up at Vallery. 'From London – in reply to my signal.' He turned it over in his hand two or three times. 'I suppose I have to open it some time,' he said reluctantly.

The Surgeon-Commander half-rose to his feet.

'Shall I—'

'No, no, Brooks. Why should you? Besides, it's from our mutual friend, Admiral Starr. I'm sure you'd like to hear what he's got to say, wouldn't you?'

'No, I wouldn't.' Brooks was very blunt. 'I can't imagine it'll be anything good.'

Tyndall opened the signal, smoothed it out.

'DNO to Admiral Commanding 14 ACS,' he read slowly. '*Tirpitz* reported preparing to move out. Impossible detach Fleet carrier: FR77 vital: proceed Murmansk all speed: good luck: Starr.' Tyndall paused, his mouth twisted. 'Good luck! He might have spared us that!'

For a long time the three men looked at each other, silently, without expression. Characteristically, it was Brooks who broke the silence.

'Speaking of forgiveness,' he murmured quietly, 'what I want to know is – who on God's earth, above or below it, is ever going to forgive that vindictive old bastard?'

—— 8 ——

THURSDAY NIGHT

It was still only afternoon, but the grey Arctic twilight was already thickening over the sea as the *Ulysses* dropped slowly astern. The wind had died away completely; again the snow was falling, steadily, heavily, and visibly was down to a bare cable-length. It was bitterly cold.

In little groups of three and four, officers and men made their way aft to the starboard side of the poop-deck. Exhausted, bone-chilled men, mostly sunk in private and bitter thought, they shuffled wordlessly aft, dragging feet kicking up little puffs of powdery snow. On the poop, they ranged themselves sound-lessly behind the Captain or in a line inboard and aft of the long, symmetrical row of snow-covered hummocks that heaved up roundly from the unbroken whiteness of the poop.

The Captain was flanked by three of his officers – Carslake, Etherton and the Surgeon-Commander. Carslake was by the guard-rail, the lower half of his face swathed in bandages to the eyes. For the second time in twenty-four hours he had waylaid Vallery, begged him to reconsider the decision to deprive him of his commission. On the first occasion Vallery had been adamant, almost contemptuous: ten minutes ago he had been icy and abrupt, had threatened Carslake with close arrest if he annoyed him again. And now Carslake just stared unseeingly into the snow and gloom, pale-blue eyes darkened and heavy with hate.

Etherton stood just behind Vallery's left shoulder, shivering uncontrollably. Above the white, jerking line of compressed mouth, cheek and jaw muscles were working incessantly: only his eyes were steady, dulled in sick fascination at the curious mound at his feet. Brooks, too, was tight-lipped, but there the resemblance ended: red of face and wrathful blue of eye, he fumed and seethed as can only a doctor whose orders have been openly flouted by the critically ill. Vallery, as Brooks had told him, forcibly and insubordinately, had no bloody right to be there, was all sorts of a damned fool for leaving his bunk. But, as Vallery had mildly pointed out, somebody had to conduct a funeral service, and that was the Captain's duty if the padre couldn't do it. And this day the padre couldn't do it, for it was the padre who lay dead at his feet. . . . At his feet, and at the feet of Etherton – the man who had surely killed him.

The padre had died four hours ago, just after Charlie had gone. Tyndall had been far out in his estimate. Charlie had not appeared within the hour. Charlie had not appeared until midmorning, but when he did come he had the company of three of his kind. A long haul indeed from the Norwegian coast to this, the 10th degree west of longitude, but nothing for these giant Condors – Focke-Wulf 200s – who regularly flew the great dawn to dusk half-circle from Trondheim to Occupied France, round the West Coast of the British Isles.

Condors in company always meant trouble, and these were no exception. They flew directly over the convoy, approaching from astern: the barrage from merchant ships and escorts was intense, and the bombing attack was pressed home with a marked lack of enthusiasm: the Condors bombed from a height of 7000 feet. In that clear, cold morning air the bombs were in view almost from the moment they cleared the bomb-bays: there was time to spare to take avoiding action. Almost at once the Condors had broken off the attack and disappeared to the east impressed, but apparently unharmed, by the warmth of their reception.

In the circumstances, the attack was highly suspicious. Circumspect Charlie might normally be on reconnaissance, but on the rare occasions that he chose to attack he generally did so with courage and determination. The recent sally was just too timorous, the tactics too obviously hopeless. Possibly, of course, recent entrants to the Luftwaffe were given to a discretion so signally lacking in their predecessors, or perhaps they were under strict orders not to risk their valuable craft. But probably, almost certainly, it was thought, that futile attack was only diversionary and the main danger lay elsewhere. The watch over and under the sea was intensified.

Five, ten, fifteen minutes passed and nothing had happened. Radar and Asdic screens remained obstinately clear. Tyndall finally decided that there was no justification for keeping the entire ship's company, so desperately in need of rest, at Action Stations for a moment longer and ordered the stand-down to be sounded.

Normal Defence Stations were resumed. All forenoon work had been cancelled, and officers and ratings off watch, almost to a man, went to snatch what brief sleep they could. But not all. Brooks and Nicholls had their patients to attend to: the Navigator returned to the chart-house: Marshall and his Commissioned Gunner, Mr Peters, resumed their interrupted routine rounds: and Etherton, nervous, anxious, over-sensitive and desperately eager to redeem himself for his share in the Carslake-Ralston episode, remained huddled and watchful in the cold, lonely eyrie of the Director Tower.

The sharp, urgent call from the deck outside came to Marshall and Peters as they were talking to the Leading Wireman in charge of No. 2 Electrical Shop. The shop was on the port side of the fo'c'sle deck cross-passage which ran athwartships for'ard of the wardroom, curving aft round the trunking of 'B' turret. Four quick steps had them out of the shop, through the screen door and peering over the side through the freshly falling snow, following the gesticulating finger of an excited marine. Marshall glanced at the man, recognised him immediately: it was Charteris, the only ranker known personally to every officer in the ship – in port, he doubled as wardroom barman.

'What is it, Charteris?' he demanded. 'What are you seeing? Quickly, man!'

'There, sir! Look! Out there – no, a bit more to your right! It's – it's a sub, sir, a U-boat!'

'What? What's that? A U-boat?' Marshall half-turned as the Rev. Winthrop, the padre, squeezed to the rail between himself and Charteris. 'Where? Where is it? Show me, show me!'

'Straight ahead, padre. I can see it now – but it's a damned funny shape for a U-boat – if you'll excuse the language,' Marshall added hastily. He caught the war-like, un-Christian gleam in Winthrop's eyes, smothered a laugh and peered through the snow at the strange squat shape which had now drifted almost abreast of them.

High up in the Tower, Etherton's restless, hunting eyes had already seen it, even before Charteris. Like Charteris, he immediately thought it was a U-boat caught surfacing in a snowstorm – the pay-off of the attack by the Condors: the thought that Asdic or radar would certainly have picked it up never occurred to him. Time, speed – that was the essence, before it vanished. Unthinkingly, he grabbed the phone to the for'ard multiple pom-pom.

'Director – pom-pom!' he barked urgently. 'U-boat, port 60. Range 100 yards, moving aft. Repeat, port 60. Can you see it? . . . No, no, port 60 – 70 now!' he shouted desperately. 'Oh, good, good! Commence tracking.'

'On target, sir,' the receiver crackled in his ear.

'Open fire – continuous!'

'Sir – but, sir – Kingston's not here. He went—'

'Never mind Kingston!' Etherton shouted furiously. Kingston, he knew, was Captain of the Gun. 'Open fire, you fools – now! I'll take responsibility.' He thrust the phone back on the rest, moved across to the observation panel. . . . The realization, sickening, shocking, fear seared through his mind and he lunged desperately for the phone.

'Belay the last order!' he shouted wildly. 'Cease fire! Cease fire! Oh, my God, my God, my God!' Through the receiver came the staccato, angry bark of the two-pounder. The receiver dropped from his hand, crashed against the bulkhead. It was too late.

It was too late because he had committed the cardinal sin – he had forgotten to order the removal of the muzzle-covers – the metal plates that sealed off the flash-covers of the guns when not in use. And the shells were fused to explode on contact. . . .

The first shell exploded inside its barrel, killing the trainer and seriously wounding the communication number: the other three smashed through their flimsy covers and exploded within a second of each other, a few feet from the faces of the four watchers on the fo'c'sle deck.

All four were untouched, miraculously untouched by the flying, screaming metal. It flew outwards and downwards, a red-hot iron hail sizzling into the sea. But the blast of the explosion was backwards, and the power of even a few pounds of high explosive detonating at arm's length is lethal.

The padre died instantly, Peters and Charteris within seconds, and all from the same cause – telescoped occiputs. The blast hurled them backwards off their feet, as if flung by a giant hand, the backs of their heads smashing to an eggshell pulp against the bulkhead. The blood seeped darkly into the snow, was obliterated in a moment.

Marshall was lucky, fantastically so. The explosion – he said afterwards that it was like getting in the way of the driving piston of the Coronation Scot – flung him through the open door behind him, ripped off the heels of both shoes as they caught on the storm-sill: he braked violently in mid-air, described a complete somersault, slithered along the passage and smashed squarely into the trunking of 'B' turret, his back framed by the four big spikes of the butterfly nuts securing an inspection hatch. Had he been standing a foot to the right or the left, had his heels been two inches higher as he catapulted through the doorway, had he hit the turret a hair's-breadth to the left or right – Lieutenant Marshall had no right to be alive. The laws of chance said so, overwhelmingly. As it was, Marshall was now sitting up in the Sick Bay, strapped, broken ribs making breathing painful, but otherwise unharmed.

The upturned lifeboat, mute token of some earlier tragedy on the Russian Convoys, had long since vanished into the white twilight.

Captain Vallery's voice, low and husky, died softly away. He stepped back, closing the Prayer Book, and the forlorn notes of the bugle echoed briefly over the poop and died in the blanketing snow. Men stood silently, unmovingly, as, one by one, the thirteen figures shrouded in weighted canvas slid down the tipped plank, down from under the Union Flag, splashed heavily into the Arctic and were gone. For long seconds, no one moved. The unreal, hypnotic effect of that ghostly ritual of burial held tired, sluggish minds in unwilling thrall, held men oblivious to cold and discomfort. Even when Etherton half-stepped forward, sighed, crumpled down quietly, unspectacularly in the snow, the trance-like hiatus continued. Some ignored him, others glanced his way, incuriously. It seemed absurd, but it struck Nicholls, standing in the background, that they might have stayed there indefinitely, the minds and the blood of men slowing up, coagulating, freezing, while they turned to pillars of ice. Then suddenly, with exacerbating abruptness, the spell was shattered: the strident scream of the Emergency Stations whistle seared through the gathering gloom.

It took Vallery about three minutes to reach the bridge. He rested often, pausing on every second or third step of the four ladders that reached up to the bridge: even so, the climb drained the last reserves of his frail strength. Brooks had to half-carry him through the gate. Vallery clung to the binnacle, fighting for breath through foam-flecked lips; but his eyes were alive, alert as always, probing through the swirling snow.

'Contact closing, closing: steady on course, interception course: speed unchanged.' The radar loudspeaker was muffled, impersonal; but the calm precise tones of Lieutenant Bowden were unmistakable.

'Good, good! We'll fox him yet!' Tyndall, his tired, sagging face lit up in almost beaming anticipation, turned to the Captain. The prospect of action always delighted Tyndall.

'Something coming up from the SSW, Captain. Good God above, man, what are you doing here?' He was shocked at Vallery's appearance. 'Brooks! Why in heaven's name—?'

'Suppose *you* try talking to him?' Brooks growled wrathfully.

118

He slammed the gate shut behind him, stalked stiffly off the bridge.

'What's the matter with him?' Tyndall asked of no one in particular. 'What the hell am I supposed to have done?'

'Nothing, sir,' Vallery pacified him. 'It's all my fault – disobeying doctor's orders and what have you. You were saying—?'

'Ah, yes. Trouble, I'm afraid, Captain.' Vallery smiled secretly as he saw the satisfaction, the pleased anticipation creep back into the Admiral's face. 'Radar reports a surface vessel approaching, big, fast, more or less on interception course for us.'

'And not ours, of course?' Vallery murmured. He looked up suddenly. 'By jove, sir, it couldn't be—?'

'The *Tirpitz*?' Tyndall finished for him. He shook his head in decision. 'My first thought, too, but no. Admiralty and Air Force are watching her like a broody hen over her eggs. If she moves a foot, we'll know. . . . Probably some heavy cruiser.'

'Closing. Closing. Course unaltered.' Bowden's voice, clipped, easy, was vaguely reminiscent of a cricket commentator's. 'Estimated speed 24, repeat 24 knots.'

His voice crackled into silence as the WT speaker came to life. 'WT – bridge. WT – bridge. Signal from convoy: *Stirling* – Admiral. Understood. Wilco. Out.'

'Excellent, excellent! From Jeffries,' Tyndall explained. 'I sent him a signal ordering the convoy to alter course to NNW. That should take 'em well clear of our approaching friend.'

Vallery nodded. 'How far ahead is the convoy, sir?'

'Pilot!' Tyndall called and leaned back expectantly.

'Six – six and a half miles.' The Kapok Kid's face was expressionless.

'He's slipping,' Tyndall said mournfully. 'The strain's telling. A couple of days ago he'd have given us the distance to the nearest yard. Six miles – far enough, Captain. He'll never pick 'em up. Bowden says he hasn't even picked us up yet, that the intersection of courses must be pure coincidence. . . . I gather Lieutenant Bowden has a poor opinion of German radar.'

'I know. I hope he's right. For the first time the question is of rather more than academic interest.' Vallery gazed to the South, his binoculars to his eyes: there was only the sea, the thinning snow. 'Anyway, this came at a good time.'

Tyndall arched a bushy eyebrow.

'It was strange, down there on the poop.' Vallery was hesitant. 'There was something weird, uncanny in the air. I didn't like it, sir. It was desperately – well, almost frightening. The snow, the silence, the dead men – thirteen dead men – I can only guess how the men felt, about Etherton, about anything. But it wasn't good – don't know how it would have ended—'

'Five miles,' the loudspeaker cut in. 'Repeat, five miles. Course, speed, constant.'

'Five miles,' Tyndall repeated in relief. Intangibles bothered him. 'Time to trail our coats a little, Captain. We'll soon be in what Bowden reckons is his radar range. Due east, I think – it'll look as if we're covering the tail of the convoy and heading for the North Cape.'

'Starboard 10,' Vallery ordered. The cruiser came gradually round, met, settled on her new course: engine revolutions were cut down till the *Ulysses* was cruising along at 26 knots.

One minute, five passed, then the loudspeaker blared again. 'Radar – bridge. Constant distance, altering on interception course.'

'Excellent! Really excellent!' The Admiral was almost purring. 'We have him, gentlemen. He's missed the convoy. . . . Commence firing by radar!'

Vallery reached for the Director handset.

'Director? Ah, it's you, Courtney . . . good, good . . . you just do that.'

Vallery replaced the set, looked across at Tyndall.

'Smart as a whip, that boy. He's had "X" and "Y" lined up, tracking for the past ten minutes. Just a matter of pressing a button, he says.'

'Sounds uncommon like our friends here.' Tyndall jerked his head in the direction of the Kapok Kid, then looked up in surprise. 'Courtney? Did you say "Courtney"? Where's Guns?'

'In his cabin, as far as I know. Collapsed on the poop. Anyway, he's in no fit state to do his job. . . . Thank God I'm not in that boy's shoes. I can imagine . . .'

The *Ulysses* shuddered, and the whip-like crash of 'X' turret drowned Vallery's voice as the 5.25 shells screamed away into the twilight. Seconds later, the ship shook again as the guns of 'Y' turret joined in. Thereafter the guns fired alternately, one shell at a time, every half-minute: there was no point in wasting ammunition when the fall of shot could not be observed; but it was probably the bare minimum necessary to infuriate the enemy and distract his attention from everything except the ship ahead.

The snow had thinned away now to a filmy curtain of gauze that blurred, rather than obscured the horizon. To the west, the clouds were lifting, the sky lightening in sunset. Vallery ordered 'X' turret to cease fire, to load with star-shell.

Abruptly, the snow was gone and the enemy was there, big and menacing, a black featureless silhouette with the sudden flush of sunset striking incongruous golden gleams from the water creaming high at her bows.

'Starboard 30!' Vallery snapped. 'Full ahead. Smoke-screen!' Tyndall nodded compliance. It was no part of his plan to become embroiled with a German heavy cruiser or pocket battleship . . . especially at an almost point-blank range of four miles.

On the bridge, half a dozen pairs of binoculars peered aft, trying to identify the enemy. But the fore-and-aft silhouette against the reddening sky was difficult to analyse, exasperatingly vague and ambiguous. Suddenly, as they watched, white gouts of flame lanced out from the heart of the silhouette: simultaneously, the starshell burst high up in the air, directly above the enemy, bathing him in an intense, merciless white glare, so that he appeared strangely naked and defenceless.

An illusory appearance. Everyone ducked low, in reflex instinct, as the shells whistled just over their heads and plunged into the sea ahead. Everyone, that is, except the Kapok Kid. He bent an impassive eye on the Admiral as the latter slowly straightened up.

'Hipper Class, sir,' he announced. '10,000 tons, 8-inch guns, carries aircraft.'

Tyndall looked at his unsmiling face in long suspicion. He cast around in his mind for a suitably crushing reply, caught sight of the German cruiser's turrets belching smoke in the sinking glare of the starshell.

'My oath!' he exclaimed. 'Not wasting much time, are they? And damned good shooting!' he added in professional admiration as the shells hissed into the sea through the *Ulysses*'s boiling wake, about 150 feet astern. 'Bracketed in the first two salvoes. They'll straddle us next time.'

The *Ulysses* was still heeling round, the black smoke beginning to pour from the after funnel, when Vallery straightened, clapped his binoculars to his eyes. Heavy clouds of smoke were mushrooming from the enemy's starboard deck, just for'ard of the bridge.

'Oh, well done, young Courtney!' he burst out. 'Well done indeed!'

'Well done indeed!' Tyndall echoed. 'A beauty! Still, I don't think we'll stop to argue the point with them. . . . Ah! Just in time, gentlemen! Gad, that was close!' The stern of the *Ulysses,* swinging round now almost to the north, disappeared from sight as a salvo crashed into the sea, dead astern, one of the shells exploding in a great eruption of water.

The next salvo – obviously the hit on the enemy cruiser hadn't affected her fire-power – fell a cable length's astern. The German was now firing blind. Engineer Commander Dodson was making smoke with a vengeance, the oily, black smoke flattening down on the surface of the sea, rolling, thick, impenetrable. Vallery doubled back on course, then headed east at high speed.

For the next two hours, in the dusk and darkness, they played cat and mouse with the 'Hipper' class cruiser, firing occasionally, appearing briefly, tantalisingly, then disappearing behind a smoke-screen, hardly needed now in the coming night. All the time, radar was their eyes and their ears and never played them false. Finally, satisfied that all danger to the convoy was gone, Tyndall laid a double screen in a great curving 'U,' and vanished to the south-west, firing a few final shells, not so much in token of farewell as to indicate direction of departure.

Ninety minutes later, at the end of a giant half-circle to port, the *Ulysses* was sitting far to the north, while Bowden and his men tracked the progress of the enemy. He was reported as moving steadily east, then, just before contact was lost, as altering course to the south-east.

Tyndall climbed down from his chair, numbed and stiff. He stretched himself luxuriantly.

'Not a bad night's work, Captain, not bad at all. What do you bet our friend spends the night circling to the south and east at high speed, hoping to come up ahead of the convoy in the morning?' Tyndall felt almost jubilant, in spite of his exhaustion. 'And by that time FR77 should be 200 miles to the north of him. . . . I suppose, Pilot, you have worked out intersection courses for rejoining the convoy at all speeds up to a hundred knots?'

'I think we should be able to regain contact without much difficulty,' said the Kapok Kid politely.

'It's when he is at his most modest,' Tyndall announced, 'that he sickens me most. . . . Heavens above, I'm frozen to death. . . . Oh, damn! Not more trouble, I hope?'

The communication rating behind the compass platform picked up the jangling phone, listened briefly.

'For you, sir,' he said to Vallery. 'The Surgeon Lieutenant.'
'Just take the message, Chrysler.'

'Sorry, sir. Insists of speaking to you himself.' Chrysler handed the receiver into the bridge. Vallery smothered an exclamation of annoyance, lifted the receiver to his ear.

'Captain, here. Yes, what is it? . . . What? . . . *What!* Oh, God, no! . . . Why wasn't I told? . . . Oh, I see. Thank you, thank you.'

Vallery handed the receiver back, turned heavily to Tyndall. In the darkness, the Admiral felt, rather than saw the sudden weariness, the hunched defeat of the shoulders.

'That was Nicholls.' Vallery's voice was flat, colourless. 'Lieutenant Etherton shot himself in his cabin, five minutes ago.'

At four o'clock in the morning, in heavy snow, but in a calm sea, the *Ulysses* rejoined the convoy.

By mid-morning of that next day, a bare six hours later Admiral Tyndall had become an old weary man, haggard, haunted by remorse and bitter self-criticism, close, very close, to despair. Miraculously, in a matter of hours, the chubby cheeks had collapsed in shrunken flaccidity, draining blood had left the florid cheeks a parchment grey, the sunken eyes had dulled in blood and exhaustion. The extent and speed of the change wrought in that tough and jovial sailor, a sailor seemingly impervious to the most deadly vicissitudes of war, was incredible: incredible and disturbing in itself, but infinitely more so in its wholly demoralising effect on the men. To every arch there is but one keystone . . . or so any man must inevitably think.

Any impartial court of judgment would have cleared Tyndall of all guilt, would have acquitted him without a trial. He had done what he thought right, what any commander would have done in his place. But Tyndall sat before the merciless court of his own conscience. He could not forget that it was he who had re-routed the convoy so far to the north, that it was he who had ignored official orders to break straight for the North Cape, that it was exactly on latitude 70 N – where their Lordships had told him they would be – that FR77 had, on that cold, clear windless dawn, blundered straight into the heart of the heaviest concentration of U-boats encountered in the Arctic during the entire course of the war.

The wolf-pack had struck at its favourite hour – the dawn – and from its favourite position – the north-east, with the dawn in its eyes. It struck cruelly, skilfully and with a calculated ferocity. Admittedly, the era of Kapitan Leutnant Prien – his U-boat long ago sent to the bottom with all hands by the destroyer *Wolverine* –and his illustrious contemporaries, the heyday of the great U-boat Commanders, the high noon of individual brilliance and great personal gallantry, was gone. But in its place – and generally acknowledged to be even more dangerous, more deadly – were the concerted, highly integrated mass attacks of the wolf-packs, methodical, machine-like, almost reduced to a formula, under a single directing command.

The *Cochella,* third vessel in the port line, was the first to go. Sister ship to the *Vytura* and the *Varella,* also accompanying her in FR77, the *Cochella* carried over 3,000,000 gallons of 100-octane petrol. She was hit by at least three torpedoes: the first two broke her almost in half, the third triggered off a stupendous detonation that literally blew her out of existence. One moment she was there, sailing serenely through the limpid twilight of sunrise: the next moment she was gone. Gone, completely, utterly gone, with only a seething ocean, convulsed in boiling white, to show where she had been: gone, while stunned eardrums and stupefied minds struggled vainly to grasp the significance of what had happened: gone, while blind reflex instinct hurled men into whatever shelter offered as a storm of lethal metal swept over the fleet.

Two ships took the full force of the explosion. A huge mass of metal – it might have been a winch – passed clear through the superstructure of the *Sirrus,* a cable-length away on the starboard: it completely wrecked the radar office. What happened to the other ship immediately astern, the impossibly-named *Tennessee Adventurer,* was not clear, but almost certainly her wheelhouse and bridge had been severely damaged: she had lost steering control, was not under command.

Tragically, this was not at first understood, simply because it was not apparent. Tyndall, recovering fast from the sheer physical shock of the explosion, broke out the signal for an emergency turn to port. The wolf-pack, obviously, lay on the port hand, and the only action to take to minimise further losses, to counter the enemy strategy, was to head straight towards them. He was reasonably sure that the U-boats would be bunched – generally, they strung out only for the slow convoys. Besides, he had adopted this tactic several times in the past with a high degree of success. Finally, it cut the U-boats' target to an impossible tenth, forcing on them the alternative of diving or the risk of being trampled under.

With the immaculate precision and co-ordination of Olympic equestrians, the convoy heeled steadily over to starboard, slewed majestically round, trailing curved, white wakes phosphorescently alive in the near-darkness that still clung to the surface of the sea. Too late, it was seen that the *Tennessee Adventurer* was not under command. Slowly, then with dismaying speed, she came round to the east, angling directly for another merchantman, the *Tobacco Planter*. There was barely time to think, to appreciate the inevitable: frantically, the *Planter*'s helm went hard over in an attempt to clear the other astern, but the wildly swinging *Adventurer*, obviously completely out of control, matched the *Planter*'s tightening circle, foot by inexorable foot, blind malice at the helm.

She struck the *Planter* with sickening violence just for'ard of the bridge. The *Adventurer*'s bows, crumpling as they went, bit deeply into her side, fifteen, twenty feet in a chaos of tearing, rending metal: the stopping power of 10,000 tons deadweight travelling at 15 knots is fantastic. The wound was mortal, and the *Planter*'s own momentum, carrying her past, wrenched her free from the lethal bows, opening the wound to the hungry sea and hastened her own end. Almost at once she began to fill, to list heavily to starboard. Aboard the *Adventurer*, someone must have taken over command: her engine stopped, she lay motionless alongside the sinking ship, slightly down by the head.

The rest of the convoy cleared the drifting vessels, steadied west by north. Far out on the starboard hand, Commander Orr, in the *Sirrus*, clawed his damaged destroyer round in a violent turn, headed back towards the crippled freighters. He had gone less than half a mile when he was recalled by a vicious signal from the flagship. Tyndall was under no illusions. The *Adventurer*, he knew, might remain there all day, unharmed – it was obvious that the *Planter* would be gone in a matter of minutes – but that would be a guarantee neither of the absence of U-boats nor of the sudden access of misguided enemy chivalry: the enemy would be there, would wait to the last possible second before dark in the hope that some rescue destroyer would heave to alongside the *Adventurer*.

In that respect, Tyndall was right. The *Adventurer* was torpedoed just before sunset. Three-quarters of the ship's company escaped in lifeboats, along with twenty survivors picked up from the *Planter*. A month later the frigate *Esher* found them, in three lifeboats tied line ahead, off the bitter, iron coast of Bear Island, heading steadily north. The Captain, alert and upright, was still sitting in the stern-sheets, empty eye-sockets searching for some lost horizon, a withered claw locked to the tiller. The rest were sitting or lying about the boats, one actually standing, his arm cradled around the mast, and all with shrunken sun-blackened lips drawn back in hideous mirth. The log-book lay beside the Captain, empty: all had frozen to death on that first night. The young frigate commander had cast them adrift, watched them disappear over the northern rim of the world, steering for the Barrier. And the Barrier is the region of the great silence, the seas of incredible peace, so peaceful, so calm, so cold that they may be there yet, the dead who cannot rest. A mean and shabby end for the temple of the spirit. . . . It is not known whether the Admiralty approved the action of the captain of the frigate.

But in the major respect, that of anticipating enemy disposition, the Admiral was utterly wrong. The wolf-pack commander had outguessed him and it was arguable that Tyndall should have foreseen this. His tactic of swinging an entire convoy into the face of a torpedo attack was well known to the enemy: it was also well known that his ship was the *Ulysses*, and the *Ulysses*, the only one of her kind, was familiar, by sight or picture silhouette, to every U-boat commander in the German Navy: and it had been reported, of course, that it was the *Ulysses* that was leading FR77 through to Murmansk. Tyndall should have expected, expected and forestalled the long overdue counter.

For the submarine that had torpedoed the *Cochella* had been the last, not the first, of the pack. The others had lain to the south of the U-boat that had sprung the trap, and well to the west of the track of FR77 – clear beyond the reach of Asdic. And when the convoy wheeled to the west, the U-boats lined up leisurely firing tracks as the ships steamed up to cross their bows at right angles. The sea was calm, calm as a millpond, an extraordinary deep, Mediterranean blue. The snow-squalls of the night had passed away. Far to the north-east a brilliant sun was shouldering itself clear of the horizon, its level rays striking a great band of silver across the Arctic, highlighting the ships, shrouded white in snow, against the darker sea and sky beyond. The conditions were ideal, if one may use the word 'ideal' to describe the prologue to a massacre.

Massacre, an almost total destruction there must inevitably have been but for the warning that came almost too late. A warning given neither by radar nor Asdic, nor by any of the magically efficient instruments of modern detection, but simply by the keen eyes of an eighteen-year-old Ordinary Seaman – and the God-sent rays of the rising sun.

'Captain, sir! Captain, sir!' It was young Chrysler who shouted. His voice broke in wild excitement, his eyes were glued to the powerful binoculars clamped on the port searchlight control position. 'There's something flashing to the south, sir! It flashed twice – there it goes again!'

'Where, boy?' Tyndall shouted. 'Come on, where, where?' In his agitation, Chrysler had forgotten the golden rule of the reporting look-out – bearing must come first.

'Port 50, sir – no, port 60. . . . I've lost sight of it now, sir.'

Every pair of glasses on the bridge swung round on the given bearing. There was nothing to be seen, just nothing at all. Tyndall shut his telescope slowly, shrugged his shoulders eloquent in disbelief.

'Maybe there *is* something,' said the Kapok Kid doubtfully. 'How about the sea catching a periscope making a quick circle sweep?'

Tyndall looked at him, silent, expressionless, looked away, stared straight ahead. To the Kapok Kid he seemed strange, different. His face was set, stonily impassive, the face of a man with twenty ships and 5000 lives in his keeping, the face of a man who has already made one wrong decision too many.

'There they go again!' Chrysler screamed. 'Two flashes – no, *three* flashes!' He was almost beside himself with excitement, literally dancing in an agony of frustration. 'I did see them, sir, I *did*. I *did*. Oh, please, sir, please!'

Tyndall had swung round again. Ten long seconds he gazed at Chrysler, who had left his binoculars, and was gripping the gate in gauntleted hands, shaking it in anguished appeal. Abruptly, Tyndall made up his mind.

'Hard aport, Captain. Bentley – the signal!'

Slowly, on the unsupported word of an eighteen-year-old, FR77 came round to the south, slowly, just too slowly. Suddenly, the sea was alive with running torpedoes – three, five, ten – Vallery counted thirty in as many seconds. They were running shallow and their bubbling trails, evil, ever-lengthening, rose swiftly to the surface and lay there milkily on the glassy sea, delicately evanescent shafts for arrowheads so lethal.

Parallel in the centre, they fanned out to the east and west to embrace the entire convoy. It was a fantastic sight: no man in that convoy had ever seen anything remotely like it.

In a moment the confusion was complete. There was no time for signals. It was every ship for itself in an attempt to avoid wholesale destruction: and confusion was worse confounded by the ships in the centre and outer lines, that had not yet seen the wakes of the streaking torpedoes.

Escape for all was impossible: the torpedoes were far too closely bunched. The cruiser *Stirling* was the first casualty. Just when she seemed to have cleared all danger – she was far ahead where the torpedoes were thickest – she lurched under some unseen hammer-blow, slewed round crazily and steamed away back to the east, smoke hanging heavily over her poop. The *Ulysses*, brilliantly handled, heeled over on maximum rudder and under the counter-thrusting of her great screws, slid down an impossibly narrow lane between four torpedoes, two of them racing by a bare boat's length from either side: she was still a lucky ship. The destroyers, fast, highly manœuvrable, impeccably handled, bobbed and weaved their way to safety with almost contemptuous ease, straightened up and headed south under maximum power.

The merchant ships, big, clumsy, relatively slow, were less fortunate. Two ships in the port line, a tanker and a freighter, were struck: miraculously, both just staggered under the numbing shock, then kept on coming. Not so the big freighter immediately behind them, her holds crammed with tanks, her decks lined with them. She was torpedoed three times in three seconds: there was no smoke, no fire no spectacular after-explosion: sieved and ripped from stern to stem, she sank quickly, quietly, still on even keel, dragged down by the sheer weight of metal. No one below decks had even the slightest chance of escaping.

A merchantman in the centre line, the *Belle Isle*, was tor-pedoed amidships. There were two separte explosions – probably she had been struck twice – and she was instantly on fire. Within seconds, the list to port was pronounced, increasing momen-tarily: gradually her rails dipped under, the outslung lifeboats almost touching the surface of the sea. A dozen, fifteen men were seen to be slipping, sliding down the sheering decks and hatch-covers, already half-submerged, towards the nearest lifeboat. Desperately they hacked at belly-band securing ropes, piled into the lifeboat in grotesquely comical haste, pushed it clear of the dipping davits, seized the oars and pulled frantically away. From beginning to end, hardly a minute had elapsed.

Half a dozen powerful strokes had them clear beyond their ship's counter: two more took them straight under the swinging bows of the *Walter A. Baddeley*, her companion tank-carrier in the starboard line. The consummate seamanship that had saved the *Baddeley* could do nothing to save the lifeboat: the little boat crumpled and splintered like a matchwood toy, catapulting screaming men into the icy sea.

As the big, grey hull of the *Baddeley* slid swifty by them, they struck out with insane strength that made nothing of their heavy Arctic clothing. At such times, reason vanishes: the thought that if, by some God-given miracle, they were to escape the guillotine of the *Baddeley*'s single great screw, they would do so only to die minutes later in the glacial cold of the Arctic, never occurred to them. But, as it happened, death came by neither metal nor cold. They were still struggling, almost abreast the poop, vainly trying to clear the rushing, sucking vortex of water, when the torpedoes struck the *Baddeley*, close together and simultaneously, just for'ard of the rudder.

For swimming men who have been in the close vicinity of an underwater high explosion there can be no shadow of hope: the effect is inhuman, revolting, shocking beyond conception: in such cases, experienced doctors, pathologists even, can with difficulty bring themselves to look upon what were once human beings. . . . But for these men, as so often in the Arctic, death was kind, for they died unknowing.

The *Walter A. Baddeley*'s stern had been almost completely blown off. Hundreds of tons of water were already rushing in the great, gaping hole below the counter, racing through cross-bulkheads fractured by the explosion, smashing open engine-boiler room watertight doors buckled by the blast, pulling her down by the stern, steadily, relentlessly, till her taffrail dipped salute to the waiting Arctic. For a moment, she hung there. Then, in quick succession from deep inside the hull, came a muffled explosion, the ear-shattering, frightening roar of escaping high-pressure steam and the thunderous crash of massive boilers rending away from their stools as the ship upended. Almost immediately the shattered stern lurched heavily, sunk lower and lower till the poop was completely gone, till the dripping forefoot was tilted high above the sea. Foot by foot the angle of tilt increased, the stern plunged a hundred, two hundred feet under the surface of the sea, the bows rearing almost as high against the blue of the sky, buoyed up by half a million cubic feet of trapped air.

The ship was exactly four degrees off the vertical when the end came. It was possible to establish this angle precisely, for it was just at that second, half a mile away aboard the *Ulysses*, that the shutter clicked, the shutter of the camera in Lieutenant Nicholl's gauntleted hands.

A camera that captured an unforgettable picture – a stark, simple picture of a sinking ship almost vertically upright against a pale-blue sky. A picture with a strange lack of detail, with the exception only of two squat shapes, improbably suspended in mid-air: these were 30-ton tanks, broken loose from their fore-deck lashings, caught in midflight as they smashed down on the bridge structure, awash in the sea. In the background was the stern of the *Belle Isle,* the screw out of the water, the Red Duster trailing idly in the peaceful sea.

Bare seconds after the camera had clicked, the camera was blown from Nicholl's hands, the case crumpling against a bulk-head, the lens shattering but the film still intact. Panic-stricken the seamen in the lifeboat may have been, but it wasn't un-reasoning panic: in No. 2 hold, just for'ard of the fire, the *Belle Isle* had been carrying over 1000 tons of tank ammunition. . . . Broken cleanly in two, she was gone inside a minute: the *Baddeley's* bows, riddled by the explosion, slid gently down behind her.

The echoes of the explosion were still rolling out over the sea in ululating diminuendo when they were caught up and flung back by a series of muffled reports from the South. Less than two miles away, the *Sirrus, Vectra* and *Viking,* dazzling white in the morning sun, were weaving a crazily intricate pattern over the sea, depth-charges cascading from either side of their poop-decks. From time to time, one or other almost disappeared behind towering mushrooms of erupting water and spray, reappearing magically as the white columns fell back into the sea.

To join in the hunt, to satisfy the flaming, primitive lust for revenge – that was Tyndall's first impulse. The Kapok Kid looked at him furtively and wondered, wondered at the hunched rigidity, the compressed lipless mouth, the face contorted in white and bitter rage – a bitterness directed not least against himself. Tyndall twisted suddenly in his seat.

'Bentley! Signal the *Stirling* – ascertain damage.' The *Stirling* was more than a mile astern now, but coming round fast, her speed at least twenty knots.

'Making water after engine-room,' Bentley read eventually. 'Store-rooms flooded, but hull damage slight. Under control. Steering gear jammed. On emergency steering. Am all right.'

'Thank God for that! Signal, "Take over: proceed east." Come on, Captain, let's give Orr a hand to deal with these murdering hounds!'

The Kapok Kid looked at him in sudden dismay.

'Sir!'

'Yes, yes, Pilot! What is it?' Tyndall was curt, impatient.

'How about that first U-boat?' Carpenter ventured. 'Can't be much more than a mile to the south, sir. Shouldn't we—?'

'God Almighty!' Tyndall swore. His face was suffused with anger. 'Are you trying to tell me. . . .?' He broke off abruptly, stared at Carpenter for a long moment. 'What did you say, Pilot?'

'The boat that sunk the tanker, sir,' the Kapok Kid said carefully. 'She could have reloaded by now and she's in a perfect position—'

'Of course, of course,' Tyndall muttered. He passed a hand across his eyes, flickered a glance at Vallery. The Captain had his head averted. Again the hand passed across the tired eyes. 'You're quite right, Pilot, quite right.' He paused, then smiled. 'As usual, damn you!'

The *Ulysses* found nothing to the north. The U-boat that had sunk the *Cochella* and sprung the trap had wisely decamped. While they were quartering the area, they heard the sound of gunfire, saw the smoke erupting from the *Sirrus's* 4.7s.

'Ask him what all the bloody fuss is about,' Tyndall demanded irritably. The Kapok Kid smiled secretly: the old man had life in him yet.

'*Vectra* and *Viking* damaged, probably destroyed U-boat,' the message read. '*Vectra* and self sunk surfaced boat. How about you?'

'How about you!' Tyndall exploded. 'Damn his confounded insolence! How about you? He'll have the oldest, bloody minesweeper in Scapa for his next command. . . . This is all your fault, Pilot!'

'Yes, sir. Sorry, sir. Maybe he's only asking in a spirit of – ah – anxious concern.'

'How would you like to be his Navigator in his next command?' said Tyndall dangerously. The Kapok Kid retired to his charthouse.

'Carrington!'

'Sir?' The First Lieutenant was his invariable self, clear-eyed, freshly shaven, competent, alert. The sallow skin – hall-mark of all men who have spent too many years under tropical suns – was unshadowed by fatigue. He hadn't slept for three days.

'What do you make of that?' He pointed to the north-west. Curiously woolly grey clouds were blotting out the horizon; before them the sea dusked to indigo under wandering catspaws from the north.

'Hard to say, sir,' Carrington said slowly. 'Not heavy weather, that's certain. . . . I've seen this before, sir – low, twisting cloud blowing up on a fine morning with a temperature rise. Very common in the Aleutians and the Bering Sea, sir – and there it means fog, heavy mist.'

'And you, Captain?'

'No idea, sir.' Vallery shook his head decisively. The plasma transfusion seemed to have helped him. 'New to me – never seen it before.'

'Thought not,' Tyndall grunted. 'Neither have I – that's why I asked Number One first. . . . If you think it's fog that's coming up, Number One, let me know, will you? Can't afford to have convoy and escorts scattered over half the Arctic if the weather closes down. Although, mind you,' he added bitterly, 'I think they'd be a damned sight safer without us!'

'I can tell you now, sir.' Carrington had that rare gift – the ability to make a confident, quietly unarguable assertion without giving the slightest offence. 'It's fog.'

'Fair enough.' Tyndall never doubted him. 'Let's get the hell out of it. Bentley – signal the destroyers: "Break off engagement. Rejoin convoy." And Bentley – add the word "Immediate." ' He turned to Vallery. 'For Commander Orr's benefit.'

Within the hour, merchant ships and escorts were on station again, on a north-east course at first to clear any further packs on latitude 70. To the south-east, the sun was still bright: but the first thick, writhing tendrils of the mist, chill and dank, were already swirling round the convoy. Speed had been reduced to six knots: all ships were streaming fog-buoys.

Tyndall shivered, climbed stiffly from his chair as the stand-down sounded. He passed through the gate, stopped in the passage outside. He laid a glove on Chrysler's shoulder, kept it there as the boy turned round in surprise.

'Just wanted a squint at these eyes of yours, laddie,' he smiled. 'We owe them a lot. Thank you very much – we will not forget.' He looked a long time into the young face, forgot his own exhaustion and swore softly in sudden compassion as he saw the red-rimmed eyes, the white, maculated cheeks stained with embarrassed pleasure.

'How old are you, Chrysler?' he asked abruptly.

'Eighteen, sir . . . in two days' time.' The soft West Country voice was almost defiant.

'He'll be eighteen – in two days' time!' Tyndall repeated slowly to himself. 'Good God! Good God above!' He dropped his hand, walked wearily aft to the shelter, entered, closed the door behind him.

'He'll be eighteen – in two days' time,' he repeated, like a man in a daze.

Vallery propped himself up on the settee. 'Who? Young Chrysler?'

Tyndall nodded unhappily.

'I know.' Vallery was very quiet. 'I know how it is. . . . He did a fine job today.'

Tyndall sagged down in a chair. His mouth twisted in bitterness.

'The only one. . . . Dear God, what a mess!' He drew heavily on a cigarette, stared down at the floor. 'Ten green bottles, hanging on a wall,' he murmured absently.

'I beg your pardon, sir?'

'Fourteen ships left Scapa, eighteen St John – the two components of FR77,' Tyndall said softly. 'Thirty-two ships in all. And now' – he paused – 'now there are seventeen – and three of these damaged. I'm counting the *Tennessee Adventurer* as a dead duck.' He swore savagely. 'Hell's teeth, how I hate leaving ships like that, sitting targets for any murdering . . .' He stopped short, drew on his cigarette again, deeply. 'Doing wonderfully, amn't I?'

'Ah, nonsense, sir!' Vallery interrupted, impatient, almost angry. 'It wasn't any fault of yours that the carriers had to return.'

'Meaning that the rest was my fault?' Tyndall smiled faintly, lifted a hand to silence the automatic protest. 'Sorry, Dick, I know you didn't mean that – but it's true, it's true. Six merchant boys gone in ten minutes – six! And we shouldn't have lost one of them.' Head bent, elbows on knees, he screwed the heels of his palms into exhausted eyes. 'Rear-Admiral Tyndall, master strategist,' he went on softly. 'Alters convoy course to run smack into a heavy cruiser, alter it again to run straight into the biggest wolf-pack I've ever known – and just where the

Admiralty said they would be. . . . No matter what old Starr does to me when I get back, I've no kick coming. Not now, not after this.'

He rose heavily to his feet. The light of the single lamp caught his face. Vallery was shocked at the change.

'Where to, now, sir?' he asked.

'The bridge. No, no, stay where you are, Dick.' He tried to smile, but the smile was a grimace that flickered only to die. 'Leave me in peace while I ponder my next miscalculation.'

He opened the door, stopped dead as he heard the unmistakable whistling of shells close above, heard the EAS signal screaming urgently through the fog. Tyndall turned his head slowly, looked back into the shelter.

'It looks,' he said bitterly, 'as if I've already made it.'

9

FRIDAY MORNING

The fog, Tyndall saw, was all around them now. Since that last heavy snowfall during the night, the temperature had risen steadily, quickly. But it had beguiled only to deceive: the clammy, icy feathers of the swirling mist now struck doubly chill.

He hurried through the gate, Vallery close behind him. Turner, steel helmet trailing, was just leaving for the After Tower. Tyndall stretched out his hand, stopped him.

'What is it, Commander?' he demanded. 'Who fired? Where? Where did it come from?'

'I don't know, sir. Shells came from astern, more or less. But I've a damned good idea who it is.' His eyes rested on the Admiral a long, speculative moment. 'Our friend of last night is back again.' He turned abruptly, hurried off the bridge.

Tyndall looked after him, perplexed, uncomprehending. Then he swore, softly, savagely, and jumped for the radar handset.

'Bridge. Admiral speaking. Lieutenant Bowden at once!' The loudspeaker crackled into immediate life.

'Bowden speaking, sir.'

'What the devil are you doing down there?' Tyndall's voice was low, vicious. 'Asleep, or what? We are being attacked Lieutenant Bowden. By a surface craft. This may be news to

you.' He broke off, ducked low as another salvo screamed overhead and crashed into the water less than half a mile ahead:
the spray cascaded over the decks of a merchantman, glimpsed
momentarily in a clear lane between two rolling fog-banks. Tyndall straightened up quickly, snarled into the mouth-piece. 'He's
got our range, and got it accurately. In God's name, Bowden,
where is he?'

'Sorry, sir.' Bowden was cool, unruffled. 'We can't seem to
pick him up. We still have the *Adventurer* on our screens, and
there appears to be a very slight distortion on his bearing, sir
– approximately 300. . . . I suggest the enemy ship is still screened
by the *Adventurer* or, if she's closer, is on the *Adventurer*'s direct bearing.'

'How near?' Tyndall barked.

'Not near, sir. Very close to the *Adventurer*. We can't distinguish either by size or distance.'

Tyndall dangled the transmitter from his hand. He turned
to Vallery.

'Does Bowden really expect me to believe that yarn?' he asked
angrily. 'A million to one coincidence like that – an enemy ship
accidentally chose and holds the only possible course to screen
her from our radar. Fantastic!'

Vallery looked at him, his face without expression.

'Well?' Tyndall was impatient. 'Isn't it?'

'No, sir,' Vallery answered quietly. 'It's not. Not really. And
it wasn't accidental. The U-pack would have radioed her, given
our bearing and course. The rest was easy.'

Tyndall gazed at him through a long moment of comprehension, screwed his eyes shut and shook his head in short fierce
jerks. It was a gesture compounded of self-criticism, the death
of disbelief, the attempt to clear a woolly, exhausted mind. Hell,
a six-year-old could have seen that. . . . A shell whistled into the
sea a bare fifty yards to port. Tyndall didn't flinch, might never
have seen or heard it.

'Bowden?' He had the transmitter to his mouth again.

'Sir?'

'Any change in the screen?'

'No, sir. None.'

'And are you still of the same opinion?'

'Yes, sir! Can't be anything else.'

'And cose to the *Adventurer*, you say?'

'Very close, I would say.'

'But, good God, man, the *Adventurer* must be ten miles astern by now!'

'Yes, sir. I know. So is the bandit.'

'What! Ten miles! But, but—'

'He's firing by radar, sir,' Bowden interrupted. Suddenly the metallic voice sounded tired. 'He must be. He's also tracking by radar, which is why he's keeping himself in line with our bearings on the *Adventurer*. And he's extremely accurate . . . I'm afraid, Admiral, that his radar is at least as good as ours.'

The speaker clicked off. In the sudden strained silence on the bridge, the crash of breaking ebonite sounded unnaturally loud as the transmitter slipped from Tyndall's hand, fractured in a hundred pieces. The hand groped forward, he clutched at a steam pipe as if to steady himself. Vallery stepped towards him, arms outstretched in concern, but Tyndall brushed by unseeingly. Like an old spent man, like a man from whose ancient bones and muscles all the pith has long since drained, he shuffled slowly across the bridge, oblivious of a dozen mystified eyes, dragged himself up on to his high stool.

You fool, he told himself bitterly, savagely, oh, you bloody old fool! He would never forgive himself, never, never, never! All along the line he had been out-thought, out-guessed and out-manœuvred by the enemy. They had taken him for a ride, made an even bigger bloody fool out of him than his good Maker had ever intended. Radar! Of course, that was it! The blind assumption that German radar had remained the limited, elementary thing that Admiralty and Air Force Intelligence had reported it to be last year! Radar – and as good as the British. As good as the *Ulysses*'s – and everybody had believed that the *Ulysses* was incomparably the most efficient – indeed the only efficient – radar ship in the world. As good as our own – probably a damned sight better. But had the thought ever occurred to him? Tyndall writhed in sheer chagrin, in agony of spirit, and knew the bitter taste of self-loathing. And so, this morning, the pay-off: six ships, three hundred men gone to the bottom. May God forgive you, Tyndall, he though dully, may God forgive you. You sent them there. . . . Radar!

Last night, for instance. When the *Ulysses* had been laying a false trail to the east, the German cruiser had obligingly tagged behind, the perfect foil to his, Tyndall's genius. Tyndall groaned in mortification. Had tagged behind, firing wildly, erratically each time the *Ulysses* had disappeared behind a smoke-screen. Had done so to conceal the efficiency of her radar, to conceal the fact that, during the first half-hour at least, she must have been tracking the escaping convoy as it disappeared to the NNW – a process made all the easier by the fact that he, Tyndall, had expressly forbidden the use of the zig-zag!

And then, when the *Ulysses* had so brilliantly circled, first to the south and then to the north again, the enemy must have had her on his screen – constantly. And later, the biter bit with a vengeance, the faked enemy withdrawal to the south-east. Almost certainly, he, too, had circled to the north again, picked up the disappearing British cruiser on the edge of his screen, worked out her intersection course as a cross check on the convoy's, and radioed ahead to the wolf-pack, positioning them almost to the foot.

And now, finally, the last galling blow to whatever shattered remnants of his pride were left him. The enemy had opened fire at extreme range, but with extreme accuracy – a dead give-away to the fact that the firing was radar-controlled. And the only reason for it must be the enemy's conviction that the *Ulysses*, by this time, must have come to the inevitable conclusion that the enemy was equipped with a highly sensitive radar transmitter. The inevitable conclusion! Tyndall had never even begun to suspect it. Slowly, oblivious to the pain, he pounded his fist on the edge of the windscreen. God, what a blind, crazy stupid fool he'd been! Six ships, three hundred men. Hundreds of tanks and planes, millions of gallons of fuel lost to Russia; how many more thousands of dead Russians, soldiers and civilians, did that represent? And the broken, sorrowing families, he thought incoherently, families throughout the breadth of Britain: the telegram boys cycling to the little houses in the Welsh valleys, along the wooded lanes of Surrey, to the lonely reek of the peat-fire, remote in the Western Isles, to the lime-washed cottages of Donegal and Antrim: the empty homes across the great reaches of the New World, from Newfoundland and Maine to the far slopes of the Pacific. These families would never know that it was he, Tyndall, who had so criminally squandered the lives of husbands, brothers, sons – and that was worse than no consolation at all.

'Captain Vallery?' Tyndall's voice was only a husky whisper. Vallery crossed over, stood beside him, coughing painfully as the swirling fog caught nose and throat, lancinated inflamed lungs. It was a measure of Tyndall's distressed preoccupation that Vallery's obvious suffering quite failed to register.

'Ah, there you are. Captain, this enemy cruiser must be destroyed.'

Vallery nodded heavily. 'Yes, sir. How?'

'How?' Tyndall's face, framed in the moisture-beaded hood of his duffel, was haggard and grey: but he managed to raise a ghost of a smile. 'As well hung for a sheep. . . . I propose to detach the escorts –including ourselves – and nail him.' He stared out blindly into the fog, his mouth bitter. 'A simple tactical exercise – maybe within even my limited compass.' He broke off suddenly, stared over the side then ducked hurriedly: a shell had exploded in the water – a rare thing – only yards away, erupting spray showering down on the bridge.

'We – the *Stirling* and ourselves – will take him from the south,' he continued, 'soak up his fire and radar. Orr and his death-or-glory boys will approach from the north. In this fog, they'll get very close before releasing their torpedoes. Conditions are all against a single ship – he shouldn't have much chance.'

'All the escorts,' Vallery said blankly. 'You propose to detach *all* the escorts?'

'That's exactly what I propose to do, Captain.'

'But – but – perhaps that's exactly what he wants,' Vallery protested.

'Suicide? A glorious death for the Fatherland? Don't you believe it!' Tyndall scoffed. 'That sort of thing went out with Langesdorff and Middelmann.'

'No, sir!' Vallery was impatient. 'He wants to pull us off, to leave the convoy uncovered.'

'Well, what of it?' Tyndall demanded. 'Who's going to find them in this lot?' He waved an arm at the rolling, twisting fog-banks. 'Dammit, man, if it weren't for their fog-buoys, even our ships couldn't see each other. So I'm damned sure no one else could either.'

'No?' Vallery countered swiftly. 'How about another German cruiser fitted with radar? Or even another wolf-pack? Either could be in radio contact with our friend astern – and he's got our course to the nearest minute!'

'In radio contact? Surely to God our WT is monitoring all the time?'

'Yes, sir. They are. But I'm told its not easy on the VHF ranges.'

Tyndall grunted non-committally, said nothing. He felt desperately tired and confused; he had neither the will nor the ability to pursue the argument further. But Vallery broke in on the silence, the vertical lines between his eyebrows etched deep with worry.

'And why's our friend sitting steadily on our tails, pumping the odd shell among us, unless he's concentrating on driving us along a particular course? It reduces his chance of a hit by 90 per cent – and cuts out half his guns.'

'Maybe he's expecting us to reason like that, to see the obvious.' Tyndall was forcing himself to think, to fight his way through a mental fog no less nebulous and confusing than the dank mist that swirled around him. 'Perhaps he's hoping to panic us into altering course – to the north, of course – where a U-pack *may* very well be.'

'Possible, possible,' Vallery conceded. 'On the other hand, he may have gone a step further. Maybe he wants us to be too clever for our own good. Perhaps he expects us to see the obvious, to avoid it, to continue on our present course – and so do exactly what he wants us to do. . . . He's no fool, sir – we know that now.'

What was it that Brooks had said to Starr back in Scapa, a lifetime ago? 'That fine-drawn feeling . . . that exquisite agony . . . every cell in the brain stretched taut to breaking point, pushing you over the screaming edge of madness.' Tyndall wondered dully how Brooks could have known, could have been so damnably accurate in his description. Anyway, he knew now, knew what it was to stand on the screaming edge. . . . Tyndall appreciated dimly that he was at the limit. That aching, muzzy forehead where to think was to be a blind man wading through a sea of molasses. Vaguely he realized that this must be the first – or was it the last? – symptom of a nervous breakdown. . . . God only knew there had been plenty of them aboard the *Ulysses* during the past months. . . . But he was still the Admiral. . . . He must *do* something, *say* something.

'It's no good guessing, Dick,' he said heavily. Vallery looked at him sharply – never before had old Giles called him anything but 'Captain' on the bridge. 'And we've got to do something. We'll leave the *Vectra* as a sop to our consciences. No more.' He smiled wanly. 'We must have at least two destroyers for the dirty work. Bentley – take this signal for WT. "To all escort vessels and Commander Fletcher on the *Cape Hatteras* . . ." '

Within ten minutes, the four warships, boring south-east through the impenetrable wall of fog, had halved the distance that lay between them and the enemy. The *Stirling, Viking* and *Sirrus* were in constant radio communication with the *Ulysses* – they had to be, for they travelled as blind men in an invious world of grey and she was their eyes and their ears.

'Radar – bridge. Radar – bridge.' Automatically, every eye swung round, riveted on the loudspeaker. 'Enemy altering course to south: increasing speed.'

'Too late!' Tyndall shouted hoarsely. His fists were clenched, his eyes alight with triumph. 'He's left it too late!'

Vallery said nothing. The seconds ticked by, the *Ulysses* knifed her way through cold fog and icy sea. Suddenly, the loudspeaker called again.

'Enemy 180° turn. Heading south-east. Speed 28 knots.'

'28 knots? He's on the run!' Tyndall seemed to have gained a fresh lease on life. 'Captain, I propose that the *Sirrus* and *Ulysses* proceed south-east at maximum speed, engage and slow the enemy. Ask WT to signal Orr. Ask Radar enemy's course.'

He broke off, waited impatiently for the answer.

'Radar – bridge. Course 312. Steady on course. Repeat, steady on course.'

'Steady on course,' Tyndall echoed. 'Captain, commence firing by radar. We have him, we have him!' he cried exultantly. 'He's waited too long! We have him, Captain!'

Again Vallery said nothing. Tyndall looked at him, half in perplexity, half in anger. 'Well, don't you agree?'

'I don't know, sir.' Vallery shook his head doubtfully. 'I don't know at all. Why did he wait so long? Why didn't he turn and run the minute we left the convoy?'

'Too damn' sure of himself!' Tyndall growled.

'Or too sure of something else,' Vallery said slowly. 'Maybe he wanted to make good and sure that we *would* follow him.'

Tyndall growled again in exasperation, made to speak then lapsed into silence as the *Ulysses* shuddered from the recoil of 'A' turret. For a moment, the billowing fog on the fo'c'sle cleared, atomised by the intense heat and flash generated by the exploding cordite. In seconds, the grey shroud had fallen once more.

Then, magically it was clear again. A heavy fog-bank had rolled over them, and through a gap in the next they caught a glimpse of the *Sirrus* dead on the beam, a monstrous bone in her teeth, scything to the south-east at something better than 34 knots. The *Stirling* and the *Viking* were already lost in the fog astern.

'He's too close,' Tyndall snapped. 'Why didn't Bowden tell us? We can't bracket the enemy this way. Signal the *Sirrus*: "Steam 317 five minutes." Captain, same for us. 5 south, then back on course.'

He had hardly sunk back in his chair, and the *Ulysses*, mist-shrouded again, was only beginning to answer her helm when the WT loudspeaker switched on.

'WT – bridge. WT – bridge—'

The twin 5.25s of 'B' turret roared in deafening unison, flame and smoke lancing out through the fog. Simultaneously, a tremendous crash and explosion heaved up the duckboards beneath the feet of the men in the bridge catapulting them all ways, into each other, into flesh-bruising, bone-breaking metal, into the dazed confusion of numbed minds and bodies fighting to reorientate themselves under the crippling handicap of stunning shock, of eardrums rended by the blast, of throat and nostrils stung by acrid fumes, of eyes blinded by dense black smoke. Throughtout it all, the calm impersonal voice of the WT transmitter repeated its unintelligible message.

Gradually the smoke cleared away. Tyndall pulled himself drunkenly to his feet by the rectifying arm of the binnacle: the explosion had blown him clean out of his chair into the centre of the compass platform. He shook his head, dazed, uncomprehending. Must be tougher than he'd imagined: all that way – and he couldn't remember bouncing. And that wrist, now – that lay over at a damned funny angle. His own wrist, he realized with mild surprise. Funny, it didn't hurt a bit. And Carpenter's face there, rising up before him: the bandages were blown off, the gash received on the night of the great storm gaping wide again, the face masked with blood. . . . That girl at Henley, the one he was always talking about – Tyndall wondered, inconsequently, what she would say if she saw him now. . . . Why doesn't the WT transmitter stop that insane yammering? . . . Suddenly his mind was clear.

'My God! Oh, God!' He stared in disbelief at the twisted duckboards, the fractured asphalt beneath his feet. He released his grip on the binnacle, lurched forward into the windscreen: his sense of balance had confirmed what his eyes had rejected: the whole compass platform tilted forward at an angle of 15 degrees.

'What is it, Pilot?' His voice was hoarse, strained, foreign even to himself. 'In God's name, what's happened? A breech explosion in "B" turret?'

'No, sir.' Carpenter drew his forearm across his eyes: the kapok sleeve came away covered in blood. 'A direct hit, sir – smack in the superstructure.'

'He's right, sir.' Carrington had hoisted himself far over the windscreen, was peering down intently. Even at that moment, Tyndall marvelled at the man's calmness, his almost inhuman control. 'And a heavy one. It's wrecked the for'ard pom-pom and there's a hole the size of a door just below us. . . . It must be pretty bad inside, sir.'

Tyndall scarcely heard the last words. He was kneeling over Vallery, cradling his head in his one good arm. The Captain lay crumpled against the gate, barely conscious, his stertorous breathing interrupted by rasping convulsions as he choked on his own blood. His face was deathly white.

'Get Brooks up here, Chrysler – the Surgeon-Commander, I mean!' Tyndall shouted. 'At once!'

'WT – bridge. WT – bridge. Please acknowledge. Please acknowledge.' The voice was hurried, less impersonal, anxiety evident even in its metallic anonymity.

Chrysler replaced the receiver, looked worriedly at the Admiral.

'Well?' Tyndall demanded. 'Is he on his way?'

'No reply, sir.' The boy hesitated. 'I think the line's gone.'

'Hell's teeth!' Tyndall roared. 'What are you doing standing there, then? Go and get him. Take over, Number One, will you? Bentley – have the Commander come to the bridge.'

'WT – bridge. WT – bridge.' Tyndall glared up at the speaker in exasperation, then froze into immobility as the voice went on. 'We have been hit aft. Damage Control reports coding-room destroyed. Number 6 and 7 Radar Offices destroyed. Canteen wrecked. After control tower severely damaged.'

'The After control tower!' Tyndall swore, pulled off his gloves, wincing at the agony of his broken hand. Carefully, he pillowed Vallery's head on the gloves, rose slowly to his feet. 'The After Tower! And Turner's there! I hope to God . . .'

He broke off, made for the after end of the bridge at a stumbling run. Once there he steadied himself, his hand on the ladder rail, and peered apprehensively aft.

At first he could see nothing, not even the after funnel and mainmast. The grey, writhing fog was too dense, too maddeningly opaque. Then suddenly, for a mere breath of time, an icy catspaw cleared away the mist, cleared away the dark, convoluted smoke-pall above the after superstructure. Tyndall's hand tightened convulsively on the rail, the knuckles whitening to ivory.

The after superstructure had disappeared. In its place was a crazy mass of jumbled twisted steel, with 'X' turret, normally invisible from the bridge, showing up clearly beyond, apparently unharmed. But the rest was gone – radar offices, coding-room, police office, canteen, probably most of the after galley. Nothing, nobody could have survived there. Miraculously, the truncated mainmast still stood, but immediately aft of it, perched crazily on top of this devil's scrapheap, the After Tower, fractured and grotesquely askew, lay over at an impossible angle of 60°, its range-finder gone. And Commander Turner had been in there. . . . Tyndall swayed dangerously on top of the steel ladder, shook his head again to fight off the fog clamping down on his mind. There was a heavy, peculiarly dull ache just behind his forehead, and the fog seemed to be spreading from there. . . . A lucky ship, they called the *Ulysses*. Twenty months on the worst run and in the worst waters in the world and never a scratch. . . . But Tyndall had always known that some time, some place, her luck would run out.

He heard hurried steps clattering up the steel ladder, forced his blurred eyes to focus themselves. He recognised the dark, lean face at once: it was Leading Signalman Davies, from the flag deck. His face was white, his breathing short and quick. He opened his mouth to speak, then checked himself, his eyes staring at the handrail.

'Your hand, sir!' He switched his startled gaze from the rail to Tyndall's eyes. 'Your hand! You've no gloves on, sir!'

'No?' Tyndall looked down as if faintly astonished he had a hand. 'No, I haven't, have I? Thank you, Davies.' He pulled his hand off the smooth frozen steel, glanced incuriously at the raw, bleeding flesh. 'It doesn't matter. What is it, boy?'

'The Fighter Direction Room, sir!' Davies's eyes were dark with remembered horror. 'The shell exploded in there. It's – it's just gone, sir. And the Plot above . . .' He stopped short, his jerky voice lost in the crash of the guns of 'A' turret. Somehow it seemed strangely unnatural that the main armament still remained effective. 'I've just come from the FDR and the Plot, sir,' Davies continued, more calmly now. 'They – well, they never had a chance.'

'Including Commander Westcliffe?' Dimly, Tyndall realized the futility of clutching at straws.

'I don't know, sir. It's – it's just bits and pieces in the FDR, if you follow me. But if he was there—'

'He would be,' Tyndall interrupted heavily. 'He never left it during Action Stations . . .'

He stopped abruptly, broken hands clenched involuntarily as the high-pitched scream and impact explosion of HE shells blurred into shattering cacophony, appalling in its closeness.

'My God!' Tyndall whispered. 'That was close! Davies! What the hell! . . .'

His voice choked off in an agonised grunt, arms flailing wildly at the empty air, as his back crashed against the deck of the bridge, driving every last ounce of breath from his body. Wordlessly, convulsively, propelled by desperately thrusting feet and launched by the powerful back-thrust of arms pivoting on the handrails, Davies had just catapulted himself up the last three steps of the ladder, head and shoulders socketing into the Admiral's body with irresistible force. And now Davies, too, was down, stretched his length on the deck, spreadeagled across Tyndall's legs. He lay very still.

Slowly, the cruel breath rasping his tortured lungs, Tyndall surfaced from the black depths of unconsciousness. Blindly, instinctively he struggled to sit up, but his broken hand collapsed under the weight of his body. His legs didn't seem to be much help either: they were quite powerless, as if he were paralysed from the waist down. The fog was gone now, and blinding flashes of colour, red, green and white were coruscating brilliantly across the darkening sky. Starshells? Was the enemy using a new type of starshell? Dimly, with a great effort of will, he realized that there must be some connection between these dazzling flashes and the now excruciating pain behind his forehead. He reached up the back of his right hand: his eyes were still screwed tightly shut. . . . Then the realisation faded and was gone.

'Are you all right, sir?' Don't move. We'll soon have you out of this!' The voice, deep, authoritative, boomed directly above the Admiral's head. Tyndall shrank back, shook his head in imperceptible despair. It was Turner who was speaking, and Turner, he knew, was gone. Was this, then, what it was like to be dead, he wondered dully. This frightening, confused world of blackness and blinding light at the same time, a dark-bright world of pain and powerlessness and voices from the past?

Then suddenly, of their own volition almost, his eyelids flickered and were open. Barely a foot above him were the lean, piratical features of the Commander, who was kneeling anxiously at his side.

'Turner! Turner?' A questioning hand reached out in tentative hope, clutched gratefully, obvious to the pain, at the reassuring solidity of the Commander's arm. 'Turner! It *is* you! I thought—'

'The After Tower, eh?' Turner smiled briefly. 'No, sir – I wasn't within a mile of it. I was coming here, just climbing up to the fo'c'sle deck, when that first hit threw me back down to the main deck. . . . How are you, sir?'

'Thank God! Thank God! I don't know how I am. My legs . . . What in the name of heaven is that?'

His eyes focusing normally again, widened in baffled disbelief. Just above Turner's head, angling for'ard and upward to port, a great white tree-trunk stretched as far as he could see in either direction. Reaching up, he could just touch the massive bole with his hand.

'The foremast, sir,' Turner explained. 'It was sheared clean off by that last shell, just above the lower yardarm. The back blast flung it on to the bridge. Took most of the AA tower with it, I'm afraid – and caved in the Main Tower. I don't think young Courtney could have had much chance. . . . Davies saw it coming – I was just below him at the time. He was very quick—'

'Davies!' Tyndall's dazed mind had forgotten all about him. 'Of course! Davies!' It must be Davies who was pinioning his legs. He craned his neck forward, saw the huddled figure at his feet, the great weight of the mast lying across his back. 'For God's sake, Commander, get him out of that!'

'Just lie down, sir, till Brooks gets here. Davies is all right.'

'All right? All right!' Tyndall was almost screaming, oblivious to the silent figures who were gathering around him. 'Are you mad, Turner? The poor bastard must be in agony!' He struggled frantically to rise, but several pairs of hands held him down, firmly, carefully.

'He's all right, sir.' Turner's voice was surprisingly gentle. 'Really he is, sir. He's all right. Davies doesn't feel a thing. Not any more.' And all at once the Admiral knew and he fell back limply to the deck, his eyes closed in shocked understanding.

His eyes were still shut when Brooks appeared, doubly welcome in his confidence and competence. Within seconds, almost, the Admiral was on his feet, shocked, badly bruised, but otherwise unharmed. Doggedly, and in open defiance of Brooks,

Tyndall demanded that he be assisted back to the bridge. His eyes lit up momentarily as he saw Vallery standing shakily on his feet, a white towel to his mouth. But he said nothing. His head bowed, he hoisted himself painfully into his chair.

'WT – bridge. WT – bridge. Please acknowledge signal.'

'Is that bloody idiot still there?' Tyndall demanded querulously. 'Why doesn't someone—?'

'You've only been gone a couple of minutes, sir,' the Kapok Kid ventured.

'Two minutes!' Tyndall stared at him, lapsed into silence. He glanced down at Brooks, busy bandaging his right hand. 'Have you nothing better to do, Brooks?' he asked harshly.

'No, I haven't,' Brooks replied truculently. 'When shells explode inside four walls, there isn't much work left for a doctor . . . except signing death certificates,' he added brutally. Vallery and Turner exchanged glances. Vallery wondered if Brooks had any idea how far through Tyndall was.

'WT – bridge. WT – bridge. *Vectra* repeats request for instruction. Urgent. Urgent.'

'The *Vectra*!' Vallery glanced at the Admiral, silent now and motionless, and turned to the bridge messenger. 'Chrysler! Get through to WT. Any way you can. Ask them to repeat the first message.'

He looked again at Turner, following the Admiral's sick gaze over the side. He looked down, recoiled in horror, fighting down the instant nausea. The gunner in the sponson below – just another boy like Chrysler – must have seen the falling mast, must have made a panic-stricken attempt to escape. He had barely cleared his cockpit when the radar screen, a hundred square feet of meshed steel carrying the crushing weight of the mast as it had snapped over the edge of the bridge, had caught him fairly and squarely. He lay still now, mangled, broken, something less than human, spreadeagled in outflung crucifixion across the twin barrels of his Oerlikon.

Vallery turned away, sick in body and mind. God, the craziness, the futile insanity of war. Damn that German cruiser, damn those German gunners, damn them, damn them! . . . But why should he? They, too, were only doing a job – and doing it terribly well. He gazed sightlessly at the wrecked shambles of his bridge. What damnably accurate gunnery! He wondered, vaguely, if the *Ulysses* had registered any hits. Probably not, and now, of course, it was impossible. It was impossible now because the *Ulysses*, still racing south-east through the fog,

146

was completely blind, both radar eyes gone, victims to the weather and the German guns. Worse still, all the Fire Control towers were damaged beyond repair. If this goes on, he thought wryly, all we'll need is a set of grappling irons and a supply of cutlasses. In terms of modern naval gunnery, even although her main armament was intact, the *Ulysses* was hopelessly crippled. She just didn't have a chance. What was it that Stoker Riley was supposed to have said – 'being thrown to the wolves'? Yes, that was it – 'thrown to the wolves.' But only a Nero, he reflected wearily, would have blinded a gladiator before throwing him into the arena.

All firing had ceased. The bridge was deadly quiet. Silence, complete silence, except for the sound of rushing water, the muffled roar of the great engine-room intake fans, the monotonous, nerve-drilling pinging of the Asdic – and these, oddly enough, only served to deepen the great silence.

Every eye, Vallery saw, was on Admiral Tyndall. Old Giles was mumbling something to himself, too faint to catch. His face, shockingly grey, haggard and blotched, still peered over the side. He seemed fascinated by the sight of the dead boy. Or was it the smashed Radar screen? Had the full significance of the broken scanner and wrecked Director Towers dawned on him yet? Vallery looked at him for a long moment, then turned away: he knew that it had.

'WT – bridge. WT – bridge.' Everyone on the bridge jumped, swung round in nerve-jangled startlement. Everyone except Tyndall. He had frozen into a graven immobility.

'Signal from *Vectra*. First Signal. Received 0952.' Vallery glanced at his watch. Only six minutes ago! Impossible!

'Signal reads: Contacts, contacts, 3, repeat 3. Amend to 5. Heavy concentration of U-boats, ahead and abeam. Am engaging." '

Every eye on the bridge swung back to Tyndall. His, they knew, the responsibility, his the decision – taken alone, against the advice of his senior officer – to leave the convoy almost unguarded. Impersonally, Vallery admired the baiting, the timing, the springing of the trap. How would old Giles react to this, the culmination of a series of disastrous miscalculations – miscalculations for which, in all fairness, he could not justly be blamed. . . . But he would be held accountable. The iron voice of the loudspeaker broke in on his thoughts.

'Second signal reads: "In close contact. Depth-charging. Depth-charging. One vessel torpedoed, sinking. Tanker torpedoed, damaged, still afloat, under command. Please advise. Please assist. Urgent. Urgent!" '

The speaker clicked off. Again that hushed silence, strained, unnatural. Five seconds it lasted, ten, twenty – then everyone stiffened, looked carefully away.

Tyndall was climbing down from his chair. His movements were stiff, slow with the careful faltering shuffle of the very old. He limped heavily. His right hand, startling white in its snowy sheath of bandage, cradled his broken wrist. There was about him a queer, twisted sort of dignity, and if his face held any expression at all, it was the far-off echo of a smile. When he spoke, he spoke as a man might talk to himself, aloud.

'I am not well,' he said. 'I am going below.' Chrysler, not too young to have an inkling of the tragedy, held open the gate, caught Tyndall as he stumbled on the step. He glanced back over his shoulder, a quick, pleading look, caught and understood Vallery's compassionate nod. Side by side, the old and the young, they moved slowly aft. Gradually, the shuffling died away and they were gone.

The shattered bridge was curiously empty now, the men felt strangely alone. Giles, the cheerful, buoyant, indestructible Giles was gone. The speed, the extent of the collapse was not for immediate comprehension: the only sensation at the moment was that of being unprotected and defenceless and alone.

'Out of the mouths of babes and sucklings . . .' Inevitably, the first to break the silence was Brooks. 'Nicholls always maintained that . . .' He stopped short, his head shaking in slow incredulity. 'I must see what I can do,' he finished abruptly, and hurried off the bridge.

Vallery watched him go, then turned to Bentley. The Captain's face, haggard, shadowed with grizzled beard, the colour of death in the weird half-light of the fog, was quite expressionless.

'Three signals, Chief. First to *Vectra*. "Steer 360°. Do not disperse. Repeat, do not disperse. Am coming to your assistance." ' He paused, then went on: 'Sign it, "Admiral, 14 ACS." Got it? . . . Right. No time to code it. Plain language. Send one of your men to the WT at once.'

'Second: To *Stirling*, *Sirrus* and *Viking*. "Abandon pursuit immediate. Course north-east. Maximum speed." Plain language also.' He turned to the Kapok Kid. 'How's your forehead, Pilot? Can you carry on?'

'Of course, sir.'

'Thank you, boy. You heard me? Convoy re-routed north –
say in a few minutes' time, at 1015. 6 knots. Give me an intersection course as soon as possible.'

'Third signal, Bentley: To *Stirling, Sirrus* and *Viking*:
"Radar out of action. Cannot pick you up on screen. Stream fog-
buoys. Siren at two-minute intervals." Have that message coded.
All acknowledgements to the bridge at once. Commander!'

'Sir?' Turner was at his elbow.

'Hands to defence stations. It's my guess the pack will have
gone before we get there. Who'll be off watch?'

'Lord only knows,' said Turner frankly. 'Let's call it port.'

Vallery smiled faintly. 'Port it is. Organise two parties. First
of port to clear away all loose wreckage: over the side with the
lot – keep nothing. You'll need the blacksmith and his mate,
and I'm sure Dodson will provide you with an oxy-acetylene
crew. Take charge yourself. Second of port as burial party.
Nicholls in charge. All bodies recovered to be laid out in the
canteen when it's clear. . . . Perhaps you could give me a full
report of casualties and damage inside the hour?'

'Long before that, sir. . . . Could I have a word with you in
private?'

They walked aft. As the shelter door shut behind them, Vallery looked at the Commander curiously, half-humorously. 'Another mutiny, perhaps, Commander?'

'No, sir.' Turner unbuttoned his coat, his hand struggling
into the depths of a hip-pocket. He dragged out a flat half-
bottle, held it up to the light. 'Thank the Lord for that!' he
said piously. 'I was afraid it got smashed when I fell. . . . Rum,
sir. Neat. I know you hate the stuff, but never mind. Come on,
you need this!'

Vallery's brows came down in a straight line.

'Rum. Look here, Commander, do you—?'

'To hell with KRs and AFOs!' Turner interrupted rudely.
'Take it – you need it badly! You've been hurt, you've lost a
lot more blood and you're almost frozen to death.' He uncorked
it, thrust the bottle into Vallery's reluctant hands. 'Face facts.
We need you – more than ever now – and you're almost dead
on your feet – and I mean dead on your feet,' he added brutally.
'This might keep you going a few more hours.'

'You put things so nicely,' Vallery murmured. 'Very well.
Against my better judgment . . .'

He paused, the bottle to his mouth.

'And you give me an idea, Commander. Have the bosun

break out the rum. Pipe "Up spirits." Double ration to each man. They, too, are going to need it.' He swallowed, pulled the bottle away, and the grimace was not for the rum.

'Especially,' he added soberly, 'the burial party.'

—— 10 ——

FRIDAY AFTERNOON

The switch clicked on and the harsh fluorescent light flooded the darkening surgery. Nicholls woke with a start, one hand coming up automatically to shield exhausted eyes. The light hurt. He screwed his eyes to slits, peered painfully at the hands of his wrist-watch. Four o'clock! Had he been asleep that long? God, it was bitterly cold!

He hoisted himself stiffly forward in the dentist's chair, twisted his head round. Brooks was standing with his back to the door, snow-covered hood framing his silver hair, numbed fingers fumbling with a packet of cigarettes. Finally he managed to pull one out. He looked up quizzically over a flaring match-head.

'Hallo, there, Johnny! Sorry to waken you, but the skipper wants you. Plenty of time, though.' He dipped the cigarette into the dying flame, looked up again. Nicholls, he thought with sudden compassion, looked ill, desperately tired and over-strained; but no point in telling him so. 'How are you? On second thoughts, don't tell me! I'm a damned sight worse myself. Have you any of that poison left?'

'Poison, sir?' The levity was almost automatic, part of their relationship with each other. 'Just because you make one wrong diagnosis? The Admiral will be all right—'

'Gad! The intolerance of the very young – especially on the providentially few occasions that they happen to be right. . . . I was referring to that bottle of bootleg hooch from the Isle of Mull.'

'Coll,' Nicholls corrected. 'Not that it matters – you've drunk it all, anyway,' he added unkindly. He grinned tiredly at the Commander's crestfallen face, then relented. 'But we do have a bottle of Talisker left.' He crossed over to the poison cupboard, unscrewed the top of a bottle marked 'Lysol.' He heard, rather than saw, the clatter of glass against glass, wondered vaguely, with a kind of clinical detachment, why his hands were shaking so badly.

Brooks drained his glass, sighed in bliss as he felt the grateful warmth sinking down inside him.

'Thank you, my boy. Thank you. You have the makings of a first-class doctor.'

'You think so, sir? I don't. Not any longer. Not after today.' He winced, remembering. 'Forty-four of them, sir, over the side in ten minutes, one after the other, like – like so many sacks of rubbish.'

'Forty-four?' Brooks looked up. 'So many, Johnny?'

'Not really, sir. That was the number of missing. About thirty, rather, and God only knows how many bits and pieces. . . . It was a brush and shovel job in the FDR.' He smiled, mirthlessly. 'I had no dinner, today. I don't think anybody else in the burial party had either. . . . I'd better screen that porthole.'

He turned away quickly, walked across the surgery. Low on the horizon, through the thinly-falling snow, he caught intermittent sight of an evening star. That meant that the fog was gone – the fog that had saved the convoy, had hidden them from the U-boats when it had turned so sharply to the north. He could see the *Vectra*, her depth-charge racks empty and nothing to show for it. He could see the *Vytura*, the damaged tanker, close by, almost awash in the water, hanging grimly on to the convoy. He could see four of the Victory ships, big, powerful, reassuring, so pitifully deceptive in their indestructible permanence. . . . He slammed the scuttle, screwed home the last butterfly nut, then swung round abruptly.

'Why the hell don't we turn back?' he burst out. 'Who does the old man think he's kidding – us or the Germans? No air cover, no radar, not the faintest chance of help! The Germans have us pinned down to an inch now – and it'll be easier still for them as we go on. And there's a thousand miles to go!' His voice rose. 'And every bloody enemy ship, U-boat and plane in the Arctic smacking their lips and waiting to pick us off at their leisure.' He shook his head in despair. 'I'll take my chance with anybody else, sir. You know that. But this is just murder – or suicide. Take your pick, sir. It's all the same when you're dead.'

'Now, Johnny, you're not—'

'*Why* doesn't he turn back?' Nicholls hadn't even heard the interruption. 'He's only got to give the order. What does he want? Death or glory? What's he after? Immortality at my expense, at *our* expense?' He swore, bitterly. 'Maybe Riley was right. Wonderful headlines. "Captain Richard Vallery, DSO, has been posthumously awarded—" '

'Shut up!' Brooks's eye was as chill as the Arctic ice itself, his voice a biting lash.

'You dare to talk of Captain Vallery like that!' he said softly. 'You dare to besmirch the name of the most honourable . . .' He broke off, shook his head in wrathful wonder. He paused to pick his words carefully, his eyes never leaving the other's white, strained face.

'He is a good officer, Lieutenant Nicholls, maybe even a great officer: and that just doesn't matter a damn. What does matter is that he is the finest gentleman – I say "gentleman" – I've ever known, that ever walked the face of this graceless, God-forsaken earth. He is not like you or me. He is not like anybody at all. He walks alone, but he is never lonely, for he has company all the way . . . men like Peter, like Bede, like St Francis of Assisi.' He laughed shortly. 'Funny, isn't it – to hear an old reprobate like myself talk like this? Blasphemy, even, you might call it – except that the truth can never be blasphemy. And I *know*.'

Nicholls said nothing. His face was like a stone.

'Death, glory, immortality,' Brooks went on relentlessly. 'These were your words, weren't they? Death?' He smiled and shook his head again. 'For Richard Vallery, death doesn't exist. Glory? Sure, he wants glory, we all want glory, but all the *London Gazettes* and Buckingham Palaces in the world can't give *him* the kind of glory he wants: Captain Vallery is no longer a child, and only children play with toys. . . . As for immortality.' He laughed, without a trace of rancour now, laid a hand on Nicholls's shoulder. 'I ask you, Johnny – wouldn't it be damned stupid to ask for what he has already?'

Nicholls said nothing. The silence lengthened and deepened, the rush of air from the ventilation louvre became oppressively loud. Finally, Brooks coughed, looked meaningfully at the 'Lysol' bottle.

Nicholls filled the glasses, brought them back. Brooks caught his eyes, held them, and was filled with sudden pity. What was that classical understatement of Cunningham's during the German invasion of Crete – 'It is inadvisable to drive men beyond a certain point.' Trite but true. True even for men like Nicholls. Brooks wondered what particular private kind of hell that boy had gone through that morning, digging out the shattered, torn bodies of what had once been men. And, as the doctor in charge, he would have had to examine them all – or all the pieces he could find. . . .

'Next step up and I'll be in the gutter.' Nicholls's voice was very low. 'I don't know what to say, sir. I don't know what made me say it. . . . I'm sorry.'

'Me too,' Brooks said sincerely. 'Shooting off my mouth like that! And I mean it.' He lifted his glass, inspected the contents lovingly. 'To our enemies, Johnny: their downfall and confusion, and don't forget Admiral Starr.' He drained the glass at a gulp, set it down, looked at Nicholls for a long moment.

'I think you should hear the rest, too, Johnny. You know, why Vallery doesn't turn back.' He smiled wryly. 'It's not because there are as many of these damned U-boats behind us as there are in front – which there undoubtedly are.' He lit a fresh cigarette, went on quietly:

'The Captain radioed London this morning. Gave it as his considered opinion that FR77 would be a goner – "annihilated" was the word he used and, as a word, they don't come any stronger – long before it reached the North Cape. He asked at least to be allowed to go north about, instead of east for the Cape. . . . Pity there was no sunset to-night, Johnny,' he added half-humourously. 'I would have liked to see it.'

'Yes, yes,' Nicholls was impatient. 'And the answer?'

'Eh! Oh, the answer. Vallery expected it immediately.' Brooks shrugged. 'It took four hours to come through.' He smiled, but there was no laughter in his eyes. 'There's something big, something on a huge scale brewing up somewhere. It can only be some major invasion – this under your hat, Johnny?'

'Of course, sir!'

'What it is I haven't a clue. Maybe even the long-awaited Second Front. Anyway, the support of the Home Fleet seems to be regarded as vital to success. But the Home Fleet is tied up – by the *Tirpitz*. And so the orders have gone out – get the *Tirpitz*. Get it at all costs.' Brooks smiled, and his face was very cold. 'We're big fish, Johnny, we're important people. We're the biggest, juiciest bait ever offered up the biggest, juiciest prize in the world today – although I'm afraid the trap's a trifle rusty at the hinges. . . . The signal came from the First Sea Lord – and Starr. The decision was taken at Cabinet level. We go on. We go east.'

'We are the "all costs," ' said Nicholls flatly. 'We are expendable.'

'We are expendable,' Brooks agreed. The speaker above his head clicked on, and he groaned. 'Hell's bells, here we go again!'

He waited until the clamour of the Dusk Action Stations' bugle had died away, stretched out a hand as Nicholls hurried for the door.

'Not you, Johnny. Not yet. I told you, the skipper wants you. On the bridge, ten minutes after Stations begin.'

'What? On the bridge? What the hell for?'

'Your language is unbecoming to a junior officer,' said Brooks solemnly. 'How did the men strike you today?' he went on inconsequently. 'You were working with them all morning. Their usual selves?'

Nicholls blinked, then recovered.

'I suppose so.' He hesitated. 'Funny, they seemed a lot better a couple of days ago, but – well, now they're back to the Scapa stage. Walking zombies. Only more so – they can hardly walk now.' He shook his head. 'Five, six men to a stretcher. Kept tripping and falling over things. Asleep on their feet – eyes not focusing, too damned tired to look where they're going.'

Brooks nodded. 'I know, Johnny, I know. I've seen it myself.'

'Nothing mutinous, nothing sullen about them any more.' Nicholls was puzzled, seeking tiredly to reduce nebulous, scattered impressions to a homogeneous coherence. 'They've neither the energy not the initiative left for a mutiny now, anyway, I suppose, but it's not that. Kept muttering to themselves in the FDR.: "Lucky bastard." "He died easy" – things like that. Or "Old Giles – off his bleedin' rocker." And you can imagine the shake of the head. But no humour, none, not even the grisly variety you usually . . .' He shook his own head. 'I just don't know, sir. Apathetic, indifferent, hopeless – call 'em what you like. I'd call 'em lost.'

Brooks looked at him a long moment, then added gently:

'Would you now?' He mused. 'And do you know, Johnny, I think you'd be right. . . . Anyway,' he continued briskly, 'get up there. Captain's going to make a tour of the ship.'

'What!' Nicholls was astounded. 'During action stations? Leave the bridge?'

'Just that.'

'But – but he can't, sir. It's – it's unprecedented!'

'So's Captain Vallery. That's what I've been trying to tell you all evening.'

'But he'll kill himself!' Nicholls protested wildly.

'That's what I said,' Brooks agreed wryly. 'Clinically, he's dying. He should be dead. What keeps him going God only knows – literally. It certainly isn't plasma or drugs. . . . Once in a while, Johnny, it's salutary for us to appreciate the limits of medicine. Anyway, I talked him into taking you with him. . . . Better not keep him waiting.'

For Lieutenant Nicholls, the next two hours were borrowed from purgatory. Two hours, the Captain took to his inspection, two hours of constant walking, of climbing over storm-sills and tangled wreckage of steel, of squeezing and twisting through impossibly narrow apertures, of climbing and descending a hundred ladders, two hours of exhausting torture in the bitter, heart-sapping cold of a sub-zero temperature. But it was a memory that was to stay with him always, that was never to return without filling him with warmth, with a strange and wonderful gratitude.

They started on the poop – Vallery, Nicholls and Chief Petty Officer Hartley – Vallery would have none of Hastings, the Master-At-Arms, who usually accompanied the Captain on his rounds. There was something oddly reassuring about the big, competent Chief. He worked like a Trojan that night, opening and shutting dozens of watertight doors, lifting and lowering countless heavy hatches, knocking off and securing the thousand clips that held these doors and hatches in place, and before ten minutes had passed, lending a protesting Vallery the support of his powerful arm.

They climbed down the long, vertical ladder to 'Y' magazine, a dim and gloomy dungeon thinly lit with pinpoints of garish light. Here were the butchers, bakers and candlestick makers – the non-specialists in the purely offensive branches. 'Hostilities only' ratings, almost to a man, in charge of a trained gunner, they had a cold, dirty and unglamorous job, strangely neglected and forgotten – strangely, because so terribly dangerous. The four-inch armour encasing them offered about as much protection as a sheet of newspaper to an eight-inch armour-piercing shell or a torpedo. . . .

The magazine walls – walls of shells and cartridge cases – were soaking wet, dripping constantly visibly, with icy condensation. Half the crew were leaning or lying against the racks, blue, pinched, shivering with cold, their breath hanging heavily in the chill air: the others were trudging heavily round and round the hoist, feet splashing in pools of water, lurching, stumbling with sheer exhaustion, gloved hands buried in their pockets, drawn, exhausted faces sunk on their chests. Zombies, Nicholls thought wonderingly, just living zombies. Why don't they lie down?

Gradually, everyone became aware of Vallery's presence, stopped walking or struggling painfully erect, eyes too tired, minds too spent for either wonder or surprise.

'As you were, as you were,' Vallery said quickly. 'Who's in charge here?'

'I am sir.' A stocky overalled figure walked slowly forward, halted in front of Vallery.

'Ah, yes. Gardiner, isn't it?' He gestured to the men circling the hoist. 'What in the world is all this for, Gardiner?'

'Ice,' said Gardiner succinctly. 'We have to keep the water moving or it'll freeze in a couple of minutes. We can't have ice on the magazine floor, sir.'

'No, no, of course not! But – but the pumps, the draincocks?'

'Solid!'

'But surely – this doesn't go on all the time?'

'In flat weather – all the time, sir.'

'Good God!' Vallery shook his head incredulously, splashed his way to the centre of the group, where a slight, boyish figure was coughing cruelly into a corner of an enormous green and white muffler. Vallery placed a concerned arm across the shaking shoulders.

'Are you all right, boy?'

'Yes, sir. 'Course Ah am!' He lifted a thin white face racked with pain. 'Ah'm fine,' he said indignantly.

'What's your name?'

'McQuater, sir.'

'And what's your job, McQuater?'

'Assistant cook, sir.'

'How old are you?'

'Eighteen, sir.' Merciful heavens, Vallery thought, this isn't a cruiser I'm running – it's a nursery!

'From Glasgow, eh?' He smiled.

'Yes, sir.' Defensively.

'I see.' He looked down at the deck, at McQuater's boots half-covered in water. 'Why aren't you wearing your seaboots?' he asked abruptly.

'We don't get issued with them, sir.'

'But your feet, man! They must be soaking!'

'Ah don't know, sir. Ah think so. Anyway,' McQuater said simply, 'it doesna matter. Ah canna feel them.'

Vallery winced. Nicholls, looking at the Captain, wondered if he realised the distressing, pathetic picture he himself presented with his sunken, bloodless face, red, inflamed eyes, his mouth and nose daubed with crimson, the inevitable dark and sodden hand-towel clutched in his left glove. Suddenly unaccountably, Nicholls felt ashamed of himself: that thought, he knew, could never occur to this man.

Vallery smiled down at McQuater.

'Tell me son, honestly – are you tired?'

'Ah am that – Ah mean, aye, aye, sir.'

'Me too,' Vallery confessed. 'But – you can carry on a bit longer?'

He felt the frail shoulders straighten under his arm.

' 'Course Ah can, sir!' The tone was injured, almost truculent. ' '*Course* Ah can!'

Vallery's gaze travelled slowly over the group, his dark eyes glowing as he heard a murmured chorus of assent. He made to speak, broke off in a harsh coughing and bent his head. He looked up again, his eyes wandering once more over the circle of now-anxious faces, then turned abruptly away.

'We won't forget you,' he murmured indistinctly. 'I promise you, we won't forget you.' He splashed quickly away, out of the pool of water, out of the pool of light, into the darkness at the foot of the ladder.

Ten minutes later, they emerged from 'Y' turret. The night sky was cloudless now, brilliant with diamantine stars, little chips of frozen fire in the dark velvet of that fathomless floor. The cold was intense. Captain Vallery shivered involuntarily as the turret door slammed behind them.

'Hartley?'

'Sir?'

'I smelt rum in there!'

'Yes, sir. So did I.' The Chief was cheerful, unperturbed. 'Proper stinking with it. Don't worry about it though, sir. Half the men in the ship bottle their rum ration, keep it for action stations.'

'Completely forbidden in regulations, Chief. You know that as well as I do!'

'I know. But there's no harm, sir. Warms 'em up – and if it gives them Dutch courage, all the better. Remember that night the for'ard pom-pom got two Stukas?'

'Of course.'

'Canned to the wide. Never have done it otherwise. . . . And now, sir, they *need* it.'

'Suppose you're right, Chief. They do and I don't blame them.' He chuckled. 'And don't worry about my knowing – I've always known. But it smelled like a saloon bar in there. . . .'

They climbed up to 'X' turret – the marine turret – then down to the magazine. Wherever he went, as in 'Y' magazine, Vallery left the men the better for his coming. In personal contact, he had some strange indefinable power that lifted men above themselves, that brought out in them something they had never known to exist. To see dull apathy and hopelessness slowly give way to resolution, albeit a kind of numbed and desperate resolve, was to see something that baffled the understanding. Physically and mentally, Nicholls knew, these men had long since passed the point of no return.

Vaguely, he tried to figure it out, to study the approach and technique. But the approach varied every time, he saw, was no more than a natural reaction to different sets of circumstances as they presented themselves, a reaction utterly lacking in calculation or finesse. There *was* no technique. Was pity, then, the activating force, pity for the heart-breaking gallantry of a man so clearly dying? Or was it shame – if *he* can do it, if *he* can still drive that wasted mockery of a body, if he can kill himself just to come to see if *we're* all right – if he can do that and smile – then, by God, we can stick it out, too? That's it, Nicholls said to himself, that's what it is, pity and shame, and he hated himself for thinking it, and not because of the thought, but because he knew he lied. . . . He was too tired to think anyway. His mind was woolly, fuzzy round the edges, his thoughts disjointed, uncontrolled. Like everyone else's. Even Andy Carpenter, the last man you would suspect of it – he felt that way, too, and admitted it. . . . He wondered what the Kapok Kid would have to say to this. . . . The Kid was probably wandering too, but wandering in his own way, back as always on the banks of the Thames. He wondered what the girl in Henley was like. Her name started with 'J' – Joan, Jean – he didn't know: the Kapok Kid had a big golden 'J' on the right breast of his kapok suit – *she* had put it there. But what was she like? Blonde and gay, like the Kid himself? Or dark and kind and gentle, like St Francis of Assisi? St Francis of Assisi? Why in the world did he – ah, yes, old Socrates had been talking about him. Wasn't he the man of whom Axel Munthe . . .

'Nicholls! Are you all right?' Vallery's voice was sharp with anxiety.

'Yes, of course, sir.' Nicholls shook his head, as if to clear it. 'Just gathering wool. Where to now, sir?'

'Engineers' Flat, Damage Control parties, Switchboard, Number 3 Low Power room – no, of course, that's gone – Noyes was killed there, wasn't he? . . . Hartley, I'd appreciate it if you'd let my feet touch the deck occasionally. . . .'

All these places they visited in turn and a dozen others besides – not even the remotest corner, the most impossible of access, did Vallery pass by, if he knew a man was there, closed up to his action station.

They came at last to the engine and boiler-room, to the gulping pressure changes on unaccustomed eardrums as they went through the airlocks, to the antithetically breath-taking blast of heat as they passed inside. In 'A' boiler-room, Nicholls insisted on Vallery's resting for some minutes. He was grey with pain and weakness, his breathing very distressed. Nicholls noticed Hartley talking in a corner, was dimly aware of someone leaving the boiler-room.

Then his eyes caught sight of a burly, swarthy stoker, with bruised cheeks and the remnants of a gorgeous black eye, stalking across the floor. He carried a canvas chair, set it down with a thump behind Vallery.

'A seat, sir,' he growled.

'Thank you, thank you.' Vallery lowered himself gratefully, then looked up in surprise. 'Riley?' he murmured, then switched his glance to Hendry, the Chief Stoker. 'Doing his duty with a minimum of grace, eh?'

Hendry stirred uncomfortably.

'He did it off his own bat, sir.'

'I'm sorry,' Vallery said sincerely. 'Forgive me, Riley. Thank you very much.' He stared after him in puzzled wonder, looked again at Hendry, eyebrows lifted in interrogation.

Hendry shook his head.

'Search me, sir. I've no idea. He's a queer fish. Does things like that. He'd bend a lead pipe over your skull without batting an eyelid – and he's got a mania for looking after kittens and lame dogs. Or if you get a bird with a broken wing – Riley's your man. But he's got a low opinion of his fellowmen, sir.'

Vallery nodded slowly, without speaking, leaned against the canvas back and closed his eyes in exhaustion. Nicholls bent over him.

'Look, sir,' he urged quietly, 'why not give it up? Frankly, sir, you're killing yourself. Can't we finish this some other time?'

'I'm afraid not, my boy.' Vallery was very patient. 'You don't understand. "Some other time" will be too late.' He turned to Hendry. 'So you think you'll manage all right, Chief?'

'Don't you worry about us, sir.' The soft Devon voice was grim and gentle at the same time. 'Just you look after yourself. The stokers won't let you down, sir.'

Vallery rose painfully to his feet, touched him lightly on the arm. 'Do you know, Chief, I never thought you would. . . . Ready, Hartley?' He stopped short, seeing a giant duffel-coated figure waiting at the foot of the ladder, the face below the hood dark and sombre. 'Who's that? Oh, I know. Never thought stokers got so cold,' he smiled.

'Yes, sir, it's Petersen,' Hartley said softly. 'He's coming with us.'

'Who said so? And – and Petersen? Wasn't that—?'

'Yes, sir. Riley's – er – lieutenant in the Scapa business. . . Surgeon Commander's orders, sir. Petersen's going to give us a hand.'

'Us? Me, you mean.' There was no resentment, no bitterness in Vallery's voice. 'Hartley, take my advice – never let yourself get into the hands of the doctors. . . . You think he's safe?' he added half-humorously.

'He'd probably kill the man who looked sideways at you,' Hartley stated matter-of-factly. 'He's a good man, sir. Simple, easily led – but good.'

At the foot of the ladder, Petersen stepped aside to let them pass, but Vallery stopped, looked up at the giant towering six inches above him, into the grave, blue eyes below the flaxen hair.

'Hallo, Petersen. Hartley tells me you're coming with us. Do you really want to? You don't have to, you know.'

'Please, Captain.' The speech was slow and precise, the face curiously dignified in unhappiness. 'I am very sorry for what has happened—'

'No, no!' Vallery was instantly contrite. 'You misunderstand. It's a bitter night up top. But I would like it very much if you would come. Will you?'

Petersen stared at him, then began slowly to smile, his face darkening with pleasure. As the Captain set foot on the first

160

step, the giant arm came round him. The sensation, as Vallery described it later, was very much like going up in a lift.

From there they visited Engineer Commander Dodson in his engine-room, a cheerful, encouraging, immensely competent Dodson, an engineer to his finger-tips in his single-minded devotion to the great engines under his care. Then aft to the Engineer's Flat, up the companionway between the wrecked Canteen and the Police Office, out on to the upper deck. After the heat of the boiler-room, the 100° drop in temperature, a drop that strangled breath with the involuntary constriction of the throat and made a skin-crawling mockery of 'Arctic clothing,' was almost literally paralysing.

The starboard torpedo tubes – the only ones at the standby – were only four paces away. The crew, huddled in the lee of the wrecked bosun's store – the one destroyed by the *Blue Ranger's* shells – were easily located by the stamping of frozen feet, the uncontrollable chattering of teeth.

Vallery peered into the gloom. 'LTO there?'

'Captain, sir?' Surprise, doubt in the voice.

'Yes. How are things going?'

'All right, sir.' He was still off-balance, hesitant. 'I think young Smith's left foot is gone, sir – frostbite.'

'Take him below – at once. And organise your crew into ten minute watches: one to keep a telephone watch here, the other four in the Engineers' Flat. From now on. You understand?' He hurried away, as if to avoid the embarrassment of thanks, the murmurs of smiling gladness.

They passed the torpedo shop, where the spare torpedoes and compressed air cylinders were stored, climbed the ladder to the boat-deck. Vallery paused a moment, one hand on the boat-winch, the other holding the bloody scarf, already frozen almost solid, to mouth and nose. He could just distinguish the shadowy bulkiness of merchantmen on either side: their masts, though, were oddly visible, swinging lazily, gently against the stars as the ships rolled to a slight swell, just beginning. He shuddered, pulled his scarf higher round his neck. God, it was cold! He moved for'ard, leaning heavily on Petersen's arm. The snow, three to four inches deep, cushioned his footsteps as he came up behind an Oerlikon gun. Quietly, he laid a hand on the shoulder of the hooded gunner hunched forward in his cockpit.

'Things all right, gunner?'

No reply. The man appeared to stir, moved forward, then fell still again.

'I said, "Are you all right?" ' Vallery's voice had hardened. He shook the gunner by the shoulder, turned impatiently to Hartley.

'Asleep, Chief! At Action Stations! We're all dead from lack of sleep, I know – but his mates below are depending on him. There's no excuse. Take his name!'

'Take his name!' Nicholls echoed softly, bent over the cockpit. He shouldn't speak like this, he knew, but he couldn't help it. 'Take his name,' he repeated. 'What for? His next of kin? This man is dead.'

The snow was beginning to fall again, cold and wet and feathery, the wind lifting a perceptible fraction. Vallery felt the first icy flakes, unseen in the darkness, brushing his cheeks, heard the distant moan of the wind in the rigging, lonely and forlorn. He shivered.

'His heater's gone.' Hartley withdrew an exploratory hand, straightened up. He seemed tired. 'These Oerlikons have black heaters bolted to the side of the cockpit. The gunners lean against them, sir, for hours at a time. . . . I'm afraid the fuse must have blown. They've been warned against this, sir, a thousand times.'

'Good God! Good God!' Vallery shook his head slowly. He felt old, terribly tired. 'What a useless, futile way to die. . . . Have him taken to the Canteen, Hartley.'

'No good, sir.' Nicholls straightened up also. 'It'll have to wait. What with the cold and the quick onset of rigor mortis – well, it'll have to wait.'

Vallery nodded assent, turned heavily away. All at once, the deck 'speaker aft of the winch blared into raucous life, a rude desecration that shattered the chilled hush of the evening.

'Do you hear there? Do you hear there? Captain, or notify Captain, to contact bridge immediately, please.' Three times the message was repeated, then the 'speaker clicked off.

Quickly Vallery turned to Hartley.

'Where's the nearest phone, Chief?'

'Right here, sir.' Hartley turned back to the Oerlikon, stripped earphones and chest mouthpiece from the dead man. 'That is, if the AA tower is still manned?'

'What's left of it is.'

'Tower? Captain to speak to bridge. Put me through.' He handed the receiver to Vallery. 'Here you are, sir.'

'Thank you. Bridge? Yes, speaking. . . . Yes, yes. . . . Very good. Detail the *Sirrus*. . . . No, Commander, nothing I can do anyway – just maintain position, that's all.' He took the handset off, handed it back to Hartley.

'Asdic contact from *Viking*,' he said briefly. 'Red 90.' He turned, looked out over the dark sea, realized the futility of his instinctive action, and shrugged. 'We've sent the *Sirrus* after him. Come on.'

Their tour of the boat-deck gun-sites completed with a visit to the midships' pom-pom crew, bone-chilled and shaking with cold, under the command of the bearded Doyle, respectfully sulphurous in his outspoken comments on the weather, they dropped down to the main deck again. By this time Vallery was making no protest at all, not even of the most token kind, against Petersen's help and support. He was too glad of them. He blessed Brooks for his foresight and thoughtfulness, and was touched by the rare delicacy and consideration that prompted the big Norwegian to withdraw his supporting arm whenever they spoke to or passed an isolated group of men.

Inside the port screen door and just for'ard of the galley, Vallery and Nicholls, waiting as the others knocked the clamps off the hatch leading down to the stokers' mess, heard the muffled roar of distant depth-charges – there were four in all – felt the pressure waves strike the hull of the *Ulysses*. At the first report Vallery had stiffened, head cocked in attention, eyes fixed on infinity, in the immemorial manner of a man whose ears are doing the work for all the senses. Hesitated a moment, shrugged, bent his arm to hook a leg over the hatch coaming. There was nothing he could do.

In the centre of the stokers' mess was another, heavier hatch. This, too, was opened. The ladder led down to the steering position, which, as in most modern warships, was far removed from the bridge, deep in the heart of the ship below the armour-plating. Here, for a couple of minutes, Vallery talked quietly to the quartermaster, while Petersen, working in the confined space just outside, opened the massive hatch – 450 lbs. of steel, actuated by a counter-balancing pulley weight – which gave access to the hold, to the very bottom of the *Ulysses*, to the Transmitting Station and No. 2 Low Power Room.

A mazing, confusing mystery of a place, this Low Power Room, confusing to the eye and ear. Round every bulkhead, interspersed with scores of switches, breakers and rheostats, were ranged tiered banks of literally hundreds of fuses, baffling to the untrained eye in their myriad complexity. Baffling, too, was the function of a score or more of low-power generators, nerve-drilling in the frenetic dissonance of their high-pitched hums. Nicholls straightened up at the foot of the ladder and shuddered involuntarily. A bad place, this. How easily could mind and nerves slide over the edge of insanity under the pounding, insistent clamour of the desynchronised cacophony!

Just then there were only two men there – an Electric Artificer and his assistant, bent over the big Sperry master gyro, making some latitude adjustment to the highly complex machinery of the compass. They looked up quickly, tired surprise melting into tired pleasure. Vallery had a few words with them – speech was difficult in that bedlam of sound – then moved over to the door of the TS.

He had his glove on the door handle when he froze to complete stillness. Another pattern had exploded, much closer this time, two cable lengths distant, at most. Depth-charges, they knew, but only because reason and experience told them: deep down in the heart of an armour-plated ship there is no sense of explosion, no roar of erruption from a detonating depth-charge. Instead, there is a tremendous, metallic clang, peculiarly tinny in calibre, as if some giant with a giant sledge had struck the ship's side and found the armour loose.

The pattern was followed almost immediately by another two explosions, and the *Ulysses* was still shuddering under the impact of the second when Vallery turned the handle and walked in. The others filed in after the Captain, Petersen closing the door softly behind him. At once the clamour of the electric motors died gratefully away in the hushed silence of the TS.

The TS, fighting heart of the ship, lined like the Low Power Room though it was by banks of fuses, was completely dominated by the two huge electronic computing tables occuping almost half the floor space. These, the vital links between the Fire Control Towers and the turrets, were generally the scene of intense, controlled activity: but the almost total destruction of the towers that morning had made them all but useless, and the undermanned TS was strangely quiet. Altogether, there were only eight ratings and an officer manning the tables.

The air in the TS, a TS prominently behung with 'No Smoking' notices, was blue with tobacco smoke hanging in a flat, lazily drifting cloud near the deckhead – a cloud which spiralled thinly down to smouldering cigarette ends. For Nicholls there was something oddly reassuring in these burning cigarettes: in the unnatural bow-taut stillness, in the inhuman immobility of the men, it was the only guarantee of life.

He looked, in a kind of detached curiosity, at the rating nearest him. A thin, dark-haired man, he was sitting hunched forward, his elbow on the table, the cigarette clipped between his fingers a bare inch from his half-open mouth. The smoke was curling up, lacing its smarting path across vacant, sightless eyes oblivious to the irritation, the ash on the cigarette, itself almost two inches in length, drooping slightly. Vaguely, Nicholls wondered how long he had been sitting there motionless, utterly motionless . . . and why?

Expectancy, of course. That was it – expectancy. It was too obvious. Waiting, just waiting. Waiting for what? For the first time it struck Nicholls, struck him with blinding clarity, what it was to wait, to wait with the bowstring of the nerves strung down at inhuman tension, strung down far beyond quivering to the tautened immobility of snapping point, to wait for the torpedo that would send them crashing into oblivion. For the first time he realized why it was that men who could, invariably it seemed, find something complainingly humorous in any place and every place never joked about the TS. A death trap is not funny. The TS was twenty feet below water level: for'ard of it was 'B' magazine, aft of it 'A' boiler-room, on either side of it were fuel tanks, and below it was the unprotected bottom, prime target for acoustic mines and torpedoes. They were ringed, surrounded, by the elements, the threat of death, and it needed only a flash, a wandering spark, to trigger off the annihilating reality. . . . And above them, in the one in a thousand chance of survival, was a series of hatches which could all too easily warp and lock solid under the metal-twisting shock of an explosion. Besides, the primary idea was that the hatches, deliberately heavy in construction, should *stay* shut in the event of damage, to seal off the flooded compartments below. The men in the TS knew this.

'Good-evening. Everything all right down here?' Vallery's voice, quiet and calm as ever, sounded unnaturally loud. Startled faces, white and strained, twisted round, eyes opening in astonishment: the depth-charging, Nicholls realized, had masked their approach.

'Wouldn't worry too much about the racket outside,' Vallery went on reassuringly. 'A wandering U-boat, and the *Sirrus* is after him. You can thank your stars you're here and not in that sub.'

No one else had spoken. Nicholls, watching them, saw their eyes flickering back from Vallery's face to the forbidden cigarettes, understood their discomfort, their embarrassment at being caught red-handed by the Captain.

'Any reports from the main tower, Brierley?' he asked the officer in charge. He seemed unaware of the strain.

'No, sir. Nothing at all. All quiet above.'

'Fine!' Vallery sounded positively cheerful. 'No news is good news.' He brought his hand out from his pocket, proffered his cigarette case to Brierley. 'Smoke? And you Nicholls?' He took one himself replaced the case, absently picked up a box of matches lying in front of the nearest gunner and if he noticed the gunner's startled disbelief, the slow beginnings of a smile, the tired shoulders slumping fractionally in a long, soundless sigh of relief, he gave no sign.

The thunderous clanging of more depth-charges drowned the rasping of the hatch, drowned Vallery's harsh, convulsive coughing as the smoke reached his lungs. Only the reddening of the sodden hand-towel betrayed him. As the last vibration died away, he looked up, concern in his eyes.

'Good God! Does it always sound like that down here?'

Brierley smiled faintly. 'More or less, sir. Usually more.'

Vallery looked slowly round the men in the TS, nodded for'ard.

' "B" magazine there, isn't it?'

'Yes, sir.'

'And nice big fuel tanks all around you?'

Brierley nodded. Every eye was on the captain.

'I see. Frankly, I'd rather have my own job – wouldn't have yours for a pension. . . . Nicholls, I think we'll spend a few minutes down here, have our smoke in peace. Besides,' – he grinned – 'think of the increased fervour with which we'll count our blessings when we get out of here!'

He stayed five minutes, talking quietly to Brierley and his men. Finally, he stubbed out his cigarette, took his leave and started for the door.

'Sir.' The voice stopped him on the threshold, the voice of the thin dark gunner whose matches he had borrowed.

'Yes, what is it?'

'I thought you might like this.' He held out a clean, white towel. 'That one you've got is – well, sir, I mean it's—'

'Thank you.' Vallery took the towel without any hesitation. 'Thank you very much.'

Despite Petersen's assistance, the long climb up to the upper deck left Vallery very weak. His feet were dragging heavily.

'Look, sir, this is madness!' Nicholls was desperately anxious. 'Sorry, sir, I didn't mean that, but – well, come and see Commander Brooks, please!'

'Certainly.' The reply was a husky whisper. 'Our next port of call anyway.'

Half a dozen paces took them to the door of the Sick Bay. Vallery insisted on seeing Brooks alone. When he came out of the surgery after some time, he seemed curiously refreshed, his step lighter. He was smiling, and so was Brooks. Nicholls lagged behind as the Captain left.

'Give him anything, sir?' he asked. 'Honest to God, he's killing himself!'

'He took something, not much.' Brooks smiled softly. 'I know he's killing himself, so does he. But he knows why, and I know why, and he knows I know why. Anyway, he feels better. Not to worry, Johnny!'

Nicholls waited at the top of the ladder outside the Sick Bay, waited for the Captain and others to come up from the telephone exchange and No. 1 Low Power Room. He stood aside as they climbed the coaming, but Vallery took his arm, walked him slowly for'ard past the Torpedo Office, nodding curtly to Carslake, in nominal charge of a Damage Control party, Carslake, face still swathed in white, looked back with eyes wild and staring and strange, his gaze almost devoid of recognition. Vallery hesitated, shook his head, then turned to Nicholls, smiling.

'BMA in secret session, eh?' he queried. 'Never mind, Nicholls, and don't worry. *I'm* the one who should be worrying.'

'Indeed, sir? Why?'

Vallery shook his head again. 'Rum in the gun turrets, cigarettes in the TS, and now a fine old whisky in a "Lysol" bottle. Thought Commander Brooks was going to poison me – and what a glorious death! Excellent stuff, and the Surgeon Commander's apologies to you for broaching your private supplies.'

Nicholls flushed darkly, began to stammer an apology but Vallery cut him off.

'Forget it, boy, forget it. What does it matter? But it makes me wonder what we're going to find next. An opium den in the Capstan Flat, perhaps, or dancing girls in "B" turret?'

But they found nothing in these or any other places, except cold, misery and hunger-haunted exhaustion. As ever, Nicholls saw, they – or rather, Vallery – left the men the better of their coming. But they themselves were now in a pretty bad state, Nicholls realized. His own legs were made of rubber, he was exhausted by continuous shivering: where Vallery found the strength to carry on, he couldn't even begin to imagine. Even Petersen's great strength was flagging, not so much from half-carrying Vallery as from the ceaseless hammering of clips frozen solid on doors and hatches.

Leaning against a bulkhead, breathing heavily after the ascent from 'A' magazine, Nicholls looked hopefully at the Captain. Vallery saw the look, interpreted it correctly, and shook his head, smiling.

'Might as well finish it, boy. Only the Capstan Flat. Nobody there anyway, I expect, but we might as well have a look.'

They walked slowly round the heavy machinery in the middle of the Capstan Flat, for'ard past the Battery Room and Sailmaker's Shop, past the Electrical Workshop and cells to the locked door of the Painter's Shop, the most for'ard compartment in the ship.

Vallery reached his hand forward, touched the door symbloically, smiled tiredly and turned away. Passing the cell door, he casually flicked open the inspection port, glanced in perfunctorily and moved on. Then he stopped dead, wheeled round and flung open the inspection port again.

'What in the name of – Ralston! What on earth are you doing here?' he shouted.

Ralston smiled. Even through the thick plate glass it wasn't a pleasant smile and it never touched the blue eyes. He gestured to the barred grille, indicating that he could not hear.

Impatiently, Vallery twisted the grille handle.

'What are you doing here, Ralston?' he demanded. The brows were drawn down heavily over blazing eyes. 'In the cells – and at this time! Speak up, man! Tell me!' Nicholls looked at Vallery in slow surprise. The old man – angry! It was unheard of! Shrewdly, Nicholls decided that he'd rather not be the object of Vallery's fury.

'I was locked up here, sir.' The words were innocuous enough, but their tone said, 'What a damned silly question.' Vallery flushed faintly.

'When?'

'At 1030 this morning, sir.'

'And by whom, may I inquire?'

'By the Master-At-Arms, sir.'

'On what authority?' Vallery demanded furiously.

Ralston looked at him a long moment without speaking. His face was expressionless. 'On yours, sir.'

'Mine!' Vallery was incredulous. 'I didn't tell him to lock you up!'

'You never told him not to,' said Ralston evenly. Vallery winced: the oversight, the lack of consideration was his, and that hurt badly.

'Where's your night Action Station?' he asked sharply.

'Port tubes, sir.' That, Vallery realized, explained why only the starboard crew had been closed up.

'And why – why have you been left here during Action Stations? Don't you know it's forbidden, against all regulations?'

'Yes, sir.' Again the hint of the wintry smile. 'I know. But does the Master-At-Arms know?' He paused a second, smiled again. 'Or maybe he just forgot,' he suggested.

'Hartley!' Vallery was on balance again, his tone level and grim. 'The Master-At-Arms here, immediately: see that he brings his keys!' He broke into a harsh bout of coughing, spat some blood into the towel, looked at Ralston again.

'I'm sorry about this, my boy,' he said slowly. 'Genuinely sorry.'

'How's the tanker?' Ralston asked softly.

'What? What did you say?' Vallery was unprepared for the sudden switch. 'What tanker?'

'The one that was damaged this morning, sir.'

'Still with us.' Vallery was puzzled. 'Still with us, but low in the water. Any special reason for asking?'

'Just interested, sir.' The smile was wary, but this time it was a smile. 'You see—'

He stopped abruptly as a deep, muffled roar crashed through the silent night, the pressure blast listing the *Ulysses* sharply to starboard. Vallery lurched, staggered and would have fallen but for Petersen's sudden arm. He braced himself against the righting roll, looked at Nicholls in sudden dismay. The sound was all too familiar.

Nicholls gazed back at him, sorry to his heart for this fresh burden for a dying man, and nodded slowly, in reluctant agreement with the unspoken thought in Vallery's eyes.

'Afraid you're right, sir. Torpedo. Somebody's stopped a packet.'

'Do you hear there!' The capstan flat speaker was hurried, intense, unnaturally loud in the aftermath of silence. 'Do you hear there! Captain on the bridge: urgent. Captain on the bridge: urgent. Captain on the bridge: urgent. . . .'

—— I I ——

FRIDAY EVENING

Bent almost double, Captain Vallery clutched the handrail of the port ladder leading up to the fo'c'sle. Desperately, he tried to look out over the darkened water, but he could see nothing. A mist, a dark and swirling and roaring mist flecked with blood, a mist shot through with dazzling light swam before his eyes and he was blind. His breath came in great whooping gasps that racked his tortured lungs: his lower ribs were clamped in giant pincers, pincers that were surely crushing him. That stumbling, lurching run from the forepeak, he dimly realized, had all but killed him. Close, too damn' close, he thought. I must be more careful in future. . . .

Slowly his vision cleared, but the brilliant light remained. Heavens above, Vallery thought, a blind man could have seen all there was to see here. For there was nothing to be seen but the tenebrous silhouette, so faint as to be almost imagined, of a tanker deep, deep in the water – and a great column of flame, hundreds of feet in height, streaking upwards from the heart of the dense mushroom of smoke that obscured the bows of the torpedoed ship. Even at the distance of half a mile, the roaring of the flames was almost intolerable. Vallery watched appalled. Behind him he could hear Nicholls swearing, softly, bitterly, continuously.

Vallery felt Petersen's hand on his arm. 'Does the Captain wish to go up to the bridge?'

'In a moment, Petersen, in a moment. Just hang on.' His mind was functioning again, his eyes, conditioned by forty years' training, automatically sweeping the horizon. Funny, he thought, you can hardly see the tanker – the *Vytura,* it must be – she's shielded by that thick pall of smoke, probably; but the other ships in the convoy, white, ghost-like, sharply etched against the indigo blue of the sky, were bathed in that deadly glare. Even the stars had died.

He became aware that Nicholls was no longer swearing in repetitious montony, that he was talking to him.

'A tanker, isn't it, sir? Hadn't we better take shelter? Remember what happened to that other one!'

'What one?' Vallery was hardly listening.

'The *Cochella*. A few days ago, I think it was. Good God, no! It was only this morning!'

'When tankers go up, they go up, Nicholls.' Vallery seemed curiously far away. 'If they just burn, they may last long enough. Tankers die hard, terribly hard, my boy: they live where any other ship would sink.'

'But – but she must have a hole the size of a house in her side!' Nicholls protested.

'No odds,' Vallery replied. He seemed to be waiting, watching for something. 'Tremendous reserve buoyancy in these ships. Maybe 27 sealed tanks, not to mention coffer-dams, pump-rooms, engine-rooms. . . . Never heard of the Nelson device for pumping compressed air into a tanker's oil tanks to give it buoyancy, to keep it afloat? Never heard of Captain Dudley Mason and the *Ohio*? Never heard of . . .' He broke off suddenly, and when he spoke again, the dreaming lethargy of the voice was gone.

'I thought so!' he exclaimed, his voice sharp with excitement. 'I thought so! The *Vytura*'s still under way, still under command! Good God, she must still be doing almost 15 knots! The bridge, quick!'

Vallery's feet left the deck, barely touched it again till Petersen set him down carefully on the duckboards in front of the startled Commander. Vallery grinned faintly at Turner's astonishment, at the bushy eyebrows lifting over the dark, lean buccaneer's face, leaner, more recklessly chiselled than ever in the glare of the blazing tanker. If ever a man was born 400 years too late, Vallery thought inconsequentially; but what a man to have around!

'It's all right, Commander.' He laughed shortly. 'Brooks thought I needed a Man Friday. That's Stoker Petersen. Over-enthusiastic, maybe a trifle apt to take orders too literally. . . . But he was a Godsend to me tonight. . . . But never mind me.' He jerked his thumb towards the tanker, blazing even more whitely now, difficult to look at, almost, as the noonday sun. 'How about him?'

'Makes a bloody fine lighthouse for any German ship or plane that happens to be looking for us,' Turner growled. 'Might as well send a signal to Trondheim giving our lat. and long.'

'Exactly,' Vallery nodded. 'Besides setting up some beautiful targets for the sub that got the *Vytura* just now. A dangerous fellow, Commander. That was a brilliant piece of work – in almost total darkness, too.'

'Probably a scuttle somebody forgot to shut. We haven't the ships to keep checking them all the time. And it wasn't so damned brilliant, at least not for him. The *Viking*'s in contact right now, sitting over the top of him. . . . I sent her right away.'

'Good man!' Vallery said warmly. He turned to look at the burning tanker, looked back at Turner, his face set. 'She'll have to go, Commander.'

Turner nodded slowly. 'She'll have to go,' he echoed.

'It *is* the *Vytura*, isn't it?'

'That's her. Same one that caught it this morning.'

'Who's the master?'

'Haven't the foggiest,' Turner confessed. 'Number One, Pilot? Any idea where the sailing list is?'

'No, sir.' The Kapok Kid was hesitant, oddly unsure of himself. 'Admiral had them, I know. Probably gone, now.'

'What makes you think that?' Vallery asked sharply.

'Spicer, his pantry steward, was almost choked with smoke this afternoon, found him making a whacking great fire in his bath,' the Kapok Kid said miserably. 'Said he was burning vital documents that must not fall into enemy hands. Old newspapers, mostly, but I think the list must have been among them. It's nowhere else.'

'Poor old . . .' Turner remembered just in time that he was speaking to the Admiral, broke off, shook his head in compassionate wonder. 'Shall I send a signal to Fletcher on the *Cape Hatteras*?'

'Never mind.' Vallery was impatient. 'There's no time. Bentley – to the master, *Vytura*: "Please abandon ship immediately: we are going to sink you." '

Suddenly Vallery stumbled, caught hold of Turner's arm.

'Sorry,' he apologised. 'I'm afraid my legs are going. Gone, rather.' He smiled up wryly at the anxious faces. 'No good pretending any longer, is there? Not when your legs start a mutiny on their own. Oh, dear God, I'm done!'

172

'And no bloody wonder!' Turner swore. 'I wouldn't treat a mad dog the way you treat yourself! Come on, sir. Admiral's chair for you – now. If you don't, I'll get Petersen to you,' he threatened, as Vallery made to protest. The protest died in a smile, and Vallery meekly allowed himself to be helped into a chair. He sighed deeply, relaxed into the God-sent support of the back and arms of the chair. He felt ghastly, powerless, his wasted body a wide sea of pain, and deadly cold; all these things, but also proud and grateful – Turner had never even suggested that he go below.

He heard the gate crash behind him, the murmur of voices, then Turner was at his side.

'The Master-At-Arms, sir. Did you send for him?'

'I certainly did.' Vallery twisted in his chair, his face grim. 'Come here, Hastings!'

The Master-At-Arms stood at attention before him. As always, his face was a mask, inscrutable, expressionless, almost inhuman in that fierce light.

'Listen carefully.' Vallery had to raise his voice above the roar of the flames: the effort even to speak was exhausting. 'I have no time to talk to you now. I will see you in the morning. Meantime, you will release Leading Seaman Ralston immediately. You will then hand over your duties, your papers and your keys to Regulating Petty Officer Perrat. Twice, now, you have overstepped the limits of your authority: that is insolence, but it can be overlooked. But you have also kept a man locked in cells during Action Stations. The prisoner would have died like a rat in a trap. You are no longer Master-At-Arms of the *Ulysses*. That is all.'

For a couple of seconds Hastings stood rigidly in shocked unbelieving silence, then the iron discipline snapped. He stepped forward, arms raised in appeal, the mask collapsed in contorted bewilderment.

'Relieved of my duties? Relieved of my duties! But, sir, you can't do that! You can't ...'

His voice broke off in a gasp of pain as Turner's iron grip closed over his elbow.

'Don't say "can't" to the Captain,' he whispered silkily in his ear. 'You heard him? Get off the bridge!'

The gate clicked behind him. Carrington said, conversationally: 'Somebody's using his head aboard the *Vytura* – fitted a red filter to his Aldis. Couldn't see it otherwise.'

Immediately the tension eased. All eyes were on the winking

red light, a hundred feet aft of the flames, and even then barely distinguishable. Suddenly it stopped.

'What does he say, Bentley?' Vallery asked quickly.

Bentley coughed apologetically. 'Message reads: "Are you hell. Try it and I will ram you. Engine intact. We can make it." '

Vallery closed his eyes for a moment. He was beginning to appreciate how old Giles must have felt. When he looked up again, he had made his decision.

'Signal: "You are endangering entire convoy. Abandon ship at once. Repeat, at once." ' He turned to the Commander, his mouth bitter. 'I take off my hat to him. How would *you* like to sit on top of enough fuel to blow you to Kingdom Come. . . . Must be oil in some of his tanks. . . . God, how I hate to have to threaten a man like that!'

'I know, sir,' Turner murmured. 'I know how it is. . . . Wonder what the *Viking*'s doing out there? Should be hearing from her now?'

'Send a signal,' Vallery ordered. 'Ask for information.' He peered aft, searched briefly for the Torpedo Lieutenant. 'Where's Marshall?'

'Marshall?' Turner was surprised. 'In the Sick Bay, of course. Still on the injured list, remember – four ribs gone?'

'Of course, of course!' Vallery shook his head tiredly, angry with himself. 'And the Chief Torpedo Gunner's Mate – Noyes, isn't it? – he was killed yesterday in Number 3. How about Vickers?'

'He was in the FDR.'

'In the FDR,' Vallery repeated slowly. He wondered why his heart didn't stop beating. He was long past the stage of chilled bone and coagulating blood. His whole body was a great block of ice. . . . He had never known that such cold could exist. It was very strange, he thought, that he was no longer shivering. . . .

'I'll do it myself, sir,' Turner interrupted his wandering. 'I'll take over the bridge Torpedo Control – used to be the worst Torps. officer on the China Station.' He smiled faintly. 'Perhaps the hand has not lost what little cunning it ever possessed!'

'Thank you.' Vallery was grateful. 'You just do that.'

'We'll have to take him from starboard,' Turner reminded him. 'Port control was smashed this morning – foremast didn't

174

do it any good. . . . I'll go check the Dumaresq.[1] . . . Good God!'
His hand gripped Vallery's shoulder with a strength that made
him wince. 'It's the Admiral, sir! He's coming on the bridge!'

Incredulously, Vallery twisted round in his chair. Turner was
right. Tyndall was coming through the gate, heading purposefully towards him. In the deep shadow cast by the side of the
bridge, he seemed disembodied. The bare head, sparsely
covered with thin, straggling wisps of white, the grey, pitifully-
shrunken face, the suddenly stooped shoulders, unaccountably
thin under black oilskins, all these were thrown into harsh
relief by the flames. Below, nothing was visible. Silently, Tyndall padded his way across the bridge, stood waiting at Vallery's
side.

Slowly, leaning on Turner's ready arm, Vallery climbed
down. Unsmiling, Tyndall looked at him, nodded gravely,
hoisted himself into his seat. He picked up the binoculars from
the ledge before him, slowly quartered the horizon.

It was Turner who noticed it first.

'Sir! You've no gloves on, sir!'

'What? What did you say?' Tyndall replaced the glasses,
looked incredulously at his blood-stained, bandaged hands. 'Ah!
Do you know, I *knew* I had forgotten something. That's the
second time. Thank you, Commander.' He smiled courteously,
picked up the binoculars again, resumed his quartering of the
horizon. All at once Vallery felt another, deadlier chill pass
through him, and it had nothing to do with the bitter chill of
the Arctic night.

Turner hesitated helplessly for a second, then turned quickly
to the Kapok Kid.

'Pilot! Haven't I seen gauntlets hanging in your chart-
house?'

'Yes, sir. Right away!' The Kapok Kid hurried off the bridge.
Turner looked up at the Admiral again.

'Your head, sir – you've nothing on. Wouldn't you like a
duffel coat, a hood, sir?'

'A hood?' Tyndall was amused. 'What in the world for? I'm
not cold. . . . If you'll excuse me, Commander?' He turned the
binoculars full into the glare of the blazing *Vytura*. Turner
looked at him again, looked at Vallery, hesitated, then walked
aft.

---

[1] The Dumaresq was a miniature plotting table on which such relevant factors
as corresponding speeds and courses were worked out to provide firing tracks
for the torpedoes.

Carpenter was on his way back with the gloves when the WT loudspeaker clicked on.

'WT – bridge. WT – bridge. Signal from *Viking*: "Lost contact. Am continuing search." '

'Lost contact!' Vallery exclaimed. Lost contact – the worst possible thing that could have happened! A U-boat out there, loose, unmarked, and the whole of FR77 lit up like a fairground. A fairground, he thought bitterly, clay pipes in a shooting gallery and with about as much chance of hitting back once contact had been lost. Any second now. . . .

He wheeled round, clutched at the binnacle for support. He had forgotten how weak he was, how the tilting of the shattered bridge affected balance.

'Bentley! No reply from the *Vytura* yet?'

'No, sir,' Bentley was as concerned as the Captain, as aware of the desperate need for speed. 'Maybe his power's gone – no, no, no, there he is now, sir!'

'Captain, sir.'

Vallery looked round. 'Yes, Commander, what is it? Not more bad news, I hope?'

' 'Fraid so, sir. Starboard tubes won't train – jammed solid.'

'Won't train,' Vallery snapped irritably. 'That's nothing new, surely. Ice, frozen snow. Chip it off, use boiling water, blow-lamps, any old—'

'Sorry, sir.' Turner shook his head regretfully. 'Not that. Rack and turntable buckled. Must have been either the shell that got the bosun's store or Number 3 Low Power Room – immediately below. Anyway – kaput!'

'Very well, then!' Vallery was impatient. 'It'll have to be the port tubes.'

'No bridge control left, sir,' Turner objected. 'Unless we fire by local control?'

'No reason why not, is there?' Vallery demanded. 'After all, that's what torpedo crews are trained for. Get on to the port tubes – I assume the communication line there is still intact – tell them to stand by.'

'Yes, sir.'

'And Turner?'

'Sir?'

'I'm sorry.' He smiled crookedly. 'As old Giles used to say of himself, I'm just a crusty old curmudgeon. Bear with me, will you?'

Turner grinned sympathetically, then sobered quickly. He jerked his head forward.

'How is he, sir?'

Vallery looked at the Commander for a long second, shook his head, almost imperceptibly. Turner nodded heavily and was gone.

'Well, Bentley? What does he say?'

'Bit confused, sir,' Bentley apologised. 'Couldn't get it all. Says he's going to leave the convoy, proceed on his own. Something like that, sir.'

Proceed on his own! That was no solution, Vallery knew. He might still burn for hours, a dead give-away, even on a different course. But to proceed on his own! An unprotected crippled, blazing tanker – and a thousand miles to Murmansk, the worst thousand miles in all the world! Vallery closed his eyes. He felt sick to his heart. A man like that, and a ship like that – and he had to destroy them both!

Suddenly Tyndall spoke.

'Port 30!' he ordered. His voice was loud, authoritative. Vallery stiffened in dismay. Port 30! They'd turn into the *Vytura*.

There was a couple of seconds' silence, then Carrington, Officer of the Watch, bent over the speaking-tube, repeated: 'Port 30.' Vallery started forward, stopped short as he saw Carrington gesturing at the speaking-tube. He'd stuffed a gauntlet down the mouthpiece.

'Midships!'

'Midships, sir!'

'Steady! Captain?'

'Sir?'

'That light hurts my eyes,' Tyndall complained. 'Can't we put that fire out?'

'We'll try, sir.' Vallery walked across, spoke softly. 'You look tired, sir. Wouldn't you like to go below?'

'What? Go below! Me!'

'Yes, sir. We'll send for you if we need you,' he added persuasively.

Tyndall considered this for a moment, shook his head grimly.

'Won't do, Dick. Not fair to you. . . .' His voice trailed away and he muttered something that sounded like 'Admiral Tyndall,' but Vallery couldn't be sure.

'Sir? I didn't catch—'

'Nothing!' Tyndall was very abrupt. He looked away towards the *Vytura*, exclaimed in sudden pain, flung up an arm to protect his eyes. Vallery, too, started back, eyes screwed up to shut out the sudden blinding flash of flame from the *Vytura*.

The explosion crashed in their ears almost simultaneously, the blast of the pressure wave sent them reeling. The *Vytura* had been torpedoed again, right aft, close to her engine-room, and was heavily on fire there. Only the bridge island, amidships, was miraculously free from smoke and flames. Even in the moment of shock, Vallery thought, 'She must go now. She can't last much longer.' But he knew he was deluding himself, trying to avoid the inevitable, the decision he must take. Tankers, as he'd told Nicholls, died hard, terribly hard. Poor old Giles, he thought unaccountably, poor old Giles.

He moved aft to the port gate. Turner was shouting angrily into the telephone.

'You'll damn' well do what you're told, do you hear? Get them out immediately! Yes, I said "immediately"!'

Vallery touched his arm in surprise. 'What's the matter, Commander?'

'Of all the bloody insolence!' Turner snorted. 'Telling *me* what to do!'

'Who?'

'The LTO on the tubes. Your friend Ralston!' said Turner wrathfully.

'Ralston! Of course!' Vallery remembered now. 'He told me that was his night Action Stations. What's wrong?'

'What's wrong: Says he doesn't think he can do it. Doesn't like to, doesn't wish to do it, if you please. Blasted insubordination!' Turner fumed.

Vallery blinked at him. 'Ralston – are you sure? But of course you are. . . . I wonder. . . . That boy's been through a very private hell, Turner. Do you think—'

'I don't know what to think!' Turner lifted the phone again. 'Tubes nine-oh? At last! . . . What? What did you say? . . . Why don't we . . . Gunfire! Gunfire!' He hung up the receiver with a crash, swung round on Vallery.

'Asks me, pleads with me, for gunfire instead of torpedoes!' He's mad, he must be! But mad or not, I'm going down there to knock some sense into that mutinous young devil!' Turner was angrier than Vallery had ever seen him. 'Can you get Carrington to man this phone, sir?'

'Yes, yes, of course!' Vallery himself had caught up some of Turner's anger. 'Whatever his sentiments, this is no time to express them!' he snapped. 'Straighten him up. . . . Maybe I've been too lenient, too easy, perhaps he thinks we're in his debt, at some psyhcological disadvantage, for the shabby treatment he's received. . . . All right, all right, Commander!' Turner's mounting impatience was all too evident. 'Off you go. Going in to attack in three or four minutes.' He turned abruptly, passed in to the compass platform.

'Bentley!'

'Sir?'

'Last signal—'

'Better have a look, sir,' Carrington interrupted. 'He's slowing up.'

Vallery stepped forward, peered over the windscreen. The *Vytura*, a roaring mass of flames was falling rapidly astern.

'Clearing the davits, sir!' the Kapok Kid reported excitedly. 'I think – yes, yes, I can see the boat coming down!'

'Thank God for that!' Vallery whispered. He felt as though he had been granted a new lease of life. Head bowed, he clutched the screen with both hands – reaction had left him desperately weak. After a few seconds he looked up.

'WT code signal to *Sirrus*,' he ordered quietly. ' "Circle well astern. Pick up survivors from the *Vytura*'s lifeboat." '

He caught Carrington's quick look and shrugged. 'It's a better than even risk, Number One, so to hell with Admiralty orders. God,' he added with sudden bitterness, 'wouldn't I love to see a boatload of the "no-survivors-will-be-picked-up" Whitehall warriors drifting about in the Barents Sea!' He turned away, caught sight of Nicholls and Petersen.

'Still here, are you, Nicholls? Hadn't you better get below?'

'If you wish, sir.' Nicholls hesitated, nodded forward towards Tyndall.

'I thought, perhaps—'

'Perhaps you're right, perhaps you're right.' Vallery shook his head in weary perplexity. 'We'll see. Just wait a bit, will you?' He raised his voice. 'Pilot!'

'Sir?'

'Slow ahead both!'

'Slow ahead both, sir!'

Gradually, then more quickly, way fell off the *Ulysses* and she dropped slowly astern of the convoy. Soon, even the last ships in the lines were ahead of her, thrashing their way to the northeast. The snow was falling more thickly now, but still the ships were bathed in that savage glare, frighteningly vulnerable in their naked helplessness.

Seething with anger, Turner brought up short at the port torpedoes. The tubes were out, their evil, gaping mouths, highlighted by the great flames, pointing out over the intermittent
refulgence of the rolling swell. Ralston, perched high on the unprotected control position above the central tube, caught his
eye at once.

'Ralston!' Turner's voice was harsh, imperious. 'I want to
speak to you!'

Ralston turned round quickly, rose, jumped on to the deck.
He stood facing the Commander. They were of a height, their
eyes on a level, Ralston's still, blue, troubled, Turner's dark
and stormy with anger.

'What the hell's the matter with you, Ralston?' Turner
ground out. 'Refusing to obey orders, is that it?'

'No, sir.' Ralston's voice was quiet, curiously strained. 'That's
not true.'

'Not true!' Turner's eyes were narrowed, his fury barely in
check. 'Then what's all this bloody claptrap about not wanting
to man the tubes? Are you thinking of emulating Stoker Riley?
Or have you just taken leave of your senses – if any?'

Ralston said nothing.

The silence, a silence all too easily interpreted as dumb insolence, infuriated Turner. His powerful hands reached out,
grasped Ralston's duffel coat. He pulled the rating towards him,
thrust his face close to the other's.

'I asked a question, Ralston,' he said softly. 'I haven't had an
answer. I'm waiting. What *is* all this?'

'Nothing, sir.' Distress in his eyes, perhaps, but no fear. 'I – I
just don't want to, sir. I hate to do it – to send one of our own
ships to the bottom!' The voice was pleading now, blurred
with overtones of desperation: Turner was deaf to them. 'Why
does she have to go, sir!' he cried. 'Why? Why? Why?'

'None of your bloody business – but as it so happens she's
endangering the entire convoy!' Turner's face was still within
inches of Ralston's. 'You've got a job to do, orders to obey. Just
get up there and obey them! Go on!' he roared, as Ralston
hesitated. 'Get up there! He fairly spat the words out.

Ralston didn't move.

'There are other LTOs, sir!' His arms lifted high in appeal,
something in the voice cut through Turner's blind anger: he
realized, almost with shock, that this boy was desperate.
'Couldn't *they*—?'

'Let someone else do the dirty work, eh? That's what you

mean, isn't it?' Turner was bitingly contemptuous. 'Get them to do what you won't do yourself, you – you contemptible young bastard! Communications Number? Give me your set. I'll take over from the bridge.' He took the phone, watched Ralston climb slowly back up and sit hunched forward, head bent over the Dumaresq.

'Number One? Commander speaking. All set here. Captain there?'

'Yes, sir. I'll call him.' Carrington put down the phone, walked through the gate.

'Captain, sir. Commander's on the—'

'Just a moment!' The upraised hand, the tenseness of the voice stopped him. 'Have a look. No. 1. What do you think?' Vallery pointed towards the *Vytura*, past the oil-skinned figure of the Admiral. Tyndall's head was sunk on his chest, and he was muttering incoherently to himself.

Carrington followed the pointing finger. The lifeboat, dimly visible through the thickening snow, had slipped her falls while the *Vytura* was still under way. Crammed with men, she was dropping quickly astern under the great twisting column of flame – dropping far too quickly astern as the First Lieutenant suddenly realized. He turned round, found Vallery's eyes, bleak and tired and old, on his own. Carrington nodded slowly.

'She's picking up, sir. Under way, under command. . . . What are you going to do, sir?'

'God help me, I've no choice. Nothing from the *Viking*, nothing from the *Sirrus*, nothing from our Asdic – and that U-boat's still out there. . . . Tell Turner what's happened. Bentley!'

'Sir?'

'Signal the *Vytura*.' The mouth, whitely compressed, belied the eyes – eyes dark and filled with pain. ' "Abandon ship. Torpedoing you in three minutes. Last signal." Port 20, Pilot!'

'Port 20 it is, sir.'

The *Vytura* was breaking off tangentially, heading north. Slowly, the *Ulysses* came round, almost paralleling her course, now a little astern of her.

'Half-ahead, Pilot!'

'Half-ahead it is, sir.'

'Pilot!'

'Sir?'

'What's Admiral Tyndall saying? Can you make it out?'

181

Carpenter bent forward, listened, shook his head. Little flurries of snow fell off his fur helmet.

'Sorry, sir. Can't make him out – too much noise from the *Vytura*. . . . I think he's humming, sir.'

'Oh, God!' Vallery bent his head, looked up again, slowly, painfully. Even so slight an effort was labour intolerable.

He looked across to the *Vytura*, stiffened to attention. The red Aldis was winking again. He tried to read it, but it was too fast: or perhaps his eyes were just too old, or tired: or perhaps he just couldn't think any more. . . . There was something weirdly hypnotic about that tiny crimson light flickering between these fantastic curtains of flame, curtains sweeping slowly, ominously together, majestic in their inevitability. And then the little red light had died, so unexpectedly, so abruptly, that Bentley's voice reached him before the realization.

'Signal from the *Vytura*, sir.'

Vallery tightened his grip on the binnacle. Bentley guessed the nod, rather than saw it.

'Message reads: "Why don't you — off. Nuts to the Senior Service. Tell him I send all my love." ' The voice died softly away, and there was only the roaring of the flames, the lost pinging of the Asdic.

'All my love.' Vallery shook his head in silent wonderment. 'All my love! He's crazy! He must be. "All my love," and I'm going to destroy him. . . . Number One!'

'Sir?'

'Tell the Commander to stand by!'

Turner repeated the message from the bridge, turned to Ralston.

'Stand by, LTO!' He looked out over the side, saw that the *Vytura* was slightly ahead now, that the *Ulysses* was still angling in on an interception course. 'About two minutes now, I should say.' He felt the vibration beneath his feet dying away, knew the *Ulysses* was slowing down. Any second now, and she'd start slewing away to starboard. The receiver crackled again in his ear, the sound barely audible above the roaring of the flames. He listened, looked up. ' "X" and "Y" only. Medium settings. Target 11 knots.' He spoke into the phone. 'How long?'

'How long, sir?' Carrington repeated.

'Ninety seconds,' Vallery said huskily. 'Pilot – starboard 10.' He jumped, startled, as he heard the crash of falling bincoulars, saw the Admiral slump forward, face and neck striking cruelly on the edge of the windscreen, the arms dangling loosely from the shoulders.

'Pilot!'

But the Kapok Kid was already there. He slipped an arm under Tyndall, took most of the dead weight off the biting edge of the screen.

'What's the matter, sir?' His voice was urgent, blurred with anxiety. 'What's wrong?'

Tyndall stirred slightly, his cheek lying along the edge of the screen.

'Cold, cold, cold,' he intoned. The quavering tones were those of an old, a very old man.

'What? What did you say, sir?' the Kapok Kid begged.

'Cold. I'm cold. I'm terribly cold! My feet, my feet!' The old voice wandered away, and the body slipped into a corner of the bridge, the grey face upturned to the falling snow.

Intuition, an intuition amounting to a sudden sick certainty, sent the Kapok Kid plunging to his knees. Vallery heard the muffled exclamation, saw him straighten up and swing round, his face blank with horror.

'He's – he's got nothing on, sir,' he said unsteadily. 'He's barefoot! They're frozen – frozen solid!'

'Barefoot?' Vallery repeated unbelievingly. 'Barefoot! It's not possible!'

'And pyjamas, sir! That's all he's wearing!'

Vallery lurched forward, peeling off his gloves. He reached down, felt his stomach turn over in shocked nausea as his fingers closed on ice-chilled skin. Bare feet! And pyjamas! Bare feet – no wonder he'd padded so silently across the duckboards! Numbly, he remembered that the last temperature reading had shown 35° of frost. And Tyndall, feet caked in frozen snow and slush, had been sitting there for almost five minutes! . . . He felt great hands under his armpits, felt himself rising effortlessly to his feet. Petersen. It *could* only be Petersen, of course. And Nicholls behind him.

'Leave this to me, sir. Right, Petersen, take him below.' Nicholls's brisk, assured voice, the voice of a man competent in his own element, steadied Vallery, brought him back to the present, and the demands of the present, more surely than anything else could have done. He became aware of Carrington's clipped, measured voice, reeling off course, speed, directions, saw the *Vytura* 50° off the port bow, dropping slowly, steadily aft. Even at that distance, the blast of heat was barely tolerable

– what in the name of heaven was it like on the bridge of the *Vytura?*

'Set course, Number One,' he called. 'Local control.'

'Set course, local control.' Carrington might have been on a peace-time exercise in the Solent.

'Local control,' Turner repeated. He hung up the set, looked round. 'You're on your own, Ralston,' he said softly.

There was no reply. The crouched figure on the control position, immobile as graved stone, gave no sign that he had heard.

'Thirty seconds!' Turner said sharply. 'All lined up?'

'Yes, sir.' The figure stirred. 'All lined up.' Suddenly, he swung round, in desperate, final appeal. 'For God's sake, sir! Is there no other—'

'Twenty seconds!' Turner said viciously. 'Do you want a thousand lives on your lily-livered conscience? And if you miss...'

Ralston swung slowly back. For a mere breath of time, his face was caught full in the harsh glare of the *Vytura*: with sudden shock, Turner saw that the eyes were masked with tears. Then he saw the lips move. 'Don't worry, sir. I won't miss.' The voice was quite toneless, heavy with nameless defeat.

Perplexed, now, rather than angry, and quite uncomprehending, Turner saw the left sleeve come up to brush the eyes, saw the right hand stretch forward, close round the grip of 'X' firing lever. Incongruously, there sprang to Turner's mind the famous line of Chaucer, 'In goon the spears full sadly in arrest.' In the closing of that hand there was the same heart-stopping decision, the same irrevocable finality.

Suddenly, so suddenly that Turner started in spite of himself, the hand jerked convulsively back. He heard the click of the tripping lever, muffled roar in the explosion chamber, the hiss of compressed air, and the torpedo was gone, its evil sleekness gleaming fractionally in the light of the flames before it crashed below the surface of the sea. It was hardly gone before the tubes shuddered again and the second torpedo was on its way.

For five, ten seconds Turner stared out, fascinated, watching the arrowing wakes of bubbles vanish in the distance. A total of 1500 lbs. of Amatol in these warheads – God help the poor bastards aboard the *Vytura*. ... The deck 'speaker clicked on.

'Do you hear there? Do you hear there? Take cover immediately! Take cover immediately!' Turner stirred, tore his eyes away from the sea, looked up, saw that Ralston was still crouched in his seat.

'Come down out of there, you young fool!' he shouted. 'Want to be riddled when the *Vytura* goes up? Do you hear me?'

Silence. No word, no movement, only the roaring of the flames.

'Ralston!'

'I'm all right, sir.' Ralston's voice was muffled: he did not even trouble to turn his head.

Turner swore, leapt up on the tubes, dragged Ralston from his seat, pulled him down to the deck and into shelter. Ralston offered no resistance: he seemed sunk in a vast apathy, an un-caring indifference.

Both torpedoes struck home. The end was swift, curiously unspectacular. Listeners – there were no watchers – on the *Ulysses* tensed themselves for the shattering detonation, but the detonation never came. Broken-backed and tired of fighting, the *Vytura* simply collapsed in on her stricken mid-ships, lay gradually, wearily over on her side and was gone.

Three minutes later, Turner open the door of the Captain's shelter, pushed Ralston in before him.

'Here you are, sir,' he said grimly. 'Thought you might like to see what a conscientious objecter looks like!'

'I certainly do!' Vallery laid down the log-book, turned a cold eye on the torpedoman, looked him slowly up and down. 'A fine job, Ralston, but it doesn't excuse your conduct. Just a minute, Commander.'

He turned back to the Kapok Kid. 'Yes, that seems all right, Pilot. It'll make good reading for their lordships,' he added bitterly. 'The ones the Germans don't get, we finish off for them. . . . Remember to signal the *Hatteras* in the morning, ask for the name of the master of the *Vytura*.'

'He's dead. . . . You needn't trouble yourself!' said Ralston bitterly, then staggered as the Commander's open hand smashed across his face. Turner was breathing heavily, his eyes dark with anger.

'You insolent young devil!' he said softly. 'That was just a little too much from you.'

Ralston's hand came up slowly, fingering the reddening weal on his cheek.

'You misunderstand me, sir.' There was no anger, the voice was a fading murmur, they had to strain to catch his words.

'The master of the *Vytura* – I can tell you his name. It's Ralston. Captain Michael Ralston. He was my father.'

—— 12 ——

SATURDAY

To all things an end, to every night its dawn; even to the longest night when dawn never comes, there comes at last the dawn. And so it came for FR77, as grey, as bitter, as hopeless as the night had been long. But it came.

It came to find the convoy some 350 miles north of the Arctic Circle, steaming due east along the 72nd- parallel of latitude, half-way between Jan Mayen and the North Cape. 8° 45' east, the Kapok Kid reckoned, but he couldn't be sure. In heavy snow and with ten-tenth cloud, he was relying on dead reckoning: he had to, for the shell that had destroyed the FDR had wrecked the Automatic Pilot. But roughly 600 nautical miles to go. 600 miles, 40 hours, and the convoy – or what would be left of it by that time – would be in the Kola Inlet, steaming up-river to Polyarnoe and Murmansk . . . 40 hours.

It came to find the convoy – 14 shops left in all – scattered over three square miles of sea and rolling heavily in the deepening swell from the NNE: 14 ships, for another had gone in the deepest part of the night. Mine, torpedo? Nobody knew, nobody ever would know. The *Sirrus* had stopped, searched the area for an hour with hooded ten-inch signalling lamps. There had been no survivors. Not that Commander Orr had expected to find any – not with the air temperature 6° below zero.

It came after a sleepless night of never-ending alarms, of continual Asdic contacts, of constant depth-charging that achieved nothing. Nothing, that is, from the escorts' point of view: but for the enemy, it achieved a double-edged victory. It kept exhausted men at Action Stations all night long, blunting, irreparably perhaps, the last vestiges of the knife-edged vigilance on which the only hope – it was never more – of survival in the Arctic depended. More deadly still, it had emptied the last depth-charge rack in the convoy. . . . It was a measure of the intensity of the attack, of the relentlessness of the persecution, that this had never happened before. But it had happened now. There was not a single depth-charge left – not one.

The fangs were drawn, the defences were down. It was only a matter of time before the wolf-packs discovered that they could strike at will. . . .

And with the dawn, of course, came dawn Action Stations, or what would have been dawn stations had the men not already been closed up for fifteen hours, fifteen endless hours of intense cold and suffering, fifteen hours during which the crew of the *Ulysses* had been sustained by cocoa and one bully-beef sandwich, thin, sliced and stale, for there had been no time to bake the previous day. But dawn stations were profoundly significant in themselves: they prolonged the waiting another interminable two hours – and to a man rocking on his feet from unimaginable fatigue, literally holding convulsively jerking eyelids apart with finger and thumb while a starving brain, which is less a brain than a well of fine-drawn agony, begs him to let go, let go just for a second, just this once and never again, even a minute is brutal eternity: and they were still more important in that they were recognised as the Ithuriel hour of the Russian Convoys, the testing time when every man stood out clearly for what he was. And for the crew of a mutiny ship, for men already tried and condemned, for physically broken and mentally scourged men who neither could nor would ever be the same again in body or mind, the men of the *Ulysses* had no need to stand in shame. Not all, of course, they were only human; but many had found, or were finding, that the point of no return was not necessarily the edge of the precipice: it could be the bottom of the valley, the beginning of the long climb up the far slope, and when a man had once begun that climb he never looked back to that other side.

For some men, neither precipice nor valley ever existed. Men like Carrington, for instance. Eighteen consecutive hours on the bridge now, he was still his own indestructible self, alert with that relaxed watchfulness that never flagged, a man of infinite endurance, a man who could never crack, who you knew could never crack, for the imagination baulked at the very idea. Why he was what he was, no man could tell. Such, too, were men like Chief Petty Officer Hartley, like Chief Stoker Hendry, like Colour-Sergeant Evans and Sergeant MacIntosh; four men strangely alike, big, tough, kindly, no longer young, steeped in the traditions of the Service. Taciturn, never heard to speak of themselves, they were under no illusions as to their importance: they knew – as any Naval officer would be the first to admit – that, as the senior NCOs, they, and not any officer,

187

were the backbone of the Royal Navy; and it was from their heavy sense of responsibility that sprung their rock-like stability. And then of course, there were men – a handful only – like Turner and the Kapok Kid and Dodson, whom dawn found as men above themselves, men revelling in danger and exhaustion, for only thus could they realize themselves, for only this had they been born. And finally, men like Vallery, who had collapsed just after midnight, and was still asleep in the shelter, and Surgeon Commander Brooks: wisdom was their sheet anchor, a clear appreciation of the relative insignificance both of themselves and the fate of FR77, a coldly intellectual appraisal of, married to an infinite compassion for, the follies and suffering of mankind.

At the other end of the scale, dawn found men – a few dozen, perhaps – gone beyond recovery. Gone in selfishness, in self-pity and in fear, like Carslake, gone because their armour, the trappings of authority, had been stripped off them, like Hastings, or gone, like Leading SBA Johnson and a score of others, because they had been pushed too far and had no sheet anchor to hold them.

And between the two extremes were those – the bulk of the men – who had touched zero and found that endurance can be infinite – and found in this realization the springboard for recovery. The other side of the valley *could* be climbed, but not without a staff. For Nicholls, tired beyond words from a long night standing braced against the operating table in the surgery, the staff was pride and shame. For Leading Seaman Doyle, crouched miserably into the shelter of the for'ard funnel, watching the pinched agony, the perpetual shivering of his young midships pom-pom crew, it was pity; he would, of course, have denied this, blasphemously. For young Spicer, Tyndall's devoted pantry-boy, it was pity, too – pity and a savage grief for the dying man in the Admiral's cabin. Even with both legs amputated below the knee, Tyndall should not have been dying. But the fight, the resistance was gone, and Brooks knew old Giles would be glad to go. And for scores, perhaps for hundreds, for men like the tubercular-ridden McQuater, chilled to death in sodden clothes, but no longer staggering drunkenly round the hoist in 'Y' turret, for the heavy rolling kept the water on the move: like Petersen, recklessly squandering his giant strength in helping his exhausted mates: like Chrysler, whose keen young eyes, invaluable now that Radar was gone, never ceased to scan the horizons: for men like these, the staff was Vallery, the tremen-

dous respect and affection in which he was held, the sure knowledge that they could never let him down.

These, then, were the staffs, the intangible sheet anchors
that held the *Ulysses* together that bleak and bitter dawn –
pride, pity, shame, affection, grief – and the basic instinct for
self-preservation although the last, by now, was an almost
negligible factor. Two things were never taken into the slightest account as the springs of endurance: never mentioned,
never even considered, they did not exist for the crew of the
Ulysses: two things the sentimentalists at home, the gallant
leader writers of the popular press, the propagandising pur-
veyors of nationalistic claptrap would have had the world believe to be the source of inspiration and endurance – hatred of
the enemy, love of kinsfolk and country.

There was no hatred of the enemy. Knowledge is the prelude
to hate, and they did not know the enemy. Men cursed the
enemy, respected him, feared him and killed him if they could:
if they didn't, the enemy would kill them. Nor did men see
themselves as fighting for King and country: they saw the
necessity for war, but objected to camouflaging this necessity
under a spurious cloak of perfervid patriotism: they were just
doing what they were told, and if they didn't, they would be
stuck against a wall and shot. Love of kinsfolk – that had some
validity, but not much. It was natural to want to protect your
kin, but this was an equation where the validity varied according to the factor of distance. It was a trifle difficult for a man
crouched in his ice-coated Oerlikon cockpit off the shores of
Bear Island to visualise himself as protecting that rose-covered
cottage in the Cotswolds. . . . But for the rest, the synthetic
national hatreds and the carefully cherished myth of King and
country, these are nothing and less than nothing when mankind stands at the last frontier of hope and endurance: for only
the basic, simple human emotions, the positive ones of love and
grief and pity and distress, can carry a man across that last
frontier.

Noon, and still the convoy, closed up in tight formation now,
rolled eastwards in the blinding snow. The alarm halfway
through dawn stations had been the last that morning. Thirty-
six hours to go, now, only thirty-six hours. And if this weather
continued, the strong wind and blinding snow that made flying
impossible, the near-zero visibility and heavy seas that would

blind any periscope . . . there was always that chance. Only thirty-six hours.

Admiral John Tyndall died a few minutes after noon. Brooks, who had sat with him all morning, officially entered the cause of death as 'post-operative shock and exposure.' The truth was that Giles had died because he no longer wished to live. His professional reputation was gone: his faith, his confidence in himself were gone, and there was only remorse for the hundreds of men who had died: and with both legs gone, the only life he had ever known, the life he had so loved and cherished and to which he had devoted forty-five glad and unsparing years, that life, too, was gone for ever. Giles died gladly, willingly. Just on noon he recovered consciousness, looked at Brooks and Vallery with a smile from which every trace of madness had vanished. Brooks winced at the grey smile, mocking shadow of the famous guffaw of the Giles of another day. Then he closed his eyes and muttered something about his family – Brooks knew he had no family. His eyes opened again, he saw Vallery as if for the first time, rolled his eyes till he saw Spicer. 'A chair for the Captain, my boy.' Then he died.

He was buried at two o'clock, in the heart of a blizzard. The Captain's voice, reading the burial service, was shredded away by snow and wind: the Union flag was flapping emptily on the tilted board before the men knew he was gone: the bugle notes were broken and distant and lost, far away and fading like the horns of Elfland: and then the men, two hundred of them at least, turned silently away and trudged back to their frozen mess-decks.

Barely half an hour later, the blizzard had died, vanished as suddenly as it had come. The wind, too, had eased, and though the sky was still dark and heavy with snow, though the seas were still heavy enough to roll 15,000-ton ships through a 30° arc, it was clear that the deterioration in the weather had stopped. On the bridge, in the turrets, in the mess-decks, men avoided each other's eyes and said nothing.

Just before 1500, the *Vectra* picked up an Asdic contact. Vallery received the report, hesitated over his decision. If he sent the *Vectra* to investigate, and if the *Vectra* located the U-boat accurately and confined herself, as she would have to do, to describing tight circles above the submarine, the reason for this freedom from depth-charging would occur to the U-boat captain within minutes. And then it would only be a matter of time – until he decided it was safe to surface and use his radio

– that every U-boat north of the Circle would know that FR77 could be attacked with impunity. Further, it was unlikely that any torpedo attack would be made under such weather conditions. Not only was periscope observation almost impossible in the heavy seas, but the U-boat itself would be a most unstable firing platform: wave motion is not confined to the surface of the water – the effects can be highly uncomfortable and unstabilising thirty, forty, fifty feet down – and are appreciable, under extreme conditions, at a depth of almost a hundred feet. On the other hand, the U-boat captain might take a 1000–1 chance, might strike home with a lucky hit. Vallery ordered the *Vectra* to investigate.

He was too late. The order would have been too late anyway. The *Vectra* was still winking acknowledgment of the signal, had not begun to turn, when the rumble of a heavy explosion reached the bridge of the *Ulysses*. All eyes swept round a full circle of the horizon, searching for smoke and flame, for the canted deck and slewing ship that would show where the torpedo had gone home. They found no sign, none whatsoever, until almost half a minute had passed. Then they noticed, almost casually, that the *Electra,* leading ship in the starboard line, was slowing up, coming to a powerless stop, already settling in the water on an even keel, with no trace of tilt either for'ard or aft. Almost certainly, she had been holed in the engineroom.

The Aldis on the *Sirrus* had begun to flash. Bentley read the message, turned to Vallery.

'Commander Orr requests permission to go alongside, port side, take off survivors.'

'Port, is it?' Turner nodded. 'The sub's blind side. It's a fair chance, sir – in a calm sea. As it is . . .' He looked over at the *Sirrus,* rolling heavily in the beam sea, and shrugged. 'Won't do her paintwork any good.'

'Her cargo?' Vallery asked. 'Any idea? Explosives?' He looked round, saw the mute headshakes, turned to Bentley.

'Ask *Electra* if she's carrying any explosives as cargo.'

Bentley's Aldis chattered, fell silent. After half a minute, it was clear that there was going to be no reply.

'Power gone, perhaps, or his Aldis smashed,' the Kapok Kid ventured. 'How about one flag for explosives, two for none?'

Vallery nodded in satisfaction. 'You heard, Bentley?'

He looked over the starboard quarter as the message went out. The *Vectra* was almost a mile distant rolling, one minute, pitching the next as she came round in a tight circle. She had found the killer, and her depth-charge racks were empty.

Vallery swung back, looked across to the *Electra.* Still no reply, nothing. . . . Then he saw two flags fluttering up to the yardarm.

'Signal the *Sirrus,*' he ordered. ' "Go ahead: exercise extreme care." '

Suddenly, he felt Turner's hand on his arm.

'Can you hear 'em?' Turner asked.

'Hear what?' Vallery demanded.

'Lord only knows. It's the *Vectra.* Look!'

Vallery followed the pointing finger. At first, he could see nothing, then all at once he saw little geysers of water leaping up in the *Vectra*'s wake, geysers swiftly extinguished by the heavy seas. Then, faintly, his straining ear caught the faraway murmur of underwater explosions, all but inaudible against the wind.

'What the devil's the *Vectra* doing?' Vallery demanded. 'And what's she using?'

'Looks like fireworks to me,' Turner grunted. 'What do you think, Number One?'

'Scuttling charges – 25-pounders,' Carrington said briefly.

'He's right, sir,' Turner admitted. 'Of course that's what they are. Mind you, he might as well be using fireworks,' he added disparagingly.

But the Commander was wrong. A scuttling charge has less than a tenth part of the disruptive power of a depth-charge – but one lodged snugly in the conning-tower or exploding alongside a steering plane could be almost as lethal. Turner had hardly finished speaking when a U-boat – the first the *Ulysses* had seen above water for almost six months – proposed high above the surface of the sea, hung there for two or three seconds, then crashed down on even keel, wallowing wickedly in the troughs between the waves.

The dramatic abruptness of her appearance – one moment the empty sea, the next a U-boat rolling in full view of the entire convoy – took every ship by surprise – including the *Vectra.* She was caught on the wrong foot, moving away on the outer leg of a figure-of-eight turn. Her pom-pom opened up immediately, but the pom-pom, a notoriously inaccurate gun in the best of circumstances, is a hopeless proposition on the rolling, heeling deck of a destroyer making a fast turn in heavy weather: the Oerlikons registered a couple of hits on the conning-tower, twin Lewises peppered the hull with as much effect as a horde of angry hornets; but by the time the *Vectra* was round, her main armament coming to bear, the U-boat had disappeared slowly under the surface.

In spite of this, the *Vectra's* 4.7s opened up, firing into the sea where the U-boat had submerged, but stopping almost immediately when two shells in succession had ricocheted off the water and whistled dangerously through the convoy. She steadied on course, raced over the position of the submerged U-boat: watchers on the *Ulysses*, binoculars to their *Vectra's* poop-deck hurling more scuttling charges over the eyes, could just distinguish duffel-coated figures on the side. Almost at once, the *Vectra's* helm went hard over and she clawed her way back south again, guns at maximum depression pointing down over her starboard side.

The U-boat must have been damaged, more severely this time, by either the shells or the last charges. Again she surfaced, even more violently than before, in a seething welter of foam, and again the *Vectra* was caught on the wrong foot, for the submarine had surfaced off her port bow, three cable-lengths away.

And this time, the U-boat was up to stay. Whatever Captain and crew lacked, it wasn't courage. The hatch was open, and men were swarming over the side of the conning-tower to man the gun, in a token gesture of defiance against crushing odds.

The first two men over the side never reached the gun – breaking, sweeping waves, waves that towered high above the submarine's deck, washed them over the side and they were gone. But others flung themselves forward to take their places, frantically training their gun through a 90° arc to bear on the onrushing bows of the *Vectra*. Incredibly – for the seas were washing over the decks, seas which kept tearing the men from their posts, and the submarine was rolling with impossible speed and violence – their first shell, fired over open sights, smashed squarely into the bridge of the *Vectra*. The first shell and the last shell, for the crew suddenly crumpled and died, sinking down by the gun or pitching convulsively over the side.

It was a massacre. The *Vectra* had two Bolton-Paul Defiant night-fighter turrets, quadruple hydraulic turrets complete with astrodome, bolted to her fo'c'sle, and these had opened up simultaneously, firing, between them, something like a fantastic total of 300 shells every ten seconds. That often misused cliché 'hail of lead' was completely accurate here. It was impossible for a man to live two seconds on the exposed deck of that U-boat, to hope to escape that lethal storm. Man after man kept flinging himself over the coaming in suicidal gallantry, but none reached the gun.

Afterwards, no one aboard the *Ulysses* could say when they first realized that the *Vectra*, pitching steeply through the heavy seas, was going to ram the U-boat. Perhaps her Captain had never intended to do so. Perhaps he had expected the U-boat to submerge, had intended to carry away conning-tower and periscope standard, to make sure that she could not escape again. Perhaps he had been killed when that shell had struck the bridge. Or perhaps he had changed his mind at the last second, for the *Vectra*, which had been arrowing in on the conning-tower, suddenly slewed sharply to starboard.

For an instant, it seemed that she might just clear the U-boat's bows, but the hope died the second it was born. Plunging heavily down the sheering side of a gaping trough, the *Vectra's* forefoot smashed down and through the hull of the submarine, some thirty feet aft of the bows, slicing through the toughened steel of the pressure hull as if it were cardboard. She was still plunging, still driving down, when two shattering explosions, so close together as to be blurred into one giant blast, completely buried both vessels under a sky-rocketing mushroom of boiling water and twisted steel. The why of the explosion was pure conjecture; but what had happened was plain enough. Some freak of chance must have triggered off the TNT – normally an extremely stable and inert disruptive – in a warhead in one of the U-boat's tubes: and then the torpedoes in the storage racks behind and possibly, probably even, the for'ard magazine of the *Vectra* had gone up in sympathetic detonation.

Slowly, deliberately almost, the great clouds of water fell back into the sea, and the *Vectra* and the U-boat – or what little was left of them – came abruptly into view. To the watchers on the *Ulysses*, it was inconceivable that either of them should still be afloat. The U-boat was very deep in the water, seemed to end abruptly just for'ards of the gun platform: the *Vectra* looked as if some great knife had sheared her athwartships, just for'ard of the bridge. The rest was gone, utterly gone. And throughout the convoy unbelieving minds were still wildly rejecting the evidence of their eyes when the shattered hull of the *Vectra* lurched into the same trough as the U-boat, rolled heavily, wearily, over on top of her, bridge and mast cradling the conning-tower of the submarine. And then the water closed over them and they were gone, locked together to the bottom of the sea.

The last ships in the convoy were two miles away now, and in the broken seas, at that distance, it was impossible to see whether there were any survivors. It did not seem likely. And if there were, if there were men over there, struggling, swimming, shouting for help in the murderous cold of that glacial sea, they would be dying already. And they would have been dead long before any rescue ship could even have turned round. The convoy steamed on, beating steadily east. All but two, that is – the *Electra* and the *Sirrus*.

The *Electra* lay beam on to the seas, rolling slowly, sluggishly, dead in the water. She had now a list of almost 15° to port. Her decks, fore and aft of the bridge, were lined with waiting men. They had given up their attempt to abandon ship by lifeboat when they had seen the *Sirrus* rolling up behind them, fine on the port quarter. A boat had been swung out on its davits, and with the listing of the *Electra* and the rolling of the sea it had proved impossible to recover it. It hung now far out from the ship's side, swinging wildly at the end of its davits about twenty feet above the sea. On his approach, Orr had twice sent angry signals, asking the falls to be cut. But the lifeboat remained there, a menacing pendulum in the track of the *Sirrus*: panic, possibly, but more likely winch brakes jammed solid with ice. In either event, there was no time to be lost: another ten minutes and the *Electra* would be gone.

The *Sirrus* made two runs past in all – Orr had no intention of stopping alongside, of being trampled under by the 15,000-ton deadweight of a toppling freighter. On his first run he steamed slowly by at five knots, at a distance of twenty feet – the nearest he dared go with the set of the sea rolling both ships towards each other at the same instant.

As the *Sirrus's* swinging bows slid up past the bridge of the *Electra*, the waiting men began to jump. They jumped as the *Sirrus's* fo'c'sle reared up level with their deck, they jumped as it plunged down fifteen, twenty feet below. One man carrying a suitcase and Burberry stepped nonchalantly across both sets of guard-rails during the split second that they were relatively motionless to each other: other crashed sickeningly on to the ice-coated steel deck far below, twisting ankles, fracturing legs and thighs, dislocating hip-joints. And two men jumped and missed; above the bedlam of noise, men heard the blood-chilling, bubbling scream of one as the swinging hulls crushed the life out of him, the desperate, terror-stricken cries of the other as the great, iron wall of the *Electra* guided him into the screws of the *Sirrus*.

It was just then that it happened and there could be no possible reflection on Commander Orr's seamanship: he had handled the *Sirrus* brilliantly. But even his skill was helpeless against these two successive freak waves, twice the size of the others. The first flung the *Sirrus* close in to the *Electra*, then passing under the *Electra*, lurched her steeply to port as the second wave heeled the *Sirrus* far over to starboard. There was a grinding, screeching crash. The *Sirrus's* guard-rails and upper side plates buckled and tore along a 150-foot length: simultaneously, the lifeboat smashed endwise into the front of the bridge, shattering into a thousand pieces. Immediately, the telegraphs jangled, the water boiled whitely at the *Sirrus's* stern – shocked realisation of its imminence and death itself must have been only a merciful hair's-breadth apart for the unfortunate man in the water – and then the destroyer was clear, sheering sharply away from the *Electra*.

In five minutes the *Sirrus* was round again. It was typical of Orr's ice-cold, calculating nerve and of the luck that never deserted him that he should this time choose to rub the *Sirrus's* shattered starboard side along the length of the *Electra* – she was too low in the water now to fall on him – and that he should do so in a momentary spell of slack water. Willing hands caught men as they jumped, cushioned their fall. Thirty seconds and the destroyer was gone again and the decks of the *Electra* were deserted. Two minutes later and a muffled roar shook the sinking ship – her boilers going. And then she toppled slowly over on her side: masts and smokestack lay along the surface of the sea, dipped and vanished: the straight-back of bottom and keel gleamed fractionally, blackly, against the grey of sea and sky, and was gone. For a minute, great gouts of air rushed turbulently to the surface. By and by the bubbles grew smaller and smaller and then there were no more.

The *Sirrus* steadied on course, crowded decks throbbing as she began to pick up speed, to overtake the convoy. Convoy No. FB77. The convoy the Royal Navy would always want to forget. Thirty-six ships had left Scapa and St John's. Now there were twelve, only twelve. And still almost thirty-two hours to the Kola Inlet....

Moodily, even his tremendous vitality and zest temporarily subdued, Turner watched the *Sirrus* rolling up astern. Abruptly he turned away, looked furtively, pityingly at Captain Vallery, no more now than a living skeleton driven by God only knew what mysterious force to wrest hour after impossible hour from death. And for Vallery now, death, even the hope of it, Turner suddenly realized, must be infinitely sweet. He looked, and saw the shock and sorrow in that grey mask, and he cursed, bitterly, silently. And then these tired, dull eyes were on him and Turner hurriedly cleared his throat.

'How many survivors does that make in the *Sirrus* now?' he asked.

Vallery lifted weary shoulders in the ghost of a shrug.

'No idea, Commander. A hundred, possibly more. Why?'

'A hundred,' Turner mused. 'And no-survivors-will-be-picked-up. I'm just wondering what old Orr's going to say when he dumps that little lot in Admiral Starr's lap when we get back to Scapa Flow!'

—— 13 ——

SATURDAY AFTERNOON

The *Sirrus* was still a mile astern when her Aldis started flickering. Bentley took the message, turned to Vallery.

'Signal, sir. "Have 25–30 injured men aboard. Three very serious cases, perhaps dying. Urgently require doctor." '

'Acknowledge,' Vallery said. He hesitated a moment, then: 'My compliments to Surgeon-Lieutenant Nicholls. Ask him to come to the bridge.' He turned to the Commander, grinned faintly. 'I somehow don't see Brooks at his athletic best in a breeches buoy on a day like this. It's going to be quite a crossing.'

Turner looked again at the *Sirrus*, occasionally swinging through a 40° arc as she rolled and crashed her way up from the west.

'It'll be no picnic,' he agreed. 'Besides, breeches buoys aren't made to accommodate the likes of our venerable chief surgeon.' Funny, Turner thought, how matter-of-fact and offhand everyone was: nobody had as much as mentioned the *Vectra* since she'd rammed the U-boat.

The gate creaked. Vallery turned round slowly, acknowledged Nicholls's sketchy salute.

'The *Sirrus* needs a doctor,' he said without preamble. 'How do you fancy it?'

Nicholls steadied himself against the canted bridge and the rolling of the cruiser. Leave the *Ulysses* – suddenly, he hated the thought, was amazed at himself for his reaction. He, Johnny Nicholls, unique, among the officers anyway, in his thorough-going detestation and intolerance of all things naval – to feel like that! Must be going soft in the head. And just as suddenly he knew that his mind wasn't slipping, knew why he wanted to stay. It was not a matter of pride or principle or sentiment: it was just that – well, just that he belonged. The feeling of belonging – even to himself he couldn't put it more accurately, more clearly than that, but it affected him strangely, powerfully. Suddenly he became aware that curious eyes were on him, looked out in confusion over the rolling sea.

'Well?' Vallery's voice was edged with impatience.

'I don't fancy it at all,' Nicholls said frankly. 'But of course I'll go, sir. Right now?'

'As soon as you can get your stuff together,' Vallery nodded.

'That's now. We have an emergency kit packed all the time.' He cast a jaundiced eye over the heavy sea again. 'What am I supposed to do sir – jump?'

'Perish the thought!' Turner clapped him on the back with a large and jovial hand. 'You haven't a thing to worry about,' he boomed cheerfully, 'you positively won't feel a thing – these, if I recall rightly, were your exact words to me when you extracted that old molar of mine two-three weeks back.' He winced in painful recollection. 'Breeches buoy, laddie, breeches buoy!'

'Breeches buoy!' Nicholls protested. 'Haven't noticed the weather, have you? I'll be going up and down like a blasted yo-yo!'

'The ignorance of youth.' Turner shook his head sadly. 'We'll be turning into the sea, of course. It'll be like a ride in a Rolls, my boy! We're going to rig it now.' He turned away. 'Chrysler – get on to Chief Petty Officer Hartley. Ask him to come up to the bridge.'

Chrysler gave no sign of having heard. He was in his usual favourite position these days – gloved hands on the steam pipes, the top half of his face crushed into the rubber eyepiece of the powerful binoculars on the starboard searchlight control. Every few seconds a hand would drop, revolve the milled training rack a fraction. Then again the complete immobility.

'Chrysler!' Turner roared. 'Are you deaf?'

Three, four, five more seconds passed in silence. Every eye was on Chrysler when he suddenly jerked back, glanced down at the bearing indicator, then swung round. His face was alive with excitement.

'Green one-double-oh!' he shouted. 'Green one-double-oh! Aircraft. Just on the horizon!' He fairly flung himself back at his binoculars. 'Four, seven – no, *ten*! Ten aircraft!' he yelled.

'Green one-double-oh?' Turner had his glasses to his eyes. 'Can't see a thing! Are you sure, boy?' he called anxiously.

'Still the same, sir.' There was no mistaking the agitated conviction in the young voice.

Turner was through the gate and beside him in four swift steps. 'Let me have a look,' he ordered. He gazed through the glasses, twisted the training rack once or twice, then stepped back slowly, heavy eyebrows lowering in anger.

'There's something bloody funny here, young man!' he growled. 'Either your eyesight or your imagination? And if you ask me—'

'He's right,' Carrington interrupted calmly. 'I've got 'em, too.'

'So have I, sir!' Bentley shouted.

Turner wheeled back to the mounted glasses, looked through them briefly, looked round at Chrysler.

'Remind me to apologise some day!' he smiled, and was back on the compass platform before he had finished speaking.

'Signal to convoy,' Vallery was saying rapidly. 'Code H. Full ahead, Number One. Bosun's mate? Broadcaster: stand by all guns. Commander?'

'Sir?'

'Independent targets, independent fire all AA guns? Agreed? And the turrets?'

'Couldn't say yet. . . . Chrysler, can you make out—'

'Condors, sir,' Chrysler anticipated him.

'Condors!' Turner stared in disbelief. 'A dozen Condors! Are you sure that . . . Oh, all right, all right!' he broke off hastily. 'Condors they are.' He shook his head in wonderment, turned to Vallery. 'Where's my bloody tin hat? Condors, he says!'

'So Condors they are,' Vallery repeated, smiling. Turner marvelled at the repose, the unruffled calm.

'Bridge targets, independent fire control for all turrets?' Vallery went on.

'I think so, sir.' Turner looked at the two communication ratings just aft of the compass platform – one each on the group phones to the for'ard and after turrets. 'Ears pinned back, you two. And hop to it when you get the word.'

Vallery beckoned to Nicholls.

'Better get below, young man,' he advised. 'Sorry your little trip's been postponed.'

'I'm not,' Nicholls said bluntly.

'No?' Vallery was smiling. 'Scared?'

'No, sir,' Nicholls smiled back. 'Not scared. And you know I wasn't.'

'I know you weren't,' Vallery agreed quietly. 'I know – and thank you.'

He watched Nicholls walk off the bridge, beckoned to the WT messenger, then turned to the Kapok Kid.

'When was our last signal to the Admiralty, Pilot? Have a squint at the log.'

'Noon yesterday,' said the Kapol Kid readily.

'Don't know what I'll do without you,' Vallery murmured. 'Present position?'

'72.20 north, 13.40 east.'

'Thank you.' He looked at Turner. 'No point in radio silence now, Commander?'

Turner shook his head.

'Take this message,' Vallery said quickly. 'To DNO, London. ... How are our friends doing, Commander?'

'Circling well to the west, sir. Usual high altitude, gambit from the stern, I suppose,' he added morosely. 'Still,' he brightened, 'cloud level's barely a thousand feet.'

Vallery nodded. 'FR77, 1600. 72.20, 13.40. Steady on 090. Force 9, north, heavy swell: Situation desperate. Deeply regret Admiral Tyndall died 1200 today. Tanker *Vytura* torpedoed last night, sunk by self. *Washington State* sunk 0145 today. *Vectra* sunk 1515, collision U-boat. *Electra* sunk 1530. Am being heavily attacked by twelve, minimum twelve, Focke-Wulf 200s." A reasonable assumption, I think, Commander,' he said wryly, 'and it'll shake their Lordships. They're of the opinion there aren't so many Condors in the whole of Norway. "Imperative send help. Air cover essential. Advise immediately." Get that off at once, will you?'

'Your nose, sir!' Turner said sharply.

'Thank you.' Vallery rubbed the frostbite, dead white in the haggard grey and blue of his face, gave up after a few seconds: the effort was more trouble than it was worth, drained away too much of his tiny reserves of strength. 'My God, it's bitter, Commander!' he murmured quietly.

Shivering, he pulled himself to his feet, swept his glasses over FR77. Code H was being obeyed. The ships were scattered over the sea apparently at random, broken out from the two lines ahead which would have made things far too simple for bomb-aimers in aircraft attacking from astern. They would have to aim now for individual targets. Scattered, but not too scattered – close enough together to derive mutual benefit from the convoy's concerted barrage. Vallery nodded to himself in satisfaction and twisted round, his glasses swivelling to the west.

There was no mistaking them now, he thought – they were Condors, all right. Almost dead astern now, massive wingtips dipping, the big four-engined planes banked slowly, ponderously to starboard, then straightened on a 180° overtaking course. And they were climbing, steadily climbing.

Two things were suddenly clear to Vallery, two things the *enemy* obviously knew. They had known where to find FR77 – the Luftwaffe was not given to sending heavy bombers out over the Arctic on random hazard: they hadn't even bothered to send Charlie on reconnaissance. For a certainty, some submarine had located them earlier on, given their position and course: at any distance at all, their chance of seeing a periscope in that heavy sea had been remote. Further, the Germans *knew* that the *Ulysses's* radar was gone. The Focke-Wulfs were climbing to gain the low cloud, would break cover only seconds before it was time to bomb. Against radar-controlled fire, at such close range, it would have been near suicide. But they *knew* it was safe.

Even as he watched, the last of the labouring Condors climbed through the low, heavy ceiling, was completely lost to sight. Vallery shrugged wearily, lowered his binoculars.

'Bentley?'

'Sir?'

'Code R. Immediate.'

The flags fluttered up. For fifteen, twenty seconds – it seemed ten times as long as that to the impatient Captain – nothing happened. And then, like rolling toy marionettes under the hand of a master puppeteer, the bows of every ship in the convoy began to swing round – those to the port of the *Ulysses* to the north, those to the starboard to the south. When the Condors broke through – two minutes, at the most, Vallery reckoned, they would find beneath them only the empty sea. Empty, that is, except for the *Ulysses* and the *Stirling*, ships admirably equipped to take care of themselves. And then the Condors would find themselves under heavy cross-fire from the merchant ships and destroyers, and too late – at that low altitude, much too late – to alter course for fore-and-aft bombing runs on the freighters. Vallery smiled wryly to himself. As a defensive tactic, it was little enough, but the best he could do in the circumstances. . . . He could hear Turner barking orders through the loudspeaker, was more than content to leave the defence of the ship in the Commander's competent hands. If only he himself didn't feel so tired. . . .

Ninety seconds passed, a hundred, two minutes – and still no sign of the Condors. A hundred eyes stared out into the cloud-wrack astern: it remained obstinately, tantalisingly grey and featureless.

Two and a half minutes passed. Still there was nothing.

'Anybody seen anything?' Vallery asked anxiously. His eyes never left that patch of cloud astern. 'Nothing? Nothing at all?' The silence remained, oppressive, unbroken.

Three minutes. Three and a half. Four. Vallery looked away to rest his straining eyes, caught Turner looking at him, caught the growing apprehension, the slow dawn and strengthening of surmise in the lean face. Wordlessly, at the same instant, they swung round, staring out into the sky ahead.

'That's it!' Vallery said quickly. 'You're right, Commander, you must be!' He was aware that everyone had turned now, was peering ahead as intently as himself. 'They've by-passed us, they're going to take us from ahead. Warn the guns! Dear God, they almost had us!' he whispered softly.

'Eyes skinned, everyone!' Turner boomed. The apprehension was gone, the irrepressible joviality, the gratifying anticipation of action was back again. 'And I mean everyone! We're all in the same boat together. No joke intended. Fourteen days' leave to the first man to sight a Condor!'

'Effective as from when?' the Kapok Kid asked dryly.

Turner grinned at him. Then the smile died, the head lifted sharply in sudden attention.

'Can you hear 'em?' he asked. His voice was soft, almost as if he feared the enemy might be listening. 'They're up there, somewhere – damned if I can tell where, though. If only that wind—'

The vicious, urgent thudding of the boat-deck Oerlikons stopped him dead in mid-sentence, had him whirling round and plunging for the broadcast transmitter in one galvanic, concerted movement. But even then he was too late – he would have been too late anyway. The Condors – the first three in line ahead, were already visible – were already through the cloud, 500 feet up and barely half a mile away – dead astern. *Astern.* The bombers must have circled back to the west as soon as they had reached the clouds, completely fooled them as to their intentions. . . . Six seconds – six seconds is time and to spare for even a heavy bomber to come less than half a mile in a shallow dive. There was barely time for realisation, for the first bitter welling of mortification and chagrin when the Condors were on them.

It was almost dusk, now, the weird half-light of the Arctic twilight. Tracers, glowing hot pinpoints of light streaking out through the darkening sky, were clearly seen, at first swinging erratically, fading away to extinction in the far distance, then steadying, miraculously dying in the instant of birth as they sank home into the fuselages of the swooping Condors. But time was too short – the guns were on target for a maximum of two seconds – and these giant Focke-Wulfs had a tremendous capacity for absorbing punishment. The leading Condor levelled out about three hundred feet, its medium 250-kilo bombs momentarily parallelling its line of flight, then arching down lazily towards the *Ulysses*. At once the Condor pulled its nose up in maximum climb, the four great engines labouring in desynchronised clamour, as it sought the protection of the clouds.

The bombs missed. They missed by about thirty feet, exploding on contact with the water just abaft the bridge. For the men in the TS, engine-and boiler-rooms, the crash and concussion must have been frightful – literally earshattering. Waterspouts, twenty feet in diameter at their turbulent bases, streaked up whitely into the twilight, high above the truncated masts, hung there momentarily, then collapsed in drenching cascades on the bridge and boat-deck aft, soaking, saturating, every gunner on the pom-pom and in the open Oerlikon cockpits. The temperature stood at 2° above zero – 30° of frost.

More dangerously, the blinding sheets of water completely unsighted the gunners. Apart from a lone Oerlikon on a sponson below the starboard side of the bridge, the next Condor pressed home its attack against a minimum of resistance. The approach was perfect, dead fore-and-aft on the centre line; but the pilot overshot, probably in his anxiety to hold course. Three bombs this time: for a second, it seemed that they must miss, but the first smashed into the fo'c'sle between the breakwater and the capstan, exploding in the flat below, heaving up the deck in a tangled wreckage of broken steel. Even as the explosion died, the men on the bridge could hear a curious clanking rattle: the explosion must have shattered the fo'c'sle capstan and Blake stopper simultaneously, and sheared the retaining shackle on the anchor cable, and the starboard anchor, completely out of control, was plummeting down to the depths of the Arctic.

The other bombs fell into the sea directly ahead, and from the *Stirling*, a mile ahead, it seemed that the *Ulysses* disappeared under the great column of water. But the water subsided, and the *Ulysses* steamed on, apparently unharmed. From dead ahead, the sweeping lift of the bows hid all damage, and there was neither flames nor smoke – hundreds of gallons of water, falling from the sky and pouring in through the great jagged holes in the deck, had killed any fire there was. The *Ulysses* was still a lucky ship. . . . And then, at last, after twenty months of the fantastic escapes, the fabulous good fortune that had made her a legend, a byword for immunity throughout all the north, the luck of the *Ulysses* ran out.

Ironically, the *Ulysses* brought disaster on herself. The main armament, the 5.25s aft, had opened up now, was pumping its 100-lb. shells at the diving bombers, at point-blank range and over equivalent of open sights. The very first shell from 'X' turret sheared away the starboard wing of the third Condor between the engines, tore it completely away to spin slowly like a fluttering leaf into the darkly-rolling sea. For a fraction of a second the Folke-Wulf held on course, then abruptly the nose tipped over and the giant plane screamed down in an almost vertical dive, her remaining engines inexplicably accelerating to a deafening crescendo as she hurtled arrow-straight for the deck of the *Ulysses*.

There was no time to take any avoiding action, no time to think, no time even to hope. A cluster of jettisoned bombs crashed in to the boiling wake – the *Ulysses was* already doing upwards of thirty knots – and two more crashed through the poop-deck, the first exploding in the after seamen's mess-deck, the other in the marines' mess-deck. One second later, with a tremendous roar and in a blinding sheet of gasoline flame, the Condor itself, at a speed of upwards of three hundred m.p.h., crashed squarely into the front of 'Y' turret.

Incredibly, that was the last attack on the *Ulysses* – incredibly, because the *Ulysses* was defenceless now, wide open to any air attack from astern. 'Y' turret was gone, 'X' turret, still magically undamaged, was half-buried under the splintered wreckage of the Condor, blinded by the smoke and leaping flame. The boat-deck Oerlikons, too, had fallen silent. The gunners, half-drowned under the deluge of less than a minute ago, were being frantically dragged from their cockpits: a difficult enough task at any time, it was almost impossible with their clothes already frozen solid, their duffels cracking and crackling like splintering matchwood as the men were dragged over the side of their cock-pits. With all speed, they were rushed below, thrust into the galley passage to thaw, literally to thaw: agony, excruciating agony, but the only alternative to the quick and certain death which would have come to them in their ice-bound cockpits.

The remaining Condors had pulled away in a slow climbing turn to starboard. They were surrounded, bracketed fore and aft and on either side, by scores of woolly, expanding puffs of exploding AA shells, but they flew straight through these, charmed, unhurt. Already, they were beginning to disappear into the clouds, to settle down on a south-east course for home. Strange, Vallery thought vaguely, one would have expected them to hammer home their initial advantage of surprise, to concentrate on the crippled *Ulysses*: certainly, thus far the Con-dor crews had shown no lack of courage. . . . He gave it up, turned his attention to more immediate worries. And there was plenty to worry about.

The *Ulysses* was heavily on fire aft – a deck and mess-deck fire, admittedly, but potentially fatal for all that – 'X' and 'Y' magazines were directly below. Already, dozens of men from the damage control parties were running aft, stumbling and falling on the rolling ice-covered deck, unwinding the hose drums be-hind them, occasionally falling flat on their faces as two ice-bound coils locked together, the abruptly tightening hose jerk-ing them off their feet. Others stumbled past them, carrying the big, red foam-extinguishers on their shoulders or under their arms. One unfortunate seaman – AB Ferry, who had left the Sick Bay in defiance of strict orders – running down the port alley past the shattered Canteen, slipped and fell abreast 'X' turret: the port wing of the Condor, even as it had sheared off and plunged into the sea, had torn away the guard-rails here, and Ferry, hands and feet scrabbling frantically at the smooth ice of the deck, his broken arm clawing uselessly at one of the remaining stanchions, slid slowly, inevitably over the side and was gone. For a second, the high-pitched, fear-stricken shriek rose thin and clear above the roaring of the flames, died abruptly as the water closed over him. The propellers were almost immediately below.

The men with the extinguishers were the first into action, as, indeed, they had to be when fighting a petrol fire – water would only have made matters worse, have increased the area of the fire by washing the petrol in all directions, and the petrol, being lighter than water, immiscible and so floating to the top, would have burned as furiously as ever. But the foam-extinguishers were of only limited efficiency, not so much because several release valves had jammed solid in the intense cold as because of the intense white heat which made close approach almost impossible, while the smaller carbontet. extinguishers, directed against electrical fires below, were shockingly ineffective: these extinguishers had never been in action before and the crew of the *Ulysses* had known for a long time of the almost magical properties of the extinguisher liquid for removing the most obstinate stains and marks in clothes. You may convince a WT rating of the lethal nature of 2000 volts: you may convince a gunner of the madness of matches in a magazine: you may convince a torpedoman of the insanity of juggling with fulminate of mercury: but you will never convince any of them of the criminal folly of draining off just a few drops of carbon-tetrachloride. . . . Despite stringent periodical checks, most of the extinguishers were only half-full. Some were completely empty.

The hoses were little more effective. Two were coupled up to the starboard mains and the valves turned: the hoses remained lifeless, empty. The starboard salt-water line had frozen solid – common enough with fresh-water systems, this, but not with salt. A third hose on the port side was coupled up, but the release valve refused to turn: attacked with hammers and crowbars, it sheered off at the base – at extremely low temperatures, molecular changes occur in metals, cut tensile strength to a fraction – the high-pressure water drenching everyone in the vicinity. Spicer, the dead Admiral's pantry-boy, a stricken-eyed shadow of his former cheerful self, flung away his hammer and wept in anger and frustration. The other port valve worked, but it took an eternity for the water to force its way through the flattened frozen hose.

Gradually, the deck fire was brought under control – less through the efforts of the firefighters than the fact that there was little inflammable material left after the petrol had burnt off. Hoses and extinguishers were then directed through the great jagged rents on the poop to the fires roaring in the mess-deck below, while two asbestos-suited fighters clambered over and struggled through the red-hot, jangled mass of smoking wreckage on the poop. Nicholls had one of the suits, Leading Telegraphist Brown, a specialist in rescue work, the other.

Brown was the first on the scene. Picking his way gingerly, he climbed up to the entrance of 'Y' turret. Watchers in the port and starboard alleyways saw him pause there, fighting to tie back the heavy steel door – it had been crashing monotonously backwards and forwards with the rolling of the cruiser. Then they saw him step inside. Less than ten seconds later they saw him appear at the door again, on his knees and clutching desperately at the side for support. His entire body was arching convulsively and he was being violently sick into his oxygen mask.

Nicholls saw this, wasted time neither on 'Y' turret nor on the charred skeletons still trapped in the incinerated fuselage of the Condor. He climbed quickly up the vertical steel ladders to 'X' gun-deck, moved round to the back and tried to open the door. The clips were jammed, immovable – whether from cold or metal distortion he did not know. He looked round for some lever, stepped aside as he saw Doyle, duffel coat smouldering, haggard face set and purposeful under the beard, approaching with a sledge in his hand. A dozen heavy, well-directed blows – the clanging, Nicholls thought, must be almost intolerable inside the hollow amplifier of the turret – and the door was open. Doyle secured it, stepped aside to let Nicholls enter.

Nicholls climbed inside. There had been no need to worry about that racket outside, he thought wryly. Every man in the turret was stone dead. Colour-Sergeant Evans was sitting bolt upright in his seat, rigid and alert in death as he had been in life: beside him lay Foster, the dashing, fiery Captain of Marines, whom death became so ill. The rest were all sitting or lying quietly at their stations, apparently unharmed and quite unmarked except for an occasional tiny trickle of blood from ear and mouth, trickles already coagulated in the intense cold – the speed of the *Ulysses* had carried the flames aft, away from the turret. The concussion must have been tremendous, death instantaneous. Heavily, Nicholls bent over the communications number, gently detached his headset, and called the bridge.

Vallery himself took the message, turned back to Turner. He looked old, defeated.

'That was Nicholls,' he said. Despite all he could do, the shock and sorrow showed clearly in every deeply-etched line in that pitiably wasted face. ' "Y" turret is gone – no survivors. "X" turret seems intact – but everyone inside is dead. Concussion, he says. Fires in the after mess-deck still not under control. . . . Yes, boy, what is it?'

' "Y" magazine, sir,' the seaman said uncertainly. 'They want to speak to the gunnery officer.'

'Tell them he's not available,' Vallery said shortly. 'We haven't time . . .' He broke off, looked up sharply. 'Did you say "Y" magazine? Here, let me have that phone.'

He took the receiver, pushed back the hood of his duffel coat.

'Captain speaking, "Y" magazine. What is it? . . . What? Speak up man, I can't hear you. . . . Oh, damn!' He swung round on the bridge LTO. 'Can you switch this receiver on to the relay amplifier? I can't hear a . . . Ah, that's better.'

The amplifier above the chart-house crackled into life – a peculiarly throaty, husky life, doubly difficult to understand under the heavy overlay of a slurred Glasgow accent.

'Can ye hear me now?' the speaker boomed.

'I can hear you.' Vallery's own voice echoed loudly over the amplifier. 'McQuater, isn't it?'

'Aye, it's me, sir. How did ye ken?' Even through the 'speaker the surprise was unmistakable. Shocked and exhausted though he was, Vallery found himself smiling.

'Never mind that now, McQuater. Who's in charge down there – Gardiner, isn't it?'

'Yes, sir. Gardiner.'

'Put him on, will you?' There was a pause.

'Ah canna, sir. Gardiner's deid.'

'Dead!' Vallery was incredulous. 'Did you say "dead," Mc-Quater?'

'Aye, and he's no' the only one.' The voice was almost truculent, but Vallery's ear caught the faint tremor below. 'Ah was knocked oot masel', but Ah'm fine now.'

Vallery paused, waited for the boy's bout of hoarse, harsh coughing to pass.

'But – but – what happened?'

'How should Ah know – Ah mean, Ah dinna ken – Ah don't know, sir. A helluva bang and then – ach, Ah'm no' sure whit happened. . . . Gardiner's mooth's all blood.'

'How – how many of you are left?'

'Just Barker, Williamson and masel', sir. Naebody else – just us.'

'And – and they're all right, McQuater?'

'Ach, they're fine. But Barker thinks he's deein'. He's in a gey bad wey. Ah think he's gone clean aff his trolley, sir.'

'He's *what*?'

'Loony, sir,' McQuater explained patiently. 'Daft. Some bluidy nonsense aboot goin' to meet his Maker, and him wi' naething behind him but a lifetime o' swindlin' his fellow-man.' Vallery heard Turner's sudden chuckle, remembered that Barker was the canteen manager. 'Williamson's busy shovin' cartridges back into the racks – floor's littered with the bluidy things.'

'McQuater!' Vallery's voice was sharp, automatic in reproof.

'Aye, Ah'm sorry, sir. Ah clean forgot. . . . Whit's to be done, sir?'

'Done about what?' Vallery demanded impatiently.

'This place, sir. "Y" magazine. Is the boat on fire ootside? It's bilin' in here – hotter than the hinges o' hell!'

'What! What did you say?' Vallery shouted. This time he forgot to reprimand McQuater. 'Hot, did you say? How hot? Quickly, boy!'

'Ah canna touch the after bulkheid, sir,' McQuater answered simply. 'It 'ud tak 'the fingers aff me.'

'But the sprinklers – what's the matter with them?' Vallery shouted. 'Aren't they working? Good God, boy, the magazine will go up any minute!'

'Aye.' McQuater's voice was noncommittal. 'Aye, Ah kinna thought that might be the wey o' it. No, sir, the sprinklers arena workin' – and it's already 20 degrees above the operatin' temperature, sir.'

'Don't just stand there,' Vallery said desperately. 'Turn them on by hand! The water in the sprinklers can't possibly be frozen if it's as hot as you say it is. Hurry, man, hurry. If the mag. goes up, the *Ulysses* is finished. For God's sake, hurry!'

'Ah've tried them, sir,' McQuater said softly. 'It's nae bluidy use. They're solid!'

'Then break them open! There must be a tommy bar lying about somewhere. Smash them open, man! Hurry!'

'Aye, richt ye are, sir. But – but if Ah do that, sir, how am Ah to shut the valves aff again?' There was a note almost of quiet desperation in the boy's voice – some trick of reproduction in the amplifier, Vallery guessed.

'You can't! It's impossible! But never mind that!' Vallery said impatiently, his voice ragged with anxiety. 'We'll pump it all out later. Hurry, McQuater, hurry!'

There was a brief silence followed by a muffled shout and a soft thud, then they heard a thin metallic clanging echoing through the amplifier, a rapid, staccato succession of strokes. McQuater must have been raining a veritable hail of blows on the valve handles. Abruptly, the noise ceased.

Vallery waited until he heard the phone being picked up, called anxiously: 'Well, how is it? Sprinklers all right?'

'Goin' like the clappers, sir.' There was a new note in his voice, a note of pride and satisfaction. 'Ah've just crowned Barker wi' the tommy bar,' he added cheerfully.

'You've *what*?'

'Laid oot old Barker,' said McQuater distinctly. 'He tried to stop me. Windy auld bastard. . . . Ach, he's no' worth mentionin'. . . . My they sprinklers are grand things, sir. Ah've never seen them workin' before. Place is ankle deep a'ready. And the steam's fair sizzlin' aff the bulkheid!'

'That's enough!' Vallery's voice was sharp. 'Get out at once – and make sure that you take Barker with you.'

'Ah saw a picture once. In the Paramount in Glasgow, Ah think. Ah must've been flush.' The tone was almost conversational, pleasurably reminiscent. Vallery exchanged glances with Turner, saw that he too, was fighting off the feeling of unreality. '*Rain*, it was cried. But it wasnae hauf as bad as this. There certainly wisnae hauf as much bluidy steam! Talk aboot the hothouse in the Botanic Gardens!'

'McQuater!' Vallery roared. 'Did you hear me? Leave at once, I say! At once, do you hear?'

'Up to ma knees a'ready!' McQuater said admiringly. 'It's gey cauld. . . . Did you say somethin' sir?'

'I said, "Leave at once!" ' Vallery ground out. 'Get out!'

'Aye, Ah see. "Get oot." Aye. Ah thought that was what ye said. Get oot. Well, it's no that easy. As a matter o' fact, we canna. Hatchway's buckled and the hatch-cover, too – jammed deid solid, sir.'

The echo from the speaker boomed softly over the shattered bridge, died away in frozen silence. Unconsciously, Vallery lowered the telephone, his eyes wandering dazedly over the bridge. Turner, Carrington, the Kapot Kid, Bentley, Chrysler and the others – they were all looking at him, all with the same curiously blank intensity blurring imperceptibly into the horror of understanding – and he knew that their eyes and faces only mirrored his own. Just for a second, as if to clear his mind, he screwed his eyes tightly shut, then lifted the phone again.

'McQuater! McQuater! Are you still there?.'

'Of course Ah'm here!' Even through the speaker, the voice was peevish, the asperity unmistakable. 'Where the hell—?'

'Are you sure it's jammed, boy?' Vallery cut in desperately. 'Maybe if you took a tommy-bar to the clips—'

'Ah could take a stick o' dynamite to the bluidy thing and it 'ud make no difference,' McQuater said matter-of-factly. 'Onywey, it's just aboot red-hot a'ready – the hatch, Ah mean. There must be a bluidy great fire directly ootside it.'

'Hold on a minute,' Vallery called. He turned round. 'Commander, have Dodson send a stoker to the main magazine flooding valve aft: stand by to shut off.'

He crossed over to the nearest communication number.

'Are you on to the poop phone just now? Good! Give it to me. . . . Hallo, Captain here. Is – ah, it's you, Hartley. Look, give me a report on the state of the mess-deck fires. It's desperately urgent. There are ratings trapped in "Y" magazine, the sprinklers are on and the hatch-cover's jammed. . . . Yes, yes, I'll hold on.'

He waited impatiently for the reply, gloved hand tapping mechanically on top of the phone box. His eyes swept slowly over the convoy, saw the freighters, steaming in to take up position again. Suddenly he stiffened, eyes unseeing.

'Yes, Captain speaking. . . . Yes. . . . Yes. Half an hour, maybe an hour. . . . Oh, God, no! You're quite certain? . . . No, that's all.'

He handed the receiver back, looked up slowly, his face drained of expression.

'Fire in the seamen's mess is under control,' he said dully. 'The marines' mess is an inferno – directly on top of "Y" magazine. Hartley says there isn't a chance of putting it out for an hour at least. . . . I think you'd better get down there, Number One.'

A whole minute passed, a minute during which there was only the pinging of the Asdic, the regular crash of the sea as the *Ulysses* rolled in the heavy troughs.

'Maybe the magazine's cool enough now,' the Kapok Kid suggested at length. 'Perhaps we could shut off the water long enough . . .' His voice trailed away uncertainly.

'Cool enough?' Turner cleared his throat noisily. 'How do we know? Only McQuater could tell us . . .' He stopped abruptly, as he realized the implications of what he was saying.

'We'll ask him,' Vallery said heavily. He picked up the phone again. 'McQuater?'

'Hallo!'

'Perhaps we could shut off the sprinklers outside, if it's safe. Do you think the temperature . . .?'

He broke off, unable to complete the sentence. The silence stretched out, taut and tangible, heavy with decision. Vallery wondered numbly what McQuater was thinking, what he himself would have thought in McQuater's place.

'Hing on a minute,' the speaker boomed abruptly. 'Ah'll have a look up top.'

Again that silence, again that tense unnatural silence lay heavily over the bridge. Vallery started as the speaker boomed again.

'Jings, Ah'm b——d. Ah couldna climb that ladder again for twenty-four points in the Treble Chance. . . . Ah'm on the ladder now, but Ah'm thinkin' Ah'll no' be on it much longer.'

'Never mind . . .' Vallery checked himself, aghast at what he had been about to say. If McQuater fell off, he'd drown like a rat in that flooded magazine.

'Oh, aye. The magazine.' In the intervals between the racked bouts of coughing, the voice was strangely composed. 'The shells up top are just aboot meltin'. Worse than ever, sir.'

'I see.' Vallery could think of nothing else to say. His eyes were closed and he knew he was swaying on his feet. With an effort, he spoke again. 'How's Williamson?' It was all he could think of.

'Near gone. Up to his neck and hangin' on to the racks.' McQuater coughed again. 'Says he's a message for the Commander and Carslake.'

'A – a message?'

'Uh-huh! Tell old Blackbeard to take a turn to himself and lay off the bottle,' he said with relish. The message for Carslake was unprintable.

Vallery didn't even feel shocked.

'And yourself, McQuater?' he said. 'No message, nothing you would like . . .' He stopped, consicious of the grotesque inadequacy, the futility of what he was saying.

'Me? Ach, there's naething Ah'd like . . . Well, maybe a transfer to the *Spartiate*, but Ah'm thinking maybe it's a wee bit ower late for that.[1] 'Williamson!' The voice had risen to a sudden urgent shout. 'Williamson! Hing on, boy, Ah'm coming!' They heard the booming clatter in the speaker as McQuater's phone crashed against metal, and then there was only the silence.

'McQuater!' Vallery shouted into the phone. 'McQuater! Answer me, man. Can you hear me? McQuater!' But the speaker above him remained dead, finally, irrevocably dead. Vallery shivered in the icy wind. That magazine, that flooded magazine . . . less than twenty-four hours since he had been there. He could see it now, see it as clearly as he had seen it last night. Only now he saw it dark, cavernous with only the pinpoints of emergency lighting, the water welling darkly, slowly up the sides, saw that little, pitifully wasted Scots boy with the thin shoulders and pain-filled eyes, struggling desperately to keep his mate's head above that icy water, exhausting his tiny reserves of strength with the passing of every second. Even now, the time must be running out and Vallery knew hope was gone. With a sudden clear certainty he knew that when those two went down, they would go down together. McQuater would never let go. Eighteen years old, just eighteen years old. Vallery turned away, stumbling blindly through the gate on to the shattered compass platform. It was beginning to snow again and darkness was falling all around them.

—— 14 ——

SATURDAY EVENING I

The *Ulysses* rolled on through the Arctic twilight. She rolled heavily, awkwardly, in seas of the wrong critical length, a strange and stricken sight with both masts gone, with all boats and rafts gone, with shattered fore-and-aft superstructure, with a crazily tilted bridge and broken, mangled after turret, half-buried in the skeleton of the Condor's fuselage. But despite all that, despite, too, the great garish patches of red lead and gaping black holes in fo'c'sle and poop – the latter welling with dark smoke laced with flickering lances of flame – she still remained uncan-

[1] HMS *Spartiate* was a shore establishment. Naval HQ for the West of Scotland, It was at St Enoch's Hotel, Glasgow.

nily ghost-like and graceful, a creature of her own element, inevitably at home in the Arctic. Ghost-like, graceful, and infinitely enduring . . . and still deadly. She still had her guns – and her engines. Above all, she had these great engines, engines strangely blessed with endless immunity. So, at least, it seemed . . .

Five minutes dragged themselves interminably by, five minutes during which the sky grew steadily darker, during which reports from the poop showed that the firefighters were barely holding their own, five minutes during which Vallery recovered something of his normal composure. But he was now terribly weak.

A bell shrilled, cutting sharply through the silence and the gloom. Chrysler answered it, turned to the bridge.

'Captain, sir. After engine-room would like to speak to you.'

Turner looked at the Captain, said quickly: 'Shall I take it, sir?'

'Thank you.' Vallery nodded his head gratefully. Turner nodded in turn, crossed to the phone.

'Commander speaking. Who is it? . . . Lieutenant Grierson. What is it, Grierson? Couldn't be good news for a change?'

For almost a minute Turner remained silent. The others on the bridge could hear the faint crackling of the earpiece, sensed rather than saw the taut attention, the tightening of the mouth.

'Will it hold?' Turner asked abruptly. 'Yes, yes, of course. . . . Tell him we'll do our best up here. . . . Do that. Half-hourly, if you please.'

'It never rains, et cetera,' Turner growled, replacing the phone. 'Engine running rough, temperature hotting up. Distortion in inner starboard shaft. Dodson himself is in the shaft tunnel right now. Bent like a banana, he says.'

Vallery smiled faintly. 'Knowing Dodson, I suppose that means a couple of thou out of alignment.'

'Maybe.' Turner was serious. 'What does matter is that the main shaft bearing's damaged and the lubricating line fractured.'

'As bad as that?' Vallery asked softly.

'Dodson is pretty unhappy. Says the damage isn't recent – thinks it began the night we lost our depth-charges.' Turner shook his head. 'Lord knows what stresses that shaft's undergone since. . . . I suppose to-night's performance brought it to a head. . . . The bearing will have to be lubricated by hand. Wants engine revs. at a minimum or engine shut off altogether. They'll keep us posted.'

'And no possibility of repair?' Vallery asked wryly.

'No, sir. None.'

'Very well, then. Convoy speed. And Commander?'

'Sir?'

'Hands to stations all night. You needn't tell 'em so – but, well, I think it would be wise. I have a feeling—'

'What's that!' Turner shouted. 'Look! What the hell's she doing?' His finger was stabbing towards the last freighter in the starboard line: her guns were blazing away at some unseen target, the tracers lancing whitely through the twilight sky. Even as he dived for the broadcaster, he caught sight of the *Viking*'s main armament belching smoke and jagged flame.

'All guns! Green 110! Aircraft! Independent fire, independent targets! Independent fire, independent targets!' He heard Vallery ordering starboard helm, knew he was going to bring the for'ard turrets to bear.

They were too late. Even as the *Ulysses* began to answer her helm, the enemy planes were pulling out of their approach dives. Great, clumsy shapes, these planes, forlorn and insubstantial in the murky gloom, but identifiable in a sickening flash by the clamour of suddenly racing engines. Condors, without a shadow of doubt. Condors that had outguessed them again, that gliding approach, throttles cut right back, muted roar of the engines drifting downwind, away from the convoy. Their timing, their judgment of distance, had been superb.

The freighter was bracketed twice, directly hit by at least seven bombs: in the near-darkness, it was impossible to see the bombs going home, but the explosions were unmistakable. And as each plane passed over, the decks were raked by savage bursts of machine-gun fire. Every gun position on the freighter was wide open, lacking all but the most elementary frontal protection: the Dems, Naval Ratings on the LA guns, Royal Marine Artillerymen on the HA weapons, were under no illusions as to their life expectancy when they joined the merchant ships on the Russian run. . . . For such few gunners as survived the bombing, the vicious stuttering of these machine-guns was almost certainly their last sound on earth.

As the bombs plummeted down on the next ship in line, the first freighter was already a broken-backed mass of licking, twisting flames. Almost certainly, too, her bottom had been torn out: she had listed heavily, and now slowly and smoothly broke apart just aft of the bridge as if both parts were hinged below the water-line, and was gone before the clamour of the last aero engine had died away in the distance.

Tactical surprise had been complete. One ship gone, a second slewing wildly to an uncontrolled stop, deep in the water by the head, and strangely disquieting and ominous in the entire absence of smoke, flame or any movement at all, a third heavily damaged but still under command. Not one Condor had been lost.

Turner ordered the cease-fire – some of the gunners were still firing blindly into the darkness: trigger-happy, perhaps, or just that the imagination plays weird tricks on woolly minds and sunken blood-red eyes that had known no rest for more hours and days than Turner could remember. And then, as the last Oerlikon fell silent, he heard it again – the drone of the heavy aero engines, the sound welling then ebbing again like breakers on a distant shore, as the wind gusted and died.

There was nothing anyone could do about it. The Focke-Wulf, although lost in the low cloud, was making no attempt to conceal its presence: the ominous drone was never lost for long. Clearly, it was circling almost directly above.

'What do you make of it, sir?' Turner asked.

'I don't know,' Vallery said slowly. 'I just don't know at all. No more visits from the Condors, I'm sure of that. It's just that little bit too dark – and they know they won't catch us again. Tailing us, like as not.'

'Tailing us! It'll be black as tar in half an hour!' Turner disagreed. 'Psychological warfare, if you ask me.'

'God knows,' Vallery sighed wearily. 'All I know is that I'd give all my chances, here and to come, for a couple of Corsairs, or radar, or fog, or another such night as we had in the Denmark Straits.' He laughed shortly, broke down in a fit of coughing. 'Did you hear me?' he whispered. 'I never thought I'd ask for that again. . . . How long since we left Scapa, Commander?'

Turner thought briefly. 'Five – six days, sir.'

'Six days!' He shook his head unbelievingly. 'Six days. And – and thirteen ships – we have thirteen ships now.'

' Twelve,' Turner corrected quietly. 'Another's almost gone. Seven freighters, the tanker and ourselves. Twelve . . . I wish they'd have a go at the old *Stirling* once in a while,' he added morosely.

Vallery shivered in a sudden flurry of snow. He bent forward, head bent against the bitter wind and slanting snow, sunk in unmoving thought. Presently he stirred.

'We will be off the North Cape at dawn,' he said absently. 'Things may be a little difficult, Commander. They'll throw in everything they've got.'

'We've been round there before,' Turner conceded.

'Fifty-fifty on our chances.' Vallery did not seem to have heard him, seemed to be talking to himself. '*Ulysses* and the Sirens – "it may be that the gulfs will wash us down." . . . I wish you luck, Commander.'

Turner stared at him. 'What do you mean—?'

'Oh, myself too.' Vallery smiled, his head lifting up. 'I'll need all the luck, too.' His voice was very soft.

Turner did what he had never done before, never dreamed he would do. In the near-darkness he bent over the Captain, pulled his face round gently and searched it with troubled eyes. Vallery made no protest, and after a few seconds Turner straightened up.

'Do me a favour, sir,' he said quietly. 'Go below. I can take care of things – and Carrington will be up before long. They're gaining control aft.'

'No, not to-night.' Vallery was smiling, but there was a curious finality about the voice. 'And it's no good dispatching one of your minions to summon old Socrates to the bridge. Please, Commander. I want to stay here – I want to see things to-night.'

'Yes, yes, of course.' Suddenly, strangely, Turner no longer wished to argue. He turned away. 'Chrysler! I'll give you just ten minutes to have a gallon of boiling coffee in the Captain's shelter. . . . And you're going to go in there for half an hour,' he said firmly, turning to Vallery, 'and drink the damned stuff, or – or—'

'Delighted!' Vallery muttered. 'Laced with your incomparable rum, of course?'

'Of course! Eh – oh, yes, damn that Williamson!' Turner growled irritably. He paused, went on slowly: 'Shouldn't have said that. . . . Poor bastards, they'll have had it by this time. . . .' He fell silent, then cocked his head listening. 'I wonder how long old Charlie means to keep stooging around up there,' he murmured.

Vallery cleared his throat, coughed, and before he could speak the WT broadcaster clicked on.

'WT – bridge. WT – bridge. Two messages.'

'One from the dashing Orr, for a fiver,' Turner grunted.

'First from the *Sirrus*. "Request permission to go alongside, take off survivors. As well hung for a sheep as a lamb."'

Vallery stared through the thinly falling snow, through the darkness of the night and over the rolling sea.

'In *this* sea?' he murmured. 'And as near dark as makes no difference. He'll kill himself!'

'That's nothing to what old Starr's going to do to him when he lays hands on him!' Turner said cheerfully.

'He hasn't a chance. I – I could never ask a man to do that. There's no justification for such a risk. Besides, the merchantman's been badly hit. There can't be many left alive aboard.'

Turner said nothing.

'Make a signal,' Vallery said clearly. ' "Thank you. Permission granted. Good luck." And tell WT to go ahead.'

'Second signal from London for Captain. Decoding. Messenger leaving for bridge immediately.'

'To Officer Commanding, 14 ACS, FR77,' the speaker boomed after a few seconds. ' "Deeply distressed at news. Imperative maintain 090. Battle squadron steaming SSE at full speed on interception course. Rendezvous approx. 1400 tomorrow. Their Lordships expressly command best wishes Rear-Admiral Vallery. DNO, London." '

The speaker clicked off and there was only the lost pinging of the Asdic, the throbbing monotony of the prowling Condor's engines, the lingering memory of the gladness in the broadcaster's voice.

'Uncommon civil of their Lordships,' murmured the Kapok Kid, rising to the occasion as usual. 'Downright decent, one might almost say.'

'Bloody long overdue,' Turner growled. 'Congratulations, sir,' he added warmly. 'Signs of grace at last along the banks of the Thames.' A murmur of pleasure ran round the bridge: discipline or not, no one made any attempt to hide his satisfaction.

'Thank you, thank you.' Vallery was touched, deeply touched. Promise of help at long, long last, a promise which might hold – almost certainly held – for each and every member of his crew the difference between life and death – and they could only think to rejoice in his promotion! Dead men's shoes, he thought, and thought of saying it, but dismissed the idea immediately: a rebuff, a graceless affront to such genuine pleasure.

'Thank you very much,' he repeated. 'But gentlemen, you appear to have missed the only item of news of any real significance—'

'Oh, no, we haven't,' Turner growled. 'Battle squadron – ha!

218

Too — late as usual. Oh, to be sure, they'll be in at the death – or shortly afterwards, anyway. Perhaps in time for a few survivors. I suppose the *Illustrious* and the *Furious* will be with them?'

'Perhaps. I don't know.' Vallery shook his head, smiling. 'Despite my recent – ah – elevation, I am not yet in their Lordship's confidence. But there'll be some carriers, and they could fly off a few hours away, give us air cover from dawn.'

'Oh, no, they won't,' said Turner prophetically. 'The weather will break down, make flying off impossible. See if I'm not right.'

'Perhaps, Cassandra, perhaps,' Vallery smiled. 'We'll see. . . . What was that, Pilot? I didn't quite . . .'

The Kapok Kid grinned.

'It's just occurred to me that tomorrow's going to be a big day for our junior doctor – he's convinced that no battleship ever puts out to sea except for a Spithead review in peacetime.'

'That reminds me,' Vallery said thoughtfully. 'Didn't we promise the *Sirrus*—?'

'Young Nicholls is up to his neck in work,' Turner cut in. 'Doesn't love us – the Navy rather – overmuch, but he sure loves his job. Borrowed a fire-fighting suit, and Carrington says he's already . . .' He broke off, looked up sharply into the thin, driving snow. 'Hallo! Charlie's getting damned nosy, don't you think?'

The roar of the Condor's engines was increasing every second: the sound rose to a clamouring crescendo as the bomber roared directly overhead, barely a couple of hundred feet above the broken masts, died away to a steady drone as the plane circled round the convoy.

'WT to escorts!' Vallery called quickly. 'Let him go – don't touch him! No starshells – nothing. He's trying to draw us out, to have us give away our position. . . . It's not likely that the merchant ships . . . Oh, God! The fools, the fools! Too late, too late!'

A merchantman in the port line had opened up – Oerlikons or Bofors, it was difficult to say. They were firing blind, completely blind: and in a high wind, snow and darkness, the chance of locating a plane by sound alone was impossibly remote.

The firing did not last long – ten, fifteen seconds at the outside. But long enough – and the damage was done. Charlie had pulled off, and straining apprehensive ears caught the sudden

219

deepening of the note of the engines as the boosters were cut in for maximum climb.

'What do you make of it, sir?' Turner asked abruptly.

'Trouble.' Vallery was quiet but certain. 'This has never happened before – and it's not psychological warfare, as you call it, Commander: he doesn't even rob us of our sleep – not when we're this close to the North Cape. And he can't hope to trail us long: a couple of quick course alterations and – ah!' He breathed softly. 'What did I tell you, Commander?'

With a suddenness that blocked thought, with a dazzling glare that struck whitely, cruelly at singeing eyeballs, night was transformed into day. High above the *Ulysses* a flare had burst into intense life, a flare which tore apart the falling snow like filmy, transparent gauze. Swinging wildly under its parachute with the gusting of the wind, the flare was drifting slowly seawards, towards a sea no longer invisible but suddenly black as night, towards a sea where every ship, in its glistening sheath of ice and snow, was silhouetted in dazzling whiteness against the inky backdrop of sea and sky.

'Get that flare!' Turner was barking into the transmitter. 'All Oerlikons, all pom-poms, get that flare!' He replaced the transmitter. 'Might as well throw empty beer bottles at it with the old girl rolling like this,' he muttered. 'Lord, gives you a funny feeling, this!'

'I know,' the Kapok Kid supplied. 'Like one of these dreams where you're walking down a busy street and you suddenly realize that all you're wearing is a wrist-watch. "Naked and defenceless," is the accepted term, I believe. For the non-literary, "caught with the pants down." ' Absently he brushed the snow off the quilted kapok, exposing the embroidered 'J' on the breast pocket, while his apprehensive eyes probed into the circle of darkness outside the pool of light. 'I don't like this at all,' he complained.

'Neither do I.' Vallery was unhappy. 'And I don't like Charlie's sudden disappearance either.'

'He hasn't disappeared,' Turner said grimly. 'Listen!' They listened, ears straining intently, caught the intermittent, distant thunder of the heavy engines. 'He's 'way astern of us, closing.'

Less than a minute later the Condor roared overhead again, higher this time, lost in the clouds. Again he released a flare, higher, much higher than the last, and this time squarely over the heart of the convoy.

Again the roar of the engines died to a distant murmur, again the desynchronised clamour strengthened as the Condor overtook the convoy a second time. Glimpsed only momentarily in the inverted valleys between the scudding clouds, it flew wide, this time, far out on the port hand, riding clear above the pitiless glare of the sinking flares. And, as it thundered by, flares exploded into blazing life – four of them, just below cloud level, at four-second intervals. The northern horizon was alive with light, glowing and pulsating with a fierce flame that threw every tiny detail into the starkest relief. And to the south there was only the blackness: the rim of the pool of light stopped abruptly just beyond the starboard line of ships.

It was Turner who first appreciated the significance, the implications of this. Realization struck at him with the galvanic effect of sheer physical shock. He gave a hoarse cry, fairly flung himself at the broadcast transmitter: there was no time to await permission.

' "B" turret!' he roared. 'Starshells to the south. Green 90, green 90. Urgent! Urgent! Starshells, green 90. Maximum elevation 10. Close settings. Fire when you are ready!' He looked quickly over his shoulder. 'Pilot! Can you see—?'

' "B" turret training, sir.'

'Good, good!' He lifted the transmitter again. 'All guns! All guns! Stand by to repel air attack from starboard. Probable bearing green 90. Hostiles probably torpedo-bombers.' Even as he spoke, he caught sight of the intermittent flashing of the fighting lights on the lower yardarm: Vallery was sending out an emergency signal to the convoy.

'You're right, Commander,' Vallery whispered. In the gaunt pallor, in the skin taut stretched across the sharp and fleshless bones, his face, in that blinding glare, was a ghastly travesty of humanity; it was a death's-head, redeemed only by the glow of the deep-sunken eyes, the sudden flicker of bloodless lids as the whip-lash crash of 'B' turret shattered the silence. 'You must be,' he went on slowly. 'Every ship silhouetted from the north – and a maximum run-in from the south under cover of darkness.' He broke off suddenly as the shells exploded in great overlapping globules of light, two miles to the south. 'You *are* right,' he said gently. 'Here they come.'

They came from the south, wing-tip to wing-tip, flying in three waves with four or five planes in each wave. They were coming in at about 500 feet, and even as the shells burst their noses were already dipping into the plane of the shallow attack dive of the torpedo-bomber. And as they dived, the bombers

221

fanned out, as if in search of individual targets – or what seemed, at first sight, to be individual targets. But within seconds it became obvious that they were concentrating on two ships and two ships alone – the *Stirling* and the *Ulysses*. Even the ideal double target of the cripled merchantman and the destroyer *Sirrus*, almost stopped alongside her, was strictly ignored. They were flying under orders.

'B' turret pumped out two more starshells at minimum settings, reloaded with HE. By this time, every gun in the convoy had opened up, the barrage was intense: the torpedo-bombers – curiously difficult to identify, but looking like Heinkels – had to fly through a concentrated lethal curtain of steel and high explosive. The element of surprise was gone: the starshells of the *Ulysses* had gained a priceless twenty seconds.

Five bombers were coming at the *Ulysses* now, fanned out to disperse fire, but arrowing in on a central point. They were levelling off, running in on firing tracks almost at wave-top height, when one of them straightened up a fraction too late, brushed lightly against a cresting wave-top, glanced harmlessly off, then catapulted crazily from wave-top to wave-top – they were flying at right angles to the set of the sea – before disappearing in a trough. Misjudgment of distance or the pilot's windscreen suddenly obscured by a flurry of snow – it was impossible to say.

A second later the leading plane in the middle disintegrated in a searing burst of flame – a direct hit on its torpedo warhead. A third plane, behind and to the west, sheered off violently to the left to avoid the hurtling debris, and the subsequent dropping of its torpedo was no more than an empty gesture. It ran half a cable length behind the *Ulysses*, spent itself in the empty sea beyond.

Two bombers left now, pressing home their attack with suicidal courage, weaving violently from side to side to avoid destruction. Two seconds passed, three, four – and still they came on, through the falling snow and intensely heavy fire, miraculous in their immunity. Theoretically, there is no target so easy to hit as a plane approaching directly head on: in practice, it never worked out that way. In the Arctic, the Mediterranean, the Pacific, the relative immunity of the torpedo-bombers, the high percentage of successful attacks carried out in the face of almost saturation fire, never failed to confound the experts. Tension, over-anxiety, fear – these were part of the trouble, at least: there are no half measures about a torpedo-bomber – you get him or he gets you. And there is nothing more nerve-racking – always, of course, with the outstanding exception of the screaming, near-vertical power-dive of the gull-winged Stuka dive-bomber – than to see a torpedo-bomber looming hugely, terrifyingly over the open sights of your gun and know that you have just five inexorable seconds to live. . . . And with the *Ulysses,* of course, the continuous rolling of the cruiser in the heavy cross-sea made accuracy impossible.

These last two bombers came in together, wing-tip to wing-tip. The plane nearer the bows dropped its torpedo less than two hundred yards away, pulled up in a maximum climbing turn to starboard, a fusillade of light cannon and machine-gun shells smashing into the upper works of the bridge: the torpedo hit the water obliquely, porpoised high into the air, then crashed back again nose first into a heavy wave, diving steeply into the sea: it passed under the *Ulysses.*

But seconds before that the last torpedo-bomber had made its attack – made its attack and failed and died. It had come roaring in less than ten feet above the waves, had come straight on without releasing its torpedo, without gaining an inch in height, until the crosses on the upper sides of the wings could be clearly seen, until it was less than a hundred yards away. Suddenly, desperately, the pilot had begun to climb: it was immediately obvious that the torpedo release mechanism had jammed, either through mechanical failure or icing in the intense cold: obviously, too, the pilot had intended to release the torpedo at the last minute, had banked on the sudden decrease of weight to lift him over the *Ulysses.*

The nose of the bomber smashed squarely into the for'ard funnel, the starboard wing shearing off like cardboard as it scythed across the after leg of the tripod mast. There was an instantaneous, blinding sheet of gasoline flame, but neither smoke nor explosion. A moment later the crumpled, shattered bomber, no longer a machine but a torn and flaming crucifix, plunged into the hissing sea a dozen yards away. The water had barely closed over it when a gigantic underwater explosion heeled the *Ulysses* far over to starboard, a vicious hammer-blow that flung men off their feet and shattered the lighting system on the port side of the cruiser.

Commander Turner hoisted himself painfully to his feet, shook his head to clear it of the cordite fumes and the dazed confusion left by cannon shells exploding almost at arm's length. The shock of the detonating torpedo hadn't thrown him

to the duckboards – he'd hurled himself there five seconds previously as the flaming guns of the other bomber had raked the
bridge from point-blank range.

His first thought was for Vallery. The Captain was lying on
his side, crumpled strangely against the binnacle. Dry-mouthed,
cold with a sudden chill that was not of that Polar wind, Turner
bent quickly, turned him gently over.

Vallery lay still, motionless, lifeless. No sign of blood, no
gaping wound – thank God for that! Turner peeled off a glove,
thrust a hand below duffel coat and jacket, thought he detected
a faint, a very faint beating of the heart. Gently he lifted the
head off the frozen slush, then looked up quickly. The Kapok
Kid was standing above him.

'Get Brooks up here, Pilot,' he said swiftly. 'It's urgent!'

Unsteadily, the Kapok Kid crossed over the bridge. The communication rating was leaning over the gate, telephone in his
hand.

'The Sick Bay, quickly!' the Kapok Kid ordered. 'Tell the
Surgeon Commander . . .' He stopped suddenly, guessed that
the man was still too dazed to understand. 'Here, give me that
phone!' Impatiently, he stretched out his hand and grabbed the
telephone, then stiffened in horror as the man slipped gradually
backwards, extended arms trailing stiffly over the top of the
gate until they disappeared. Carpenter opened the gate, stared
down at the dead man at his feet: there was a hole the size of
his gloved fist between the shoulder-blades.

He lay alongside the Asdic cabinet, a cabinet, the Kapok Kid
now saw for the first time, riddled and shattered with machine-
gun bullets and shells. His first thought was the numbing appreciation that the set must be smashed beyond recovery, that
their last defence against the U-boats was gone. Hard on the
heels of that came the sickening realization that there had been
an Asdic operator inside there. . . . His eyes wandered away,
caught sight of Chrysler rising to his feet by the torpedo control. He, too, was staring at the Asdic cabinet, his face drained
of expression. Before the Kapok Kid could speak, Chrysler
lurched forward, fists battering frantically, blindly at the
jammed door of the cabinet. Like a man in a dream, the Kapok
Kid heard him sobbing. . . . And then he remembered. The
Asdic operator – his name was Chrysler too. Sick to his heart,
the Kapok Kid lifted the phone again. . . .

Turner pillowed the Captain's head, moved across to the
starboard corner of the compass platform. Bentley, quiet, un-

obtrusive as always, was sitting on the deck, his back wedged between two pipes, his head pillowed peacefully on his chest. His hand under Bentley's chin, Turner gazed down into the sightless eyes, the only recognisable feature of what had once been a human face. Turner swore in savage quiet, tried to prise the dead fingers locked round the hand-grip of the Aldis, then gave up. The barred beam shone eerily across the darkening bridge.

Methodically, Turner searched the bridge-deck for further casualties. He found three others and it was no consolation at all that they must have died unknowing. Five dead men for a three-second burst – a very fair return, he thought bitterly. Standing on the after ladder, his face stilled in unbelief as he realized that he was staring down into the heart of the shattered for'ard funnel. More he could not see: the boat deck was already blurred into featureless anonymity in the dying glare of the last of the flares. He swung on his heel, returned to the compass platform.

At least, he thought grimly, there was no difficulty in seeing the *Stirling*. What was it that he had said – said less than ten minutes ago? 'I wish they'd have a go at the *Stirling* once in a while.' Something like that. His mouth twisted. They'd had a go, all right. The *Stirling*, a mile ahead, was slewing away to starboard, to the south-east, her for'ard superstructure enveloped in a writhing cocoon of white flame. He stared through his night glasses, tried to assess the damage; but a solid wall of flame masked the superstructure, from the fo'c'sle deck clear abaft the bridge. He could see nothing there, just nothing – but he could see, even in that heavy swell, that the *Stirling* was listing to starboard. It was learned later that the *Stirling* had been struck twice: she had been torpedoed in the for'ard boiler-room, and seconds later a bomber had crashed into the side of her bridge, her torpedo still slung beneath the belly of her fuselage: almost certainly, in the light of the similar occurence on the *Ulysses*, severe icing had jammed the release mechanism. Death must have been instantaneous for every man on the bridge and the decks below; among the dead were Captain Jeffries, the First Lieutenant and the Navigator.

The last bomber was hardly lost in the darkness when Carrington replaced the poop phone, turned to Hartley.

'Think you can manage now, Chief? I'm wanted on the bridge.'

'I think so, sir.' Hartley, blackened and stained with smoke and extinguisher foam, passed his sleeve wearily across his face. 'The worst is over. . . . Where's Lieutenant Carslake? Shouldn't he—?'

'Forget him,' Carrington interrupted brusquely. 'I don't know where he is, nor do I care. There's no need for us to beat about the bush, Chief – we're better without him. If he returns, *you're* still in charge. Look after things.'

He turned away, walked quickly for'ard along the port alley. On the packed snow and ice, the pad of his rubber seaboots was completely soundless.

He was passing the shattered canteen when he saw a tall, shadowy figure standing in the gap between the snow-covered lip of the outer torpedo tube and the end stanchion of the guard-rails, trying to open a jammed extinguisher valve by striking it against the stanchion. A second later, he saw another blurred form detach itself stealthily from the shadows, creep up stealthily behind the man with the extinguisher, a heavy bludgeon of wood or metal held high above his head.

'Look out!' Carrington shouted. 'Behind you!'

It was all over in two seconds – the sudden, flailing rush of the attacker, the crash as the victim, lightning fast in his re-actions, dropped his extinguisher and fell crouched to his knees, the thin piercing scream of anger and terror as the attacker catapulted over the stooping body and through the gap between tubes and rails, the splash – and then the silence.

Carrington ran up to the man on the deck, helped him to his feet. The last flare had not yet died, and it was still light enough for him to see who it was – Ralston, the LTO. Carrington gripped his arms, looked at him anxiously.

'Are you all right? Did he get you? Good God, who on earth—?'

'Thank you, sir.' Ralston was breathing quickly, but his face was almost expressionless again. 'That was too close! Thank you very much, sir.'

'But who on earth—?' Carrington repeated in wonder.

'Never saw him, sir.' Ralston was grim. 'But I know who it was – Sub-Lieutenant Carslake. He's been following me around all night, never let me out of his sight, not once. Now I know why.'

It took much to disturb the First Lieutenant's iron equa-nimity, but now he shook his head in slow disbelief.

'I knew there was bad blood!' he murmured. 'But that it

should come to this! What the Captain will say to this I just—'

'Why tell him?' Ralston said indifferently. 'Why tell any-one? Perhaps Carslake had relations. What good will it do to hurt them, to hurt anyone. Let anyone think what they like.' He laughed shortly. 'Let them think he died a hero's death fire-fighting, fell over the side, anything.' He looked down into the dark, rushing water, then shivered suddenly. 'Let him go, sir, please. He's paid.'

For a long second Carrington, too, stared down over the side, looked back at the tall boy before him. Then he clapped his arm, nodded slowly and turned away.

Turner heard the clanging of the gate, lowered the binoculars to find Carrington standing by his side, gazing wordlessly at the burning cruiser. Just then Vallery moaned softly, and Carring-ton looked down quickly at the prone figure at his feet.

'My God! The Old Man! Is he hurt badly, sir?'

'I don't know, Number One. If not, it's a bloody miracle,' he added bitterly. He stooped down, raised the dazed Captain to a sitting position.

'Are you all right, sir?' he asked anxiously. 'Do you – have you been hit?'

Vallery shuddered in a long, exhausting paroxysm of cough-ing, then shook his head feebly.

'I'm all right,' he whispered weakly. He tried to grin, a piti-ful, ghastly travesty of a smile in the reflected light from the burning Aldis. 'I dived for the deck, but I think the binnacle got in my way.' He rubbed his forehead, already bruised and discoloured. 'How's the ship, Commander?'

'To hell with the ship!' Turner said roughly. He passed an arm round Vallery, raised him carefully to his feet. 'How are things aft, Number One?'

'Under control. Still burning, but under control. I left Hart-ley in charge.' He made no mention of Carslake.

'Good! Take over. Radio Stirling, Sirrus, see how they are. Come on, sir. Shelter for you!'

Vallery protested feebly, a token protest only, for he was too weak to stand. He checked involuntarily as he saw the snow falling whitely through the barred beam of the Aldis, slowly followed the beam back to its source.

'Bentley?' he whispered. 'Don't tell me . . .' He barely caught the Commander's wordless nod, turned heavily away. They passed by the dead man stretched outside the gate, then stopped at the Asdic cabinet. A sobbing figure was crouched into the angle between the shelter and the jammed and shattered door of the hut, head pillowed on the forearm resting high against the door. Vallery laid a hand on the shaking shoulder, peered into the averted face.

'What is it? Oh, it's you, boy.' The white face had been lifted towards him. 'What's the matter, Chrysler?'

'The door, sir!' Chrysler's voice was muffled, quivering. 'The door – I can't open it.'

For the first time, Vallery looked at the cabinet, at the gashed and torn metal. His mind was still dazed, exhausted, and it was almost by a process of association that he suddenly, horrifyingly thought of the gashed and mangled operator that must lie behind that locked door.

'Yes,' he said quietly. 'The door's buckled. . . . There's nothing anyone can do, Chrysler.' He looked more closely at the grief-dulled eyes. 'Come on, my boy, there's no need—'

'My brother's in there, sir.' The words, the hopeless despair, struck Vallery like a blow. Dear God! He had forgotten. . . . Of course – Leading Asdic Operator Chrysler. . . . He stared down at the dead man at his feet, already covered with a thin layer of snow.

'Have that Aldis unplugged, Commander, will you?' he asked absently. 'And Chrysler?'

'Yes, sir.' A flat monotone.

'Go below and bring up some coffee, please.'

'Coffee, sir!' He was bewildered, uncomprehending. 'Coffee! But – but – my – my brother—'

'I know,' Vallery said gently. 'I know. Bring some coffee, will you?'

Chrysler stumbled off. When the shelter door closed behind them, clicking on the light, Vallery turned to the Commander.

'Cue for moralising on the glories of war,' he murmured quietly. '*Dulce et decorum,* and the proud privilege of being the sons of Nelson and Drake. It's not twenty-four hours since Ralston watched his father die. . . . And now this boy. Perhaps—'

'I'll take care of things,' Turner nodded. He hadn't yet forgiven himself for what he had said and done to Ralston last night, in spite of Ralston's quick friendliness, the ready acceptance of his apologies. 'I'll keep him busy out of the way till we open up the cabinet. . . . Sit down, sir. Have a swig of this.' He smiled faintly. 'Friend Williams having betrayed my guilty secret. . . . Hallo! Company.'

The light clicked off and a burly figure bulked momentarily against the grey oblong of the doorway. The door shut, and Brooks stood blinking in the sudden light, red of face and gasping for breath. His eyes focused on the bottle in Turner's hand.

'Ha!' he said at length. 'Having a bottle party, are we? All contributions gratefully received, I have no doubt.' He opened his case on a convenient table, was rummaging inside when someone rapped sharply on the door.

'Come in,' Vallery called.

A signalman entered, handed a note to Vallery. 'From London, sir. Chief says there may be some reply.'

'Thank you. I'll phone down.'

The door opened and closed again. Vallery looked up at an empty-handed Turner.

'Thanks for removing the guilty evidence so quickly,' he smiled. Then he shook his head. 'My eyes – they don't seem so good. Perhaps you would read the signal, Commander?'

'And perhaps *you* would like some decent medicine,' Brooks boomed, 'instead of that filty muck of Turner's.' He fished in his bag, produced a bottle of amber liquid. 'With all the resources of modern medicine – well, practically all, anyway – at my disposal, I can find nothing to equal this.'

'Have you told Nicholls?' Vallery was stretched out on the settee now, eyes closed, the shadow of a smile on his bloodless lips.

'Well, no,' Brooks confessed. 'But plenty of time. Have some?'

'Thanks. Let's have the good news, Turner.'

'Good news!' The sudden deadly quiet of the Commander's voice fell chilly over the waiting men. 'No, sir, it's not good news.

' "Rear-Admiral Vallery, Commanding 14 ACS, FR77." ' The voice was drained of all tone and expression. ' "*Tirpitz*, escorting cruisers, destroyers, reported moving out Alta Fjord sunset. Intense activity Alta Fjord airfield. Fear sortie under air cover. All meaures avoid useless sacrifice Merchant, Naval ships. DNO, London." ' With deliberate care Turner folded the paper, laid it on the table. 'Isn't that just wonderful,' he murmured. 'Whatever next?'

Vallery was sitting bolt upright on the settee, blind to the blood trickling down crookedly from one corner of his mouth. His face was calm, unworried.

'I think I'll have that glass, now, Brooks, if you don't mind,' he said quietly. The *Tirpitz*. The *Tirpitz*. He shook his head tiredly, like a man in a dream. The *Tirpitz* – the name that no man mentioned without a far-off echo of awe and fear, the name that had completely dominated North Atlantic naval strategy during the past two years. Moving out at last, an armoured Colossus, sister-ship to that other Titan that had destroyed the *Hood* with one single, savage blow – the *Hood,* the darling of the Royal Navy, the most powerful ship in the world – or so men had thought. What chance had *their* tiny cockle-shell cruiser. . . . Again he shook his head, angrily this time, forced himself to think of the present.

'Well, gentlemen, I suppose time bringeth all things – even the *Tirpitz*. It had to come some day. Just our ill luck – the bait was too close, too tempting.'

'My young colleague is going to be just delighted,' Brooks said grimly. 'A *real* battleship at long, long last.'

'Sunset,' Turner mused. 'Sunset. My God! he said sharply, 'even allowing for negotiating the fjord they'll be on us in four hours on this course!'

'Exactly,' Vallery nodded. 'And it's no good running north. They'll overtake us before we're within a hundred miles of them.'

'Them? Our big boys up north?' Turner scoffed. 'I hate to sound like a gramophone record, but you'll recall my earlier statement about them – too — late as usual!' He paused, swore again. 'I hope that old bastard Starr's satisfied at last!' he finished bitterly.

'Why all the gloom?' Vallery looked up quizzically, went on softly. 'We can still be back, safe and sound in Scapa in forty-eight hours. "Avoid useless sacrifice Merchant, Naval ships," he said. The *Ulysses* is probably the fastest ship in the world today. It's simple, gentlemen.'

'No, no!' Brooks moaned. 'Too much of an anti-climax. I couldn't stand it!'

'Do another PQ17?'[1] Turner smiled, but the smile never touched his eyes. 'The Royal Navy could never stand it:

[1] PQ17, a large mixed convoy – it included over 30 British, American and Panamanian ships – left Iceland for Russia under the escort of half a dozen destroyers and perhaps a dozen smaller craft, with a mixed Anglo-American cruiser and destroyer squadron in immediate support. A shadow covering force – again Anglo-American – comprising one aircraft carrier, two battleships, three cruisers and a flotilla of destroyers, lay to the north. As with FR77, they formed the spring of the trap that closed too late.

The time was midsummer, 1942, a suicidal season for the attempt, for in June and July, in these high latitudes, there is no night. About longitude 20° east, the convoy was heavily attacked by U-boats and aircraft.

Captain – Rear-Admiral Vallery would never permit it; and speaking for myself and, I'm fairly certain, this bunch of cut-throat mutineers of ours – well, I don't think we'd ever sleep so sound o' nights again.'

'Gad!' Brooks murmured. 'The man's a poet!'

'You're right, Turner.' Vallery drained his glass, lay back exhausted. 'We don't seem to have much option. . . . What if we receive orders for a – ah – high-speed withdrawal?'

'You can't read,' Turner said bluntly. 'Remember, you just said your eyes are going back on you.'

'"Souls that have toiled and wrought and fought with me," ' Vallery quoted softly. 'Thank you, gentlemen. You make things very easy for me.' He propped himself on an elbow, his mind made up. He smiled at Turner, and his face was almost boyish again.

'Inform all merchant ships, all escorts. Tell them to break north.'

Turner stared at him.

'North? Did you say "north"?' But the Admiralty—'

'North, I said,' Vallery repeated quietly. 'The Admiralty can do what they like about it. We've played along long enough. We've sprung the trap. What more can they want? This way there's a chance – an almost hopeless chance, perhaps, but a fighting chance. To go east is suicide.' He smiled again, almost

On the same day as the attack began – 4th July – the covering cruiser squadron was radioed that the *Tirpitz* had just sailed from Alta Fjord. (This was not the case: The *Tirpitz* did make a brief, abortive sortie on the afternoon of the 5th, but turned back the same evening: rumour had it that she had been damaged by torpedoes from a Russian submarine.) The support squadron and convoy escorts immediately withdrew to the west at high speed, leaving PQ17 to their fate, leaving them to scatter and make their unescorted way to Russia as best they could. The feelings of the crews of the merchant ships at this save-their-own-skins desertion and betrayal by the Royal Navy can be readily imagined. Their fears, too, can be readily imagined, but even their darkest forebodings never conceived the dreadful reality: 23 merchant ships were sent to the bottom – by U-boats and aircraft. The *Tirpitz* was not seen, never came anywhere near the convoy; but even the threat had driven the naval squadrons to flight.

The author does not know all the facts concerning PQ17, nor does he seek to interpret those he does know: still less does he seek to assign blame. Curiously enough, the only definite conclusion is that no blame can be attached to the commander of the squadron, Admiral Hamilton. He had no part of the decision to withdraw – the order came from the Admiralty, and was imperative. But one does not envy him.

It was a melancholy and bitter incident, all the more unpalatable in that it ran so directly counter to the traditions of a great Service; one wonders what Sir Philip Sydney would have thought, or, in more modern times, Kennedy of the *Rawalpindi* or Fegen of the *Jervis Bay*. But there was no doubt what the Merchant Navy thought. What they still think. From most of the few survivors, there can be no hope of forgiveness. They will, probably, always remember: the Royal Navy would desperately like to forget. It is difficult to blame either.

dreamily. 'The end is not all-important,' he said softly. 'I don't think I'll have to answer for this. Not now – not ever.'

Turner grinned at him, his face lit up. 'North, you said.'

'Inform C-in-C.' Vallery went on. 'Ask Pilot for an interception course. Tell the convoy we'll tag along behind, give 'em as much cover as we can, as long as we can. . . . As long as we can. Let us not delude ourselves. 1000 to 1 at the outside. . . . Nothing else we can do, Commander?'

'Pray,' Turner said succinctly.

'And sleep,' Brooks added. 'Why don't you have half an hour, sir?'

'Sleep!' Vallery seemed genuinely amused. 'We'll have all the time in the world to sleep, just by and by.'

'You have a point,' Brooks conceded. 'You are very possibly right.'

—— 15 ——

SATURDAY EVENING II

Messages were pouring in to the bridge now, messages from the merchant ships, messages of dismayed unbelief asking for confirmation of the *Tirpitz* breakout: from the *Stirling,* replying that the superstructure fire was now under control and that the engine-room watertight bulkheads were holding; and one from Orr of the *Sirrus,* saying that his ship was making water to the capacity of the pumps – he had been in heavy collision with the sinking merchantman – that they had taken off forty-four survivors, that the *Sirrus* had already done her share and couldn't she go home? The signal had arrived after the *Sirrus's* receipt of the bad news. Turner grinned to himself: no inducement on earth, he knew, could have persuaded Orr to leave now.

The messages kept pouring in, by visual signal or WT. There was no point in maintaining radio silence to outwit enemy monitor positions; the enemy knew where they were to a mile. Nor was there any need to prohibit light signalling – not with the *Stirling* still burning furiously enough to illuminate the sea for a mile around. And so the messages kept on coming – messages of fear and dismay and anxiety. But, for Turner, the most disquieting message came neither by lamp nor by radio.

Fully quarter of an hour had elapsed since the end of the

attack and the *Ulysses* was rearing and pitching through the head seas on her new course of 350°, when the gate of the bridge crashed open and a panting, exhausted man stumbled on to the compass platform. Turner, back on the bridge again, peered closely at him in the red glare from the *Stirling,* recognised him as a stoker. His face was masked in sweat, the sweat already caking to ice in the intense cold. And in spite of that cold, he was hatless, coatless, clad only in a pair of thin dungarees. He was shivering violently, shivering from excitement and not because of the icy wind – he was oblivious to such things.

Turner seized him by the shoulder.

'What is it, man?' he demanded anxiously. The stoker was still too breathless to speak. 'What's wrong? Quickly!'

'The TS, sir!' The breathing was so quick, so agonised, that the words blurred into a gasping exhalation. 'It's full of water!'

'The TS!' Turner was incredulous. 'Flooded! When did this happen?'

'I'm not sure, sir.' He was still gasping for breath. 'But there was a bloody awful explosion, sir, just about amid—'

'I know! I know!' Turner interrupted impatiently. 'Bomber carried away the for'ard funnel, exploded in the water, port side. But that was fifteen minutes ago, man! Fifteen minutes! Good God, they would have—'

'TS switchboard's gone, sir.' The stoker was beginning to recover, to huddle against the wind, but frantic at the Commander's deliberation and delay, he straightened up and grasped Turner's duffel without realising what he was doing. The note of urgency deepened still further. 'All the power's gone, sir. And the hatch is jammed! The men can't get out!'

'The hatch-cover jammed!' Turner's eyes narrowed in concern. 'What happened?' he rapped out. 'Buckled?'

'The counter-weight's broken off, sir. It's on top of the hatch. We can only get it open an inch. You see, sir—'

'Number One!' Turner shouted.

'Here, sir.' Carrington was standing just behind him. 'I heard. ... Why can't you open it?'

'It's the *TS* hatch!' the stoker cried desperately. 'A quarter of a bloody ton if it's an ounce, sir. You know – the one below the ladder outside the wheelhouse. Only two men can get at it at the same time. We've tried. ... Hurry, sir. *Please.*'

'Just a minute.' Carrington was calm, unruffled, infuriatingly so. 'Hartley? No, still fire-fighting. Evans, MacIntosh – dead.' He was obviously thinking aloud. 'Bellamy, perhaps?'

'What is it, Number One?' Turner burst out. He himself had caught up the anxiety, the impatience of the stoker. 'What are you trying—?'

'Hatch-cover plus pulley – 1000 lbs,' Carrington murmured. 'A special man for a special job.'

'Petersen, sir!' The stoker had understood immediately. 'Petersen!'

'Of course!' Carrington clapped gloved hands together. 'We're on our way, sir. Acetylene? No time! Stoker – crow-bars, sledges. ... Perhaps if you would ring the engine-room, sir?'

But Turner already had the phone in his hand.

Aft on the poop-deck, the fire was under control, all but in a few odd corners where the flames were fed by a fierce through draught. In the mess-decks, bulkheads, ladders, mess partitions, lockers had been twisted and buckled into strange shapes by the intense heat: on deck, the gasoline-fed flames, incinerating the two and three-quarter inch deck plating and melting the caulking as by some gigantic blow-torch, had cleanly stripped all covering and exposed the steel deck-plates, plates dull red and glowing evilly, plates that hissed and spat as heavy snowflakes drifted down to sibilant extinction.

On and below decks, Hartley and his crews, freezing one moment, reeling in the blast of heat the next, toiled like men insane. Where their wasted, exhausted bodies found the strength God only knew. From the turrets, from the Master-At-Arms's office, from mess-decks and emergency steering position, they pulled out man after man who had been there when the Condor had crashed: pulled them out, looked at them, swore, wept and plunged back into the aftermath of that holocaust, oblivious of pain and danger, tearing aside wreckage, wreckage still burning, still red-hot, with charred and broken gloves: and when the gloves fell off, they used their naked hands.

As the dead were ranged in the starboard alleyway, Leading Seaman Doyle was waiting for them. Less than half an hour previously, Doyle had been in the for'ard galley passage, rolling in silent agony as frozen body and clothes thawed out after the drenching of his pom-pom. Five minutes later, he had been back on his gun, rock-like, unflinching, as he pumped shell after shell over open sights into the torpedo bombers. And now, steady and enduring as ever, he was on the poop. A man of iron, and a face of iron, too, that night, the bearded leonine head still and impassive as he picked up one dead man after the other, walked to the guard-rail and dropped his burden gently over the side. How many times he repeated that brief journey that night, Doyle never knew: he had lost count after the first twenty or so. He had no right to do this, of course: the navy was very strong on decent burial, and this was not decent burial. But the sailmakers were dead and no man would or could have sewn up these ghastly charred heaps in the weighted and sheeted canvas. The dead don't care, Doyle thought dispassionately – let them look after themselves. So, too, thought Carrington and Hartley, and they made no move to stop him.

Beneath their feet, the smouldering mess-decks rang with hollow reverberating clangs as Nicholls and Leading Telegraphist Brown, still weirdly garbed in their white asbestos suits, swung heavy sledges against the securing clips of 'Y' magazine hatch. In the smoke and gloom and their desperate haste, they could hardly see each other, much less the clips: as often as not they missed their strokes and the hammers went spinning out of numbed hands into the waiting darkness.

Time yet, Nicholls thought desperately, perhaps there is time. The main flooding valve had been turned off five minutes ago: it was possible, barely possible, that the two trapped men inside were clinging to the ladder, above water level.

One clip, one clip only was holding the hatch-cover now. With alternate strokes of their sledges, they struck it with vicious strength. Suddenly, unexpectedly, it sheared off at its base and the hatch-cover crashed open under the explosive up-surge of the compressed air beneath. Brown screamed in agony, a single coughing shout of pain, as the bone-crashing momentum of the swinging hatch crashed into his right hip, then fell to the deck where he lay moaning quietly.

Nicholls did not even spare him a glance. He leant far through the hatch, the powerful beam of his torch stabbing downwards into the gloom. And he could see nothing, nothing at all – not what he wanted to see. All he saw was the water, dark and viscous and evil, water rising and falling, water flooding and ebbing in the eerie oilbound silence as the *Ulysses* plunged and lifted in the heavy seas.

'Below!' Nicholls called loudly. The voice, a voice, he noted impersonally, cracked and shaken with strain, boomed and echoed terrifyingly down the iron tunnel. 'Below!' he shouted again. 'Is there anybody there?' He strained his ears for the least sound, for the faintest whisper of an answer, but none came.

'McQuater!' He shouted a third time. 'Williamson! Can you

hear me?' Again he looked, again he listened, but there was only the darkness and the muffled whisper of the oil-slicked water swishing smoothly from side to side. He stared again down the light from the torch, marvelled that any surface could so quickly dissipate and engulf the brilliance of that beam. And beneath that surface. . . . He shivered. The water – even the water seemed to be dead, old and evil and infinitely horrible. In sudden anger, he shook his head to clear it of these stupid, primitive fears: his imagination – he'd have to watch it. He stepped back, straightened up. Gently, carefully, he closed the swinging hatch. The mess-deck echoed as his sledge swung down on the clips, again and again and again.

Engineer-Commander Dodson stirred and moaned. He struggled to open his eyes but his eyelids refused to function. At least, he thought that they did for the blackness around remained as it was, absolute, impenetrable, almost palpable.

He wondered dully what had happened, how long he had been there, what had happened. And the side of his head – just below the ear – that hurt abominably. Slowly, with clumsy deliberation, he peeled off his glove, reached up an exploratory hand. It came away wet and sticky: his hair, he realized with mild surprise, was thickly matted with blood. It must be blood – he could feel it trickling slowly, heavily down the side of his cheek.

And that deep, powerful vibration, a vibration overlain with an indefinable note of strain that set his engineer's teeth on edge – he could hear it, almost feel it, immediately in front of him. His bare hand reached out, recoiled in instant reflex as it touched something smooth and revolving – and burning hot.

The shaft tunnel! Of course. That's where he was – the shaft tunnel. They'd discovered fractured lubricating pipes on the port shafts too, and he'd decided to keep this engine turning. He knew they'd been attacked. Down here in the hidden bowels of the ship, sound did not penetrate: he had heard nothing of the aircraft engines: he hadn't even heard their own guns firing – but there had been no mistaking the jarring shock of the 5.25s surging back on their hydraulic recoils. And then – a torpedo perhaps, or a near miss by a bomb. Thank God he'd been sitting facing inboard when the *Ulysses* had lurched. The other way round and it would have been curtains for sure when he'd been flung across the shaft coupling and wrapped round . . .

The shaft! Dear God, the shaft! It was running almost red-hot on dry bearings! Frantically, he pawed around, picked up his emergency lamp and twisted its base. There was no light. He twisted it again with all his strength, reached up, felt the jagged edges of broken screen and bulb, and flung the useless lamp to the deck. He dragged out his pocket torch: that, too, was smashed. Desperate now, he searched blindly around for his oil can: it was lying on its side, the patent spring top beside it. The can was empty.

No oil, none. Heaven only knew how near that overstressed metal was to the critical limit. He didn't. He admitted that: even to the best engineers, metal fatigue was an incalculable unknown. But, like all men who had spent a lifetime with machines, he had developed a sixth sense for these things – and, right now, that sixth sense was jabbing at him, mercilessly, insistently. Oil – he would have to get oil. But he knew he was in bad shape, dizzy, weak from shock and loss of blood, and the tunnel was long and slippery and dangerous – and unlighted. One slip, one stumble against or over that merciless shaft. . . . Gingerly, the Engineer-Commander stretched out his hand again, rested his hand for an instant on the shaft, drew back sharply in sudden pain. He lifted his hand to his cheek, knew that it was not friction that had flayed and burnt the skin off the tips of his fingers. There was no choice. Resolutely, he gathered his legs under him, swayed dizzily to his feet, his back bent against the arching convexity of the tunnel.

It was then that he noticed it for the first time – a light, a swinging tiny pinpoint of light, imponderably distant in the converging sides of that dark tunnel, although he knew it could be only yards away. He blinked, closed his eyes and looked again. The light was still there, advancing steadily, and he could hear the shuffling of feet now. All at once he felt weak, light-headed: gratefully he sank down again, his feet safely braced once more against the bearing block.

The man with the light stopped a couple of feet away, hooked the lamp on to an inspection bracket, lowered himself carefully and sat beside Dodson. The rays of the lamp fell full on the dark heavy face, the jagged brows and prognathous jaw: Dodson stiffened in sudden surprise.

'Riley! Stoker Riley!' His eyes narrowed in suspicion and conjecture. 'What the devil are you doing here?'

'I've brought a two-gallon drum of lubricating oil,' Riley growled. He thrust a Thermos flask into the Engineer-Commander's hands. 'And here's some coffee. I'll 'tend to this – you

drink that. . . . Suffering Christ! This bloody bearing's red-hot!'
Dodson set down the Thermos with a thump.
'Are you deaf?' he asked harshly. 'Why are *you* here? Who
sent you? Your station's in "B" boiler-room!'
'Grierson sent me,' Riley said roughly. His dark face was impassive. 'Said he couldn't spare his engine-room men – too bloody
valuable. . . . Too much?' The oil, thick, viscous, was pouring
slowly on to the overheated bearing.
'*Lieutenant* Grierson!' Dodson was almost vicious, his voice a
whip-lash of icy correction. 'And that's a damned lie, Riley!
Lieutenant Grierson never sent you: I suppose you told *him*
that somebody else had sent you?'
'Drink your coffee,' Riley advised sourly. 'You're wanted in
the engine-room.'
The Engineer-Commander clenched his fist, restrained himself with difficulty.
'You damned insolent bastard!' he burst out. Abruptly, control came back and he said evenly: 'Commander's Defaulters in
the morning. You'll pay for this, Riley!'
'No, I won't.' Confound him, Dodson thought furiously, he's
actually grinning, the insolent . . .
He checked his thought.
'Why not?' he demanded dangerously.
'Because you won't report me.' Riley seemed to be enjoying
himself hugely.
'Oh so that's it!' Dodson glanced swiftly round the darkened
tunnel, and his lips tightened as he realized for the first time
how completely alone they were: in sudden certainty he looked
back at Riley, big and hunched and menacing. Smiling yet, but
no smile, Dodson thought, could ever transform that ugly brutal
face. The smile on the face of the tiger. . . . Fear, exhaustion,
never-ending strain – they did terrible things to a man and you
couldn't blame him for what he had become, or for what he was
born. . . . But his, Dodson's, first responsibility was to himself.
Grimly, he remembered how Turner had berated him, called
him all sorts of a fool for refusing to have Riley sent to prison.
'So that's it, eh?' he repeated softly. He turned himself, feet
thrusting solidly against the block. 'Don't be so sure, Riley. I
can give you twenty-five years, but—'
'Oh, for Christ's sake!' Riley burst out impatiently. 'What are
you talking about, sir? Drink your coffee – please. You're wanted
in the engine-room, I tell you!' he repeated impatiently.
Uncertainly, Dodson relaxed, unscrewed the cap of the Ther-

mos. He had a sudden, peculiar feeling of unreality, as if he were a spectator, some bystander in no way involved in this scene, this fantastic scene. His head, he realized, still hurt like hell.

'Tell me, Riley,' he asked softly, 'what makes you so sure I won't report you?'

'Oh, you can report me all right.' Riley was suddenly cheerful again. 'But I won't be at the Commander's table tomorrow morning.'

'No?' It was half-challenge, half-question.

'No,' Riley grinned. ' 'Cos there'll *be* no Commander *and* no table tomorrow morning.' He clasped his hands luxuriously behind his head. 'In fact, there'll be no nothin'.'

Something in the voice, rather than in the words, caught and held Dodson's attention. He knew, with instant conviction, that though Riley might be smiling, he wasn't joking. Dodson looked at him curiously, but said nothing.

'Commander's just finished broadcastin',' Riley continued. 'The *Tirpitz* is out – we have four hours left.'

The bald, flat statement, the complete lack of histrionics, of playing for effect, left no possible room for doubt. The *Tirpitz* – out. The *Tirpitz* – out. Dodson repeated the phrase to himself, over and over again. Four hours, just four hours to go. . . . He was surprised at his own reaction, his apparent lack of concern.

'Well?' Riley was anxious now, restive. 'Are you goin' or aren't you? I'm not kiddin', sir – you're wanted – urgent!'

'You're a liar,' Dodson said pleasantly. 'Why did you bring the coffee?'

'For myself.' The smile was gone, the face set and sullen. 'But I thought you needed it – you don't look so good to me. . . . They'll fix you up back in the engine-room.'

'And that's just where you're going, right now!' Dodson said evenly.

Riley gave no sign that he had heard.

'On your way, Riley,' Dodson said curtly. 'That's an order!'

'— off!' Riley growled. 'I'm stayin'. You don't require to have three — great gold stripes on your sleeve to handle a bloody oil can,' he finished derisively.

'Possibly not.' Dodson braced against a sudden, violent pitch, but too late to prevent himself lurching into Riley. 'Sorry, Riley. Weather's worsening, I'm afraid. Well, we – ah – appear to have reached an impasse.'

'What's that?' Riley asked suspiciously.

'A dead-end. A no-decision fight. . . . Tell me, Riley,' he asked quietly. 'What brought you here?'

'I told you!' Riley was aggrieved. 'Grierson – *Lieutenant* Grierson sent me.'

'What brought you here?' Dodson persisted. It was as if Riley had not spoken.

'That's my — business!' Riley answered savagely.

'What brought you here?'

'Oh, for Christ's sake leave me alone!' Riley shouted. His voice echoed loudly along the dark tunnel. Suddenly he turned round full-face, his mouth twisted bitterly. 'You know bloody well why I came.'

'To do me in, perhaps?'

Riley looked at him a long second, then turned away. His shoulders were hunched, his head held low.

'You're the only bastard in this ship that ever gave me a break,' he muttered. 'The only bastard I've ever *known* who ever gave me a chance,' he amended slowly. 'Bastard,' Dodson supposed, was Riley's accolade of friendship, and he felt suddenly ashamed of his last remark. 'If it wasn't for you,' Riley went on softly, 'I'd 'a' been in cells the first time, in a civvy jail the second. Remember, sir?'

Dodson nodded. 'You were rather foolish, Riley,' he admitted.

'Why did you do it?' The big stoker was intense, worried. 'God, everyone knows what I'm like—'

'Do they? I wonder. . . . I thought you had the makings of a better man than you—'

'Don't give me that bull!' Riley scoffed. '*I* know what I'm like. I know what I am. I'm no — good! Everybody says I'm no — good! And they're right. . . .' He leaned forward. 'Do you know somethin'? I'm a Catholic. Four hours from now . . .' He broke off. 'I should be on my knees, shouldn't I?' he sneered. 'Repentance, lookin' for – what do they call it?'

'Absolution?'

'Aye. That's it. Absolution. And do you know what?' He spoke slowly, emphatically. 'I don't give a single, solitary damn!'

'Maybe you don't have to,' Dodson murmured. 'For the last time, get back to that engine-room!'

'No!'

The Engineer-Commander sighed, picked up the Thermos.

'In that case, perhaps you would care to join me in a cup of coffee?'

Riley looked up, grinned, and when he spoke it was in a very creditable imitation of Colonel Chinstrap of the famous ITMA radio programme.

'Ectually, I don't mind if I do!'

Vallery rolled over on his side, his legs doubled up, his hand automatically reaching for the towel. His emaciated body shook violently, and the sound of the harsh, retching cough beat back at him from the iron walls of his shelter. God, he thought, oh, God, it's never been as bad as this before. Funny, he thought, it doesn't hurt any more, not even a little bit. The attack eased. He looked at the crimson, sodden towel, flung it in sudden disgust and with what little feeble strength was left into the darkest corner of the shelter.

'You carry this damned ship on your back!' Unbidden, old Socrates's phrase came into his mind and he smiled faintly. Well, if ever they needed him, it was now. And if he waited any longer, he knew he could never be able to go.

He sat up, sweating with the effort, swung his legs carefully over the side. As his feet touched the deck, the *Ulysses* pitched suddenly, steeply, and he fell forward against a chair, sliding helplessly to the floor. It took an eternity of time, an infinite effort to drag himself to his feet again: another effort like that, he knew, would surely kill him.

And then there was the door – that heavy, steel door. Somehow he had to open it, and he knew he couldn't. But he laid hold of the handle and the door opened, and suddenly, miraculously, he was outside, gasping as the cruel, sub-zero wind seared down through his throat and wasted lungs.

He looked fore and aft. The fires were dying, he saw, the fires on the *Stirling* and on his own poop-deck. Thank God for that at least. Beside him, two men had just finished levering the door off the Asdic cabinet, were flashing a torch inside. But he couldn't bear to look: he averted his head, staggered with outstretched hands for the gate of the compass platform.

Turner saw him coming, hurried to meet him, helped him slowly to his chair.

'You've no right to be here,' he said quietly. He looked at Vallery for a long moment. 'How are you feeling, sir?'

'I'm a good deal better, now, thanks,' Vallery replied. He smiled and went on: 'We Rear-Admirals have our responsibilities, you know, Commander: it's time I began to earn my princely salary.'

'Stand back, there!' Carrington ordered curtly. 'Into the wheel-house or up on the ladder – all of you. Let's have a look at this.'

He looked down at the great, steel hatch-cover. Looking at it, he realized he'd never before appreciated just how solid, how massive that cover was. The hatch-cover, open no more than an inch, was resting on a tommy-bar. He noticed the broken, stranded pulley, the heavy counterweight lying against the sill of the wheelhouse. So that's off, he thought: thank the Lord for that, anyway.

'Have you tried a block and tackle?' he asked abruptly.

'Yes, sir,' the man nearest him replied. He pointed to a tangled heap in a corner. 'No use, sir. The ladder takes the strain all right, but we can't get the hook under the hatch, except side-ways – and then it slips off all the time.' He gestured to the hatch. 'And every clip's either bent – they were opened by sledges – or at the wrong angle. . . . I think I know how to use a block and tackle, sir.'

'I'm sure you do,' Carrington said absently. 'Here, give me a hand, will you?'

He hooked his fingers under the hatch, took a deep breath. The seaman at one side of the cover – the other side was hard against the after bulkhead – did the same. Together they strained, thighs and backs quivering under the strain. Carring-ton felt his face turning crimson with effort, heard the blood pounding in his ears, and relaxed. They were only killing them-selves and that damned cover hadn't shifted a fraction – someone had done remarkably well to open it even that far. But even though they were tired and anything but fit, Carrington thought, two men should have been able to raise an edge of that hatch. He suspected that the hinges were jammed – or the deck buckled. If that were so, he mused, even if they could hook on a tackle, it would be of little help. A tackle was of no use when a sudden, immediate application of force was required; it always yielded that fraction before tightening up.

He sank to his knees, put his mouth to the edge of the hatch.

'Below there!' he called. 'Can you hear me?'

'We can hear you.' The voice was weak, muffled. 'For God's sake get us out of here. We're trapped like rats!'

'Is that you, Brierley? Don't worry – we'll get you out. How's the water down there?'

'Water? More bloody oil than water! There must be a fracture right through the port oil tank. I think the ring main passage must be flooded, too.'

'How deep is it?'

'Three-quarters way up already! We're standing on generators, hanging on to switchboards. One of our boys is gone already – we couldn't hold him.' Even muffled by the hatch, the strain, the near-desperation in the voice was all too obvious. 'For pity's sake, hurry up!'

'I said we'd get you out!' Carrington's voice was sharp, authoritative. The confidence was in his voice only, but he knew how quickly panic could spread down there. 'Can you push from below at all?'

'There's room for only one on the ladder,' Brierley shouted. 'It's impossible to get any pressure, any leverage upwards.' There was a sudden silence, then a series of muffled oaths.

'What's up?' Carrington called sharply.

'It's difficult to hang on,' Brierley shouted. 'There are waves two feet high down there. One of the men was washed off there. ... I think he's back again. It's pitch dark down here.'

Carrington heard the clatter of heavy footsteps above him, and straightened up. It was Petersen. In that narrow space, the blond Norwegian stoker looked gigantic. Carrington looked at him, looked at the immense span of shoulder, the great depth of chest, one enormous hand hanging loosely by his side, the other negligently holding three heavy crowbars and a sledge as if they were so many lengths of cane. Carrington looked at him, looked at the still, grave eyes so startlingly blue under the flaxen hair, and all at once he felt oddly confident, reassured.

'We can't open this, Petersen,' Carrington said baldly. 'Can you?'

'I will try, sir.' He laid down his tools, stooped, caught the end of the tommy-bar projecting beneath the corner of the cover. He straightened quickly, easily: the hatch lifted a fraction, then the bar, putty-like in its apparent malleability, bent over almost to a right angle.

'I think the hatch is jammed.' Petersen wasn't even breathing heavily. 'It will be the hinges, sir.'

He walked round the hatch, peered closely at the hinges, then grunted in satisfaction. Three times the heavy sledge, swung with accuracy and all the power of these great shoulders behind them, smashed squarely into the face of the outer hinge. On the third stroke the sledge snapped. Petersen threw away the broken shaft in disgust, picked up another, much heavier crowbar.

Again the bar bent, but again the hatch-cover lifted – an inch this time. Petersen picked up the two smaller sledges that had been used to open clips, hammered at the hinges till these sledges, too, were broken and useless.

This time he used the last two crowbars together, thrust under the same corner of the hatch. For five, ten seconds he remained bent over them, motionless. He was breathing deeply, quickly, now, then suddenly the breathing stopped. The sweat began to pour off his face, his whole body to quiver under that titanic strain: then slowly, incredibly, both crowbars began to bend.

Carrington watched, fascinated. He had never seen anything remotely like this before: he was sure no one else had either. Neither of these bars, he would have sworn, would have bent under less than half a ton of pressure. It was fantastic, but it was happening: and as the giant straightened, they were bending more and more. Then suddenly, so unexpectedly that everyone jumped, the hatch sprang open five or six inches and Petersen crashed backwards against the bulkhead, the bars falling from his hand and splashing into the water below.

Petersen flung himself back at the hatch, tigerish in his ferocity. His fingers hooked under the edge, the great muscles of his arms and shoulders lifted and locked as he tugged and pulled at that massive hatch-cover. Three times he heaved, four times, then on the fifth the hatch almost literally leapt up with a screech of tortured metal and smashed shudderingly home into the retaining latch of the vertical stand behind. The hatch was open. Petersen just stood there smiling – no one had seen Petersen smile for a long time – his face bathed in sweat, his great chest rising and falling rapidly as his starved lungs sucked in great draughts of air.

The water level in the Low Power Room was within two feet of the hatch: sometimes, when the *Ulysses* plunged into a heavy sea, the dark, oily liquid splashed over the hatch coaming into the flat above. Quickly, the trapped men were hauled to safety. Soaked in oil from head to foot, their eyes gummed and blinded, they were men overcome by reaction, utterly spent and on the verge of collapse, so far gone that even their fear could do no more than cling helplessly to the ladder, would almost certainly have slipped back into the surging blackness below; but Petersen bent over and plucked them clean out of the Low Power Room as if they had been little children.

'Take these men to the Sick Bay at once!' Carrington ordered. He watched the dripping, shivering men being helped up the ladder, then turned to the giant stoker with a smile. 'We'll all thank you later, Petersen. We're not finished yet. This hatch must be closed and battened down.'

'It will be difficult, sir,' Petersen said gravely.

'Difficult or not, it *must* be done.' Carrington was emphatic. Regularly, now, the water was spilling over the coaming, was lapping the sill of the wheelhouse. 'The emergency steering position is gone: if the wheelhouse is flooded, we're finished.'

Petersen said nothing. He lifted the retaining latch, pulled the protesting hatch-cover down a foot. Then he braced his shoulder against the latter, planted his feet on the cover and straightened his back convulsively: the cover screeched down to $45°$. He paused, bent his back like a bow, his hands taking his weight on the ladder, then pounded his feet again and again on the edge of the cover. Fifteen inches to go.

'We need heavy hammers, sir,' Petersen said urgently.

'No time!' Carrington shook his head quickly. 'Two more minutes and it'll be impossible to shut the hatch-cover against the water pressure. Hell!' he said bitterly. 'If it were only the other way round – closing from below. Even I could lever it shut!'

Again Petersen said nothing. He squatted down by the side of the hatch, gazed into the darkness beneath his feet.

'I have an idea, sir,' he said quickly. 'If two of you would stand on the hatch, push against the ladder. Yes, sir, that way – but you could push harder if you turned your back to me.'

Carrington laid the heels of his hands against the iron steps of the ladder, heaved with all his strength. Suddenly he heard a splash, then a metallic clatter, whirled round just in time to see a crowbar clutched in an enormous hand disappear below the edge of the hatch. There was no sign of Petersen. Like many big, powerful men, he was lithe and cat-like in his movements: he'd gone down over the edge of that hatch without a sound.

'Petersen!' Carrington was on his knees by the hatch. 'What the devil do you think you're doing? Come out of there, you bloody fool! Do you want to drown?'

There was no reply. Complete silence below, a silence deepened by the gentle sussuration of the water. Suddenly the quiet was broken by the sound of metal striking against metal, then by a jarring screech as the hatch dropped six inches. Before Carrington had time to think, the hatch-cover dropped farther still. Desperately, the First Lieutenant seized a crowbar, thrust it under the hatch-cover: a split second later the great steel cover thudded down on top of it. Carrington had his mouth to the gap now.

'In the name of God, Petersen,' he shouted, 'Are you sane? Open up, open up at once, do you hear?'

'I can't.' The voice came and went as the water surged over the stoker's head. 'I won't. You said yourself . . . there is no time . . . this was the only way.'

'But I never meant—'

'I know. It does not matter . . . it is better this way.' It was almost impossible to make out what he was saying. 'Tell Captain Vallery that Petersen says he is very sorry. . . . I tried to tell the Captain yesterday.'

'Sorry! Sorry for what?' Madly Carrington flung all his strength against the iron bar: the hatch-cover did not even quiver.

'The dead marine in Scapa Flow. . . . I did not mean to kill him, I could never kill any man. . . . But he angered me,' the big Norwegian said simply. 'He killed my friend.'

For a second, Carrington stopped straining at the bar. Petersen! Of course – who but Petersen could have snapped a man's neck like that. Petersen, the big, laughing Scandinavian, who had so suddenly changed overnight into a grave unsmiling giant, who stalked the deck, the mess-decks and alleyways by day and by night, who was never seen to smile or sleep. With a sudden flash of insight, Carrington saw clear through the tortured mind of that kind and simple man.

'Listen, Petersen,' he begged. 'I don't give a damn about that. Nobody shall ever know, I promise you. Please, Petersen, just—'

'It is better this way.' The muffled voice was strangely content. 'It is not good to kill a man . . . it is not good to go on living.... I know. . . . Please, it is important – you will tell my Captain – Petersen is sorry and filled with shame. . . . I do this for my Captain.' Without warning, the crowbar was plucked from Carrington's hand. The cover clanged down in position. For a minute the wheelhouse flat rang to a succession of muffled, metallic blows. Suddenly the clamour ceased and there was only the rippling surge of the water outside the wheelhouse and the creak of the wheel inside as the *Ulysses* steadied on course.

The clear sweet voice soared high and true above the subdued roar of the engine-room fans, above the whine of a hundred electric motors and the sound of the rushing of the waters. Not even the metallic impersonality of the loudspeakers could detract from the beauty of that singing voice. . . . It was a favourite device of Vallery's when the need for silence was not paramount, to pass the long, dark hours by coupling up the record-player to the broadcast system.

Almost invariably, the musical repertoire was strictly classical – or what is more often referred to, foolishly and disparagingly, as the popular classics. Bach, Beethoven, Tchaikovski, Lehar, Verdi, Delius – these were the favourites. 'No. I in B flat minor,' 'Air on a G string,' 'Moonlight on the Alster,' 'Claire de Lune,' 'The Skater's Waltz' – the crew of the *Ulysses* could never have enough of these. 'Ridiculous,' 'impossible' – it is all too easy to imagine the comments of those who equate the matelot's taste in music with the popular conception of his ethics and morals; but those same people have never heard the hushed, cathedral silence in the crowded hangar of a great aircraft carrier in Scapa Flow as Yehudi Menuhin's magic bow sang across the strings of the violin, swept a thousand men away from the harsh urgencies of reality, from the bitter memories of the last patrol or convoy, into the golden land of music.

But now a girl was singing. It was Deanna Durbin, and she was singing 'Beneath the Lights of Home,' that most heart-breakingly nostalgic of all songs. Below decks and above, bent over the great engines or huddled by their guns, men listened to the lovely voice as it drifted through the darkened ship and the falling snow, and turned their minds inwards and thought of home, thought of the bitter contrast and the morning that would not come. Suddenly, half-way through, the song stopped.

'Do you hear there?' the 'speakers boomed. 'Do you hear there? This – this is the Commander speaking.' The voice was deep and grave and hesitant: it caught and held the attention of every man in the ship.

'I have bad news for you.' Turner spoke slowly, quietly. 'I am sorry – I . . .' He broke off, then went on more slowly still. 'Captain Vallery died five minutes ago.' For a moment the 'speaker was silent, then crackled again. 'He died on the bridge, in his chair. He knew he was dying and I don't think he suffered at all. . . . He insisted – he insisted that I thank you for the way you all stood by him. "Tell them" – these were his words, as I remember – "tell them," he said, "that I couldn't have carried on without them, that they are the best crew that God ever gave a Captain.' Then he said – it was the last thing he said: "Give them my apologies. After all they've done for me – well, well, tell them I'm terribly sorry to let them down like this." That was all he said – just "Tell them I'm sorry." And then he died.'

—— 16 ——

SATURDAY NIGHT

Richard Vallery was dead. He died grieving, stricken at the thought that he was abandoning the crew of the *Ulysses*, leaving them behind, leaderless. But it was only for a short time, and he did not have to wait long. Before the dawn, hundreds more, men in the cruisers, the destroyers and the merchantmen, had died also. And they did not die as he had feared under the guns of the *Tirpitz* – another grim parallel with PQ17, for the *Tirpitz* had not left Alta Fjord. They died, primarily, because the weather had changed.

Richard Vallery was dead, and with his death a great change had come over the men of the *Ulysses*. When Vallery died, other things died also, for he took these things with him. He took with him the courage, the kindliness, the gentleness, the unshakable faith, the infinitely patient and understanding endurance, all these things which had been so peculiarly his own. And now these things were gone and the *Ulysses* was left without them and it did not matter. The men of the *Ulysses* no longer needed courage and all the adjuncts of courage, for they were no longer afraid. Vallery was dead and they did not know how much they respected and loved that gentle man until he was gone. But then they knew. They knew that something wonderful, something that had become an enduring part of their minds and memories, something infinitely fine and good, was gone and they would never know it again, and they were mad with grief. And, in war, a grief-stricken man is the most terrible enemy there is. Prudence, caution, fear, pain – for the grief-stricken man these no longer exist. He lives only to lash out blindly at the enemy, to destroy, if he can, the author of his grief. Rightly or wrongly, the *Ulysses* never thought to blame the Captain's death on any but the enemy. There was only, for them, the sorrow and the blind hate. Zombies, Nicholls had called them once, and the *Ulysses* was more than ever a ship manned by living zombies, zombies who prowled restlessly, incessantly, across the snow and ice of the heaving decks, automatons living only for revenge.

The weather changed just before the end of the middle watch, The seas did not change – FR77 was still butting into the heavy, rolling swell from the north, still piling up fresh sheets of glistening ice on their labouring fo'c'sles. But the wind dropped, and almost at once the snowstorm blew itself out, the last banks of dark, heavy cloud drifting away to the south. By four o'clock the sky was completely clear.

There was no moon that night, but the stars were out, keen and sharp and frosty as the icy breeze that blew steadily out of the north.

Then, gradually, the sky began to change. At first there was only a barely perceptible lightening on the northern rim then, slowly, a pulsating flickering band of light began to broaden and deepen and climb steadily above the horizon, climbing higher to the south with the passing of every minute. Soon that pulsating ribbon of light was paralleled by others, streamers in the most delicate pastel shades of blue and green and violet, but always and predominantly white. And always, too, these lanes of multi-coloured light grew higher and stronger and brighter: at the climax, a great band of white stretched high above the convoy, extending from horizon to horizon. . . . These were the Northern Lights, at any time a spectacle of beauty and wonder, and this night surpassing lovely: down below, in ships clearly illumined against the dark and rolling seas, the men of FR77 looked up and hated them.

On the bridge of the *Ulysses*, Chrysler of the uncanny eyesight and super-sensitive hearing, was the first to hear it. Soon everyone else heard it too, the distant roar, throbbing and intermittent, of a Condor approaching from the south. After a time they became aware that the Condor was no longer approaching, but sudden hope died almost as it was born. There was no mistaking it now – the deeper, heavier note of a Focke-Wulf in maximum climb. The Commander turned wearily to Carrington.

'It's Charlie, all right,' he said grimly. 'The bastard's spotted us. He'll already have radioed Alta Fjord and a hundred to one in anything you like that he's going to drop a marker flare at 10,000 feet or so. It'll be seen fifty miles away.'

'Your money's sake.' The First Lieutenant was withering. 'I

never bet against dead certs. . . . And then, by and by, maybe a few flares at a couple of thousand?'

'Exactly!' Turner nodded. 'Pilot, how far do you reckon we're from Alta Fjord – in flying time, I mean?'

'For a 200-knot plane, just over an hour,' the Kapok Kid said quietly. His ebullience was gone: he had been silent and dejected since Vallery had died two hours previously.

'An hour!' Carrington exclaimed. 'And they'll be here. My God, sir,' he went on wonderingly, 'they're really out to get us. We've never been bombed nor torpedoed at night before. We've never had the *Tirpitz* after us before. We never—'

'The *Tirpitz*,' Turner interrupted. 'Just where the hell *is* that ship? She's had time to come up with us. Oh, I know it's dark and we've changed course,' he added, as Carrington made to object, 'but a fast destroyer screen would have picked us – Preston!' He broke off, spoke sharply to the Signal Petty Officer. 'Look alive, man! That ship's flashing us.'

'Sorry, sir.' The signalman, swaying on his feet with exhaustion, raised his Aldis, clacked out an acknowledgment. Again the light on the merchantman began to wink furiously.

' "Transverse fracture engine bedplate," ' Preston read out. ' "Damage serious: shall have to moderate speed." '

'Acknowledge,' said Turner curtly. 'What ship is that, Preston?'

'The *Ohio Freighter*, sir.'

'The one that stopped a tin fish a couple of days back?'

'That's her, sir.'

'Make a signal. "Eessential maintain speed and position." ' Turner swore. 'What a time to choose for an engine breakdown. . . . Pilot, when do we rendezvous with the Fleet?'

'Six hours' time, sir: exactly.'

'Six hours.' Turner compressed his lips. 'Just six hours – perhaps!' he added bitterly.

'Perhaps?' Carrington murmured.

'Perhaps,' Turner affirmed. 'Depends entirely on the weather. C-in-C won't risk capital ships so near the coast unless he can fly off fighter cover against air attack. And, if you ask me, that's why the *Tirpitz* hasn't turned up yet – some wandering U-boat's tipped him off that our Fleet Carriers are steaming south. He'll be waiting on the weather. . . . What's he saying now, Preston?' The *Ohio*'s signal lamp had flashed briefly, then died.

' "Imperative slow down," ' Preston repeated. ' "Damage severe. Am slowing down." '

'He is, too,' Carrington said quietly. He looked up at Turner, at the set face and dark eyes, and knew the same thought was in the Commander's mind as was in his own. 'He's a goner, sir, a dead duck. He hasn't a chance. Not unless—'

'Unless what?' Turner asked harshly. 'Unless we leave him an escort? Leave what escort, Number One? The *Viking* – the only effective unit we've left?' He shook his head in slow decision. 'The greatest good of the greatest number: that's how it has to be. They'll know that. Preston, send "Regret cannot leave you standby. How long to effect repairs?" '

The flare burst even before Preston's hand could close on the trigger. It burst directly over FR77. It was difficult to estimate the height – probably six to eight thousand feet – but at that altitude it was no more than an incandescent pin-point against the great band of the Northern Lights arching majestically above. But it was falling quickly, glowing more brightly by the sound: the parachute, if any, could have been only a steadying drogue.

The cracking of the WT 'speaker broke through the stuttering chatter of the Aldis.

'WT – bridge. WT – bridge. Message from *Sirrus*: "Three survivors dead. Many dying or seriously wounded. Medical assistance urgent, repeat urgent." ' The 'speaker died, just as the *Ohio* started flickering her reply.

'Send for Lieutenant Nicholls,' Turner ordered briefly. 'Ask him to come up to the bridge at once.'

Carrington stared down at the dark broad seas, seas flecked with milky foam: the bows of the *Ulysses* were crashing down heavily, continuously.

'You're going to risk it, sir?'

'I must. You'd do the same, Number One. . . . What does the *Ohio* say, Preston?'

' "I understand. Too busy to look after the Royal Navy anyway. We will make up on you. Au revoir!" '

'We will make up on you. Au revoir.' Turner repeated softly. 'He lies in his teeth, and he knows it. By God!' he burst out. 'If anyone ever tells me the Yankee sailors have no guts – I'll push his perishing face in. Preston, send: "Au revoir. Good luck." . . . Number One, I feel like a murderer.' He rubbed his hand across his forehead, nodded towards the shelter where Vallery lay stretched out, and strapped to his settee. 'Month in, month out, he's been taking these decisions. It's no wonder . . .' He broke off as the gate creaked open.

'Is that you, Nicholls? There is work for you, my boy. Can't have you medical types idling around uselessly all day long.' He raised his hand. 'All right, all right,' he chuckled. 'I know. . . . How are things on the surgical front?' he went on seriously.

'We've done all we can, sir. There was very little left for us to do,' Nicholls said quietly. His face was deeply lined, haggard to the point of emaciation. 'But we're in a bad way for supplies. Hardly a single dressing left. And no anæsthetics at all – except what's left in the emergency kit. The Surgeon-Commander refuses to touch those.'

'Good, good,' Turner murmured. 'How do you feel, laddie?'

'Awful.'

'You look it,' Turner said candidly. 'Nicholls – I'm terribly sorry, boy – I want you to go over to the *Sirrus*.'

'Yes, sir.' There was no surprise in the voice: it hadn't been difficult to guess why the Commander had sent for him. 'Now?'

Turner nodded without speaking. His face, the lean strong features, the heavy brows and sunken eyes were quite visible now in the strengthening light of the plunging flare. A face to remember, Nicholls thought.

'How much kit can I take with me, sir?'

'Just your medical gear. No more. You're not travelling by Pullman, laddie!'

'Can I take my camera, my films?'

'All right.' Turner smiled briefly. 'Looking forward keenly to photographing the last seconds of the *Ulysses*, I suppose. . . . Don't forget that the *Sirrus* is leaking like a sieve. Pilot – get through to the WT. Tell the *Sirrus* to come alongside, prepare to receive medical officer by breeches buoy.'

The gate creaked again. Turner looked at the bulky figure stumbling wearily on to the compass platform. Brooks, like every man in the crew was dead on his feet; but the blue eyes burned as brightly as ever.

'My spies are everywhere,' he announced. 'What's this about the *Sirrus* shanghaiing young Johnny here?'

'Sorry, old man,' Turner apologised. 'It seems things are pretty bad on the *Sirrus*.'

'I see.' Brooks shivered. It might have been the thin threnody of the wind in the shattered rigging, or just the iceladen wind itself. He shivered again, looked upwards at the sinking flare. 'Pretty, very pretty,' he murmured. 'What are the illuminations in aid of?'

'We are expecting company,' Turner smiled crookedly. 'An

old world custom, O Socrates – the light in the window and what have you.' He stiffened abruptly, then relaxed, his face graven in granitic immobility. 'My mistake,' he murmured. 'The company has already·arrived.'

The last words were caught up and drowned in the rumbling of a heavy explosion. Turner had known it was coming – he'd · seen the thin stiletto of flame stabbing skywards just for'ard of the *Ohio Freighter*'s bridge. The sound had taken five or six seconds to reach them – the *Ohio* was already a mile distant on the starboard quarter, but clearly visible still under the luminance of the Northern Lights – the Northern Lights that had betrayed her, almost stopped in the water, to a wandering U-boat.

The *Ohio Freighter* did not remain visible for long. Except for the moment of impact, there was neither smoke, nor flame, nor sound. But her back must have been broken, her bottom torn out – and she was carrying a full cargo of nothing but tanks and ammunition. There was a curious dignity about her end – she sank quickly, quietly, without any fuss. She was gone in three minutes.

It was Turner who finally broke the heavy silence on the bridge. He turned away and in the light of the flare his face was not pleasant to see.

'Au revoir,' he muttered to no one in particular. 'Au revoir. That's what he said, the lying . . .' He shook his head angrily, touched the Kapok Kid on the arm. 'Get through to WT,' he said sharply. 'Tell the *Viking* to sit over the top of that sub till we get clear.'

'Where's it all going to end?' Brooks's face was still and heavy in the twilight.

'God knows! How I hate those murdering bastards!' Turner ground out. 'Oh, I know, I know, we do the same – but give me something I can see, something I can fight, something—'

'You'll be able to see the *Tirpitz* all right,' Carrington interrupted dryly. 'By all accounts, she's big enough.'

Turner looked at him, suddenly smiled. He clapped his arm, then craned his head back, staring up at the shimmering loveliness of the sky. He wondered when the next flare would drop.

'Have you a minute to spare, Johnny?' The Kapok Kid's voice was low. 'I'd like to speak to you.'

'Sure.' Nicholls looked at him in surprise. 'Sure, I've a minute, ten minutes – until the *Sirrus* comes up. What's wrong, Andy?'

'Just a second.' The Kapok Kid crossed to the Commander. 'Permission to go to the charthouse, sir?'

'Sure you've got your matches?' Turner smiled. 'OK. Off you go.'

The Kapok Kid smiled faintly, said nothing. He took Nicholls by the arm, led him into the charthouse, flicked on the lights and produced his cigarettes. He looked steadily at Nicholls as he dipped his cigarette into the flickering pool of flame.

'Know something, Johnny?' he said abruptly. 'I reckon I must have Scotch blood in me.'

'Scots,' Nicholls corrected. 'And perish the very thought.'

'I'm feeling – what's the word? – fey, isn't it? I'm feeling fey tonight, Johnny.' The Kapok Kid hadn't even heard the interruption. He shivered. 'I don't know why – I've never felt this way before.'

'Ah, nonsense! Indigestion, my boy,' Nicholls said briskly. But he felt strangely uncomfortable.

'Won't wash this time,' Carpenter shook his head, half-smiling. 'Besides, I haven't eaten a thing for two days. I'm on the level, Johnny.' In spite of himself, Nicholls was impressed. Emotion, gravity, earnestness – these were utterly alien to the Kapok Kid.

'I won't be seeing you again,' the Kapok Kid continued softly. 'Will you do me a favour, Johnny?'

'Don't be so bloody silly,' Nicholls said angrily. 'How the hell do you—?'

'Take this with you.' The Kapok Kid pulled out a slip of paper, thrust it into Nicholl's hands. 'Can you read it?'

'I can read it.' Nicholls had stilled his anger. 'Yes, I can read it.' There was a name and address on the sheet of paper, a girl's name and a Surrey address. 'So that's her name,' he said softly. 'Juanita . . . Juanita.' He pronounced it carefully, accurately, in the Spanish fashion. 'My favourite song and my favourite name,' he murmured.

'Is it?' the Kapok Kid asked eagerly. 'Is it indeed? And mine, Johnny.' He paused. 'If, perhaps – well, if I don't – well, you'll go to see her, Johnny?'

'What are you talking about, man?' Nicholls felt embarrassed. Half-impatiently, half-playfully, he tapped him on the chest. 'Why, with that suit on, you could *swim* from here to Murmansk. You've said so yourself, a hundred times.'

The Kapok Kid grinned up at him. The grin was a little crooked.

'Sure, sure, I know, I know – will you go, Johnny?'

'Dammit to hell, yes!' Nicholls snapped. 'I'll go – and it's high time I was going somewhere else. Come on!' He snapped off the lights, pulled back the door, stopped with his foot half-way over the sill. Slowly, he stepped back inside the charthouse, closed the door and flicked on the light. The Kapok Kid hadn't moved, was gazing quietly at him.

'I'm sorry, Andy,' Nicholls said sincerely. 'I don't know what made me—'

'Bad temper,' said the Kapok Kid cheerfully. 'You always did hate to think that I was right and you were wrong!'

Nicholls caught his breath, closed his eyes for a second. Then he stretched out his hand.

'All the best, Vasco.' It was an effort to smile. 'And don't worry. I'll see her if – well, I'll see her, I promise you. Juanita. . . . But if I find *you* there,' he went on threateningly, 'I'll—'

'Thanks, Johnny. Thanks a lot.' The Kapok Kid was almost happy. 'Good luck, boy. . . . Vaya con Dios. That's what she always said to me, what she said before I came away. "Vaya con Dios."'

Thirty minutes later, Nicholls was operating aboard the *Sirrus*.

The time was 0445. It was bitterly cold, with a light wind blowing steadily from the north. The seas were heavier than ever, longer between the crests, deeper in their gloomy troughs, and the damaged *Sirrus,* labouring under a mountain of ice, was making heavy weather of it. The sky was still clear, a sky of breath-taking purity, and the stars were out again, for the Northern Lights were fading. The fifth successive flare was drifting steadily seawards.

It was at 0445 that they heard it – the distant rumble of gun-fire far to the south – perhaps a minute after they had seen the incandescent brilliance of a burning flare on the rim of the far horizon. There could be no doubt as to what was happening. The *Viking,* still in contact with the U-boat, although power-less to do anything about it, was being heavily attacked. And the attack must have been short, sharp and deadly, for the firing ceased soon after it had begun. Ominously, nothing came through on the WT. No one ever knew what had happened to the *Viking,* for there were no survivors.

The last echo of the *Viking*'s guns had barely died away be-fore they heard the roar of the engines of the Condor, at maxi-

mum throttle in a shallow dive. For five, perhaps ten seconds
– it seemed longer than that, but not long enough for any gun
in the convoy to begin tracking him accurately – the great
Focke-Wulf actually flew beneath his own flare, and then was
gone. Behind him, the sky opened up in a blinding coruscation
of flame, more dazzling, more hurtful, than the light of the
noonday sun. So intense, so extraordinary the power of those
flares, so much did pupils contract and eyelids narrow in instinctive self-protection, that the enemy bombers were through
the circle of light and upon them before anyone fully realized
what was happening. The timing, the split-second co-operation
between marker planes and bombers were magnificent.

There were twelve planes in the first wave. There was no
concentration on one target, as before: not more than two
attacked any ship. Turner, watching from the bridge, watching
them swoop down steeply and level out before even the first
gun in the *Ulysses* had opened up, caught his breath in sudden
dismay. There was something terribly familiar about the speed,
the approach, the silhouette of these planes. Suddenly he had
it – Heinkels, by God! Heinkel 111s. And the Heinkel 111,
Turner knew, carried that weapon he dreaded above all others
– the glider bomb.

And then, as if he had touched a master switch, every gun on
the *Ulysses* opened up. The air filled with smoke, the pungent
smell of burning cordite: the din was indescribable. And all
at once, Turner felt fiercely, strangely happy. . . . To hell with
them and their glider bombs, he thought. This was war as he
liked to fight it: not the cat-and-mouse, hide-and-seek frustration of trying to outguess the hidden wolf-packs, but war out
in the open, where he could see the enemy and hate him and
love him for fighting as honest men should and do his
damnedest to destroy him. And, Turner knew, if they could
at all, the crew of the *Ulysses* would destroy him. It needed no
great sensitivity to direct the sea-change that had overtaken his
men – yes, *his* men now: they no longer cared for themselves:
they had crossed the frontier of fear and found that nothing lay
beyond it and they would keep on feeding their guts and squeezing their triggers until the enemy overwhelmed them.

The leading Heinkel was blown out of the sky, and fitting
enough it was 'X' turret that destroyed it – 'X' turret, the turret
of dead marines, the turret that had destroyed the Condor, and
was now manned by a scratch marine crew. The Heinkel behind lifted sharply to avoid the hurtling fragments of fuselage

and engines, dipped, flashed past the cruiser's bows less than a boat-length away, banked steeply to port under maximum power, and swung back in on the *Ulysses*. Every gun on the ship was caught on the wrong foot, and seconds passed before the first one was brought to bear – time and to spare for the Heinkel to angle in at 60°, drop his bomb and slew frantically away as the concentrated fire of the Oerlikons and pom-poms closed in on him. Miraculously, he escaped.

The winged bomb was high, but not high enough. It wavered, steadied, dipped, then glided forwards and downwards through the drifting smoke of the guns to strike home with a tremendous, deafening explosion that shook the *Ulysses* to her keel and almost shattered the eardrums of those on deck.

To Turner, looking aft from the bridge, it seemed that the *Ulysses* could never survive this last assault. An ex-torpedo officer and explosives expert himself, he was skilled in assessing the disruptive power of high explosive: never before had he been so close to so powerful, so devastating an explosion. He had dreaded these glider bombs, but even so he had underestimated their power: the concussion had been double, treble what he had been expecting.

What Turner did not know was that what he had heard had been not one explosion but two, but so nearly simultaneous as to be indistinguishable. The glider bomb, by a freakish chance had crashed directly into the port torpedo tubes. There had been only one torpedo left there – the other two had sent the *Vytura* to the bottom – and normally Amatol, the warhead explosive, is extremely stable and inert, even when subjected to violent shock: but the bursting bomb had been too close too powerful: sympathetic detonation had been inevitable.

Damage was extensive and spectacular: it was severe, but not fatal. The side of the *Ulysses* had been ripped open, as by a giant can-opener, almost to the water's edge: the tubes had vanished: the decks were holed and splintered: the funnel casing was a shambles, the funnel itself tilting over to port almost to fifteen degrees; but the greatest energy of the explosion had been directed aft, most of the blast expending itself over the open sea, while the galley and canteen, severely damaged already, were no more than a devil's scrapyard.

Almost before the dust and debris of the explosion had settled, the last of the Heinkels was disappearing, skimming the waves, weaving and twisting madly in evasive action, pursued and harried by a hundred glowing streams of tracer. Then, magically, they were gone, and there was only the sudden deafening silence and the flares, drooping slowly to extinction, lighting up the pall above the *Ulysses,* the dark clouds of smoke rolling up from the shattered *Stirling* and a tanker with its after superstructure almost gone. But not one of the ships in FR77 had faltered or stopped; and they had destroyed five Heinkels. A costly victory, Turner mused, if it could be called a victory; but he knew the Heinkels would be back. It was not difficult to imagine the fury, the hurt pride of the High Command in Norway: as far as Turner knew, no Russian Convoy had ever sailed so far south before.

Riley eased a cramped leg, stretched it gently so as to avoid the great spinning shaft. Carefully he poured some oil on to the bearing, carefully, so as not to disturb the Engineer Commander, propped in sleep between the tunnel wall and Riley's shoulder. Even as Riley drew back, Dodson stirred, opened heavy, gummed lids.

'Good God above!' he said wearily. 'You still here, Riley?' It was the first time either of them had spoken for hours.

'It's a — good job I *am* here,' Riley growled. He nodded towards the bearing. 'Bloody difficult to get a fire-hose down to this place, I should think!' That was unfair Riley knew: he and Dodson had been taking it in half-hour turns to doze and feed the bearing. But he felt he had to say something: he was finding it increasingly difficult to keep on being truculent to the Engineer Commander.

Dodson grinned to himself, said nothing. Finally, he cleared his throat, murmured casually: 'The *Tirpitz* is taking its time about making its appearance, don't you think?'

'Yes, sir.' Riley was uncomfortable. 'Should 'a' been here long ago, damn her!'

'Him,' Dodson corrected absently. '*Admiral von Tirpitz,* you know. . . . Why don't you give up this foolishness, Riley?'

Riley grunted, said nothing. Dodson sighed, then brightened. 'Go and get some more coffee, Riley, I'm parched!'

'No.' Riley was blunt. '*You* get it.'

'As a favour, Riley.' Dodson was very gentle. 'I'm damned thirsty!'

'Oh, all right.' The big stoker swore, climbed painfully to his feet. 'Where'll I get it?'

'Plenty in the engine-room. If it's not iced water they're swigging, it's coffee. But no iced water for me.' Dodson shivered.

Riley gathered up the Thermos, stumbled along the passage. He had only gone a few feet when they felt the *Ulysses* shudder under the recoil of the heavy armament. Although they did not know it, it was the beginning of the air attack.

Dodson braced himself against the wall, saw Riley do the same, paused a second then hurry away in an awkward, stumbling run. There was something grotesquely familiar in that awkward run, Dodson thought. The guns surged back again and the figure scuttled even faster, like a giant crab in a panic. . . . *Panic*, Dodson thought: that's it, panic-stricken. Don't blame the poor bastard – I'm beginning to imagine things myself down here. Again the whole tunnel vibrated, more heavily this time – that must be 'X' turret, almost directly above. No, I don't blame him. Thank God he's gone. He smiled quietly to himself. I won't be seeing friend Riley again – he isn't all that of a reformed character. Tiredly, Dodson settled back against the wall. On my own at last, he murmured to himself, and waited for the feeling of relief. But it never came. Instead, there was only a vexation and loneliness, a sense of desertion and a strangely empty disappointment.

Riley was back inside a minute. He came back with that same awkward crab-like run, carrying a three-pint Thermos jug and two cups, cursing fluently and often as he slipped against the wall. Panting, wordlessly, he sat down beside Dodson, poured out a cup of steaming coffee.

'Why the hell did you have to come back?' Dodson demanded harshly. 'I don't want you and—'

'You wanted coffee,' Riley interrupted rudely. 'You've got the bloody stuff. Drink it.'

At that instant the explosion and the vibration from the explosion in the port tubes echoed weirdly down the dark tunnel, the shock flinging the two men heavily against each other. His whole cup of coffee splashed over Dodson's leg: his mind was so tired, his reactions so slow, that his first realization was of how damnably cold he was, how chill that dripping tunnel. The scalding coffee had gone right through his clothes, but he could feel neither warmth nor wetness: his legs were numbed, dead below the knees. Then he shook his head, looked up at Riley.

'What in God's name was that? What's happening? Did you—?'

'Haven't a clue. Didn't stop to ask.' Riley stretched himself luxuriously, blew on his steaming coffee. Then a happy thought

struck him, and a broad cheerful grin came as near to trans-
forming that face as would ever be possible.

'It's probably the *Tirpitz*,' he said hopefully.

Three times more during that terrible night, the German
squadrons took off from the airfield at Alta Fjord, throbbed
their way nor'-nor'-west through the bitter Arctic night, over
the heaving Arctic sea, in search of the shattered remnants of
FR77. Not that the search was difficult – the Focke-Wulf Condor stayed with them all night, defied their best attempts to
shake him off. He seemed to have an endless supply of these
deadly flares, and might very well have been – in fact, almost
certainly was – carrying nothing else. And the bombers had
only to steer for the flares.

The first assault – about 0545 – was an orthodox bombing
attack, made from about 3000 feet. The planes seemed to be
Dorniers, but it was difficult to be sure, because they flew high
above a trio of flares sinking close to the water level. As an
attack, it was almost but not quite abortive, and was pressed
home with no great enthusiasm. This was understandable: the
barrage was intense. But there were two direct hits, one on a
merchantman, blowing away most of the fo'c'sle, the other on
the *Ulysses*. It sheered through the flag deck and the Admiral's
day cabin, and exploded in the heart of the Sick Bay. The Sick
Bay was crowded with the sick and dying, and, for many, that
bomb must have come as a God-sent release, for the *Ulysses* had
long since run out of anæsthetics. There were no survivors.
Among the dead was Marshall, the Torpedo Officer, Johnson,
the Leading SBA, the Master-At-Arms who had been lightly
wounded an hour before by a splinter from the torpedo tubes,
Burgess, strapped helplessly in a strait-jacket – he had suffered
concussion on the night of the great storm and gone insane.
Brown, whose hip had been smashed by the hatch-cover of 'Y'
magazine, and Brierley, who was dying anyway, his lungs saturated and rotted away with fuel oil. Brooks had not been there.

The same explosion had also shattered the telephone exchange: barring only the bridge-gun phones, and the bridge-
engine phones and speaking-tubes, all communication lines in
the *Ulysses* were gone.

The second attack at 7 a.m., was made by only six bombers
– Heinkels again, carrying glider-bombs. Obviously flying
strictly under orders, they ignored the merchantmen and concentrated their attack solely on the cruisers. It was an expensive

attack: the enemy lost all but two of their force in exchange for a single hit aft on the *Stirling*, a hit which, tragically, put both after guns out of action.

Turner, red-eyed and silent, bareheaded in that sub-zero wind, and pacing the shattered bridge of the *Ulysses*, marvelled that the *Stirling* still floated, still fought back with everything she had. And then he looked at his own ship, less a ship, he thought wearily, than a floating shambles of twisted steel still scything impossibly through those heavy seas, and marvelled all the more. Broken, burning cruisers, cruisers ravaged and devastated to the point of destruction, were nothing new for Turner: he had seen the *Trinidad* and the *Edinburgh* being literally battered to death on these same Russian convoys. But he had never seen any ship, at any time, take such inhuman, murderous punishment as the *Ulysses* and the obsolete *Stirling* and still live. He would not have believed it possible.

The third attack came just before dawn. It came with the grey half-light, an attack carried out with great courage and the utmost determination by fifteen Heinkel 111 glider-bombers. Again the cruisers were the sole targets, the heavier attack by far being directed against the *Ulysses*. Far from shirking the challenge and bemoaning their ill-luck the crew of the *Ulysses*, that strange and selfless crew of walking zombies whom Nicholls had left behind, welcomed the enemy gladly, even joyfully, for how can one kill an enemy if he does not come to you? Fear, anxiety, the near-certainty of death – these did not exist. Home and country, families, wives and sweethearts, were names, only names: they touched a man's mind, these thoughts, touched it and lifted and were gone as if they had never been. 'Tell them,' Vallery had said, 'tell them they are the best crew God ever gave a captain.' Vallery. *That* was what mattered, that and what Vallery stood for, that something that had been so inseparably a part of that good and kindly man that you never saw it because it *was* Vallery. And the crew hoisted the shells, slammed the breeches and squeezed their triggers, men uncaring, men oblivious of anything and everything, except the memory of the man who had died apologising because he had let them down, except the sure knowledge that they could not let Vallery down. Zombies, but inspired zombies, men above themselves, as men commonly are when they know the next step, the inevitable step has them clear to the top of the far side of the valley. . . .

The first part of the attack was launched against the *Stirling*.

Turner saw two Heinkels roaring in in a shallow dive, improbably surviving against heavy, concentrated fire at point-blank range. The bombs, delayed action and armour-piercing, struck the *Stirling* amidships, just below deck level, and exploded deep inside, in the boiler-room and engine-room. The next three bombers were met with only pom-pom and Lewis fire: the main armament for'ard had fallen silent. With sick apprehension. Turner realized what had happened: the explosion had cut the power to the turrets.[1] Ruthlessly, contemptuously almost, the bombers brushed aside the puny opposition: every bomb went home. The *Stirling,* Turner saw, was desperately wounded. She was on fire again, and listing heavily to starboard.

The suddenly lifting crescendo of aero engines spun Turner round to look to his own ship. There were five Heinkels in the first wave, at different heights and approach angles so as to break up the pattern of AA fire, but all converging on the after end of the *Ulysses*. There was so much smoke and noise that Turner could only gather confused, broken impressions. Suddenly, it seemed, the air was filled with glider-bombs and the tearing, staccato crash of the German cannon and guns. One bomb exploded in mid-air, just for'ard of the after funnel and feet away from it: a maiming, murderous storm of jagged steel scythed across the boat-deck, and all Oerlikons and the pom-poms fell immediately silent, their crews victim to shrapnel or concussion. Another plunged through the deck and Engineers' Flat and turned the WT office into a charnel house. The remaining two that struck were higher, smashing squarely into 'X' gun-deck and 'X' turret. The turret was split open around the top and down both sides as by a giant cleaver, and blasted off its mounting, to lie grotesquely across the shattered poop.

Apart from the boat-deck and turret gunners, only one other man lost his life in that attack, but that man was virtually irreplaceable. Shrapnel from the first bomb had burst a compressed air cylinder in the torpedo workshop, and Hartley, the man who, above all, had become the back-bone of the *Ulysses* had taken shelter there, only seconds before. . . .

---

[1] It is almost impossible for one single explosion, or even several in the same locality, to destroy or incapacitate all the dynamos in a large naval vessel, or to sever all the various sections of the Ring Main, which carries the power around the ship. When a dynamo or its appropriate section of the Ring Main suffered damage, the interlinking fuses automatically blew, isolating the damaged section. Theoretically, that is. In practice, it does not always happen that way – the fuses may not rupture and the entire system breaks down. Rumour – very strong rumour – had it that at least one of HM capital ships was lost simply because the Dynamo Fuse Release Switches – fuses of the order of 800 amps – failed to blow, leaving the capital ship powerless to defend itself.

The *Ulysses* was running into dense black smoke, now – the *Stirling* was heavily on fire, her fuel tanks gone. What happened in the next ten minutes, no one ever knew. In the smoke and flame and agony, they were moments borrowed from hell and men could only endure. Suddenly, the *Ulysses* was out in the clear, and the Heinkels, all bombs gone, were harrying her, attacking her incessantly with cannon and machine-gun, ravening wolves with their victim on its knees, desperate to finish it off. But still, here and there, a gun fired on the *Ulysses*.

Just below the bridge, for instance – there was a gun firing there. Turner risked a quick glance over the side, saw the gunner pumping his tracers into the path of a swooping Heinkel. And then the Heinkel opened up, and Turner flung himself back, knocking the Kapok Kid to the deck. Then the bomber was gone and the guns were silent. Slowly, Turner hoisted himself to his feet, peered over the side: the gunner was dead, his harness cut to ribbons.

He heard a scuffle behind him, saw a slight figure fling off a restraining hand, and climb to the edge of the bridge. For an instant, Turner saw the pale, staring face of Chrysler, Chrysler who had neither smiled nor even spoken since they had opened up the Asdic cabinet; at the same time he saw three Heinkels forming up to starboard for a fresh attack.

'Get down, you young fool!' Turner shouted. 'Do you want to commit suicide?'

Chrysler looked at him, eyes wide and devoid of recognition, looked away and dropped down to the sponson below. Turner lifted himself to the edge of the bridge and looked down.

Chrysler was struggling with all his slender strength, struggling in a strange and frightening silence, to drag the dead man from his Oerlikon cockpit. Somehow, with a series of convulsive, despairing jerks, he had him over the side, had laid him gently to the ground, and was climbing into the cockpit. His hand, Turner saw, was bare and bleeding, stripped to the raw flesh – then out of the corner of his eyes he saw the flame of the Heinkel's guns and flung himself backward.

One second passed, two, three – three seconds during which cannon shells and bullets smashed against the reinforced armour of the bridge – then, as a man in a daze, he heard the twin Oerlikons opening up. The boy must have held his fire to the very last moment. Six shots the Oerlikon fired – only six, and a great, grey shape, stricken and smoking, hurtled over the bridge barely at head height, sheared off its port wing on the Director Tower and crashed into the sea on the other side.

Chrysler was still sitting in the cockpit. His right hand was clutching his left shoulder, a shoulder smashed and shattered by a cannon shell, trying hopelessly to stem the welling arterial blood. Even as the next bomber straightened out on its strafing run, even as he flung himself backwards, Turner saw the mangled, bloody hand reach out for the trigger grip again.

Flat on the duckboards beside Carrington and the Kapok Kid, Turner pounded his fist on the deck in terrible frustration of anger. He thought of Starr, the man who had brought all this upon them, and hated him as he would never have believed he could hate anybody. He could have killed him then. He thought of Chrysler, of the excruciating hell of that gun-rest pounding into that shattered shoulder, of brown eyes glazed and shocked with pain and grief. If he himself lived, Turner swore, he would recommend that boy for the Victoria Cross. Abruptly the firing ceased and a Heinkel swung off sharply to starboard, smoke pouring from both its engines.

Quickly, together with the Kapok Kid, Turner scrambled to his feet, hoisted himself over the side of the bridge. He did it without looking, and he almost died then. A burst of fire from the third and last Heinkel – the bridge was always the favourite target – whistled past his head and shoulders: he felt the wind of their passing fan his cheek and hair. Then, winded from the convulsive back-thrust that had sent him there, he was stretched full length on the duckboards again. They were only inches from his eyes, these duckboards, but he could not see them. All he could see was the image of Chrysler, a gaping wound the size of a man's hand in his back, slumped forward across the Oerlikons, the weight of his body tilting the barrels grotesquely skywards. Both barrels had still been firing, were still firing, would keep on firing until the drums were empty, for the dead boy's hand was locked across the trigger.

Gradually, one by one, the guns of the convoy fell silent, the clamour of the aero engines began to fade in the distance. The attack was over.

Turner rose to his feet, slowly and heavily this time. He looked over the side of the bridge, stared down into the Oerlikon gunpit, then looked away, his face expressionless.

Behind him, he heard someone coughing. It was a strange, bubbling kind of cough. Turner whirled round, then stood stock-still, his hands clenched tightly at his sides.

The Kapok Kid, with Carrington kneeling helplessly at his side, was sitting quietly on the boards, his back propped against the legs of the Admiral's chair. From left groin to right shoulder through the middle of the embroidered 'J' on the chest, stretched a neat, straight, evenly-spaced pattern of round holes, stitched in by the machine-gun of the Heinkel. The blast of the shells must have hurtled him right across the bridge.

Turner stood absolutely still. The Kid, he knew with sudden sick certainty, had only seconds to live: he felt that any sudden move on his part would snap the spun-silk thread that held him on to life.

Gradually, the Kapok Kid became aware of his presence, of his steady gaze, and looked up tiredly. The vivid blue of his eyes were dulled already, the face white and drained of blood. Idly, his hand strayed up and down the punctured kapok, fingering the gashes. Suddenly he smiled, looked down at the quilted suit.

'Ruined,' he whispered. 'Bloody well ruined!' Then the wandering hand slipped down to his side, palm upward, and his head slumped forward on his chest. The flaxen hair stirred idly in the wind.

—— 17 ——

SUNDAY MORNING

The *Stirling* died at dawn. She died while still under way, still plunging through the heavy seas, her mangled, twisted bridge and superstructure glowing red, glowing white-hot as the wind and sundered oil tanks lashed the flames into an incandescent holocaust. A strange and terrible sight, but not unique: thus the *Bismarck* had looked, whitely incandescent, just before the *Shropshire's* torpedoes had sent her to the bottom.

The *Stirling* would have died anyway – but the Stukas made siccar. The Northern Lights had long since gone: now, too, the clear skies were going, and dark cloud was banking heavily to the north. Men hoped and prayed that the cloud would spread over FR77, and cover it with blanketing snow. But the Stukas got there first.

The Stukas – the dreaded gull-winged Junkers 87 dive-bombers – came from the south, flew high over the convoy, turned, flew south again. Level with, and due west of the *Ulysses*, rear ship in the convoy, they started to turn once more: then, abruptly, in the classic Stuka attack pattern, they peeled off in sequence, port wings dipping sharply as they half-rolled, turned and fell out of the sky, plummetting arrow-true for their targets.

Any plane that hurtles down in undeviating dive on waiting gun emplacements has never a chance. Thus spoke the pundits, the instructors in the gunnery school of Whale Island, and proceeded to prove to their own satisfaction the evident truth of their statement, using AA guns and duplicating the situation which would arise insofar as it lay within their power. Unfortunately, they couldn't duplicate the Stuka.

'Unfortunately,' because in actual battle, the Stuka was the only factor in the situation that really mattered. One had only to crouch behind a gun, to listen to the ear-piercing, screaming whistle of the Stuka in its near-vertical dive, to flinch from its hail of bullets as it loomed larger and larger in the sights, to know that nothing could now arrest the flight of that under-slung bomb, to appreciate the truth of that. Hundreds of men alive today – the lucky ones who endured and survived a Stuka attack – will readily confirm that the war produced nothing quite so nerve-rending, quite so demoralising as the sight and sound of those Junkers with the strange dihedral of the wings in the last seconds before they pulled out of their dive.

But one time in a hundred, maybe one time in a thousand, when the human factor of the man behind the gun ceased to operate, the pundits could be right. This was the thousandth time, for fear was a phantom that had vanished in the night: ranged against the dive-bombers were only one multiple pom-pom and half a dozen Oerlikons – the for'ard turrets could not be brought to bear – but these were enough, and more, in the hands of men inhumanly calm, ice-cool as the Polar wind itself, and filled with an almost dreadful singleness of purpose. Three Stukas in almost as many seconds were clawed out of the sky, two to crash harmlessly in the sea, a third to bury itself with tremendous impact in the already shattered day cabin of the Admiral.

The chances against the petrol tanks not erupting in searing flame or of the bomb not exploding were so remote as not to exist: but neither happened. It hardly seemed to call for comment – in extremity, courage becomes routine – when the bearded Doyle abandoned his pom-pom, scrambled up to the fo'c'sle deck, and flung himself on top of the armed bomb rolling heavily in scuppers awash with 100 per cent octane petrol. One tiny spark from Doyle's boot or from the twisted, broken steel of the Stuka rubbing and grinding against the superstructure would have been trigger enough: the contact fuse in the bomb was still undamaged, and as it slipped and skidded over the ice-bound deck, with Doyle hanging desperately on, it seemed animistically determined to smash its delicate percussion nose against a bulkhead or stanchion.

If Doyle thought of these things, he did not care. Coolly, almost carelessly, he kicked off the only retaining clip left on a broken section of the guard-rail, slid the bomb, fins first, over the edge, tipped the nose sharply to clear the detonator. The bomb fell harmlessly into the sea.

It fell into the sea just as the first bomb sliced contemptuously through the useless one-inch deck armour of the *Stirling* and crashed into the engine-room. Three, four, five, six other bombs buried themselves in the dying heart of the cruiser, the lightened Stukas lifting away sharply to port and starboard. From the bridge of the *Ulysses,* there seemed to be a weird, unearthly absence of noise as the bombs went home. They just vanished into the smoke and flame, engulfed by the inferno.

No one blow finished the *Stirling*, but a mounting accumulation of blows. She had taken too much and she could take no more. She was like a reeling boxer, a boxer over-matched against an unskilled but murderous opponent, sinking under an avalanche of blows.

Stony-faced, bitter beyond words at his powerlessness, Turner watched her die. Funny, he thought tiredly, she's like all the rest. Cruisers, he mused in a queerly detached abstraction, must be the toughest ships in the world. He'd seen many go, but none easily, cleanly, spectacularly. No sudden knock-out, no *coup de grâce* for them – always, always, they had to be battered to death. . . . Like the *Stirling*. Turner's grip on the shattered windscreen tightened till his forearms ached. To him, to all good sailors, a well-loved ship was a well-loved friend: for fifteen months, now, the old and valiant *Stirling* had been their faithful shadow, had shared the burden of the *Ulysses* in the worst convoys of the war: she was the last of the old guard, for only the *Ulysses* had been longer on the blackout run. It was not good to watch a friend die: Turner looked away, stared down at the ice-covered duckboards between his feet, his head sunk between hunched shoulders.

He could close his eyes, but he could not close his ears. He winced, hearing the monstrous, roaring hiss of boiling water and steam as the white-hot superstructure of the *Stirling* plunged deeply into the ice-chilled Arctic. For fifteen, twenty seconds that dreadful, agonised sibilation continued, then stopped in an instant, the sound sheared off as by a guillotine. When Turner looked up, slowly, there was only the rolling, empty sea ahead, the big oil-slicked bubbles rising to the top, bubbles rising only to be punctured as they broke the surface by the fine rain falling back into the sea from the great clouds of steam already condensing in that bitter cold.

The *Stirling* was gone, and the battered remnants of FR77 pitched and plunged steadily onwards to the north. There were seven ships left now – the four merchantmen, including the Commodore's ship, the tanker, the *Sirrus* and the *Ulysses*. None of them was whole: all were damaged, heavily damaged, but none so desperately hurt as the *Ulysses*. Seven ships, only seven: thirty-six had set out for Russia.

At 0800 Turner signalled the *Sirrus*: 'WT gone. Signal C-in-C course, speed, position. Confirm 0930 as rendezvous. Code.'

The reply came exactly an hour later. 'Delayed heavy seas. Rendezvous approx 1030. Impossible fly off air cover. Keep coming. C-in-C.'

'Keep coming!' Turner repeated savagely. 'Would you listen to him! "Keep coming," he says! What the hell does he expect us to do – scuttle ourselves?' He shook his head in angry despair. 'I hate to repeat myself,' he said bitterly. 'But I must. Too bloody late as usual!'[1]

Dawn and daylight had long since come, but it was growing darker again. Heavy grey clouds, formless and menacing, blotted out the sky from horizon to horizon. They were snow clouds, and, please God, the snow would soon fall: that could save them now, that and that alone.

But the snow did not come – not then. Once more, there came instead the Stukas, the roar of their engines rising and falling as they methodically quartered the empty sea in search of the

[1] It is regrettable but true – the Home Fleet squadron was almost always too late. The Admiralty could not be blamed – the capital ships were essential for the blockade of the *Tirpitz*, and they did not dare risk them close inshore against land-based bombers. The long awaited trap *did* eventually snap shut: but it caught only the heavy cruiser *Scharnhorst* and not the *Tirpitz*. It never caught the great ship. She was destroyed at her anchorage in Alta Fjord by Lancaster bombers of the Royal Air Force.

convoy – Charlie had left at dawn. But it was only a matter of time before the dive-bomber squadron found the tiny convoy; ten minutes from the time of the first warning of their approach, the leading Junkers 87 tipped over its wing and dropped out of the sky.

Ten minutes – but time for a council and plan of desperation. When the Stukas came, they found the convoy stretched out in line abreast, the tanker *Varella* in the middle, two merchant-men in close line ahead on either side of it, the *Sirrus* and the *Ulysses* guarding the flanks. A suicidal formation in submarine warters – a torpedo from port or starboard could hardly miss them all. But weather conditions were heavily against sub-marines, and the formation offered at least a fighting chance against the Stukas. It they approached from astern – their favourite attack technique – they would run into the simul-taneous massed fire of seven ships; if they approached from the sides, they must first attack the escorts, for no Stuka would present is unprotected underbelly to the guns of a warship. . . . They elected to attack from either side, five from the east, four from the west. This time, Turner noted, they were carrying long-range fuel tanks.

Turner had no time to see how the *Sirrus* was faring. Indeed, he could hardly see how his own ship was faring, for thick acrid smoke was blowing back across the bridge from the barrels of 'A' and 'B' turrets. In the gaps of sound between the crash of the 5.25s, he could hear the quick-fire of Doyle's midship pom-pom, the vicious thudding of the Oerlikons.

Suddenly, startling in its breath-taking unexpectedness, two great beams of dazzling white stabbed out through the mirk and gloom. Turner stared, then bared his teeth in fierce delight. The 44-inch searchlights! Of course! The great searchlights, still on the official secret list, capable of lighting up an enemy six miles away! What a fool he had been to forget them – Val-lery had used them often, in daylight and in dark, against attack-ing aircraft. No man could look into those terrible eyes, those flaming arcs across the electrodes and not be blinded.

Blinking against the eye-watering smoke, Turner peered aft to see who was manning the control position. But he knew who it was before he saw him. It could only be Ralston – searchlight control, Turner remembered, was his day action station: be-sides, he could think of no one other than the big, blond tor-pedoman with the gumption, the quick intelligence to burn the lamps on his own initiative.

Jammed in the corner of the bridge by the gate, Turner watched him. He forgot his ship, forgot even the bombers – he personally could do nothing about them anyway – as he stared in fascination at the man behind the controls.

His eyes were glued to the sights, his face expressionless, absolutely; but for the gradual stiffening of back and neck as the sight dipped in docile response to the delicate caress of his fingers on the wheel, he might have been carved from marble: the immobility of the face, the utter concentration was almost frightening.

There was not a flicker of feeling or emotion: never a flicker as the first Stuka weaved and twisted in maddened torment, seeking to escape that eye-staring flame, not even a flicker as it swerved violently in its dive, pulled out too late and crashed into the sea a hundred yards short of the *Ulysses*.

What was the boy thinking of? Turner wondered. His mother, his sisters, entombed under the ruins of a Croydon bungalow: of his brother, innocent victim of that mutiny – how impossible that mutiny seemed now! – in Scapa Flow: of his father, dead by his son's own hand? Turner did not know, could not even begin to guess: clairvoyantly, almost, he knew that it was too late, that no one would ever know now.

The face was inhumanly still. There wasn't a shadow of feeling as the second Stuka overshot the *Ulysses*, dropped its bomb into the open sea: not a shadow as a third blew up in mid-air: not a trace of emotion when the guns of the next Stuka smashed one of the lights . . . not even when the cannon shells of the last smashed the searchlight control, tore half his chest away. He died instantaneously, stood there a moment as if unwilling to abandon his post, then slumped back quietly on to the deck. Turner bent over the dead boy, looked at the face, the eyes upturned to the first feathery flakes of falling snow. The eyes, the face, were still the same, mask-like, expressionless. Turner shivered and looked away.

One bomb, and one only, had struck the *Ulysses*. It had struck the fo'c'sle deck just for'ard of 'A' turret. There had been no casualties, but some freak of vibration and shock had fractured the turret's hydraulic lines. Temporarily, at least, 'B' was the only effective remaining turret in the ship.

The *Sirrus* hadn't been quite so lucky. She had destroyed one Stuka – the merchantmen had claimed another – and had been hit twice, both bombs exploding in the after mess-deck. The *Sirrus*, overloaded with survivors, was carrying double her normal complement of men, and usually that mess-deck would have been crowded: during action stations it was empty. Not a man had lost his life – not a man was to lose his life on the destroyer *Sirrus*: she was never damaged again on the Russian convoys.

Hope was rising, rising fast. Less than an hour to go, now, and the battle squadron would be there. It was dark, dark with the gloom of an Arctic storm, and heavy snow was falling, hissing gently into the dark and rolling sea. No plane could find them in this – and they were almost beyond the reach of shore-based aircraft, except, of course, for the Condors. And it was almost impossible weather for submarines.

'It may be we shall touch the Happy Isles.' Carrington quoted softly.

'What?' Turner looked up, baffled. 'What did you say, Number One?'

'Tennyson.' Carrington was apologetic. 'The Captain was always quoting him. . . . Maybe we'll make it yet.'

'Maybe, maybe.' Turner was non-committal. 'Preston!'

'Yes, sir, I see it.' Preston was staring to the north where the signal lamp of the *Sirrus* was flickering rapidly.

'A ship, sir!' he reported excitedly. '*Sirrus* says naval vessel approaching from the north!'

'From the north! Thank God! Thank God!' Turner shouted exultantly. 'From the north! It must be them! They're ahead of time. . . . I take it all back. Can you see anything, Number One?'

'Not a thing, sir. Too thick – but it's clearing a bit, I think. . . . There's the *Sirrus* again.'

'What does she say, Preston?' Turner asked anxiously.

'Contact. Sub. contact. Green 30. Closing.'

'Contact! At this late hour!' Turner groaned, then smashed his fist down on the binnacle. He swore fiercely.

'By God, she's not going to stop us now! Preston, signal the *Sirrus* to stay . . .'

He broke off, looked incredulously to the north. Up there in the snow and gloom, stilettos of white flame had lanced out briefly, vanished again. Carrington by his side now, he stared unwinkingly north, saw shells splashing whitely in the water under the bows of the Commodore's ship, the *Cape Hatteras*: then he saw the flashes again, stronger, brighter this time, flashes that lit up for a fleeting second the bows and super-structure of the ship that was firing.

He turned slowly, to find that Carrington, too, had turned, was gazing at him with set face and bitter eyes. Turner, grey and haggard with exhaustion and the sour foretaste of ultimate defeat, looked in turn at his First Lieutenant in a long moment of silence.

'The answer to many questions,' he said softly. 'That's why they've been softening up the *Stirling* and ourselves for the past couple of days. The fox is in among the chickens. It's our old pal the *Hipper* cruiser come to pay us a social call.'

'It is.'

'So near and yet . . .' Turner shrugged. 'We deserved better than this. . . .' He grinned crookedly. 'How would you like to die a hero's death?'

'The very idea appals me!' boomed a voice behind him. Brooks had just arrived on the bridge.

'Me, too,' Turner admitted. He smiled: he was almost happy again. 'Have we any option, gentlemen?'

'Alas, no,' Brooks said sadly.

'Full ahead both!' Carrington called down the speaking-tube: it was by way of his answer.

'No, no,' Turner chided gently. 'Full *power*, Number One. Tell them we're in a hurry: remind them of the boasts they used to make about the *Abdiel* and the *Manxman* . . . Preston! General emergency signal: "Scatter: proceed independently to Russian ports." '

The upper deck was thick with freshly fallen snow, and the snow was still falling. The wind was rising again and, after the warmth of the canteen where he had been operating, it struck at Johnny Nicholls's lungs with sudden, searing pain: the temperature, he guessed, must be about zero. He buried his face in his duffel coat, climbed laboriously, haltingly up the ladders to the bridge. He was tired, deadly weary, and he winced in agony every time his foot touched the deck: his splinted left leg was shattered just above the ankle – shrapnel from the bomb in the after mess-deck.

Peter Orr, commander of the *Sirrus*, was waiting for him at the gate of the tiny bridge.

'I thought you might like to see this, Doc.' The voice was strangely high-pitched for so big a man. 'Rather I thought you would want to see this,' he corrected himself. 'Look at her go!' he breathed. 'Just look at her go!'

Nicholls looked out over the port side. Half a mile away on the beam, the *Cape Hatteras* was blazing furiously, slowing to a stop. Some miles to the north, through the falling snow, he could barely distinguish the vague shape of the German cruiser, a shape pinpointed by the aming guns still mercilessly pumping shells into the sinking ship. Every shot went home: the accuracy of their gunnery was fantastic.

Half a mile astern on the port quarter, the *Ulysses* was coming up. She was sheeted in foam and spray, the bows leaping almost clear of the water, then crashing down with a pistol-shot impact easily heard, even against the wind, on the bridge of the *Sirrus*, as the great engines thrust her through the water, faster, faster, with the passing of every second.

Nicholls gazed, fascinated. This was the first time he'd seen the *Ulysses* since he'd left her and he was appalled. The entire upperworks, fore and aft, were a twisted, unbelievable shambles of broken steel: both masts were gone, the smoke-stacks broken and bent, the Director Tower shattered and grotesquely askew: smoke was still pluming up from the great holes in fo'c'sle and poop, the after turrets, wrenched from their mountings, pitched crazily on the deck. The skeleton of the Condor still lay athwart 'Y' turret, a Stuka was buried to the wings in the fo'c'sle deck, and she was, he knew, split right down to the water level abreast the torpedo tubes. The *Ulysses* was something out of a nightmare.

Steadying himself against the violent pitching of the destroyer, Nicholls stared and stared, numbed with horror and disbelief. Orr looked at him, looked away as a messenger came to the bridge.

'Rendezvous 1015,' he read. '1015! Good lord, 25 minutes' time! Do you hear that, Doc? 25 minutes' time!'

'Yes, sir,' Nicholls said absently: he hadn't heard him.

Orr looked at him, touched his arm, pointed to the *Ulysses*. 'Bloody well incredible, isn't it?' he murmured.

'I wish to God I was aboard her,' Nicholls muttered miserably. 'Why did they send me—? Look! What's that?'

A huge flag, a flag twenty feet in length, was streaming out below the yardarm of the *Ulysses*, stretched taut in the wind of its passing. Nicholls had never seen anything remotely like it: the flag was enormous, red and blue and whiter than the driving snow.

'The battle ensign,' Orr murmured. 'Bill Turner's broken out the battle ensign.' He shook his head in wonder. 'To take time off to do that *now* – well, Doc., only Turner would do that. You know him well?'

Nicholls nodded silently.

'Me, too,' Orr said simply. 'We are both lucky men.'

The *Sirrus* was still doing fifteen knots, still headed for the enemy, when the *Ulysses* passed them by â cable-length away as if they were stopped in the water.

Long afterwards, Nicholls could never describe it all accurately. He had a hazy memory of the *Ulysses* no longer plunging and lifting, but battering through waves and troughs on a steady even keel, the deck angling back sharply from a rearing forefoot to the counter buried deep in the water, fifteen feet below the great boiling tortured sea of white that arched up in seething magnificence above the shattered poop-deck. He could recall, too, that 'B' turret was firing continuously, shell after shell screaming away through the blinding snow, to burst in brilliant splendour over and on the German cruiser: for 'B' turret had only starshells left. He carried, too, a vague mental picture of Turner waving ironically from the bridge, of the great ensign streaming stiffly astern, already torn and tattered at the edges. But what he could never forget, what he would hear in his heart and mind as long as he lived, was the tremendous, frightening roar of the great boiler-room intake fans as they sucked in mighty draughts of air for the starving engines. For the *Ulysses* was driving through the heavy seas under maximum power, at a speed that should have broken her shuddering back, should have burnt out the great engines. There was no doubt as to Turner's intentions: he was going to ram the enemy, to destroy him and take him with him, at a speed of just on or over forty incredible knots.

Nicholls gazed and gazed and did not know what to think: he felt sick at heart, for that ship was part of him now, his good friends, especially the Kapok Kid – for he did not know that the Kid was already dead – they, too, were part of him, and it is always terrible to see the end of a legend, to see it die, to see it going into the gulfs. But he felt, too, a strange exultation; she was dying but what a way to die! And if ships had hearts, had souls, as the old sailing men declared, surely the *Ulysses* would want it this way too.

She was still doing forty knots when, as if by magic, a great gaping hole appeared in her bows just above the water-line.

Shell-fire, possibly, but unlikely at that angle. It must have been a torpedo from the U-boat, not yet located: a sudden dip of the bows could have coincided with the upthrust of a heavy sea forcing a torpedo to the surface. Such things had happened before: rarely, but they happened. . . . The *Ulysses* brushed aside the torpedo, ignored the grievous wound, ignored the heavy shells crashing into her and kept on going.

She was still doing forty knots, driving in under the guns of the enemy, guns at maximum depression, when 'A' magazine blew up, blasted off the entire bows in one shattering detonation. For a second, the lightened fo'c'sle reared high into the air: then it plunged down, deep down, into the shoulder of a rolling sea. She plunged down and kept on going down, driving down to the black floor of the Arctic, driven down by the madly spinning screws, the still thundering engines her own executioner.

—— 18 ——

EPILOGUE

The air was warm and kind and still. The sky was blue, a deep and wonderful blue, with little puffs of cotton-wool cloud drifting lazily to the far horizon. The street-gardens, the hanging birdcage flower-baskets, spilled over with blue and yellow and red and gold, all the delicate pastel shades and tints he had almost forgotten had ever existed: every now and then an old man or a hurrying housewife or a young man with a laughing girl on his arm would stop to admire them, then walk on again, the better for having seen them. The nesting birds were singing, clear and sweet above the distant roar of the traffic, and Big Ben was booming the hour as Johnny Nicholls climbed awkwardly out of the taxi, paid off the driver and hobbled slowly up the marble steps.

His face carefully expressionless, the sentry saluted, opened the heavy swing door. Nicholls passed inside, looked around the huge hall, saw that both sides were lined with heavy, imposing doors: at the far end, beneath the great curve of the stairs and overhanging the widely convex counter of the type usually found in banks, hung a sign: 'Typist Pool: Inquiries.'

The tip-tap of the crutches sounded unnaturally loud on the

marble floor as he limped over to the counter. Very touching and melodramatic, Nicholls, he thought dispassionately: trust the audience are having their money's worth. Half a dozen typists had stopped work as if by command, were staring at him in open curiosity, hands resting limply on their machines. A trim young wren, red-haired and shirt-sleeved, came to the counter.

'Can I help you, sir?' The quiet voice, the blue eyes were soft with concern. Nicholls, catching a glimpse of himself in a mirror behind her, a glimpse of a scuffed uniform jacket over a grey fisherman's jersey, of blurred, sunken eyes and gaunt, pale cheeks, admitted wryly to himself that he couldn't blame her. He didn't have to be a doctor to know that he was in pretty poor shape.

'My name is Nicholls, Surgeon-Lieutenant Nicholls. I have an appointment—'

'Lieutenant Nicholls. . . . HMS *Ulysses*!' The girl drew in her breath sharply. 'Of course, sir. They're expecting you.' Nicholls looked at her, looked at the Wrens sitting motionless in the chairs, caught the intense, wondering expression in their eyes, the awed gaze with which one would regard beings from another planet. It made him feel vaguely uncomfortable.

'Upstairs, I suppose?' He hadn't meant to sound so brusque.

'No, sir.' The Wren came quietly round the counter. 'They – well, they heard you'd been wounded, sir,' she murmured apologetically. 'Just across the hall here, please.' She smiled at him, slowed her step to match his halting walk.

She knocked, held open the door, announced him to someone he couldn't see, and closed the door softly behind him when he had passed through.

There were three men in the room. The one man he recognised, Vice-Admiral Starr, came forward to meet him. He looked older, far older, far more tired than when Nicholls had last seen him – hardly a fortnight previously.

'How are you, Nicholls?' he asked. 'Not walking so well, I see.' Under the assurance, the thin joviality so flat and misplaced, the harsh edge of strain burred unmistakably. 'Come and sit down.'

He led Nicholls across to the table, long, big and covered with leather. Behind the table, framed against huge wall-maps, sat two men. Starr introduced them. One, big, beefy, red of face, was in full uniform, the sleeves ablaze with the broad band and four stripes of an Admiral of the Fleet: the other was a civilian, a small, stocky man with iron-grey hair, eyes still and wise and old. Nicholls recognised him immediately, would have known anyway from the deference of both the Admirals. He reflected wryly that the Navy was indeed doing him proud: such receptions were not for all. . . . But they seemed reluctant to begin the reception, Nicholls thought – he had forgotten the shock his appearance must give. Finally, the grey-haired man cleared his throat.

'How's the leg, boy?' he asked. 'Looks pretty bad to me.' His voice was low, but alive with controlled authority.

'Not too bad, thank you, sir,' Nicholls answered. 'Two, three weeks should see me back on the job.'

'You're taking two months, laddie,' said the grey-haired man quietly. 'More if you want it.' He smiled faintly. 'If anyone asks, just tell 'em I said so. Cigarette?'

He flicked the big table-lighter, sat back in his chair. Temporarily, he seemed at a loss as to what to say next. Then he looked up abruptly.

'Had a good trip home?'

'Very fair, sir. VIP treatment all the way. Moscow, Teheran, Cairo, Gib.' Nicholls's mouth twisted. 'Much more comfortable than the trip out.' He paused, inhaled deeply on his cigarette, looked levelly across the table. 'I would have preferred to come home in the *Sirrus*.'

'No doubt,' Starr broke in acidly. 'But we cannot afford to cater for the personal prejudices of all and sundry. We were anxious to have a first-hand account of FR77 – and particularly the *Ulysses* – as soon as possible.'

Nicholls's hands clenched on the edge of his chair. The anger had leapt in him like a flame, and he knew that the man opposite was watching closely. Slowly he relaxed, looked at the grey-haired man, interrogative eyebrows mutely asking confirmation.

The grey-haired man nodded.

'Just tell us all you know,' he said kindly. 'Everything – about everything. Take your time.'

'From the beginning?' Nicholls asked in a low voice.

'From the beginning.'

Nicholls told them. He would have liked to tell the story, right as it fell out, from the convoy before FR77 straight through to the end. He did his best, but it was a halting story, strangely lacking in conviction. The atmosphere, the surroundings were wrong – the contrast between the peaceful warmth of these rooms and the inhuman cold and cruelty of the Arctic was an immense gulf that could be bridged only by experience and understanding. Down here, in the heart of London, the wild, incredible tale he had to tell fell falsely, incredibly even on his own ears. Half-way through, he looked at his listeners, almost gave up. Incredulity? No, it wasn't that – at least, not with the grey-haired man and the Admiral of the Fleet. Just a baffled incomprehension, an honest failure to understand.

It wasn't so bad when he stuck to the ascertainable facts, the facts of carriers crippled by seas, of carriers mined, stranded and torpedoed: the facts of the great storm, of the desperate struggle to survive: the facts of the gradual attrition of the convoy, of the terrible dying of the two gasoline tankers, of the U-boats and bombers sent to the bottom, of the *Ulysses,* battering through the snowstorm at 40 knots, blown up by the German cruiser, of the arrival of the battle squadron, of the flight of the cruiser before it could inflict further damage, of the rounding-up of the scattered convoy, of the curtain of Russian fighters in the Barents Sea, of the ultimate arrival in the Kola Inlet of the battered remnants of FR77 – five ships in all.

It was when he came to less readily ascertainable facts, to statements that could never be verified at all, that he sensed the doubt, the something more than wonder. He told the story as calmly, as unemotionally as he could: the story of Ralston, Ralston of the fighting lights and the searchlights, of his father and family: of Riley, the ringleader of the mutiny and his re-fusal to leave the shaft tunnel: of Petersen, who had killed a marine and gladly given his own life: of McQuater and Chrys-ler and Doyle and a dozen others.

For a second, his own voice broke uncertainly as he told the story of the half-dozen survivors from the *Ulysses,* picked up by the *Sirrus* soon afterwards. He told how Brooks had given his lifejacket to an ordinary seaman, who amazingly survived fifteen minutes in that water: how Turner, wounded in head and arm, had supported a dazed Spicer till the *Sirrus* came plunging alongside, had passed a bowline round him, and was gone before anything could be done: how Carrington, that enduring man of iron, a baulk of splintered timber under his arms, had held two men above water till rescue came. Both men – Preston was one – had died later: Carrington had climbed the rope unaided, clambered over the guard-rails dangling a left-leg with the foot blown off above the ankle. Carrington would survive: Carrington was indestructible. Finally, Doyle, too, was gone: they had thrown him a rope, but he had not seen it, for he was blind.

But what the three men really wanted to know, Nicholls realized, was how the *Ulysses* had been, how a crew of mutineers had borne themselves. He had told them, he knew, things of wonder and of splendour, and they could not reconcile these with men who would take up arms against their own ship, in effect, against their own King.

So Nicholls tried to tell them, then knew, as he tried, that he could never tell them. For what was there to tell? That Vallery had spoken to the men over the broadcast system: how he had gone among them and made them almost as himself, on that grim, exhausting tour of inspection: how he had spoken of them as he died: and how, most of all, his death had made them men again? For that was all that there was to tell, and these things were just nothing at all. With sudden insight, Nicholls saw that the meaning of that strange transformation of the men of the *Ulysses,* a transformation of bitter, broken men to men above themselves, could neither be explained nor understood, for all the meaning was in Vallery, and Vallery was dead.

Nicholls felt tired, now, desperately so. He knew he was far from well. His mind was cloudy, hazy in retrospect, and he was mixing things up: his sense of chronological time was gone, he was full of hesitations and uncertainties. Suddenly he was overwhelmed by the futility of it all, and he broke off slowly, his voice trailing into silence.

Vaguely, he heard the grey-haired man ask something in a quiet voice, and he muttered aloud, unthinking.

'What was that? What did you say?' The grey-haired man was looking at him strangely. The face of the Admiral behind the table was impassive. Starr's, he saw, was open in disbelief.

'I only said, "They were the best crew God ever gave a Captain," ' Nicholls murmured.

'I see.' The old, tired eyes looked at him steadily, but there was no other comment. Fingers drumming on the table, he looked slowly at the two Admirals, then back to Nicholls again.

'Take things easy for a minute, boy. . . . If you'll just excuse us . . .'

He rose to his feet, walked slowly over to the big, bay windows at the other end of the long room, the others following. Nicholls made no move, did not even look after them: he sat slumped in the chair, looking dejectedly, unseeingly, at the crutches on the floor between his feet.

From time to time, he could hear a murmur of voices. Starr's high-pitched voice carried most clearly. 'Mutiny ship, sir . . . never the same again . . . better this way.' There was a murmured reply, too low to catch, then he heard Starr saying, '. . . finished as a fighting unit.' The grey-haired man said something rapidly, his tone sharp with disagreement, but the words were blurred. Then the deep, heavy voice of the Fleet Admiral said something about 'expiation,' and the grey-haired man nodded slowly. Then Starr looked at him over his shoulder, and Nicholls knew they were talking about him. He thought he heard the words 'not well' and 'frightful strain,' but perhaps he was imagining it.

Anyway, he no longer cared. He was anxious for one thing only, and that was to be gone. He felt an alien in an alien land, and whether they believed him or not no longer mattered. He did not belong here, where everything was so sane and commonplace and real – and withal a world of shadows.

He wondered what the Kapok Kid would have said had he been here, and smiled in fond reminiscence: the language would have been terrible, the comments rich and barbed and pungent. Then he wondered what Vallery would have said, and he smiled again at the simplicity of it all, for Vallery would have said: 'Do not judge them, for they do not understand.'

Gradually, he became aware that the murmuring had ceased, that the three men were standing above him. His smile faded, and he looked up slowly to see them looking down strangely at him, their eyes full of concern.

'I'm damnably sorry, boy,' the grey-haired man said sincerely. 'You're a sick man and we've asked far too much of you. A drink, Nicholls? It was most remiss—'

'No, thank you, sir.' Nicholls straightened himself in his chair. 'I'll be perfectly all right.' He hesitated. 'Is – is there anything else?'

'No, nothing at all.' The smile was genuine, friendly. 'You've been a great help to us, Lieutenant, a great help. And a fine report. Thank you very much indeed.'

A liar and a gentleman, Nicholls thought gratefully. He struggled to his feet, reached out for his crutches. He shook hands with Starr and the Admiral of the Fleet, and said goodbye. The grey-haired man accompanied him to the door, his hand beneath Nicholls's arm.

At the door Nicholls paused.

'Sorry to bother you but – when do I begin my leave, sir?'

'As from now,' the other said emphatically. 'And have a good time. God knows you've earned it, my boy. . . . Where are you going?'

'Henley, sir.'

'Henley! I could have sworn you were Scots.'

'I am, sir – I have no family.'

'Oh. . . . A girl, Lieutenant?'

Nicholls nodded silently.

The grey-haired man clapped him on the shoulder, and smiled gently.

'Pretty, I'll be bound?'

Nicholls looked at him, looked away to where the sentry was already holding open the street doors, and gathered up his crutches.

'I don't know, sir,' he said quietly. 'I don't know at all. I've never seen her.'

He tip-tapped his way across the marble flags, passed through the heavy doors and limped out into the sunshine.

The Guns
of Navarone

ALISTAIR
MacLEAN

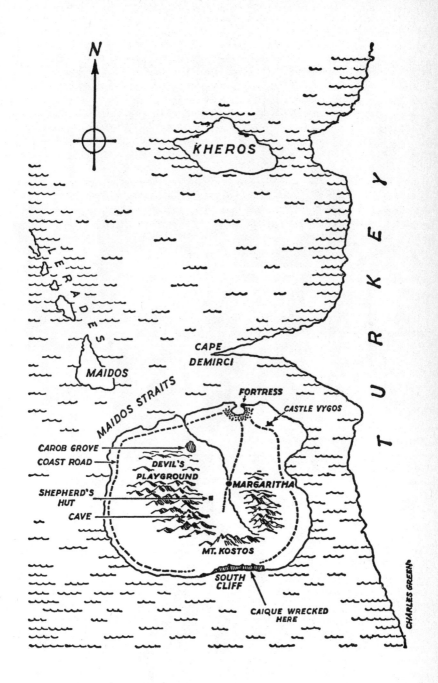

N

KHEROS

CYCLADES

MAIDOS

MAIDOS STRAITS

CAPE
DEMIRCI

FORTRESS

CASTLE VYGOS

CAROB GROVE

COAST ROAD

DEVIL'S
PLAYGROUND

MARGARITHA

SHEPHERD'S
HUT

CAVE

MT. KOSTOS

SOUTH
CLIFF

CAIQUE WRECKED
HERE

T U R K E Y

CHARLES GREEN

I

PRELUDE: SUNDAY

0100–0900

The match scratched noisily across the rusted metal of the corrugated iron shed, fizzled, then burst into a sputtering pool of
light, the harsh sound and sudden brilliance alike strangely
alien in the stillness of the desert night. Mechanically, Mallory's
eyes followed the cupped sweep of the flaring match to the
cigarette jutting out beneath the Group-Captain's clipped
moustache, saw the light stop inches away from the face, saw
too the sudden stillness of that face, the unfocused vacancy of
the eyes of a man lost in listening. Then the match was gone,
ground into the sand of the airfield perimeter.

'I can hear them,' the Group-Captain said softly. 'I can hear
them coming in. Five minutes, no more. No wind tonight –
they'll be coming in on Number Two. Come on, let's meet them
in the interrogation room.' He paused, looked quizzically at
Mallory and seemed to smile. But the darkness deceived, for
there was no humour in his voice. 'Just curb your impatience,
young man – just for a little longer. Things haven't gone too
well tonight. You're going to have all your answers, I'm afraid,
and have them all too soon.' He turned abruptly, strode off towards the squat buildings that loomed vaguely against the pale
darkness that topped the level horizon.

Mallory shrugged, then followed on more slowly, step for step
with the third member of the group, a broad, stocky figure with
a very pronounced roll in his gait. Mallory wondered sourly
just how much practice Jensen had required to achieve that
sailorly effect. Thirty years at sea, of course – and Jensen had
done exactly that – were sufficient warrant for a man to dance
a hornpipe as he walked; but that wasn't the point. As the
brilliantly successful Chief of Operations of the Subversive
Operation Executive in Cairo, intrigue, deception, imitation
and disguise were the breath of life to Captain James Jensen,
DSO, RN. As a Levantine stevedore agitator, he had won the
awed respect of the dock-labourers from Alexandretta to
Alexandria: as a camel-driver, he had blasphemously out-

camel-driven all available Bedouin competition: and no more pathetic beggar had ever exhibited such realistic sores in the bazaars and market-places of the East. Tonight, however, he was just the bluff and simple sailor. He was dressed in white from cap-cover to canvas shoes, the starlight glinted softly on the golden braid on epaulettes and cap peak.

Their footsteps crunched in companionable unison over the hard-packed sand, rang sharply as they moved on to the concrete of the runway. The hurrying figure of the Group-Captain was already almost lost to sight. Mallory took a deep breath and turned suddenly towards Jensen.

'Look, sir, just what *is* all this? What's all the flap, all the secrecy about? And why am *I* involved in it? Good lord, sir, it was only yesterday that I was pulled out of Crete, relieved at eight hours' notice. A month's leave, I was told. And what happens?'

'Well,' Jensen murmured, 'what did happen?'

'No leave,' Mallory said bitterly. 'Not even a night's sleep. Just hours and hours in the SOE Headquarters, answering a lot of silly, damnfool questions about climbing in the Southern Alps. Then hauled out of bed at midnight, told I was to meet you, and then driven for hours across the blasted desert by a mad Scotsman who sang drunken songs and asked hundreds of even more silly, damnfool questions!'

'One of my more effective disguises, I've always thought,' Jensen said smugly. 'Personally, I found the journey most entertaining!'

'One of your—' Mallory broke off, appalled at the memory of the things he had said to the elderly bewhiskered Scots captain who had driven the command vehicle. 'I – I'm terribly sorry, sir. I never realized—'

'Of course you didn't!' Jensen cut in briskly. 'You weren't supposed to. Just wanted to find out if you were the man for the job. I'm sure you are – I was pretty sure you were before I pulled you out of Crete. But where you got the idea about leave I don't know. The sanity of the SOE has often been questioned, but even *we* aren't given to sending a flying-boat for the sole purpose of enabling junior officers to spend a month wasting their substance among the flesh-pots of Cairo,' he finished dryly.

'I still don't know—'

'Patience, laddie, patience – as our worthy Group-Captain has just advocated. Time is endless. To wait, and to keep on waiting – that is to be of the East.'

'To total four hours' sleep in three days is not,' Mallory said feelingly. 'And that's all I've had. . . . Here they come!'

Both men screwed up their eyes in automatic reflex as the fierce glare of the landing light struck at them, the flare path arrowing off into the outer darkness. In less than a minute the first bomber was down, heavily, awkwardly, taxi-ing to a stand-still just beside them. The grey camouflage paint of the after fuselage and tail-planes was riddled with bullet and cannon shells, an aileron was shredded and the port outer engine out of commission, saturated in oil. The cabin Perspex was shattered and starred in a dozen places.

For a long time Jensen stared at the holes and scars of the damaged machine, then shook his head and looked away.

'Four hours' sleep, Captain Mallory,' he said quietly. 'Four hours. I'm beginning to think that you can count yourself damn' lucky to have had even that much.'

The interrogation room, harshly lit by two powerful, unshaded lights, was uncomfortable and airless. The furniture consisted of some battered wall-maps and charts, a score or so of equally scuffed chairs and an unvarnished deal table. The Group-Captain, flanked by Jensen and Mallory, was sitting behind this when the door opened abruptly and the first of the flying crews entered, blinking rapidly in the fierceness of the unaccustomed light. They were led by a dark-haired, thick-set pilot, trailing helmet and flying-suit in his left hand. He had an Anzac bush helmet crushed on the back of his head, and the word 'Australia' emblazoned in white across each khaki shoulder. Scowling, word-lessly and without permission, he sat down in front of them, produced a pack of cigarettes and rasped a match across the surface of the table. Mallory looked furtively at the Group-Captain. The Group-Captain just looked resigned. He even sounded resigned.

'Gentlemen, this is Squadron Leader Torrance. Squadron Leader Torrance,' he added unnecessarily, 'is an Australian.' Mallory had the impression that the Group-Captain rather hoped this would explain some things, Squadron Leader Tor-rance among them. 'He led tonight's attack on Navarone. Bill, these gentlemen here – Captain Jensen of the Royal Navy, Cap-tain Mallory of the Long Range Desert Group – have a very special interest in Navarone. How did things go tonight?'

Navarone! So that's why I'm here tonight, Mallory thought. Navarone. He knew it well, rather, knew of it. So did everyone who had served any time at all in the Eastern Mediterranean: a grim, impregnable iron fortress off the coast of Turkey, heavily defended by – it was thought – a mixed garrison of Germans and Italians, one of the few Ægean islands on which the Allies had been unable to establish a mission, far less recapture, at some period of the war. . . . He realized that Torrance was speaking, the slow drawl heavy with controlled anger.

'Bloody awful, sir. A fair cow, it was, a real suicide do.' He broke off abruptly, stared moodily with compressed lips through his own drifting tobacco smoke. 'But we'd like to go back again,' he went on. 'Me and the boys here. Just once. We were talking about it on the way home.' Mallory caught the deep murmur of voices in the background, a growl of agreement. 'We'd like to take with us the joker who thought this one up and shove him out at ten thousand over Navarone, without benefit of a parachute.'

'As bad as that, Bill?'

'As bad as that, sir. We hadn't a chance. Straight up, we really hadn't. First off, the weather was against us – the jokers in the Met. office were about as right as they usually are.'

'They gave you clear weather?'

'Yeah. Clear weather. It was ten-tenths over the target,' Torrance said bitterly. 'We had to go down to fifteen hundred. Not that it made any difference. We would have to have gone down lower than that anyway – about three thousand feet below sea-level then fly up the way: that cliff overhang shuts the target clean off. Might as well have dropped a shower of leaflets asking them to spike their own bloody guns. . . . Then they've got every second AA gun in the south of Europe concentrated along this narrow 50-degree vector – the only way you can approach the target, or anywhere near the target. Russ and Conroy were belted good and proper on the way in. Didn't even get half-way towards the harbour. . . . They never had a chance.'

'I know, I know.' The Group-Captain nodded heavily. 'We heard. W/T reception was good. . . . And McIlveen ditched just north of Alex?'

'Yeah. But he'll be all right. The old crate was still awash when we passed over, the big dinghy was out and it was as smooth as a millpond. He'll be all right,' Torrance repeated.

The Group-Captain nodded again, and Jensen touched his sleeve.

'May I have a word with the Squadron Leader?'

'Of course, Captain. You don't have to ask.'

'Thanks.' Jensen looked across at the burly Australian and smiled faintly.

'Just one little question, Squadron Leader. You don't fancy going back there again?'

'Too bloody right, I don't!' Torrance growled.

'Because?'

'Because I don't believe in suicide. Because I don't believe in sacrificing good blokes for nothing. Because I'm not God and I can't do the impossible.' There was a flat finality in Torrance's voice that carried conviction, that brooked no argument.

'It is impossible, you say?' Jensen persisted. 'This is terribly important.'

'So's my life. So are the lives of all these jokers.' Torrance jerked a big thumb over his shoulder. 'It's impossible, sir. At least, it's impossible for us.' He drew a weary hand down his face. 'Maybe a Dornier flying-boat with one of these new-fangled radio-controlled glider-bombs might do it and get off with it. I don't know. But I do know that nothing we've got has a snowball's chance in hell. Not,' he added bitterly, 'unless you cram a Mosquito full of TNT and order one of us to crash-dive it at four hundred into the mouth of the gun cave. That way there's always a chance.'

'Thank you, Squadron Leader – and all of you.' Jensen was on his feet. 'I know you've done your very best, no one could have done more. And I'm sorry. . . . Group-Captain?'

'Right with you, gentlemen.' He nodded to the bespectacled Intelligence officer who had been sitting behind them to take his place, led the way out through a side door and into his own quarters.

'Well, that is that, I suppose.' He broke the seal of a bottle of Talisker, brought out some glasses. 'You'll have to accept it as final, Jensen. Bill Torrance's is the senior, most experienced squadron left in Africa today. Used to pound the Ploesti oil well and think it a helluva skylark. If anyone could have done tonight's job it was Bill Torrance, and if he says it's impossible, believe me, Captain Jensen, it can't be done.'

'Yes.' Jensen looked down sombrely at the golden amber of the glass in his hand. 'Yes, I know now. I *almost* knew before, but I couldn't be sure, and I couldn't take the chance of being wrong. . . . A terrible pity that it took the lives of a dozen men to prove me right. . . . There's just the one way left, now.'

'There's just the one,' the Group-Captain echoed. He lifted his glass, shook his head. 'Here's luck to Kheros!'

'Here's luck to Kheros!' Jensen echoed in turn. His face was grim.

'Look!' Mallory begged. 'I'm completely lost. Would somebody please tell me—'

'Kheros,' Jensen interrupted. 'That was your cue call, young man. All the world's a stage, laddie, etc., and this is where you tread the boards in this particular little comedy.' Jensen's smile was quite mirthless. 'Sorry you've missed the first two acts, but don't lose any sleep over that. This is no bit part: you're going to be the star, whether you like it or not. This is it. Kheros, Act 3, Scene 1. Enter Captain Keith Mallory.'

Neither of them had spoken in the last ten minutes. Jensen drove the big Humber command car with the same sureness, the same relaxed efficiency that hall-marked everything he did: Mallory still sat hunched over the map on his knees, a large-scale Admiralty chart of the Southern Ægean illuminated by the hooded dashboard light, studying an area of the Sporades and Northern Dodecanese heavily squared off in red pencil. Finally he straightened up and shivered. Even in Egypt these late November nights could be far too cold for comfort. He looked across at Jensen.

'I think I've got it now, sir.'

'Good!' Jensen gazed straight ahead along the winding grey ribbon of dusty road, along the white glare of the headlights that cleaved through the darkness of the desert. The beams lifted and dipped, constantly, hypnotically, to the cushioning of the springs on the rutted road. 'Good!' he repeated. 'Now, have another look at it and imagine yourself standing in the town of Navarone – that's on that almost circular bay on the north of the island. Tell me, what would you see from there?'

Mallory smiled.

'I don't have to look again, sir. Four miles or so away to the east I'd see the Turkish coast curving up north and west to a point almost due north of Navarone – a very sharp promontory, that, for the coastline above curves back almost due east. Then, about sixteen miles away, due north beyond this promontory – Cape Demirci, isn't it? – and practically in a line with it I'd see the island of Kheros. Finally, six miles to the west is the island of Maidos, the first of the Lerades group. They stretch away in a north-westerly direction, maybe fifty miles.'

'Sixty.' Jensen nodded. 'You have the eye, my boy. You've got the guts and the experience – a man doesn't survive eighteen months in Crete without both. You've got one or two special qualifications I'll mention by and by.' He paused for a moment, shook his head slowly. 'I only hope you have the luck – all the luck. God alone knows you're going to need it.'

Mallory waited expectantly, but Jensen had sunk into some private reverie. Three minutes passed, perhaps five, and there was only the swish of the tyres, the subdued hum of the powerful engine. Presently Jensen stirred and spoke again, quietly, still without taking his eyes off the road.

'This is Saturday – rather, it's Sunday morning now. There are one thousand two hundred men on the island of Kheros – one thousand two hundred British soldiers – who will be dead, wounded or prisoner by next Saturday. Mostly they'll be dead.' For the first time he looked at Mallory and smiled, a brief smile, a crooked smile, and then it was gone. 'How does it feel to hold a thousand lives in your hands, Captain Mallory?'

For long seconds Mallory looked at the impassive face beside him, then looked away again. He stared down at the chart. Twelve hundred men on Kheros, twelve hundred men waiting to die. Kheros and Navarone, Kheros and Navarone. What was that poem again, that little jingle that he'd learnt all these long years ago in that little upland village in the sheeplands outside Queenstown? Chimborazo – that was it. 'Chimborazo and Cotopaxi, you have stolen my heart away.' Kheros and Navarone – they had the same ring, the same indefinable glamour, the same wonder of romance that took hold of a man and stayed with him. Kheros and – angrily, almost, he shook his head, tried to concentrate. The pieces of the jigsaw were beginning to click into place, but slowly.

Jensen broke the silence.

'Eighteen months ago, you remember, after the fall of Greece, the Germans had taken over nearly all the islands of the Sporades: the Italians, of course, already held most of the Dodecanese. Then, gradually, we began to establish missions on these islands, usually spear-headed by your people, the Long Range Desert Group or the Special Boat Service. By last September we had retaken nearly all the larger islands except Navarone – it was too damned hard a nut, so we just by-passed it –and brought some of the garrisons up to, and beyond, battalion strength.' He grinned at Mallory. 'You were lurking in your cave somewhere in the White Mountains at the time, but you'll remember how the Germans reacted?'

'Violently?'

Jensen nodded.

'Exactly. Very violently indeed. The political importance of Turkey in this part of the world is impossible to over-estimate – and she's always been a potential partner for either Axis or Allies. Most of these islands are only a few miles off the Turkish coast. The question of prestige, of restoring confidence in Germany, was urgent.'

'So?'

'So they flung in everything – paratroopers, airborne troops, crack mountain brigades, hordes of Stukas – I'm told they stripped the Italian front of dive-bombers for these operations. Anyway, they flung everything in – the lot. In a few weeks we'd lost over ten thousand troops and every island we'd ever recaptured – except Kheros.'

'And now it's the turn of Kheros?'

'Yes.' Jensen shook out a pair of cigarettes, sat silently until Mallory had lit them and sent the match spinning through the window towards the pale gleam of the Mediterranean lying north below the coast road. 'Yes, Kheros is for the hammer. Nothing that we can do can save it. The Germans have absolutely air superiority in the Ægean. . . .'

'But – but how can you be so sure that it's this week?'

Jensen sighed.

'Laddie, Greece is fairly hotching with Allied agents. We have over two hundred in the Athens-Piraeus area alone and—'

'Two hundred!' Mallory interrupted incredulously. 'Did you say—'

'I did.' Jensen grinned. 'A mere bagatelle, I assure you, compared to the vast hordes of spies that circulate freely among our noble hosts in Cairo and Alexandria.' He was suddenly serious again. 'Anyway, our information is accurate. An armada of caiques will sail from the Piraeus on Thursday at dawn and island-hop across the Cyclades, holing up in the islands at night.' He smiled. 'An intriguing situation, don't you think? We daren't move in the Ægean in the daytime or we'd be bombed out of the water. The Germans don't dare move at night. Droves of our destroyers and MTBs and gun-boats move into the Ægean at dusk: the destroyers retire to the south before dawn, the small boats usually lie up in isolated island creeks. But we can't stop them from getting across. They'll be there Saturday or Sunday – and synchronise their landings with the first of the airborne troops: they've scores of Junkers 52s waiting just outside Athens. Kheros won't last a couple of days.' No one could have listened to Jensen's carefully casual voice, his abnormal matter-of-factness and not have believed him.

Mallory believed him. For almost a minute he stared down at the sheen of the sea, at the faerie tracery of the stars shimmering across its darkly placid surface. Suddenly he swung round on Jensen.

'But the Navy, sir! Evacuation! Surely the Navy—'

'The Navy,' Jensen interrupted heavily, 'is not keen. The Navy is sick and tired of the Eastern Med. and the Ægean, sick and tired of sticking out its long-suffering neck and having it regularly chopped off – and all for sweet damn all. We've had two battleships wrecked, eight cruisers out of commission – four of them sunk – and over a dozen destroyers gone. . . . I couldn't even start to count the number of smaller vessels we've lost. And for what? I've told you – for sweet damn all! Just so's our High Command can play round-and-round-the-rugged-rocks and who's-the-king-of-the-castle with their opposite numbers in Berlin. Great fun for all concerned – except, of course, for the thousand or so sailors who've been drowned in the course of the game, the ten thousand or so Tommies and Anzacs and Indians who suffered and died on these same islands – and died without knowing why.'

Jensen's hands were whiteknuckled on the wheel, his mouth tight-drawn and bitter. Mallory was surprised, shocked almost, by the vehemence, the depth of feeling; it was so completely out of character. . . . Or perhaps it was in character, perhaps Jensen knew a very great deal indeed about what went on on the inside. . . .

'Twelve hundred men, you said, sir?' Mallory asked quietly. 'You said there were twelve hundred men on Kheros?'

Jensen flickered a glance at him, looked away again.

'Yes. Twelve hundred men.' Jensen sighed. 'You're right, laddie, of course you're right. I'm just talking off the top of my head. Of course we can't leave them there. The Navy will do its damnedest. What's two or three more destroyers – sorry, boy, sorry, there I go again. . . . Now listen, and listen carefully.

'Taking 'em off will have to be a night operation. There isn't a ghost of a chance in the daytime – not with two-three hundred Stukas just begging for a glimpse of a Royal Naval destroyer. It'll have to be destroyers – transports and tenders are too slow by half. And they can't possibly go north about the northern tip of the Lerades – they never get back to safety before daylight. It's too long a trip by hours.'

'But the Lerades is a pretty long string of islands,' Mallory ventured. 'Couldn't the destroyers go through—'

'Between a couple of them? Impossible.' Jensen shook his head. 'Mined to hell and back again. Every single channel. You couldn't take a dinghy through.'

'And the Maidos-Navarone channel. Stiff with mines also, I suppose?'

'No, that's a clear channel. Deep water – you can't moor mines in deep water.'

'So that's the route you've got to take, isn't it, sir? I mean, they're Turkish territorial waters on the other side and we—'

'We'd go through Turkish territorial waters tomorrow, and in broad daylight, if it would do any good,' Jensen said flatly. 'The Turks know it and so do the Germans. But all other things being equal, the Western channel is the one we're taking. It's a clearer channel, a shorter route – and it doesn't involve any unnecessary international complications.'

'All other things being equal?'

'The guns of Navarone.' Jensen paused for a long time, then repeated the words, slowly, expressionlessly, as one would repeat the name of some feared and ancient enemy. 'The guns of Navarone. They make everything equal. They cover the Northern entrances to both channels. We could take the twelve hundred men off Kheros tonight – if we could silence the guns of Navarone.'

Mallory sat silent, said nothing. He's coming to it now, he thought.

'These guns are no ordinary guns,' Jensen went on quietly. 'Our naval experts say they're about nine-inch rifle barrels. I think myself they're more likely a version of the 210 mm. "crunch" guns that the Germans are using in Italy – our soldiers up there hate and fear those guns more than anything on earth. A dreadful weapon – shell extremely slow in flight and damnably accurate. Anyway,' he went on grimly, 'whatever they were they were good enough to dispose of the *Sybaris* in five minutes flat.'

Mallory nodded slowly.

'The *Sybaris*? I think I heard—'

'An eight-inch cruiser we sent up there about four months ago to try conclusions with the Hun. Just a formality, a routine exercise, we thought. The *Sybaris* was blasted out of the water. There were seventeen survivors.'

'Good God!' Mallory was shocked. 'I didn't know—'

'Two months ago we mounted a large-scale amphibious attack on Navarone.' Jensen hadn't even heard the interruption. 'Commandos, Royal Marine Commandos and Jellicoe's Special Boat Service. Less than an even chance, we knew – Navarone's practically solid cliff all the way round. But then these were very special men, probably the finest assault troops in the world today.' Jensen paused for almost a minute, then went on very quietly. 'They were cut to ribbons. They were massacred almost to a man.

'Finally, twice in the past ten days – we've seen this attack on Kheros coming for a long time now – we sent in parachute saboteurs: Special Boat Service men.' He shrugged his shoulders helplessly. 'They just vanished.'

'Just like that?'

'Just like that. And then tonight – the last desperate fling of the gambler and what have you.' Jensen laughed, briefly and without humour. 'That interrogation hut – I kept pretty quiet in there tonight, I tell you. I was the 'joker' that Torrance and his boys wanted to heave out over Navarone. I don't blame them. But I had to do it, I just had to do it. I knew it was hopeless – but it had to be done.'

The big Humber was beginning to slow down now, running silently between the tumble-down shacks and hovels that line the Western approach to Alexandria. The sky ahead was already beginning to streak in the first tenuous greys of the false dawn.

'I don't think I'd be much good with a parachute,' Mallory said doubtfully. 'In fact, quite frankly, I've never ever *seen* a parachute.'

'Don't worry,' Jensen said briefly. 'You won't have to use one. You're going into Navarone the hard way.'

Mallory waited for more, but Jensen had fallen silent, intent on avoiding the large potholes that were beginning to pock the roadway. After a time Mallory asked:

'Why me, Captain Jensen?'

Jensen's smile was barely visible in the greying darkness. He swerved violently to avoid a gaping hole and straightened up again.

'Scared?'

'Certainly I'm scared. No offence intended, sir, but the way you talk you'd scare anyone. . . . But that wasn't what I meant.'

'I know it wasn't. Just my twisted humour. . . . Why you? Special qualifications, laddie, just like I told you. You speak Greek like a Greek. You speak German like a German. Skilled saboteur, first-class organiser and eighteen unscathed months in the White Mountains of Crete – a convincing demonstration of your ability to survive in enemy-held territory.' Jensen chuckled. 'You'd be surprised to know just how complete a dossier I have on you!'

'No, I wouldn't.' Mallory spoke with some feeling. 'And,' he added, 'I know of at least three other officers with the same qualifications.'

'There are others,' Jensen agreed. 'But there are no other Keith Mallorys. Keith Mallory,' Jensen repeated rhetorically. 'Who hadn't heard of Keith Mallory in the palmy, balmy days before the war? The finest mountaineer, the greatest rock climber New Zealand has ever produced – and by that, of course, New Zealanders mean the world. The human fly, the climber of the unclimbable, the scaler of vertical cliffs and impossible precipices. The entire south coast of Navarone,' said Jensen cheerfully, 'consists of one vast, impossible precipice. Nary a hand or foot-hold in sight.'

'I see,' Mallory murmured. 'I see indeed. "Into Navarone the hard way." That was what you said.'

'That was,' Jensen acknowledged. 'You and your gang – just four others. Mallory's Merry Mountaineers. Hand-picked. Every man a specialist. You meet them all tomorrow – this afternoon, rather.'

They travelled in silence for the next ten minutes, turned up right from the dock area, jounced their uncomfortable way over the massive cobbles of the Rue Soeurs, slewed round into Mohammed Ali square, passed in front of the Bourse and turned right down the Sherif Pasha.

Mallory looked at the man behind the wheel. He could see his face quite clearly now in the gathering light.

'Where to, sir?'

'To see the only man in the Middle East who can give you any help now. Monsieur Eugene Vlachos of Navarone.'

'You are a brave man, Captain Mallory.' Nervously Eugene Vlachos twisted the long, pointed ends of his black moustache. 'A brave man and a foolish one, I would say – but I suppose we cannot call a man a fool when he only obeys his orders.' His eyes left the large drawing lying before him on the table and sought Jensen's impassive face.

'Is there no other way, Captain?' he pleaded.

Jensen shook his head slowly:

'There are. We've tried them all, sir. They all failed. This is the last.'

'He must go, then?'

'There are over a thousand men on Kheros, sir.'

Vlachos bowed his head in silent acceptance, then smiled faintly at Mallory.

'He calls me "sir." Me, a poor Greek hotel-keeper and Captain Jensen of the Royal Navy calls me "sir." It make an old man feel good.' He stopped, gazed off vacantly into space, the faded eyes and tired, lined face soft with memory. 'An old man, Captain Mallory, an old man now, a poor man and a sad one. But I wasn't always, not always. Once I was just middle-aged, and rich and well content. Once I owned a lovely land, a hundred square miles of the most beautiful country God ever sent to delight the eyes of His creatures here below, and how well I loved that land!' He laughed self-consciously and ran a hand through his thick, greying hair. 'Ah, well, as you people say, I suppose it's all in the eye of the beholder. "A lovely land," I say. "That blasted rock," as Captain Jensen has been heard to describe it out of my hearing.' He smiled at Jensen's sudden discomfiture. 'But we both give it the same name – Navarone.'

Startled, Mallory looked at Jensen. Jensen nodded.

'The Vlachos family has owned Navarone for generations. We had to remove Monsieur Vlachos in a great hurry eighteen months ago. The Germans didn't care over-much for his kind of collaboration.'

'It was – how do you say – touch and go.' Vlachos nodded. 'They had reserved three very special places for my two sons and myself in the dungeons in Navarone. . . . But enough of the Vlachos family. I just wanted you to know, young man, that I spent forty years on Navarone and almost four days' – he gestured to the table – 'on that map. My information and that map you can trust absolutely. Many things will have changed, of course, but some things never change. The mountains, the bays, the passes, the caves, the roads, the houses and, above all, the fortress itself – these have remained unchanged for centuries, Captain Mallory.'

'I understand, sir.' Mallory folded the map carefully, stowed it away in his tunic. 'With this, there's always a chance. Thank you very much.'

'It is little enough, God knows.' Vlachos's fingers drummed on the table for a moment, then he looked up at Mallory. 'Captain Jensen informs me that most of you speak Greek fluently, that you will be dressed as Greek peasants and will carry forged papers. That is well. You will be – what is the word? – self-contained, will operate on your own.' He paused, then went on very earnestly.

'Please do not try to enlist the help of the people of Navarone. At all costs you must avoid that. The Germans are ruthless. I know. If a man helps you and is found out, they will destroy not only that man but his entire village – men, women and children. It has happened before. It will happen again.'

'It happened in Crete,' Mallory agreed quietly. 'I've seen it for myself.'

'Exactly.' Vlachos nodded. 'And the people of Navarone have neither the skill nor the experience for successful guerrilla operations. They have not had the chance – German surveillance has been especially severe in our island.'

'I promise you, sir—' Mallory began.

Vlachos held up his hand.

'Just a moment. If your need is desperate, really desperate, there are two men to whom you may turn. Under the first plane tree in the village square of Margaritha – at the mouth of the valley about three miles south of the fortress – you will find a man called Louki. He has been the steward of our family for many years. Louki has been of help to the British before – Captain Jensen will confirm that – and you can trust him with your life. He has a friend, Panayis: he, too, has been useful in the past.'

'Thank you, sir. I'll remember. Louki and Panayis and Margaritha – the first plane tree in the square.'

'And you will refuse all other aid, Captain?' Vlachos asked anxiously. 'Louki and Panayis – only these two,' he pleaded.

'You have my word, sir. Besides, the fewer the safer for us as well as your people.' Mallory was surprised at the old man's intensity.

'I hope so, I hope so.' Vlachos sighed heavily.

Mallory stood up, stretched out his hand to take his leave.

'You're worrying about nothing, sir. They'll never see us,' he promised confidently. 'Nobody will see us – and we'll see nobody. We're after only one thing – the guns.'

'Ay, the guns – those terrible guns.' Vlachos shook his head. 'But just suppose—'

'Please. It will be all right,' Mallory insisted quietly. 'We will bring harm to none – and least of all to your islanders.'

'God go with you tonight,' the old man whispered. God go with you tonight. I only wish I could go too.'

——— 2 ———

SUNDAY NIGHT

1900–0200

'Coffee, sir?'

Mallory stirred and groaned and fought his way up from the depths of exhausted sleep. Painfully he eased himself back on the metal-framed bucket-seat, wondering peevishly when the Air Force was going to get round to upholstering these fiendish contraptions. Then he was fully awake, tired, heavy eyes automatically focusing on the luminous dial of his wrist-watch. Seven o'clock. Just seven o'clock – he'd been asleep barely a couple of hours. Why hadn't they let him sleep on?

'Coffee, sir?' The young air-gunner was still standing patiently by his side, the inverted lid of an ammunition box serving as a tray for the cups he was carrying.

'Sorry, boy, sorry.' Mallory struggled upright in his seat, reached up for a cup of the steaming liquid, sniffed it appreciatively. 'Thank you. You know, this smells just like real coffee.'

'It is, sir.' The young gunner smiled proudly. 'We have a percolator in the galley.'

'He has a percolator in the galley.' Mallory shook his head in disbelief. 'Ye gods, the rigours of war in the Royal Air Force!' He leaned back, sipped the coffee luxuriously and sighed in contentment. Next moment he was on his feet, the hot coffee splashing unheeded on his bare knees as he stared out the window beside him. He looked at the gunner, gestured in disbelief at the mountainous landscape unrolling darkly beneath them.

'What the hell goes on here? We're not due till two hours after dark – and it's barely gone sunset! Has the pilot—?'

'That's Cyprus, sir.' The gunner grinned. 'You can just see Mount Olympus on the horizon. Nearly always, going to Castelrosso, we fly a big dog-leg over Cyprus. It's to escape observation, sir; and it takes us well clear of Rhodes.'

'To escape observation, he says!' The heavy transatlantic drawl came from the bucket-seat diagonally across the passage:

the speaker was lying collapsed – there was no other word for it
– in his seat, the bony knees topping the level of one chin by
several inches. 'My Gawd! To escape observation!' he repeated
in awed wonder. 'Dog-legs over Cyprus. Twenty miles out from
Alex by launch so that nobody ashore can see us takin' off by
plane. And then what?' He raised himself painfully in his seat,
eased an eyebrow over the bottom of the window, then fell back
again, visibly exhausted by the effort. 'And then what? Then
they pack us into an old crate that's painted the whitest white
you ever saw guaranteed visible to a blind man at a hundred
miles – 'specially now that it's gettin' dark.'

'It keeps the heat out,' the young gunner said defensively.

'The heat doesn't worry me, son.' The drawl was tireder, more
lugubrious than ever. 'I like the heat. What I don't like are
them nasty cannon shells and bullets that can ventilate a man
in all the wrong places.' He slid his spine another impossible
inch down the seat, closed his eyes wearily and seemed asleep
in a moment.

The young gunner shook his head admiringly and smiled at
Mallory.

'Worried to hell, isn't he, sir?'

Mallory laughed and watched the boy disappear for'ard into
the control cabin. He sipped his coffee slowly, looked again at
the sleeping figure across the passage. The blissful unconcern
was magnificent: Corporal Dusty Miller of the United States,
and more recently of the Long Range Desert Force, would be a
good man to have around.

He looked round at the others and nodded to himself in
satisfaction. They would all be good men to have around.
Eighteen months in Crete had developed in him an unerring
sense for assessing a man's capacity for survival in the peculiar
kind of irregular warfare in which he himself had been so long
engaged. Off-hand he'd have taken long odds on the capacity of
these four to survive. In the matter of picking an outstanding
team Captain Jensen, he reckoned, had done him proud. He
didn't know them all yet – not personally. But he was intimately
acquainted with the exhaustive dossier that Jensen held on each
one of them. These were reassuring, to say the least.

Or was there perhaps a slight question mark against Stevens?
Mallory wondered, looking across the passage at the fair-haired,
boyish figure gazing out eagerly beneath the gleaming white
wing of the Sunderland. Lieutenant Andy Stevens, RNVR, had
been chosen for this assignment for three reasons. He would

navigate the craft that was to take them to Navarone: he was a first-class Alpinist, with several outstanding climbs to his record: and, the product of the classical side of a red-brick university, he was an almost fanatical philhellene, fluent in both Ancient and Modern Greek, and had spent his last two long vacations before the war as a tourist courier in Athens. But he was young, absurdly young, Mallory thought as he looked at him, and youth could be dangerous. Too often, in that island guerrilla warfare, it had been fatal. The enthusiasm, the fire, the zeal of youth was not enough: rather, it was too much, a positive handicap. This was not a war of bugle calls and roaring engines and magnificent defiance in the clamour of battle: this was a war of patience and endurance and stability, of cunning and craft and stealth, and these were not commonly the attributes of youth. . . . But he looked as if he might learn fast.

Mallory stole another glance at Miller. Dusty Miller, he decided, had learnt it all a long, long time ago. Dusty Miller on a white charger, the bugle to his lips – no, his mind just refused to encompass the incongruity of it. He just didn't look like Sir Launcelot. He just looked as if he had been around for a long, long time and had no illusions left.

Corporal Miller had, in fact, been around for exactly forty years. By birth a Californian, by descent three parts Irish and one part Central European, he had lived and fought and adventured more in the previous quarter of a century than most men would in a dozen lifetimes. Silver-miner in Nevada, tunneller in Canada and oil-fire shooter all over the globe, he had been in Saudi Arabia when Hitler attacked Poland. One of his more remote maternal ancestors, some time around the turn of the century, had lived in Warsaw, but that had been affront enough for Miller's Irish blood. He had taken the first available plane to Britain and lied his way into the Air Force, where, to his immense disgust, and because of his age, he was relegated to the rear turret of a Wellington.

His first operational flight had been his last. Within ten minutes of taking off from the Menidi airfied outside Athens on a January night in 1941, engine failure had brought them to an ignominious though well-cushioned end in a paddy field some miles north-west of the city. The rest of the winter he had spent seething with rage in a cook-house back in Menidi. At the beginning of April he resigned from the Air Force without telling anyone and was making his way north towards the fighting and the Albanian frontier when he met the Germans coming south. As Miller afterwards told it, he reached Nauplion two blocks ahead of the nearest panzer division, was evacuated by the transport *Slamat*, sunk, picked up by the destroyer *Wryneck*, sunk, and finally arrived in Alexandria in an ancient Greek caique, with nothing left him in the world but a fixed determination never again to venture in the air or on the sea. Some months later he was operating with a long-range striking force behind the enemy lines in Libya.

He was, Mallory mused, the complete antithesis to Lieutenant Stevens. Stevens, young, fresh, enthusiastic, correct and immaculately dressed, and Miller, dried-up, lean, stringy, immensely tough and with an almost pathological aversion to spit and polish. How well the nickname 'Dusty' suited him: there could hardly have been a greater contrast. Again, unlike Stevens, Miller had never climbed a mountain in his life and the only Greek words he knew were invariably omitted from the dictionaries. And both these facts were of no importance at all. Miller had been picked for one reason only. A genius with explosives, resourceful and cool, precise and deadly in action, he was regarded by Middle East Intelligence in Cairo as the finest saboteur in southern Europe.

Behind Miller sat Casey Brown. Short, dark and compact, Petty Officer Telegraphist Brown was a Clydesider, in peacetime an installation and testing engineer in a famous yacht-builder's yard on the Gareloch. The fact that he was a born and ready-made engine-room artificer had been so blindingly obvious that the Navy had missed it altogther and stuck him in the Communications Branch. Brown's ill luck was Mallory's good fortune. Brown would act as the engineer of the boat taking them to Navarone and would maintain radio contact with base. He had also the further recommendation of being a first-class guerrilla fighter: a veteran of the Special Boat Service, he held the DCM and DSM for his exploits in the Ægan and off the coast of Libya.

The fifth and last member of the part sat directly behind Mallory. Mallory did not have to turn round to look at him. He already knew him, knew him better than he knew anyone else in the world, better even than he knew his own mother. Andrea, who had been his lieutenant for all these eighteen interminable months in Crete. Andrea of the vast bulk, the continual rumbling laughter and tragic past, with whom he had eaten, lived and slept in caves, rock-shelters and abandoned shepherds' huts while constanly harried by German patrols and aircraft – that Andrea had become his *alter ego,* his *doppelganger*: to look at Andrea was to look in a mirror to remind himself what he was like. . . . There was no question as to why Andrea had come along. He wasn't there primarily because he was a Greek himself, with an intimate knowledge of the islanders' language, thought and customs, nor even because of his perfect understanding with Mallory, although all these things helped. He was, instead, there exclusively for the protection and safety he afforded. Endlessly patient, quiet and deadly, tremendously fast in spite of his bulk, and with a feline stealth that exploded into berserker action, Andrea was the complete fighting machine. Andrea was their insurance policy against failure.

Mallory turned back to look out the window again, then nodded to himself in imperceptible satisfaction. Jensen probably couldn't have picked a better team if he'd scoured the whole Mediterranean theatre. It suddenly occurred to Mallory that Jensen probably had done just that. Miller and Brown had been recalled to Alexandria almost a month ago. It was almost as long since Stevens's relief had arrived aboard his cruiser in Malta. And if their battery-charging engine hadn't slipped down that ravine in the White Mountains, and if the sorely harassed runner from the nearest listening post hadn't taken a week to cover fifty miles of snowbound, enemy patrolled mountains and another five days to find them, he and Andrea would have been in Alexandria almost a fortnight earlier. Mallory's opinion of Jensen, already high, rose another notch. A far-seeing man who planned accordingly, Jensen must have had all his preparations for this made even before the first of the two abortive parachute landings on Navarone.

It was eight o'clock and almost totally dark inside the plane when Mallory rose and made his way for'ard to the control cabin. The captain, face wreathed in tobacco smoke, was drinking coffee: the co-pilot waved a languid hand at his approach and resumed a bored scanning of the scene ahead.

'Good evening.' Mallory smiled. 'Mind if I come in?'

'Welcome in my office any time,' the pilot assured him. 'No need to ask.'

'I only thought you might be busy. . . .' Mallory stopped and looked again at the scene of masterly inactivity. 'Just who is flying this plane?' he asked.

'George. The automatic pilot.' He waved a coffee-cup in the

direction of a black, squat box, its blurred outlines just visible in the near darkness. 'An industrious character, and makes a damn' sight fewer mistakes than that idle hound who's supposed to be on watch. . . . Anything on your mind, Captain?'

'Yes. What were your instructions for tonight?'

'Just to set you blokes down in Castelrosso when it was good and dark.' The pilot paused, then said frankly, 'I don't get it. A ship this size for only five men and a couple of hundred odd pounds of equipment. Especially to Castelrosso. Especially after dark. Last plane that came down here after dark just kept on going down. Underwater obstruction – dunno what it was. Two survivors.'

'I know. I heard. I'm sorry, but I'm under orders too. As for the rest, forget it – and I mean forget. Impress on your crew that they mustn't talk. They've never seen us.'

The pilot nodded glumly. 'We've all been threatened with court-martial already. You'd think there was a ruddy war on.'

'There is. . . . We'll be leaving a couple of cases behind. We're going ashore in different clothes. Somebody will be waiting for our old stuff when you get back.'

'Roger. And the best of luck, Captain. Official secrets, or no official secrets, I've got a hunch you're going to need it.'

'If we are, you can give us a good send-off.' Mallory grinned. 'Just set us down in one piece will you?'

'Ressure yourself, brother,' the pilot said firmly. 'Just set your mind at ease. Don't forget – I'm in this ruddy plane too.'

The clamour of the Sunderland's great engines was still echoing in their ears when the stubby little motor-boat chugged softly out of the darkness and nosed alongside the gleaming hull of the flying-boat. There was no time lost, there were no words spoken; within a minute the five men and all their gear had been embarked; within another the little boat was rubbing to a stop against the rough stone Navy jetty of Castelrosso. Two ropes were spinning up into the darkness, were caught and quickly secured by practised hands. Amidships, the rust-scaled iron ladder, recessed deep into the stone, stretched up into the star-dusted darkness above: as Mallory reached the top, a figure stepped forward out of the gloom.

'Captain Mallory?'

'Yes.'

'Captain Briggs, Army. Have your men wait here, will you? The colonel would like to see you.' The nasal voice peremptory

in its clipped affectation, was far from cordial. Mallory stirred
in slow anger, but said nothing. Briggs sounded like a man who
might like his bed or his gin, and maybe their late visitation was
keeping him from either or both. War was hell.

They were back in ten minutes, a third figure following behind them. Mallory peered at the three men standing on the
edge of the jetty, identified them, then peered around again.

'Where's Miller got to?' he asked.

'Here, boss, here.' Miller groaned, eased his back off a big,
wooden bollard, climbed wearily to his feet. 'Just restin', boss.
Recuperatin', as you might say, from the nerve-rackin' rigours
of the trip.'

'When you're all *quite* ready,' Briggs said acidly, 'Matthews
here will take you to your quarters. You are to remain on call
for the Captain, Matthews. Colonel's orders.' Briggs's tone left
no doubt that he thought the colonel's orders a piece of arrant
nonsense. 'And don't forget, Captain – two hours, the Colonel
said.'

'I know, I know,' Mallory said wearily. 'I was there when he
said it. It was to me he was talking. Remember? All right, boys,
if you're ready.'

'Our gear, sir?' Stevens ventured.

'Just leave it there. Right, Matthews, lead the way, will you?'

Matthews led the way along the jetty and up interminable
flights of steep, worn steps, the others followed in Indian file,
rubbed soles noiseless on the stone. He turned sharply right at
the top, went down a narrow, winding alley, into a passage,
climbed a flight of creaking, wooden stairs, opened the first door
in the corridor above.

'Here you are, sir. I'll just wait in the corridor outside.'

'Better wait downstairs,' Mallory advised. 'No offence, Matthews, but the less you know of this the better.'

He followed the others into the room, closing the door behind
him. It was a small, bleak room, heavily curtained. A table and
half a dozen chairs took up most of the space. Over in the far
corner the springs of the single bed creaked as Corporal Miller
stretched himself out luxuriously, hands clasped behind his
head.

'Gee!' he murmured admiringly. 'A hotel room. Just like
home. Kinda bare, though.' A thought occurred to him. 'Where
are all you other guys gonna sleep?'

'We aren't,' Mallory said briefly. 'Neither are you. We're pulling out in less than two hours.' Miller groaned. 'Come on, soldier,' Mallory went on relentlessly. 'On your feet.'

Miller groaned again, swung his legs over the edge of the bed and looked curiously at Andrea. The big Greek was quartering the room methodically, pulling out lockers, turning pictures, peering behind curtains and under the bed.

'What's he doin'?' Miller asked. 'Lookin' for dust?'

'Testing for listening devices,' Mallory said curtly. 'One of the reasons why Andrea and I have lasted so long.' He dug into the inside pocket of his tunic, a dark naval battledress with neither badge nor insignia, pulled out a chart and the map Vlachos had given him, unfolded and spread them out. 'Round the table, all of you. I know you've been bursting with curiosity for the past couple of weeks, asking yourselves a hundred questions. Well, here are all the answers. I hope you like them. . . . Let me introduce you to the island of Navarone.'

Mallory's watch showed exactly eleven o'clock when he finally sat back, folded away the map and chart. He looked quizzically at the four thoughtful faces round the table.

'Well, gentlemen, there you have it. A lovely set-up, isn't it?' He smiled wryly. 'If this was a film, my next line should be, "Any questions, men?" But we'll dispense with that because I just wouldn't have any of the answers. You all know as much as I do.'

'A quarter of a mile of sheer cliff, four hundred feet high, and he calls it the only break in the defences.' Miller, his head bent moodily over his tobacco tin, rolled a long, thin cigarette with one expert hand. 'This is just crazy, boss. Me, I can't even climb a bloody ladder without falling off.' He puffed strong, acrid clouds of smoke into the air. 'Suicidal. That's the word I was lookin' for. Suicidal. One buck gets a thousand we never get within five miles of them gawddamned guns!'

'One in a thousand, eh?' Mallory looked at him for a long time without speaking. 'Tell me, Miller, what odds are you offering on the boys on Kheros?'

'Yeah.' Miller nodded heavily. 'Yeah, the boys on Kheros. I'd forgotten about them. I just keep thinkin' about me and that damned cliff.' He looked hopefully across the table at the vast bulk of Andrea. 'Or maybe Andrea there would carry me up. He's big enough, anyway.'

Andrea made no reply. His eyes were half-closed, his thoughts could have been a thousand miles away.

'We'll tie you hand and foot and haul you up on the end of a rope,' Stevens said unkindly. 'We'll try to pick a fairly sound rope,' he added carelessly. The words, the tone, were jocular enough, but the worry on his face belied them. Mallory apart, only Stevens appreciated the almost insuperable technical difficulties of climbing a sheer, unknown cliff in the darkness. He looked at Mallory questioningly. 'Going up alone, sir or—'

'Excuse me, please.' Andrea suddenly sat forward, his deep rumble of a voice rapid in the clear, idiomatic English he had learnt during his long association with Mallory. He was scribbling quickly on a piece of paper. 'I have a plan for climbing this cliff. Here is a diagram. Does the Captain think this is possible?'

He passed the paper across to Mallory. Mallory looked at it, checked, recovered, all in one instant. There was no diagram on it. There were only two large, printed words: 'Keep talking.'

'I see,' Mallory said thoughtfully. 'Very good indeed, Andrea. This has distinct possibilities.' He reversed the paper, held it up before him so that they could all see the words. Andrea had already risen to his feet, was padding cat-footed towards the door. 'Ingenious, isn't it, Corporal Miller,' he went on conversationally. 'Might solve quite a lot of our difficulties.'

'Yeah.' The expression on Miller's face hadn't altered a fraction, the eyes were still half-closed against the smoke drifting up from the cigarette dangling between his lips. 'Reckon that might solve the problem, Andrea – and get me up in one piece, too.' He laughed easily, concentrated on screwing a curiously-shaped cylinder on to the barrel of an automatic that had magically appeared in his left hand. 'But I don't quite get that funny line and the dot at—'

It was all over in two seconds – literally. With a deceptive ease and nonchalance Andrea opened the door with one hand, reached out with the other, plucked a wildly-struggling figure through the gap, set him on the ground again and closed the door, all in one concerted movement. It had been as soundless as it had been swift. For a second the eavesdropper, a hatched-faced, swarthy Levantine in badly-fitting white shirt and blue trousers, stood there in shocked immobility, blinking rapidly in the unaccustomed light. Then his hand dived in under his shirt.

'Look out!' Miller's voice was sharp, the automatic lining up as Mallory's hand closed over his.

'Watch!' Mallory said softly.

The men at the table caught only a flicker of blued steel as the knife arm jerked convulsively back and plunged down with vicious speed. And then, incredibly, hand and knife were stopped dead in mid-air, the gleaming point only two inches from Andrea's chest. There was a sudden scream of agony, the ominous cracking of wrist bones as the giant Greek tightened his grip, and then Andrea had the blade between finger and thumb, had removed the knife with the tender, reproving care of a parent saving a well-loved but irresponsible child from himself. Then the knife was reversed, the point was at the Levantine's throat and Andrea was smiling down pleasantly into the dark and terror-stricken eyes.

Miller let out a long breath, half-sigh, half-whistle.

'Well, now,' he murmured. 'I guess mebbe Andrea has done that sort of thing before?'

'I guess maybe he has,' Mallory mimicked. 'Let's have a closer look at exhibit A, Andrea.'

Andrea brought his prisoner close up to the table, well within the circle of light. He stood there sullenly before them, a thin, ferret-faced man, black eyes dulled in pain and fear, left hand cradling his crushed wrist.

'How long do you reckon this fellow's been outside, Andrea?' Mallory asked.

Andrea ran a massive hand through his thick, dark, curling hair, heavily streaked with grey above the temples.

'I cannot be sure, Captain. I imagined I heard a noise – a kind of shuffle – about ten minutes ago, but I thought my ears were playing tricks. Then I heard the same sound a minute ago. So I am afraid—'

'Ten minutes, eh?' Mallory nodded thoughtfully, then looked at the prisoner. 'What's your name?' he asked sharply. 'What are you doing here?'

There was no reply. There were only the sullen eyes, the sullen silence – a silence that gave way to a sudden yelp of pain as Andrea cuffed the side of his head.

'The Captain is asking you a question,' Andrea said reproachfully. He cuffed him again, harder this time. 'Answer the Captain.'

The stranger broke into rapid, excitable speech, gesticulating wildly with both hands. The words were quite unintelligible. Andrea sighed, shut off the torrent by the simple expedient of almost encircling the scrawny throat with his left hand.

Mallory looked questioningly at Andrea. The giant shook his head.

'Kurdistan or Armenian, Captain, I think. But I don't understand it.'

'I certainly don't,' Mallory admitted. 'Do you speak English?' he asked suddenly.

Black, hate-filled eyes glared back at him in silence. Andrea cuffed him again.

'Do you speak English?' Mallory repeated relentlessly.

'Eenglish? Eenglish?' Shoulders and upturned palms lifted in the age-old gesture of incomprehension. 'Ka Eenglish!'

'He says he don't speak English,' Miller drawled.

'Maybe he doesn't and maybe he does,' Mallory said evenly. 'All we know is that he *has* been listening and that we can't take any chances. There are far too many lives at stake.' His voice suddenly hardened, the eyes were grim and pitiless. 'Andrea!'

'Captain?'

'You have the knife. Make it clean and quick. Between the shoulder blades!'

Stevens cried out in horror, sent his chair crashing back as he leapt to his feet.

'Good God, sir, you can't—'

He broke off and stared in amazement at the sight of the prisoner catapulting himself bodily across the room to crash into a distant corner, one arm up-curved in rigid defence, stark, unreasoning panic limned in every feature of his face. Slowly Stevens looked away, saw the triumphant grin on Andrea's face, the dawning comprehension in Brown's and Miller's. Suddenly he felt a complete fool. Characteristically, Miller was the first to speak.

'Waal, waal, whaddya know! Mebbe he *does* speaka da Eenglish after all.'

'Maybe he does,' Mallory admitted. 'A man doesn't spend ten minutes with his ear glued to a keyhole if he doesn't understand a word that's being said. . . . Give Matthews a call, will you, Brown?'

The sentry appeared in the doorway a few seconds later.

'Get Captain Briggs here, will you, Matthews?' he asked. 'At once, please.'

The soldier hesitated.

'Captain Briggs has gone to bed, sir. He left strict orders that he wasn't to be disturbed.'

'My heart bleeds for Captain Briggs and his broken slumbers,' Mallory said acidly. 'He's had more sleep in a day than I've had in the past week.' He glanced at his watch and the heavy brows

came down in a straight line over the tired, brown eyes. 'We've
no time to waste. Get him here at once. Understand? At once!'

Matthews saluted and hurried away. Miller cleared his throat
and clucked his tongue sadly.

'These hotels are all the same. The goin's-on – you'd never
believe your eyes. Remember once I was at a convention in
Cincinnati—'

Mallory shook his head wearily.

'You have a fixation about hotels, Corporal. This is a military
establishment and these are army officers' billets.'

Miller made to speak but changed his mind. The American
was a shrewd judge of people. There were those who could be
ribbed and those who could not be ribbed. An almost hopeless
mission, Miller was quietly aware, and as vital as it was, in his
opinion, suicidal; but he was beginning to understand why
they'd picked this tough, sunburnt New Zealander to lead it.

They sat in silence for the next five minutes, then looked up
as the door opened. Captain Briggs was hatless and wore a white
silk muffler round his throat in place of the usual collar and tie.
The white contrasted oddly with the puffed red of the heavy
neck and face above. These had been red enough when Mallory
had first seen them in the colonel's office – high blood pressure
and even higher living. Mallory had supposed: the extra deeper
shades of red and purple now present probably sprang from a
misplaced sense of righteous indignation. A glance at the chol-
eric eyes, gleaming light-blue prawns afloat in a sea of vermilion,
was quite enough to confirm the obvious.

'I think this is a bit much, Captain Mallory!' The voice was
high pitched in anger, more nasal than ever. 'I'm not the duty
errand-boy, you know. I've had a damned hard day and—'

'Save it for your biography,' Mallory said curtly, 'and take a
gander at this character in the corner.'

Briggs's face turned an even deeper hue. He stepped into the
room, fists balled in anger, then stopped in his tracks as his eye
hit on the crumpled, dishevelled figure still crouched in the corner of the room.

'Good God!' he ejaculated. 'Nicolai!'

'You know him.' It was a statement, not a question.

'Of course I know him!' Briggs snorted. 'Everybody knows
him. Nicolai. Our laundry-boy.'

'Your laundry-boy! Do his duties entail snooping around the
corridors at night, listening at keyholes?'

'What do you mean?'

'What I say.' Mallory was very patient. 'We caught him listening outside the door.'

'Nicolai? I don't believe it-'

'Watch it, mister,' Miller growled. 'Careful who you call a liar. We all saw him.'

Briggs stared in fascination at the black muzzle of the automatic waving negligently in his direction, gulped, looked hastily away.

'Well, what if you did?' He forced a smile. 'Nicolai can't speak a word of English.'

'Maybe not,' Mallory agreed dryly. 'But he understands it well enough.' He raised his hand. 'I've no desire to argue all night and I certainly haven't the time. Will you please have this man placed under arrest, kept in solitary confinement and incommunicado for the next week at least. It's vital. Whether he's a spy or just too damned nosy, he knows far too much. After that, do what you like. My advice is to kick him out of Castelrosso.'

'*Your advice*, indeed!' Briggs's colour returned, and with it his courage. 'Who the hell are you to give me advice or to give me orders, Captain Mallory?' There was a heavy emphasis on the word 'captain.'

'Then I'm asking it as a favour,' Mallory pleaded wearily. 'I can't explain, but it's terribly important. There are hundreds of lives—'

'Hundreds of lives!' Briggs sneered. 'Melodramatic stuff and nonsense!' He smiled unpleasantly. 'I suggest you keep that for *your* cloak-and-dagger biography, Captain Mallory.'

Mallory rose, walked round the table, stopped a foot away from Briggs. The brown eyes were still and very cold.

'I could go and see your colonel, I suppose. But I'm tired of arguing. You'll do exactly as I say or I'll go straight to Naval HQ and get on the radio-telephone to Cairo. And if I do,' Mallory went on, 'I swear to you that you'll be on the next ship home to England – and on the troop-deck, at that.'

His last words seem to echo in the little room for an interminable time: the stillness was intense. And then, as suddenly as it had arisen, the tension was gone and Briggs's face, a now curiously mottled white and red, was slack and sullen in defeat.

'All right, all right,' he said. 'No need for all these damned stupid threats – not if it means all that much to you.' The attempt to bluster, to patch up the shredded rags of his dignity, was pathetic in its transparency. 'Matthews – call out the guard.'

The torpedo-boat, great aero engines throttled back half speed, pitched and lifted, pitched and lifted with monotonous regularity as it thrust its way into the long, gentle swell from the WNW. For the hundredth time that night Mallory looked at his watch.

'Running behind time, sir?' Stevens suggested.

Mallory nodded.

'We should have stepped straight into this thing from the Sunderland – there was a hold-up.'

Brown grunted. 'Engine trouble, for a fiver.' The Clydeside accent was very heavy.

'Yes, that's right.' Mallory looked up, surprised. 'How did you know?'

'Always the same with these blasted MTB engines,' Brown growled. 'Temperamental as a film star.'

There was silence for a time in the tiny blacked-out cabin, a silence broken only by the occasional clink of a glass. The Navy was living up to its traditional hospitality.

'If we're late,' Miller observed at last, 'why doesn't the skipper open her up? They tell me these crates can do forty to fifty knots.'

'You look green enough already,' Stevens said tactlessly. 'Obviously, you've never been in an MTB full out in a heavy sea.'

Miller fell silent a moment. Clearly, he was trying to take his mind off his internal troubles. 'Captain?'

'Yes, what is it?' Mallory answered sleepily. He was stretched full length on a narrow settee, an almost empty glass in his fingers.

'None of my business, I know, boss, but – would you have carried out that threat you made to Captain Briggs?'

Mallory laughed.

'It *is* none of your business, but – well, no, Corporal, I wouldn't. I wouldn't because I couldn't. I haven't all that much authority invested in me – and I didn't even know whether there was a radio-telephone in Castelrosso.'

'Yeah. Yeah, do you know, I kinda suspected that.' Corporal Miller rubbed a stubbled chin. 'If he'd called your bluff, what would you have done, boss?'

'I'd have shot Nicolai,' Mallory said quietly. 'If the colonel had failed me. I'd have had no choice left.'

'I knew that too. I really believe you would. For the first time I'm beginning to believe we've got a chance. . . . But I kinda wish you *had* shot him – *and* little Lord Fauntleroy. I didn't like the expression on old Briggs's face when you went out that door. Mean wasn't the word. He coulda killed you then. You trampled right over his pride, boss – and to a phony like that nothin' else in the world matters.'

Mallory made no reply. He was already sound asleep, his empty glass fallen from his hand. Not even the banshee clamour of the great engines opening full out as they entered the sheltered calm of the Rhodes channel could plumb his bottomless abyss of sleep.

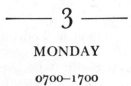

3

MONDAY

0700–1700

'My dear fellow, you make me feel dreadfully embarrassed.' Moodily the officer switched his ivory-handled flyswat against an immaculately trousered leg, pointed a contemptuous but gleaming toe-cap at the ancient caique, broadbeamed and two-masted, moored stern on to the even older and more dilapidated wooden pier on which they were standing. 'I am positively ashamed. The clients of Rutledge and Company, I assure you, are accustomed only to the best.'

Mallory smothered a smile. Major Rutledge of the Buffs, Eton and Sandhurst as to intonation, millimetrically tooth-brushed as to moustache, Savile Row as to the quite dazzling sartorial perfection of his khaki drill, was so magnificently out of place in the wild beauty of the rocky, tree-lined bluffs of that winding creek that his presence there seemed inevitable. Such was the major's casual assurance, so dominating his majestic unconcern, that it was the creek, if anything, that seemed slightly out of place.

'It *does* look as if it had seen better days,' Mallory admitted. 'Nevertheless, sir, it's exactly what we want.'

'Can't understand it, I really can't understand it.' With an irritable but well-timed swipe the major brought down a harmless passing fly. 'I've been providing chaps with everything during the past eight or nine months – caiques, launches, yachts, fishing boats, everything – but no one has ever yet specified the oldest, most dilapidated derelict I could lay hands on. Quite a job laying hands on it, too, I tell you.' A pained expression crossed his face. 'The chaps know I don't usually deal in this line of stuff.'

'What chaps?' Mallory asked curiously.

'Oh, up the islands, you know.' Rutledge gestured vaguely to the north and west.

'But – but those are enemy held—'

'So's this one. Chap's got to have his HQ somewhere.' Rutledge explained patiently. Suddenly his expression brightened. 'I say, old boy, I know just the thing for you. A boat to escape observation and investigation – that was what Cairo insisted I get. How about a German E-boat, absolutely perfect condition, one careful owner. Could get ten thou. for her at home. Thirty-six hours. Pal of mine over in Bodrum—'

'Bodrum?' Mallory questioned. 'Bodrum? But – but that's in Turkey, isn't it?'

'Turkey? Well, yes, actually, I believe it is,' Rutledge admitted. 'Chap has to get his supplies from somewhere, you know,' he added defensively.

'Thanks all the same' – Mallory smiled – 'but this is exactly what we want. We can't wait, anyway.'

'On your own heads be it!' Rutledge threw up his hands in admission of defeat. 'I'll have a couple of my men shove your stuff aboard.'

'I'd rather we did it ourselves, sir. It's – well, it's a very special cargo.'

'Right you are,' the major acknowledged. 'No questions Rutledge, they call me. Leaving soon?'

Mallory looked at his watch.

'Half an hour, sir.'

'Bacon, eggs and coffee in ten minutes?'

'Thanks very much.' Mallory grinned. 'That's one offer we'll be very glad to accept.'

He turned away, walked slowly down to the end of the pier. He breathed deeply, savouring the heady, herb-scented air of an Ægean dawn. The salt tang of the sea, the drowsily sweet perfume of honeysuckle, the more delicate, sharper fragrance of mint all subtly merged into an intoxicating whole, indefinable, unforgettable. On either side, the steep slopes, still brilliantly green with pine and walnut and holly, stretched far up to the moorland pastures above, and from these, faintly borne on the perfumed breeze, came the distant, melodic tinkling of goats' bells, a haunting, a nostalgic music, true symbol of the leisured peace the Ægean no longer knew.

Unconsciously almost, Mallory shook his head and walked more quickly to the end of the pier. The others were still sitting where the torpedo boat had landed them just before dawn. Miller, inevitably, was stretched his full length, hat tilted against the golden, level rays of the rising sun.

'Sorry to disturb you and all that, but we're leaving in half an hour; breakfast in ten minutes. Let's get the stuff aboard.' He turned to Brown. 'Maybe you'd like to have a look at the engine?' he suggested.

Brown heaved himself to his feet, looked down unenthusiastically at the weather-beaten, paint-peeled caique.

'Right you are, sir. But if the engine is on a par with this bloody wreck . . .' He shook his head in prophetic gloom and swung nimbly over the side of the pier.

Mallory and Andrea followed him, reaching up for the equipment as the other two passed it down. First they stowed away a sackful of old clothes, then the food, pressure stove and fuel, the heavy boots, spikes, mallets, rock axes and coils of wire-centred rope to be used for climbing, then, more carefully, the combined radio receiver and transmitter and the firing generator fitted with the old-fashioned plunge handle. Next came the guns – two Schmeissers, two Brens, a Mauser and a Colt – then a case containing a weird but carefully selected hodge-podge of torches, mirrors, two sets of identity papers and, incredibly, bottles of Hock, Moselle, *ouzo* and *retsima*.

Finally, and with exaggerated care, they stowed away for'ard in the forepeak two wooden boxes, one green in colour, medium sized and bound in brass, the other small and black. The green box held high explosive – TNT, amatol and a few standard sticks of dynamite, together with grenades, gun-cotton primers and canvas hosing; in one corner of the box was a bag of emery dust, another of ground glass, and a sealed jar of potassium, these last three items having been included against the possibility of Dusty Miller's finding an opportunity to exercise his unique talents as a saboteur. The black box held only detonators, percussion and electrical, detonators with fulminates so unstable that their exposed powder could be triggered off by the impact of a falling feather.

The last box had been stowed away when Casey Brown's head appeared above the engine hatch. Slowly he examined the mainmast reaching up above his head, as slowly turned for'ard to look at the foremast. His face carefully expressionless, he looked at Mallory.

'Have we got sails for these things, sir?'

'I suppose so. Why?'

'Because God only knows we're going to need them!' Brown said bitterly. 'Have a look at the engine-room, you said. This isn't an engine-room. It's a bloody scrap-yard. And the biggest, most rusted bit of scrap down there is attached to the propeller shaft. And what do you think it is? An old Kelvin two-cylinder job built more or less on my own doorstep – about thirty years ago.' Brown shook his head in despair, his face as stricken as only a Clydeside engineer's can be at the abuse of a beloved machine. 'And it's been falling to bits for years, sir. Place is littered with discarded bits and spares. I've seen junk heaps off the Gallowgate that were palaces compared to this.'

'Major Rutledge said it was running only yesterday,' Mallory said mildly. 'Anyway, come on ashore. Breakfast. Remind me we're to pick up a few heavy stones on the way back, will you?'

'Stones!' Miller looked at him in horror. 'Aboard that thing?'

Mallory nodded, smiling.

'But that gawddamned ship is sinkin' already!' Miller protested. 'What do you want stones for?'

'Wait and see.'

Three hours later Miller saw. The caique was chugging steadily north over a glassy, windless sea, less than a mile off the coast of Turkey, when he mournfully finished lashing his blue battle-dress into a tight ball and heaved it regretfully over the side. Weighted by the heavy stone he had carried aboard, it was gone from sight in a second.

Morosely he surveyed himself in the mirror propped up against the for'ard end of the wheelhouse. Apart from a deep violet sash wrapped round his lean middle and a fancifully embroidered waistcoat with its former glory mercifully faded, he was dressed entirely in black. Black lacing jackboots, black baggy trousers, black shirt and black jacket: even his sandy hair had been dyed to the same colour.

He shuddered and turned away.

'Thank Gawd the boys back home can't see me now!' he said feelingly. He looked critically at the others, dressed, with some minor variations, like himself. 'Waal, mebbe I ain't quite so bad after all. . . . Just what is all this quick-change business for, boss?'

'They tell me you've been behind the German lines twice, once as a peasant, once as a mechanic.' Mallory heaved his own ballasted uniform over the side. 'Well, now you see what the well-dressed Navaronian wears.'

'The double change, I meant. Once in the plane, and now.'

'Oh, I see. Army khaki and naval whites in Alex., blue battle-dress in Castelrosso and now Greek clothes? Could have been – almost certainly were – snoopers in Alex. or Castelrosso or Major Rutledge's island. And we've changed from lunch to plane to MTB to caique. Covering our tracks, Corporal. We just can't take any chances.'

Miller nodded, looked down at the clothes sack at his feet, wrinkled his brows in puzzlement, stooped and dragged out the white clothing that had caught his eye. He held up the long, voluminous clothes for inspection.

'To be used when passing through the local cemeteries, I suppose.' He was heavily ironic. 'Disguised as ghosts.'

'Camouflage,' Mallory explained succinctly. 'Snow-smocks.'

'What!'

'Snow. That white stuff. There are some pretty high mountains in Navarone, and we may have to take to them. So – snow-smocks.'

Miller looked stunned. Wordlessly he stretched his length on the deck, pillowed his head and closed his eyes. Mallory grinned at Andrea.

'Picture of a man getting his full quota of sunshine before battling with the Arctic wastes. . . . Not a bad idea. Maybe you should get some sleep, too. I'll keep watch for a couple of hours.'

For five hours the caique continued on its course parallel to the Turkish coast, slightly west of north and rarely more than two miles off-shore. Relaxed and warm in the still kindly November sun, Mallory sat wedged between the bulwarks of the blunt bows, his eyes ceaselessly quartering sky and horizon. Amidships, Andrea and Miller lay asleep. Casey Brown still defied all attempts to remove him from the engine-room. Occasionally – very occasionally – he came up for a breath of fresh air, but the intervals between his appearances steadily lengthened as he concentrated more and more on the aged Kelvin engine, regulating the erratic drip-fed lubrication, constantly adjusting the air intake: an engineer to his fingertips, he was unhappy about that engine: he was drowsy, too, and headachy – the narrow hatchway gave hardly any ventilation at all.

Alone in the wheelhouse – an unusual feature in so tiny a caique – Lieutenant Andy Stevens watched the Turkish coast slide slowly by. Like Mallory's, his eyes moved ceaselessly, but not with the same controlled wandering. They shifted from the coast to the chart: from the chart to the islands up ahead off the port bow, islands whose position and relation to each other changed continually and deceptively, islands gradually lifting from the sea and hardening in definition through the haze of blue refraction: from the islands to the old alcohol compass swinging almost imperceptibly on corroded gimbals, and from the compass back to the coast again. Occasionally, he peered up into the sky, or swung a quick glance through a 180-degree sweep of the horizon. But one thing his eyes avoided all the time. The chipped, fly-blown mirror had been hung up in the wheelhouse again, but it was as if his eyes and the mirror were of opposite magnetic poles: he could not bring himself to look at it.

His forearms ached. He had been spelled at the wheel twice, but still they ached, abominably: his lean, tanned hands were ivory-knuckled on the cracked wheel. Repeatedly, consciously, he tried to relax, to ease the tension that was bunching up the muscles of his arms; but always, as if possessed of independent volition, his hands tightened their grip again. There was a funny taste in his mouth, too, a sour and salty taste in a dry, parched mouth, and no matter how often he swallowed, or drank from the sun-warmed pitcher at his side, the taste and the dryness remained. He could no more exorcise them than he could that twisting, cramping ball that was knotting up his insides, just above the solar plexus, or the queer, uncontrollable tremor that gripped his right leg from time to time.

Lieutenant Andy Stevens was afraid. He had never been in action before, but it wasn't that. This wasn't the first time he had been afraid. He had been afraid all his life, ever since he could remember: and he could remember a long way back, even to his early prep-school days when his famous father, Sir Cedric Stevens, the most celebrated explorer and mountaineer of his time, had thrown him bodily into the swimming pool at home, telling him that this was the only way he could learn to swim. He could remember still how he had fought and spluttered his way to the side of the pool, panic-stricken and desperate, his nose and mouth blocked with water, the pit of his stomach knotted and constricted in that nameless, terrifying ache he was to come to know so well: how his father and two elder brothers, big and jovial and nerveless like Sir Cedric himself, had wiped the tears of mirth from their eyes and pushed him in again. . . .

His father and brothers. . . . It had been like that all through his schooldays. Together, the three of them had made his life thoroughly miserable. Tough, hearty, open-air types who worshipped at the shrine of athleticism and physical fitness, they could not understand how anyone could fail to revel in diving from a five-metre springboard or setting a hunter at a five-barred gate or climbing the crags of the Peak district or sailing a boat in a storm. All these things they had made him do and often he had failed in the doing, and neither his father nor his brothers could ever have understood how he had come to dread those violent sports in which they excelled, for they were not cruel men, nor even unkind, but simply stupid. And so to the simple physical fear he sometimes and naturally felt was added the fear of failure, the fear that he was bound to fail in whatever he had to do next, the fear of the inevitable mockery and ridicule: and because he had been a sensitive boy and feared the ridicule above all else, he had come to fear these things that provoked the ridicule. Finally, he had come to fear fear itself, and it was in a desperate attempt to overcome this double fear that he had devoted himself – this in his late teens – to crag and mountain climbing: in this he had ultimately become so proficent, developed such a reputation, that father and brothers had come to treat him with respect and as an equal, and the ridicule had ceased. But the fear had not ceased; rather it had grown by what it fed on, and often, on a particularly difficult climb, he had all but fallen to his death, powerless in the grip of sheer, unreasoning terror. But this terror he had always sought, successfully so far, to conceal. As now. He was trying to overcome, to conceal that fear now. He was afraid of failing – in what he wasn't quite sure – of not measuring up to expectation: he was afraid of being afraid: and he was desperately afraid, above all things, of being seen, of being known to be afraid. . . .

The startling, incredible blue of the Ægean; the soft, hazy silhouette of the Anatolian mountains against the washed-out cerulean of the sky; the heart-catching, magical blending of the blues and violets and purples and indigoes of the sun-soaked islands drifting lazily by, almost on the beam now; the iridescent rippling of the water fanned by the gentle, scent-laden breeze newly sprung from the south-east; the peaceful scene on deck, the reassuring, interminable thump-thump thump-thump of the old Kelvin engine. . . . All was peace and quiet and contentment and warmth and languor, and it seemed impossible that anyone could be afraid. The world and the war were very far away that afternoon.

Or perhaps, after all, the war wasn't so far away. There were occasional pin-pricks – and constant reminders. Twice a German Arado seaplane had circled curiously overhead, and a Savoia and Fiat, flying in company, had altered course, dipped to have a look at them and flown off, apparently satisfied: Italian planes, these, and probably based on Rhodes, they were almost certainly piloted by Germans who had rounded up their erstwhile Rhodian allies and put them in prison camps after the surrender of the Italian Government. In the morning they had passed within half a mile of a big German caique – it flew a German flag and bristled with mounted machine-guns and a two-pounder far up in the bows; and in the early afternoon a high-speed German launch had roared by so closely that their caique had rolled wickedly in the wash of its passing: Mallory and Andrea had shaken their fists and cursed loudly and fluently at the grinning sailors on deck. But there had been no attempts to molest or detain them: neither British nor German hesitated at any time to violate the neutrality of Turkish territorial waters, but by the strange quixotry of a tacit gentlemen's agreement hostilities between passing vessels and planes were almost unknown. Like the envoys of warring countries in a neutral capital, their behaviour ranged from the impeccably and frigidly polite to a very pointed unawareness of one another's existence.

These, then, were the pin-pricks – the visitation and by-goings, harmless though they were, of the ships and planes of the enemy. The other reminders that this was no peace but an illusion, an ephemeral and a frangible thing, were more permanent. Slowly the minute hands of their watches circled, and every tick took them nearer to that great wall of cliff, barely eight hours away, that had to be climbed somehow: and almost dead ahead now, and less than fifty miles distant, they could see the grim, jagged peaks of Navarone topping the shimmering horizon and reaching up darkly against the sapphired sky, desolate and remote and strangely threatening.

At half-past two in the afternoon the engine stopped. There had been no warning coughs or splutters or missed strokes. One moment the regular, reassuring thump-thump: the next, sudden, completely unexpected silence, oppressive and foreboding in its absoluteness.

Mallory was the first to reach the engine hatch.

'What's up, Brown?' His voice was sharp with anxiety. 'Engine broken down?'

'Not quite, sir.' Brown was still bent over the engine, his voice muffled. 'I shut it off just now.' He straightened his back, hoisted himself wearily through the hatchway, sat on deck with his feet dangling, sucking in great draughts of fresh air. Beneath the heavy tan his face was very pale.

Mallory looked at him closely.

'You look as if you had the fright of your life.'

'Not that.' Brown shook his head. 'For the past two-three hours I've been slowly poisoned down that ruddy hole. Only now I realize it.' He passed a hand across his brow and groaned. 'Top of my blinkin' head just about lifting off, sir. Carbon monoxide ain't a very healthy thing.'

'Exhaust leak?'

'Aye. But it's more than a leak now.' He pointed down at the engine. 'See that stand-pipe supporting that big iron ball above the engine – the water-cooler? That pipe's as thin as paper, must have been leaking above the bottom flange for hours. Blew out a bloody great hole a minute ago. Sparks, smoke and flames six inches long. Had to shut the damned thing off at once, sir.'

Mallory nodded in slow understanding.

'And now what? Can you repair it, Brown?'

'Not a chance, sir.' The shake of the head was very definite. 'Would have to be brazed or welded. But there's a spare down there among the scrap. Rusted to hell and about as shaky as the one that's on. . . . I'll have a go, sir.'

'I'll give him a hand,' Miller volunteered.

'Thanks, Corporal. How long, Brown, do you think?'

'Lord only knows, sir. Two hours, maybe four. Most of the nuts and bolts are locked solid with rust: have to shear or saw 'em – and then hunt for others.'

Mallory said nothing. He turned away heavily, brought up beside Stevens who had abandoned the wheelhouse and was now bent over the sail locker. He looked up questioningly as Mallory approached.

Mallory nodded. 'Just get them out and up. Maybe four hours, Brown says. Andrea and I will do our landlubbery best to help.'

Two hours later, with the engine still out of commission, they were well outside territorial waters, closing on a big island some eight miles away to the WNW. The wind, warm and oppressive now, had backed to a darkening and thundery east, and with only a lug and a jib – all the sails they had found – bent to the foremast, they could make no way at all into it. Mallory had decided to make for the island – the chances of being observed there were far less than in the open sea. Anxiously he looked at his watch then stared back moodily at the receding safety of the Turkish shore. Then he stiffened, peered closely at the dark line of sea, land and sky that lay to the east.

'Andrea! Do you see—'

'I see it, Captain.' Andrea was at his shoulder. 'Caique. Three miles. Coming straight towards us,' he added softly.

'Coming straight towards us.' Mallory acquiesced. 'Tell Miller and Brown. Have them come here.'

Mallory wasted no time when they were all assembled. 'We're going to be stopped and investigated,' he said quickly. 'Unless I'm much mistaken, it's that big caique that passed us this morning. Heaven only knows how, but they've been tipped off and they're going to be as suspicious as hell. This'll be no kid-glove, hands-in-the-pockets inspection. They'll be armed to the teeth and hunting trouble. There's going to be no half-measures. Let's be quite clear about that. Either they go under or we do: we can't possibly survive an inspection – not with all the gear *we've* got aboard. And,' he added softly, 'we're not going to dump that gear.' Rapidly he explained his plans. Stevens, leaning out from the wheelhouse window, felt the old sick ache in his stomach, felt the blood leaving his face. He was glad of the protection of the wheelhouse that hid the lower part of his body: that old familiar tremor in his leg was back again. Even his voice was unsteady.

'But, sir – sir—'

'Yes, yes, what is it, Stevens?' Even in his hurry Mallory paused at the sight of the pale, set face, the bloodless nails clenched over the sill of the window.

'You – you can't do *that*, sir!' The voice burred harshly under the sharp edge of strain. For a moment his mouth worked soundlessly, then he rushed on. 'It's massacre, sir, it's – it's just murder!'

'Shut up, kid!' Miller growled.

'That'll do, Corporal!' Mallory said sharply. He looked at the American for a long moment then turned to Stevens, his eyes cold. 'Lieutenant, the whole concept of directing a successful war is aimed at placing your enemy at a disadvantage, at *not* giving him an even chance. We kill them or they kill us. They go under or we do – and a thousand men on Kheros. It's just as simple as that, Lieutenant. It's not even a question of con-science.'

For several seconds Stevens stared at Mallory in complete

silence. He was vaguely aware that everyone was looking at him. In that instant he hated Mallory, could have killed him. He hated him because – suddenly he was aware that he hated him only for the remorseless logic of what he said. He stared down at his clenched hands. Mallory, the idol of every young mountaineer and cragsman in pre-war England, whose fantastic climbing exploits had made world headlines, in '38 and '39: Mallory, who had twice been baulked by the most atrocious ill-fortune from surprising Rommel in his desert headquarters: Mallory, who had three times refused promotion in order to stay with his beloved Cretans who worshipped him the other side of idolatry. Confusedly these thoughts tumbled through his mind and he looked up slowly, looked at the lean, sunburnt face, the sensitive, chiselled mouth, the heavy, dark eyebrows bar-straight over the lined brown eyes that could be so cold or so compassionate, and suddenly he felt ashamed, knew that Captain Mallory lay beyond both his understanding and his judgment.

'I am very sorry, sir.' He smiled faintly. 'As Corporal Miller would say, I was talking out of turn.' He looked aft at the caique arrowing up from the south-east. Again he felt the sick fear, but his voice was steady enough as he spoke. 'I won't let you down, sir.'

'Good enough. I never thought you would.' Mallory smiled in turn, looked at Miller and Brown. 'Get the stuff ready and lay it out, will you? Casual, easy and keep it hidden. They'll have the glasses on you.'

He turned away, walked for'ard. Andrea followed him.

'You were very hard on the young man.' It was neither criticism nor reproach – merely statement of fact.

'I know.' Mallory shrugged. 'I didn't like it either. . . . I had to do it.'

'I think you had,' Andrea said slowly. 'Yes, I think you had. But it was hard. . . . Do you think they'll use the big guns in the bows to stop us?'

'Might – they haven't turned back after us unless they're pretty sure we're up to something fishy. But the warning shot across the bows – they don't go in for that Captain Teach stuff normally.'

Andrea wrinkled his brows.

'Captain Teach?'

'Never mind.' Mallory smiled. 'Time we were taking up position now. Remember, wait for me. You won't have any trouble in hearing my signal,' he finished dryly.

The creaming bow-wave died away to a gentle ripple, the throb of the heavy diesel muted to a distant murmur as the German boat slid alongside, barely six feet away. From where he sat on a fish-box on the port of the fo'c'sle, industriously sewing a button on to the old coat lying on the deck between his legs, Mallory could see six men, all dressed in the uniform of the regular German Navy – one crouched behind a belted Spandau mounted on its tripod just aft of the two-pounder, three others bunched amidships each armed with an automatic machine carbine – Schmeissers, he thought – the captain, a hard, cold-faced young lieutenant with the Iron Cross on his tunic, looking out the open door of the wheelhouse and, finally, a curious head peering over the edge of the engine-room hatch. From where he sat, Mallory couldn't see the poop-deck – the intermittent ballooning of the lug-sail in the uncertain wind blocked his vision; but from the restricted fore-and-aft lateral sweep of the Spandau, hungrily traversing only the for'ard half of their one caique, he was reasonably sure that there was another machine-gunner similarly engaged on the German's poop.

The hard-faced young lieutenant – a real product of the Hitler Jugend that one, Mallory thought – leaned out of the wheelhouse, cupped his hand to his mouth.

'Lower your sails!' he shouted.

Mallory stiffened, froze to immobility. The needle had jammed hard into the palm of his hand, but he didn't even notice it. The lieutenant had spoken in English! Stevens was so young, so inexperienced. He'd fall for it, Mallory thought with a sudden sick certainty, he's bound to fall for it.

But Stevens didn't fall for it. He opened the door, leaned out, cupped his hand to his ear and gazed vacantly up to the sky, his mouth wide open. It was so perfect an imitation of dull-witted failure to catch or comprehend a shouted message that it was almost a caricature. Mallory could have hugged him. Not in his actions alone, but in his dark, shabby clothes and hair as blackly counterfeit as Miller's, Stevens was the slow, suspicious island fisherman to the life.

'Eh?' he bawled.

'Lower your sails! We are coming aboard!' English again, Mallory noted; a persistent fellow this.

Stevens stared at him blankly, looked round helplessly at Andrea and Mallory: their faces registered a lack of comprehension as convincing as his own. He shrugged his shoulders in despair.

'I am sorry, I do not understand German,' he shouted. 'Can you not speak my language?' Stevens's Greek was perfect, fluent and idiomatic. It was also the Greek of Attica, not of the islands; but Mallory felt sure that the lieutenant wouldn't know the difference.

He didn't. He shook his head in exasperation, called in slow, halting Greek: 'Stop your boat at once. We are coming aboard.'

'Stop my boat!' The indignation was so genuine, the accompanying flood of furious oaths so authentic, that even the lieutenant was momentarily taken aback. 'And why should I stop my boat for you, you – you—'

'You have ten seconds,' the lieutenant interrupted. He was on balance again, cold, precise. 'Then we will shoot.'

Stevens gestured in admission of defeat and turned to Andrea and Mallory.

'Our conquerors have spoken,' he said bitterly. 'Lower the sails.'

Quickly they loosened the sheets from the cleats at the foot of the mast. Mallory pulled the jib down, gathered the sail in his arms and squatted sullenly on the deck – he knew a dozen hostile eyes were watching him – close by the fish-box. The sail covering his knees and the old coat, his forearms on his thighs, he sat with head bowed and hands dangling between his knees, the picture of heart-struck dejection. The lug-sail, weighted by the boom at the top, came down with a rush. Andrea stepped over it, walked a couple of uncertain paces aft, then stopped, huge hands hanging emptily by his sides.

A sudden deepening of the muted throbbing of the diesel, a spin of the wheel and the big German caique was rubbing alongside. Quickly, but carefully enough to keep out of the line of fire of the mounted Spandaus – there was a second clearly visible now on the poop – the three men armed with the Schmeissers leapt aboard. Immediately one ran forward, whirled round level with the foremast, his automatic carbine circling gently to cover all of the crew. All except Mallory – and he was leaving Mallory in the safe hands of the Spandau gunner in the bows. Detachedly, Mallory admired the precision, the timing, the clockwork inevitability of an old routine.

He raised his head, looked around him with a slow, peasant indifference. Casey Brown was squatting on the deck abreast the engine-room, working on the big ball-silencer on top of the hatch-cover. Dusty Miller, two paces farther for'ard and with his brows furrowed in concentration, was laboriously cutting a section of metal from a little tin box, presumably to help in the engine repairs. He was holding the wire-cutting pliers in his left hand – and Miller, Mallory knew, was right-handed. Neither Stevens nor Andrea had moved. The man beside the foremast still stood there, eyes unwinking. The other two were walking slowly aft, had just passed Andrea, their carriage relaxed and easy, the bearing of men who knew they have everything so completely under control that even the idea of trouble is ridiculous.

Carefully, coldly and precisely, at point-blank range and through the folds of both coat and sail, Mallory shot the Spandau machine-gunner through the heart, swung the still chattering Bren round and saw the guard by the mast crumple and die, half his chest torn away by the tearing slugs of the machine-gun. But the dead man was still on his feet, still had not hit the deck, when four things happened simultaneously. Casey Brown had had his hand on Miller's silenced automatic, lying concealed beneath the ball-silencer, for over a minute. Now he squeezed the trigger four times, for he wanted to mak' siccar; the after machine-gunner leaned forward tiredly over his tripod, lifeless fingers locked on the firing-guard. Miller crimped the three-second chemical fuse with the pliers, lobbed the tin box into the enemy engine-room, Stevens spun the armed stick-grenade into the opposite wheelhouse and Andrea, his great arms reaching out with all the speed and precision of striking cobras, swept the Schmeisser gunners' heads together with sickening force. And then all five men had hurled themselves to the deck and the German caique was erupting in a roar of flame and smoke and dying débris: gradually the echoes faded away over the sea and there was left only the whining stammer of the Spandau, emptying itself uselessly skyward; and then the belt jammed and the Ægean was as silent as ever, more silent than it had ever been.

Slowly, painfully, dazed by the sheer physical shock and the ear-shattering proximity of the twin explosions, Mallory pushed himself off the wooden deck and stood shakily on his feet. His first conscious reaction was that of surprise, incredulity almost: the concussive blast of a grenade and a couple of lashed blocks of TNT, even at such close range, was far beyond anything he had expected.

The German boat was sinking, sinking fast. Miller's homemade bomb must have torn the bottom out of the engine-room. She was heavily on fire amidships, and for one dismayed instant

Mallory had an apprehensive vision of towering black columns of smoke and enemy reconnaissance planes. But only for an instant: timbers and planking, tinder-dry and resinous, were burning furiously with hardly a trace of smoke, and the flaming, crumpling deck was already canted over sharply to port: she would be gone in seconds. His eyes wandered to the shattered skeleton of the wheelhouse, and he caught his breath suddenly when he saw the lieutenant impaled on the splintered wreck of the wheel, a ghastly, mangled caricature of what had once been a human being, decapitated and wholly horrible: vaguely, some part of Mallory's mind registered the harsh sound of retching, violent and convulsive, coming from the wheelhouse, and he knew Stevens must have seen it too. From deep within the sinking caique came the muffled roar of rupturing fuel tanks: a flame-veined gout of oily black smoke erupted from the engine-room and the caique miraculously struggled back on even keel, her gunwales almost awash, and then the hissing waters had overflowed and overcome the decks and the twisting flames, and the caique was gone, her slender masts sliding vertically down and vanishing in a turbulent welter of creaming foam and oil-filmed bubbles. And now the Ægean was calm and peaceful again, as placid as if the caique had never been, and almost as empty: a few charred planks and an inverted helmet drifted lazily on the surface of the shimmering sea.

With a conscious effort of will, Mallory turned slowly to look to his own ship and his own men. Brown and Miller were on their feet, staring down in fascination at where the caique had been, Stevens was standing at the wheelhouse door. He, too, was unhurt, but his face was ashen: during the brief action he had been a man above himself, but the aftermath, the brief glimpse he'd had of the dead lieutenant had hit him badly. Andrea, bleeding from a gash on the cheek, was looking down at the two Schmeisser gunners lying at his feet. His face was expressionless. For a long moment Mallory looked at him, looked in slow understanding.

'Dead?' he asked quietly.

Andrea inclined his head.

'Yes.' His voice was heavy. 'I hit them too hard.'

Mallory turned away. Of all the men he had ever known, Andrea, he thought, had the most call to hate and to kill his enemies. And kill them he did, with a ruthless efficiency appalling in its single-mindedness and thoroughness of execution. But he rarely killed without regret, without the most bitter self-condemnation, for he did not believe that the lives of his fellow-men were his to take. A destroyer of his fellow-man, he loved his fellow-man above all things. A simple man, a good man, a killer with a kindly heart, he was for ever troubled by his consicence, ill at ease with his inner self. But over and above the wonderings and the reproaches, he was informed by an honesty of thought, by a clear-sighted wisdom which sprang from and transcended his innate simplicity. Andrea killed neither for revenge, nor from hate, nor nationalism, nor for the sake of any of the other 'isms' which self-seekers and fools and knaves employ as beguilement to the battlefield and justication for the slaughter of millions too young and too unknowing to comprehend the dreadful futility of it all. Andrea killed simply that better men might live.

'Anybody else hurt?' Mallory's voice was deliberately brisk, cheerful. 'Nobody? Good! Right, let's get under way as fast as possible. The farther and the faster we leave this place behind, the better for all of us.' He looked at his watch. 'Almost four o'clock – time for our routine check with Cairo. Just leave that scrap-yard of yours for a couple of minutes, Chief. See if you can pick them up.' He looked at the sky to the east, a sky now purply livid and threatening, and shook his head. 'Could be that the weather forecast might be worth hearing.'

It was. Reception was very poor – Brown blamed the violent static on the dark, convoluted thunderheads steadily creeping up astern, now overspreading almost half the sky – but adequate. Adequate enough to hear information they had never expected to hear, information that left them silenced, eyes stilled in troubled speculation. The tiny loud-speaker boomed and faded, boomed and faded, against the scratchy background of static.

'Rhubarb calling Pimpernel! Rhubarb calling Pimpernel!' These were the respective code names for Cairo and Mallory. 'Are you receiving me?'

Brown tapped an acknowledgment. The speaker boomed again.

'Rhubarb calling Pimpernel. Now X minus one. Repeat, X minus one.' Mallory drew in his breath sharply. X – dawn on Saturday – had been the assumed date for the German attack on Kheros. It must have been advanced by one day – and Jensen was not the man to speak without certain knowledge. Friday, dawn – just over three days.

'Send "X minus one understood," ' Mallory said quietly.

'Forecast, East Anglia,' the impersonal voice went on: the

Northern Sporades, Mallory knew. 'Severe electrical storms probable this evening, with heavy rainfall. Visibility poor. Temperature falling, continuing to fall next twenty-four hours. Winds east to south-east, force six, locally eight, moderating early tomorrow.'

Mallory turned away, ducked under the billowing lug-sail, walked slowly aft. What a set-up, he thought, what a bloody mess. Three days to go, engine u. s. and a first-class storm building up. He thought briefly, hopefully, of Squadron Leader Torrance's low opinion of the backroom boys of the Met. Office, but the hope was never really born. It couldn't be, not unless he was blind. The steep-piled buttresses of the thunderheads towered up darkly terrifying, now almost directly above.

'Looks pretty bad, huh?' The slow nasal drawl came from immediately behind him. There was something oddly reassuring about that measured voice, about the steadiness of the washed-out blue of the eyes enmeshed in a spider's web of fine wrinkles.

'It's not so good,' Mallory admitted.

'What's all this force eight business, boss?'

'A wind scale,' Mallory explained. 'If you're in a boat this size and you're good and tired of life, you can't beat a force eight wind.'

Miller nodded dolefully.

'I knew it. I might have known. And me swearing they'd never get me on a gawddamned boat again.' He brooded a while, sighed, slid his legs over the engine-room hatchway, jerked his thumb in the direction of the nearest island, now less than three miles away. 'That doesn't look so hot, either.'

'Not from here,' Mallory agreed. 'But the chart shows a creek with a right-angle bend. It'll break the sea and the wind.'

'Inhabited?'

'Probably.'

'Germans?'

'Probably.'

Miller shook his head in despair and descended to help Brown. Forty minutes later, in the semi-darkness of the overcast evening and in torrential rain, lance-straight and strangely chill, the anchor of the caique rattled down between the green walls of the forest, a dank and dripping forest, hostile in its silent indifference.

4

MONDAY EVENING

1700–2330

'Brilliant!' said Mallory bitterly. 'Ruddy well brilliant! "Come into my parlour said the spider to the fly." ' He swore in chagrin and exasperated disgust, eased aside the edge of the tarpaulin that covered the for'ard hatchway, peered out through the slackening curtain of rain and took a second and longer look at the rocky bluff that elbowed out into the bend of the creek, shutting them off from the sea. There was no difficulty in seeing now, none at all: the drenching cloudburst had yielded to a gentle drizzle, and grey and white cloud streamers, shredding in the lifting wind, had already pursued the blackly towering cumulonimbus over the far horizon. In a clear band of sky far to the west, the sinking, flame-red sun was balanced on the rim of the sea. From the shadowed waters of the creek it was invisible, but its presence unmistakable from the gold-shot gauze of the falling rain, high above their heads.

The same golden rays highlighted the crumbling old watch-tower on the very point of the cliff, a hundred feet above the river. They burnished its fine-grained white Parian marble, mellowed it to a delicate rose: they gleamed on the glittering steel, the evil mouths of the Spandau machine-guns reaching out from the slotted embrasures in the massive walls, illumined the hooked cross of the swastika on the flag that streamed out stiffly from the staff above the parapet. Solid even in its decay, impregnable in its position, commanding in its lofty outlook, the tower completely dominated both waterborne approaches, from the sea and, upriver, down the narrow, winding channel that lay between the moored caique and the foot of the cliff.

Slowly, reluctantly almost. Mallory turned away and gently lowered the tarpaulin. His face was grim as he turned round to Andrea and Stevens, ill-defined shadows in the twilit gloom of the cabin.

'Brilliant!' he repeated. 'Sheer genius. Mastermind Mallory. Probably the only bloody creek within a hundred miles – and in a hundred islands – with a German guard post on it. And of course I had to go and pick it. Let's have another look at that chart, will you, Stevens?'

Stevens passed it across, watched Mallory study it in the pale light filtering in under the tarpaulin, leaned back against the bulkhead and drew heavily on his cigarette. It tasted foul, stale and acrid, but the tobacco was fresh enough, he knew. The old, sick fear was back again, as strongly as ever. He looked at the great bulk of Andrea across from him, felt an illogical resentment towards him for having spotted the emplacement a few minutes ago. They'll have cannon up there, he thought dully, they're bound to have cannon – couldn't control the creek otherwise. He gripped his thigh fiercely, just above the knee, but the tremor lay too deep to be controlled: he blessed the merciful darkness of the tiny cabin. But his voice was casual enough as he spoke.

'You're wasting your time, sir, looking at that chart and blaming yourself. This is the only possible anchorage within hours of sailing time from here. With that wind there was nowhere else we could have gone.'

'Exactly. That's just it.' Mallory folded the chart, handed it back. 'There was nowhere else we could have gone. There was nowhere else anyone could have gone. Must be a very popular port in a storm, this – a fact which must have become apparent to the Germans a long, long time ago. That's why I should have known they were almost bound to have a post here. However, spilt milk, as you say.' He raised his voice. 'Chief!'

'Hallo!' Brown's muffled voice carried faintly from the depths of the engine-room.

'How's it going?'

'Not too bad, sir. Assembling it now.'

Mallory nodded in relief.

'How long?' he called. 'An hour?'

'Aye, easy, sir.'

'An hour.' Again Mallory glanced through the tarpaulin, looked back at Andrea and Stevens. 'Just about right. We'll leave in an hour. Dark enough to give us some protection from our friends up top, but enough light left to navigate our way out of this damned corkscrew of a channel.'

'Do you think they'll try to stop us, sir?' Stevens's voice was just too casual, too matter of fact. He was pretty sure Mallory would notice.

'It's unlikely they'll line the banks and give us three hearty cheers,' Mallory said dryly. 'How many men do you reckon they'll have up there, Andrea?'

'I've seen two moving around,' Andrea said thoughtfully.

'Maybe three or four altogether, Captain. A small post. The Germans don't waste men on these.'

'I think you're about right,' Mallory agreed. 'Most of them'll be in the garrison in the village – about seven miles from here, according to the chart, and due west. It's not likely—'

He broke off sharply, stiffened in rigid attention. Again the call came, louder this time, imperative in its tone. Cursing himself for his negligence in not posting a guard – such carelessness would have cost him his life in Crete – Mallory pulled the tarpaulin aside, clambered slowly on to the deck. He carried no arms, but a half-empty bottle of Moselle dangled from his left hand; as part of a plan prepared before they had left Alexandria, he'd snatched it from a locker at the foot of the tiny companionway.

He lurched convincingly across the deck, grabbed at a stay in time to save himself from falling overboard. Insolently he stared down at the figure on the bank, less than ten yards away – it hadn't mattered about a guard, Mallory realized, for the soldier carried his automatic carbine slung over his shoulder – insolently he tilted the wine to his mouth and swallowed deeply before condescending to talk to him.

He could see the mounting anger in the lean, tanned face of the young German below him. Mallory ignored it. Slowly, an inherent contempt in the gesture, he dragged the frayed sleeve of his black jacket across his lips, looked the soldier even more slowly up and down in a minutely provocative inspection as disdainful as it was prolonged.

'Well?' he asked truculently in the slow speech of the islands. 'What the hell do you want?'

Even in the deepening dusk he could see the knuckles whitening on the stock of the carbine, and for an instant Mallory thought he had gone too far. He knew he was in no danger – all noise in the engine-room had ceased, and Dusty Miller's hand was never far from his silenced automatic – but he didn't want trouble. Not just yet. Not while there were a couple of manned Spandaus in that watch-tower.

With an almost visible effort the young soldier regained his control. It needed little help from the imagination to see the draining anger, the first tentative stirrings of hesitation and bewilderment. It was the reaction Mallory had hoped for. Greeks – even half-drunk Greeks – didn't talk to their overlords like that – not unless they had an overpoweringly good reason.

'What vessel is this?' The Greek was slow and halting but passable. 'Where are you bound for?'

Mallory tilted the bottle again, smacked his lips in noisy satisfaction. He held the bottle at arm's length, regarded it with a loving respect.

'One thing about you Germans,' he confided loudly. 'You do know how to make a fine wine. I'll wager *you* can't lay your hands on this stuff, eh? And the swill they're making up above' – the island term for the mainland – 'is so full of resin that it's only good for lighting fires.' He thought for a moment. 'Of course, if you know the right people in the islands, they *might* let you have some ouzo. But some of us can get ouzo *and* the best Hocks *and* the best Moselles.'

The soldier wrinkled his face in disgust. Like almost every fighting man he despised Quislings, even when they were on his side: in Greece they were very few indeed.

'I asked you a question,' he said coldly. 'What vessel, and where bound?'

'The caique *Aigion*,' Mallory replied loftily. 'In ballast, for Samos. Under orders,' he said significantly.

'Whose orders?' the solder demanded. Shrewdly Mallory judged the confidence as superficial only. The guard was impressed in spite of himself.

'Herr Commandant in Vathy. General Graebel,' Mallory said softly. 'You will have heard of the Herr General before, yes?' He was on safe ground here, Mallory knew, The reputation of Graebel, both as a paratroop commander and an iron disciplinarian, had spread far beyond these islands.

Even in the half-light Mallory could have sworn that the guard's complexion turned paler. But he was dogged enough.

'You have papers? Letters of authority?'

Mallory sighed wearily, looked over his shoulder.

'Andrea!' he bawled.

'What do you want?' Andrea's great bulk loomed through the hatchway. He had heard every word that passed, had taken his cue from Mallory: a newly-opened wine bottle was almost engulfed in one vast hand and he was scowling hugely. 'Can't you see I'm busy?' he asked surlily. He stopped short at the sight of the German and scowled again, irritably. 'And what does this halfling want?'

'Our passes and letters of authority from Herr General. They're down below.'

Andrea disappeared, grumbling deep in his throat. A rope

was thrown ashore, the stern pulled in against the sluggish current and the papers passed over. The papers – a set different from those to be used if emergency arose in Navarone – proved to be satisfactory, eminently so. Mallory would have been surprised had they been anything else. The preparation of these, even down to the photostatic facsimile of General Graebel's signature, was all in the day's work for Jensen's bureau in Cairo.

The soldier folded the papers, handed them back with a muttered word of thanks. He was only a kid, Mallory could see now – if he was more than nineteen his looks belied him. A pleasant, open-faced kid – of a different stamp altogether from the young fanatics of the SS Panzer Division – and far too thin. Mallory's chief reaction was one of relief: he would have hated to have to kill a boy like this. But he had to find out all he could. He signalled to Stevens to hand him up the almost empty crate of Moselle. Jensen, he mused, had been very thorough indeed: the man had literally thought of everything. . . . Mallory gestured in the direction of the watch-tower.

'How many of you are up there?' he asked.

The boy was instantly suspicious. His face had tightened up, stilled in hostile surmise.

'Why do you want to know?' he asked stiffly.

Mallory groaned, lifted his hands in despair, turned sadly to Andrea.

'You see what it is to be one of them?' he asked in mournful complaint. 'Trust nobody. Think everyone is as twisted as . . .' He broke off hurriedly, turned to the soldier again. 'It's just that we don't want to have the same trouble every time we come in here,' he explained. 'We'll be back in Samos in a couple of days, and we've still another case of Moselle to work through. General Graebel keeps his – ah – special envoys well supplied. . . . It must be thirsty work up there in the sun. Come on, now, a bottle each. How many bottles?'

The reassuring mention that they would be back again, the equally reassuring mention of Graebel's name, plus, probably, the attraction of the offer and his comrades' reaction if he told them he had refused it, tipped the balance, overcame scruples and suspicions.

'There are only three of us,' he said grudgingly.

'Three it is,' Mallory said cheerfully. 'We'll bring you some Hock next time we return.' He tilted his own bottle. '*Prosit!*' he said, an islander proud of airing his German, and then, more proudly still, '*Auf Wiedersehen!*'

The boy murmured something in return. He stood hesitating for a moment, slightly shame-faced, then wheeled abruptly, walked off slowly along the river bank, clutching his bottles of Moselle.

'So!' Mallory said thoughtfully. 'There are only three of them. That should make things easier—'

'Well done sir!' It was Stevens who interrupted, his voice warm, his face alive with admiration. 'Jolly good show!'

'Jolly good show!' Miller mimicked. He heaved his lanky length over the coaming of the engine hatchway. ' "Good" be damned! I couldn't understand a gawddamned word, but for my money that rates an Oscar. That was terrific, boss!'

'Thank you, one and all,' Mallory murmured. 'But I'm afraid the congratulations are a bit premature.' The sudden chill in his voice struck at them, so that their eyes aligned along his pointing finger even before he went on. 'Take a look,' he said quietly.

The young soldier had halted suddenly about two hundred yards along the bank, looked into the forest on his left in startled surprise, then dived in among the trees. For a moment the watchers on the boat could see another soldier, talking excitedly to the boy and gesticulating in the direction of their boat, and then both were gone, lost in the gloom of the forest.

'That's torn it!' Mallory said softly. He turned away. 'Right, that's enough. Back to where you were. It would look fishy if we ignored that incident altogether, but it would look a damned sight fishier if we paid too much attention to it. Don't let's appear to be holding a conference.'

Miller slipped down into the engine-room with Brown, and Stevens went back to the little for'ard cabin. Mallory and Andrea remained on deck, bottles in their hands. The rain had stopped now, completely, but the wind was still rising, climbing the scale with imperceptible steadiness, beginning to bend the tops of the tallest of the pines. Temporarily the bluff was affording them almost complete protection. Mallory deliberately shut his mind to what it must be like outside. They had to put out to sea – Spandaus permitting – and that was that.

'What do you think has happened, sir?' Steven's' voice carried up from the gloom of the cabin.

'Pretty obvious, isn't it?' Mallory asked. He spoke loudly enough for all to hear. 'They've been tipped off. Don't ask me how. This is the second time – and their suspicions are going to be considerably reinforced by the absence of a report from the caique that was sent to investigate us. She was carrying a wire-less aerial, remember?'

'But why should they get so damned suspicious all of a sud-den?' Miller asked. 'It doesn't make sense to me, boss.'

'Must be in radio contact with their HQ. Or a telephone – probably a telephone. They've just been given the old tic-tac. Consternation on all sides.'

'So mebbe they'll be sending a small army over from their HQ to deal with us,' Miller said lugubriously.

Mallory shook his head definitely. His mind was working quickly and well, and he felt oddly certain, confident of himself.

'No, not a chance. Seven miles as the crow flies. Ten, maybe twelve miles over rough hill and forest tracks – and in pitch darkness. They wouldn't think of it.' He waved his bottle in the direction of the watch-tower. 'Tonight's their big night.'

'So we can expect the Spandaus to open up any minute?' Again the abnormal matter-of-factness of Stevens's voice.

Mallory shook his head a second time.

'They won't. I'm positive of that. No matter how suspicious they may be, how certain they are that we're the big bad wolf, they are going to be shaken to the core when that kid tells them we're carrying papers and letters of authority signed by General Graebel himself. For all they know, curtains for us may be the firing squad for them. Unlikely, but you get the general idea. So they're going to contact HQ, and the commandant on a small island like this isn't going to take a chance on rubbing out a bunch of characters who may be the special envoys of the Herr General himself. So what? So he codes a message and radios it to Vathy in Samos and bites his nails off to the elbow till a message comes back saying Graebel has never heard of us and why the hell haven't we all been shot dead?' Mallory looked at the luminous dial of his watch. 'I'd say we have at least half an hour.'

'And meantime we all sit around with our little bits of paper and pencil and write out our last wills and testaments.' Miller scowled. 'No percentage in that, boss. We gotta *do* somethin'.'

Mallory grinned.

'Don't worry, Corporal, we are going to do something. We're going to hold a nice little bottle party, right here on the poop.'

The last words of their song – a shockingly corrupted Grecian version of 'Lilli Marlene,' and their third song in the past few minutes – died away in the evening air. Mallory doubted whether more than faint snatches of the singing would be carried to the watch-tower against the wind, but the rhythmical stamping of feet and waving of bottles were in themselves sufficient evidence of drunken musical hilarity to all but the totally blind and deaf. Mallory grinned to himself as he thought of the complete confusion and uncertainty the Germans in the tower must have been feeling then. This was not the behaviour of enemy spies, especially enemy spies who know that suspicions had been aroused and that their times was running out.

Mallory tilted the bottle to his mouth, held it there for several seconds, then set it down again, the wine untasted. He looked round slowly at the three men squatting there with him on the poop, Miller, Stevens and Brown. Andrea was not there, but he didn't have to turn his head to look for him. Andrea, he knew, was crouched in the shelter of the wheelhouse, a waterproof bag with grenades and a revolver strapped to his back.

'Right!' Mallory said crisply. 'Now's your big chance for *your* Oscar. Let's make this as convincing as we can.' He bent forward, jabbed his finger into Miller's chest and shouted angrily at him.

Miller shouted back. For a few moment they sat there, gesticulating angrily and, to all appearances, quarrelling furiously with each other. Then Miller was on his feet, swaying in drunken inbalance as he leaned threateningly over Mallory, clenched fists ready to strike. He stood back as Mallory struggled to his feet, and in a moment they were fighting fiercely, raining apparently heavy blows on each other. Then a haymaker from the American sent Mallory reeling back to crash convincingly against the wheelhouse.

'Right, Andrea.' He spoke quietly, without looking round. 'This is it. Five seconds. Good luck.' He scrambled to his feet, picked up a bottle by the neck and rushed at Miller, upraised arm and bludgeon swinging fiercely down. Miller dodged, swung a vicious foot, and Mallory roared in pain as his shins caught on the edge of the bulwarks. Silhouetted against the pale gleam of the creek, he stood poised for a second, arms flailing wildly, then plunged heavily, with a loud splash, into the waters of the creek.

For the next half-minute – it would take about that time for Andrea to swim underwater round the next upstream corner of the creek – everything was a confusion and a bedlam of noise. Mallory trod water as he tried to pull himself aboard: Miller had seized a boathook and was trying to smash it down on his head: and the others, on their feet now, had flung their arms round Miller, trying to restrain him: finally they managed to knock him off his feet, pin him to the deck and help the dripping Mallory aboard. A minute later, after the immemorial fashion of drunken men, the two combatants had shaken hands with one another and were sitting on the engine-room hatch, arms round each other's shoulders and drinking in perfect amity from the same freshly-opened bottle of wine.

'Very nicely done,' Mallory said approvingly. 'Very nicely indeed. An Oscar, definitely, for Corporal Miller.'

Dusty Miller said nothing. Taciturn and depressed, he looked moodily at the bottle in his hand. At last he stirred.

'I don't like it, boss,' he muttered unhappily. 'I don't like the set-up one little bit. You shoulda let me go with Andrea. It's three to one up there, and they're waiting and ready.' He looked accusingly at Mallory. 'Dammit to hell, boss, you're always telling us how desperately important this mission is!'

'I know,' Mallory said quietly. 'That's why I didn't send you with him. That's why none of us has gone with him. We'd only be a liability to him, get in his way.' Mallory shook his head. 'You don't know Andrea, Dusty.' It was the first time Mallory had called him that: Miller was warmed by the unexpected familiarity, secretly pleased. 'None of you know him. But I know him.' He gestured towards the watch-tower, its square-cut lines in sharp silhouette against the darkening sky. 'Just a big, fat, good-natured chap, always laughing and joking.' Mallory paused, shook his head again, went on slowly. 'He's up there now, padding through that forest like a cat, the biggest and most dangerous cat you'll ever see. Unless they offer no resistance – Andrea never kills unnecessarily – when I send him up there after these three poor bastards I'm executing them just as surely as if they were in the electric chair and I was pulling the switch.'

In spite of himself Miller was impressed, profoundly so.

'Known him a long time, boss, huh?' It was half question, half statement.

'A long time. Andrea was in the Albanian war – he was in the regular army. They tell me the Italians went in terror of him – his long-range patrols against the Iulia division, the Wolves of Tuscany, did more to wreck the Italian morale in Albania than any other single factor. I've heard a good many stories about them – not from Andrea – and they're all incredible. And they're all true. But it was afterwards I met him, when we were trying to hold the Servia Pass. I was a very junior liaison lieutenant in the Anzac brigade at the time. Andrea' – he paused deliberately for effect – 'Andrea was a lieutenant-colonel in the 19th Greek Motorised Division.'

'A *what?*' Miller demanded in astonishment. Stevens and Brown were equally incredulous.

'You heard me. Lieutenant-colonel. Outranks me by a fairish bit, you might say.' He smiled at them, quizzically. 'Puts Andrea in rather a different light, doesn't it?'

They nodded silently but said nothing. The genial, hail-fellow Andrea – a good-natured, almost simple-minded buffoon – a senior army officer. The idea had come too suddenly, was too incongruous for easy assimilation and immediate comprehension. But, gradually, it began to make sense to them. It explained many things about Andrea to them – his repose, his confidence, the unerring sureness of his lightning reactions, and, above all, the implicit faith Mallory had in him, the respect he showed for Andrea's opinions whenever he consulted him, which was frequently. Without surprise now, Miller slowly recalled that he'd never yet heard Mallory give Andrea a direct order. And Mallory never hesitated to pull his rank when necessary.

'After Servia,' Mallory went on, 'everything was pretty confused. Andrea had heard that Trikkala – a small country town where his wife and three daughters lived – had been flattened by the Stukas and Heinkels. He reached there all right, but there was nothing he could do. A land-mine had landed in the front garden and there wasn't even rubble left.'

Mallory paused, lit a cigarette. He stared through the drifting smoke at the fading outlines of the tower.

'The only person he found there was his brother-in-law, George. George was with us in Crete – he's still there. From George he heard for the first time of the Bulgarian atrocities in Thrace and Macedonia – and his parents lived there. So they dressed in German uniforms – you can imagine how Andrea got those – commandeered a German army truck and drove to Protosami.' The cigarette in Mallory's hand snapped suddenly, was sent spinning over the side. Miller was vaguely surprised: emotion, or rather, emotional displays, were so completely foreign to that very tough New Zealander. But Mallory went on quietly enough.

'They arrived in the evening of the infamous Protosami massacre. George has told me how Andrea stood there, clad in his German uniform and laughing as he watched a party of nine or ten Bulgarian soldiers lash couples together and throw them into the river. The first couple in were his father and step-mother, both dead.'

'My Gawd above!' Even Miller was shocked out of his usual equanimity. 'It's just not possible—'

'You know nothing,' Mallory interrupted impatiently. 'Hundreds of Greeks in Macedonia died the same way – but usually alive when they were thrown in. Until you know how the Greeks hate the Bulgarians, you don't even begin to know what hate is. . . . Andrea shared a couple of bottles of wine with the soldiers, found out that they had killed his parents earlier in the afternoon – they had been foolish enough to resist. After dusk he followed them up to an old corrugated-iron shed where they were billeted for the night. All he had was a knife. They left a guard outside. Andrea broke his neck, went inside, locked the door and smashed the oil lamp. George doesn't know what happened except that Andrea went berserk. He was back outside in two minutes, completely sodden, his uniform soaked in blood from head to foot. There wasn't a sound, not even a groan to be heard from the hut when they left, George says.'

He paused again, but this time there was no interruption, nothing said. Stevens shivered, drew his shabby jacket closer round his shoulders: the air seemed to have become suddenly chill. Mallory lit another cigarette, smiled faintly at Miller, nodded towards the watch-tower.

'See what I mean by saying we'd only be a liability to Andrea up there?'

'Yeah. Yeah, I guess I do,' Miller admitted. 'I had no idea, I had no idea. . . . Not *all* of them, boss! He couldn't have killed—'

'He did,' Mallory interrupted flatly. 'After that he formed his own band, made life hell for the Bulgarian outposts in Thrace. At one time there was almost an entire division chasing him through the Rhodope mountains. Finally he was betrayed and captured, and he, George and four others were shipped to Stavros – they were to go on to Salonika for trial. They overpowered their guards – Andrea got loose among them on deck at night – and sailed the boat to Turkey. The Turks tried to intern him – they might as well have tried to intern an earthquake. Finally he arrived in Palestine, tried to join the Greek Commando Battalion that was being formed in the Middle East – mainly veterans of the Albanian campaign, life himself.' Mallory laughed mirthlessly. 'He was arrested as a deserter. He was released eventually, but there was no place for him in the new Greek Army. But Jensen's bureau heard about him, knew he was a natural for Subversive Operations . . . And so we went to Crete together.'

Five minutes passed, perhaps ten, but nobody broke the silence. Occasionally, for the benefit of any watchers, they went through the motions of drinking; but even the half-light was fading now and Mallory knew they could only be half-seen blurs, shadowy and indistinct, from the heights of the watch-tower. The caique was beginning to rock in the surge from the open sea round the bluff. The tall, reaching pines, black now as midnight cypress and looming impossibly high against the the star-dusted cloud wrack that scudded palely overhead, were closing in on them from either side, sombre, watchful and vaguely threatening, the wind moaning in lost and mourn-ful requiem through their swaying topmost branches. A bad night, an eerie and an aminous night, pregnant with that in-definable foreboding that reaches down and touches the well-springs of the nameless fears, the dim and haunting memories of a million years ago, the ancient racial superstitions of man-kind: a night that sloughed off the tissue veneer of civilisation and the shivering man complains that someone is walking over his grave.

Suddenly, incongruously, the spell was shattered and Andrea's cheerful hail from the bank had them all on their feet in a moment. They heard his booming laugh and even the forests seemed to shrink back in defeat. Without waiting for the stern to be pulled in, he plunged into the creek, reached the caique in half a dozen powerful strokes and hoisted himself easily aboard. Grinning down from his great height, he shook himself like some shaggy mastiff and reached out a hand for a con-venient wine bottle.

'No need to ask how things went, eh?' Mallory asked, smiling.

'None at all. It was just too easy. They were only boys, and they never even saw me.' Andrea took another long swig from the bottle and grinned in sheer delight. 'And I didn't lay a finger on them,' he went on triumphantly. 'Well, maybe a couple of little taps. They were all looking down here, staring out over the parapet when I arrived. Held them up, took their guns of them and locked them in a cellar. And then I bent their Spandaus – just a little bit.'

This is it, Mallory thought dully, this is the end. This is the finish of everything, the strivings, the hopes, the fears, the loves and laughter of each one of us. This is what it all comes to. This is the end, the end for us, the end for a thousand boys on Kheros. In unconscious futility his hand came up, slowly wiped lips salt from the spray bulleting off the wind-flattened wave-tops, then lifted farther to shade bloodshot eyes that peered out hopelessly into the storm-filled darkness ahead. For a moment the dullness lifted, and an almost intolerable bitterness welled through his mind. All gone, everything – everything except the guns of Navarone. The guns of Navarone. They would live on, they were indestructible. Damn them, damn them, damn them! Dear God, the blind waste, the terrible uselessness of it all!

The caique was dying, coming away at the seams. She was literally being pounded to death, being shaken apart by the constant battering shocks of wind and sea. Time and time again the poop-deck dipped beneath the foam-streaked cauldron at the stern, the fo'c'sle rearing crazily into the air, dripping fore-foot showing clear: then the plummetting drop, the shotgun, shuddering impact as broad-beamed bows crashed vertically down into the cliff-walled trough beyond, an explosive collision that threw so unendurable a strain on the ancient timbers and planks and gradually tore them apart.

It had been bad enough when they'd cleared the creek just as darkness fell, and plunged and wallowed their way through a quartering sea on a northward course for Navarone. Steering the unwieldly old caique had become difficult in the extreme: with the seas fine on the starboard quarter she had yawed wildly and unpredictably through a fifty degree arc, but at least her seams had been tight then, the rolling waves overtaking her in regular formation and the wind settled and steady somewhere east of south. But now all that was gone. With half a dozen planks sprung from the stem-post and working loose from the apron, and leaking heavily through the stuffing-gland of the propeller shaft, she was making water far faster than the ancient, vertical hand-pump could cope with: the wind-truncated seas were heavier, but broken and confused, sweeping down on them now from this quarter, now from that: and the wind itself, re-doubled in its shrieking violence, veered and backed insanely from south-west to south-east. Just then it was steady from the south, driving the unmanageable craft blindly on to the closing iron cliffs of Navarone, cliffs that loomed invisibly ahead, some-where in that all-encompassing darkness.

Momentarily Mallory straightened, tried to ease the agony of the pincers that were clawing into the muscles of the small of his back. For over two hours now he had been bending and straightening, bending and straightening, lifting a thousand buckets that Dusty Miller filled interminably from the well of the hold. God only knew how Miller felt. If anything, he had the harder job of the two and he had been violently and almost continuously seasick for hours on end. He looked ghastly, and he must have been feeling like death itself: the sustained effort, the sheer iron will-power to drive himself on in that condition reached beyond the limits of understanding. Mallory shook his head wonderingly. 'My God, but he's tough, that Yank.' Unbidden, the words framed themselves in his mind, and he shook his head in anger, vaguely conscious of the complete inadequacy of the words.

Fighting for his breath, he looked aft to see how the others were faring. Casey Brown, of course, he couldn't see. Bent double in the cramped confines of the engine-room, he, too, was constantly sick and suffering a blinding headache from the oil fumes and exhaust gases still filtering from the replacement stand-pipe, neither of which could find any escape in the unventilated engine-room: but, crouched over the engine, he had not once left his post since they had cleared the mouth of the creek, had nursed the straining, ancient Kelvin along with the loving care, the exquisite skill of a man born into a long and proud tradition of engineering. That engine had only to falter once, to break down for the time in which a man might draw a deep breath, and the end would be as immediate as it was violent. Their steerage way, their lives, depended entirely on the continuous thrust of that screw, the laboured thudding of that rusted old two-cylinder. It was the heart of the boat, and when that heart stopped beating the boat died too, slewed broadside on and foundering in the waiting chasms between the waves.

For'ard of the engine-room, straddle-legged and braced against the corner pillar of the splintered skeleton that was all that remained of the wheelhouse, Andrea laboured unceasingly at the pump, never once lifting his head, obvious of the crazy lurching of the deck of the caique, obvious, too, of the biting wind and stinging, sleet-cold spray that numbed bare arms and moulded the sodden shirt to the hunched and massive shoulders. Ceaselessly, tirelessly, his arm thrust up and down, up and down, with the metronomic regularity of a piston. He had been there for close on three hours now, and he looked as if he could go on for ever. Mallory, who had yielded him the pump in complete exhaustion after less than twenty minutes' cruel labour, wondered if there was any limit to the man's endurance.

He wondered, too, about Stevens. For four endless hours now Andy Stevens had fought and overcome a wheel that leapt and struggled in his hands as if possessed of a convulsive life and will of its own – the will to wrench itself out of exhausted hands and turn them into the troughs: he had done a superb job, Mallory thought, had handled the clumsy craft magnificently. He peered at him closely, but the spray lashed viciously across his eyes and blinded him with tears. All he could gather was a vague impression of a tightly-set mouth, sleepless, sunken eyes and little patches of skin unnaturally pale against the mask of blood that covered almost the entire face from hairline to throat. The twisting, towering comber that had stove in the planks of the wheelhouse and driven in the windows with such savage force had been completely unexpected: Stevens hadn't had a chance. The cut above the right temple was particularly bad, ugly and deep: the blood still pulsed over the ragged edge of the wound, dripped monotonously into the water that sloshed and gurgled about the floor of the wheelhouse.

Sick to his heart, Mallory turned away, reached down for another bucket of water. What a crew, he thought to himself, what a really terrific bunch of – of . . . He sought for words to describe them, even to himself, but he knew his mind was far too tired. It didn't matter anyway, for there were no words for men like that, nothing that could do them justice.

He could almost taste the bitterness in his mouth, the bitterness that washed in waves through his exhausted mind. God, how wrong it was, how terribly unfair! Why did such men have to die, he wondered savagely, why did they have to die so uselessly. Or maybe it wasn't necessary to justify dying, even dying ingloriously empty of achievement. Could one not die for intangibles, for the abstract and the ideal? What had the martyrs at the stake achieved? Or what was the old tag – *dulce et decorum est pro patria mori*. If one lives well, what matter how one dies. Unconsciously his lips tightened in quick revulsion and he thought of Jensen's remarks about the High Command playing who's-the-king-of-the-castle. Well, they were right bang in the middle of their playground now, just a few more pawns sliding into the limbo. Not that it mattered – they had thousands more left to play with.

For the first time Mallory thought of himself. Not with bitterness or self-pity or regret that it was all over. He thought of himself only as the leader of this party, his responsibility for the present situation. It's my fault, he told himself over and over again, it's all my fault. I brought them here, I made them come. Even while one part of his mind was telling him that he'd had no option, that his hand had been forced, that if they had remained in the creek they would have been wiped out long before the dawn, irrationally he still blamed himself the more. Shackleton, of all the men that ever lived, maybe Ernest Shackleton could have helped them now. But not Keith Mallory. There was nothing he could do, no more than the others were doing, and they were just waiting for the end. But he was the leader, he thought dully, he should be planning something, he should be doing something. . . . But there was nothing he could do. There was nothing anyone on God's earth could do. The sense of guilt, of utter inadequacy, settled and deepened with every shudder of the ancient timbers.

He dropped his bucket, grabbed for the security of the mast as a heavy wave swept over the deck, the breaking foam quicksilver in its seething phosphorescence. The waters swirled hungrily round his legs and feet, but he ignored them, stared out into the darkness. The darkness – that was the devil of it. The old caique rolled and pitched and staggered and plunged, but as if disembodied, in a vacuum. They could see nothing – not where the last wave had gone, nor where the next was coming from. A sea invisible and strangely remote, doubly frightening in its palpable immediacy.

Mallory stared down into the hold, was vaguely conscious of the white blur of Miller's face: he had swallowed some seawater and was retching painfully, salt water laced with blood. But Mallory ignored it, involuntarily: all his mind was concentrated elsewhere, trying to reduce some fleeting impression, as vague as it had been evanescent, to a coherent realization. It seemed desperately urgent that he should do so. Then another and still heavier wave broke over the side and all at once he had it.

The wind! The wind had dropped away, was lessening with every second that passed. Even as he stood there, arms locked round the mast as the second wave fought to carry him away, he remembered how often in the high hills at home he had stood at the foot of a precipice as an onrushing wind, seeking the path of least resistance, had curved and lifted up the sheer face, leaving him standing in a pocket of relative immunity. It was a common enough mountaineering phenomenon. And these two freak waves – the surging backwash! The significance struck at him like a blow. The cliffs! They were on the cliffs of Navarone!

With a hoarse, wordless cry of warning, reckless of his own safety, he flung himself aft, dived full length through the swirling waters for the engine-room hatchway.

'Full astern!' he shouted. The startled white smudge that was Casey Brown's face twisted up to his. 'For God's sake, man, full astern! We're heading for the cliffs!'

He scrambled to his feet, reached the wheelhouse in two strides, hand pawing frantically for the flare pocket.

'The cliffs, Stevens! We're almost on them! Andrea – Miller's still down below!'

He flicked a glance at Stevens, caught the slow nod of the set, blood-masked face, followed the line of sight of the expressionless eyes, saw the whitely phosphorescent line ahead, irregular but almost continuous, blooming and fading, blooming and fading, as the pounding seas smashed against and fell back from cliffs still invisible in the darkness. Desperately his hands fumbled with the flare.

And then, abruptly, it was gone, hissing and spluttering along the near-horizontal trajectory of its flight. For a moment, Mallory thought it had gone out, and he clenched his fists in impotent bitterness. Then it smashed against the rock face, fell back on to a ledge about a dozen feet above the water, and lay there smoking and intermittently burning in the driving rain, in the heavy spray that cascaded from the booming breakers.

The light was feeble, but it was enough. The cliffs were barely fifty yards away, black and wetly shining in the fitful radiance of the flare – a flare that illuminated a vertical circle of less than five yards in radius, and left the cliff below the ledge shrouded in the treacherous dark. And straight ahead, twenty, maybe fifteen yards from the shore, stretched the evil length of a reef, gap-toothed and needle-pointed, vanishing at either end into the outer darkness.

'Can you take her through?' he yelled at Stevens.

'God knows! I'll try!' He shouted something else about 'steerage way,' but Mallory was already half-way to the for'ard cabin. As always in an emergency, his mind was racing ahead with that abnormal sureness and clarity of thought for which he could never afterwards account.

Grasping spikes, mallet and a wire-cored rope, he was back on deck in seconds. He stood stock still, rooted in the almost intolerable tension as he saw the towering, jagged rock bearing down upon them, fine on the starboard bow, a rock that reached half way to the wheelhouse. It struck the boat with a crash that sent him to his knees, rasped and grated along half the length of the buckled, splintered gunwales: and then the caique had rolled over to port and she was though, Stevens frantically spinning the wheel and shouting for full astern.

Mallory's breath escaped in a long, heavy sigh of relief – he had been quite unaware that he had stopped breathing – and he hurriedly looped the coil of rope round his neck and under his left shoulder and stuck spikes and hammer in his belt. The caique was slewing heavily round now, port side to, plunging and corkscrewing violently as she began to fall broadside into the troughs of the waves, waves shorter and steeper than ever under the double thrust of the wind and the waves and the backwash recoiling from the cliffs: but she was still in the grip of the sea and her own momentum, and the distance was closing with frightening speed. It's a chance I have to take, Mallory repeated to himself over and over again; it's a chance I have to take. But that little ledge remote and just inaccessible, was fate's last refinement of cruelty, the salt in the wound of extinction, and he knew in his heart of hearts that it wasn't a chance at all, but just a suicidal gesture. And then Andrea had heaved the last of the fenders – worn truck tyres – outboard, and was towering above him, grinning down hugely into his face: and suddenly Mallory wasn't so sure any more.

'The ledge?' Andrea's vast, reassuring hand was on his shoulder.

Mallory nodded, knees bent in readiness, feet braced on the plunging, slippery deck.

'Jump for it,' Andrea boomed. 'Then keep your legs stiff.'

There was no time for any more. The caique was swinging in broadside to, teetering on the crest of a wave, as high up the cliff as she would ever be, and Mallory knew it was now or never. His hands swung back behind his body, his knees bent farther, and then, in one convulsive leap he had flung himself upwards, fingers scrabbling on the wet rock of the cliff, then hooking over the rim of the ledge. For an instant he hung there at the length of his arms, unable to move, wincing as he heard the foremast crash against the ledge and snap in two, then his fingers left the ledge without their own volition, and he was almost half-way over, propelled by one gigantic heave from below.

He was not up yet. He was held only by the buckle of his belt, caught on the edge of the rock, a buckle now dragged up to his breastbone by the weight of his body. But he did not paw frantically for a handhold, or wriggle his body or flail his legs in the air – and any of these actions would have sent him crashing down again. At last, and once again, he was a man utterly at home in his own element. The greatest rock climber of his time, men called him, and this was what he had been born for.

Slowly, methodically, he felt the surface of the ledge, and almost at once he discovered a crack running back from the face. It would have been better had it been parallel to the face – and more than the width of a matchstick. But it was enough for Mallory. With infinite care he eased the hammer and a couple of spikes from his belt, worked a spike into the crack to obtain a minimal purchase, slid the other in some inches nearer, hooked his left wrist round the first, held the second spike with the fingers of the same hand and brought up the hammer in his free hand. Fifteen seconds later he was standing on the ledge.

Working quickly and surely, catlike in his balance on the slippery, shelving rock, he hammered a spike into the face of the cliff, securely and at a downward angle, about three feet above the ledge, dropped a clove hitch over the top and kicked the rest of the coil over the ledge. Then, and only then, he turned round and looked below him.

Less than a minute had passed since the caique had struck, but already she was a broken-masted, splintered shambles, sides caving in and visibly disintegrating as he watched. Every seven or eight seconds a giant comber would pick her up and fling her bodily against the cliff, the heavy truck tyres taking up only a fraction of the impact that followed, the sickening, rending crash that reduced the gunwales to matchwood, holed and split the sides and cracked the oaken timbers: and then she would roll clear, port side showing, the hungry set pouring in through the torn and ruptured planking.

Three men were standing by what was left of the wheelhouse. *Three* men – suddenly, he realized that Casey Brown was missing, realized, too, that the engine was still running, its clamour rising and falling then rising again, at irregular intervals. Brown was edging the caique backwards and forwards along the cliff, keeping her as nearly as humanly possible in the same position, for he knew their lives depended on Mallory – and on himself. 'The fool!' Mallory swore. 'The crazy fool!'

The caique surged back in a receding trough, steadied, then

swept in against the cliff again, heeling over so wildly that the roof of the wheelhouse smashed and telescoped against the wall of the cliff. The impact was so fierce, the shock so sudden, that Stevens lost both hand-grip and footing and was catapulted into the rock face, upflung arms raised for protection. For a moment he hung there, as if pinned against the wall, then fell back into the sea, limbs and head relaxed, lifeless in his limp acquiescence. He should have died then, drowned under the hammer-blows of the sea or crushed by the next battering-ram collision of caique and cliff. He should have died and he would have died but for the great arm that hooked down and plucked him out of the water like a limp and sodden rag doll and heaved him inboard a bare second before the next bludgeoning impact of the boat against the rock would have crushed the life out of him.

'Come on, for God's sake!' Mallory shouted desperately. 'She'll be gone in a minute! The rope – use the rope!' He saw Andrea and Miller exchange a few quick words, saw them shake and pummel Stevens and stand him on his feet, dazed and retching sea-water, but conscious. Andrea was speaking in his ear, emphasising something and guiding the rope into his hands, and then the caique was swinging in again, Stevens automatically shortening his grip on the rope. A tremendous boost from below by Andrea, Mallory's long arm reaching out and Stevens was on the ledge, sitting with his back to the cliff and hanging on to the spike, dazed still and shaking a muzzy head, but safe.

'You're next, Miller!' Mallory called. 'Hurry up, man – jump for it!'

Miller looked at him and Mallory could have sworn that he was grinning. Instead of taking the rope from Andrea, he ran for'ard to the cabin.

'Just a minute, boss!' he bawled. 'I've forgotten my toothbrush.'

He reappeared in a few seconds, but without the toothbrush. He was carrying the big, green box of explosives, and before Mallory had appreciated what was happening the box, all fifty pounds of it, was curving up into the air, upthrust by the Greek's tireless arms. Automatically Mallory's hands reached for and caught it. He over-balanced, stumbled and toppled forward, still clutching the box, then was brought up with a jerk. Stevens, still clutching the spike, was on his feet now, free hand hooked in Malloy's belt: he was shivering violently, with cold and exhaustion and an oddly fear-laced excitement. But, like Mallory, he was a hillman at home again.

Mallory was just straightening up when the waterproofed radio set came soaring up. He caught it, placed it down, looked over the side.

'Leave that bloody stuff alone!' he shouted furiously. 'Get up here yourself – now!'

Two coils of rope landed on the ledge beside him, then the first of the rucksacks with the food and clothing. He was vaguely aware that Stevens was trying to stack the equipment in some sort of order.

'Do you hear me?' Mallory roared. 'Get up here at once! That's an order. The boat's sinking, you bloody idiots!'

The caique *was* sinking. She was filling up quickly and Casey Brown had abandoned the flooded Kelvin. But she was a far steadier platform now, rolling through a much shorter arc, less violent in her soggy, yielding collisions with the cliff wall. For a moment Mallory thought the sea was dropping away, then he realized that the tons of water in the caique's hold had drastically lowered her centre of gravity, were acting as a counter-balancing weight.

Miller cupped a hand to his ear. Even in the near darkness of the sinking flare his face had an oddly greenish pallor.

'Can't hear a word you say, boss. Besides, she ain't sinkin' yet.' Once again he disappeared into the for'ard cabin.

Within thirty seconds, with all five men working furiously, the remainder of the equipment was on the ledge. The caique was down by the stern, the poop-deck covered and water pouring down the engine-room hatchway as Brown struggled up the rope, the fo'c'sle awash as Miller grabbed the rope and started after him, and as Andrea reached up and swung in against the cliff his legs dangled over an empty sea. The caique had foundered, completely gone from sight: no drifting flotsam, not even an air bubble marked where she had so lately been.

The ledge was narrow, not three feet wide at its broadest, tapering off into the gloom on either side. Worse still, apart from the few square feet where Stevens had piled the gear, it shelved sharply outwards, the rock underfoot treacherous and slippery. Backs to the wall, Andrea and Miller had to stand on their heels, hands outspread and palms inward against the cliff, pressing in to it as closely as possible to maintain their balance. But in less than a minute Mallory had another two spikes hammered in about twenty inches above the ledge, ten feet apart and joined with a rope, a secure lifeline for all of them.

Wearily Miller slid down to a sitting position, leaned his chest in heartfelt thankfulness against the safe barrier of the rope. He fumbled in his breast pocket, produced a pack of cigarettes and handed them round, oblivious to the rain that soaked them in an instant. He was soaking wet from the waist downwards and both his knees had been badly bruised against the cliff wall: he was bitterly cold, drenched by heavy rain and the sheets of spray that broke continually over the ledge: the sharp edge of the rock bit cruelly into the calves of his legs, the tight rope constricted his breathing and he was still ashen-faced and exhausted from long hours of labour and seasickness: but when he spoke, it was with a voice of utter sincerity.

'My Gawd!' he said reverently. 'Ain't this wonderful!'

—— 5 ——

MONDAY NIGHT

0100—0200

Ninety minutes later Mallory wedged himself into a natural rock chimney on the cliff face, drove in a spike beneath his feet and tried to rest his aching, exhausted body. Two minutes' rest, he told himself, only two minutes while Andrea comes up: the rope was quivering and he could just hear, above the shrieking of the wind that fought to pluck him off the cliff face, the metallic scraping as Andrea's boots struggled for a foothold on that wicked overhang immediately beneath him, the overhang that had all but defeated him, the obstacle that he had impossibly overcome only at the expense of torn hands and body completely spent, of shoulder muscles afire with agony and breath that rasped in great gulping inhalations into his starving lungs. Deliberately he forced his mind away from the pains that racked his body, from its insistent demands for rest, and listened again to the ringing of steel against rock, louder this time, carrying clearly even in the gale. . . . He would have to tell Andrea to be more careful on the remaining twenty feet or so that separated them from the top.

At least, Mallory thought wryly, no one would have to tell him to be quiet. He couldn't have made any noise with his feet if he'd tried – not with only a pair of torn socks as cover for his bruised and bleeding feet. He'd hardly covered the first twenty feet of the climb when he'd discovered that his climbing boots were quite useless, had robbed his feet of all sensitivity, the ability to locate and engage the tiny toe-holds which afforded the only sources of purchase. He had removed them with great difficulty, tied them to his belt by the laces – and lost them, had them torn off, when forcing his way under a projecting spur of rock.

The climb itself had been a nightmare, a brutal, gasping agony in the wind and the rain and the darkness, an agony that had eventually dulled the danger and masked the suicidal risks in climbing that sheer unknown face, in interminable agony of hanging on by fingertips and toes, of driving in a hundred spikes, of securing ropes then inching on again up into the darkness. It was a climb such as he had not ever made before, such as he knew he would not ever make again, for this was insanity. It was a climb that had extended him to the utmost of his great skill, his courage and his strength, and then far beyond that again, and he had not known that such reserves, such limitless resources, lay within him or any man. Nor did he know the wellspring, the source of that power that had driven him to where he was, within easy climbing reach of the top. The challenge to a mountaineer, personal danger, pride in the fact that he was probably the only man in southern Europe who could have made the climb, even the sure knowledge that time was running out for the men on Kheros – it was none of these things, he knew that: in the last twenty minutes it had taken him to negotiate that overhang beneath his feet his mind had been drained of all thought and all emotion, and he had climbed only as a machine.

Hand over hand up the rope, easily, powerfully, Andrea hauled himself over the smoothly swelling convexity of the overhang, legs dangling in mid-air. He was festooned with heavy coils of rope, girdled with spikes that protruded from his belt at every angle and lent him the incongruous appearance of a comic-opera Corsican bandit. Quickly he hauled himself up beside Mallory, wedged himself in the chimney and mopped his sweating forehead. As always, he was grinning hugely.

Mallory looked at him, smiled back. Andrea, he reflected, had no right to be there. It was Stevens's place, but Stevens had still been suffering from shock, had lost much blood: besides, it required a first-class climber to bring up the rear, to coil up the ropes as he came and to remove the spikes – there must be no trace left of the ascent: or so Mallory had told him, and Stevens had reluctantly agreed, although the hurt in his face had been easy to see. More than ever now Mallory was glad he had resisted the quiet plea in Stevens's face: Stevens was undoubtedly a fine climber, but what Mallory had required that night was not another mountaineer but a human ladder. Time and time again during the ascent he had stood on Andrea's back, his shoulders, his upturned palm and once – for at least ten seconds and while he was still wearing his steel-shod boots – on his head. And not once had Andrea protested or stumbled or yielded an inch. The man was indestructible, as tough and enduring as the rock on which he stood. Since dusk had fallen that evening, Andrea had laboured unceasingly, done enough work to kill two ordinary men, and, looking at him then, Mallory realized, almost with despair, that even now he didn't look particularly tired.

Mallory gestured at the rock chimney, then upwards at its shadowy mouth limned in blurred rectangular outline against the pale glimmer of the sky. He leant forward, mouth close to Andrea's ear.

'Twenty feet, Andrea,' he said softly. His breath was still coming in painful gasps. 'It'll be no bother – it's fissured on my side and the chances are that it goes up to the top.'

Andrea looked up the chimney speculatively, nodded in silence.

'Better with your boots off,' Mallory went on. 'And any spikes we use we'll work in by hand.'

'Even on a night like this – high winds and rain, cold and black as a pig's inside – and on a cliff like this?' There was neither doubt nor question in Andrea's voice: rather it was acquiescence, unspoken confirmation of an unspoken thought. They had been so long together, had reached such a depth of understanding that words between them were largely superfluous.

Mallory nodded, waited while Andrea worked home a spike, looped his ropes over it and secured what was left of the long ball of twine that stretched four hundred feet below to the ledge where the others waited. Andrea then removed boots and spikes, fastening them to the ropes, eased the slender, double-edged throwing-knife in its leather shoulder scabbard, looked across at Mallory and nodded in turn.

The first ten feet were easy. Palms and back against one side of the chimney and stocking-soled feet against the other, Mallory jack-knifed his way upwards until the widening sheer of the walls defeated him. Legs braced against the far wall, he worked in a spike as far up as he could reach, grasped it with both hands, dropped his legs across and found a toe-hold in the crevice. Two minutes later his hands hooked over the crumbling edge of the precipice.

Noiselessly and with an infinite caution he fingered aside earth and grass and tiny pebbles until his hands were locked on the solid rock itself, bent his knee to seek lodgment for the final toe-hold, then eased a wary head above the cliff-top, a movement imperceptible in its slow-motion, millimetric stealth. He stopped moving altogether as soon as his eyes had cleared the level of the cliff, stared out into the unfamiliar darkness, his whole being, the entire field of consciousness, concentrated into his eyes and his ears. Illogically, and for the first time in all that terrifying ascent, he became acutely aware of his own danger and helplessness, and he cursed himself for his folly in not borrowing Miller's silenced automatic.

The darkness below the high horizon of the lifting hills beyond was just one degree less than absolute: shapes and angles, heights and depressions were resolving themselves in nebulous silhouette, contours and shadowy profiles emerging reluctantly from the darkness, a darkness suddenly no longer vague and unfamiliar but disturbingly reminiscent in what it revealed, clamouring for recognition. And then abruptly, almost with a sense of shock, Mallory had it. The cliff-top before his eyes was exactly as Monsieur Vlachos had drawn and described it – the narrow, bare strip of ground running parallel to the cliff, the jumble of huge boulders behind them and then, beyond these, the steep scree-strewn lower slopes of the mountains. The first break they'd had yet, Mallory thought exultantly – but what a break! The sketchiest navigation but the most incredible luck, right bang on the nose of the target – the highest point of the highest, most precipitous cliffs in Navarone: the one place where the Germans never mounted a guard, because the climb was impossible! Mallory felt the relief, the high elation wash through him in waves. Jubilantly he straightened his leg, hoisted himself halfway over the edge, arms straight, palms down on the top of the cliff. And then he froze into immobility, petrified as the solid rock beneath his hands, his heart thudding painfully in his throat.

One of the boulders had moved. Seven, maybe eight yards away, a shadow had gradually straightened, detached itself stealthily from the surrounding rock, was advancing slowly towards the edge of the cliff. And then the shadow was no longer 'it.' There could be no mistake now – the long jackboots, the long greatcoat beneath the waterproof cape, the close-fitting helmet were all too familiar. Damn Vlachos! Damn Jensen! Damn all the know-alls who sat at home, the pundits of Intelligence who gave a man wrong information and sent him out to die. And in the same instant Mallory damned himself for his own carelessness, for he had been expecting this all along.

For the first two or three seconds Mallory had lain rigid and unmoving, temporarily paralysed in mind and body: already the guard had advanced four or five steps, carbine held in readiness before him, head turned sideways as he listened into the high, thin whine of the wind and the deep and distant booming of the surf below, trying to isolate the sound that had aroused his suspicions. But now the first shock was over and Mallory's mind was working again. To go up on to the top of the cliff would be suicidal: ten to one the guard would hear him scrambling over the edge and shoot him out of hand: and if he did get up he had neither the weapons nor, after that exhausting climb, the strength to tackle an armed, fresh man. He would have to go back down. But he would have to slide down slowly, an inch at a time. At night, Mallory knew, side vision is even more acute than direct, and the guard might catch a sudden movement out of the corner of his eye. And then he would only have to turn his head and that would be the end: even in that darkness, Mallory realized, there could be no mistaking the bulk of his silhouette against the sharp line of the edge of the cliff.

Gradually, every movement as smooth and controlled as possible, every soft and soundless breath a silent prayer, Mallory slipped gradually back over the edge of the cliff. Still the guard advanced, making for a point about five yards to Mallory's left, but still he looked away, his ear turned into the wind. And then Mallory was down, only his finger-tips over the top, and Andrea's great bulk was beside him, his mouth to his ear.

'What is it? Somebody there?'

'A sentry,' Mallory whispered back. His arms were beginning to ache from the strain. 'He's heard something and he's looking for us.'

Suddenly he shrank away from Andrea, pressed himself as closely as possible to the face of the cliff, was vaguely aware of Andrea doing the same thing. A beam of light, hurtful and dazzling to eyes so long accustomed to the dark, had suddenly stabbed out at an angle over the edge of the cliff, was moving slowly along towards them. The German had his torch out, was methodically examining the rim of the cliff. From the angle of the beam, Mallory judged that he was walking along a couple of feet from the edge. On that wild and gusty night he was taking no chances on the crumbly, treacherous top-soil of the cliff: even more likely, he was taking no chances on a pair of sudden hands reaching out for his ankles and jerking him to a mangled death on the rocks and reefs four hundred feet below.

Slowly, inexorably, the beam approached. Even at that slant, it was bound to catch them. With a sudden sick certainly Mallory realized that the German wasn't just suspicious: he *knew* there was someone there, and he wouldn't stop looking until he found them. And there was nothing they could do, just nothing at all. . . . Then Andrea's head was close to his again.

'A stone,' Andrea whispered. 'Over there, behind him.'

Cautiously at first, then frantically, Mallory pawed the cliff-top with his right hand. Earth, only earth, grass roots and tiny pebbles – there was nothing even half the size of a marble. And then Andrea was thrusting something against him and his hand closed over the metallic smoothness of a spike: even in that moment of desperate urgency, with the slender, searching beam only a few feet away, Mallory was conscious of a sudden brief anger with himself – he had still a couple of spikes stuck in his belt and had forgotten all about them.

His arm swung back, jerked convulsively forward, sent the spike spinning away into the darkness. One second passed, then another, he knew he had missed, the beam was only inches from Andrea's shoulders, and then the metallic clatter of the spike striking a boulder fell upon his ear like a benison. The beam wavered for a second, stabbed out aimlessly into the darkness and then whipped round, probing into the boulders to the left. And then the sentry was running towards them, slipping and stumbling in his haste, the barrel of the carbine gleaming in the light of the torch held clamped to it. He'd gone less than ten yards when Andrea was over the top of the cliff like a great, black cat, was padding noiselessly across the ground to the shelter of the nearest boulder. Wraith-like, he fitted in behind it and was gone, a shadow long among shadows.

The sentry was about twenty yards away now, the beam of his torch darting fearfully from boulder to boulder when Andrea struck the haft of his knife against a rock, twice. The sentry whirled round, torch shining along the line of the boulders, then started to run clumsily back again, the skirts of the greatcoat fluttering grotesquely in the wind. The torch was swinging wildly now, and Mallory caught a glimpse of a white, straining face, wide-eyed and fearful, incongruously at variance with the gladiatorial strength of the steel helmet above. God only knew, Mallory thought, what wild and panic-stricken thoughts were passing through his confused mind: noises from the cliff-top, metallic sound from either side among the boulders, the long, eerie vigil, afraid and companionless, on a deserted cliff edge on a dark and tempest-filled night in a hostile land – suddenly Mallory felt a deep stab of compassion for this man, a man like himself, someone's well-loved husband or brother or son who was only doing a dirty and dangerous job as best he could and because he was told to, compassion for his loneliness and his anxieties and his fears, for the sure knowledge that before he had drawn breath another three times he would be dead. . . . Slowly, gauging his time and distance, Mallory raised his head.

'Help!' he shouted. 'Help me! I'm falling!'

The soldier checked in mid-stride and spun round, less than five feet from the rock that hid Andrea. For a second the beam of his torch waved wildly around, then settled on Mallory's head. For another moment he stood stock still, then the carbine in his right hand swung up, the left hand reached down for the barrel. Then he grunted once, a violent and convulsive exhalation of breath, and the thud of the hilt of Andrea's knife striking home against the ribs carried clearly to Mallory's ears, even against the wind. . . .

Mallory stared down at the dead man, at Andrea's impassive face as he wiped the blade of his knife on the greatcoat, rose slowly to his feet, sighed and slid the knife back in its scabbard.

'So, my Keith!' Andrea reserved the punctilious 'Captain' for company only. 'This is why our young lieutenant eats his heart out down below.'

'That is why,' Mallory acknowledged. 'I knew it – or I almost knew it. So did you. Too many coincidences – the German caique investigating, the trouble at the watch-tower – and now this.' Mallory swore, softly and bitterly. 'This is the end of our little friend Captain Briggs of Castelrosso. He'll be cashiered within the month. Jensen will make certain of that.'

Andrea nodded.

'He let Nicolai go?'

'Who else could have known that we were to have landed here, tipped off everyone all along the line?' Mallory paused, dismissed the thought, caught Andrea by the arm. 'The Germans are thorough. Even although they must know it's almost an impossibility to land on a night like this, they'll have a dozen

sentries scattered along the cliffs.' Unconsciously Mallory had
lowered his voice. 'But they wouldn't depend on one man to
cope with five. So—'

'Signals,' Andrea finished for him. 'They must have some way
of letting the others know. Perhaps flares—'

'No, not that,' Mallory disagreed. 'Give their position away.
Telephone. It has to be that. Remember how they were in Crete
– miles of field telephone wire all over the shop?'

Andrea nodded, picked up the dead man's torch, hooded it in
his huge hand and started searching. He returned in less than a
minute.

'Telephone it is,' he announced softly. 'Over there, under the
rocks.'

'Nothing we can do about it,' Mallory said. 'If it does ring,
I'll have to answer or they'll come hot-footing along. I only hope
to heaven they haven't got a bloody password. It would be just
like them.'

He turned away, stopped suddenly.

'But someone's got to come sometime – a relief, sergeant of
the guard, something like that. Probably he's supposed to make
an hourly report. Someone's bound to come – and come soon.
My God, Andrea, we'll have to make it fast!'

'And this poor devil?' Andrea gestured to the huddled shadow
at his feet.

'Over the side with him.' Mallory grimaced in distaste. 'Won't
make any difference to the poor bastard now, and we can't leave
any traces. The odds are they'll think he's gone over the edge –
this top soil's as crumbly and treacherous as hell. . . . You might
see if he's any papers on him – never know how useful they
might be.'

'Not half as useful as these boots on his feet.' Andrea waved
a large hand towards the scree-strewn slopes. 'You are not going
to walk very far there in your stocking soles.'

Five minutes later Mallory tugged three times on the string
that stretched down into the darkness below. Three answering
tugs came from the ledge, and then the cord vanished rapidly
down over the edge of the overhang, drawing with it the long,
steel-cored rope that Mallory paid out from the coil on the top
of the cliff.

The box of explosives was the first of the gear to come up.
The weighted rope plummetted straight down from the point of
the overhang, and padded though the box was on every side
with lashed rucksacks and sleeping-bags it still crashed terrify-

ingly against the cliff on the inner arc of every wind-driven swing of the pendulum. But there was no time for finesse, to wait for the diminishing swing of the pendulum after each tug. Securely anchored to a rope that stretched around the base of a great boulder, Andrea leaned far out over the edge of the precipice and reeled in the seventy-pound deadweight as another man would a trout. In less than three minutes the ammunition box lay beside him on the cliff-top; five minutes later the firing generator, guns and pistols, wrapped in a couple of other sleeping-bags and their lightweight, reversible tent – white on one side, brown and green camouflage on the other – lay beside the explosives.

A third time the rope went down into the rain and the darkness, a third time the tireless Andrea hauled it in, hand over hand. Mallory was behind him, coiling in the slack of the rope, when he heard Andrea' sudden exclamation: two quick strides and he was at the edge of the cliff, his hand on the big Greek's arm.

'What's up, Andrea? Why have you stopped—?'

He broke off, peered through the gloom at the rope in Andrea's hand, saw that it was being held between only finger and thumb. Twice Andrea jerked the rope up a foot or two, let it fall again: the weightless rope swayed wildly in the wind.

'Gone?' Mallory asked quietly.

Andrea nodded without speaking.

'Broken?' Mallory was incredulous. 'A wire-cored rope?'

'I don't think so.' Quickly Andrea reeled in the remaining forty feet. The twine was still attached to the same place, about a fathom from the end. The rope was intact.

'Somebody tied a knot.' Just for a moment the giant's voice sounded tired. 'They didn't tie it too well.'

Mallory made to speak, then flung up an instinctive arm as a great, forked tongue of flame streaked between the cliff-top and unseen clouds above. Their cringing eyes were still screwed tight shut, their nostrils full of the acrid, sulphurous smell of burning, when the first volley of thunder crashed in Titan fury almost overhead, a deafening artillery to mock the pitiful efforts of embattled man, doubly terrifying in the total darkness that followed that searing flash. Gradually the echoes pealed and faded inland in diminishing reverberations, were lost among the valleys of the hills.

'My God!' Mallory murmured. 'That was close. We'd better make it fast, Andrea – this cliff is liable to be lit up like a fair-

ground any minute. . . . What was in that last load you were
bringing up?' He didn't really have to ask – he himself had
arranged for the breaking up of the equipment into three separate loads before he'd left the ledge. It wasn't even that he suspected his tired mind of playing tricks on him; but it was tired
enough, too tired, to probe the hidden compulsion, the nameless hope that prompted him to grasp at nameless straws that
didn't even exist.

'The food,' Andrea said gently. '*All* the food, the stove, the
fuel – and the compasses.'

For five, perhaps ten seconds, Mallory stood motionless. One
half of his mind, conscious of the urgency, the desperate need
for haste, was jabbing him mercilessly: the other half held him
momentarily in a vast irresolution, an irresolution of coldness
and numbness that came not from the lashing wind and sleety
rain but from his own mind, from the bleak and comfortless
imaginings of lost wanderings on that harsh and hostile island,
with neither food nor fire. . . . And then Andrea's great hand
was on his shoulder, and he was laughing softly.

'Just so much less to carry, my Keith. Think how grateful our
tired friend Corporal Miller is going to be. . . . This is only a
little thing.'

'Yes,' Mallory said. 'Yes, of course. A little thing.' He turned
abruptly, tugged the cord, watched the rope disappear over the
edge.

Fifteen minutes later, in drenching, torrential rain, a great,
sheeting downpour almost constantly illuminated by the jagged,
branching stilettos of the forked lightning, Casey Brown's be-
draggled head came into view over the edge of the cliff. The
thunder, too, emptily cavernous in that flat and explosive intensity of sound that lies at the heart of a thunderstorm, was
almost continuous: but in the brief intervals, Casey's voice,
rich in his native Clydeside accent, carried clearly. He was expressing himself fluently in basic Anglo-Saxon, and with cause.
He had had the assistance of two ropes on the way up – the one
stretched from spike to spike and the one used for raising supplies, which Andrea had kept pulling in as he made the ascent.
Casey Brown had secured the end of this round his waist with
a bowline, but the bowline had proved to be nothing of the
sort but a slip-knot, and Andrea's enthusiastic help had almost
cut him in half. He was still sitting on the cliff-top, exhausted
head between his knees, the radio still strapped to his back,

when two tugs on Andrea's rope announced that Dusty Miller was on his way up.

Another quarter of an hour elapsed, an interminable fifteen minutes when, in the lulls between the thunderclaps, every slightest sound was an approaching enemy patrol, before Miller materialised slowly out of the darkness, half-way down the rock chimney. He was climbing steadily and methodically, then checked abruptly at the cliff-top, groping hands pawing uncertainly on the top-soil of the cliff. Puzzled, Mallory bent down, peered into the lean face: both the eyes were clamped tightly shut.

'Relax, Corporal,' Mallory advised kindly. 'You have arrived.'

Dusty Miller slowly opened his eyes, peered round at the edge of the cliff, shuddered and crawled quickly on hands and knees to the shelter of the nearest boulders. Mallory followed and looked down at him curiously.

'What was the idea of closing your eyes coming over the top?'

'I did not,' Miller protested.

Mallory said nothing.

'I closed them at the bottom,' Miller explained wearily. 'I opened them at the top.'

Mallory looked at him incredulously.

'What! All the way?'

'It's like I told you, boss,' Miller complained. 'Back in Castelrosso. When I cross a street and step up on to the sidewalk I gotta hang on to the nearest lamp-post. More or less.' He broke off, looked at Andrea leaning far out over the side of the cliff, and shivered again. 'Brother! Oh, brother! Was I scared!'

Fear. Terror. Panic. Do the thing you fear and the death of fear is certain. Do the thing you fear and the death of fear is certain. Once, twice, a hundred times, Andy Stevens repeated the words to himself, over and over again, like a litany, A psychiatrist had told him that once and he'd read it a dozen times since. Do the thing you fear and the death of fear is certain. The mind is a limited thing, they had said. It can only hold one thought at a time, one impulse to action. Say to yourself, I am brave, I am overcoming this fear, this stupid, unreasoning panic which has no origin except in my own mind, and because the mind *can* only hold one thought at a time, and because thinking and feeling are one, then you *will* be brave, you *will* overcome and the fear will vanish like a shadow in the night. And so Andy Stevens said these things to himself, and the shadows only lengthened and deepened, lengthened and deepened, and the icy claws of fear dug ever more savagely into his dull exhausted mind, into his twisted, knotted stomach.

His stomach. That knotted ball of jangled, writhing nerve-ends beneath the solar plexus. No one could ever know how it was, how it felt, except those whose shredded minds were going, collapsing into complete and final breakdown. The waves of panic and nausea and faintness that flooded up through a suffocating throat to a mind dark and spent and sinewless, a mind fighting with woollen fingers to cling on to the edge of the abyss, a tired and lacerated mind, only momentarily in control, wildly rejecting the clamorous demands of a nervous system, which had already taken far too much, that he should let go, open the torn fingers that were clenched so tightly round the rope. It was just that easy. 'Rest after toil, port after stormy seas.' What was that famous stanza of Spenser's? Sobbing aloud, Stevens wrenched out another spike, sent it spinning into the waiting sea three hundred long feet below, pressed himself closely into the face and inched his way despairingly upwards.

Fear. Fear had been at his elbow all his life, his constant companion, his *alter ego,* at his elbow, or in close prospect or immediate recall. He had become accustomed to that fear, at times almost reconciled, but the sick agony of this night lay far beyond either tolerance or familiartiy. He had never know anything like this before, and even in his terror and confusion he was dimly aware that the fear did not spring from the climb itself. True, the cliff was sheer and almost vertical, and the lightning, the ice-cold rain, the darkness and the bellowing thunder were a waking nightmare. But the climb, technically, was simple: the rope stretched all the way to the top and all he had to do was to follow it and dispose of the spikes as he went. He was sick and bruised and terribly tired, his head ached abominably and he had lost a great deal of blood: but then, more often than not, it is in the darkness of agony and exhaustion that the spirit of man burns most brightly.

Andy Stevens was afraid because his self-respect was gone. Always before, that had been his sheet anchor, had tipped the balance against his ancient enemy – the respect in which other men had held him, the respect he had had for himself. But now these were gone, for his two greatest fears had been realized – he was known to be afraid, he had failed his fellow-man. Both in the fight with the German caique and when anchored above the watch-tower in the creek, he had known that Mallory and

Andrea knew. He had never met such men before, and he had known all along that he could never hide his secrets from such men. He should have gone up that cliff with Mallory, but Mallory had made excuses and taken Andrea instead – Mallory *knew* he was afraid. And twice before, in Castelrosso and when the German boat had closed in on them, he had almost failed his friends – and tonight he had failed them terribly. He had not been thought fit to lead the way with Mallory – and it was he, the sailor of the party, who had made such a botch of tying that last knot, had lost all the food and the fuel that had plummetted into the sea a bare ten feet from where he had stood on the ledge . . . and a thousand men on Kheros were depending on a failure so abject as himself. Sick and spent, spent in mind and body and spirit, moaning aloud in his anguish of fear and self-loathing, and not knowing where one finished and the other began, Andy Stevens climbed blindly on.

The sharp, high-pitched call-up buzz of the telephone cut abruptly through the darkness on the cliff-top. Mallory stiffened and half-turned, hands clenching involuntarily. Again it buzzed, the jarring stridency carrying clearly above the bass rumble of the thunder, fell silent again. And then it buzzed again and kept on buzzing, peremptory in its harsh insistance.

Mallory was half-way towards it when he checked in mid-step, turned slowly round and walked back towards Andrea. The big Greek looked at him curiously.

'You have changed your mind?'

Mallory nodded but said nothing.

'They will keep on ringing until they get an answer,' Andrea murmured. 'And when they get no answer, they will come. They will come quickly and soon.'

'I know, I know.' Mallory shrugged. 'We have to take that chance – certainty rather. The question is – how long will it be before anyone turns up.' Instinctively he looked both ways along the windswept cliff-top: Miller and Brown were posted one on either side about fifty yards away, lost in the darkness. 'It's not worth the risk. The more I think of it, the poorer I think my chances would be of getting away with it. In matters of routine the old Hun tends to be an inflexible sort of character. There's probably a set way of answering the phone, or the sentry has to identify himself by name, or there's a password – or maybe my voice would give me away. On the other hand the sentry's gone without trace, all our gear is up and so's everyone except Stevens. In other words, we've practically made it. We've landed – and nobody knows we're here.'

'Yes.' Andrea nodded slowly. 'Yes, you are right – and Stevens should be up in two or three minutes. It would be foolish to throw away everything we've gained.' He paused, then went on quietly: 'But they are going to come running.' The phone stopped ringing as suddenly as it had started. 'They are going to come now.'

'I know. I hope to hell Stevens . . .' Mallory broke off, spun on his heel, said over his shoulder, 'Keep your eye open for him, will you? I'll warn the others we're expecting company.'

Mallory moved quickly along the cliff-top, keeping well away from the edge. He hobbled rather than walked – the sentry's boots were too small for him and chafed his toes cruelly. Deliberately he closed his mind to the thought of how his feet would be after a few hours' walking over rough territory in these boots: time enough for the reality, he thought grimly, without the added burden of anticipation. . . . He stopped abruptly as something hard and metallic pushed into the small of his back.

'Surrender or die!' The drawling, nasal voice was positively cheerful: after what he had been through on the caique and the cliff face, just to set feet on solid ground again was heaven enough for Dusty Miller.

'Very funny,' Mallory growled. 'Very funny indeed.' He looked curiously at Miller. The American had removed his oilskin cape – the rain had ceased as abruptly as it had come – to reveal a jacket and braided waistcoat even more sodden and saturated than his trousers. It didn't make sense. But there was no time for questions.

'Did you hear the phone ringing just now?' he asked.

'Was that what it was? Yeah, I heard it.'

'The sentry's phone. His hourly report, or whatever it was, must have been overdue. We didn't answer it. They'll be hot-footing along any minute now, suspicious as hell and looking for trouble. Maybe your side, maybe Brown's. Can't approach any other way unless they break their necks climbing over these boulders.' Mallory gestured at the shapeless jumble of rocks behind them. 'So keep your eyes skinned.'

'I'll do that, boss. No shootin', huh?'

'No shooting. Just get back as quickly and quietly as you can and let us know. Come back in five minutes anyway.'

Mallory hurried away, retracing his steps. Andrea was

stretched full length on the cliff-top, peering over the edge. He twisted his head round as Mallory approached.

'I can hear him. He's just at the overhang.'

'Good.' Mallory moved on without breaking step. 'Tell him to hurry, please.'

Ten yards farther on Mallory checked, peered into the gloom ahead. Somebody was coming along the cliff-top at a dead run, stumbling and slipping on the loose gravelly soil.

'Brown?' Mallory called softly.

'Yes, sir. It's me.' Brown was up to him now, breathing heavily, pointing back in the direction he had just come. 'Somebody's coming, and coming fast! Torches waving and jumping all over the place – must be running.'

'How many?' Mallory asked quickly.

'Four or five at least.' Brown was still gasping for breath. 'Maybe more – four or five torches, anyway. You can see them for yourself.' Again he pointed backwards, then blinked in puzzlement. 'That's bloody funny! They're all gone.' He turned back swiftly to Mallory. 'But I can swear—'

'Don't worry,' Mallory said grimly. 'You saw them all right. I've been expecting visitors. They're getting close now and taking no chances. . . . How far away?'

'Hundred yards – not more than a hundred and fifty.'

'Go and get Miller. Tell him to get back here fast.'

Mallory ran back along the cliff edge and knelt beside the huge length of Andrea.

'They're coming, Andrea,' he said quickly. 'From the left. At least five, probably more. Two minutes at the most. Where's Stevens? Can you see him?'

'I can see him.' Andrea was magnificently unperturbed. 'He is just passing the overhang . . .' The rest of his words were lost, drowned in a sudden, violent thunderclap, but there was no need for more. Mallory could see Stevens now, climbing up the rope, strangely old and enfeebled in action, hand over hand in paralysing slowness, half-way now between the overhang and the foot of the chimney.

'Good God!' Mallory swore. 'What's the matter with him? He's going to take all day . . .' He checked himself, cupped his hands to his mouth. 'Stevens! Stevens!' But there was no sign that Stevens had heard. He still kept climbing with the same unnatural over-deliberation, a robot in slow motion.

'He is very near the end,' Andrea said quietly. 'You see he

does not even lift his head. When a climber does not lift his head, he is finished.' He stirred. 'I will go down for him.'

'No.' Mallory's hand was on his shoulder. 'Stay here. I can't risk you both. . . . Yes, what is it?' He was aware that Brown was back, bending over him, his breath coming in great heaving gasps.

'Hurry, sir; hurry, for God's sake!' A few brief words but he had to suck in two huge gulps of air to get them out. 'They're on top of us!'

'Get back to the rocks with Miller,' Mallory said urgently. 'Cover us. . . . Stevens! Stevens!' But again the wind swept up the face of the cliff, carried his words away.

'Stevens! For God's sake, man! Stevens!' His voice was low-pitched, desperate, but this time some quality in it must have reached through Stevens's fog of exhaustion and touched his consciousness, for he stopped climbing and lifted his head, hand cupped to his ear.

'Some Germans coming!' Mallory called through funnelled hands, as loudly as he dared. 'Get to the foot of the chimney and stay there. Don't make a sound. Understand?'

Stevens lifted his hand, gestured in tired acknowledgment, lowered his head, started to climb up again. He was going even more slowly now, his movements fumbling and clumsy.

'Do you think he understands?' Andrea was troubled.

'I think so. I don't know.' Mallory stiffened and caught Andrea's arm. It was beginning to rain again, not heavily yet, and through the drizzle he'd caught sight of a hooded torch beam probing among the rocks thirty yards away to his left. 'Over the edge with the rope,' he whispered. 'The spike at the bottom of the chimney will hold it. Come on – let's get out of here!'

Gradually, meticulous in their care not to dislodge the smallest pebble, Mallory and Andrea inched back from the edge, squirmed round and headed back for the rocks, pulling themselves along on their elbows and knees. The few yards were interminable and without even a gun in his hand Mallory felt defenceless, completely exposed. An illogical feeling, he knew, for the first beam of light to fall on them meant the end not for them but for the man who held the torch. Mallory had complete faith in Brown and Miller. . . . That wasn't important. What mattered was the complete escape from detection. Twice during the last endless few feet a wandering beam reached out towards them, the second a bare arm's length away: both times they pressed their faces into the sodden earth, lest the pale blur of their faces betray them, and lay very still. And then, all at once it seemed, they were among the rocks and safe.

In a moment Miller was beside them, a half-seen shadow against the darker dusk of the rocks around them.

'Plenty of time, plenty of time,' he whispered sarcastically. 'Why didn't you wait another half-hour? 'He gestured to the left, where the flickering of torches, the now clearly audible murmur of guttural voices, were scarcely twenty yards away. 'We'd better move farther back. They're looking for him among the rocks.'

'For him or for his telephone,' Mallory murmured in agreement. 'You're right anyway. Watch your guns on these rocks. Take the gear with you. . . . And if they look over and find Stevens we'll have to take the lot. No time for fancy work and to hell with the noise. Use the automatic carbines.'

Andy Stevens had heard, but he had not understood. It was not that he panicked, was too terrified to understand, for he was no longer afraid. Fear is of the mind, but his mind had ceased to function, drugged by the last stages of exhaustion, crushed by the utter, damnable tiredness that held his limbs, his whole body, in leaden thrall. He did not know it, but fifty feet below he had struck his head against a spur of rock, a sharp, wicked projection that had torn his gaping temple wound open to the bone. His strength drained out with the pulsing blood.

He had heard Mallory, had heard something about the chimney he had now reached, but his mind had failed to register the meaning of the words. All that Stevens knew was that he was climbing, and that one always kept on climbing until one reached the top. That was what his father had always impressed upon him, his brothers too. You must reach the top.

He was half-way up the chimney now, resting on the spike that Mallory had driven into the fissure. He hooked his fingers in the crack, bent back his head and stared up towards the mouth of the chimney. Ten feet away, no more. He was conscious of neither surprise nor elation. It was just there: he had to reach it. He could hear voices, carrying clearly from the top. He was vaguely surprised that his friends were making no attempt to help him, that they had thrown away the rope that would have made those last few feet so easy, but he felt no bitterness, no emotion at all: perhaps they were trying to test him. What did it matter anyway – he had to reach the top.

He reached the top. Carefully, as Mallory had done before him, he pushed aside the earth and tiny pebbles, hooked his fingers over the edge, found the same toe-hold as Mallory had and levered himself upwards. He saw the flickering torches, heard the excited voices, and then for an instant the curtain of fog in his mind lifted and a last tidal wave of fear washed over him and he knew that the voices were the voices of the enemy and that they had destroyed his friends. He knew now that he was alone, that he had failed, that this was the end, one way or another, and that it had all been for nothing. And then the fog closed over him again, and there was nothing but the emptiness of it all, the emptiness and the futility, the overwhelming lassitude and despair and his body slowly sinking down the face of the cliff. And then the hooked fingers – they, too, were slipping away, opening gradually, reluctantly as the fingers of a drowning man releasing their final hold on a spar of wood. There was no fear now, only a vast and heedless indifference as his hands slipped away and he fell like a stone, twenty vertical feet into the cradling bottle-neck at the foot of the chimney.

He himself made no sound, none at all: the soundless scream of agony never passed his lips, for the blackness came with the pain: but the straining ears of the men crouching in the rocks above caught clearly the dull sickening crack as his right leg fractured cleanly in two, snapping like a rotten bough.

6

MONDAY NIGHT

0200–0600

The German patrol was everything that Mallory had feared – efficient, thorough and very, very painstaking. It even had imagination, in the person of its young and competent sergeant, and that was more dangerous still.

There were only four of them, in high boots, helmets and green, grey and brown mottled capes. First of all they located the telephone and reported to base. Then the young sergeant sent two men to search another hundred yards or so along the cliff, while he and the fourth soldier probed among the rocks that paralleled the cliff. The search was slow and careful, but the two men did not penetrate very far into the rocks. To Mallory, the sergeant's reasoning was obvious and logical. If the sentry had gone to sleep or taken ill, it was unlikely that he would have gone far in among that confused jumble of boulders. Mallory and the others were safely back beyond their reach.

And then came what Mallory had feared – an organised, methodical inspection of the cliff-top itself: worse still, it began with a search along the very edge. Securely held by his three men with interlinked arms – the last with a hand hooked round his belt – the sergeant walked slowly along the rim, probing every inch with the spot-lit beam of a powerful torch. Suddenly he stopped short, exclaimed suddenly and stooped, torch and face only inches from the ground. There was no question as to what he had found – the deep gouge made in the soft, crumbling soil by the climbing rope that had been belayed round the boulder and gone over the edge of the cliff. . . . Softly, silently, Mallory and his three companions straightened to their knees or to their feet, gun barrels lining along the tops of boulders or peering out between cracks in the rocks. There was no doubt in any of their minds that Stevens was lying there helplessly in the crutch of the chimney, seriously injured or dead. It needed only one German carbine to point down that cliff face, however carelessly, and these four men would die. They would have to die.

The sergeant was stretched out his length now, two men holding his legs. His head and shoulders were over the edge of the cliff, the beam from his torch stabbing down the chimney. For ten, perhaps fifteen seconds, there was no sound on the cliff-top, no sound at all, only the high, keening moan of the wind and the swish of the rain in the stunted grass. And then the sergeant had wriggled back and risen to his feet, slowly shaking his head. Mallory gestured to the others to sink down behind the boulders again, but even so the sergeant's soft Bavarian voice carried clearly in the wind.

'It's Ehrich all right, poor fellow.' Compassion and anger blended curiously in the voice. 'I warned him often enough about his carelessness, about going too near the edge of that cliff. It is very treacherous.' Instinctively the sergeant stepped back a couple of feet and looked again at the gouge in the soft earth. 'That's where his heel slipped – or maybe the butt of his carbine. Not that it matters now.'

'Is he dead, do you think, Sergeant?' The speaker was only a boy, nervous and unhappy.

'It's hard to say. . . . Look for yourself.'

Gingerly the youth lay down on the cliff-top, peering cautiously over the lip of the rock. The other soldiers were talking among themselves, in short staccato sentences when Mallory turned to Miller, cupped his hands to his mouth and the American's ear. He could contain his puzzlement no longer.

'Was Stevens wearing his dark suit when you left him?' he whispered.

'Yeah,' Miller whispered back. 'Yeah, I think he was.' A pause. 'No, dammit, I'm wrong. We both put on our rubber camouflage capes about the same time.'

Mallory nodded. The waterproofs of the Germans were almost identical with their own: and the sentry's hair, Mallory remembered, had been jet black – the same colour as Stevens's dyed hair. Probably all that was visible from above was a crumpled, cape-shrouded figure and a dark head. The sergeant's mistake in identity was more than understandable: it was inevitable.

The young soldier eased himself back from the edge of the cliff and hoisted himself carefully to his feet.

'You're right, Sergeant. It *is* Ehrich.' The boy's voice was unsteady. 'He's alive, I think. I saw his cape move, just a little. It wasn't the wind, I'm sure of that.'

Mallory felt Andrea's massive hand squeezing his arm, felt the quick surge of relief, then elation, wash through him. So Stevens *was* alive! Thank God for that! They'd save the boy yet. He heard Andrea whispering the news to the others, then grinned wryly to himself, ironic at his own gladness. Jensen definitely would not have approved of this jubilation. Stevens had already done his part, navigated the boat to Navarone, and climbed the cliff: and now he was only a crippled liability, would be a drag on the whole party, reduce what pitful chances of success remained to them. For a High Command who pushed the counters around crippled pawns slowed up the whole game, made the board so damnably untidy. It was most inconsiderate of Stevens not to have killed himself so that they could have disposed of him neatly and without trace in the deep and hungry waters that boomed around the foot of the cliff. . . . Mallory clenched his hands in the darkness and swore to himself that the boy would live, come home again, and to hell with total war and all its inhuman demands. . . . Just a kid, that was all, a scared and broken kid and the bravest of them all.

The young sergeant was issuing a string of orders to his men, his voice was quick, crisp and confident. A doctor, splints, rescue stretcher, anchored sheer-legs, ropes, spikes – the trained, well-ordered mind missed nothing. Mallory waited tensely, wondering how many men, if any, would be left on guard, for the guards would have to go and that would inevitably betray them. The question of their quick and silent disposal never entered his mind – a whisper in Andrea's ear and the guards would have no more chance than penned lambs against a marauding wolf. Less chance even than that – the lambs could always run and cry out before the darkness closed over them.

The sergeant solved the problem for them. The assured competence, the tough, unsentimental ruthlessness that made the German NCO the best in the world gave Mallory the chance he never expected to have. He had just finished giving his orders when the young soldier touched him on the arm, then pointed over the edge.

'How about poor Ehrich, Sergeant?' he asked uncertainly. 'Shouldn't – don't you think one of us ought to stay with him?'

'And what could you do if you did stay – hold his hand?' the sergeant asked acidly. 'If he stirs and falls, then he falls, that's all, and it doesn't matter then if a hundred of us are standing up here watching him. Off you go, and don't forget the mallets and pegs to stay the sheer-legs.'

The three men turned and went off quickly to the east without another word. The sergeant walked over to the phone, reported briefly to someone, then set off in the opposite direction – to check the next guard post, Mallory guessed. He was still in sight, a dwindling blur in the darkness, when Mallory whispered to Brown and Miller to post themselves on guard again: and they could still hear the measured crunch of his firm footfalls on a patch of distant gravel as their belayed rope went snaking over the edge of the cliff, Andrea and Mallory sliding swiftly down even before it had stopped quivering.

Stevens, a huddled, twisted heap with a gashed and bleeding cheek lying cruelly along a razor-sharp spur of rock, was still unconscious, breathing stertorously through his open mouth. Below the knee his right leg twisted upwards and outwards against the rock at an impossible angle. As gently as he could, braced against either side of the chimney and supported by Andrea, Mallory lifted and straightened the twisted limb. Twice, from the depths of the dark stupor of his unconsciousness, Stevens moaned in agony, but Mallory had no option but to carry on, his teeth clenched tight until his jaws ached. Then slowly, with infinite care, he rolled up the trouser leg, winced and screwed his eyes shut in momentary horror and nausea as he saw the dim whiteness of the shattered tibia sticking out through the torn and purply swollen flesh.

'Compound fracture, Andrea.' Gently his exploring fingers slid down the mangled leg, beneath the lip of the jackboot, stopped suddenly as something gave way beneath his feather touch. 'Oh, my God!' he murmured. 'Another break, just above the ankle. This boy is in a bad way, Andrea.'

'He is indeed,' Andrea said gravely. 'We can do nothing for him here?'

'Nothing. Just nothing. We'll have to get him up first.' Mallory straightened, gazed up bleakly at the perpendicular face of the chimney. 'Although how in the name of heaven—'

'I will take him up.' There was no suggestion in Andrea's voice either of desperate resolve or consciousness of the almost incredible effort involved. It was simply a statement of intention, the voice of a man who never questioned his ability to do what he said he would. 'If you will help me to raise him, to tie him to my back. . . .'

'With his broken leg loose, dangling from a piece of skin and torn muscle?' Mallory protested. 'Stevens can't take much more. He'll die if we do this.'

'He'll die if we don't,' Andrea murmured.

Mallory stared down at Stevens for a long moment, then nodded heavily in the darkness.

'He'll die if we don't,' he echoed tiredly. 'Yes, we have to do this.' He pushed outwards from the rock, slid half a dozen feet down the rope and jammed a foot in the crutch of the chimney just below Stevens's body. He took a couple of turns of rope round his waist and looked up.

'Ready, Andrea?' he called softly.

'Ready.' Andrea stooped, hooked his great hands under Stevens's armpits and lifted slowly, powerfully, as Mallory pushed from below. Twice, three times before they had him up, the boy moaned deep down in his tortured throat, the long, quivering 'Aahs' of agony setting Mallory's teeth on edge: and then his dangling, twisted leg had passed from Mallory's reach and he was held close and cradled in Andrea's encircling arm, the rain-lashed, bleeding mask of a face lolling grotesquely backwards, forlorn and lifeless with the dead pathos of a broken doll. Seconds later Mallory was up beside them, expertly lashing Stevens's wrists together. He was swearing softly, as his numbed hands looped and tightened the rope, softly, bitterly, continuously, but he was quite unaware of this: he was aware only of the broken head that lolled stupidly against his shoulder, of the welling, rain-thinned blood that filmed the upturned face, of the hair above the gashed temple emerging darkly fair as the dye washed slowly out. Inferior bloody boot-blacking, Mallory thought savagely: Jensen shall know of this – it could cost a man's life. And then he became aware of his own thoughts and swore again, still more savagely and at himself this time, for the utter triviality of what he was thinking.

With both hands free – Stevens's bound arms were looped round his neck, his body lashed to his own – Andrea took less than thirty seconds to reach the top; if the dragging, one hundred and sixty pound deadweight on his back made any difference to Andrea's climbing speed and power, Mallory couldn't detect it. The man's endurance was fantastic. Once, just once, as Andrea scrambled over the edge of the cliff, the broken leg caught on the rock, and the crucifying torture of it seared through the merciful shell of insensibility, forced a brief shriek of pain from his lips, a hoarse, bubbling whisper of sound all the more horrible for its muted agony. And then Andrea was standing upright and Mallory was behind him, cutting swiftly at the ropes that bound the two together.

'Straight into the rocks with him, Andrea, will you?' Mallory whispered. 'Wait for us at the first open space you come to.' Andrea nodded slowly and without raising his head, his hooded eyes bent over the boy in his arms, like a man sunk in thought. Sunk in thought or listening, and all unawares Mallory, too, found himself looking and listening into the thin, lost moaning of the wind, and there was nothing there, only the lifting, dying threnody and the chill of the rain hardening to an ice-cold sleet. He shivered, without knowing why, and listened again; then he shook himself angrily, turned abruptly towards the cliff face and started reeling in the rope. He had it all up, lying round his feet in a limp and rain-sodden tangle when he remembered about the spike still secured to the foot of the chimney, the hundreds of feet of rope suspended from it.

He was too tired and cold and depressed even to feel exasperated with himself. The sight of Stevens and the knowledge of how it was with the boy had affected him more than he knew. Moodily, almost, he kicked the rope over the side again, slid down the chimney, untied the second rope and sent the spike spinning out into the darkness. Less than ten minutes later, the wetly-coiled ropes over his shoulder, he led Miller and Brown into the dark confusion of the rocks.

They found Stevens lying under the lee of a huge boulder, less than a hundred yards inland, in a tiny, cleared space barely the size of a billiard table. An oilskin was spread beneath him on the sodden, gravelly earth, a camouflage cape covered most of his body: it was bitterly cold now, but the rock broke the force of the wind, sheltered the boy from the driving sleet. Andrea looked up as the three men dropped into the hollow and lowered their gear to the ground; already, Mallory could see, Andrea had rolled the trouser up beyond the knee and cut the heavy jackboot away from the mangled leg.

'Sufferin' Christ!' The words, half-oath, half-prayer, were torn involuntarily from Miller: even in the deep gloom the shattered leg looked ghastly. Now he dropped on one knee and stooped low over it. 'What a mess!' he murmured slowly. He looked up over his shoulder. 'We've gotta do something about that leg, boss, and we've no damned time to lose. This kid's a good candidate for the mortuary.'

'I know. We've got to save him, Dusty, we've just *got* to.' All at once this had become terribly important to Mallory. He dropped down on his knees. 'Let's have a look at him.'

Impatiently Miller waved him away.

'Leave this to me, boss.' There was a sureness, a sudden authority in his voice that held Mallory silent. 'The medicine pack, quick – and undo that tent.'

'You sure you can handle this?' God knew, Mallory thought, he didn't really doubt him – he was conscious only of gratitude, of a profound relief, but he felt he had to say something. 'How are you going—'

'Look, boss,' Miller said quietly. 'All my life I've worked with just three things – mines, tunnels and explosives. They're kinda tricky things, boss. I've seen hundreds of busted arms and legs – and fixed most of them myself.' He grinned wryly in the darkness. 'I was boss myself, then – just one of my privileges, I reckon.'

'Good enough!' Mallory clapped him on the shoulder. 'He's all yours, Dusty. But the tent!' Involuntarily he looked over his shoulder in the direction of the cliff. 'I mean—'

'You got me wrong, boss.' Miller's hands, steady and precise with the delicate certainty of a man who has spent a lifetime with high explosive, were busy with a swab and disinfectant. 'I

376

wasn't fixin' on settin' up a base hospital. But we need tent-poles – splints for his legs.'

'Of course, of course. The poles. Never occurred to me for splints – and I've been thinking of nothing else for—'

'They're not too important, boss.' Miller had the medicine pack open now, rapidly selecting the items he wanted with the aid of a hooded torch. 'Morphine – that's the first thing, or this kid's goin' to die of shock. And then shelter, warmth, dry clothin'—'

'Warmth! Dry clothing!' Mallory interrupted incredulously. He looked down at the unconscious boy, remembering how Stevens had lost them the stove and all the fuel, and his mouth twisted in bitterness. His own executioner. . . . 'Where in God's name are we going to find them?'

'I don't know, boss,' Miller said simply. 'But we gotta find them. And not just to lessen shock. With a leg like this and soaked to the skin, he's bound to get pneumonia. And then as much sulfa as that bloody great hole in his leg will take – one touch of sepsis in the state this kid's in . . .' His voice trailed away into silence.

Mallory rose to his feet.

'I reckon you're the boss.' It was a very creditable imitation of the American's drawl, and Miller looked up quickly, surprise melting into a tired smile, then looked away again. Mallory could hear the chatter of his teeth as he bent over Stevens, and sensed rather than saw that he was shivering violently, continuously, but oblivious to it all in his complete concentration on the job in hand. Miller's clothes, Mallory remembered again, were completely saturated: not for the first time, Mallory wondered how he had managed to get himself into such a state with a waterproof covering him.

'You fix him up. I'll find a place.' Mallory wasn't as confident as he felt: still, on the scree-strewn, volcanic slopes of these hills behind, there ought to be a fair chance of finding a rock shelter, if not a cave. Or there would have been in day-light: as it was they would just have to trust to luck to stumble on one. . . . He saw that Casey Brown, grey-faced with exhaustion and illness – the after-effects of carbon monoxide poisoning are slow to disappear – had risen unsteadily to his feet and was making for a gap between the rocks.

'Where are you going, Chief?'

'Back for the rest of the stuff, sir.'

'Are you sure you can manage?' Mallory peered at him closely. 'You don't look any too fit to me.'

'I don't feel it either,' Brown said frankly. He looked at Mallory. 'But with all respects, sir, I don't think you've seen yourself recently.'

'You have a point,' Mallory acknowledged. 'All right then, come on. I'll go with you.'

For the next ten minutes there was silence in the tiny clearing, a silence broken only by the murmurs of Miller and Andrea working over the shattered leg, and the moans of the injured man as he twisted and struggled feebly in his dark abyss of pain: then gradually the morphine took effect and the struggling lessened and died away altogether, and Miller was able to work rapidly, without fear of interruption. Andrea had an oilskin outstretched above them. It served a double purpose – it curtained off the sleet that swept round them from time to time and blanketed the pinpoint light of the rubber torch he held in his free hand. And then the leg was set and bandaged and as heavily splinted as possible and Miller was on his feet, straightening his aching back.

'Thank Gawd that's done,' he said wearily. He gestured at Stevens. 'I feel just the way that kid looks.' Suddenly he stiffened, stretched out a warning arm. 'I can hear something, Andrea,' he whispered.

Andrea laughed. 'It's only Brown coming back, my friend. He's been coming this way for over a minute now.'

'How do you know it's Brown?' Miller challenged. He felt vaguely annoyed with himself and unobtrusively shoved his ready automatic back into his pocket.

'Brown is a good man among rocks,' Andrea said gently; 'but he is tired. But Captain Mallory . . .' He shrugged. 'People call me "the big cat" I know, but among the mountains and rocks the captain is more than a cat. He is a ghost, and that was how men called him in Crete. You will know he is here when he touches you on the shoulder.'

Miller shivered in a sudden icy gust of sleet.

'I wish you people wouldn't creep around so much,' he complained. He looked up as Brown came round the corner of a boulder, slow with the shambling, stumbling gait of an exhausted man. 'Hi, there, Casey. How are things goin'?'

'Not too bad.' Brown murmured his thanks as Andrea took the box of explosives off his shoulder and lowered it easily to the ground. 'This is the last of the gear. Captain sent me back with

it. We heard voices some way along the cliff. He's staying behind
to see what they say when they find Stevens gone.' Wearily he
sat down on top of the box. 'Maybe he'll get some idea of what
they're going to do next, if anything.'

'Seems to me he could have left you there and carried that
damned box back himself,' Miller growled. Disappointment in
Mallory made him more outspoken than he'd meant to be. 'He's
much better off than you are right now, and I think it's a bit
bloody much . . .' He broke off and gasped in pain as Andrea's
finger caught his arm like giant steel pincers.

'It is not fair to talk like that, my friend,' Andrea said reproachfully. 'You forget, perhaps, that Brown here cannot talk
or understand a word of German?'

Miller rubbed his bruised arm tenderly, shaking his head in
slow self-anger and condemnation.

'Me and my big mouth,' he said ruefully. 'Always talkin' outa
turn Miller, they call me. Your pardon, one and all. . . . And
what is next on the agenda, gentlemen?'

'Captain says we're to go straight on into the rocks and up the
right shoulder of this hill here.' Brown jerked a thumb in the
direction of the vague mass, dark and strangely foreboding, that
towered above and beyond them. 'He'll catch us up within fifteen
minutes or so.' He grinned tiredly at Miller. 'And we're to leave
this box and a rucksack for him to carry.'

'Spare me,' Miller pleaded. 'I feel only six inches tall as it is.'
He looked down at Stevens, lying quietly under the darkly
gleaming wetness of the oilskins, then up at Andrea. 'I'm afraid,
Andrea—'

'Of course, of course!' Andrea stooped quickly, wrapped the
oil skins round the unconscious boy and rose to his feet, as effor-
lessly as if the oilskins had been empty.

'I'll lead the way,' Miller volunteered. 'Mebbe I can pick an
easy path for you and young Stevens.' He swung generator and
rucksacks on to his shoulder, staggering under the sudden
weight; he hadn't realized he was so weak. 'At first, that is,' he
amended. 'Later on, you'll have to carry us both.'

Mallory had badly miscalculated the time it would require to
overtake the others; over an hour had elapsed since Brown had
left him, and still there were no signs of the others. And with
seventy pounds on his back, he wasn't making such good time
himself.

It wasn't all his fault. The returning German patrol, after the first shock of discovery, had searched the cliff-top again, methodically and with exasperating slowness. Mallory had waited tensely for someone to suggest descending and examining the chimney — the gouge-marks of the spikes on the rock would have been a dead giveaway – but nobody even mentioned it. With the guard obviously fallen to his death. it would have been a pointless thing to do anyway. After an unrewarding search, they had debated for an unconscionable time as to what they should do next. Finally they had done nothing. A replacement guard was left, and the rest made off along the cliff, carrying their rescue equipment with them.

The three men ahead had made surprisingly good time, although the conditions, admittedly, were now much easier. The heavy fall of boulders at the foot of the slope had petered out after another fifty yards, giving way to broken scree and rain-washed rubble. Possibly he had passed them, but it seemed unlikely: in the intervals between these driving sleet showers – it was more like hail now – he was able to scan the bare shoulder of the hill, and nothing moved. Besides, he knew that Andrea wouldn't stop until he reached what promised at least a bare minimum of shelter, and as yet these exposed windswept slopes had offered nothing that even remotely approached that.

In the end, Mallory almost literally stumbled upon both men and shelter. He was negotiating a narrow, longitudinal spine of rock, had just crossed its razor-back, when he heard the murmur of voices beneath him and saw a tiny glimmer of light behind the canvas stretching down from the overhang of the far wall of the tiny ravine at his feet.

Miller started violently and swung round as he felt the hand on his shoulder; the automatic was half-way out of his pocket before he saw who it was and sunk back heavily on the rock behind him.

'Come, come, now! Trigger-happy.' Thankfully Mallory slid his burden from his aching shoulders and looked across at the softly laughing Andrea. 'What's so funny?'

'Our friend here.' Andrea grinned again. 'I told him that the first thing he would know of your arrival would be when you touched him on the shoulder. I don't think he believed me.'

'You might have coughed or somethin',' Miller said defensively. 'It's my nerves, boss,' he added plaintively. 'They're not what they were forty-eight hours ago.'

Mallory looked at him disbelievingly, made to speak, then stopped short as he caught sight of the pale blur of a face propped up against a rucksack. Beneath the white swathe of a bandaged forehead the eyes were open, looking steadily at him. Mallory took a step forward, sank down on one knee.

'So you've come round at last!' He smiled into the sunken parchment face and Stevens smiled back, the bloodless lips whiter than the face itself. He looked ghastly. 'How do you feel, Andy?'

'Not too bad, sir. Really I'm not.' The bloodshot eyes were dark and filled with pain. His gaze fell and he looked down vacantly at his bandaged leg, looked up again, smiled uncertainly at Mallory. 'I'm terribly sorry about all this, sir. What a bloody stupid thing to do.'

'It wasn't a stupid thing.' Mallory spoke with slow, heavy emphasis. 'It was criminal folly.' He knew everyone was watching them, but knew, also, that Stevens had eyes for him alone. 'Criminal, unforgivable folly,' he went on quietly, '– and I'm the man in the dock. I'd suspected you'd lost a lot of blood on the boat, but I didn't know you had these big gashes on your forehead. I should have made it my business to find out.' He smiled wryly. 'You should have heard what these two insubordinate characters had to say to me about it when they got to the top. . . . And they were right. You should never have been asked to bring up the rear in the state you were in. It was madness.' He grinned again. 'You should have been hauled up like a sack of coals like the intrepid mountaineering team of Miller and Brown. . . . God knows how you ever made it – I'm sure you'll never know.' He leaned forward, touched Stevens's sound knee. 'Forgive me, Andy. I honestly didn't realize how far through you were.'

Stevens stirred uncomfortably, but the dead pallor of the high-boned cheeks was stained with embarrassed pleasure.

'Please, sir,' he pleaded. 'Don't talk like that. It was just one of these things.' He paused, eyes screwed shut and indrawn breath hissing sharply through his teeth as a wave of pain washed up from his shattered leg. Then he looked at Mallory again. 'And there's no credit due to me for the climb,' he went on quietly. 'I hardly remember a thing about it.'

Mallory looked at him without speaking, eyebrows arched in mild interrogation.

'I was scared to death every step of the way up,' Stevens said simply. He was conscious of no surprise, no wonder that he was saying the thing he would have died rather than say. 'I've never been so scared in all my life.'

Mallory shook his head slowly from side to side, stubbled chin rasping in his cupped palm. He seemed genuinely puzzled. Then he looked down at Stevens and smiled quizzically.

'Now I know you *are* new to this game, Andy.' He smiled again. 'Maybe you think I was laughing and singing all the way up that cliff? Maybe you think *I* wasn't scared?' He lit a cigarette and gazed at Stevens through a cloud of drifting smoke. 'Well, I wasn't. "Scared" isn't the word – I was bloody well terrified. So was Andrea here. We knew too much not to be scared.'

'Andrea!' Stevens laughed, then cried out as the movement triggered off a crepitant agony in his bone-shattered leg. For a moment Mallory thought he had lost consciousness, but almost at once he spoke again, his voice husky with pain. 'Andrea!' he whispered. 'Scared! I don't believe it.'

'Andrea *was* afraid.' The big Greek's voice was very gentle. 'Andrea *is* afraid. Andrea is always afraid. That is why I have lived so long.' He stared down at his great hands. 'And why so many have died. They were not so afraid as I. They were not afraid of everything a man could be afraid of, there was always something they forgot to fear, to guard against. But Andrea was afraid of everything – and he forgot nothing. It is as simple as that.'

He looked across at Stevens and smiled.

'There are no brave men and cowardly men in the world, my son. There are only brave men. To be born, to live, to die – that takes courage enough in itself, and more than enough. We are all brave men and we are all afraid, and what the world calls a brave man, he, too, is brave and afraid like all the rest of us. Only he is brave for five minutes longer. Or sometimes ten minutes, or twenty minutes – or the time it takes a man sick and bleeding and afraid to climb a cliff.'

Stevens said nothing. His head was sunk on his chest, and his face was hidden. He had seldom felt so happy, seldom so at peace with himself. He had known that he could not hide things from men like Andrea and Mallory, but he had not known that it would not matter. He felt he should say something, but he could not think what and he was deathly tired. He knew, deep down, that Andrea was speaking the truth, but not the whole truth; but he was too tired to care, to try to work things out.

Miller cleared his throat noisily.

'No more talkin', Lieutenant,' he said firmly. 'You gotta lie down, get yourself some sleep.'

Stevens looked at him, then at Mallory in puzzled inquiry.

'Better do what you're told, Andy,' Mallory smiled. 'Your surgeon and medical adviser talking. He fixed your leg.'

'Oh! I didn't know. Thanks, Dusty. Was it very – difficult?' Miller waved a deprecatory hand.

'Not for a man of my experience. Just a simple break,' he lied easily. 'Almost let one of the others do it. . . . Give him a hand to lie down, will you, Andrea?' He jerked his head towards Mallory. 'Boss?'

The two men moved outside, turning their backs to the icy wind.

'We gotta get a fire, dry clothing, for that kid,' Miller said urgently. 'His pulse is about 140, temperature 103. He's runnin' a fever, and he's losin' ground all the time.'

'I know, I know,' Mallory said worriedly. 'And there's not a hope of getting any fuel on this damned mountain. Let's go in and see how much dried clothing we can muster between us.'

He lifted the edge of the canvas and stepped inside. Stevens was still awake, Brown and Andrea on either side of him. Miller was on his heels.

'We're going to stay here for the night,' Mallory announced, 'so let's make things as snug as possible. Mind you,' he admitted, 'we're a bit too near the cliff for comfort, but old Jerry hasn't a clue we're on the island, and we're out of sight of the coast. Might as well make ourselves comfortable.'

'Boss . . .' Miller made to speak, then fell silent again. Mallory looked at him in surprise, saw that he, Brown and Stevens were looking at one another, uncertainty, then doubt and a dawning, sick comprehension in their eyes. A sudden anxiety, the sure knowledge that something was far wrong, struck at Mallory like a blow.

'What's up?' he demanded, sharply. 'What is it?'

'We have bad news for you, boss,' Miller said carefully. 'We should have told you right away. Guess we all thought that one of the others would have told you. . . . Remember that sentry you and Andrea shoved over the side?'

Mallory nodded, sombrely. He knew what was coming.

'He fell on top of that reef twenty-thirty feet or so from the cliff,' Miller went on. 'Wasn't much of him left, I guess, but what was was jammed between two rocks. He was really stuck good and fast.'

'I see,' Mallory murmured. 'I've been wondering all night how you managed to get so wet under your rubber cape.'

'I tried four times, boss,' Miller said quietly. 'The others had a rope round me.' He shrugged his shoulders. 'Not a chance. Them gawddamned waves just flung me back against the cliff every time.'

'It will be light in three or four hours,' Mallory murmured. 'In four hours they will know we are on the island. They will see him as soon as it's dawn and send a boat to investigate.'

'Does it really matter, sir,' Stevens suggested. 'He could still have fallen.'

Mallory eased the canvas aside and looked out into the night. It was bitterly cold and the snow was beginning to fall all around them. He dropped the canvas again.

'Five minutes,' he said absently. 'We will leave in five minutes.' He looked at Stevens and smiled faintly. 'We are forgetful too. We should have told you. Andrea stabbed the sentry through the heart.'

The hours that followed were hours plucked from the darkest nightmare, endless, numbing hours of stumbling and tripping and falling and getting up again, of racked bodies and aching, tortured muscles, of dropped loads and frantic pawing around in the deepening snow, of hunger and thirst and all-encompassing exhaustion.

They had retraced their steps now, were heading WNW back across the shoulder of the mountain – almost certainly the Germans would think they had gone due north, heading for the centre of the island. Without compass, stars or moon to guide, Mallory had nothing to orientate them but the feel of the slope of the mountain and the memory of the map Vlachos had shown them in Alexandria. But by and by he was reasonably certain that they had rounded the mountain and were pushing up some narrow gorge into the interior.

The snow was the deadly enemy. Heavy, wet and feathery, it swirled all around them in a blanketing curtain of grey, sifted down their necks and jackboots, worked its insidious way under their clothes and up their sleeves, blocked their eyes and ears and mouths, pierced and then anæsthetised exposed faces, and turned gloveless hands into leaden lumps of ice. benumbed and all but powerless. All suffered, and suffered badly, but Stevens most of all. He had lost consciousness again within minutes of leaving the cave and clad in clinging, sodden clothes as he was, he now lacked even the saving warmth generated by physical activity. Twice Andrea had stopped and felt for the beating of the heart, for he thought that the boy had died: but he could feel nothing for there was no feeling left in his hands, and he could only wonder and stumble on again.

About five in the morning, as they were climbing up the steep valley head above the gorge, a treacherous, slippery slope with only a few stunted carob trees for anchor in the sliding scree, Mallory decided that they must rope up for safety's sake. In single file they scrambled and struggled up the ever-steepening slope for the next twenty minutes: Mallory, in the lead, did not even dare to think how Andrea was getting on behind him. Suddenly the slope eased, flattened out completely, and almost before they realized what was happening they had crossed the high divide, still roped together and in driving, blinding snow with zero visibility, and were sliding down the valley on the other side.

They came to the cave at dawn, just as the first grey stirrings of a bleak and cheerless day struggled palely through the lowering, snow-filled sky to the east. Monsieur Vlachos had told them that the south of Navarone was honey-combed with caves, but this was the first they had seen, and even then it was no cave but a dark, narrow tunnel in a great heap of piled volcanic slabs, huge, twisted layers of rock precariously poised in a gully that threaded down the slope towards some broad and unknown valley a thousand, two thousand feet, beneath them, a valley still shrouded in the gloom of night.

It was no cave, but it was enough. For frozen, exhausted, sleep-haunted men, it was more than enough, it was more than they had ever hoped for. There was room for them all, the few cracks were quickly blocked against the drifting snow, the entrance curtained off by the boulder-weighted tent. Somehow, impossibly almost in the cramped darkness, they stripped Stevens of his sea- and rain-soaked clothes, eased him into a providentially zipped sleeping-bag, forced some brandy down his throat and cushioned the bloodstained head on some dry clothing. And then the four men, even the tireless Andrea, slumped down to the sodden, snow-chilled floor of the cave and slept like men already dead, oblivious alike of the rocks on the floor, the cold, their hunger and their clammy, saturated clothing, oblivious even to the agony of returning circulation in their frozen hands and faces.

—— 7 ——

TUESDAY

1500–1900

The sun, rime-ringed and palely luminous behind the drifting cloud-wrack, was far beyond its zenith and dipping swiftly westwards to the snowlimned shoulder of the mountain when Andrea lifted the edge of the tent, pushed it gently aside and peered out warily down the smooth sweep of the mountainside. For a few moments he remained almost motionless behind the canvas, automatically easing cramped and aching leg muscles, narrowed, roving eyes gradually accustoming themselves to the white glare of the glistening, crystalline snow. And then he had flitted noiselessly out of the mouth of the tunnel and reached far up the bank of the gully in half a dozen steps; stretched full length against the snow, he eased himself smoothly up the slope, lifted a cautious eye over the top.

Far below him stretched the great, curved sweep of an almost perfectly symmetrical valley – a valley born abruptly in the cradling embrace of steep-walled mountains and falling away gently to the north. That towering, buttressed giant on his right that brooded darkly over the head of the valley, its peak hidden in the snow clouds – there could be no doubt about that, Andrea thought. Mt Kostos, the highest mountain in Navarone: they had crossed its western flank during the darkness of the night. Due east and facing his own at perhaps five miles' distance, the third mountain was barely less high: but its northern flank fell away more quickly, debouching on to the plains that lay to the north-east of Navarone. And about four miles away to the north-north-east, far beneath the snowline and the isolated shepherds' huts, a tiny, flat-roofed township lay in a fold in the hills, along the bank of the little stream that wound its way through the valley. That could only be the village of Margaritha.

Even as he absorbed the topography of the valley, his eyes probing every dip and cranny in the hills for a possible source of danger, Andrea's mind was racing back over the last two minutes of time, trying to isolate, to remember the nature of the alien sound that had cut through the cocoon of sleep and brought him instantly to his feet, alert and completely awake, even before his conscious mind had time to register the memory of the sound. And then he heard it again, three times in as many seconds, the high-pitched, lonely wheep of a whistle, shrill peremptory blasts that echoed briefly and died along the lower slopes of Mt Kostos: the final echo still hung faintly on the air as Andrea pushed himself backwards and slid down to the floor of the gully.

He was back on the bank within thirty seconds, cheek muscles contracting involuntarily as the ice-chill eyepieces of Mallory's Zeiss-Ikon binoculars screwed into his face. There was no mistaking them now, he thought grimly, his first, fleeting impression had been all too accurate. Twenty-five, perhaps thirty soldiers in all, strung out in a long, irregular line, they were advancing slowly across the flank of Kostos, combing every gully, each jumbled confusion of boulders that lay in their path. Every man was clad in a snow-suit, but even at a distance of two miles they were easy to locate: the arrow-heads of their strapped skis angled up above shoulders and hooded heads: startingly black against the sheer whiteness of the snow, the skis bobbed and weaved in disembodied drunkenness as the men slipped and stumbled along the scree-strewn slopes of the mountain. From time to time a man near the centre of the line pointed and gestured with an alpenstock, as if co-ordinating the efforts of the search party. The man with the whistle, Andrea guessed.

'Andrea!' The call from the cave mouth was very soft. 'Anything wrong?'

Finger to his lips, Andrea twisted round in the snow. Mallory was standing by the canvas screen. Dark-jowled and crumple-clothed, he held up one hand against the glare of the snow while the other rubbed the sleep from his blood-shot eyes. And then he was limping forward in obedience to the crooking of Andrea's finger, wincing in pain at every step he took. His toes were swollen and skinned, gummed together with congealed blood. He had not had his boots off since he had taken them from the feet of the dead German sentry: and now he was almost afraid to remove them, afraid of what he would find. . . . He clambered slowly up the bank of the gully and sank down in the snow beside Andrea.

'Company?'

'The very worst of company,' Andrea murmured. 'Take a look, my Keith.' He handed over the binoculars, pointed down to the lower slopes of Mt Kostos. 'Your friend Jensen never told us that they were here.'

Slowly, Mallory quartered the slopes with the binoculars. Suddenly the line of searchers moved into his field of vision. He raised his head, adjusted the focus impatiently, looked briefly once more, then lowered the binoculars with a restrained deliberation of gesture that held a wealth of bitter comment.

'The WGB,' he said softly.

'A Jaeger battalion,' Andrea conceded. 'Alpine Corps – their finest mountain troops. This is most inconvenient, my Keith.'

Mallory nodded, rubbed his stubbled chin.

'If anyone can find us, they can. And they'll find us.' He lifted the glasses to look again at the line of advancing men. The painstaking thoroughness of the search was disturbing enough: but even more threatening, more frightening, was the snail-like relentlessness, the inevitability of the approach of these tiny figures. 'God knows what the Alpenkorps is doing here,' Mallory went on. 'It's enough that they are here. They must know that we've landed and spent the morning searching the eastern saddle of Kostos – that was the obvious route for us to break into the interior. They've drawn a blank there, so now they're working their way over to the other saddle. They must be pretty nearly certain that we're carrying a wounded man with us and that we can't have got very far, It's only going to be a matter of time, Andrea.'

'A matter of time,' Andrea echoed. He glanced up at the sun, a sun all but invisible in a darkening sky. 'An hour, an hour and a half at the most. They'll be here before the sun goes down. And we'll still be here.' He glanced quizzically at Mallory. 'We cannot leave the boy. And we cannot get away if we take the boy – and then he would die anyway.'

'We will not be here,' Mallory said flatly. 'If we stay we all die. Or finish up in one of these nice little dungeons that Monsieur Vlachos told us about.'

'The greatest good of the greatest number,' Andrea nodded slowly. 'That's how it has to be, has it not, my Keith? The greatest number. That is what Captain Jensen would say.' Mallory stirred uncomfortably, but his voice was steady enough when he spoke.

'That's how I see it, too, Andrea. Simple proportion – twelve hundred to one. You know it has to be this way.' Mallory sounded tired.

'Yes, I know. But you are worrying about nothing.' Andrea smiled. 'Come, my friend. Let us tell the others the good news.'

Miller looked up as the two men came in, letting the canvas screen fall shut behind them. He had unzipped the side of Stevens's sleeping-bag and was working on the mangled leg. A pencil flashlight was propped on a rucksack beside him.

'When are we goin' to do somethin' about this kid, boss?' The voice was abrupt, angry, like his gesture towards the sleep-drugged boy beside him. 'This damned waterproof sleeping-bag is soaked right through. So's the kid – and he's about frozen stiff: his leg feels like a side of chilled beef. He's gotta have heat, boss, a warm room and hot drinks – or he's finished. Twenty-four hours.' Miller shivered and looked slowly round the broken walls of the rock-shelter. 'I reckon he'd have less than an even chance in a first-class general hospital. . . . He's just wastin' his time keepin' on breathin' in this gawdamned ice-box.'

Miller hardly exaggerated. Water from the melting snow above trickled continuously down the clammy, green-lichened walls of the cave or dripped directly on to the half-frozen gravelly slush on the floor of the cave. With no through venti-lation and no escape for the water accumulating at the sides of the shelter, the whole place was dank and airless and terribly chill.

'Maybe he'll be hospitalised sooner than you think,' Mallory said dryly. 'How's his leg?'

'Worse.' Miller was blunt. 'A helluva sight worse. I've just chucked in another handful of sulpha and tied things up again. That's all I can do, boss, and it's just a waste of time anyway. . . . What was that crack about a hospital?' he added suspiciously.

'That was no crack,' Mallory said soberly, 'but one of the more unpleasant facts of life. There's a German search party heading this way. They mean business. They'll find us, all right.'

Miller swore. 'That's handy, that's just wonderful,' he said bitterly. 'How far away, boss?'

'An hour, maybe a little more.'

'And what are we goin' to do with Junior, here? Leave him? It's his only chance, I reckon.'

Stevens comes with us.' There was a flat finality in Mallory's voice. Miller looked at him for a long time in silence: his face was very cold.

'Stevens comes with us,' Miller repeated. 'We drag him along with us until he's dead – that won't take long – and then we leave him in the snow. Just like that, huh?'

'Just like that, Dusty.' Absently Mallory brushed some snow off his clothes, and looked up again at Miller. 'Stevens knows too much. The Germans will have guessed why we're on the island, but they won't know how we propose to get inside the fortress – and they don't know when the Navy's coming through. But Stevens does. They'll make him talk. Scopolamine will make anyone talk.'

'Scopolamine! On a dying man?' Miller was openly incredulous.

'Why not? I'd do the same myself. If you were the German commandant and you knew that your big guns and half the men in your fortress were liable to be blown to hell any moment, you'd do the same.'

Miller looked at him, grinned wryly, shook his head.

'Me and my—'

'I know. You and your big mouth.' Mallory smiled and clapped him on the shoulder. 'I don't like it one little bit more than you do, Dusty.' He turned away and crossed to the other side of the cave. 'How are you feeling, Chief?'

'Not too bad, sir.' Casey Brown was only just awake, numbed and shivering in sodden clothes. 'Anything wrong?'

'Plenty,' Mallory assured him. 'Search party moving this way. We'll have to pull out inside half an hour.' He looked at his watch. 'Just on four o'clock. Do you think you could raise Cairo on the set?'

'Lord only knows,' Brown said frankly. He rose stiffly to his feet. 'The radio didn't get just the best of treatment yesterday. I'll have a go.'

'Thanks, Chief. See that your aerial doesn't stick up above the sides of the gully.' Mallory turned to leave the cave, but halted abruptly at the sight of Andrea squatting on a boulder just beside the entrance. His head bent in concentration, the big Greek had just finished screwing telescopic sights on to the barrel of his 7.92 mm. Mauser and was now deftly wrapping a sleeping-bag lining round its barrel and butt until the entire rifle was wrapped in a white cocoon.

Mallory watched him in silence. Andrea glanced up at him, smiled, rose to his feet and reached out for his ruck-sack. Within thirty seconds he was clad from head to toe in his mountain camouflage suit, was drawing tight the purse-strings of his snow-hood and easing his feet into the rucked elastic anklets of his canvas boots. Then he picked up the Mauser and smiled slightly.

'I thought I might be taking a little walk, Captain,' he said apologetically. 'With your permission, of course.'

Mallory nodded his head several times in slow recollection.

'You said I was worrying about nothing,' he murmured. 'I should have known. You might have told me, Andrea.' But the protest was automatic, without significance. Mallory felt neither anger nor even annoyance at this tacit arrogation of his authority. The habit of command died hard in Andrea: on such occasions as he ostensibly sought approval for or consulted about a proposed course of action it was generally as a matter of courtesy and to give information as to his intentions. Instead of resentment, Mallory could feel only an overwhelming relief and gratitude to the smiling giant who towered above him: he had talked casually to Miller about driving Stevens till he died and then abandoning him, talked with an indifference that masked a mind sombre with bitterness at what he must do, but even so he had not known how depressed, how sick at heart this decision had left him until he knew it was no longer necessary.

'I am sorry.' Andrea was half-contrite, half-smiling. 'I should have told you. I thought you understood. . . . It is the best thing to do, yes?'

'It is the only thing to do,' Mallory said frankly. 'You're going to draw them off up the saddle?'

'There is no other way. With their skis they would overtake me in minutes if I went down into the valley. I cannot come back, of course, until it is dark. You will be here?'

'Some of us will.' Mallory glanced across the shelter where a waking Stevens was trying to sit up, heels of his palms screwing into his exhausted eyes. 'We must have food and fuel, Andrea,' he said softly. 'I am going down into the valley tonight.'

'Of course, of course. We must do what we can.' Andrea's face was grave, his voice only a murmur. 'As long as we can. He is only a boy, a child almost. . . . Perhaps it will not be long.' He pulled back the curtain, looked out at the evening sky. 'I will be back by seven o'clock.'

'Seven o'clock,' Mallory repeated. The sky, he could see, was darkening already, darkening with the gloom of coming snow. and the lifting wind was beginning to puff little clouds of air-spun, flossy white into the little gully. Mallory shivered and caught hold of the massive arm. 'For God's sake, Andrea,' he urged quietly, 'look after yourself!'

'Myself?' Andrea smiled gently, no mirth in his eyes, and as gently he disengaged his arm. 'Do not think about me.' The voice was very quiet, with an utter lack of arrogance. 'If you must speak to God, speak to Him about these poor devils who are looking for us.' The canvas dropped behind him and he was gone.

For some moments Mallory stood irresolutely at the mouth of the cave, gazing out sightlessly through the gap in the curtain. Then he wheeled abruptly, crossed the floor of the shelter and knelt in front of Stevens. The boy was propped up against Miller's anxious arm, the eyes lack-lustre and expressionless, bloodless cheeks deep-sunken in a grey and parchment face. Mallory smiled at him: he hoped the shock didn't show in his face.

'Well, well, well. The sleeper awakes at last. Better late than never.' He opened his waterproof cigarette case, proffered it to Stevens. 'How are you feeling now, Andy?'

'Frozen, sir.' Stevens shook his head at the case and tried to grin back at Mallory, a feeble travesty of a smile that made Mallory wince.

'And the leg?'

'I think it must be frozen, too.' Stevens looked down incuriously at the sheathed whiteness of his shattered leg. 'Anyway, I can't feel a thing.'

'Frozen!' Miller's sniff was a masterpiece of injured pride. 'Frozen, he says! Gawddamned ingratitude. It's the first-class medical care, if I do say so myself!'

Stevens smiled, a fleeting, absent smile that flickered over his face and was gone. For long moments he kept staring down at his leg, then suddenly lifted his head and looked directly at Mallory.

'Look, sir, there's no good kidding ourselves.' The voice was soft, quite toneless. 'I don't want to seem ungrateful and I hate even the idea of cheap heroics, but – well, I'm just a damned great millstone round your necks and—'

'Leave you, eh?' Mallory interrupted. 'Leave you to die of the cold or be captured by the Germans. Forget it, laddie. We can look after you – and these ruddy guns – at the same time.'

'But, sir—'

'You insult us, Lootenant.' Miller sniffed again. 'Our feelings are hurt. Besides, as a professional man I gotta see my case through to convalescence, and if you think I'm goin' to do that in any gawddamned dripping German dungeon, you can—'

'Enough!' Mallory held up his hand. 'The subject is closed.' He saw the stain high up on the thin cheeks, the glad light that touched the dulled eyes, and felt the self-loathing and the shame well up inside him, shame for the gratitude of a sick man who did not know that their concern stemmed not from solicitude but from fear that he might betray them. . . . Mallory bent forward and began to unlace his high packboots. He spoke without looking up.

'Dusty.'

'Yeah?'

'When you're finished boasting about your medical prowess, maybe you'd care to use some of it. Come and have a look at these feet of mine, will you? I'm afraid the sentry's boots haven't done them a great deal of good.'

Fifteen painful minutes later Miller snipped off the rough edges of the adhesive bandage that bound Mallory's right foot, straightened up stiffly and contemplated his handiwork with pride.

'Beautiful, Miller, beautiful,' he murmured complacently. 'Not even in John Hopkins in the city of Baltimore . . .' He broke off suddenly, frowned down at the thickly bandaged feet and coughed apologetically. 'A small point has just occurred to me, boss.'

'I thought it might eventually,' Mallory said grimly. 'Just how do you propose to get my feet into these damned boots again?' He shivered involuntarily as he pulled on a pair of thick woollen socks, matted and sodden with melted snow, picked up the German sentry's boots, held them at arm's length and examined them in disgust. 'Sevens, at the most – and a darned small sevens at that!'

'Nines,' Stevens said laconically. He handed over his own jackboots, one of them slit neatly down the sides where Andrea had cut it open. 'You can fix that tear easily enough, and they're no damned good to me now. No arguments, sir, please.' He began to laugh softly, broke off in a sharply indrawn hiss of pain as the movement jarred the broken bones, took a couple of deep, quivering breaths, then smiled whitely. 'My first – and probably my last – contribution to the expedition. What sort of medal do you reckon they'll give me for that, sir?'

Mallory took the boots, looked at Stevens a long moment in silence, then turned as the tarpaulin was pushed aside. Brown stumbled in, lowered the transmitter and telescopic aerial to the floor of the cave and pulled out a tin of cigarettes. They slipped from his frozen fingers, fell into the icy mud at his feet, became brown and sodden on the instant. He swore, briefly, and without enthusiasm, beat his numbed hands across his chest, gave it up and sat down heavily on a convenient boulder. He looked tired and cold and thoroughly miserable.

Mallory lit a cigarette and passed it across to him.

'How did it go, Casey? Manage to raise them at all?'

'They managed to raise me – more or less. Reception was lousy.' Brown drew the grateful tobacco smoke deep down into his lungs. 'And I couldn't get through at all. Must be that damned great hill to the south there.'

'Probably,' Mallory nodded. 'And what news from our friends in Cairo? Exhorting us to greater efforts? Telling us to get on with the job?'

'No news at all. Too damn' worried about the silence at this end. Said that from now on they were going to come through every four hours, acknowledgment or no. Repeated that about ten times, then signed off.'

'That'll be a great help,' Miller said acidly. 'Nice to know they're on our side. Nothin' like moral support.' He jerked his thumb towards the mouth of the cave. 'Reckon them blood-hounds would be scared to death if they knew. . . . Did you take a gander at them before you came in?'

'I didn't have to,' Brown said morosely. 'I could hear them – sounded like the officer in charge shouting directions.' Mechanically, almost, he picked up his automatic rifle, eased the clip in the magazine. 'Must be less than a mile away now.'

The search party, more closely bunched by this time, was less than a mile, was barely half a mile distant from the cave when the Oberleutnant in charge saw that the right wing of his line, on the steeper slopes to the south, was lagging behind once more. Impatiently he lifted his whistle to his mouth for the three sharp peremptory blasts that would bring his weary men stumbling into line again. Twice the whistle shrilled out its imperative urgency, the piercing notes echoing flatly along the snowbound slopes and dying away in the valley below: but the third *wheep* died at birth, caught up again and tailed off in a wailing, eldritch diminuendo that merged with dreadful harmony into a long bubbling scream of agony. For two or three seconds the Oberleutnant stood motionless in his tracks, his face shocked and contorted: then he jack-knifed violently forward and pitched down into the crusted snow. The burly sergeant beside him stared down at the fallen officer, looked up in sudden horrified understanding, opened his mouth to shout, sighed and toppled wearily over the body at his feet, the evil, whip-lash crack of the Mauser in his ears as he died.

High up on the western slopes of Mount Kostos, wedged in the V between two great boulders, Andrea gazed down the darkening mountainside over the depressed telescopic sights of his rifle and pumped another three rounds into the wavering, disorganised line of searchers. His face was quite still, as immobile as the eyelids that never flickered to the regular crashing of his Mauser, and drained of all feeling. Even his eyes reflected the face, eyes neither hard nor pitiless, but simply empty and almost frighteningly remote, a remoteness that mirrored his mind, a mind armoured for the moment against all thought and sensation, for Andrea knew that he must not think about this thing. To kill, to take the life of his fellows, that was the supreme evil, for life was a gift that it was not his to take away. Not even in fair fight. And this was murder.

Slowly Andrea lowered the Mauser, peered through the drifting gun-smoke that hung heavily in the frosty evening air. The enemy had vanished, completely, rolled behind scattered boulders or burrowed frantically into the blanketing anonymity of the snow. But they were still there, still potentially as dangerous as ever. Andrea knew that they would recover fast from the death of their officer – there were no finer, no more tenacious fighters in Europe than the ski-troops of the Jaeger mountain battalion – and would come after him, catch him and kill him if humanly possible. That was why Andrea's first case had been to kill their officer – he might not have come after him, might have stopped to puzzle out the reason for this unprovoked flank attack.

Andrea ducked low in reflex instinct as a sudden burst of automatic fire whined in murderous ricochet off the boulders before him. He had expected this. It was the old classic infantry attack pattern – advance under covering fire, drop, cover your mate and come again. Swiftly Andrea rammed home another charge into the magazine of his Mauser, dropped flat on his face and inched his way along behind the low line of broken rock that extended fifteen or twenty yards to his right – he had chosen his ambush point with care – and then petered out. At the far end he pulled his snow hood down to the level of his brows and edged a wary eye round the corner of the rock.

Another heavy burst of automatic fire smashed into the boulders he had just left, and half a dozen men – three from either side of the line – broke cover, scurried along the slope in a stumbling, crouching run, then pitched forward into the snow again. *Along* the slope – the two parties had run in opposite directions. Andrea lowered his head and rubbed the back of a massive hand across the stubbled grizzle of his chin. Awkward, damned awkward. No frontal attack for the foxes of the WGB. They were extending their lines on either side, the points hooking round in a great, encircling half-moon. Bad enough for himself, but he could have coped with that – a carefully reconnoitred escape gully wound up the slope behind him. But he hadn't forseen what was obviously going to happen: the curving crescent of line to the west was going to sweep across the rock-shelter where the others lay hidden.

Andrea twisted over on his back and looked up at the evening sky. It was darkening by the moment darkening with the gloom of coming snow, and daylight was beginning to fail. He twisted again and looked across the great swelling shoulder of Mount Kostos, looked at the few scattered rocks and shallow depressions that barely dimpled the smooth convexity of the slope. He took a second quick look round the rock as the rifles of the WGB opened up once more, saw the same encircling manœuvre being executed again, and waited no longer. Firing blindly downhill, he half-rose to his feet and flung himself out into the open, finger squeezing on the trigger, feet driving desperately into the frozen snow as he launched himself towards the nearest rock-cover, forty yards away if an inch. Thirty-five yards to go, thirty, twenty and still not a shot fired, a slip, a stumble on the sliding scree a catlike recovery, ten yards, still miraculously immune, and then he had dived into shelter to land on chest and stomach with a sickening impact that struck cruelly into his ribs and emptied his lungs with an explosive gasp.

Fighting for breath, he struck the magazine cover, rammed home another charge, risked a quick peep over the top of the rock and catapulted himself to his feet again, all inside ten seconds. The Mauser held across his body opened up again, firing downhill at vicious random, for Andrea had eyes only for the smoothly-treacherous ground at his feet, for the scree-lined depression so impossibly far ahead. And then the Mauser was empty, useless in his hand, and every gun far below had opened up, the shells whistling above his head or blinding him with spurting gouts of snow as they ricocheted off the solid rock. But twilight was touching the hills, Andrea was only a blur, a swiftly-flitting blur against a ghostly background, and uphill accuracy was notoriously difficult at any time. Even so, the massed fire from below was steadying and converging, and Andrea waited no longer. Unseen hands plucking wickedly at the flying tails of his snow-smock, he flung himself almost horizontally forward and slid the last ten feet face down into the waiting depression.

Stretched full length on his back in the hollow, Andrea fished out a steel mirror from his breast pocket and held it gingerly above his head. At first he could see nothing, for the darkness was deeper below and the mirror misted from the warmth of his body. And then the film vanished in the chill mountain air and he could see two, three and then half a dozen men breaking cover, heading at a clumsy run straight up the face of the hill – and two of them had come from the extreme right of the line. Andrea lowered the mirror and relaxed with a long sigh of relief, eyes crinkling in a smile. He looked up at the sky, blinked as the first feathery flakes of falling snow melted on his eyelids and smiled again. Almost lazily he brought out another charger for the Mauser, fed more shells into the magazine.

'Boss?' Miller's voice was plaintive.

'Yes? What is it?' Mallory brushed some snow off his face and the collar of his smock and peered into the white darkness ahead.

'Boss, when you were in school did you ever read any stories about folks gettin' lost in a snowstorm and wanderin' round and round in circles for days?'

'We had exactly the same book in Queenstown,' Mallory conceded.

'Wanderin' round and round until they died?' Miller persisted.

'Oh, for heaven's sake!' Mallory said impatiently. His feet, even in Stevens's roomy boots, hurt abominably. 'How can we be wandering in circles if we're going downhill all the time? What do you think we're on – a bloody spiral staircase?'

Miller walked on in hurt silence, Mallory beside him, both men ankle-deep in the wet, clinging snow that had been falling so silently, so persistently, for the past three hours since Andrea had drawn off the Jaegar search party. Even in mid-winter in the White Mountains in Crete Mallory could recall no snowfall so heavy and continuous. So much for the Isles of Greece and the eternal sunshine that gilds them yet, he thought bitterly. He hadn't reckoned on this when he'd planned on going down to Margaritha for food and fuel, but even so it wouldn't have made any difference to his decision. Although in less pain now, Stevens was becoming steadily weaker, and the need was desperate.

With moon and stars blanketed by the heavy snow-clouds – visibility, indeed, was hardly more than ten feet in any direction – the loss of their compasses had assumed a crippling importance. He didn't doubt his ability to find the village – it was simply a matter of walking downhill till they came to the stream that ran through the valley, then following that north till they came to Margaritha – but if the snow didn't let up their chances of locating that tiny cave again in the vast sweep of the hillsides ...

Mallory smothered an exclamation as Miller's hand closed round his upper arm, dragged him down to his knees in the snow. Even in that moment of unknown danger he could feel a slow stirring of anger against himself, for his attention had been wandering along with his thoughts. . . . He lifted his hand as vizor against the snow, peered out narrowly through the wet, velvety curtain of white that swirled and eddied out of the darkness before him. Suddenly he had it – a dark, squat shape only feet away. They had all but walked straight into it.

'It's the hut,' he said softly in Miller's ear. He had seen it early in the afternoon, half-way between their cave and Margaritha, and almost in a line with both. He was conscious of relief, an increase in confidence: they would be in the village in less than half an hour. 'Elementary navigation, my dear Corporal,' he murmured. 'Lost and wandering in circles, my foot! Just put your faith ...'

He broke off as Miller's fingers dug viciously into his arm, as Miller's head came close to his own.

'I heard voices, boss.' The words were a mere breath of sound.

'Are you sure?' Miller's silenced gun, Mallory noticed, was still in his pocket.

Miller hesitated.

'Dammit to hell, boss. I'm sure of nothin',' he whispered irritably. 'I've been imaginin' every damn' thing possible in the past hour!' He pulled the snow hood off his head, the better to listen, bent forward for a few seconds then sank back again. 'Anyway, I'm sure I *thought* I heard somethin'.'

'Come on. Let's take a look-see.' Mallory was on his feet again. 'I think you're mistaken. Can't be the Jaeger boys – they were half-way back across Mount Kostos when we saw them. And the shepherds only use these places in the summer months.' He slipped the safety catch of his Colt .455, walked slowly, at a half-crouch, towards the nearest wall of the hut, Miller at his shoulder.

They reached the hut, put their ears against the frail, tar-paper walls. Ten seconds passed, twenty, half a minute, then Mallory relaxed.

'Nobody at home. Or if they are, they're keeping mighty quiet. But no chances, Dusty. You go that way. I'll go this. Meet at the door – that'll be on the opposite side, facing into the valley. . . . Walk wide at the corners – never fails to baffle the unwary.'

A minute later both men were inside the hut, the door shut behind them. The hooded beam of Mallory's torch probed into every corner of the ramshackle cabin. It was quite empty – an earthen floor, a rough wooden bunk, a dilapidated stove with a rusty lantern standing on it, and that was all. No table, no chair, no chimney, not even a window.

Mallory walked over to the stove, picked up the lamp and sniffed it.

'Hasn't been used for weeks. Still full of kerosene, though. Very useful in that damn' dungeon up there – if we can ever find the place. . . .'

He froze into a sudden listening immobility, eyes unfocused and head cocked slightly to one side. Gently, ever so gently, he set the lamp down, walked leisurely across to Miller.

'Remind me to apologise at some future date,' he murmured. 'We have company. Give me your gun and keep talking.'

'Castelrosso again,' Miller complained loudly. He hadn't even raised an eyebrow. 'This is downright monotonous. A Chinaman – I'll bet it's a Chinaman this time.' But he was already talking to himself.

The silenced automatic balanced at his wait, Mallory walked noiselessly round the hut, four feet out from the walls. He had passed two corners, was just rounding the third when, out of the corner of his eye, he saw a vague figure behind him rising up swiftly from the ground and lunging out with upraised arm. Mallory stepped back quickly under the blow, spun round, swung his balled fist viciously and backwards into the stomach of his attacker. There was a sudden explosive gasp of agony as the man doubled up, moaned and crumpled silently to the ground. Barely in time Mallory arrested the downward, clubbing swipe of his reversed automatic.

Gun reversed again, the butt settled securely in his palm,

Mallory stared down unblinkingly at the huddled figure, at the primitive wooden baton still clutched in the gloved right hand, at the unmilitary looking knapsack strapped to his back. He kept his gun lined up on the fallen body, waiting: this had been just too easy, too suspicious. Thirty seconds passed and still the figure on the ground hadn't stirred. Mallory took a short step forward and carefully, deliberately and none too gently kicked the man on the outside of the right knee. It was an old trick, and he'd never known it to fail – the pain was brief, but agonising. But there was no movement, no sound at all.

Quickly Mallory stooped, hooked his free hand round the knapsack shoulder straps, straightened and made for the door, half-carrying, half-dragging his captive. The man was no weight at all. With a proportionately much heavier garrison than ever in Crete, there would be that much less food for the islanders, Mallory mused compassionately. There would be very little indeed. He wished he hadn't hit him so hard.

Miller met him at the open door, stooped wordlessly, caught the unconscious man by the ankles and helped Mallory dump him unceremoniously on the bunk in the far corner of the hut.

'Nice goin', boss,' he complimented. 'Never heard a thing. Who's the heavyweight champ?'

'No idea.' Mallory shook his head in the darkness. 'Just skin and bones, that's all, just skin and bones. Shut the door, Dusty, and let's have a look at what we've got.'

8

TUESDAY

1900–0015

A minute passed, two, then the little man stirred, moaned and pushed himself to a sitting position. Mallory held his arm to steady him, while he shook his bent head, eyes screwed tightly shut as he concentrated on clearing the muzziness away. Finally he looked up slowly, glanced from Mallory to Miller and back at Mallory again in the feeble light of the newly-lit shuttered lantern. Even as the men watched, they could see the colour returning to the swarthy cheeks, the indignant bristling of the heavy, dark moustache, the darkening anger in the eyes. Suddenly the man reached up, tore Mallory's hand away from his arm.

'Who are you?' He spoke in English, clear, precise, with hardly a trace of accent.

'Sorry, but the less you know the better.' Mallory smiled, deliberately to rob the words of offence. 'I mean that for your own sake. How are you feeling now?'

Tenderly the little man massaged his midriff, flexed his leg with a grimace of pain.

'You hit me very hard.'

'I had to.' Mallory reached behind him and picked up the cudgel the man had been carrying. 'You tried to hit me with this. What did you expect me to do – take my hat off so you could have a better swipe at me?'

'You are very amusing.' Again he bent his leg, experimentally, looking up at Mallory in hostile suspicion. 'My knee hurts me,' he said accusingly.

'First things first. Why the club?'

'I meant to knock you down and have a look at you,' he explained impatiently. 'It was the only safe way. You might have been one of the WGB. . . . Why is my knee—?'

'You had an awkward fall,' Mallory said shamelessly. 'What are you doing here?'

'Who are you?' the little man countered.

Miller coughed, looked ostentatiously at his watch.

'This is all very entertainin', boss—'

'True for you, Dusty. We haven't all night.' Quickly Mallory reached behind him, picked up the man's rucksack, tossed it across to Miller. 'See what's in there, will you?' Strangely, the little man made no move to protest.

'Food!' Miller said reverently. 'Wonderful, wonderful food. Cooked meat, bread, cheese – and wine.' Reluctantly Miller closed the bag and looked curiously at their prisoner. 'Helluva funny time for a picnic.'

'So! An American, a Yankee.' The little man smiled to himself. 'Better and better!'

'What do you mean?' Miller asked suspiciously.

'See for yourself,' the man said pleasantly. He nodded casually to the far corner of the room. 'Look there.'

Mallory spun round, realized in a moment that he had been tricked, jerked back again. Carefully he leaned forward and touched Miller's arm.

'Don't look round too quickly, Dusty. And don't touch your gun. It seems our friend was not alone.' Mallory tightened his lips, mentally cursed himself for his obtuseness. Voices – Dusty had said there had been voices. Must be even more tired than he had thought. . . .

A tall, lean man blocked the entrance to the doorway. His face was shadowed under an enveloping snow-hood, but there was no mistaking the gun in his hand. A short Lee Enfield rifle, Mallory noted dispassionately.

'Do not shoot!' The little man spoke rapidly in Greek. 'I am almost sure that they are those whom we seek, Panayis.'

Panayis! Mallory felt the wave of relief wash over him. That was one of the names Eugene Vlachos had given him, back in Alexandria

'The tables turned, are they not?' The little man smiled at Mallory, the tired eyes crinkling, the heavy black moustache lifting engagingly at one corner. 'I ask you again, who are you?'

'SOE,' Mallory answered unhesitatingly.

The man nodded in satisfaction. 'Captain Jensen sent you?'

Mallory sank back on the bunk and sighed in long relief.

'We are among friends, Dusty.' He looked at the little man before him. 'You must be Louki – the first plane tree in the square in Margaritha?'

The little man beamed. He bowed, stretched out his hand.

'Louki. At your service, sir.'

'And this of course, is Panayis?'

The tall man in the doorway, dark, saturnine, unsmiling, inclined his head briefly but said nothing.

'You have us right!' The little man was beaming with delight. 'Louki and Panayis. They know about us in Alexandria and Cairo, then?' he asked proudly.

'Of course!' Mallory smothered a smile. 'They spoke highly of you. You have been of great help to the Allies before.'

'And we will again,' Louki said briskly. 'Come, we are wasting time. The Germans are on the hills. What help can we give you?'

'Food, Louki. We need food – we need it badly.'

'We have it!' Proudly, Louki gestured at the rucksacks. 'We were on our way up with it.'

'You were on your way. . . .' Mallory was astonished. 'How did you know where we were – or even that we were on the island?'

Louki waved a deprecating hand.

'It was easy. Since first light German troops have been moving south through Margaritha up into the hills. All morning they combed the east col of Kostos. We knew someone must have landed, and that the Germans were looking for them. We heard, too, that the Germans had blocked the cliff path on the south coast, at both ends. So you must have come over the west col. They would not expect that – you fooled them. So we came to find you.'.

'But you would never have found us—'

'We would have found you.' There was complete certainty in the voice. 'Panayis and I – we know every stone, every blade of grass in Navarone.' Louki shivered suddenly, stared out bleakly through the swirling snow. 'You couldn't have picked worse weather.'

'We couldn't have picked better,' Mallory said grimly.

'Last night, yes,' Louki agreed. 'No one would expect you in that wind and rain. No one would hear the aircraft or even dream that you would try to jump—'

'We came by sea,' Miller interrupted. He waved a negligent hand. 'We climbed the south cliff.'

'What? The south cliff!' Louki was frankly disbelieving. 'No one could climb the south cliff, It is impossible!'

'That's the way we felt when we were about half-way up,' Mallory said candidly. 'But Dusty, here, is right. That's how it was.'

Louki had taken a step back: his face was expressionless.

'I say it is impossible,' he repeated flatly.

'He is telling the truth, Louki,' Miller cut in quietly. 'Do you never read newspapers?'

'Of course I read newspapers!' Louki bristled with indignation. 'Do you think I am – how you say – illiterate?'

'Then think back to just before the war,' Miller advised. 'Think of mountaineerin' – and the Himalayas. You must have seen his picture in the papers – once, twice, a hundred times.' He looked at Mallory consideringly. 'Only he was a little prettier in those days. You must remember. This is Mallory, Keith Mallory of New Zealand.'

Mallory said nothing. He was watching Louki, the puzzlement, the comical screwing up of the eyes, head cocked to one side: then, all at once, something clicked in the little man's memory and his face lit up in a great, crinkling smile that swamped every last trace of suspicion. He stepped forward, hand oustretched in welcome.

'By heaven, you are right! Mallory! Of course I know Mallory!' He grabbed Mallory's hand, pumped it up and down with great enthusiasm. 'It is indeed as the American says. You need a shave. . . . And you look older.'

'I feel older,' Mallory said gloomily. He nodded at Miller. 'This is Corporal Miller, an American citizen.'

'Another famous climber?' Louki asked eagerly. 'Another tiger of the hills, yes?'

'He climbed the south cliff as it has never been climbed before,' Mallory answered truthfully. He glanced at his watch, then looked directly at Louki. 'There are others up in the hills. We need help, Louki. We need it badly and we need it at once. You know the danger if you are caught helping us?'

'Danger?' Louki waved a contemptuous hand. 'Danger to Louki and Panayis, the foxes of Navarone? Impossible! We are the ghosts of the night.' He hitched his pack higher up on his shoulders. 'Come. Let us take this food to your friends.'

'Just a minute.' Mallory's restraining hand was on his arm. 'There are two other things. We need heat – a stove and fuel, and we need—'

'Heat! A stove!' Louki was incredulous. 'Your friends in the hills – what are they? A band of old women?'

'And we also need bandages and medicine,' Mallory went on patiently. 'One of our friends has been terribly injured. We are not sure, but we do not think he will live.'

'Panayis!' Louki barked. 'Back to the village.' Louki was speaking in Greek now. Rapidly he issued his orders, had Mallory describe where the rock-shelter was, made sure that Panayis understood, then stood a moment in indecision, pulling at an end of his moustache. At length he looked up at Mallory.

'Could you find this cave again by yourself?'

'Lord only knows,' Mallory said frankly. 'I honestly don't think so.'

'Then I must come with you. I had hoped – you see, it will be a heavy load for Panayis – I have told him to bring bedding as well – and I don't think—'

'I'll go along with him,' Miller volunteered. He thought of his back-breaking labours on the caique, the climb up the cliff, their forced march through the mountains. 'The exercise will do me good.'

Louki translated his offer to Panayis – taciturn, apparently, only because of his complete lack of English – and was met by what appeared to be a torrent of protest. Miller looked at him in astonishment.

'What's the matter with old sunshine here?' he asked Mallory. 'Doesn't seem any too happy to me.'

'Says he can manage OK and wants to go by himself,' Mallory interpreted. 'Thinks you'll slow him up on the hills.' He shook his head in mock wonder. 'As if any man could slow Dusty Miller up!'

'Exactly!' Louki was bristling with anger. Again he turned to Panayis, fingers stabbing the empty air to emphasise his words. Miller turned looked apprehensively at Mallory.

'What's he tellin' him now, boss?'

'Only the truth,' Mallory said solemnly. 'Saying he ought to be honoured at being given the opportunity of marching with Monsieur Miller, the world-famous American climber.' Mallory grinned. 'Panayis will be on his mettle tonight – determined to prove that a Navaronian can climb as well and as fast as any man.'

'Oh, my Gawd!' Miller moaned.

'And on the way back, don't forget to give Panayis a hand up the steeper bits.'

Miller's reply was luckily lost in a sudden flurry of snow-laden wind.

That wind was rising steadily now, a bitter wind that whipped the heavy snow into their bent faces and stung the tears from their blinking eyes. A heavy, wet snow that melted as it touched, and trickled down through every gap and ching in their clothing until they were wet and chilled and thoroughly miserable. A clammy, sticky snow that built up layer after energy-sapping layer under their leaden-footed boots, until they stumbled along inches above the ground, leg muscles aching from the sheer accumulated weight of snow. There was no visibility worthy of the name, not even of a matter of feet, they were blanketed, swallowed up by an impenertable cocoon of swirling grey and white, unchanging, featureless: Louki strode on diagonally upwards across the slope with the untroubled certainty of a man walking up his own garden path.

Louki seemed as agile as a mountain goat, and as tireless. Nor was his tongue less nimble, less unwearied than his legs. He talked incessantly, a man overjoyed to be in action again, no matter what action so long as it was against the enemy. He told Mallory of the last three attacks on the island and how they had so bloodily failed – the Germans had been somehow fore-warned of the seaborne assault, had been waiting for the Special Boat Service and the Commandos with everything they had and had cut them to pieces, while the two airborne groups had had the most evil luck, been delivered up to the enemy by mis-judgment, by a series of unforeseeable coincidences; or how Panayis and himself had on both occasions narrowly escaped with their lives – Panayis had actually been captured the last time, had killed both his guards and escaped unrecognised; of the disposition of the German troops and check-points through-out the island, the location of the road blocks on the only two roads; and finally, of what little he himself knew of the layout of the fortress of Navarone itself. Panayis, the dark one, could tell him more of that, Louki said: twice Panayis had been in-side the fortress, once for an entire night: the guns, the control rooms, the barracks, the officers' quarters, the magazine, the turbo rooms, the sentry points – he knew where each one lay, to the inch.

Mallory whistled softly to himself. This was more than he had ever dared hope for. They had still to escape the net of searchers, still to reach the fortress, still to get inside it. But once inside – and Panayis must know how to get inside. . . . Un-consciously Mallory lengthened his stride, bent his back to the slope.

'Your friend Panayis must be quite something,' he said slowly. 'Tell me more about him, Louki.'

'What can I tell you?' Louki shook his head in a little flurry of snowflakes. 'What do I know of Panayis? What does anyone know of Panayis? That he has the luck of the devil, the courage of a madman and that sooner the lion will lie down with the lamb, the starving wolf spare the flock, than Panayis breathe the same air as the Germans? We all know that, and we knew nothing of Panayis. All I know is that I thank God I am no German, with Panayis on the island. He strikes by stealth, by night, by knife and in the back.' Louki crossed himself. 'His hands are full of blood.'

Mallory shivered involuntarily. The dark, sombre figure of Panayis, the memory of the expressionless face, the hooded eyes, were beginning to fascinate him.

'There's more to him than that, surely,' Mallory argued. 'After all, you are both Navaronians—'

'Yes, yes, that is so.'

'This is a small island, you've lived together all your lives—'

'Ah, but that is where the Major is wrong!' Mallory's promotion in rank was entirely Louki's own idea: despite Mallory's protests and explanations he seemed determined to stick to it. 'I, Louki, was for many years in foreign lands, helping Monsieur Vlachos. Monsier Vlachos,' Louki said with pride, 'is a very important Government official.'

'I know,' Mallory nodded. 'A consul. I've met him. He is a very fine man.'

'You have met him! Monsieur Vlachos?' There was no mistaking the gladness, the delight in Louki's voice. 'That is good! That is wonderful! Later you must tell me more. He is a great man. Did I ever tell you—'

'We were speaking about Panayis,' Mallory reminded him gently.

'Ah, yes, Panayis. As I was saying, I was away for a long time. When I came back, Panayis was gone. His father had died, his mother had married again and Panayis had gone to live with his stepfather and two little stepsisters in Crete. His stepfather, half-fisherman, half-farmer, was killed in fighting the Germans near Candia – this was in the beginning. Panayis took over the boat of his father, helped many of the Allies to escape until he was caught by the Germans, strung up by his wrists in the village square – where his family lived – not far from Casteli. He was flogged till the white of his ribs, of his backbone, was there for all to see, and left for dead. Then they burnt the village and Panayis's family – disappeared. You understand, Major?'

'I understand,' Mallory said grimly. 'But Panayis—'

'He should have died. But he is tough, that one, tougher than a knot in an old carob tree. Friends cut him down during the night, took him away into the hills till he was well again. And then he arrived back in Navarone, God knows how. I think he came from island to island in a small rowing-boat. He never says why he came back – I think it gives him greater pleasure to kill on his own native island. I do not know, Major. All I know is that food and sleep, the sunshine, women and wine – all these are nothing and less than nothing to the dark one.' Again Louki crossed himself. 'He obeys me, for I am the steward of the Vlachos family, but even I am afraid of him. To kill, to keep on killing, then kill again – that is the very breath of his being.' Louki stopped momentarily, sniffed the air like a hound seeking some fugitive scent, then kicked the snow off his boots

and struck off up the hill at a tangent. The little man's un-
hesitating sureness of direction was uncanny.

'How far to go now, Louki?'

'Two hundred yards, Major. No more.' Louki blew some
snow off his heavy, dark moustache and swore. 'I shall not be
sorry to arrive.'

'Nor I.' Mallory thought of the miserable, draughty shelter
in the dripping rocks almost with affection. It was becoming
steadily colder as they climbed out of the valley, and the wind
was rising, climbing up the register with a steady, moaning
whine: they had to lean into it now, push hard against it, to
make any progress. Suddenly both men stopped, listened, looked
at each other, heads bent against the driving snow. Around them
there was only the white emptiness and the silence: there was
no sign of what had caused the sudden sound.

'You heard something, too?' Mallory murmured.

'It is only I.' Mallory spun round as the deep voice boomed
out behind him and the bulky, white-smocked figure loomed
out of the snow. 'A milk wagon on a cobbled street is as nothing
compared to yourself and your friend here. But the snow
muffled your voices and I could not be sure.'

Mallory looked at him curiously. 'How come you're here,
Andrea?'

'Wood,' Andrea explained. 'I was looking for firewood. I was
high up on Kostos at sunset when the snow lifted for a moment.
I could have sworn I saw an old hut in a gully not far from
here – it was dark and square against the snow. So I left—'

'You are right,' Louki interrupted. 'The hut of old Leri, the
mad one. Leri was a goatherd. We all warned him, but Leri
would listen and speak to no man, only to his goats. He died
in his hut, in a landslide.'

'It is an ill wind . . .' Andrea murmured. 'Old Leri will keep
us warm tonight.' He checked abruptly as the gully opened up
at his feet, then dropped quickly to the bottom, sure-footed as
a mountain sheep. He whistled twice, a double high-pitched
note, listening intently into the snow for the answering whistle,
walked swiftly up the gully. Casey Brown, gun lowered, met
them at the entrance to the cave and held back the canvas screen
to let them pass inside.

The smoking tallow candle, guttering heavily to one side in the
icy draught, filled every corner of the cave with dark and flickering shadows from its erratic flame. The candle itself was almost

gone, the dripping wick bending over tiredly till it touched the rock, and Louki, snow-suit cast aside, was lighting another stump of candle from the dying flame. For a moment, both candles flared up together, and Mallory saw Louki clearly for the first time – a small, compact figure in a dark-blue jacket black-braided at the seams and flamboyantly frogged at the breast, the jacket tightly bound to his body by the crimson *tsanta* or cummerbund and, above, the swarthy, smiling face, the magnificent moustache that he flaunted like a banner. A Laughing Cavalier of a man, a miniature d'Artagnan splendidly behung with weapons. And then Mallory's gaze travelled up to the lined, liquid eyes, eyes dark and sad and permanently tired, and his shock, a slow, uncomprehending shock had barely time to register before the stub of the candle had flared up and died and Louki had sunk back into the shadows.

Stevens was stretched in a sleeping-bag, his breathing harsh and shallow and quick. He had been awake when they had arrived but had refused all food and drink, and turned away and drifted off into an uneasy jerky sleep. He seemed to be suffering no pain at all now: a bad sign, Mallory thought bleakly, the worst possible. He wished Miller would return. . . .

Casey Brown washed down the last few crumbs of bread with a mouthful of wine, rose stiffly to his feet, pulled the screen aside and peered out mournfully at the falling snow. He shuddered, let the canvas fall, lifted up his transmitter and shrugged into the shoulder straps, gathered up a coil of rope, a torch and a groundsheet. Mallory looked at his watch: it was fifteen minutes to midnight. The routine call from Cairo was almost due.

'Going to have another go, Casey? I wouldn't send a dog out on a night like this.'

'Neither would I,' Brown said morosely. 'But I think I'd better sir. Reception is far better at night and I'm going to climb uphill a bit to get a clearance from that damned mountain there: I'd be spotted right away if I tried to do that in daylight.'

'Right you are, Casey. You know best.' Mallory looked at him curiously. 'What's all the extra gear for?'

'Putting the set under the groundsheet then getting below it myself with the torch,' Brown explained. 'And I'm pegging the rope here, going to pay it out on my way up. I'd like to be able to get back some time.'

'Good enough,' Mallory approved. 'Just watch it a bit higher up. This gully narrows and deepens into a regular ravine.'

'Don't you worry about me, sir,' Brown said firmly. 'Nothing's going to happen to Casey Brown.' A snow-laden gust of wind, the flap of the canvas and Brown was gone.

'Well, if Brown can do it . . .' Mallory was on his feet now, pulling his snow-smock over his head. 'Fuel, gentlemen – old Leri's hut. Who's for a midnight stroll?'

Andrea and Louki were on their feet together, but Mallory shook his head.

'One's enough. I think someone should stay to look after Stevens.'

'He's sound asleep,' Andrea murmured. 'He can come to no harm in the short time we are away.'

'I wasn't thinking of that. It's just that we can't take the chance of him falling into German hands. They'd make him talk, one way or another. It would be no fault of his – but they'd make him talk. It's too much of a risk.'

'Pouf!' Louki snapped his fingers. 'You worry about nothing, Major. There isn't a German within miles of here. You have my word.'

Mallory hesitated, then grinned. 'You're right. I'm getting the jumps.' He bent over Stevens, shook him gently. The boy stirred and moaned, opened his eyes slowly.

'We're going out for some firewood,' Mallory said. 'Back in a few minutes. You be OK?'

'Of course, sir. What can happen? Just leave a gun by my side – and blow out the candle.' He smiled. 'Be sure to call out before you come in!'

Mallory stooped, blew out the candle. For an instant the flame flared then died and every feature, every person in the cave was swallowed up in the thick darkness of a winter midnight. Abruptly Mallory turned on his heel and pushed out through the canvas into the drifting, wind-blown snow already filling up the floor of the gully, Andrea and Louki close behind.

It took them ten minutes to find the ruined hut of the old goatherd, another five for Andrea to wrench the door off its shattered hinges and smash it up to manageable lengths, along with the wood from the bunk and table, another ten to carry back with them to the rock-shelter as much wood as they could conveniently rope together and carry. The wind, blowing straight north off Kostos, was in their faces now – faces numbed with the chill, wet lash of the driving snow, and blowing almost at gale force: they were not sorry to reach the gully again, drop down gratefully between the sheltering walls.

Mallory called softly at the mouth of the cave. There was no reply, no movement from inside. He called again, listened intently as the silent seconds went by, turned his head and looked briefly at Andrea and Louki. Carefully, he laid his bundle of wood in the snow, pulled out his Colt and torch, eased aside the curtain, lamp switch and Colt safety-catch clicking as one.

The spotlight beam lit up the floor at the mouth of the cave, passed on, settled, wavered, probed into the farthest corner of the shelter, returned again to the middle of the cave and steadied there as if the torch were clamped in a vice. On the floor there was only a crumpled, empty sleeping-bag. Andy Stevens was gone.

9

TUESDAY NIGHT

0015–0200

'So I was wrong,' Andrea murmured. 'He wasn't asleep.'

'He certainly wasn't,' Mallory agreed firmly. 'He fooled me too – *and* he heard what I said.' His mouth twisted. 'He knows now why we're so anxious to look after him. He knows now that he was right when he spoke about a mill-stone. I should hate to feel the way he must be feeling right now.'

Andrea nodded. 'It is not difficult to guess why he has gone.'

Mallory looked quickly at his watch, pushed his way out of the cave.

'Twenty minutes – he can't have been gone more than twenty minutes. Probably a bit less to make sure we were well clear. He can only drag himself – fifty yards at the most. We'll find him in four minutes. Use your torches and take the hoods off – nobody will see us in this damn' blizzard. Fan out uphill – I'll take the gully in the middle.'

'Uphill?' Louki's hand was on his arm, his voice puzzled. 'But his leg—'

'Uphill, I said,' Mallory broke in impatiently. 'Stevens has brains – and a damn' sight more guts than he thinks we credit him with. He'll figure we'll think he's taken the easy way.' Mallory paused a moment then went on sombrely: 'Any dying man who drags himself out in this lot is going to do nothing the easy way. Come on!'

They found him in exactly three minutes. He must have suspected that Mallory wouldn't fall for the obvious. or he had heard them stumbling up the slope, for he had managed to burrow his way in behind the overhanging snowdrift that sealed off the space beneath a projecting ledge just above the rim of the gully. An almost perfect place of concealment, but his leg betrayed him: in the probing light of his torch Andrea's sharp eyes caught the tiny trickle of blood seeping darkly through the surface of the snow. He was already unconscious when they uncovered him, from cold or exhaustion or the agony of his shattered leg: probably from all three.

Back in the cave again, Mallory tried to pour some ouzo – the fiery, breath-catching local spirit – down Stevens's throat. He had a vague suspicion that this might be dangerous – or perhaps it was only dangerous in cases of shock, his memory was confused on that point – but it seemed better than nothing. Stevens gagged, spluttered and coughed most of it up again, but some at least stayed down. With Andrea's help Mallory tightened the loosened splints on the leg, staunched the oozing blood, and spread below and above the boy every dry covering he could find in the cave. Then he sat back tiredly and fished out a cigarette from his waterproof case. There was nothing more he could do until Dusty Miller returned with Panayis from the village. He was pretty sure there was nothing that Dusty could do for Stevens either. There was nothing anybody could do for him.

Already Louki had a fire burning near the mouth of the cave, the old tinder-dry wood blazing up in a fierce crackling blaze with hardly a wisp of smoke. Almost at once its warmth began to spread throughout the cave, and the three men edged gratefully nearer. From half a dozen points in the roof thin, steadily-increasing streams of water from the melting snows above began to splash down on the gravelly floor beneath: with these and with the heat of the blaze the ground was soon a quagmire. But, especially to Mallory and Andrea, these discomforts were a small price to pay for the privilege of being warm for the first time in over thirty hours. Mallory felt the glow seep through him like a benison, felt his entire body relax, his eyelids grow heavy and drowsy.

Back propped against the wall, he was just drifting off to

sleep, still smoking that first cigarette, when there was a gust of wind, a sudden chilling flurry of snow and Brown was inside the cave, wearily slipping the transmitter straps from his shoulders. Lugubrious as ever, his tired eyes lit up momentarily at the sight of the fire. Blue-faced and shuddering with cold – no joke, Mallory thought grimly, squatting motionless for half an hour on that bleak and frozen hillside – he hunched down silently by the fire, dragged out the inevitable cigarette and gazed moodily into the flames, oblivious alike of the clouds of steam that almost immediately enveloped him, of the acrid smell of his singeing clothes. He looked utterly despondent. Mallory reached for a bottle, poured out some of the heated *retsimo* – mainland wine heavily reinforced with resin – and passed it across to Brown.

'Chuck it straight down the hatch,' Mallory advised. 'That way you won't taste it.' He prodded the transmitter with his foot and looked up at Brown again. 'No dice this time either?'

'Raised them no bother, sir.' Brown grimaced at the sticky sweetness of the wine. 'Reception was first class – both here and in Cairo.'

'You got through!' Mallory sat up, leaned forward eagerly. 'And were they pleased to hear from their wandering boys tonight?'

'They didn't say. The first thing they told me was to shut up and stay that way.' Brown poked moodily at the fire with a steaming boot. 'Don't ask me how, sir, but they've been tipped off that enough equipment for two or three small monitoring stations has been sent here in the past fortnight.'

Mallory swore.

'Monitoring stations! That's damned handy, that is!' He thought briefly of the fugitive, nomad existence these same monitoring stations had compelled Andrea and himself to lead in the White Mountains of Crete. 'Dammit, Casey, on an island like this, the size of a soup plate, they can pin-point us with their eyes shut!'

'Aye, they can that, sir,' Brown nodded heavily.

'Have you heard anything of these stations, Louki?' Mallory asked.

'Nothing, Major; nothing.' Louki shrugged. 'I am afraid I do not even know what you are talking about.'

'I don't suppose so. Not that it matters – it's too late now. Let's have the rest of the good news, Casey.'

'That's about it, sir. No sending for me – by order. Restricted to code abbreviations – affirmative, negative, repetitive, wilco and such-like. Continuous sending only in emergency or when concealment's impossible anyway.'

'Like from the condemned cell in these ducky little dungeons in Navarone,' Mallory murmured. ' "I died with my boots on, ma." '

'With all respects, sir, that's not funny,' Brown said morosely. 'Their invasion fleet – mainly caiques and E-boats – sailed this morning from the Piraeus,' he went on. 'About four o'clock this morning. Cairo expects they'll be holding up in the Cyclades somewhere tonight.'

'That's very clever of Cairo. Where the hell else could they hole up?' Mallory lit a fresh cigarette and looked bleakly into the fire. 'Anyway, it's nice to know they're on the way. That the lot, Casey?'

Brown nodded silently.

'Good enough, then. Thanks a lot for going out. Better turn in, catch up with some sleep while you can. . . . Louki reckons we should be down in Margaritha before dawn, hole up there for the day – he's got some sort of abandoned well all lined up for us – and push on to the town of Navarone tomorrow night.'

'My God!' Brown moaned. 'Tonight a leaking cave. To-morrow night an abandoned well – half-full of water, probably. Where are we staying in Navarone, sir. The crypt in the local cemetery?'

'A singularly apt lodging, the way things are going,' Mallory said dryly. 'We'll hope for the best. We're leaving before five.' He watched Brown lie down beside Stevens and transferred his attention to Louki. The little man was seated on a box on the opposite side of the fire, occasionally turning a heavy stone to be wrapped in cloth and put to Stevens's number feet, and blissfully hugging the flames. By and by he became aware of Mallory's close scrutiny and looked up.

'You look worried, Major.' Louki seemed vexed. 'You look – what is the word? – concerned. You do not like my plan, no? I thought we had agreed—'

'I'm not worried about your plan,' Mallory said frankly. 'I'm not even worried about you. It's that box you're sitting on. Enough HE in it to blow up a battleship – and you're only three feet from that fire. It's not just too healthy, Louki.'

Louki shifted uneasily on his seat, tugged at one end of his moustache.

'I have heard that you can throw this TNT into a fire and that it just burns up nicely, like a pine full of sap.'

'True enough,' Mallory acquiesced. 'You can also bend it, break it, file it, saw it, jump on it and hit it with a sledge-hammer, and all you'll get is the benefit of the exercise. But if it starts to sweat in a hot, humid atmosphere – and then the exudation crystallises. Oh, brother! And it's getting far too hot and sticky in this hole.

'Outside with it!' Louki was on his feet, backing farther into the cave. 'Outside with it!' He hesitated. 'Unless the snow, the moisture—'

'You can also leave it immersed in salt water for ten years without doing it any harm,' Mallory interrupted didactically. 'But there are some primers there that might come to grief – not to mention that box of detonators beside Andrea. We'll just stick the lot outside, under a cape.'

'Pouf! Louki has a far better idea!' The little man was already slipping into his cloak. 'Old Leri's hut! The very place. Exactly! We can pick it up there whenever we want – and if you have to leave here in a hurry you do not have to worry about it.' Before Mallory could protest, Louki had bent over the box lifted it with an effort, half-walked, half-staggered round the fire, making for the screen. He had hardly taken three steps when Andrea was by his side, had relieved him firmly of the box and tucked it under one arm.

'If you will permit me—'

'No, no!' Louki was affronted. 'I can manage easily. It is nothing.'

'I know, I know,' Andrea said pacifically. 'But these explosives – they must be carried a certain way. I have been trained,' he explained.

'So? I did not realize. Of course it must be as you say! I, then, will bring the detonators.' Honour satisfied, Louki thankfully gave up the argument, lifted the little box and scuttled out of the cave close on Andrea's heels.

Mallory looked at his watch. One o'clock exactly. Miller and Panayis should be back soon, he thought. The wind had passed its peak and the snow was almost gone: the going would be all that easier, but there would be tracks in the snow. Awkward, these tracks, but not fatal – they themselves would be gone before light, cutting straight downhill for the foot of the valley. The snow wouldn't lie there – and even if there were patches they could take to the stream that wound through the valley, leaving no trace behind.

The fire was sinking and the cold creeping in on them again. Mallory shivered in his still wet clothes, threw some more wood on the fire, watched it blaze up, and flood the cave with light. Brown, huddled on a groundsheet, was already asleep. Stevens, his back to him, was lying motionless, his breathing short and quick. God only knew how long the boy would stay alive: he was dying, Miller said, but 'dying' was a very indefinite term: when a man, a terribly injured, dying man, made up his mind not to die he became the toughest, most enduring creature on earth. Mallory had seen it happen before. But maybe Stevens didn't want to live. To live, to overcome these desperate injuries – that would be to prove himself to himself, and to others, and he was young enough, and sensitive enough and had been hurt and had suffered so much in the past that that could easily be the most important thing in the world to him: on the other hand, he knew what an appalling handicap he had become – he had heard Mallory say so; he knew, too, that Mallory's primary concern was not for his welfare but the fear that he would be captured, crack under pressure and tell everything – he had heard Mallory say so; and he knew that he had failed his friends. It was all very difficult, impossible to say how the balance of contending forces would work out eventually. Mallory shook his head, sighed, lit a fresh cigarette and moved closer to the fire.

Andrea and Louki returned less than five minutes later, and Miller and Panayis were almost at their heels. They could hear Miller coming some distance away, slipping falling and swearing almost continuously as he struggled up the gully under a large and awkward load. He practically fell across the threshold of the cave and collapsed wearily by the fire. He gave the impression of a man who had been through a very great deal indeed. Mallory grinned sympathetically at him.

'Well, Dusty, how did it go? Hope Panayis here didn't slow you up too much.'

Miller didn't seem to hear him. He was gazing incredulously at the fire, lantern jaw drooping open as its significance slowly dawned on him.

'Hell's teeth! Would you look at that!' He swore bitterly. 'Here I spend half the gawddamned night climbing up a gawddamned mountain with a stove and enough kerosene to bath a

bloody elephant. And what do I find?' He took a deep breath
.to tell them what he found, then subsided into a strangled.
seething silence.

'A man your age should watch his blood pressure,' Mallory
advised him. 'How did the rest of it go?'

'Okay, I guess.' Miller had a mug of ouzo in his hand and
was beginning to brighten up again. 'We got the beddin', the
medicine kit—'

'If you'll give me the bedding I will get our young friend
into it now,' Andrea interrupted.

'And food?' Mallory asked.

'Yeah. We got the grub, boss. Stacks of it. This guy Panayis
is a wonder. Bread, wine, goat-cheese, garlic sausages, rice –
everything.'

'Rice?' It was Mallory's turn to be incredulous. 'But you
can't get the stuff in the islands nowadays, Dusty.'

'Panayis can.' Miller was enjoying himself hugely now. 'He
got it from the German commandant's kitchen. Guy by the
name of Skoda.'

'The German commandant's – you're joking!'

'So help me, boss, that's Gospel truth.' Miller drained half
the ouzo at a gulp and expelled his breath in a long, gusty sigh
of satisfaction. 'Little ol' Miller hangs around the back door,
knees knockin' like Carmen Miranda's castanets, ready for a
smart take off in any direction while Junior here goes in and
cracks the joint. Back home in the States he'd make a fortune
as a cat-burglar. Comes back in about ten minutes, luggin' that
damned suitcase there.' Miller indicated it with a casual wave
of his hand. 'Not only cleans out the commandant's pantry, but
also borrows his satchel to carry the stuff in. I tell you, boss,
associatin' with this character gives me heart attacks.'

'But – but how about guards, about sentries?'

'Taken the night off, I guess, boss. Old Panayis is like a clam
– never says a word, and even then I can't understand him. My
guess is that everybody's out lookin' for us.'

'There and back and you didn't meet a soul.' Mallory filled
him a mug of wine. 'Nice going, Dusty.'

'Panayis's doin', not mine. I just tagged along. Besides. we
did run into a couple of Panayis's pals – he hunted them up
rather. Musta given him the tip-off about somethin'. He was
hoppin' with excitement just afterwards, tried to tell me all
about it.' Miller shrugged his shoulders sadly. 'We weren't
operatin' on the same wave-length, boss.'

Mallory nodded across the cave. Louki and Panayis were close together, Louki doing all the listening, while Panayis talked rapidly in a low voice, gesticulating with both hands.

'He's still pretty worked up about something,' Mallory said thoughtfully. He raised his voice. 'What's the matter, Louki?'

'Matter enough, Major.' Louki tugged ferociously at the end of his moustache. 'We will have to be leaving soon – Panayis wants to go right away. He has heard that the German garrison is going to make a house-to-house check in our village during the night – about four o'clock, Panayis was told.'

'Not a routine check, I take it?' Mallory asked.

'This has not happened for many months. They must think that you have slipped their patrols and are hiding in the village.' Louki chuckled. 'If you ask me, I don't think they know *what* to think. It is nothing to you, of course. You will not be there – and even if you were they would not find you: and it will make it all the safer for you to come to Margaritha afterwards. But Panayis and I – we must not be found out of our beds. Things would go hard with us.'

'Of course, of course. We must take no risks. But there is plenty of time. You will go down in an hour. But first, the fortress.' He dug into his breast pocket, brought out the map Eugene Vlachos had drawn for him, turned to Panayis and slipped easily into the island Greek. 'Come, Panayis. I hear you know the fortress as Louki here knows his own vegetable patch. I already know much, but I want you to tell me everything about it – the layout, guns, magazines, power rooms, barracks, sentries, guard routine, exits, alarm systems, even where the shadows are deep and the others less deep – just everything. No matter how tiny and insignificant the details may seem to you, nevertheless you must tell me. If a door opens outwards instead of inwards, you must tell me: that could save a thousand lives.'

'And how does the Major mean to get inside?' Louki asked.

'I don't know yet. I cannot decide until I have seen the fortress.' Mallory was aware of Andrea looking sharply at him, then looking away. They had made their plans on the MTB for entering the fortress. But it was the keystone upon which everything depended, and Mallory felt that this knowledge should be confined to the fewest number possible.

For almost half an hour Mallory and the three Greeks huddled over the chart in the light of the flames, Mallory checking on what he had been told, meticulously pencilling in all the fresh information that Panayis had to give him – and

Panayis had a very great deal to tell. It seemed almost impossible that a man could have assimilated so much in two brief visits to the fortress – and clandestine visits in the darkness, at that. He had an incredible eye and capacity for detail; and it was a burning hatred of the Germans, Mallory felt certain, that had imprinted these details on an all but photographic memory. Mallory could feel his hopes rising with every second that passed.

Casey Brown was awake again. Tired though he was, the babble of voices had cut through an uneasy sleep. He crossed over to where Andy Stevens, half-awake now, lay propped against the wall, talking rationally at times, incoherently at others. There was nothing for him to do there, Brown saw: Miller, cleaning, dusting and rebandaging the wounds had had all the help he needed – and very efficient help at that – from Andrea. He moved over to the mouth of the cave, listened blankly to the four men talking in Greek, moved out past the screen for a breath of the cold, clean night air. With seven people inside the cave and the fire burning continuously, the lack of almost all ventilation had made it uncomfortably warm.

He was back in the cave in thirty seconds, drawing the screen tightly shut behind him.

'Quiet, everybody!' he whispered softly. He gestured behind him. 'There's something moving out there, down the slope a bit. I heard it twice, sir.'

Panayis swore softly, twisted to his feet like a wild cat. A foot-long, two-edged throwing knife gleamed evilly in his hand and he had vanished through the canvas screen before anyone could speak. Andrea made to follow him, but Mallory stretched out his hand.

'Stay where you are, Andrea. Our friend Panayis is just that little bit too precipitate,' he said softly. 'There may be nothing – or it might be some diversionary move. . . . Oh, damn!' Stevens had just started babbling to himself in a loud voice. 'He would start talking now. Can't you do something . . .'

But Andrea was already bent over the sick boy, holding his hand in his own, smoothing the hot forehead and hair with his free hand and talking to him soothingly, softly, continuously, At first he paid no attention, kept on talking in a rambling, inconsequential fashion about nothing in particular; gradually, however. the hypnotic effect of the stroking hand, the gentle caressing murmur took effect, and the babbling died away to a barely aduible muttering ceased altogether. Suddenly his eyes opened and he was awake and quite rational.

'What is it, Andrea? Why are you—?'

'Shh!' Mallory held up his hand. 'I can hear someone—'

'It's Panayis, sir.' Brown had his eye at a crack in the curtain. 'Just moving up the gully.'

Seconds later, Panayis was inside the cave, squatting down by the fire. He looked thoroughly disgusted.

'There is no one there,' he reported. 'Some goats I saw, down the hill, but that was all.' Mallory translated to the others.

'Didn't sound like goats to me.' Brown said doggedly. 'Different kind of sound altogether.'

'I will take a look,' Andrea volunteered. 'Just to make sure. But I do not think the dark one would make a mistake.' Before Mallory could say anything he was gone, as quickly and silently as Panayis. He was back in three minutes, shaking his head. 'Panayis is right. There is no one. I did not even see the goats.'

'And that's what it must have been, Casey,' Mallory said. 'Still, I don't like it. Snow almost dropped, wind dropping and the valley probably swarming with German patrols – I think it's time you two were away. For God's sake, be careful. If anyone tries to stop you, shoot to kill. They'll blame it on us anyway.'

'Shoot to kill!' Louki laughed dryly. 'Unnecessary advice, Major, when the dark one is with us. He never shoots any other way.'

'Right, away you go. Damned sorry you've got yourselves mixed up in all this – but now that you are, a thousand thanks for all you've done. See you at half-past six.'

'Half-past six,' Louki echoed. 'The olive grove on the bank of the stream, south of the village. We will be waiting there.'

Two minutes later they were lost to sight and sound and all was still inside the cave again, except for the faint crackling of the embers of the dying fire. Brown had moved out on guard, and Stevens had already fallen into a restless, pain-filled sleep. Miller bent over him for a moment or two, then moved softly across the cave to Mallory. His right hand held a crumpled heap of bloodstained bandages. He held them out towards Mallory.

'Take a sniff at that, boss,' he asked quietly. 'Easy does it.'

Mallory bent forward, drew away sharply, his nose wrinkled in immediate disgust.

'Good lord, Dusty! That's vile!' He paused, paused in sure, sick certainty. He knew the answer before he spoke. 'What on earth is it?'

'Gangrene.' Miller sat down heavily by his side, threw the

bandages into the fire. All at once he sounded tired, defeated. 'Gas gangrene, Spreadin' like a forest fire – and he would have died anyway. I'm just wastin' my time.'

──── IO ────

TUESDAY NIGHT

0400–0600

The Germans took them just after four o'clock in the morning, while they were still asleep. Bone-tired and deep-drugged with this sleep as they were, they had no chance, not the slightest hope of offering any resistance. The conception. timing and execution of the coup were immaculate. Surprise was complete.

Andrea was the first awake. Some alien whisper of sound had reached deep down to that part of him that never slept, and he twisted round and elbowed himself off the ground with the same noiseless speed as his hand reached out for his ready-cocked and loaded Mauser. But the white beam of the powerful torch lancing through the blackness of the cave had blinded him, frozen his stretching hand even before the clipped bite of command from the man who held the torch.

'Still! All of you!' Faultless English, with barely a trace of accent, and the voice glacial in its menace. 'You move, and you die!' Another torch switched on, a third, and the cave was flooded with light. Wide awake, now, and motionless Mallory squinted painfully into the dazzling beams: in the back-wash of reflected light, he could just discern the vague, formless shapes crouched in the mouth of the cave, bent over the dulled barrels of automatic rifles.

'Hands clasped above the heads and back to the wall!' A certainty, an assured competence in the voice that made for instant obedience. 'Take a good look at them, Sergeant.' Almost conversational now, the tone, but neither torch nor gun barrel had wavered a fraction. 'No shadow of expression in their faces, not even a flicker of the eyes. Dangerous men, Sergeant. The English choose their killers well!'

Mallory felt the grey bitterness of defeat wash through him in an almost tangible wave, he could taste the sourness of it in the back of his mouth. For a brief, heart-sickening second he allowed himself to think of what must now inevitably happen and as soon as the thought had come he thrust it savagely away. Every-thing, every action, every thought, every breath must be on the present. Hope was gone, but not irrecoverably gone: not so long as Andrea lived. He wondered if Casey Brown had seen or heard them coming, and what had happened to him: he made to ask, checked himself just in time. Maybe he was still at large.

'How did you manage to find us?' Mallory asked quietly.

'Only fools burn juniper wood,' the officer said contemptu-ously. 'We have been on Kostos all day and most of the night. A dead man could have smelt it.'

'On Kostos?' Miller shook his head. 'How could—?'

'Enough!' The officer turned to someone behind him. 'Tear down that screen,' he ordered in German, 'and keep us covered on either side.' He looked back into the cave, gestured almost imperceptibly with his torch. 'All right, you three. Outside – and you had better be careful. Please believe me that my men are praying for an excuse to shoot you down, you murdering swine!' The venomous hatred in his voice carried utter con-viction.

Slowly, hands still clasped above their heads, the three men stumbled to their feet. Mallory had taken only one step when the whip-lash of the German's voice brought him up short.

'Stop!' He stabbed the beam of his torch down at the un-conscious Stevens, gestured abruptly at Andrea. 'One side, you! Who is this?'

'You need not fear from him,' Mallory said quietly. 'He is one of us but he is terribly injured. He is dying.'

'We will see,' the officer said tightly. 'Move to the back of the cave!' He waited until the three men had stepped over Stevens, changed his automatic rifle for a pistol, dropped to his knees and advanced slowly, torch in one hand, gun in the other, well below the line of fire of the two soldiers who advanced unbidden at his heels. There was no inevitability, a cold professionalism about it all that made Mallory's heart sink.

Abruptly the officer reached out his gun-hand, tore the covers off the boy. A shuddering tremor shook the whole body, his head rolled from side to side as he moaned in unconscious agony. The officer bent quickly over him, the hard, clean lines of the face, the fair hair beneath the hood high-lit in the beam of his own torch. A quick look at Stevens's pain-twisted, emaciated features, a glance at the shattered leg, a brief, distasteful wrinkling of the nose as he caught the foul stench of the gangrene, and he had hunched back on his heels, gently replacing the covers over the sick boy.

'You speak the truth.' he said softly. 'We are not barbarians. I have no quarrel with a dying man. Leave him there.' He rose to his feet, walked slowly backwards. 'The rest of you outside.'

The snow had stopped altogether, Mallory saw, and stars were beginning to twinkle in the clearing sky. The wind, too, had fallen away and was perceptibly warmer. Most of the snow would be gone by midday, Mallory guessed.

Carelessly, incuriously, he looked around him. There was no sign of Casey Brown. Inevitably Mallory's hopes began to rise. Petty Officer Brown's recommendation for this operation had come from the very top. Two rows of ribbons to which he was entitled but never wore bespoke his gallantry, he had a formidable reputation as a guerrilla fighter – and he had had an automatic rifle in his hand. If he were somewhere out there. . . . Almost as if he had divined his hopes, the German smashed them at a word.

'You wonder where your sentry is, perhaps?' he asked mockingly. 'Never fear, Englishman, he is not far from here, asleep at his post. Very sound asleep. I'm afraid.'

'You've killed him?' Mallory's hands clenched until his palms ached.

The other shrugged his shoulder in vast indifference.

'I really couldn't say. It was all too easy. One of my men lay in the gully and moaned. A masterly performance – really pitiable – he almost had me convinced. Like a fool your man came to investigate. I had another man waiting above, the barrel of his rifle in his hand. A very effective club, I assure you. . . .'

Slowly Mallory unclenched his fists and stared bleakly down the gully. Of course Casey would fall for that, he was bound to after what had happened earlier in the night. He wasn't going to make a fool of himself again, cry 'wolf' twice in succession: inevitably, he had gone to check first. Suddenly the thought occurred to Mallory that maybe Casey Brown *had* heard something earlier on, but the thought vanished as soon as it had come. Panayis did not look like the man to make a mistake: and Andrea never made a mistake; Mallory turned back to the officer again.

'Well, where do we go from here?'

'Margaritha, and very shortly. But one thing first.' The German, his own height to an inch, stood squarely in front of him, levelled revolver at waist height, switched-off torch dangling loosely from his right hand. 'Just a little thing, Englishman. Where are the explosives?' He almost spat the words out.

'Explosives?' Mallory furrowed his brows in perplexity. 'What explosives?' he asked blankly, then staggered and fell to the ground as the heavy torch swept round in a vicious half-circle, caught him flush on the side of the face. Dizzily he shook his head and climbed slowly to his feet again.

'The explosives.' The torch was balanced in the hand again, the voice silky and gentle. 'I asked you where they were.'

'I don't know what you are talking about.' Mallory spat out a broken tooth, wiped some blood off his smashed lips. 'Is this the way the Germans treat their prisoners?' he asked contemptuously.

'Shut up!'

Again the torch lashed out. Mallory was waiting for it, rode the blow as best he could: even so the torch caught him heavily high up on the cheek-bone, just below the temple, stunning him with his jarring impact. Seconds passed, then he pushed himself slowly off the snow, the whole side of his face afire with agony, his vision blurred and unfocused.

'We fight a clean war!' The officer was breathing heavily, in barely controlled fury. 'We fight by the Geneva Conventions. But these are for soldiers, not for murdering spies—'

'We are no spies!' Mallory interrupted. He felt as if his head was coming apart.

'Then where are your uniforms?' the officer demanded. 'Spies, I say – murdering spies who stab in the back and cut men's throats!' The voice was trembling with anger. Mallory was at a loss – nothing spurious about this indignation.

'Cut men's throats?' He shook his head in bewilderment. 'What the hell are you talking about?'

'My own batman. A harmless messenger, a boy only – and he wasn't even armed. We found him only an hour ago. Ach, I waste my time!' He broke off as he turned to watch two men coming up the gully. Mallory stood motionless for a moment, cursing the ill luck that had led the dead man across the path of Panayis – it could have been no one else – then turned to see what had caught the officers attention. He focused his aching eyes with difficulty, looked at the bent figure struggling up the slope, urged on by the ungentle prodding of a bayoneted rifle. Mallory let go a long, silent breath of relief. The left side of

Brown's face was caked with blood from a gash above the temple, but he was otherwise unharmed.

'Right! Sit down in the snow, all of you!' He gestured to several of his men. 'Bind their hands!'

'You are going to shoot us now, perhaps?' Mallory asked quietly. It was suddenly, desperately urgent that he should know: there was nothing they could do but die, but at least they could die on their feet, fighting; but if they weren't to die just yet, almost any later opportunity for resistance would be less suicidal than this.

'Not yet, unfortunately. My section commander in Margaritha, Hauptmann Skoda, wishes to see you first – maybe it would be better for you if I *did* shoot you now. Then the Herr Commandant in Navarone – Officer Commanding of the whole island.' The German smiled thinly. 'But only a postponement, Englishman. You will be kicking your heels before the sun sets. We have a short way with spies in Navarone.'

'But, sir! Captain!' Hands raised in appeal, Andrea took a step forward, brought up short as two rifle muzzles ground into his chest.

'Not Captain – Lieutenant,' the officer corrected him. 'Oberleutnant Turzig, at your service. What is it you want, fat one?' he asked contemptuously.

'Spies! You said spies! I am no spy!' The words rushed and tumbled over one another, as if he could not get them out fast enough. 'Before God, I am no spy! I am not one of them.' The eyes were wide and staring, the mouth working soundlessly between the gasped-out sentences. 'I am only a Greek, a poor Greek. They forced me to come along as an interpreter. I swear it, Lieutenant Turzig, I swear it!'

'You yellow bastard!' Miller ground out viciously, then grunted in agony as a rifle butt drove into the small of his back, just above the kidney. He stumbled, fell forward on his hands and knees, realized even as he fell that Andrea was only playing a part, that Mallory had only to speak half a dozen words in Greek to expose Andrea's lie. Miller twisted on his side in the snow, shook his fist weakly and hoped that the contorted pain on his face might be mistaken for fury. 'You two-faced, double-crossing dago! You gawddamned swine, I'll get you . . .' There was a hollow, sickening thud and Miller collapsed in the snow: the heavy ski-boot had caught him just behind the ear.

Mallory said nothing. He did not even glance at Miller. Fists balled helplessly at his sides and mouth compressed, he glared steadily at Andrea through narrowed slits of eyes. He knew the lieutenant was watching him, felt he must back Andrea up all the way. What Andrea intended he could not even begin to guess – but he would back him to the end of the world.

'So!' Turzig murmured thoughtfully. 'Thieves fall out, eh?' Mallory thought he detected the faintest overtones of doubt, of hesitancy, in his voice, but the lieutenant was taking no chances. 'No matter, fat one. You have cast your lot with these assassins. What is it the English say? "You have made your bed, you must lie on it." ' He looked at Andrea's vast bulk dispassionately. 'We may need to strengthen a special gallows for you.'

'No, no, no!' Andrea's voice rose sharply, fearfully, on the last word. 'It is true what I tell you! I am not one of them, Lieutenant Turzig, before God I am not one of them!' He wrung his hands in distress, his great moon-face contorted in anguish. 'Why must I die for no fault of my own? I didn't want to come. I am no fighting man, Lieutenant Turzig!'

'I can see that,' Turzig said dryly. 'A monstrous deal of skin to cover a quivering jelly-bag your size – and every inch of it precious to you.' He looked at Mallory, and at Miller, still lying face down in the snow. 'I cannot congratulate your friends on their choice of companion.'

'I can tell you everything, Lieutenant, I can tell you everything!' Andrea pressed forward excitedly, eager to consolidate his advantage, to reinforce the beginnings of doubt. 'I am no friend of the Allies – I will prove it to you – and then perhaps—'

'You damned Judas!' Mallory made to fling himself forward, but two burly soldiers caught him and pinioned his arms from behind. He struggled briefly, then relaxed, looked balefully at Andrea. 'If you dare to open your mouth, I promise you you'll never live to—'

'Be quiet!' Turzig's voice was very cold. 'I have had enough of recrimination, of cheap melodrama. Another word and you join your friend in the snow there.' He looked at him a moment in silence, then swung back to Andrea. 'I promise nothing. I will hear what you have to say.' He made no attempt to disguise the repugnance in his voice.

'You must judge for yourself.' A nice mixture of relief, earnestness and the dawn of hope, of returning confidence. Andrea paused a minute and gestured dramatically at Mallory, Miller and Brown. 'These are no ordinary soldiers – they are Jellicoe's men, of the Special Boat Service!'

'Tell me something I couldn't have guessed myself,' Turzig growled. 'The English Earl has been a thorn in our flesh these many months past. If that is all you have to tell me, fat one—'

'Wait!' Andrea held up his hand. 'They are still no ordinary men but a specially picked force – an assault unit, they call themselves – flown last Sunday night from Alexandria to Castelrosso. They left that same night from Castelrosso in a motorboat.'

'A torpedo boat,' Turzig nodded. 'So much we know already. Go on.'

'You know already! But how—'

'Never mind how. Hurry up!'

'Of course, Lieutenant, of course.' Not a twitch in his face betrayed Andrea's relief. This had been the only dangerous point in his story. Nicolai, of course, had warned the Germans, but never thought it worth while mentioning the presence of a giant Greek in the party. No reason, of course. why he should have selected him for special mention – but if he had done, it would have been the end.

'The torpedo boat landed them somewhere in the islands, north of Rhodes. I do not know where. There they stole a caique, sailed it up through Turkish waters, met a big German patrol boat – and sunk it.' Andrea paused for effect. 'I was less than half a mile away at the time in my fishing boat.'

Turzig leaned forward. 'How did they manage to sink so big a boat?' Strangely, he didn't doubt that it had been sunk.

'They pretended to be harmless fishermen like myself. I had just been stopped, investigated and cleared,' Andrea said virtuously. 'Anyway, your patrol boat came alongside this old caique. Close alongside. Suddenly there were guns firing on both sides, two boxes went flying through the air – into the engine-room of your boat, I think. Pouf!' Andrea threw up his hands dramatically. 'That was the end of that!'

'We wondered . . .' Turzig said softly. 'Well, go on.'

'You wondered what, Lieutenant?' Turzig's eyes narrowed and Andrea hurried on.

'Their interpreter had been killed in the fight. They tricked me into speaking English – I spent many years in Cyprus – kidnapped me, let my sons sail the boat—'

'Why should they want an interpreter?' Turzig demanded suspiciously. 'There are many British officers who speak Greek.'

'I am coming to that,' Andrea said impatiently. 'How in God's name do you expect me to finish my story if you keep interrupt-

ing all the time? Where was I? Ah, yes. They forced me to come
along, and their engine broke down. I don't know what happened – I was kept below. I think we were in a creek somewhere, repairing the engine, and then there was a wild bout of
drinking – you will not believe this, Lieutenant Turzig, that
men on so desperate a mission should get drunk – and then we
sailed again.'

'On the contrary, I do believe you.' Turzig was nodding his
head slowly, as if in secret understanding. 'I believe you indeed.'

'You do?' Andrea contrived to look disappointed. 'Well, we
ran into a fearful storm, wrecked the boat on the south cliff
of this island and climbed—'

'Stop!' Turzig had drawn back sharply, suspicion flaring in
his eyes. 'Almost I believed you! I believed you because we
know more than you think, and so far you have told the truth.
But not now. You are clever, fat one, but not so clever as you
think. One thing you have forgotten – or maybe you do not
know. We are of the *Wurttembergische Gebirgsbataillon* – we
know mountains, my friend, better than any troops in the world.
I myself am a Prussian, but I have climbed everything worth
climbing in the Alps and Transylvania – and I tell you that
the south cliff cannot be climbed. It is impossible!'

'Impossible perhaps for you.' Andrea shook his head sadly.
'These cursed Allies will beat you yet. They are clever, Lieutenant Turzig, damnably clever!'

'Explain yourself,' Turzig ordered curtly.

'Just this. They knew men thought the south cliff could not
be climbed. So they determined to climb it. You would never
dream that this could be done, that an expedition could land
on Navarone that way. But the Allies took a gamble, found a
man to lead the expedition. He could not speak Greek, but that
did not matter, for what they wanted was a man who could
climb – and so they picked the greatest rock-climber in the
world today.' Andrea paused for effect, flung out his arm
dramatically. 'And this is the man they picked, Lieutenant
Turzig! You are a mountaineer yourself and you are bound to
know him. His name is Mallory – Keith Mallory of New Zealand!'

There was a sharp exclamation, the click of a switch, and
Turzig had taken a couple of steps forward, thrust the torch
almost into Mallory's eyes. For almost ten seconds he stared into
the New Zealander's averted, screwed-up face, then slowly
lowered his arm, the harsh spotlight limning a dazzling white

circle in the snow at his feet. Once, twice, half a dozen times Turzig nodded his head in slow understanding.

'Of course!' he murmured. 'Mallory – Keith Mallory! Of course I know him. There's not a man in my *Abteilung* but has heard of Keith Mallory.' He shook his head. 'I should have known him, I should have known him at once.' He stood for some time with his head bent, aimlessly screwing the toe of his right boot into the soft snow, then looked up abruptly. 'Before the war, even during it, I would have been proud to have known you, glad to have met you. But not here, not now. Not any more. I wish to God they had sent someone else.' He hesitated, made to carry on, then changed his mind, turned wearily to Andrea. 'My apologies, fat one. Indeed you speak the truth. Go on.'

'Certainly!' Andrea's round moon face was one vast smirk of satisfaction. 'We climbed the cliff as I said – although the boy in the cave there was badly hurt – and silenced the guard. Mallory killed him,' Andrea added unblushingly. 'It was a fair fight. We spent most of the night crossing the divide and found this cave before dawn. We were almost dead with hunger and cold. We have been here since.'

'And nothing has happened since?'

'On the contrary.' Andrea seemed to be enjoying himself hugely, revelling in being the focus of attention. 'Two people came up to see us. Who they were I do not know – they kept their faces hidden all the time – nor do I know where they came from.'

'It is as well that you admitted that,' Turzig said grimly. 'I knew someone had been here. I recognised the stove – it belongs to Hauptmann Skoda!'

'Indeed?' Andrea raised his eyebrows in polite surprise. 'I did not know. Well, they talked for some time and—'

'Did you manage to overhear anything they were talking about?' Turzig interrupted. The question came so naturally, so spontaneously, that Mallory held his breath. It was beautifully done. Andrea would walk into it – he couldn't help it. But Andrea was a man inspired that night.

'Overhear them!' Andrea clamped his lips shut in sorely-tried forbearance, gazed heavenwards in exasperated appeal. 'Lieutenant Turzig, how often must I tell you that I am the interpreter? They *could* only talk through me. Of course I know what they were talking about. They are going to blow up the big guns in the harbour.'

'I didn't think they had come here for their health!' Turzig said acidly.

'Ah, but you don't know that they have the plans of the fortress. You don't know that Kheros is to be invaded on Saturday morning. You don't know that they are in radio contact with Cairo all the time. You don't know that destroyers of the British Navy are coming through the Maidos Straits on Friday night as soon as the big guns have been silenced. You don't know—'

'Enough!' Turzig clapped his hands together, his face alight with excitement. 'The Royal Navy, eh? Wonderful, wonderful! *That* is what we want to hear. But enough! Keep it for Hauptmann Skoda and the Kommandant in the fortress. We must be off. But first – one more thing. The explosives – where are they?'

Andrea's shoulders slumped in dejection. He spread out his arms, palms upward.

'Alas, Lieutenant Turzig, I do not know. They took them out and hid them – some talk about the cave being too hot.' He waved a hand towards the western col, in the diametrically opposite direction to Leri's hut. 'That way, I think. But I cannot be sure, for they would not tell me.' He looked bitterly at Mallory. 'These Britishers are all the same. They trust nobody.'

'Heaven only knows that I don't blame them for that!' Turzig said feelingly. He looked at Andrea in disgust. 'More than ever I would like to see you dangling from the highest scaffold in Navarone. But Herr Kommandant in the town is a kindly man and rewards informers. You may yet live to betray some more comrades.'

'Thank you, thank you, thank you! I knew you were fair and just. I promise you, Lieutenant Turzig—'

'Shut up!' Turzig said contemptuously. He switched into German. 'Sergeant, have these men bound. And don't forget the fat one! Later we can untie him, and he can carry the sick man back to the post. Leave a man on guard. The rest of you come with me – we must find those explosives.'

'Could we not make one of them tell us, sir?' the sergeant ventured.

'The only man who would tell us, can't. He's already told us all he knows. As for the rest – well, I was mistaken about them, Sergeant.' He turned to Mallory, inclined his head briefly, spoke in English. 'An error of judgment, Herr Mallory. We are all very tired. I am almost sorry I struck you.' He wheeled abruptly, climbed swiftly up the bank. Two minutes later only a solitary soldier was left on guard.

For the tenth time Mallory shifted his position uncomfortably, strained at the cord that bound his hands together behind his back, for the tenth time recognised the futility of both these actions. No matter how he twisted and turned, the wet snow soaked icily through his clothes until he was chilled to the bone and shaking continually with the cold; and the man who had tied these knots had known his job all too well. Mallory wondered irritably if Turzig and his men meant to spend all night searching for the explosives: they had been gone for more than half an hour already.

He relaxed, lay back on his side in the cushioning snow of the gully bank, and looked thoughtfully at Andrea who was sitting upright just in front of him. He had watched Andrea, with bowed head and hunched and lifting shoulders, making one single, titanic effort to free himself seconds after the guard had gestured them to sit down, had seen the cords bite and gouge until they had almost disappeared in his flesh, the fractional slump of his shoulders as he gave up. Since then the giant Greek had sat quite still and contented himself with scowling at the sentry in the injured fashion of one who has been grievously wronged. That solitary test of the strength of his bonds had been enough. Oberleutnant Turzig had keen eyes, and swollen, chafed and bleeding wrists would have accorded ill with the character Andrea had created for himself.

A masterly creation, Mallory mused, all the more remarkable for its spontaneity, its improvisation. Andrea had told so much of the truth, so much that was verifiable or could be verified, that belief in the rest of his story followed almost automatically. And at the same time he had told Turzig nothing of importance, nothing the Germans could not have found out for themselves – except the proposed evacuation of Kheros by the Navy. Wryly Mallory remembered his dismay, his shocked unbelief when he heard Andrea telling of it – but Andrea had been far ahead of him. There was a fair chance that the Germans might have guessed anyway – they would reason, perhaps, that an assault by the British on the guns of Navarone at the same time as the German assault on Kheros would be just that little bit too co-incidental: again, escape for them all quite clearly depended upon how thoroughly Andrea managed to convince his captors that he was all he claimed, and the relative freedom of action that he could thereby gain – and there was no doubt at all that it was the news of the proposed evacuation that had tipped the scales with Turzig: and the fact that Andrea had given Saturday as the invasion date would only carry all the more weight, as that had been Jensen's original date – obviously false information fed to his agents by German counter-Intelligence, who had known it impossible to conceal the invasion preparations themselves; and finally, if Andrea hadn't told Turzig of the destroyers, he might have failed to carry conviction, they might all yet finish on the waiting gallows in the fortress, the guns would remain intact and destroy the naval ships anyway.

It was all very complicated, too complicated for the state his head was in. Mallory sighed and looked away from Andrea towards the other two. Brown and a now conscious Miller were both sitting upright, hands bound behind their backs, staring down into the snow, occasionally shaking muzzy heads from side to side. Mallory could appreciate all too easily how they felt – the whole right-hand side of his face ached cruelly, continuously. Nothing but aching, broken heads everywhere. Mallory thought bitterly. He wondered how Andy Stevens was feeling, glanced idly past the sentry towards the dark mouth of the cave, stiffened in sudden, almost uncomprehending shock.

Slowly, with an infinitely careful carelessness, he let his eyes wander away from the cave, let them light indifferently on the sentry who sat on Brown's transmitter, hunched watchfully over the Schmeisser cradled on his knees, finger crooked on the trigger. Pray God he doesn't turn round, Mallory said to himself over and over again, pray God he doesn't turn round. Let him sit like that just for a little while longer, only a little while longer. . . . In spite of himself, Mallory felt his gaze shifting, being dragged back again towards that cave-mouth.

Andy Stevens was coming out of the cave. Even in the dim starlight every movement was terribly plain as he inched forward agonisingly on chest and belly, dragging his shattered leg behind him. He was placing his hands beneath his shoulders, levering himself upwards and forwards while his head dropped below his shoulders with pain and the exhaustion of the effort, lowering himself slowly on the soft and sodden snow, then repeating the same heart-sapping process over and over again. Exhausted and pain-filled as the boy might be, Mallory thought, his mind was still working: he had a white sheet over his shoulders and back as camouflage against the snow, and he carried a climbing spike in his right hand. He must have heard at least some of Turzig's conversation: there were two or three guns in the cave, he could easily have shot the guard without coming out at all – but he must have known that the sound of a shot would have brought the Germans running, had them back at the cave long before he could have crawled across the gully, far less cut loose any of his friends.

Five yards Stevens had to go, Mallory estimated, five yards at the most. Deep down in the gully where they were, the south wind passed them by, was no more than a muted whisper in the night; that apart, there was no sound at all, nothing but their own breathing, the occasional stirring as someone stretched a cramped or frozen leg. He's bound to hear him if he comes any closer, Mallory thought desperately, even in that soft snow he's bound to hear him.

Mallory bent his head, began to cough loudly, almost continuously. The sentry looked at him, in surprise first, then in irritation as the coughing continued.

'Be quiet!' the sentry ordered in German. 'Stop that coughing at once!'

'*Hüsten? Hüsten?* Coughing, is it? I can't help it,' Mallory protested in English. He coughed again, louder, more persistently than before. 'It is your Oberleutnant's fault,' he gasped. 'He has knocked out some of my teeth.' Mallory broke into a fresh paroxysm of coughing, recovered himself with an effort. 'Is it my fault that I'm choking on my own blood?' he demanded.

Stevens was less than ten feet away now, but his tiny reserves of strength were almost gone. He could no longer raise himself to the full stretch of his arms, was advancing only a few pitiful inches at a time. At length he stopped altogether, lay still for half a minute. Mallory thought he had lost consciousness, but by and by he raised himself up again, to the full stretch this time, had just begun to pivot himself forward when he collapsed, fell heavily in the snow. Mallory began to cough again, but he was too late. The sentry leapt off his box and whirled round all in one movement, the evil mouth of the Schmeisser lined 'up on the body almost at his feet. Then he relaxed as he realized who it was, lowered the barrel of his gun.

'So!' he said softly. 'The fledgling has left its nest. Poor little fledgling!' Mallory winced as he saw the backswing of the gun ready to smash down on Stevens's defenceless head, but the sentry was a kindly enough man, his reaction had been purely automatic. He arrested the swinging butt inches above the tortured face, bent down and almost gently removed the spike from the feebly threatening hand, sent it spinning over the edge of the gully. Then he lifted Stevens carefully by the shoulders, slid in the bunched-up sheet as pillow for the unconscious head against the bitter cold of the snow, shook his head wonderingly, sadly, went back to his seat on the ammunition box.

Hauptmann Skoda was a small, thin man in his late thirties, neat, dapper, debonair and wholly evil. There was something innately evil about the long, corded neck that stretched up scrawnily above his padded shoulders, something repellent about the incongruously small bullet head perched above. When the thin, bloodless lips parted in a smile, which was often, they revealed a perfect set of teeth: far from lighting his face, the smile only emphasised the sallow skin stretched abnormally taut across the sharp nose and high cheek-bones, puckered up the sabre scar that bisected the left cheek from eyebrow to chin: and whether he smiled or not, the pupils of the deep-set eyes remained always the same, still and black and empty. Even at that early hour – as it was not yet six o'clock – he was immaculately dressed, freshly shaven, the wetly-gleaming hair – thin, dark, heavily indented above the temples – brushed straight back across his head. Seated behind a flat-topped table, the sole article of furniture in the bench-lined guardroom, only the upper half of his body was visible: even so, one instinctively knew that the crease of the trousers, the polish of the jack-boots, would be beyond reproach.

He smiled often, and he was smiling now as Oberleutnant Turzig finished his report. Leaning far back in his chair, elbows on the arm-rests, Skoda steepled his lean fingers under his chin, smiled benignly round the guardroom. The lazy, empty eyes missed nothing – the guard at the door, the two guards behind the bound prisoners, Andrea sitting on the bench where he had just laid Stevens – one lazy sweep of those eyes encompassed them all.

'Excellently done, Oberleutnant Turzig!' he purred. 'Most efficient, really most efficient!' He looked speculatively at the three men standing before him, at their bruised and blood-caked faces, switched his glance to Stevens, lying barely conscious on the bench, smiled again and permitted himself a fractional lift of his eyebrows. 'A little trouble, perhaps, Turzig? The prisoners were not too – ah – co-operative?'

'They offered no resistance, sir, no resistance at all,' Turzig said stiffly. The tone, the manner, were punctilious, correct, but the distaste, the latent hostility were mirrored in his eyes. 'My men were maybe a little enthusiastic. We wanted to make no mistake.'

'Quite right, Lieutenant, quite right,' Skoda murmured approvingly. 'These are dangerous men and one cannot take chances with dangerous men.' He pushed back his chair, rose easily to his feet, strolled round the table and stopped in front of Andrea. 'Except maybe this one, Lieutenant?'

'He is dangerous only to his friends,' Turzig said shortly. 'It is as I told you, sir. He would betray his mother to save his own skin.'

'And claiming friendship with us, eh?' Skoda asked musingly. 'One of our gallant allies. Lieutenant.' Skoda reached out a gentle hand, brought it viciously down and across Andrea's cheek, the heavy signet ring on his middle finger tearing skin and flesh. Andrea cried out in pain, clapped one hand to his bleeding face and cowered away, his right arm raised above his head in blind defence.

'A notable addition to the armed forces of the Third Reich,' Skoda murmured. 'You were not mistaken, Lieutenant. A poltroon – the instinctive reaction of a hurt man is an infallible guide. It is curious,' he mused, 'how often very big men are thus. Part of nature's compensatory process, I suppose. . . . What is your name, my brave friend?'

'Papagos.' Andrea muttered sullenly. 'Peter Papagos.' He took his hand away from his cheek, looked at it with eyes slowly widening with horror, began to rub it across his trouser leg with jerky, hurried movements, the repugnance on his face plain for every man to see. Skoda watched him with amusement.

'You do not like to see blood, Papagos, eh?' he suggested. 'Especially your own blood?'

A few seconds passed in silence, then Andrea lifted his head suddenly, his fat face screwed up in misery. He looked as if he were going to cry.

'I am only a poor fisherman, your Honour!' he burst out. 'You laugh at me and say I do not like blood, and it is true. Nor do I like suffering and war. I want no part of any of these things!' His great fists were clenched in futile appeal, his face puckered in woe, his voice risen an octave. It was a masterly exhibition of despair, and even Mallory found himself almost believing in it. 'Why wasn't I left alone?' he went on pathetically. 'God only knows I am no fighting man—'

'A highly inaccurate statement,' Skoda interrupted dryly. 'That fact must be patently obvious to every person in the room by this time.' He tapped his teeth with a jade cigarette-holder. 'A fisherman you call yourself—'

'He's a damned traitor!' Mallory interrupted. The commandant was becoming just that little bit too interested in Andrea. At once Skoda wheeled round, stood in front of Mallory with his hands clasped behind his back, teetering on heels and toes, and looked him up and down in mocking inspection.

'So!' he said thoughtfully. 'The great Keith Mallory! A rather different proposition from our fat and fearful friend on the bench there, eh, Lieutenant?' He did not wait for an answer. 'What rank are you. Mallory?'

'Captain,' Mallory answered briefly.

'Captain Mallory, eh? Captain Keith Mallory, the greatest mountaineer of our time, the idol of pre-war Europe, the conqueror of the world's most impossible climbs.' Skoda shook his head sadly. 'And to think that it should all end like this. . . . I doubt whether posterity will rank your last climb as among your greatest: there are only ten steps leading to the gallows in the fortress of Navarone.' Skoda smiled. 'Hardly a cheerful thought, is it, Captain Mallory?'

'I wasn't even thinking about it,' the New Zealander answered pleasantly. 'What worries me is your face.' He frowned. 'Somewhere or other I'm sure I've seen it or something like it before.' His voice trailed off into silence.

'Indeed?' Skoda was interested. 'In the Bernese Alps, perhaps? Often before the war—'

'I have it now!' Mallory's face cleared. He knew the risk he was taking, but anything that concentrated attention on himself to the exclusion of Andrea was justified. He beamed at Skoda. 'Three months ago, it was, in the zoo in Cairo. A plains buzzard that had been captured in the Sudan. A rather old and mangy buzzard, I'm afraid,' Mallory went on apologetically. 'but exactly the same scrawny neck, the same beaky face and bald head—'

Mallory broke off abruptly, swayed back out of reach as Skoda, his face livid and gleaming teeth bared in rage. swung at him with his fist. The blow carried with it all Skoda's wiry strength, but anger blurred his timing and the fist swung harmlessly by: he stumbled, recovered, then fell to the floor with a shout of pain as Mallory's heavy boot caught him flush on the thigh, just above the knee. He had barely touched the floor when he was up like a cat, took a pace forward and collapsed heavily again as his injured leg gave way under him.

There was a moment's shocked stillness throughout the room, then Skoda rose painfully, supporting himself on the edge of the heavy table. He was breathing quickly, the thin mouth a hard, white line, the great sabre scar flaming redly in the sallow face drained now of all colour. He looked neither at Mallory nor anyone else, but slowly, deliberately, in an almost frightening silence, began to work his way round to the back of the table, the scuffling of his sliding palms on the leather top rasping edgily across over-tautened nerves.

Mallory stood quite still, watching him with expressionless face, cursing himself for his folly. He had overplayed his hand. There was no doubt in his mind – there could be no doubt in the mind of anyone in that room – that Skoda meant to kill him; and he, Mallory would not die. Only Skoda and Andrea would die: Skoda from Andrea's throwing knife – Andrea was rubbing blood from his face with the inside of his sleeve, fingertips only inches from the sheath – and Andrea from the guns of the guards, for the knife was all he had. You fool, you fool, you bloody stupid fool. Mallory repeated to himself over and over again. He turned his head slightly and glanced out of the corner of his eye at the sentry nearest him. Nearest him – but still six or seven feet away. The sentry would get him, Mallory knew, the blast of the slugs from the Schmeisser would tear him in half before he could cover the distance. But he would try. He must try. It was the least he owed to Andrea.

Skoda reached the back of the table, opened a drawer and lifted out a gun. An automatic, Mallory noted with detachment – a little, blue-metal, snub-nosed toy – but a murderous toy, the kind of gun he would have expected Skoda to have. Unhurriedly Skoda pressed the release button, checked the magazine, snapped it home with the palm of his hand, flicked off the safety catch and looked at Mallory. The eyes hadn't altered in the slightest – they were cold, dark and empty as ever. Mallory flicked a glance at Andrea and tensed himself for one convulsive fling backwards. Here it comes, he thought savagely, this is how bloody fools like Keith Mallory die – and then all of a sudden, and unknowingly, he relaxed, for his eyes were still on Andrea and he had seen Andrea doing the same, the huge hand slipping down unconcernedly from the neck, empty of any sign of knife.

There was a scuffle at the table and Mallory was just in time to see Turzig pin Skoda's gun-hand to the table-top.

'Not that, sir!' Turzig begged. 'For God's sake, not that way!'

'Take your hands away.' Skoda whispered. The staring, empty
eyes never left Mallory's face. 'Take your hands away, I say –
unless you want to go the same way as Captain Mallory.'

'You can't kill him, sir!' Turzig persisted doggedly. 'You just
can't. Herr Kommandant's orders were very clear, Hauptmann
Skoda. The leader must be brought to him alive.'

'He was shot while trying to escape,' Skoda said thickly.

'It's no good.' Turzig shook his head. 'We can't kill them all
– and the other prisoners would talk.' He released his grip on
Skoda's hands. 'Alive, Herr Kommandant said, but he didn't
say how much alive.' He lowered his voice confidentially. 'Perhaps we may have some difficulty in making Captain Mallory
talk,' he suggested.

'What? What did you say?' Abruptly the death's head smile
flashed once more, and Skoda was completely on balance again.
'You are over-zealous, Lieutenant. Remind me to speak to you
about it some time. You underestimate me: that was exactly
what I was trying to do – frighten Mallory into talking. And
now you've spoilt it all.' The smile was still on his face, the
voice light, almost bantering, but Mallory was under no
illusions. He owed his life to the young WGB lieutenant – how
easily one could respect, form a friendship with a man like
Turzig if it weren't for this damned, crazy war. . . . Skoda was
standing in front of him again: he had left his gun on the
table.

'But enough of this fooling, eh, Captain Mallory?' The German's teeth fairly gleamed in the bright light from the naked
lamps overhead. 'We haven't all night, have we?'

Mallory looked at him, then turned away in silence. It was
warm enough, stuffy almost, in that little guardroom, but he
was conscious of a sudden, nameless chill; he knew all at once,
without knowing why, but with complete certainty, that this
little man before him was utterly evil.

'Well, well, well, we are not quite so talkative now, are we,
my friend?' He hummed a little to himself, looked up abruptly,
the smile broader than ever. 'Where are the explosives, Captain
Mallory?'

'Explosives?' Mallory lifted an interrogatory eyebrow. 'I don't
know what you are talking about.'

'You don't remember, eh?'

'I don't know what you are talking about.'

'So.' Skoda hummed to himself again and walked over in front of Miller. 'And what about you, my friend?'

'Sure I remember,' Miller said easily. 'The captain's got it all wrong.'

'A sensible man!' Skoda purred – but Mallory could have sworn to an undertone of disappointment in the voice. 'Proceed, my friend.'

'Captain Mallory has no eye for detail,' Miller drawled. 'I was with him that day. He is malignin' a noble bird. It was a vulture, not a buzzard.'

Just for a second Skoda's smile slipped, then it was back again, as rigidly fixed and lifeless as if it had been painted on.

'Very, very witty men, don't you think, Turzig? What the British would call music-hall comedians. Let them laugh while they may, until the hangman's noose begins to tighten. . . .' He looked at Casey Brown. 'Perhaps you—'

'Why don't you go and take a running jump to yourself?' Brown growled.

'A running jump? The idiom escapes me, but I fear it is hardly complimentary.' Skoda selected a cigarette from a thin case, tapped it thoughtfully on a thumb nail. 'Hmm. Not just what one might call too co-operative, Lieutenant Turzig.'

'You won't get these men to talk, sir.' There was a quiet finality in Turzig's voice.

'Possibly not, possibly not.' Skoda was quite unruffled. 'Nevertheless, I shall have the information I want, and within five minutes.' He walked unhurriedly across to his desk, pressed a button, screwed his cigarette into its jade holder, and leaned against the table, an arrogance, a careless contempt in every action, even to the leisurely crossing of the gleaming jackboots.

Suddenly a side door was flung open and two men stumbled into the room, prodded by a rifle barrel. Mallory caught his breath, felt his nails dig savagely into the palms of his hands. Louki and Panayis! Louki and Panayis, bound and bleeding, Louki from a cut above the eye, Panayis from a scalp wound. So they'd got them too, and in spite of his warnings. Both men were shirt-sleeved; Louki, minus his magnificently frogged jacket, scarlet *stanta* and the small arsenal of weapons that he carried stuck beneath it, looked strangely pathetic and woebegone – strangely, for he was red-faced with anger, the moustache bristling more ferociously than ever. Mallory looked at him with eyes empty of all recognition, his face expressionless.

'Come now, Captain Mallory,' Skoda said reproachfully. 'Have you no word of greeting for two old friends? No? Or perhaps you are just overwhelmed?' he suggested smoothly. 'You had not expected to see them so soon again, eh, Captain Mallory?'

'What cheap trick is this?' Mallory asked contemptuously. 'I've never seen these men before in my life.' His eyes caught those of Panayis, held there involuntarily: the black hate that stared out of those eyes, the feral malevôlence – there was something appalling about it.

'Of course not,' Skoda sighed wearily. 'Oh, of course not. Human memory is so short, is it not, Captain Mallory.' The sigh was pure theatre – Skoda was enjoying himself immensely, the cat playing with the mouse. 'However, we will try again.' He swung round, crossed over to the bench where Stevens lay, pulled off the blanket and, before anyone could guess his intentions, chopped the outside of his right hand against Stevens's smashed leg, just below the knee. . . . Stevens's entire body leapt in a convulsive spasm, but without even the whisper of a moan: he was still fully conscious, smiling at Skoda, blood trickling down his chin from where his teeth had gashed his lower lip.

'You shouldn't have done that, Hauptmann Skoda,' Mallory said. His voice was barely a whisper, but unnaturally loud in the frozen silence of the room. 'You are going to die for that, Hauptmann Skoda.'

'So? I am going to die, am I?' Again he chopped his hand against the fractured leg, again without reaction. 'Then I may as well die twice over – eh, Captain Mallory? This young man is very, very tough – but the British have soft hearts, have they not, my dear Captain?' Gently his hand slid down Stevens's leg, closed round the stockinged ankle. 'You have exactly five seconds to tell me the truth, Captain Mallory, and then I fear I will be compelled to re-arrange these splints – *Gott in Himmel!* What's the matter with that great oaf?'

Andrea had taken a couple of steps forward, was standing only a yard away, swaying on his feet.

'Outside! Let me outside!' His breath came in short, fast gasps. He bowed his head, one hand to his throat, one over his stomach. 'I cannot stand it! Air! Air! I must have air!'

'Ah, no, my dear Papagos, you shall remain her and enjoy – Corporal! Quickly!' He had seen Andrea's eyes roll upwards until only the whites showed. 'The fool is going to faint! Take him away before he falls on top of us!'

Mallory had one fleeting glimpse of the two guards hurrying forwards, of the incredulous contempt on Louki's face, then he flicked a glance at Miller and Brown, caught the lazy droop of the American's eyelid in return, the millimetric inclination of Brown's head. Even as the two guards came up behind Andrea and lifted the flaccid arms across their shoulders, Mallory glanced half-left, saw the nearest sentry less than four feet away now, absorbed in the spectacle of the toppling giant. Easy, dead easy – the gun dangling by his side: he could hit him between wind and water before he knew what was happening. . . .

Fascinated, Mallory watched Andrea's forearms slipping nervelessly down the shoulders of the supporting guards till his wrists rested loosely beside their necks, palms facing inwards. And then there was the sudden leap of the great shoulder muscles and Mallory had hurled himself convulsively sidewards and back, his shoulder socketing with vicious force into the guard's stomach, inches below the breast-bone: an explosive *ouf!* of agony, the crash against the wooden walls of the room and Mallory knew the guard would be out of action for some time to come.

Even as he dived. Mallory had heard the sickening thud of heads being swept together. Now, as he twisted round on his side, he had a fleeting glimpse of another guard thrashing feebly on the floor under the combined weights of Miller and Brown, and then of Andrea tearing an automatic rifle from the guard who had been standing at his right shoulder: the Schmeisser was cradled in his great hands, lined up on Skoda's chest even before the unconscious man had hit the floor.

For one second, maybe two, all movement in the room ceased, every sound sheared off by a knife edge: the silence was abrupt, absolute – and infinitely more clamorous than the clamour that had gone before. No one moved, no one spoke, no one even breathed: the shock, the utter unexpectedness of what had happened held them all in thrall.

And then the silence erupted in a staccato crashing of sound, deafening in that confined space. Once, twice, three times, wordlessly, and with great care, Andrea shot Hauptmann Skoda through the heart. The blast of the shells lifted the little man off his feet, smashed him against the wall of the hut, pinned him there for one incredible second, arms outflung as though nailed against the rough planks in spreadeagle crucifixion; and then he collapsed, fell limply to the ground a grotesque and broken doll that struck its heedless head against the edge of the bench before coming to rest on its back on the floor. The eyes

441

were still wide open, as cold, as dark, as empty in death as they had been in life.

His Schmeisser waving in a gentle arc that covered Turzig and the sergeant, Andrea picked up Skoda's sheath knife, sliced through the ropes that bound Mallory's wrists.

'Can you hold this gun, my Captain?'

Mallory flexed his stiffened hands once or twice, nodded, took the gun in silence. In three steps Andrea was behind the blind side of the door leading to the ante-room, pressed to the wall, waiting, gesturing to Mallory to move as far back as possible out of the line of sight.

Suddenly the door was flung open. Andrea could just see the tip of the rifle barrel projecting beyond it.

'Oberleutnant Turzig! *Was ist los? Wer schoss . . .*' The voice broke off in a coughing grunt of agony as Andrea smashed the sole of his foot against the door. He was round the outside of the door in a moment, caught the man as he fell, pulled him clear of the doorway and peered into the adjacent hut. A brief inspection, then he closed the door, bolted it from the inside.

'Nobody else there, my Captain,' Andrea reported. 'Just the one gaoler, it seems.'

'Fine! Cut the others loose, will you, Andrea?' He wheeled round towards Louki, smiled at the comical expression on the little man's face, the tentative, spreading, finally ear-to-ear grin that cut through the baffled incredulity.

'Where do the men sleep, Louki – the soldiers, I mean?'

'In a hut in the middle of the compound, Major. This is the officers' quarters.'

'Compound? You mean—?'

'Barbed wire,' Louki said succinctly. 'Ten feet high – and all the way round.'

'Exits?'

'One and one only. Two guards.'

'Good! Andrea – everybody into the side room. No, not you, Lieutenant. You sit down here.' He gestured to the chair behind the big desk. 'Somebody's bound to come. Tell him you killed one of us – trying to escape. Then send for the guards at the gate.'

For a moment Turzig didn't answer. He watched unseeingly as Andrea walked past him, dragging two unconscious soldiers by their collars. Then he smiled. It was a wry sort of smile.

'I am sorry to disappoint you, Captain Mallory. Too much has been lost already through my blind stupidity. I won't do it.'

'Andrea!' Mallory called softly.

'Yes?' Andrea stood in the ante-room doorway.

'I think I hear someone coming. Is there a way out of that side room?'

Andrea nodded silently.

'Outside! The front door. Take your knife. If the Lieutenant . . .' But he was talking to himself. Andrea was already gone, slipping out through the back door, soundless as a ghost.

'You will do exactly as I say,' Mallory said softly. He took position himself in the doorway to the side room, where he could see the front entrance between door and jamb: his automatic rifle was trained on Turzig. 'If you don't, Andrea will kill the man at the door. Then we will kill you and the guards inside. Then we will knife the sentries at the gate. Nine dead men – and all for nothing, for we will escape anyway. . . . Here he is now.' Mallory's voice was barely a whisper, eyes pitiless in a pitiless face. 'Nine dead men, Lieutenant – and just because your pride is hurt.' Deliberately, the last sentence was in German, fluent, colloquial, and Mallory's mouth twisted as he saw the almost imperceptible sag of Turzig's shoulders. He knew he had won, that Turzig had been going to take a last gamble on his ignorance of German, that this last hope was gone.

The door burst open and a soldier stood on the threshold, breathing heavily. He was armed, but clad only in a singlet and trousers, oblivious of the cold.

'Lieutenant! Lieutenant!' He spoke in German. 'We heard the shots—'

'It is nothing, Sergeant.' Turzig bent his head over an open drawer, pretended to be searching for something to account for his solitary presence in the room. 'One of our prisoners tried to escape. . . . We stopped him.'

'Perhaps the medical orderly—'

'I'm afraid we stopped him rather permanently.' Turzig smiled tiredly. 'You can organise a burial detail in the morning. Meantime, you might tell the guards at the gate to come here for a minute. Then get to bed yourself – you'll catch your death of cold!'

'Shall I detail a relief guard—'

'Of course not!' Turzig said impatiently. 'It's just for a minute. Besides, the only people to guard against are already in here.' His lips tightened for a second as he realized what he had said, the unconscious irony of the words. 'Hurry up, man! We haven't got all night!' He waited till the sound of the running footsteps died away, then looked steadily at Mallory. 'Satisfied?'

'Perfectly. And my very sincere apologies,' Mallory said quietly. 'I hate to do a thing like this to a man like you.' He looked round the door as Andrea came into the room. 'Andrea, ask Louki and Panayis if there's a telephone switchboard in this block of huts. Tell them to smash it up and any receivers they can find.' He grinned. 'Then hurry back for our visitors from the gate. I'd be lost without you on the reception committee.'

Turzig's gaze followed the broad retreating back.

'Captain Skoda was right. I still have much to learn.' There was neither bitterness nor rancour in his voice. 'He fooled me completely, that big one.'

'You're not the first,' Mallory reassured him. 'He's fooled more people than I'll ever know. . . . You're not the first,' he repeated. 'But I think you mus' be just about the luckiest.'

'Because I'm still alive?'

'Because you're still alive,' Mallory echoed.

Less than ten minutes later the two guards at the gates had joined their comrades in the back room, captured, disarmed, bound and gagged with a speed and noiseless efficiency that excited Turzig's professional admiration, chagrined though he was. Securely tied hand and foot, he lay in a corner of the room, not yet gagged.

'I think I understand now why your High Command chose you for this task, Captain Mallory. If anyone could succeed, you would – but you must fail. The impossible must always remain so. Nevertheless, you have a great team.'

'We get by,' Mallory said modestly. He took a last look round the room, then grinned down at Stevens.

'Ready to take off on your travels again, young man, or do you find this becoming rather monotonous?'

'Ready when you are, sir.' Lying on a stretcher which Louki had miraculously procured, he sighed in bliss. 'First-class travel, this time, as befits an officer. Sheer luxury. I don't mind how far we go!'

'Speak for yourself,' Miller growled morosely. He had been allocated first stint at the front or heavy end of the stretcher. But the quirk of his eyebrows robbed the words of all offence.

'Right, then, we're off. One last thing. Where is the camp radio, Lieutenant Turzig?'

'So you can smash it, I suppose?'

'Precisely.'

'I have no idea.'

'What if I threaten to blow your head off?'

'You won't.' Turzig smiled, though the smile was a trifle lopsided. 'Given certain circumstances, you would kill me as you would a fly. But you wouldn't kill a man for refusing such information.'

'You haven't as much to learn as your late and unlamented captain thought,' Mallory admitted. 'It's not all that important. . . . I regret we have to do all this. I trust we do not meet again – not at least, until the war is over. Who knows, some day we might even go climbing together.' He signed to Louki to fix Turzig's gag and walked quickly out of the room. Two minutes later they had cleared the barracks and were safely lost in the darkness and the olive groves that stretched to the south of Margaritha.

When they cleared the groves, a long time later, it was almost dawn. Already the black silhouette of Kostos was softening in the first feathery greyness of the coming day. The wind was from the south, and warm, and the snow was beginning to melt on the hills.

I I

WEDNESDAY

1400–1600

All day long they lay hidden in the carob grove, a thick clump of stunted, gnarled trees that clung grimly to the treacherous, scree-strewn slope abutting what Louki called the 'Devil's Play-ground.' A poor shelter and an uncomfortable one, but in every other way all they could wish for: it offered concealment, a first-class defensive position immediately behind, a gentle breeze drawn up from the sea by the sun-baked rocks to the south, shade from the sun that rode from dawn to dusk in a cloudless sky – and an incomparable view of a sun-drenched, shimmering Ægean.

Away to their left, fading through diminishing shades of blue and indigo and violet into faraway nothingness, stretched the islands of the Lerades, the nearest of them, Maidos, so close that they could see isolated fisher cottages sparkling whitely in the sun: through that narrow, intervening gap of water would pass the ships of the Royal Navy in just over a day's time. To the right, and even farther away, remote, featureless, back-dropped by the towering Anatolian mountains, the coast of Turkey hooked north and west in a great curving scimitar: to the north itself, the thrusting spear of Cape Demirci, rock-rimmed but dimpled with sandy coves of white, reached far out into the placid blue of the Ægean: and north again beyond the Cape, haze-blurred in the purple distance, the island of Kheros lay dreaming on the surface of the sea.

It was a breath-taking panorama, a heart-catching beauty sweeping majestically through a great semi-circle over the sunlit sea. But Mallory had no eyes for it, had spared it only a passing glance when he had come on guard less than half an hour pre-viously, just after two o'clock. He had dismissed it with one quick glance, settled by the bole of a tree, gazed for endless minutes, gazed until his eyes ached with strain at what he had so long waited to see. Had waited to see and come to destroy – the guns of the fortress of Navarone.

The town of Navarone – a town of from four to five thousand people, Mallory judged – lay sprawled round the deep, volcanic crescent of the harbour, a crescent so deep, so embracing, that it was almost a complete circle with only a narrow bottleneck of an entrance to the north-west, a gateway dominated by searchlights and mortar and machine-gun batteries on either side. Less that three miles distant to the north-east from the carob grove, every detail, every street, every building, every caique and launch in the harbour were clearly visible to Mal-lory and he studied them over and over again until he knew them by heart: the way the land to the west of the harbour sloped up gently to the olive groves, the dusty streets running down to the water's edge: the way the ground rose more sharply to the south, the streets now running parallel to the water down to the old town: the way the cliffs to the east – cliffs pock-marked by the bombs of Torrance's Liberator Squadron – stretched a hundred and fifty sheer feet above the water, then curved dizzily out over and above the harbour, and the great mound of volcanic rock towering above that again, a mound barricaded off from the town below by the high wall that ended flush with the cliff itself: and, finally, the way the twin rows of AA guns, the great radar scanners and the barracks of the for-tress, squat, narrow-embrasured, built of big blocks of masonry, dominated everything in sight – including that great, black gash in the rock, below the fantastic overhang of the cliff.

Unconsciously, almost, Mallory nodded to himself in slow understanding. This was the fortress that had defied the Allies for eighteen long months, that had dominated the entire naval strategy in the Sporades since the Germans had reached out from the mainland into the isles, that had blocked all naval activity in that 2000 square mile triangle between the Lerades and the Turkish coast. And now, when he saw it, it all made sense. Impregnable to land attack – the commanding fortress saw to that: impregnable to air attack – Mallory realized just how suicidal it had been to send out Torrance's squadron against the great guns protected by that jutting cliff, against those bristling rows of anti-aircraft guns: and impregnable to sea attack – the waiting squadrons of the Luftwaffe on Samos saw to that. Jensen had been right – only a guerrilla sabotage mission stood any chance at all: a remote chance, an all but suicidal chance, but still a chance, and Mallory knew he couldn't ask for more.

Thoughtfully he lowered the binoculars and rubbed the back of his hand across his aching eyes. At last he felt he knew exactly what he was up against, was grateful for the knowledge, for the opportunity he'd been given of this long-range reconnaissance, this familarising of himself with the terrain, the geography of the town. This was probably the one vantage point in the whole island that offered such an opportunity together with concealment and near immunity. No credit to himself, the leader of the mission, he reflected wryly, that they had found such a place: it had been Louki's idea entirely.

And he owed a great deal more than that to the sad-eyed little Greek. It had been Louki's idea that they first move up-valley from Margaritha, to give Andrea time to recover the explosives from old Leri's hut, and to make certain there was no immediate hue and cry and pursuit – they could have fought a rearguard action up through the olive groves, until they had lost themselves in the foothills of Kostos: it was he who had guided them back past Margaritha when they had doubled on their tracks, had halted them opposite the village while he and Panayis had slipped wraith-like through the lifting twilight, picked up outdoor clothes for themselves, and, on the return journey, slipped into the *Abteilung* garage, torn away the coil ignitions of the German command car and truck – the only transport in Margaritha – and smashed their distributors for good measure; it was Louki who had led them by a sunken ditch right up to the road-block guard post at the mouth of the valley – it had been almost ludicrously simple to disarm the sentries, only one of whom had been awake – and, finally, it was Louki who had insisted that they walk down the muddy centre of the valley track till they came to the metalled road, less than two miles from the town itself. A hundred yards down this they had branched off to the left across a long, sloping field of lava that left no trace behind, arrived in the carob copse just on sunrise.

And it had worked. All these carefully engineered pointers, pointers that not even the most sceptical could have ignored and denied, had worked magnificently. Miller and Andrea, who had shared the forenoon watch, had seen the Navarone garrison spending long hours making the most intensive house-to-house search of the town. That should make it doubly, trebly safe for them the following day, Mallory reckoned: it was unlikely that the search would be repeated, still more unlikely that, if it were, it would be carried out with a fraction of the same enthusiasm. Louki had done his work well.

Mallory turned his head to look at him. The little man was still asleep – wedged on the slope behind a couple of tree-trunks, he hadn't stirred for five hours. Still dead tired himself, his legs aching and eyes smarting with sleeplessness, Mallory could not find it in him to grudge Louki a moment of his rest. He'd earned it all – and he'd been awake all through the previous night. So had Panayis, but Panayis was already awakening, Mallory saw, pushing the long, black hair out of his eyes: awake, rather, for his transition from sleep to full awareness was immediate, as fleeting and as complete as a cat's. A dangerous man, Mallory knew, a desperate man, almost, and a bitter enemy, but he knew nothing of Panayis, nothing at all. He doubted if he ever would.

Farther up on the slope, almost in the centre of the grove, Andrea had built a high platform of broken branches and twigs against a couple of carob poles maybe five feet apart, gradually filling up the space between slope and trees until he had a platform four feet in width, as nearly level as he could make it. Andy Stevens lay on this, still on his stretcher, still conscious. As far as Mallory could tell, Stevens hadn't closed his eyes since they had been marched away by Turzig from their cave in the mountains. He seemed to have passed beyond the need for sleep, or had crushed all desire for it. The stench from the gangrenous

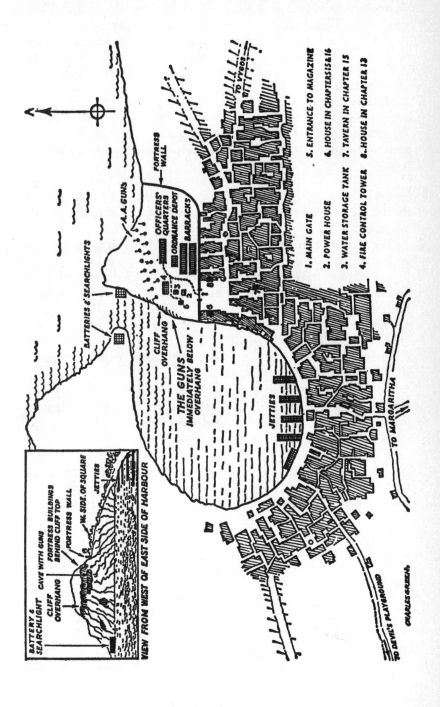

TO VIGOS

FORTRESS WALL

A.A. GUNS

OFFICERS' QUARTERS

ORDNANCE DEPOT

BARRACKS

BATTERIES & SEARCHLIGHTS

CLIFF OVERHANG

THE GUNS
IMMEDIATELY BELOW
OVERHANG

JETTIES

TO MARGARITHA

TO DEVIL'S PLAYGROUND

CHARLES GREEN

1. MAIN GATE
2. POWER HOUSE
3. WATER STORAGE TANK
4. FIRE CONTROL TOWER.
5. ENTRANCE TO MAGAZINE
6. HOUSE IN CHAPTERS 15 & 16
7. TAVERN IN CHAPTER 15
8. HOUSE IN CHAPTER 13

BATTERY &
SEARCHLIGHT   CAVE WITH GUNS
CLIFF
OVERHANG   FORTRESS BUILDINGS
BEHIND CLIFF TOP

FORTRESS WALL

W. SIDE OF SQUARE

JETTIES

VIEW FROM WEST OF EAST SIDE OF HARBOUR

leg was nauseating, appalling, poisoned all the air around. Mallory and Miller had had a look at the leg shortly after their arrival in the copse, uncovered it, examined it, smiled at one another tied it up again and assured Stevens that the wound was closing. Below the knee, the leg had turned almost completely black.

Mallory lifted his binoculars to have another look at the town, but lowered them almost at once as someone came sliding down the slope, touched him on the arm. It was Panayis, upset, anxious, almost angry looking. He gesticulated towards the westering sun.

'The time, Captain Mallory?' He spoke in Greek, his voice low, sibilant, urgent – an inevitable voice, Mallory thought, for the lean, dark mysteriousness of the man. 'What is the time?' he repeated.

'Half-past two, or thereabouts.' Mallory lifted an interrogatory eyebrow. 'You are concerned, Panayis. Why?'

'You should have wakened me. You should have wakened me hours ago!' He *was* angry, Mallory decided. 'It is my turn to keep watch.'

'But you had no sleep last night,' Mallory pointed out reasonably. 'It just didn't seem fair—'

'It is my turn to keep watch, I tell you!' Panayis insisted stubbornly.

'Very well, then. If you insist.' Mallory knew the high, fierce pride of the islanders too well to attempt to argue. 'Heaven only knows what we would have done without Louki and yourself. . . . I'll stay and keep you company for a while.'

'Ah, so that is why you let me sleep on!' There was no disguising the hurt in the eyes, the voice. 'You do not trust Panayis—'

'Oh, for heaven's sake!' Mallory began in exasperation, checked himself and smiled. 'Of course we trust you. Maybe I should go and get some more sleep anyway; you are kind to give me the chance. You will shake me in two hours' time?'

'Certainly, certainly!' Panayis was almost beaming. 'I shall not fail.'

Mallory scrambled up to the centre of the grove and stretched out lazily along the ledge he had levelled out for himself. For a few idle moments he watched Panayis pacing restlessly to and fro just inside the perimeter of the grove, lost interest when he saw him climbing swiftly up among the branches of a tree, seeking a high lookout vantage point and decided he might as well follow his advice and get some sleep while he could.

'Captain Mallory! Captain Mallory!' An urgent, heavy hand was shaking his shoulder. 'Wake up! Wake up!'

Mallory stirred, rolled over on his back, sat up quickly, opening his eyes as he did so. Panayis was stooped over him, the dark, saturnine face alive with anxiety. Mallory shook his head to clear away the mists of sleep and was on his feet in one swift, easy movement.

'What's the matter, Panayis?'

'Planes!' he said quickly. 'There is a squadron of planes coming our way!'

'Planes? What planes? Whose planes?'

'I do not know, Captain. They are yet far away. But—'

'What direction?' Mallory snapped.

'They come from the north.'

Together they ran down to the edge of the grove. Panayis gestured to the north, and Mallory caught sight of them at once, the afternoon sun glinting off the sharp dihedral of the wings. Stukas, all right, he thought grimly. Seven – no, eight of them – less than three miles away, flying in two echelons of four, two thousand, certaintly not more than twenty-five hundred feet. . . . He became aware that Panayis was tugging urgently at his arm.

'Come, Captain Mallory!' he said excitedly. 'We have no time to lose!' He pulled Mallory round, pointed with outstretched arm at the gaunt, shattered cliffs that rose steeply behind them, cliffs crazily riven by rock-jumbled ravines that wound their aimless way back into the interior – or stopped as abruptly as they had begun. 'The Devil's Playground! We must get in there at once! At once, Captain Mallory!'

'Why on earth should we?' Mallory looked at him in astonishment. 'There's no reason to suppose that they're after us. How can they be? No one knows we're here.'

'I do not care!' Panayis was stubborn in his conviction. 'I know. Do not ask me how I know, for I do not know that myself. Louki will tell you – Panayis knows these things. I know, Captain Mallory, I *know*!'

Just for a second Mallory stared at him, uncomprehending. There was no questioning the earnestness, the utter sincerity – but it was the machine-gun staccato of the words that tipped the balance of instinct against reason. Almost without realizing it, certainly without realizing why, Mallory found himself running uphill, slipping and stumbling in the scree. He found the others already on their feet, tense, expectant, shrugging on their packs, the guns already in their hands.

'Get to the edge of the trees up there!' Mallory shouted. 'Quickly! Stay there and stay under cover – we're going to have to break for that gap in the rocks.' He gestured through the trees at a jagged fissure in the cliff-side, barely forty yards from where he stood, blessed Louki for his foresight in choosing a hideout with so convenient a bolt-hole. 'Wait till I give the word. Andrea!' He turned round, then broke off, the words unneeded. Andrea had already scooped up the dying boy in his arms, just as he lay in stretcher and blankets and was weaving his way uphill in and out among the trees.

'What's up, Boss?' Miller was by Mallory's side as he plunged up the slope. 'I don't see nothin'.'

'You can hear something if you'd just stop talking for a moment,' Mallory said grimly. 'Or just take a look up there.'

Miller, flat on his stomach, now and less than a dozen feet from the edge of the grove, twisted round and craned his neck upwards. He picked up the planes immediately.

'Stukas!' he said incredulously. 'A squadron of gawddamned Stukas! It can't be, boss!'

'It can and it is,' Mallory said grimly. 'Jensen told me that Jerry has stripped the Italian front of them – over two hundred pulled out in the last few weeks.' Mallory squinted up at the squadron, less than half a mile away now. 'And he's brought the whole damn' issue down to the Ægean.'

'But they're not lookin' for us,' Miller protested.

'I'm afraid they are,' Mallory said grimly. The two bomber echelons had just dove-tailed into line ahead formation. 'I'm afraid Panayis was right.'

'But – but they're passin' us by—'

'They aren't.' Mallory said flatly. 'They're here to stay. Just keep your eyes on that leading plane.'

Even as he spoke, the flight-commander tilted his gull-winged Junkers 87 sharply over to port, half-turned, fell straight out of the sky in a screaming power-dive, plummeting straight for the carob grove.

'Leave him alone!' Mallory shouted. 'Don't fire!' The Stukas, airbrakes at maximum depression, had steadied on the centre of the grove. Nothing could stop him now – but a chance shot might bring him down directly on top of them: the chances were poor enough as it was. . . . 'Keep your hands over your heads – and your heads down!'

He ignored his own advice, his gaze following the bomber every foot of the way down. Five hundred, four hundred, three, the rising crescendo of the heavy engine was beginning to hurt his ears, and the Stuka was pulling sharply out of its plunging fall, its bomb gone.

Bomb! Mallory sat up sharply, screwing up his eyes against the blue of the sky. Not one bomb but dozens of them, clustered so thickly that they appeared to be jostling each other as they arrowed into the centre of the grove, striking the gnarled and stunted trees, breaking off branches and burying themselves to their fins in the soft and shingled slope. Incendiaries! Mallory had barely time to realize that they had been spared the horror of a 500-kilo HE bomb when the incendiaries erupted into hissing, guttering life, into an incandescent magnesium whiteness that reached out and completely destroyed the shadowed gloom of the carob grove. Within a matter of seconds the dazzling coruscation had given way to thick, evil-smelling clouds of acrid black smoke, smoke laced with flickering tongues of red, small at first then licking and twisting resinously upwards until entire trees were enveloped in a cocoon of flame. The Stuka was still pulling upwards out of its dive, had not yet levelled off when the heart of the grove, old and dry and tindery, was fiercely ablaze.

Miller twisted up and round, nudging Mallory to catch his attention through the crackling roar of the flames.

'Incendiaries, boss,' he announced.

'What did you think they were using?' Mallory asked shortly. 'Matches? They're trying to smoke us out, to burn us out, get us in the open. High explosive's not so good among trees. Ninety-nine times out of a hundred this would have worked.' He coughed as the acrid smoke bit into his lungs, peered up with watering eyes through the tree-tops. 'But not this time. Not if we're lucky. Not if they hold off another half-minute or so. Just look at that smoke!'

Miller looked. Thick, convoluted, shot through with fiery sparks, the rolling cloud was already a third of the way across the gap between grove and cliff, borne uphill by the wandering catspaws from the sea. It was the complete, the perfect smokescreen. Miller nodded.

'Gonna make a break for it, huh, boss?'

'There's no choice – we either go, or we stay and get fried

or blown into very little bits. Probably both.' He raised his voice. 'Anybody see what's happening up top?'

'Queuing up for another go at us, sir,' Brown said lugubriously. 'The first bloke's still circling around.'

'Waiting to see how we break cover. They won't wait long. This is where we take off.' He peered uphill through the rolling smoke, but it was too thick, laced his watering eyes until everything was blurred through a misted sheen of tears. There was no saying how far uphill the smoke-bank had reached, and they couldn't afford to wait until they were sure. Stuka pilots had never been renowned for their patience.

'Right, everybody!' he shouted. 'Fifteen yards along the tree-line to that wash, then straight up into the gorge. Don't stop till you're at least a hundred yards inside. Andrea, you lead the way. Off you go!' He peered through the blinding smoke. 'Where's Panayis?'

There was no reply.

'Panayis!' Mallory called. 'Panayis!'

'Perhaps he went back for somethin'.' Miller had stopped, half-turned. 'Shall I go—'

'Get on your way!' Mallory said savagely. 'And if anything happens to young Stevens I'll hold you . . .' But Miller, wisely, was already gone, Andrea stumbling and coughing by his side.

For a couple of seconds Mallory stood irresolute, then plunged back downhill towards the centre of the grove. Maybe Panayis had gone back for something – and he couldn't understand English. Mallory had hardly gone five yards when he was forced to halt and fling his arm up before his face: the heat was searing. Panayis couldn't be down there; no one could have been down there, could have lived for seconds in that furnace. Gasping for air, hair singeing and clothes smoldering with fire, Mallory clawed his way back up the slope, colliding with trees, slipping, falling, then stumbling desperately to his feet again.

He ran along to the east end of the wood. No one there. Back to the other end again, towards the wash, almost completely blind now, the super-heated air searing viciously through throat and lungs till he was suffocating, till his breath was coming in great, whooping, agonised breaths. No sense in waiting longer, nothing he could do, nothing anyone could do except save himself. There was a noise in his ears, the roaring of the flames, the roaring of his own blood – and the screaming, heart-stopping roar of a Stuka in a power-dive. Desperately he flung himself

forward over the sliding scree, stumbled and pitched headlong
down to the floor of the wash.

Hurt or not, he did not know and he did not care. Sobbing
aloud for breath, he rose to his feet, forced his aching legs to
drive him somehow up the hill. The air was full of the thunder
of engines, he knew the entire squadron was coming in to the
attack, and then he had flung himself uncaringly to the ground
as the first of the high explosive bombs erupted in its concussive
blast of smoke and flame – erupted not forty yards away, to his
left and ahead of him. *Ahead* of him! Even as he struggled
upright again, lurched forward and upward once more, Mallory cursed himself again and again and again. You madman,
he thought bitterly, confusedly, you damned crazy madman.
Sending the others out to be killed. He should have thought of
it – oh, God, he should have thought of it, a five-year-old could
have thought of it. Of course Jerry wasn't going to bomb the
grove: they had seen the obvious, the inevitable, as quickly as
he had, were dive-bombing the pall of smoke between the grove
and the cliff! A five-year-old – the earth exploded beneath his
feet, a giant hand plucked him up and smashed him to the
ground and the darkness closed over him.

—— 1 2 ——

WEDNESDAY

1600–1800

Once, twice, half a dozen times, Mallory struggled up from the
depths of a black, trance-like stupor and momentarily touched
the surface of consciousness only to slide back into the darkness
again. Desperately, each time, he tried to hang on to these fleeting moments of awareness, but his mind was like the void, dark
and sinewless, and even as he knew that his mind was slipping
backwards again, loosing its grip on reality, the knowledge was
gone, and there was only the void once more. Nightmare, he
thought vaguely during one of the longer glimmerings of comprehension, I'm having a nightmare, like when you know you
are having a nightmare and that if you could open your eyes it
would be gone, but you can't open your eyes. He tried it now,
tried to open his eyes, but it was no good, it was still as dark

as ever and he was still sunk in this evil dream, for the sun had been shining brightly in the sky. He shook his head in slow despair.

'Aha! Observe! Signs of life at last!' There was no mistaking the slow, nasal drawl. 'Ol' Medicine Man Miller triumphs again!' There was a moment's silence, a moment in which Mallory was increasingly aware of the diminishing thunder of aero engines, the acrid, resinous smoke that stung his nostrils and eyes, and then an arm had passed under his shoulders and Miller's persuasive voice was in his ear. 'Just try a little of this, boss. Ye olde vintage brandy. Nothin' like it anywhere.'

Mallory felt the cold neck of the bottle, tilted his head back, took a long pull. Almost immediately he had jerked himself upright and forward to a sitting position, gagging, spluttering and fighting for breath as the raw, fiery ouzo bit into the mucous membrane of cheeks and throat. He tried to speak but could do no more than croak, gasp for fresh air and stare indignantly at the shadowy figure that knelt by his side. Miller, for his part, looked at him with unconcealed admiration.

'See, boss? Just like I said – nothin' like it.' He shook his head admiringly. 'Wide awake in an instant, as the literary boys would say. Never saw a shock and concussion victim recover so fast!'

'What the hell are you trying to do?' Mallory demanded. The fire had died down in his throat, and he could breathe again. 'Poison me?' Angrily he shook his head, fighting off the pounding ache, the fog that still swirled round the fringes of his mind. 'Bloody fine physician you are! Shock, you say, yet the first thing you do is administer a dose of spirits—'

'Take your pick,' Miller interrupted grimly. 'Either that or a damned sight bigger shock in about fifteen minutes or so when brother Jerry gets here.'

'But they've gone away. I can't hear the Stukas any more.'

'This lot's comin' up from the town,' Miller said morosely. 'Louki's just reported them. Half a dozen armoured cars and a couple of trucks with field guns the length of a telegraph pole.'

'I see.' Mallory twisted round, saw a gleam of light at a bend in the wall. A cave – a tunnel, almost. Little Cyprus, Louki had said some of the older people had called it – the Devil's Playground was riddled with a honeycomb of caves. He grinned wryly at the memory of his momentary panic when he thought his eyes had gone and turned again to Miller. 'Trouble again, Dusty, nothing but trouble. Thanks for bringing me round.'

'Had to,' Miller said briefly. 'I guess we couldn't have carried you very far, boss.'

Mallory nodded. 'Not just the flattest of country hereabouts.'

'There's that, too.' Miller agreed. 'What I really meant is that there's hardly anyone left to carry you. Casey Brown and Panayis have both been hurt, boss.'

'What! Both of them?' Mallory screwed his eyes shut, shook his head in slow anger. 'My God, Dusty, I'd forgotten all about the bomb – the bombs.' He reached out his hand, caught Miller by the arm. 'How – how bad are they?' There was so little time left, so much to do.

'How bad?' Miller shook out a pack of cigarettes and offered one to Mallory. 'Not bad at all – if we could get them into hospital. But hellish painful and cripplin' if they gotta start hikin' up and down those gawddamned ravines hereabouts. First time I've seen canyon floors more nearly vertical than the walls themselves.'

'You still haven't told me—'

'Sorry, boss, sorry. Shrapnel wounds, both of them, in exactly the same place – left thigh, just above the knee. No bones gone, no tendons cut. I've just finished tying up Casey's leg – it's a pretty wicked-lookin' gash. He's gonna know all about it when he starts walkin'.'

'And Panayis?'

'Fixed his own leg.' Miller said briefly. 'A queer character. Wouldn't even let me look at it, far less bandage it. I reckon he'd have knifed me if I'd tried.'

'Better to leave him alone anyway,' Mallory advised. 'Some of these islanders have strange taboos and superstitions. Just as long as he's alive. Though I still don't see how the hell he managed to get here.'

'He was the first to leave,' Miller explained. 'Along with Casey. You must have missed him in the smoke. They were climbin' together when they got hit.'

'And how did I get here?'

'No prizes for the first correct answer.' Miller jerked a thumb over his shoulder at the huge form that blocked half the width of the cave. 'Junior here did his St Bernard act once again. I wanted to go with him, but he wasn't keen. Said he reckoned it would be difficult to carry both of us up the hill. My feelin's were hurt considerable.' Miller sighed. 'I guess I just wasn't born to be a hero, that's all.'

Mallory smiled. 'Thanks again, Andrea.'

'Thanks!' Miller was indignant. 'A guy saves your life and all you can say is "thanks"!'

'After the first dozen times or so you run out of suitable speeches,' Mallory said dryly. 'How's Stevens?'

'Breathin'.'

Mallory nodded forward towards the source of light, wrinkled his nose. 'Just round the corner, isn't he?'

'Yeah, it's pretty grim,' Miller admitted. 'The gangrene's spread up beyond the knee.'

Mallory rose groggily to his feet, picked up his gun. 'How is he really, Dusty?'

'He's dead, but he just won't die. He'll be gone by sundown. Gawd only knows what's kept him goin' so far.'

'It may sound presumptuous,' Mallory murmured; 'but I think I know too.'

'The first-class medical attention?' Miller said hopefully.

'Looks that way, doesn't it?' Mallory smiled down at the still kneeling Miller. 'But that wasn't what I meant at all. Come, gentlemen, we have some business to attend to.'

'Me, all I'm good for is blowin' up bridges and droppin' a handful of sand in engine bearin's,' Miller announced. 'Strategy and tactics are far beyond my simple mind. But I still think those characters down there are pickin' a very stupid way of committin' suicide. It would be a damned sight easier for all concerned if they just shot themselves.'

'I'm inclined to agree with you.' Mallory settled himself more firmly behind the jumbled rocks in the mouth of the ravine that opened on the charred and smoking remains of the carob grove directly below and took another look at the Alpenkorps troops advancing in extended order up the steep, shelterless slope. 'They're no children at this game. I bet they don't like it one little bit, either.'

'Then why the hell are they doin' it, boss?'

'No option, probably. First off, this place can only be attacked frontally.' Mallory smiled down at the little Greek lying between himself and Andrea. 'Louki here chose the place well. It would require a long detour to attack from the rear – and it would take them a week to advance through that devil's scrap-heap behind us. Secondly, it'll be sunset in a couple of hours, and they know they haven't a hope of getting us after it's dark. And finally – and I think this is more important than the other two reasons put together – it's a hundred to one that the commandant in the town is being pretty severely prodded by his High Command. There's too much at stake, even in the one in a thousand chance of us getting at the guns. They can't afford to have Kheros evacuated under their noses, to lose—'

'Why not?' Miller interrupted. He gestured largely with his hands. 'Just a lot of useless rocks—'

'They can't afford to lose face with the Turks,' Mallory went on patiently. 'The strategic importance of these islands in the Sporades is negligible, but their political importance is tremendous. Adolph badly needs another ally in these parts. So he flies in Alpenkorps troops by the thousand and the Stukas by the hundred, the best he has – and he needs them desperately on the Italian front. But you've got to convince your potential ally that you're a pretty safe bet before you can persuade him to give up his nice, safe seat on the fence and jump down on your side.'

'Very interestin',' Miller observed. 'So?'

'So the Germans are going to have no compunction about thirty or forty of their best troops being cut into little pieces. It's no trouble at all when you're sitting behind a desk a thousand miles away. . . . Let 'em come another hundred yards or so closer. Louki and I will start from the middle and work out: you and Andrea start from the outside.'

'I don't like it, boss.' Miller complained.

'Don't think that I do either,' Mallory said quietly. 'Slaughtering men forced to do a suicidal job like this is not my idea of fun – or even of war. But if we don't get them, they get us.' He broke off and pointed across the burnished sea to where Kheros lay peacefully on the hazed horizon, striking golden glints off the western sun. 'What do you think they would have us do, Dusty?'

'I know, I know, boss.' Miller stirred uncomfortably. 'Don't rub it in.' He pulled his woollen cap low over his forehead and stared bleakly down the slope. 'How soon do the mass executions begin?'

'Another hundred yards, I said.' Mallory looked down the slope towards the coast road and grinned suddenly, glad to change the topic. 'Never saw telegraph poles shrink so suddenly before, Dusty.'

Miller studied the guns drawn up on the roads behind the two trucks and cleared his throat.

'I was only sayin' what Louki told me,' he said defensively.

'What Louki told you!' The little Greek was indignant. 'Before God, Major, the Americano is full of lies!'

'Ah, well, mebbe I was mistaken,' Miller said magnanimously. He squinted again at the guns, forehead lined in puzzlement. 'That first one's a mortar, I reckon. But what in the universe that other weird-looking contraption can be—'

'Also a mortar,' Mallory explained. 'A five-barrelled job, and very nasty. The *Nebelwerfer* or Moanin' Minnie. Howls like all the lost souls in hell. Guaranteed to turn the knees to jelly, especially after nightfall – but it's still the other one you have to watch. A six-inch mortar, almost certainly using fragmentation bombs – you use a brush and shovel for clearing up afterwards.'

'That's right,' Miller growled. 'Cheer us all up.' But he was grateful to the New Zealander for trying to take their minds off what they had to do. 'Why don't they use them?'

'They will,' Mallory assured him. 'Just as soon as we fire and they find out where we are.'

'Gawd help us,' Miller muttered. 'Fragmentation bombs, you said!' He lapsed into gloomy silence.

'Any second now,' Mallory said softly. 'I only hope that our friend Turzig isn't among this lot.' He reached out for his field-glasses but stopped in surprise as Andrea leaned across Louki and caught him by the wrist before he could lift the binoculars. 'What's the matter, Andrea?'

'I would not be using these, my Captain. They have betrayed us once already. I have been thinking, and it can be nothing else. The sunlight reflecting from the lenses . . .'

Mallory stared at him, slowly released his grip on the glasses, nodded several times in succession.

'Of course, of course! I had been wondering. . . . Someone has been careless. There was no other way, there *could* have been no other way. It would only require a single flash to tip them off.' He paused, remembering, then grinned wryly. 'It could have been myself. All this started just after I had been on watch – and Panayis didn't have the glasses.' He shook his head in mortification. 'It *must* have been me, Andrea.'

'I do not believe it,' Andrea said flatly. 'You couldn't make a mistake like that, my Captain.'

'Not only could, but did, I'm afraid. But we'll worry about that afterwards.' The middle of the ragged line of advancing soldiers, slipping and stumbling on the treacherous scree, had almost reached the lower limits of the blackened, stunted remains of the copse. 'They've come far enough. I'll take the white helmet in the middle, Louki.' Even as he spoke he could hear the soft scrape as the three others slid their automatic barrels across and between the protective rocks on front of them, could feel the wave of revulsion that washed through his mind. But his voice was steady enough as he spoke, relaxed and almost casual. 'Right. Let them have it now!'

His last words were caught up and drowned in the tearing, rapid-fire crash of the automatic carbines. With four machine-guns in their hands – two Brens and two 9 mm. Schmeissers – it was no war, as he had said, but sheer, pitiful massacre, with the defenceless figures on the slope below, figures still stunned and uncomprehending, jerking, spinning round and collapsing like marionettes in the hands of a mad puppeteer, some to die where they fell, others to roll down the steep slope, legs and arms flailing in the grotesque disjointedness of death. Only a couple stood still where they had been hit, vacant surprise mirrored in their lifeless faces, then slipped down tiredly to the stony ground at their feet. Almost three seconds had passed before the handful of those who still lived – about a quarter of the way in from either end of the line where the converging streams of fire had not yet met – realized what was happening and flung themselves desperately to the ground in search of the cover that didn't exist.

The phrenetic stammering of the machine-guns stopped abruptly and in unison, the sound sheared off as by a guillotine. The sudden silence was curiously oppressive, louder, more ob-trusive than the clamour that had gone before. The gravelly earth beneath his elbows grated harshly as Mallory shifted his weight slightly, looked at the two men to his right, Andrea with his impassive face empty of all expression, Louki with the sheen of tears in his eyes. Then he became aware of the low murmur-ing to his left, shifted round again. Bitter-mouthed, savage, the American was swearing softly and continuously, oblivious to the pain as he pounded his fist time and again into the sharp-edged gravel before him.

'Just one more, Gawd.' The quiet voice was almost a prayer. 'That's all I ask. Just one more.'

Mallory touched his arm. 'What is it, Dusty?'

Miller looked round at him, eyes cold and still and empty of all recognition, then he blinked several times and grinned, a cut and bruised hand automatically reaching for his cigarettes.

'Jus' daydreamin', boss,' he said easily. 'Jus' daydreamin'.'
He shook out his pack of cigarettes. 'Have one?'

'That inhuman bastard that sent these poor devils up that
hill,' Mallory said quietly. 'Make a wonderful picture seen over
the sights of your rifle, wouldn't he?'

Abruptly Miller's smile vanished and he nodded.

'It would be all of that.' He risked a quick peep round one
of the boulders, eased himself back again. 'Eight, mebbe ten
of them still down there, boss,' he reported. 'The poor bastards
are like ostriches – trying to take cover behind stones the size
of an orange. . . . We leave them be?'

'We leave them be!' Mallory echoed emphatically. The
thought of any more slaughter made him feel almost physically
sick. 'They won't try again.' He broke off suddenly, flattened
himself in reflex instinct as a burst of machine-gun bullets
struck the steep-walled rock above their heads and whined up
the gorge in vicious ricochet.

'Won't try again, huh?' Miller was already sliding his gun
around the rock in front of him when Mallory caught his arm
and pulled him back.

'Not them? Listen!' Another burst of fire, then another, and
now they could hear the savage chatter of the machine-gun, a
chatter rhythmically interrupted by a weird, half-human sighing
as its belt passed through the breech. Mallory could feel the
prickling of the hairs on the nape of his neck.

'A Spandau. Once you've heard a Spandau you can never
forget it. Leave it alone – it's probably fixed on the back of one
of the trucks and can't do us any harm. . . . I'm more worried
about these damned mortars down there.'

'I'm not,' Miller said promptly. 'They're not firing at us.'

'That's why I'm worried. . . . What do you think, Andrea?'

'The same as you, my Captain. They are waiting. This Devil's
Playground, as Louki calls it, is a madman's maze, and they can
only fire as blind men—'

'They won't be waiting much longer,' Mallory interrupted
grimly. He pointed to the north. 'Here come their eyes.'

At first only specks above the promontory of Cape Demirci,
the planes were soon recognisable for what they were, droning
in slowly over the Ægean at about fifteen hundred feet. Mallory
looked at them in astonishment, then turned to Andrea.

'Am I seeing things, Andrea?' He gestured at the first of the
two planes, a high-winged little monoplane fighter. 'That can't
be a PZL?'

'It can be and it is,' Andrea murmured. 'An old Polish plane we had before the war,' he explained to Miller. 'And the other is an old Belgian plane – Breguets, we called them.' Andrea shaded his eyes to look again at the two planes, now almost directly overhead. 'I thought they had all been lost during the invasion.'

'Me too,' Mallory said. 'Must have patched up some bits and pieces. Ah, they've seen us – beginning to circle. But why on earth they use these obsolete death traps—'

'I don't know and I don't care,' Miller said rapidly. He had just taken a quick look round the boulder in front of him. 'These damned guns down there are just linin' up on us, and muzzle-on they look a considerable sight bigger than telegraph poles. Fragmentation bombs, you said! Come on, boss, lets get the hell outa here!'

Thus the pattern was set for the remainder of that brief November afternoon, for the grim game of tip-and-run, hide-and-seek among the ravines and shattered rocks of the Devil's Playground. The planes held the key to the game, cruised high overhead observing every move of the hunted group below, relaying the information to the guns on the coast road and the company of Alpenkorps that had moved up through the ravine above the carob grove soon after the planes reported that the positions there had been abandoned. The two ancient planes were soon replaced by a couple of modern Henschels – Andrea said that the PZL couldn't remain airborne for more than an hour anyway.

Mallory was between the devil and the deep sea. Inaccurate though the mortars were, some of the deadly fragmentation bombs found their way into the deep ravines where they took temporary shelter, the blast of metal lethal in the confined space between the sheering walls. Occasionally they came so close that Mallory was forced to take refuge in some of the deep caves that honeycombed the walls of the canyons. In these they were safe enough, but the safety was an illusion that could lead only to ultimate defeat and capture; in the lulls, the Alpenkorps, whom they had fought off in a series of brief, skirmishing rearguard actions during the afternoon, could approach closely enough to trap them inside. Time and time again Mallory and his men were forced to move on to widen the gap between themselves and their pursuers, following the indomitable Louki wherever he chose to lead them, and taking their chance, often a very slender and desperate chance, with the mortar bombs. One bomb arced into a ravine that led into the interior, burying itself in the gravelly ground not twenty yards ahead of them, by far the nearest anything had come during the afternoon. By one chance in a thousand, it didn't explode. They gave it as wide a berth as possible, almost holding their breaths until they were safely beyond.

About half an hour before sunset they struggled up the last few boulder-strewn yards of a steeply-shelving ravine floor, halted just beyond the shelter of the projecting wall where the ravine dipped again and turned sharply to the right and the north. There had been no more mortar bombs since the one that had failed to explode. The six-inch and the weirdly-howling *Nebelwerfer* had only a limited range, Mallory knew, and though the planes still cruised overhead, they cruised uselessly: the sun was dipping towards the horizon and the floors of the ravines were already deep-sunk in shadowed gloom, invisible from above. But the Alpenkorps, tough, dogged, skilful soldiers, soldiers living only for the revenge of their massacred comrades, were very close behind. And they were highly-trained mountain troops, fresh, resilient, the reservoir of their energies barely tapped: whereas his own tiny band, worn out from continuous days and sleepless nights of labour and action. . . .

Mallory sank to the ground near the angled turn of the ravine where he could keep lookout, glanced at the others with a deceptive casualness that marked his cheerless assessment of what he saw. As a fighting unit they were in a pretty bad way. Both Panayis and Brown were badly crippled, the latter's face grey with pain. For the first time since leaving Alexandria, Casey Brown was apathetic, listless and quite indifferent to everything: this Mallory took as a very bad sign. Nor was Brown helped by the heavy transmitter still strapped to his back – with point-blank truculence he had ignored Mallory's categorical order to abandon it. Louki was tired, and looked it: his physique, Mallory realized now, was no match for his spirit, for the infectious smile that never left his face, for the panache of that magnificently upswept moustache that contrasted so oddly with the sad, tired eyes above. Miller, like himself, was tired, but, like himself, could keep on being tired for a long time yet. And Stevens was still conscious but even in the twilit gloom of the canyon floor his face looked curiously transparent, while the nails, lips and eyelids were drained of blood. And Andrea, who had carried him up and down all these killing canyon tracks – where there had been tracks – for almost two interminable hours, looked as he always did: immutable, indestructible.

Mallory shook his head, fished out a cigarette, made to strike a light, remembered the planes still cruising overhead and threw the match away. Idly his gaze travelled north along the canyon and he slowly stiffened, the unlit cigarette crumpling and shredding between his fingers. This ravine bore no resemblance to any of the others through which they had so far passed – it was broader, dead straight, at least three times as long – and, as far as he could see in the twilight, the far end was blocked off by an almost vertical wall.

'Louki!' Mallory was on his feet now, all weariness forgotten. 'Do you know where you are? Do you know this place?'

'But certainly, Major!' Louki was hurt. 'Have I not told you that Panayis and I, in the days of our youth—'

'But this is a cul-de-sac, a dead-end!' Mallory protested. 'We're boxed in, man, we're trapped!'

Louki grinned impudently and twirled a corner of his moustache. The little man was enjoying himself.

'So? The Major does not trust Louki, is that it?' He grinned again, relented, patted the wall by his side. 'Panayis and I, we have been working this way all afternoon. Along this wall there are many caves. One of them leads through to another valley that leads down to the coast road.'

'I see, I see.' Relief washing through his mind, Mallory sank down on the ground again. 'And where does this other valley come out?'

'Just across the strait from Maidos.'

'How far from the town?'

'About five miles, Major, maybe six. Not more.'

'Fine, fine! And you're sure you can find this cave?'

'A hundred years from now and my head in a goat-skin bag!' Louki boasted.

'Fair enough!' Even as he spoke, Mallory catapulted himself violently to one side, twisted in mid-air to avoid falling across Stevens and crashed heavily into the wall between Andrea and Miller. In a moment of unthinking carelessness he had exposed himself to view from the ravine they had just climbed: the burst of machine-gun fire from its lower end – a hundred and fifty yards away at the most – had almost blown his head off. Even as it was, the left shoulder of his jacket had been torn away, the shell just grazing his shoulder. Miller was already kneeling by his side. fingering the gash, running a gently exploratory hand across his back.

'Careless, damn' careless,' Mallory murmured. 'But I didn't think they were so close.' He didn't feel as calm as he sounded. If the mouth of that Schmeisser had been another sixteenth of an inch to the right, he'd have had no head left now.

'Are you all right, boss?' Miller was puzzled. 'Did they—'

'Terrible shots,' Mallory assured him cheerfully. 'Couldn't hit a barn.' He twisted round to look at his shoulder. 'I hate to sound heroic, but this really is just a scratch. . . .' He rose easily to his feet, and picked up his gun. 'Sorry and all that, gentlemen, but it's time we were on our way again. How far along is this cave, Louki?'

Louki rubbed his bristly chin, the smile suddenly gone. He looked quickly at Mallory, then away again.

'Louki!'

'Yes, yes, Major. The cave.' Louki rubbed his chin again. 'Well, it is a good way along. In fact, it is at the end,' he finished uncomfortably.

'The *very* end?' asked Mallory quietly.

Louki nodded miserably, stared down at the ground at his feet. Even the ends of his moustache seemed to droop.

'That's handy,' Mallory said heavily. 'Oh, that's very handy!' He sank down to the ground again. 'Helps us no end, that does.'

He bowed his head in thought and didn't even lift it as Andrea poked a Bren round the angle of the rock, and fired a short downhill burst more in token of discouragement than in any hope of hitting anything. Another ten seconds passed, then Louki spoke again, his voice barely audible.

'I am very, very sorry. This is a terrible thing. Before God, Major, I would not have done it but that I thought they were still far behind.'

'It's not your fault, Louki.' Mallory was touched by the little man's obvious distress. He touched his ripped shoulder jacket. 'I thought the same thing.'

'Please!' Stevens put his hand on Mallory's arm. 'What's wrong? I don't understand.'

'Everybody else does, I'm afraid, Andy. It's very, very simple. We have half a mile to go along this valley here – and not a shred of cover. The Alpenkorps have less than two hundred yards to come up that ravine we've just left.' He paused while Andrea fired another retaliatory short burst, then continued. 'They'll do what they're doing now – keep probing to see if

we're still here. The minute they judge we're gone, they'll be
up here in a flash. They'll nail us before we're half-way, quarter
way to the cave – you know we can't travel fast. And they're
carrying a couple of Spandaus – they'll cut us to ribbons.'

'I see,' Stevens murmured. 'You put it all so nicely, sir.'

'Sorry, Andy, but that's how it is.'

'But could you not leave two men as a rear-guard, while the
rest—'

'And what happens to the rear-guard?' Mallory interrupted
dryly.

'I see what you mean,' he said in a low voice. 'I hadn't thought
of that.'

'No, but the rear-guard would. Quite a problem, isn't it?'

'There is no problem at all,' Louki announced. 'The Major
is kind, but this is all my fault. I will—'

'You'll do damn all of the kind!' Miller said savagely. He
tore Louki's Bren from his hand and laid it on the ground. 'You
heard what the boss said – it wasn't your fault.' For a moment
Louki stared at him in anger, then turned dejectedly away. He
looked as if he were going to cry. Mallory, too, stared at the
American, astonished at the sudden vehemence, so completely
out of character. Now that he came to think of it, Dusty had
been strangely taciturn and thoughtful during the past hour or
so – Mallory couldn't recall his saying a word during all that
time. But time enough to worry about that later on. . . .

Casey Brown eased his injured leg, looked hopefully at Mallory. 'Couldn't we stay here till it's dark – real dark – then make
our way—'

'No good. The moon's almost full tonight – and not a cloud
in the sky. They'd get us. Even more important, we have to get
into the town between sunset and curfew tonight. Our last
chance. Sorry, Casey, but it's no go.'

Fifteen seconds, half a minute passed, and passed in silence,
then they all started abruptly as Andy Stevens spoke.

'Louki *was* right, you know,' he said pleasantly. The voice
was weak, but filled with a calm certainty that jerked every eye
towards him. He was propped up on one elbow, Louki's Bren
cradled in his hands. It was a measure of their concentration
on the problem on hand that no one had heard or seen him
reach out for the machine-gun. 'It's all very simple,' Stevens
went on quietly. 'Just let's use our heads, that's all. . . . The
gangrene's right up past the knee, isn't it, sir?'

Mallory said nothing: he didn't know what to say, the

complete unexpectedness had knocked him off balance. He was vaguely aware that Miller was looking at him, his eyes begging him to say 'No.'

'Is it or isn't it?' There was a patience. a curious under-standing in the voice, and all of a sudden Mallory knew what to say.

'Yes,' he nodded. 'It is.' Miller was looking at him in horror.

'Thank you, sir.' Stevens was smiling in satisfaction. 'Thank you very much indeed. There's no need to point out all the advantages of my staying here.' There was an assurance in his voice no one had ever heard before, the unthinking authority of a man completely in charge of a situation. 'Time I did some-thing for my living anyway. No fond farewells, please. Just leave me a couple of boxes of ammo, two or three thirty-six grenades and away you go.'

'I'll be damned if we will!' Miller was up on his feet, making for the boy, then brought up abruptly as the Bren centred on his chest.

'One step nearer and I'll shoot you,' Stevens said calmly. Miller looked at him in long silence, sank slowly back to the ground.

'I would, you know,' Stevens assured him. 'Well, goodbye, gentlemen. Thank you for all you've done for me.'

Twenty seconds, thirty, a whole minute passed in a queer, trance-like silence, then Miller heaved himself to his feet again, a tall, rangy figure with tattered clothes and a face curiously haggard in the gathering gloom.

'So long, kid. I guess – waal, mebbe I'm not so smart after all.' He took Stevens's hand, looked down at the wasted face for a long moment, made to say something else, then changed his mind. 'Be seein' you,' he said abruptly, turned and walked off heavily down the valley. One by one the others followed him, wordlessly, except for Andrea who stopped and whispered in the boy's ear, a whisper that brought a smile and a nod of com-plete understanding, and then there was only Mallory left. Stevens grinned up at him.

'Thank you, sir. Thanks for not letting me down. You and Andrea – you understand. You always did understand.'

'You'll – you'll be all right, Andy?' God, Mallory thought, what a stupid, what an insane thing, to say.

'Honest, sir, I'm OK.' Stevens smiled contentedly. 'No pain left – I can't feel a thing. It's wonderful!'

'Andy, I don't—'

'It's time you were gone, sir. The others will be waiting. Now if you'll just light me a gasper and fire a few random shots down that ravine . . .'

Within five minutes Mallory had overtaken the others, and inside fifteen they had all reached the cave that led to the coast. For a moment they stood in the entrance, listening to the intermittent firing from the other end of the valley, then turned wordlessly and plunged into the cave. Back where they had left him, Andy Stevens was lying on his stomach, peering down into the now almost dark ravine. There was no pain left in his body, none at all. He drew deeply on a cupped cigarette, smiled as he pushed another clip home into the magazine of the Bren. For the first time in his life Andy Stevens was happy and content beyond his understanding, a man at last at peace with himself. He was no longer afraid.

——— 13 ———

WEDNESDAY EVENING

1800–1915

Exactly forty minutes later they were safely in the heart of the town of Navarone, within fifty yards of the great gates of the fortress itself.

Mallory, gazing out at the gates and the still more massive arch of stone that encased them, shook his head for the tenth time and tried to fight off the feeling of disbelief and wonder that they should have reached their goal at last – or as nearly as made no difference. They had been due a break some time, he thought, the law of averages had been overwhelmingly against the continuation of the evil fortune that had dogged them so incessantly since they had arrived on the island. It was only right, he kept telling himself, it was only just that this should be so: but even so, the transition from that dark valley where they had left Andy Stevens to die to this tumbledown old house on the east side of the town square of Navarone had been so quick, so easy, that it still lay beyond immediate understanding or unthinking acceptance.

Not that it had been too easy in the first fifteen minutes or so, he remembered. Panayis's wounded leg had given out on him immediately after they had entered the cave, and he had collapsed; he must have been in agony, Mallory had thought, with his torn, roughly-bandaged leg, but the failing light and the dark, bitter impassive face had masked the pain. He had begged Mallory to be allowed to remain where he was, to hold off the Alpenkorps when they had overcome Stevens and reached the end of the valley, but Mallory had roughly refused him permission. Brutally he had told Panayis that he was far too valuable to be left there – and that the chances of the Alpenkorps picking that cave out of a score of others were pretty remote. Mallory had hated having to talk to him like that, but there had been no time for gentle blandishments, and Panayis must have seen his point for he had made neither protest nor struggle when Miller and Andrea picked him up and helped him to limp through the cave. The limp, Mallory had noticed, had been much less noticeable then, perhaps because of the assistance, perhaps because now that he had been baulked of the chance of killing a few more Germans it had been pointless to exaggerate his hurt.

They had barely cleared the mouth of the cave on the other side and were making their way down the tree-tufted, sloping valley side towards the sea, the dark sheen of the Ægean clearly visible in the gloom, when Louki, hearing something, had gestured them all to silence. Almost immediately Mallory, too, heard it, a soft guttural voice occasionally lost in the crunch of approaching feet on gravel, had seen that they were providentially screened by some stunted trees, given the order to stop and sworn in quick anger as he had heard the soft thud and barely muffled cry behind them. He had gone back to investigate and found Panayis stretched on the ground unconscious. Miller, who had been helping him along, had explained that Mallory had halted them so suddenly that he'd bumped into Panayis, that the Greek's bad leg had given beneath him, throwing him heavily, his head striking a stone as he had fallen. Mallory had stooped down in instantly renewed suspicion – Panayis was a throw-back, a natural-born killer, and he was quite capable of faking an accident if he thought he could turn it to his advantage, line a few more of the enemy up on the sights of his rifle . . . but there had been no fake about that: the bruised and bloodied gash above the temple was all too real.

The German patrol, having had no inkling of their presence, moved noisily up the valley till they had finally gone out of earshot. Louki had thought that the commandant in Navarone was becoming desperate, trying to seal off every available exit from the Devil's Playground. Mallory had thought it unlikely, but had not stayed to argue the point. Five minutes later they had cleared the mouth of the valley, and in another five had not only reached the coast road but silenced and bound two sentries – the drivers, probably – who had been guarding a truck and command car parked by the roadside. stripped them of denims and helmets and bundled them out of sight behind some bushes.

The trip into Navarone had been ridiculously simple, but the entire lack of opposition was easily understandable, because of the complete unexpectedness of it all. Seated beside Mallory on the front seat, clad, like Mallory, in captured clothes. Louki had driven the big car, and driven it magnificently, an accomplishment so unusual to find in a remote Ægean island that Mallory had been completely mystified until Louki had reminded him that he had been Eugene Vlachos's Consulate chauffeur for many years. The drive into town had taken less than twelve minutes – not only did the little man handle the car superbly, but he knew the road so well that he got the utmost possible out of the big machine, most of the time without benefit of any lights at all.

Not only a simple journey, but quite uneventful. They had passed several parked trucks at intervals along the road, and less than two miles from the town itself had met a group of about twenty soldiers marching in the opposite direction in column of twos. Louki had slowed down – it would have been highly suspicious had he accelerated, endangering the lives of the marching men – but had switched on the powerful headlights, blinding them, and blown raucously on the horn, while Mallory had leaned out of the right-hand window, sworn at them in perfect German and told them to get out of his damned way. This they had done, while the junior officer in charge had come smartly to attention, throwing up his hand in punctilious salute.

Immediately afterwards they had run through an area of high-walled, terraced market gardens, passed between a decaying Byzantine church and a whitewashed orthodox monastery that faced each other incongruously across the same dusty road, then almost at once were running through the lower part of the old town. Mallory had had a vague impression of narrow, winding, dim-lit streets only inches wider than the car itself, hugely cobbled and with almost knee-high pavements, then Louki was

making his way up an arched lane, the car climbing steeply all
the time. He had stopped abruptly, and Mallory had followed
his quick survey of the darkened lane: completely deserted
though over an hour yet to curfew. Beside them had been a
flight of white stone steps innocent of any hand-rail, running up
parallel to the wall of a house, with a highly ornamented lattice-
work grill protecting the outside landing at the top. A still
groggy Panayis had led them up these stairs, through to a house
– he had known exactly where he was – across a shallow roof,
down some more steps, through a dark courtyard and into this
ancient house where they were now. Louki had driven the car
away even before they reached the top of the stairs; it was only
now that Mallory remembered that Louki hadn't thought it
worth while to say what he intended to do with the car.

Still gazing out of the windowless hole in the wall at the fortress gate, Mallory found himself hoping intensely that nothing
would happen to the sad-eyed little Greek, and not only because
in his infinite resource and local knowledge he had been invaluable to them and was likely to prove so again; all these considerations apart, Mallory had formed the deepest affection for him,
for his unvarying cheerfulness, his enthusiasm, his eagerness to
help and to please, above all for his complete disregard of self. A
thoroughly lovable little man, and Mallory's heart warmed to
him. More than he could say for Panayis, he thought sourly, and
then immediately regretted the thought: it was no fault of Panayis's that he was what he was, and in his own dark and bitter way
he had done as much for them as Louki. But the fact remained
that he was sadly lacking in Louki's warm humanity.

He lacked also Louki's quick intelligence, the calculated oppor-
tunism that amounted almost to genius. It had been a brilliant
idea on Louki's part, Mallory mused, that they should take over
this abandoned house: not that there had been any difficulty in
finding an empty house – since the Germans had taken over the
old castle the inhabitants of the town had left in their scores for
Margaritha and other outlying villages, none more quickly than
those who had lived in the town square itself; the nearness of the
fortress wall that formed the north side of the square had been
more than many of them could stomach, with the constant
coming and going of their conquerors through the fortress gates,
the sentries marching to and fro, the never ceasing reminders
that their freedom was a vanished thing. So many gone that
more than half the houses on the west side of the square – those
nearest the fortress – were now occupied by German officers. But

this same enforced close observation of the fortress's activities had been exactly what Mallory had wanted. When the time came to strike they had only yards to go. And although any competent garrison commander would always be prepared against the unexpected. Mallory considered it unlikely indeed that any reasonable man could conceive of a sabotage group so suicidally minded as to spend an entire day within a literal stones' throw of the fortress wall.

Not that the house as such had much to recommend it. As a home, a dwelling place, it was just about as uncomfortable as possible, as dilapidated as it could be without actually falling down. The west side of the square – the side perched precariously on the cliff-top – and the south side were made up of fairly modern buildings of whitewashed stone and Parian granite, huddled together in the invariable fashion of houses in these island towns, flat-roofed to catch as much as possible of the winter rains. But the east side of the square, where they were, was made up of antiquated timber and turf houses, of the kind much more often found in remote mountain villages.

The beaten earth floor beneath his feet was hummocky, uneven, and the previous occupants had used one corner of it – obviously – for a variety of purposes, not least as a refuse dump. The ceiling was of rough-hewn, blackened beams, more or less covered with planks, these in turn being covered with a thick layer of trodden earth: from previous experience of such houses in the White Mountains, Mallory knew that the roof would leak like a sieve whenever the rain came on. Across one end of the room was a solid ledge some thirty inches high, a ledge that served, after the fashion of similar structures in Eskimo igloos, as bed, tables or settee as the occasion demanded. The room was completely bare of furniture.

Mallory started as someone touched him on the shoulder and turned round. Miller was behind him, munching away steadily, the remains of a bottle of wine in his hand.

'Better get some chow, boss,' he advised. 'I'll take a gander through this hole from time to time.'

'Right you are, Dusty. Thanks.' Mallory moved gingerly towards the back of the room – it was almost pitch dark inside and they dared not risk a light – and felt his way till he brought up against the ledge. The tireless Andrea had gone through their provisions and prepared a meal of sorts – dried figs, honey, cheese, garlic sausages and pounded roast chestnuts. A horrible mixture, Mallory thought, but the best Andrea could do: besides he was too hungry, ravenously so, to worry about such niceties as the pleasing of his palate. And by the time he had washed it down with some of the local wine that Louki and Panayis had provided the previous day, the sweetly-resinous rawness of the drink had obliterated every other taste.

Carefully, shielding the match with his hand, Mallory lit a cigarette and began to explain for the first time his plan for entering the fortress. He did not have to bother lowering his voice – a couple of looms in the next house, one of the few occupied ones left on that side of the square, clacked incessantly throughout the evening. Mallory had a shrewd suspicion that this was more of Louki's doing, although it was difficult to see how he could have got word through to any of his friends. But Mallory was content to accept the situation as it was, to concentrate on making sure that the others understood his instructions.

Apparently they did, for there were no questions. For a few minutes the talk became general, the usually taciturn Casey Brown having the most to say, complaining bitterly about the food, the drink, his injured leg and the hardness of the bench where he wouldn't be able to sleep a wink all night long. Mallory grinned to himself but said nothing; Casey Brown was definitely on the mend.

'I reckon we've talked enough, gentlemen.' Mallory slid off the bench and stretched himself. God, he was tired! 'Our first and last chance to get a decent night's sleep. Two hour watches – I'll take the first.'

'By yourself?' It was Miller calling softly from the other end of the room. 'Don't you think we should share watches, boss? One for the front, one for the back. Besides, you know we're all pretty well done up. One man by himself might fall asleep.' He sounded so anxious that Mallory laughed.

'Not a chance, Dusty. Each man will keep watch by the window there and if he falls asleep he'll damn' soon wake up when he hits the floor. And it's because we're so darned bushed that we can't afford to have anyone lose sleep unnecessarily. Myself first, then you, then Panayis, then Casey, then Andrea.'

'Yeah, I suppose that'll be OK,' Miller conceded grudgingly. He put something hard and cold into his hand. Mallory recognised it at once – it was Miller's most cherished possession, his silenced automatic.

'Just so's you can fill any nosy customers full of little holes without wakin' the whole town.' He ambled off to the back of the room, lit a cigarette, smoked it quietly for a few moments, then swung his legs up on the bench. Within five minutes everyone except the silently watchful man at the window was sound asleep.

Two or three minutes later Mallory jerked to unmoving attention as he heard a stealthy sound outside – from the back of the house, he thought. The clacking of the looms next door had stopped, and the house was very still. Again there came the noise, unmistakable this time, a gentle tapping at the door at the end of the passage that led from the back of the room.

'Remain there, my Captain.' It was Andrea's soft murmur, and Mallory marvelled for the hundredth time at Andrea's ability to rouse himself from the deepest of sleeps at the slightest alien sound: the violence of a thunderstorm would have left him undisturbed. 'I will see to it. It must be Louki.'

It was Louki. The little man was panting, near exhaustion, but extraordinarily pleased with himself. Gratefully he drank the cup of wine that Andrea poured for him.

'Damned glad to see you back again!' Mallory said sincerely. 'How did it go? Someone after you?'

Mallory could almost see him drawing himself up to his full height in the darkness.

'As if any of these clumsy fools could see Louki, even on a moonlit night, far less catch him,' he said indignantly. He paused to draw some deep breaths. 'No, no, Major, I knew you would be worried about me so I ran back all the way. Well, nearly all the way,' he amended. 'I am not so young as I was, Major Mallory.'

'All the way from where?' Mallory asked. He was glad of the darkness that hid his smile.

'From Vygos. It is an old castle that the Franks built there many generations ago, about two miles from here along the coast road to the east.' He paused to drink another mouthful of wine. 'More than two miles, I would say – and I only walked twice, a minute at a time, on the way back.' Mallory had the impression that Louki already regretted his momentary weakness in admitting that he was no longer a young man.

'And what did you do there?' Mallory asked.

'I was thinking, after I left you,' Louki answered indirectly. 'Me, I am always thinking,' he explained. 'It is a habit of mine. I was thinking that when the soldiers who are looking for us out in the Devil's Playground find out that the car is gone, they will know that we are no longer in that accursed place.'

'Yes.' Mallory agreed carefully. 'Yes, they will know that.'

'Then they will say to themselves, "Ha, those *verdammt Eng-landers* have little time left." They will know that we will know that they have little hope of catching us in the island – Panayis and I, we know every rock and tree and path and cave. So all they can do is to make sure that we do not get into the town – they will block every road leading in, and tonight is our last chance to get in. You follow me?' he asked anxiously.

'I am trying very hard.'

'But first' – Louki spread his hands dramatically – 'but first they will make sure we are not in the town. They would be fools to block the roads if we were already in the town. They *must* make sure we are not in the town. And so – the search. The very great search. With – how do you say? – the teeth-comb!'

Mallory nodded his head in slow understanding.

'I'm afraid he's right, Andrea.'

'I, too, fear so,' Andrea said unhappily. 'We should have thought of this. But perhaps we could hide – the roof-tops or—'

'With a teeth-comb, I said!' Louki interrupted impatiently. 'But all is well. I, Louki, have thought it all out. I can smell rain. There will be clouds over the moon before long, and it will be safe to move. . . . You do not want to know what I have done with the car, Major Mallory?' Louki was enjoying himself immensely.

'Forgotten all about it,' Mallory confessed. 'What *did* you do with the car?'

'I left it in the courtyard of Vygos castle. Then I emptied all the petrol from the tank and poured it over the car. Then I struck a match.'

'You did *what*?' Mallory was incredulous.

'I struck a match. I think I was standing too near the car, for I do not seem to have any eyebrows left.' Louki sighed. 'A pity – it was such a splendid machine.' Then he brightened. 'But before God, Major, it burned magnificently.'

Mallory stared at him.

'Why on earth—?'

'It is simple,' Louki explained patiently. 'By this time the men out in the Devil's Playground must know that their car has been stolen. They see the fire. They hurry back to – how do you say?'

'Investigate?'

'So. Investigate. They wait till the fire dies down. They investigate again. No bodies, no bones in the car, so they search the castle. And what do they find?'

There was silence in the room.

'Nothing!' Louki said impatiently. 'They find nothing. And then they search the countryside for half a mile around. And what do they find? Again nothing. So then they know that they have been fooled, and that we are in the town, and will come to search the town.'

'With the teeth-comb,' Mallory murmured.

'With the teeth-comb. And what do they find?' Louki paused, then hurried on before anyone could steal his thunder. 'Once again, they will find nothing,' he said triumphantly. 'And why? For by then the rain will have come, the moon will have vanished, the explosives will be hidden – and we will be gone!'

'Gone where?' Mallory felt dazed.

'Where but to Vygos castle, Major Mallory. Never while night follows day will they think to look for us there!'

Mallory looked at him in silence for long seconds without speaking, then turned to Andrea.

'Captain Jensen's only made one mistake so far,' he murmured. 'He picked the wrong man to lead this expedition. Not that it matters anyway. With Louki here on our side, how can we lose?'

Mallory lowered his rucksack gently to the earthen roof, straightened and peered up into the darkness, both hands shielding his eyes from the first drizzle of rain. Even from where they stood – on the crumbling roof of the house nearest the fortress on the east side of the square – the walls stretched fifteen, perhaps twenty feet above their heads; the wickedly out- and down-curving spikes that topped the wall were all but lost in the darkness.

'There she is, Dusty,' Mallory murmured. 'Nothing to it.'

'Nothin' to it!' Miller was horrified. 'I've – I've gotta get over *that*?'

'You'd have a ruddy hard time going through it,' Mallory answered briefly. He grinned, clapped Miller on the back and prodded the rucksack at his feet. 'We chuck this rope up, the hook catches, you shin smartly up—'

'And bleed to death on those six strands of barbed wire,' Miller interrupted. 'Louki says they're the biggest barbs he's ever seen.'

'We'll use the tent for padding,' Mallory said soothingly.

'I have a very delicate skin, boss,' Miller complained. 'Nothin' short of a spring mattress—'

'Well, you've only an hour to find one,' Mallory said indifferently. Louki had estimated that it would be at least an hour before the search party would clear the northern part of the town, give himself and Andrea a chance to begin a diversion. 'Come on, let's cache this stuff and get out of here. We'll shove the rucksacks in this corner and cover 'em with earth. Take the rope out first, though; we'll have no time to start undoing the packs when we get here.'

Miller dropped to his knees, hands fumbling with straps, then exclaimed in sudden annoyance.

'This can't be the pack,' he muttered in disgust. Abruptly his voice changed. 'Here, wait a minute, though.'

'What's up, Dusty?'

Miller didn't answer immediately. For a few seconds his hands explored the contents of the pack, then he straightened.

'The slow-burnin' fuse, boss.' His voice was blurred with anger, with a vicious anger that astonished Mallory. 'It's gone!'

'What!' Mallory stooped, began to search through the pack. 'It can't be, Dusty, it just *can't*! Dammit to hell, man, you packed the stuff yourself!'

'Sure, I did, boss,' Miller grated, 'And then some crawlin' bastard comes along behind my back and unpacks it again.'

'Impossible!' Mallory protested. 'It's just downright impossible, Dusty. *You* closed that rucksack – I saw you do it in the grove this morning – and Louki has had it all the time. And I'd trust Louki with my life.'

'So would I, boss.'

'Maybe we're both wrong,' Mallory went on quietly. 'Maybe you did miss it out. We're both helluva tired, Dusty.'

Miller looked at him queerly, said nothing for a moment then began to swear again. 'It's my own fault, boss, my own gawddamned fault.'

'What do you mean, your own fault? Heavens above, man, I was there when . . .' Mallory broke off, rose quickly to his feet and stared through the darkness at the south side of the square. A single shot had rung out there, the whiplash crack of a carbine followed the thin, high whine of a ricochet, and then silence.

Mallory stood quite still, hands clenched by his sides. Over ten minutes had passed since he and Miller had left Panayis to guide Andrea and Brown to the Castle Vygos – they should have been well away from the square by this time. And almost certainly Louki wouldn't be down there. Mallory's instructions to him had been explicit – to hide the remainder of the TNT blocks in the roof and then wait there to lead himself and Miller to the keep. But something could have gone wrong, something could always go wrong. Or a trap, maybe a ruse. But what kind of trap?

The sudden off-beat stammering of a heavy machine-gun stilled his thoughts, and for a moment or two he was all eyes and straining ears. And then another, and lighter machine-gun, cut in, just for a few seconds: as abruptly as they had started, both guns died away, together. Mallory waited no longer.

'Get the stuff together again,' he whispered urgently. 'We're taking it with us. Something's gone wrong.' Within thirty seconds they had ropes and explosives back in their knapsacks, had strapped them on their backs and were on their way.

Bent almost double, careful to make no noise whatsoever, they ran across the roof-tops towards the old house where they had hidden earlier in the evening, where they were now to rendezvous with Louki. Still running, they were only feet away from the house when they saw his shadowy figure rise up, only it wasn't Louki, Mallory realized at once, for it was too tall for Louki and without breaking step he catapulted the horizontal driving weight of his 180 pounds at the unknown figure in a homicidal tackle, his shoulder catching the man just below the breast-bone, emptying every last particle of air from the man's lungs with an explosive, agonised *whoosh*. A second later both of Miller's sinewy hands were clamped round the man's neck, slowly choking him to death.

And he would have choked to death, neither of the two men were in any mind for half-measures, had not Mallory, prompted by some fugitive intuition, stooped low over the contorted face, the staring, protruding eyes, choked back a cry of sudden horror.

'Dusty!' he whispered hoarsely. 'For God's sake stop! Let him go! It's Panayis!'

Miller didn't hear him. In the gloom his face was like stone, his head sunk farther and farther between hunching shoulders as he tightened his grip, strangling the Greek in a weird savage silence.

'It's Panayis, you bloody fool, Panayis!' Mallory's mouth was at the American's ear, his hands clamped round the other's wrists as he tried to drag him off Panayis's throat. He could hear the muffled drumming of Panayis's heels on the turf of the roof, tore at Miller's wrists with all his strength: twice before he had heard that sound as a man had died under Andrea's great hands, and he knew with sudden certainty that Panayis would go the same way, and soon, if he didn't make Miller understand. But all at once Miller understood, relaxed heavily, straightened up still kneeling, hands hanging limply by his sides. Breathing deeply he stared down in silence at the man at his feet.

'What the hell's the matter with you?' Mallory demanded softly. 'Deaf or blind or both?'

'Just one of these things, I guess.' Miller rubbed the back of a hand across his forehead, his face empty of expression. 'Sorry, boss, sorry.'

'Why the hell apologise to me?' Mallory looked away from him, looked down at Panayis: the Greek was sitting up now, hands massaging his bruised throat, sucking in long draughts of air in great, whooping gasps. 'But maybe Panayis here might appreciate—'

'Apologies can wait,' Miller interrupted brusquely. 'Ask him what's happened to Louki.'

Mallory looked at him for a moment, made no reply, changed his mind, translated the question. He listened to Panayis's halting answer – it obviously hurt him even to try to speak – and his mouth tightened in a hard, bitter line. Miller watched the fractional slump of the New Zealander's shoulders, felt he could wait no longer.

'Well, what is it, boss? Somethin's happened to Louki, is that it?'

'Yes,' Mallory said tonelessly. 'They'd only got as far as the lane at the back when they found a small German patrol blocking their way. Louki tried to draw them off and the machine-gunner got him through the chest. Andrea got the machine-gunner and took Louki away. Panayis says he'll die for sure.'

—— 14 ——

WEDNESDAY NIGHT

1915–2000

The three men cleared the town without any difficult, striking out directly across country for the castle Vygos and avoiding the main road. It was beginning to rain now, heavily, persistently, and the ground was mired and sodden, the few ploughed fields they crossed almost impassable. They had just struggled their way through one of these and could just see the dim outline of the keep – less than a cross-country mile from the town instead of Louki's exaggerated estimate – when they passed by an abandoned earthen house and Miller spoke for the first time since they had left the town square of Navarone.

'I'm bushed, boss.' His head was sunk on his chest, and his breathing was laboured. 'Ol' man Miller's on the downward path, I reckon, and the legs are gone. Couldn't we squat inside here for a couple of minutes, boss, and have a smoke?'

Mallory looked at him in surprise thought how desperately weary his own legs felt and nodded in reluctant agreement. Miller wasn't the man to complain unless he was near exhaustion.

'Okay, Dusty, I don't suppose a minute or two will harm.' He translated quickly into Greek and led the way inside, Miller at his heels complaining at length about his advancing age. Once inside, Mallory felt his way across to the inevitable wooden bunk, sat down gratefully, lit a cigarette then looked up in puzzlement. Miller was still on his feet, walking slowly round the hut, tapping the walls as he went.

'Why don't you sit down?' Mallory asked irritably. 'That was why you came in here in the first place, wasn't it?'

'No, boss, not really.' The drawl was very pronounced. 'Just a low-down trick to get us inside. Two-three very special things I want to show you.'

'Very special? What the devil are you trying to tell me?'

'Bear with me, Captain Mallory,' Miller requested formally. 'Bear with me just a few minutes. I'm not wastin' your time. You have my word, Captain Mallory.'

'Very well.' Mallory was mystified, but his confidence in Miller remained unshaken. 'As you wish. Only don't be too long about it.'

'Thanks, boss.' The strain of formality was too much for Miller. 'It won't take long. There'll be a lamp or candles in here – you said the islanders never leave an abandoned house without 'em?'

'And a very useful superstition it's been to us, too.' Mallory reached under the bunk with his torch. straightened his back. 'Two or three candles here.'

'I want a light, boss. No windows – I checked. OK?'

'Light one and I'll go outside to see if there's anything showing.' Mallory was completely in the dark about the American's
intentions. He felt Miller didn't want him to say anything, and
there was a calm surety about him that precluded questioning.
Mallory was back in less than a minute. 'Not a chink to be seen
from the outside,' he reported.

'Fair enough. Thanks, boss.' Miller lit a second candle, then
slipped the rucksack straps from his shoulders, laid the pack on
the bunk and stood in silence for a moment.

Mallory looked at his watch, looked back at Miller.

'You were going to show me something,' he prompted.

'Yeah, that's right. Three things, I said.' He dug into the
pack, brought out a little black box hardly bigger than a match-
box. 'Exhibit A, boss.'

Mallory looked at it curiously. 'What's that?'

'Clockwork fuse.' Miller began to unscrew the back panel.
'Hate the damned things. Always make me feel like one of those
Bolshevik characters with a dark cloak, a moustache like Louki's
and carryin' one of those black cannon-ball things with a sput-
terin' fuse stickin' outa it. But it works.' He had the back off the
box now, examining the mechanism in the light of his torch.
'But this one doesn't, not any more,' he added softly. 'Clock's
OK, but the contact arm's been bent right back. This thing
could tick till Kingdom Come and it couldn't even set off a
firework.'

'But how on earth—?'

'Exhibit B.' Miller didn't seem to hear him. He opened the
detonator box, gingerly lifted a fuse from its felt and cotton-
wool bed and examined it closely under his torch. Then he
looked at Mallory again. 'Fulminate of mercury, boss. Only
seventy-five grains, but enough to blow your fingers off. Unstable as hell, too – the littlest tap will set it off.' He let it fall
to the ground, and Mallory winced and drew back involuntarily
as the American smashed a heavy heel down on top of it. But
there was no explosion, nothing at all.

'Ain't workin' so good either, is it, boss? A hundred to one
the rest are all empty, too.' He fished out a pack of cigarettes,
lit one, and watched the smoke eddy and whirl about the heat
of the candles. He slid the cigarettes into his pocket.

'There was a third thing you were going to show me,' Mallory
said quietly.

'Yeah, I was goin' to show you somethin' else.' The voice was
very gentle, and Mallory felt suddenly cold. 'I was goin' to show

you a spy, a traitor, the most vicious, twistin', murderin', double-crossin' bastard I've ever known.' The American had his hand in his pocket now, the silenced automatic sitting snugly against his palm, the muzzle trained over Panayis's heart. He went on, more gently than ever. 'Judas Iscariot had nothin' on the boy-friend here, boss. . . Take your coat off, Panayis.'

'What the devil are you doing? Are you crazy?' Mallory started forward, half-angry, half-amazed, but brought up sharply against Miller's extended arm, rigid as a bar of iron. 'What bloody nonsense is this? He doesn't understand English!'

'Don't he, though? Then why was he out of the cave like a flash when Casey reported hearin' sounds outside . . . and why was he the first to leave the carob grove this afternoon if he didn't understand your order? Take your coat off, Judas, or I'll shoot you through the arm. I'll give you two seconds.'

Mallory made to throw his arms round Miller and bring him to the ground, but halted in mid-step as he caught the look on Panayis's face – teeth bared, murder glaring out from the coal-black eyes. Never before had Mallory seen such malignity in a human face, a malignity that yielded abruptly to shocked pain and disbelief as the .32 bullet smashed into his upper arm, just below the shoulder.

'Two seconds and then the other arm,' Miller said woodenly. But Panayis was already tearing off his jacket, the dark, bestial eyes never leaving Miller's face. Mallory looked at him, shivered involuntarily, looked at Miller. Indifference, he thought, that was the only word to describe the look on the American's face. Indifference. Unaccountably, Mallory felt colder than ever.

'Turn round!' The automatic never wavered.

Slowly Panayis turned round. Miller stepped forward, caught the black shirt by the collar, ripped it off his back with one convulsive jerk.

'Waal, waal, now, whoever woulda thought it?' Miller drawled. 'Surprise, surprise, surprise! Remember, boss, this was the character that was publicly flogged by the Germans in Crete, flogged until the white of his ribs showed through. His back's in a helluva state, isn't it?'

Mallory looked but said nothing. Completely off balance, his mind was in a kaleidescopic whirl, his thoughts struggling to adjust themselves to a new set of circumstances, a complete re-versal of all his previous thinking. Not a scar, not a single blem-ish, marked the dark smoothness of that skin.

'Just a natural quick healer,' Miller murmured. 'Only a

nasty, twisted mind like mine would think that he had been
a German agent in Crete, became known to the Allies as a fifth
columnist, lost his usefulness to the Germans and was shipped
back to Navarone by fast motor-launch under cover of night.
Floggin'! Island-hoppin' his way back here in a row-boat! Just
a lot of bloody eyewash!' Miller paused, and his mouth twisted.
'I wonder how many pieces of silver he made in Crete before
they got wise to him?'

'But heavens above, man, you're not going to condemn someone just for shooting a line!' Mallory protested. Strangely, he
didn't feel nearly as vehement as he sounded. 'How many survivors would there be among the Allies if—?'

'Not convinced yet, huh?' Miller waved his automatic negligently at Panayis. 'Roll up the left trouser leg, Iscariot. Two
seconds again.'

Panayis did as he was told. The black venomous eyes never
looked away from Miller's. He rolled the dark cloth up to the
knee.

'Farther yet? That's my little boy,' Miller encouraged him.
'And now take that bandage off – right off.' A few seconds
passed, then Miller shook his head sadly. 'A ghastly wound,
boss, a ghastly wound!'

'I'm beginning to see your point,' Mallory said thoughtfully.
The dark sinewy leg wasn't even scratched. 'But why on
earth—?'

'Simple. Four reasons at least. Junior here is a treacherous,
slimy bastard – no self-respectin' rattlesnake would come within a mile of him – but he's a clever bastard. He faked his leg
so he could stay in the cave in the Devil's Playground when the
four of us went back to stop the Alpenkorps from comin' up
the slope below the carob grove.'

'Why? Frightened he'd stop something?'

Miller shook his head impatiently.

'Junior here's scared o' nothin'. He stayed behind to write a
note. Later on he used his leg to drop behind us some place,
and leave the note where it could be seen. Early on, this must
have been. Note probably said that we would come out at such
and such a place, and would they kindly send a welcomin' committee to meet us there. They sent it, remember: it was their
car we swiped to get to town. . . . That was the first time I got
real suspicious of the boyfriend: after he'd dropped behind he
made up on us again quick – too damn' quick for a man with a

game leg. But it wasn't till I opened that rucksack in the square this evenin' that I really knew.'

'You only mentioned two reasons,' Mallory prompted.

'Comin' to the others. Number three – he could fall behind when the welcomin' committee opened up in front – Iscariot here wasn't goin' to get himself knocked off before he collected his salary. And number four – remember that real touchin' scene when he begged you to let him stay at the far end of the cave that led into the valley we came out? Goin' to do his Horatio-on-the-bridge act?'

'Going to show them the right cave to pick, you mean.'

'Check. After that he was gettin' pretty desperate. I still wasn't sure, but I was awful suspicious, boss. Didn't know what he might try next. So I clouted him good and hard when that last patrol came up the valley.'

'I see,' Mallory said quietly. 'I see indeed.' He looked sharply at Miller. 'You should have told me. You had no right—'

'I was goin' to, boss. But I hadn't a chance – Junior here was around all the time. I was just startin' to tell you half an hour back, when the guns started up.'

Mallory nodded in understanding. 'How did you happen on all this in the first place, Dusty?'

'Juniper,' Miller said succinctly. 'Remember that's how Turzig said he came to find us? He smelt the juniper.'

'That's right. We *were* burning juniper.'

'Sure we were. But he said he smelt it on Kostos – and the wind was blowin' off Kostos all day long.'

'My God,' Mallory whispered. 'Of course, of course! And I missed it completely.'

'But Jerry knew we were there. How? Waal, he ain't got second sight no more than I have. So he was tipped off – he was tipped off by the boy-friend here. Remember I said he'd talked to some of his pals in Margaritha when we went down there for the supplies?' Miller spat in disgust. 'Fooled me all along the line. Pals? I didn't know how right I was. Sure they were his pals – his German pals! And that food he said he got from the commandant's kitchen – he got it from the kitchen all right. Almost certainly he goes in and asks for it – and old Skoda hands him his own suitcase to stow it in.'

'But the German he killed on the way back to the village? Surely to God—'

'Panayis killed him.' There was a tired certainty in Miller's voice. 'What's another corpse to Sunshine here. Probably stumbled on the poor bastard in the dark and had to kill him. Local colour. Louki was there, remember, and he couldn't have Louki gettin' suspicious. He would have blamed it on Louki anyway. The guy ain't human. . . . And remember when he was flung into Skoda's room in Margaritha along with Louki, blood pourin' from a wound in his head?'

'Mallory nodded.

'High-grade ketchup. Probably also from the commandant's kitchen,' Miller said bitterly. 'If Skoda had failed by every other means, there would still have been the boy-friend here as a stool-pigeon. Why he never asked Louki where the explosives were I don't know.'

'Obviously he didn't know Louki knew.'

'Mebbe. But one thing the bastard did know – how to use a mirror. Musta heliographed the garrison from the carob grove and given our position. No other way, boss. Then sometime this morning he must have got hold of my rucksack, whipped out all the slow fuse and fixed the clock fuse and detonators. He should have had his hands blown off tamperin' with them fulmi-nates. Lord only knows where he learnt to handle the damn' things.'

'Crete,' Mallory said positively. 'The Germans would see to that. A spy who can't also double as a saboteur is no good to them.'

'And he was very good to them,' Miller said softly. 'Very, very good. They're gonna miss their little pal. Iscariot here was a very smart baby indeed.'

'He was. Except tonight. He should have been smart enough to know that at least one of us would be suspicious—'

'He probably was,' Miller interrupted. 'But he was misin-formed. I think Louki's unhurt. I think Junior here talked Louki into letting him stay in his place – Louki was always a bit scared of him – then he strolled across to his pals at the gate, told 'em to send a strong-arm squad out to Vygos to pick up the others, asked them to fire a few shots – he was very strong on local colour, was our loyal little pal – then strolls back across the square, hoists himself up on the roof and waits to tip off his pals as soon as we came in the back door. But Louki forgot to tell him just one thing – that we were goin' to rendezvous on the roof of the house, not inside. So the boy-friend here lurks away for all he's worth up top, waiting to signal his friends. Ten to one that he's got a torch in his pocket.'

Mallory picked up Panayis's coat and examined it briefly. 'He has.'

'That's it, then.' Miller lit another cigarette, watched the match burn down slowly to his fingers, then looked up at Panayis. 'How does it feel to know that you're goin' to die, Panayis, to feel like all them poor bastards who've felt just as you're feeling now, just before they died – all the men in Crete, all the guys in the sea-borne and air landings on Navarone who died because they thought you were on their side? How does it feel, Panayis?'

Panayis said nothing. His left hand clutching his torn right arm, trying to stem the blood, he stood there motionless, the dark, evil face masked in hate, the lips still drawn back in that less than human snarl. There was no fear in him, none at all, and Mallory tensed himself for the last, despairing attempt for life that Panayis must surely make, and then he had looked at Miller and knew there would be no attempt, because there was a strange sureness and inevitability about the American, an utter immobility of hand and eye that somehow precluded even the thought, far less the possibility, of escape.

'The prisoner has nothin' to say.' Miller sounded very tired. 'I suppose I should say somethin'. I suppose I should give out with a long spiel about me bein' the judge, the jury and the executioner, but I don't think I'll bother myself. Dead men make poor witnesses. . . . Meebe it's not your fault, Panayis, mebbe there's an awful good reason why you came to be what you are. Gawd only knows. I don't, and I don't much care. There are too many dead men. I'm goin' to kill you, Panayis. and I'm goin' to kill you now.' Miller dropped his cigarette, ground it into the floor of the hut. 'Nothin' at all to say?'

And he had nothing at all to say, the hate, the malignity of the black eyes said it all for him and Miller nodded, just once, as if in secret understanding. Carefully, accurately, he shot Panayis through the heart, twice, blew out the candles, turned his back and was half-way towards the door before the dead man had crashed to the ground.

'I am afraid I cannot do it, Andrea.' Louki sat back wearily, shook his head in despair. 'I am very sorry, Andrea. The knots are too tight.'

'No matter.' Andrea rolled over from his side to a sitting position, tried to ease his tightly-bound legs and wrists. 'They are cunning, these Germans, and wet cords can only be cut.'

Characteristically, he made no mention of the fact that only a couple of minutes previously he had twisted round to reach the cords on Louki's wrists and undone them with half a dozen tugs of his steel-trap fingers. 'We will think of something else.'

He looked away from Louki, glanced across the room in the faint light of the smoking oil-lamp that stood by the grille door, a light so yellow, so dim that Casey Brown, trussed like a barn-yard fowl and loosely secured, like himself, by a length of rope to the iron hooks suspended from the roof, was no more than a shapeless blur in the opposite corner of the stone-flagged room. Andrea smiled to himself, without mirth. Taken prisoner again, and for the second time that day – and with the same ease and surprise that gave no chance at all of resistance: completely un-suspecting, they had been captured in an upper room, seconds after Casey had finished talking to Cairo. The patrol had known exactly where to find them – and with their leader's assurance that it was all over, with his gloating explanation of the part Panayis had played, the unexpectedness, the success of the coup was all too easy to understand. And it was difficult not to be-lieve his assurance that neither Mallory nor Miller had a chance. But the thought of ultimate defeat never occurred to Andrea.

His gaze left Casey Brown, wandered round the room, took in what he could see of the stone walls and floor, the hooks, the ventilation ducts, the heavy grille door. A dungeon, a torture dungeon, one would have thought, but Andrea had seen such places before. A castle, they called this place, but it was really only an old keep, no more than a manor house built round the crenellated towers. And the long-dead Frankish nobles who had built these keeps had lived well. No dungeon this, Andrea knew, but simply the larder where they had hung their meat and game, and done without windows and light for the sake of . . .

The light! Andrea twisted round, looking at the smoking oil-lamp, his eyes narrowing.

'Louki!' he called softly. The little Greek turned round to look at him.

'Can you reach the lamp?'

'I think so. . . . Yes, I can.'

'Take the glass off.' Andrea whispered. 'Use a cloth – it will be hot. Then wrap it in the cloth, hit it on the floor – gently. The glass is thick – you can cut me loose in a minute or two.'

Louki stared at him for an uncomprehending moment, then nodded in understanding. He shuffled across the floor – his legs were still bound – reached out, then halted his hand abruptly, only inches from the glass. The peremptory, metallic clang had been only feet away, and he raised his head slowly to see what had caused it.

He could have stretched out his hand, touched the barrel of the Mauser that protruded threateningly through the bars of the grille door. Again the guard rattled the rifle angrily between the bars, shouted something he didn't understand.

'Leave it alone, Louki,' Andrea said quietly. His voice was tranquil, unshadowed by disappointment. 'Come back here. Our friend outside is not too pleased.' Obediently Louki moved back, heard the guttural voice again, rapid and alarmed this time, the rattle as the guard withdrew his rifle quickly from the stones outside as he raced up the passage.

'What's the matter with our little friend?' Casey Brown was as lugubrious, as weary as ever. 'He seems upset.'

'He is upset.' Andrea smiled. 'He's just realized that Louki's hands are untied.'

'Well, why doesn't he tie them up again?'

'Slow in the head he may be, but he is no fool,' Andrea explained. 'This could be a trap and he's gone for his friends.'

Almost at once they heard a thud, like the closing of a distant door, the sound of more than one pair of feet running down the passage, the tinny rattling of keys on a ring, the rasp of a key against the lock, a sharp click, the squeal of rusty hinges and then two soldiers were in the room, dark and menacing with their jackboots and ready guns. Two or three seconds elapsed while they looked around them, accustoming their eyes to the gloom, then the man nearest the door spoke.

'A terrible thing, boss, nothin' short of deplorable! Leave 'em alone for a couple of minutes and see what happens? The whole damn's bunch tied up like Houdini on an off night!'

There was a brief, incredulous silence, then all three were sitting upright, staring at them. Brown recovered first.

'High time, too,' he complained. 'Thought you were never going to get here.'

'What he means is that he thought we were never going to see you again,' Andrea said quietly. 'Neither did I. But here you are, safe and sound.'

'Yes,' Mallory nodded. 'Thanks to Dusty and his nasty suspicious mind that cottoned on to Panayis while all the rest of us were asleep.'

'Where is he?' Louki asked.

'Panayis?' Miller waved a negligent hand. 'We left him behind – he met with a sorta accident.' He was across at the other side of the door now, carefully cutting the cords that pinioned Brown's injured leg, whistling tunelessly as he sawed away with his sheath knife. Mallory, too, was busy, slicing through Andrea's bonds, explaining rapidly what had happened, listening to the big Greek's equally concise account of what had befallen the other in the keep. And then Andrea was on his feet, massaging his numbed hands, looking across at Miller.

'That whistling, my Captain. It sounds terrible and, what is worse, it is very loud. The guards—'

'No worry there,' Mallory said grimly. 'They never expected to see Dusty and myself again. . . . They kept a poor watch.' He turned round to look at Brown, now hobbling across the floor.

'How's the leg, Casey?'

'Fine, sir.' Brown brushed it aside as of no importance. 'I got through to Cairo, tonight, sir. The report—'

'It'll have to wait, Casey. We must get out as fast as we can. You all right, Louki?'

'I am heart-broken, Major Mallory. That a countryman of mine – a trusted friend—'

'That too, will have to wait. Come on!'

'You are in a great hurry,' Andrea protested mildly. They were already out in the passage, stepping over the cell guard lying in a crumpled heap on the floor. 'Surely if they're all like our friend here—'

'No danger from this quarter,' Mallory interrupted impatiently. 'The soldiers in the town – they're bound to know by now that we've either missed Panayis or disposed of him. In either case they'll know that we're certain to come hot-footing out here. Work it out for yourself. They're probably half-way here already, and if they do come . . .' He broke off, stared a the smashed generator and the ruins of Casey Brown's transmitter set lying in one corner of the entrance hall. 'Done a pretty good job on these, haven't they?' he said bitterly.

'Thank the lord,' Miller said piously. 'All the less to tote around, is what I say. If you could only see the state of my back with that damned generator—'

'Sir!' Brown had caught Mallory's arm, an action so foreign to the usually punctilious petty officer that Mallory halted in surprise. 'Sir, it's terribly important – the report, I mean. You *must* listen, sir!'

The action, the deadly earnestness, caught and held Mallory's full attention. He turned to face Brown with a smile.

'OK, Casey, let's have it,' he said quietly. 'Things can't possibly be any worse than they are now.'

'They can, sir.' There was something tired, defeated about Casey Brown, and the great, stone hall seemed strangely chill. 'I'm afraid they can, sir. I got through tonight. First-class reception. Captain Jensen himself, and he was hopping mad. Been waiting all day for us to come on the air. Asked how things were, and I told him that you were outside the fortress just then, and hoped to be inside the magazine in an hour or so.'

'Go on.'

'He said that was the best news he'd ever had. He said his information had been wrong, he'd been fooled, that the invasion fleet didn't hole up overnight in the Cyclades, that they had come straight through under the heaviest air and E-boat escort ever seen in the Med., and are due to hit the beaches on Kheros some time before dawn tomorrow. He said our destroyers had been waiting to the south all day, moved up at dusk and were waiting word from him to see whether they would attempt the passage of the Maidos Straits. I told him maybe something could go wrong, but he said not with Captain Mallory and Miller inside and besides he wasn't – he couldn't risk the lives of twelve hundred men on Kheros just on the off chance that he might be wrong.' Brown broke off suddenly and looked down miserably at his feet. No one else in the hall moved or made any sound at all.

'Go on,' Mallory repeated in a whisper. His face was very pale.

'That's all, sir. That's all there is. The destroyers are coming through the Straits at midnight.' Brown looked down at his luminous watch. 'Midnight. Four hours to go.'

'Oh, God! Midnight!' Mallory was stricken, his eyes for the moment unseeing, ivory-knuckled hands clenched in futility and despair. 'They're coming through at midnight! God help them! God help them all now!'

—— 15 ——

WEDNESDAY NIGHT

2000–2115

Eight-thirty, his watch said. Eight-thirty. Exactly half an hour to curfew. Mallory flattened himself on the roof, pressed himself as closely as possible against the low retaining wall that almost touched the great, sheering sides of the fortress, swore softly to himself. It only required one man with a torch in his hand to look over the top of the fortress wall – a cat-walk ran the whole length of the inside of the wall, four feet from the top – and it would be the end of them all. The wandering beam of a torch and they were bound to be seen, it was impossible not to be seen: he and Dusty Miller – the American was stretched out behind him clutching the big truck battery in his arms – were wide open to the view of anyone who happened to glance down that way. Perhaps they should have stayed with the others a couple of roofs away, with Casey and Louki, the one busy tying spaced knots in a rope, the other busy splicing a bent wire hook on to a long bamboo they had torn from a bamboo hedge just outside the town, where they had hurriedly taken shelter as a convoy of three trucks had roared past them heading for the castle Vygos.

Eight thirty-two. What the devil was Andrea doing down there, Mallory wondered irritably and at once regretted his irritation. Andrea wouldn't waste an unnecessary second. Speed was vital, haste fatal. It seemed unlikely that there would be any officers inside – from what they had seen, practically half the garrison were combing either the town or the countryside out in the direction of Vygos – but if there were and even one gave a cry it would be the end.

Mallory stared down at the burn on the back of his hand, thought of the truck they had set on fire and grinned wryly to himself. Setting the truck on fire had been his only contribution to the night's performance so far. All the other credit went to either Andrea or Miller. It was Andrea who had seen in this house on the west side of the square – one of several adjoining houses used as officer's billets – the only possible answer to their problem. It was Miller, now lacking all time-fuses, clockwork, generator and every other source of electric power who had suddenly stated that he must have a battery, and again it was Andrea, hearing the distant approach of a truck, who had blocked the entrance to the long driveway to the keep with heavy stones from the flanking pillars, forcing the soldiers to abandon their truck at the gates and run up the drive towards their house. To overcome the driver and his mate and bundle them senseless into a ditch had taken seconds only, scarcely more time than it had taken Miller to unscrew the terminals of the heavy battery, find the inevitable jerri-can below the tail-board and pour the contents over engine, cab and body. The truck had gone up in a roar and *whoosh* of flames: as Louki had said earlier in the night, setting petrol-soaked vehicles on fire was not without its dangers – the charred patch on his hand stung painfully – but, again as Louki had said it had burned magnificently. A pity, in a way – it had attracted attention to their escape sooner than was necessary – but it had been vital to destroy the evidence, the fact that a battery was missing. Mallory had too much experience of and respect for the Germans ever to underrate them: they could put two and two together better than most.

He felt Miller tug at his ankle, started, twisted round quickly. The American was pointing beyond him, and he turned again and saw Andrea signalling to him from the raised trap in the far corner: he had been so engrossed in his thinking, the giant Greek so catlike in his silence, that he had completely failed to notice his arrival. Mallory shook his head, momentarily angered at his own abstraction, took the battery from Miller, whispered to him to get the others, then edged slowly across the roof, as noiselessy as possible. The sheer deadweight of the battery was astonishing, it felt as if it weighed a ton, but Andrea plucked it from his hands, lifted it over the trap coaming, tucked it under one arm and nimbly descended the stairs to the tiny hall-way as if it weighed nothing at all.

Andrea moved out through the open doorway to the covered balcony that overlooked the darkened harbour, almost a hundred vertical feet beneath. Mallory, following close behind, touched him on the shoulder as he lowered the battery gently to the ground.

'Any trouble?' he asked softly.

'None at all, my Keith.' Andrea straightened. 'The house is empty. I was so surprised that I went over it all, twice, just to make sure.'

'Fine! Wonderful! I suppose the whole bunch of them are

out scouring the country for us – interesting to know what they would say if they were told we were sitting in their front parlour?'

'They would never believe it,' Andrea said without hesitation. 'This is the last place they would ever think to look for us.'

'I've never hoped so much that you're right!' Mallory murmured fervently. He moved across to the latticed railing that enclosed the balcony, gazed down into the blackness beneath his feet and shivered. A long, long drop and it was very cold; that sluicing, vertical rain chilled one to the bone. . . . He stepped back, shook the railing.

'This thing strong enough, do you think?' he whispered.

'I don't know, my Keith. I don't know at all.' Andrea shrugged. 'I hope so.'

'I hope so,' Mallory echoed. 'It doesn't really matter. This is how it has to be.' Again he leaned far out over the railing, twisted his head to the right and upwards. In the rain-filled gloom of the night he could just faintly make out the still darker gloom of the mouth of the cave housing the two great guns, perhaps forty feet away from where he stood, at least thirty feet higher – and all vertical cliff-face between. As far as accessibility went, the cave mouth could have been on the moon.

He drew back, turned round as he heard Brown limping on to the balcony.

'Go to the front of the house and stay there, Casey, will you? Stay by the window. Leave the front door unlocked. If we have any visitors let them in.'

'Club 'em, knife 'em, no guns,' Brown murmured. 'Is that it, sir?'

'That's it, Casey.'

'Just leave this little thing to me,' Brown said grimly. He hobbled away through the doorway.

Mallory turned to Andrea. 'I make it twenty-three minutes.'

'I, too. Twenty-three minutes to nine.'

'Good luck,' Mallory murmured. He grinned at Miller. 'Come on, Dusty. Opening time.'

Five minutes later, Mallory and Miller were seated in a *taverna* just off the south side of the town square. Despite the garish blue paint with which the *tavernaris* had covered everything in sight, walls, tables, chairs, shelves all in the same execrably vivid colour (blue and red for the wine shops, green for the sweetmeat shops was the almost invariable rule throughout the islands) –

it was a gloomy, ill-lit place, as gloomy almost as the stern, righteous, magnificently-moustached heroes of the Wars of Independence whose dark, burning eyes glared down at them from a dozen faded prints scattered at eye-level along the walls. Between each pair of portraits was a brightly-coloured wall advertisement for Fix's beer: the effect of the décor, taken as a whole, was indescribable, and Mallory shuddered to think what it would have been like had the *tavernaris* had at his disposal any illumination more powerful than the two smoking oil-lamps placed on the counter before him.

As it was, the gloom suited him well. Their dark clothes, braided jackets, *tsantas* and jackboots looked genuine enough, Mallory knew, and the black-fringed turbans Louki had mysteriously obtained for them looked as they ought to look in a tavern where every islander there – about eight of them – wore nothing else on their heads. Their clothes had been good enough to pass muster with the *tavernaris* – but then even the keeper of a wine shop could hardly be expected to know every man in a town of five thousand, and a patriotic Greek, as Louki had declared this man to be, wasn't going to lift even a faintly suspicious eyebrow as long as there were German soldiers present. And there were Germans present – four of them, sitting round a table near the counter. Which was why Mallory had been glad of the semi-darkness. Not, he was certain, that he and Dusty Miller, had any reason to be physically afraid of these men. Louki had dismissed them contemptuously as a bunch of old women – headquarters clerks, Mallory guessed – who came to this tavern every night of the week. But there was no point in sticking out their necks unnecessarily.

Miller lit one of the pungent, evil-smelling local cigarettes, wrinkling his nose in distaste.

'Damn' funny smell in this joint, boss.'

'Put your cigarette out,' Mallory suggested.

'You wouldn't believe it, but the smell I'm smelling is a damn' sight worse than that.'

'Hashish,' Mallory said briefly. 'The curse of these island ports.' He nodded over towards a dark corner. 'The lads of the village over there will be at it every night in life. It's all they live for.'

'Do they have to make that gawddamned awful racket when they're at it?' Miller asked peevishly. 'Toscanini should see this lot!'

Mallory looked at the small group in the corner, clustered

round the young man playing a *bouzouko* – a long-necked mandolin – and singing the haunting, nostalgic *rembetika* songs of the hashish smokers of the Piraeus. He supposed the music did have a certain melancholy, lotus-land attraction, but right then it jarred on him. One had to be in a certain twilit, untroubled mood to appreciate that sort of thing; and he had never felt less untroubled in his life.

'I suppose it *is* a bit grim,' he admitted. 'But at least it lets us talk together, which we couldn't do if they all packed up and went home.'

'I wish to hell they would,' Miller said morosely. 'I'd gladly keep my mouth shut.' He picked distastefully at the *meze* – a mixture of chopped olives, liver, cheese and apples – on the plate before him: as a good American and a bourbon drinker of long standing he disapproved strongly of the invariable Greek custom of eating when drinking. Suddenly he looked up and crushed his cigarette against the table top. 'For Gawd's sake, boss, how much longer?'

Mallory looked at him, then looked away. He knew exactly how Dusty Miller felt, for he felt that way himself – tense, keyed-up, every nerve strung to the tautest pitch of efficiency. So much depended on the next few minutes; whether all their labour and their suffering had been necessary, whether the men on Kheros would live or die, whether Andy Stevens had lived and died in vain. Mallory looked at Miller again, saw the nervous hands, the deepened wrinkles round the eyes, the tightly compressed mouth, white at the outer corners, saw all these signs of strain, noted them and discounted them. Excepting Andrea alone, of all the men he had ever known he would have picked the lean, morose American to be his companion that night. Or maybe even including Andrea. 'The finest saboteur in southern Europe' Captain Jensen had called him back in Alexandria. Miller had come a long way from Alexandria, and he had come for this alone. Tonight was Miller's night.

Mallory looked at his watch.

'Curfew in fifteen minutes,' he said quietly. 'The balloon goes up in twelve minutes. For us, another four minutes to go.'

Miller nodded, but said nothing. He filled his glass again from the beaker in the middle of the table, lit a cigarette. Mallory could see a nerve twitching high up in his temple and wondered dryly how many twitching nerves Miller could see in his own face. He wondered, too, how the crippled Casey Brown was getting on in the house they had just left. In many ways he had the most responsible job of all – and at the critical moment he would have to leave the door unguarded, move back to the balcony. One slip up there. . . . He saw Miller look strangely at him and grinned crookedly. This had to come off, it just had to: he thought of what must surely happen if he failed, then shied away from the thought. It wasn't good to think of these things, not now not at this time.

He wondered if the other two were at their posts, unmolested; they should be, the search party had long passed through the upper part of the town; but you never knew what could go wrong, there was so much that could go wrong, and so easily. Mallory looked at his watch again: he had never seen a second hand move so slowly. He lit a last cigarette, poured a final glass of wine, listened without really hearing to the weird, keening threnody of the *rembetika* song in the corner. And then the song of the hashish singers died plaintively away, the glasses were empty and Mallory was on his feet.

'Time bringeth all things,' he murmured. 'He we go again.'

He sauntered easily towards the door, calling good night to the *tavernaris*. Just at the doorway he paused, began to search impatiently through his pockets as if he had lost something: it was a windless night, and it was raining, he saw, raining heavily, the lances of rain bouncing inches off the cobbled street – and the street itself was deserted as far as he could see in either direction. Satisfied, Mallory swung round with a curse, forehead furrowed in exasperation, started to walk back towards the table he had just left, right hand now delving into the capacious inner pocket of his jacket. He saw without seeming to that Dusty Miller was pushing his chair back, rising to his feet. And then Mallory had halted, his face clearing and his hands no longer searching. He was exactly three feet from the table where the four Germans were sitting.

'Keep quite still!' He spoke in German, his voice low but as steady, as menacing, as the Navy Colt .455 balanced in his right hand. We are desperate men. If you move we will kill you.'

For a full three seconds the soldiers sat immobile, expressionless except for the shocked widening of their eyes. And then there was a quick flicker of the eyelids from the man sitting nearest the counter, a twitching of the shoulder and then a grunt of agony as the .32 bullet smashed into his upper arm. The soft thud of Miller's silenced automatic couldn't have been heard beyond the doorway.

'Sorry, boss,' Miller apologised. 'Mebbe he's only sufferin' from St Vitus' Dance.' He looked with interest at the pain-twisted face, the blood welling darkly between the fingers clasped tightly over the wound. 'But he looks kinda cured to me.'

'He is cured,' Mallory said grimly. He turned to the inn-keeper, a tall, melancholy man with a thin face and mandarin moustache that drooped forlornly over either corner of his mouth, spoke to him in the quick, colloquial speech of the islands. 'Do these men speak Greek?'

The *tavernaris* shook his head. Completely unruffled and unimpressed, he seemed to regard armed hold-ups in his tavern as the rule rather than the exception.

'Not them!' he said contemptuously. 'English a little, I think – I am sure. But not our language. That I do know.'

'Good. I am a British Intelligence officer. Have you a place where I can hide these men?'

'You shouldn't have done this,' the *tavernaris* protested mildly. 'I will surely die for this.'

'Oh, no, you won't.' Mallory had slid across the counter, his pistol boring into the man's midriff. No one could doubt that the man was being threatened – and violently threatened – no one, that is, who couldn't see the broad wink that Mallory had given the inn-keeper. 'I'm going to tie you up with them. All right?'

'All right. There is a trap-door at the end of the counter here. Steps lead down to the cellar.'

'Good enough. I'll find it by accident.' Mallory gave him a vicious and all too convincing shove that sent the man stagger-ing, vaulted back across the counter, walked over to the *rem-betika* singers at the far corner of the room.

'Go home,' he said quickly. 'It is almost curfew time anyway. Go out the back way, and remember – you have seen nothing, no one. You understand?'

'We understand.' It was the young *bouzouko* player who spoke. He jerked his thumb at his companions and grinned. 'Bad men – but good Greeks. Can we help you?'

'No!' Mallory was emphatic. 'Think of your families – these soldiers have recognised you. They must know you well – you and they are here most nights, is that not so?'

The young man nodded.

'Off you go, then. Thank you all the same.'

A minute later, in the dim, candle-lit cellar, Miller prodded the soldier nearest him – the one most like himself in height and build. 'Take your clothes off!' he ordered.

'English pig!' the German snarled.

'Not *English*,' Miller protested. 'I'll give you thirty seconds to get your coat and pants off.'

The man swore at him, viciously, but made no move to obey. Miller sighed. The German had guts, but time was running out. He took a careful bead on the soldier's hand and pulled the trigger. Again the soft *plop* and the man was staring down stupidly at the hole torn in the heel of his left hand.

'Mustn't spoilt the nice uniforms, must we?' Miller asked conversationally. He lifted the automatic until the soldier was staring down the barrel of the gun. 'The next goes between the eyes.' The casual drawl carried complete conviction. 'It won't take me long to undress you, I guess.' But the man had already started to tear his uniform off, sobbing with anger and the pain of his wounded hand.

Less than another five minutes had passed when Mallory, clad like Miller in German uniform, unlocked the front door of the tavern and peered cautiously out. The rain, if anything, was heavier than ever – and there wasn't a soul in sight. Mallory beckoned Miller to follow and locked the door behind him. Together the two men walked up the middle of the street, making no attempt to seek either shelter or shadows. Fifty yards took them into the town square, where they turned right along the south side of the square, then left along the east side, not breaking step as they passed the old house where they had hidden earlier in the evening, not even as Louki's hand appeared mysteriously behind the partly opened door, a hand weighted down with two German Army rucksacks – rucksacks packed with rope, fuses, wire and high explosive. A few yards farther on they stopped suddenly, crouched down behind a couple of huge wine barrels outside a barber's shop, gazed at the two armed guards in the arched gateway, less than a hundred feet away, as they shrugged into their packs and waited for their cue.

They had only moments to wait – the timing had been split-second throughout. Mallory was just tightening the waist-belt of his rucksack when a series of explosions shook the centre of the town, not three hundred yards away, explosions followed by the vicious rattle of a machine-gun, then by further explosions. Andrea was doing his stuff magnificently with his grenades and home-made bombs.

Both men suddenly shrank back as a broad, white beam of

light stabbed out from a platform high above the gateway, a beam that paralleled the top of the wall to the east, showed up every hooked spike and strand of barbed wire as clearly as sunlight. Mallory and Miller looked at each other for a fleeting moment, their faces grim. Panayis hadn't missed a thing: they would have been pinned on these strands like flies on fly-paper and cut to ribbons by machine-guns.

Mallory waited another half-minute, touched Miller's arm, rose to his feet and started running madly across the square, the long hooked bamboo pressed close to his side, the American pounding behind him. In a few seconds they had reached the gates of the fortress, the startled guards running the last few feet to meet them.

'Every man to the Street of Steps!' Mallory shouted. 'Those damned English saboteurs are trapped in a house down there! We've got to have some mortars. Hurry, man, hurry, in the name of God!'

'But the gate!' one of the two guards protested. 'We cannot leave the gate!' The man had no suspicions, none at all: in the circumstances – the near darkness, the pouring rain, the German-clad soldier speaking perfect German, the obvious truth that there was a gun-battle being fought near-hand – it would have been remarkable had he shown any signs of doubt.

'Idiot!' Mallory screamed at him. '*Dummkopf!* What is there to guard against here? The English swine are in the Street of Steps. They must be destroyed! For God's sake, hurry!' he shouted desperately. 'If they escape again it'll be the Russian Front for all of us!'

Mallory had his hand on the man's shoulder now, ready to push him on his way, but his hand fell to his side unneeded. The two men were already gone, running pell-mell across the square, had vanished into the rain and the darkness already. Seconds later Mallory and Miller were deep inside the fortress of Navarone.

Everywhere there was complete confusion – a bustling, purposeful confusion as one would expect with the seasoned troops of the Alpenkorps, but confusion nevertheless, with much shouting of orders, blowing of whistles, starting of truck engines, sergeants running to and fro chivvying their men into marching order or into the waiting transports. Mallory and Miller ran too, once or twice through groups of men milling round the tailboard of a truck. Not that they were in any desperate hurry for themselves, but nothing could have been more conspicuous – and suspicious – than the sight of a couple of men walking calmly along in the middle of all that urgent activity. And so they ran, heads down or averted whenever they passed through a pool of light, Miller cursing feelingly and often at the unaccustomed exercise.

They skirted two barrack blocks on their right, then the power-house on their left, then an ordnance depot on their right and then the *Abteilung* garage on their left. They were climbing, now, almost in darkness, but Mallory knew where he was to the inch: he had so thoroughly memorised the closely tallying descriptions given him by Vlachos and Panayis that he would have been confident of finding his way with complete accuracy, even if the darkness had been absolute.

'What's that, boss?' Miller had caught Mallory by the arm, was pointing to a large, uncompromisingly rectangular building that loomed gauntly against the horizon. 'The local hoosegow?'

'Water storage tank,' Mallory said briefly. 'Panayis estimates there's half a million gallons in there – magazine flooding in an emergency. The magazines are directly below.' He pointed to a squat, box-like, concrete structure a little farther on. 'The only entrance to the magazine. Locked and guarded.'

They were approaching the senior officers' quarters now – the commandant had his own flat on the second storey, directly overlooking the massive, reinforced ferro-concrete control tower that controlled the two great guns below. Mallory suddenly stopped, picked up a handful of dirt, rubbed it on his face and told Miller to do the same.

'Disguise,' he explained. 'The experts would consider it a bit on the elementary side, but it'll have to do. The lighting's apt to be a bit brighter inside this place.'

He went up the steps to the officers' quarters at a dead run, crashed through the swing doors with a force that almost took them off their hinges. The sentry at the keyboard looked at him in astonishment, the barrel of his submachine-gun lining up on the New Zealander's chest.

'Put that thing down, you damned idiot!' Mallory snapped furiously. 'Where's the commandant? Quickly, you oaf! It's life or death!'

'Herr – Herr Kommandant?' the sentry stuttered. 'He's left – they are all gone, just a minute ago.'

'What? All gone?' Mallory was staring at him with narrowed, dangerous eyes. 'Did you say "all gone"?' he asked softly.

'Yes. I – I'm sure they're . . .' He broke off abruptly as Mallory's eyes shifted to a point behind his shoulder.

'Then who the hell is that?' Mallory demanded savagely.

The sentry would have been less than human not to fall for it. Even as he was swinging round to look, the vicious judo cut took him just below the left ear. Mallory had smashed open the glass of the keyboard before the unfortunate guard had hit the floor, swept all the keys – about a dozen in all – off their rings and into his pocket. It took them another twenty seconds to tape the man's mouth and hands and lock him in a convenient cupboard; then they were on their way again, still running.

One more obstacle to overcome, Mallory thought as they pounded along in the darkness, the last of the triple defences. He did not know how many men would be guarding the locked door to the magazine, and in that moment of fierce exaltation he didn't particularly care. Neither, he felt sure, did Miller. There were no worries now, no taut-nerved tensions or nameless anxieties. Mallory would have been the last man in the world to admit it, or even believe it, but this was what men like Miller and himself had been born for.

They had their hand-torches out now, the powerful beams swinging in wide arcs as they plunged along, skirting the massed batteries of AA guns. To anyone observing their approach from the front, there could have been nothing more calculated to disarm suspicion than the sight and sound of the two men running towards them without any attempt at concealment, one of them shouting to the other in German, both with lit torches whose beams lifted and fell, lifted and fell as the men's arms windmilled by their sides. But these same torches were deeply hooded, and only a very alert observer indeed would have noticed that the downward arc of the light never passed backwards beyond the runners' feet.

Suddenly Mallory saw two shadows detaching themselves from the darker shadow of the magazine entrance, steadied his torch for a brief second to check. He slackened speed.

'Right!' he said softly. 'Here they come – only two of them. One each – get as close as possible first. Quick and quiet – a shout, a shot, and we're finished. And for God's sake don't start clubbing 'em with your torch. There'll be no lights on in that magazine and I'm not going to start crawling around there with a box of bloody matches in my hand!' He transferred his torch to his left hand, pulled out his Navy Colt, reversed it, caught it by the barrel, brought up sharply only inches away from the guards now running to meet them.

'Are you all right?' Mallory gasped. 'Anyone been here? Quickly, man, *quickly*!'

'Yes, yes, we're all right.' The man was off guard, apprehensive. 'What in the name of God is all that noise—'

'Those damned English saboteurs!' Mallory swore viciously. 'They've killed the guards and they're inside! Are you sure no one's been here? Come, let me see.'

He pushed his way past the guard, probed his torch at the massive padlock, then straightened his back.

'Thank heaven for that anyway!' He turned round, let the dazzling beam of his torch catch the man square in the eyes, muttered an apology and switched off the light, the sound of the sharp click lost in the hollow, soggy thud of the heel of his Colt catching the man behind the ear, just below the helmet. The sentry was still on his feet, just beginning to crumple, when Mallory staggered as the second guard reeled into him, staggered, recovered, clouted him with the colt for good measure, then stiffened in sudden dismay as he heard the vicious hissing *plop* of Miller's automatic, twice in rapid succession.

'What the hell—'

'Wily birds, boss,' Miller murmured. 'Very wily indeed. There was a third character in the shadows at the side. Only way to stop him.' Automatic cocked in his ready hand, he stooped over the man for a moment, then straightened. 'Afraid he's been stopped kinda permament, boss.' There was no expression in his voice.

'Tie up the others.' Mallory had only half heard him, he was already busy at the magazine door, trying a succession of keys in the lock. The third key fitted, the lock opened and the heavy steel door gave easily to his touch. He took a last swift look round, but there was no one in sight, no sound but the revving engine of the last of the trucks clearing the fortress gates, the distant rattle of machine-gun fire. Andrea was doing a magnificent job – if only he didn't overdo it, leave his withdrawal till it was too late. . . . Mallory turned quickly, switched on his torch, stepped inside the door. Miller would follow when he was ready.

A vertical steel ladder fixed to the rock led down to the floor of the cave. On either side of the ladder were hollow lift-shafts, unprotected even by a cage, oiled wire ropes glistening in the middle, a polished metal runner at each side of the square to guide and steady the spring-loaded side-wheels of the lift itself. Spartan in their simplicity but wholly adequate, there was no mistaking these for anything but what they were – the shell hoist shafts going down to the magazine.

Mallory reached the solid floor of the cave and swept his torch round through a 180-degree arc. This was the very end of that great cave that opened out beneath the towering overhang of rock that dominated the entire harbour. Not the natural end, he saw after a moment's inspection, but a man-made addition: the volcanic rock around him had been drilled and blasted out. There was nothing here but the two shafts descending into the pitchy darkness and another steel ladder, also leading to the magazine. But the magazine could wait: to check that there were no more guards down here and to ensure an emergency escape route – these were the two vital needs of the moment.

Quickly Mallory ran along the tunnel, flipping his torch on and off. The Germans were past-masters of booby traps – explosive booby traps – for the protection of important installations, but the chances were that they had none in that tunnel – not with several hundred tons of high explosive stored only feet away.

The tunnel itself, dripping-damp and duck-board floored, was about seven feet high and even wider, but the central passage was very narrow – most of the space was taken up by the roller conveyors, one on either side, for the great cartridge and shells. Suddenly the conveyors curved away sharply to the left and right, the sharply-sheering tunnel roof climbed steeply up into the near-darkness of the vaulted dome above, and, almost at his feet, their burnished steel caught in the beam from his torch, twin sets of parallel rails, inbedded in the solid stone and twenty feet apart, stretched forward into the lightened gloom ahead, the great, gaping mouth of the cave. And just before he switched off the torch – searchers returning from the Devil's Playground might easily catch the pinpoint of light in the darkness – Mallory had a brief glimpse of the turn-tables that crowned the far end of these shining rails and, crouched massively above, like some nightmare monsters from an ancient and other world, the evil, the sinister silhouettes of the two great guns of Navarone.

Torch and revolver dangling loosely in his hands, only dimly aware of the curious tingling in the tips of his fingers, Mallory walked slowly forward. Slowly, but not with the stealthy slowness, the razor-drawn expectancy of a man momentarily anticipating trouble – there was no guard in the cave, Mallory was quite sure of that now – but with that strange, dream-like slow-ness, the half-belief of a man who has accomplished something he had known all along he could never accomplish, with the slowness of a man at last face to face with a feared but long-sought enemy. I'me here at last, Mallory said to himself over and over again. I'm here at last, I've made it, and these are the guns of Navarone: these are the guns I came to destroy, the guns of Navarone, and I have come at last. But somehow he couldn't quite believe it. . . .

Slowly still Mallory approached the guns, walked half-way round the perimeter of the turn-table of the gun on the left, examined it as well as he could in the gloom. He was staggered by the sheer size of it, the tremendous girth and reach of the barrel that stretched far out into the night. He told himself that the experts thought it was only a nine-inch crunch gun, that the crowding confines of the caves were bound to exaggerate its size. He told himself these things, discounted them: twelve-inch bore if an inch, that gun was the biggest thing he had ever seen. Big? Heavens above, it was gigantic! The fools, the blind crazy fools who had sent the *Sybaris* out against these . . .

The train of thought was lost, abruptly. Mallory stood quite still, one hand resting against the massive gun carriage and tried to recall the sound that had jerked him back to the present. Immobile, he listened for it again, eyes closed the better to hear, but the sound did not come again, and suddenly he knew that it was no sound at all but the absence of sound that had cut through his thoughts, triggered off some unconscious warning bell. The night was suddenly very silent, very still: down in the heart of the town the guns had stopped firing.

Mallory swore softly to himself. He had already spent far too much time day-dreaming, and time was running short. It *must* be running short – Andrea had withdrawn, it was only a matter of time until the Germans discovered that they had been duped. And then they would come running – and there was no doubt where they would come. Swiftly Mallory shrugged out of his rucksack, pulled out the hundred-foot wire-cored rope coiled inside. Their emergency escape route – whatever else he did he must make sure of that.

The rope looped round his arm, he moved forward cautiously, seeking a belay, but had only taken three steps when his right knee-cap struck something hard and unyielding. He checked the exclamation of pain, investigated the obstacle with his free hand, realized immediately what it was – an iron railing stretched waist-high across the mouth of the cave. Of course!' There had been bound to be something like that, some barrier to prevent people from falling over the edge, especially in the darkness of the night. He hadn't been able to pick it up with the binoculars from the carob grove that afternoon – close though it was to the entrance, it had been concealed in the gloom of the cave. But he should have thought of it.

Quickly Mallory felt his way along to the left, to the very end of the railing, crossed it, tied the rope securely to the base of the vertical stanchion next to the wall, paid out the rope as he moved gingerly to the lip of the cave mouth. And then, almost at once, he was there and there was nothing below his probing foot but a hundred and twenty feet of sheer drop to the land-locked harbour of Navarone.

Away to his right was a dark, formless blur lying on the water, a blur that might have been Cape Demirci: straight ahead, across the darkly velvet sheen of the Maidos Straits, he could see the twinkle of far-away lights – it was a measure of the enemy's confidence that they permitted these lights at all, or, more likely, these fisher cottages were useful as a bearing marker for the guns at night: and to the left, surprisingly near, barely thirty feet away in a horizontal plane, but far below the level where he was standing, he could see the jutting end of the outside wall of the fortress where it abutted on the cliff, the roofs of the houses on the west side of the square beyond that, and, beyond that again, the town itself curving sharply downwards and outwards, to the south first, then to the west, close-girdling and matching the curve of the crescent harbour. Above – but there was nothing to be seen above, that fantastic overhang above blotted out more than half the sky; and below, the darkness was equally impenetrable, the surface of the harbour inky and black as night. There were vessels down there, he knew, Grecian caiques and German launches, but they might have been a thousand miles away for any sign he could see of them.

The brief, all encompassing glance had taken barely ten seconds, but Mallory waited no longer. Swiftly he bent down, tied a double bowline in the end of the rope and left it lying on the edge. In an emergency they could kick it out into the darkness. It would be thirty feet short of the water, he estimated – enough to clear any launch or masted caique that might be moving about the harbour. They could drop the rest of the way, maybe a bone-breaking fall on to the deck of a ship, but they would have to risk it. Mallory took one last look down into the

Stygian blackness and shivered: he hoped to God that he and Miller wouldn't have to take that way out.

Dusty Miller was kneeling on the duck-boards by the top of the ladder leading down to the magazine as Mallory came running back up the tunnel, his hands busy with wires, fuses, detonators and explosives. He straightened up as Mallory approached.

'I reckon this stuff should keep 'em happy, boss.' He set the hands of the clockwork fuse, listened appreciatively to the barely audible hum, then eased himself down the ladder. 'In here among the top two rows of cartridges, I thought.'

'Wherever you say,' Mallory acquiesced. 'Only don't make it too obvious – or too difficult to find. Sure there's no chance of them suspecting that we knew the clock and fuses were dud?'

'None in the world,' Miller said confidently. 'When they find this here contraption they'll knock holes in each other's back congratulatin' themselves – and they'll never look any further.'

'Fair enough.' Mallory was satisfied. 'Lock the door up top?'

'Certainly I locked the door!' Miller looked at him reproachfully. 'Boss, sometimes I think . . .'

But Mallory never heard what he thought. A metallic reverberating clangour echoed cavernously through the cave and magazine, blotting out Miller's words, then died away over the harbour. Again the sound came, while the two men stared bleakly at one another, then again and again, then escaped for a moment of time.

'Company,' Mallory murmured. 'Complete with sledgehammers. Dear God, I only hope that door holds.' He was already running along the passage towards the guns, Miller close behind him.

'Company!' Miller was shaking his head as he ran. 'How in the hell did they get here so soon?'

'Our late lamented little pal,' Mallory said savagely. He vaulted over the railing, edged back to the mouth of the cave. 'And we were suckers enough to believe he told the whole truth. But he never told us that opening that door up top triggered of an alarm bell in the guard-room.'

─── 16 ───

WEDNESDAY NIGHT

2115–2345

Smoothly, skilfully, Miller paid out the wire-cored rope– double-turned round the top rail – as Mallory sank out of sight into the darkness. Fifty feet had gone, he estimated, fifty-five, sixty, then there came the awaited sharp double tug on the signal cord looped round his wrist and he at once checked the rope, stooped and tied it securely to the foot of the stanchion.

And then he had straightened again, belayed himself to the rail with the rope's end, leaned far out over the edge, caught hold of the rope with both hands as far down as he could reach and began slowly, almost imperceptibly at first, then with gradually increasing momentum, to swing man and rope from side to side, pendulum-wise. As the swings of the pendulum grew wider, the rope started to twist and jump in his hands, and Miller knew that Mallory must be striking outcrops of rock, spinning uncontrollably as he bounced off them. But Miller knew that he couldn't stop now, the clanging of the sledges behind him was almost continuous: he only stooped the lower over the rope, flung all the strength of his sinewy arms and shoulders into the effort of bringing Mallory nearer and still nearer to the rope that Brown would by now have thrown down from the balcony of the house where they had left him.

Far below, half-way between the cave mouth and the invisible waters of the harbour, Mallory swung in a great arc through the rain-filled darkness of the sky, forty rushing, bone-bruising feet between the extremities of the swings. Earlier he had struck his head heavily on an outcrop of rock, all but losing consciousness and his grip on the rope. But he knew where to expect that projection now and pushed himself clear each time as he approached it, even although this made him spin in a complete circle every time. It was as well, he thought, that it was dark, that he was independent of sight anyway: the blow had re-opened an old wound Turzig had given him, his whole upper face was masked with blood, both eyes completely gummed.

But he wasn't worried about the wound, about the blood in his eyes. The rope – that was all that mattered. Was the rope there? Had anything happened to Casey Brown? Had he been jumped before he could get the rope over the side? If he had, then all hope was gone and there was nothing they could do, no other way they could span the forty sheer feet between house and cave. It just *had* to be there. But if it were there, why couldn't he find it? Three times now, at the right extremity of a swing, he had reached out with his bamboo pole, heard the hook scrape emptily, frustratingly, against the bare rock.

And then, the fourth time, stretched out to the straining limit of both arms, he felt the hook catch on! Immediately he jerked the pole in, caught the rope before he dropped back on the downward swing, jerked the signal cord urgently, checked himself gradually as he fell back. Two minutes later, near exhaustion from the sixty-foot climb up the wet, slippery rope, he crawled blindly over the lip of the cave and flung himself to the ground, sobbing for breath.

Swiftly, without speaking, Miller bent down, slipped the twin loops of the double bowline from Mallory's legs, undid the knot, tied it to Brown's rope, gave the latter a tug and watched the joined ropes disappear into the darkness. Within two minutes the heavy battery was across, underslung from the two ropes, lowered so far by Casey Brown then hauled up by Mallory and Miller. Within another two minutes, but with infinitely more caution, this time, the canvas bag with the nitro, primers and detonators, had been pulled across, lay on the stone floor beside the battery.

All noise had ceased, the hammering of the sledges against the steel door had stopped completely. There was something threatening, foreboding about the stillness, the silence was more menacing than all the clamour that had gone before. Was the door down, the lock smashed, the Germans waiting for them in the gloom of the tunnel, waiting with cradled machine-carbines that would tear the life out of them? But there was no time to wonder, no time to wait, no time now to stop to weigh the chances. The time for caution was past, and whether they lived or died was of no account any more.

The heavy Colt .455 balanced at his waist, Mallory climbed over the safety barrier, padded silently past the great guns and through the passage, his torch clicking on half-way down its length. The place was deserted, the door above still intact. He climbed swiftly up the ladder, listened at the top. A subdued murmur of voices, he thought he heard, and a faint hissing sound on the other side of the heavy steel door, but he couldn't be sure. He leaned forward to hear better, the palm of his hand against the door, drew back with a muffled exclamation of pain. Just above the lock, the door was almost red-hot. Mallory dropped down to the floor of the tunnel just as Miller came staggering up with the battery.

'That door's as hot as blazes. They must be burning—'

'Did you hear anything?' Miller interrupted.

'There was a kind of hissing—'

'Oxy-acetylene torch,' Miller said briefly. 'They'll be burnin' out the lock. It'll take time – that door's made of armoured steel.'

'Why don't they blow it in – gelignite or whatever you use for that job?'

'Perish the thought,' Miller said hastily. 'Don't even *talk* about it, boss. Sympathetic detonation's a funny thing – there's an even chance that the whole damned lot would go up. Give me a hand with this thing, boss, will you?'

Within seconds Dusty Miller was again a man absorbed in his own element, the danger outside, the return trip he had yet to make across the face of the cliff, completely forgotten for the moment. The task took him four minutes from beginning to end. While Mallory was sliding the battery below the floored well of the lift, Miller squeezed in between the shining steel runners of the lift shaft itself, stopped to examine the rear one with his torch and establish, by the abrupt transition from polished to dull metal, exactly where the spring-loaded wheel of the shell-hoist came to rest. Satisfied, he pulled out a roll of sticky black tape, wound it a dozen times round the shaft, stepped back to look at it: it was quite invisible.

Quickly he taped the ends of two rubber-covered wires on the insulated strip, one at either side, taped these down also until nothing was visible but the bared steel cores at the tips, joined these to two four-inch strips of bared wire, taped these also, top and bottom, to the insulated shaft, vertically and less than half an inch apart. From the canvas bag he removed the TNT, the primer and the detonator – a bridge mercury detonater lugged and screwed to his own specification – fitted them together and connected one of the wires from the steel shaft to a lug on the detonator, screwing it firmly home. The other wire from the shaft he led to the positive terminal on the battery, and a third wire from the negative terminal to the detonator. It only required the ammunition hoist to sink down into the magazine – as it would do as soon as they began firing – and the spring-loaded wheel would short out the bare wires, completing the circuit and triggering off the detonator. A last check on the position of the bared vertical wires and he sat back satisfied. Mallory had just descended the ladder from the tunnel. Miller tapped him on the leg to draw his attention, negligently waving the steel blade of his knife within an inch of the exposed wires.

'Are you aware, boss,' he said conversationally, 'that if I touched this here blade across those terminals, the whole gawd-damned place would go up in smithereens.' He shook his head musingly. 'Just one little slip of the hand, just one teeny little touch and Mallory and Miller are among the angels.'

'For God's sake put that thing away!' Mallory snapped nervously. 'And let's get the hell out of here. They've got a complete half-circle cut through that door already!'

Five minutes later Miller was safe – it had been a simple matter of sliding down a 45-degree tautened rope to where Brown waited. Mallory took a last look back into the cave, and his mouth twisted. He wondered how many soldiers manned the guns and magazine during action stations. One thing, he thought, they'll never know anything about it, the poor bastards. And then he thought, for the hundredth time, of all the men on Kheros and the destroyers, and his lips tightened and he looked away. Without another backward glance he slipped over the edge, dropped down into the night. He was half-way there, at the very lowest point of the curve and about to start climbing again, when he heard the vicious, staccato rattle of machine-gun fire directly overhead.

It was Miller who helped him over the balcony rail, an apprehensive-looking Miller who glanced often over his shoulder in the direction of the gun-fire – and the heaviest concentration of fire, Mallory realized with sudden dismay, was coming from their own, the west side of the square, only three or four houses away. Their escape route was cut off.

'Come on, boss!' Miller said urgently. 'Let's get away from this joint. Gettin' downright unhealthy round these parts.'

Mallory jerked his head in the direction of the fire. 'Who's down there?' he asked quickly.

'A German patrol.'

'Then how in the hell can we get away?' Mallory demanded. 'And where's Andrea?'

'Across the other side of the square, boss. That's who those birds along there are firing at.'

'The other side of the square!' He glanced at his watch.

'Heavens above, man, what's he doing there?' He was moving through the house now, speaking over his shoulder. 'Why did you let him go?'

'I didn't let him go, boss,' Miller said carefully. 'He was gone when I came. Seems that Brown here saw a big patrol start a house to house search of the square. Started on the other side and were doin' two or three houses at a time. Andrea – he'd come back by this time – thought it a sure bet that they'd work right round the square and get here in two or three minutes, so he took off like a bat across the roofs.'

'Going to draw them off?' Mallory was at Louki's side staring out of the window. 'The crazy fool! He'll get himself killed this time – get himself killed for sure! There are soldiers everywhere. Besides, they won't fall for it again. H tricked them once up in the hills, and the Germans—'

'I'm not so sure, sir,' Brown interrupted excitedly. 'Andrea's just shot out the searchlight on his side. They'll think for certain that we're going to break out over the wall and – look, sir, look! There they go!' Brown was almost dancing with excitement, the pain of his injured leg forgotten. 'He's done it, sir, he's done it!'

Sure enough, Mallory saw, the patrol had broken away from their shelter in the house to their right and were running across the square in extended formation, their heavy boots clattering on the cobbles, stumbling, falling, recovering again as they lost footing on the slippery wetness of the uneven stones. At the same time Mallory could see torches flickering on the roofs of the houses opposite, the vague forms of men crouching low to escape observation and making swiftly for the spot where Andrea had been when he had shot out the great Cyclops eye of the searchlight. ·

'They'll be on him from every side.' Mallory spoke quietly enough, but his fists clenched until the nails cut into the palms of his hands. He stood stock-still for some seconds, stooped quickly and gathered a Schmeisser up from the floor. 'He hasn't a chance. I'm going after him.' He turned abruptly, brought up with equal suddenness: Miller was blocking his way to the door.

'Andrea left word that we were to leave him be, that he'd find his own way out.' Miller was very calm, very respectful. 'Said that no one was to help him, not on any account.'

'Don't try to stop me. Dusty.' Mallory spoke evenly, mechanically almost. He was hardly aware that Dusty Miller was there. He only knew that he must get out at once, get to Andrea's side, give him what help he could. They had been together too long, he owed too much to the smiling giant to let him go so easily. He couldn't remember how often Andrea had come after *him*, more than once when he had thought hope was gone. . . . He put his hand against Miller's chest.

'You'll only be in his way, boss.' Miller said urgently. 'That's what you said . . .'

Mallory pushed him aside, strode for the door, brought up his fist to strike as hands closed round his upper arm. He stopped just in time, looked down into Louki's worried face.

'The American is right,' Louki said insistently. 'You must not go. Andrea said you were to take us down to the harbour.'

'Go down yourselves,' Mallory said brusquely. 'You know the way, you know the plans.'

'You would let us all go, let us all—'

'I'd let the whole damn' world go if I could help him.' There was an utter sincerity in the New Zealander's voice. 'Andrea would never let me down.'

'But you would let him down,' Louki said quietly. 'Is that it, Major Mallory?'

'What the devil do you mean?'

'By not doing as he wishes. He may be hurt, killed even, and if you go after him and are killed too, that makes it all useless. He would die for nothing. Is it thus you would repay your friend?'

'All right, all right, you win,' Mallory said irritably.

'That is how Andrea would want it,' Louki murmured. 'Any other way you would be—'

'Stop preaching at me! Right, gentlemen, lets be on our way.' He was back on balance again, easy, relaxed, the primeval urge to go out and kill well under control. 'We'll take the high road – over the roofs. Dig into that kitchen stove there, rub the ashes all over your hands and faces. See that there's nothing white on you anywhere. And no talking!'

The five-minute journey down to the harbour wall – a journey made in soft-footed silence with Mallory hushing even the beginnings of a whisper – was quite uneventful. Not only did they see no soldiers, they saw no one at all. The inhabitants of Navarone were wisely obeying the curfew, and the streets were completely deserted. Andrea had drawn off pursuit with a vengeance. Mallory began to fear that the Germans had taken him, but just as they reached the water's edge he heard the gunfire again, a good deal farther away this time, in the very north-east corner of the town, round the back of the fortress.

Mallory stood on the low wall above the harbour, looked at his companions, gazed out over the dark oiliness of the water. Through the heavy rain he could just distinguish, to his right and left, the vague blurs of caiques moored stern on to the wall. Beyond that he could see nothing.

'Well, I don't suppose we can get much wetter than we are right now,' he observed. He turned to Louki, checked something the little man was trying to say about Andrea. 'You sure you can find it all right in the darkness?' 'It, was the comman-dant's personal launch, a thirty-six foot ten-tonner always kept moored to a buoy a hundred feet off-shore. The engineer, who doubled as guard, slept aboard, Louki had said.

'I am already there,' Louki boasted. 'Blindfold me as you will and I—'

'All right, all right,' Mallory said hastily. 'I'll take your word for it. Lend me your hat, will you, Casey?' He jammed the automatic into the crown of the hat, pulled it firmly on to his head, slid gently into the water and struck out by Louki's side.

'The engineer,' Louki said softly. 'I think he will be awake, Major.'

'I think so, too,' Mallory said grimly. Again there came the chatter of machine-carbines, the deeper whiplash of a Mauser. 'So will everyone else in Navarone, unless they're deaf or dead. Drop behind as soon as we see the boat. Come when I call.'

Ten seconds, fifteen passed, then Louki touched Mallory on the arm.

'I see it,' Mallory whispered. The blurred silhouette was less than fifteen yards away. He approached silently, neither legs nor arms breaking water, until he saw the vague shape of a man standing on the poop, just aft of the engine-room hatch-way. He was immobile, staring out in the direction of the for-tress and the upper town: Mallory slowly circled round the stern of the boat and came up behind him, on the other side. Carefully he removed his hat, took out the gun, caught the low gunwale with his left hand. At the range of seven feet he knew he couldn't possibly miss, but he couldn't shoot the man, not then. The guard-rails were token affairs only, eighteen inches high at the most, and the splash of the man falling into the water would almost certainly alert the guards at the harbour mouth emplacements.

'If you move I will kill you!' Mallory said softly in German.

The man stiffened. He had a carbine in his hand, Mallory saw.

'Put the gun down. Don't turn round.' Again the man obeyed, and Mallory was out of the water and on to the deck, in seconds, neither eye nor automatic straying from the man's back. He stepped softly forward, reversed the automatic, struck, caught the man before he could fall overboard and lowered him quietly to the deck. Three minutes later all the others were safely aboard.

Mallory followed the limping Brown down to the engine-room, watched him as he switched on his hooded torch, looked around with a professional eye, looked at the big, gleaming, six-cylinder in line Diesel engine.

'This,' said Brown reverently, 'is an engine. What a beauty! Operates any number of cylinders you like. I know the type, sir.'

'I never doubted but you would. Can you start her up, Casey?'

'Just a minute till I have a look round, sir.' Brown had all the unhurried patience of the born engineer. Slowly, methodically, he played the spotlight round the immaculate interior of the engine-room, switched on the fuel and turned to Mallory. 'A dual control job, sir. We can take her from up top.'

He carried out the same painstaking inspection in the wheel-house, while Mallory waited impatiently. The rain was easing off now, not much, but sufficiently to let him see the vague outlines of the harbour entrance. He wondered for the tenth time if the guards there had been alerted against the possibility of an attempted escape by boat. It seemed unlikely – from the racket Andrea was making, the Germans would think that escape was the last thing in their minds. . . . He leaned forward, touched Brown on the shoulder.

'Twenty past eleven, Casey,' he murmured. 'If these destroyers come through early we're apt to have a thousand tons of rock falling on our heads.'

'Ready now, sir,' Brown announced. He gestured at the crowded dash-board beneath the screen. 'Nothing to it really.'

'I'm glad you think so,' Mallory murmured fervently. 'Start her moving, will you? Just keep it slow and easy.'

Brown coughed apologetically. 'We're still moored to the buoy. And it might be a good thing, sir, if we checked on the fixed guns, searchlights, signalling lamps, life-jackets and buoys. It's useful to know where these things are,' he finished deprecatingly.

Mallory laughed softly, clapped him on the shoulder.

'You'd make a great diplomat, Chief. We'll do that.' A landsman first and last, Mallory was none the less aware of the gulf
that stretched between him and a man like Brown, made no
bones about acknowledging it to himself. 'Will you take her
out, Casey?'

'Right, sir. Would you ask Louki to come here – I think it's
steep to both sides, but there may be snags or reefs. You never
know.'

Three minutes later the launch was half-way to the harbour
mouth, purring along softly on two cylinders, Mallory and
Miller, still clad in German uniform, standing on the deck
for'ard of the wheelhouse, Louki crouched low inside the wheelhouse itself. Suddenly, about sixty yards away, a signal lamp
began to flash at them, its urgent clacking quite audible in the
stillness of the night.

'Dan'l Boone Miller will now show how it's done,' Miller
muttered. He edged closer to the machine-gun on the starboard
bow. 'With my little gun I shall . . .'

He broke off sharply, his voice lost in the sudden clacking
from the wheelhouse behind him, the staccato off-beat chattering
of a signal shutter triggered by professional fingers. Brown had
handed the wheel over to Louki, was morsing back to the harbour entrance, the cold rain lancing palely through the flickering beams of the lamp. The enemy lamp had stopped but now
began again.

'My, they got a lot to say to each other,' Miller said admiringly. 'How long do the exchange of courtesies last, boss?'

'I should say they are just about finished.' Mallory moved
back quickly to the wheelhouse. They were less than a hundred
feet from the harbour entrance. Brown had confused the enemy,
gained precious seconds, more time than Mallory had ever
thought they could gain. But it couldn't last. He touched Brown
on the arm.

'Give her everything you've got when the balloon goes up.'
Two seconds later he was back in position in the bows,
Schmeisser ready in his hands. 'Your big chance, Dan'l Boone.
Don't give the searchlights a chance to line up – they'll blind
you.'

Even as he spoke, the light from the signal lamp at the harbour mouth cut off abruptly and two dazzling white beams, one
from either side of the harbour entrance, stabbed blindingly
through the darkness, bathing the whole harbour in their savage
glare – a glare that lasted for only a fleeting second of time,

yielded to a contrastingly Stygian darkness as two brief bursts of machine-gun fire smashed them into uselessness. From such short range it had been almost impossible to miss.

'Get down, everyone!' Mallory shouted. 'Flat on the deck!'

The echoes of the gunfire were dying away, the reverberations fading along the great sea wall of the fortress when Casey Brown cut in all six cylinders of the engine and opened the throttle wide, the surging roar of the big Diesel blotting out all other sounds in the night. Five seconds, ten seconds, they were passing through the entrance, fifteen, twenty, still not a shot fired, half a minute and they were well clear, bows lifting high out of the water, the deep-dipped stern trailing its long, seething ribbon of phosphorescent white as the engine crescendoed to its clamorous maximum power and Brown pulled the heeling craft sharply round to starboard, seeking the protection of the steep-walled cliffs.

'A desperate battle, boss, but the better men won.' Miller was on his feet now, clinging to a mounted gun for support as the deck canted away beneath his feet. 'My grandchildren shall hear of this.'

'Guards probably all up searching the town. Or maybe there *were* some poor blokes behind these searchlights. Or maybe we just took 'em all by surprise.' Mallory shook his head. 'Anyway you take it, we're just plain damn' lucky.'

He moved aft, into the wheelhouse. Brown was at the wheel, Louki almost crowing with delight.

'That was magnificent, Casey,' Mallory said sincerely. 'A first-class job of work. Cut the engine when we come to the end of the cliffs. Our job's done. I'm going ashore.'

'You don't have to, Major.'

Mallory turned. 'What's that?'

'You don't have to. I tried to tell you on the way down, but you kept telling me to be quiet.' Louki sounded injured, turned to Casey. 'Slow down, please. The last thing Andrea told me, Major, was that we were to come this way. Why do you think he let himself be trapped against the cliffs to the north instead of going out into the country, where he could have hidden easily?'

'Is this true, Casey?' Mallory asked.

'Don't ask me, sir. Those two – they always talk in Greek.'

'Of course, of course.' Mallory looked at the low cliffs close of the starboard beam, barely moving now with the engine shut right down, looked back at Louki. 'Are you quite sure . . .'

He stopped in mid-sentence, jumped out through the wheel-house door. The splash – there had been no mistaking the noise – had come from almost directly ahead. Mallory, Miller by his side, peered into the darkness, saw a dark head surfacing above the water less than twenty feet away, leaned far over with out-stretched arm as the launch slid slowly by. Five seconds later Andrea stood on the deck, dripping mightily and beaming all over his great moon face. Mallory led him straight into the wheelhouse, switched on the soft light of the shaded chart-lamp.

'By all that's wonderful, Andrea, I never thought to see you again. How did it go?'

'I will soon tell you,' Andrea laughed. 'Just after—'

'You've been wounded!' Miller interrupted. 'Your shoulder's kinda perforated.' He pointed to the red stain spreading down the sea-soaked jacket.

'Well, now, I believe I have.' Andrea affected vast surprise. 'Just a scratch, my friend.'

'Oh, sure, sure, just a scratch! It would be the same if your arm had been blown off. Come on down to the cabin – this is just a kindergarten exercise for a man of my medical skill.'

'But the captain—'

'Will have to wait. And your story. Ol' Medicine Man Miller permits no interference with his patients. Come on!'

'Very well, very well,' Andrea said docilely. He shook his head in mock resignation, followed Miller out of the cabin.

Brown opened up to full throttle again, took the launch north almost to Cape Demirci to avoid any hundred to one chance the harbour batteries might make, turned due east for a few miles then headed south into the Maidos Straits. Mallory stood by his side in the wheelhouse, gazing out over the dark, still waters. Suddenly he caught a gleam of white in the distance, touched Brown's arm and pointed for'ard.

'Breakers ahead, Casey, I think. Reefs perhaps?'

Casey looked in long silence, finally shook his head.

'Bow-wave,' he said unemotionally. 'It's the destroyers coming through.'

—— 17 ——

WEDNESDAY NIGHT

MIDNIGHT

Commander Vincent Ryan, RN, Captain (Destroyers) and Commanding Officer of His Majesty's lastest S-class destroyer *Sirdar*, looked round the cramped chart-room and tugged thoughtfully at his magnificent Captain Kettle beard. A scruffier, a more villainous, a more cut and battered-looking bunch of hard cases he had never seen, he reflected, with the possible exception of a Bias Bay pirate crew he had helped round up when a very junior officer on the China Station. He looked at them more closely, tugged his beard again, thought there was more to it than mere scruffiness. He wouldn't care to be given the task of rounding this lot up. Dangerous, highly dangerous, he mused, but impossible to say why, there was only this quietness, this relaxed watchfulness that made him feel vaguely uncomfortable. His 'hatchet-men,' Jensen had called them: Captain Jensen picked his killers well.

'Any of you gentlemen care to go below.' he suggested. 'Plenty of hot water, dry clothes – and warm bunks. We won't be using them tonight.'

'Thank you very much, sir.' Mallory hesitated. 'But we'd like to see this through.'

'Right then, the bridge it is,' Ryan said cheerfully. The *Sirdar* was beginning to pick up speed again, the deck throbbing beneath their feet. 'It is at your own risk, of course.'

'We lead charmed lives,' Miller drawled. 'Nothin' ever happens to us.'

The rain had stopped and they could see the cold twinkling of stars through broadening rifts in the clouds. Mallory looked around him, could see Maidos broad off the port bow and the great bulk of Navarone slipping by to starboard. Aft, about a cable length away, he could just distinguish two other ships, high-curving bow-waves piled whitely against tenebrious silhouettes. Mallory turned to the captain.

'No transports, sir?'

'No transports.' Ryan felt a vague mixture of pleasure and embarrassment that this man should call him 'sir.' 'Destroyers only. This is going to be a smash-and-grab job. No time for dawdlers tonight – and we're behind schedule already.'

'How long to clear the beaches?'

'Half an hour.'

'What! Twelve hundred men?' Mallory was incredulous.

'More.' Ryan sighed. 'Half the ruddy inhabitants want to come with us, too. We could still do it in half an hour, but we'll probably take a bit longer. We'll embark all the mobile equipment we can.'

Mallory nodded, let his eye travel along the slender outlines of the *Sirdar*. 'Where are you going to put 'em all, sir.'

'A fair question,' Ryan admitted. 'Five p.m. on the London Underground will be nothing compared to this little lot. But we'll pack them in somehow.'

Mallory nodded again and looked across the dark waters at Navarone. Two minutes, now, three at the most, and the fortress would open behind that headland. He felt a hand touch his arm, half-turned and smiled down at the sad-eyed little Greek by his side.

'Not long now, Louki,' he said quietly.

'The people, Major,' he murmured. 'The people in the town. Will they be all right?'

'They'll be all right. Dusty says the roof of the cave will go straight up. Most of the stuff will fall into the harbour.'

'Yes, but the boats—?'

'Will you stop worrying! There's nobody aboard them – you know they have to leave at curfew time.' He looked round as someone touched his arm.

'Captain Mallory, this is Lieutenant Beeston, my gunnery officer.' There was a slight coolness in Ryan's voice that made Mallory think that he wasn't overfond of his gunnery officer. 'Lieutenant Beeston is worried.'

'I *am* worried!' The tone was cold, aloof, with an indefinable hint of condescension. 'I understand that you have advised the captain not to offer any resistance?'

'You sound like a BBC communiqué,' Mallory said shortly. 'But you're right. I did say that. You couldn't locate the guns except by searchlight and that would be fatal. Similarily with gunfire.'

'I'm afraid I don't understand.' One could almost see the lift of the eyebrows in the darkness.

'You'd give away your position,' Mallory said patiently. 'They'd nail you first time. Give 'em two minutes and they'd nail you anyway. I have good reason to believe that the accuracy of their gunners is quite fantastic.'

'So has the Navy, Ryan interjected quietly. 'Their third shell got the *Sybaris*'s B magazine.'

'Have you got any idea why this should be, Captain Mallory?' Beeston was quite unconvinced.

'Radar-controlled guns,' Mallory said briefly. 'They have two huge scanners atop the fortress.'

'The *Sirdar* had radar installed last month,' Beeston said stiffly. 'I imagine we could register some hits ourselves if—'

'You could hardly miss.' Miller drawled out the words, the tone dry and provocitive. 'It's a helluva big island, Mac.'

'Who – who are you?' Beeston was rattled. 'What the devil do you mean?'

'Corporal Miller.' The American was unperturbed. 'Must be a very selective instrument, Lootenant, that can pick out a cave in a hundred square miles of rock.'

There was a moment's silence, then Beeston muttered something and turned away.

'You've hurt Guns's feelings, Corporal,' Ryan murmured. 'He's very keen to have a go – but we'll hold our fire. . . . How long till we clear that point, Captain?'

'I'm not sure.' He turned. 'What do you say, Casey?'

'A minute, sir. No more.'

Ryan nodded, said nothing. There was a silence on the bridge, a silence only intensified by the sibilant rushing of the waters, the weird, lonesome pinging of the Asdic. Above, the sky was steadily clearing, and the moon, palely luminous, was struggling to appear through a patch of thinning cloud. Nobody spoke, nobody moved. Mallory was conscious of the great bulk of Andrea beside him, of Miller, Brown and Louki behind. Born in the heart of the country, brought up on the foothills of the Southern Alps, Mallory knew himself as a landsman first and last, an alien to the sea and ships: but he had never felt so much at home in his life, never really known till now what it was to belong. He was more than happy, Mallory thought vaguely to himself, he was content. Andrea and his new friends and the impossible well done – how could a man be but content? They weren't all going home, Andy Stevens wasn't coming with them, but strangely he could feel no sorrow, only a gentle melancholy. . . . Almost as if he had divined what Mallory was thinking, Andrea leaned towards him, towering over him in the darkness.

'He should be here,' he murmured. 'Andy Stevens should be here. That is what you are thinking, is it not?'

Mallory nodded and smiled, and said nothing.

'It doesn't really matter, does it, my Keith?' No anxiety, no questioning, just a statement of fact. 'It doesn't really matter.'

'It doesn't matter at all.'

Even as he spoke, he looked up quickly. A light, a bright orange flame had lanced out from the sheering wall of the fortress; they had rounded the headland and he hadn't even noticed it. There was a whistling roar – Mallory thought incongruously of an express train emerging from a tunnel – directly overhead, and the great shell had crashed into the sea just beyond them. Mallory compressed his lips, unconsciously tightened his clenched fists. It was easy now to see how the *Sybaris* had died.

He could hear the gunnery officer saying something to the captain, but the words failed to register. They were looking at him and he at them and he did not see them. His mind was strangely detached. Another shell, would that be next? Or would the roar of the gunfire of that first shell come echoing across the sea? Or perhaps . . . Once again, he was back in that dark magazine entombed in the rocks, only now he could see men down there, doomed, unknowing men, could see the overhead pulleys swinging the great shells and cartridges towards the well of the lift, could see the shell hoist ascending slowly, the bared, waiting wires less than half an inch apart, the shining, spring-loaded wheel running smoothly down the gleaming rail, the gentle bump as the hoist . . .

A white pillar of flame streaked up hundreds of feet into the night sky as the tremendous detonation tore the heart out of the great fortress of Navarone. No after-fire of any kind, no dark, billowing clouds of smoke, only that one blinding white column that lit up the entire town for a single instant of time, reached up incredibly till it touched the clouds, vanished as if it had never been. And then, by and by, came the shock waves, the solitary thunderclap of the explosion, staggering even at that distance, and finally the deep-throated rumbling as thousands of tons of rock toppled majestically into the harbour – thousands of tons of rock and the two great guns of Navarone.

The rumbling was still in their ears, the echoes fading away far out across the Ægean, when the clouds parted and the moon broke through, a full moon silvering the darkly-rippling waters to starboard, shining iridescently through the spun phosphorescence of the *Sirdar*'s boiling wake. And dead ahead, bathed in the white moonlight, mysterious, remote, the island of Kheros lay sleeping on the surface of the sea.

Where Eagles Dare

ALISTAIR MacLEAN

The vibrating clangour from the four great piston engines set
teeth on edge and made an intolerable assault on cringing eardrums. The decibel-level, Smith calculated, must have been
about that found in a boiler factory, and one, moreover, that
was working on overtime rates, while the shaking cold in that
cramped, instrument-crowded flight-deck was positively Siberian. On balance, he reflected, he would have gone for the
Siberian boiler factory any time because, whatever its draw-
backs, it wasn't liable to fall out of the sky or crash into a mountain-side which, in its present circumstances, seemed a likely
enough, if not imminent contingency for all that the pilot of
their Lancaster bomber appeared to care to the contrary, Smith
looked away from the darkly opaque world beyond the windscreens where the wipers fought a useless battle with the driving
snow and looked again at the man in the left-hand captain's
seat.

Wing Commander Cecil Carpenter was as completely at home
in his environment as the most contented oyster in his shell in
Whitstable Bay. Any comparison with a Siberian boiler factory
he would have regarded as the ravings of an unhinged mind.
Quite clearly, he found the shuddering vibration as soothing as
the ministrations of the gentlest of masseurs, the roar of the
engines positively soporific and the ambient temperature just
right for a man of his leisured literary tastes. Before him, at a
comfortable reading distance, a book rested on a hinged contraption which he had swung out from the cabin's side. From
what little Smith could occasionally see of the lurid cover, de-
picting a blood-stained knife plunged into the back of a girl
who didn't seem to have any clothes on, the Wing Commander
held the more serious contemporary novelists in a fine contempt. He turned a page.

'Magnificent,' he said admiringly. He puffed deeply on an
ancient briar that smelt like a fumigating plant. 'By heavens,
this feller can write. Banned, of course, young Tremayne' –
this to the fresh-faced youngster in the co-pilot's seat – 'so I
can't let you have it till you grow up.' He broke off, fanned the
smoke-laden air to improve the visibility, and peered accusingly

at his co-pilot. 'Flying Officer Tremayne, you have that look of pained apprehension on your face again.'

'Yes, sir. That's to say, no, sir.'

'Part of the malaise of our time,' Carpenter said sorrowfully. 'The young lack so many things, like appreciation of a fine pipe tobacco or faith in their commanding officers.' He sighed heavily, carefully marked the place in his book, folded the rest away and straightened in his seat. 'You'd think a man would be entitled to some peace and quiet on his own flight-deck.'

He slid open his side screen. An icy gust of snow-laden wind blew into the flight-deck, carrying with it the suddenly deepened roar from the engines. Carpenter grimaced and thrust his head outside, shielding his eyes with a gauntleted right hand. Five seconds later he shook his head dispiritedly, screwed his eyes shut as he winced in what appeared to be considerable pain, withdrew his head, closed the screen, brushed the snow away from his flaming red hair and magnificent handlebar moustache, and twisted round to look at Smith.

'It is no small thing, Major, to be lost in a blizzard in the night skies over war-torn Europe.'

'Not again, sir,' Tremayne said protestingly.

'No man is infallible, my son.'

Smith smiled politely. 'You mean you don't know where we are, sir?'

'How should I?' Carpenter slid down in his seat, half-closed his eyes and yawned vastly. 'I'm only the driver. We have a navigator and the navigator has a radar set and I've no faith in either of them.'

'Well, well.' Smith shook his head. 'To think that they lied to me at the Air Ministry. They told me you'd flown some three hundred missions and knew the continent better than any taxi driver knows his London.'

'A foul *canard* put about by unfriendly elements who are trying to prevent me from getting a nice safe job behind a desk in London.' Carpenter glanced at his watch. 'I'll give you exactly thirty minutes' warning before we shove you out over the dropping zone.' A second glance at his watch and a heavy frown. 'Flying Officer Tremayne, your gross dereliction of duty is endangering the entire mission.'

'Sir?' An even deeper apprehension in Tremayne's face.

'I should have had my coffee exactly three minutes ago.'

'Yes, sir. Right away, sir.'

Smith smiled again, straightened from his cramped position

behind the pilots' seats, left the flight-deck and moved aft into the Lancaster's fuselage. Here in this cold, bleak and forbidding compartment, which resembled nothing so much as an iron tomb, the impression of the Siberian boiler factory was redoubled The noise level was so high as to be almost intolerable, the cold was intense and metal-ribbed metal walls, dripping with condensation, made no concessions whatsoever to creature comfort Nor did the six metal-framed canvas seats bolted to the floor, functionalism gone mad. Any attempt to introduce those sadistically designed instruments of torture in HM penitentiaries would have caused a national outcry.

Huddled in those six chairs sat six men, probably, Smith reflected, the six most miserable men he'd ever seen. Like himself, each of the six was dressed in the uniform of the German Alpine Corps. Like himself, each man wore two parachutes. All were shivering constantly, stamping their feet and beating their arms, and their frozen breath hung heavy in the ice-chill air. Facing them, along the upper starboard side of the fuselage, ran a taut metal wire which passed over the top of the doorway. On to this wire were clipped snap-catches, wires from which led down to folded parachutes resting on top of an assortment of variously shaped bundles, the contents of only one of which could be identified by the protruding ends of several pairs of skis.

The nearest parachutist, a dark intense man with Latin features, looked up at Smith's arrival. He had never, Smith thought, seen Edward Carraciola look quite so unhappy.

'Well?' Carraciola's voice was just as unhappy as his face. 'I'll bet he's no more bloody idea where we are than I have.'

'He does seem to navigate his way across Europe by opening his window and sniffing the air from time to time,' Smith admitted. 'But I wouldn't worry—'

He broke off as a sergeant air-gunner entered from the rear, carrying a can of steaming coffee and enamel mugs.

'Neither would I, sir.' The sergeant smiled tolerantly. 'The Wing Commander has his little ways. Coffee, gentlemen? Back at the base he claims that he reads detective novels all the time and depends upon one of the gunners telling him from time to time where we are.'

Smith cradled frozen hands round the coffee mug. 'Do *you* know where we are?'

'Of course, sir.' He seemed genuinely surprised, then nodded to the metal rungs leading to the upper machine-gun turret. 'Just nip up there, sir, and look down to your right.'

Smith lifted an enquiring eyebrow, handed over his mug, climbed the ladder and peered down to his right through the Perspex dome of the turret cupola. For a few seconds only the darkness filled his eyes then gradually, far below and seen dimly through the driving snow, he could make out a ghostly luminescence in the night, a luminescence which gradually resolved itself into a criss-cross pattern of illuminated streets. For a brief moment only Smith's face registered total disbelief then quickly returned to its normal dark stillness.

'Well, well.' He retrieved his coffee. 'Somebody should tell them down there. The lights are supposed to be out all over Europe.'

'Not in Switzerland, sir,' the sergeant explained patiently. 'That's Basle.'

'Basle?' Smith stared at him. 'Basle! Good God, he's gone seventy or eighty miles off course. The flight plan routed us north of Strasbourg.'

'Yes, sir.' The sergeant air-gunner was unabashed. 'The Wing Commander says he doesn't understand flight plans.' He grinned, half apologetically. 'To tell the truth, sir, this is our milk-run into the Vorarlberg. We fly east along the Swiss frontier, then south of Schaffhausen—'

'But that's over Swiss territory!'

'Is it? On a clear night you can see the lights of Zurich. They say Wing Commander Carpenter has a room permamently reserved for him there in the Baur-au-Lac.'

'What?'

'He says if it's a choice between a prisoner-of-war camp in Germany and interment in Switzerland he knows which side of the frontier he's coming down on . . . After that we fly down the Swiss side of Lake Constance, turn east at Lindau, climb to eight thousand to clear the mountains and it's only a hop, skip and jump to the Weissspitze.'

'I see,' Smith said weakly. 'But – don't the Swiss object?'

'Frequently, sir. Their complaints always seem to coincide with the nights we're around those parts. Wing Commander Carpenter claims it's some ill-intentioned Luftwaffe pilot trying to discredit him.'

'What else?' Smith asked, but the sergeant was already on his way to the flight-deck. The Lancaster lurched as it hit an infrequent air pocket, Smith grabbed a rail to steady himself and Lieutenant Morris Schaffer, of the American Office of Strategic Services and Smith's second-in-command, cursed fluently as the better part of a cup of scalding coffee emptied itself over his thigh.

'That's all I need,' he said bitterly. 'I've no morale left. I wish to God we *would* crash-land in Switzerland. Think of all those lovely Wienerschnitzels and Apfelstrudels. After a couple of years living among you Limeys, Spam and powdered eggs and an ounce of margarine a day, that's what Mama Schaffer's little boy requires. Building up.'

'You'd also live a damn' sight longer, friend,' Carraciola observed morosely. He transferred his gaze to Smith, gave him a long considering look. 'The whole set-up stinks, Major.'

'I don't think I understand,' Smith said quietly.

'Suicidal, is what I mean. What a bunch. Just look at us.' He gestured to the three men sitting nearest to him on his left: Olaf Christiansen, a flaxen-haired first cousin of Leif Ericsson, Lee Thomas, a short dark Welshman – both those men seemed slightly amused – and Torrance-Smythe, as languidly aristocratic-looking as any ci-devant French count that ever rode a tumbrel, a doleful ex-Oxford don who clearly wished he were back among the University cloisters. 'Christiansen, Thomas, old Smithy and myself. 'We're just a bunch of civil servants, filing clerks—'

'I know very well what you are,' Smith said quietly.

'Or yourself.' In the de-synchronised thunder of the engines the soft-voiced interruption had gone unnoticed. 'A major in the Black Watch. No doubt you cut quite a dash playing the bagpipes at El Alamein, but why the hell *you* to command us? No offence. But this is no more in your line than it is ours. Or Lieutenant Schaffer here. An airborne cowboy—'

'I hate horses,' Schaffer said loudly. 'That's why I had to leave Montana.'

'Or take George here.' Carraciola jerked a thumb in the direction of the last member of the party, George Harrod, a stocky army sergeant radio-operator with an expression of profound resignation on his face. 'I'll bet he's never as much as made a parachute jump in his life before.'

'I have news for you,' Harrod said stoically. 'I've never even been in a plane before.'

'He's never even been in a plane before,' Carraciola said despairingly. 'My God, what a bunch of no-hopers! All we need is a team composed of specialist Alpinists, Commandos, mountaineers and safe-breakers and what do we have?' He shook his head slowly. 'We have us.'

Smith said gently: 'We were all the Colonel could get. Be fair. He told us yesterday that the one thing in the world that he didn't have was time.'

Carraciola made no reply, none of the others spoke, but Smith didn't have to be any clairvoyant to know what was in the minds of all of them. They were thinking what he was thinking, like himself they were back several hours in time and several hundred miles in space in that Admiralty Operations Room in London where Vice-Admiral Rolland, ostensibly Assistant Director of Naval Operations but in fact the long-serving head of MI6, the counter-espionage branch of the British Secret Service, and his deputy, Colonel Wyatt-Turner, had gravely and reluctantly briefed them on what they had as gravely and reluctantly admitted to be a mission born from the sheerest desperation.

'Deucedly sorry and all that, chaps, but time is of the essence.' Wyatt-Turner, a big, red-faced, heavily moustached colonel, tapped his cane against a wall-map of Germany, pointing to a spot just north of the Austrian border and a little west of Garmisch-Partenkirchen. 'Our man was brought down here at 2 a.m. this morning but SHAEF, in their all-knowing wisdom, didn't let us know until 10 a.m. Damned idiots! Damned idiots for not letting us know until so late and double-damned idiots for ignoring our advice in the first place. Gad, will they never learn to listen to us?' He shook his head in anger, tapped the map again. 'Anyway, he's here. Schloss Adler. The castle of the eagle. Believe me, it's well named, only an eagle could get there. Our job—'

Smith said: 'How are you so sure he's there, sir?'

'We're sure. Mosquito he was in crash-landed only ten miles away. The pilot got off a radio message just before a German patrol closed in.' He paused, smiled grimly, continued: 'Schloss Adler, Major Smith, is the combined HQ of the German Secret Service and the Gestapo in South Germany. Where else would they take him?'

'Where indeed? How was he brought down, sir?'

'Through the most damnable ill-luck. We carried out a saturation raid on Nürnberg last night and there shouldn't have been a German fighter within a hundred miles of the Austrian border. But a wandering Messerschmidtt patrol got

532

him. That's unimportant. What's important is getting him out before he talks.'

'He'll talk,' Thomas said sombrely. 'They all do. *Why* did they disregard our advice, sir? We told them two days ago.'

'The whys don't matter,' Wyatt-Turner said tiredly. 'Not any more. The fact that he'll talk does. So we get him out. *You* get him out.'

Torrance-Smythe cleared his throat delicately. 'There are paratroops, sir.'

'Scared, Smithy?'

'Naturally, sir.'

'The Schloss Adler is inaccessible and impregnable. It would require a battalion of paratroops to take it.'

'Of course,' Christiansen said, 'the fact that there's no time to mount a massed paratroop attack has no bearing on the matter.' Christiansen appeared positively cheerful, the proposed operation obviously appealed vastly to him.

Wyatt-Turner gave him the benefit of his icy blue stare then decided to ignore him.

'Secrecy and stealth are the only hope,' he went on. 'And you gentlemen are – I trust – secretive and stealthy. You are experts at that and experts at survival behind enemy lines where all of you have spent considerable periods of time, Major Smith, Lieutenant Schaffer and Sergeant Harrod here in their professional capacities, the rest of you in – um – other duties. With the—'

'That was a damned long time ago, sir,' Carraciola interrupted. 'At least for Smithy, Thomas, Christiansen and myself. We're out of touch now. We don't know the latest developments in weapons and combat techniques. And God only knows we're out of training. After a couple of years behind a desk it takes me all my time to run fifty yards after a bus.'

'You'll have to get fit fast, won't you?' Wyatt-Turner said coldly. 'Besides, what matters most is, that with the exception of Major Smith, you all have an extensive knowledge of Western Europe. You all speak fluent German. You'll find your combat training – on the level you'll be engaged in – as relevant today as it was five years ago. You are men with exceptional records of resourcefulness, ability and ingenuity. If anyone has a chance, you have. You're all volunteers, of course.'

'Of course,' Carraciola echoed, his face carefully deadpan. Then he looked speculatively at Wyatt-Turner. 'There is, of course, another way, sir.' He paused, then went on very quietly indeed. 'A way with a hundred per cent guarantee of success.'

'Neither Admiral Rolland nor I claim to be infallible,' Wyatt-Turner said slowly. 'We have missed an alternative? You have the answer to our problems?'

'Yes. Whistle up a Pathfinder squadron of Lancasters with 10-ton blockbuster bombs. Do *you* think *anyone* in the Schloss Adler would ever talk again?'

'I don't think so.' Admiral Rolland spoke gently and for the first time, moving from the wall-map to join the group. Admiral Rolland always spoke gently. When you wielded the almost incredible range of power that he did, you didn't have to talk loudly to make yourself heard. He was a short, grey-haired man, with a deeply trenched face and an air of immense authority. 'No,' he repeated, 'I don't think so. Nor do I think that your grasp of the realities of the situation is any match for your total ruthlessness. The captured man, Lieutenant General Carnaby, is an American. If we were to destroy him General Eisenhower would probably launch his Second Front against us instead of against the Germans.' He smiled deprecatingly, as though to remove rebuke from his voice. 'There are certain – um – niceties to be observed in our relationship with out Allies. Wouldn't you agree?'

Carraciola didn't agree or disagree. He had, apparently, nothing to say. Neither did anyone else. Colonel Wyatt-Turner cleared his throat.

'That's it then, gentlemen. Ten o'clock tonight at the airfield. No more questions, I take it?'

'Yes, sir, there bloody well is, begging the Colonel's pardon, sir.' Sergeant George Harrod not only sounded heated, he looked it, too. 'What's all this about? Why's this geezer so bloody important? Why the hell do we have to risk our necks—'

'That'll do, Sergeant.' Wyatt-Turner's voice was sharp, authoritative. 'You know all you require to know—'

'If we're sending a man to what may be his death, Colonel, I think he has the right to know why,' Admiral Rolland interrupted gently, almost apologetically. 'The rest know. He should too. It's painfully simple, Sergeant. General Carnaby is the overall co-ordinator of planning for the exercise known as Operation Overlord – the Second Front. It would be absolutely true to say that he knows more about the Allied preparations for the Second Front than any man alive.

'He set off last night to meet his opposite numbers in the

Middle East, Russia and the Italian Front to co-ordinate final plans for the invasion of Europe. The rendezvous was in Crete – the only meeting point the Russians would accept. They haven't a plane fast enough to out-run the German fighters. The British Mosquito can – but it didn't last night.'

Silence lay heavy in the austere operations room. Harrod rubbed his hand across his eyes, then shook his head slowly, as if to clear it. When he spoke again all the truculence, all the anger had vanished from his voice. His words came very slowly.

'And if the General talks—'

'He'll talk,' Rolland said. The voice was soft, but it carried total conviction. 'As Mr Thomas has just said, they all talk. He won't be able to help himself. A mixture of mescalin and scopolamine.'

'And he'll tell them all the plans for the Second Front.' The words came as from a man in a dream. 'When, where, how – Good God, sir, we'll have to call the whole thing off!'

'Precisely. We call it off. No Second Front this year. Another nine months on the war, another million lives needlessly lost. You understand the urgency, Sergeant, the sheer desperate urgency of it all?'

'I understand, sir. Now I understand.' Harrod turned to Wyatt-Turner. 'Sorry I spoke like that, sir. I'm afraid – well, I'm a bit edgy, sir.'

'We're all a bit edgy, Sergeant. Well, the airfield at ten o'clock and we'll check the equipment.' He smiled without humour. 'I'm afraid the uniforms may not fit too well. This is early closing day in Savile Row.'

Sergeant Harrod huddled more closely into his bucket seat, beat freezing hands against freezing shoulders, morosely surveyed his uniform, wrinkled like an elephant's legs and about three sizes too big for him, then raised his voice above the clamour of the Lancaster's engines.

'Well,' he said bitterly, 'he was right about the bloody uniforms, anyway.'

'And wrong about everything else,' Carraciola said heavily. 'I still say we should have sent in the Lancasters.'

Smith, still standing against the starboard fuselage, lit a cigarette and eyed him speculatively. He opened his mouth to speak when it occurred to him that he had seen men in more receptive mood. He looked away without saying anything.

In the flight-deck, now slid so impossibly far forward in his seat that the back of his head rested on the back of his seat, Wing Commander Carpenter was still deeply and contentedly preoccupied with pipe, coffee and literature. Beside him, Flying Officer Tremayne was obviously failing to share his mood of pleasureable relaxation. He was, in fact, keeping a most anxious watch, his eyes constantly shifting from the instrument panel to the opaque darkness beyond the windscreen to the recumbent figure of his superior officer who appeared to be in danger of dropping off to sleep at any moment. Suddenly Tremayne sat far forward in his seat, stared for long seconds through the windscreen ahead of him then turned excitedly to Carpenter.

'There's Schaffhausen down there, sir!'

Carpenter groaned heavily, closed his book, swung back the hinged book-rest, finished his coffee, levered himself upright with another groan, slid open his side-screen and made an elaborate pretence of examining the loom of light far below, without, however, actually going to the lengths of exposing his face to the wind and the driving snow outside. He closed the screen and looked at Tremayne.

'By heavens,' he said admiringly, 'I believe you're right. It's a great comfort to have you along, my boy, a great comfort.' He switched on the intercom while Tremayne looked suitably abashed. 'Major Smith? Yes. Thirty minutes to go.' He switched off and turned again to Tremayne. 'Right. South-east down the old Bodensee. And for God's sake keep to the Swiss side.'

Smith hung up the headphones and looked quizzically at the six seated men.

'That's it, then. Half an hour. Let's hope it's warmer down there than it is up here.'

No one had any comment to make on that. No one seemed to have any hope either. Soundlessly, wordlessly, they looked without expression at one another, then pulled themselves stiffly to their frozen feet. Then very slowly, very awkwardly, their numbed hands and cramped conditions making things almost impossibly awkward for them, they prepared themselves for the drop. They helped each other strap loads on their backs, beneath the high-mounted parachutes, then struggled into their white waterproof snow trousers. Sergeant Harrod went one better. He pulled a voluminous snow-smock over his head, zipped it up with difficulty and drew the hood over his head. He turned round questioningly as a hand tapped the hummocked outline below his white smock.

'I hardly like to say this,' Schaffer said diffidently, 'but I really don't reckon your radio is going to stand the shock of landing, Sergeant.'

'Why not?' Harrod looked more lugubrious than ever. 'It's been done before.'

'Not by you, it hasn't. By my reckoning you're going to hit the ground with a terminal velocity of a hundred and eighty miles an hour. Not to put too fine a point on it, I think you're going to experience some difficulty in opening your chute.'

Harrod looked at him, looked at his other five smockless companions, then nodded slowly and touched his own smock.

'You mean I put this on *after* we reach the ground?'

'Well,' Schaffer said consideringly, 'I really think it would help.' He grinned at Harrod, who grinned back almost cheerfully. Even Carraciola's lips twitched in the beginnings of a smile. The release of tension within that frozen fuselage was almost palpable.

'Well, well, time I earned my wing-commander's pay while you stripling pilots sit and gaze in rapt admiration.' Carpenter studied his watch. 'Two fifteen. Time we changed places.'

Both men unhooked their safety belts and awkwardly changed over. Carpenter fastidiously adjusted the right-hand seat's back rest until it was exactly right for him, manœuvered his parachute to its position of maximum comfort, fastened his seat-belt, unhooked and adjusted on his head a combined earphones and microphone set and made a switch.

'Sergeant Johnson?' Carpenter never bothered with the regulation call-up formalities. 'Are you awake?'

Back in the navigator's tiny and extremely uncomfortable recess, Sergeant Johnson was very much awake. He had been awake for hours. He was bent over a glowing greenish radar screen, his eyes leaving it only to make rapid reference to the charts, an Ordnance map, a picture and a duplicate compass, altimeter and air-speed indicator. He reached for the switch by his side.

'I'm awake, sir.'

'If you fly us into the side of the Weissspitze,' Carpenter said threateningly, 'I'll have you reduced to aircraftman. Aircraftman second class, Johnson.'

'I wouldn't like that. I make it nine minutes, sir.'

'For once we're agreed on something. So do I.' Carpenter switched off, slid open the starboard screen and peered out. Although there was just the faintest wash of moonlight in the night

537

sky, visibility might as well have been zero. It was a greyly opaque world, a blind world, with nothing to be seen but the thinly driving snow. He withdrew his head, brushed away the snow from his huge moustache, closed the screen, looked regretfully at his pipe and carefully put it away in his pocket.

For Tremayne, the stowage of the pipe was the final proof that the Wing Commander was clearing the decks for action. He said unhappily: 'A bit dicey, isn't it, sir? Locating the Weissspitze in this lot, I mean?'

'Dicey?' Carpenter sounded almost jovial. 'Dicey? I don't see why? It's as big as a mountain. In fact, it *is* a mountain. We can't miss it, my dear boy.'

'That's what I mean.' He paused, a pause with more meaning in it. 'And this plateau on the Weissspitze that we have to drop them on. Only three hundred yards wide, sir. Mountain above it, cliff below it. And those adiabatic mountain winds, or whatever you call them, blowing in any old unpredictable direction. A fraction to the south and we'll hit the mountain, a fraction to the north and they'll fall down that whacking great cliff and like as not all break their necks. Three hundred yards!'

'What do you want?' Carpented demanded expansively. 'Heathrow Airport? Three hundred yards? All the room in the world, my boy. We land this old crate on runways a tenth of that width.'

'Yes, sir. I've always found runway landing lights a great help, sir. At seven thousand feet up the side of the Weissspitze—'

He broke off as a buzzer rang. Carpenter made a switch. 'Johnson?'

'Yes, sir.' Johnson was huddled more closely than ever over his radar screen where the revolving scanner-line had picked up a white spot immediately to the right of centre of the screen. 'I have it, sir. Right where it should be.' He looked away from the screen and made a quick check on the compass. 'Course oh-nine-three, sir.'

'Good lad.' Carpenter smiled at Tremayne, made a tiny course alteration and began to whistle softly to himself. 'Have a look out your window, laddie. My moustache is beginning to get all waterlogged.'

Tremayne opened his window, strained his head as far as possible, but still there was only this grey and featurelesss opacity. He withdrew his head, silently shook it.

'No matter. It must be there somewhere,' Carpenter said

reasonably. He spoke into the intercom. 'Sergeant? Five minutes. Hook up.'

'Hook up!' The sergeant air-gunner repeated the order to the seven men standing in line along the starboard side of the fuselage. 'Five minutes.'

Silently they clipped their parachute snap catches on to the overhead wire, the sergeant air-gunner carefully checking each catch. Nearest the door and first man to jump was Sergeant Harrod. Behind him stood Lieutenant Schaffer whose experience with the OSS had made him by far the most experienced parachutist of the group and whose unenviable task it was to keep an eye on Harrod. He was followed by Carraciola, then Smith – as leader he preferred to be in the middle of the group – then Christiansen, Thomas and Torrance-Smythe. Behind Torrance-Smythe two young aircraftmen stood ready to slide packaged equipment and parachutes along the wire and heave them out as swiftly as possible after the last man had jumped. The sergeant air-gunner took up position by the door. The tension was back in the air again.

Twenty-five feet forward of where they were standing, Carpenter slid open his side screen for the fifth time in as many minutes. The now downward drooping moustache had lost much of its splendid panache but the Wing Commander had obviously decided that there were more urgent considerations in life than waterlogged moustaches. He was wearing goggles now, continuously brushing away snow and moisture with a chamois leather, but the view ahead – or lack of view – remained obstinately the same, still that greyly driving snow looming out of and vanishing into that greyly impenetrable opacity, still nothingness. He closed the screen.

A call-up buzzer rang. Carpenter made a switch, listened, nodded.

'Three minutes,' he said to Tremayne. 'Oh-nine-two.'

Tremayne made the necessary minute course adjustment. He no longer looked through the side-screen, he no longer even looked at the screen ahead of him. His whole being was concentrated upon flying that big bomber, his all-exclusive attention, his total concentration, on three things only: the compass, the altimeter, and Carpenter. A degree too far to the south and the Lancaster would crash into the side of the Weissspitze: a couple of hundred feet too low and the same thing would happen: a missed signal from Carpenter and the mission was over before it had begun. The young, the absurdly young face was expressionless, the body immobile as he piloted the Lancaster with a hair-trigger precision that he had never before achieved. Only his eyes moved, in a regular, rhythmic, unvarying pattern: the compass, the altimeter, Carpenter, the compass, the altimeter, Carpenter: and never longer than a second on each.

Again Carpenter slid open his side-screen and peered out. Again he had the same reward, the opacity, the grey nothingness. With his head still outside he lifted his left hand, palm downwards, and made a forward motion. Instantly Tremayne's hand fell on the throttle levers and eased them forward. The roar of the big engines died away to a more muted thunder.

Carpenter withdrew his head. If he was concerned, no trace of it showed in his face. He resumed his soft whistling, calmly, almost leisurely, scanned the instrument panel, then turned his head to Tremayne. He said conversationally:

'When you were in flying school, ever hear tell of a strange phenomenon known as stalling speed?'

Tremayne started, glanced hurriedly at the instrument panel and quickly gave a fraction more power to the engines. Carpenter smiled, looked at his watch and pressed a buzzer twice.

The bell rang above the head of the sergeant air-gunner standing by the fuselage door. He looked at the tense, expectant faces before him and nodded.

'Two minutes, gentlemen.'

He eased the door a few inches to test whether it was moving freely. With the door only fractionally open the suddenly deepened roar from the engines was startling but nowhere nearly as dismaying as the snow-laden gust of icy wind that whistled into the fuselage. The parachutists exchanged carefully expressionless glances, glances correctly interpreted by the sergeant who closed the door and nodded again.

'I agree, gentlemen. No night for man nor beast.'

Wing Commander Carpenter, his head once again poked through the side-screen, didn't think so either. Five seconds' exposure to that arctic wind and driving snow and your face was full of porcupine quills: fifteen seconds and the totally numbed skin conveyed no sensation at all, it was when you withdrew your head and waited for the exquisite pain of returning circulation that the fun really started: but this time Carpenter was determined not to withdraw his head until he had complete justification for doing so: and the only justification would be the sighting of the Weissspitze. Mechanically, industriously, he rubbed the chamois leather across his goggles, stared unblinkingly into the greyly swirling gloom and hoped that he saw the Weissspitze before the Weissspitze saw him.

Inside, Tremayne's eyes continued on their rhythmic, unvarying pattern of movement: the compass, the altimeter, Carpenter, the compass, the altimeter, Carpenter. But now his gaze was resting fractionally longer on Carpenter each time, waiting for the sudden signal that would galvanise him into throwing the big Lancaster into a violent bank to port, the only avoiding action they could possibly take. Carpenter's left hand was moving, but he wasn't giving any signal, the fingers of his left hand were drumming gently on his knee. This, Tremayne suddenly and incredulously realized, was probably the highest state of excitement that Carpenter was capable of achieving.

Ten seconds passed. Five. And another five. Tremayne was conscious that, even in that ice-cold cabin, the sweat was pouring down his face. The urge to pull the bomber away to the left, to avoid the shattering, annihilating collision that could be only seconds away now, was almost overpowering. He was aware of a fear, a fear bordering on a reason-abdicating panic, such as he had never previously guessed at, let alone experienced. And then he became aware of something else. Th drumming of Carpenter's left fingers had abruply ceased.

Carpenter had it now. It was more imagined than real, more guessed at than seen, but he had it now. Then gradually, almost imperceptibly, ahead and a little to the right of the direction of flight, he became aware of something more solidly tangible than wishful thinking beginning to materialise out of the nothingness. And then, suddenly, it wasn't materialising any more, it was solidly, unmistakably there, the smooth, unbroken side of an almost vertically towering mountain soaring up at a dizzy 80° until it vanished in the grey darkness above. Carpenter withdrew his head, leaving the screen open this time, and pressed his head-switch.

'Sergeant Johnson?' The words came out stiffly, mechanically, not because of any crisis of emotion that the Wing Commander was passing through but because his entire face, lips included, was so frozen that he could no longer articulate properly.

'Sir?' Johnson's voice over the intercom was disembodied, empty, but even the metallic impersonality of that single word could not disguise the bow-taut tension behind it.

Carpenter said: 'I think Flying Officer Johnson a much nicer name.'

'Sir?'

'Relax. I have it. You can go back to sleep.' He switched off, took a quick look through the side-screen, reached up and touched an overhead switch.

Above the starboard door in the fuselage, a red light came on. The sergeant air-gunner laid his hand on the door.

'One minute, gentlemen.' He jerked the door wide open, securing it on its standing latch, and a miniature blizzard howled into the belly of the Lancaster. 'When the red light turns green—'

He left the sentence unfinished, partly because those few words were crystal clear in themselves, partly because he had to shout so loudly to make himself heard over the combined roar of wind and engines that any superfluity of words was only that much wasted effort.

No one else said anything, mainly because of the near impossibility of making oneself heard. In any event, the parachutists' silently exchanged glances conveyed more eloquently than words the very obvious thought that was in the minds of all of them: if it was like that inside, what the hell was it like outside? At a gesture from the sergeant, they moved up in line to the open door. Sergeant Harrod in the lead. On his face was the expression of a Christian martyr meeting his first and last lion.

The Lancaster, like some great black pterodactyl from out of the primeval past, roared on through the driving snow alongside the smoothly precipitous side of the Weissspitze. That sheer wall of ice-encrusted rock seemed very close indeed. Tremayne was convinced that it was impossibly close. He stared through the still open screen by Carpenter's head and would have sworn that the starboard wing-tip must be brushing the side of the mountain. Tremayne could still feel the sweat that bathed his face but his lips were as dry as ashes. He licked them, surreptitiously, so that Carpenter would not see him, but it didn't do any good at all: as dry as ashes they remained.

Sergeant Harrod's lips weren't dry, but that was only because his face was taking the full brunt of the horizontally driving snowstorm that lashed along the bomber's fuselage. Otherwise, he shared Tremayne's sentiments and apprehensions to a very marked degree. He stood in the doorway, gripping the fuselage on each side to hold him in position against the gale of wind, his storm-lashed face showing no fear, just a peculiarly resigned expression. His eyes were turned to the left, looking forward with an almost hypnotised fixity at that point in space where it seemed that at any second now the starboard wing-tip must strike against the Weissspitze.

Inside the fuselage, the red lamp still burned. The sergeant air-gunner's hand fell on Harrod's shoulder in an encouraging gesture. It took Harrod all of three seconds to free himself from his thrall-like fixation with that starboard wing-tip and take a half step back inside. He reached up and firmly removed the sergeant's hand.

'Don't shove, mate.' He had to shout to make himself heard. 'If I'm to commit suicide, let me do it in the old-fashioned way. By my own hand.' He again took up position by the open door.

At the same instant Carpenter took a last quick look through the side-screen and made the gesture that Tremayne had been waiting for, been praying for, a slight turning motion of the left hand. Quickly Tremayne banked the big bomber, as quickly straightened up again.

Slowly, the mountain-side fell away. The mountain-brushing episode had been no mere bravado or folly, Carpenter had been deliberately lining up for his pre-determined course across the narrow plateau. Once again, and for the last time, he had his head outside, while his left hand slowly – interminably slowly, it seemed to Tremayne – reached up for the button on the bulk-head above the screen, located it, paused, then pressed it.

Sergeant Harrod, head craned back at a neck-straining angle, saw the red light turn to green, brought his head down, screwed shut his eyes and, with a convulsive jerk of his arms, launched himself out into the snow and the darkness, not a very expert launching, for instead of jumping out he had stepped out and was already twisting in mid-air as the parachute opened. Schaffer was the next to go, smoothly, cleanly, feet and knees together, then Carraciola followed by Smith.

Smith glanced down below him and his lips tightened. Just dimly visible in the greyness beneath, Harrod, a very erratic human pendulum, was swinging wildly across the sky. The parachute cords were already badly twisted and his clumsily desperate attempts to untwist them resulted only in their becoming more entangled than ever. His left-hand cords were pulled too far down, air was spilling from the parachute, and, still swaying madly, he was side-slipping to his left faster than any man Smith had even seen side-slip a parachute before. Smith stared after the rapidly disappearing figure and hoped to God that he didn't side-slip his way right over the edge of the precipice.

Grim-faced, he stared upwards to see how the others had fared. Thank God, there was no worry there. Christiansen, Thomas and Smithy all there, so close as to be almost touching, all making perfectly normal descents.

Even before the last of the parachutists, Torrance-Smythe, had cleared the doorway, the sergeant air-gunner was running towards the after end of the fuselage. Swiftly he flung aside a packing-case, dragging a tarpaulin away, reached down and pulled a huddled figure upright. A girl, quite small, with wide dark eyes and delicate features. One would have looked for the figure below to be as petite as the features, but it was enveloped in bulky clothes over which had been drawn a snow-suit. Over the snow-suit she wore a parachute. She was almost numb with cold and cramp but the sergeant had his orders.

'Come on, Miss Ellison.' His arm round her waist, he moved quickly towards the doorway. 'Not a second to lose.'

He half led, half carried her there, where an aircraftman was just heaving the second last parachute and container through the doorway. The sergeant snapped the parachute catch on to the wire. Mary Ellison half-turned as if to speak to him, then turned away abruptly and dropped into the darkness. The last parachute and container followed at once.

For a long moment the sergeant stared down into the darkness. Then he rubbed his chin with the palm of his hand, shook his head in disbelief, stepped back and pulled the heavy door to. The Lancaster, its four engines still on reduced power, droned on into the snow and the night. Almost immediately, it was lost to sight and, bare seconds later, the last faint throb of its engines died away in the darkness.

2

Smith reached his hands far up into the parachute shrouds, hauled himself sharply upwards and made a perfect knees-bent, feet-together landing in about two feet of snow. The wind tugged fiercely at his parachute. He struck the quick release harness clasp, collapsed the parachute, pulled it in, rolled it up and pressed it deeply into the snow, using for weight the pack he had just shrugged off his shoulders.

Down there at ground level – if seven thousand feet up on the Weissspitze could be called ground level – the snowfall was comparatively slight compared to that blizzard they'd experienced jumping from the Lancaster but, even so, visibility was almost as bad as it had been up above, for there was a twenty-knot wind blowing and the dry powdery snow was drifting quite heavily. Smith made a swift 360° sweep of his horizon but there was nothing to be seen, nobody to be seen.

With fumbling frozen hands he clumsily extracted a torch and whistle from his tunic. Facing alternately east and west, he bleeped on the whistle and flashed his torch. The first to appear was Thomas, then Schaffer, then, with two minutes altogether, all of the others with the exception of Sergeant Harrod.

'Pile your chutes there and weight them,' Smith ordered. 'Yes, bed them deep. Anyone seen Sergeant Harrod?' A shaking of heads. 'Nobody? No sight of him at all?'

'Last I saw of him,' Schaffer said, 'he was going across my bows like a destroyer in a heavy sea.

'I saw a bit of that,' Smith nodded. 'The shrouds were twisted?'

'Put a corkscrew to shame. But I'd have said there was no danger of the chute collapsing. Not enough time. We were almost on the ground before I lost sight of him.'

'Any idea where he landed, then?'

'Roughly. He'll be all right, Major. A twisted ankle, a bump on the head. Not to worry.'

'Use your torches, Smith said abruptly. 'Spread out. Find him.'

With two men on one side of him, three on the other, all within interlocking distance of their torch beams, Smith searched through the snow, his flash-light raking the ground ahead of him. If he shared Schaffer's optimism about Harrod, his face didn't show it. It was set and grim. Three minutes passed and then came a shout from the right. Smith broke into a run.

Carraciola it was who had called and was now standing at the farther edge of a wind-swept outcrop of bare rock, his torch shining downwards and slightly ahead. Beyond the rock the ground fell away abruptly to a depth of several feet and in this lee a deep drift had formed. Half-buried in its white depths, Sergeant Harrod lay spread-eagled on his back, his feet almost touching the rock, his face upturned to the falling snow, his eyes open. He did not seem to notice the snow falling on his eyes.

They were all there now, staring down at the motionless man. Smith jumped down into the drift, dropped to his knees, slid an arm under Harrod's shoulders and began to lift him to a sitting position. Harrod's head lolled back like that of a broken rag doll. Smith lowered him back into the snow and felt for the pulse in the throat. Still kneeling, Smith straightened, paused for a moment with bent head then climbed wearily to his feet.

'Dead?' Carraciola asked.

'He's dead. His neck is broken. Smith's face was without expression. 'He must have got caught up in the shrouds and made a bad landing.'

'It happens,' Schaffer said. 'I've known it happen.' A long pause, then: 'Shall I take the radio, sir?'

Smith nodded. Schaffer dropped to his knees and began to fumble for the buckle of the strap securing the radio to Harrod's back.

Smith said: 'Sorry, no, not that way. There's a key around his neck, under his tunic. It fits the lock under the flap of the breast buckle.'

Schaffer located the key, unlocked the buckle after some difficulty, eased the straps off the dead man's shoulders and finally managed to work the radio clear. He rose to his feet, the radio dangling from his hand, and looked at Smith.

'Second thoughts, what's the point. Any fall hard enough to break his neck wouldn't have done the innards of this radio any good.'

Wordlessly, Smith took the radio, set it on the rock, extended the antenna, set the switch to 'Transmit', and cranked the call-up handle. The red tell-tale glowed, showing the transmission circuit to be in order. Smith turned the switch to receive, turned up the volume, moved the tuning knob, listened briefly to some static-laden music, closed up the radio set and handed it back to Schaffer.

'It made a better landing than Sergeant Harrod,' Smith said briefly. 'Come on.

'We bury him, Major?' Carraciola asked.

'No need.' Smith shook his head and gestured with his torch at the drifting snow. 'He'll be buried within the hour. Let's find the supplies.'

'Now, for God's sake don't lose your grip!' Thomas said urgently.

'That's the trouble with you Celts,' Schaffer said reprovingly. 'No faith in anyone. There is no cause for alarm. Your life is in the safe hands of Schaffer and Christiansen. Not to worry.'

'What else do you think I'm worrying about?'

'If we all start sliding,' Schaffer said encouragingly, 'we won't let you go until the last possible minute.'

Thomas gave a last baleful glance over his shoulder and then began to edge himself out over the black lip of the precipice. Schaffer and Christiansen had an ankle apiece, and they in turn were anchored by the others. As far as the beam of Thomas's torch could reach, the cliff stretching down into the darkness was absolutely vertical, black naked rock with the only fissures in sight blocked with ice and with otherwise never a hand- or foot-hold.

'I've seen all I want to,' he said over his shoulder. They pulled him back and he edged his way carefully up to their supply pile before getting to his feet. He prodded the pack with the skis protruding from one end.

'Very handy,' he said morosely. 'Oh, very handy for this lot indeed.'

'As steep as that?' Smith asked.

'Vertical. Smooth as glass and you can't see the bottom. How deep do you reckon it is, Major?'

'Who knows?' Smith shrugged. 'We're seven thousand feet up. Maps never give details at this altitude. Break out that nylon.'

The proper supply pack was located and the nylon produced, one thousand feet of it coiled inside a canvas bag as it had come from the makers. It had very little more diameter than a clothes line but its wire core made it immensely strong and every yard of it had been fully tested to its rated breaking strain – its actual breaking strain was much higher – before leaving the factory. Smith tied a hammer to one end, and with two of the men holding him securely, paid it out over the edge, counting his arm spans as he let it go. Several times the hammer snagged on some unseen obstruction but each time Smith managed to swing it free. Finally the rope went completely slack and, despite all Smith's efforts, it remained that way.

'Well.' Smith moved back from the edge. 'That seems to be about it.'

'And if it isn't, hey?' Christiansen asked. 'If it's caught on a teensy-weensy ledge a thousand feet above damn all?'

'I'll let you know,' Smith said shortly.

'You measured it off,' Carraciola said. 'How deep?'

'Two hundred feet.'

'Eight hundred feet left, eh?' Thomas grinned. 'We'll need it all to tie up the garrison of the Schloss Adler.'

No one was amused. Smith said: 'I'll need a piton and two walkie-talkies.'

Fifteen feet back from the edge of the cliff they cleared away the snow and hammered an angled piton securely into the bare rock. Smith made a double bowline at one end of the nylon, slipped his legs through the loops, unclasped his belt then fastened it tightly round both himself and the rope and slipped a walkie-talkie over his shoulder. The rope was then passed round the piton and three men, backs to the cliff, wrapped it round their hands and prepared to take the weight. Schaffer stood by with the other walkie-talkie.

Smith checked that there were no sharp or abrasive edges on the cliff-top, wriggled cautiously over and gave the signal to be lowered. The descent itself was simple. As Thomas had said, it was a vertical drop and all he had to do was to fend himself off from the face as the men above paid out the rope. Once only, passing an overhang, he spun wildly in space, but within ten seconds regained contact with the rock face again. Mountaineering made easy, Smith thought. Or it seemed easy: perhaps, he thought wryly, it was as well that he couldn't see what stretched beneath him.

His feet passed through eighteen inches of snow and rested on solid ground. He flashed his torch in a semi-circle, from cliff wall to cliff wall. If it was a ledge, it was a very big one for, as far as his eye and torch could reach, it appeared to be a smooth plateau sloping gently outwards from the cliff. The cliff wall itself was smooth, unbroken, except for one shallow fissure, a few feet wide, close by to where he stood. He climbed out of the double bowline and made the switch on the walkie-talkie.

'OK so far. Haul up the rope. Supplies first, then yourselves.'

The rope snaked upwards into the darkness. Within five minutes all the equipment had been lowered in two separate loads. Christiansen appeared soon afterwards.

'What's all the fuss about this Alpine stuff, then?' he asked cheerfully. 'My grandmother could do it.'

'Maybe we should have brought your grandmother along instead,' Smith said sourly. 'We're not down yet. Take your torch and find out how big this ledge is and the best way down and for God's sake don't go falling over any precipices.'

Christiansen grinned and moved off. Life was for the living and Christiansen gave the impression of a man thoroughly enjoying himself. While he was away reconnoitring, all the others came down in turn until only Schaffer was left. His plaintive voice came over the walkie-talkie.

'And how am I supposed to get down? Hand over hand for two hundred feet? Frozen hand over frozen hand for two hundred feet on a rope this size? You'd better stand clear. Somebody should have thought of this.'

'Somebody did,' Smith said patiently. 'Make sure the rope is still round the piton then kick the other eight hundred feet over the edge.'

'There's always an answer.' Schaffer sounded relieved.

They had just lowered him to the ground when Christiansen returned.

'It's not so bad,' he reported. 'There's another cliff ahead of us, maybe fifty yards away, curving around to the east. At least I think it's a cliff. I didn't try to find out how deep or how steep. I'm married. But the plateau falls away gently to the west there. Seems it might go on a fair way. Trees, too. I followed the line of them for two hundred yards.'

'Trees? At this altitude?'

'Well, no masts for a tall ship. Scrub pine. They'll give shelter, hiding.'

'Fair enough,' Smith nodded. 'We'll bivouac there.'

'So close?' The surprised tone in Schaffer's voice showed that he didn't think much of the idea. 'Shouldn't we get as far down this mountain as possible tonight, Major?'

'No need. If we start at first light we'll be well below the main tree line by dawn.'

'I agree with Schaffer,' Carraciola said reasonably. 'Let's get as much as we can behind us. What do you think, Olaf?' This to Christiansen.

'It doesn't matter what Christiansen thinks.' Smith's voice was quiet but cold as the mountain air itself. 'Nor you, Carraciola. This isn't a round-table seminar, it's a military operation. Military operations have leaders. Like it or not, Admiral Rolland put me in charge. We stay here tonight. Get the stuff across.'

The five men looked speculatively at one another, then

stooped to lift the supplies. There was no longer any question as to who was in charge.

'We pitch the tents right away, boss?' Schaffer asked.

'Yes.' In Schaffer's book, Smith reflected, 'boss' was probably a higher mark of respect than either 'Major' or 'sir'. 'Then hot food, hot coffee and a try for London on the radio. Haul that rope down, Christiansen. Come the dawn, we don't want to start giving heart attacks to any binocular-toting characters in the Schloss Adler.'

Christiansen nodded, began to haul on the rope. As the free end rose into the air, Smith gave a shout, jumped towards Christiansen and caught his arm. Christiansen, startled, stopped pulling and looked round.

'Jesus!' Smith drew the back of his hand across his forehead. 'That was a close one.'

'What's up?' Schaffer asked quickly.

'Two of you. Hoist me up. Quickly! Before that damn rope disappears.'

Two of them hoisted him into the air. Smith reached up and caught the dangling end of the rope, dropped to earth, taking the rope with him and then very carefully, very securely, tied it to the other end of the rope.

'Now that you've *quite* finished—' Torrance-Smyth said politely.

'The radio.' Smith let out a long sigh of relief. 'There's only one list of frequencies, call signs and code. Security. And that one list is inside Sergeant Harrod's tunic.'

'Mind if I mop my brow, too, boss?' Schaffer enquired.

'I'll go get it for you if you like,' Christiansen enquired.

'Thanks. But it's my fault and I'll get it. Besides, I'm the only person here who's done any climbing – or so I believe from Colonel Wyatt-Turner – and I think you'd find that cliff rather more awkward to climb than descend. No hurry. Let's bivouac and eat first.'

'If you can't do better than this, Smithy,' Schaffer said to Torrance-Smythe, 'you can have a week's notice. Starting from a week ago.' He scraped the bottom of his metal plate and shuddered. 'I was brought up in a Christian home, so I won't tell you what this reminds me of.'

'It's not my fault,' Torrance-Smyth complained. 'They packed the wrong size tin-openers.' He stirred the indeterminate-looking goulash in the pot on top of the butane stove and looked hopefully at the men seated in a rough semi-circle in the dimly-lit tent. 'Anyone for any more?'

'That's not funny,' Schaffer said severely.

'Wait till you try his coffee,' Smith advised, 'and you'll be wondering what you were complaining about.' He rose, poked his head through the door to take a look at the weather, looked inside again. 'May take me an hour. But if it's been drifting up there ...'

The seated men, suddenly serious, nodded. If it had been drifting up there it might take Smith a very long time indeed to locate Sergeant Harrod.

'It's a bad night,' Schaffer said. 'I'll come and give you a hand.'

'Thanks. No need. I'll haul myself up and lower myself down. A rope round a piton is no elevator, but it'll get me there and back and two are no better than one for that job. But I'll tell you what you can do.' He moved out and reappeared shortly afterwards carrying the radio which he placed in front of Schaffer. 'I don't want to go all the way up there to get the code-book just to find that some hob-nailed idiot has fallen over this and given it a heart attack. Guard it with your life, Lieutenant Schaffer.'

'Aye, aye, sir,' Schaffer said solemnly.

With a hammer and a couple of spare pitons hanging from his waist, Smith secured himself to the rope, with double bowline and belt as before, grabbed the free end of the rope and began to haul himself up. Smith's statement to the others that this was a job for a moutaineer seemed hardly accurate for the amount of mountaineering skill required was minimal. It was gruelling physical labour, no more. Most of the time, with his legs almost at right angles to his body, he walked up the vertical cliff face: on the stretch of the overhang, with no assistance for his arms, he twice had to take a turn of the free end of the rope and rest until the strength came back to aching shoulder and forearm muscles: and by the time he finally dragged himself, gasping painfully and sweating like a man in a sauna bath, over the edge of the cliff, exhaustion was very close indeed. He had overlooked the crippling effect of altitude to a man unaccustomed to it.

He lay face down for several minutes until breathing and pulse returned to something like normal – or what was normal for seven thousand feet – rose and examined the piton round which the nylon passed. It seemed firm enough but, for good measure, he gave it another few heavy blows with the hammer, undid the double bowline round his legs and secured the end of the rope to the piton with a round turn and two half-hitches, hauling on the rope until the knot locked tight.

He moved a few feet farther away from the cliff edge, cleared away the snow and lightly hammered in one of the spare pitons he had brought with him. He tested it with his hand to see if it broke clear easily. It did. He tapped it in lightly a second time and led round it the part of the rope that was secured to the firmly anchored first piton. Then he walked away, moving up the gently sloping plateau, whistling 'Lorelei'. It was, as Smith himself would have been the first to admit, a far more tuneful whistle, but recognisable for all that. A figure appeared out of the night and came running towards him, stumbling and slipping in the deep snow. It was Mary Ellison. She stopped short a yard away and put her hands on her hips.

'Well!' He could hear her teeth chattering uncontrollably with the cold. 'You took your time about it, didn't you?'

'Never wasted a minute,' Smith said defensively. 'I had to have a hot meal and coffee first.'

'You had to have – you beast, you selfish beast!' She took a quick step forward and flung her arms around his neck. 'I hate you.'

'I know.' He pulled off a gauntlet and gently touched her disengaged cheek. 'You're frozen.'

'You're frozen, he says! Of course I'm frozen. I almost *died* in that plane. Why couldn't you have supplied some hot water bottles – or – or an electrically heated suit or – or something? I thought you loved me!'

'I can't help what you think,' Smith said kindly, patting her on the back. 'Where's your gear?'

'Fifty yards. And *stop* patting me in that – that avuncular fashion.'

'Language, language,' Smith said. 'Come on, let's fetch it.'

They trudged upwards through the deep snow, Mary holding his arm tightly. She said curiously: 'What on earth excuse did you give for coming back up here? Lost a cuff-link?'

'There was something I had to come for, something apart from you, although I gave a song-and-dance act of having forgotten about it until the last moment, until it was almost too late. The radio code-book inside Sergeant Harrod's tunic.'

'He – he lost it? He dropped it? How – how could he have

been so criminally careless!' She stopped, puzzled. 'Besides, it's chained—'

'It's still inside Sergeant Harrod's tunic,' Smith said sombrely. 'He's up here, dead.'

'Dead?' She stopped and clutched him by the arms. After a long pause, she repeated: 'He's dead! That – that nice man. I heard him saying he'd never jumped before. A bad landing?'

'So it seems.'

They located the kit-bag in silence and Smith carried it back to the edge of the cliff. Mary said: 'And now? The code-book?'

'Let's wait a minute. I want to watch this rope.'

'Why the rope?'

'Why not?'

'Don't tell me,' Mary said resignedly. 'I'm only a little girl. I suppose you know what you're doing.'

'I wish to God I did,' Smith said feelingly.

They waited, again in silence, side by side on the kit-bag. Both stared at the rope in solemn concentration as if nylon ropes at seven thousand feet had taken on a special meaningfulness denied nylon ropes elsewhere. Twice Smith tried to light a cigarette and twice it sputtered to extinction in the drifting snow. The minutes passed, three, maybe four: they felt more like thirty or forty. He became conscious that the girl beside him was shivering violently – he guessed that she had her teeth clamped tight to prevent their chattering – and was even more acutely conscious that his entire left side – he was trying to shelter her from the wind and snow – was becoming numb. He rose to leave when suddenly the rope gave a violent jerk and the piton farther from the cliff edge was torn free. The loop of the rope slid quickly down past the piton to which it was anchored and kept on going till it was brought up short by its anchor. Whatever pressure was on the rope increased until the nylon bit deeply into the fresh snow on the cliff-edge. Smith moved across and tested the pressure on the rope, at first gingerly and tentatively then with all his strength. The rope was bar-taut and remained bar-taut. But the piton held.

'What – what on earth—' Mary began, then broke off. Her voice was an unconscious whisper.

'Charming, charming,' Smith murmured. 'Someone down there doesn't like me. Surprised?'

'If – if that spike hadn't held we'd never have got down again.' The tremor in her voice wasn't all due to the cold.

'It's a fair old jump,' Smith conceded.

He took her arm and they moved off. The snow was heavier now and even with the aid of their torches visibility was no more than six feet, but, by using the rocky out-crop as a bearing, it took Smith no more than two minutes to locate Sergeant Harrod, now no more than a featureless mound buried in the depths of the snow-drift. Smith brushed aside the covering shroud of white, undid the dead man's tunic, recovered the code-book, hung the chain round his neck and buttoned the book securely inside his own Alpenkorps uniform.

Then came the task of turning Sergeant Harrod over on his side. Unpleasant Smith had expected it to be, and it was: impossible he hadn't expected it to be, and it wasn't – not quite. But the effort all but defeated him, the dead man was stiff as a board, literally froze solid into the arms outflung position into which he had fallen. For a second time that night Smith could feel the sweat mingling with the melted snow on his face. But by and by he had him over, the frozen right arm pointing up into the snow-filled sky. Smith knelt, brought his torch close and carefully examined the back of the dead man's head.

'What are you trying to do?' Mary asked. 'What are you looking for?' Again her voice was a whisper.

'His neck is broken. I want to find out just *how* it was broken.' He glanced up at the girl. 'You don't have to look.'

'Don't worry.' She turned away. 'I'm not going to.'

The clothes, like the man, were frozen stiff. The hood covering Harrod's head crackled and splintered in Smith's gauntleted hands as he pulled it down, exposing the back of the head and neck. Finally, just below the collar of the snow smock, Smith found what he was searching for – a red mark at the base of the neck where the skin was broken. He rose, caught the dead man's ankles and dragged him a foot or two down the slope.

'What now?' In spite of herself Mary was watching again, in reluctant and horrified fascination. 'What are you looking for now?'

'A rock,' Smith said briefly. There was a cold edge to the words and although Mary knew it wasn't intended for her, it was an effective discouragement to any further questioning.

Smith cleared the snow for two feet around where Harrod's head had lain. With hand and eyes he examined the ground with meticulous care, rose slowly to his feet, took Mary's arm and began to walk away. After a few steps he hesitated, stopped, turned back to the dead man and turned him over again so that the right arm was no longer pointing towards the sky.

Half-way back to the cliff-edge, Smith said abruptly:

'Something struck Harrod on the back of the neck. I thought it might have been a rock. But there was no rock where he lay, only turf.'

'There was a rocky outcrop near by.'

'You don't break your neck on a rocky outcrop, then stand up and jump out into a snow-drift. Even had he rolled over into the drift, he could never have finished with his head seven feet out from the rock. He was struck by some hard metallic object, either the butt of a gun or the haft of a knife. The skin is broken but there is no bruising for the neck was broken immediately afterwards. When he was unconscious. To make us think it was an accident. It must have happened on the rock – there was no disturbance in the snow round Harrod – and it must have happened while he was upright. A tap on the neck, a quick neck-twist, then he fell or was pushed over the edge of the outcrop. Wonderful stuff, stone,' Smith finished bitterly. 'It leaves no footprints.'

Mary stopped and stared at him.

'Do you realize what you're saying?' She caught his speculative and very old-fashioned look, took his arm and went on quickly: 'No, I mean the implications. I'm sorry, I'm sorry, of course you do. John, I – I'm scared. Even all those months with you in Italy – well you know, nothing like this—' She broke off, then continued: 'Couldn't there – couldn't there be some other explanation?'

'Like he hit himself on the back of the head or the abominable snowman got him?'

She looked at him steadily, her dark eyes far too large in what could be seen of her hooded face. 'I don't deserve that, John. I *am* frightened.'

'Me, too.'

'I don't believe you.'

'Well, if I'm not, it's damn well time I started to be.'

Smith checked his descent when he estimated he was about forty feet from the base of the cliff. He took two turns of the nylon round his left leg, clamped it with his right, took a turn round his left arm, pulled off his right gauntlet with his teeth, stuffed it inside his tunic, eased out his Luger, slid the safety catch and went on his way again, checking his speed of descent with his gauntleted left hand. It was a reasonable enough expectation that whoever had tried to pull down the rope would be waiting there to finish off the job.

But there was no reception committee waiting, not, at least, at the spot where he touched down. He traversed a quick circle with his torch. There was nobody there and nothing there and the footprints that must have been there were long obscured by the drifting snow. Gun in one hand, torch in the other, he moved along the cliff face for thirty yards then moved out in a semi-circle until he arrived back at the cliff face. The rope-puller had evidently opted for discretion. Smith returned to the rope and jerked it. In two minutes he had Mary's kit-bag down and, a few minutes later, Mary herself. As soon as she had stepped out of the double bowline, Smith undid the knot, pulled the rope down from the top of the cliff and coiled it. So numbed and frozen were his hands by this time that the operation took him nearly fifteen minutes.

Rope over one shoulder, her kit-bag in the other, Smith led Mary to the fissure in the cliff side.

'Don't pitch the tent,' Smith said. 'Unroll it, put your sleeping bag on one half, get into it and pull the other half of the tent over you. Half an hour and you'll be covered with drifting snow. The snow will not only keep you warm, it'll hide you from any somnambulists. I'll be along in the morning before we leave.'

He walked away, stopped, looked back. Mary was still standing where he had left her, looking after him. There was no sag to her shoulders, no particular expression to her face, but for all that she looked oddly defenceless, lonely and forlorn, a quality as undefinable as it was unmistakable. Smith hesitated, then went back to her, unrolled her tent and sleeping bag, waited till she had climbed in, zipped up the bag and pulled the other half of the tent up to her chin. She smiled at him. He fixed the sleeping bag hood, pulled a corner of the tent over it and left, all without saying a word.

Locating his own tent was simple enough, a steady light burnt inside it. Smith beat the snow from his clothes, stooped and entered. Christiansen, Thomas and Carraciola were in their sleeping bags and were asleep or appeared to be. Torrance-Smythe was checking over their store of plastic explosives, fuses, detonators and grenades, while Schaffer was reading a paperback – in German – smoking a cigarette – also German – and faithfully guarding the radio. He put down the book and looked at Smith.

'OK?'

'OK.' Smith produced the code-book from his tunic. 'Sorry I was so long, but I thought I'd never find him. Drifting pretty badly up there.'

'We've arranged to take turns on watch,' Schaffer said. 'Half an hour each. It'll be dawn in three hours.'

Smith smiled. 'What are you guarding against in these parts?'

'The abominable snowman.'

The smile left Smith's face as quickly as it had come. He turned his attention to Harrod's code-book and spent about ten minutes in memorising call-up signals and wave-frequencies and writing a message out in code. Before he had finished Schaffer had turned into his sleeping bag, leaving Torrance-Smythe on watch. Smith folded the message, tucked it in a pocket, rose, took the radio and a rubber ground-sheet to protect it from the snow.

'I'm going to move out a bit,' he said to Torrance-Smythe. 'Reception is lousy among trees. Besides, I don't want to wake everybody up. Won't be long.'

Two hundred yards from the tent, after having stopped twice and changed direction twice, Smith knelt with his back – and the rubber ground-sheet – to the drifting snow. He extended a fourteen feet telescopic aerial, adjusted a pre-selected call-up and cranked a handle. Four times he cranked the handle and on the fifth he got results. Someone was keeping a very close radio watch indeed.

'This is Danny Boy,' the set speaker crackled. The signal was faint and intermittent, but just comprehensible. 'Danny Boy replying to you. Over.'

Smith spoke into the mouth microphone. 'This is Broadsword. Can I speak to Father Machree or Mother Machree? Over.'

'Sorry. Unavailable. Over.'

'Code,' Smith said. 'Over.'

'Ready.'

Smith extracted the paper from his pocket and shone his torch on it. There were two lines containing meaningless jumbles of letters and, below that, the plain language translation, which read: 'SAFE LANDING HARROD DEAD WEATHER FINE PLEASE AWAIT MESSAGE 0800 GMT.' Smith read off the corresponding code figures and finished off: 'Have that delivered to Father Machree by 0700. Without fail.'

Torrance-Smythe looked up at Smith's return.

'Back already?' Surprise in his voice. 'You got through?'

'Not a chance,' Smith said disgustedly. 'Too many bloody mountains around.'

'Didn't try for very long, did you?'

'Two and a half minutes.' It was Smith's turn to look surprised. 'Surely you know that's the safe maximum?'

'You think there may be radio monitoring stations hereabouts?'

'Oh, no, not at all.' Smith's voice was heavy with sarcasm. 'You wouldn't expect to find radio monitors in the Schloss Adler, would you now?'

'Well, now.' Torrance-Smythe smiled tiredly. 'I believe someone did mention it was the southern HQ of the German Secret Service. Sorry, Major. It's not that I'm growing old, though there's that, too. It's just that what passes for my mind is so gummed up by cold and lack of sleep that I think it's stopped altogether.'

Smith pulled off his boots and snow-suit, climbed into his sleeping bag and pulled the radio close to him.

'Then it's time you had some sleep. My explosives expert is going to be no good to me if he can't tell a detonator from a door-knob. Go on. Turn in. I'll keep watch.'

'But we had arranged—'

'Arguments, arguments,' Smith sighed. 'Insubordination on every hand.' He smiled. 'Straight up, Smithy, I'm wide awake. I know I won't sleep tonight.'

One downright lie, Smith thought, and one statement of incontrovertible truth. He wasn't wide awake, he was physically and mentally exhausted and on the slightest relaxation of will-power oblivion would have overtaken him in seconds. But that he wouldn't sleep that night was beyond doubt: no power on earth would have let him sleep that night but, in the circumstances, it was perhaps wiser not to say so to Torrance-Smythe.

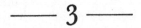

— 3 —

The pre-dawn greyness was in the sky. Smith and his men had broken camp. Tent and sleeping bags were stored away and the cooking utensils – after a very sketchy breakfast scarcely deserving of the name – were being thrust into haversacks. There was no conversation, none at all: it wasn't a morning for speaking. All of them, Smith thought, looked more drawn, more exhausted, than they had done three hours ago: he wondered how he himself, who had had no sleep at all, must look. It was as well, he reflected, that mirrors were not part of their commando equipment. He looked at his watch.

'We'll leave in ten minutes,' he announced. 'Should give us plenty of time to be down in the tree line before sun-up. Assuming there are no more cliffs. Back in a moment. Visibility is improving and I think I'll go recce along the cliff edge. With any luck, maybe I can see the best way down.'

'And if you haven't any luck?' Carraciola asked sourly.

'We've still that thousand feet of nylon rope,' Smith said shortly.

He pulled on his snow-suit and left, angling off in the direction of the cliff. As soon as he was beyond the belt of the scrub pines and out of sight of the camp he changed direction uphill and broke into a run.

A single eye appeared under a lifted corner of snow-covered canvas as Mary Ellison heard the soft crunch of running footsteps in the snow. She heard the first two bars of a tuneless whistling of 'Lorelei' unzipped her sleeping bag and sat up. Smith was standing above her.

'Not already!' she said protestingly.

'Yes already. Come on. Up!'

'I haven't slept a wink.'

'Neither have I. I've been watching that damned radio all night – and watching to check that no somnambulists took a stroll in this direction.'

'You kept awake. You did that for me?'

'I kept awake. We're off. Start in five minutes. Leave your tent and kit-bag here, you won't be requiring them again. Take some food, something to drink, that's all. And for God's sake, don't get too close to us.' He glanced at his watch. 'We'll stop at 7 a.m. Check your watch. Exactly 7 a.m. And *don't* bump into us.'

'What do you think I am?' But Smith didn't tell her what he thought she was. He had already gone.

A thousand feet farther down the side of the Weissspitze the trees were something worth calling trees, towering conifers that soared sixty and seventy feet up into the sky. Into the clear sky, for the snow had stopped falling now. It was dawn.

The slope of the Weissspitze was still very steep, perhaps one in four or five. Smith, with his five men strung out behind him in single file, slipped and stumbled almost constantly: but the deep snow, Smith reflected, at least cushioned their frequent falls and as a mode of progress it was a damn sight preferable to shinning down vertical cliff-faces, on an impossible thin clothesline. The curses of his bruised companions were almost continuous but serious complaints were marked by their total absence: there was no danger, they were making excellent time and they were now completely hidden in the deep belt of pines.

Two hundred yards behind them Mary Ellison carefully picked her way down the tracks made by the men below her. She slipped and fell only very occasionally for, unlike the men, she was carrying no over-balancing gear on her back. Nor had she any fear of being observed, of coming too close to Smith and the others: in still, frosty air on a mountain sound carries with a preternatural clarity and from the sound of the voices farther down the slope she could judge her distance from them to a nicety. For the twentieth time she looked at her watch: it was twenty minutes to seven.

Some time later, for much more than the twentieth time, Smith checked his watch again. It was exactly 7 o'clock. The dawn had gone and the light of full day-time filtered down through the snow-bent boughs of the conifers. Smith stopped and held up his hand, waiting until the other five had caught up with him.

'We must be half-way down now.' He shrugged off the heavy pack on his back and lowered it gratefully into the snow. 'I think it's time we had a look at the scenery.'

They piled their gear and moved off to the right. Within a minute the pines started to thin out and at a signal from Smith they all dropped to hands and knees and crawled forward the last few yards towards the edge of the belt of pines. Smith carried a telescope in his hand: Christiansen and Thomas both wore binoculars. Zeiss binoculars. Admiral Rolland had left nothing to chance. Beyond the last of the pines a mound of snow obstructed their view of the valley below. Shrouded from top to toe, in the all enveloping white of their snow-smocks, they completed the last few feet on their elbows and knees.

What lay below them was something out of a fairy tale, an impossibly beautiful scene from an impossibly beautiful fairy tale, a fairy tale set aeons back in the never-never land of the age of dreams, a kindlier land, a nobler land than man had ever known since first he had set his hand against his brother. A land that never was, Smith thought, a land that never was: but there it lay before them, the golden land that never was, the home of that most dreaded organisation in the entire world, the German Gestapo. The impeccable incongruity of it all, Smith reflected, passed all belief.

The valley was bowl-shaped, open to the north, hemmed in by steeply rising hills to the east and west, closed off by the towering bulk of the Weissspitze to the south.

A scene of fantastic beauty. Nine thousand, seven hundred and ten feet in height, the second highest mountain in Germany, the Weisspitze soared up menacingly like another north wall of the Eiger, its dazzling whiteness caught in the morning sun, its starkly lovely outline sharply etched against the now cloudless blue of the sky. High up near the cone-shaped summit could be seen the line of black rock marking the cliff Smith and his men had descended during the night with, just below it, a much greater cliff-face on the plateau above which they had spent the night.

Directly opposite where they lay, and almost exactly on the same level, was the Schloss Adler itself. The castle of the eagle had been aptly named, an impregnable fortress, an inaccessible eyrie set between mountain and sky.

Just below the spot where the steep-sided slopes of the Weissspitze began to flatten out northwards into the head of the valley, a geological freak, known as a volcanic plug, jutted two hundred vertical feet up into the sparkling, ice-cold air. It was on this that the Schloss Adler had been built. The northern, western and eastern sides of this volcanic plug were sheer, perpendicular walls of rock, walls that swept up smoothly, without intermission or break into the structure of the castle itself: from where they lay, it was impossible to say where the one ended and the other began. To the south, a steeply-sloping ridgeback connected the plug to the equally sloping ramparts of the Weissspitze.

The castle itself was another dream, the dream of the apotheosis of medievalism. This dream, Smith was aware, was as illusory as the golden age of its setting. It wasn't medieval at all, it had been built as late as the mid-nineteenth century to the express order of one of the madder of the Bavarian monarchs who had suffered from a comprehensive list of delusions, of which grandeur had not been the least. But, delusions or not, he had had, as the deluded so often have – to the dismay and

561

consternation of their allegedly saner brethren – impeccable taste. The castle was perfect for the valley, the valley for the castle. Any other combination would have been inconceivable.

The Schloss Adler was built in the form of a hollow square. It was towered, battlemented and crenellated, its most imposing aspects, two perfectly circular towers, the one to the east higher than that to the west, facing down the valley towards the north. Two smaller, but still magnificent towers, lay at the southern corners, facing the looming bulk of the Weissspitze. From where Smith lay, at some slight level above that of the castle, he could just see into the open square in its middle, outside access to which was obtained by a pair of huge iron gates at the rear. The sun had not yet climbed sufficiently high above the eastern hills for its rays to strike the castle directly, but, for all that, its incredibly white walls gleamed and glittered as if made of the most iridescent marble.

Below the soaring northern ramparts of the castle the valley fell away steeply to the Blau See, beautiful pine-fringed jewel of a lake of the deepest and most sparkling blue, a colour which with the green of the pines, the white dazzle of the snow and the brilliant, lighter blue of the sky above formed a combination of breath-taking loveliness. Impossibly lovely, Smith thought, a completely faithful colour reproduction of the scene would have had everybody shouting 'fake'.

From where they lay they could see that the belt of pines in which they lay hidden extended almost all the way down to the lake. Getting down there unobserved would be no problem at all. An almost exactly matching line of pines swept down the opposite – the eastern – side of the valley. From the lake those two long sweeps of pines, climbing steadily upwards as they marched to the south, must have appeared like a pair of great curving horns almost meeting at the top of the lower of the two cliff-faces on the Weissspitze.

A small village lay at the head of the lake. Basically it consisted of a single wide street, perhaps two hundred yards in length, a railway station, two inevitable churches perched on two inevitable knolls and a thin scattering of houses climbing up the steep slopes on either side of the village. From the southern end of the village a road curved up the far side of the valley till it reached the ridge-back to the south of the castle: this ridge-back it ascended by a series of hairpin bends, the last of which led to the great doors guarding the forecourt at the back of the castle. The road, just then, was completely blocked by snow and sole access to the castle was obviously by means of the *Luftseilbahn,* an aerial cableway. Two cables stretched from the village straight up to the castle, crossing three supporting pylons en route. Even as they watched, a cable-car was completing the last section of its journey up to the castle. At a distance of not much more than a hundred feet from the glittering walls of the Schloss Adler it appeared to be climbing almost vertically.

On the Blau See, about a mile beyond the village, lay a very large group of regularly spaced huts, arranged in rectangular patterns. It bore an uncommonly close resemblance to a military encampment.

'Well, I'll be damned!' With an almost physical effort of will, Schaffer forced himself to look away and Smith could see the wonder reflected in his eyes. 'Is this for real, boss?'

It wasn't a question that called for an answer. Schaffer had summed up their collective feeling pretty well and there was nothing that anyone could add that wouldn't seem and sound superfluous. Prone in the snow, they watched in silence as the cable-car climbed agonisingly slowly up the last fifty feet towards the castle. It seemed as if it would never make it and Smith could almost palpably sense the empathy of his companions and himself as they willed that little car on the last few feet of its journey. But make it it did and it disappeared from sight under the roof of the cable header station that has been built into the western foot of the castle. The tension relaxed and Schaffer cleared his throat.

'Boss,' he said diffidently, 'there are a couple of minor points that occur to me. Requiring elucidation, one might say. First of all, if I didn't know better I'd say that was a military barracks down by that little old lake there.'

'You don't know better. That *is* a military barracks down by that little old lake there. And no ordinary military barracks either, I might say. That's the training HQ of the Jäger battalions of the Wehrmacht's Alpenkorps.'

'Oh, my gosh! The Alpine Corps! If I'd known this I'd never have come along. The Alpine Corps! Why didn't someone tell Ma Schaffer's nearest and dearest?'

'I thought you knew,' Smith said mildly. 'Why do you think we're not dressed as German sailors or Red Cross nurses?'

Schaffer unzipped his snow-smock, minutely examined his Alpenkorps uniform as if seeing it for the first time, then zipped it up again. He said carefully: 'You mean to say we're going to mingle, careless like, with the German Army.' He paused, looked wide-eyed at Smith's smiling nod, then went on incredulously: 'But – but we'll be recognised as strangers!'

'Training troops come and go all the time,' Smith said offhandedly. 'What's six new faces among six hundred new faces?'

'This is terrible,' Schaffer said gloomily.

'Worse than horses?' Smith smiled. 'After all, the Alpenkorps don't buck and trample all over you.'

'Horses don't carry machine-guns,' Schaffer said morosely.

'And your second point?'

'Ah, yes. The second point. There's the little matter of the old Schloss itself. Kinda forgotten our helicopter, haven't we? How do we get in?'

'A good point,' Smith conceded. 'We'll have to think about it. But I'll tell you this. If Colonel Wyatt-Turner can penetrate the German High Command and, more important, get away again, this should be a piece of cake for us.'

'He did what?' Schaffer demanded.

'Didn't you know?'

'How should I know?' Schaffer was irritated. 'Never met the guy till yesterday.'

'He spent the years '40 to '43 inside Germany. Served in the Wehrmacht for part of the time. Ended up in the GHQ in Berlin. Says he knows Hitler quite well.'

'Well, I'll be damned.' Schaffer paused for a long moment, finally arrived at a conclusion. 'The guy,' he said moodily, 'must be nuts.'

'Maybe. But if he can do it, we can. We'll figure a way. Let's get back among the trees.'

They inched their way back into cover, leaving Christiansen behind with Smith's telescope to keep watch. After they'd made a temporary camp, heated and drunk some coffee, Smith announced his intention of trying to contact London again.

He unpacked the radio and sat down on a kit-bag a few feet distant from the others. The switch that cut in the transmitter circuit was on the left hand side of the radio, the side remote from where the other four men were sitting. Smith switched on with a loud positive click, cranked the call-up handle with his left hand. With the very first crank his left hand moved the transmitting switch from 'On' to 'Off', the whirring of the call-up blanketing the sound. Smith cranked away diligently at intervals, stopping from time to time to make minute adjustments to the controls, then finally gave up and sat back, shaking his head in disgust.

'You'll never make it with all those trees around,' Torrance-Smythe observed.

'That must be it,' Smith agreed. 'I'll try the other side of the wood. Might have better luck there.'

He slung the transmitter over his shoulder and trudged off through the deep snow, cutting straight across to the other side of the belt of pines. When he thought he was safely out of eye-shot of the men at the camp, he checked with a quick look over his shoulder. They were out of sight. He turned more than ninety degrees left and hurried up the hill until he cut the tracks that he and his men had made on the way down. He followed the tracks uphill, whistling 'Lorelei', but whistling softly: in that frosty air, sound travelled dangerously far. He stopped whistling when Mary appeared from where she had been hiding behind a fallen pine.

'Hallo, darling,' she said brightly.

'We'll have less of the "darlings",' Smith said briskly. 'It's 8 a.m. Father Machree awaits. And keep your voice down.'

He sat on the fallen tree, cranked the handle and established contact almost immediately. The transmission from London was still very faint but clearer than it had been in the earlier hours of the morning.

'Father Machree is waiting,' the radio crackled. 'Hold. Hold.'

Smith held and the unmistakable voice of Admiral Rolland took over from the London operator.

'Position please, Broadsword.'

Smith consulted the piece of paper in his hand, again in code and plain language. The message read: WOODS DUE WEST CASTLE DESCENDING W.H. THIS EVENING. Smith read out the corresponding code letters.

There was a pause, presumably while Rolland was having the message decoded, then his voice came again.

'Understood. Proceed. Harrod killed accidentally?'

'No. Over.'

'By the enemy? Over.'

'No. What is the weather report? Over.'

'Deteriorating. Freshening winds, strong later. Snow. Over.'

Smith looked up at the still and cloudless sky above. He assumed that Rolland hadn't got his forecasts mixed up. He said: 'Time of next broadcast uncertain. Can you stand by? Over.'

'Am remaining HQ until operation complete,' Rolland said. 'Good luck. Goodbye.'

Smith closed up the radio and said thoughtfully to Mary: 'I didn't much care for the way he said goodbye there.'

In the naval Operations room in Whitehall, Admiral Rolland and Colonel Wyatt-Turner, one on either side of the radio operator manning a huge transceiver, looked at each other with heavy faces.

'So the poor devil was murdered,' Wyatt-Turner said flatly.

'A high price to pay for confirmation that we were right,' Rolland said sombrely. 'Poor devil, as you say. The moment we gave him that radio to carry we signed a death-warrant. I wonder who's next. Smith himself?'

'Not Smith.' Wyatt-Turner shook his head positively. 'Some people have a sixth sense. Smith has a seventh, eighth and ninth and a built-in radar set for danger. Smith can survive under any circumstances I can conceive of. I didn't pick him with a pin, sir. He's the best agent in Europe.'

'Except possibly yourself. And don't forget, Colonel, there may possibly be circumstances that even you can't conceive of.'

'Yes, that's so.' He looked directly at Rolland. 'What do you reckon his chances are, sir?'

'Chances?' Rolland's eyes were remote, unseeing. 'What do you mean, chances? He doesn't have any.'

Almost precisely the same thought was in Smith's mind as he lit a cigarette and looked at the girl beside him, careful not to let his thoughts show in his face. Not until that first sight he'd just had of the castle had the full realization of the apparent impossibility of their task struck him. Had he known what the precise physical situation had been, he doubted very much whether he would have come. Deep in the furthest recesses of his mind, he knew, although he would not admit it to himself, that there really was no room for the element of doubt. He wouldn't have come. But he had come. He was here and he had better do something about it.

He said to Mary: 'Have you had a squint at the old Schloss yet?'

'It's a fantastic place. How on earth do we ever get General Carnaby out of there?'

'Easy. We'll take a walk up there tonight, get inside and take him away.'

Mary stared at him in disbelief and waited for him to amplify his statement. He didn't. Finally, she said: 'That's all?'

'That's all.'

'The simplicity of true genius. You must have spent a lot of time working that one out.' When he still didn't reply, she went on, elaborately sarcastic: 'In the first place, of course, there'll be no trouble about getting in. You just go up to the main door and knock.'

'More or less. Then the door – or window – opens, I smile at you, say thank you and pass inside.'

'You what?'

'I smile and say thank you. Even in wartime, there's no reason why the little courtesies—'

'Please!' She was thoroughly exasperated now. 'If you can't talk sense—'

'*You* are going to open the door for *me*,' Smith explained patiently.

'Are you feeling all right?'

'The staff shortage in Germany is acute. The Schloss Adler is no exception. You're just the type they're looking for. Young, intelligent, good-looking, you can cook, polish, sew on Colonel Kramer's buttons—'

'Who's Colonel Kramer?' Her tone as much as her face showed the bewilderment in her mind.

'Deputy Chief of the German Secret Service.'

Mary said with conviction: 'You must be mad.'

'If I wasn't I wouldn't be doing this job.' He glanced at his watch. 'I've been gone too long and I fear that I'm surrounded by the odd suspicious mind. We move off at five. Exactly five. Down in the village there's a *Gasthaus* on the east side of the main street called "Zum Wilden Hirsch." "The Wild Deer." Remember it, "Zum Wilden Hirsch." We don't want you wandering into the wrong pub. Behind it there's a shed used as a beer cellar. It's always kept locked but there will be a key in the door tonight. I'll meet you there at exactly eight o'clock.'

He turned to go, but she caught him by the arm.

'How do you know all this?' she asked tensely. 'About the *Gasthaus* and the bottle store and the key being there and about Colonel Kramer and—'

'Ah, ah!' Smith shook his head admonishingly and touched her lips with his forefinger.

'Hand-book for spies, golden rule number one.' She drew away from him and stared down at the snow-covered ground,

567

her voice low and bitter. 'Never ever tell anyone anything unless you have to.' She paused and looked up. 'Not even me?'

'Especially not you, poppet.' He patted her lightly on the
cheek. 'Don't be late.'

He walked away down the slope leaving her looking after
him with an expressionless face.

Lieutenant Schaffer lay stretchted out and almost buried in the
deep snow, half-hidden behind the bole of a pine, with a telescope to his eye. He twisted as he heard the soft crunch of
snow behind him and saw Smith approaching on his hands and
knees.

'Couldn't you knock or something?' Schaffer asked irritably.

'Sorry. Something you wanted to show me, so the boys say.'

'Yeah.' Schaffer handed Smith the telescope. 'Take a gander
at this lot. Thought it might interest you.'

Smith took the telescope and fingered the very precise adjustment until he achieved maximum definition.

'Lower down,' Schaffer said. 'At the foot of the rock.'

Smith traversed the telescope down the sides of the Schloss
Adler and the sheer walls of the volcanic plug until the fine
cross-hairs came to rest on the snow-covered slopes at the foot.
Moving across the slope he could see two soldiers with slung
machine-carbines and, not on leashes, four dogs.

'My, my,' Smith murmured thoughtfully. 'I see what you
mean.'

'Those are Dobermann pinchers, boss.'

'Well, they aren't toy poodles and that's a fact,' Smith agreed.
He moved the telescope a little way up the walls of the volcanic
plug, held it there.

'*And* floodlights?' he added softly.

He lowered the telescope again, past the patrolling soldiers
and dogs, till it came to rest on a high wire fence that appeared
to go all the way around the base of the volcanic plug.

'*And* a dinky little fence.'

'Fences,' Schaffer said pontifically, 'are made to be cut or
climbed.'

'You try cutting or climbing this one, laddie, and you'll be
cooked to a turn in nothing flat. A standard design, using a
standard current of 2300 volt, single-phase, 60 cycle AC. All the
best electric chairs have it.'

Schaffer shook his head. 'Amazing the lengths some folks will
go to protect their privacy.'

'Fences, floods and Dobermanns,' Smith said. 'I don't think that combination will stop us, do you, Lieutenant?'

'Of course not. Stop us? Of course not!' He paused for some moments, then burst out: 'How in God's name do you propose—'

'We'll decide when the time comes,' Smith said easily.

'You mean you'll decide,' Schaffer said complainingly. 'Play it pretty close to the cuff, don't you?'

'That's because I'm too young to die.'

'Why me, for God's sake?' Schaffer demanded after a long pause. 'Why pick me for this job? This isn't my line of country, Major.'

'God knows,' Smith said frankly. 'Come to that, why me?'

Schaffer was in the middle of giving him a long and pointedly disbelieving look when he suddenly stiffened and cocked his head up to the sky in the direction of the unmistakably rackety whirr of a helicopter engine. Both men picked it up at once. It was coming from the north, over the Blau See, and heading directly towards them. It was a big military version and, even at that distance, the swastika markings were clearly distinguishable. Schaffer started to move backwards towards the line of pines.

'Exit Schaffer,' he announced hurriedly. 'The bloodhounds are out for us.'

'I don't think so,' Smith said. 'Stay where you are and pull your smock over your head.'

Quickly they pulled their white smocks over their heads until only their eyes, and Smith's telescope, partly buried in the snow, could be seen. From thirty yards in any direction, including straight up, they must have been quite invisible.

The helicopter swept up the valley still maintaining a course directly towards the spot where the two men lay hidden. When it was only a few hundred yards away even Smith began to feel uneasy and wondered if by some evil mischance the enemy knew or suspected their presence. They were bound to have heard the engines of the Lancaster, muted though they had been, during the night. Had some suspicious and intelligent character – and there would be no lack of those in the Schloss Adler – come up with the right answer to the question of the presence of this errant bomber in one of the most unlikely places in all Germany? Could picked members of the Alpenkorps be combing the pine woods even at that moment – and he, Smith, had been so confident that he hadn't even bothered to post a guard.

Then, abruptly, when the helicopter was almost directly over-head, it side-slipped sharply to its left, sank down over the castle courtyard, hovered for a few moments and slowly descended. Smith surreptitiously mopped his forehead and applied his eye to the telescope.

The helicopter had landed. The rotor stopped, steps de-scended and a man climbed down to the courtyard floor. From his uniform, Smith decided, a very senior officer. Then he sud-denly realized that it was a very very senior officer indeed. His face tightened as he pushed the telescope across to Schaffer. 'Take a good look,' he advised.

Schaffer took a good look, lowered the telescope as the man passed through a doorway. 'Pal of yours, boss?'

'I know him. Reichsmarschall Julius Rosemeyer. The Wehr-macht Chief of Staff.'

'My very first Reichsmarschall and me without my telescopic rifle,' Schaffer said regretfully. 'I wonder what his highness wants.'

'Same as us,' Smith said briefly.

'General Carnaby?'

'When you're going to ask the Allies' overall co-ordinator of planning a few questions about the Second Front you don't send just the corporal of the guard to interview him.'

'You don't think they might have come to take old Carnaby away?' Schaffer asked anxiously.

'Not a chance. The Gestapo never gives up its prisoners. In this country the Wehrmacht does what the Gestapo says.'

'Or else?'

'Or else. Off you go – they've more coffee on the brew back there. Send someone to relieve me in an hour.'

Admiral Rolland's weather forecast for the sea turned out to be perfectly correct. As the endless shivering hours dragged slowly by the weather steadily deteriorated. By noon the sun was gone and a keen wind sprung up from the east. By early afternoon snow had begun to fall from the darkened sky, slowly at first then with increasing severity as the east wind steadily increased in strength and became bitingly cold. It looked like being a bad night, Smith thought. But a bad night that reduced visibility to near-zero and kept people indoors was what they wanted: it would have been difficult for them to saunter up to the Schloss Adler bathed in the warm light of a harvest moon. Smith checked his watch.

'Time to go.' He climbed stiffly to his feet and beat his arms to restore circulation. 'Call Thomas, will you.'

Rucksacks and kit-bags were slung and shouldered. Thomas, who had been keeping watch, appeared carrying Smith's telescope. Thomas was very far from being his usual cheerful self, and it wasn't just the fact that he'd spent the last hour exposed to the full force of wind and snow that had left him in such ill-humour.

'Is that damned radio working yet?' he asked Smith.

'Not a hope. Six tries, six failures. Why?'

'I'll tell you why,' Thomas said bitterly. 'Pity we couldn't get the Admiral to change his mind about the paratroops. A full troop train just got in, that's all.'

'Well, that's fine,' Smith said equably. 'The old hands will think we're new boys and the new boys will think we're old hands. Very convenient.'

Thomas looked thoughtfully at Smith.

'Very, *very* convenient.' He hesitated, then went on: 'How about loosening up a bit, Major?'

'What do you mean?'

'Come off it,' Carraciola said roughly. 'You know damn well what he means. It's our lives. Why do we have to go down into that damned village? And how do you intend to get Carnaby out? If we're to commit suicide, tell us why. You owe us that.'

'I owe you nothing,' Smith said flatly. 'I'll tell you nothing. And if you know nothing you can't talk. You'll be told when the time comes.'

'You, Smith,' Torrance-Smythe said precisely, 'are a cold-blooded devil.'

'It's been said before,' Smith said indifferently.

The village railway station was a small, two-track, end-of-the-line depot. Like all end-of-the-line depots it was characterised by rust, dilapidation, the barest functionalism of design and an odd pessimistically-expectant air of waiting for someone to come along and finish it off properly. At any time, its air of desolation was total. That night, completely deserted, with a high, gusting wind driving snow through pools of light cast by dim and swaying electric lamps, the ghostly impression of a place abandoned by man and by the world was almost overwhelming. It suited Smith's purpose perfectly.

He led his five snow-smock clad men quickly across the tracks and into the comparative shelter of the station buildings. They filed silently past the closed bookstall, the freight office, the booking office, flitted quickly into the shadows beyond and stopped.

Smith lowered the radio, shrugged off his rucksack, removed snow-smock and trousers and sauntered casually alongside the tracks – the thrifty Bavarians regardèd platforms as a wasteful luxury. He stopped outside a door next to a bolted hatch which bore above it the legend GEPACK ANNAHME. He tried the door. It was locked. He made a quick survey to check that he was unobserved, stooped, examined the keyhole with a pencil flash, took a bunch of oddly shaped keys from his pockets and had the door opened in seconds. He whistled softly and was almost at once joined by the others, who filed quickly inside, already slipping off their packs as they went. Schaffer, bringing up the rear, paused and glanced up at the sign above the hatch.

'My God!' He shook his head. 'The left luggage office!'

'Where else?' Smith asked reasonably. He ushered Schaffer in, closed and locked the door behind him. Hooding his pencil torch until only a finger-width beam emerged, he passed by the luggage racks till he came to the far end of the room where a bay window was set in the wall. It was a perfectly ordinary sash window and he examined it very minutely, careful that at no time the pinpoint of light touched the glass to shine through to the street beyond. He turned his attention to the vertical wooden planking at the side of the window, took out his sheath knife and levered a plank away to expose a length of twin-cored flex stapled vertically to the wall. He split the cores, sliced through each in turn, replaced the plank and tested the lower sash of the window. It moved easily up and down.

'An interesting performance,' Schaffer observed. 'What was all that in aid of?'

'It's not always convenient to enter by the front door. Or, come to that, leave by it either.'

'A youth mis-spent in philandering or burgling,' Schaffer said sadly. 'How did you know it was wired for sound?'

'Even a small country station will have valuables stored in its left luggage office from time to time,' Smith said patiently. 'But it will *not* have a full-time baggage attendant. The attendant, booking clerk, ticket-collector, porter and station-master are probably all one man. So it's kept locked. But there's no point in barring the front door if your bag-snatcher can climb in through the back window. So your back window is grilled or wired. No grille – and a badly-fitting plank. Obvious.'

'Obvious to you, maybe,' Carraciola said sourly. 'All this – ah – expertise with skeleton keys and burglar alarms. The Black Watch you said you were in?'

'That's right.'

'Very odd training they give you in those Scottish regiments. Very odd indeed.'

' "Thorough" is the word you're searching for,' Smith said kindly. 'Let's go and have a drink.'

'Let's do that,' Carraciola said heavily. 'Remind me to get mine down in one go or ten gets you one that I'll never live to finish it.'

'It would be a shame to waste good beer,' Smith agreed. He waited until the last man was out, locked the door behind him and rejoined them as they walked out of the main station entrance under the 'Bahnhof' sign. They were now no longer carrying rucksacks or wearing snow-smocks. All were dressed in the uniforms of soldiers of a Jäger battalion, Smith as a major, Schaffer as a lieutenant and the other four as sergeants. Their uniforms were no longer as immaculately crease-free as they might have been nor for that matter, as Sergeant Harrod had observed, did they fit as well as they might have done. But in a village street or crowded bar, at night-time, they should pass muster. Or so Smith devoutly hoped.

It was a typical main street in a typical high alpine village. The buildings lining either side of the street, solid, rugged, four-square buildings, looked as if they had been defying the bitter Bavarian winters for a long long time and intended going on doing so for as long again. Nearly all the houses were of the wooden chalet type, with great sweeping eaves and balconies running the full width of the front of the houses. A few were of comparatively modern construction, with shingled walls, large double-glazed windows and fancy wrought-iron grille-work, but most were very old and low, planked with rough adze-cut wood, and having the interlocking wall-beams projecting at the corners.

There were no street lamps but neither was there any attempt at a blackout. Elongated rectangles of light from uncurtained windows patterned the snow-packed streets. Beyond the far or southern end of the street, intermittently seen through the sweeping curtains of snow, a cluster of bright lights seemed to hang suspended in the sky. Instinctively, almost, Smith stopped to gaze at this distant constellation and his men stopped with him. The lights of the Schloss Adler, the castle of the eagle, seemed impossibly remote, as unattainable as the mountains of the moon. Wordlessly, the men looked at them in long silence, then at one another, then, by mutual and still silent consent, moved on their way again, their boots crunching crisply in the beaten snow, their frozen breaths wisping away in the chill night wind.

The main street – the only street – was deserted, quite empty of life. Inevitably so, on so bitter a night. But if the street was deserted, the village was anything but: the sounds of laughter and singing and the babel of voices filled the night air and the nose-to-tail row of parked German trucks along one side of the street showed clearly enough just who was responsible for the singing and the laughter. For the training troops in the military barracks on the Blau See there was only one centre of entertainment for twenty miles around and this village was it: the *Gasthäuser* and *Weinstuben* were jammed to the doors with soldiers of the Alpenkorps, probably the most highly trained combat troops in Europe.

Schaffer said plaintively: 'I don't really feel like a drink, boss.'

'Nonsense,' Smith said encouragingly. 'You're just shy at the thought of meeting strangers.' He stopped in front of a *Gasthaus* with the legend 'Drei Könige' above the door. 'Here's a likely looking place, now. Hang on a minute.'

He climbed the steps, opened the door and looked inside. Down in the street the other five looked at one another, the same mingled apprehension and expectancy mirrored in every eye. Austrian *Schrammel* music, hauntingly and nostalgically evocative of a kindlier and happier age, flooded through the open doorway. The expressions on the faces of the men below didn't change. There was a time and a place for *Schrammel* music and this wasn't it.

Smith shook his head, closed the door and rejoined his men. 'Packed,' he said. 'Not even standing room.' He nodded across the street to another hostelry, the 'Eichhof,' a small, squat, beetle-browed building with adze-cut corner beams and an air of advanced dilapidation. 'Let's see what this has to offer.'

But the 'Eichhof' had nothing to offer, Regretfully but firmly Smith closed its front door and turned away.

'Jammed,' he announced. 'Besides, a low-class dump unsuitable for officers and NCOs of the Wehrmacht. But this next place looks more promising, don't you think?'

From the pointed silence it was apparent that the other five didn't think anything of the kind, and, in fact, apart from the factor of size, the third *Weinstube* looked remarkably like the ones Smith had just passed up. 'Zum Wilden Hirsch', it was called, and above the sign was a snow-shrouded wooden carving of a wild deer.

Smith walked up the half-dozen steps to the front door and opened it. He winced as the blast of sound reached him, an almost physical assault upon the eardrums. Heaven knew the last two *Weinstuben* had been clamorous enough but compared to this place they now seemed, in retrospect, to have been invested in a cathedral silence. To the blaring accompaniment of a battery of discordant accordions what appeared, from the sheer volume of sound, to be an entire regiment were giving 'Lili Marlene' all they had. Smith glanced at his men, nodded and passed inside.

As the others followed, Schaffer paused in the doorway as Christiansen took his arm and said wonderingly: 'You think he thinks this *isn't* packed?'

'They must,' Schaffer conceded, 'have had them packed six deep in the other joints.'

—— 4 ——

They weren't exactly stacked six deep inside 'Zum Wilden Hirsch' but they might well have been if the music-swaying crowd of elbow-jostling customers has assumed the horizontal instead of the perpendicular. He had never, Smith thought, seen so many people in one bar before. There must have been at least four hundred of them. To accommodate a number of that order called for a room of no ordinary dimensions, and this one wasn't. It was a very big room indeed. It was also a very very old room.

The floor of knotted pine sagged, the walls sagged and the massive smoke-blackened beams on the roof seemed to be about ready to fall down at any moment. In the middle of the room stood a huge black wood-burning stove, a stove stoked with such ferocious purpose that the cast-iron top cover glowed dull red. From just below the cover two six-inch twenty-foot long black-enamelled stove pipes led off to points high up on opposite sides of the room – a primitive but extremely efficient form of central heating. The three-sided settees – half booths – lining three walls of the room were of oak darkened by age and smoke and unknown centuries of customers, each booth having recessed holes for stowing newspapers rolled round slats of wood. The twenty or so tables scattered across the floor had hand-cut wooden tops of not less than three inches in thickness with chairs to match. Most of the back of the room was taken up by a solid oaken bar with a coffee-machine at one end, and, behind the bar, swing doors that presumably led to the kitchen. What little illumination there was in the room came from ceiling-suspended and very sooty oil lamps, each one with its generations-old patch of coal-black charred wood in the roof above.

Smith transferred his attention from the room to the customers in the room, a clientele of a composition such as one might expect to find in a high Alpine village with a military encampment at its back door. In one corner were a group of obvious locals, men with still, lean, aquiline, weather-beaten faces, unmistakably men of the mountains, many of them in intricately embroidered leather jackets and Tyrolean hats. They spoke little and drank quietly, as did another small group at the back of the room, perhaps a dozen or so nondescript civilians, clearly not locals, who drank sparingly from small Schnapps glasses. But ninety per cent of the customers were soldiers of the German Alpenkorps, some seated, many more standing, but all giving of their very best with 'Lili Marlene', and nearly all of them enthusiastically waving their pewter-capped litre Steinbechers in the air, happily oblivious, in that moment of tearfully nostalgic romanticism, of the fact that the amount of beer finding its way to comrades' uniforms and the floor was about the equivalent of a moderately heavy rainstorm.

Behind the bar was the obvious proprietor, a gargantuan three-hundred pounder with an impressive moon-like face and several girls busy filling trays with Steinbechers. Several others moved about the room, collecting or serving beer-mugs. One of them approaching in his direction caught Smith's eye.

It would have been surprising if she hadn't. It would have been surprising if she hadn't caught the attention of every man there. But there was no surprise. She did. She would have won any Miss Europe contest hands down if she had had a face other than her own which, though pleasant and plump, was rather plain. But any possible lack of attraction in that cheerfully smiling face was more than over-compensated for elsewhere. She was dressed in a gaily-patterned dirndl and Tyrolean blouse, had a hand-span waist, and hour-and-a-half-glass figure and an obvious predilection for low-cut blouses, that in terms of attracting local custom, must have been worth a fortune to the gigantic proprietor behind the bar. She drew a great deal of attention from the assembled soldiery, not all of it just consisting of admiring glances: if she weren't wearing armour-plating, Smith reflected, she must be permanently black and blue. She approached Smith, brushed back her blonde hair and smiled, the gesture as provocative as the smile.

'Can I help you, sir?'

'Dark beer, please,' Smith said politely. 'Six.'

'With pleasure, sir.' Again the provocative smile, this time accompanied by a half-appraising, half-lingering look from cornflower blue eyes, then she turned and walked away, if her method of locomotion could strictly be described as walking. Schaffer, a slightly dazed expression on his face, stared after her, then caught Smith by the arm.

'*Now* I know why I left Montana, boss.' His voice held something of the dazed quality on his face. 'It wasn't because of the horses after all.'

'Your mind on the job if you don't mind, Lieutenant.' Smith looked thoughtfully after the girl, rubbed his chin and said slowly: 'Barmaids know more about what's going on in their own manor than any chief of police – and that one looks as if she might know more than most. Yes, I'll do that.'

'Do what?' Schaffer asked suspiciously.

'Try to get next to her.'

'I saw her first,' Schaffer said plaintively.

'You can have the next dance,' Smith promised. The levity of the words were belied by the cool watchful expression on his face as his eyes constantly travelled the room. 'When you get your drinks, circulate. See if you can hear any mention of Carnaby or Reichsmarschall Rosemeyer.'

He caught sight of an empty chair by a corner table, moved across and sat in it, nodding politely to a rather bleary-eyed Alpenkorps captain deep in what appeared to be rather patronising conversation with two lieutenants. The captain showed no more than a brief recognition of his presence and, as far as Smith could tell, no other person present was showing the slightest interest in either himself or his companions. The accordion band finished its stint more or less on the same note and at the same time and the singing of 'Lili Marlene' died away. For long seconds there was a profound and nostalgic silence, four hundred men alone with Lili Marlene under the barrack gate lantern, then, as if on cue, a babel of voices broke out all over the room: four hundred men with unfinished litre mugs do not remain sentimental for overly long.

He caught sight of the girl returning with six Steinbechers on a tray, pushing her way through the crowd and fending off admirers with a practised hand. She gave drinks to Smith's men who immediately but unostentatiously broke up and began to wander away into different parts of the room. The girl looked around, located Smith, smiled brightly, crossed to his table, and put the Steinbecher on it. Before she could straighten. Smith put his arm around her waist and pulled her on to his knee. The Jäger captain across the table broke off his conversation, stared across in startled disapproval, opened his mouth as if to speak, caught Smith's discouraging glance, decided to mind his own business and resumed his conversation. Smith, in his turn, looked away, squeezed the girl's waist, patted her knee and smiled what he hoped was a winning smile.

'And what might your name be, my Alpine rose?' His voice had a slightly slurred edge to it.

'Heidi.' She struggled to rise, but didn't really put her heart into it. 'Please, Major. I have work to do.'

'There is no more important work than entertaining soldiers of the Fatherland,' Smith said loudly. Holding Heidi firmly to forestall any attempt at escape, he took a long pull at his beer, then continued, quietly now, the mug still in front of his face: 'Shall I sing you a song?'

'What song?' Heidi asked warily. 'I hear too much singing.'

'I whistle better than I sing. Listen.' He whistled, very softly the first two bars of 'Lorelei'. 'Do you like that?'

Heidi stiffened and stared but immediately relaxed and smiled at him coquettishly.

'It's very nice, Major. And I'm sure you have a beautiful singing voice, too.'

Smith put his Steinbecher down with an unsteady bang that brought more disapproval from the other side of the table then lifted his hand to wipe the froth from his lips. Heidi smiled down at him, but the wary eyes weren't smiling.

Smith said from behind his hand: 'The men at the bar? The civilians? *Don't* turn round.'

'Gestapo.' She made another apparently futile attempt to free herself. 'From the castle.'

'One's a lip-reader.' Smith had the Steinbecher in front of his face again. 'I can tell. They're watching. Your room in five minutes. Hit me good and hard.'

Heidi stared at him in bewilderment, then yelped in pain as he pinched her, far from gently. She drew back, her right hand came over in a round-house swing and the sound of the slap could be heard clear across the crowded room, cutting sharply through the deep buzz of conversation. The voices died away, Steinbechers remained poised half-way towards lips, and every eye in the room turned until it was focused on the scene of the disturbance. Smith now had the exclusive and undivided attention of close on four hundred German soldiers which was exactly how he wanted it: no man anxious to avoid attention at all costs would ever do anything to incur the slightest risk of drawing that unwanted attention.

Heidi pushed herself to her feet, rubbed herself tenderly, snatched up the note which Smith had earlier placed on the table and stalked haughtily away. Smith, his already reddening face discomfited and tight in anger, rose, made to leave the table then halted when confronted by the Jäger captain who had already risen from his side of the table. He was a spruce, erect youngster, very much of the Hitler Jügend type, punctilious and correct but at that moment rather suffering from the effect of too many Steinbechers. Beneath the redly-dulled eyes lay a gleam which bespoke the not uncommon combination of self-importance and officious self-righteousness.

'Your conduct does not become an officer of the Wehrmacht,' he said loudly.

Smith did not reply at once. The embarrassed anger faded from his face to be replaced by an expressionlessly penetrating stare. He gazed unwinkingly into the captain's eyes for so long that the other finally looked away. When Smith's voice came it was too quiet to be heard even at the next table.

'*Herr* Major, when you talk to me, little man.' The tone was glacial: so now were also the eyes. 'Major Bernd Himmler. You may have heard of me?'

He paused significantly and the young captain seemed to shrink perceptibly before his eyes. Himmler, head of the Gestapo, was the most feared man in Germany. Smith could have been any relative of Himmler, possibly even his son.

'Report to me at 8 a.m. tomorrow morning,' Smith said curtly. He swung away without waiting for an answer. The Alpenkorps captain, suddenly very sober indeed, nodded wordlessly and sank wearily into his chair. As Smith strode towards the door the hubbub of conversation resumed. For the soldiers stationed in that remote military outpost, drinking beer, very large quantities of beer, was the only pastime: such incidents were no sooner seen than forgotten.

On his way to the door Smith stopped briefly by Schaffer and said: 'Well, I fouled that one up.'

'You could have handled it differently,' Schaffer conceded, then went on curiously: 'What did you say to him? The young Alpine Corps captain, I mean.'

'I gave him to understand that I was Himmler's son.'

'The Gestapo boss?' Schaffer asked incredulously. 'God above, you took a chance.'

'I couldn't afford to take a chance,' Smith said cryptically. 'I'll go try the "Eichhof". Better luck there, maybe. Back in ten minutes. Less.'

He left Schaffer looking uncertainly after him, made an urgent negative move of his hand towards Carraciola, who was approaching him, and passed outside. He moved a few paces along the wooden boardwalk, stopped and glanced briefly up and down the snow-filled street. It was deserted in both directions. He turned and walked quickly up a narrow alleyway which paralleled the side of 'Zum Wilden Hirsch'. At the rear stood a small wooden hut. Smith checked again that he was unobserved, opened the door quietly.

'Eight o'clock,' he said into the darkness. 'Come on.'

There was a rustle of clothes and Mary appeared in the doorway. She was shivering violently, her face blue-tinged with the extreme cold. She looked questioningly at Smith but he took her arm without a word and led her quickly to the back door of the *Gasthaus*. They entered a small hallway, dimly lit by an oil lamp, crossed it, climbed a flight of stairs, moved along a corridor and stopped at the second door on the right. They passed swiftly inside, Smith closing the door behind him.

It was a small room, plainly furnished, but from the chintz soft furnishings and toilet articles on a dressing-table, very obviously a feminine room. Mary sat down on the bed, hugging herself tightly to try to restore some warmth and looked up at Smith without any admiration in her face.

'I hope you're enjoying your little game,' she said bitterly. 'Seem to know your way around, don't you?'

'Instinct,' Smith explained. He stooped over the low-burning oil lamp by the bed, turned up the flame, glanced briefly about the room, located a battered leather case in one corner, swung it to the bed and snapped open the lid. The case contained women's clothing. He pulled Mary to her feet and said: 'Don't waste time. Take off your clothes. And when I say that, I mean your clothes. Every last stich. Then get into that top outfit there. You'll find everything you need.'

Mary stared at him.

'Those clothes? Why on earth must I—'

'Don't *argue*. Now!'

'Now it is,' she said resignedly. 'You might at least turn your back.'

'Relax,' Smith said wearily. 'I have other things on my mind.' He crossed to the window, stood peering out through a crack in the chintz curtains and went on: 'Now, hurry. You're supposed to be coming off the bus from Steingaden that arrives in twenty minutes' time. You'll be carrying that case, which contains the rest of your clothes. Your name is Maria Schenk, you're from Düsseldorf, a cousin of a barmaid that works here, and you've had TB and been forced to give up your factory job and go to the mountains for your health. So you've got this new job, through this barmaid, in the Schloss Adler. And you have identity papers, travel permit, references and letters in appropriately post-marked envelopes to prove all of it. They're in that handbag in the case. Think you got all that?'

'I – I think so,' she said uncertainly. 'But if you'd only tell me—'

'For God's sake!' Smith said impatiently. 'Time, girl, time! Got it or not?'

'Maria Schenk, Düsseldorf, factory, TB, cousin here, Steingaden – yes, I have it.' She broke off to pull a ribbed blue wool dress over her head, smoothed it down and said wonderingly: 'It's a perfect fit! You'd think this dress was made for me!'

'It *was* made for you.' Smith turned round to inspect her. '36-26-36 or whatever. We – um – broke into your flat and borrowed a dress to use as a model. Thorough, that's us.'

'You broke into my flat?' she asked slowly.

'Well, now, you wouldn't want to go around like a refugee from a jumble sale,' Smith said reasonably. He looked at the dress with an approving eye. 'Does something for you.'

'I'd like to do something for you,' she said feelingly. Her eyes mirrored her bafflement, her total lack of understanding. 'But – but it must have taken *weeks* to prepare those clothes – and those papers!'

'Like enough,' Smith agreed. 'Our Forgery Section did a very special job on those papers. Had to, to get you into the lion's den.'

'Weeks,' Mary said incredulously. 'Weeks! But General Carnaby's plane crashed only yesterday morning.' She stared at him, registering successive expressions of confusion, accusation and, finally, downright anger. 'You *knew* it was going to crash!'

'Right first time, my poppet,' Smith said cheerfully. He gave her an affectionate pat. 'We rigged it.'

'*Don't* do that,' she snapped, then went on carefully, her face still tight with anger: 'There really *was* a plane crash?'

'Guaranteed. The plane crash-landed on the airfield HQ of the Bavarian Mountain Rescue pilots. Place called Oberhausen, about five miles from here. The place we'll be leaving from, incidentally.'

'The place we'll be leaving—' She broke off, gazed at him a long moment then shook her head almost in despair. 'But – but in the plane I overheard you telling the men that if the mission failed or you had to split up that you were all to make a rendezvous at Frauenfeld, over the Swiss border.'

'Did you now?' There was mild interest in Smith's voice. 'I must be getting confused. Anyway, this Mosquito put down on the Oberhausen airfield riddled with machine-gun bullet holes. British machine-gun bullet holes, but what the hell, holes are holes.'

'And you'd risk the life of an American general – and all the plans for the Second Front—'

'Well, now, that's why I'm in such a hurry to get inside the Schloss Adler.' Smith cleared his throat. 'Not before they get his secrets out of him but before they find out that he's *not* an American general and knows no more about the Second Front than I do about the back of the moon.'

'What! He's a plant?'

'Name of Jones,' Smith nodded. 'Cartwright Jones. American actor. As a Thespian he's pretty second rate but he's a dead ringer for Carnaby.'

She looked at him with something like horror in her eyes.

'You'd risk an innocent—'

'He's getting plenty,' Smith interrupted. 'Twenty-five thousand dollars for a one-night stand. The peak of his professional career.'

There came a soft double knock on the door. A swift sliding movement of Smith's hand and a gun was suddenly there, a

Mauser automatic, cocked and ready to go. Another swift movement and he was silently by the door, jerking it open. Smith put his gun away. Heidi came in, Smith shutting the door behind her.

'Well, cousins, here we are,' he announced. 'Mary – now Maria – and Heidi. I'm off.'

'You're off!' Mary said dazedly. 'But – but what am I supposed to *do*?'

'Heidi will tell you.'

Mary looked uncertainly at the other girl. 'Heidi?'

'Heidi. Our top secret agent in Bavaria since 1941.'

'Our – top—' Mary shook her head. 'I don't believe it!'

'Nobody would.' Smith surveyed Heidi's opulent charms with an admiring eye. 'Brother, what a disguise!'

Smith opened the back door of the *Gasthaus* with a cautious hand, moved swiftly outside and remained stock-still in the almost total darkness, waiting for his eyes to become accustomed to the change of light. The snow, he thought, was heavier than when they had first entered 'Zum Wilden Hirsch' and the wind had certainly freshened. It was bitingly cold.

Satisfied that he was unobserved, Smith turned to the left, took two steps and bit off an exclamation as he tripped over some unseen object and fell his length in the snow. He rolled over three times in the snow just in case any bystander might have a knife or gun and homicidal ideas about using them, then got to his feet with cat-like speed, his Mauser in one hand, his pencil-flash in the other. He snapped on the torch and swung round in a 360° turn. He was alone.

Alone, that was, but for the crumpled form over which he had tripped, an Alpenkorps sergeant lying face-down in the snow, a form lying still and curiously relaxed in that huddled shapelessness of death.

Smith stooped and rolled the figure over to expose the great red stain in the snow were the body had been lying. The pencil-flash rested briefly on the front of the tunic, a tunic gashed and soaked in blood. The beam of the torch moved up to the face. No more cloisters for this don, Smith thought in irrational emptiness, no more honey still for tea, and the fault is all mine and I can see it in his face. The already dulled and faded eyes of Torrance-Smythe stared up at him in the sightless reproach of death.

Smith straightened to his feet, his face remote and withdrawn, and quartered the immediate ground area with his light. There were no signs of a struggle but struggle there must have been, for some tunic buttons had been ripped off and the high collar torn open. Smithy had not died easily. Flash still in hand, Smith walked slowly along to the mouth of the narrow alleyway, then stopped. A confusion of footprints, dark smears of blood in the trodden snow, dark bare patches on the wooden walls of the *Gasthaus* where struggling men had staggered heavily against it – here was where the struggle had been. Smith switched off the light, returned both torch and gun to their hiding-places and stepped out into the street. On the one side was 'Zum Wilden Hirsch' with the sound of singing once again emanating from it, on the other side a brightly-lit telephone kiosk outside a Post Office. In the kiosk, talking animatedly on the telephone, was a uniformed figure, a soldier Smith had never seen before. The street itself was deserted.

Schaffer leaned negligently against the bar, the picture of complete and careless relaxation. His face belied him. It was grim and shocked and he was savagely shedding a cigarette between his fingers.

'Smithy!' Schaffer's voice was a low and vicious whisper. 'Not Smithy! You *sure*, boss?'

'I'm sure.' Smith's face still held the same remote and withdrawn expression, almost as if all feeling had been drained from him. 'You say he left in a hurry three minutes after I'd gone. So he wasn't after me. Who else left?'

'No idea.' Schaffer snapped the cigarette in half, dropped it to the floor. 'The place is packed. And there's another door. I *can't* believe it. Why old Smithy? *Why* Torrance-Smythe. He was the cleverest of us all.'

'That's why he's dead,' Smith said somberly. 'Now listen carefully. It's time you knew the score.'

Schaffer looked at him steadily and said: 'It's more than time.'

Smith began to speak in a very low voice, in fluent completely idiomatic German, careful that his back was turned to the Gestapo officers at the far end of the bar. After a minute or two he saw Heidi returning to the room through the doorway behind the bar but ignored her as she ignored him. Almost immediately afterwards a gradual diminution in the babel of talk, followed by an almost complete silence, made him fall quiet himself and follow the direction of the gaze of hundreds of soldiers all of whom were looking towards the door.

There was a reason for the silence, especially good reason, Smith thought, for soldiers almost totally cut off from woman-kind. Mary Ellison, clad in a belted rain-coat, with a scarf over her head and a battered suitcase in her hand, was standing in the doorway. The silence seemed to deepen. Women are rare at any time in a high Alpine *Gastbaus*, unaccompanied young women even rarer and beautiful young women on their own virtually unknown. For some moments Mary stood there uncertainly, as if unsure of her welcome or not knowing what to do. Then she dropped her bag, and her face lit up as she caught sight of Heidi, a face transformed with joy. Marlene Dietrich in *The Blue Angel,* Smith thought inconsequentially. With a face and a fig-ure and an acting talent like that, she could have had Hollywood tramping a path of beaten gold to her doorstep . . . Through the silent room she and Heidi ran toward one another and embraced.

'My dear Maria! My dear Maria!' There was a break in Heidi's voice that made Smith reflect that Hollywood might have been well advised to tramp out two paths of beaten gold. 'So you came after all!'

'After all these years!' Mary hugged the other girl and kissed her again. 'It's wonderful to see you again, Cousin Heidi! Won-derful, wonderful, wonderful! Of *course* I came. Why ever not?'

'Well!' Heidi made no effort to lower her voice as she looked around significantly. 'They're a pretty rough lot, hereabouts. You should carry a gun, always. Hunter battalion, they call themselves. They're well named!'

The soldiers broke out into a roar of laughter and the normal hubbub of sound resumed almost at once. Arm in arm, Heidi led Mary across to the small group of civilians standing at the far end of the bar. She stopped in front of the man in the centre of the group, a dark, wiry, intelligent-faced man who looked very very tough indeed, and performed the introductions.

'Maria, this is Captain von Brauchitsch. He – um – works in the Schloss Adler. Captain, my cousin, Maria Schenk.'

Von Brauchitsch bowed slightly.

'You are fortunate in your cousins, Heidi. We were expect-ing you, Miss Schenk.' He smiled. 'But not someone as beautiful as this.'

Mary smiled in turn, her face puzzled. 'You were expecting—'

'He was expecting,' Heidi said dryly. 'It is the captain's business to know what is going on.'

'Don't make me sound so sinister, Heidi. You'll frighten Miss

Schenk.' He glanced at his watch. 'The next cable-car leaves in ten minutes. If I might escort the young lady—'

'The young lady is going to my room first,' Heidi said firmly. 'For a wash-up and a Kaffee-Schnapps. Can't you see that she's half-dead with cold?'

'I do believe her teeth are chattering,' von Brauchitsch said with a smile. 'I thought it might have been me. Well, the cable-car after the next one, then.'

'And I'm going with her,' Heidi announced.

'Both of you?' Von Brauchitsch shook his head and smiled again. Von Brauchitsch was always smiling. 'My lucky night.'

'Permits, travel documents, identity cards and letters you have,' Heidi said. She fished up some papers from the recesses of her Tyrolean blouse and handed them to Mary who was sitting across from her on the bed in her room. 'Plan of the castle and instructions. Do your homework well then give them back to me. I'll take them up. You might be searched – they're a suspicious bunch up there. And drink up that Schnapps – first thing von Brauchitsch will do is to smell your breath. Just to check. He checks everything. He's the most suspicious of the lot.'

'He seemed a very pleasant man to me,' Mary said mildly.

'He's a very unpleasant Gestapo officer,' Heidi said dryly.

When Heidi returned to the bar, Smith and Schaffer had been rejoined by Carraciola, Thomas and Christiansen. All five appeared to be carefree in their drinking and chatting inconsequentially, but their low and urgent voices were evidence enough of the desperate worry in their minds. Or in the minds of some of them.

'You haven't seen old Smithy, then?' Smith asked quietly. 'None of you saw him go? Then where in hell has he got to?'

There was no reply, but the shrugs and worried frowns were reply enough. Christiansen said: 'Shall I go and have a look?'

'I don't think so,' Smith said. 'I'm afraid it's too late to go anywhere now.'

Both doors of 'Zum Wilden Hirsch' had suddenly burst open and half a dozen soldiers were coming quickly in through either door. All had slung machine-carbines, Schmeissers, at the ready. They fanned out along the walls and waited, machine-carbines horizontal, fingers on triggers, their eyes very calm, very watchful.

'Well, well,' Christiansen murmured. 'It was a nice war.'

The sudden and total silence was emphasised rather than broken by the crisp footfalls on the wooden floor as a full colonel of the Wehrmacht came striding into the room and looked coldly around him. The gargantuan proprietor of the *Gasthaus* came hurrying round from the back of the bar, tripping over chairs in the anxiety and fear limned so unmistakably clearly in his round pumpkin of a face.

'Colonel Weissner!' It required no acute ear to catch the shake in the proprietor's voice. 'What in God's name—'

'No fault of yours, mein Herr.' The colonel's words were reassuring which was more than the tone of his voice was. 'But you harbour enemies of the state.'

'Enemies of the state.' In a matter of seconds the proprietor's complexion had changed from a most unbecoming puce to an even more unbecoming washed-out grey while his voice now quavered like a high-C tuning fork. 'What? I? I. Josef Wartmann—'

'Please.' The colonel held up his hand for silence. 'We are looking for four or five Alpenkorps deserters from the Stuttgart military prison. To escape, they killed two officers and a guard-room sergeant. They were known to be heading this way.'

Smith nodded and said in Schaffer's ear: 'Very clever. Very clever indeed.'

'Now then,' Weissner continued briskly. 'If they're here, we'll soon have them. I want the senior officers present of drafts thirteen, fourteen and fifteen to come forward.' He waited until two majors and a captain came forward and stood at attention before him. 'You know all your officers and men by sight?'

The three officers nodded.

'Good. I wish you—'

'No need, Colonel.' Heidi had come round from behind the bar and now stood before Weissner, hands clasped respectfully behind her back. 'I know the man you're after. The ringleader.'

'Ah!' Colonel Weissner smiled. 'The charming—'

'Heidi, Herr Colonel. I have waited table on you up in the Schloss Adler.'

Weissner bowed gallantly. 'As if one could ever forget.'

'That one.' Her face full of a combination of righteous indignation and devotion to duty, Heidi pointed a dramatically accusing finger at Smith. 'That's the one, Herr Colonel. He – he pinched me!'

'My dear Heidi!' Colonel Weissner smiled indulgently. 'If

we were to convict every man who ever harboured thoughts of—'

'Not that, Herr Colonel. He asked me what I knew or had heard about a man called General Cannabee – I think.'

'General Carnaby!' Colonel Weissner was no longer smiling. He glanced at Smith, motioned guards to close in on him, then glanced back at Heidi. 'What did you tell him?'

'Herr Colonel!' Heidi was stiff with outraged dignity. 'I hope I am a good German. *And* I value my engagements at the Schloss Adler.' She half-turned and pointed across the room. 'Captain von Brauchitsch of the Gestapo will vouch for me.'

'No need. We will not forget this, my dear child.' He patted her affectionately on the cheek, then turned to Smith, the temperature of his voice dropping from warm to sub-zero. 'Your accomplices, sir, and at once.'

'At once, my dear Colonel?' The look he gave Heidi was as glacial as the Colonel's voice. 'Surely not. Let's get our priorities straight. First, her thirty pieces of silver. Then us.'

'You talk like a fool,' Colonel Weissner said contemptuously. 'Heidi is a true patriot.'

'I'm sure she is,' Smith said bitterly.

Mary, her face still and shocked, stared down from the uncurtained crack in Heidi's dark room as Smith and the four others were led out of the front door of 'Zum Wilden Hirsch' and marched off down the road under heavy escort to where several command cars were parked on the far side of the street. Brusquely, efficiently, the prisoners were bundled into two of the cars, engines started up and within a minute both cars were lost to sight round a bend in the road. For almost a minute aferwards Mary stood there, staring out unseeingly on the swirling snow, then pulled the curtains together and turned back towards the darkened room.

She said in a whisper: 'How did it happen?'

A match scratched as Heidi lit and turned up the flame of the oil lamp.

'I can't guess.' Heidi shrugged. 'Someone, I don't know who, must have tipped Colonel Weissner off. But I put the finger on him.'

Mary stared at her. 'You – you—'

'He'd have been found out in another minute anyway. They were strangers. But it strengthens our hand. I – and you – are now above suspicion.'

588

'Above suspicion!' Mary looked at her in disbelief then went on, almost wildly: 'But there's no point in going ahead now!'

'Is there not?' Heidi said thoughtfully. 'Somehow, I feel sorrier for Colonel Weissner than I do for Major Smith. Is not our Major Smith a man of resource? Or do our employers in Whitehall lie to us? When they told me he was coming here, they told me not to worry, to trust him implicitly. A man of infinite resource – those were their exact words – who can extricate himself from positions of utmost difficulty. They have a funny way of talking in Whitehall. But already I trust him. Don't you?'

There was no reply. Mary stared at the floor, her eyes bright with unshed tears. Heidi touched her arm and said softly. 'You love him as much as that?'

Mary nodded in silence.

'And does he love you?'

'I don't know. I just don't know. He's been too long in this business – even if he did know,' she said bitterly, 'he probably wouldn't tell himself.'

Heidi looked at her for a moment, shook her head and said: 'They should never have sent you. How can you hope to—' She broke off, shook her head again, and went on: 'It's too late now. Come on. We mustn't keep von Brauchitsch waiting.'

'But – but if he doesn't come? If he can't escape – and how *can* he escape?' She gestured despairingly at the papers lying on the bed. 'They're bound to check with Düsseldorf first thing in the morning about those forged references.'

Heidi said without any particular expression in her voice: 'I don't think he'd let *you* down, Mary.'

'No,' Mary said dolefully. 'I don't suppose he would.'

The big black Mercedes command car swept along the snow-packed road that paralleled the Blau See, the windscreen wipers just coping with the thickly-swirling snow that rushed greyly back at the windscreen through powerful headlight beams. It was an expensive car and a very comfortable one, but neither Schaffer up front nor Smith in the rear seat experienced any degree of comfort whatsoever, either mental or physical. On the mental side there was the bitter prospect of the inevitable firing squad and the knowledge that their mission was over even before it had properly begun: on the physical side they were cramped in the middle of their seats, Schaffer flanked by driver and guard, Smith by Colonel Weissner and guard, and both

Smith and Schaffner were suffering from pain in the lower ribs: the owners of the Schmeisser machine-pistols, the muzzles of which were grinding into the captives' sides, had no compunction about letting their presence be known.

They were now, Smith estimated, half-way between village and barracks. Another thirty seconds and they would be through the barrack gates. Thirty seconds. No more.

'Stop this car!' Smith's voice was cold, authoritative with an odd undertone of menace. 'Immediately, do you hear? I must think.'

Colonel Weissner, startled, turned and stared at him. Smith ignored him completely. His face reflected an intensely frowning concentration, a thin-lipped anger barely under control, the face of a man to whom the thought of disobedience of his curt instruction was unthinkable: most certainly not the face of a man going to captivity and death. Weissner hesitated, but only fractionally. He gave an order and the big car began to slow.

'You oaf! You utter idiot!' Smith's tone, shaking with anger, was low and vicious, so low that only Weissner could hear it. 'You've almost certainly ruined everything and, by God, if you have, Weissner, you'll be without a regiment tomorrow!'

The car pulled into the roadside and stopped. Ahead, the red tail lights of the command car in front vanished into a snow-filled darkness. Weissner said brusquely, but with a barely perceptible tremor of agitation in his voice: 'What the devil are you talking about?'

'You knew about this American general, Carnaby?' Smith's face, eyes narrowed and teeth bared in anger, was within six inches of Weissner's. 'How?' He almost spat the word out.

'I dined in the Schloss Adler last night. I—'

Smith looked at him in total incredulity.

'Colonel Paul Kramer told you? He actually talked to you about him?' Weissner nodded wordlessly 'Admiral Canaris' Chief of Staff! And now everybody knows. God in heaven, heads will roll for this.' He screwed the heels of his palms into his eyes, lowered his hands wearily to his thighs, gazed ahead unseeingly and shook his head, very slowly. 'This is too big, even for me.' He fished out his pass and handed it to Weissner, who examined it in the beam of a none too steady torch. 'Back to the barracks at once! I must get through to Berlin immediately. My uncle will know what to do.'

'Your uncle?' By what seemed a great effort of will Weissner

590

looked up from the pass he held in his hand: his voice was no steadier than the torch. *'Heinrich* Himmler?'

'Who do you think?' Smith snarled. 'Mickey Mouse?' He dropped his voice to a low murmur. 'I trust you never have the privilege of meeting him, Colonel Weissner.' He gave Weissner the benefit of a long and speculative look singularly lacking in any encouragement, then turned away and prodded the driver, none too lightly, in the back. 'The barracks – and make it quick!'

The car moved off. Anything that the nephew of the dreaded Heinrich Himmler, Chief of the Gestapo, said was good enough for the driver.

Smith turned to the guard by his side. 'Take that damned thing out of my ribs!'

Angrily, he snatched the gun away. The guard, who had also heard of Himmler, meekly yielded up the machine-pistol. One second later he was doubled up in helpless retching agony as the butt of the Schmeisser smashed into his stomach and another second later Colonel Weissner was pinned against the window of his Mercedes as the muzzle of the Schmeisser ground into his right ear.

Smith said: 'If your men move, you die.'

'Okay.' Schaffer's calm voice from the front seat. 'I have their guns.'

'Stop the car,' Smith ordered.

The car came to a halt. Through the windscreen Smith could see the lights of the barracks guard-room, now less than two hundred yards away. He gave Weissner a prod with the Schmeisser muzzle.

'Out!'

Weissner's face was a mask of chagrined rage but he was too experienced a soldier even to hesitate. He got out.

'Three paces from the car,' Smith said. 'Face down on the snow. Hands clasped behind your head. Schaffer, your gun on your guard. Out beside the General, you.' This with his gun muzzle in the driver's neck.

Twenty seconds later, Schaffer at the wheel, they were on their way, leaving three men face downwards in the snow and the fourth, Smith's erstwhile guard, still doubled up in agony by the roadside.

'A creditable effort, young Himmler,' Schaffer said approvingly.

'I'll never be that lucky again,' Smith said soberly. 'Take

591

your time passing the barracks. We don't want any of the sentries getting the wrong idea.'

At a steady twenty miles an hour they passed the main gates and then the secondary gates, apparently, as far as Smith could see, without exciting any comment. Just behind the three-pointed star on the car's radiator flew a small triangular pennant, the Camp Commandant's personal standard, and no one, it was safe to assume, would question the comings and goings of Colonel Weissner.

For half a mile or so beyond the secondary gates the road ran northwards in a straight line with, on the left, a sheer hundred-foot cliff dropping down into the waters of the Blau See, and, to the right, a line of pines, not more than fifty yards wide, backing up against another vertical cliff-face which soared up until lost in the snow and the darkness.

At the end of the half-mile straight, the road ahead swept sharply to the right to follow an indentation in the Blau See's shore-line, a dangerous corner marked by white fencing which would normally have been conspicuous enough by night-time but which was at the moment all but invisible against the all-enveloping background of snow. Schaffer braked for the corner. A thoughtful expression crossed his face and he applied still heavier pressure to the brake pedal and glanced at Smith.

'An excellent idea.' It was Smith's turn to be approving. 'We'll make an agent out of you yet.'

The Mercedes stopped. Smith gathered up the Schmeissers and pistols they had taken from Weissner and his men and got out. Schaffer wound down the driver's window, released the hand-brake, engaged gear and jumped out as the car began to move. With his right arm through the window Schaffer walked and then, as the car began to gather speed, ran along beside the Mercedes, his hand on the steering wheel. Twenty feet from the cliff edge he gave a last steering correction, jerked the quadrant hand throttle wide open and leapt aside as the car accelerated. The wooden fence never had a chance. With a splintering crash barely audible above the roaring of the engine at maximum revs in first gear, the Mercedes went through the barrier as if it had been made of cardboard, shot out over the edge of the cliff and disappeared from sight.

Smith and Schaffer reached the safety of an unbroken stretch of fencing and peered down just in time to see the car, upside down now and its headlamps still blazing, strike the surface of the lake with an oddly flat explosive sound, like distant gunfire. A column of water and weirdly phosphorescent spray reached half-way up the cliff side. When it subsided, they could at once locate from an underwater luminescence the position of the sinking car: the headlamps were still burning. Smith and Schaffer looked at each other then Smith thoughtfully removed his peaked cap and sent it sailing over the edge. The strong gusting wind blew the cap in against the cliff face, but it tumbled on down and landed, inside up, on still surfacing bubbles iridescently glittering from the light now far below. Then the light went out.

'So who cares?' Schaffer straightened up from the fencing and shrugged his shoulders. 'Wasn't our car. Back to the village, hey?'

'Not on your life,' Smith said emphatically. 'And I mean that – literally. Come on. Other way.'

Clutching their recently acquired weapons, they ran round the corner in the direction in which the car had been travelling. They had covered less than seventy yards when they heard the sound of car engines and saw wavering beams lighting up the splintered fence. Seconds later Smith and Schaffer were off the road, hidden in the pines and moving slowly back in the direction of a command car and two armoured cars that had now pulled up at the broken barrier.

'That's it, then, Herr Colonel.' An Alpenkorps sergeant with shoulder-slung gun peered gingerly over the edge of the cliff. 'Going too fast, saw it too late – or never saw it at all. The Blau See is over a hundred metres deep here, Herr Colonel. They're gone.'

'Maybe they're gone and maybe they're not. I wouldn't trust that lot as far as my front door.' Colonel Weissner's voice carried clearly and sounded bitter. 'They may have faked it and doubled back. Send one party of men straight into the pines there as far as the cliff wall. Five metre spacing. Let them use their torches. Then another party of men five hundred metres in the car back towards the camp. You go with them, Sergeant. Again spread out to the cliff-face. Let them come together. And be quick.'

Schaffer, from his hiding-place behind the bole of a pine, looked thoughtfully at Smith.

'I have to concede a point, boss, it's perhaps as well we didn't go straight back to the village. Cunning old devil, isn't he?'

'And what does that make me?' Smith murmured.

'Okay, okay. I'll concede that point, too.'

Five minutes passed. Comparatively little of the falling snow penetrated the thickly-matted branches of the pines and the two men could clearly see the occasional flicker of torches as the line of men nearest them moved away to the south, their lights probing behind tree-trunks and under windfalls as they searched for the two escaped prisoners. Colonel Weissner paced up and down, slowly, beside his command car, his head bowed as if immersed in thought. From time to time he consulted his watch. As Smith watched, he moved out to the unbroken fencing and remained there, peering down towards the surface of the Blau See.

By and by Smith and Schaffer could hear the distant sound of muffled voices and within a minute the sergeant moved into the beam of the command car headlamps, approached Colonel Weissner and saluted.

'Not even a footprint, Herr Colonel.'

Weissner straightened and turned.

'There wouldn't be,' he said sombrely. 'I've just seen a hat floating in the water. A squalid end for such brave men, Sergeant. A squalid end.'

5

The cable-car moved slowly out of the lower station at the beginning of its long climb up to the castle. An impossible climb, Mary thought, a dangerous and impossible climb. Peering through the front windows she could just distinguish the outline of the first pylon through the thinly-driving snow. The second and third pylons were invisible, but the intermittently shining cluster of lights suspended impossibly high in the sky showed clearly enough where they had to go. People have made it before, she thought dully, we'll probably make it, too. The way she felt then, with the bottom gone from her world, she didn't particularly care whether she made it or not.

The cable-car was a twelve-passenger vehicle, painted bright red outside, well-lit inside. There were no seats, only grab-rails along the two sides. That the grab-rails were very necessary became immediately and alarmingly obvious. The wind was now very strong and the car began to sway alarmingly only seconds after clearing the shelter of the lower station.

Apart from two soldiers and an apparent civilian, the only other passengers consisted of von Brauchitsch, Mary and Heidi, the last now with a heavy woollen coat and cossack fur hat over her ordinary clothes. Von Brauchitsch, holding on to the grab-rail with one hand, had his free arm round Mary's shoulders. He gave them a reassuring squeeze and smiled down at her.

'Scared?' he asked.

'No.' And she wasn't, she hadn't enough emotion left to be scared, but even with no hope left she was supposed to be a professional. 'No, I'm not scared. I'm terrified. I feel sea-sick already. Does – does this cable ever break.'

'Never.' Von Brauchitsch was reassurance itself. 'Just hang on to me and you'll be all right.'

'That's what he used to say to me,' Heidi said coldly.

'Fräulein,' von Brauchitsch explained patiently, 'I am gifted beyond the average, but I haven't yet managed to grow a third arm. Guests first.'

With a cupped cigarette in his hand, Schaffer leaned against the base of an unmistakable telephone pole and gazed thoughtfully into the middle distance. There was reason both for the hooded cigarette and the thoughtful expression. Less than a hundred yards away from where he stood at the edge of the pines bordering the road running alongside the shore of the Blau See he could see guards, clearly illuminated by over-head lights, moving briskly to and fro in the vicinity of the barrack gates. Dimly seen behind them were the outline of the barracks themselves.

Schaffer shifted his stance and gazed upwards. The snow was almost gone now, the moon was threatening to break through, and he had no difficulty at all in distinguishing the form of Smith, his legs straddled across the lowest cross-bar.

Smith was busily employed with a knife, a specially designed commando knife which, among other advanced features, had a built-in wire cutter. Carefully, methodically, he brought the wire-cutter to bear. With eight consecutive snips eight consecutive telephone wires fell to the ground. Smith closed and pocketed his knife, disentangled his legs from the cross-bar, wrapped his arms round the pole and slid down to he ground. He grinned at Schaffer.

'Every little helps,' he said.

'Should hold them for a while,' Schaffer agreed. Once more they gathered up their guns and moved off to the east, vanishing into the pine woods which bordered the rear of the barracks.

The cable-car swayed more alarmingly than ever. It had now entered upon the last near-vertical lap of its journey. With von Brauchitsch's arm still around her shoulders, with her face still pressed against the front windows of the car, Mary stared up at the towering battlements, white as the driving snow, and thought that they reached up almost to the clouds themselves. As she watched, a break came in the wisping clouds and the whole fairy-tale castle was bathed in bright moonlight. Fear touched her eyes, she moistened her lips and gave an involuntary shiver. Nothing escaped von Brauchitsch's acute perception. He gave her shoulders another reassuring squeeze, perhaps the twentieth in that brief journey.

'Not to worry, Fräulein. It will be all right.'

'I hope so.' Her voice was the ghost of a whisper.

The same unexpected moonlight almost caught Smith and Schaffer. They had just crossed the station tracks and were moving stealthily along towards the left luggage office when the moon broke through. But they were still in the shadows of the over-hanging station roof. They pressed back into those shadows and peered along the tracks, past the hydraulic bumpers which marked the end of the line. Clearly now, sharply-limned as if in full daylight, red etched against the white, they could see one cable-car approaching the lower station, the other climbing the last few vertical feet towards the header station and, above that, the dazzling outline of the Schloss Adler glittering under the bright moon.

'That helps,' Schaffer said bitterly. 'That helps a lot.'

'Sky's still full of clouds,' Smith said mildly. He bent to the keyhole of the left luggage office, used his skeleton keys and moved inside. Schaffer followed, closing the door.

Smith located their rucksacks, cut a length of rope from the nylon, wrapped it round his waist and began stuffing some hand grenades and plastic explosives into a canvas bag. He raised his head as Schaffer diffidently cleared his throat.

'Boss?' This with an apprehensive glance through the window.

'Uh-huh?'

'Boss, has it occurred to you that Colonel Weissner probably knows all about this cache by this time? What I mean is, we may have company soon.'

'We may indeed,' Smith admitted. 'Surprised if we don't have. That's why I've cut this itsy-bitsy piece of rope off the big coil and why I'm taking the explosives and grenades only from my rucksack and yours. It's a very big coil – and no one knows what's inside our rucksacks. So it's unlikely that anything will be missed.'

'But the radio—'

'If we broadcast from here we might be caught in the act. If we take it away and they find it gone they'll know that that car at the bottom of the Blau See is empty. Is that it?'

'More or less.'

'So we compromise. We remove it, but we return it here after we've broadcast from a safe place.'

'What do you mean "safe place",' Schaffer demanded plaintively. The darkly saturnine face was unhappy. 'There isn't a safe place in Bavaria.'

'There's one not twenty yards away. Last place they'd look.' He tossed Schaffer a bunch of skeleton keys. 'Ever been inside a Bavarian ladies' cloakroom?'

Schaffer fielded the keys, stared at Smith, shook his head and left. Quickly he moved down the tracks, his torch flashing briefly on and off. Finally his torch settled on a doorway with, above it, the legend DAMEN.

Schaffer looked at it, pursed his lips, shrugged his shoulders and got to work on the lock.

Slowly, with apparently infinite labour, the cable-car completed the last few feet of its ascent and passed in under the roof of the Schloss Adler header station. It juddered to a halt, the front door opened and the passengers disembarked. They moved from the header station – built into the north-west base of the castle – up through a steeply-climbing twenty-five foot tunnel which had heavy iron doors and guards at either end. Passing the top gateway, they emerged into the courtyard, the entrance of which was sealed off by a massively-barred iron gate guarded by heavily armed soldiers and Dobermann pinchers. The courtyard itself was brightly illuminated by the light of dozens of uncurtained interior windows. In the very centre of the courtyard stood the helicopter which had that morning brought Reichsmarschall Rosemeyer to the Schloss Adler. Under the cover of a heavy tarpaulin – momentarily unnecessary because of the cessation of the snow – a dungareed figure, possibly the pilot, worked on the helicopter engine with the aid of a small but powerful arc-lamp.

Mary turned to von Brauchitsch, still holding a proprietary grip on her arm, and smiled ruefully.

'So many soldiers. So many men – and, I'm sure, so few women. What happens if I want to escape from the licentious soldiery?'

'Easy.' Von Brauchitsch really did have, Mary thought dully, a most charming smile. 'Just jump from your bedroom window. One hundred metres straight down and there you are. Free!'

The ladies' cloakroom in the station was a superlatively nondescript place, bleakly furnished with hard-backed benches, chairs, deal tables and a sagging wooden floor. The Spartans would have turned up their noses at it, in its sheer lack of decorative inspiration it could have been surpassed only by its counterpart in England. The expiring remains of a fire burnt dully in a black enamel stove.

Smith was seated by the central table, radio beside him, consulting a small book by the light of a hooded pencil-flash and writing on a slip of paper. He checked what he had written, straightened and handed the book to Schaffer.

'Burn it. Page by page.'

'Page by page? All?' Surprise in the saturnine face. 'You won't be requiring this any more?'

Smith shook his head and began to crank the radio handle.

There was a very much better fire in the Operations Room in Whitehall, a pine-log fire with a healthy crackle and flames of a respectable size. But the two men sitting on either side of the fire were a great deal less alert than the two men sitting by the dying embers of the fire in the Bavarian Alps. Admiral Rolland and Colonel Wyatt-Turner were frankly dozing, eyes shut, more asleep than awake. But they came to full wakefulness, jerking upright, almost instantly, when the long-awaited call-sign came through on the big transceiver manned by the civilian operator at the far end of the room. They glanced at each other, heaved themselves out of their deep arm-chairs.

'Broadsword calling Danny Boy.' The voice on the radio was faint but clear. 'Broadsword calling Danny Boy. You hear me? Over.'

The civilian operator spoke into his microphone, 'We hear you. over.'

'Code. Ready? Over.'

'Ready. Over.'

Rolland and Wyatt-Turner were by the operator's shoulder now, his eyes fixed on his pencil as he began to make an instantaneous transcription of the meaningless jumble of letters beginning to come over the radio. Swiftly the message was spelt out: TORRANCE-SMYTH MURDERED. THOMAS CHRISTIANSEN AND CARRACIOLA CAPTURED.

As if triggered by an unheard signal, the eyes of Rolland and Wyatt-Turner lifted and met. Their faces were strained and grim. Their eyes returned to the flickering pencil.

ENEMY BELIEVE SCHAFFER AND SELF DEAD, the message continued. EFFECTING ENTRY INSIDE THE HOUR. PLEASE HAVE TRANSPORT STANDING BY NINETY MINUTES. OVER.

Admiral Rolland seized the microphone from the operator.

'Broadsword! Broadsword! Do you know who I am, Broadswords?'

'I know who you are, sir. Over.'

'Pull out, Broadsword. Pull out now. Save yourselves. Over.'

'You – must – be – joking.' The words were spoken in slow motion, a perceptible pause between each pair. 'Over.'

'You heard me.' Rolland's voice was almost as slow and distinct. 'You *heard* me. That was an order, Broadsword.'

'Mary is already inside. Over and out.'

The transceiver went dead.

'He's gone, sir,' the operator said quietly.

'He's gone,' Rolland repeated mechanically. 'Dear God, he's gone.'

Colonel Wyatt-Turner moved away and sat down heavily in his chair by the fire. For such a big, burly man he appeared curiously huddled and shrunken. He looked up dully as Admiral Rolland sank into the opposite chair.

'It's all my fault.' The Colonel's voice was barely distinguishable. 'All my fault.'

'We did what we had to do. All *our* fault, Colonel. It was my idea.' He gazed into the fire. 'Now this – this on top of everything else.'

'Our worst day,' Wyatt-Turner agreed heavily. 'Our worst day ever. Maybe I'm too old.'

'Maybe we're all too old.' With his right forefinger Rolland

599

began to tick off the fingers of his left hand. 'HQ Commander-in-Chief, Porstmouth. Secret alarm triggered. Nothing missing.'

'Nothing taken,' Wyatt-Turner agreed wearily. 'But the vigil emulsion plates show photostatic copies taken.'

'Two. Southampton. Barge-movement duplicates missing. Three, Plymouth. Time-lock in the naval HQ inoperative. We don't know what this means.'

'We can guess.'

'We can guess. Dover. Copy of a section of the Mulberry Harbour plans missing. An error? Carelessness? We'll never know. Five, Bradley's HQ guard sergeant missing. Could mean anything.'

'Could mean everything. All the troop movements for Overlord's Omaha beach are there.'

'Lastly, seven OS reports today. France, Belgium, Netherlands. Four demonstrably false. Other three unverifiable.'

For long moments there was a heavy, a defeated silence, finally broken by Wyatt-Turner.

'If there was ever any doubt, there's none now.' He spoke without looking up, his eyes gazing emptily into the fire. 'The Germans have almost total penetration here – and we have almost none on the continent. And now this – Smith and his men, I mean.'

'Smith and his men,' Rolland echoed. 'Smith and his men. We can write them off.'

Wyatt-Turner dropped his voice, speaking so softly that the radio operator couldn't overhear.

'And Operation Overlord, sir?'

'Operation Overlord,' Rolland murmured. 'Yes, we can write that off, too.'

'Intelligence is the first arm of modern warfare,' Wyatt-Turner said bitterly. 'Or has someone said that before?'

'No intelligence, no war.' Admiral Rolland pressed an intercom button. 'Have my car brought round. Coming, Colonel? To the airfield?'

'And a lot farther than that. If I have your permission, sir.'

'We've discussed it.' Admiral Rolland shrugged. 'I understand how you feel. Kill yourself if you must.'

'I've no intention.' Wyatt-Turner crossed to a cupboard and took out a Sten gun, turned to Rolland and smiled: 'We may encounter hostiles, sir.'

'You may indeed.' There was no answering smile on the Admiral's face.

'You heard what the man said?' Smith switched off the transmitter, telescoped the aerial and glanced across at Schaffer. 'We can pull out now.'

'Pull out now? Pull out now?' Schaffer was outraged. 'Don't you realize that if we do they'll get to Mary inside twelve hours.' He paused significantly, making sure he had all Smith's attention. 'And if they get to her they're bound to get to Heidi ten minutes later.'

'Come off it, Lieutenant,' Smith said protestingly. 'You've only seen her once, for five minutes.'

'So?' Schaffer was looking positively belligerent. 'How often did Paris see Helen of Troy? How often did Antony see Cleopatra. How often did Romeo—' He broke off then went on defiantly: 'And I don't care if she is a traitor spying on her own people.'

'She was born and brought up in Birmingham,' Smith said wearily.

'So who cares? I draw the line at nothing. Even if she is a Limey—' He paused. 'English?'

'Come on,' Smith said. 'Let's return this radio. We may have callers soon.'

'We mustn't be raising too many eyebrows,' Schaffer agreed.

They returned the radio, locked the left luggage office and were just moving towards the station exit when they were halted by the sound of truck engines and a siren's ululation. They pressed back against a wall as headlights lit up the station entrance. The leading truck came to a skidding halt not ten yards away.

Schaffer looked at Smith. 'Discretion, I think?'

'Discretion, indeed. Behind the booking office.'

The two men moved swiftly alongside the tracks and hid in the deep shadows behind the booking office. A sergeant, the one who had organised the search along the Blau See, came running through the entrance, followed by four soldiers, located the left luggage office, tried the door handle, reversed his machine-pistol and hammered the lock without effect, reversed his gun again, shot away the lock and passed inside, torch in hand. He appeared at the doorway almost at once.

'Tell the captain. They didn't lie. The Engländers' gear is here!' One of the soldiers left and the sergeant said to the three remaining men: 'Right. Get their stuff out and load it up.'

'There goes my last pair of cotton socks,' Schaffer murmured mournfully as their rucksacks were taken away. 'Not to mention my toothbrush and—'

He broke off as Smith caught his arm. The sergeant had stopped the man carrying the radio, taken it from him, placed his hand on it and stood quite still. He was directly under one of the small swinging electric lights and the expression on his face could clearly be seen to change from puzzlement to disbelief to complete and shocked understanding.

'Kapitan!' the sergeant shouted. 'Kapitan.'

An officer came hurrying through the station entrance.

'The radio, Kapitan! It's warm, very warm! It's been in use inside the last five minutes.'

'In the last five minutes? Impossible!' He stared at the sergeant. 'Unless—'

'Yes, Herr Kapitan. Unless.'

'Surround the station,' the officer shouted. 'Search every room.'

'Oh God!' Schaffer moaned. 'Why can't they leave us alone?'

'Quickly,' Smith said softly. He took Schaffer's arm and they moved through the dark shadows till they reached the ladies' cloakroom. Carefully not to rattle his skeleton keys, Smith had the door open in seconds. They passed inside and locked the door behind them.

'This won't look so good in my obituary,' Schaffer said dolefully. There was a perceptible edge of strain under the lightly-spoken words.

'What won't?'

'Gave his life for his country in a ladies' lavatory in Upper Bavaria. How can a man RIP with that on his mind? . . . What's our friend outside saying?'

'If you shut up we might hear.'

'And when I say everywhere, I mean everywhere.' The German captain was barking out his commands in the best parade-ground fashion. 'If a door is locked, break it open. If you can't break it open, shoot the lock away. And if you don't want to die in the next five minutes, never forget that these are violent and extremely dangerous men almost certainly armed with stolen Schmeisser machine-pistols, apart from their own weapons. Make no attempt to capture them. Shoot on sight and shoot to kill.'

'You heard?' Smith said.

'I'm afraid I did.' There was a perceptible click as Schaffer cocked his machine-pistol.

They stood side-by-side in the darkness listening to the sounds of the search, the calling of voices, the hammering of rifle butts on wood, the splintering of yielding doors, the occasional short burst of machine-gun fire where a door, presumably, had failed to yield to more conventional methods of persuasion. The sounds of the approaching search grew very close.

'They're getting warm,' Schaffer murmured.

Schaffer had underestimated the temperature. Just as he finished speaking an unseen hand closed on the outer door handle and rattled the door furiously. Smith and Schaffer moved silently and took up position pressed close against the wall, one on either side of the door.

The rattling ceased. A heavy crashing impact from the outside shook the door on its hinges. A second such impact and the woodwork in the jamb by the lock began to splinter. Two more would do it, Smith thought, two more.

But there were no more.

'*Gott in Himmel*, Hans!' The voice beyond the door held – or appeared to hold – a mixture of consternation and outrage. 'What are you thinking of? Can't you read?'

'Can't I—' The second voice broke off abruptly and when it came again it was in tones of defensive apology. 'DAMEN! *Mein Gott!* DAMEN!' A pause. 'If you, had spent as many years on the Russian Front as I have—' His voice faded as the two men moved away.

'God bless our common Anglo-Saxon heritage,' Schaffer murmured fervently.

'What are you talking about?' Smith demanded. He had released his tense grip on the Schmeisser and realized that the palms of his hands were damp.

'This misplaced sense of decency,' Schaffer explained.

'A far from misplaced and highly developed sense of self-preservation,' Smith said dryly. 'Would *you* like to come searching for a couple of reputed killers, like us, knowing that the first man to find us would probably be cut in half by a burst of machine-gun fire? Put yourself in their position. How do you think those men feel. How would you feel?'

'I'd feel very unhappy,' Schaffer said candidly.

'And so do they. And so they seize on any reasonable excuse not to investigate. Our two friends who have just left have no idea whatsoever whether we're in here or not and, what's more, the last thing they want to do is to find out.'

'Stop making with the old psychology. All that matters is that Schaffer is saved. Saved!'

'If you believe that,' Smith said curtly, 'you deserve to end up with a blindfold round your eyes.'

'How's that again?' Schaffer asked apprehensively.

'You and I,' Smith explained patiently, 'are not the only people who can put ourselves in the places of the searchers. You can bet your life that the captain can and more than likely the sergeant, too – you saw how quickly he caught on to the damn' radio. By and by one or other is going to come by, see this closed and undamaged door, blow his top and insist on a few of his men being offered the chance to earn a posthumous Iron Cross. What I mean is, Schaffer is not yet saved.'

'What do we do, boss?' Schaffer said quietly. 'I don't feel so funny any more.'

'We create a diversion. Here are the keys – this one. Put it in the lock and hold it ready to turn. We'll be leaving in a hurry – troops of this calibre can't be fooled for long.'

He dug into his knapsack, fished out a hand-grenade, crossed the cloakroom into the washroom and, in almost total darkness, felt his way across it to where the window at the back should have been, finally located it from the source of a faint wash of light. He pressed his nose against the glass but could see nothing, cursed softly as he realized a washroom window would always certainly be frosted, located the latch and slowly swung the window wide. With infinite caution, a fraction of an inch at a time, he thrust his head slowly through the window.

Nobody blew his head off. There were soldiers immediately to be seen, it was true, soldiers armed and at the ready, but they weren't looking in his direction: there were five of them, spread out in an arc of a circle, perhaps fifteen yards from the station entrance, and every machine-pistol was trained on that entrance. Waiting for the rabbits to bolt, Smith thought.

What was of much more interest was the empty truck parked only feet away from the window where he was: it was the reflected light from its side-lights that had enabled him to locate the window. Hoping that the truck was built along conventional lines, Smith armed the grenade, counted three, lobbed it under the back wheels of the truck and ducked behind the shelter of the washroom wall.

The two explosions – grenade and petrol tank – went off so almost simultaneously as to be indistinguishable in time. Shattered glass from the window above showered down on his head and his ear-drums hurt fiercely both from the roar of sound and the proximity to the explosive shock-wave. Smith made no attempt to inspect the damage he had done, less from the urgent need for haste to leave there than from the very obvious fact that the remains of the truck outside had burst into flames and to have lifted his head above that window-sill would have been a swift form of illuminated suicide: not that he could have done so in any event for the wind-driven flames from the truck were already beginning to lick through the shattered washroom window. On hands and knees Smith scuttled across the washroom floor, not rising till he had reached the cloakroom. Schaffer, who had his hand on the key and the door already open a fraction of an inch turned at Smith's approach.

'To the hills, boss?' he enquired.

'To the hills.'

The track-side of the station was, predictably, deserted: those who had not automatically run to investigate the source of the explosion would have as automatically assumed that the explosion was in some way connected with an escape attempt or resistance on the part of the hunted men. However it was, the result was the satisfactory same.

They ran along the tracks till they came to the bumpers at the end of the line, skirted these and continued running until they were safely among the scatter of houses that rose steeply up the hill-side on the eastern side of the village. They stopped to take breath and looked back the way they had come.

The station was on fire, not yet heavily on fire, but, with flames rising six to eight feet and black smoke billowing into the night sky, obviously already beyond any hope of extinction.

Schaffer said: 'They're not going to be very pleased.'

'I shouldn't think so.'

'What I mean is, they're really going to go after us now. With everything they have. They've Dobermann pinchers up at the castle and I've no doubt they have them at the camp too. They've only to bring them to the station, sniff our gear, have them circle the station, pick up our scent and that's it. Smith and Schaffer torn to shreds. I'll take on the Alpenkorps by numbers, but I draw the line at Dobermann pinchers, boss.'

'I thought it was horses you were scared of?' Smith said mildly.

'Horses, Dobermann pinchers, you name it, I'm scared of it. All it's got to have is four feet.' He looked gloomily at the burning station. 'I'd make a rotten vet.'

'No worry,' Smith assured him. 'We won't be here long enough for any of your four-footed pals to come bothering you.'

'No?' Schaffer looked at him suspiciously.

'The castle,' Smith said patiently. 'That's what we're here for. Remember?'

'I hadn't forgotten.' The flames from the blazing station were now licking thirty, forty feet up in the air. 'You gone and ruined a perfectly good station, you know that?'

'As you would say yourself,' Smith reminded him, 'it wasn't our station to start with. Come on. We've a call to make then we'll go see what kind of reception awaits us at the Schloss Adler.'

Mary Ellison was just at that moment discovering what the reception in the Schloss Adler was like. In her case it was none too pleasant. Von Brauchitsch and Heidi beside her, she was gazing around the great hall of the castle, stone walls, stone flags, a dark oaken roof, when a door at the end of the hall opened and a girl came towards them. There was an arrogance, a crisp authority about her: she marched, rather than walked.

But a very beautiful girl, Mary had to admit to herself, big, blonde, blue-eyed and beautiful. She could have been a pin-up girl for the Third Reich. At the moment, the blue eyes were very cold.

'Good-evening, Anne-Marie,' von Brauchitsch said. There was a marked lack of cordiality in his voice. 'This is the new girl, Fräulein Maria Schenk. Maria, this is the Colonel's secretary, in charge of all female staff.'

'Took your time about getting here, didn't you, Schenk?' If Anne-Marie had a soft, lilting, mellifluous voice she wasn't bothering to use it just then. She turned to Heidi and gave her an icy up-and-down. 'And why you? Just because we let you wait table when the Colonel has company—'

'Heidi is this girl's cousin,' von Brauchitsch interrupted brusqeuly. '*And* she has my permission.' The cold implication that she should confine herself to her duties was unmistakable.

Anne-Marie glared at him but made no attempt to press the point. Very few people would have done. Von Brauchitsch was just that sort of person.

'In here, Schenk.' Anne-Marie nodded to a side door. 'I have a few questions to ask.'

Mary looked at Heidi, then at von Brauchitsch, who shrugged

and said: 'Routine investigation, Fräulein. I'm afraid you must.'

Mary preceded Anne-Marie through the doorway. The door was firmly closed behind them. Heidi and von Brauchitsch looked at each other. Heidi compressed her lips and the expression that momentarily flitted over her face about matched the one Anne-Marie had been wearing: von Brauchitsch made the age-old helpless gesture of lifting his shoulders high, palms of the hands turned up.

Within half a minute the reason for von Brauchitsch's helpless gesture became obvious. Through the door there came first the sound of a raised voice, a brief scuffle then a sharp cry of pain. Von Brauchitsch exchanged another resigned glance with Heidi, then turned as he heard heavy footsteps behind him. The man approaching was burly, weather-beaten, middle-aged and in civilian clothes: but although not in uniform he could never have been mistaken for anything other than an army officer. The heavy blue-shaven jowls, bull-neck, close-cropped hair and piercing blue eyes made him almost a caricature of the World War I Prussian Uhlan cavalry officer. That he was by no means as fossilised as he appeared was quite evident from the distinctly respectful manner in which von Brauchitsch addressed him.

'Good evening, Colonel Kramer.'

'Evening, Captain. Evening, Fräulein.' He had an unexpectedly gentle and courteous voice. 'You wear an air of expectancy?'

Before either could answer, the door opened and Anne-Marie and Mary entered: Mary gave the impression of having been pushed into the room. Anne-Marie was slightly flushed and breathing rather heavily, but otherwise her beautiful Aryan self. Mary's clothes were disordered, her hair dishevelled and it was obvious that she had been crying. Her cheeks were still tear-stained.

'We'll have no more trouble with *her*,' Anne-Marie announced with satisfaction. She caught sight of Kramer and the change in her tone was perceptible. 'Interviewing new staff, Colonel.'

'In your usual competent fashion, I see,' Colonel Kramer said dryly. He shook his head. 'When will you learn that respectable young girls do not like being forcibly searched and having their underclothes examined to see if they were made in Piccadilly or Gorki Street?'

'Security regulations,' Anne-Marie said defensively.

'Yes, yes.' Kramer's voice was brusque. 'But there are other ways.' He turned away impatiently. The engaging of female staff was not the problem of the deputy chief of the German Secret Service. While Heidi was helping Mary to straighten her clothes, he went on, to von Brauchitsch: 'A little excitement in the village tonight?'

'Nothing for us.' Von Brauchitsch shrugged. 'Deserters.'

Kramer smiled.

'That's what I told Colonel Weissner to say. I think our friends are British agents.'

'What!'

'After General Carnaby, I shouldn't wonder,' Kramer said carelessly. 'Relax, Captain. It's over. Three of them are coming up for interrogation within the hour. I'd like you to be present later on. I think you'll find it most entertaining and – ah – instructive.'

'There were five of them, sir. I saw them myself when they were rounded up in "Zum Wilden Hirsch".'

'There *were* five,' Colonel Kramer corrected. 'Not now. Two of them – the leader and one other – are in the Blau See. They commandeered a car and went over a cliff.'

Mary, her back to the men and Anne-Marie, smoothed down her dress and slowly straightened. Her face was stricken. Anne-Marie turned, saw Mary's curiously immobile position and was moving curiously towards her when Heidi took Mary's arm and said quickly: 'My cousin looks ill. May I take her to her room?'

'All right.' Anne-Maria waved her hand in curt dismissal. 'The one you use when you are here.'

The room was bleak, monastic, linoleum-covered, with a made-up iron bed, chair, tiny dressing-table, a hanging cupboard and nothing else. Heidi locked the door behind them.

'You heard?' Mary said emptily. Her face was as drained of life as her voice.

'I heard – and I don't believe it.'

'Why should they lie?'

'*They* believe it.' Heidi's tone was impatient, almost rough. 'It's time you stopped loving and started thinking. The Major Smiths of this world don't drive over cliff edges.'

'Talk is easy, Heidi.'

'So is giving up. *I* believe he is alive. And if he is, and if he comes here and you're gone or not there to help him, you know what he'll be then?' Mary made no reply, just gazed emptily into Heidi's face. 'He'll be dead. He'll be dead because you let him down. Would *he* let *you* down?'

Mary shook her head dumbly.

'Now then,' Heidi went on briskly. She reached first under her skirt then down the front of her blouse and laid seven objects on the table. 'Here we are. Lilliput .21 automatic, two spare magazines, ball of string, lead weight, plan of the castle and the instructions.' She crossed to a corner of the room, raised a loose floor-board, placed the articles beneath it and replaced the board. 'They'll be safe enough there.'

Mary looked at her for a long moment and showed her first spark of interest in an hour.

'You *knew* that board was loose,' she said slowly.

'Of course. I loosened it myself, a fortnight ago.'

'You – you knew about this as far back as then?'

'Whatever else?' Heidi smiled. 'Good luck, cousin.'

Mary sank on to the bed and sat there motionless for ten minutes after Heidi had gone, then rose wearily to her feet and crossed to her window. Her window faced to the north and she could see the line of pylons, the lights of the village and, beyond that, the darkened waters of the Blau See. But what dominated the entire scene were the redly-towering flames and billowing clouds of black smoke reaching up from some burning building at the far end of the village. For a hundred yards around it night had been turned into day and even if there had been a local fire brigade to hand it would have been clearly impossible for them to approach anywhere near the flames. When that first fire went out all that would be left would be smoking ashes. Mary wondered vaguely what it might mean.

She opened her window and leaned out, but cautiously. Even for a person as depressed as she was, there was no temptation to lean too far: castle walls and volcanic plug stretched vertically downwards for almost three hundred feet. She felt slightly dizzy.

To the left and below a cable-car left the castle header station and started to move down to the valley below. Heidi was in that car, leaning out a partially opened window and hopefully waving but Mary's eyes had again blurred with tears and she did not see her. She closed the window, turned away, lay down heavily on the bed and wondered again about John Smith, whether he were alive or dead. And she wondered again about the significance of that fire in the valley below.

Smith and Schaffer skirted the backs of the houses, shops and *Weinstuben* on the east side of the street, keeping to the dark shadows as far as it was possible. Their precautions, Smith realized, were largely superfluous: the undoubted centre of attraction that night was the blazing station and the street leading to it was jammed with hundreds of soldiers and villagers. It must, Smith thought, be a conflagration of quite some note, for although they could no longer see the fire itself, only the red glow in the sky above it, they could clearly hear the roaring crackle of the flames, flames three hundred yards away and with the wind blowing in the wrong direction. As a diversion, it was a roaring success.

They came to one of the few stone buildings in the village, a large barn-like affair with double doors at the back. The yard abutting the rear doors looked like an automobile scrap-yard. There were half-a-dozen old cars lying around, most of them without tyres, some rusted engines, dozens of small useless engine and body parts and a small mountain of empty oil drums. They picked their way carefully through the debris and came to the doors.

Schaffer used skeleton keys to effect and they were inside, doors closed and both torches on, inside fifteen seconds.

One side of the garage was given over to lathes or machine tools of one kind or another, but the rest of the floor space was occupied by a variety of vehicles, mostly elderly. What caught and held Smith's immediate attention, however, was a big yellow bus parked just inside the double front doors. It was a typically Alpine post-bus, with a very long overhang at the back to help negotiate mountain hairpin bends: the rear wheels were so far forward as to be almost in the middle of the bus. As was also common with Alpine post-buses in winter, it had a huge angled snow-plough bolted on to the front of the chasis. Smith looked at Schaffer.

'Promising, you think?'

'If I was optimistic enough to think we'd ever get back to this place,' Schaffer said sourly, 'I'd say it was very promising. You knew about this?'

'What do you think I am? A bus-diviner? Of course I knew about it.'

Smith climbed into the driver's seat. The keys were in the ignition. Smith switched on and watched the fuel gauge climb up to the half-full mark. He located the headlamps switch and turned it on. They worked. He pressed the starter button and the engine caught at once. Smith killed it immediately. Schaffer watched the performance with interest.

'I suppose you know you need a PSV licence to drive one of those, boss?'

'I have one around somewhere. Leave half the explosives in the back of the bus. And hurry. Heidi might be down with the next car.'

Smith climbed down from the driver's seat, went to the front doors, unbolted both, top and bottom, and pushed gently. The doors gave an inch, then stopped.

'Padlocked,' Smith said briefly.

Schaffer surveyed the massive steel plough on the front of the bus and shook his head sorrowfully.

'Poor old padlock,' he said.

The snow had stopped but the wind from the west was now very strong. The cold was intense. Masses of ragged dark cloud hurried across the sky and the entire valley was alternatively cast into the deepest shadow or bathed in contrastingly dazzling light as the moon was alternatively obscured by the clouds or shone through the shifting gaps between them. But there was no alternating light and shade at the far end of the village: the station still burnt furiously enough to render the moon's best efforts pretty ineffectual.

A cable-car was coming slowly down the valley, less than a hundred yards now from the lower station. Impelled by the powerfully gusting wind, it swung wildly, terrifyingly, across the night sky. But as it approached the end of its journey the motion quickly dampened down and disappeared altogether as it approached the station.

The cable-car jerked to a stop. Heidi, the only passenger, climbed out: understandably enough, she was looking rather pale. She walked down the steps at the back of the station, reached ground level then stopped dead as she heard the softly-whistled first few notes of 'Lorelei', She whirled round, then slowly approached two shapes, clad all in white, huddled by the side of the station.

'The Major Smiths of this world *don't* drive off cliff-tops,' she said calmly. She paused, then stepped forward suddenly and gave each man a quick hug and kiss on the cheek. 'But you had me a little worried there.'

'You just keep on worrying like that,' Schaffer said. 'No need to worry about him, though.'

Heidi waved a hand in the direction of the other end of the village. From the cable-car station on the lower slopes they had an excellent if distant view of the fire. 'Are you responsible for this?' she asked.

'It was a mistake,' Smith explained.

'Yeah. His hand slipped,' Schaffer added.

'You two should audition for a turn on vaudeville,' Heidi said dryly. Suddenly serious she said: 'Mary thinks you're both gone.'

'Weissner doesn't,' Smith said. 'The car that went over the cliff went without us. They're on to us.'

'Hardly surprising,' she murmured. 'Or hadn't you noticed the size of the fire.' She paused, then went on bleakly: 'They're not the only ones who are on to you. Kramer knows you're British agents after General Carnaby.'

'Well, well, well,' Smith said thoughtfully. 'I wonder what little bird has been whispering in Kramer's shell-like ear. One with a very long-range voice, methinks.'

'What *are* you talking about?'

'Nothing. It's not important.'

'It's not important! But don't you *see*?' Her voice was imploring, almost despairing. 'They *know* – or will any minute – that you're alive. They *know* who you are. They'll be expecting you up there.'

'Ah, but you overlook the subtleties, my dear Heidi,' Schaffer put in. 'What they *don't* know is that *we* are expecting *them* to be expecting *us*. At least, that's what I think I mean.'

'You're whistling in the dark, Lieutenant. And one last thing: your friends are being brought up to the castle any time now.'

'For interrogation?' Smith asked.

'I don't expect they've been asked up for tea,' she said acidly.

'Fair enough,' Smith nodded. 'We'll go up with them.'

'In the same car?' The words didn't question Smith's sanity, but the tone and expression did.

'Not "in". With.' Smith peered at his watch. 'The post-bus in Sulz's garage. Be there in eighty minutes. And oh! – bring a couple of crates of empty beer bottles.'

'Bring a couple of – oh, all right.' She shook her head in conviction. 'You're both mad.'

'Shines through in our every word and gesture,' Schaffer agreed, then, suddenly serious, added: 'Say a prayer for us, honey. And if you don't know any prayers, keep your fingers crossed till they ache.'

'Please come back,' she said. There was a catch in her voice. She hesitated, made to say more, turned and walked quickly away. Schaffer looked after her admiringly as she walked down the street.

'There goes the future Mrs Schaffer,' he announced. 'Bit tetchy and snappy, perhaps.' He pondered. 'But funny, I thought she was near crying at the end there.'

'Maybe you'd be tetchy and snappy and tearful if you'd been through what she's been in the past two and a half years,' Smith said sourly.

'Maybe she'd be less tetchy and tearful if she knew a bit more about what's going on.'

'I haven't the time to explain everything to everybody.'

'You can say that again. Devious, boss. That's the word for you.'

'Like enough.' Smith glanced at his watch. 'I wish to God they'd hurry up.'

'Speak for yourself.' Schaffer paused. 'When we – well, if we – get away, is she coming with us?'

'Is who coming with us?'

'Heidi, of course!'

'Heidi, of course. If we make it – and we can only do it through Mary, and Mary was introduced by—'

'Say no more.' He stared after the retreating figure and shook his head. 'She'll be a sensation in the Savoy Grill,' he said dreamily.

—— 6 ——

The seconds crawled by and became minutes, and the minutes in turn piled up with agonising slowness until almost quarter of an hour had passed. Brilliant moonshine and a contrastingly almost total darkness had alternated a score of times as the low, tattered, black clouds scudded across the valley, and the cold deepened until it reached down into the bones of the two watchers in the shadows. And still they waited. They waited because they had to: they couldn't reach the Schloss Adler without company and company was a long time in coming.

And they waited in silence, each man alone with his own thoughts. What was in Schaffer's mind Smith couldn't guess.

Probably he was blissfully envisaging himself as the instigator of a series of uncontrollable stampedes in a selection of the better known hostelries in the West End of London. Smith's own thoughts were much more pragmatic and concerned solely with the immediate future. He was becoming concerned, and seriously concerned, about the intense cold and how it would affect their chances of making the trip up to the castle intact. Stamp their feet and flail their arms as they might, that numbing cold tightened its grip on them with every minute that passed. What they were about to do needed both physical strength and quick reactions in full measure, and that glacial cold was swiftly draining them of both. Briefly and bleakly he wondered what odds any reasonable bookmaker would have given against their chances of reaching the castle but dismissed the thought still-born. When no other option offered there was no point in figuring the percentages, and, besides, they were due to find out immediately: the long-awaited company was at hand.

Two Alpenkorps command cars, the leading one with wailing siren and flashing headlamps, swept up the village street just as the moon broke through the cloud-wrack once again, flooding the valley with light. Smith and Schaffer looked up at the moon, then at each other and then, wordlessly, moved back and pressed more deeply into the shadows on the west side of the lower station. The two metallic clicks seemed unnaturally loud as thy eased forward the safety catches of their Schmeisser machine-pistols.

Engines stopped and headlamps faded and died almost on the same instant as the two cars pulled up beneath the steps. Men hurried out and lined up briefly before advancing single file up the station steps. A dozen altogether, Smith counted, an officer, eight guards and Carraciola, Thomas and Christiansen. All eight guards had their guns at the ready, which seemed a rather superfluous precaution as the three prisoners had their hands manacled behind their backs. Ergo, the guns weren't there to guard the prisoners but against any rescue attempt by Smith and Schaffer. He and Schaffer, Smith thought wryly, must be acquiring quite a reputation for themselves. But, nonetheless, a reassuring spectacle: if the Germans had known the true reason for his, Smith's, presence in Bavaria, they would also have known that they could have taken the three prisoners up with only a pea-shooter for protection and still have remained free from molestation.

The last of the twelve men passed inside the lower station. Smith touched Schaffer's arm. They slung their Schmeissers, scrambled quickly but quietly on to the ice-covered and steeply-sloping roof of the station and silently and with no little difficulty crawled forwards and upwards to the front edge of the roof under which the cable-car would appear as it moved out at the beginning of its long haul towards the castle. They were, Smith knew, terribly exposed: snow-suits or not, a casual passer-by in the street below had only to glance upwards and their detection was certain. Fortunately, there appeared to be no casual passers-by: the free entertainment provided by the burning station was drawing a full house. And then, as the cable began to move, the moon disappeared behind clouds.

They waited, tensely, till the leading edge of the cable-car appeared, swung their legs over the lip of the roof, waited till the suspension bracket passed beneath them, reached down for the cable, allowed themselves to be pulled off the roof, fell across the cable and lowered themselves gently until their feet touched the roof of the cable-car.

Mary walked softly along the dimly-lit, stone-flagged passage, counting off doors as she went. Outside the fifth she stopped, put her ear to it, stooped, glanced through the key-hole, knocked quietly and waited for a response. There was none. She knocked again, more loudly, with the same result. She turned the handle and found the door locked. From her small handbag she produced a set of skeleton keys. When the door yielded, she slipped quickly inside, closed the door and switched on the light.

The room was a considerable improvement on the one she had been given, although furnished with the same regulation iron bedstead. It was close-carpeted, boasted a couple of arm-chairs, and had a small chair with an Oberleutnant's uniform on it, a large wardrobe and a chest of drawers with a holstered belt, gun and binoculars resting on its glass top.

Mary locked the door, withdrew the key, crossed the room, lifted the lower sash window and looked down. She was, she saw, directly above the roof of the cable-car header station, a very steeply downward sloping roof the upper edge of which was built into the castle wall itself. She withdrew her head, removed from her handbag a ball of string with a heavy bolt attached to one end, laid it on the bed, picked up the binoculars and took up station by the window. Shivering in the bitter night wind, she adjusted the focus of the field-glasses, then traversed down the line of the aerial cables. And then she had it, dimly seen but unmistakable, the squat black outline of the cable-car, now half-way between the bottom and middle pylons, swaying madly, frighteningly, across the sky in the high and gusting wind.

Smith and Schaffer lay stretched out on the roof, clutching desperately to the suspension bracket, the only anchorage available. The roof was solidly coated with white-sheeted ice, they could find no purchase anywhere for their feet, and their bodies slid uncontrollably in all directions with the violent buffeting of the car beneath them. The sheer physical strain on hands and arms and shoulders was even worse than Smith had feared: and the worst was yet to come.

Schaffer twisted his head and peered downwards. It was a dizzy, vertiginous and frankly terrifying spectacle. The entire valley below seemed to be swinging through a forty-five degree arc. One second he was looking at the line of pines that bordered the western slope of the valley, then the floor of the valley rushed by beneath them and seconds later he was staring at the line of pines that swept up the eastern side of the valley. He twisted his head upwards, but that was no improvement; the lights of the Schloss Adler careened wildly through the same dizzy arc: it was like being on a combination of a roller-coaster, big dipper and runaway Ferris wheel with the notable exception, Schaffer thought bleakly, that the coaster, dipper and Ferris wheel were provided with safety belts and other securing devices designed to prevent the occupant from parting company with his machine. The wind howled its high and lonely threnody through the cables and the suspension bracket. Schaffer looked away, screwed his eyes shut, lowered his head between his outstretched arms and moaned.

'Still think the horse the world's worst form of transport?' Smith asked. His lips were close to Schaffer's ear.

'Give me my boots and saddle,' Schaffer said, then, even more despairingly, 'Oh, no! Not again!'

Once more, without any warning, the moon had broken through, flooding the two men in its pale cold light. Gauging the time when the strain on their arms was least, they pulled the snow hoods far over their heads and tried to flatten themselves even more closely on to the roof.

In the Schloss Adler two people were watching the wild upward progress of the cable-car, now brilliantly illuminated by the moon. Through Mary's field-glasses two clearly distinguishable shapes of men could be seen stretched out on the cable-car roof. For half a minute she kept the glasses trained on them, then slowly turned away, her eyes wide, almost staring, her face empty of expression. Fifty feet above her head a sentry with slung gun patrolling the battlements stopped and gazed down at the cable-car crawling up the valley. But he didn't gaze for long. Although booted, gauntleted and muffled to the ears, he shook with the cold. It was no night for idle spectating. He looked away indifferently and resumed his brisk sentry-go.

Indifference was a quality that was conspicuously lacking on top of the cable-car. The cable-car was on the last lap now, the section between the last pylon and the castle header station. Soon the moment of truth. A minute from then, Smith thought, and they could both well be lying broken and lifeless on the rocks two hundred feet below.

He twisted his head upwards. The cold moon still sailed across a clear gap in the sky but was closing rapidly towards another bank of cloud. The castle battlements, with the header station at the base, seemed almost vertically above his head. So steeply was the car rising on this last section that the volcanic plug itself was now less than fourteen yards away. His gaze followed the volcanic plug downwards till it reached its base: down there, on the slopes below, patrolling guards and their Dobermann pinchers were barely the size of beetles.

'Suits her, doesn't it?' Schaffer said suddenly. Harsh edges of strain burried in his voice and his face was tight and desperate. 'A lovely name.'

'What are you talking about?' Smith demanded.

'Heidi.'

'Oh, my God!' Smith stared up at the rapidly closing header station. 'Her name is Ethel.'

'You didn't have to tell me.' Schaffer tried to sound aggrieved but it didn't quite come off. He followed Smith's upward gaze and, after a long pause, said very slowly: 'Jesus! Look at the slope of that goddamned roof!'

'I've been looking.' Smith eased his knife from its sheath and made a quick grab at the suspension bracket as a particularly violent swing almost broke his grip with his other hand. 'Get your knife ready. And for God's sake don't lose it.'

The moon slid behind a black patch of cloud and the valley

was flooded with darkness. Slowly, carefully, as the cable-car approached the header station and the swaying motion dampened down, Smith and Schaffer eased their way to the after end of the car, rose gingerly but swiftly to their feet and grabbed the cable with their free hands while their feet tried to find what precarious hold they could on the treacherously ice-sheathed roof.

The front of the car passed under the lip of the header station roof. A moment later the suspension bracket followed and Smith lunged forward and upwards, flinging himself bodily on to the roof. His right arm struck downwards and the knife blade pierced the coating of ice and imbedded itself firmly in the wood beneath. Less than a second later Schaffer had landed beside him, the downward arcing knife making contact at exactly the same instant as himself.

The blade broke off at the hilt. Schaffer opened his hand, dropped the haft and clawed desperately at the ice. The dragging nails ripped through the encrusting ice, quite failing to hold him. He reached his left hand to his mouth, tore off the gauntlet and dug both hands in with all the strength that was in him. He slowed, but not enough. His scrabbling toes failed to find any more purchase and he knew he was sliding out over the edge – and that when he went the first thing to halt his fall would be the rock-pile two hundred and fifty feet beneath at the base of the volcanic plug.

Smith had been badly winded by his fall. Several seconds elapsed before he realized that Schaffer wasn't where he should have been – lying on the roof beside him. He twisted round, saw the white blur of Schaffer's strained and desperate face, had a vague impression of Schaffer's eight finger-nails scoring their way through the ice as his body, already up to mid-thigh, slid inexorably over the edge and brought his left hand flashing down with a speed and power that, even in those circumstances, made Schaffer grunt in pain as the vice-like grip clamped over his right wrist.

For some seconds they lay like that, spreadeagled and motionless on the sloping roof, the lives of both dependent on the slim imbedded blade of Smith's knife; then Schaffer, urged by Smith's quivering left arm, began to inch his way slowly upwards. Thirty seconds later and he was level with Smith.

'This is a knife I have, not an ice-axe,' Smith said hoarsely. 'Won't take much more of this. Have you another knife?'

Schaffer shook his head. Momentarily, speech was beyond him.

'Piton?'

The same shake of the head.

'Your torch?'

Schaffer nodded, reached under the cumbersome snow-smock with his left hand and eventually managed to wriggle his torch free.

'Unscrew the bottom,' Smith said. 'Throw it away – and the battery.' Schaffer brought his left hand across to where his right was pinioned by Smith, removed base and battery, flattened the now empty cylinder base a little, reversed his grip and gouged the torch into the ice, downwards and towards himself. He moved his right hand and Smith released his grip. Schaffer remained where he was. Smith smiled and said: 'Try holding me.'

Schaffer caught Smith's left wrist. Tentatively, his hand still hooked in readiness, Smith removed his hand from the haft of the knife. Schaffer's imbedded torch held firm. Cautiously at first, then with increasing confidence as the sharp blade cut through the protective sheathing of ice, Smith carved out a secure handhold in the wooden roof of the station, passed his knife to Schaffer, wriggled out of his snow-smock, undid a few turns of the knotted rope round his waist and secured the free end to Schaffer's belt. He said: 'With the knife and torch, think you can make it?'

'Can I make it?' Schaffer tested both knife and torch and smiled, a pretty strained effort, but his first for some time. 'After what I've been through – well, ever seen a monkey go up a coconut palm tree?'

Fifty feet above their heads, Mary withdrew from the window and laid the binoculars on the chest of drawers. Her hands shook and the metal of the binoculars rattled like castanets against the glass top. She returned to the window and began to pay out the weighted string.

Smith came up the last few feet of the sloping roof at the end of the rope, caught Schaffer's hand, stood upright on the flat inner section of the roof and at once began to unwind the rest of the knotted rope from his waist. Schaffer, although the temperature was far below freezing, wiped his brow like a man in a heat-wave.

'Brother!' He mopped his brow some more. 'If I can ever do you a favour, like lending you a car-fare—'

Smith grinned, clapped his shoulder, reached up into the gloom, caught the weighted end of the suspended string and quickly bent the nylon on to it. He gave two gentle tugs and the rope began to move upwards as Mary hauled it in through the window. Smith waited until two more gentle return tugs indicated that the rope was securely fastened and began to climb.

He was half-way up to the window when the moon broke through. In his Alpenkorps uniform he was perfectly silhouetted against the gleaming white of the castle walls. He hung there motionless, not daring to move, not so much as even daring to glance upwards or downwards lest the movement attract some hostile attention.

Twenty-five feet below him Schaffer peered cautiously over the edge of the header station roof. The guards and dogs were still patrolling the area round the roof of the volcanic plug. They had only to give one casual upwards glance and Smith's discovery was inevitable. Then some hair-prickling sixth sense made Schaffer look sharply upwards and he became very still indeed. The sentry, another circuit of the battlements completed, was standing with hands splayed out on the parapet, gazing out over the valley, perhaps watching the now dying flames from the burnt-out station: he had to lower his eyes only a fraction and that was that. Slowly, with his right hand, Schaffer brought up the Luger with the long perforated silencer screwed to its muzzle and laid it, in the best police fashion, across his left wrist. He had no doubt he could kill his man with one shot, the only question was when best to do it, how to weigh the balance of possibilities. If he waited until the man sighted them, he might give a warning shout or thrust himself back into cover before Schaffer could kill him. If he shot the sentry before he sighted them, then there would be no question of either escape or warning. But there was the possibility that the man might pitch forward over the battlements, crash off the roof of the header station and fall into the valley below, close by the patrolling men and dogs. A possibility only, Schaffer decided, not a probability: the slamming effect of the Luger shell would almost certainly knock him backwards off his feet. Schaffer had never before gunned down an unsuspecting man, but he coldly prepared to do so now. He lined up the luminous sight on the man's breast-bone and began to squeeze the trigger.

The moon went behind a cloud.

Slowly, stiffly, Schaffer lowered his gun. Schaffer, once again, wiped sweat from his forehead. He had the feeling that he wasn't through with brow-mopping for the night.

Smith reached the window, clambered over the sill, gave the rope two tugs as a signal for Schaffer to start climbing and passed into the room. It was almost totally dark inside, he'd just time to make out the iron bedstead which had been dragged to the window as anchorage for the rope when a pair of arms wound tightly round his neck and someone started murmuring incoherently in his ear.

'Easy on, easy on,' Smith protested. He was still breathing heavily and needed all the air he could get, but summoned enough energy to bend and kiss her. 'Unprofessional conduct, what's more. But I won't report it this time.'

She was still clinging to him, silent now, when Lieutenant Schaffer made his appearance, dragging himself wearily over the sill and collapsing on the iron bedstead. He was breathing very heavily indeed and had about him the air of one who has suffered much.

'Have they no elevators in this dump?' he demanded. It took him two breaths to get the words out.

'Out of training,' Smith said unsympathetically. He crossed to the door and switched on the light, hurriedly switched it off again. 'Damn. Get the rope in then pull the curtains.'

'This is the way they treated them in the Roman galleys,' Schaffer said bitterly. But he had the rope inside and the curtains closed in ten seconds. As Smith was manœuvering the bed back into its original position, Schaffer was stuffing the nylon into their canvas bag, a bag, which, in addition to snowsuits and Schmeissers, contained some hand grenades and a stock of plastic explosives. He had just finished tying the neck of the bag when a key scraped in the lock.

Smith motioned Mary to stay where she was as he moved quickly to take up position behind the door: Schaffer, for all his alleged exhaustion, had dropped flat to the floor behind the bed with all the speed and silence of a cat. The door opened and a young Oberleutnant strode into the room, stopping short as he saw Mary, her hand to her mouth. His face registered astonishment, an astonishment almost immediately replaced by an anticipatory half-smile as he stepped forward beyond the opened door. Smith's arm came down and the young officer's eyes turned up in his head.

Smith studied the plans of the castle given him by Mary while Schaffer trussed up the Oberleutnant with the nylon, gagged him with tape and shoved him, jack-knifed, into the bottom of the cupboard. For good measure he pulled the top of the bed against the door.

'Ready when you are, boss.'

'That's now. I have my bearings. First left, down the stairs, third left. The gold drawing-room. Where Colonel Kramer holds court. Complete with minstrels' gallery.'

'What's a minstrel's gallery?' Schaffer enquired.

'A gallery for minstrels. Then the next right-hander takes us to the east wing. Down again, second left. Telephone exchange.'

'Why there?' Schaffer asked. 'We've already cut the lines.'

'Not the ones between here and the barracks, we haven't. Want them to whistle up a regiment of Alpenkorps?' He turned to Mary. 'Helicopter still here?'

'It was when I arrived.'

'The helicopter?' Schaffer showed his puzzlement. 'What gives with the whirlybird, then?'

'This gives with the whirlybird. They could use it either to whip Caranaby out of here – they *might* just be nervous if they think we're on the loose – or they might use it to block our getaway.'

'*If* we get away.'

'There's that. How are you on immobilising helicopters, Lieutenant Schaffer? Your report states that you were an up-and-coming racing driver and a very competent mechanic before they scraped the bottom of the barrel and dragged you in.'

'I volunteered,' Schaffer said with dignity. 'About the competence, I dunno. But give me a four-pound hammer and I'll sure as little fishes immobilise anything from a bull-dozer to a bicycle.'

'And without the four-pounder? This is not a boiler-makers' convention.'

'I have been known to use finesse.'

Smith said to Mary: 'How can we get a sight of this machine?'

'Just five paces that way.' She pointed to the door. 'Every passage window in the Schloss Adler opens on to the courtyard.'

Smith opened the door, glanced up and down the passage and crossed to an opposite window. Schaffer was by his side.

The comings and goings of the moon made no difference to the state of illumination in the Schloss Adler courtyard. Two big overhead arc lamps burned by the heavily-barred entrance gates. A third burned at the opposite end of the courtyard, over the main doorway leading into the castle itself. At a height of about ten feet, four waterproof storm lamps were fastened to the east and west walls of the courtyard. Lights burned from a dozen windows on the east and northern sides. And the brightest light of all came from an arc-lamp that had been rigged above the helicopter and under the temporary protection of a stretched tarpaulin. A figure in green overalls and a high-peaked cap was working on the helicopter's engine. Smith touched Schaffer's arm and they moved back into the room where Mary was waiting, closing the door behind them.

'Seems a straightforward operation,' Schaffer said. 'Fixing it so that the chopper doesn't fly again, I mean. I cross to the main gates, overpower the four men on guard, strangle the four Dobermann pinchers, knock off two or three other characters – armed characters – who appear to be patrolling the place all the time, overpower about twenty soldiers who appear to be drinking beer in some sort of canteen across the way, dispose of the guy who's working on the engine and *then* immobilise the chopper. I mean, just immobilising the chopper itself wouldn't be anything, really, would it?'

'We'll think of something,' Smith said soothingly.

'I'll bet you think of something,' Schaffer said moodily. 'That's what I'm afraid of.'

'Time's a-wasting. We won't need those any more.'

Smith folded the plan, handed it to Mary, then frowned as she put it in her bag. 'You know better than that. The Lilliput: it should be on your person, not in the bag. Here.' He handed her the Mauser he'd taken from Colonel Weissner. 'This in your bag. Hide the Lilliput on you.'

'When I get to my room I will,' she said primly.

'All those leering Yankee lieutenants around,' Schaffer said sadly. 'Thank heavens I'm a changed man.'

'His mind is set on higher things,' Smith explained. He glanced at his watch. 'Give us thirty minutes.'

They slipped cautiously through the doorway then strode briskly and confidently along the passage, making no attempt to conceal their presence. The bag with the Schmeissers, rope, grenades and explosives Smith swung carelessly from one hand. They passed a bespectacled soldier carrying a sheaf of papers and a girl carrying a laden tray, neither of whom paid any attention to them. They turned right at the end of the passage, reached a circular flight of stairs and went down three floors until they came to the level of the courtyard. A short broad passage, with two doors on either side, took them to the main door leading out to the courtyard.

Smith opened the door and looked out. The scene was very much as Schaffer had feelingly described it, with far too many armed guards and police dogs around for anyone's peace of mind. The overalled mechanic was still at work on the helicopter's engine. Smith quietly closed the door and turned his attention to the nearest right-hand door in the passage. It was locked. He said to Schaffer: 'Keep an eye open at the end of the passage there.'

Schaffer went. As soon as he was in position, Smith brought out skeleton keys. The third key fitted and the door gave under his hand. He signalled Schaffer to return.

With the door closed and locked behind them, they looked around the room, a room faintly but for their purposes adequately lit by the backwash of light shining through the unshuttered window from the courtyard. It was, quite apparently, the fire-fighting HQ of the castle. The walls were hung with drums of rolled hoses, asbestos suits, helmets and fire-axes: wheeled handpumps, CO_2 cylinders and a variety of smaller cylinders for fighting oil and electrical fires took up much of the floor space.

'Ideal,' Smith murmured.

'Couldn't be better,' Schaffer agreed. 'What are you talking about?'

'If we leave anyone in here,' Smith explained, 'he's unlikely to be discovered unless there's an actual outbreak of fire. Agreed? So.' He took Schaffer by the arm and led him to the window. 'The lad working on the chopper there. About your size, wouldn't you say?'

'I wouldn't know,' Schaffer said. 'And if you've got in mind what I think you have in mind, then I don't want to know, either.'

Smith drew the shutters, crossed to the door and switched on the overhead light.

'You got any better ideas?'

'Give me time,' he complained.

'I can't give you what we haven't got. Take your jacket off and keep your Luger lined up on that door. I'll be back in a minute.'

Smith left, closing but not locking the door behind him. He passed through the outer doorway, walked a few paces across the courtyard, halted at the base of a set of steps leading up to the helicopter and looked up at the man working above him, a tall rangy man with a thin intelligent face and a lugubrious expression on it. If he'd been working bare-handed with metal tools in that freezing temperature, Smith thought, he'd have had a lugubrious expression on his face, too.

'You the pilot?' Smith asked.

'You wouldn't think so, would you?' the overalled man said bitterly. He laid down a spanner and blew on his hands. 'Back in Tempelhof I have two mechanics for this machine, one a farm-hand from Swabia, the other a blacksmith's assistant from the Harz. If I want to keep alive I do my own mechanics. What do you want?'

'Not me. Reichsmarschall Rosemeyer. The phone.'

'The Reichsmarschall?' The pilot was puzzled. 'I was speaking to him less than fifteen minutes ago.'

'A call just came through from the Chancellory in Berlin. It seems urgent.' Smith let a slight note of impatience creep into his voice. 'You better hurry. Through the main door there, then the first on the right.'

Smith stood aside as the pilot clambered down, looked casually around him. A guard with a leashed Dobermann was no more than twenty feet away, but paying no attention to them: with his pinched bluish face sunk deep in his upturned collar, his hands thrust down into his great-coat pockets and his frozen breath hanging heavily in the air, he was too busy concentrating on his own miseries to have time to spare for ridiculous suspicions. Smith turned to follow the pilot through th main door, unobtrusively unholstering his Luger and gripping it by the barrel.

Smith hadn't intended chopping down the pilot with his gun butt but was left with no option. As soon as the pilot had passed through the side door and seen Schaffer's Luger pointing at his chest from a distance of four feet his shoulders lifted – the preliminary, Smith knew, not to violence or resistance but to a shout for help. Schaffer caught him as he pitched forward and lowered him to the floor.

Quickly they unzipped the overall from the unconscious man, bound and gagged him and left him lying in a corner. The overall was hardly a perfect fit for Schaffer, but, then, overalls are rarely a perfect fit for anybody. Schaffer switched the pilot's hat for his own, pulled the peak low over his eyes and left.

Smith switched off the light, unshuttered the window, raised the lower sash and stood, Luger in hand, just far enough back from the window so as not to be seen from outside. Schaffer was already climbing the steps up to the helicopter. The guard was now only feet from the base of the ladder. He'd his hands out of his pockets now and was flailing his arms across his shoulders in an attempt to keep warm.

Thirty seconds later Schaffer climbed down the ladder again, carrying some pieces of equipment in his left hand. He reached the ground, lifted the piece of equipment for a closer inspection, shook his head in disgust, lifted his right hand in a vague half-greeting to the uncaring German guard and headed for the main door again. By the time he reached the fire-fighting room, Smith had the window shuttered again and the light on.

'That was quick,' Smith said approvingly.

'Fear lent him wings, as the saying goes,' Schaffer said sourly. 'I'm always quick when I'm nervous. Did you see the size of the teeth in that great slavering monster out there?' He held up the piece of equipment for inspection, dropped it to the floor and brought his heel down on it. 'Distributor cap. I'll bet they haven't another in Bavaria. Not for that engine. And now, I suppose, you want me to go and impersonate the telephone operator.'

'No. We don't want to exhaust all your Thespian stamina.'

'My what?' Schaffer asked suspiciously. 'That sounds kinda like a nasty crack to me.'

'Your acting resources. The only other impersonation you'll be called to make tonight is that of Lieutenant Schaffer, OSS, the innocent American abroad.'

'That shouldn't be too difficult,' Schaffer said bitterly. He draped the overalls he'd just removed over the unconscious pilot. 'A cold night. Anyway, the telephone exchange.'

'Soon. But I'd like to check first how far they've got with old Carnaby-Jones. Let's take a look.'

Two floors higher up and midway along the central passage Smith stopped outside a doorway. At a nod from him, Schaffer reached for a light switch. Except for a faint glow of light at either end, the passage was now completely dark. Smith laid a gentle hand on the door-knob and quietly eased the door open. Fifteen inches, no more. Both men swiftly slid through the narrow gap, Smith quickly and softly closing the door to again.

The room, if so enormous a chamber could be called a room, must have been at least seventy feet long by thirty wide. The farther end of the room was brightly and warmly lit by three large chandeliers: comparatively, the end of the room where Smith and Schaffer stood was shrouded in near darkness.

They stood, not on the floor, but on a platform some dozen feet above the floor. It was a massive and grotesquely carved oaken minstrels' gallery which completely spanned the thirty-foot width of that end and ran perhaps a quarter of the way down both the longer sides of the room. There were rows of wooden benches, an organ on one side of the door through which they had just passed, a battery of organ pipes on the other. Whoever had built that place had obviously liked the organ and choir-singing: or maybe he just thought he did. From the centre of the front of the gallery, opposite the rear door, a flight of steps with intricately scrolled wooden banisters led down to what was very obviously the gold drawing-room.

It was aptly named, Smith thought. Everything in it was gold or golden or gilt. The enormous wall-to-wall carpet was deep gold in colour, the thickness of the pile would have turned a polar bear green with envy. The heavy baroque furniture, all twisted snakes and gargoyles' heads, was gilt, the huge couches and chairs covered in a dusty gold lamé. The chandeliers were gilded and, above the enormous white and gilt-plated fireplace, in which a crackling pine log fire burned, hung an almost equally enormous white and gilt-plated mirror. The great heavy curtains could have been made from beaten gold. The ceiling-high oak panelling, was a mistake, it continued to look obstinately like oak panelling, maybe the original covering gold paint had worn off. All in all, Smith reflected, it was a room only a mad Bavarian monarch could have conceived of, far less lived in.

Three men were seated comfortably round the great fire, to all appearances having an amicable discussion over after-dinner coffee and brandy, which was being served to them from – almost inevitably – a golden trolley by Anne-Marie. Anne-Marie, like the panelling was a disappointment: instead of a gold lamé dress she wore a long white silk sheath gown which, admittedly, went very well with her blonde colouring and snow-tan. She looked as if she were about to leave for the opera.

The man with his back to him Smith had never seen before but, because he immediately recognised who the other men were, knew who this man must be: Colonel Paul Kramer, Deputy Chief of the German Secret Service, regarded by MI6 as having the most brilliant and formidable brain in German

Intelligence. The man to watch, Smith knew, the man to fear. It was said of Kramer that he never made the same mistake twice – and that no one could remember when he'd last made a mistake for the first time.

As Smith watched, Colonel Kramer stirred, poured some more brandy from a Napoleon bottle by his side and looked first at the man on his left, a tall, ageing, but still good-looking man in the uniform of a Reichsmarschall of the Wehrmacht – at that moment, wearing a very glum expression on his face – then at the man seated opposite, an iron-grey-haired and very distinguished looking character in the uniform of a lieutenant general of the US Army. Without a comptometer to hand, it was difficult to say which of the two generals was wearing the more decorations.

Kramer sipped his brandy and said wearily: 'You make things very difficult for me, General Carnaby. Very, very difficult indeed.'

'The difficulties are of your own making, my dear Kramer,' Cartwright Jones said easily. 'Yours and General Rosemeyer's here . . . There *is* no difficulty.' He turned to Anne-Maria and smiled. 'If I might have some more of that excellent brandy, my dear. My word, we've nothing like this in SHAEF. Marooned in your Alpine redoubt or not, you people know how to look after yourselves.'

In the gloom at the back of the minstrels' gallery, Schaffer nudged Smith with his elbow.

'What gives with old Carnaby-Jones knocking back the Napoleon, then?' he asked in a low indignant murmur. 'Why isn't he being turned on a spit or having the French fits coming out of scopolamine?'

'Sssh!' Smith's nudge carried a great deal more weight and authority than Schaffer's had done.

Jones smiled his thanks as Anne-Marie poured him some more brandy, sipped from the glass, sighed in satisfaction and continued: 'Or have you forgotten, General Rosemeyer, that Germany is also a signatory to The Hague conventions?'

'I haven't forgotten,' Rosemeyer said uncomfortably. 'And if I had my way . . . General, my hands are tied. I have my orders from Berlin.'

'And you can tell Berlin all they're entitled to know,' Jones said easily. 'I am General – Lieutenant General – George Carnaby, United States Army.'

'And Chief Co-ordinator of Planning for the Second Front,' Rosemeyer added morosely.

'The Second Front?' Jones asked with interest. 'What's that?'

Rosemeyer said heavily and with earnest gravity: 'General, I've done all I can. You must believe me. For thirty-six hours now, I've held off Berlin. I've persuaded – I've *tried* to persuade the High Command that the mere *fact* of your capture will compel the Allies to alter all their invasion plans. But this, it seems, is not enough. For the last time, may I request—'

'General George Carnaby,' Jones said calmly. 'United States Army.'

'I expected nothing else,' Rosemeyer admitted tiredly. 'How could I expect anything else from a senior army officer? I'm afraid the matter is now in Colonel Kramer's hands.'

Jones sipped some more brandy and eyed Kramer thoughtfully. 'The Colonel doesn't seem very happy about it either.'

'I'm not,' Kramer said. 'But the matter is out of my hands, too. I also have my orders. Anne-Marie will attend to the rest of it.'

'*This* charming young lady?' Jones was politely incredulous. 'A maestro of the thumb-screw?'

'Of the hypodermic syringe,' Kramer said shortly. 'She used to be a trained nurse.' A bell rang and Kramer picked up a phone by his side. 'Yes? Ah! They have, of course, been searched? Very good. Now.' He looked across at Jones. 'Well, well, well. Some interesting company coming up, General. Very interesting indeed. Parachutists. A rescue team – for you. I'm sure you'll be delighted to meet one another.'

'I really can't imagine what you're talking about,' Jones said idly.

'The rescue team we've seen before,' Smith murmured to Schaffer. 'And no doubt we'll be renewing old acquaintances before long. Come on.'

'What? Now?' Schaffer jerked an urgent thumb in the direction of Jones. 'Just when they're going to get to work on him?'

'Out of your social depth, Lieutenant,' Smith whispered. 'They're civilised. First, they finish the brandy. *Then* the works.'

'It's like I said,' Schaffer said mournfully. 'I'm from Montana.'

The two men left as quietly as they had come and as quietly closed the door behind them. Against the loom of light at either end of the corridor, they could see that the passage-way was clear. Smith switched on the light. They walked briskly along the passage, dropped down a flight of stairs, turned left and halted outside a doorway which bore above it the legend TELEFON ZENTRALE.

'Telephone exchange,' Schaffer said.

Smith shook his head in admiration, put his ear to the door, dropped to one knee, peered through the keyhole and, while still in that position, softly tried the handle. Whatever slight sound he made was masked by the muffled sound of a voice speaking over a telephone. The door was locked. Smith slowly released the handle, straightened and shook his head.

'Suspicious bunch of devils,' Schaffer said sourly. 'The skeletons.'

'The operator would hear us. Next door.'

Next door wasn't locked. The door gave before Smith's pressure on the handle. The room beyond was in total darkness and appeared to be empty.

'*Moment, bitte!*' a cold voice said behind them.

Quickly, but not too quickly, Smith and Schaffer turned round. A few feet away stood a soldier, levelled carbine in his hand, his eyes moving in active suspicion from the two men to the kit-bag in Smith's hands. Smith glared at the man, raised an imperative forefinger to his lips.

'*Dummkopf!*' Smith's voice was a low furious whisper through clenched teeth. '*Silenz! Engländer!*'

He turned away impatiently and peered tensely through the partly-opened doorway. Again he held up an imperious hand that commanded silence. After a few more seconds he straightened, lips compressed, looked significantly at Schaffer and moved slightly to one side. Schaffer took his position and started peering in turn. Curiosity, Smith could see, was replacing suspicion in the soldier's face. Schaffer straightened and said softly: 'What in God's name do we do?'

'I don't know,' Smith said in a worried whisper. 'Colonel Kramer told me he wanted them alive. But—'

'What is it?' the soldier demanded in a voice as low as their own. With the mention of Colonel Kramer the last of his suspicions had gone. 'Who is it?'

'You still here,' Smith said irritably. 'All right, go on. Have a look. But be quick!'

The soldier, his face and eyes now alight with intense curiosity and what might have been dreams of rapid promotion, moved forward on tiptoe as Schaffer courteously stepped to one side to let him see. A pair of Lugers grinding simultaneously into both temples effectively put an end to any idea of rapid military advancement that he might briefly have entertained. He was propelled, stumbling, into the room and, by the time he'd picked himself up and turned round, the door was closed, the light on and both pistols lined at his head.

'Those are silencers you see on our guns,' Smith said quietly. 'No heroics, no shooting. Dying for the Fatherland is one thing, dying uselessly for no reason at all is another and very stupid thing. Don't you agree?'

The soldier looked at them, calculated his chances, accepted the fact that he had none and nodded. Schaffer produced a length of rope and said: 'You may be over-eager, son, but you're no fool. Lie down with your hands behind your back.'

The room, Smith saw, was small and lined with metal shelves and filing cabinets. Some sort of storage room for office records. The chances of anyone coming along weren't high and it was, anyway, a chance they had to take. He waited till Schaffer had bound and gagged the prisoner, put his Luger away, helped Schaffer to bind the man to two of the metal poles supporting the shelves, turned to the window, slid up the lower sash and peered out.

The valley to the north stretched out before him, the lights of the village and the smouldering embers of the railway station visible through very gently falling snow. Smith looked to his right. The lighted window of the telephone exchange was only a few feet away. From the window a heavy lead-sheathed cable attached to a wire almost equally as heavy stretched down the castle wall into the darkness.

'That the one?' Schaffer was by his side now.

'That's the one. Let's have the rope.'

Smith eased his legs into a double bowline, wriggled over the window-sill and cautiously lowered himself to the full extent of his arms while Schaffer, standing by the window with the rope belayed round one of the stanchions of the shelving, took the strain. Smith released his grip on the sill and was lowered jerkily by Schaffer till he was about ten or twelve feet down. Then, using a free hand and both feet to fend himself off from the wall he began to swing himself in a pendulum arc across the face of the castle, an assist from Schaffer up above adding momentum to his swing. On the fifth swing the fingers of his left hand hooked round the lead cable and wire. As Schaffer eased off tension on the rope Smith got both hands round the cable and quickly climbed up the few feet to the window above. He was almost certain that the lead cable he had in his hands *was* the telephone outlet, but only almost: he had no desire to slice the blade of his knife through high-powered electricity supply lines.

He hitched a wary eye over the window-sill, saw that the telephone operator, his back almost directly to him, was talking animatedly on the phone, lifted himself another six inches, observed a cable of what appeared to be exactly similar dimensions to the one he was holding running along the skirting-board to some point behind the exchange and then not reappearing again. He lowered himself a couple of feet, grasped cable and wire firmly with his left hand, inserted the point of his knife between cable and wire a few inches below that and started sawing. A dozen powerful saw-cuts and he was through.

He replaced the knife in its sheath, hoisted himself up again and had another look through the window. The operator was still animated, but this time not with his voice but with a hand which he was using furiously to crank a handle at the side of the exchange. After a few seconds of this profitless exercise he gave up and just sat there staring at the switchboard and shaking his head in bafflement. Smith made a signal to Schaffer, released his grip on the cable and swung back across the castle wall.

Mary glanced at her watch for the tenth time in less than as many minutes, stubbed out the half-cigarette she'd been nervously smoking, rose from her chair, opened her hand-bag, checked that the safety catch of the Mauser inside was in the off position, closed the bag and crossed the room. She had just turned the handle and begun to open the door when knuckles rapped on the outside. She hesitated, glanced at the bag in her hand and looked round almost wildly to see where she could dispose of it. But it was too late to dispose of anything. The door opened and a cheerfully smiling von Brauchitsch stood framed in the doorway.

'Ah, Fräulein!' He glanced at the bag and smiled again. 'Lucky me! Just in time to escort you wherever you're going.'

'To escort me—' She broke off and smiled. 'My business is of no consequence. It can wait. You wanted to see me, Captain?'

'Naturally.'

'What about?'

'What about, she says! About nothing, that's what. Unless you call yourself nothing. Just to see you. Is that a crime? The prettiest girl we've seen—' He smiled again, this man who was always smiling, and took her arm. 'Come, a little Bavarian hospitality. Coffee. We have an armoury that's been converted into the finest *Kaffeestube*—'

'But – but my duties?' Mary said uncertainly. 'I must see the Colonel's secretary—'

'That one! Let her wait!' There was a marked lack of cordiality in von Brauchitsch's voice. 'You and I have a lot to talk about.'

'We have?' It was impossible to resist the infectious smile, not to reply in kind. 'Such as?'

'Düsseldorf.'

'Düsseldorf?'

'Of course! That's my home town, too.'

'Your home town, too!' She smiled again and gave his arm the briefest of squeezes. 'How small a world. That *will* be nice.'

She wondered vaguely, as she walked along, how one could smile and smile and, inside, feel as chilled as the tomb.

—— 7 ——

For the second time in fifteen minutes Smith and Schaffer stopped at the doorway outside the gold room's minstrels' gallery, switched out the passage light, paused, listened, then passed silently inside. This time, however, Smith reached through the crack of the almost closed door and switched the light back on again. He did not expect to be using that door again, that night or any night, and he had no wish to raise any eyebrows, however millimetric the raising: survival was a matter of the infinitely careful consideration of all possible dangers, no matter how remote that possibility might at times appear.

This time, Smith and Schaffer did not remain at the back of the minstrels' gallery. They moved slowly to the front, till they had come to the head of the broad flight of stairs leading down to the floor of the gold room and then sat down on the front oaken benches, one on each side of the gallery's passageway. They were still shrouded in deep gloom, completely invisible from below.

Colonel Kramer's stock of VSOP Napoleon brandy was certainly taking a beating that night, Smith reflected. The

Colonel, Reichsmarschall Rosemeyer, Jones and Anne-Marie had been joined by three others – Carraciola, Thomas and Christiansen. Those last three were no longer manacled and under heavy guard. On the contrary there was no sign of any guard, and the three men were sitting deeply relaxed and side by side on one of the massive gold lamé-covered couches, glasses of brandy, and no small ones at that, in their hands. Even Anne-Marie now held a glass in her hand. It appeared to be an occasion for a celebration of some note.

Kramer lifted his glass towards the three men seated in the couch.

'Your health, gentlemen. Your very good health.' He turned to the Reichsmarschall. 'Three of the best in Europe, sir.'

'I suppose they are necessary,' Rosemeyer said in resigned distaste. 'At least, their courage is beyond dispute. Your health, gentlemen.'

'Your health, gentlemen,' Jones said bitterly. He sat forward in his chair and hurled his glass into the fire. The glass shattered and there was a momentary tongue of flame as the brandy ignited. '*That's* how I drink the health of double agents.'

Schaffer leaned across the passage-way and whispered: 'I thought you said he couldn't act?'

'Nobody's ever paid him twenty-five thousand bucks a night before,' Smith said sardonically.

'Tut, tut, General. Best Venetian glass.' Kramer shook his head deprecatingly then smiled. 'But an understandable fit of pique. When your heroic rescuers turn out to be, well, birds of a different feather—'

'Double agents!' In his contempt, Jones almost spat out the words.

Kramer smiled again, tolerantly, and turned to the three men on the couch.

'And the return trip, gentlemen? As well organised as your outward journey?'

'That's about the one thing the close-mouthed so-and-so told us,' Carraciola said with some bitterness. 'A Mosquito bomber is to come to pick us up. Salen, a little village north of Frauenfeld in Switzerland. There's a little civilian airfield just to the north of Salen.'

Schaffer bent across the passage again and said in an admiring whisper: 'You really are a fearful liar.'

'So Salen it is,' Kramer was saying. 'We know all about it. The Swiss are very good at looking the wrong way when it suits them: but for reasons of our own we find it convenient not to protest too much. Odd things happen at Salen . . . However. A little message to London. Arrange pick-up times and so forth. Then a helicopter to the border – so much easier than walking, gentlemen – a rubber dinghy for the Rhine and then a short walk. You'll be back in Whitehall, reporting General Carnaby's transfer to Berlin, before you know it.'

'Back in London?' Thomas shook his head in slow emphasis. 'Not on your nelly, Colonel. With Smith and that Yank still at large? What happens if they find out what's really happening? What happens if they remain at large? What happens if they get a message through to London—'

'What do you take us for?' Kramer said tiredly. 'You will also, of course, be reporting the unfortunate demise of your leader. As soon as we located that still-warm radio set in the left luggage office we put on bloodhounds from the barracks. Your precious Major Smith was the last man to handle that set and he left a pretty clear trail. The hounds traced him along the east side of the village as far as a garage and then up to the lower station of the *Luftseilbahn*.'

'The cable-car?' Thomas was frankly disbelieving.

'The cable-car. Our Major Smith is either a very foolhardy or a very dangerous man – I must confess I know nothing of him. And there, at the lower station, the hounds completely lost the scent. The handlers circled the station with the hounds and then brought them into the cable-car itself. But the trail was cold. Our quarry appeared to have vanished into thin air.

'It was then that one of the searchers had the original idea of examining the thin air, so to speak. He climbed up and examined the roof of the lower station. Surprise, surprise, unmistakable signs in the snow and ice that two men had been up there before him. From that it was only a logical step to examine the roof of the cable-car itself, and sure enough—'

'They're inside!' Christiansen exclaimed.

'And won't get out again.' Colonel Kramer leaned back comfortably in his chair. 'Have no fear, gentlemen. Every exit is blocked – including the header station. We've doubled the guards outside and the rest have just begun to carry out a floor to floor search.'

In the gloom of the minstrels' gallery Smith and Schaffer exchanged thoughtful glances.

'I don't know,' Thomas said uneasily. 'He's a resourceful devil—'

Kramer held up a hand.

'Fifteen minutes. I guarantee it.' He shifted his glance to Jones. 'I don't pretend to look forward to this, General, but shall we get on with your – ah – medication?'

Jones glared at Carraciola, Christiansen and Thomas and said, very slowly and distinctly: 'You – bloody – swine!'

'Against all my principles, General Carnaby,' Rosemeyer said uncomfortably. 'But if we could only dispense with force—'

'Principles? You make me sick!' Jones stood up and made a strangled noise in his throat. 'The hell with you all! The Hague Conventions! Principles! Officers and gentlemen of the Third bloody Reich!' He stripped off his uniform jacket, rolled up a sleeve and sat down again.

There was a brief and uncomfortable silence, then Kramer nodded to Anne-Marie who put down her glass and moved off to a side door leading off the gold drawing-room. It was obvious to everyone that Anne-Marie wasn't feeling in the least uncomfortable: the half-smile on her face was as near to that of pleasurable anticipation as she could permit herself in the presence of Rosemeyer and Kramer.

Again Smith and Schaffer exchanged glances, no longer thoughtful glances, but the glances of men who know what they have to do and are committed to doing it. Carefully, silently, they eased themselves up from the choir-stalls, adjusted the straps of their shoulder-slung Schmeissers until the machine-pistols were in the horizontal position then started slowly down the stairs, well apart and as close as possible to their respective banisters, to minimise the danger of creaking treads.

They were half-day down, just beginning to emerge from the dark gloom of the gallery, when Anne-Marie re-entered the room. She was carrying a small stainless steel tray: on the tray were a glass beaker, a phial containing some colourless liquid and a hypodermic syringe. She set the tray down on an occasional table close to Jones and broke the phial into the narrow beaker.

Smith and Schaffer had reached the foot of the stairs and were now advancing towards the group round the fire-place. They had now completely emerged from the shadows, and were in full view of anyone who cared to turn his head. But no one cared to turn his head, every seated person in the drawing-room was engrossed in the scene before him, watching in varying degrees of willing or unwilling fascination as Anne-Marie carefully filled the hypodermic syringe and held it up to the light to examine it. Smith and Schaffer continued to advance, their footfalls soundless on the luxuriously deep pile of the gold carpet.

Carefully, professionally, but with the trace of the smile still on her lips, Anne-Marie swabbed an area of Jones's forearm with cotton wool soaked in alcohol and then, as the watchers unconsciously bent forward in their seats, picked up Jones's wrist in one hand and the hypodermic in the other. The hypodermic hovered over the swabbed area as she located the vein she wanted.

'Just a waste of good scopolamine, my dear,' Smith said. 'You won't get anything out of him.'

There was a moment's frozen and incredulous stillness, the hypodermic syringe fell soundlessly to the floor, then everyone whirled round to stare at the two advancing figures, carbines moving gently from side to side. Predictably, Colonel Kramer was the first to recover and react. Almost imperceptibly, his hand began to drift to a button on a panel beside his chair.

'That button, Colonel,' Smith said conversationally.

Slowly, reluctantly, Kramer's hand retreated from the button.

'On the other hand,' Smith went on cordially, 'why not? By all means, if you wish.'

Kramer glanced at him in narrow-eyed and puzzled suspicion.

'You will notice, Colonel,' Smith continued by way of explanation, 'that my gun is not pointing at you. It is pointed at him' – he swung his gun to cover Carraciola – 'at him,' – the gun moved to Thomas – 'at him,' – it covered Christiansen – 'and at him!' Smith swung round abruptly and ground the muzzle of the Schmeisser into Schaffer's ribs. 'Drop that gun! Now!'

'Drop the gun?' Schaffer stared at him in shock and baffled consternation. 'What in the name of God—'

Smith stepped swiftly forward and, without altering his grip on his gun, lifted the barrel sharply upwards and drove the butt of the Schmeisser into Schaffer's stomach. Schaffer grunted in agony, doubled forward with both hands clutched over his midriff, then, seconds later, obviously in great pain, began to straighten slowly. Glaring at Smith, the dark eyes mad in his face, he slipped the shoulder strap and the Schmeisser fell to the carpet.

'Sit there.' With the muzzle of his gun Smith gestured to a chair half-way between Rosemeyer's and the couch where the three men were sitting.

Schaffer said slowly, painfully: 'You goddamned lousy, dirty, double-crossing—'

'That's what they all say. You're not even original.' The contempt in Smith's voice gave way to menace. 'That chair, Schaffer.'

Schaffer lowered himself with difficulty into his chair, rubbed his solar plexus and said, 'You —. If I live to be a hundred—'

'If you live to be a hundred you'll do nothing,' Smith said contemptuously. 'In your own idiom, Schaffer, you're a punk and a petty second-rate one at that.' He settled himself confortably in a chair beside Colonel Kramer. 'A simple-minded American,' he explained carelessly. 'Had him along for local colour.'

'I see,' Kramer said. It was obvious that he did not see. He went on uncertainly: 'If we might have an explanation—'

Smith waved him negligently to silence.

'All in good time, my dear Kramer, all in good time. As I was saying, my dear Anna-Marie—'

'How did you know her name was Anne-Marie?' Kramer asked sharply.

Smith smiled enigmatically, ignored him completely, and continued: 'As I was saying, scopolamine is a waste of time. All scopolamine will do, as you're all aware, is to reveal the truth about our friend here, which is that he is not Lieutenant General George Carnaby, Chief Co-ordinator of Planning for the Second Front, but a certain Cartwright Jones, an American actor being paid precisely twenty-five thousand dollars to impersonate General Carnaby.' He looked over to Jones and bowed. 'My congratulations, Mr Jones. A very creditable performance. Pity you'll have to spend the rest of the war in a concentration camp.'

Kramer and Rosemeyer were on their feet, the others leaning far forward on the couch, an almost exactly identical expression of disbelief showing in every face. If Cartwright Jones had been earth's first visitor from outer space he couldn't possibly have been the object of more incredulous consternation.

'Well, well, well,' Smith said with interest. 'Surprise, surprise, surprise.' He tapped Kramer on the arm and gestured in the direction of Carraciola, Thomas and Christiansen. 'Odd, wouldn't you say, Kramer? They seem just as astonished as you are?'

'Is this true?' Rosemeyer demanded hoarsely of Jones. 'What he says? Do you deny—'

In a voice that was no more than a whisper, Jones said: 'How – how in God's name – who *are* you, sir?'

'A stranger in the night.' Smith waved a hand. 'Dropped in in the passing, you might say. Maybe the Allies will let you have that twenty-five thousand after the war. I wouldn't bank on it though. If international law allows you to shoot a captured enemy soldier dressed as a civilian, maybe the opposite holds good too.' Smith stretched and politely patted a yawn to extinction. 'And now, Anne-Marie, if I could – with your permission, my dear Kramer – have a glass of that excellent Napoleon. Clinging to the roofs of cable-cars works the devil with my circulation.'

The girl hesitated, looked at Kramer and Rosemeyer, found neither encouragement nor discouragement, shrugged, poured a glass and handed it to Smith, who sniffed the bouquet approvingly, drank a little and bowed again to Jones.

'My congratulations, sir. You are a connoisseur.' He sipped again, turned to Kramer and said sadly: 'To think you have been wasting such excellent liquor on enemies of the Third Reich.'

'Don't listen to him, Colonel Kramer, don't listen to him!' Carraciola shouted wildly. 'It's a bluff! He's just trying—'

Smith lined up his gun on Carraciola's chest and said softly: 'Keep quiet or I'll make you quiet, you damned traitor. You'll have your chance – *and* we'll see who's bluffing.' He lowered his gun to his knees and went on tiredly: 'Colonel Kramer, I don't fancy talking and having to keep a gun on this unlovely trio all the time. Have you a guard you can trust? A man who won't talk afterwards, I mean?'

He sat back in his chair, sipped his brandy and ignored the malevolent stares from his four erstwhile colleagues. Kramer looked at him for a very long moment, then nodded thoughtfully and reached for a phone.

The armoury – now converted into a *Kaffeestube* – of the Schloss Adler was very much in keeping with the remainder of the castle, something out of a medieval dream or nightmare, according to how individual tastes and inclinations lay. It was a large, darkly-panelled, stone-flagged room with enormous adze-cut smoke-blackened beams and walls behung with ancient and rusty suits of armour, ancient and rusty weapons of all kinds and scores of armorial bearings, some of which could have been genuine. Three-sided half-booths lined the walls and half-a-dozen slab-topped monastery refectory tables, flanked by massive oak benches, paralleled the shorter axis of the room. The oil lamps, suspended by iron chains from the ceiling, were turned low, lending the atmosphere in the armoury an air of intimacy or brooding menace, according to one's original mood on entering. There was no doubt in Mary's mind as to its effect upon her. Her gaze followed half-a-dozen heavily armed and jack-booted men who were just leaving the armoury, then came back reluctantly to the man sitting close beside her in the corner booth.

'Well, what did I tell you?' von Brauchitsch said expansively. 'Coffee to match the surroundings!'

Coffee to match the surroundings, Mary thought, would have tasted of hemlock. She said: 'What did those men want? They seemed to be looking for someone.'

'Forget them. Concentrate on von Brauchitsch.'

'But you spoke to them. What did they *want*?'

'They say there are spies in the castle!' Von Brauchitsch threw his head back, laughed, and spread his hands palms up. 'Imagine! Spies in the Schloss Adler! The Gestapo HQ! They must have flown in on their broom-sticks. The military commandant is an old woman. He has spies in about once a week. Now what was I saying about Düsseldorf?' He broke off, glancing at her empty coffee cup. 'My apologies, my dear Fräulein. Come, more coffee.'

'No, really. I must go.'

Von Brauchitsch laughed again and put his hand on hers.

'Go where? There *is* nowhere to go inside the Schloss Adler. Nonsense, nonsense.' He turned in his seat and called: 'Fräulein! Two more coffees. And with Schnapps, this time.'

While he was ordering, Mary glanced quickly at her watch and a momentary expression of desperation crossed her face, but by the time von Brauchitsch turned back she was smiling sweetly at him. She said: 'You were saying about Düsseldorf—'

The company in the gold drawing-room had now been increased by one, a tall, cold-faced and hard-eyed sergeant who held a carbine cradled in a pair of strong and very capable looking hands. He was standing behind the couch on which Carraciola, Thomas and Christiansen were seated, and he was giving them his entire attention, apart from a frequent sideways glance at Schaffer. He had about him a reassuring air of competence.

'A very much more civilised arrangement,' Smith said approvingly. He rose, leaving his Schmeisser lying on the floor, crossed to the brandy decanter on the sideboard, poured himself another drink and made his way back to the fireplace where he placed his glass on the mantelpiece.

'This will take but minutes, only,' Smith said in a soft and ominous voice. 'Anne-Marie, bring in three more capsules of scopolamine.' He smiled at her. 'And I needn't remind *you* to bring the hypodermics.'

'Colonel Kramer!' Carraciola said desperately. 'This is madness! Are you going to allow—'

'Guard!' Smith's voice was harsh. 'If that man talks again, silence him!'

The guard jabbed his carbine muzzle none too lightly into Carraciola's back. Carraciola subsided, fuming, his fists clenched till the ivory showed.

'What do you take Reichsmarschall Rosemeyer and Colonel Kramer for?' Smith demanded cuttingly. 'Credulous fools? Little children? Imbeciles of your own calibre, who imagine you can get away with a cretinous masquerade of this nature? The scopolamine will be used *after* I have established my own bonafides and *after* I have disproved yours. Anne-Marie?'

Anne-Marie smiled and marched away. It was not every night that she got the chance to administer three injections of scopolamine. Then she stopped and turned, eyebrows raised in interrogation, as Smith called her name again.

'One moment, Fräulein.' Smith, brandy glass in hand, was staring unseeingly into the middle distance and the watchers could see a slow smile coming to his face, a smile obviously heralding the birth of a new idea and one that pleased him very much. 'Of course, of course,' Smith said softly. 'And bring three note-books will you, my dear?'

'*Three* note-books?' Colonel Kramer's tone was neutral, his eyes watchful. '*Three* capsules? You give the impression that we have *four* enemies of the Reich here.'

'Only three enemies that matter,' Smith said in weary patience. 'The American?' The fact that he neither bothered to glance at Schaffer nor even permit a trace of contempt to creep into his voice showed unmistakably his opinion of the American. 'He doesn't even know what day of the week it is. Now then.' He picked up a cigar from an inlaid marquetry box, lit it and sipped some more brandy. 'Let's be fair and establish my bonafides first. Pointers first, then proof. In the best judicial fashion.

'First, why did I invite another guard in and lay down my own gun?' He paused and went on sarcastically: 'Of course! Because I wanted to increase the odds against myself. Secondly, why didn't I kill Colonel Weissner and his men when I had them at my mercy – if, that is, I'm an enemy of the Third Reich – earlier this evening? I had some difficulty, I might tell you, in restraining our fire-eating young American here from turning himself into a one-man firing squad. Very aggressive, he was.'

'I'll damned well tell you why,' Carraciola said viciously. 'Because you knew the shots would be heard!'

Smith sighed, lifted the flap of his jacket, produced an automatic and fired. The sound of the impact of the bullet thudding into the couch inches from Carraciola's shoulder completely blanketed the soft plop made by the automatic itself. Smith carelessly threw the silenced Luger into a nearby empty chair and smiled quizzically at Carraciola.

'Didn't know I had that, did you? I didn't kill Colonel Weissner because German does not kill German.'

'You are German?' Kramer's eyes were still watchful but the tone perhaps a shade less neutral.

'Johann Schmidt, at your service.' This with a little bow and click of the heels. 'Captain John Smith of the Black Watch.'

'From the Rhineland, by your accent?'

'Heidelberg.'

'But that is *my* home town.'

'Indeed?' Smith smiled his interest. 'Then I think we have a mutual friend.'

Momentarily, a faraway look came to Kramer's eyes and he said softly, apparently apropos of nothing: 'The columns of Charlemagne.'

'Ah, and the fountain in the courtyard of the dear old Friedrichsbau,' Smith said nostalgically. He glanced at Kramer, and the nostalgia gave way to a pseudo-mournful reproof. 'How could you, my dear Colonel? To proceed. Why – third point, I think – why did I stage this elaborate car accident – because I *knew* those three impostors wouldn't dare come into the open until they thought I was dead. Anyway, if I *were* the impostor, would I have come back when I knew the game was up? Anyway, to come back for what?' He smiled wearily and nodded at Jones. 'To rescue *another* impostor?'

Kramer said thoughtfully: 'I must say I'm rather beginning to look forward to hearing what our three friends here have to say.'

'I'll tell you *now* what I've bloody well got to say.' Christiansen was on his feet, ignoring the guard's gun, his voice shaking with fury. 'He's fooling you, he's fooling all of us. He's a damned liar and you're too damned stupid to see the wool over your eyes. A tissue of — lies, from beginning to end—'

'That will do!' Kramer's hand was up, his eyes bleak, his tone icy. 'You condemn yourselves from your own mouths. Every statement made so far by this officer is demonstrably true. Sergeant Hartmann' – this to the guard with the carbine – 'if any of those men speak again, do you think you could silence him without silencing him permanently?'

Hartmann produced a small woven-leather truncheon from his tunic and slipped the looped thong over his wrist.

'You know I can, Herr Colonel.'

'Good. Pray continue, Captain Schmidt.'

'Thank you. I hadn't finished.' Smith felt like pouring himself another brandy, a celebration brandy or, alternatively, pinning a medal on Christiansen for having so unerringly if unwittingly exposed the chink in Kramer's armour, a wounded intellectual vanity, the lacerated professional pride of a brilliant man being reminded of his capacity for being duped by one of those who had already duped him. 'For the same excellent reason I came here by the roof of the cable-car – they'd *never* have come into the open if they'd known I was here – and alive. Incidentally, Kramer, hasn't it occurred to you that it's impossible to enter the Schloss Adler from the roof of the header station without the assistance of a rope and someone inside?'

'Damnation!' Coming so soon after Christiansen's reminder of his fallibility, Smith's question left Kramer's self-confidence badly shaken. 'I never thought—'

'Von Brauchitsch,' Smith said carelessly. 'He had his orders direct from Berlin.' He placed his glass on the mantelpiece, walked across and stood before the three spies. 'Tell me, how did I know Jones was an impostor? Why did you *not* know he was one? And If I'm not what I claim to be then what in God's name am I doing here at all? Perhaps you would like to explain that?'

The three men glanced up at him in baleful silence.

'Perhaps they would indeed,' Kramer said heavily. He came and stood by Smith, staring down at the three men with an oddly expressionless gaze that was more disturbing than any show of anger could ever have been. After another and longer silence he said: 'Captain Schmidt, this has gone far enough.'

'Not yet.'

'I require no more,' Kramer persisted.

'I promised you proof – those were but the pointers. A proof to satisfy the Deputy Chief of the German Secret Service – and that proof is in three parts. A yes or no, Colonel Kramer, if you please. Do you or do you not know the name of our top man in Britain?' Kramer nodded. 'Then suppose we ask them?'

The three men on the couch looked at each other, then at Smith. They looked in silence. Thomas licked dry lips, a movement that did not go unnoticed by Kramer. Smith produced a small red note-book from his tunic pocket, removed a rubber band, tore out the central page, then carefully replaced the band on the book and the book in his pocket. He wrote something on the page and handed it to Kramer, who glanced at it and nodded. Smith took the paper from him, walked across to the fire and burned it.

'Now then,' Smith said. 'You have here, in the Schloss Adler, the most powerful radio transmitter in Central Europe—'

'You are singularly well-informed, Captain Schmidt,' Kramer said wryly.

'Smith. I live Smith. I breathe Smith. I *am* Smith. Put a radio-telephone call through to Field-Marshal Kesselring's HQ in Northern Italy. Ask for his Chief of Military Intelligence.'

Kramer said softly: 'The mutual friend you mentioned?'

'An old alumnus of Heidelberg University,' Smith nodded. 'Colonel Wilhelm Wilner.' He smiled. 'Willi-Willi.'

'You know that? Then it will not be necessary to call him.'

'Admiral Canaris would like you to.'

'And you know my chief, too?' Kramer's voice was even softer.

'My self-esteem urges me to say that I do – but modesty and the truth compels me to admit I don't,' Smith said disarmingly. 'I just work for him.'

'I'm convinced already, convinced beyond all doubt,' Rosemeyer said. 'But do as he says, Colonel.'

Kramer did as he was told. He put a call through to the radio room, hung up and waited patiently. Smith lay back in his armchair, brandy in one hand, cigar in the other, the picture of relaxed confidence. If Schaffer and the three men on the couch beside him were either relaxed or confident they entirely failed to show it. Behind them their guard watched his four charges hopefully, as if eager to show his expertise with a blackjack. If either Rosemeyer or Jones were thinking any thoughts at all, those thoughts didn't break through to the surface. Anne-Marie, not quite knowing what was going on, hovered around indecisively, a tentative smile of anticipation still on her face. She was the only person who moved during the period of waiting and that only because Smith crooked a finger at her and indicated his empty brandy glass: so complete was the ascendancy he had achieved that she obeyed the unspoken command without hesitation and brought back a very generous measure of brandy which she sat down by his side-table to the accompaniment of a winning smile. Smith gave her a winning smile in return. But no one spoke, not once, during that seemingly interminable wait.

The phone bell rang.

Kramer lifted it and, after a few preliminary exchanges, presumably with operators, said: 'Colonel Wilhelm Wilner. My dear friend, Willi-Willi. How are you.' After the introductory courtesies were over, Kramer said: 'We have an agent here who claims to know you. A Captain John Smith. Have you ever – ah, so you know him? Good, good!' A pause, then he continued: 'Could you describe him?'

He listened intently, looking at Smith as a voice crackled over the receiver. Suddenly he beckoned to Smith, who rose and crossed over to where Kramer was sitting.

'Your left hand,' Kramer said to Smith, took it in his own, then spoke into the phone. 'Yes, the tip of the little finger is missing . . . and the right forearm has what?' Smith bared his right forearm without being told. 'Yes, yes, two parallel scars, three centimetres apart . . . What's that? . . . Tell him he's a traitor?'

'And tell him he's a renegade,' Smith smiled.

'And you're a renegade,' Kramer said on the phone. 'Chambertin, you say. Ah! Thank you, thank you. Goodbye, my old friend.' He replaced the receiver.

'We both prefer French wine,' Smith said apologetically and by way of explanation.

'Our top double agent in the Mediterranean,' Kramer said wonderingly. 'And I'd never even heard of you.'

'Maybe that's why he is what he is,' Rosemeyer said dryly.

'I've been lucky.' Smith shrugged then said briskly: 'Well, then. My credentials?'

'Impeccable,' Kramer said. 'My God, they're impeccable.'

'So,' Smith said grimly. 'Now for our friends' credentials. As you know, Christiansen, Thomas and Carraciola – the real Christiansen, Thomas and Carraciola – while working for—'

'What in God's name are you talking about?' Christiansen

shouted. He was on his feet, his face suffused with uncontrollable anger. 'The real Christiansen—' His eyes turned up as Hartmann's blackjack caught him behind the ear and he sagged to the floor.

'He was warned,' Kramer said grimly. 'You didn't hit him too hard, Sergeant?'

'A two-minute tap,' Hartmann said reassuringly.

'Good. I think you may now proceed without interruption, my dear Schmidt.'

'Smith,' Smith corrected him. 'As I was saying, our real agents while working for the British counter-espionage have not only been responsible for the deep infiltration of the German Secret Service into the British espionage network in France and the Low Countries but have also set up an excellent chain of spies in England – a most successful ring, as Admiral Canaris well knows.'

'It's not my territory,' Kramer said. 'But that, of course, I know.'

Smith said coldly: 'To your feet, you impostors, and sit at the table there. Sergeant, lend a hand to that man on the floor there. He appears to be coming round.'

Their faces baffled and uncomprehending, Carraciola and Thomas made their way towards the table and sat down, where they were shortly joined by a very shaky and sick-looking Christiansen. The sergeant remained by him just long enough to ensure that he didn't fall off his chair, then took three paces back and covered them all with his carbine again.

From the other side of the table Smith flung down in front of the three men the little note-books that Anne-Marie had brought. Then he produced his own elastic-banded note-book from his pocket and laid it on the small table beside Kramer.

'If they are who they claim to be,' Smith said quietly, 'it would be reasonable, would it not, my dear Kramer, to expect them to be able to write the names and the addresses or contacts of our agents in England and of the British agents who have been supplanted on the Continent by our men.' He paused significantly. 'And then compare their lists with the genuine one in my book there.'

'It would indeed,' Kramer said slowly. 'Proof at one stroke. Masterly, my dear Captain Schmidt – Smith, I mean.' He smiled, almost wanly. 'I'm afraid I'm not myself tonight. But tell me, Captain.' He touched the banded note-book by his side.

'This list of agents – I mean, carrying it around on your person. Does this not contravene every rule we have?'

'Of course it does. Rules can only be broken by the man who made them. You think that even I would dare without his authority? Admiral Walter Canaris will be in his Berlin office now.' Smith nodded towards the telephone.

'What do you take me for.' Kramer smiled and turned to the three men at the table. 'Well, you heard.'

'There's something terribly far wrong—' Carraciola began despairingly.

'There is indeed,' Kramer interrupted bleakly.

'I don't *doubt* Smith's bona-fides.' Carraciola was almost in anguish now. 'Not any more. But there's been some ghastly mistake—'

'You are the ones who have made it,' Smith said curtly.

'Write,' Kramer commanded. 'Sergeant Hartmann.'

Sergeant Hartmann stepped forward, his leather-thonged blackjack at the ready. The three men bent their heads and wrote.

—— 8 ——

The armoury was almost deserted now. Some time previously, a couple of sergeants had entered, moved around among the coffee tables and taken at least a score of grumbling men away for unspecified duties. Mary did not have to guess at what those unspecified duties might be. She glanced secretly at her watch for what must have been the twentieth time, rubbed her forehead wearily, rose to her feet and smiled palely at von Brauchitsch.

'I'm so sorry, Captain. I must go. I really must go. A most dreadful headache.'

'I *am* sorry, my dear Maria.' A troubled contrition had replaced his habitual smile. 'You should have told me earlier. You don't look at all well. A long journey from the Rhineland, then all this Schnapps—'

'I'm afraid I'm not used to it,' Mary said ruefully. 'I'll be all right when I've lain down.'

'Of course, of course. Come, my dear, let me escort you to your room.'

'No, no!' Then, realizing she had spoken with uncalled-for

vehemence, she smiled again and touched his hand. 'I'll be all right. Really I will.'

'Captain von Brauchitsch knows what's best.' The face was serious but friendly, the voice authoritative but with an underlying tone of humour, and Mary knew there was no answer to it. 'I positively insist. Come along.'

He tucked her arm protectively under his and led her from the armoury.

Arm in arm they walked along the passage-way leading from the armoury-cum-*Kaffeestube* towards the central block of the castle. The passage-way, in contrast to the last time they had walked along there, was completely deserted and Mary commented on the fact.

'It's the witches on their broomsticks,' von Brauchitsch laughed. 'The commandant hasn't caught them yet, but give him another few years and you never know. All those poor souls you saw being hauled out of the armoury are now probably poking about the eaves or climbing up the flagpoles. You never know where spies get to nowadays.'

'You seem to treat the possibility lightly enough,' Mary said.

'I'm a Gestapo officer. I'm paid and trained to use my head, not an overheated imagination,' he said curtly, then squeezed her arm and apologised. 'Sorry, that tone of voice was aimed at someone else, not you.' He halted abruptly, peered out a window into the courtyard and said: 'Now that is strange.'

'What's strange?'

'The helicopter there,' von Brauchitsch said thoughtfully. 'Army regulations state that High Command helicopters must be kept in instant readiness at all times. But that one has part of its engine cover dismantled and a tarpaulin stretched in position over it. Wouldn't call that instant readiness, would you?'

'I suppose helicopters need repairing from time to time the same as any other machine.' Her throat was suddenly dry and she wished von Brauchitsch wouldn't hold her so closely: he was bound to notice her accelerating heart-beat. 'What's so unusual about that?'

'What's so unusual is that there was no one working on that machine almost half an hour ago when we first passed by here,' von Brauchitsch said. 'Unheard of for a Reichsmarschall's personal pilot to walk away and leave a job half done.'

'Would it be unheard of for him to take a piece of mechanism inside and repair it under cover?' Mary asked sweetly. 'Or perhaps you haven't seen a thermometer tonight?'

'I'm getting as bad as the old commandant and his witch-hunts,' von Brauchitsch said sadly. He moved on, shaking his head. 'You see before you a horrible example of the dangers of being too long in my business: the obvious answer is far too obvious for shrewd and cunning intellects like ours. I must remember that later on tonight.'

'You're going to exercise this great mind again tonight?' Mary asked lightly.

'In there, as a matter of fact.' Von Brauchitsch nodded as they passed by an ornate door. 'The gold drawing-room.' He glanced at his watch. 'In twenty minutes! So soon! Your charming company, Fräulein.'

'Thank you, kind sir. You – you have an appointment?' Her heart was back at its old tricks again.

'An evening of musical appreciation. Even the Gestapo has its finer side. We are going to listen to a nightingale sing.' He quickened his pace. 'Sorry, Fräulein, but I've just remembered I've one or two reports to prepare.'

'I'm sorry if I've kept you from your work, Captain,' she said demurely. How much does he know, she thought wildly, how much does he suspect, what action has he suddenly decided to take? The von Brauchitschs of this world didn't just suddenly remember anything for the excellent reason that they never forgot it in the first place. 'It's been most kind of you.'

'The pleasure was one-sided,' von Brauchitsch protested gallantly. 'Mine and mine alone.' He stopped outside her bedroom door, took her hand in his and smiled. 'Goodnight, my dear Maria. You really are the most charming girl.'

'Goodnight.' She returned smile for smile. 'And thank you.'

'We really must get to know each other better,' von Brauchitsch said in farewell. He opened her door, bowed, kissed her hand, gently closed the door behind her and rubbed his chin thoughtfully. 'Very much better, my dear Maria,' he said softly to himself. 'Very much better indeed.'

Carraciola, Thomas and Christiansen bent over their notebooks and scribbled furiously. At least the first two did: Christiansen had not yet recovered from the blow on the head and was making heavy weather of his writing. Kramer, who was standing apart with Smith and talking to him in low tones, looked at them in curiosity and with just a trace of uneasiness.

'They seem to be finding plenty of inspiration from somewhere,' he said carefully.

'The spectacle of an open grave is often thought-provoking,' Smith said cynically.

'I am afraid I don't quite follow.'

'Do you know what those men will be fifteen minutes from now?'

'I'm tired,' Kramer said. He sounded it. 'Please don't play with words, Captain Schmidt.'

'Smith. In fifteen minutes they'll be dead. And they know it. They're fighting desperately for extra minutes to live: when you have as little time as they have, even a minute is a prize snatched from eternity. Or the last despairing fling of the ruined gambler. Call it what you like.'

'You wax lyrical, Captain,' Kramer grumbled. He paced up and down for almost a minute, no longer troubling to watch the men at the table, then stopped and planted himself squarely in front of Smith. 'All right,' he said wearily. 'I've been on the spit long enough. I confess I'm baffled. Out with it. What in God's name is behind all this?'

'The simplicity of true genius, my dear Kramer. Admiral Rolland, the head of MI6. And he *is* a genius, make no mistake.'

'So he's a genius,' Kramer said impatiently. 'Well?'

'Carraciola, Thomas and Christiansen were caught three weeks ago. Now, as you are aware, they were concerned only with north-west Europe and were not known here.'

'By reputation, they were.'

'Yes, yes. But only that. Admiral Rolland reckoned that if three full-briefed men impersonated our three captured men and were despatched here for a perfectly plausible reason, they would be *persona grata* of some note, honoured guests and completely accepted by you. And, of course, once they were accepted by you, they could operate inside the Schloss Adler with complete security and safety.'

'And?'

'Well, don't you see?' It was Smith's turn to be impatient. 'Rolland knew that if General Carnaby—' he broke off and scowled across the room at Carnaby-Jones – 'or that impostor masquerading as General Carnaby were taken here, his opposite number in the German Army would be sent to interrogate him.' Smith smiled. 'Even in Britain they are aware that the prophet must go to the mountain, not the mountain to the prophet: the Army calls upon the Gestapo, not vice versa.'

'Go on, go on!'

'The Wehrmacht Chief of Staff, Reichsmarschall Julius Rose-meyer, would have been just as priceless to the Allies as General Carnaby to us.'

'The Reichsmarschall!' Kramer spoke in a shocked whisper, his eyes straying across the room to Rosemeyer. 'Kidnap!'

'Your precious trusted agents there,' Smith said savagely. 'And they would have got away with it.'

'My God! God in heaven! It's – it's diabolical!'

'Isn't it?' Smith said. 'Isn't is just?'

Kramer left him abruptly, crossed the room to Rosemeyer and sat down in the chair beside him. For perhaps two minutes they talked together in low tones, occasionally glancing in Smith's direction. Kramer it was, Smith could see, who did most of the talking, Rosemeyer who did all of the reacting. Kramer, Smith reflected, must be putting it across rather well: a printed diagram could have been no clearer than the successive ex-pressions of curiosity, puzzlement, astonishment and, finally, shocked realization that reflected on Rosemeyer's face. After some seconds' silence, both men rose to their feet and walked across to where Smith stood. The Reichsmarschall, Smith saw, was a little paler than normal, and when he spoke it required neither a sensitive ear nor imagination to detect a slight tremor in his voice.

He said: 'This is an incredible story, Captain Smith, in-credible. But inevitable. It must be. The only explanation that can cover all the facts, put all the pieces of the jig-saw together.' He attempted a smile. 'To change the metaphor, I must say that it comes as a considerable shock to find that one is the missing key in a baffling code. I am eternally in your debt, Captain Smith.'

'Germany is eternally in your debt,' Kramer said. 'You have done her a great service. We shall not forget this. I am sure the Führer will personally wish to honour you with some mark of his esteem.'

'You are too kind, gentlemen,' Smith murmured. 'To do my duty is reward enough.' He smiled faintly. 'Perhaps our Führer will give me two or three weeks' leave – the way I feel tonight my nerves aren't what they were. But if you gentlemen will excuse me – my present task is not yet completed.'

He moved away and walked slowly up and down, brandy glass in hand, behind the three men bent over the table. From time to time he glanced at one of the note-books and smiled in weary cynicism, neither the smile nor the significance of the smile going unremarked by anyone in the room except the three writing men. He stopped behind Thomas, shook his head in disbelief and said, 'My God!'

'Let's finish it now!' Rosemeyer demanded impatiently.

'If you please, Reichsmarschall, let us play this charade out to the bitter end.'

'You have your reasons?'

'I must certainly have.'

Briskly, but not hurriedly, von Brauchitsch walked away from Mary's room, his footfalls echoing crisply on the stone-flagged corridor. Once round the corner of the corridor he broke into a run.

He reached the courtyard and ran across to the helicopter. There was no one there. Quickly he ran up a few steps and peered through the Perspex cupola of the cockpit. He reached ground again and hailed the nearest guard, who came stumbling across, a leashed Dobermann trailing behind him.

'Quickly,' von Brauchitsch snapped. 'Have you seen the pilot?'

'No, Herr Major,' the guard answered nervously. He was an elderly man, long past front-line service and held the Gestapo in great fear. 'Not for a long time.'

'What do you mean by a long time?' von Brauchitsch demanded.

'I don't know. That's to say,' the guard added hastily, 'half an hour. More. Three-quarters, I would say, Herr Major.'

'Damnation,' von Brauchitsch swore. 'So long. Tell me, when the pilot is carrying out repairs is there a place near here he uses as a work-shop?'

'Yes, sir.' The guard was eager to oblige with some positive information. 'That door there, sir. The old grain store.'

'Is he in there now?'

'I don't know, Herr Major.'

'You should know,' von Brauchitsch said coldly. 'It's your job to keep your eyes open. Well, just don't stand there, oaf! Go and find out!'

The elderly guard trotted away while von Brauchitsch, shaking his head angrily over his impatience with the old soldier, crossed the courtyard and questioned the guards at the gate, three tough, competent, young storm-troopers who, unlike the patrol guard, could be guaranteed not to miss anything. He received the same negative answer there.

He strode back towards the helicopter and intercepted the elderly guard running from the old grain store.

'There's nobody there, Herr Major.' He was slightly out of breath and highly apprehensive at being the bearer of what might be ill news. 'It's empty.'

'It would be,' von Brauchitsch nodded. He patted the old shoulder and smiled. 'No fault of yours, my friend. You keep a good watch.'

Unhurriedly, almost, now, he made for the main entrance door, pulling out a set of master keys as he went. He struck oil with the first door he opened. The pilot lay there, still unconscious, the smashed distributor cap lay beside him, the pair of overalls lying on top of him a mute but entirely sufficient explanation of the way in which the distributor cap had been removed without detection. Von Brauchitsch took a torch from a long rack on the wall, cut the pilot's bonds, freed his gag and left him lying there with the door wide open. The passage outside was a heavily travelled one, and someone was bound to be along soon.

Von Brauchitsch ran up the stairs to the passage leading to the bedrooms, slowed down, walked easily, casually past Mary's bedroom and stopped at the fifth door beyond that. He used his master keys and passed inside. switching on the light as he went in. He crossed the room, lifted the lower sash window and nodded when he saw that nearly all the snow on the sill had been brushed or rubbed away. He leaned farther out, switched on his torch and flashed the beam downwards. The roof of the header station was fifty feet directly below and the markings and footprints in the snow told their own unmistakable story.

Von Brauchitsch straightened, looked at the odd position of the iron bedstead against the wardrobe door and tugged the bed away. He watched the wardrobe door burst open and the bound and gagged figure inside roll to the floor without as much as hoisting an eyebrow. This had been entirely predictable. From the depths of the bound man's groans it was obvious that he was coming round. Von Brauchitsch cut him free, removed his gag and left. There were more urgent matters demanding his attention than holding the hands of young Oberleutnants as they held their heads and groaned their way back to consciousness.

He stopped outside Mary's room, put his ear to the door and

listened. No sound. He put his eye to the keyhole and peered. No light. He knocked. No reply. He used his master keys and passed inside. No Mary.

'Well, well, well,' von Brauchitsch murmured. 'Very interesting indeed.'

'Finished?' Smith asked.

Thomas nodded. Christiansen and Carraciola glowered. But all three were sitting back and it was obvious that all three were, in fact, finished. Smith walked along behind them, reaching over their shoulders for the note-books. He took them across the room and laid them on the little table by Kramer's chair.

'The moment of truth,' Smith said quietly. 'One book should be enough.'

Kramer, reluctantly almost, picked up the top book and began to read. Slowly he began to leaf his way through the pages. Smith drained his glass and sauntered unconcernedly across the room to the decanter on the sideboard. He poured some brandy, carefully recapped the bottle, walked a few aimless steps and halted. He was within two feet of the guard with the carbine.

He sipped his brandy and said to Kramer: 'Enough?'

Kramer nodded.

'Then compare it with my original.'

Kramer nodded. 'As you say, the moment of truth.'

He picked up the note-book, slid off the rubber band and opened the cover. The first page was blank. So was the next. And the next . . . Frowning, baffled, Kramer lifted his eyes to look across the room to Smith.

Smith's brandy glass was falling to the ground as Smith himself, with a whiplash violent movement of his body brought the side of his right hand chopping down on the guard's neck. The guard toppled as if a bridge had fallen on him. Glasses on the sideboard tinkled in the vibration of his fall.

Kramer's moment of utter incomprehension vanished. The bitter chagrin of total understanding flooded his face. His hand stretched out towards the alarm button.

'Uh-uh! Not the buzzer, Mac!' The blow that had struck down the guard had held no more whiplash than the biting urgency in Schaffer's voice. He was stretched his length on the floor where he'd dived to retrieve the Schmeisser now trained, rock steady, on Kramer's heart. For the second time that night, Kramer's hand withdrew from the alarm button.

Smith picked up the guard's carbine, walked across the room and changed it for his silenced Luger. Schaffer, his gun still trained on Kramer, picked himself up from the floor and glared at Smith.

'A second-rate punk,' he said indignantly. 'A simple-minded American. That's what you said. Don't know what goddamned day of the week it is, do I?'

'All I could think of on the spur of the moment,' Smith said apologetically.

'That makes it even worse,' Schaffer complained. 'And did you have to clobber me so goddamned realistically?'

'Local colour. What are you complaining about? It worked.' He walked across to Kramer's table, picked up the three note-books and buttoned them securely inside his tunic. He said to Schaffer: 'Between them, they shouldn't have missed any-thing... Well, time to be gone. Ready, Mr Jones?'

'And hurry about it,' Schaffer added. 'We have a street-car to catch. Well, anyhow, a cable-car.'

'It's a chicken farm in the boondocks for me.' Jones looked completely dazed and he sounded exactly the same way. 'Acting? My God, I don't know anything about it.'

'This is all you want?' Kramer was completely under control again, calm, quiet, the total professional. 'Those books? just those books?'

'Well, just about. Lots of nice names and addresses. A bed-time story for MI6.'

'I see.' Kramer nodded his understanding. 'Then those men are, of course, what they claim to be?'

'They've been under suspicion for weeks. Classified infor-mation of an invaluable nature was going out and false – and totally valueless – information was coming in. It took two months' work to pin-point the leakages and channels of false information to one or more of the departments controlled by those men. But we knew we could never prove it on them – **we** weren't even sure if there was more than one traitor and had **no** idea who that one might be – and, in any event, proving it with-out finding out their contacts at home and abroad would have been useless. So we – um – thought this one up.'

'You mean, *you* thought it up, Captain Smith,' Rosemeyer said.

'What does it matter?' Smith said indifferently.

'True. It doesn't. But something else does.' Rosemeyer smiled faintly. 'When Colonel Kramer asked you if the books were all you wanted, you said "just about". Indicating that there was possibly something else. It is your hope to kill two birds with one stone, to invite me to accompany you?'

'If you can believe that, Reichsmarschall Rosemeyer,' Smith said unkindly, 'it's time you handed your baton over to someone else. I have no intention of binding you hand and foot and carrying you over the Alps on my shoulder. The only way I could take you is at the point of a gun and I very much fear that you are a man of honour, a man to whom the safety of his skin comes a very long way behind his loyalty to his country. If I pointed this gun at you and said to get up and come with us or be gunned down, nobody in this room doubts that you'd just keep on sitting. So we must part.'

'You are as complimentary as you are logical.' Rosemeyer smiled, a little, bitter smile. 'I wish the logic had struck me as forcibly when we were discussing this very subject a few minutes ago.'

'It is perhaps as well it didn't,' Smith admitted.

'But – but Colonel Wilner?' Kramer said. 'Field-Marshal Kesselring's Chief of Intelligence. Surely he's not—'

'Rest easy. Willi-Willi is not on our pay-roll. What he said he believed to be perfectly true. He believes me to be the top double-agent in Italy. I've been feeding him useless, false and out-of-date information for almost two years. Tell him so, will you?'

'Kind of treble agent, see?' Schaffer said in a patient explaining tone. 'That's one better than double.'

'Heidelberg?' Kramer asked.

'Two years at the University. Courtesy of the – um – Foreign Office.'

Kramer shook his head. I still don't understand—'

'Sorry. We're going.'

'In fact, we're off,' Schaffer said. 'Read all about it in the post-war memoirs of Pimpernel Schaffer—'

He broke off as the door opened wide. Mary stood framed in the doorway and the Mauser was very steady in her hand. She let it fall to her side with a sigh of relief.

'Took your time about getting here, didn't you?' Smith said severely. 'We were beginning to get a little worried about you.'

'I'm sorry. I just couldn't get away. Von Brauchitsch—'

'No odds, young lady.' Schaffer made a grandiose gesture with his right arm. 'Schaffer was here.'

'The new girl who arrived tonight!' Kramer whispered. He looked slightly dazed. 'The cousin of that girl from the—'

'None else,' Smith said. 'She's the one who has been helping me to keep Willi-Willi happy for a long time past. *And* she's the one who opened the door for us tonight.'

'Boss,' Schaffer said unhappily. 'Far be it for me to rush you—'

'Coming now.' Smith smiled at Rosemeyer. 'You were right, the books weren't all I wanted. You were right, I did want company. But unlike you, Reichsmarschall, those I want have a high regard for their own skins and are entirely without honour. And so they will come.' His gun waved in the direction of Carraciola, Thomas and Christiansen. 'On your feet, you three. You're coming with us.'

'Coming with us?' Schaffer said incredulously. 'To England?'

'To stand trial for treason. It's no part of my duties to act as public executioner . . . God alone knows how many hundreds and thousands of lives they've cost already. Not to mention Torrance-Smyth and Sergeant Harrod.' He looked at Carraciola, and his eyes were very cold. 'I'll never know, but I think you were the brains. It was you who killed Harrod back up there on the mountain. If you could have got that radio code-book you could have cracked our network in South Germany. That would have been something, our network here has never been penetrated. The radio code-book was a trap that didn't spring . . . And you got old Smithy. You left the pub a couple of minutes after I did tonight and he followed you. But he couldn't cope with a man—'

'Drop those guns.' Von Brauchitsch's voice was quiet and cold and compelling. No one had heard or seen the stealthy opening of the door. He stood just inside, about four feet from Mary and he had a small-calibre automatic in his right hand. Smith whirled round, his Luger lining up on the doorway, hesitated a fatal fraction of a second because Mary was almost directly in line with von Brauchitsch. Von Brauchitsch, his earlier gallantry of the evening abruptly yielding to a coldly professional assessment of the situation, had no such inhibitions. There was a sharp flat crack, the bullet passed through Mary's sleeve just above the elbow and Smith exclaimed in pain as he clutched his bleeding hand and heard his flying Luger strike against some unidentified furniture. Mary tried to turn round but von Brauchitsch was too quick and too strong. He jumped forward, hooked his arm round her and caught her wrist with the gun and thrust his own over her shoulder. She tried to struggle free.

Von Brauchitsch squeezed her wrist, she cried out in pain, her hand opened and her gun fell to the floor. Von Brauchitsch seemed to notice none of this, his unwinking right eye, the only vulnerable part of him that could be seen behind Mary's gun, was levelled along the barrel of his automatic.

Schaffer dropped his gun.

'You shouldn't have tried it,' von Brauchitsch said to Smith. 'An extremely silly thing to do . . . In your circumstances, I'd have done exactly the same silly thing.' He looked at Kramer. 'Sorry for the delay, Herr Colonel. But I *thought* the young lady was very anxious and restive. *And* she knows precious little about her native Düsseldorf. *And* she doesn't know enough not to let people hold her hand when she's telling lies – as she does most of the time.' He released the girl and half turned her round, smiling down at her. 'A delightful hand, my dear – but what a fascinating variation of pulse rates.'

'I don't know what you're talking about and I don't care.' Kramer gave vent to a long luxurious sigh and drooped with relief. 'Well *done,* my boy, well done. My God! Another minute—' He heaved himself to his feet, crossed over to Schaffer, prudently keeping clear of von Brauchitsch's line of fire, searched him for hidden weapons, found none, did the same to Smith with the same results, handed him a white handkerchief to stem the flow of blood, looked at Mary and hesitated. 'Well, I don't see how she very well can be, but . . . I wonder. Anne-Marie?'

'Certainly, Herr Colonel. It will be a pleasure. We've met before and she knows my methods. Don't you, my dear?' With a smile as nearly wolf-like as any beautiful Aryan could give, Anne-Marie walked across to Mary and struck her viciously across the face. Mary cried in pain, staggered back against the wall and crouched there, eyes too wide in a pale face, palms pressed behind her for support from the wall, a trickle of blood coming from the corner of her mouth. 'Well?' Anne-Marie demanded. 'Have you a gun.'

'Anne-Marie!' There was protest and aversion in Kramer's face. 'Must you—'

'I know how to deal with cheap little spies like her!' She turned to Mary and said: 'I'm afraid they don't like watching how I get results. In there!'

She caught Mary by the hair, pulled her to the side door, opened it and pushed her violently inside. The sound of her body crashing to the floor and another gasp of pain came together. Anne-Marie closed the door behind them.

For the next ten seconds or so there could be clearly heard the sound of blows and muffled cries of pain. Von Brauchitsch waved Smith and Schaffer back with his gun, advanced, hitched a seat on the edge of one of the big arm-chairs, winced as he listened to the sound of the struggle and said to Kramer dryly: 'I somehow think the young lady would have preferred me to search her. There's a limit to the value of false modesty.'

'I'm afraid Anne-Marie sometimes lets her enthusiasm carry her away,' Kramer conceded. His mouth was wrinkled in distaste.

'Sometimes?' Von Brauchitsch winced again as more sounds filtered through the door, the crash of a body against a wall, a shriek of pain, low sobbing moans, then silence. 'Always. When the other girl is as young and beautiful as herself.'

'It's over now,' Kramer sighed. 'It's all over now.' He looked at Smith and Schaffer. 'We'll fix that hand first, then – well, one thing about the Schloss Adler, there are no shortage of dungeons.' He broke off, the fractional widening of his eyes matching a similar slumping of his shoulders, and he said carefully to von Brauchitsch: 'You are far too good a man to lose, Captain. It would seem that we were wasting our sympathy on the wrong person. There's a gun four feet from you pointing at the middle of your back.'

Von Brauchitsch, his gun-hand resting helplessly on his thigh, turned slowly round and looked over his shoulder. There was indeed a gun pointing at the middle of his back, a Lilliput .21 automatic, and the hand that held it was disconcertingly steady, the dark eyes cool and very watchful. Apart from the small trickle of blood from her cut lip and rather dishevelled hair, Mary looked singularly little the worse for wear.

'It's every parent's duty,' Schaffer said pontifically, 'to encourage his daughter to take up Judo.' He took the gun from von Brauchitsch's unresisting hand, retrieved his own Schmeisser, walked across to the main door and locked it. 'Far too many folk coming in here without knocking.' On his way back he looked through the open door of the room, whistled, grinned and said to Mary: 'It's a good job I have my thoughts set on someone else. I wouldn't like to be married to you if you lost your temper. That's a regular sickbay dispensary in there. Fix the Major's hand as best you can. I'll watch them.' He hoisted his Schmeisser and smiled almost blissfully: 'Oh, brother, how I'll watch them.'

And he watched them. While Mary attended to Smith's injured hand in the small room where Anne-Marie had so lately met her Waterloo, Schaffer herded his six charges into one of the massive couches, took up position by the mantelpiece, poured himself some brandy, sipped it delicately and gave the prisoners an encouraging smile from time to time. There were no answering smiles. For all Schaffer's nonchalance and light-hearted banter there was about him not only a coldly discouraging competence with the weapon in his hand but also the unmistakable air of one who would, when the need arose and without a second's hesitation, squeeze the trigger and keep on squeezing it. Being at the wrong end of a Schmeisser machine-pistol does not make for an easy cordiality in relationships.

Smith and Mary emerged from the side room, the latter carrying a cloth-covered tray. Smith was pale and had his right hand heavily bandaged. Schaffer looked at the hand then lifted an enquiring eyebrow to Mary.

'Not so good.' She looked a little pale herself. 'Forefinger and thumb are both smashed. I've patched it as best I can but I'm afraid it's a job for a surgeon.'

'If I can survive Mary's first aid,' Smith said philosophically, 'I can survive anything. We have a more immediate little problem here.' He tapped his tunic. 'Those names and addresses here. Might be an hour or two before we get them through to England and then another hour or two before those men can be rounded up.' He looked at the men seated on the couch. '*You* could get through to them in a lot less than that and warn them. So we have to ensure your silence for a few hours.'

'We could ensure it for ever, boss,' Schaffer said carelessly.

'That won't be necessary. As you said yourself, it's a regular little dispensary in there.' He removed the tray cloth to show bottles and hypodermic syringes. He held up a bottle in his left hand. 'Nembutal. You'll hardly feel the prick.'

Kramer stared at him. 'Nembutal? I'll be damned if I do.'

Smith said in a tone of utter conviction: 'You'll be dead if you don't.'

—— 9 ——

Smith halted outside the door marked RADIO RAUM, held up his hand for silence, looked at the three scowling captives and said: 'Don't even *think* of tipping anyone off or raising the alarm. I'm not all that keen on taking you back to England. Lieutenant Schaffer, I think we might immobilise those men a bit more.'

'We might at that,' Schaffer agreed. He went behind each of the three men in turn, ripped open the top buttons on their tunics and pulled the tunics down their backs until their sleeves reached their elbows and said in the same soft voice: 'That'll keep their hands out of trouble for a little.'

'But not their feet. Don't let them come anywhere near you,' Smith said to Mary. 'They've nothing to lose. Right, Lieutenant, when you're ready.'

'Ready now.' Carefully, silently, Schaffer eased open the door of the radio room. It was a large, well-lit, but very bleak room, the two main items of furniture being a massive table by the window on the far wall and, on the table, an almost equally massive transceiver in gleaming metal: apart from two chairs and a filing cabinet the room held nothing else, not even as much as a carpet to cover the floorboards.

Perhaps it was the lack of a carpet that betrayed them. For the first half of Schaffer's stealthy advance across the room the operator, his back to them, sat smoking a cigarette in idle unconcern, listening to soft Austrian *Schrammel* music coming in over his big machine: suddenly, alerted either by the faintest whisper of sound from a creaking floorboard or just by some sixth sense, he whirled round and jumped to his feet. And he thought as quickly as he moved. Even as he raised his arms high in apparently eager surrender, he appeared to move slightly to his right, shifting the position of his right foot. There came the sudden strident clamour of an alarm bell ringing in the passage outside, Schaffer leapt forward, his Schmeisser swinging, and the operator staggered back against his transceiver then slid unconscious to the floor. But Schaffer was too late. The bell rang and kept on ringing.

'That's all I need!' Smith swore bitterly. 'That's all I bloody well need.' He ran through the radio room door out into the passage, located the glass-cased alarm bell some feet away and struck it viciously with the butt of his Schmeisser. The shattered glass tinkled to the floor and the clangour abruptly ceased.

'Inside!' Smith gestured to the open doorway of the radio room. 'All of you. Quickly.' He ushered them all inside, looked around, saw a side door leading off to the right and said to Mary: 'Quickly. What's in there? Schaffer!'

'Horatio hold the bridge,' Schaffer murmured. He moved across and took up position at the radio room door. 'We could have done without this, boss.'

'We could do without a lot of things in this world,' Smith said wearily. He glanced at Mary. 'Well?'

'Storage rooms for radio spares, looks like.'

'You and Jones take those three in there. If they breathe, kill them.'

Jones looked down at the gun held gingerly in his hand and said: 'I am not a serviceman, sir.'

'I have news for you,' Smith said. 'Neither am I.'

He crossed hurriedly to the transceiver, sat down and studied the confusing array of dials, knobs and switches. For fully twenty seconds he sat there, just looking.

Schaffer said from the doorway: 'Know how to work it, boss?'

'A fine time to ask me,' Smith said. 'We'll soon find out, won't we?' He switched the machine to 'Send', selected the ultra short wave band and lined up his transmitting frequency. He opened another switch and picked up a microphone.

'Broadsword calling Danny Boy,' he said. 'Broadsword calling Danny Boy. Can you hear me? Can you hear me?'

Nobody heard him or gave indication of hearing him. Smith altered the transmitting frequency fractionally and tried again. And again. And again. After the sixth or seventh repetition, Smith started as a crash of machine-pistol fire came from the doorway. He twisted round. Schaffer was stretched full length on the floor, smoke wisping from the barrel of his Schmeisser.

'We got callers, boss,' Schaffer said apologetically. 'Don't think I got any but I sure as hell started their adrenalin moving around.'

'Broadsword calling Danny Boy,' Smith said urgently, insistingly. 'Broadsword calling Danny Boy. For God's sake, why don't they answer?'

'They can't come round the corner of the passage without being sawn in half.' Schaffer spoke comfortably from his uncomfortable horizontal position on the floor. 'I can hold them off to Christmas. So what's the hurry?'

'Broadsword calling Danny Boy. Broadsword calling Danny Boy. How long do you think it's going to be before someone cuts the electricity?'

'For God's sake, Danny Boy,' Schaffer implored. 'Why don't you answer? Why don't you answer?'

'Danny Boy calling Broadsword.' The voice on the radio was calm and loud and clear, so free from interference that it might have come from next door. 'Danny Boy—'

'One hour, Danny Boy,' Smith interrupted. 'One hour. Understood? Over.'

'Understood. You have it, Broadsword?' The voice was unmistakably that of Admiral Rolland's. 'Over.'

'I have it,' Smith said. 'I have it all.'

'All sins are forgiven. Mother Machree coming to meet you. Leaving now.'

There came another staccato crash of sound as Schaffer loosed off another burst from his Schmeisser. Admiral Rolland's voice on the radio said: 'What was that?'

'Static,' Smith said. He didn't bother to switch off. He rose, took three paces back and fired a two-second burst from his machine-pistol, his face twisting in pain as the recoil slammed into his shattered hand. No one would ever use that particular radio again. He glanced briefly at Schaffer, but only briefly: the American's face, though thoughtful, was calm and unworried: there were those who might require helpful words, encouragement and reassurance, but Schaffer was not one of them. Smith moved swiftly across to the window and lifted the lower sash with his left hand.

The moon was almost obscured behind some darkly drifting cloud. A thin weak light filtered down into the half-seen obscurity of the valley below. Once again the snow was beginning to fall, gently. The air was taut, brittle, in the intensity of its coldness, an Arctic chill that bit to the bone. The icy wind that gusted through the room could have come off the polar ice-cap.

They were on the east side of the castle, Smith realized, the side rem.te from the cable-car header station. The base of the volcanic plug was shrouded in a gloom so deep that it was impossible to be sure whether or not the guards and Dobermanns were patrolling down there: and, for the purposes of present survival, it didn't really matter. Smith withdrew from the window, pulled the nylon from the kit-bag, tied one end securely to the metal leg of the radio table, threw the remainder of the rope out into the night then, with his left hand, thoroughly scuffed and rubbed away the frozen encrusted snow on both the window-sill and for two or three feet beneath it: it would, he thought, have to be a hypercritical eye that didn't immediately register the impression that there had been fairly heavy and recent traffic over the sill. He wondered, vaguely, whether the rope reached as far as the ground and dismissed the thought as soon as it had occurred to him: again, it didn't really matter.

He crossed the room to where Schaffer lay spread-eagled in the doorway. The key was in the lock on the inside of the door and the lock, he observed with satisfaction, was on the same massive scale as everything else in the Schloss Adler. He said to Schaffer: 'Time to close the door.'

'Let's wait till they show face again then discourage them some more,' Schaffer suggested. 'It's been a couple of minutes since the last lad peeked his head round the corner there. Another peek, another salvo from Schaffer and it might give us another couple of minutes' grace – enough time to make it feasible for us to have shinned down that little rope there and make our getaway.'

'I should have thought of that.' An icy snow-laden gust of wind blew across the room, from open window through open door, and Smith shivered. 'My God, it's bitter!'

'Loss of blood,' Schaffer said briefly, then added, unsympathetically: 'And all that brandy you guzzled back there. When it comes to opening pores—'

He broke off and lay very still, lowering his head a fraction to sight along the barrel of his Schmeisser. He said softly: 'Give me your torch, boss.'

'What is it?' Smith whispered. He handed Schaffer the torch.

'Discretion,' Schaffer murmured. He switched on the torch and placed it on the floor, pushing it as far away from himself as he could. 'I reckon if I were in their place I'd be discreet, too. There's a stick poking round the corner of the passage and the stick has a mirror tied to it. Only, they haven't got it angled right.'

Smith peered cautiously round the door jamb, just in time to see stick and suspended mirror being withdrawn from sight, presumably to make adjustments. A few seconds later and the stick appeared again, this time with the mirror angled at more or less forty-five degrees. Mirror and stick disintegrated under the flatly staccato hammering of Schaffer's machine-pistol. Schaffer stood up, took careful aim at the single overhead light illuminating the passage and fired one shot. Now the sole light in the passage came from the torch on the floor, the light from which would not only effectively conceal from the Germans at the far end of the passage what was going on at the radio room door but, indeed, make it very difficult to decide whether or not the door itself was open or shut.

Smith and Schaffer moved back into the radio room, soundlessly closed the door behind them and as soundlessly turned the key in the lock. Schaffer used the leverage of his Schmeisser to bend the key so that it remained firmly jammed in the wards of the lock.

They waited. At least two minutes passed, then they heard the sound of excited voices at the far end of the passage followed almost at once by the sound of heavy boots pounding down the passage. They moved away from the door, passed inside the radio spares room, leaving just a sufficient crack in the doorway to allow a faint backwash of light to filter through. Smith said softly: 'Mary, you and Mr Jones for Thomas there. A gun in each temple.' He took Christiansen for himself, forced him to kneel and ground his gun into the back of his neck. Schaffer backed Carraciola against a wall, the muzzle of his Schmeisser pressed hard against his teeth. At the other end of the machine-pistol Schaffer smiled pleasantly, his teeth a pale gleam in the near darkness. The stillness inside the little room was complete.

The half-dozen Germans outside the radio room door bore no resemblance to the elderly guard von Brauchitsch had interrogated in the courtyard. They were elite soldiers of the Alpenkorps, ruthless men who had been ruthlessly trained. No one made any move to approach the door handle or lock: the machine-like efficiency with which they broached that door without risk to themselves was clearly the result of a well-drilled procedure for handling situations of precisely this nature.

At a gesture from the Oberleutnant in charge, a soldier stepped forward and with two diagonal sweeps emptied the magazine of his machine-pistol through the door. A second used his machine-pistol to stitch a neat circle in the wood, reversed his gun and knocked in the wooden circle with the butt. A third armed two grenades and lobbed them accurately through the hole provided while a fourth shot away the lock. The soldiers pressed back on each side of the door. The two flat cracks of the exploding grenades came almost simultaneously and smoke came pouring through the circular hole in the door.

The door was kicked open and the men rushed inside. There

665

was no longer any need to take precautions – any men who had been in the same confined space as those two exploding grenades would be dead men now. For a moment there was confusion and hesitation until the blue acrid smoke was partially cleared away by the powerful cross-draught then the Oberleutnant, locating the source of this draught with the aid of a small hand-torch, ran across to the open window, checked at the sight of the rope disappearing over the sill, leaned out the window, rubbed his now-streaming eyes and peered downwards along the beam of his torch. The beam reached perhaps half-way down the side of the volcanic plug. There was nothing to be seen. He caught the rope in his free hand and jerked it savagely: it was as nearly weightless as made no difference. For a moment he focused his torch on the disturbed snow on the window-ledge then swung back into the room.

'*Gott in Himmel!*' he shouted. 'They've got away. They're down already! Quickly, the nearest phone!'

'Well, now.' Schaffer listened to the fading sound of running footsteps, removed the muzzle of his Schmeisser from Carraciola's teeth and smiled approvingly. 'That was a good boy.' Gun in Carraciola's back, he followed Smith out into the wrecked radio room and said thoughtfully: 'It isn't going to take them too long to find out there are no footprints in the snow down there.'

'It's going to take them even less time to discover that this rope is gone.' Swiftly, ignoring the stabbing pain in his right hand, Smith hauled the nylon in through the window. 'We're going to need it. *And* we're going to need some distractions.'

'I'm distracted enough as it is,' Schaffer said.

'Take four or five plastic explosives, each with different fuse length settings. Chuck them into rooms along the corridor there.'

'Distractions coming up.' Schaffer extracted some plastic explosives from the kit-bag, cut the slow-burning RDX fuses off to varying lengths, crimped on the chemical igniters, said, 'Consider it already done,' and left.

The first three rooms he came to were locked and he wasted neither time nor the precious ammunition of his silenced Luger in trying to open them. But each of the next five rooms was unlocked. In the first three, all bedrooms, he placed charges in a Dresden fruit bowl, under an officer's cap and under a pillow: in the fourth room, a bathroom, he placed it behind a WC and in the fifth, a store-room, high up on a shelf beside some highly inflammable-looking cardboard cartons.

Smith, meanwhile, had ushered the others from the still

smoke-filled, eye-watering, throat-irritating atmosphere of the
radio room into the comparatively purer air of the passageway
beyond, and was waiting the return of Schaffer when his face
became suddenly thoughtful at the sight of some fire-fighting
gear – a big CO_2 extinguisher, buckets of sand and a fireman's
axe – on a low platform by the passage wall.

'You *are* slipping, Major Smith.' Mary's eyes were red-rimmed
and her tear-streaked face white as paper, but she could still
smile at him. 'Distractions, you said. I've had the same thought
myself, and I'm only me.'

Smith gave her a half-smile, the way his hand hurt he felt he
couldn't afford the other half, and tried the handle of a door
beside the low platform, a door lettered AKTEN RAUM – Records
Office. Such a door, inevitably, was locked. He took the Luger
in his left hand, placed it against the lock, squeezed the trigger
and went inside.

It certainly looked like a Records Office. The room was heavily
shelved and piled ceiling-high with files and papers. Smith
crossed to the window, opened it wide to increase the draught
then scattered large piles of paper on the floor and put a match
to them. The paper flared up at once, the flames feet high within seconds.

'Kinda forgot this, didn't you?' Schaffer had returned and was
bearing with him the large CO_2 cylinder. He crossed to the window. 'Gardyloo or mind your heads or whatever the saying is.'

The cylinder disappeared through the open window. The
room was already so furiously ablaze that Schaffer had difficulty
in finding his way back to the door again. As he stumbled out,
his clothes and hair singed and face smoke-blackened, a deep-
toned bell far down in the depths of the Schloss Adler began to
ring with a strident urgency. 'For God's sake, what next,' Schaffer
said in despair. 'The fire brigade?'

'Just about,' Smith said bitterly. 'Damn it, why couldn't I
have checked first? Now they know where we are.'

'A heat-sensing device linked to an indicator?'

'What else? Come on.'

They ran along the central passage-way, driving the prisoners
in front of them, dropped down a central flight of stairs and
were making for the next when they heard the shouting of voices
and the clattering of feet on treads as soldiers came running up
from the castle courtyard.

'Quickly! In behind there!' Smith pointed to a curtained

alcove. 'Hurry up! Oh, God – I've forgotten something!' He turned and ran back the way he had come.

'Where the hell has he—' Schaffer broke off as he realized the approaching men were almost upon them, whirled and jabbed the nearest prisoner painfully with the muzzle of his Schmeisser. 'In that alcove. Fast.' In the dim light behind the curtains he changed his machine-pistol for the silenced Luger. 'Don't even think of touching those curtains. With the racket that bell's making, they won't even hear you die.'

Nobody touched the curtains. Jack-booted men, gasping heavily for breath, passed by within feet of them. They clattered furiously up the next flight of stairs, the one Smith and the others had just descended, and then the footsteps stopped abruptly. From the next shouted words it was obvious that they had just caught sight of the fire and had abruptly and for the first time realized the magnitude of the task they had to cope with.

'Emergency! Sergeant, get on that phone!' It was the voice of the Oberleutnant who had led the break-in to the radio room. 'Fire detail at the double! Hoses, more CO_2 cylinders. Where in God's name is Colonel Kramer. Corporal! Find Colonel Kramer at once.'

The corporal didn't answer, the sound of jutting heels striking the treads as he raced down the stairs was answer enough. He ran by the alcove and ran down the next flight of stairs until the sound of his footfalls was lost in the metallic clamour of the alarm bell. Schaffer risked a peep through a crack in the curtains just as Smith came running up on tiptoe.

'Where the hell have you been?' Schaffer's voice was low and fierce.

'Come on, come on! Out of it!' Smith said urgently. 'No, Jones, not down that flight of stairs, you want to meet a whole regiment of Alpenkorps coming up it? Along the passage to the west wing. We'll use the side stairs. For God's sake, hurry. This place will be like Piccadilly Circus in a matter of seconds.'

Schaffer pounded along the passage beside Smith and when he spoke again the anxiety-born fierceness of tone had a certain plaintive equality to it. 'Well, where the bloody hell have you been?'

'The man we left tied up in the room beside the telephone exchange. The Records Office is directly above. I just remembered. I cut him free and dragged him out to the passage. He'd have burnt to death.'

'You did that, did you?' Schaffer said wonderingly. 'You do think of the most goddamned unimportant things, don't you?'

'It's a point of view. Our friend lying in the passage back there wouldn't share your sentiments. Right, down those stairs and straight ahead. Mary, you know the door.'

Mary knew the door. Fifteen paces from the foot of the stairs she stopped. Smith spared a glance through the passage window on his left. Already smoke and flame were showing through the windows and embrasures in the north-east tower of the castle. In the courtyard below, dozens of soldiers were running around, most of them without what appeared to be any great sense of purpose or direction. One man there wasn't running. He was the overalled helicopter pilot and he was standing very still indeed, bent low over the engine. As Smith watched he slowly straightened, lifted his right arm and shook his fist in the direction of the burning tower.

Smith turned away and said to Mary: 'Sure this is the room? Two stories below the window we came in?'

Mary nodded. 'No question. This is it.'

Smith tried the door handle: the room was locked. The time for skeleton keys and such-like finesse was gone: he placed the barrel of his Luger against the lock.

The corporal despatched by his Oberleutnant to locate Colonel Kramer was faced by the same problem when he turned the handle of the gold drawing-room, for when Smith and the others had left there for the last time Schaffer had locked the door and thoughtfully thrown the key out a convenient passage window. The corporal first of all knocked respectfully. No reply. He knocked loudly, with the same lack of result. He depressed the handle and used his shoulder and all he did was to hurt his shoulder. He battered at the lock area with the butt of his Schmeisser but the carpenters who had built the Schloss Adler doors had known what they were about. He hesitated, then brought his machine-pistol right way round and fired a burst through the lock, praying to heaven that Colonel Kramer wasn't sleeping in a chair in direct line with the keyhole.

Colonel Kramer was sleeping all right, but nowhere near the direct line of the keyhole. He was stretched out on the gold carpet with a considerately-placed pillow under his head. The corporal advanced slowly into the drawing-room, his eyebrows reaching for his hair and his face almost falling apart in shocked disbelief. Reichsmarschall Rosemeyer was stretched out beside the Colonel. Von Brauchitsch and a sergeant were sprawled in arm-chairs, heads lolling on their shoulders, while Anne-Marie – a very dishevelled and somewhat bruised-looking Anne-Marie – was stretched out on one of the big gold-lamé couches.

Like a man in a daze, still totally uncomprehending, the corporal approached Kramer, knelt by his side and then shook him by the shoulder, with gentle respect at first and then with increasing vigour. After some time it was borne in upon him that he could shake the Colonel's shoulder all night and that would be all he would have for it.

And then, illogically and for the first time, he noticed that all the men were without jackets, and that everyone, including Anne-Marie, had their left sleeves rolled up to the elbow. He looked slowly around the drawing-room and went very still as his gaze rested on a tray with bottles, beakers and hypodermic syringes. Slowly, on the corporal's face, shocked incomprehension was replaced by an equally shocked understanding. He took off through the doorway like the favourite in the Olympics 100 métres final.

Schaffer tied the nylon rope round the head of the iron bedstead, tested the security of the knot, lifted the lower sash window, pushed the rope through and peered unhappily down the valley. At the far end of the village a pulsating red glow marked the smouldering embers of what had once been the railway station. The lights of the village itself twinkled clearly. Immediately below and to the right of where he stood could be seen four patrolling guards with as many dogs – Kramer hadn't spoken idly when he'd said the outside guards had been doubled – and the ease with which he could spot them Schaffer found all too readily understandable when he twisted his head and stared skywards through the thinly driving snow. The moon had just emerged from behind a black bar of cloud and was sailing across a discouragingly large stretch of empty sky. Even the stars could be seen.

'I'm going to feel a mite conspicuous out there, boss,' Schaffer said complainingly. 'And there's a wolf-pack loose down below there.'

'Wouldn't matter if they had a battery of searchlights trained on this window,' Smith said curtly. 'Not now. We've no option. Quickly!'

Schaffer nodded dolefully, eased himself through the window, grasped the rope and halted momentarily as a muffled explosion came from the eastern wing of the castle.

'Number one,' Schaffer said with satisfaction. 'Bang goes a bowl of Dresden fruit – or a Dresden bowl of fruit. I do hope,' he added anxiously, 'that there's nobody using the toilet next door to where that bang just went off.'

Smith opened his mouth to make impatient comment but Schaffer was already gone. Fifteen feet only and he was standing on the roof of the header station. Smith eased himself awkwardly over the sill, wrapped the rope round his right forearm, took the strain with his left hand and looked at Mary. She gave him an encouraging smile, but there was nothing encouraging about her expression when she transferred her gaze back to the three men who were lined up facing a wall, their hands clasped behind their necks. Carnaby-Jones was also covering them but, in his case, he held the gun as if it might turn and bite him at any moment.

Smith joined Schaffer on the roof of the header station. Both men crouched low to minimise the chances of being spotted from below. For the first ten feet out from the wall the roof was quite flat then dropped away sharply at an angle of thirty degrees. Smith thoughtfully regarded this steep slope and said: 'We don't want a repeat performance of what happened to us last time we were out there. We could do with a good piton to hammer into the castle wall here. Or the roof. Some sort of belay for our rope.'

'Pitons we don't need. Look at this.' With his bare hands Schaffer scraped at the snow-encrusted roof of the header station to reveal a fine wire netting and, below that, iron bars covering a pane of plate glass perhaps two feet by one. 'Skylights, I believe they're called. Those bars look pretty firm to me.'

He laid both hands on one of the bars and tugged firmly. It remained secure. Smith laid his left hand on the same bar and they pulled together. It still remained secure. Schaffer grinned in satisfaction, passed the rope round the bar and made no mistake about the knot he tied. Smith sat down on the roof and put his hand to the rope. Schaffer caught his wrist and firmly broke Smith's grip.

'No, you don't.' Schaffer lifted Smith's right hand: the thick wrapping of bandages were already sodden, saturated with blood. 'You can win your VC next time out. This time, you'd never make it. This one is on me.' He paused and shook his

671

head in wonder. 'My God, Schaffer, you don't know what you're saying.'

He removed the kit-bag he'd been carrying round his neck, crawled to the break in the roof, gripped the rope and slid smoothly down the sloping surface. As he approached the roof edge he turned round with infinite care until he was pointing head downwards. Slowly, inch by almost imperceptible inch, the rope above him caught securely between his feet, he lowered himself still farther until his head was projecting over the edge of the roof. He peered downwards.

He was, he discovered, directly above one of the cables. Two hundred feet below, but to his left, this time, guards and Dobermanns were floundering uphill through the deep snow at the best speed they could make, heading for the main entrance, to the castle courtyard. The word had gone out, Schaffer realized, and every available man was being pulled in either to fight the fire or to help in the search for the men who had started the fire. Which meant, Schaffer concluded, that some of the garrison must have checked the state of the ground beneath the radio room window and found there nothing but virgin and undisturbed snow . . .

He twisted his head and looked upwards. There was no sign of any guard patrolling the battlements, which was what he would have expected: there was no point in keeping a posted lookout for an enemy without when every indication pointed to the fact that the enemy was still within.

Schaffer eased himself downwards another perilous six inches till head and shoulders were over the edge of the roof. Only two things mattered now: was there a winch attendant or guard inside the header station and, if there were, could he, Schaffer, hold on to the rope with one hand while with the other he wriggled his Luger free and shoot the guard? Schaffer doubted it. His OSS training had been wide-ranging and intensive but no one had ever thought it necessary that they should master the techniques of a high-wire circus acrobat. His mouth very dry and his heart pounding so heavily as to threaten to dislodge his precarious hand- and toe-holds, Schaffer craned his head and looked inside.

There was neither guard nor winch attendant inside: or, if there were any such, he was so well concealed that Schaffer couldn't see him. But logic said that no one would be hiding there for there was no conceivable reason why anyone should be hiding: logic also said that any person who might have been there would, like the patrolling guards below and the sentry on the battlements, have been called inside the castle to help fight fire and enemy. All Schaffer could see was a cable-car, heavy winching machinery and heavy banks of lead-acid batteries: he was soon convinced that that was all that there was to see. No cause for concern.

But what he did see, something that did dismay him considerably, was that there was only one way for him to get into the station. There was no possibility of his sliding down the rope on to the floor of the station for the excellent reason that the roof of the station, in typically Alpine eaves fashion, overhung the floor by at least six feet. The only way in was by dropping down on to the *Luftseilbahn's* heavy steel cable then overhanding himself up inside the station. Schaffer wasted no time in considering whether this was physically possible. It *had* to be possible. There was no other way in.

Carefully and with no little difficulty Schaffer inched himself back up the rope and the slope of the roof until he was about three feet clear of the edge. He eased his foot-grip on the rope and swung round through 180° until he was once more facing up the slope with his legs now dangling over the edge. He looked up. The crouched figure of Smith showed tension in every line although the face was as expressionless as ever. Schaffer lifted one hand, made a circle with thumb and forefinger, then eased himself over the edge until his searching feet found the cable.

He eased himself farther until he was sitting astride the cable, transferred his grip to the cable and swung down until he was suspended by hands and feet and looked up towards the moon. As a view, Schaffer reflected, it was vastly preferable to contemplating that two hundred foot drop down into the valley below. He started to climb.

He almost failed to make it. For every six inches he made up the cable, he slid back five. The cable was covered by a diabolically slippery coating of oil and sheath ice and only by clenching his fists till his forearms ached could he make any kind of progress at all and the fact that the cable stretched up at forth-five degrees made the difficult the well-nigh impossible. Such a means of locomotion would have been suicidal for the virtually one-handed Smith and quite impossible for either Mary or Carnaby-Jones. Once, after he had made about twelve feet, Schaffer looked down to gauge his chances if he let go and dropped down to the floor beneath, and rapidly concluded that the chances were either that he would break both legs or, if he landed at all awkwardly, would pitch out two hundred feet down to the valley below. As Schaffer later recounted it, this last possibility combined with the vertiginous view of the long long way to the floor of the valley, did him more good than an extra pair of arms. Ten seconds later, sweating and gasping like a long distance runner and very close to the last stages of exhaustion, he hauled himself on to the roof of the cable-car.

He lay there for a full minute until the trembling in his arms eased and pulse and breathing rates returned to not more than a man in a high fever might expect to have, lowered himself quietly and wearily to the floor, took out his Luger, slid the safety catch and began to make a quick check that the header station really was empty of the enemy, a superfluous precaution, reason told him, any concealed person would have been bound both to see and hear his entry, but instinct and training went deeper than reason. There was no one there. He looked behind winches, electric motors and batteries. He had the place to himself.

The next thing was to ensure that he continued to have the place to himself. At the lower end of the sloping archway leading up to the castle courtyard, the heavy iron door stood wide. He passed through this doorway and padded softly up the cobbled pathway until he came to the courtyard exit. Here, too, was another iron gate, as wide open as the other. Schaffer moved as far forward as the shadowing safety of the tunnel's overhang permitted and looked cautiously around the scene before him.

There was certainly, he had to admit, plenty to be seen and under more auspicious circumstances it would have done his heart good. The courtyard scene was as frenzied as the earlier glimpse they had had from the passage, but this time the action was much more purposive and controlled. Shouting, gesticulating figures were supervising the unrolling of hoses, the coupling-up of hydrants, the relays of men carrying extinguishers and buckets of sand. The main gates stood open and unguarded, even the sentries must have been pressed into action: not that the unguarded doors offered any warmly beckoning escape route. Only a suicide would have tried making his escape through a courtyard crowded with sixty or seventy scurrying Alpenkorps troops.

Over to his left the helicopter still stood forlorn and useless. There was no sign of the pilot. Suddenly a loud flat explosion echoed inside the confining walls of the square. Schaffer lifted his head to locate its source, saw fresh clouds of smoke billowing from an upper window in the east wing and briefly wondered which of his diversionary explosives that might be. But only for a brief moment. Some instinct made him glance to his right and his face went very still. The men he'd seen floundering up the slope outside, guards with the Dobermann pinchers, were coming through the main gate, the clouds of frozen breath trailing in the air behind them evidence enough of their exhausting run uphill through that knee-high snow. Schaffer backed away slowly and silently: German soldiers he could cope with or avoid but Dobermanns were out of his class. He swung the heavy iron door to, careful not to make the least whisper of sound, slid home two heavy bolts, ran quickly down the arched passageway, closed and padlocked the lower door and put the key in his pocket.

He looked up, startled, at a loud crashing of glass and the subsequent tinkle as the shattered fragments tinkled to the floor. Automatically, the barrel of his Luger followed his glance.

'Put that cannon away,' Smith said irritably. Schaffer could clearly see his face now, pressed close to the iron bars. 'Who do you think is up here – Kramer and company?'

'It's my nerves,' Schaffer explained coldly. 'You haven't been through what Lieutenant Schaffer's just been through. How are things up there?'

'Carraciola and friends are face down on the roof, freezing to death in the snow and Mary has the Schmeisser on them. Jones is still up there. Won't even put his head outside. Says he's no head for heights. I've given up arguing with him. How are things your end?'

'Quiet. If anyone is having any passing thoughts about the cable-car, there are no signs of it. Both doors to the courtyard are locked. They're iron and even if someone does start having suspicious thoughts, they should hold them for a while. And, boss, the way I came in is strictly for the birds. And I mean strictly. What you need is wings. Your hand the way it is you could never make it. Mary and the old boy couldn't try it. Carraciola and the rest – well, who cares about Carraciola and the rest.'

'What winch controls are there?' Smith asked.

'Well, now.' Schaffer approached the winch. 'A small lever marked "*Normal*" and "*Notfall*"—'

'Are there batteries down there?' Smith interrupted.

'Yeah. Any amount.'

'Put the lever to "*Notfall*" – "Emergency." They could cut off the main power from inside the castle.'

'OK, it's done. Then there are Start and Stop buttons, a big mechanical handbrake and a gear lever affair marked "Forwards" and "Backwards". With a neutral position.'

'Start the motor,' Smith ordered. Schaffer pressed the 'Start' button and a generator whined into life, building up to its maximum revolutions after perhaps ten seconds. 'Now release the brake and select forward gear. If it works, stop the car and try the other gear.'

Schaffer released the brake and engaged gear, sliding the gear handle progressively over successive stops. The car moved forward, gently at first, but gathering speed until it was clear of the header station roof. After a few more feet Schaffer stopped the car, engaged reverse gear and brought the car back up into its original position. He looked up at Smith. 'Smooth, huh?'

'Lower it down till it's half-way past the edge of the roof. We'll slide down the rope on to the top of the cable-car then you can bring us up inside.'

'Must be all the fish you eat,' Schaffer said admiringly. He set the car in motion.

'I'm sending Carraciola, Thomas and Christiansen down first,' Smith said. 'I wouldn't care for any of us to be on the top of the same cable-car as that lot. Think you can hold them till we get down?'

'You don't improve morale by being insulting to subordinate officers,' Schaffer said coldly.

'I didn't know you'd any left. While you're doing that I'll have another go at persuading Juliet up there to come and join us.' He prodded Carraciola with a far from gentle toe. 'You first. Down that rope and on to the top of the cable-car.'

Carraciola straightened until he was kneeling, glanced down the slope of the roof to the depths of the valley beyond.

'You're not getting me on that lot. Not ever.' He shook his head in finality, then stared up at Smith, his black eyes implacable in their hate. 'Go on, shoot me. Kill me now.'

'I'll kill you if you ever try to escape,' Smith said. 'Don't you know that, Carraciola?'

'Sure I know it. But you won't kill me in cold blood, just standing here. You're a man of principle, aren't you, Major? Ethics, that's the word. The kind of noble sucker who risks his life to free an enemy soldier who might burn to death. Why don't you shoot, Major?'

'Because I don't have to.' With his left hand Smith grabbed
Carraciola's hair and jerked his head back till Carraciola, gasping with the pain of it, was staring skywards, while he reversed
the grip on his Luger and raised it high. Nausea and pain
flooded through him as the ends of the broken finger-bone grated
together, but none of this showed in his face. 'I just knock you
out, tie a rope round your waist and lower you down over the
edge, maybe eight or ten feet. Schaffer eases out the car till it
touches you, then he climbs in the back door, goes to the front
door and hauls you inside. You can see my right hand's not too
good, maybe I won't be able to tie a secure enough knot round
you, maybe I won't be able to hold you, maybe Schaffer might
let you go when he's hauling you inside. I don't much care,
Carraciola.'

'You double-dealing bastard!' Tears of pain filled Carraciola's
eyes and his voice was low and venomous. 'I swear to God I'll
live to make you wish you'd never met me.'

'Too late.' Smith thrust him away contemptuously and Carraciola had to grab wildly at the rope to prevent himself from
sliding over the break of the roof. 'I've been wishing that ever
since I found out who and what you really are. Vermin soil my
hands. Move now or I damn well will shoot you. Why the hell
should I bother taking you back to England?'

Carraciola believed him. He slid down the rope until first
his feet then his hands found the security of the supporting
bracket of the cable-car. Smith gestured with his gun towards
Thomas. Thomas went without a word. Ten seconds later
Christiansen followed him. Smith watched the cable-car begin
to move up inside the station, then looked upwards to the window from which the rope dangled.

'Mr Jones?'

'I'm still here.' Carnaby-Jones's voice had a quaver to it and
he didn't as much as venture to risk a glance over the window-
sill.

'Not for much longer, I hope,' Smith said seriously. 'They'll
be coming for you, Mr Jones. They'll be coming any moment
now. I hate to say this, but I must. It is my duty to warn you
what will happen to you, an enemy spy. You'll be tortured, Mr
Jones – not simply everyday tortures like pulling out your teeth
and toe-nails, but unspeakable tortures I can't mention with
Miss Ellison here – and then you'll finish in the gas chambers.
If you're still alive.'

Mary clutched his arm. 'Would they – would they really do that?'

'Good God, no!' Smith stared at her in genuine surprise. 'What on earth would they want to do that for?' He raised his voice again: 'You'll die in a screaming agony, Mr Jones, an agony beyond your wildest dreams. And you'll take a long time dying. Hours. Maybe days. And screaming. Screaming all the time.'

'What in God's name am I to do?' The desperate voice from above was no longer quavering, it vibrated like a broken bedspring. 'What *can* I do?'

'You can slide down that rope,' Smith said brutally. 'Fifteen feet. Fifteen little feet, Mr Jones. My God, you could do that in a pole vault.'

'I can't.' The voice was a wail. 'I simply can't.'

'Yes, you can,' Smith urged. 'Grab the rope now, close your eyes, out over the sill and down. Keep your eyes closed. We can catch you.'

'I can't! I can't!'

'Oh God!' Smith said despairingly. 'Oh, my God! It's too late now.'

'It's too – what in heaven's name do you mean?'

'The lights are going on along the passage,' Smith said, his voice low and tense. 'And that window. And the next. They're coming for you, Mr Jones, they're coming now. Oh God, when they strip you off and strap you down on the torture table—'

Two seconds later Carnaby-Jones was over the sill and sliding down the nylon rope. His eyes were screwed tightly shut. Mary said, admiringly: 'You really are the most fearful liar ever.'

'Schaffer keeps telling me the same thing,' Smith admitted. 'You can't all be wrong.'

The cable-car, with the three men clinging grimly to the suspension bracket, climbed slowly up into the header station and jerked to a halt. One by one the three men, under the persuasion of Schaffer's gently waving Luger, lowered themselves the full length of their arms and dropped the last two or three feet to the floor. The last of them, Thomas, seemed to land awkwardly, exclaimed in muffled pain and fell heavily sideways. As he fell, his hands shot out and grabbed Schaffer by the ankles. Schaffer, immediately off-balance, flung up his arms in an attempt to maintain equilibrium and, before he could even begin to bring his arms down again, was winded by a diving rugby tackle by Christiansen. He toppled backwards, his back smashing into a generator with an impact that drove from his lungs what little breath had been left in them. A second later and Christiansen had his gun, driving the muzzle cruelly into a throat gasping for air.

Carraciola was already at the lower iron door, shaking it fiercely. His eye caught sight of the big padlock in its hasp. He swung round, ran back towards Schaffer, knocked aside the gun in Christiansen's hand and grabbed Schaffer by the throat.

'That padlock. Where's the key to that bloody padlock?' The human voice can't exactly emulate the hiss of a snake, but Carraciola's came pretty close to it then. 'That door has been locked from the inside. You're the only person who could have done it. *Where is that key?*'

Schaffer struggled to a sitting position, feebly pushing aside Carraciola's hand. 'I can't breathe!' The moaning, gasping breathing lent credence to the words. 'I can't breathe. I – I'm going to be sick.'

'Where *is* that damned key?' Carraciola demanded.

'Oh God, I feel ill!' Schaffer hoisted himself slowly to a kneeling position, his head bent, retching sounds coming from his throat. He shook his head from side to side, as if to clear away the muzziness, then slowly raised it, his eyes unfocused. He mumbled: 'What do you want? What did you say?'

'The key!' If the need for silence hadn't been paramount, Carraciola's voice would have been a frustrated scream of rage. Half-a-dozen times, in brutal and rapid succession, he struck Schaffer across the face with the palm and back of his hand. 'Where is that key?'

'Easy on, easy on!' Thomas caught Carraciola's hand. 'Don't be such a damned fool. You want him to talk, don't you?'

'The key. Yes, the key.' Schaffer hoisted himself wearily to his feet and stood there swaying eyes half-closed, face ashen, blood trickling from both corners of his mouth. 'The batteries there, I think I hid them behind the batteries. I don't know, I can't think. No, wait.' The words came in short, anguished gasps. 'I didn't. I meant to, but I didn't.' He fumbled in his pocket, eventually located the key and brought it out, offering it vaguely in Carraciola's direction. Carraciola, the beginnings of a smile on his face, reached out for the key but, before he could reach it Schaffer abruptly straightened and with a convulsive jerk of his arm sent the key spinning through the open end of the station to land in the valley hundreds of feet below.

Carraciola stared after the vanished key in total incredulity then, his suffused and enraged face mute evidence of his complete loss of self-control, stooped, picked up Schaffer's fallen Schmeisser and swung it viciously across the American's head and face. Schaffer fell like a tree.

'Well,' Thomas said acidly. 'Now that we've got that out of our system, we can shoot the lock away.'

'You can commit suicide with ricochets – that door's iron, man.' Carraciola had indeed got it out of his system for he was back on balance again. He paused, then smiled slowly. 'What the hell are we all thinking of? Let's play it clever. If we did get through that door the first thing we'd probably collect would be a chestful of machine-gun bullets. Remember, the only people who know who we really are have bloody great doses of Nembutal inside them and are liable to remain unconscious for a long time. To the rest of the garrison we're unknowns – and to the few who saw us arrive, we're prisoners. In both cases we're automatically enemies.'

'So?' Thomas was impatient.

'So, as I say, we play it clever. We go down in this cable-car and play it clever again. We phone old Weissner. We ask him to phone the Schloss Adler, tell him where Smith is and, in case Smith does manage to get down to the village on the other cable-car after us, we ask him to have a reception committee waiting for him at the lower station. Then we go to the barracks – they're bound to have a radio there – and get in touch with you know who. Flaws?'

'Nary a flaw.' Christiansen grinned. 'And then we all live happily ever afterwards. Come on, what are we waiting for?'

'Into the cable-car, you two.' Carraciola waited until they had boarded, walked across the floor until he was directly under the smashed skylight and called: 'Boss!' Schaffer's silenced Luger was in his hand.

On the roof above Smith stiffened, handed the trembling Carnaby-Jones – his eyes were still screwed shut – over to the care of Mary, took two steps towards the skylight and stopped. It was Wyatt-Turner who had said of Smith that he had a built-in radar set against danger and Carraciola's voice had just started it up into instantaneous operation and had it working with a clarity and precision that would have turned Decca green with envy.

'Schaffer?' Smith called softly. 'Lieutenant Schaffer? Are you there?'

'Right here, boss.' Mid-west accent, Schaffer to the life. Smith's radar-scope went into high and had it been geared to warning bells he'd have been deafened for life. He dropped to hands and knees and crawled soundlessly forward. He could see the floor of the station now. The first thing that came into his vision was a bank of batteries, then an outflung hand, then, gradually the rest of the spread-eagled form of Schaffer. Another few inches forward and he sensed as much as saw a long finger pointing in his direction and flung himself to one side. The wind from the Luger's shell rifled his hair. Down below someone cursed in anger and frustration.

'That's the last chance you'll ever have, Carraciola,' Smith said. From where he lay he could just see Schaffer's face – or the bloody mask that covered his face. It was impossible to tell whether he was alive or dead. He looked dead.

'Wrong again. Merely the postponement of a pleasure. We're leaving now, Smith. I'm going to start the motor. Want Schaffer to get his— Christiansen has the Schmeisser on him. Don't try anything.'

'You make for that control panel,' Smith said, 'and your first step into my line of vision will be your last. I'll cut you down, Carraciola. Schaffer's dead. I can see he's dead.'

'He's damn all of the kind dead. He's just been clobbered by a gun butt.'

'I'll cut you down,' Smith said monotonously.

'Goddam it, I tell you he's not dead!' Carraciola was exasperated now.

'I'm going to kill you,' Smith said quietly. 'If I don't, the first guards through that door surely will. You can see what we've done to their precious Schloss Adler – it's well alight. Can't you guess the orders that have gone out – shoot on sight. Any stranger, shoot on sight – and shoot to kill. You're a stranger, Carraciola.'

'For God's sake, will you listen to me?' There was desperation in the voice now. 'I can prove it. He *is* alive. What can you see from up there?'

The signal strengths of Smith's danger radar set began to fade. He said: 'I can see Schaffer's head.'

'Watch it, then.' There was a thud and a silenced Luger bounced to a stop a few inches from Schaffer's head. A moment later Carraciola himself came into Smith's field of vision. He looked up at Smith and at the Schmeisser muzzle staring down at him and said: 'You won't be needing that.' He stooped over

Schaffer, pinched his nose with one hand and clamped his other hand over the mouth. Within seconds the unconscious man, fighting for the air that would not come, began to move his head and to raise feeble hands in the direction of his face. Carraciola took his hands away, looked up at Smith and said: 'Don't forget, Christiansen has still that Schmeisser on him.'

Carraciola walked confidently across to the control panel, made the generator switch, released the mechanical handbrake and engaged gear, pushing the lever all the way across. The cable-car leapt forward with a violent jerk. Carraciola ran for it, jumped inside, turned and slammed the door of the cable-car.

On the roof above, Smith laid down his useless Schmeisser and pushed himself wearily to his feet. His face was bleak and bitter.

'Well, that's it, then,' Mary said. Her voice was unnaturally calm. 'Finish. All finish. Operation Overlord – and us. If that matters.'

'It matters to me.' Smith took out his silenced automatic and held it in his good left hand. 'Keep an eye on Junior here.'

——— 10 ———

'No!' For perhaps two dazed, incredulous seconds that were the longest seconds she had ever known, Mary had quite failed to gather Smith's intention: when shocked understanding did come, her voice rose to a scream. 'No! No! For God's sake, no!'

Smith ignored the heart-broken voice, the desperate clutching hand and walked to the end of the flat section of the roof. At the lower edge of the steeply sloping roof section the leading edge of the cable-car had just come into view: a cable-car with, inside it, three men who were exchanging delighted grins and thumping one another joyously on the back.

Smith ran down the ice-coated pitch of the roof, reached the edge and jumped. The cable-car was already seven or eight feet beyond him and almost as far below. Had the cable-car not been going away from him he must surely have broken both legs. As it was, he landed with a jarring teeth-rattling crash, a crash that caused the cable-car to shudder and sway and his legs to buckle and slide from beneath him on the ice-coated roof.

His injured right hand failed to find a purchase on the suspension bracket and in his blindly despairing grab with his left hand he was forced to drop his Luger. It slid to the edge of the roof and fell away into the darkness of the valley below. Smith wrapped both arms round the suspension bracket and fought to draw some whooping gasps of air into his starving lungs: he had been completely winded by the fall.

In their own way, the three men inside the cable-car were as nearly stunned as Smith himself. The smiles had frozen on their faces and Christiansen's arm was still poised in mid-air where it had been arrested by the sound and the shock of Smith's landing on the cable-car roof. Carraciola, predictably, was the first to recover and react. He snatched the Schmeisser from Christiansen and pointed it upwards.

The cable-car was now forty to fifty feet clear of the castle and the high wind was beginning to swing it, pendulum-like, across the sky. Smith, weakened by the impact of the fall, the pain in his hand and the loss of blood, hung on grimly and dizzily to the suspension bracket, his body athwart the roof of the car. He felt sick and exhausted and there seemed to be a mist in front of his eyes.

From shoulder to knee and only inches from his body a venomous burst of machine-pistol fire stitched a pattern of holes in the cable-car roof: the mists cleared away from Smith's eyes more quickly than he would have believed possible. A Schmeisser magazine held far more shells than that. They would wait a second or two to see if a falling body passed any of the side windows – with that violently swinging transverse movement it was virtually impossible for anyone to fall off over the leading or trailing ends of the car – and if none came, then they would fire again. But where? What would be the next area of roof chosen for treatment? Would the gunman fire at random or to a systematic pattern? It was impossible to guess. Perhaps at that very moment the muzzle of the Schmeisser was only two inches from the middle of his spine. The very thought was enough to galvanise Smith into a quick roll that stretched him out over the line of holes that had just been made. It was unlikely that the gunman would fire in exactly the same place again, but even that was a gamble, the gunman might figure just as Smith was doing and traverse the same area again. But he wasn't figuring the same as Smith, the next burst was three feet away towards the trailing end of the car.

Using the suspension bracket as support, Smith pulled himself to his feet until he was quite vertical, hanging on to the cable itself. This way, the possible target area was lessened by eighty per cent. Quickly, soundlessly, sliding his hands along the cable, he moved forward until he was standing at the very front of the car.

The cable-car's angle of arc through the sky was increasing with every swing of the pendulum. The purchase for his feet was minimal, all the strain came on his arms, and by far the greater part of that on his sound left arm. There was nothing smoothly progressive about the cable-car's sideways motion through the sky, it jumped and jerked and jarred and jolted like a Dervish dancer in the last seconds before total collapse. The strain on the left arm was intolerable, it felt as if the shoulder sinews were being torn apart: but shoulder sinews are reparable whereas the effects of a Schmeisser blast at point blank range were not. And it seemed, to Smith, highly unlikely that anybody would waste a burst on the particular spot where he was standing, the obvious position for any roof passenger who didn't want to be shaken off into the valley below was flat out on the roof with his arms wrapped for dear life round one of the suspension arm's support brackets.

His reasoning was correct. There were three more bursts, none of which came within feet of him, and then no more. Smith knew that he would have to return to the comparative security of the suspension arm and return there soon. He was nearly gone. The grip of his left hand on the cable was weakening, this forced him to strengthen the grip of his right hand and the resulting agony that travelled like an electric shock from his hand up his arm clear to the right hand side of his head served only to compound the weakness. He would have to get back, and he would have to get back now. He prayed that the Schmeisser's magazine was empty.

And then, and for another reason, he knew that he had no option but to go now: and he knew his prayer hadn't been answered. The leading door of the cable-car opened and a head and a hand appeared. The head was Carraciola's: the hand held the Schmeisser. Carraciola was looking upwards even as he leaned out and he saw Smith immediately: he leaned farther out still, swung the Schmeisser one-handedly until the stock rested on his shoulder and squeezed the trigger.

Under the circumstances accurate aiming was impossible but at a distance of four feet accurate aiming was the last thing that mattered. Smith had already let go of the cable and was flinging himself convulsively backward when the first of the bullets ripped off his left hand epaulette. The second grazed his left shoulder, a brief burning sensation, but the rest of the burst passed harmlessly over his head. He landed heavily, stretched out blindly, located and grasped one of the suspension arms and scuttled crab-like round the base of the suspension arm until he had it and what little pathetic cover it offered between him and Carraciola.

For Carraciola was coming after him and Carraciola was coming to mak' siccar. He had the gun still in his hand and that gun could have very few shells indeed left in the magazine: it would be no part of Carraciola's plan to waste any of those shells. Even as Smith watched, Carraciola seemed to rise effortlessly three feet into the air – a feat of levitation directly attributable to the powerful boost given him by Thomas and Christiansen – jack-knifed forward at hip level and flattened his body on top of the cable-car roof: his legs still dangled over the leading edge. A suicidal move, Smith thought in brief elation, Carraciola had made a fatal mistake: with neither hand hold nor purchase on that ice-coated roof, he must slide helplessly over the edge at the first jerk or jolt of the cable-car. But the elation was brief indeed for Carraciola had made no mistake. He had known what Smith hadn't: where to find a secure lodgment for his hand on the smooth expanse of that roof. Within seconds his scrabbling fingers had found safety – a gash in the cable-car roof that had been torn open by one of the bursts from the Schmeisser. Carraciola's fingers hooked securely and he pulled himself forward until he was in a kneeling position, his toes hooked over the leading edge.

Smith reached up with his wounded hand and clawed desperately for a grenade in the canvas bag slung over his left shoulder, at the same time pushing himself as far back as his anchoring left hand, clutched round a suspension bracket, would permit: at that range a grenade could do almost as much damage to himself as to Carraciola. His legs slid back until his feet projected over the trailing edge and he cried out in pain as a tremendous pressure, a bone-breaking, skin tearing pressure, was applied to his shins, half-way between knees and feet: someone had him by the ankles and that someone seemed determined to separate his feet from the rest of his body. Smith twisted his head round but all he could see was a pair of hands round his ankles, knuckles bone-white in the faint wash of moonlight. And no one man's weight, Smith realized, could have caused that agonising pain in his shins. His companion must had had him by the waist, whether to increase the pressure or to ensure his safety if Smith did slide over the end. The reasons were immaterial: the effect was the same. He tried to draw up his legs but with a pinning weight of well over 200 lbs., any movement was quite impossible.

Smith risked a quick glance forward, but Carraciola hadn't moved, the cable-car was now half-way between the header station and the top pylon, the pendulum swing was at its maximum and Carraciola, still in his kneeling position, was hanging on for his life. Smith abandoned his attempt to reach for a grenade which could now serve no purpose whatsoever, unsheathed his knife, clasped the haft in the three good fingers of his right hand, twisted round and tried to strike at those hands that were causing him such excruciating agony. He couldn't get within fifteen inches of them.

His legs were breaking: his left arm was breaking: and his clenched grip on the support was slowly beginning to open. He had only seconds to go, Smith knew, and so he had nothing in the world to lose. He changed his grip on his knife, caught the tip of the blade between his broken thumb and the rest of his fingers, turned and threw the knife as powerfully and as accurately as his smashed hand and pain-dimmed eyes would permit. The stinging pain in his left ankle and the scream of pain from the trailing door were simultaneous: immediately, all the pressure on his ankles vanished: a second later, Christiansen, whom Thomas had managed to drag back inside the cable-car, was staring stupidly at the knife that transfixed his right wrist.

In that one instant Smith had won and he had lost. Or so it most surely seemed, for he was defenceless now: Carraciola had bided his time, calculated his changes and flung himself forward until he had reached the safety of the suspension bracket. Now he pulled himself slowly to his feet, his left arm round the suspension arm itself, his left leg twined securely round one of the brackets. The Schmeisser pointed into Smith's face.

'Only one bullet left.' Carraciola's smile was almost pleasant. 'I had to make sure, you see.'

Perhaps he hadn't lost, Smith thought, perhaps he hadn't lost after all. Because of the pinioning effect of Christiansen's hands on his ankles he'd been unaware, until now, how much less difficult it had become to maintain position on that ice-sheathed roof, unaware how much the pendulum swaying of the cable-car had been reduced. And it seemed that, even now, Carraciola was still unaware of it, or, if the change of motion had registered with him, the reason for it had not. With a conscious effort of will Smith shifted his by now half-hypnotised gaze from the staring muzzle of the Schmeisser to a point just over Carraciola's shoulder. The suspension arm of the first pylon was less than twenty feet away.

'Too bad, Smith.' Carraciola steadied the barrel of his machine pistol. 'Comes to us all. Be seeing you.'

'Look behind you,' Smith said.

Carraciola half-smiled in weary disbelief that anyone should try that ancient one on him. Smith glanced briefly, a second time, over Carraciola's shoulder, winced and looked away. The disbelief vanished from Carraciola's face as if a light had been switched off. Some sixth sense or instantaneous flash of comprehension or just some sudden certainty of knowledge made him twist round and glance over his shoulder. He cried out in terror, the last sound he ever made. The steel suspension arm of the pylon smashed into his back. Both his back and inter-twined leg broke with a simultaneous crack that could have been heard a hundred yards away. One second later he was swept from the roof of the cable-car but by that time Carraciola was already dead. From the open rearward door of the car, Thomas and Christiansen, their shocked faces mirroring their stunned disbelief, watched the broken body tumbling down into the darkness of the valley below.

Shaking like a man with the ague and moving like an old man in a dream, Smith slowly and painfully hauled himself forward until he was in a sitting position with an arm and leg wound round one of the after arms of the supporting bracket. Still in the same dream-like slow motion he lifted his head and gazed down the valley. The other cable-car, moving up-valley on its reciprocal course, had just passed the lower-most of the three pylons. With luck, his own cable-car might be the first to arrive at the central pylon. With luck. Not, of course, that the question of luck entered into it any more: he had no options or alternatives left, he had to do what he had to do and luck was the last factor to be taken into consideration.

From his kit-bag Smith extracted two packets of plastic explosives and wedged them firmly between the roof of the car and the two after arms of the suspension bracket, making sure that the tear strip igniters were exposed and ready to hand.

Then he braced himself, sitting upright, against the suspension bracket, using both arms and legs to anchor himself and prepared to sit it out once more as the cable-car, approaching midsection of its second lap between the first and central pylons, steadily increased its swaying angle of arc across the night sky.

It was foolish of him, he knew, to sit like that. The snow had momentarily stopped, and the full moon, riding palely in an empty sky, was flooding the valley with a wash of ghostly light. Sitting as he was he must, he realized, be clearly visible from either the castle or the lower station: but apart from the fact that he doubted whether concealment mattered any longer he knew there was nothing he could do about it, there wasn't the strength left in his one good arm to allow him to assume the prone spread-eagled position that he and Schaffer had used on the way up.

He wondered about Schaffer, wondered about him in a vaguely woolly detached way for which exhaustion, loss of blood and the bitter cold were almost equally responsible. He wondered about the others, too, about the elderly man and the girl perched on top of the header station roof, about the two men inside the cable-car: but Mary and Carnaby-Jones were helpless to do anything to help and the chances of the unarmed Thomas and Christiansen carrying out another roof-top sortie were remote indeed: Carraciola had carried a Schmeisser, and they had seen what had happened to Carraciola. Schaffer, it was Schaffer who mattered.

Schaffer was feeling even more vague and woolly than Smith, if for different reasons. He was waking, slowly and painfully, from a very bad dream and in this dream he could taste salt in his mouth and hear a soft urgent feminine voice calling his name, calling it over and over again. In normal times Schaffer would have been all for soft feminine voices, urgent or not, but he wished that this one would stop for it was all part of the bad dream and in this bad dream someone had split his head in half and he knew the pain wouldn't go until he woke up. He moaned, put the palms of his hands on the floor and tried to prop himself up. It took a long time, it took an eternity, for someone had laid one of the girders from the Forth bridge across his back, but at last he managed to straighten both his arms, his head hanging down between them. His head didn't feel right, it didn't even feel like his head, for, apart from the fact that there seemed to be a butcher's cleaver stuck in it, it seemed to be stuffed with cotton wool, grey and fuzzy round the edges. He shook his head to clear it and this was a mistake for the top of his head fell off. Or so it felt to Schaffer as the blinding coruscation of multi-coloured lights before his eyes arranged themselves into oddly kaleidoscopic patterns. He opened his eyes and the patterns dimmed and the lights began to fade: gradually, beneath his eyes the pattern of floorboards began to resolve themselves, and, on the board, the outlines of hands. His own hands.

He was awake, but this was one of those bad dreams which stayed with you even when you were awake. He could still taste salt – the salt of blood – his head still felt as if one incautious shake would have it rolling across the floor and that soft and urgent voice was still calling.

'Lieutenant Schaffer! Lieutenant Schaffer! Wake up, Lieutenant, wake up! Can you hear me?'

He'd heard that voice before, Schaffer decided, but he couldn't place it. It must have been a long time ago. He twisted his head to locate the source of the voice – it seemed to come from above – and the kaleidoscopic whirligig of colours were back in position again, revolving more quickly than ever. Head-shaking and head-twisting, Schaffer decided, were contra-indicated. He returned his head slowly to its original position, managed to get his knees under him, crawled forward in the direction of some dimly-seen piece of machinery and hauled himself shakily to his feet.

'Lieutenant! Lieutenant Schaffer! I'm up here.'

Schaffer turned and lifted his head in an almost grotesque slow motion and this time the whole universe of brightly dancing stars was reduced to the odd constellation or two. He recognised the voice from the distant past now, it was that of Mary Ellison, he even thought he recognised the pale strained face looking down from above, but he couldn't be sure, his eyes weren't focusing as they should. He wondered dizzily what the hell she was doing up there staring down at him through what appeared to be the bars of a shattered sky-light: his mind, he dimly realized, was operating with all the speed and subtle fluency of a man swimming upstream against a river of black molasses.

'Are you – are you all right?' Mary asked.

Schaffer considered this ridiculous question carefully. 'I expect I shall be,' he said with great restraint. 'What happened?'

'They hit you with your own gun.'

'That's right.' Schaffer nodded and immediately wished he hadn't. He gingerly fingered a bruise on the back of his head. 'In the face. I must have struck my head as—' He broke off and turned slowly to face the door. 'What was that?'

'A dog. It sounded like a dog barking.'

'That's what I thought.' His voice slurred and indistinct, he staggered drunkenly across to the lower iron door and put his ear to it. 'Dogs,' he said. 'Lots of dogs. And lots and lots of hammering. Sledge-hammers, like enough.' He left the door and walked back to the centre of the floor, still staggering slightly. 'They're on to us and they're coming for us. Where's the Major?'

'He went after them.' The voice was empty of all feeling. 'He jumped on to the top of the cable-car.'

'He did, eh?' Schaffer received the news as if Smith's action had been the most natural and inevitable thing in the world. 'How did he make out?'

'How did he make—' There was life back in her voice now, a shocked anger at Schaffer's apparent callousness. She checked herself and said: 'There was a fight and I think someone fell off the roof. I don't know who it was.'

'It was one of them,' Schaffer said positively.

'One of – how can you say that?'

'The Major Smiths of this world don't drive over the edge of a cliff, Quotation from the future Mrs Schaffer. The Major Smiths of this world don't fall off the roofs of cable-cars. Quotation from the future Mrs Schaffer's future husband.'

'You're recovering,' Mary said coldly. 'But I think you're right. There's still someone sitting on top of the cable-car and it wouldn't be one of them, would it?'

'How do you know there's someone sitting—'

'Because I can see him,' she said impatiently. 'It's bright moonlight. Look for yourself.'

Schaffer looked for himself, then rubbed a weary forearm across aching eyes. 'I have news for you, love,' he said. 'I can't even see the damn' cable-car.'

The cable-car was ten yards away from the central pylon. Smith, upright now, stooped, tore off the two friction fuses, straightened and, holding the cable in his left hand, took up position just on the inner side of the car roof. At the last moment he released his grip on the cable and stretched both arms out before him to break the impact of his body against the suspension arm.

The ascending car on the other cable was now almost as close to the central pylon as his own. It didn't seem possible that he could make it in time.

The impact of the horizontal suspension arm drove the thought from his mind and all the breath from his body; had it not been for the buffering effect of his outstretched arms, Smith was sure, some of his ribs must have gone. As it was, he was almost completely winded but he forced himself to ignore the pain and his heaving lungs' demand for oxygen, swung his feet up till they rested on the lower cross-girder, hooked his hands round the upper girder and made his way quickly across to the other side. At least, his hands and his feet moved quickly, but the steel was so thickly coated in clear smooth ice that his scrabbling feet could find almost no purchase whatsoever on the lower girder. He had reached no farther than the middle when the ascending car began to pass under its suspension arm. For the first time that night Smith blessed the brightness of the moon. He took two more slipping, sliding steps and launched himself towards the ice-coated cable that glittered so brightly in the pale moonlight.

His left hand caught the cable, his right arm hooked over it and the cable itself caught him high up on the chest. He had made no mistake about the location of his hand and arm, but his sliding take-off had caused his bady to fall short and the cable slid up under his chin with a jerk that threatened to decapitate him. His legs swung out far beneath him, swung back and touched the roof as he lowered himself to the full extent of his left arm. He released his grip on the cable, dropped on all fours and reached out blindly but successfully for one of the arms of the suspension bracket. For long seconds he knelt there, retching uncontrollably as he was flooded by the nausea and pain from his throat and still winded lungs: then, by and by, the worst of it passed and he lay face down on the floor as the cable-car began to increase its pendulum swing with the increasing distance from the central pylon. He would not have believed that a man could be so totally exhausted and yet still have sufficient residual strength and sufficient self-preservation instinct to hang on to that treacherous and precarious hand-hold on that ice-coated roof.

Long seconds passed and some little measure of strength began to return to his limbs and body. Wearily, he hauled himself up into a sitting position, twisted round and gazed back down the valley.

The cable-car he had so recently abandoned was now hardly more than fifty yards from the lowermost plyon. Thomas and Christiansen sat huddled in the middle, the latter wrapping a makeshift bandage round his injured hand. Both fore and aft doors were still open as they were when the abortive attack on Smith had been made. That neither of the two men had ventured near the extremities of the car to try to close either of the doors was proof enough of the respect, if not fear, in which Smith was now held.

From the roof of the cable-car came a brilliant flash of light, magnesium-blinding in its white intensity: simultaneously there came the sound of two sharp explosions, so close together as to be indistinguishable in time. The two rear supports of the suspension bracket broke and the car, suspended now by only the two front supports, tilted violently, the front going up, the rear down.

Inside, the angle of the floor of the car changed in an instant from the horizontal to at least thirty degrees. Christiansen was flung back towards the still open rear door. He grabbed despairingly at the side – but he grabbed with his wounded hand. Soundlessly, he vanished through the open doorway and as soundlessly fell to the depths of the valley below.

Thomas, with two sound hands and faster reactions, had succeeded in saving himself – for the moment. He glanced up and saw where the roof was beginning to buckle and break as the forward two suspension arm support brackets, now subjected to a wrenching lateral pressure they had never been designed to withstand, began to tear their retaining bolts free. Thomas struggled up the steeply inclined floor till he stood in the front doorway: because of the tilt of the car, now almost 45° as the front supports worked loose, the leading edge of the roof was almost touching the car. Thomas reached up, grabbed the cable with both hands, and had just cleared his legs from the doorway when the two front supports tore free from the roof in a rending screech of metal. The cable-car fell away, slowly turning end over end.

Despite the cable's violent buffeting caused by the sudden release of the weight of the car, Thomas had managed to hang on. He twisted round and saw the suspension arm of the lowest pylon only feet away. The sudden numbing of all physical and mental faculties was accurately and shockingly reflected in the frozen fear of his face, the lips drawn back in a snarling rictus of terror. The knuckles of the hands gleamed like burnished ivory. And then, suddenly, there were no hands there, just the suspension arm and the empty wire and a long fading scream in the night.

As his cable-car approached the header station, Smith edged well forward to clear the lip of the roof. From where he crouched it was impossible to see the east wing of the Schloss Adler but if the columns of dense smoke now drifting across the valley were anything to go by, the fire seemed to have an unshakable hold. Clouds were again moving across the moon and this could be both a good thing and a bad thing: a good thing in that it would afford them cover and help obscure those dense clouds of smoke, a bad thing in that it was bound to high-light the flames from the burning castle. It could only be a matter of time, Smith reflected, before the attention of someone in the village or the barracks beyond was caught by the fire or the smoke. Or, he thought grimly, by the increasing number of muffled explosions coming from the castle itself. He wondered what might be the cause of them: Schaffer hadn't had the time to lay all those distractions.

The roof of the cable-car cleared the level of the floor of the header station and Smith sagged in relief as he saw the figure standing by the controls of the winch. Schaffer. A rather battered and bent Schaffer, it was true, an unsteady Schaffer, a Schaffer with one side of his face masked in blood, a Schaffer who from his peering and screwed-up expression had obviously some difficulty in focusing his gaze. But undoubtedly Schaffer and as nearly a going concern as made no odds. Smith felt energy flow back into him, he hadn't realized just how heavily he had come to depend on the American: with Schaffer by his side it was going to take a great deal to stop them now.

Smith glanced up as the roof of the header station came into view. Mary and Carnaby-Jones were still there, pressed back against the castle wall. He lifted a hand in greeting, but they gave no sign in return. Ghosts returning from the dead, Smith thought wryly, weren't usually greeted by a wave of the hand.

Schaffer, for all the trouble he was having with his eyes and his still obviously dazed condition, seemed to handle the winch controls immaculately. It may have been – and probably was – the veriest fluke, but he put the gear level in neutral and applied the brake to bring the cable-car to rest exactly half-way in under the lip of the roof. First Mary and then Jones came sliding down the nylon rope on to the roof of the car, Jones with his eyes screwed tightly shut. Neither of them spoke a word, not even when Schaffer had brought them up inside and they had slid down on to the floor of the station.

'Hurry! Hurry!' Smith flung open the rear door of the cable-car. 'Inside, all of you!' He retrieved Schaffer's Luger from the floor, then whirled round as he heard the furious barking of dogs followed by the sound of heavy sledges battering against the iron door leading from the station. The first of the two defences must have been carried away: now the second was under siege.

Mary and a stumbling Schaffer were already inside the cable-car. Jones, however, had made no move to go. He stood there, Smith's Schmeisser in his hand, listening to the furious hammering on the door. His face seemed unconcerned. He said, apologetically: 'I'm not very good at heights, I'm afraid. But this is different.'

'Get inside!' Smith almost hissed the words.

'No.' Jones shook his head. 'You hear. They'll be through any minute. I'll stay.'

'For God's sake!' Smith shouted in exasperation.

'I'm twenty years older than any of you.'

'Well, there's that.' Smith nodded consideringly, held out his right hand, said, 'Mr Jones. Good luck,' brought across his left hand and half-dragged, half-carried the dazed Jones into the cable-car. Smith moved quickly across to the controls, engaged gear all the way, released the handbrake and ran after the moving car.

As they moved out from below the roof of the station, the sound of the assault on the inner door seemed to double in its intensity. In the Schloss Adler, Smith reflected, there would be neither pneumatic chisels nor oxy-acetylene equipment for there could be no conceivable call for either, but, even so, it didn't seem to matter: with all the best will in the world a couple of iron hasps couldn't for long withstand an attack of that nature. Thoughtfully, Smith closed the rear door. Schaffer was seated, his elbows on his knees, his head in his hands. Mary was kneeling on the floor, Jones's head in her lap, looking down at the handsome silvery-haired head. He couldn't see her expression but was dolefully certain that she was even then preparing a homily about the shortcomings of bullies who went around clobbering elderly and defenceless American actors. Almost two minutes passed in complete silence before Carnaby-Jones stirred, and, when he did, Mary herself stirred and looked up at Smith. To his astonishment, she had a half-smile on her face.

'It's all right,' she said. 'I've counted ten. In the circumstances, it was the only argument to use.' She paused and the smile faded. 'I though you were gone then.'

'You weren't the only one. After this I retire. I've used up a lifetime's luck in the past fifteen minutes. You're not looking so bright yourself.'

'I'm not feeling so bright.' Her face was pale and strained as she braced herself against the wild lurching of the cable-car. 'If you want to know, I'm sea-sick. I don't go much on this form of travel.'

Smith tapped the roof. 'You want to try travelling steerage on one of those,' he said feelingly. 'You'd never complain about first-class travel again. Ah! Pylon number two coming up. Almost half-way.'

'*Only* half-way.' A pause. 'What happens if they break through that door up there?'

'Reverse the gear lever and up we go.'

'Like it or not?'

'Like it or not.'

Carnaby-Jones struggled slowly to a sitting position, gazed uncomprehendingly around him until he realized where he was, rubbed his jaw tenderly and said to Smith: 'That was a dirty trick.'

'It was all of that,' Smith acknowledged. 'I'm sorry.'

'I'm not.' Jones smiled shakily. 'Somehow, I don't really think I'm cut out to be a hero.'

'Neither am I, brother, neither am I,' Schaffer said mournfully. He lifted his head from his hands and looked slowly around. His eyes were still glassy and only partially focusing but a little colour was returning to his right cheek, the one that wasn't masked in blood. 'Our three friends. What became of our three friends?'

'Dead.'

'Dead?' Schaffer groaned and shook his head. 'Tell me about it sometime. But not now.'

'He doesn't know what he's missing,' Smith said unsympathetically. 'The drama of it all escapes him, which is perhaps just as well. Is the door up above there still standing or are the hinges or padlocks going? Is someone rushing towards the winch controls – Is there—'

'Stop it!' Mary's voice was sharp, high-pitched and carried overtones of hysteria. 'Stop talking like that!'

'Sorry,' Smith said contritely. He reached out and touched her shoulder. 'Just whistling in the dark, that's all. Here comes the last pylon. Another minute or so and we're home and dry.'

'Home and dry,' Schaffer said bitterly. 'Wait till I have that Savoy Grill menu in my hand. *Then* I'll be home and dry.'

'Some people are always thinking of their stomachs,' Smith observed. At that moment he was thinking of his own and it didn't feel any too good. No stomach does when it feels as if it has a solid lead ball, a chilled lead ball lodged in it with an icy hand squeezing from the outside. His heart was thumping slowly, heavily, painfully in his chest and he was having difficulty in speaking for all the saliva seemed to have evaporated from his mouth. He became suddenly aware that he was unconsciously leaning backward, bracing himself for the moment when the cable-car jerked to a stand-still then started climbing back up to the Schloss Adler again. I'll count to ten, he said to himself, then if we get that far without being checked, I'll count to nine, and then – And then he caught sight of Mary's face, a dead-white, scared and almost haggard face that made her look fifteen years older than she was, and felt suddenly ashamed of himself. He sat on the bench, and squeezed her shoulder. 'We'll be all right,' he said confidently. All of a sudden he found it easy to speak again. 'Uncle John has just said so, hasn't he? You wait and see.'

She looked up at him, trying to smile. 'Is Uncle John always right?'

'Always,' Smith said firmly.

Twenty seconds passed. Smith rose to his feet, walked to the front of the cable-car and peered down. Though the moon was obscured he could just dimly discern the shape of the lower section. He turned to look at the others. They were all looking at him.

'Not much more than a hundred feet to go,' Smith said. 'I'm going to open that door in a minute. Well, a few seconds. By that time we won't be much more than fifteen feet above the ground. Twenty, at the most. If the car stops, we jump. There's two or three feet of snow down there. Should cushion our fall enough to give an even chance of not breaking anything.'

Schaffer parted his lips to make some suitable remark, thought better of it and returned head to hands in weary silence. Smith opened the leading door, did his best to ignore the icy blast of wind that gusted in through the opening, and looked vertically downwards, realizing that he had been over-optimistic in his assessment of the distance between cable-car and ground. The distance was at least fifty feet, a distance sufficient to arouse in even the most optimistic mind dismaying thoughts of fractured femurs and tibias. And then he dismissed the thought, for an even more dismaying factor had now to be taken into consideration: in the far distance could be heard the sound of sirens, in the far distance could be seen the wavering beams of approaching headlamps. Schaffer lifted his head. The muzziness had now left him, even if his sore head had not.

'Enter, left, reinforcements,' he announced. 'This wasn't on the schedule, boss. Radio gone, telephone gone, helicopter gone—'

'Just old-fashioned.' Smith pointed towards the rear window. 'They're using smoke signals.'

'Jeez!' Schaffer stared out the rear windows, his voice awestruck. 'For stone, it sure burns good!'

Schaffer was in no way exaggerating. For stone, it burnt magnificently. The Schloss Adler was well and truly alight, a conflagration in which smoke had suddenly become an inconsiderable and, indeed, a very minor element. It was wreathed in flames, almost lost to sight in flames, towering flames that now reached up almost to the top of the great round tower to the north-east. Perched on its volcanic plug half-way up the mountain-side against the dimly seen back-drop of the unseen heights of the Weissspitze, the blazing castle, its effulgence now beginning to light up the entire valley and quite drowning out the pale light of a moon again showing through, was an incredibly fantastic sight from some equally incredible and fantastic fairy tale.

'One trusts that they are well insured,' Schaffer said. He was on his feet now, peering down towards the lower station. 'How far, boss? And how far down?'

'Thirty feet. Maybe twenty-five. And fifteen feet down.' The lights of the leading cars were passing the still smouldering embers of the station. 'We have it made, Lieutenant Schaffer.'

'We have it made.' Schaffer cursed and staggered as the car jerked to a violent and abrupt stop. 'Almost, that is.'

'All out!' Smith shouted. 'All out!'

'There speaks the eternal shop steward,' Schaffer said. 'Stand back, I've got two good hands.' He brushed by Smith, clutched the door jamb with his left hand, pulled Mary towards him, transferred his grip from waist to wrist and dropped her out through the leading door, lowering her as far as the stretch of his left arm would permit. When he let her go, she had less than three feet to fall. Within three seconds he had done the same with Carnaby-Jones. The cable-car jerked and started to move back up the valley. Schaffer practically bundled Smith out of the car, wincing in pain as he momentarily took all of Smith's two hundred pound weight, then slid out of the doorway himself, hung momentarily from the doorway at the full stretch of his arms, then dropped six feet into the soft yielding snow. He staggered, but maintained balance.

Smith was beside him. He had fished out a plastic explosive from the bag on his back and torn off the friction fuse. He handed the package to Schaffer and said: 'You have a good right arm.'

'I have a good right arm. Horses, no. Baseball, yes.' Schaffer took aim and lobbed the explosive neatly through the doorway of the disappearing cable-car. 'Like that?'

'Like that. Come on.' Smith turned and, catching Mary by the arm while Schaffer hustled Carnaby-Jones along, ran down the side of the lower station and into the shelter of the nearest house bare seconds before a command car, followed by several trucks crammed with soldiers, slid to a skidding halt below the lower station. Soldiers piled out of the trucks, following an officer, clearly identifiable as Colonel Weissner, up the steps into the lower station.

The castle burned more fiercely than ever, a fire obviously totally out of control. Suddenly, there was the sharp crack of an explosion and the ascending cable-car burst into flames. The car, half-way up to the first pylon, swung in great arcs across the valley, its flames fanned by the wind, and climbed steadily upwards into the sky until its flame was lost in the greater flame of the Schloss Adler.

Crouched in the shelter of the house, Schaffer touched Smith's arm. 'Sure you wouldn't like to go and burn down the station as well?'

'Come on,' Smith said. 'The garage.'

——— I I ———

Colonel Wyatt-Turner leaned over in the co-pilot's seat, pressed his face against the side-screen and stared down unhappily at the ground. The Mosquito bomber, all engines and plywood, was, he was well aware, the fastest warplane in the world: even so, he hadn't been prepared for anything quite so fast as this.

Normal flying, of course, imparts no sensation of speed, but then, Wing Commander Carpenter wasn't engaged in normal flying; he was engaged in what Wyatt-Turner regarded as highly abnormal flying and flying, moreover, that was liable to bring them to disaster at any second. Carpenter was giving a ground-level performance of some spectacular note, skimming across fields, brushing tree-tops, skirting small hills that stood in his way, and Wyatt-Turner didn't like any of it one little bit. What he liked even less was the appalling speed of their own moon-shadow flitting over the ground beneath them; and what he liked least of all was the increasing number of occasions on which plane and shadow came within almost touching distance of each other. In an effort to keep his mind off what must inevitably happen when and if the gap were finally closed he withdrew his almost mesmerised stare and glanced at his watch.

'Twenty-five minutes.' He looked at the relaxed figure in the pilot's seat, at the world-weary face that contrasted so oddly with the magnificent panache of the red handlebar moustache. 'Can you make it in time?'

'I can make it,' Carpenter said comfortably. 'Point is, will they?'

'God only knows. I don't see how they can. Both the Admiral and I are convinced that they're trapped in the Schloss Adler. Besides, the whole countryside must be up in arms by this time. What chance *can* they have?'

'And that is why you came?'

'I sent them,' Wyatt-Turner said emptily. He glanced through the side-screen and recoiled as plane and shadow seemed to touch as they skimmed over the top of a pine forest. He said plaintively: 'Must you fly so close to the damned ground?'

'Enemy radar, old chap,' Carpenter said soothingly. 'We're safer down here among the bushes.'

Smith, with Mary and Jones behind him and Schaffer bringing

up the rear, skirted the backs of the houses on the east side of the village street and cautiously made their way through the automobile junkyard to the rear double doors of Sulz's garage. Smith had his skeleton keys in his hand and was just reaching for the padlock when one of the doors opened quietly inwards. Heidi stood there. She stared at them as if they were creatures from another world, then up at the burning castle, then word-lessly, questioningly, at Smith.

'All here in black and white.' Smith patted his tunic. 'Into the bus.'

Smith waited till they had filed through the door, closed it, crossed to a small barred window at the front of the garage and peered out cautiously.

The street was packed with a milling crowd of people, most of them soldiers, nearly all unarmed men who had come hurry-ing out from the various *Weinstuben* to watch the burning Schloss Adler. But there were plenty of armed soldiers nearby – two truck-loads not thirty yards from the garage, not to men-tion three more truck-loads even farther up the street at the foot of the lower station. Farther down the street a motor-cycle patrol was parked outside 'Zum Wilden Hirsch'. The one real physical obstacle in the way of their escape was a small com-mand car, manned, parked directly outside the doors of Sulz's garage. Smith looked at the car thoughtfully, decided that this was an obstacle that could be overcome. He withdrew from the window and crossed over to the doors to check that the four bolts were still withdrawn.

Mary and Carnaby-Jones had already made their way into the bus. As Heidi went to follow, Schaffer caught her by the shoulders, kissed her briefly and smiled at her. She looked at him in surprise.

'Well, aren't you glad to see me?' Schaffer demanded. 'I've had a *terrible* time up there. Good God, girl, I might have been killed.'

'Not as handsome as you were two hours ago.' She smiled, gently touched his face when Carraciola's handiwork with the Schmeisser had left its bloody mark, and added over her shoulder as she climbed into the bus: 'And that's as long as you've known me.'

'Two hours! I've aged twenty years tonight. And that, lady, is one helluva long courtship. Oh, God!' He watched in wearily resigned despair as Smith climbed into the driver's seat and switched on the ignition. 'Here we go for another twenty. On the floor, everyone.'

'How about you?' Heidi asked.

'Me?' Schaffer's surprise seemed genuine. He smashed the front window with the butt of the Schmeisser, reversed the gun, released the trigger and knelt on the floor. 'I'm the conductor. It's against regulations.'

The middle finger of Smith's blood-stained, bandaged hand reached for the starter button and the big diesel caught at once. Smith started to back towards the rear of the garage. Two perfectly good cars, a Mercedes and an Opel, lay in his way and by the time that Smith – whose expression betrayed no awareness of their presence – reached the back of the garage neither were fit for anything other than the scrap-heap that lay beyond the rear doors. Smith stopped, engaged first gear, revved up the engine and let in the clutch with a bang. The bus jerked forward, gathering speed as it went.

Smith aimed the angled point of the massive snow-plough at the junction of the double doors and for all the resistance the doors offered they might have been made of brown paper. With a splintering crash that sent shattered door-planks flying through the air like so much confetti, the bus roared out into the street, Smith spinning the wheel violently to the right as they careened into the crowded thoroughfare.

Crowded the thoroughfare might have been, but the pedestrians, the rubber-neckers gazing at the funeral pyre of the Schloss Adler, had had at least sufficient warning given them by the accelerating clamour of the post-bus's diesel to fling themselves clear as the bus came crashing through the doors. But the command car had no such opportunity for escape. Before either of the two occupants of the front seat – a sergeant with his hands resting lightly on the wheel, a major with a radio telephone in one hand, a thin cigar with a long ash in the other – were properly aware of what was happening, their car was swept up and carried away on the post-bus's snow-plough. For fifteen, perhaps even twenty yards, the command car was carried along, precariously balanced, on the broad blade of the snow-plough, before dropping off to one side. Miraculously enough, it landed on even keel, all four wheels still on the ground. The dazed major still had the telephone in one hand, the cigar in the other: he hadn't even lost the ash from his cigar.

Farther down the street, outside 'Zum Wilden Hirsch', a group of Alpenkorps motor-cyclists standing just outside the door stared incredulously up the street. Their first reaction, their immediate conclusion was either that Zep Salzmann, the highly popular driver of the post-bus, had gone mad or that the accelerator had jammed on the floor-boards. Disillusionment was rapid. They heard the unmistakable sound of an engine changing up quickly through the gears and caught a brief glimpse of Smith hunched over the steering wheel and of Schaffer crouched behind, the Schmeisser sticking out through the right-hand shattered windscreen: then the post-bus's headlamps switched on and they could see no more. But they had seen enough. One quick command from their sergeant and the motor-cycle patrol leapt for their machines, began to kick them into life.

But Smith also had seen enough. He blew a warning blast on his town horn, twisted the wheel and slewed the bus into the side of the street. His intentions were unmistakable and the motor-cycle patrol's decision to elect for discretion in lieu of suicidal valour was as immediate as it was automatic. They frantically abandoned their machines and flung themselves for their lives up the steps of 'Zum Wilden Hirsch'.

There was a thunderous series of metallic bangs interspersed with the eldritch screeches of torn and tortured metal as the snow-plough smashed into the motor-cycles and swept them along in its giant maw. As Smith straightened out into the middle of the road again several of them slid off the angled blade and crashed with a great splintering of wood and buckling of metal into the boarded sidewalk: the machines were no longer recognisable as motor-cycles. Two of them, however still remained perched on the blade.

The post-bus was still accelerating with Smith's accelerator foot flat on the floor-boards. The headlamps were flashing rapidly, alternately main beam and dipped, and the streets ahead were clearing with corresponding rapidity: but the moment when the last few straggling pedestrians were galvanised into jumping for safety came when Smith switched on the Alpine horn.

In the mountains, the Alpine post-bus has absolute priority over every other vehicle in the road and its penetrating and stentorian three-toned post-horn is the symbol of its total authority, of its unquestioned right to complete priority at all times. The sound of that horn – whether the post-bus is in sight or not – is the signal for all vehicles or pedestrians to stop or move well into the side of the road, a signal that is immediately and automatically obeyed, for the absolute entitlement to the right of way of the official post-bus is deeply ingrained into the minds of all Alpine dwellers, and has been from earliest childhood. A magic wand might have made a better job of clearing that village street, but not all that much better; vehicles and pedestrians alike pressed into the sides of the street as if some powerful magnetic affinity had just been developed between them and the walls of the houses. The expression on faces ranged from astonishment to blank incomprehension. Hostility there was none: there had been no time for any to develop for events were moving far too swiftly and comprehension hadn't even begun to overtake the events. The bus had now reached the end of the village street and still not one shot had been fired.

At the sharp left-hand corner at the foot of the street the two remaining motor-cycles slid off the snow-plough and smashed into a low stone wall: two more absolute certainties, Smith thought inconsequentially, for the automobile cemetery behind Sulz's garage. Ahead of him now he could see the road stretch almost arrow-straight alongside the dark waters of the Blau See. He switched off the Alpine horn button, changed his mind and switched it on again: that horn was worth a pair of machine-guns any day.

'Don't you know any other tunes?' Schaffer asked irritably. He shivered in the icy blast from the smashed front window, and sat on the floor to get what little shelter he could. 'Give me a call when you require my services. A mile from now, I'd say.'

'What do you mean, a mile from now?'

'The barrack gates. That guy in the command car had a radio phone.'

'He had, had he?' Smith spared him a brief glance. 'Why didn't you shoot him?'

'I'm a changed man, boss.' Schaffer sighed. 'Something splendid has just come into my life.'

'Besides, you didn't have a chance.'

'Besides, as you say, I didn't have a chance.' Schaffer twisted round and looked through the rear windows of the bus for signs of pursuit, but the road behind them was empty. For all that, Schaffer reflected, the rearward view was one not lacking in interest: the Schloss Adler, now completely enveloped in flames, a reddish-white inferno by this time lighting up for half a mile around the startling incongruity of its snow and ice covered setting, was clearly beyond saving: arsonist's dream or fireman's nightmare, the castle was finished: before dawn it would be an empty and desolate shell, a gaunt and blackened ruin to haunt and desecrate for generations to come the loveliest fairy-tale valley he had ever seen.

Schaffer shortened his gaze and tried to locate the three others, but all were on the floor, under seats and completely concealed. He cursed as the shaking and shuddering bus lurched violently, throwing him against the right-hand front door, then straightened and peered at the illuminated dashboard.

'God save us all,' he said piously. 'Ninety!'

'Kilometres,' Smith said patiently.

'Ah!' Schaffer said as he watched Smith's foot move quickly from accelerator to brake, hoisted a wary eye over the lower edge of the shattered windscreen and whistled softly. The barrack gates were barely two hundred yards away: both the area around the guard-house and the parade ground beyond were brilliantly illuminated by overhead flood-lamps: scores of armed soldiers seemed to be running around in purposeless confusion, a totally erroneous impression as Schaffer almost immediately realized. They were running towards and scrambling aboard trucks and command cars and they weren't wasting any time about it either.

'A hive of activity and no mistake,' Schaffer observed. 'I wonder—' He broke off, his eyes widening. A giant tank came rumbling into view past the guard-house, turned right on to the road, stopped, swivelled 180° on its tracks, completely blocking the road: the gun turret moved fractionally until it was lined up on the headlights of the approaching bus. 'Oh, my gosh!' Schaffer's shocked whisper was just audible over the fading sound of the post-bus's diesel. 'A Tiger tank. And that's an 88-millimetre cannon, boss.'

'It's not a pop-gun, and that's a fact,' Smith agreed. 'Flat on the floor.' He reached forward, pulled a switch, and the eighteen-inch long semaphore indicator began to wave gently up and down. Smith first dipped his main headlights, then switched them off altogether, covering the last thirty yards on side-lamps alone and praying that all those signs of peaceful normality might help to keep nervous fingers away from the firing button of the most lethal tank cannon ever devised.

The fingers, for whatever reason, left the button alone. Smith slowed to a walking pace, turned right through the guard-house gates and stopped. Taking care to keep his injured right hand well out of sight, he wound down his window and leaned out, left elbow over the sill as three guards, led by a sergeant and all with machine-pistols at the ready, closed in on the driver's cab.

'Quickly!' Smith shouted. 'Telephone. Surgeon to the sickbay.' He jerked his thumb over his shoulder. 'Colonel Weissner. They got him twice. Through the lungs. For God's sake, don't just *stand* there!'

'But – but the post-bus!' the sergeant protested. 'We had a call from—'

'Drunk, by God!' Smith swore savagely. 'He'll be court-martialled in the morning.' His voice dropped menacingly. 'And you, if the Colonel dies. Move!'

Smith engaged gear and drove off, still at walking pace. The sergeant, reassured by the sight of a major's uniform, the fact that the bus was moving into the barracks, the slow speed with which it was moving and, above all, by the authoritative clamour of the Alpine horn which Smith still had not switched off, ran for the nearest phone.

Still crawling along in first gear, Smith carefully edged the post-bus through the press of men and machines, past a column of booted and gauntleted soldiers mounted on motor-cycles, past armoured vehicles and trucks, all with engines already running, some already moving towards the gates – but not moving as quickly towards the gates as Smith would have wished. Ahead of the post-bus was a group of officers, most of them obviously senior, talking animatedly. Smith slowed down the bus even more and leaned from the window.

'They're trapped!' he called excitedly. 'Upstairs in "Zum Wilden Hirsch". They've got Colonel Weissner as hostage. Hurry, for God's sake!'

He broke off as he suddenly recognised one of the officers as the Alpenkorps captain to whom in his temporary capacity of Major Bernd Himmler, he'd spoken in 'Zum Wilden Hirsch' earlier that evening. A second later the recognition was mutual, the captain's mouth fell open in total incredulity and before he had time to close it Smith's foot was flat on the accelerator and the bus heading for the southern gates, soldiers flinging themselves to both sides to avoid the scything sweep of the giant snow-plough. Such was the element of surprise that fully thirty yards had been covered before most of the back windows of the bus were holed and broken, the shattering of glass mingling with the sound of the ragged fusillade of shots from behind. And then Smith, wrenching desperately on the wheel, came careering through the southern gates back on to the main road, giving them at least temporary protection from the sharp-shooters on the parade ground.

But they had, it seemed, only changed from the frying pan to the fire. Temporary protection they might have obtained from one enemy – but from another and far deadlier enemy they had no protection at all. Smith all but lost control of the bus as something struck a glancing blow low down on his cab door, ricocheted off into the night with a viciously screaming whine and exploded in a white flash of snow-flurried light less than fifty yards ahead.

'The Tiger tank,' Schaffer shouted. 'That goddamned 88-millimetre—'

'Get down!' Smith jack-knifed down and to one side of the wheel until his eyes were only an inch above the foot of the windscreen. 'That one was low. The next one—'

The next one came through the top of the back door, traversed the length of the bus and exited through the front of the roof, just above the windscreen. This time there was no explosion.

'A dud?' Schaffer said hopefully. 'Or maybe a dummy practice—'

'Dummy nothing!' Upright again, Smith was swinging the bus madly, dangerously, from side to side of the road in an attempt to confuse the tank gunner's aim. 'Armour-piercing shells, laddie, designed to go through two inches of steel plate in a tank before they explode.' He winced and ducked low as a third shell took out most of the left-hand windows of the bus, showering himself and Schaffer with a flying cloud of shattered glass fragments. 'Just let one of those shells strike a chassis member, instead of thin sheet metal, or the engine block, or the snow-plough—'

'Don't!' Schaffer begged. 'Just let it creep up on me all unbeknownst, like.' He paused, then continued: 'Taking his time, isn't he? Lining up for the Sunday one.'

'No.' Smith glanced in the rear-view mirror and steadied the wildly swaying bus up on a steadier course. 'Never thought I'd be glad to see a few car-loads or truck loads of Alpenkorps coming after me.' He changed into top gear and pushed the accelerator to the floor. 'I'm happy to make an exception this time.'

Schaffer turned and looked through the shattered rear windows. He could count at least three pairs of headlights on the road behind them, with two others swinging out through the southern gates: between them, they effectively blotted the post-bus from the view of the tank gunner.

'Happy isn't the word for it. Me, I'm ecstatic. Tiger tanks are one thing but little itsy-bitsy trucks are another.' Schaffer strode rapidly down the central aisle, passing by Mary, Heidi and Carnaby-Jones, all of whom were struggling rather shakily to their feet, and looked at the crates stacked in the rear seats.

'Six crates!' he said to Heidi. 'And we asked for only two. Honey, you're going to make me the happiest man alive.' He opened the rear door and began to empty the contents of the crate on to the road. A few of the bottles just bounced harmlessly on ridges of hard-packed snow, but the speed of the bus was now such that most of them shattered on impact.

The first of the two leading pursuit cars was within three hundred yards of the bus when it ran into the area of broken glass. From Schaffer's point of view it was impossible to tell what exactly happened, but such indications as could be gathered by long-range sight and sound were satisfying enough. The headlights of the leading car suddenly began to slew violently from side to side, the screeching of brakes was clearly audible above the sound of the post-bus's diesel, but not nearly as loud as the rending crash of metal as the second car smashed into the rear of the first. For a few seconds both cars seemed locked together, then they skidded wildly out of control, coming to rest with the nose of the first car in the right hand ditch, the tail of the second in the left hand ditch. The headlamps of both cars had failed just after the moment of impact but there was more than sufficient illumination from the lamps of the first of the trucks coming up behind them to show that the road was completely blocked.

'Neat,' Schaffer said admiringly. 'Very neat, Schaffer.' He called to Smith: 'That'll hold them, boss.'

'Sure, it'll hold them,' Smith said grimly. 'It'll hold them for all of a minute. You can't burst heavy truck tyres that way and it won't take them long to bull-doze those cars out of the way. Heidi?'

Heidi walked forward, shivering in the icy gale blowing through both the shattered front and side windows. 'Yes, Major?'

'How far to the turn off?'

'A mile.'

'And to the wooden bridge – what do you call it, Zur Alten Brücke?'

'Another mile.'

'Three minutes. At the most, that.' He raised his voice. 'Three minutes, Lieutenant. Can you do it?'

'I can do it.' Schaffer was already lashing together packages of plastic explosives. He used transparent adhesive tape, leaving long streamers dangling from the bound packages. He had just secured the last package in position when he lurched heavily as the post-bus, now clear of the Blau See and running through a pine forest, swung abruptly to the left on to a side road.

'Sorry,' Smith called. 'Almost missed that one. Less than a mile, Lieutenant.'

'No panic,' Schaffer said cheerfully. He fished out a knife to start cutting the fuses to their shortest possible length, then went very still indeed as he glanced through where the rear windows had once been. In the middle distance were the vertically wavering beams of powerful headlights, closing rapidly. The cheerfulness left Schaffer's voice. 'Well, maybe there is a little bit panic, at that. I've got bad news, boss.'

'And I have a rear mirror. How far, Heidi?'

'Next corner.'

While Schaffer worked quickly on the fuses, Smith concentrated on getting the post-bus round the next corner as quickly as possible without leaving the road. And then they were on and round the corner and the bridge was no more than a hundred yards away.

It was not, Smith thought, a bridge he would have chosen to have crossed with a bicycle, much less a six ton bus. Had it been a bridge crossing some gently meandering stream, then, yes, possibly: but not a bridge such as this one was, a fifty-foot bridge surfaced with untied railway sleepers, spanning a ravine two hundred feet in depth and supported by trestles, very ancient wooden trestles which, from what little he could see of them from his acute angle of approach, he wouldn't have trusted to support the tables at the vicar's garden party.

Smith hit this elderly and decrepit edifice at forty miles per hour. A more cautious and understandable approach might have been to crawl over it at less than walking pace but Smith's conviction that the less time he spent on each ancient sleeper the better was as instantaneous as it was complete. The heavy snow chains on each tyre bit into and dislodged each successive sleeper with a terrifying rumble, the post-bus bounced up and down as if on a giant cake-walk while the entire structure of the bridge swayed from side to side like the bridge of a destroyer at speed in a heavy cross-sea. It had been Smith's original intention to stop in the middle of the bridge but once embarked upon the crossing he would no more have done so than dallied to pick up an edelweiss in the path of an Alpine avalanche. Ten feet from the edge of the bridge he stamped on the brakes and skidded to a sliding halt, on solid ground again, in less than twenty yards.

Schaffer had already the back door open and the two packages of plastic explosives in his hands before the bus stopped. Five seconds after hitting the road he was back on the bridge again, skipping nimbly over a dozen dislodged sleepers until he had arrived at the main supports of the central trestle. It took him less than twenty seconds to tape one package to the right hand support, cross the bridge and tape the second package to the left hand support. He heard the deepening roar of a rapidly approaching engine, glanced up, saw the swathe of unseen head-lamp beams shining round the corner they had just passed, tore off the ignition fuse, crossed the bridge, tore off the other and raced for the bus. Smith had already the bus in gear and was moving away when Schaffer flung himself through the back doorway and was hauled inside by helping hands.

Schaffer twisted round till he was sitting on the passage-way, his legs dangling through the open doorway, just in time to see the headlamps of the pursuing car sweep into sight round the corner. It was now less than a hundred yards from the bridge, and accelerating. For a brief, almost panic-stricken, moment, Schaffer wondered wildly if he had cut the fuses short enough, he hadn't realized the following car had been quite as close as it was: and from the tense and strained expressions on the faces of the two girls and the man beside him, expressions sensed rather than seen, he knew that exactly the same thought was in their minds.

The two loud, flat detonations, each fractionally preceded by the brilliant white flash characteristic of the plastic explosive, came within one second of each other. Baulks of timber and railway sleepers were hurled forty feet into the air, spinning lazily around in a curious kind of slow motion, many of them falling back again on to the now tottering support structure with an impact sufficient to carry away the central trestle. One moment, a bridge: the next, an empty ravine with, on the far side of it, the wildly swinging headlamp beams as the driver flung his car from side to side in a nothing-to-be-lost attempt to prevent the car from sliding over the edge of the ravine. It seemed certain that he must fail until the moment when the car, sliding broadside on along the road, struck a large rock, rolled over twice and came to a halt less than six feet from the edge of the ravine.

Schaffer shook his head in wonder, rose, closed the rear door, sat in the back seat, lit a cigarette, tossed the spent match through the smashed rear window and observed: 'You're a lucky lot to have me around.'

'All this and modesty too,' Heidi said admiringly.

'A rare combination,' Schaffer acknowledged. 'You'll find lots of other pleasant surprises in store for you as we grow old together. How far to this airfield now?'

'Five miles. Perhaps eight minutes. But this is the only road in. With the bridge gone, there's no hurry now.'

'That's as maybe. Schaffer is anxious to be gone. Tell me, honey, were *all* those beer bottles empty?'

'The ones we threw away were.'

'I just simply don't deserve you,' Schaffer said reverently.

'We're thinking along the same lines at last,' Heidi said acidly.

Schaffer grinned, took two beer bottles and went forward to relieve Smith, who moved out only too willingly with the bus still in motion. Smith's right hand, Schaffer saw, hadn't a scrap of bandage left that wasn't wholly saturated in blood and the face was very pale. But he made no comment.

Three minutes later they were out of the forest, running along through open farm-land, and five minutes after that, acting on Heidi's directions, Schaffer swung the bus through a narrow gateway on the left hand side of the road. The headlamps successively illuminated two small hangars, a narrow, cleared runway stretching into the distance and, finally, a bullet-riddled Mosquito bomber with a crumpled under-carriage.

'Ain't that a beautiful sight, now?' Schaffer nodded at the damaged plane. 'Carnaby-Jones's transport?'

Smith nodded. 'It began with a Mosquito and it will end – we hope – in a Mosquito. This is Oberhausen airfield HQ of the Bavarian Mountain Rescue pilots.'

'Three cheers for the Bavarian Mountain Rescue pilots.' Schaffer stopped the bus facing up the length of the runway, switched off the lights and turned off the engine. They sat silently in the darkness, waiting.

Colonel Wyatt-Turner glanced through the side-screen and breathed with relief as, for the first time that night, the ground fell away sharply beneath the Mosquito. He said sarcastically: 'Losing your nerve, Wing Commander?'

'I lost that September 3rd, 1939,' Carpenter said cheerfully.

'Got to climb. Can't expect to see any recognition signals down among the bushes there.'

'You're sure we're on the right course?'

'No question. That's the Weissspitze there. Three minutes' flying time.' Carpenter paused and went on thoughtfully. 'Looks uncommon like Guy Fawkes night up there, don't you think.'

The Wing Commander was hardly exaggerating. In the far distance the silhouette of the Weissspitze was but dimly seen, but there was no mistaking the intensity of the great fire blazing half-way up the mountain-side. Occasionally, great gouts of red flame and what looked like gigantic fireworks could be seen soaring high above the main body of the fire.

'Explosives or boxes of ammunition going up, I'd say,' Carpenter said pensively. 'That's the Schloss Adler, of course. Were any of your boys carrying matches?'

'They must have been.' Wyatt-Turner stared impassively at the distant blaze. 'It's quite a sight.'

'It's all of that,' Carpenter agreed. He touched Wyatt-Turner's arm and pointed forwards and down. 'But there's a sight that's finer far, the most beautiful sight I've ever seen.'

Wyatt-Turner followed the pointing finger. Less than two miles away, about five hundred feet below, a pair of headlamps were flashing regularly on and off, once every two seconds. With a conscious effort of will he looked away and glanced briefly at Carpenter, but almost at once was back on the flashing head-lamps. He stared at them hypnotically and shook his head in slow and total disbelief.

Schaffer had the headlights switched on main beam, illuminating the runway, and the post-bus engine running as the black squat shape of the Mosquito, air-brakes fully extended, lined up for its approach to the runway, and had the bus itself moving, accelerating quickly through the gears, as the Mosquito sank down over the top of the bus and settled down beautifully without the slightest suspicion of a bounce.

Within a minute Schaffer brought the bus to a skidding halt only yards from the now stationary plane. Half a minute later, with all five of them safely inside the plane, Carpenter had the Mosquito turned through 180° and was standing hard on the brakes as he brought the engines up to maximum revolutions. And then they were on their way, gathering speed so rapidly that they were air-borne two hundred yards before the end of the runway. For the first mile of their climb Carpenter kept the plane heading almost directly towards the blazing castle that now redly illuminated the entire valley, then the funeral pyre of the Schloss Adler vanished for the last time as the Mosquito banked and headed for the north-west and home.

—— I 2 ——

Wing Commander Carpenter took the Mosquito up to five thousand feet and kept it there. The time for dodging around among the bushes was past for, on the outward journey, Carpenter had been concerned only that no German station pick him up long enough to form even a rough guess as to where he was going. But now he didn't care if every radar station in the country knew where he was going: he was going home to England, mission accomplished, and there wasn't a warplane in Europe that could catch him. Wing Commander Carpenter pulled luxuriously at his evil-smelling briar. He was well content.

His five newly-acquired passengers were, perhaps, a fraction less content. They lacked Carpenter's well-upholstered pilot's seat. The interior of the Mosquito made no concessions whatsoever to passenger comfort. It was bleak, icy, cramped – it didn't require much space to carry a 4000 lb. bomb load, the Mosquito's maximum – and totally devoid of seating in any form. The three men and the two girls squatted uncomfortably on thin palliasses, the expressions on their faces pretty accurately reflecting their acute discomfort. Colonel Wyatt-Turner, still holding across his knees the Sten gun he'd had at the ready in case any trouble had developed on the ground or the flashing lights of the truck had been a German ruse, was sitting sideways in the co-pilot's seat so that he could see and talk to the pilot and the passengers at the same time. He had accepted without question or apparent interest Smith's brief explanation of the two girls' presence as being necessary to escape Gestapo vengeance. Colonel Wyatt-Turner had other and weightier matters on his mind.

Smith looked up from the bleeding mangled hand that Mary was re-bandaging with the plane's first aid kit and said to the Colonel: 'It was good of you to come in person to meet us, sir.'

'It wasn't good of me at all,' Wyatt-Turner said frankly. 'I'd have gone mad if I'd stayed another minute in London – I *had* to know. It was I who sent you all out here.' He sat without speaking for some time, then went on heavily: 'Torrance-Smythe gone, Sergeant Harrod, and now, you say, Carraciola, Christiansen and Thomas. All dead. A heavy price, Smith, a terrible price. My best men.'

'All of them, sir?' Smith asked softly.

'I'm getting old.' Wyatt-Turner shook his head wearily and drew a hand across his eyes. 'Did you find out who—'

'Carraciola.'

'Carraciola! Ted Carraciola? Never! I can't believe it.'

'*And* Christiansen.' Smith's voice was still quiet, still even. '*And* Thomas.'

'And Christiansen? And Thomas?' He looked consideringly at Smith. 'You've been through a lot, Major Smith. You're not well.'

'I'm not as well as I was,' Smith admitted. 'But I was well enough when I killed them?'

'You – *you* killed them?'

'I've killed a traitor before now. You know that.'

'But – but traitors! All three of them. Impossible. I can't believe it! I *won't* believe it!'

'Then maybe you'll believe this, sir.' Smith produced one of the note-books from his tunic and handed it to Wyatt-Turner. 'The names and addresses or contacts of every German agent in southern England *and* the names of all British agents in north-west Europe who have been supplanted by German agents. You will recognise Carraciola's writing. He wrote this under duress.'

Slowly, like a man in a dream, Wyatt-Turner reached out and took the note-book. For three minutes he examined the contents, leafing slowly, almost reluctantly through the pages, then finally laid the book down with a sigh.

'This is the most important document in Europe, the most important document I have even seen.' Wyatt-Turner sighed. 'The nation is deeply in your debt, Major Smith.'

'Thank you, sir.'

'Or would have been. It's a great pity it will never have the chance to express its gratitude.' He lifted the Sten from his knees and pointed it at Smith's heart. 'You will do nothing foolish, will you, Major Smith?'

'What in God's name—' Carpenter twisted in his seat and stared at Wyatt-Turner in startled and total disbelief.

'Concentrate on your flying, my dear Wing Commander.' Wyatt-Turner waved the Sten gently in Carpenter's direction. 'Your course will do for the present. We'll be landing at Lille airport within the hour.'

'The guy's gone nuts!' Schaffer's voice was a shocked whisper.

'If he has,' Smith said drily, 'he went nuts some years ago. Ladies and gentlemen, I give you the most dangerous spy in Europe, the most successful double agent of all time.' He paused for reaction, but the silence remained unbroken: the enormity of the revelation of Wyatt-Turner's duplicity was too great for immediate comprehension. Smith continued: 'Colonel Wyatt-Turner, you will be court-martialled this afternoon, sentenced, removed to the Tower then taken out, blind-folded and shot at eight o'clock tomorrow morning.'

'You knew?' Wyatt-Turner's affable self-confidence had completely deserted him and his voice, low and strained, was barely distinguishable above the clamour of the engines. 'You knew about me?'

'I knew about you,' Smith nodded. 'But we all knew about you, didn't we, Colonel? Three years, you claimed, behind the German lines, served with the Wehrmacht and finally penetrated the Berlin High Command. Sure you did. With the help of the Wehrmacht and the High Command. But when the tide of war turned and you could no longer feed the Allies with false and misleading reports about proposed German advances, then you were allowed to escape back to England to feed the Germans true and accurate reports about Allied plans – *and* give them all the information they required to round up British agents in north-west Europe. How many million francs do you have in your numbered account in Zurich, Colonel?'

Wing Commander Carpenter stared straight ahead through the windscreen and said very slowly: 'Frankly, old chap, this is preposterous.'

'Try batting an eyelid and see just how preposterous that Sten gun is,' Smith suggested. He looked at Wyatt-Turner again. 'You underestimated Admiral Rolland, I'm afraid. He's had his suspicions about you and the four section leaders of Department C for months. But he was wrong about Torrance-Smythe.'

'Guess away.' Wyatt-Turner had recovered his composure and most of his self-confidence. 'It'll pass the time till we get to Lille.'

'Unfortunately for you, there is no guess-work. Admiral Rol-

land recalled me – and Mary – from Italy: he could no longer
be sure of anyone in London. You know how corruption
spreads? Played it very clever, did the Admiral. He told you he
had his suspicions about one of his section leaders, but didn't
know which. So, when General Carnaby crashed, he put up to
you the idea of sending the section officers to the rescue – and
made damn sure that you never once had the opportunity of
talking to any of them in private before they took off.'

'That – that was why I was called in?' Schaffer looked as if
he had been sand-bagged. 'Because you couldn't trust—'

'For all we knew, MI6 was riddled . . . Well, Colonel, you
weren't too happy until Rolland asked *you* to pick the leader.
So you picked me. Rolland knew you would. You'd only just
met me for the first time, but you knew from Kesselring's
military intelligence chief, through your pal Admiral Canaris,
that I was their top double agent. Or thought you did. Rolland
was the only man on either side who knew I wasn't. For you, I
was the ideal choice. Rolland made certain that you didn't have
the chance of talking to *me* either, but you weren't worried.
You knew that I would know what to do.' Smith smiled bleakly.
'I'm happy to say I did. It must have been quite a shock to your
system this afternoon when he told you what I really was.'

'You knew that? You knew all that?' Wyatt-Turner's new-
found composure had vanished, his voice was quiet and vicious.
He lifted the Sten slightly. 'What goes on, Smith?'

'All pre-arranged to force your hand. We had everything –
except proof – about you. I got that proof this evening. Colonel
Kramer *knew* that we were coming, *knew* we were after General
Carnaby.' He nodded towards Jones. 'Incidentally meet Cartwright Jones, an American actor.'

'What?' Wyatt-Turner forced out the word as if a pair of
powerful hands were squeezing on his wind-pipe.

'General Carnaby is spending a quiet weekend at the Admiral's country house in Wiltshire. As a stand-in, Mr Jones was
quite admirable. He had them all as deceived as that faked
plane crash – you will have realized by now that it was a deliberate crash-landing.' Wyatt-Turner tried to speak, but the
words failed to come: his mouth was working and the colour
had drained from his ruddy face. 'And why did Kramer know?
He knew because you had informed Berlin as soon as Rolland
had put the plan to you. *Nobody else had the chance to. And*
he knew that we would be in "Zum Wilden Hirsch" this even-

ing. He knew because I told you on the radio broadcast this morning and you lost no time in passing the good word on.'

'Are you sure?' Heidi asked. 'Couldn't the informant have been whichever of the men – Carraciola or Christiansen or Thomas – who killed Torrance-Smythe. There's a phone box just outside the inn.'

'I know. No, he didn't have time. I left the inn for exactly seven minutes. Three minutes after I'd left, Torrance-Smythe did the same – to follow one of the three others he'd just seen leaving. Smithy was clever and he knew something was far wrong. He—'

'*How* did he know?' Schaffer demanded.

'We'll never be sure. I think we'll find that he was a highly-skilled lip-reader. Anyway, he caught the man he'd seen leaving in the phone booth outside the Post Office – before he'd had time to get through to either Weissner or Kramer. There was a fight to the death. By the time the killer had dragged Smithy around to the back and returned to the booth, someone else was occupying it. I saw him. So the killer had to go back into the inn. Kramer it was who told Weissner – and the Colonel here who told Kramer.'

'Very interesting.' There was a sneer in Wyatt-Turner's voice, but a sneer belied by the deep unease in his face. 'Fascinating, in fact. Quite finished, Major Smith?'

'Finished.' Smith sighed. 'You just had to come to meet us, hadn't you, Colonel? This was the last door to life left open to you. In my final broadcast I told the Admiral "I have it all". He told you what that meant – all the names, all the addresses. We could never have got at you through Carraciola, Christiansen or Thomas – they were too close to you in MI6, you were too cagey and they never knew who they were working for. You used intermediaries – and all their names are in that book. You *knew* they'd put the finger on you – when it's a choice between taking a walk to the gallows and talking – well, it's not much of a choice, is it?'

Wyatt-Turner didn't answer. He turned to Carpenter and said: 'Lay off a course for Lille airport.'

'Don't bother,' Smith said.

Wyatt-Turner lined his Sten on Smith. 'Give me one good reason why I shouldn't shoot you now.'

'I can do that,' Smith nodded. 'Why do you think that Admiral Rolland accompanied you to the airport. He never has before.'

'Go on.' Wyatt's voice was hard, abrupt, but his eyes were sick, sick with the sudden certainty of defeat and death.

'To make quite certain that you took that Sten and only that Sten with you. Tell me, can you see two parallel scores where the stock meets the barrel?'

Wyatt-Turner stared at him for a long moment then glanced down quickly at the Sten. There were two unmistakable parallel scratches exactly where Smith had said they would be. Wyatt-Turner looked up again, his face contorted, desperation replacing the sickness in his eyes.

'That's right,' Smith said. 'I personally filed off the firing pin exactly thirty-six hours ago.' With his left hand Smith reached awkwardly under his tunic flap and brought out his silenced Luger. Wyatt-Turner, with his Sten lined up on Smith's head and the muzzle less than three feet from Smith's face, squeezed the trigger time and again, and each convulsive contraction of his forefinger was rewarded by a dry and empty click. With a stunned almost uncomprehending expression on his face, Wyatt-Turner slowly lowered the Sten to the floor, then quickly whirled in his seat, jerked open the door and threw the notebook out into the night. He turned and smiled bleakly at Smith.

'The most important document in Europe, I believe I called it.'

'So you did.' Smith handed his gun to Schaffer, reached under his tunic and brought out two more books. 'Duplicates.'

'Duplicates!' The smile slowly faded from the heavily-jowled face, leaving it frozen in defeat. 'Duplicates,' he whispered. He looked slowly around them all and then finally back at Smith, who had retrieved his gun from Schaffer. He said: 'Are you going to shoot me?'

'No.'

Wyatt-Turner nodded, slid back the door to its widest extent and said: 'Can you really see me in the Tower?' He stepped forward into the doorway.

'No.' Smith shook his head. 'No, I can't see that.'

'Mind the step,' said Schaffer. His voice was cold and empty, his face was carved from stone.

'Well, now, time to make a call.' Smith slid shut the door, scrambled painfully into the co-pilot's seat and looked at Mary. 'The Admiral must be getting worried by this time.'

'Time to make a call,' Mary repeated mechanically. She stared

at him as if seeing a ghost. 'How can you sit there – just after
– how can you be so *calm*?'

'Because it's no shock to me, silly. I *knew* he was going to die.'

'You knew – of course, of course,' she murmured.

'Now then,' Smith went on, deliberately brisk-voiced as he
took her hand. 'You realize what this means, don't you?'

'Do I realize what what means?' She was still ashen-faced.

'You and I are all washed up,' Smith explained patiently.
'Finished. In Italy, in north-west Europe. I won't even be
allowed to fight as a soldier because if I were captured I'd still
be shot as a spy.'

'So?'

'So, for us, the war is over. For the first time we can think
of ourselves. OK?' He squeezed her hand and she smiled shakily
in reply. 'OK. Wing Commander, may I use your radio?'

'So that's the way he went.' Admiral Rolland, telephone in hand
and standing by the big transceiver in his London Operations
HQ, looked old and very very tired. 'Maybe it's all for the best,
Smith. And you have all the information you want?'

Smith's voice crackled over the earphone. 'Everything, sir.'

'Magnificent, magnificent! I have all the police forces in the
country alerted. As soon as we get that book . . . There's a car
waiting for you at the airport. See you in an hour.'

'Yes, sir. There's one thing, sir, a small thing. I want to get
married this morning.'

'You what?' Grey bushy eyebrows lifted towards the mane
of white hair.

'I want to get married,' Smith explained slowly and patiently.
'To Miss Mary Ellison.'

'But you can't,' Rolland protested. 'This morning! Impossible! There are such things as banns, permits, the registrar's
office will be shut today—'

'After all I've done for you,' Smith interrupted reproachfully.

'Blackmail, sir! You play on an old man's gratitude. Downright blackmail!' Rolland banged down the phone, smiled
tiredly and picked up another phone. 'Operator? Put me
through to the Forgery Section.'

Wing Commander Carpenter, his pipe well alight and by his
elbow a cup of coffee newly poured from a vacuum flask, was
his old imperturbable self again. Smith talked quietly to Mary
while Jones had his eyes closed and appeared to be asleep.

Farther aft in the fuselage, Schaffer had his arm around Heidi, who was making no attempt to fight him off.

'Right,' Schaffer said. 'So we go to this pub tonight, see—'

'You said the Savoy Grill,' Heidi reminded him.

'A rose by any other name . . . So we go to this pub, and we'll have paté, smoked trout, sirloin of Aberdeen-Angus—'

'Aberdeen-Angus!' Heidi looked at him in amusement. 'Forgotten the war, haven't you? Forgotten rationing? More like a sirloin of horse meat.'

'Honey.' Schaffer took her hands and spoke severely and earnestly. 'Honey, don't ever again mention that word to me. I'm allergic to horses.'

'You eat them?' Heidi gazed at him in astonishment. 'In Montana?'

'I fall off them,' Schaffer said moodily. 'Everywhere.'

Force Ten from Navarone

ALISTAIR MacLEAN

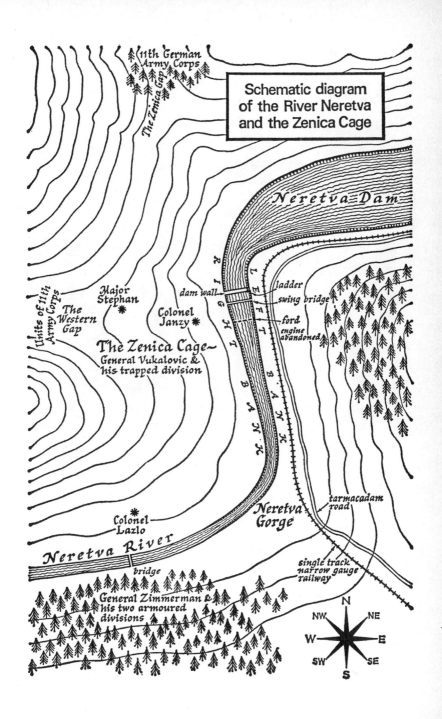

Schematic diagram
of the River Neretva
and the Zenica Cage

I

PRELUDE: THURSDAY

0000–0600

Commander Vincent Ryan, RN, Captain (Destroyers) and commanding officer of His Majesty's latest S-class destroyer *Sirdar,* leaned his elbows comfortably on the coaming of his bridge, brought up his night-glasses and gazed out thoughtfully over the calm and silvered waters of the moonlit Aegean.

He looked first of all due north, straight out over the huge and smoothly sculpted and whitely phosphorescent bow-wave thrown up by the knife-edged forefoot of his racing destroyer: four miles away, no more, framed in its backdrop of indigo sky and diamantine stars, lay the brooding mass of a darkly cliff-girt island: the island of Kheros, for months the remote and beleaguered outpost of two thousand British troops who had expected to die that night, and who would now not die.

Ryan swung his glasses through 180° and nodded approvingly. This was what he liked to see. The four destroyers to the south were in such perfect line astern that the hull of the leading vessel, a gleaming bone in its teeth, completely obscured the hulls of the three ships behind. Ryan turned his binoculars to the east.

It was odd, he thought inconsequentially, how unimpressive, even how disappointing, the aftermath of either natural or man-made disaster could be. Were it not for that dull red glow and wisping smoke that emanated from the upper part of the cliff and lent the scene a vaguely Dantean aura of primeval menace and foreboding, the precipitous far wall of the harbour looked as it might have done in the times of Homer. That great ledge of rock that looked from that distance so smooth and regular and somehow inevitable could have been carved out by the wind and weather of a hundred million years: it could equally well have been cut away fifty centuries ago by the masons of Ancient Greece seeking marble for the building of their Ionian temples: what was almost inconceivable, what almost passed rational comprehension, was the fact that ten minutes ago that ledge had not been there at all, that there had been in its place tens of thousands of tons of rock, the most impregnable German fortress in the Aegean and, above all, the two great guns of Navarone, now all buried for ever three hundred feet under the sea. With a slow shake of his head Commander Ryan lowered his binoculars and turned to look at the men responsible for achieving more in five minutes than nature could have done in five million years.

Captain Mallory and Corporal Miller. That was all he knew of them, that and the fact that they had been sent on this mission by an old friend of his, a naval captain by the name of Jensen who, he had learnt only twenty-four hours previously – and that to his total astonishment – was the Head of Allied Intelligence in the Mediterranean. But that was all he knew of them and maybe he didn't even know that. Maybe their names weren't Mallory and Miller. Maybe they weren't even a captain and a corporal. They didn't look like any captain or corporal he'd ever seen. Come to that, they didn't look like any soldiers he'd ever seen. Clad in salt-water- and blood-stained German uniforms, filthy, unshaven, quiet and watchful and remote, they belonged to no category of men he'd ever encountered: all he could be certain of as he gazed at the blurred and blood-shot sunken eyes, the gaunt and trenched and stubbled-grey faces of two men no longer young, was that he had never before seen human beings so far gone in total exhaustion.

'Well, that seems to be about it,' Ryan said. 'The troops on Kheros waiting to be taken off, our flotilla going north to take them off and the guns of Navarone no longer in any position to do anything about our flotilla. Satisfied, Captain Mallory?'

'That was the object of the exercise,' Mallory agreed.

Ryan lifted his glasses again. This time, almost at the range of night vision, he focused on a rubber dinghy closing in on the rocky shore-line to the west of Navarone harbour. The two figures seated in the dinghy were just discernible, no more. Ryan lowered his glasses and said thoughtfully:

'Your big friend – and the lady with him – doesn't believe in hanging about. You didn't – ah – introduce me to them, Captain Mallory.'

'I didn't get the chance to. Maria and Andrea. Andrea's a colonel in the Greek army: 19th Motorized Division.'

'Andrea *was* a colonel in the Greek army,' Miller said. 'I think he's just retired.'

'I rather think he has. They were in a hurry, Commander, because they're both patriotic Greeks, they're both islanders and there is much for both to do in Navarone. Besides, I understand they have some urgent and very personal matters to attend to.'

'I see.' Ryan didn't press the matter, instead he looked out again over the smoking remains of the shattered fortress. 'Well, that seems to be that. Finished for the evening, gentlemen?'

Mallory smiled faintly. 'I think so.'

'Then I would suggest some sleep.'

'What a wonderful word that is.' Miller pushed himself wearily off the side of the bridge and stood there swaying as he drew an exhausted forearm over blood-shot, aching eyes. 'Wake me up in Alexandria.'

'Alexandria?' Ryan looked at him in amusement. 'We won't be there for thirty hours yet.'

'That's what I meant,' Miller said.

Miller didn't get his thirty hours. He had, in fact, been asleep for just over thirty minutes when he was wakened by the slow realization that something was hurting his eyes: after he had moaned and feebly protested for some time he managed to get one eye open and saw that that something was a bright overhead light let into the deck-head of the cabin that had been provided for Mallory and himself. Miller propped himself up on a groggy elbow, managed to get his second eye into commission and looked without enthusiasm at the other two occupants of the cabin: Mallory was seated by a table, apparently transcribing some kind of message, while Commander Ryan stood in the open doorway.

'This is outrageous,' Miller said bitterly. 'I haven't closed an eye all night.'

'You've been asleep for thirty-five minutes,' Ryan said. 'Sorry. But Cairo said this message for Captain Mallory was of the greatest urgency.'

'It is, is it?' Miller said suspiciously. He brightened. 'It's probably about promotions and medals and leave and so forth.' He looked hopefully at Mallory, who had just straightened after decoding the message. 'Is it?'

'Well, no. It starts off promisingly enough, mind you, warmest congratulations and what-have-you, but after that the tone of the message deteriorates a bit.'

Mallory re-read the message: SIGNAL RECEIVED WARMEST CONGRATULATIONS MAGNIFICENT ACHIEVEMENT. YOU BLOODY FOOLS WHY YOU LET ANDREA GET AWAY? ESSENTIAL CONTACT HIM IMMEDIATELY. WILL EVACUATE BEFORE DAWN UNDER DIVERSIONARY

AIR ATTACK AIR STRIP ONE MILE SOUTH-EAST MANDRAKOS. SEND CE VIA SIRDAR. URGENT 3 REPEAT URGENT 3. BEST LUCK. JENSEN.

Miller took the message from Mallory's outstretched hand, moved the paper to and fro until he had brought his bleary eyes into focus, read the message in horrified silence, handed it back to Mallory and stretched out his full length on his bunk. He said, 'Oh, my God!' and relapsed into what appeared to be a state of shock.

'That about sums it up,' Mallory agreed. He shook his head wearily and turned to Ryan. 'I'm sorry, sir, but we must trouble you for three things. A rubber dinghy, a portable radio transmitter and an immediate return to Navarone. Please arrange to have the radio lined up on a pre-set ferquency to be constantly monitored by your WT room. When you receive a CE signal, transmit it to Cairo.'

'CE?' Ryan asked.

'Uh-huh. Just that.'

'And that's all?'

'We could do with a bottle of brandy,' Miller said. 'Something – anything – to see us through the rigours of the long night that lies ahead.'

Ryan lifted an eyebrow. 'A bottle of five-star, no doubt, Corporal?'

'Would you,' Miller asked morosely, 'give a bottle of three-star to a man going to his death?'

As it happened, Miller's gloomy expectations of an early demise turned out to be baseless – for that night, at least. Even the expected fearful rigours of the long night ahead proved to be no more than minor physical inconveniences.

By the time the *Sirdar* had brought them back to Navarone and as close in to the rocky shores as was prudent, the sky had become darkly overcast, rain was falling and a swell was beginning to blow up from the south-west so that it was little wonder to either Mallory or Miller that by the time they had paddled their dinghy within striking distance of the shore, they were in a very damp and miserable condition indeed: and it was even less wonder that by the time they had reached the boulder-strewn beach itself, they were soaked to the skin, for a breaking wave flung their dinghy against a sloping shelf of rock, overturning their rubber craft and precipitating them both into the sea. But this was of little enough account in itself: their Schmeisser machine-pistols, their radio, their torches were securely wrapped in waterproof bags and all of those were safely salvaged. All in all, Mallory reflected, an almost perfect three-point landing compared to the last time they had come to Navarone by boat, when their Greek caique, caught in the teeth of a giant storm, had been battered to pieces against the jaggedly vertical – and supposedly unclimbable – South Cliff of Navarone.

Slipping, stumbling and with suitably sulphuric comments, they made their way over the wet shingle and massively rounded boulders until their way was barred by a steeply-angled slope that soared up into the near-darkness above. Mallory unwrapped a pencil torch and began to quarter the face of the slope with its narrow, concentrated beam. Miller touched him on the arm.

'Taking a bit of a chance, aren't we? With that thing, I mean?'

'No chance,' Mallory said. 'There won't be a soldier left on guard on the coasts tonight. They'll all be fighting the fires in the town. Besides, who is left for them to guard against? We are the birds and the birds, duty done, have flown. Only a madman would come back to the island again.'

'I know what we are,' Miller said with feeling. 'You don't have to tell me.'

Mallory smiled to himself in the darkness and continued his search. Within a minute he had located what he had been hoping to find – an angled gully in the slope. He and Miller scrambled up the shale- and rock-strewn bed of the gully as fast as the treacherous footing and their encumbrances would permit: within fifteen minutes they had reached the plateau above and paused to take their breath. Miller reached inside the depths of his tunic, a discreet movement that was at once followed by a discreet gurgling.

'What are you doing?' Mallory enquired.

'I thought I heard my teeth chattering. What's all this "urgent 3 repeat urgent 3" business in the message, then?'

'I've never seen it before. But I know what it means. Some people, somewhere, are about to die.'

'I'll tell you two for a start. And what if Andrea won't come? He's not a member of our armed forces. He doesn't have to come. *And* he said he was getting married right away.'

Mallory said with certainty: 'He'll come.'

'What makes you so sure?'

'Because Andrea is the one completely responsible man I've ever met. He has two great responsibilities – one to others, one to himself. That's why he came back to Navarone – because he knew the people needed him. And that's why he'll leave Navarone when he sees this "urgent 3" signal, because he'll know that someone, in some other place, needs him even more.'

Miller retrieved the brandy bottle from Mallory and thrust it securely inside his tunic again. 'Well, I can tell you this. The future Mrs Andrea Stavros isn't going to be very happy about it.'

'Neither is Andrea Stavros and I'm not looking forward to telling him,' Mallory said candidly. He peered at his luminous watch and swung to his feet. 'Mandrakos in half an hour.'

In precisely thirty minutes, their Schmeissers removed from their waterproof bags and now shoulder-slung at hip level, Mallory and Miller moved swiftly but very quietly from shadow to shadow through the plantations of carob trees on the outskirts of the village of Mandrakos. Suddenly, from directly ahead, they heard the unmistakable clink of glasses and bottlenecks.

For the two men a potentially dangerous situation such as this was so routine as not even to warrant a glance at each other. They dropped silently to their hands and knees and crawled forward, Miller sniffing the air appreciatively as they advanced: the Greek resinous spirit *ouzo* has an extraordinary ability to permeate the atmosphere for a considerable distance around it. Mallory and Miller reached the edge of a clump of bushes, sank prone and looked ahead.

From their richly-befrogged waistcoats, cummerbunds and fancy headgear, the two characters propped against the bole of a plane tree in the clearing ahead were obviously men of the island: from the rifles across their knees, their role appeared to be that of guards of some kind: from the almost vertical angle at which they had to tip the *ouzo* bottle to get at what little was left of its contents, it was equally apparent that they weren't taking their duties too seriously, nor had been for some considerable time past.

Mallory and Miller withdrew somewhat less stealthily than they had advanced, rose and glanced at each other. Suitable comment seemed lacking. Mallory shrugged and moved on, circling around to his right. Twice more, as they moved swiftly into the centre of Mandrakos, flitting from the shadow of carob grove to carob grove, from the shadow of plane tree to plane tree, from the shadow of house to house, they came upon but easily avoided other ostensible sentries, all busy interpreting their duties in a very liberal fashion. Miller pulled Mallory into a doorway.

'Our friends back there,' he said, 'What were they celebrating?'

'Wouldn't you? Celebrate, I mean. Navarone is useless to the Germans now. A week from now and they'll all be gone.'

'All right. So why are they keeping a watch?' Miller nodded to a small, whitewashed Greek Orthodox church standing in the centre of the village square. From inside came a far from subdued murmur of voices. Also from inside came a great deal of light escaping through very imperfectly blacked-out windows. 'Could it be anything to do with that?'

Mallory said: 'Well, there's one sure way to find out.'

They moved quietly on, taking advantage of all available cover and shadow until they came to a still deeper shadow caused by two flying buttresses supporting the wall of the ancient church. Between the buttresses was one of the few more successfully blacked-out windows with only a tiny chink of light showing along the bottom edge. Both men stooped and peered through the narrow aperture.

The church appeared even more ancient inside than on the outside. The high unpainted wooden benches, adze-cut oak from centuries long gone, had been blackened and smoothed by untold generations of church-goers, the wood itself cracked and splintered by the ravages of time: the whitewashed walls looked as if they required buttresses within as well as without, crumbling to an extinction that could not now be long delayed: the roof appeared to be in imminent danger of falling in at any moment.

The now even louder hum of sound came from islanders of almost every age and sex, many in ceremonial dress, who occupied nearly every available seat in the church: the light came from literally hundreds of guttering candles, many of them ancient and twisted and ornamented and evidently called out for this special occasion, that lined the walls, the central aisle and the altar: by the altar itself, a priest, a bearded patriarch in Greek Orthodox robes, waited impassively.

Mallory and Miller looked interrogatively at each other and were on the point of standing upright when a very deep and very quiet voice spoke behind them.

'Hands behind the necks,' it said pleasantly. 'And straighten very slowly. I have a Schmeisser machine-pistol in my hands.'

Slowly and carefully, just as the voice asked, Mallory and Miller did as they were told.

'Turn round. Carefully, now.'

So they turned round, carefully. Miller looked at the massive dark figure who indeed had, as he'd claimed, a machine-pistol in his hands, and said irritably: 'Do you mind? Point that damned thing somewhere else.'

The dark figure gave a startled exclamation, lowered the gun to his side and bent forward, the dark, craggy, lined face expressing no more than a passing flicker of surprise. Andrea Stavros didn't go in very much for registering unnecessary emotional displays and the recovery of his habitual composure was instantaneous.

'The German uniforms,' he explained apologetically. 'They had me fooled.'

'You could have fooled me, too,' Miller said. He looked incredulously at Andrea's clothes, at the unbelievably baggy black trousers, the black jackboots, the intricately ornamented black waistcoat and violently purple cummerbund, shuddered and closed his eyes in pain. 'Been visiting the Mandrakos pawnshop?'

'The ceremonial dress of my ancestors,' Andrea said mildly. 'You two fall overboard?'

'Not intentionally,' Mallory said. 'We came back to see you.'

'You could have chosen a more convenient time.' He hesitated, glanced at a small lighted building across the street and took their arms. 'We can talk in here.'

He ushered them in and closed the door behind him. The room was obviously, from its benches and Spartan furnishings, some sort of communal meeting-place, a village hall: illumination came from three rather smoky oil-lamps, the light from which was most hospitably reflected by the scores of bottles of spirit and wine and beer and glasses that took up almost every available inch of two long trestle tables. The haphazardly unaesthetic layout of the refreshments bespoke a very impromptu and hastily improvised preparation for a celebration: the serried rows of bottles heralded the intention of compensating for lack of quality by an excess of quantity.

Andrea crossed to the nearest table, picked up three glasses and a bottle of *ouzo*, and began to pour drinks. Miller fished out his brandy and offered it, but Andrea was too preoccupied to notice. He handed them the *ouzo* glasses.

'Health.' Andrea drained his glass and went on thoughtfully: 'You did not return without a good reason, my Keith.'

Silently, Mallory removed the Cairo radio message from its

waterproof oilskin wallet and handed it to Andrea, who took it half-unwillingly, then read it, scowling blackly.

He said: 'Urgent 3 means what I think it means?'

Again Mallory remained silent, merely nodding as he watched Andrea unwinkingly.

'This is most inconvenient for me.' The scowl deepened. '*Most* inconvenient. There are many things for me to do in Navarone. The people will miss me.'

'It's also inconvenient for me,' Miller said. 'There are many things *I* could profitably be doing in the West End of London. They miss me, too. Ask any barmaid. But that's hardly the point.'

Andrea regarded him for an impassive moment, then looked at Mallory. '*You* are saying nothing.'

'I've nothing to say.'

The scowl slowly left Andrea's face, though the brooding frown remained. He hesitated, then reached again for the bottle of *ouzo*. Miller shuddered delicately.

'Please.' He indicated the bottle of brandy.

Andrea smiled, briefly and for the first time, poured some of Miller's five-star into their glasses, re-read the message and handed it back to Mallory. 'I must think it over. I have some business to attend to first.'

Mallory looked at him thoughtfully. 'Business?'

'I have to attend a wedding.'

'A wedding?' Miller said politely.

'Must you two repeat everything I say? A wedding.'

'But who do *you* know?' Miller asked. 'And at this hour of night.'

'For some people in Navarone,' Andrea said drily, 'the night is the only safe time.' He turned abruptly, walked away, opened the door and hesitated.

Mallory said curiously: 'Who's getting married?'

Andrea made no reply. Instead he walked back to the nearest table, poured and drained a half-tumbler of the brandy, ran a hand through his thick dark hair, straightened his cummerbund, squared his shoulders and walked purposefully towards the door. Mallory and Miller stared after him, then at the door that closed behind him: then they stared at each other.

Some fifteen minutes later they were still staring at each other, this time with expressions which alternated between the merely bemused and slightly stunned.

They were seated in the back seat of the Greek Orthodox church – the only part of any pew in the entire church not now occupied by islanders. From where they sat, the altar was at least sixty feet away but as they were both tall men and sitting by the central aisle, they had a pretty fair view of what was going on up there.

There was, to be accurate, nothing going on up there any more. The ceremony was over. Gravely, the Orthodox priest bestowed his blessing and Andrea and Maria, the girl who had shown them the way into the fortress of Navarone, turned with the slow dignity becoming the occasion, and walked down the aisle. Andrea bent over, tenderness and solicitousness both in expression and manner, and whispered something in her ear, but his words, it would have seemed, bore little relation to the way in which they were expressed for half-way down the aisle a furious altercation broke out between them. Between, perhaps, is not the right word: it was less an altercation than a very one-sided monologue. Maria, her face flushed and dark eyes flashing, gesticulating and clearly mad through, was addressing Andrea in far from low tones of not even barely-controlled fury: Andrea, for his part, was deprecatory, placatory, trying to hush her up with about the same amount of success as Canute had in holding back the tide, and looking apprehensively around. The reaction of the seated guests varied from disbelief through open-mouthed astonishment and bafflement to downright horror: clearly all regarded the spectacle as a highly unusual aftermath to a wedding ceremony.

As the couple approached the end of the aisle opposite the pew where Mallory and Miller were seated, the argument, if such it could be called, raged more furiously than ever. As they passed by the end pew, Andrea, hand over his mouth, leaned over towards Mallory.

'This,' he said, *sotto voce*, 'is our first married quarrel.'

He was given time to say no more. An imperative hand seized his arm and almost literally dragged him through the church doorway. Even after they had disappeared from sight, Maria's voice, loud and clear, could still be heard by everyone within the church. Miller turned from surveying the empty doorway and looked thoughtfully at Mallory.

'Very high-spirited girl, that. I wish I understood Greek. What was she saying there?'

Mallory kept his face carefully expressionless. 'What about my honeymoon?'

'Ah!' Miller's face was equally dead-pan. 'Don't you think we'd better follow them?'

'Why?'

'Andrea can take care of most people.' It was the usual masterly Miller understatement. 'But he's stepped out of his class this time.'

Mallory smiled, rose and went to the door, followed by Miller, who was in turn followed by an eager press of guests understandably anxious to see the second act of this unscheduled entertainment: but the village square was empty of life.

Mallory did not hesitate. With the instinct born from the experience of long association with Andrea, he headed across the square to the communal hall where Andrea had made the earlier of his two dramatic statements. His instincts hadn't betrayed him. Andrea, with a large glass of brandy in his hand and moodily fingering a spreading patch of red on his cheek, looked up as Mallory and Miller entered.

He said moodily: 'She's gone home to her mother.'

Miller glanced at his watch. 'One minute and twenty-five seconds,' he said admiringly. 'A world record.'

Andrea glowered at him and Mallory moved in hastily.

'You're coming, then.'

'Of course I'm coming,' Andrea said irritably. He surveyed without enthusiasm the guests now swarming into the hall and brushing unceremoniously by as they headed, like the camel for the oasis, towards the bottle-laden tables. 'Somebody's got to look after you two.'

Mallory looked at his watch. 'Three and a half hours yet before that plane is due. We're dead on our feet, Andrea. Where can we sleep – a safe place to sleep. Your perimeter guards are drunk.'

'They've been that way ever since the fortress blew up,' Andrea said. 'Come, I'll show you.'

Miller looked around the islanders, who, amid a loud babel of cheerful voices, were already quite exceptionally busy with bottles and glasses. 'How about your guests?'

'How about them, then?' Andrea surveyed his compatriots morosely. 'Just look at that lot. Ever known a wedding reception yet where anybody paid any attention to the bride and groom? Come.'

They made their way southwards through the outskirts of Mandrakos to the open countryside beyond. Twice they were challenged by guards, twice a scowl and growl from Andrea sent them back hurriedly to their *ouzo* bottles. It was still raining heavily, but Mallory's and Miller's clothes were already so saturated that a little more rain could hardly make any appreciable difference to the way they felt, while Andrea, if anything, seemed even more oblivious of it. Andrea had the air of a man who had other things on his mind.

After fifteen minutes' walk, Andrea stopped before the swing doors of a small, dilapidated and obviously deserted roadside barn.

'There's hay inside,' he said. 'We'll be safe here.'

Mallory said: 'Fine. A radio message to the *Sirdar* to send her CE message to Cairo and—'

'CE?' Andrea asked. 'What's that?'

'To let Cairo know we've contacted you and are ready for pick-up . . . And after that, three lovely long hours' sleep.'

Andrea nodded. 'Three hours it is.'

'Three *long* hours,' Mallory said meditatively.

A smile slowly broke on Andrea's craggy face as he clapped Mallory on the shoulder.

'In three long hours,' he said, 'a man like myself can accomplish a great deal.'

He turned and hurried off through the rain-filled night. Mallory and Miller looked after him with expressionless faces, looked at each other, still with the same expressionless faces, then pushed open the swing doors of the barn.

The Mandrakos airfield would not have received a licence from any Civil Air Board anywhere in the world. It was just over half a mile long, with hills rising steeply at both ends of the alleged runway, not more than forty yards wide and liberally besprinkled with a variety of bumps and potholes virtually guaranteed to wreck any undercarriage in the aviation business. But the RAF had used it before so it was not impossible that they might be able to use it at least once again.

To the south, the airstrip was lined with groves of carob trees. Under the pitiful shelter afforded by one of those, Mallory, Miller and Andrea sat waiting. At least Mallory and Miller did, hunched, miserable and shivering violently in their still sodden clothes. Andrea, however, was stretched out luxuriously with his hands behind his head, oblivious of the heavy drips of rain that fell on his upturned face. There was about him an air of satisfaction, of complacency almost, as he gazed at the first greyish tinges appearing in the sky to the east over the black-walled massif of the Turkish coast.

Andrea said: 'They're coming now.'

Mallory and Miller listened for a few moments, then they too heard it – the distant, muted roar of heavy aircraft approaching. All three rose and moved out to the perimeter of the airstrip. Within a minute, descending rapidly after their climb over the mountains to the south and at a height of less than a thousand feet, a squadron of eighteen Wellingtons, as much heard as seen in the light of early dawn, passed directly over the airstrip, heading for the town of Navarone. Two minutes later, the three watchers both heard the detonations and saw the brilliant orange mushrooming of light as the Wellingtons unloaded their bombs over the shattered fortress to the north. Sporadic lines of upward-flying tracers, obviously exclusively small-arm, attested to the ineffectuality, the weakness of the ground defences. When the fortress had blown up, so had all the anti-aircraft batteries in the town. The attack was short and sharp: less than two minutes after the bombardment had started it ceased as abruptly as it had begun and then there was only the fading dying sound of de-synchronized engines as the Wellingtons pulled away, first to the north and then the west, across the still-dark waters of the Aegean.

For perhaps a minute the three watchers stood silent on the perimeter of the Mandrakos airstrip, then Miller said wonderingly: 'What makes us so important?'

'I don't know,' Mallory said. 'But I don't think you're going to enjoy finding out.'

'And that won't be long now.' Andrea turned round and looked towards the mountains to the south. 'Hear it?'

Neither of the others heard it, but they did not doubt that, in fact, there was something to hear. Andrea's hearing was on a par with his phenomenal eyesight. Then, suddenly, they could hear it, too. A solitary bomber – also a Wellington – came sinking in from the south, circled the perimeter area once as Mallory blinked his torch upwards in rapidly successive flashes, lined up its approach, landed heavily at the far end of the airstrip and came taxiing towards them, bumping heavily across the atrocious surface of the airfield. It halted less than a hundred yards from where they stood: then a light started winking from the flight-deck.

Andrea said: 'Now, don't forget. I've promised to be back in a week.'

'Never make promises,' Miller said severely. 'What if we aren't back in a week? What if they're sending us to the Pacific?'

'Then when we get back I'll send you in first to explain.'

Miller shook his head. 'I don't really think I'd like that.'

'We'll talk about your cowardice later on,' Mallory said. 'Come on. Hurry up.'

The three men broke into a run towards the waiting Wellington.

The Wellington was half an hour on the way to its destination, wherever its destination was, and Andrea and Miller, coffee-mugs in hand, were trying, unsuccessfully, to attain a degree of comfort on the lumpy palliasses on the fuselage floor when Mallory returned from the flight-deck. Miller looked up at him in weary resignation, his expression characterized by an entire lack of enthusiasm and the spirit of adventure.

'Well, what did you find out?' His tone of voice made it abundantly clear that what he had expected Mallory to find out was nothing short of the very worst. 'Where to, now? Rhodes? Beirut? The flesh-pots of Cairo?'

'Termoli, the man says.'

'Termoli, is it? Place I've always wanted to see.' Miller paused. 'Where the hell's Termoli?'

'Italy, so I believe. Somewhere on the south Adriatic coast.'

'Oh, no!' Miller turned on his side and pulled a blanket over his head. 'I *hate* spaghetti.'

—— 2 ——

THURSDAY

1400–2330

The landing on Termoli airfield, on the Adriatic coast of Southern Italy, was every bit as bumpy as the harrowing take-off from the Mandrakos airstrip had been. The Termoli fighter air-base was officially and optimistically listed as newly-constructed but in point of fact was no more than half-finished and felt that way for every yard of the excruciating touch-down and the jack-rabbit run-up to the prefabricated control-tower at the eastern end of the field. When Mallory and Andrea swung down to terra firma, neither of them looked particularly happy: Miller, who came a very shaky last, and who was widely known to have an almost pathological loathing and detestation of all conceivable forms of transport, looked very ill indeed.

Miller was given time neither to seek nor receive commiseration. A camouflaged British 5th Army jeep pulled up alongside the plane, and the sergeant at the wheel, having briefly established their identity, waved them inside in silence, a silence which he stonily maintained on their drive through the shambles of the war-torn streets of Termoli. Mallory was unperturbed by the apparent unfriendliness. The driver was obviously under the strictest instructions not to talk to them, a situation which Mallory had encountered all too often in the past. There were not, Mallory reflected, very many groups of untouchables, but his, he knew, was one of them: no one, with two or three rare exceptions, was ever permitted to talk to them. The process, Mallory knew, was perfectly understandable and justifiable, but it was an attitude that did tend to become increasingly wearing with the passing of the years. It tended to make for a certain lack of contact with one's fellow-men.

After twenty minutes, the jeep stopped below the broad-flagged steps of a house on the outskirts of the town. The jeep driver gestured briefly to an armed sentry on the top of the steps who responded with a similarly perfunctory greeting. Mallory took this as a sign that they had arrived at their destination and, not wishing to violate the young sergeant's vow of silence, got out without being told. The others followed and the jeep at once drove off.

The house – it looked more like a modest palace – was a rather splendid example of late Renaissance architecture, all colonnades and columns and everything in veined marble, but Mallory was more interested in what was inside the house than what it was made of on the outside. At the head of the steps their path was barred by the young corporal sentry armed with a Lee-Enfield .303. He looked like a refugee from high school.

'Names, please.'

'Captain Mallory.'

'Identity papers? Pay-books?'

'Oh, my God,' Miller moaned. 'And me feeling so sick, too.'

'We have none,' Mallory said gently. 'Take us inside, please.'

'My instructions are—'

'I know, I know,' Andrea said soothingly. He leaned across, effortlessly removed the rifle from the corporal's desperate grasp, ejected and pocketed the magazine and returned the rifle. 'Please now.'

Red-faced and furious, the youngster hesitated briefly, looked at the three men more carefully, turned, opened the door behind him and gestured for the three to follow him.

Before them stretched a long, marble-flagged corridor, tall leaded windows on one side, heavy oil paintings and the occasional set of double-leather doors on the other. Half-way down the passage Andrea tapped the corporal on the shoulder and handed the magazine back without a word. The corporal took it, smiling uncertainly, and inserted it into his rifle without a word. Another twenty paces and he stopped before the last pair of leather doors, knocked, heard a muffled acknowledgment and pushed open one of the doors, standing aside to let the three men pass him. Then he moved out again, closing the door behind him.

It was obviously the main drawing-room of the house – or palace – furnished in an almost medieval opulence, all dark oak, heavily brocaded silk curtains, leather upholstery, leather-bound books, what were undoubtedly a set of Old Masters on the walls and a flowing sea of dull bronze carpeting from wall to wall. Taken all in all, even a member of the old-pre-war Italian nobility wouldn't have turned up his nose at it.

The room was pleasantly redolent with the smell of burning pine, the source of which wasn't difficult to locate: one could have roasted a very large ox indeed in the vast and crackling fireplace at the far end of the room. Close by this fireplace stood three young men who bore no resemblance whatsoever to the rather ineffectual youngster who had so recently tried to prevent their entry. They were, to begin with, a good few years older, though still young men. They were heavily-built, broad-shouldered characters and had about them a look of tough and hard-bitten competence. They were dressed in the uniform of that elite of combat troops, the Marine Commandos, and they looked perfectly at home in those uniforms.

But what caught and held the unwavering attention of Mallory and his two companions was neither the rather splendidly effete decadence of the room and its furnishings nor the wholly unexpected presence of the three commandos: it was the fourth figure in the room, a tall, heavily built and commanding figure who leaned negligently against a table in the centre of the room. The deeply-trenched face, the authoritative expression, the splendid grey beard and the piercing blue eyes made him a prototype for the classic British naval captain, which, as the immaculate white uniform he wore indicated, was precisely what he was. With a collective sinking of their hearts, Mallory, Andrea and Miller gazed again, and with a marked lack of enthusiasm, upon the splendidly piratical figure of Captain Jensen, RN, Chief of Allied Intelligence, Mediterranean, and the man who had so recently sent them on their suicidal mission to the island of Navarone. All three looked at one another and shook their heads in slow despair.

Captain Jensen straightened, smiled his magnificent sabre-toothed tiger's smile and strode forward to greet them, his hand outstretched.

'Mallory! Andrea! Miller!' There was a dramatic five-second pause between the words. 'I don't know what to say! I just don't know what to say! A magnificent job, a magnificent—' He broke off and regarded them thoughtfully. 'You – um – don't seem all that surprised to see me, Captain Mallory?'

'I'm not. With respect, sir, whenever and wherever there's dirty work afoot, one looks to find—'

'Yes, yes, yes. Quite, quite. And how are you all?'

'Tired,' Miller said firmly. 'Terribly tired. We need a rest. At least, I do.'

Jensen said earnestly: 'And that's exactly what you're going to have, my boy. A rest. A long one. A *very* long one.'

'A *very* long one?' Miller looked at him in frank incredulity.

'You have my word,' Jensen stroked his beard in momentary diffidence. 'Just as soon, that is, as you get back from Yugoslavia.'

'Yugoslavia!' Miller stared at him.

'Tonight.'

'Tonight!'

'By parachute.'

'By *parachute*!'

Jensen said with forbearance: 'I am aware, Corporal Miller, that you have had a classical education and are, moreover, just returned from the Isles of Greece. But we'll do without the Ancient Greek Chorus bit, if you don't mind.'

Miller looked moodily at Andrea. 'Bang goes your honeymoon.'

'What was that?' Jensen asked sharply.

'Just a private joke, sir.'

Mallory said in mild protest: 'You're forgetting, sir, that none of us has ever made a parachute jump.'

'I'm forgetting nothing. There's a first time for everything. What do you gentlemen know about the war in Yugoslavia?'

'What war?' Andrea said warily.

'Precisely.' There was satisfaction in Jensen's voice.

'I heard about it,' Miller volunteered. 'There's a bunch of what-do-you-call-'em – Partisans, isn't it – offering some kind of underground resistance to the German occupation troops.'

'It is probably as well for you,' Jensen said heavily, 'that the Partisans cannot hear you. They're not underground, they're very much over ground and at the latest count there were 350,000 of them tying down twenty-eight German and Bulgarian divisions in Yugoslavia.' He paused briefly. 'More, in fact, than the combined Allied armies are tying down here in Italy.'

'Somebody should have told me,' Miller complained. He brightened. 'If there's 350,000 of them around, what would they want us for?'

Jensen said acidly: 'You must learn to curb your enthusiasm, Corporal. The fighting part of it you may leave to the Partisans – and they're fighting the cruellest, hardest, most brutal war in Europe today. A ruthless, vicious war with no quarter and no surrender on either side. Arms, munitions, food, clothes – the Partisans are desperately short of all of those. But they have those twenty-eight divisions pinned down.'

'I don't want any part of that,' Miller muttered.

Mallory said hastily: 'What do you want us to do, sir?'

'This.' Jensen removed his glacial stare from Miller. 'Nobody appreciates it yet, but the Yugoslavs are our most important Allies in Southern Europe. Their war is our war. And they're fighting a war they can never hope to win. Unless—'

Mallory nodded. 'The tools to finish the job.'

'Hardly original, but true. The tools to finish the job. We are the *only* people who are at present supplying them with rifles, machine-guns, ammunition, clothing and medical supplies. And those are not getting through.' He broke off, picking up a cane, walked almost angrily across the room to a large wall-map hanging between a couple of Old Masters and rapped the tip of the bamboo against it. 'Bosnia-Herzegovina, gentlemen. West-Central Yugoslavia. We've sent in four British Military Missions in the past two months to liaise with the Yugoslavs – the Partisan Yugoslavs. The leaders of all four missions have disappeared without trace. Ninety percent of our recent airlift supplies have fallen into German hands. They have broken all our radio codes and have established a network of agents in Southern Italy here with whom they are apparently able to communicate as and when they wish. Perplexing questions, gentlemen. Vital questions. I want the answers. Force 10 will get me the answers.'

'Force 10?' Mallory said politely.

'The code name for your operation.'

'Why that particular name?' Andrea asked.

'Why not? Ever heard of *any* code name that had *any* bearing on the operation on hand? It's the whole essence of it, man.'

'It wouldn't, of course,' Mallory said woodenly, 'have anything to do with a frontal attack on something, a storming of some vital place.' He observed Jensen's total lack of reaction and went on in the same tone: 'On the Beaufort Scale, Force 10 means a storm.'

'A storm!' It is very difficult to combine an exclamation and a moan of anguish in the same word, but Miller managed it without any difficulty. 'Oh, my God, and all I want is a flat calm, and that for the rest of my life.'

'There are limits to my patience, Corporal Miller,' Jensen said. 'I may – I say *may* – have to change my mind about a re-commendation I made on your behalf this morning.'

'On my behalf?' Miller said guardedly.

'For the Distinguished Conduct Medal.'

'*That* should look nice on the lid of my coffin,' Miller muttered.

'What was that?'

'Corporal Miller was just expressing his appreciation.' Mallory moved closer to the wall-map and studied it briefly. 'Bosnia-Herzegovina – well, it's a fair-sized area, sir.'

'Agreed. But we can pin-point the spot – the approximate location of the disappearances – to within twenty miles.'

Mallory turned from the map and said slowly: 'There's been a lot of homework on this one. That raid this morning on Navarone. The Wellington standing by to take us here. All preparations – I infer this from what you've said – laid on for tonight. Not to mention—'

'We've been working on this for almost two months. You three were supposed to have come here some days ago. But – ah – well, you know.'

'We know.' The threatened withholding of his DCM had left Miller unmoved. 'Something else came up. Look, sir, why us? We're saboteurs, explosive experts, combat troops – this is a job for undercover espionage agents who speak Serbo-Croat or whatever.'

'You must allow me to be the best judge of that.' Jensen gave them another flash of his sabre-toothed smile. 'Besides, you're lucky.'

'Luck deserts tired men,' Andrea said. 'And we are very tired.'

'Tired or not, I can't find another team in Southern Europe to match you for resource, experience and skill.' Jensen smiled again. 'And luck. I have to be ruthless, Andrea. I don't like it, but I have to. But I take the point about your exhaustion. That's why I have decided to send a back-up team with you.'

Mallory looked at the three young soldiers standing by the hearth, then back to Jensen, who nodded.

'They're young, fresh and just raring to go. Marine Commandos, the most highly trained combat troops we have today. Remarkable variety of skills, I assure you. Take Reynolds, here.' Jensen nodded to a very tall, dark sergeant in his late twenties, a man with a deeply-tanned aquiline face. 'He can do anything from underwater demolition to flying a plane. And he will be flying a plane tonight. And, as you can see, he'll come in handy for carrying any heavy cases you have.'

Mallory said mildly: 'I've always found that Andrea makes a pretty fair porter, sir.'

Jensen turned to Reynolds. 'They have their doubts. Show them you can be of some use.'

Reynolds hesitated, then stooped, picked up a heavy brass poker and proceeded to bend it between his hands. Obviously, it wasn't an easy poker to bend. His face turned red, the veins stood out on his forehead and the tendons in his neck, his arms quivered with the strain, but slowly, inexorably, the poker was bent into a figure 'U'. Smiling almost apologetically, Reynolds handed the poker over to Andrea. Andrea took it reluctantly. He hunched his shoulders, his knuckles gleamed white but the poker remained in its 'U' shape. Andrea looked up at Reynolds, his expression thoughtful, then quietly laid the poker down.

'See what I mean?' Jensen said. 'Tired. Or Sergeant Groves here. Hot-foot from London, via the Middle East. Ex-air navigator, with all the latest in sabotage, explosives and electrics. For booby-traps, time-bombs and concealed microphones, a human mine-detector. And Sergeant Saunders here – a top-flight radio-operator.'

Miller said morosely to Mallory: 'You're a toothless old lion and you're over the hill.'

'Don't talk rubbish, Corporal!' Jensen's voice was sharp. 'Six is the ideal number. You'll be duplicated in every department, and those men are *good*. They'll be invaluable. If it's any salve to your pride, they weren't originally picked to go with you:. they were picked as a reserve team in case you – um – well—'

'I see.' The lack of conviction in Miller's voice was total.

'All clear, then?'

'Not quite,' Mallory said. 'Who's in charge?'

Jensen said in genuine surprise: 'You are, of course.'

'So.' Mallory spoke quietly and pleasantly. 'I understand the training emphasis today – especially in the Marine Commandos – is on initiative, self-reliance, independence in thought and action. Fine – if they happen to be caught out on their own.' He smiled, almost deprecatingly. 'Otherwise I shall expect immediate, unquestioning and total compliance with orders. My orders. Instant and total.'

'And if not?' Reynolds asked.

'A superfluous question, Sergeant. You know the wartime penalty for disobeying an officer in the field.'

'Does that apply to your friends, too?'

'No.'

Reynolds turned to Jensen. 'I don't think I like that, sir.'

Mallory sank wearily into a chair, lit a cigarette, nodded at Reynolds and said, 'Replace him.'

'What!' Jensen was incredulous.

'Replace him, I said. We haven't even left and already he's questioning my judgment. What's it going to be like in action? He's dangerous. I'd rather carry a ticking time-bomb with me.'

'Now, look here, Mallory—'

'Replace him or replace me.'

'And me,' Andrea said quietly.

'And me,' Miller added.

There was a brief and far from companionable silence in the room, then Reynolds approached Mallory's chair.

'Sir.'

Mallory looked at him without encouragement.

'I'm sorry,' Reynolds went on. 'I stepped out of line. I will never make the same mistake twice. I *want* to go on this trip, sir.'

Mallory glanced at Andrea and Miller. Miller's face registered only his shock at Reynold's incredibly foolhardy enthusiasm for action. Andrea, impassive as ever, nodded almost imperceptibly. Mallory smiled and said: 'As Captain Jensen said, I'm sure you'll be a great asset.'

'Well, that's it, then.' Jensen affected not to notice the almost palpable relaxation of tension in the room. 'Sleep's the thing now. But first I'd like a few minutes – report on Navarone, you know.' He looked at the three sergeants. 'Confidential, I'm afraid.'

'Yes, sir,' Reynolds said. 'Shall we go down to the field, check flight plans, weather, parachutes and supplies?'

Jensen nodded. As the three sergeants closed the double doors behind them, Jensen crossed to a side door, opened it and said: 'Come in, General.'

The man who entered was very tall, very gaunt. He was probably about thirty-five, but looked a great deal older. The care, the exhaustion, the endless privations inseparable from too many years' ceaseless struggle for survival had heavily silvered the once-black hair and deeply etched into the swarthy, sunburnt face the lines of physical and mental suffering. The eyes were dark and glowing and intense, the hypnotic eyes of a man inspired by a fanatical dedication to some as yet unrealized ideal. He was dressed in a British Army officer's uniform, bereft of insignia and badges.

Jensen said: 'Gentlemen, General Vukalovic. The general is second-in-command of the Partisan forces in Bosnia-Herzegovina. The RAF flew him out yesterday. He is here as a Partisan doctor seeking medical supplies. His true identity is known only to us. General, those are your men.'

Vukalovic looked them over severally and steadily, his face expressionless. He said: 'Those are tired men, Captain Jensen. So much depends . . . too tired to do what has to be done.'

'He's right, you know,' Miller said earnestly.

'There's maybe a little mileage left in them yet,' Jensen said mildly. 'It's a long haul from Navarone. Now then—'

'Navarone?' Vukalovic interrupted. 'These – these are the men—'

'An unlikely-looking lot, I agree.'

'Perhaps I was wrong about them.'

'No, you weren't, General,' Miller said. 'We're exhausted. We're completely—'

'Do you mind?' Jensen said acidly. 'Captain Mallory, with two exceptions the General will be the only person in Bosnia who knows who you are and what you are doing. Whether the General reveals the identity of the others is entirely up to him. General Vukalovic will be accompanying you to Yugoslavia, but not in the same plane.'

'Why not?' Mallory asked.

'Because his plane will be returning. Yours won't.'

'Ah!' Mallory said. There was a brief silence while he, Andrea and Miller absorbed the significance behind Jensen's words. Abstractedly, Andrea threw some more wood on the sinking fire and looked around for a poker: but the only poker was the one that Reynolds had already bent into a 'U'-shape. Andrea picked it up. Absent-mindedly, effortlessly, Andrea straightened it out, poked the fire into a blaze and laid the poker down, a performance Vukalovic watched with a very thoughtful expression on his face.

Jensen went on: 'Your plane, Captain Mallory, will not be returning because your plane is expendable in the interests of authenticity.'

'Us, too?' Miller asked.

'You won't be able to accomplish very much, Corporal Miller, without actually putting your feet on the ground. Where you're going, no plane can possibly land: so you jump – and the plane crashes.'

'That sounds very authentic,' Miller muttered.

Jensen ignored him. 'The realities of total war are harsh beyond belief. Which is why I sent those three youngsters on their way – I don't want to dampen their enthusiasm.'

'Mine's water-logged,' Miller said dolefully.

'Oh, do be quiet. Now, it would be fine if, by way of a bonus, you could discover why eighty percent of our air-drops fall into German hands, fine if you could locate and rescue our captured mission leaders. But not important. Those supplies, those agents are militarily expendable. What are not expendable are the seven thousand men under the command of General Vukalovic here, seven thousand men trapped in an area called the Zenica Cage, seven thousand starving men with almost no ammunition left, seven thousand men with no future.'

'We can help them?' Andrea asked heavily. 'Six men?'

Jensen said candidly: 'I don't know.'

'But you have a plan?'

'Not yet. Not as such. The glimmerings of an idea. No more.' Jensen rubbed his forehead wearily. 'I myself arrived from Alexandria only six hours ago.' He hesitated, then shrugged. 'By tonight, who knows? A few hours' sleep this afternoon might transform us all. But, first, the report on Navarone. It would be pointless for you three other gentlemen to wait – there are sleeping-

quarters down the hall. I daresay Captain Mallory can tell me
all I want to know.'

Mallory waited until the door closed behind Andrea, Miller
and Vukalovic and said: 'Where shall I begin my report, sir?'

'What report?'

'Navarone, of course.'

'The hell with Navarone. That's over and done with.' He
picked up his cane, crossed to the wall, pulled down two more
maps. 'Now, then.'

'You – you *have* a plan,' Mallory said carefully.

'Of course I have a plan,' Jensen said coldly. He rapped the
map in front of him. 'Ten miles north of here. The Gustav Line.
Right across Italy along the line of the Sangro and Liri rivers.
Here the Germans have the most impregnable defensive positions in the history of modern warfare. Monte Cassino here – our
finest Allied divisions have broken on it, some for ever. And here
– the Anzio beach-head. Fifty thousand Americans fighting for
their lives. For five solid months now we've been battering our
heads against the Gustav Line and the Anzio perimeter. Our
losses in men and machines – incalculable. Our gains – not one
solitary inch.'

Mallory said diffidently: 'You mentioned something about
Yugoslavia, sir.'

'I'm coming to that,' Jensen said with restraint. 'Now, our
only hope of breaching the Gustav Line is by weakening the
German defensive forces and the only way we can do *that* is by
persuading them to withdraw some of their front-line divisions.
So we practise the Allenby technique.'

'I see.'

'You don't see at all. General Allenby, Palestine, 1918. He
had an east-west line from the Jordan to the Mediterranean. He
planned to attack from the west – so he convinced the Turks the
attack was coming from the east. He did this by building up in
the east a huge city of army tents occupied by only a few hundred men who came out and dashed around like beavers whenever enemy planes came over on reconnaissance. He did this by
letting the same planes see large army truck convoys pouring to
the east all day long – what the Turks didn't know was that the
same convoys poured back to the west all night long. He even
had fifteen thousand canvas dummies of horses built. Well, we're
doing the same.'

'Fifteen thousand canvas horses?'

'Very, very amusing.' Jensen rapped the map again. 'Every

airfield between here and Bari is jammed with dummy bombers and gliders. Outside Foggia is the biggest military encampment in Italy – occupied by two hundred men. The harbours of Bari and Taranto are crowded with assault landing-craft, the whole lot made of plywood. All day long columns of trucks and tanks converge on the Adriatic coast. If you, Mallory, were in the German High Command, what would you make of this?'

'I'd suspect an airborne and sea invasion of Yugoslavia. But I wouldn't be sure.'

'The German reaction exactly,' Jensen said with some satisfaction. 'They're badly worried, worried to the extent that they have already transferred two divisions from Italy to Yugoslavia to meet the threat.'

'But they're not certain?'

'Not quite. But almost.' Jensen cleared his throat. 'You see, our four captured mission leaders were all carrying unmistakable evidence pointing to an invasion of Central Yugoslavia in early May.'

'They carried evidence—' Mallory broke off, looked at Jensen for a long and speculative moment, then went on quietly: 'And how *did* the Germans manage to capture them all?'

'We told them they were coming.'

'You did what!'

'Volunteers all, volunteers all,' Jensen said quickly. There were, apparently, some of the harsher realities of total war that even he didn't care to dwell on too long. 'And it will be your job, my boy, to turn near-conviction into absolute certainty.' Seemingly oblivious of the fact that Mallory was regarding him with a marked lack of enthusiasm, he wheeled round dramatically and stabbed his cane at a large-scale map of Central Yugoslavia.

'The valley of the Neretva,' Jensen said. 'The vital sector of the main north-south route through Yugoslavia. Whoever controls this valley controls Yugoslavia – and no one knows this better than the Germans. If the blow falls, they know it must fall here. They are fully aware that an invasion of Yugoslavia is on the cards, they are terrified of a link-up between the Allies and the Russians advancing from the east and they *know* that any such link-up must be along this valley. They already have two armoured divisions along the Neretva, two divisions that, in the event of invasion, could be wiped out in a night. From the north – here – they are trying to force their way south to the Neretva with a whole army corps – but the only way is through the Zenica Cage here. And Vukalovic and his seven thousand men block the way.'

'Vukalovic knows about this?' Mallory asked. 'About what you really have in mind, I mean?'

'Yes. And the Partisan command. They know the risks, the odds against them. They accept them.'

'Photographs?' Mallory asked.

'Here.' Jensen pulled some photographs from a desk drawer, selected one and smoothed it out on the table. 'This is the Zenica Cage. Well-named: a perfect cage, a perfect trap. To the north and west, impassable mountains. To the east, the Neretva dam and the Neretva gorge. To the south, the Neretva river. To the north of the cage here, at the Zenica gap, the German 11th Army Corps is trying to break through. To the west here – they call it the West Gap – more units of the 11th trying to do the same. And to the south here, over the river and hidden in the trees, two armoured divisions under a General Zimmermann.'

'And this?' Mallory pointed to a thin black line spanning the river just north of the two armoured divisions.

'That,' Jensen said thoughtfully, 'is the bridge at Neretva.'

Close-up, the bridge at Neretva looked vastly more impressive than it had done in the large-scale photograph: it was a massively cantilevered structure in solid steel, with a black asphalt roadway laid on top. Below the bridge rushed the swiftly-flowing Neretva, greenish-white in colour and swollen with melting snow. To the south there was a narrow strip of green meadowland bordering the river and, to the south of this again, a dark and towering pine forest began. In the safe concealment of the forest's gloomy depths, General Zimmermann's two armoured divisions crouched waiting.

Parked close to the edge of the wood was the divisional command radio truck, a bulky and very long vehicle so beautifully camouflaged as to be invisible at more than twenty paces.

General Zimmermann and his ADC, Captain Warburg, were at that moment inside the truck. Their mood appeared to match the permanent twilight of the woods. Zimmermann had one of those high-foreheaded, lean and aquiline and intelligent faces which so rarely betray any emotion, but there was no lack of emotion now, no lack of anxiety and impatience as he removed his cap and ran his hand through his thinning grey hair. He said to the radio-operator seated behind the big receiver:

'No word, yet? Nothing?'

'Nothing, sir.'

'You are in constant touch with Captain Neufeld's camp?'

'Every minute, sir.'

'And his operator is keeping a continuous radio watch?'

'All the time, sir. Nothing. Just nothing.'

Zimmermann turned and descended the steps, followed by Warburg. He walked, head down, until he was out of earshot of the truck, then said: 'Damn it! Damn it! God damn it all!'

'You're as sure as that, sir.' Warburg was tall, good-looking, flaxen-haired and thirty, and his face at the moment reflected a nice balance of apprehension and unhappiness. 'That they're coming?'

'It's in my bones, boy. One way or another it's coming, coming for all of us.'

'You can't be *sure*, sir,' Warburg protested.

'True enough.' Zimmermann sighed. 'I can't be sure. But I'm sure of this. If they do come, if the 11th Army Group can't break through from the north, if we can't wipe out those damned Partisans in the Zenica Cage—'

Warburg waited for him to continue, but Zimmermann seemed lost in reverie. Apparently apropos of nothing, Warburg said: 'I'd like to see Germany again, sir. Just once more.'

'Wouldn't we all, my boy, wouldn't we all.' Zimmermann walked slowly to the edge of the wood and stopped. For a long time he gazed out over the bridge at Neretva. Then he shook his head, turned and was almost at once lost to sight in the dark depths of the forest.

The pine fire in the great fireplace in the drawing-room in Termoli was burning low. Jensen threw on some more logs, straightened, poured two drinks and handed one to Mallory.

Jensen said: 'Well?'

'That's the plan?' No hint of his incredulity, of his near-despair, showed in Mallory's impassive face. 'That's *all* of the plan?'

'Yes.'

'Your health.' Mallory paused. 'And mine.' After an even longer pause he said reflectively: 'It should be interesting to watch Dusty Miller's reactions when he hears about this little lot this evening.'

As Mallory had said, Miller's reactions were interesting, even if wholly predictable. Some six hours later, clad now, like Mallory and Andrea, in British Army uniform, Miller listened in visibly growing horror as Jensen outlined what he considered should be their proposed course of action in the next twenty-four hours or so. When he had finished, Jensen looked directly at Miller and said: 'Well? Feasible?'

'Feasible?' Miller was aghast. 'It's suicidal!'

'Andrea?'

Andrea shrugged, lifted his hands palms upwards and said nothing.

Jensen nodded and said: 'I'm sorry, but I'm fresh out of options. We'd better go. The others are waiting at the airstrip.'

Andrea and Miller left the room, began to walk down the long passage-way. Mallory hesitated in the doorway, momentarily blocking it, then turned to face Jensen who was watching him with a surprised lift of the eyebrows.

Mallory said in a low voice: 'Let me tell Andrea, at least.'

Jensen looked at him for a considering moment or two, shook his head briefly and brushed by into the corridor.

Twenty minutes later, without a further word being spoken, the four men arrived at the Termoli airstrip to find Vukalovic and two sergeants waiting for them: the third, Reynolds, was already at the controls of his Wellington, one of two standing at the end of the airstrip, propellors already turning. Ten minutes later both planes were airborne, Vukalovic in one, Mallory, Miller, Andrea, and the three sergeants in the other, each plane bound for its separate destination.

Jensen, alone on the tarmac, watched both planes climbing, his straining eyes following them until they disappeared into the overcast darkness of the moonless sky above. Then, just as General Zimmermann had done that afternoon, he shook his head in slow finality, turned and walked heavily away.

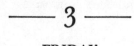

3

FRIDAY

0030–0200

Sergeant Reynolds, Mallory reflected, certainly knew how to handle a plane, especially this one. Although his eyes showed him to be always watchful and alert, he was precise, competent, calm and relaxed in everything he did. No less competent was Groves: the poor light and cramped confines of his tiny plotting-table clearly didn't worry him at all and as an air navigator he was quite clearly as experienced as he was proficient. Mallory peered forward through the windscreen, saw the white-capped waters of the Adriatic rushing by less than a hundred feet beneath their fuselage, and turned to Groves.

'The flight-plan calls for us to fly as low as this?'

'Yes. The Germans have radar installations on some of the outlying islands off the Yugoslav coast. We start climbing when we reach Dalmatia.'

Mallory nodded his thanks, turned to watch Reynolds again. He said curiously: 'Captain Jensen was right about you. As a pilot. How on earth does a Marine Commando come to learn to drive one of those things?'

'I've had plenty of practice,' Reynolds said. 'Three years in the RAF, two of them as sergeant-pilot in a Wellington bomber squadron. One day in Egypt I took a Lysander up without per-mission. People did it all the time – but the crate I'd picked had a defective fuel gauge.'

'You were grounded?'

'With great speed.' He grinned. 'There were no objections when I applied for a service transfer. I think they felt I wasn't somehow quite right for the RAF.'

Mallory looked at Groves. 'And you?'

Groves smiled broadly. 'I was his navigator in that old crate. We were fired on the same day.'

Mallory said consideringly: 'Well, I should think that might be rather useful.'

'What's useful?' Reynolds asked.

'The fact that you're used to this feeling of disgrace. It'll en-able you to act your part all the better when the time comes. If the time comes.'

Reynolds said carefully: 'I'm not quite sure—'

'Before we jump, I want you – all of you – to remove every distinguishing badge or emblem or rank on your clothes.' He gestured to Andrea and Miller at the rear of the flight-deck to indicate that they were included as well, then looked at Reynolds again. 'Sergeants' stripes, regimental flashes, medal ribbons – the lot.'

'Why the hell should I?' Reynolds, Mallory thought, had the lowest boiling-point he'd come across in quite some time. 'I *earned* those stripes, those ribbons, that flash. I don't see—'

Mallory smiled. 'Disobeying an officer on active service?'

'Don't be so damned touchy,' Reynolds said.

'Don't be so damned touchy, *sir*.'

'Don't be so damned touchy, *sir*.' Reynolds suddenly grinned. 'OK, so who's got the scissors?'

'You see,' Mallory explained, 'the last thing we want to happen is to fall into enemy hands.'

'Amen,' Miller intoned.

'But if we're to get the information we want we're going to have to operate close to or even inside their lines. We might get caught. So we have our cover story.'

Groves said quietly: 'Are we permitted to know just what that cover story is, sir?'

'Of course you are,' Mallory said in exasperation. He went on earnestly: 'Don't you realize that, on a mission like this, survival depends on one thing and one thing only – complete and mutual trust? As soon as we start having secrets from each other — we're finished.'

In the deep gloom at the rear of the flight-deck, Andrea and Miller glanced at each other and exchanged their wearily cynical smiles.

As Mallory left the flight-deck for the fuselage, his right hand brushed Miller's shoulder. After about two minutes Miller yawned, stretched and made his way aft. Mallory was waiting towards the rear of the fuselage. He had two pieces of folded paper in his hand, one of which he opened and showed to Miller, snapping on a flash-light at the same time. Miller stared at it for some moments, then lifted an eyebrow.

'And what is this supposed to be?'

'It's the triggering mechanism for a 1500-pound submersible mine. Learn it by heart.'

Miller looked at it without expression, then glanced at the other paper Mallory held.

'And what have you there?'

Mallory showed him. It was a large-scale map, the central feature of which appeared to be a winding lake with a very long eastern arm which bent abruptly at right-angles into a very short southern arm, which in turn ended abruptly at what appeared to be a dam wall. Beneath the dam, a river flowed away through a winding gorge.

Mallory said: 'What does it look like to you? Show them both to Andrea and tell him to destroy them.'

Mallory left Miller engrossed in his homework and moved forward again to the flight-deck. He bent over Groves's chart table. 'Still on course?'

'Yes, sir. We're just clearing the southern tip of the island of Hvar. You can see a few lights on the mainland ahead.' Mallory followed the pointing hand, located a few clusters of lights, then reached out a hand to steady himself as the Wellington started to climb sharply. He glanced at Reynolds.

'Climbing now, sir. There's some pretty lofty stuff ahead. We should pick up the Partisan landing lights in about half an hour.'

'Thirty-three minutes,' Groves said. 'One-twenty, near enough.'

For almost half an hour Mallory remained on a jump-seat in the flight-deck, just looking ahead. After a few minutes Andrea disappeared and did not reappear. Miller did not return. Groves navigated, Reynolds flew, Saunders listened in to his portable transceiver and nobody talked at all. At one-fifteen Mallory rose, touched Saunders on the shoulders, told him to pack up his gear and headed aft. He found Andrea and a thoroughly miserable-looking Miller with their parachute snap-catches already clipped on to the jumping wire. Andrea had the door pulled back and was throwing out tiny pieces of shredded paper which swirled away in the slipstream. Mallory shivered in the suddenly intense cold. Andrea grinned, beckoned him to the open doorway and pointed downwards. He yelled in Mallory's ear: 'There's a lot of snow down there.'

There was indeed a lot of snow down there. Mallory understood now Jensen's insistence on not landing a plane in those parts. The terrain below was rugged in the extreme, consisting almost entirely of a succession of deep and winding valleys and steep-sided mountains. Maybe half of the landscape below was covered in dense forests of pine trees: all of it was covered in what appeared to be a very heavy blanket of snow. Mallory drew back into the comparative shelter of the Wellington's fuselage and glanced at his watch.

'One-sixteen.' Like Andrea, he had to shout.

'Your watch is a little fast, maybe?' Miller bawled unhappily. Mallory shook his head, Miller shook his. A bell rang and Mallory made his way to the flight-deck, passing Saunders going the other way. As Mallory entered, Reynolds looked briefly over his shoulder, then pointed directly ahead. Mallory bent over his shoulder and peered forwards and downwards. He nodded.

The three lights, in the form of an elongated V, were still some miles ahead, but quite unmistakable, Mallory turned, touched Groves on the shoulder and pointed aft. Groves rose and left. Mallory said to Reynolds: 'Where are the red and green jumping lights?'

Reynolds indicated them.

'Press the red light. How long?'

'Thirty seconds. About.'

Mallory looked ahead again. The lights were less than half as distant as they had been when first he'd looked. He said to Reynolds: 'Automatic pilot. Close the fuel switches.'

'Close the – for the petrol that's left—'

'Shut off the bloody tanks! And get aft. Five seconds.'

Reynolds did as he was told. Mallory waited, briefly made a last check of the landing lights ahead, pressed the green light button, rose and made his way swiftly aft. By the time he reached the jump door, even Reynolds, the last of the first five, was gone. Mallory clipped on his snap-catch, braced his hands round the edge of the doorway and launched himself out into the bitter Bosnian night.

The sudden jarring impact from the parachute harness made him look quickly upwards: the concave circle of a fully open parachute was a reassuring spectacle. He glanced downwards and saw the equally reassuring spectacle of another five open parachutes, two of which were swaying quite wildly across the sky – just as was his own. There were some things, he reflected, about which he, Andrea and Miller had a great deal to learn. Controlling parachute descents was one of those things.

He looked up and to the east to see if he could locate the Wellington, but it was no longer visible. Suddenly, as he looked and listened, both engines, almost in perfect unison, cut out. Long seconds passed when the only sound was the rush of wind in his ears, then there came an explosively metallic sound as the bomber crashed either into the ground or into some unseen mountainside ahead. There was no fire or none that he could see: just the crash, then silence. For the first time that night, the moon broke through.

Andrea landed heavily on an uneven piece of ground, rolled over twice, rose rather experimentally to his feet, discovered he was still intact, pressed the quick-release button of his parachute, then automatically, instinctively – Andrea had a built-in computer for assuring survival – swung through a complete 360°

circle. But no immediate danger threatened, or none that he could see. Andrea made a more leisurely survey of their landing spot.

They had, he thought grimly, been most damnably lucky. Another hundred yards to the south and they'd have spent the rest of the night, and for all he knew, the rest of the war, clinging to the tops of the most impossibly tall pine trees he had ever seen. As it was, luck had been with them and they had landed in a narrow clearing which abutted closely on the rocky scarp of a mountainside.

Or rather, all but one. Perhaps fifty yards from where Andrea had landed, an apex of the forest elbowed its way into the clearing. The outermost tree in this apex had come between one of the parachutists and terra firma. Andrea's eyebrows lifted in quizzical astonishment, then he broke into an ambling run.

The parachutist who had come to grief was dangling from the lowermost bough of the pine. He had his hands twisted in the shrouds, his legs bent, knees and ankles close together in the classic landing position, his feet perhaps thirty inches from the ground. His eyes were screwed tightly shut. Corporal Miller seemed acutely unhappy.

Andrea came up and touched him on the shoulder, gently. Miller opened his eyes and glanced at Andrea, who pointed downwards. Miller followed his glance and lowered his legs, which were then four inches from the ground. Andrea produced a knife, sliced through the shreds and Miller completed the remainder of his journey. He straightened his jacket, his face splendidly impassive, and lifted an enquiring elbow. Andrea, his face equally impassive, pointed down the clearing. Three of the other four parachutists had already landed safely: the fourth, Mallory, was just touching down.

Two minutes later, just as all six were coming together some little distance away from the most easterly landing flare, a shout announced the appearance of a young soldier running towards them from the edge of the forest. The parachutists' guns came up and were almost immediately lowered again: this was no occasion for guns. The soldier was trailing his by the barrel, excitedly waving his free hand in greeting. He was dressed in a faded and tattered near-uniform that had been pillaged from a variety of armies, had long flowing hair, a cast to his right eye and a straggling ginger beard. That he was welcoming them, was beyond doubt. Repeating some incomprehensible greeting over and over again, he shook hands all round and then a second time, the huge grin on his face reflecting his delight.

Within thirty seconds he'd been joined by at least a dozen others, all bearded, all dressed in the same nondescript uniforms, no two of which were alike, all in the same almost festive mood. Then, as at a signal almost, they fell silent and drew slightly apart as the man who was obviously their leader appeared from the edge of the forest. He bore little resemblance to his men. He differed in that he was completely shaven and wore a uniform, a British battledress, which appeared to be all of one piece. He differed in that he was not smiling: he had about him the air of one who was seldom if ever given to smiling. He also differed from the others in that he was a hawk-faced giant of a man, at least six feet four inches in height, carrying no fewer than four wicked-looking Bowie-type knives in his belt – an excess of armament that on another man might have looked incongruous or even comical but which on this man provoked no mirth at all. His face was dark and sombre and when he spoke it was in English, slow and stilted, but precise.

'Good evening.' He looked round questioningly. 'I am Captain Droshny.'

Mallory took a step forward. 'Captain Mallory.'

'Welcome to Yugoslavia, Captain Mallory – Partisan Yugoslavia.' Droshny nodded towards the dying flare, his face twitched in what may have been an attempt at a smile, but he made no move to shake hands. 'As you can see, we were expecting you.'

'Your lights were a great help,' Mallory acknowledged.

'Thank you.' Droshny stared away to the east, then back to Mallory, shaking his head. 'A pity about the plane.'

'All war is a pity.'

Droshny nodded. 'Come. Our headquarters is close by.'

No more was said. Droshny, leading, moved at once into the shelter of the forest. Mallory, behind him, was intrigued by the footprints, clearly visible in the now bright moonlight, left by Droshny in the deep snow. They were, thought Mallory, most peculiar. Each sole left three V-shaped marks, the heel one: the right hand side of the leading V on the right sole had a clearly defined break in it. Unconsciously, Mallory filed away this little oddity in his mind. There was no reason why he should have done so other than that the Mallorys of this world always observe and record the unusual. It helps them to stay alive.

The slope steepened, the snow deepened and the pale moonlight filtered thinly down through the spreading, snow-laden branches of the pines. The light wind was from the east: the cold was intense. For almost ten minutes no voice was heard, then Droshny's came, softly but clearly and imperative in its staccato urgency.

'Be still.' He pointed dramatically upward. 'Be still! Listen!'

They stopped, looked upward and listened intently. At least, Mallory and his men looked upward and listened intently, but the Yugoslavs had other things on their minds: swiftly, efficiently and simultaneously, without either spoken or gestured command being given, they rammed the muzzles of their machine-guns and rifles into the sides and backs of the six parachutists with a force and uncompromising authority that rendered any accompanying orders quite superfluous.

The six men reacted as might have been expected. Reynolds, Groves and Saunders, who were rather less accustomed to the vicissitudes of fate than their three older companions, registered a very similar combination of startled anger and open-mouthed astonishment. Mallory looked thoughtful. Miller lifted a quizzical eyebrow. Andrea, predictably, registered nothing at all: he was too busy exhibiting his usual reaction to physical violence.

His right hand, which he had instantly lifted half-way to his shoulder in an apparent token of surrender, clamped down on the barrel of the rifle of the guard to his left, forcing it away from him, while his left elbow jabbed viciously into the solar plexus of the guard to his left, who gasped in pain and staggered back a couple of paces. Andrea, with both hands now on the rifle of the other guard, wrenched it effortlessly free, lifted it high and brought the barrel down in one continuous blur of movement. The guard collapsed as if a bridge had fallen on him. The winded guard to the left, still bent and whooping in agony, was trying to line up his rifle when the butt of Andrea's rifle struck him in the face: he made a brief coughing sound and fell senseless to the forest floor.

It took all of the three seconds that this action had lasted for the Yugoslavs to release themselves from their momentary thrall of incredulity. Half-a-dozen soldiers flung themselves on Andrea, bearing him to the ground. In the furious, rolling struggle that followed, Andrea laid about him in his usual willing fashion, but when one of the Yugoslavs started pounding him on the head with the barrel of a pistol, Andrea opted for discretion and lay still. With two guns in his back and four hands on either arm Andrea was dragged to his feet: two of his captors already looked very much the worse for wear.

Droshny, his eyes bleak and bitter, came up to Andrea, unsheathed one of his knives and thrust its point against Andrea's throat with a force savage enough to break the skin and draw blood that trickled on to the gleaming blade. For a moment it seemed that Droshny would push the knife home to the hilt, then his eyes moved sideways and downwards to look at the two huddled men lying in the snow. He nodded to the nearest man.

'How are they?'

A young Yugoslav dropped to his knees, looked first at the man who had been struck by the rifle-barrel, touched his head briefly, examined the second man, then stood up. In the filtered moonlight, his face was unnaturally pale.

'Josef is dead. I think his neck is broken. And his brother – he's breathing – but his jaw seems to be—' The voice trailed away uncertainly.

Droshny transferred his gaze back to Andrea. His lips drew back, he smiled the way a wolf smiles and leaned a little harder on the knife.

'I *should* kill you now. I *will* kill you later.' He sheathed his knife, held up his clawed hands in front of Andrea's face, and shouted: 'Personally. With those hands.'

'With those hands.' Slowly, meaningfully, Andrea examined the four pairs of hands pinioning his arms, then looked contemptuously at Droshny. He said: 'Your courage terrifies me.'

There was a brief and unbelieving silence. The three young sergeants stared at the tableau before them with faces reflecting various degrees of consternation and incredulity. Mallory and Miller looked on impassively. For a moment or two, Droshny looked as if he hadn't heard aright, then his face twisted in savage anger as he struck Andrea back-handed across the face. Immediately a trickle of blood appeared at the right-hand corner of Andrea's mouth but Andrea himself remained unmoving, his face without expression.

Droshny's eyes narrowed. Andrea smiled again, briefly. Droshny struck again, this time with the back of the other hand. The effect was as before, with the exception that this time the trickle of blood came from the left-hand corner of the mouth. Andrea smiled again but to look into his eyes was to look into an open grave. Droshny wheeled and walked away, then halted as he approached Mallory.

'You *are* the leader of those men, Captain Mallory?'

'I am.'

'You're a very – *silent* leader, Captain?'

'What am I to say to a man who turns his guns on his friends and allies?' Mallory looked at him dispassionately. 'I'll talk to your commanding officer, not to a madman.'

Droshny's face darkened. He stepped forward, his arm lifted to strike. Very quickly, but so smoothly and calmly that the movement seemed unhurried, and totally ignoring the two rifle-muzzles pressing into his side, Mallory lifted his Luger and pointed it at Droshny's face. The click of the Luger safety-catch being released came like a hammer-blow in the suddenly unnatural intensity of silence.

And unnatural intensity of silence there was. Except for one little movement, so slow as to be almost imperceptible, both Partisans and parachutists had frozen into a tableau that would have done credit to the frieze on an Ionic temple. The three sergeants, like most of the Partisans, registered astonished incredulity. The two men guarding Mallory looked at Droshny with questioning eyes. Droshny looked at Mallory as if he were mad. Andrea wasn't looking at anyone, while Miller wore that look of world-weary detachment which only he could achieve. But it was Miller who made that one little movement, a movement that now came to an end with his thumb resting on his Schmeisser's safety-release. After a moment or two he removed his thumb: there would come a time for Schmeissers, but this wasn't it.

Droshny lowered his hand in a curious slow-motion gesture and took two paces backwards. His face was still dark with anger, the dark eyes cruel and unforgiving, but he had himself well in hand. He said: 'Don't you know we have to take precautions? Till we are satisfied with your identity?'

'How should I know that?' Mallory nodded at Andrea. 'Next time you tell your men to take precautions with my friend here, you might warn them to stand a little farther back. He reacted the only way he knows how. And I know why.'

'You can explain later. Hand over your guns.'

'No.' Mallory returned the Luger to its holster.

'Are you mad? I can take them from you.'

'That's so,' Mallory said reasonably. 'But you'd have to kill us first, wouldn't you? I don't think you'd remain a captain very long, my friend.'

Speculation replaced anger in Droshny's eyes. He gave a sharp order in Serbo-Croat and again his soldiers levelled their guns at Mallory and his five companions. But they made no attempt to remove the prisoners' guns. Droshny turned, gestured and started moving up the steeply-sloping forest floor again. Droshny wasn't, Mallory reflected, a man likely to be given to taking too many chances.

For twenty minutes they scrambled awkwardly up the slippery hillside. A voice called out from the darkness ahead and Droshny answered without breaking step. They passed by two sentries armed with machine-carbines and, within a minute, were in Droshny's HQ.

It was a moderately-sized military encampment – if a wide circle of rough-hewn adze-cut cabins could be called an encampment – set in one of those very deep hollows in the forest floor that Mallory was to find so characteristic of the Bosnian area. From the base of this hollow grew two concentric rings of pines far taller and more massive than anything to be found in western Europe, massive pines whose massive branches interlocked eighty to a hundred feet above the ground, forming a snow-shrouded canopy of such impenetrable density that there wasn't even a dusting of snow on the hard-packed earth of the camp compound: by the same token, the same canopy also effectively prevented any upward escape of light: there was no attempt at any blackout in several illuminated cabin windows and there were even some oil-lamps suspended on outside hooks to illuminate the compound itself. Droshny stopped and said to Mallory:

'You come with me. The rest of you stay here.'

He led Mallory towards the door of the largest hut in the compound. Andrea, unbidden, slipped off his pack and sat on it, and the others, after various degrees of hesitation, did the same. Their guards looked them over uncertainly, then withdrew to form a ragged but watchful semi-circle. Reynolds turned to Andrea, the expression on his face registering a complete absence of admiration and goodwill.

'You're crazy.' Reynolds's voice came in a low, furious whisper. 'Crazy as a loon. You could have got yourself killed. You could have got us all killed. What are you, shell-shocked or something?'

Andrea did not reply. He lit one of his obnoxious cigars and regarded Reynolds with mild speculation or as near an approach to mildness as it was possible for him to achieve.

'Crazy isn't half the word for it.' Groves, if anything, was even more heated than Reynolds. 'Or didn't you *know* that was a Partisan you killed? Don't you *know* what that means? Don't you *know* people like that must always take precautions?'

Whether he knew or not, Andrea wasn't saying. He puffed at

his cigar and transferred his peaceable gaze from Reynolds to Groves.

Miller said soothingly: 'Now, now. Don't be like that. Maybe Andrea *was* a mite hasty but—'

'God help us all,' Reynolds said fervently. He looked at his fellow-sergeants in despair. 'A thousand miles from home and help and saddled with a trigger-happy bunch of has-beens.' He turned back to Miller and mimicked: ' "Don't be like that." '

Miller assumed his wounded expression and looked away.

The room was large and bare and comfortless. The only concession to comfort was a pine fire crackling in a rough hearthplace. The only furniture consisted of a cracked deal table, two chairs and a bench.

Those things Mallory noted only subconsciously. He didn't even register when he heard Droshny say: 'Captain Mallory. This is my commanding officer.' He seemed to be too busy staring at the man seated behind the table.

The man was short, stocky and in his mid-thirties. The deep lines around eyes and mouth could have been caused by weather or humour or both: just at that moment he was smiling slightly. He was dressed in the uniform of a captain in the German Army and wore an Iron Cross at his throat.

—— 4 ——

FRIDAY

0200–0330

The German captain leaned back in his chair and steepled his fingers. He had the air of a man enjoying the passing moment.

'Hauptmann Neufeld, Captain Mallory.' He looked at the places on Mallory's uniform where the missing insignia should have been. 'Or so I assume. You are surprised to see me?'

'I am *delighted* to meet you, Hauptmann Neufeld.' Mallory's astonishment had given way to the beginnings of a long, slow smile and now he sighed in deep relief. 'You just can't imagine *how* delighted.' Still smiling, he turned to Droshny, and at once the smile gave way to an expression of consternation. 'But who *are* you? Who is this man, Hauptmann Neufeld? Who in the

name of God are those men out there? They must be – they
must be—'

Droshny interrupted heavily: 'One of his men killed one of
my men tonight.'

'What!' Neufeld, the smile now in turn vanishing from his
face, stood abruptly: the backs of his legs sent his chair crashing
to the floor. Mallory ignored him, looked again at Droshny.

'*Who are you?* For God's sake, tell me!'

Droshny said slowly: 'They call us Cetniks.'

'Cetniks? Cetniks? What on earth are Cetniks?'

'You will forgive me, Captain, if I smile in weary disbelief.'
Neufeld was back on balance again, and his face had assumed a
curiously wary impassivity, an expression in which only the eyes
were alive: things, Mallory reflected, unpleasant things could
happen to people misguided enough to underrate Hauptmann
Neufeld. 'You? The leader of a special mission to this country
and you haven't been well enough briefed to know that the
Cetniks are our Yugoslav allies?'

'Allies? Ah!' Mallory's face cleared in understanding.
'Traitors? Yugoslav Quislings? Is that it?'

A subterranean rumble came from Droshny's throat and he
moved towards Mallory, his right hand closing round the haft of
a knife. Neufeld halted him with a sharp word of command and
a brief downward-chopping motion of his hand.

'And what do you mean by a special mission?' Mallory demanded. He looked at each man in turn and smiled in wry
understanding. 'Oh, we're special mission all right, but not in
the way you think. At least, not in the way I think you think.'

'No?' Neufeld's eyebrow-raising technique, Mallory reflected,
was almost on a par with Miller's. 'Then why do you think we
were expecting you?'

'God only knows,' Mallory said frankly. 'We thought the
Partisans were. That's why Droshny's man was killed, I'm
afraid.'

'That's why Droshny's man—' Neufeld regarded Mallory with
his warily impassive eyes, picked up his chair and sat down
thoughtfully. 'I think, perhaps, you had better explain yourself.'

As befitted a man who had adventured far and wide in the West
End of London, Miller was in the habit of using a napkin when
at meals, and he was using one now, tucked into the top of his
tunic, as he sat on his rucksack in the compound of Neufeld's
camp and fastidiously consumed some indeterminate goulash

from a mess-tin. The three sergeants, seated near by, briefly observed this spectacle with open disbelief, then resumed a low-voiced conversation. Andrea, puffing the inevitable nostril-wrinkling cigar and totally ignoring half-a-dozen watchful and understandably apprehensive guards, strolled unconcernedly about the compound, poisoning the air wherever he went. Clearly through the frozen night air came the distant sound of someone singing a low-voiced accompaniment to what appeared to be guitar music. As Andrea completed his circuit of the compound, Miller looked up and nodded in the direction of the music.

'Who's the soloist?'

Andrea shrugged. 'Radio, maybe.'

'They want to buy a new radio. My trained ear—'

'Listen.' Reynolds's interrupting whisper was tense and urgent. 'We've been talking.'

Miller performed some fancy work with his napkin and said kindly: 'Don't. Think of the grieving mothers and sweethearts you'd leave behind you.'

'What do you mean?'

'About making a break for it is what I mean,' Miller said. 'Some other time, perhaps?'

'Why not now?' Groves was belligerent. 'They're off guard—'

'Are they now.' Miller sighed. 'So young, so young. Take another look. You don't think Andrea *likes* exercise, do you?'

The three sergeants took another look, furtively, surreptitiously, then glanced interrogatively at Andrea.

'Five dark windows,' Andrea said. 'Behind them, five dark men. With five dark machine-guns.'

Reynolds nodded and looked away.

'Well now.' Neufeld, Mallory noted, had a great propensity for steepling his fingers: Mallory had once known a hanging judge with exactly the same propensity. 'This *is* a most remarkably odd story you have to tell us, my dear Captain Mallory.'

'It is,' Mallory agreed. 'It would have to be, wouldn't it, to account for the remarkably odd position in which we find ourselves at this moment.'

'A point, a point.' Slowly, deliberately, Neufeld ticked off other points on his fingers. 'You have for some months, you claim, been running a penicillin and drug-running ring in the south of Italy. As an Allied liaison officer you found no difficulty in obtaining supplies from American Army and Air Force bases.'

'We found a little difficulty towards the end,' Mallory admitted.

'I'm coming to that. Those supplies, you also claim, were funnelled through to the Wehrmacht.'

'I wish you wouldn't keep using the word "claim" in that tone of voice,' Mallory said irritably. 'Check with Field-Marshal Kesselring's Chief of Military Intelligence in Padua.'

'With pleasure.' Neufeld picked up a phone, spoke briefly in German and replaced the receiver.

Mallory said in surprise: 'You have a direct line to the outside world? From *this* place?'

'I have a direct line to a hut fifty yards away where we have a very powerful radio transmitter. So. You further claim that you were caught, court-martialled and were awaiting the confirmation of your death sentence. Right?'

'If your espionage system in Italy is all we hear it is, you'll know about it to-morrow,' Mallory said drily.

'Quite, quite. You then broke free, killed your guards and overheard agents in the briefing-room being briefed on a mission to Bosnia.' He did some more finger-steepling. 'You may be telling the truth at that. What did you say their mission was?'

'I didn't say. I didn't really pay attention. It had something to do with locating missing British mission leaders and trying to break your espionage set-up. I'm not sure. We had more important things to think about.'

'I'm sure you had,' Neufeld said distastefully. 'Such as your skins. What happened to your epaulettes, Captain? The medal ribbons? The buttons?'

'You've obviously never attended a British court-martial, Hauptmann Neufeld.'

Neufeld said mildly: 'You could have ripped them off yourself.'

'And then, I suppose, emptied three-quarters of the fuel from the tanks before we stole the plane?'

'Your tanks were only a quarter full?' Mallory nodded. 'And your plane crashed without catching fire?'

'We didn't mean to crash,' Mallory said in a weary patience. 'We meant to land. But we were out of fuel – and, as we know now, at the wrong place.'

Neufeld said absently: 'Whenever the Partisans put up landing flares we try a few ourselves – *and* we knew that you – or someone – were coming. No petrol, eh?' Again Neufeld spoke briefly on the telephone, then turned back to Mallory. 'All very satisfactory – if true. There just remains to explain the death of Captain Droshny's man here.'

'I'm sorry about that. It was a ghastly blunder. But surely you can understand. The last thing we wanted was to land among you, to make direct contact with you. We've heard what happens to British parachutists dropping over German territory.'

Neufeld steepled his fingers again. 'There is a state of war. Proceed.'

'Our intention was to land in Partisan territory, slip across the lines and give ourselves up. When Droshny turned his guns on us we thought the Partisans were on to us, that they had been notified that we'd stolen the plane. And that could mean only one thing for us.'

'Wait outside. Captain Droshny and I will join you in a moment.'

Mallory left. Andrea, Miller and the three sergeants were sitting patiently on their rucksacks. From the distance there still came the sound of distant music. For a moment Mallory cocked his head to listen to it, then walked across to join the others. Miller patted his lips delicately with his napkin and looked up at Mallory.

'Had a cosy chat?'

'I spun him a yarn. The one we talked about in the plane.' He looked at the three sergeants. 'Any of you speak German?'

All three shook their heads.

'Fine. Forget you speak English too. If you're questioned you know nothing.'

'If I'm not questioned,' Reynolds said bitterly, 'I still don't know anything.'

'All the better,' Mallory said encouragingly. 'Then you can never tell anything, can you?'

He broke off and turned round as Neufeld and Droshny appeared in the doorway. Neufeld advanced and said: 'While we're waiting for some confirmation, a little food and wine, perhaps.' As Mallory had done, he cocked his head and listened to the singing. 'But first of all, you must meet our minstrel boy.'

'We'll settle for just the food and wine,' Andrea said.

'Your priorities are wrong. You'll see. Come.'

The dining-hall, if it could be dignified by such a name, was about forty yards away. Neufeld opened the door to reveal a crude and makeshift hut with two rickety trestle tables and four benches set on the earthen floor. At the far end of the room the inevitable pine fire burnt in the inevitable stone hearth-place.

Close to the fire, at the end of the farther table, three men –obviously, from their high-collared coats and guns propped by their sides, some kind of temporarily off-duty guards – were drinking coffee and listening to the quiet singing coming from a figure seated on the ground by the fire.

The singer was dressed in a tattered anorak type jacket, an even more incredibly tattered pair of trousers and a pair of knee boots that gaped open at almost every possible seam. There was little to be seen of his face other than a mass of dark hair and a large pair of rimmed dark spectacles.

Beside him, apparently asleep with her head on his shoulder, sat a girl. She was clad in a high-collared British Army great-coat in an advanced state of dipalidation, so long that it completely covered her tucked-in legs. The uncombed platinum hair spread over her shoulders would have done justice to any Scandinavian, but the broad cheekbones, dark eyebrows and long dark lashes lowered over very pale cheeks were unmistakably Slavonic.

Neufeld advanced across the room and stopped by the fireside. He bent over the singer and said: 'Petar, I want you to meet some friends.'

Petar lowered his guitar, looked up, then turned and touched the girl on the arm. Instantly, the girl's head lifted and her eyes, great dark sooty eyes, opened wide. She had the look, almost, of a hunted animal. She glanced around her, almost wildly, then jumped quickly to her feet, dwarfed by the greatcoat which reached almost to her ankles, then reached down to help the guitarist to his feet. As he did so, he stumbled: he was obviously blind.

'This is Maria,' Neufeld said. 'Maria, this is Captain Mallory.'

'Captain Mallory.' Her voice was soft and a little husky: she spoke in almost accentless English. 'You are English, Captain Mallory?'

It was hardly, Mallory thought, the time or the place for proclaiming his New Zealand ancestry. He smiled. 'Well, sort of.'

Maria smiled in turn. 'I've always wanted to meet an Englishman.' She stepped forward towards Mallory's outstretched hand, brushed it aside and struck him, open-handed and with all her strength, across the face.

'Maria!' Neufeld stared at her. 'He's on our side.'

'An Englishman *and* a traitor!' She lifted her hand again but the swinging arm was suddenly arrested in Andrea's grip. She struggled briefly, futilely, then subsided, dark eyes glowing in an angry face. Andrea lifted his free hand and rubbed his own cheek in fond recollection.

He said admiringly: 'By heavens, she reminds me of my own Maria,' then grinned at Mallory. 'Very handy with their hands, those Yugoslavs.'

Mallory rubbed his cheek ruefully with his hand and turned to Neufeld. 'Perhaps Petar – that's his name—'

'No.' Neufeld shook his head definitely. 'Later. Let's eat now.' He led the way across to the table at the far end of the room, gestured the others to seats, sat down himself and went on: 'I'm sorry. That was my fault. I should have known better.'

Miller said delicately: 'Is she – um – all right?'

'A wild animal, you think?'

'She'd make a rather dangerous pet, wouldn't you say?'

'She's a graduate of the University of Belgrade. Languages. With honours, I'm told. Some time after graduation she returned to her home in the Bosnian mountains. She found her parents and two small brothers butchered. She – well, she's been like this ever since.'

Mallory shifted in his seat and looked at the girl. Her eyes, dark and unmoving and unwinking, were fixed on him and their expression was less than encouraging. Mallory turned back to Neufeld.

'Who did it? To her parents, I mean,'

'The Partisans,' Droshny said savagely. 'Damn their black souls, the Partisans. Maria's people were our people. Cetniks.'

'And the singer?' Mallory asked.

'Her elder brother.' Neufeld shook his head. 'Blind from birth. Wherever they go, she leads him by the hand. She is his eyes: she is his life.'

They sat in silence until food and wine were brought in. If an army marched on its stomach, Mallory thought, this one wasn't going to get very far: he had heard that the food situation with the Partisans was close to desperate, but, if this were a representative sample, the Cetniks and Germans appeared to be in little better case. Unenthusiastically, he spooned – it would have been impossible to use a fork – a little of the greyish stew, a stew in which little oddments of indefinable meat floated forlornly in a mushy gravy of obscure origin, glanced across at Andrea and marvelled at the gastronomic fortitude that lay behind the already almost empty plate. Miller averted his eyes from the plate before him and delicately sipped the rough red wine. The three sergeants, so far, hadn't even looked at their food: they were too occupied in looking at the girl by the fireside. Neufeld saw their interest, and smiled.

'I do agree, gentlemen, that I've never seen a more beautiful girl and heaven knows what she'd look like if she had a wash. But she's not for you, gentlemen. She's not for any man. She's wed already.' He looked at the questioning faces and shook his head. 'Not to any man. To an ideal – if you can call death an ideal. The death of the Partisans.'

'Charming,' Miller murmured. There was no other comment, for there was none to make. They ate in a silence broken only by the soft singing from the fireside, the voice was melodious enough, but the guitar sounded sadly out of tune. Andrea pushed away his empty plate, looked irritably at the blind musician and turned to Neufeld.

'What's that he's singing?'

'An old Bosnian love-song, I've been told. Very old and very sad. In English you have it too.' He snapped his fingers, 'Yes, that's it. "The girl I left behind me".'

'Tell him to sing something else,' Andrea muttered. Neufeld looked at him, puzzled, then looked away as a German sergeant entered and bent to whisper in his ear. Neufeld nodded and the sergeant left.

'So.' Neufeld was thoughtful. 'A radio report from the patrol that found your plane. The tanks *were* empty. I hardly think we need await confirmation from Padua, do you, Captain Mallory?'

'I don't understand.'

'No matter. Tell me, have you ever heard of a General Vukalovic?'

'General which?'

'Vukalovic.'

'He's not on our side,' Miller said positively. 'Not with a name like that.'

'You must be the only people in Yugoslavia who *don't* know him. Everybody else does. Partisans, Cetniks, Germans, Bulgarians, everyone. He is one of their national heroes.'

'Pass the wine,' Andrea said.

'You'd do better to listen.' Neufeld's tone was sharp. 'Vukalovic commands almost a division of Partisan infantry who have been trapped in a loop of the Neretva river for almost three months. Like the men he leads, Vukalovic is insane. They have no shelter, none. They are short of weapons, have almost no ammunition left and are close to starvation. Their army is dressed in rags. They are finished.'

'Then why don't they escape?' Mallory asked.

'Escape is impossible. The precipices of the Neretva cut them off to the east. To the north and west are impenetrable mountains. The only conceivable way out is to the south, over the bridge at Neretva. And we have two armoured divisions waiting there.'

'No gorges?' Mallory asked. 'No passes through the mountains?'

'Two. Blocked by our best combat troops.'

'Then why don't they give up?' Miller asked reasonably. 'Has no one told them the rules of war?'

'They're insane, I tell you,' Neufeld said. 'Quite insane.'

At that precise moment in time, Vukalovic and his Partisans were proving to some other Germans just how extraordinary their degree of insanity was.

The Western Gap was a narrow, tortuous, boulder-strewn and precipitously walled gorge that afforded the only passage through the impassable mountains that shut off the Zenica Cage to the east. For three months now German infantry units – units which had recently included an increasing number of highly-skilled Alpine troops – had been trying to force the pass: for three months they had been bloodily repulsed. But the Germans never gave up trying and on this intensely cold night of fitful moonlight and gently, intermittently falling snow, they were trying again.

The Germans carried out their attack with the coldly professional skill and economy of movement born of long and harsh experience. They advanced up the gorge in three fairly even and judiciously spaced lines: the combination of white snow-suits, of the utilization of every scrap of cover and of confining their brief forward rushes to those moments when the moon was temporarily obscured made it almost impossible to see them. There was, however, no difficulty in locating them: they had obviously ammunition and to spare for machine-pistols and rifles alike and the fire-flashes from those muzzles were almost continuous. Almost as continuous, but some distance behind them, the sharp flat cracks of fixed mountain pieces pin-pointed the source of the creeping artillery barrage that preceded the Germans up the boulder-strewn slope of that narrow defile.

The Yugoslav Partisans waited at the head of the gorge, entrenched behind a redoubt of boulders, hastily piled stones and splintered tree-trunks that had been shattered by German artillery fire. Although the snow was deep and the east wind full of little knives, few of the Partisans wore greatcoats. They were clad in an extraordinary variety of uniforms, uniforms that had belonged in the past to members of British, German, Italian, Bulgarian and Yugoslav armies: the one identifying feature that all had in common was a red star sewn on to the right-hand side of their forage caps. The uniforms, for the most part, were thin and tattered, offering little protection against the piercing cold, so that the men shivered almost continuously. An astonishing proportion of them appeared to be wounded: there were splinted legs, arms in slings and bandaged heads everywhere. But the most common characteristic among this rag-tag collection of defenders was their pinched and emaciated faces, faces where the deeply etched lines of starvation were matched only by the calm and absolute determination of men who have no longer anything to lose.

Near the centre of the group of defenders, two men stood in the shelter of the thick bole of one of the few pines still left standing. The silvered black hair, the deeply trenched – and now even more exhausted – face of General Vukalovic was unmistakable. But the dark eyes glowed as brightly as ever as he bent forward to accept a cigarette and light from the officer sharing his shelter, a swarthy, hook-nosed man with at least half of his black hair concealed under a blood-stained bandage. Vukalovic smiled.

'Of course I'm insane, my dear Stephan. You're insane – or you would have abandoned this position weeks ago. We're all insane. Didn't you know?'

'I know this.' Major Stephan rubbed the back of his hand across a week-old growth of beard, 'Your parachute landing, an hour ago. That was insane. Why, you—' He broke off as a rifle fired only feet away, moved to where a thin youngster, not more than seventeen years of age, was peering down into the white gloom of the gorge over the sights of a Lee-Enfield. 'Did you get him?'

The boy twisted and looked up. A child. Vukalovic thought despairingly, no more than a child: he should still have been at school. The boy said: 'I'm not sure, sir.'

'How many shells have you left. Count them.'

'I don't have to. Seven.'

'Don't fire till you are sure.' Stephan turned back to Vukalovic. 'God above, General, you were almost blown into German hands.'

'I'd have been worse off without the parachute,' Vukalovic said mildly.

'There's so little time.' Stephan struck a clenched fist against a palm. 'So little time left. You were crazy to come back. They need you far more—' He stopped abruptly, listened for a fraction of a second, threw himself at Vukalovic and brought them both crashing heavily to the ground as a whining mortar shell buried itself among loose rocks a few feet away, exploding on impact. Close by a man screamed in agony. A second mortar shell landed, then a third and a fourth, all within thirty feet of one another.

'They've got the range now, damn them.' Stephan rose quickly to his feet and peered down the gorge. For long seconds he could see nothing, for a band of dark cloud had crossed the face of the moon: then the moon broke through and he could see the enemy all too clearly. Because of some almost certainly pre-arranged signal, they were no longer making any attempt to seek cover: they were pounding straight up the slope with all the speed they could muster, machine-carbines and rifles at the ready in their hands – and as soon as the moon broke through they squeezed the triggers of those guns. Stephan threw himself behind the shelter of a boulder.

'Now!' he shouted. 'Now!'

The first ragged Partisan fusillade lasted for only a few seconds, then a black shadow fell over the valley. The firing ceased.

'Keep firing,' Vukalovic shouted. 'Don't stop now. They're closing in.' He loosed off a burst from his own machine-pistol and said to Stephan. 'They know what they are about, our friends down there.'

'They should.' Stephan armed a stick grenade and spun it down the hill. 'Look at all the practice we've given them.'

The moon broke through again. The leading German infantry were no more than twenty-five yards away. Both sides exchanged hand-grenades, fired at point-blank range. Some German soldiers fell, but many more came on, flinging themselves on the redoubt. Matters became temporarily confused. Here and there bitter hand-to-hand fighting developed. Men shouted at each other, cursed each other, killed each other. But the redoubt remained unbroken. Suddenly, dark heavy clouds again rolled over the moon, darkness flooded the gorge and everything slowly fell quiet. In the distance the thunder of artillery and mortar fire fell away to a muted rumble, then finally died.

'A trap?' Vukalovic said softly to Stephan. 'You think they will come again?'

'Not tonight.' Stephan was positive. 'They're brave men, but—'

'But not insane?'

'But not insane.'

Blood poured down over Stephan's face from a re-opened wound in his face, but he was smiling. He rose to his feet and turned as a burly sergeant came up and delivered a sketchy salute.

'They've gone, Major. We lost seven of ours this time, and fourteen wounded.'

'Set pickets two hundred metres down,' Stephan said. 'He turned to Vukalovic. 'You heard, sir? Seven dead. Fourteen hurt.'

'Leaving how many?'

'Two hundred. Perhaps two hundred and five.'

'Out of four hundred.' Vukalovic's mouth twisted. 'Dear God, out of four hundred.'

'And sixty of those are wounded.'

'At least you can get them down to the hospital now.'

'There is no hospital,' Stephan said heavily. 'I didn't have time to tell you. It was bombed this morning. Both doctors killed. All our medical supplies – poof! Like that.'

'Gone? All gone? Vukalovic paused for a long moment. 'I'll have some sent up from HQ. The walking wounded can make their own way to HQ.'

'The wounded won't leave, sir. Not any more.'

Vukalovic nodded in understanding and went on: 'How much ammunition?'

'Two days. Three, if we're careful.'

'Sixty wounded.' Vukalovic shook his head in slow disbelief. 'No medical help whatsoever for them. Ammunition almost gone. No food. No shelter. And they won't leave. Are they insane, too?'

'Yes, sir.'

'I'm going down to the river,' Vukalovic said. 'To see Colonel Lazlo at HQ.'

'Yes, sir.' Stephan smiled faintly. 'I doubt if you'll find his mental equilibrium any better than mine.'

'I don't suppose I will,' Vukalovic said.

Stephan saluted and turned away, mopping blood from his face, walked a few short swaying steps then knelt down to comfort a badly wounded man. Vukalovic looked after him expressionlessly, shaking his head: then he, too, turned and left.

Mallory finished his meal and lit a cigarette. He said. 'So what's going to happen to the Partisans in the Zenica Cage, as you call it?'

'They're going to break out,' Neufeld said. 'At least, they're going to try to.'

'But you've said yourself that's impossible.'

'Nothing is too impossible for those mad Partisans to try. I wish to heaven,' Neufeld said bitterly, 'that we were fighting a normal war against normal people, like the British or Americans. Anyway, we've had information – reliable information – that an attempted break-out is imminent. Trouble is, there are those two passes – they might even try to force the bridge at Neretva – and we don't know where the break-out is coming.'

'This is very interesting.' Andrea looked sourly at the blind musician who was still giving his rendering of the same old Bosnian love-song. 'Can we get some sleep now?'

'Not tonight, I'm afraid.' Neufeld exchanged a smile with Droshny. '*You* are going to find out for us where this break-out is coming.'

'We are?' Miller drained his glass and reached for the bottle. 'Infectious stuff, this insanity.'

Neufeld might not have heard him. 'Partisan HQ is about ten kilometres from here. You are going to report there as the bona-fide British mission that has lost its way. Then, when you've found out their plans, you tell them that you are going to their main HQ at Drvar, which of course, you don't. You come back here instead. What could be simpler?'

'Miller's right,' Mallory said with conviction. 'You *are* mad.'

'I'm beginning to think there's altogether too much talk of this madness.' Neufeld smiled. 'You would prefer, perhaps, that Captain Droshny here turned you over to his men. I assure you, they are most unhappy about their – ah – late comrade.'

'You can't ask us to do this!' Mallory was hard-faced in anger. 'The Partisans are bound to get a radio message about us. Sooner or later. And then – well, you know what then. You just can't ask this of us.'

'I can and I will.' Neufeld looked at Mallory and his five companions without enthusiasm. 'It so happens that I don't care for dope-peddlers and drug-runners.'

'I don't think your opinion will carry much weight in certain circles,' Mallory said.

'And that means?'

'Kesselring's Director of Military Intelligence isn't going to like this at all.'

'If you don't come back, they'll never know. If you do—' Neufeld smiled and touched the Iron Cross at his throat – 'they'll probably give me an oak leaf to this.'

'Likeable type, isn't he?' Miller said to no one in particular.

'Come, then.' Neufeld rose from the table. 'Petar?'

The blind singer nodded, slung his guitar over his shoulder and rose to his feet, his sister rising with him.

'What's this, then?' Mallory asked.

'Guides.'

'*Those* two?'

'Well,' Neufeld said reasonably, 'you can't very well find your own way there, can you? Petar and his sister – well, his sister – know Bosnia better than the foxes.'

'But won't the Partisans—' Mallory began, but Neufeld interrupted.

'You don't know your Bosnia. These two wander wherever they like and no one will turn them from their door. The Bosnians believe, and God knows with sufficient reason, that they are accursed and have the evil eye on them. This is a land of superstition, Captain Mallory.'

'But – but how will they know where to take us?'

'They'll know.' Neufeld nodded to Droshny, who talked rapidly to Maria in Serbo-Croat: she in turn spoke to Petar, who made some strange noises in his throat.

'That's an odd language,' Miller observed.

'He's got a speech impediment,' Neufeld said shortly. 'He was born with it. He can sing, but not talk – it's not unknown. Do you wonder people think they are cursed?' He turned to Mallory. 'Wait outside with your men.'

Mallory nodded, gestured to the others to precede him. Neufeld, he noted, was immediately engaged in a short, low-voiced discussion with Droshny, who nodded, summoned one of his Cetniks and dispatched him on some errand. Once outside, Mallory moved with Andrea slightly apart from the others and murmured something in his ear, inaudible to all but Andrea, whose nodded acquiescence was almost imperceptible.

Neufeld and Droshny emerged from the hut, followed by Maria who was leading Petar by the hand. As they approached

Mallory's group, Andrea walked casually towards them, smoking the inevitable noxious cigar. He planted himself in front of a puzzled Neufeld and arrogantly blew smoke into his face.

'I don't think I care for you very much, Hauptmann Neufeld,' Andrea announced. He looked at Droshny. 'Nor for the cutlery salesman here.'

Neufeld's face immediately darkened, became tight in anger. But he brought himself quickly under control and said with restraint: 'Your opinion of me is of no concern to me.' He nodded to Droshny. 'But do not cross Captain Droshny's path, my friend. He is a Bosnian and a proud one – and the best man in the Balkans with a knife.'

'The best man—' Andrea broke off with a roar of laughter, and blew smoke into Droshny's face. 'A knife-grinder in a comic opera.'

Droshny's disbelief was total but of brief duration. He bared his teeth in a fashion that would have done justice to any Bosnian wolf, swept a wickedly-curved knife from his belt and threw himself on Andrea, the gleaming blade hooking viciously upwards, but Andrea, whose prudence was exceeded only by the extraordinary speed with which he could move his vast bulk, was no longer there when the knife arrived. But his hand was. It caught Droshny's knife wrist as it flashed upward and almost at once the two big men crashed heavily to the ground, rolling over and over in the snow while they fought for possession of the knife.

So unexpectedly, so wholly incredible the speed with which the fight had developed from nowhere that, for a few seconds, no one moved. The three young sergeants, Neufeld and the Cetniks registered nothing but utter astonishment. Mallory, who was standing close behind the wide-eyed girl, rubbed his chin thoughtfully while Miller, delicately tapping the ash off the end of his cigarette, regarded the scene with a sort of weary interest.

Almost at the same instant, Reynolds, Groves and two Cetniks flung themselves upon the struggling pair on the ground and tried to pull them apart. Not until Saunders and Neufeld lent a hand did they succeed. Droshny and Andrea were pulled to their feet, the former with contorted face and hatred in his eyes, Andrea calmly resuming the smoking of the cigar which he'd somehow picked up after they had been separated.

'You madman!' Reynolds said savagely to Andrea. 'You crazy maniac. You – you're a bloody psychopath. You'll get us all killed.'

'That wouldn't surprise me at all,' Neufeld said thoughtfully. 'Come. Let us have no more of this foolishness.'

He led the way from the compound, and as he did so they were joined by a group of half-a-dozen Cetniks, whose apparent leader was the youth with the straggling ginger beard and cast to his eye, the first of the Cetniks to greet them when they had landed.

'Who are they and what are they for?' Mallory demanded of Neufeld. 'They're not coming with us.'

'Escort,' Neufeld explained. 'For the first seven kilometres only.'

'Escorts? What would we want with escorts? We're in no danger from you, nor, according to what you say, will we be from the Yugoslav Partisans.'

'We're not worried about you,' Neufeld said drily. 'We're worried about the vehicle that is going to take you most of the way there. Vehicles are very few and very precious in this part of Bosnia – and there are many Partisan patrols about.'

Twenty minutes later, in a now moonless night and with snow falling, they reached a road, a road which was little more than a winding track running through a forested valley floor. Waiting for them there was one of the strangest four-wheeled contraptions Mallory or his companions had ever seen, an incredibly ancient and battered truck which at first sight, from the vast clouds of smoke emanating from it, appeared to be on fire. It was, in fact, a very much pre-war wood-burning truck, of a type at one time common in the Balkans. Miller regarded the smoke-shrouded truck in astonishment and turned to Neufeld.

'You call this a vehicle?'

'You call it what you like. Unless you'd rather walk.'

'Ten kilometres? I'll take my chance on asphyxiation.' Miller climbed in, followed by the others, till only Neufeld and Droshny remained outside.

Neufeld said: 'I shall expect you back before noon.'

'If we ever come back,' Mallory said. 'If a radio message has come through—'

'You can't make an omelette without breaking eggs,' Neufeld said indifferently.

With a great rattling and shaking and emission of smoke and steam, all accompanied by much red-eyed coughing from the canvas-covered rear, the truck jerked uncertainly into motion and moved off slowly along the valley floor, Neufeld and Droshny gazing after it. Neufeld shook his head. 'Such clever little men.'

'Such *very* clever little men,' Droshny agreed. 'But I want the big one, Captain.'

Neufeld clapped him on the shoulder. 'You shall have him, my friend. Well, they're out of sight. Time for you to go.'

Droshny nodded and whistled shrilly ·between his fingers. There came the distant whirr of an engine starter, and soon an elderly Fiat emerged from behind a clump of pines and approached along the hard-packed snow of the road, its chains clanking violently, and stopped beside the two men. Droshny climbed into the front passenger seat and the Fiat moved off in the wake of the truck.

5

FRIDAY

0300–0500

For the fourteen people jammed on the narrow side benches under the canvas-hooped roof, the journey could hardly be called pleasurable. There were no cushions on the seats just as there appeared to be a total absence of springs on the vehicle, and the torn and badly fitting hood admitted large quantities of icy night air and eye-smarting smoke in about equal proportions. At least, Mallory thought, it all helped considerably to keep them awake.

Andrea was sitting directly opposite him, seemingly oblivious of the thick choking atmosphere inside the truck, a fact hardly surprising considering that the penetrating power and the pungency of the smoke from the truck was of a lower order altogether than that emanating from the black cheroot clamped between Andrea's teeth. Andrea glanced idly across and caught Mallory's eye. Mallory nodded once, a millimetric motion of the head that would have gone unremarked by even the most suspicious. Andrea dropped his eyes until his gaze rested on Mallory's right hand, lying loosely on his knee. Mallory sat back and sighed, and as he did his right hand slipped until his thumb was pointing directly at the floor. Andrea puffed out another Vesuvian cloud of acrid smoke and looked away indifferently.

For some kilometres the smoke-enshrouded truck clattered and screeched its way along the valley floor, then swung off to the left on to an even narrower track, and began to climb. Less than two minutes later, with Droshny sitting impassively in the front passenger seat, the pursuing Fiat made a similar turn off.

The slope was now so steep and the spinning driving wheels losing so much traction on the frozen surface of the track that the ancient wood-burning truck was reduced to little more than walking pace. Inside the truck, Andrea and Mallory were as watchful as ever, but Miller and the three sergeants seemed to be dozing off, whether through exhaustion or incipient asphyxiation it was difficult to say. Maria and Petar, hand in hand, appeared to be asleep. The Cetniks, on the other hand, could hardly have been more wide awake, and were making it clear for the first time that the rents and holes in the canvas cover had not been caused by accident: Droshny's six men were now kneeling on the benches with the muzzles of their machine-pistols thrust through the apertures in the canvas. It was clear that the truck was now moving into Partisan territory, or, at least, what passed for no-man's-land in that wild and rugged territory.

The Cetnik farthest forward in the truck suddenly withdrew his face from a gap in the canvas and rapped the butt of his gun against the driver's cab. The truck wheezed to a grateful halt, the ginger-bearded Cetnik jumped down, checked swiftly for any signs of ambush, then gestured the others to disembark, the repeatedly urgent movements of his hand making it clear that he was less than enamoured of the idea of hanging around that place for a moment longer than necessity demanded. One by one Mallory and his companions jumped down on to the frozen snow. Reynolds guided the blind singer down to the ground, then reached up a hand to help Maria as she clambered over the tail-board. Wordlessly, she struck his hand aside and leapt nimbly to the ground: Reynolds stared at her in hurt astonishment. The truck, Mallory observed, had stopped opposite a small clearing in the forest. Backing and filling and issuing denser clouds of smoke than ever, it used this space to turn around in a remarkably short space of time and clanked its way off down the forest path at a considerably higher speed than it had made the ascent. The Cetniks gazed impassively from the back of the departing truck, made no gesture of farewell.

Maria took Petar's hand, looked coldly at Mallory, jerked her head and set off up a tiny footpath leading at right-angles from the track. Mallory shrugged and set off, followed by the three sergeants. For a moment or two Andrea and Miller remained where they were, gazing thoughtfully at the corner round which the truck had just disappeared. Then they, too, set off, talking in low tones to each other.

The ancient wood-burning truck did not maintain its initial impetus for any lengthy period of time. Less than four hundred yards after rounding the corner which blocked it from the view of Mallory and his companions it braked to a halt. Two Cetniks, the ginger-bearded leader of the escort and another black-bearded man, jumped over the tail-board and moved at once into the protective covering of the forest. The truck rattled off once more, its belching smoke hanging heavily in the freezing night air.

A kilometre farther down the track, an almost identical scene was taking place. The Fiat slid to a halt, Droshny scrambled from the passenger's seat and vanished among the pines. The Fiat reversed quickly and moved off down the track.

The track up through the heavily wooded slope was very narrow, very winding: the snow was no longer hard-packed, but soft and deep and making for very hard going. The moon was quite gone now, the snow, gusted into their faces by the east wind, was becoming steadily heavier and the cold was intense. The path frequently arrived at a V-shaped branch but Maria, in the lead with her brother, never hesitated: she knew, or appeared to know, exactly where she was going. Several times she slipped in the deep snow, on the last occasion so heavily that she brought her brother down with her. When it happened yet again, Reynolds moved forward and took the girl by the arm to help her. She struck out savagely and drew her arm away. Reynolds stared at her in astonishment, then turned to Mallory.

'What the devil's the matter with – I mean, I was only trying to help—'

'Leave her alone,' Mallory said. 'You're one of them.'

'I'm one of—'

'You're wearing a British uniform. That's all the poor kid understands. Leave her be.'

Reynolds shook his head uncomprehendingly. He hitched his pack more securely on his shoulders, glanced back down the trail, made to move on, then glanced backwards again. He caught Mallory by the arm and pointed.

Andrea had already fallen thirty yards behind. Weighed down by his rucksack and Schmeisser and weight of years, he was very obviously making heavy weather of the climb and was falling steadily behind by the second. At a gesture and word from Mallory the rest of the party halted and peered back down through the driving snow, waiting for Andrea to make up on them. By this time Andrea was beginning to stumble almost drunkenly and clutched at his right side as if in pain. Reynolds looked at Groves: they both looked at Saunders: all three slowly shook their heads. Andrea came up with them and a spasm of pain flickered across his face.

'I'm sorry.' The voice was gasping and hoarse. 'I'll be all right in a moment.'

Saunders hesitated, then advanced towards Andrea. He smiled apologetically, then reached out a hand to indicate the rucksack and Schmeisser.

'Come on, Dad. Hand them over.'

For the minutest fraction of a second a flicker of menace, more imagined than seen, touched Andrea's face, then he shrugged off his rucksack and wearily handed it over. Saunders accepted it and tentatively indicated the Schmeisser.

'Thanks.' Andrea smiled wanly. 'But I'd feel lost without it.'

Uncertainly, they resumed their climb, looking back frequently to check on Andrea's progress. Their doubts were well-founded. Within thirty seconds Andrea had stopped, his eyes screwed up and bent almost double in pain. He said, gaspingly: 'I must rest . . . Go on. I'll catch up with you.'

Miller said solicitously: 'I'll stay with you.'

'I don't need anybody to stay with me,' Andrea said surlily. 'I can look after myself.'

Miller said nothing. He looked at Mallory and jerked his head in an uphill direction. Mallory nodded, once, and gestured to the girl. Reluctantly, they moved off, leaving Andrea and Miller behind. Twice, Reynolds looked back over his shoulder, his expression an odd mixture of worry and exasperation: then he shrugged his shoulders and bent his back to the hill.

Andrea, scowling blackly and still clutching his ribs, remained bent double until the last of the party had rounded the nearest uphill corner, then straightened effortlessly, tested the wind with a wetted forefinger, established that it was moving uptrail, produced a cigar, lit it and puffed in deep and obvious contentment. His recovery was quite astonishing, but it didn't appear to astonish Miller, who grinned and nodded downhill. Andrea grinned in return, made a courteous gesture of precedence.

Thirty yards down-trail, at a position which gave them an uninterrupted view of almost a hundred yards of the track below them they moved into the cover of the bole of a giant pine. For about two minutes they stood there, staring downhill and listening intently, then suddenly Andrea nodded, stooped and carefully laid his cigar in a sheltered dry patch of ground behind the bole of the pine.

They exchanged no words: there was need of none. Miller crawled round to the downhill-facing front of the pine and carefully arranged himself in a spread-eagled position in the deep snow, both arms outflung, his apparently sightless face turned up to the falling snow. Behind the pine, Andrea reversed his grip on his Schmeisser, holding it by the barrel, produced a knife from the recesses of his clothing and stuck it in his belt. Both men remained as motionless as if they had died there and frozen solid over the long and bitter Yugoslav winter.

Probably because his spread-eagled form was sunk so deeply in the soft snow as to conceal most of his body, Miller saw the two Cetniks coming quite some time before they saw him. At first they were no more than two shapeless and vaguely ghostlike forms gradually materializing from the falling snow: as they drew nearer, he identified them as the Cetnik escort leader and one of his men.

They were less than thirty yards away before they saw Miller. They stopped, stared, remained motionless for at least five seconds, looked at each other, unslung their machine-pistols and broke into a stumbling uphill run. Miller closed his eyes. He didn't require them any more, his ears gave him all the information he wanted, the closing sound of crunching footsteps in the snow, the abrupt cessation of those, the heavy breathing as a man bent over him.

Miller waited until he could actually feel the man's breath in his face, then opened his eyes. Not twelve inches from his own were the eyes of the ginger-bearded Cetnik. Miller's outflung arms curved upwards and inwards, his sinewy fingers hooked deeply into the throat of the startled man above him.

Andrea's Schmeisser had already reached the limit of its backswing as he stepped soundlessly round the bole of the pine. The black-bearded Cetnik was just beginning to move to help his friend when he caught sight of Andrea from the corner of one eye, and flung up both arms to protect himself. A pair of straws would have served him as well. Andrea grimaced at the sheer physical shock of the impact, dropped the Schmeisser, pulled out his knife and fell upon the other Cetnik still struggling desperately in Miller's stranglehold.

Miller rose to his feet and he and Andrea stared down at the two dead men. Miller looked in puzzlement at the ginger-bearded man, then suddenly stooped, caught the beard and tugged. It came away in his hand, revealing beneath it a clean-shaven face and a scar which ran from the corner of a lip to the chin.

Andrea and Miller exchanged speculative glances, but neither made comment. They dragged the dead men some little way off the path into the concealment of some undergrowth. Andrea picked up a dead branch and swept away the drag-marks in the snow and, by the base of the pine, all traces of the encounter: inside the hour, he knew, the brushmarks he had made would have vanished under a fresh covering of snow. He picked up his cigar and threw the branch deep into the woods. Without a backward glance, the two men began to walk briskly up the hill.

Had they given this backyard glance, it was barely possible that they might have caught a glimpse of a face peering round the trunk of a tree farther downhill. Droshny had arrived at the bend in the track just in time to see Andrea complete his brushing operations and throw the branch away: what the meaning of this might be he couldn't guess.

He waited until Andrea and Miller has disappeared from his sight, waited another two minutes for good measure and safety, then hurried up the track, the expression on his swarthy brigand's face nicely balanced between puzzlement and suspicion. He reached the pine where the two Cetniks had been ambushed, briefly quartered the area, then followed the line of brush-marks leading into the woods, the puzzlement on his face giving way first to pure suspicion, then the suspicion to complete certainty.

He parted the bushes and peered down at the two Cetniks lying half-buried in a snow-filled gully with that curiously huddled shapelessness that only the dead can achieve. After a few moments he straightened, turned and looked uphill in the direction in which Andrea and Miller had vanished: his face was not pleasant to look upon.

Andrea and Miller made good time up the hill. As they approached one of the innumerable bends in the trail they heard up ahead the sound of a softly-played guitar, curiously muffled and softened in tone by the falling snow. Andrea slowed up, threw away his cigar, bent forward and clutched his ribs. Solicitously, Miller took his arm.

The main party, they saw, was less than thirty yards ahead. They, too, were making slow time: the depth of snow and the increasing slope of the track made any quicker movement impossible. Reynolds glanced back – Reynolds was spending a great deal of his time in looking over his shoulder, he appeared to be in a highly apprehensive state – caught sight of Andrea and Miller and called out to Mallory who halted the party and waited for Andrea and Miller to make up with them. Mallory looked worriedly at Andrea.

'Getting worse?'

'How far to go?' Andrea asked hoarsely.

'Must be less than a mile.'

Andrea said nothing, he just stood there breathing heavily and wearing the stricken look of a sick man contemplating the prospect of another upward mile through deep snow. Saunders, already carrying two rucksacks, approached Andrea diffidently, tentatively. He said: 'It would help, you know, if—'

'I know.' Andrea smiled painfully, unslung his Schmeisser and handed it to Saunders. 'Thanks, son.'

Petar was still softly plucking the strings of his guitar, an indescribably eerie sound in those dark and ghostly pine woods. Miller looked at him and said to Mallory: 'What's the music while we march for?'

'Petar's password, I should imagine.'

'Like Neufeld said? Nobody touches our singing Cetnik?'

'Something like that.'

They moved on up the trail. Mallory let the others pass by until he and Andrea were bringing up the rear. Mallory glanced incuriously at Andrea, his face registering no more than a mild concern for the condition of his friend. Andrea caught his glance and nodded fractionally: Mallory looked away.

Fifteen minutes later they were halted, at gun-point, by three men, all armed with machine-pistols, who simply appeared to have materialized from nowhere, a surprise so complete that not even Andrea could have done anything about it – even if he had had his gun. Reynolds looked urgently at Mallory, who smiled and shook his head.

'It's all right. Partisans – look at the red star on their forage caps. Just outposts guarding one of the main trails.'

And so it proved. Maria talked briefly to one of the soldiers, who listened, nodded and set off up the path, gesturing to the party to follow him. The other two Partisans remained behind, both men crossing themselves as Petar again strummed gently on his guitar. Neufeld, Mallory reflected, hadn't exaggerated about the degree of awed respect and fear in which the blind singer and his sister were held.

They came to Partisan HQ inside another ten minutes, an HQ curiously similar in appearance and choice of location to Hauptmann Neufold's camp: the same rough circle of crude huts set deep in the same *jamba* – depression – with similar massive pines towering high above. The guide spoke to Maria and she turned coldly to Mallory, the disdain on her face making it very plain how much against the grain it went for her to speak to him at all.

'We are to go to the guest hut. You are to report to the commandant. This soldier will show you.'

The guide beckoned in confirmation. Mallory followed him across the compound to a fairly large, fairly well-lit hut. The guide knocked, opened the door and waved Mallory inside, he himself following.

The commandant was a tall, lean, dark man with that aquiline, aristocratic face so common among the Bosnian mountainmen. He advanced towards Mallory with outstretched hand and smiled.

'Major Broznik, and at your service. Late, late hours, but as you see we are still up and around. Although I must say I did expect you before this.'

'I don't know what you're talking about.'

'You don't know – you *are* Captain Mallory, are you not?'

'I've never heard of him.' Mallory gazed steadily at Broznik, glanced briefly sideways at the guide, then looked back to Broznik again. Broznik frowned for a moment, then his face cleared. He spoke to the guide, who turned and left. Mallory put out his hand.

'Captain Mallory, at your service. I'm sorry about that, Major Broznik, but I insist we must talk alone.'

'You trust no one? Not even in *my* camp?'

'No one.'

'Not even your own men?'

'I don't trust them not to make mistakes. I don't trust myself not to make mistakes. I don't trust *you* not to make mistakes.'

'Please?' Broznik's voice was as cold as his eyes.

'Did you ever have two of your men disappear, one with ginger hair, the other with black, the ginger-haired man with a cast to his eye and a scar running from mouth to chin?'

Broznik came closer. 'What do you know about those men?'

'Did you? Know them, I mean?'

Broznik nodded and said slowly: 'They were lost in action. Last month.'

'You found their bodies?'

'No.'

'There were no bodies to be found. They had deserted – gone over to the Cetniks.'

'But they *were* Cetniks – converted to our cause.'

'They'd been re-converted. They followed us tonight. On the orders of Captain Droshny. I had them killed.'

'You – had – them – killed?'

'Think, man,' Mallory said wearily. 'If they had arrived here – which they no doubt intended to do a discreet interval after our arrival – we wouldn't have recognized them and you'd have welcomed them back as escaped prisoners. They'd have reported our every movement. Even if we had recognized them after they had arrived here and done something about it, you may have *other* Cetniks here who would have reported back to their masters that we had done away with their watch-dogs. So we disposed of them very quietly, no fuss, in a very remote place, then hid them.'

'There are no Cetniks in my command, Captain Mallory.'

Mallory said drily: 'It takes a very clever farmer, Major, to see two bad apples on the top of the barrel and be quite certain that there are none lower down. No chances. None. Ever.' Mallory smiled to remove any offence from his words and went on briskly: 'Now, Major, there's some information that Hauptmann Neufeld wants.'

To say that the guest hut hardly deserved so hospitable a title would have been a very considerable understatement. As a shelter for some of the less-regarded domesticated animals it might have been barely acceptable: as an overnight accommodation for human beings it was conspicuously lacking in what our modern effete European societies regard as the minimum essentials for civilized living. Even the Spartans of ancient Greece would have considered it as too much of a good thing. One rickety trestle table, one bench, a dying fire and lots of hard-packed earthen floor. It fell short of being a home from home.

There were six people in the hut, three standing, one sitting, two stretched out on the lumpy floor. Petar, for once without his sister, sat on the floor, silent guitar clasped in his hands, gazing sightlessly into the fading embers. Andrea, stretched in apparently luxurious ease in a sleeping-bag, peacefully puffed at what, judging from the frequent suffering glances cast in his direction, appeared to be a more than normally obnoxious cigar. Miller, similarly reclining, was reading what appeared to be a slender volume of poetry. Reynolds and Groves, unable to sleep, stood idly by the solitary window, gazing out abstractedly into the dimly-lit compound: they turned as Saunders removed his radio transmitter from its casing and made for the door.

With some bitterness Saunders said: 'Sleep well.'

'Sleep well?' Reynolds raised an eyebrow. 'And where are you going?'

'Radio hut across there. Message to Termoli. Mustn't spoil your beauty sleep when I'm transmitting.'

Saunders left. Groves went and sat by the table, cradling a weary head in his hands. Reynolds remained by the window, watched Saunders cross the compound and enter a darkened hut on the far side. Soon a light appeared in the window as Saunders lit a lamp.

Reynolds's eyes moved in response to the sudden appearance of an oblong of light across the compound. The door to Major Broznik's hut had opened and Mallory stood momentarily framed there, carrying what appeared to be a sheet of paper in his hand. Then the door closed and Mallory moved off in the direction of the radio hut.

Reynolds suddenly became very watchful, very still. Mallory had taken less than a dozen steps when a dark figure detached itself from the even darker shadow of a hut and confronted him. Quite automatically, Reynolds's hand reached for the Luger at his belt, then slowly withdrew. Whatever this confrontation signified for Mallory it certainly wasn't danger, for Maria, Reynolds knew, did not carry a gun. And unquestionably it was Maria who was now in such apparent close conversation with Mallory.

Bewildered now, Reynolds pressed his face close against the glass. For almost two minutes he stared at this astonishing spectacle of the girl who had slapped Mallory with such venom, who had lost no opportunity of displaying an animosity bordering on hatred, now talking to him not only animatedly but also clearly very amicably. So total was Reynold's baffled incomprehension at this inexplicable turn of events that his mind moved into a trance-like state, a spell that was abruptly snapped when he saw Mallory put a reassuring arm around her shoulder and pat her in a way that might have been comforting or affectionate or both but which in any event clearly evoked no resentment on the part of the girl. This was still inexplicable: but the only interpretation that could be put upon it was an uncompromisingly sinister one. Reynolds whirled round and silently and urgently beckoned Groves to the window. Groves rose quickly, moved to the window and looked out, but by the time he had done so there was no longer any sign of Maria: Mallory was alone, walking across the compound towards the radio hut, the paper still in his hand. Groves glanced questioningly at Reynolds.

'They were together,' Reynolds whispered. 'Mallory and Maria. I saw them! They were talking?'

'What? You sure?'

'God's my witness. I *saw* them, man. He even had his arm around – Get away from this window – Maria's coming.'

Without haste, so as to arouse no comment from Andrea or Miller, they turned and walked unconcernedly towards the table and sat down. Seconds later, Maria entered and, without looking at or speaking to anyone, crossed to the fire, sat by Petar and took his hand. A minute or so later Mallory entered, and sat on a palliasse beside Andrea, who removed his cigar and glanced at him in mild enquiry. Mallory casually checked to see that he wasn't under observation, then nodded. Andrea returned to the contemplation of his cigar.

Reynolds looked uncertainly at Groves, then said to Mallory: 'Shouldn't we be setting a guard, sir?'

'A guard?' Mallory was amused. 'Whatever for? This is a Partisan camp, Sergeant. Friends, you know. And, as you've seen, they have their own excellent guard system.'

'You never know—'

'*I* know. Get some sleep.'

Reynolds went on doggedly: 'Saunders is alone over there. I don't like—'

'He's coding and sending a short message for me. A few minutes, that's all.'

'But—'

'Shut up,' Andrea said. 'You heard the captain?'

Reynolds was by now thoroughly unhappy and uneasy, an unease which showed through in his instantly antagonistic irritation.

'Shut up? Why should I shut up? I don't take orders from you. And while we're telling each other what to do, you might put out that damned stinking cigar.'

Miller wearily lowered his book of verse.

'I quite agree about the damned cigar, young fellow. But do bear in mind that you are talking to a ranking colonel in the army.'

Miller reverted to his book. For a few moments Reynolds and Groves stared open-mouthed at each other, then Reynolds stood up and looked at Andrea.

'I'm extremely sorry, sir. I – I didn't realize—'

Andrea waved him to silence with a magnanimous hand and resumed his communion with his cigar. The minutes passed in silence. Maria, before the fire, had her head on Petar's shoulder, but otherwise had not moved: she appeared to be asleep. Miller shook his head in rapt admiration of what appeared to be one of the more esoteric manifestations of the poetic muse, closed his book reluctantly and slid down into his sleeping-bag. Andrea ground out his cigar and did the same. Mallory seemed to be already asleep. Groves lay down and Reynolds, leaning over the table, rested his forehead on his arms. For five minutes, perhaps longer, Reynolds remained like this, uneasily dozing off, then he lifted his head, sat up with a jerk, glanced at his watch, crossed to Mallory and shook him by the shoulder. Mallory stirred.

'Twenty minutes,' Reynolds said urgently. 'Twenty minutes and Saunders isn't back yet.'

'All right, so it's twenty minutes,' Mallory said patiently. 'He could take that long to make contact, far less transmit the message.'

'Yes, sir. Permission to check, sir?'

Mallory nodded wearily and closed his eyes. Reynolds picked up his Schmeisser, left the hut and closed the door softly behind him. He released the safety-catch on his gun and ran across the compound.

The light still burned in the radio hut. Reynolds tried to peer through the window but the frost of that bitter night had made it completely opaque. Reynolds moved around to the door. It was slightly ajar. He set his finger to the trigger and opened the door in the fashion in which all Commandos were trained to open doors – with a violent kick of his right foot.

There was no one in the radio hut, no one, that is, who could bring him to any harm. Slowly, Reynolds lowered his gun and walked in in a hesitant, almost dream-like fashion, his face masked in shock.

Saunders was leaning tiredly over the transmitting table, his head resting on it at an unnatural angle, both arms dangling limply towards the ground. The hilt of a knife protruded between his shoulder-blades: Reynolds noted, almost subconsciously, that there was no trace of blood: death had been instantaneous. The transmitter itself lay on the floor, a twisted and mangled mass of metal that was obviously smashed beyond repair. Tentatively, not knowing why he did so, he reached out and touched the dead man on the shoulder: Saunders seemed to stir, his cheek slid along the table and he toppled to one side, falling heavily across the battered remains of the transmitter. Reynolds stooped low over him. Grey parchment now, where a bronzed tan had been, sightless, faded eyes uselessly guarding a mind now flown. Reynolds swore briefly, bitterly, straightened and ran from the hut.

Everyone in the guest hut was asleep, or appeared to be. Reynolds crossed to where Mallory lay, dropped to one knee and shook him roughly by the shoulder. Mallory stirred, opened weary eyes and propped himself up on one elbow. He gave Reynolds a look of unenthusiastic enquiry.

'Among friends, you said!' Reynolds voice was low, vicious, almost a hissing sound. 'Safe, you said. Saunders will be all right, you said. You *knew*, you said. You bloody well knew.'

Mallory said nothing. He sat up abruptly on his palliasse, and the sleep was gone from his eyes. He said: 'Saunders?'

Reynolds said. 'I think you'd better come with me.'

In silence the two men left the hut, in silence they crossed the deserted compound and in silence they entered the radio hut. Mallory went no farther than the doorway. For what was probably no more than ten seconds but for what seemed to Reynolds to be an unconsciously long time, Mallory stared at the dead man and the smashed transmitter, his eyes bleak, his face registering no emotional reaction. Reynolds mistook the expression, or lack of it, for something else, and could suddenly no longer contain his pent-up fury.

'Well, aren't you bloody well going to do something about it instead of standing there all night?'

'Every dog's entitled to his one bite,' Mallory said mildly. 'But don't talk to me like that again. Do what, for instance?'

'Do what?' Reynolds visibly struggled for his self-control. 'Find the nice gentleman who did this.'

'Finding him will be very difficult.' Mallory considered. 'Impossible, I should say. If the killer came from the camp here, then he'll have gone to earth in the camp here. If he came from outside, he'll be a mile away by this time and putting more distance between himself and us every second. Go and wake Andrea and Miller and Groves and tell them to come here. Then go and tell Major Broznik what's happened.'

'I'll tell them what's happened,' Reynolds said bitterly. 'And I'll also tell them it never *would* have happened if you'd listened to me. But oh no, you wouldn't listen, would you?'

'So you were right and I was wrong. Now do as I ask you.'

Reynolds hesitated, a man obviously on the brink of outright revolt. Suspicion and defiance alternated in the angry face. Then some strange quality in the expression in Mallory's face tipped the balance for sanity and compliance and he nodded in sullen antagonism, turned and walked away.

Mallory waited until he had rounded the corner of the hut, brought out his torch and started, not very hopefully, to quarter the hard-packed snow outside the door of the radio hut. But almost at once he stopped, stooped, and brought the head of the torch close to the surface of the ground.

It was a very small portion of footprint indeed, only the front half of the sole of a right foot. The pattern showed two V-shaped marks, the leading V with a cleanly-cut break in it. Mallory, moving more quickly now, followed the direction indicated by the pointed toe-print and came across two more similar indentations, faint but unmistakable, before the frozen snow gave way to the frozen earth of the compound, ground so hard as to be incapable of registering any footprints at all. Mallory retraced his steps, carefully erasing all three prints with the toe of his boot and reached the radio hut only seconds before he was joined by Reynolds, Andrea, Miller and Groves. Major Broznik and several of his men joined them soon after.

They searched the interior of the radio hut for clues as to the killer's identity, but clues there were none. Inch by inch they searched the hard-packed snow surrounding the hut, with the same completely negative results. Reinforced, by this time, by perhaps sixty or seventy sleepy-eyed Partisan soldiers, they carried out a simultaneous search of all the buildings and of the woods surrounding the encampment: but neither the encampment nor the surrounding woods had any secrets to yield.

'We may as well call it off,' Mallory said finally. 'He's got clean away.'

'It looks that way,' Major Broznik agreed. He was deeply troubled and bitterly angry that such a thing should have happened in his encampment. 'We'd better double the guards for the rest of the night.'

'There's no need for that,' Mallory said. 'Our friend won't be back.'

'There's no need for that,' Reynolds mimicked savagely. 'There was no need for that for poor Saunders, you said. And where's Saunders now? Sleeping comfortably in his bed? Is he hell! No need—'

Andrea muttered warningly and took a step nearer Reynolds, but Mallory made a brief conciliatory movement of his right hand. He said: 'It's entirely up to you, of course, Major. I'm sorry that we have been responsible for giving you and your men so sleepless a night. See you in the morning.' He smiled wryly. 'Not that that's so far away.' He turned to go, found his way blocked by Sergeant Groves, a Groves whose normally cheerful countenance now mirrored the tight hostility of Reynolds's.

'So he's got clear away, has he? Away to hell and gone. And that's the end of it, eh?'

Mallory looked at him consideringly. 'Well, no. I wouldn't quite say that. A little time. We'll find him.'

'A little time? Maybe even before he dies of old age?'

Andrea looked at Mallory. 'Twenty-four hours?'

'Less.'

Andrea nodded and he and Mallory turned and walked away towards the guest hut. Reynolds and Groves, with Miller slightly behind them, watched the two men as they went, then looked at each other, their faces still bleak and bitter.

'Aren't they a nice warm-hearted couple now? Completely broken up about old Saunders.' Groves shook his head. 'They don't care. They just don't care.'

'Oh, I wouldn't say that,' Miller said diffidently. 'It's just that they don't *seem* to care. Not at all the same thing.'

'Faces like wooden Indians,' Reynolds muttered. 'They never even said they were *sorry* that Saunders was killed.'

'Well,' Miller said patiently, 'it's a cliché, but different people react in different ways. Okay, so grief and anger is the natural reaction to this sort of thing, but if Mallory and Andrea spent their time in reacting in that fashion to all the things that have happened to *them* in their lifetimes, they'd have come apart at the seams years ago. So they don't react that way any more. They do things. Like they're going to do things to your friend's killer. Maybe you didn't get it, but you just heard a death sentence being passed.'

'How do *you* know?' Reynolds said uncertainly. He nodded in the direction of Mallory and Andrea who were just entering the guest hut. 'And how did *they* know? Without talking, I mean.'

'Telepathy.'

'What do you mean – "telepathy"?'

'It would take too long,' Miller said wearily. 'Ask me in the morning.'

FRIDAY

0800–1000

Crowning the tops of the towering pines, the dense, interlocking snow-laden branches formed an almost impenetrable canopy that effectively screened Major Broznik's camp, huddled at the foot of the *jamba*, from all but the most fleeting glimpses of the sky above. Even at high noon on a summer's day, it was never more than a twilit dusk down below: on a morning such as this, an hour after dawn with snow falling gently from an overcast sky, the quality of light was such as to be hardly distinguishable from a starlit midnight. The interior of the dining hut, where Mallory and his company were at breakfast with Major Broznik, was gloomy in the extreme, the darkness emphasized rather than alleviated by the two smoking oil-lamps which formed the only primitive means of illumination.

The atmosphere of gloom was significantly deepened by the behaviour and expression of those seated round the breakfast table. They ate in a moody silence, heads lowered, for the most part not looking at one another: the events of the previous night had clearly affected them all deeply but none so deeply as Reynolds and Groves in whose faces was still unmistakably reflected the shock caused by Saunders's murder. They left their food untouched.

To complete the atmosphere of quiet desperation, it was clear that the reservations held about the standard of the Partisan early-morning cuisine were of a profound and lasting nature. Served by two young *partisankas* – women members of Marshal Tito's army – it consisted of *polenta*, a highly unappetizing dish made from ground corn, and *raki*, a Yugoslav spirit of unparalled fierceness. Miller spooned his breakfast with a marked lack of enthusiasm.

'Well,' he said to no one in particular, 'it makes a change, I'll say that.'

'It's all we have,' Broznik said apologetically. He laid down his spoon and pushed his plate away from him. 'And even that I can't eat. Not this morning. Every entrance to the *jamba* is guarded, yet there was a killer loose in my camp last night. But maybe he *didn't* come in past the guards, maybe he was already inside. Think of it – a traitor in my own camp. And if there is, I can't even find him. I can't even believe it!'

Comment was superfluous, nothing could be said that hadn't been said already, nobody as much as looked in Broznik's direction: his acute discomfort, embarrassment and anger were apparent to everyone in his tone of voice. Andrea, who had already emptied his plate with apparent relish, looked at the two untouched plates in front of Reynolds and Groves and then enquiringly at the two sergeants themselves, who shook their heads. Andrea reached out, brought their plates before him and set to with every sign of undiminished appetite. Reynolds and Groves looked at him in shocked disbelief, possibly awed by the catholicity of Andrea's tastes, more probably astonished by the insensitivity of a man who could eat so heartily only a few hours after the death of one of his comrades. Miller, for his part, looked at Andrea in near horror, tried another tiny portion of his *polenta* and wrinkled his nose in delicate distaste. He laid down his spoon and looked morosely at Petar who, guitar slung over his shoulder, was awkwardly feeding himself.

Miller said irritably: 'Does he *always* wear that damned guitar?'

'Our lost one,' Broznik said softly. 'That's what we call him. Our poor blind lost one. Always he carries it or has it by his side. Always. Even when he sleeps – didn't you notice last night? That guitar means as much to him as life itself. Some weeks ago, one of our men, by way of a joke, tried to take it from him: Petar, blind though he is, almost killed him.'

'He must be stone tone deaf,' Miller said wonderingly. 'It's the most god-awful guitar I ever heard.'

Broznik smiled faintly. 'Agreed. But don't you understand? He can feel it. He can touch it. It's his own. It's the only thing left to him in the world, a dark and lonely and empty world. Our poor lost one.'

'He could at least tune it,' Miller muttered.

'You are a good man, my friend. You try to take our minds off what lies ahead this day. But no man can do that.' He turned to Mallory. 'Any more than you can hope to carry out your crazy scheme of rescuing your captured agents and breaking up the German counter-espionage network here. It is insanity. Insanity!'

Mallory waved a vague hand. 'Here you are. No food. No artillery. No transport. Hardly any guns – and practically no ammunition for those guns. No medical supplies. No tanks. No planes. No hope – and you keep on fighting. That makes you sane?'

'Touché.' Broznik smiled, pushed across the bottle of *raki*, waited until Mallory had filled his glass. 'To the madmen of this world.'

'I've just been talking to Major Stephan up at the Western Gap,' General Vukalovic said. 'He thinks we're all mad. Would you agree, Colonel Lazlo?'

The man lying prone beside Vukalovic lowered his binoculars. He was a burly, sun-tanned, thick-set, middle-aged man with a magnificent black moustache that had every appearance of being waxed. After a moment's consideration, he said: 'Without a doubt, sir.'

'Even you?' Vukalovic said protestingly. 'With a Czech father?'

'He came from the High Tatra,' Lazlo explained. 'They're all mad there.'

Vukalovic smiled, settled himself more comfortably on his elbows, peered downhill through the gap between two rocks, raised his binoculars and scanned the scene to the south of him, slowly raising his glasses as he did so.

Immediately in front of where he lay was a bare, rocky hillside, dropping gently downhill for a distance of about two hundred feet. Beyond its base it merged gradually into a long flat grassy plateau, no more than two hundred yards wide at its maximum, but stretching almost as far as the eye could see on both sides, on the right-hand side stretching away to the west, on the left curving away to the east, north-east and finally north.

Beyond the edge of the plateau, the land dropped abruptly to form the bank of a wide and swiftly flowing river, a river of that peculiarly Alpine greenish-white colour, green from the melting ice-water of spring, white from where it foamed over jagged rocks and overfalls in the bed of the river. Directly to the south of where Vukalovic and Lazlo lay, the river was spanned by a green-and-white-painted and very solidly-constructed canti-levered steel bridge. Beyond the river, the grassy bank on the far side rose in a very easy slope for a distance of about a hundred yards to the very regularly defined limit of a forest of giant pines which stretched away into the southern distance. Scattered through the very outermost of the pines were a few dully metal-lic objects, unmistakably tanks. In the farthest distance, beyond the river and beyond the pines, towering, jagged mountains dazzled in their brilliant covering of snow and above that again, but more to the south-east, an equally white and dazzling sun shone from an incongruously blue patch in an otherwise snow-cloud-covered sky.

Vukalovic lowered his binoculars and sighed.

'No idea at all how many tanks are across in the woods there?'

'I wish to heaven I knew.' Lazlo lifted his arms in a small, helpless gesture. 'Could be ten. Could be two hundred. We've no idea. We've sent scouts, of course, but thy never came back. May-be they were swept away trying to cross the Neretva.' He looked at Vukalovic, speculation in his eyes. 'Through the Zenica Gap, through the Western Gap or across that bridge there – you don't know where the attack is coming from, do you, sir?'

Vukalovic shook his head.

'But you expect it soon?'

'Very soon.' Vukalovic struck the rocky ground with a clenched fist. 'Is there *no* way of destroying that damned bridge?'

'There have been five RAF attacks,' Lazlo said heavily. 'To date, twenty-seven planes lost – there are two hundrd AA guns along the Neretva and the nearest Messerschmitt station only ten minutes flying time away. The German radar picks up the British bombers crossing our coast – and the Messerschmitts are here, waiting, by the time they arrive. And don't forget that the bridge is set in rock on either side.'

'A direct hit or nothing?'

'A direct hit on a target seven metres wide from three thou-sand metres. It is impossible. And a target so camouflaged that you can hardly see it five hundred metres away on land. Doubly impossible.'

'And impossible for us,' Vukalovic said bleakly.

'Impossible for us. We made our last attempt two nights ago.'

'You made – I told you not to.'

'You *asked* us not to. But of course I, Colonel Lazlo, knew better. They started firing star-shells when our troops were half-way across the plateau, God knows how they knew they were coming. Then the searchlights—'

'Then the shrapnel shells,' Vukalovic finished. 'And the Oerlikons. Casualties?'

'We lost half a battalion.'

'Half a battalion! And tell me, my dear Lazlo, what would have happened in the unlikely event of your men reaching the bridge?'

'They had some amatol blocks, some hand-grenades—'

'No fireworks?' Vukalovic asked in heavy sarcasm. 'That might have helped. That bridge is built of steel set in reinforced concrete, man! You were mad even to try.'

'Yes, sir,' Lazlo looked away. 'Perhaps you ought to relieve me.'

'I think I should.' Vukalovic looked closely at the exhausted face. 'In fact I would. But for one thing.'

'One thing?'

'All my other regimental commanders are as mad as you are. And if the Germans do attack – maybe even tonight?'

'We stand here. We are Yugoslavs and we have no place to go. What else can we do?'

'What else? Two thousand men with pop-guns, most of them weak and starving and lacking ammunition, against what may perhaps be two first-line German armoured divisions. And you stand here. You could always surrender, you know.'

Lazlo smiled. 'With respect, General, this is no time for facetiousness.'

Vukalovic clapped his shoulder. 'I didn't think it funny, either. I'm going up to the dam, to the north-eastern redoubt. I'll see if Colonel Janzy is as mad as you are. And Colonel?'

'Sir?'

'If the attack comes, I may give the order to retreat.'

'Retreat!'

'Not surrender. Retreat. Retreat to what, one hopes, may be victory.'

'I am sure the General knows what he is talking about.'

'The General isn't.' Oblivious to possible sniper fire from across the Neretva, Vukalovic stood up in readiness to go. 'Ever heard of a man called Captain Mallory. Keith Mallory, a New Zealander?'

'No.' Lazlo said promptly. He paused, then went on: 'Wait a minute, though. Fellow who used to climb mountains?'

'That's the one. But he has also, I'm given to understand,

other accomplishments.' Vukalovic rubbed a stubby chin. 'If all I hear about him is true, I think you could quite fairly call him a rather gifted individual.'

'And what about this gifted individual?' Lazlo asked curiously.

'Just this.' Vukalovic was suddenly very serious, even sombre. 'When all things are lost and there is no hope left, there is always, somewhere in the world, one man you can turn to. There may be only that one man. More often than not there *is* only that one man. But that one man is always there.' He paused reflectively. 'Or so they say.'

'Yes, sir,' Lazlo said politely. 'But about this Keith Mallory—'

'Before you sleep tonight, pray for him. I will.'

'Yes, sir. And about us? Shall I pray for us, too?'

'That,' said Vukalovic, 'wouldn't be at all a bad idea.'

The sides of the *jamba* leading upwards from Major Broznik's camp were very steep and very slippery and the ascending cavalcade of men and ponies were making very heavy going of it. Or most of them were. The escort of dark stocky Bosnian Partisans, to whom such terrain was part and parcel of existence, appeared quite unaffected by the climb: and it in no way appeared to interfere with Andrea's rhythmic puffing of his usual vile-smelling cigar. Reynolds noticed this, a fact which fed fresh fuel to the already dark doubts and torments in his mind.

He said sourly: 'You seem to have made a remarkable recovery in the night-time, Colonel Stavros, sir.'

'Andrea.' The cigar was removed. 'I have a heart condition. It comes and it goes.' The cigar was replaced.

'I'm sure it does,' Reynolds muttered. He glanced suspiciously, and for the twentieth time, over his shoulder. 'Where the hell is Mallory?'

'Where the hell is *Captain* Mallory,' Andrea chided.

'Well, where?'

'The leader of an expedition has many responsibilities,' Andrea said. 'Many things to attend to. Captain Mallory is probably attending to something at this very moment.'

'You can say that again,' Reynolds muttered.

'What was that?'

'Nothing.'

Captain Mallory was, as Andrea had so correctly guessed, attending to something at that precise moment. Back in Broznik's office, he and Broznik were bent over a map spread out on the trestle table. Broznik pointed to a spot near the northern limit of the map.

'I agree. This *is* the nearest possible landing strip for a plane. But it is very high up. At this time of year there will still be almost a metre of snow up there. There are other places, better places.'

'I don't doubt that for a moment.' Mallory said. 'Faraway fields are always greener, maybe even faraway airfields. But I haven't the time to go to them.' He stabbed his forefinger on the map. 'I want a landing-strip here and only here by nightfall. I'd be most grateful if you'd send a rider to Konjic within the hour and have my request radioed immediately to your partisan HQ at Drvar.'

Broznik said drily: 'You are accustomed to asking for instant miracles, Captain Mallory?'

'This doesn't call for miracles. Just a thousand men. The feet of a thousand men. A small price for seven thousand lives?' He handed Broznik a slip of paper. 'Wavelength and code. Have Konjic transmit it as soon as possible.' Mallory glanced at his watch. 'They have twenty minutes on me already. I'd better hurry.'

'I suppose you'd better,' Broznik said hurriedly. He hesitated, at a momentary loss for words, then went on awkwardly: 'Captain Mallory, I – I—'

'I know. Don't worry. The Mallorys of this world never make old bones anyway. We're too stupid.'

'Aren't we all, aren't we all?' Broznik gripped Mallory's hand. 'Tonight, I make a prayer for you.'

Mallory remained silent for a moment, then nodded.

'Make it a long one.'

The Bosnian scouts, now, like the remainder of the party, mounted on ponies, led the winding way down through the gentle slopes of the thickly-forested valley, followed by Andrea and Miller riding abreast, then by Petar, whose pony's bridle was in the hand of his sister. Reynolds and Groves, whether by accident or design, had fallen some little way behind and were talking in soft tones.

Groves said speculatively: 'I wonder what Mallory and the Major are talking about back there?'

Reynolds's mouth twisted in bitterness. 'It's perhaps as well we don't know.'

'You may be right at that. I just don't know.' Groves paused, went on almost pleadingly: 'Broznik is on the up-and-up. I'm sure of it. Being what he is, he *must* be.'

'That's as may be. Mallory too, eh?'

'*He* must be, too.'

'Must?' Reynolds was savage. 'God alive, man, I tell you I saw him with my own eyes.' He nodded towards Maria, some twenty yards ahead, and his face was cruel and hard. 'That girl hit him – and *how* she hit him – back in Neufeld's camp and the next thing I see is the two of them having a cosy little lovey-dovey chat outside Broznik's hut. Odd, isn't it? Soon after, Saunders was murdered. Coincidence, isn't it? I tell you, Groves, Mallory could have done it himself. The girl *could* have had time to do it before she met Mallory – except that it would have been physically impossible for her to drive a six-inch knife home to the hilt. But Mallory could have done it all right. He'd time enough – and opportunity enough – when he handed that damned message into the radio hut.'

Groves said protestingly: 'Why in God's name should he do that?'

'Because Broznik had given him some urgent information. Mallory *had* to make a show of passing this information back to Italy. But maybe sending that message was the last thing he wanted. Maybe he stopped it in the only way he knew how – and smashed the transmitter to make sure no one else could send a message. Maybe that's why he stopped me from mounting a guard or going to see Saunders – to prevent me from discovering the fact that Saunders was already dead – in which case, of course, because of the time factor, suspicion would have automatically fallen on him.'

'You're imagining things.' Despite his discomfort, Groves was reluctantly impressed by Reynolds's reasoning.

'You think so? That knife in Saunders's back – did I imagine that too?'

Within half an hour, Mallory had rejoined the party. He jogged past Reynolds and Groves, who studiously ignored him, past Maria and Petar, who did the same, and took up position behind Andrea and Miller.

It was in this order, for almost an hour, that they passed through the heavily-wooded Bosnian valleys. Occasionally, they came to clearings in the pines, clearings that had once been the site of human habitation, small villages or hamlets. But now there were no humans, no habitations, for the villages had ceased to exist. The clearings were all the same, chillingly and depressingly the same. Where the hard-working but happy Bosnians had once lived in their simple but sturdy homes, there were now only the charred and blackened remains of what had once been thriving communities, the air still heavy with the acrid smell of ancient smoke, the sweet-sour stench of corruption and death, mute testimony to the no-quarter viciousness and total ruthlessness of the war between the Germans and the Partisan Yugoslavs. Occasionally, here and there, still stood a few small, stone-built houses which had not been worth the expenditure of bombs or shells or mortars or petrol: but few of the larger buildings had escaped complete destruction. Churches and schools appeared to have been the primary targets: on one occasion, as evidenced by some charred steel equipment that could have come only from an operating theatre, they passed by a small cottage hospital that had been so razed to the ground that no part of the resulting ruins was more than three feet high. Mallory wondered what would have happened to the patients occupying the hospital at the time: but he no longer wondered at the hundreds of thousands of Yugoslavs – 350,000 had been the figure quoted by Captain Jensen, but, taking women and children into account, the number must have been at least a million – who had rallied under the banner of Marshal Tito. Patriotism apart, the burning desire for liberation and revenge apart, there was no place else left for them to go. They were a people, Mallory realized, with literally nothing left, with nothing to lose but their lives which they apparently held of small account, but with everything to gain by the destruction of the enemy: were he a German soldier, Mallory reflected, he would not have felt particularly happy about the prospect of a posting to Yugoslavia. It was a war which the Wehrmacht could never win, which the soldiers of no Western European country could ever have won, for the peoples of the high mountains are virtually indestructible.

The Bosnian scouts, Mallory observed, looked neither to left nor right as they passed through the lifeless shattered villages of their countrymen, most of whom were now almost certainly dead. They didn't *have* to look, he realized: they had their memories, and even their memories would be too much for them. If it were possible to feel pity for an enemy, then Mallory at that moment felt pity for the Germans.

By and by they emerged from the narrow winding mountain track on to a narrow, but comparatively wide road, wide enough, at least, for single-file vehicular traffic. The Bosnian scout in the lead threw up his hand and halted his pony.

'Unofficial no-man's-land, it would seem,' Mallory said. 'I think this is where they turfed us off the truck this morning.'

Mallory's guess appeared to be correct. The Partisans wheeled their horses, smiled widely, waved, shouted some unintelligible words of farewell and urged their horses back the way they had come.

With Mallory and Andrea in the lead and the two sergeants bringing up the rear, the seven remaining members of the party moved off down the track. The snow had stopped now, the clouds above had cleared away and the sunlight was filtering down between the now thinning pines. Suddenly Andrea, who had been peering to his left, reached out and touched Mallory on the arm. Mallory followed the direction of Andrea's pointing hand. Downhill, the pines petered out less than a hundred yards away and through the trees could be glimpsed some distant object, a startling green in colour. Mallory swung round in his saddle.

'Down there. I want to take a look. *Don't* move below the tree-line.'

The ponies picked their delicate sure-footed way down the steep and slippery slope. About ten yards from the tree-line and at a signal from Mallory, the riders dismounted and advanced cautiously on foot, moving from the cover of one pine to the next. The last few feet they covered on hands and knees, then finally stretched out flat in the partial concealment of the boles of the lowermost pines. Mallory brought out his binoculars, cleared the cold-clouded lenses and brought them to his eyes.

The snow-line, he saw, petered out some three or four hundred yards below them. Below that again was a mixture of fissured and eroded rock-faces and brown earth and beyond that again a belt of sparse and discouraged-looking grass. Along the lower reaches of this belt of grass ran a tarmacadam road, a road which struck Mallory as being, for that area, in remarkably good condition: the road was more or less exactly paralleled, at a distance of about a hundred yards, by a single-track and extremely narrow-gauge railway: a grass-grown and rusted line that looked as if it hadn't been used for many years. Just beyond the line the land dropped in a precipitous cliff to a narrow winding lake, the farther margin of which was marked by far more towering precipices leading up without break and with hardly any variation in angle to rugged snow-capped mountains.

From where he lay Mallory was directly overlooking a right-angled bend in the lake, a lake which was almost incredibly beautiful. In the bright clear sparkling sunlight of that spring morning it glittered and gleamed like the purest of emeralds. The smooth surface was occasionally ruffled by errant catspaws of wind, catspaws which had the effect of deepening the emerald colour to an almost translucent aquamarine. The lake itself was nowhere much more than a quarter of a mile in width, but obviously miles in length: the long right-hand arm, twisting and turning between the mountains, stretched to the east almost as far as the eye could see: to the left, the short southern arm, hemmed in by increasingly vertical walls which finally appeared almost to meet overhead, ended against the concrete ramparts of a dam. But what caught and held the attention of the watchers was the incredible mirrored gleam of the far mountains in that equally incredible emerald mirror.

'Well, now,' Miller murmured, 'that *is* nice.' Andrea gave him a long expressionless look, then turned his attention to the lake again.

Groves's interest momentarily overcame his animosity.

'What lake is that, sir?'

Mallory lowered the binoculars. 'Haven't the faintest idea. Maria?' She made no answer. Maria! What – lake – is – that?'

'That's the Neretva dam,' she said sullenly. 'The biggest in Yugoslavia.'

'It's important, then?'

'It is important. Whoever controls that controls Central Yugoslavia.'

'And the Germans control it, I suppose?'

'They control it. *We* control it.' There was more than a hint of triumph in her smile. 'We – the Germans – have got it completely sealed off. Cliffs on both sides. To the east there – the upper end – they have a boom across a gorge only ten yards wide. And that boom is patrolled night and day. So is the dam wall itself. The only way in is by a set of steps – ladders, rather – fixed to the cliff face just below the dam.'

Mallory said drily: 'Very interesting information – for a parachute brigade. But we've other and more urgent fish to fry. Come on.' He glanced at Miller, who nodded and began to ease his way back up the slope, followed by the two sergeants, Maria and Petar. Mallory and Andrea lingered for a few moments longer.

'I wonder what it's like,' Mallory murmured.

'What's what like?' Andrea asked.
'The other side of the dam.'
'And the ladder let into the cliff?'
'And the ladder let into the cliff.'

From where General Vukalovic lay, high on a cliff-top on the right-hand or western side of the Neretva gorge, he had an excellent view of the ladder let into the cliff: he had, in fact, an excellent view of the entire outer face of the dam wall and of the gorge which began at the foot of the wall and extended southwards for almost a mile before vanishing from sight round an abrupt right-hand corner.

The dam wall itself was quite narrow, not much more than thirty yards in width, but very deep, stretching down in a slightly V-formation from between overhanging cliff-faces to the greenish-white torrent of water foaming from the outlet pipes at the base. On top of the dam, at the eastern end and on a slight eminence, were the control station and two small huts, one of which, judging from the clearly visible soldiers patrolling the top of the wall, was almost certainly a guard-room. Above those buildings the walls of the gorge rose quite vertically for about thirty feet, then jutted out in a terrifying overhang.

From the control-room, a zig-zag, green-painted iron ladder, secured by brackets to the rock face, led down to the floor of the gorge. From the base of the ladder a narrow path extended down the gorge for a distance of about a hundred yards, ending abruptly at a spot where some ancient landslide had gouged a huge scar into the side of the gorge. From here a bridge spanned the river to another path on the right-hand bank.

As bridges go, it wasn't much, an obviously very elderly and rickety wooden swing bridge which looked as if its own weight would be enough to carry it into the torrent at any moment: what was even worse, it seemed, at first glance, as if its site had been deliberately picked by someone with an unhinged mind, for it lay directly below an enormous boulder some forty feet up the landslide, a boulder so clearly in a highly precarious state of balance that none but the most foolhardy would have lingered in the crossing of the bridge. In point of fact, no other site would have been possible.

From the western edge of the bridge, the narrow, boulder-strewn path followed the line of the river, passing by what looked like an extremely hazardous ford, and finally curving away from sight with the river.

General Vukalovic lowered his binoculars, turned to the man
at his side and smiled.

'All quiet on the eastern front, eh, Colonel Janzy?'

'All quiet on the eastern front,' Janzy agreed. He was a small,
puckish, humorous-looking character with a youthful face and
incongruous white hair. He twisted round and gazed to the
north. 'But not so quiet on the northern front, I'm afraid.'

The smile faded from Vukalovic's face as he turned, lifted his
binoculars again and gazed to the north. Less than three miles
away and clearly visible in the morning sunlight, lay the heavily
wooded Zenica Gap, for weeks a hotly contested strip of territory
between Vukalovic's northern defensive forces, under the command of Colonel Janzy, and units of the invading German 11th
Army Corps. At that moment frequent puffs of smoke could be
seen, to the left a thick column of smoke spiralled up to form a
dark pall against the now cloudless blue of the sky, while the
distant rattle of small-arms fire, punctuated by the occasional
heavier boom of artillery, was almost incessant. Vukalovic
lowered his glasses and looked thoughtfully at Janzy.

'The softening-up before the main attack?'

'What else? The final assault.'

'How many tanks?'

'It's difficult to be sure. Collating reports, my staff estimate a
hundred and fifty.'

'One hundred and fifty!'

'That's what they make it – and at least fifty of those are Tiger
tanks.'

'Let's hope to heaven your staff can't count.' Vukalovic rubbed
a weary hand across his bloodshot eyes: he'd had no sleep during
the night just gone, no esleep during the night previous to that.
'Let's go and see how many *we* can count.'

Maria and Petar led the way now, with Reynolds and Groves,
clearly in no mood for other company, bringing up the rear almost fifty yards behind. Mallory, Andrea and Miller rode
abreast along the narrow road. Andrea looked at Mallory, his
eyes speculative.

'Saunders's death? Any idea?'

Mallory shook his head. 'Ask me something else.'

'The message you'd given him to send. What was it?'

'A report of our safe arrival in Broznik's camp. Nothing more.'

'A psycho,' Miller announced. 'The handy man with the
knife, I mean. Only a psycho would kill for that reason.'

'Maybe he didn't kill for that reason,' Mallory said mildly. 'Maybe he thought it was some other kind of message.'

'Some other kind of message?' Miller lifted an eyebrow in the way that only he knew how. 'Now what kind—' He caught Andrea's eye, broke off and changed his mind about saying anything more. Both he and Andrea gazed curiously at Mallory who seemed to have fallen into a mood of intense introspection.

Whatever its reason, the period of deep preoccupation did not last for long. With the air of a man who has just arrived at a conclusion about something, Mallory lifted his head and called to Maria to stop, at the same time reining in his own pony. Together they waited until Reynolds and Groves had made up on them.

'There are a good number of options open to us,' Mallory said, 'but for better or worse this is what I have decided to do.' He smiled faintly. 'For better, I think, if for no other reason than that this is the course of action that will get us out of here fastest. I've talked to Major Broznik and found out what I wanted. He tells me—'

'Got your information for Neufeld, then, have you?' If Reynolds was attempting to mask the contempt in his voice he made a singularly poor job of it.

'The hell with Neufeld,' Mallory said without heat. 'Partisan spies have discovered where the four captured Allied agents are being held.'

'They have?' Reynolds said. 'Then why don't the Partisans do something about it?'

'For a good enough reason. The agents are held deep in German territory. In an impregnable block-house high up in the mountains.'

'And what are *we* going to do about the Allied agents held in this impregnable block-house?'

'Simple.' Mallory corrected himself. 'Well, in theory it's simple. We take them out of there and make our break tonight.'

Reynolds and Groves stared at Mallory, then at each other in frank disbelief and consternation. Andrea and Miller carefully avoided looking at each other or at anyone else.

'You're mad!' Reynolds spoke with total conviction.

'You're mad, *sir*,' Andrea said reprovingly.

Reynolds looked uncomprehendingly at Andrea, then turned back to Mallory again.

'You must be!' he insisted. 'Break? Break for where, in heaven's name?'

'For home. For Italy.'

'Italy!' It took Reynolds all of ten seconds to digest this startling piece of information, then he went on sarcastically: 'We're going to fly there, I suppose?'

'Well, it's a long swim across the Adriatic, even for a fit youngster like you. How else?'

'Flying?' Groves seemed slightly dazed.

'Flying. Not ten kilometres from here is a high – a very high mountain plateau, mostly in Partisan hands. There'll be a plane there at nine o'clock tonight.'

In the fashion of people who have failed to grasp something they have just heard, Groves repeated the statement in the form of a question. 'There'll be a plane there at nine o'clock tonight? You've just arranged this?'

'How could I? We've no radio.'

Reynolds's distrustful face splendidly complemented the scepticism in his voice. 'But *how* can you be sure – well, at nine o'clock?'

'Because, starting at six o'clock this evening, there'll be a Wellington bomber over the airstrip every three hours for the next week if necessary.'

Mallory kneed his pony and the party moved on, Reynolds and Groves taking up their usual position well to the rear of the others. For some time Reynolds, his expression alternating between hostility and speculation, stared fixedly at Mallory's back: then he turned to Groves.

'Well, well, well. Isn't that very convenient indeed. We just *happen* to be sent to Broznik's camp. He just *happens* to know where the four agents are held. It just *happens* that an airplane will be over a certain airfield at a certain time – and it also so happens that I know for an absolute certainty that there are no airfields up in the high plateau. Still think everything clean and above-board?'

It was quite obvious from the unhappy expression on Groves's face that he thought nothing of the kind. He said: 'What in God's name are we going to do?'

'Watch our backs.'

Fifty yards ahead of them Miller cleared his throat and said delicately to Mallory: 'Reynolds seems to have lost some of his – um – earlier confidence in you, sir.'

Mallory said drily: 'It's not surprising. He thinks I stuck that knife in Saunders's back.'

This time Andrea and Miller did exchange glances, their faces

registering expressions as close to pure consternation as either
of those poker-faced individuals was capable of achieving.

7

FRIDAY

1000—1200

Half a mile from Neufeld's camp they were met by Captain
Droshny and some half-dozen of his Cetniks. Droshny's welcome
was noticably lacking in cordiality but at least he managed, at
what unknown cost, to maintain some semblance of inoffensive
neutrality.

'So you came back?'

'As you can see,' Mallory agreed.

Droshny looked at the ponies. 'And travelling in comfort.'

'A present from our good friend Major Broznik.' Mallory
grinned. 'He thinks we're heading for Konjic on them.'

Droshny didn't appear to care very much what Major Broznik
had thought. He jerked his head, wheeled his horse and set off at
a fast trot for Neufeld's camp.

When they had dismounted inside the compound, Droshny
immediately led Mallory into Neufeld's hut. Neufeld's welcome,
like Droshny's, was something less than ecstatic, but at least he
succeeded in imparting a shade more benevolence to his neutrality. His face held, also, just a hint of surprise, a reaction
which he explained at once.

'Candidly, Captain, I did not expect to see you again. There
were so many – ah – imponderables. However, I am delighted to
see you – you would not have returned without the information
I wanted. Now then, Captain Mallory, to business.'

Mallory eyed Neufeld without enthusiasm. 'You're not a very
business-like partner, I'm afraid.'

'I'm not?' Neufeld said politely. 'In what way?'

'Business partners don't tell lies to each other. Sure you said
Vukalovic's troops are massing. So they are indeed. But not, as
you said, to break out. Instead, they're massing to defend themselves against the final German attack, the assault that is to
crush them once and for all, and this assault they believe to be
imminent.'

'Well, now, you surely didn't expect me to give away our military secrets – which you might, I say just might, have relayed to the enemy – before you had proved yourselves, Neufeld said reasonably. 'You're not that naïve. About this proposed attack. Who gave you the information.'

'Major Broznik.' Mallory smiled in recollection. 'He was very expansive.'

Neufeld leaned forward, his tension reflected in the sudden stillness of his face, in the way his unblinking eyes held Mallory's. 'And did they say where they expected this attack to come?'

'I only know the name. The bridge at Neretva.'

Neufeld sank back into his chair, exhaled a long soundless sigh of relief and smiled to rob his next words of any offence. 'My friend, if you weren't British, a deserter, a renegade and a dope-peddler, you'd get the Iron Cross for this. By the way,' he went on, as if by casual afterthought, 'you've been cleared from Padua. The bridge at Neretva? You're sure of this?'

Mallory said irritably: 'If you doubt my word—'

'Of course not, of course not. Just a manner of speaking.' Neufeld paused for a few moments, then said softly: 'The bridge at Neretva.' The way he spoke them, the words sounded almost like a litany.

Droshny said softly: 'This fits in with all we suspected.'

'Never mind what you suspected,' Mallory said rudely. 'To *my* business now, if you don't mind. We have done well, you would say? We have fulfilled your request, got the precise information you wanted?' Neufeld nodded. 'Then get us the hell out of here. Fly us deep into some German-held territory. Into Austria or Germany itself, if you like – the farther away from here the better. You know what will happen to us if we ever again fall into British or Yugoslav hands?'

'It's not hard to guess,' Neufeld said almost cheerfully. 'But you misjudge us, my friend. Your departure to a place of safety has already been arranged. A certain Chief of Military Intelligence in northern Italy would very much like to make your personal acquaintance. He has reason to believe that you can be of great help to him.'

Mallory nodded his understanding.

General Vukalovic trained his binoculars on the Zenica Gap, a narrow and heavily-wooded valley floor lying between the bases of two high and steep-shouldered mountains, mountains almost identical in both shape and height.

The German 11th Army Corps tanks among the pines were not difficult to locate, for the Germans had made no attempt either to camouflage or conceal them, measure enough, Vukalovic thought grimly, of the Germans' total confidence in themselves and in the outcome of the battle that lay ahead. He could clearly see soldiers working on some stationary vehicles: other tanks were backing and filling and manœuvring into position as if making ready to take up battle formation for the actual attack: the deep rumbling roar of the heavy engines of Tiger tanks was almost incessant.

Vukalovic lowered his glasses, jotted down a few more pencil marks on a sheet of paper already almost covered with similar pencil marks, performed a few exercises in addition, laid paper and pencil aside with a sigh and turned to Colonel Janzy, who was similarly engaged.

Vukalovic said wryly: 'My apologies to your staff, Colonel. They can count just as well as I can.'

For once, Captain Jensen's piratical swagger and flashing, confident smile were not very much in evidence: at that moment, in fact, they were totally absent. It would have been impossible for a face of Jensen's generous proportions ever to assume an actually haggard appearance, but the set, grim face displayed unmistakable signs of strain and anxiety and sleeplessness as he paced up and down the 5th Army Operations Headquarters in Termoli in Italy.

He did not pace alone. Beside him, matching him step for step, a burly grey-haired officer in the uniform of a lieutenant-general in the British Army accompanied him backwards and forwards, the expression on his face an exact replica of that on Jensen's. As they came to the farther end of the room, the General stopped and glanced interrogatively at a head-phone-wearing sergeant seated in front of a large RCA transceiver. The sergeant slowly shook his head. The two men resumed their pacing.

The General said abruptly: 'Time is running out. You do appreciate, Jensen, that once you launch a major offensive you can't possibly stop it?'

'I appreciate it,' Jensen said heavily. 'What are the latest reconnaissance reports, sir?'

'There is no shortage of reports, but God alone knows what to make of them all.' The General sounded bitter. 'There's intense activity all along the Gustav Line, involving – as far as we can make out – two Panzer divisions, one German infantry division, one Austrian infantry division and two Jaeger battalions – their crack Alpine troops. They're not mounting an offensive, that's for sure – in the first place, there's no possibility of their making an offensive from the area in which they are manœuvring and in the second place if they *were* contemplating an offensive they'd take damn good care to keep all their preparations secret.'

'All this activity, then? If they're not planning an attack.'

The General sighed. 'Informed opinion has it that they're making all preparations for a lightning pull-out. Informed opinion! All that concerns me is that those blasted divisions are still in the Gustav Line. Jensen, *what has gone wrong?*'

Jensen lifted his shoulders in a gesture of helplessness. 'It was arranged for a radio rendezvous every two hours from four a.m.—'

'There have been no contacts whatsoever.'

Jensen said nothing.

The General looked at him, almost speculatively. 'The best in Southern Europe, you said.'

'Yes, I did say that.'

The General's unspoken doubts as to the quality of the agents Jensen had selected for operation Force 10 would have been considerably heightened if he had been at that moment present with those agents in the guest hut in Hauptmann Neufeld's camp in Bosnia. They were exhibiting none of the harmony, understanding and implicit mutual trust which one would have expected to find among a team of agents rated as the best in the business. There was, instead, tension and anger in the air, an air of suspicion and mistrust so heavy as to be almost palpable. Reynolds, confronting Mallory, had his anger barely under control.

'I want to know now!' Reynolds almost shouted the words.

'Keep your voice down,' Andrea said sharply.

'I want to know now,' Reynolds repeated. This time his voice was little more than a whisper, but none the less demanding and insistent for that.

'You'll be told when the time comes.' As always, Mallory's voice was calm and neutral and devoid of heat. 'Not till then. What you don't know, you can't tell.'

Reynolds clenched his fists and advanced a step. 'Are you damn well insinuating that—'

Mallory said with restraint: 'I'm insinuating nothing. I was right, back in Termoli, Sergeant. You're no better than a ticking time-bomb.'

'Maybe.' Reynolds's fury was out of control now. 'But at least there's something honest about a bomb.'

'Repeat that remark,' Andrea said quietly.

'What?'

'Repeat it.'

'Look, Andrea—'

'Colonel Stavros, sonny.'

'Sir.'

'Repeat it and I'll guarantee you a minimum of five years for insubordination in the field.'

'Yes, sir.' Reynolds's physical effort to bring himself under control was apparent to everyone. 'But *why* should he *not* tell us his plans for this afternoon and at the same time let us all know that we'll be leaving from this Ivenici place tonight?'

'Because our plans are something the Germans can do something about,' Andreas said patiently. 'If they find out. If one of us talked under duress. But they can't do anything about Ivenici – that's in Partisan hands.'

Miller pacifically changed the subject. He said to Mallory: 'Seven thousand feet up, you say. The snow must be thigh-deep up there. How in God's name does anyone hope to clear all that lot away?'

'I don't know,' Mallory said vaguely. 'I suspect somebody will think of something.'

And, seven thousand feet up on the Ivenici plateau, somebody had indeed thought of something.

The Ivenici plateau was a wilderness in white, a bleak and desolate and, for many months of the year, a bitterly cold and howling and hostile wilderness, totally inimical to human life totally intolerant of human presence. The plateau was bounded to the west by a five-hundred-foot-high cliff-face, quite vertical in some parts, fractured and fissured in others. Scattered along its length were numerous frozen waterfalls and occasional lines of pine trees, impossibly growing on impossibly narrow ledges, their frozen branches drooped and laden with the frozen snow of six long months gone by. To the east the plateau was bounded

813

by nothing but an abrupt and sharply defined line marking the top of another cliff-face which dropped away perpendicularly into the valleys below.

The plateau itself consisted of a smooth, absolutely level, unbroken expanse of snow, snow which at that height of 2000 metres and in the brilliant sunshine gave off a glare and dazzling reflection which was positively hurtful to the eyes. In length, it was perhaps half a mile: in width, nowhere more than a hundred yards. At its southern end, the plateau rose sharply to merge with the cliff-face which here tailed off and ran into the ground.

On this prominence stood two tents, both white, one small, the other a large marquee. Outside the small tent stood two men, talking. The taller and older man, wearing a heavy greatcoat and a pair of smoked glasses, was Colonel Vis, the commandant of a Sarajevo-based brigade of Partisans: the younger, slighter figure was his adjutant, a Captain Vlanovich. Both men were gazing out over the length of the plateau.

Captain Vlanovich said unhappily: 'There must be easier ways of doing this, sir.'

'You name it, Boris, my boy, and I'll do it.' Both in appearance and voice Colonel Vis gave the impression of immense calm and competence. 'Bull-dozers, I agree, would help. So would snow-ploughs. But you will agree that to drive either of them up vertical cliff-faces in order to reach here would call for considerable skill on the part of the drivers. Besides, what's an army for, if not for marching?'

'Yes, sir,' Vlanovich said, dutifully and doubtfully.

Both men gazed out over the length of the plateau to the north.

To the north, and beyond, for all around a score of encircling mountain peaks, some dark and jagged and sombre, others rounded and snow-capped and rose-coloured, soared up into the cloudless washed-out pale blue of the sky. It was an immensely impressive sight.

Even more impressive was the spectacle taking place on the plateau itself. A solid phalanx of a thousand uniformed soldiers, perhaps half in the buff grey of the Yugoslav army, the rest in a motley array of other countries' uniforms, were moving, at a snail-pace, across the virgin snow.

The phalanx was fifty people wide but only twenty deep, each line of fifty linked arm-in-arm, heads and shoulders bowed forward as they laboriously trudged at a painfully slow pace through the snow. That the pace was so slow was no matter for wonder, the leading line of men were ploughing their way through waist-deep snow, and already the signs of strain and exhaustion were showing in their faces. It was killingly hard work, work which, at that altitude, doubled the pulse rate, made a man fight for every gasping breath, turned a man's legs into leaden and agonized limbs where only the pain could convince him that they were still part of him.

And not only men. After the first five lines of soldiers, there were almost as many women and girls in the remainder of the phalanx as there were men, although everyone was so muffled against the freezing cold and biting winds of those high altitudes that it was impossible almost to tell man from woman. The last two lines of the phalanx were composed entirely of *partisankas* and it was significantly ominous of the murderous labour still to come that even they were sinking knee-deep in the snow.

It was a fantastic sight, but a sight that was far from unique in wartime Yugoslavia. The airfields of the lowlands, completely dominated by the armoured divisions of the Wehrmacht, were permanently barred to the Yugoslavs and it was thus that the Partisans constructed many of their airstrips in the mountains. In snow of this depth and in areas completely inaccessible to powered mechanical aids, there was no other way open to them.

Colonel Vis looked away and turned to Captain Vlanovich.

'Well, Boris, my boy, do you think you're up here for the winter sports? Get the food and soup kitchens organized. We'll use up a whole week's rations of hot food and hot soup in this one day.'

'Yes, sir.' Vlanovich cocked his head, then removed his ear-flapped fur cap the better to listen to the newly-begun sound of distant explosions to the north. 'What on earth is that?'

Vis said musingly: 'Sound does carry far in our pure Yugo-slavian mountain air, does it not?'

'Sir? Please?'

'That, my boy,' Vis said with considerable satisfaction, 'is the Messerschmitt fighter base at Novo Derventa getting the biggest plastering of its lifetime.'

'Sir?'

Vis sighed in long-suffering patience. 'I'll make a soldier of you some day. Messerschmitts, Boris, are fighters, carrying all sorts of nasty cannons and machine-guns. What, at this moment, is the finest fighter target in Yugoslavia?'

'What is—' Vlanovich broke off and looked again at the trudging phalanx. 'Oh!'

' "Oh," indeed. The British Air Force have diverted six of their best Lancaster heavy bomber squadrons from the Italian front just to attend to our friends at Novo Derventa.' He in turn removed his cap, the better to listen. 'Hard at work, aren't they? By the time they're finished there won't be a Messerschmitt able to take off from that field for a week. If, that is to say, there are any left to take off.'

'If I might venture a remark, sir?'

'You may so venture, Captain Vlanovich.'

'There are other fighter bases.'

'True.' Vis pointed upwards. 'See anything?'

Vlanovich craned his neck, shielded his eyes against the brilliant sun, gazed into the empty blue sky and shook his head.

'Neither do I,' Vis agreed. 'But at seven thousand metres – and with their crews even colder than we are – squadrons of Beaufighters will be keeping relief patrol up there until dark.'

'Who – who *is* he, sir? Who can ask for all our soldiers down here, for squadrons of bombers and fighters?'

'Fellow called Captain Mallory, I believe.'

'A *captain*? Like me?'

'A captain. I doubt, Boris,' Vis went on kindly, 'whether he's quite like you. But it's not the rank that counts. It's the name. Mallory.'

'Never heard of him.'

'You will, my boy, you will.'

'But – but this man Mallory. What does he want all this *for*?'

'Ask him when you see him tonight.'

'When I – he's coming here tonight?'

'Tonight. If,' Vis added sombrely, 'he lives that long.'

Neufeld, followed by Droshny, walked briskly and confidently into his radio hut, a bleak, ramshackle lean-to furnished with a table, two chairs, a large portable transceiver and nothing else. The German corporal seated before the radio looked up enquiringly at their entrance.

'The Seventh Armoured Corps HQ at the Neretva bridge,' Neufeld ordered. He seemed in excellent spirits. 'I wish to speak to General Zimmermann personally.'

The corporal nodded acknowledgment, put through the call-sign and was answered within seconds. He listened briefly, looked up at Neufeld. 'The General is coming now, sir.'

Neufeld reached out a hand for the ear-phones, took them and nodded towards the door. The corporal rose and left the hut while Neufeld took the vacated seat and adjusted the headphones to his satisfaction. After a few seconds he automatically straightened in his seat as a voice came crackling over the ear-phones.

'Hauptmann Neufeld here, Herr General. The Englishmen have returned. Their information is that the Partisan division in the Zenica Cage is expecting a full-scale attack from the south across the Neretva bridge.'

'Are they now?' General Zimmermann, comfortably seated in a swivel chair in the back of the radio truck parked on the tree-line due south of the Neretva bridge, made no attempt to conceal the satisfaction in his voice. The canvas hood of the truck was rolled back and he removed his peaked cap the better to enjoy the pale spring sunshine. 'Interesting, very interesting. Anything else.'

'Yes,' Neufeld's voice crackled metallically over the loud-speaker. 'They've asked to be flown to sanctuary. Deep behind our lines, even to Germany. They feel – ah – unsafe here.'

'Well, well, well. Is that how they feel.' Zimmermann paused, considered, then continued. 'You are fully informed of the situation, Hauptmann Neufeld? You are aware of the delicate balance of – um – niceties involved?'

'Yes, Herr General.'

'This calls for a moment's thought. Wait.'

Zimmermann swung idly to and fro in his swivel chair as he pondered his decision. He gazed thoughtfully but almost unseeingly to the north, across the meadows bordering the south bank of the Neretva, the river spanned by the iron bridge, then the meadows on the far side rising steeply to the rocky redoubt which served as the first line of defence for Colonel Lazlo's Partisan defenders. To the east, as he turned, he could look up the green-white rushing waters of the Neretva, the meadows on either side of it narrowing until, curving north, they disappeared suddenly at the mouth of the cliff-side gorge from which the Neretva emerged. Another quarter turn and he was gazing into the pine forest to the south, a pine forest which at first seemed innocuous enough and empty of life – until, that was, one's eyes became accustomed to the gloom and scores of large rectangular shapes, effectively screened from both observation from the air and from the northern bank of the Neretva by camouflage canvas, camouflage nets and huge piles of dead branches. The sight of those camouflaged spearheads of his two Panzer divisions somehow helped Zimmermann to make up his mind. He picked up the microphone.

'Hauptmann Neufeld? I have decided on a course of action and you will please carry out the following instructions precisely . . .'

Droshny removed the duplicate pair of ear-phones that he had been wearing and said doubtfully to Neufeld: 'Isn't the General asking rather a lot of us?'

Neufeld shook his head reassuringly. 'General Zimmermann *always* knows what he is doing. His psychological assessment of the Captain Mallorys of this world is invariably a hundred per cent right.'

'I hope so.' Droshny was unconvinced. 'For our sakes, I hope so.'

They left the hut. Neufeld said to the radio-operator: 'Captain Mallory in my office, please. And Sergeant Baer.'

Mallory arrived in the office to find Neufeld, Droshny and Baer already there. Neufeld was brief and business-like.

'We've decided on a ski-plane to fly you out – there're the only planes that can land in those damned mountains. You'll have time for a few hours sleep – we don't leave till four. Any questions?'

'Where's the landing-strip?'

'A clearing. A kilometre from here. Anything else?'

'Nothing. Just get us out of here, that's all.'

'You need have no worry on that score,' Neufeld said emphatically. 'My one ambition is to see you safely on your way. Frankly, Mallory, you're just an embarrassment to me and the sooner you're on your way the better.'

Mallory nodded and left. Neufeld turned to Baer and said: 'I have a little task for you. Sergeant Baer. Little but very important. Listen carefully.'

Mallory left Neufeld's hut, his face pensive, and walked slowly across the compound. As he approached the guest hut, Andrea emerged and passed wordlessly by, wreathed in cigar smoke and scowling. Mallory entered the hut where Petar was again playing the Yugoslavian version of 'The girl I left behind me.' It seemed to be his favourite song. Mallory glanced at Maria,

Reynolds and Groves, all sitting silently by, then at Miller who was reclining in his sleeping-bag with his volume of poetry.

Mallory nodded toward the doorway. 'Something's upset our friend.'

Miller grinned and nodded in turn towards Petar. 'He's playing Andrea's tune again.'

Mallory smiled briefly and turned to Maria. 'Tell him to stop playing. We're pulling out late this afternoon and we all need all the sleep we can get.'

'We can sleep in the plane,' Reynolds said sullenly. 'We can sleep when we arrived at our destination – wherever that may be.'

'No, sleep now.'

'Why now?'

'Why now?' Mallory's unfocused eyes gazed into the far distance. He said in a quiet voice: 'For now is all the time there may be.'

Reynolds looked at him strangely. For the first time that day his face was empty of hostility and suspicion. There was puzzled speculation in his eyes, and wonder and the first faint beginnings of understanding.

On the Ivenici plateau, the phalanx moved on, but they moved no more like human beings. They stumbled along now in the advanced stages of exhaustion, automatons, no more, zombies resurrected from the dead, their faces twisted with pain and unimaginable fatigue, their limbs on fire and their minds benumbed. Every few seconds someone stumbled and fell and could not get up again and had to be carried to join scores of others already lying in an almost comatose condition by the side of the primitive runway, where *partisankas* did their best to revive their frozen and exhausted bodies with mugs of hot soup and liberal doses of *raki*.

Captain Vlanovich turned to Colonel Vis. His face was distressed, his voice low and deeply earnest.

'This is madness, Colonel, madness! It's – it's impossible, you can see it's impossible. We'll never – look, sir, two hundred and fifty dropped out in the first two hours. The altitude, the cold, sheer physical exhaustion. It's madness.'

'All war is madness,' Vis said calmly. 'Get on the radio. We require five hundred more men.'

—— 8 ——

FRIDAY

1500–2115

Now it had come, Mallory knew. He looked at Andrea and Miller and Reynolds and Groves and knew that they knew it too. In their faces he could see very clearly reflected what lay at the very surface of his own mind, the explosive tension, the hair-trigger alertness straining to be translated into equally explosive action. Always it came, this moment of truth that stripped men bare and showed them for what they were. He wondered how Reynolds and Groves would be: he suspected they might acquit themselves well. It never occurred to him to wonder about Miller and Andrea, for he knew them too well: Miller, when all seemed lost, was a man above himself, while the normally easy-going, almost lethargic Andrea was transformed into an unrecognizable human being, an impossible combination of an icily calculating mind and berserker fighting machine entirely without the remotest parallel in Mallory's knowledge or experience. When Mallory spoke his voice was as calmly impersonal as ever.

'We're due to leave at four. It's now three. With any luck we'll catch them napping. Is everything clear?'

Reynolds said wonderingly, almost unbelievingly: 'You mean if anything goes wrong we're to shoot our way out?'

'You're to shoot and shoot to kill. That, Sergeant, is an order.'

'Honest to God,' Reynolds said, 'I just don't know what's going on.' The expression on his face clearly indicated that he had given up all attempts to understand what was going on.

Mallory and Andrea left the hut and walked casually across the compound towards Neufeld's hut. Mallory said: 'They're on to us, you know.'

'I know. Where are Petar and Maria?'

'Asleep, perhaps? They left the hut a couple of hours ago. We'll collect them later.'

'Later may be too late . . . They are in great peril, my Keith.'

'What can a man do, Andrea? I've thought of nothing else in the past ten hours. It's a crucifying risk to have to take, but I have to take it. They are expendable, Andrea. You know what it would mean if I showed my hand now.'

'I know what it would mean,' Andrea said heavily. 'The end of everything.'

They entered Neufeld's hut without benefit of knocking. Neufeld, sitting behind his desk with Droshny by his side, looked up in irritated surprise and glanced at his watch.

He said curtly: 'Four o'clock, I said, not three.'

'Our mistake,' Mallory apologized. He closed the door. 'Please do not be foolish.'

Neufeld and Droshny were not foolish, few people would have been while staring down the muzzles of two Lugers with perforated silencers screwed to the end: they just sat there, immobile, the shock slowly draining from their faces. There was a long pause then Neufeld spoke, the words coming almost haltingly.

'I have been seriously guilty of underestimating—'

'Be quiet. Broznik's spies have discovered the whereabouts of the four captured Allied agents. We know roughly where they are. You know precisely where they are. You will take us there. Now.'

'You're mad,' Neufeld said with conviction.

'We don't require you to tell us that.' Andrea walked round behind Neufeld and Droshny, removed their pistols from their holsters, ejected the shells and replaced the pistols. He then crossed to a corner of the hut, picked up two Schmeisser machine-pistols, emptied them, walked back round to the front of the table and placed the Schmeissers on its top, one in front of Neufeld, one in front of Droshny.

'There you are, gentlemen,' Andrea said affably. 'Armed to the teeth.'

Droshny said viciously: 'Suppose we decide not to come with you?'

Andrea's affability vanished. He walked unhurriedly round the table and rammed the Luger's silencer with such force against Droshny's teeth that he gasped in pain. 'Please—' Andrea's voice was almost beseeching – '*please* don't tempt me.'

Droshny didn't tempt him. Mallory moved to the window and peered out over the compound. There were, he saw, at least a dozen Cetniks within thirty feet of Neufeld's hut, all of them armed. Across the other side of the compound he could see that the door to the stables was open indicating that Miller and the two sergeants were in position.

'You will walk across the compound to the stables,' Mallory said. 'You will talk to nobody, warn nobody, make no signals.

We will follow about ten yards behind.'

'Ten yards behind. What's to prevent us making a break for it. You wouldn't dare hold a gun on us out there.'

'That's so,' Mallory agreed. 'From the moment you open this door you'll be covered by three Schmeissers from the stables. If you try anything – *anything* – you'll be cut to pieces. That's why we're keeping well behind you – we don't want to be cut to pieces too.'

At a gesture from Andrea, Neufeld and Droshny slung their empty Schmeissers in angry silence. Mallory looked at them consideringly and said: 'I think you'd better do something about your expressions. They're a dead giveaway that something is wrong. If you open that door with faces like that, Miller will cut you down before you reach the bottom step. Please try to believe me.'

They believed him and by the time Mallory opened the door had managed to arrange their features into a near enough imitation of normality. They went down the steps and set off across the compound to the stables. When they had reached half-way Andrea and Mallory left Neufeld's hut and followed them. One or two glances of idle curiosity came their way, but clearly no one suspected that anything was amiss. The crossing to the stables was completely uneventful.

So also, two minutes later, was their departure from the camp. Neufeld and Droshny, as would have been proper and expected, rode together in the lead, Droshny in particular looking very warlike with his Schmeisser, pistol and the wickedly-curved knives at his waist. Behind them rode Andrea, who appeared to be having some trouble with the action of his Schmeisser, for he had it in his hands and was examining it closely: he certainly wasn't looking at either Droshny or Neufeld and the fact that the gun-barrel, which Andrea had sensibly pointed towards the ground, had only to be lifted a foot and the trigger pressed to riddle the two men ahead was a preposterous idea that would not have occurred to even the most suspicious. Behind Andrea, Mallory and Miller rode abreast: like Andrea, they appeared unconcerned, even slightly bored. Reynolds and Groves brought up the rear, almost but not quite attaining the degree of nonchalance of the other three: their still faces and restlessly darting eyes betrayed the strain they were under. But their anxiety was needless for all seven passed from the camp not only unmolested but without as much as even an enquiring glance being cast in their direction.

They rode for over two and a half hours, climbing nearly all the time, and a blood-red sun was setting among the thinning pines to the west when they came across a clearing set on, for once, a level stretch of ground. Neufeld and Droshny halted their ponies and waited until the others came up with them. Mallory reined in and gazed at the building in the middle of the clearing, a low, squat, immensely strong-looking blockhouse, with narrow, heavily barred windows and two chimneys, from one of which smoke was coming.

'This the place?' Mallory asked.

'Hardly a necessary question.' Neufeld's voice was dry, but the underlying resentment and anger unmistakable. 'You think I spent all this time leading you to the wrong place?'

'I wouldn't put it past you,' Mallory said. He examined the building more closely. 'A hospitable-looking place.'

'Yugoslav Army ammunition dumps were never intended as first-class hotels.'

'I dare say not,' Mallory agreed. At a signal from him they urged their ponies forward into the clearing, and as they did so two metal strips in the facing wall of the block-house slid back to reveal a pair of embrasures with machine-pistols protruding. Exposed as they were, the seven mounted men were completely at the mercy of those menacing muzzles.

'Your men keep a good watch,' Mallory acknowledged to Neufeld. 'You wouldn't require many men to guard and hold a place like this. How many are there?'

'Six,' Neufeld said reluctantly.

'Seven and you're a dead man,' Andrea warned.

'Six.'

As they approached, the guns – almost certainly because the men behind them had identified Neufeld and Droshny – were withdrawn, the embrasures closed, the heavy metal front door opened. A sergeant appeared in the doorway and saluted respectfully, his face registering a certain surprise.

'An unexpected pleasure, Hauptmann Neufeld,' the sergeant said. 'We had no radio message informing us of your arrival.'

'It's out of action for the moment.' Neufeld waved them inside but Andrea gallantly insisted on the German officer taking precedence, reinforcing his courtesy with a threatening hitch of his Schmeisser. Neufeld entered, followed by Droshny and the other five men.

The windows were so narrow that the burning oil-lamps were obviously a necessity, the illumination they afforded being almost doubled by a large log fire blazing in the hearth. Nothing could ever overcome the bleakness created by four rough-cut stone walls, but the room itself was surprisingly well furnished with a table, chairs, two armchairs and a sofa: there were even some pieces of carpet. Three doors led off from the room, one heavily barred. Including the sergeant who had welcomed them, there were three armed soldiers in the room. Mallory glanced at Neufeld who nodded, his face tight in suppressed anger.

Neufeld said to one of the guards: 'Bring out the prisoners.' The guard nodded, lifted a heavy key from the wall and headed for the barred door. The sergeant and the other guard were sliding the metal screens back across the embrasures. Andrea walked casually towards the nearest guard, then suddenly and violently shoved him against the sergeant. Both men cannoned into the guard who had just inserted the key into the door. The third man fell heavily to the ground: the other two, thought staggering wildly, managed to retain a semblance of balance or at least remain on their feet. All three twisted round to stare at Andrea, anger and startled incomprehension in their faces, and all three remained very still, and wisely so. Faced with a Schmeisser machine-pistol at three paces, the wise man always remains still.

Mallory said to the sergeant: 'There are three other men. Where are they?'

There was no reply: the guard glared at him in defiance. Mallory repeated the question, this time in fluent German: the guard ignored him and looked questioning at Neufeld, whose lips were tight-shut in a mask of stone.

'Are you mad?' Neufeld demanded of the sergeant. 'Can't you see those men are killers? Tell him.'

'The night guards. They're asleep.' The sergeant pointed to a door. 'That one.'

'Open it. Tell them to walk out. Backwards and with their hands clasped behind their necks.'

'Do exactly as you're told,' Neufeld ordered.

The sergeant did exactly what he was told and so did the three guards who had been resting in the inner room, who walked out as they had been instructed, with obviously no thought of any resistance in their minds. Mallory turned to the guard with the key who had by this time picked himself up somewhat shakily from the floor, and nodded to the barred door.

'Open it.'

The guard opened it and pushed the door wide. Four British officers moved out slowly and uncertainly into the outer room.

Long confinement indoors had made them very pale, but apart from this prison pallor and the fact that they were rather thin they were obviously unharmed. The man in the lead, with a major's insignia and a Sandhurst moustache – and, when he spoke, a Sandhurst accent – stopped abruptly and stared in disbelief at Mallory and his men.

'Good God above! What on earth are you chaps—'

'Please.' Mallory cut him short. 'I'm sorry, but later. Collect your coats, whatever warm gear you have, and wait outside.'

'But – but where are you taking us?'

'Home. Italy. Tonight. Please hurry!'

'Italy. You're talking—'

'Hurry!' Mallory glanced in some exasperation at his watch. 'We're late already.'

As quickly as their dazed condition would allow, the four officers collected what warm clothing they had and filed outside. Mallory turned to the sergeant again. 'You must have ponies here, a stable.'

'Round the back of the block-house,' the sergeant said promptly. He had obviously made a rapid readjustment to the new facts of life.

'Good lad,' Mallory said approvingly. He looked at Groves and Reynolds. 'We'll need two more ponies. Saddle them up, will you?'

The two sergeants left. Under the watchful guns of Mallory and Miller, Andrea searched each of the six guards in turn, found nothing, and ushered them all into the cell, turning the heavy key and hanging it up on the wall. Then, just as carefully, Andrea searched Neufeld and Droshny: Droshny's face, as Andrea carelessly flung his knives into a corner of the room, was thunderous.

Mallory looked at the two men and said: 'I'd shoot you if necessary. It's not. You won't be missed before morning.'

'They might not be missed for a good few mornings,' Miller pointed out.

'So they're over-weight anyway,' Mallory said indifferently. He smiled. 'I can't resist leaving you with a last little pleasant thought, Hauptmann Neufeld. Something to think about until someone comes and finds you.' He looked consideringly at Neufeld, who said nothing, then went on: 'About that information I gave you this morning, I mean.'

Neufeld looked at him guardedly. 'What about the information you gave me this morning?'

825

'Just this. It wasn't, I'm afraid, quite accurate. Vukalovic expects the attack from the *north,* through the Zenica Gap, not across the bridge at Neretva from the south. There are, we know, close on two hundred of your tanks massed in the woods just to the north of the Zenica Gap – but there won't be at two a.m. this morning when your attack is due to start. Not after I've got through to our Lancaster squadrons in Italy. Think of it, think of the target. Two hundred tanks bunched in a tiny trap a hundred and fifty yards wide and not more than three hundred yards long. The RAF will be there at 1.30. By two this morning there won't be a single tank left in commission.'

Neufeld looked at him for a long moment, his face very still, then said, slowly and softly: 'Damn you! Damn you! Damn you!'

'Damning is all you'll have for it,' Mallory said agreeably. 'By the time you are released – hopefully assuming that you will be released – it will be all over. See you after the war.'

Andrea locked the two men in a side room and hung the key up by the one to the cell. Then they went outside, locked the outer door, hung the key on a nail by the door, mounted their ponies – Groves and Reynolds had already two additional ones saddled – and started climbing once again, Mallory, map in hand, studying in the fading light of dusk the route they had to take.

Their route took them up alongside the perimeter of a pine forest. Not more than half a mile after leaving the blockhouse, Andrea reined in his pony, dismounted, lifted the pony's right foreleg and examined it carefully. He looked up at the others who had also reined in their ponies.

'There's a stone wedged under the hoof,' he announced. 'Looks bad – but not too bad. I'll have to cut it out. Don't wait for me – I'll catch you up in a few minutes.'

Mallory nodded, gave the signal to move on. Andrea produced a knife, lifted the hoof and made a great play of excavating the wedged stone. After a minute or so, he glanced up and saw that the rest of the party had vanished round a corner of the pine wood. Andrea put away his knife and led the pony; which quite obviously had no limp whatsoever into the shelter of the wood and tethered it there, then moved on foot some way down the hill towards the block-house. He sat down behind the bole of a convenient pine and removed his binoculars from their case.

He hadn't long to wait. The head and shoulders of a figure appeared in the clearing below peering out cautiously from behind the trunk of a tree. Andrea flat in the snow now and with the icy rims of the binoculars clamped hard against his eyes, had no difficulty at all in making an immediate identification: Sergeant Baer, moon-faced, rotund and about seventy pounds overweight for his unimpressive height, had an unmistakable physical presence which only the mentally incapacitated could easily forget.

Baer withdrew into the woods, then reappeared shortly afterwards leading a string of ponies, one of which carried a bulky covered object strapped to a pannier bag. Two of the following ponies had riders, both of whom had their hands tied to the pommels of their saddles. Petar and Maria, without a doubt. Behind them appeared four mounted soldiers. Sergeant Baer beckoned them to follow him across the clearing and within moments all had disappeared from sight behind the block-house. Andrea regarded the now empty clearing thoughtfully, lit a fresh cigar and made his way uphill towards his tethered pony.

Sergeant Baer dismounted, produced a key from his pocket, caught sight of the key suspended from the nail beside the door, replaced his own, took down the other, opened the door with it and passed inside. He glanced around, took down one of the keys hanging on the wall and opened a side door with it. Hauptmann Neufeld emerged, glanced at his watch and smiled.

'You have been very punctual, Sergeant Baer. You have the radio?'

'I have the radio. 'It's outside.'

'Good, good, good.' Neufeld looked at Droshny and smiled again. 'I think it's time for us to make our rendezvous with the Ivenici plateau.'

Sergeant Baer said respectfully: 'How can you be so sure that it is the Ivenici plateau, Hauptmann Neufeld?'

'How can I be so sure? Simple, my dear Baer. Because Maria – you have her with you?'

'But of course, Hauptmann Neufeld.'

'Because Maria told me. The Ivenici plateau it is.'

Night had fallen on the Ivenici plateau, but still the phalanx of exhausted soldiers was trudging out the landing-strip for the plane. The work was not by this time so cruelly and physically exacting, for the snow was now almost trampled and beaten hard and flat; but, even allowing for the rejuvenation given by the influx of another five hundred fresh soldiers, the overall level of utter weariness was such that the phalanx was in no better condition than its original members who had trudged out the first outline of the airstrip in the virgin snow.

The phalanx, too, had changed its shape. Instead of being fifty wide by twenty deep it was now twenty wide by fifty deep: having achieved a safe clearance for the wings of the aircraft, they were now trudging out what was to be as close as possible an iron-hard surface for the landing wheels.

A three-quarters moon, intensely white and luminous, rode low in the sky, with scattered bands of cloud coming drifting down slowly from the north. As the successive bands moved across the face of the moon, the black shadows swept lazily across the surface of the plateau: the phalanx, at one moment bathed in silvery moonlight, was at the next almost lost to sight in the darkness. It was a fantastic scene with a remarkably faery-like quality of eeriness and foreboding about it. In fact it was, as Colonel Vis had just unromantically mentioned to Captain Vlanovich, like something out of Dante's *Inferno*, only a hundred degrees colder. At least a hundred degrees, Vis had amended: he wasn't sure how hot it was in hell.

It was this scene which, at twenty minutes to nine in the evening, confronted Mallory and his men when they topped the brow of a hill and reined in their ponies just short of the edge of the precipice which abutted on the western edge of the Ivenici plateau. For at least two minutes they sat there on their ponies, not moving, not speaking, mesmerized by the other-world quality of a thousand men with bowed heads and bowed shoulders, shuffling exhaustedly across the level floor of the plain beneath, mesmerized because they all knew they were gazing at a unique spectacle which none of them had ever seen before and would never see again. Mallory finally broke free from the trance-like condition, looked at Miller and Andrea, and slowly shook his head in an expression of profound wonder conveying his disbelief, that his refusal to accept the reality of what his own eyes told him was real and actual beyond dispute. Miller and Andrea returned his look with almost identical negative motions of their own heads. Mallory wheeled his pony to the right and led the way along the cliff-face to the point where the cliff ran into the rising ground below.

Ten minutes later they were being greeted by Colonel Vis.

'I did not expect to see you, Captain Mallory.' Vis pumped his hand enthusiastically. 'Before God, I did not expect to see you. You – and your men – must have a remarkable capacity for survival.'

'Say that in a few hours,' Mallory said drily, 'and I would be very happy indeed to hear it.'

'But it's all over now. We expect the plane—' Vis glanced at his watch – 'in exactly eight minutes. We have a bearing surface for it and there should be no difficulty in landing and taking off provided it doesn't hang around too long. You have done all that you came to do and achieved it magnificently. Luck has been on your side.'

'Say that in a few hours,' Mallory repeated.

'I'm sorry.' Vis could not conceal his puzzlement. You expect something to happen to the plane?'

'I don't expect anything to happen to the plane. But what's gone, what's past, is – was, rather – only the prologue.'

'The – the prologue?'

'Let me explain.'

Neufeld, Droshny and Sergeant Baer left their ponies tethered inside the woodline and walked up the slight eminence before them, Sergeant Baer making heavy weather of their uphill struggle through the snow because of the weight of the large portable transceiver strapped to his back. Near the summit they dropped to their hands and knees and crawled forward till they were within a few feet of the edge of the cliff overlooking the Ivenici plateau. Neufeld unslung his binoculars and then replaced them: the moon had just moved out from behind a dark barred cloud highlighting every aspect of the scene below: the intensely sharp contrast afforded by black shadow and snow so deeply and gleamingly white as to be almost phosphorescent made the use of binoculars superfluous.

Clearly visible and to the right were Vis's command tents and, near by, some hastily erected soup kitchens. Outside the smallest of the tents could be seen a group of perhaps a dozen people, obviously, even at that distance, engaged in close conversation. Directly beneath where they lay, the three men could see the phalanx turning round at one end of the runway and beginning to trudge back slowly, so terribly slowly, so terribly tiredly, along the wide path already tramped out. As Mallory and his men had been, Neufeld, Droshny and Baer were momentarily caught and held by the weird and other-worldly dark grandeur of the spectacle below. Only by a conscious act of will could Neufeld bring himself to look away and return to the world of normality and reality.

'How very kind,' he murmured, 'of our Yugoslav friends to go to such lengths on our behalf.' He turned to Baer and indicated the transceiver. 'Get through to the General, will you?'

Baer unslung his transceiver, settled it firmly in the snow, extended the telescopic aerial, pre-set the frequency and cranked the handle. He made contact almost at once, talked briefly then handed the microphone and head-piece to Neufeld, who fitted on the phones and gazed down, still half mesmerized, at the thousand men and women moving antlike across the plain below. The head-phones cracked suddenly in his ears and the spell was broken.

'Herr General?'

'Ah. Hauptmann Neufeld.' In the ear-phones the General's voice was faint but very clear, completely free from distortion or static. 'Now then. About my psychological assessment of the English mind?'

'You have mistaken your profession, Herr General. Everything has happened exactly as you forecast. You will be interested to know, sir, that the Royal Air Force is launching a saturation bombing attack on the Zenica Gap at precisely 1.30 a.m. this morning.'

'Well, well, well,' Zimmermann said thoughtfully. 'That is interesting. But hardly surprising.'

'No, sir.' Neufeld looked up as Droshny touched him on the shoulder and pointed to the north. 'One moment, sir.'

Neufeld removed the ear-phones and cocked his head in the direction of Droshny's pointing arm. He lifted his binoculars but there was nothing to be seen. But unquestionably there was something to be heard – the distant clamour of aircraft engines, closing. Neufeld readjusted the ear-phones.

'We have to give the English full marks for punctuality, sir. The plane is coming in now.'

'Excellent, excellent. Keep me informed.'

Neufeld eased off one ear-phone and gazed to the north. Still nothing to be seen, the moon was now temporarily behind a cloud, but the sound of the aircraft engines was unmistakably closer. Suddenly, somewhere down on the plateau, came three sharp blasts on a whistle. Immediately, the marching phalanx broke up, men and women stumbling off the runway into the deep snow on the eastern side of the plateau, leaving behind them, obviously by pre-arrangement, about eighty men who spaced themselves out on either side of the runway.

'They're organized, I'll say that for them,' Neufeld said admiringly.

Droshny smiled his wolf's smile. 'All the better for us, eh?'

'Everybody seems to be doing their best to help us tonight,' Neufeld agreed.

Overhead, the dark and obscuring band of cloud drifted away to the south and the white light of the moon raced across the plateau. Neufeld could immediately see the plane, less than half a mile away, its camouflaged shape sharply etched in the brilliant moonlight as it sank down towards the end of the runway. Another sharp blast of the whistle and at once the men lining both sides of the runway switched on hand-lamps – a superfluity, really, in those almost bright as day perfect landing conditions, but essential had the moon been hidden behind cloud.

'Touching down now,' Neufeld said into the microphone. 'It's a Wellington bomber.'

'Let's hope it makes a safe landing,' Zimmermann said.

'Let's hope so indeed, sir.'

The Wellington made a safe landing, a perfect landing considering the extremely difficult conditions. It slowed down quickly, then steadied its speed as it headed towards the end of the runway.

Neufeld said into the microphone: 'Safely down, Herr General, and rolling to rest.'

'Why doesn't it stop?' Droshny wondered.

'You can't accelerate a plane over snow as you can over a concrete runway,' Neufeld said. 'They'll require every yard of the runway for the take-off.'

Quite obviously, the pilot of the Wellington was of the same opinion. He was about fifty yards from the end of the runway when two groups of people broke from the hundreds lining the edge of the runway, one group heading for the already opened door in the side of the bomber, the other heading for the tail of the plane. Both groups reached the plane just as it rolled to a stop at the very end of the runway, a dozen men at once flinging themselves upon the tail unit and beginning to turn the Wellington through 180°.

Droshny was impressed. 'By heavens, they're not wasting much time, are they?'

'They can't afford to. If the plane stays there any time at all it'll start sinking in the snow.' Neufeld lifted his binoculars and spoke into the microphone.

'They're boarding now, Herr General. One, two, three . . . seven, eight, nine. Nine it is.' Neufeld sighed in relief and at the relief of tension. 'My warmest congratulations, Herr General. Nine it is, indeed.'

The plane was already facing the way it had come. The pilot stood on the brakes, revved the engines up to a crescendo, then twenty seconds after it had come to a halt the Wellington was on its way again, accelerating down the runway. The pilot took no chances, he waited till the very far end of the airstrip before lifting the Wellington off, but when he did it rose cleanly and easily and climbed steadily into the night sky.

'Airborne, Herr General,' Neufeld reported. 'Everything perfectly according to plan.' He covered the microphone, looked after the disappearing plane, then smiled at Droshny. 'I think we should wish them *bon voyage*, don't you?'

Mallory, one of the hundreds lining the perimeter of the airstrip, lowered his binoculars. 'And a very pleasant journey to them all.'

Colonel Vis shook his head sadly. 'All this work just to send five of my men on a holiday to Italy.'

'I dare say they needed a break,' Mallory said.

'The hell with them. How about us?' Reynolds demanded. In spite of the words, his face showed no anger, just a dazed and total bafflement. 'We should have been aboard that damned plane.'

'Ah. Well. I changed my mind.'

'Like hell you changed your mind,' Reynolds said bitterly.

Inside the fuselage of the Wellington, the moustached major surveyed his three fellow-escapees and the five Partisan soldiers, shook his head in disbelief and turned to the captain by his side.

'A rum do, what?'

'Very rum, indeed, sir,' said the captain. He looked curiously at the papers the major held in his hand. 'What have you there?'

'A map and papers that I'm to give to some bearded naval type when we land back in Italy. Odd fellow, that Mallory, what?'

'Very odd indeed, sir,' the captain agreed.

Mallory and his men, together with Vis and Vlanovich, had detached themselves from the crowd and were now standing outside Vis's command tent.

Mallory said to Vis: 'You have arranged for the ropes? We must leave at once.'

'What's all the desperate hurry, sir?' Groves asked. Like Reynolds, much of his resentment seemed to have gone to be replaced by a helpless bewilderment. 'All of a sudden, like, I mean?'

'Petar and Maria,' Mallory said grimly. 'They're the hurry.'

'What about Petar and Maria?' Reynolds asked suspiciously. 'Where do they come into this?'

'They're being held captive in the ammunition block-house. And when Neufeld and Droshny get back there—'

'Get back there,' Groves said dazedly. 'What do you mean, get back there. We – we left them locked up. And how in God's name do you know that Petar and Maria are being held in the block-house. How can they be? I mean, they weren't there when we left there – and that wasn't so long ago.'

'When Andrea's pony had a stone in its hoof on the way up here from the block-house, it didn't have a stone in its hoof. Andrea was keeping watch.'

'You see,' Miller explained, 'Andrea doesn't trust anyone.'

'He saw Sergeant Baer taking Petar and Maria there,' Mallory went on. 'Bound. Baer released Neufeld and Droshny and you can bet your last cent our precious pair were up on the cliff-side there checking that we really did fly out.'

'You don't tell us very much, do you, sir?' Reynolds said bitterly.

'I'll tell you this much,' Mallory said with certainty. 'If we don't get there soon, Maria and Petar are for the high jump. Neufeld and Droshny don't *know* yet, but by this time they must be pretty convinced that it was Maria who told me where those four agents were being kept. They've always known who we really were – Maria told them. Now they know who Maria is. Just before Droshny killed Saunders—'

'Droshny?' Reynolds's expression was that of a man who has almost given up all attempt to understand. 'Maria?'

'I made a miscalculation.' Mallory sounded tired. 'We all make miscalculations, but this was a bad one.' He smiled, but the smile didn't touch his eyes. 'You will recall that you had a few harsh words to say about Andrea here when he picked that fight with Droshny outside the dining hut in Neufeld's camp?'

'Sure I remember. It was one of the craziest—'

'You can apologize to Andrea at a later and more convenient time,' Mallory interrupted. 'Andrea provoked Droshny because I asked him to. I knew that Neufeld and Droshny were up to no good in the dining hut after we had left and I wanted a moment to ask Maria what they had been discussing. She told me that they intended to send a couple of Cetniks after us into Broznik's camp – suitably disguised, of course – to report on us. They were two of the men acting as our escort in that wood-burning truck. Andrea and Miller killed them.'

'Now you tell us,' Groves said almost mechanically. 'Andrea and Miller killed them.'

'What I didn't know was that Droshny was also following us. He saw Maria and myself together.' He looked at Reynolds. 'Just as you did. I didn't know at the time that he'd seen us, but I've known for some hours now. Maria has been as good as under sentence of death since this morning. But there was nothing I could do about it. Not until now. If I'd shown my hand, we'd have been finished.'

Reynolds shook his head. 'But you've just said that Maria betrayed us—'

'Maria,' Mallory said, 'is a top-flight British espionage agent. English father, Yugoslav mother. She was in this country even before the Germans came. As a student in Belgrade. She joined the Partisans, who trained her as a radio-operator, then arranged for her defection to the Cetniks. The Cetniks had captured a radio-operator from one of the first British missions. They – the Germans, rather – trained her to imitate this operator's hand – every radio-operator has his own unmistakable style – until their styles were quite indistinguishable. And her English, of course, was perfect. So then she was in direct contact with Allied Intelligence in both North Africa and Italy. The Germans thought they had us completely fooled: it was, in fact, the other way round.'

Miller said complainingly: 'You didn't tell me any of this, either.'

'I've so much on my mind. Anyway, she was notified direct of the arrival of the last four agents to be parachuted in. She, of course, told the Germans. And all those agents carried information reinforcing the German belief that a second front – a full-scale invasion – of Yugoslavia was imminent.'

Reynolds said slowly: 'They knew we were coming too?'

'Of course. They knew everything about us all along, what we really were. What they didn't know, of course, is that we knew they knew and though what they knew of us was true it was only part of the truth.'

Reynolds digested this. He said, hesitating: 'Sir?'

'Yes?'

'I could have been wrong about you, sir.'

'It happens,' Mallory agreed. 'From time to time, it happens. You were wrong, Sergeant, of course you were, but you were wrong from the very best motives. The fault is mine. Mine alone. But my hands were tied.' Mallory touched him on the shoulder. 'One of these days you might get round to forgiving me.'

'Petar?' Groves asked. 'He's not her brother?'

Petar is Petar. No more. A front.'

'There's still an awful lot—' Reynolds began, but Mallory interrupted him.

'It'll have to wait. Colonel Vis, a map, please.' Captain Vlanovich brought one from the tent and Mallory shone a torch on it. 'Look. Here. The Neretva dam and the Zenica Cage. I told Neufeld that Broznik had told me that the Partisans believe that the attack is coming across the Neretva bridge from the south. But, as I've just said, Neufeld knew – he knew even before we had arrived – who and what we *really* were. So he was convinced I was lying. He was convinced that I was convinced that the attack was coming through the Zenica Gap to the north here. Good reason for believing that, mind you: there are two hundred German tanks up there.'

Vis stared at him. 'Two hundred!'

'One hundred and ninety of them are made of plywood. So the only way Neufeld – and, no doubt, the German High Command – could ensure that this useful information got through to Italy was to allow us to stage this rescue bid. Which, of course, they very gladly did, assisting us in every possible way even to the extent of gladly collaborating with us in permitting themselves to be captured. They *knew*, of course, that we had no option left but to capture them and force them to lead us to the block-house – an arrangement they had ensured by previously seizing and hiding away the only other person who could have helped us in this – Maria. And, of course, knowing this in advance, they had arranged for Sergeant Baer to come and free them.'

'I see.' It was plain to everyone that Colonel Vis did not see at all. 'You mentioned an RAF saturation attack on the Zenica Gap. This, of course, will now be switched to the bridge?'

'No. You wouldn't have us break our word to the Wehrmacht, would you? As promised, the attack comes on the Zenica Gap. As a diversion. To convince them, in case they have any last doubts left in their minds, that we have been fooled. Besides, you know as well as I do that that bridge is immune to high-level air attack. It will have to be destroyed in some other way.'

'In what way?'

'We'll think of something. The night is young. Two last things, Colonel Vis. There'll be another Wellington in at midnight and a second at 3 a.m. Let them both go. The next in, at 6 a.m., hold it against our arrival. Well, our possible arrival. With any luck we'll be flying out before dawn.'

'With any luck,' Vis said sombrely.

'And radio General Vukalovic, will you? Tell him what I've told you, the exact situation. And tell him to begin intensive small-arms fire at one o'clock in the morning.'

'What are they supposed to fire at?'

'They can fire at the moon for all I care.' Mallory swung aboard his pony. 'Come on, let's be off.'

'The moon,' General Vukalovic agreed, 'is a fair-sized target, though rather a long way off. However, if that's what our friend wants, that's what he shall have.' Vukalovic paused for a moment, looked at Colonel Janzy who was sitting beside him on a fallen log in the woods to the south of the Zenica Gap, then spoke again into the radio mouth-piece.

'Anyway, many thanks, Colonel Vis. So the Neretva bridge it is. And you think it will be unhealthy for us to remain in the immediate vicinity of this area after 1 a.m. Don't worry, we won't be here.' Vukalovic removed the head-phones and turned to Janzy. 'We pull out, quietly, at midnight. We leave a few men to make a lot of noise.'

'The ones who are going to fire at the moon?'

'The ones who are going to fire at the moon. Radio Colonel Lazlo at Neretva, will you? Tell him we'll be with him before the attack. Then radio Major Stephan. Tell him to leave just a holding force, pull out of the Western Gap and make his way to Colonel Lazlo's HQ.' Vukalovic paused for a thoughtful moment. 'We should be in for a few very interesting hours, don't you think?'

'Is there any chance in the world for this man Mallory?' Janzy's tone carried with it its own answer.

'Well, look at it this way,' Vukalovic said reasonably. 'Of course there's a chance. There has to be a chance. It is, after all, my dear Janzy, a question of options – and there are no other options left open to us.'

Janzy made no reply but nodded several times in slow succession as if Vukalovic had just said something profound.

—— 9 ——

FRIDAY 2115 –

SATURDAY 0040

The pony-back ride downhill through the thickly wooded forests from the Ivenici plateau to the block-house took Mallory and his men barely a quarter of the time it had taken them to make the ascent. In the deep snow the going underfoot was treacherous to a degree, collision with the bole of a pine was always an imminent possibility and none of the five riders made any pretence towards being an experienced horseman, with the inevitable result that slips, stumbles and heavy falls were as frequent as they were painful. Not one of them escaped the indignity of involuntarily leaving his saddle and being thrown headlong into the deep snow, but it was the providential cushioning effect of that snow that was the saving of them, that and, more often, the sure-footed agility of their mountain ponies: whatever the reason or combination of reasons, bruises and winded falls there were in plenty, but broken bones, miraculously, there were none.

The block-house came in sight. Mallory raised a warning hand, slowing them down until they were about two hundred yards distant from their objective, where he reined in, dismounted and led his pony into a thick cluster of pines, followed by the others. Mallory tethered his horse and indicated to the others to do the same.

Miller said complainingly: 'I'm sick of this damned pony but I'm sicker still of walking through deep snow. Why don't we just ride on down there?'

'Because they'll have ponies tethered down there. They'll start whinnying if they hear or see or smell other ponies approaching.'

'They might start whinnying anyway.'

'And there'll be guards on watch,' Andrea pointed out. 'I don't think, Corporal Miller, that we could make a very stealthy and unobtrusive approach on pony-back.'

'Guards. Guarding against what? As far as Neufeld and company are concerned, we're halfway over the Adriatic at this time.'

'Andrea's right,' Mallory said. 'Whatever else you may think about Neufeld, he's a first-class officer who takes no chances.

837

There'll be guards.' He glanced up to the night sky where a narrow bar of cloud was just approaching the face of the moon. 'See that?'

'I see it,' Miller said miserably.

'Thirty seconds, I'd say. We make a run for the far gable end of the block-house – there are no embrasures there. And for God's sake, once we get there, keep dead quiet. If they hear anything, if they as much as suspect that we're outside, they'll bar the doors and use Petar and Maria as hostages. Then we'll just have to leave them.'

'You'd do that, sir?' Reynolds asked.

'I'd do that. I'd rather cut a hand off, but I'd do that. I've no choice, Sergeant.'

'Yes, sir. I understand.'

The dark bar of cloud passed over the moon. The five men broke from the concealment of the pines and pounded downhill through the deep clogging snow, heading for the farther gable-wall of the block-house. Thirty yards away, at a signal from Mallory, they slowed down lest the sound of their crunching, running footsteps be heard by any watchers who might be keeping guard by the embrasures and completed the remaining distance by walking as quickly and quietly as possible in single file, each man using the footprints left by the man in front of him.

They reached the blank gable-end undetected, with the moon still behind the cloud. Mallory did not pause to congratulate either himself or any of the others. He at once dropped to his hands and knees and crawled round the corner of the block-house, pressing close in to the stone wall.

Four feet from the corner came the first of the embrasures. Mallory did not bother to lower himself any deeper into the snow – the embrasures were so deeply recessed in the massive stone walls that it would have been quite impossible for any watcher to see anything at a lesser distance than six feet from the embrasure. He concentrated, instead, on achieving as minimal a degree of sound as was possible, and did so with success, for he safely passed the embrasure without any alarm being raised. The other four were equally successful even although the moon broke from behind the cloud as the last of them, Groves, was directly under the embrasure. But he, too, remained undetected.

Mallory reached the door. He gestured to Miller, Reynolds and Groves to remain prone where they were: he and Andrea rose silently to their feet and pressed their ears close against the door.

Immediately they heard Droshny's voice, thick with menace, heavy with hatred.

'A traitress! That's what she is. A traitress to our cause. Kill her now!'

'Why did you do it, Maria?' Neufeld's voice, in contrast to Droshny's, was measured, calm, almost gentle.

'Why did she do it?' Droshny snarled. 'Money. That's why she did it. What else?'

'Why?' Neufeld was quietly persistent. 'Did Captain Mallory threaten to kill your brother?'

'Worse than that.' They had to strain to catch Maria's low voice. 'He threatened to kill me. Who would have looked after my blind brother then?'

'We waste time,' Droshny said impatiently. 'Let me take them both outside.'

'No.' Neufeld's voice, still calm, admitted of no argument. 'A blind boy? A terrified girl? What are you, man?'

'A Cetnik!'

'And I'm an officer of the Wehrmacht.'

Andrea whispered in Mallory's ear: 'Any minute now and someone's going to notice our foot-tracks in the snow.'

Mallory nodded, stood aside and made a small gesturing motion of his hand. Mallory was under no illusions as to their respective capabilities when it came to bursting open doors leading into rooms filled with armed men. Andrea was the best in the business – and proceeded to prove it in his usual violent and lethal fashion.

A twist of the door handle, a violent kick with the sole of the right foot and Andrea stood framed in the doorway. The wildly swinging door had still not reached the full limit of travel on its hinges when the room echoed to the flat staccato chatter of Andrea's Schmeisser: Mallory, peering over Andrea's shoulder through the swirling cordite smoke, saw two German soldiers, lethally cursed with over-fast reactions, slumping wearily to the floor. His own machine-pistol levelled, Mallory followed Andrea into the room.

There was no longer any call for Schmeissers. None of the other soldiers in the room was carrying any weapon at all while Neufeld and Droshny, their faces frozen into expressions of total incredulity, were clearly, even if only momentarily, incapable of any movement at all, far less being capable of the idea of offering any suicidal resistance.

Mallory said to Neufeld: 'You've just bought yourself your

life.' He turned to Maria, nodded towards the door, waited until she had led her brother outside, then looked again at Neufeld and Droshny and said curtly: 'Your guns.'

Neufeld managed to speak, although his lips moved in a strangely mechanical fashion. 'What in the name of God—'

Mallory was in no mind for small talk. He lifted his Schmeisser. 'Your guns.'

Neufeld and Droshny, like men in a dream, removed their pistols and dropped them to the floor.

'The keys.' Droshny and Neufeld looked at him in almost uncomprehending silence. 'The keys,' Mallory repeated. 'Now. Or the keys won't be necessary.'

For several seconds the room was completely silent, then Neufeld stirred, turned to Droshny and nodded. Droshny scowled – as well as any man can scowl when his face is still overspread with an expression of baffled astonishment and homicidal fury – reached into his pocket and produced the keys. Miller took them, unlocked and opened wide the cell door wordlessly and with a motion of his machine-pistol invited Neufeld, Droshny, Baer and the other soldiers to enter, waited until they had done so, swung shut the door, locked it and pocketed the key. The room echoed again as Andrea squeezed the trigger of his machine-pistol and destroyed the radio beyond any hope of repair. Five seconds later they were all outside, Mallory, the last man to leave, locking the door and sending the key spinning to fall yards away, buried from sight in the deep snow.

Suddenly he caught sight of the number of ponies tethered outside the block-house. Seven. Exactly the right number. He ran across to the embrasure outside the cell window and shouted: 'Our ponies are tethered two hundred yards uphill just inside the pines. Don't forget.' Then he ran quickly back and ordered the other six to mount. Reynolds looked at him in astonishment.

'You think of this, sir? At such a time?'

'I'd think of this at any time.' Mallory turned to Petar, who had just awkwardly mounted his horse, then turned to Maria. 'Tell him to take off his glasses.'

Maria looked at him in surprise, nodded in apparent understanding and spoke to her brother, who looked at her uncomprehendingly, then ducked his head obediently, removed his dark glasses and thrust them deep inside his tunic. Reynolds looked on in astonishment, then turned to Mallory.

'I don't understand, sir.'

Mallory wheeled his pony and said curtly: 'It's not necessary that you do.'

'I'm sorry, sir.'

Mallory turned his pony again and said, almost wearily: 'It's already eleven o'clock, boy, and almost already too late for what we have to do.'

'Sir.' Reynolds was deeply if obscurely pleased that Mallory should call him boy. 'I don't really want to know, sir.'

'You've asked. We'll have to go as quickly as our ponies can take us. A blind man can't see obstructions, can't balance himself according to the level of the terrain, can't anticipate in advance how he should brace himself for an unexpectedly sharp drop, can't lean in the saddle for a corner his pony knows is coming. A blind man, in short, is a hundred times more liable to fall off in a downhill gallop than we are. It's enough that a blind man should be blind for life. It's too much that we should expose him to the risk of a heavy fall with his glasses on, to expose him to the risk of not only being blind but of having his eyes gouged out and being in agony for life.'

'I hadn't thought – I mean – I'm sorry, sir.'

'Stop apologizing, boy. It's really my turn, you know – to apologize to you. Keep an eye on him, will you?'

Colonel Lazlo, binoculars to his eyes, gazed down over the moon-lit rocky slope below him towards the bridge at Neretva. On the southern bank of the river, in the meadows between the south bank and the beginning of the pine forest beyond, and, as far as Lazlo could ascertain, in the fringes of the pine forest itself, there was a disconcertingly ominous lack of movement, of any sign of life at all. Lazlo was pondering the disturbingly sinister significance of this unnatural peacefulness when a hand touched his shoulder. He twisted, looked up and recognized the figure of Major Stephan, commander of the Western Gap.

'Welcome, welcome. The General has advised me of your arrival. Your battalion with you?'

'What's left of it.' Stephan smiled without really smiling. 'Every man who could walk. And all those who couldn't.'

'God send we don't need them all tonight. The General has spoken to you of this man Mallory?' Major Stephan nodded, and Lazlo went on: 'If he fails? If the Germans cross the Neretva tonight—'

'So?' Stephan shrugged. 'We were all due to die tonight anyway.'

841

'A well-taken point,' Lazlo said approvingly. He lifted his binoculars and returned to his contemplation of the bridge at Neretva.

So far, and almost incredibly, neither Mallory nor any of the six galloping behind him had parted company with their ponies. Not even Petar. True, the incline of the slope was not nearly as steep as it had been from the Ivenici plateau down to the block-house, but Reynolds suspected it was because Mallory had imperceptibly succeeded in slowing down the pace of their earlier headlong gallop. Perhaps, Reynolds thought vaguely, it was because Mallory was subconsciously trying to protect the blind singer, who was riding almost abreast with him, guitar firmly strapped over his shoulder, reins abandoned and both hands clasped desperately to the pommel of his saddle. Unbidden, almost, Reynold's thoughts strayed back to that scene inside the block-house. Moments later, he was urging his pony forwards until he had drawn alongside Mallory.

'Sir?'

'What is it?' Mallory sounded irritable.

'A word, sir. It's urgent. Really it is.'

Mallory threw up a hand and brought the company to a halt. He said curtly: 'Be quick.'

'Neufeld and Droshny, sir.' Reynolds paused in a moment's brief uncertainty, then continued. 'Do you reckon they know where you're going?'

'What's that to do with anything?'

'Please.'

'Yes, they do. Unless they're complete morons. And they're not.'

'It's a pity, sir,' Reynolds said reflectively, 'that you hadn't shot them after all.'

'Get to the point,' Mallory said impatiently.

'Yes, sir. You reckoned Sergeant Baer released them earlier on?'

'Of course.' Mallory was exercising all his restraint. 'Andrea saw them arrive. I've explained all this. They – Neufeld and Droshny – had to go up to the Ivenici plateau to check that we'd really gone.'

'I understand that, sir. So you knew that Baer was following us. How did he get into the block-house?'

Mallory's restraint vanished. He said in exasperation: 'Because I left both keys hanging outside.'

'Yes, sir. You were expecting him. But Sergeant Baer didn't know you were expecting him – and even if he did he wouldn't be expecting to find keys so conveniently to hand.'

'Good God in heaven! Duplicates!' In bitter chagrin, Mallory smacked the fist of one hand into the palm of the other. 'Imbecile! Imbecile! Of *course* he would have his own keys!'

'And Droshny,' Miller said thoughtfully, 'may know a short-cut.'

'That's not all of it.' Mallory was completely back on balance again, outwardly composed, the relaxed calmness of the face the complete antithesis of his racing mind. 'Worse still, he may make straight for his camp radio and warn Zimmermann to pull his armoured divisions back from the Neretva. You've earned your passage tonight, Reynolds. Thanks, boy. How far to Neufeld's camp, do you think, Andrea?'

'A mile.' The words came over Andrea's shoulder, for Andrea, as always in situations which he knew called for the exercise of his highly specialized talents, was already on his way.

Five minutes later they were crouched at the edge of the forest less than twenty yards from the perimeter of Neufeld's camp. Quite a number of the huts had illuminated windows, music could be heard coming from the dining hut and several Cetnik soldiers were moving about in the compound.

Reynolds whispered to Mallory: 'How do we go about it, sir?'

'We don't do anything at all. We just leave it to Andrea.'

Groves spoke, his voice low. 'One man? Andrea? We leave it to one man?'

Mallory sighed. 'Tell them, Corporal Miller.'

'I'd rather not. Well, if I have to. The fact is,' Miller went on kindly, 'Andrea is rather good at this sort of thing.'

'So are we,' Reynolds said. 'We're commandos. We've been trained for this sort of thing.'

'And very highly trained, no doubt,' said Miller approvingly. 'Another half-dozen years' experience and half a dozen of you might be just about able to cope with him. Although I doubt it very much. Before the night is out, you'll learn – I don't mean to be insulting, Sergeants – that you are little lambs to Andrea's wolf.' Miller paused and went on sombrely: 'Like whoever happens to be inside that radio hut at this moment.'

'Like whoever happens—' Groves twisted round and looked behind him. 'Andrea? He's gone. I didn't see him go.'

'No one ever does,' Miller said. 'And those poor devils won't ever see him come.' He looked at Mallory. 'Time's a-wasting.'

Mallory glanced at the luminous hands of his watch. 'Eleven-thirty. Time *is* a-wasting.'

For almost a minute there was a silence broken only by the restless movements of the ponies tethered deep in the woods behind them, then Groves gave a muffled exclamation as Andrea materialized beside him. Mallory looked up and said: 'How many?'

Andrea held up two fingers and moved silently into the woods towards his pony. The others rose and followed him, Groves and Reynolds exchanging glances which indicated more clearly than any words could possibly have done that they could have been even more wrong about Andrea than they had ever been about Mallory.

At precisely the moment that Mallory and his companions were remounting their ponies in the woods fringing Neufeld's camp, a Wellington bomber came sinking down towards a well-lit airfield – the same airfield from which Mallory and his men had taken off less than twenty-four hours previously. Termoli, Italy. It made a perfect touch-down and as it taxied along the runway an army radio truck curved in on an interception course, turning to parallel the last hundred yards of the Wellington's run down. In the left-hand front seat and in the right-hand back seat of the truck sat two immediately recognizable figures: in the front, the piratical splendidly bearded figure of Captain Jensen, in the back the British lieutenant-general with whom Jensen had recently spent so much time in pacing the Termoli Operations Room.

Plane and truck came to a halt at the same moment. Jensen, displaying a surprising agility for one of his very considerable bulk, hopped nimbly to the ground and strode briskly across the tarmac and arrived at the Wellington just as its door opened and the first of the passengers, the moustached major, swung to the ground.

Jensen nodded to the papers clutched in the major's hand and said without preamble: 'Those for me?' The major blinked uncertainly, then nodded stiffly in return, clearly irked by this abrupt welcome for a man just returned from durance vile. Jensen took the papers without a further word, went back to his seat in the jeep, brought out a flashlight and studied the papers briefly. He twisted in his seat and said to the radio-operator seated beside the General: 'Flight plan as stated. Target as indicated. Now.' The radio-operator began to crank the handle.

Some fifty miles to the south-east, in the Foggia area, the buildings and runways of the RAF heavy bomber base echoed and reverberated to the thunder of scores of aircraft engines: at the dispersal area at the west end of the main runway several squadrons of Lancaster heavy bombers were lined up ready for take-off, obviously awaiting the signal to go. The signal was not long in coming.

Half-way down the airfield, but well to one side of the main runway, was parked a jeep identical to the one in which Jensen was sitting in Termoli. In the back seat a radio-operator was crouched over a radio, ear-phones to his head. He listened intently, then looked up and said matter-of-factly: 'Instructions as stated. Now. Now. Now.'

'Instructions as stated,' a captain in the front seat repeated. 'Now. Now. Now.' He reached for a wooden box, produced three Very pistols, aimed directly across the runway and fired each in turn. The brilliantly arcing flares burst into incandescent life, green, red and green again, before curving slowly back to earth. The thunder at the far end of the airfield mounted to a rumbling crescendo and the first of the Lancasters began to move. Within a few minutes the last of them had taken off and was lifting into the darkly hostile night skies of the Adriatic.

'I did say, I believe,' Jensen remarked conversationally and comfortably to the General in the back seat, 'that they are the best in the business. Our friends from Foggia are on their way.'

'The best in the business. Maybe. I don't know. What I do know is that those damned Germans and Austrian divisions are still in position in the Gustav Line. Zero hour for the assault on the Gustav Line is—' he glanced at his watch —'in exactly thirty hours.'

'Time enough,' Jensen said confidently.

'I wish I shared this blissful confidence.'

Jensen smiled cheerfully at him as the jeep moved off, then faced forward in his seat again. As he did, the smile vanished completely from his face and his fingers beat a drum tattoo on the seat beside him.

The moon had broken through again as Neufeld, Droshny and their men came galloping into camp and reined in ponies so covered with steam from their heaving flanks and distressed breathing as to have a weirdly insubstantial appearance in the pale moonlight. Neufeld swung from his pony and turned to Sergeant Baer.

'How many ponies left in the stables?'

'Twenty. About that.'

'Quickly. And as many men as there are ponies. Saddle up.'

Neufeld gestured to Droshny and together they ran towards the radio hut. The door, ominously enough on that icy night, was standing wide open. They were still ten feet short of the door when Neufeld shouted: 'The Neretva bridge at once. Tell General Zimmermann—'

He halted abruptly in the doorway, Droshny by his shoulder. For the second time that evening the faces of both men reflected their stunned disbelief, their total uncomprehending shock.

Only one small lamp burned in the radio hut, but that one small lamp was enough. Two men lay on the floor in grotesquely huddled positions, the one lying partially across the other: both were quite unmistakably dead. Beside them, with its face-plate ripped off and interior smashed, lay the mangled remains of what had once been a transmitter. Neufeld gazed at the scene for some time before shaking his head violently as if to break the shocked spell and turned to Droshny.

'The big one,' he said quietly. 'The big one did this.'

'The big one,' Droshny agreed. He was almost smiling. 'You will remember what you promised, Hauptmann Neufeld? The big one. He's for me.'

'You shall have him. Come. They can be only minutes ahead.' Both men turned and ran back to the compound where Sergeant Baer and a group of soldiers were already saddling up the ponies.

'Machine-pistols only,' Neufeld shouted. 'No rifles. It will be close-quarter work tonight. And Sergeant Baer?'

'Hauptmann Neufeld?'

'Inform the men that we will not be taking prisoners.'

As those of Neufeld and his men had been, the ponies of Mallory and his six companions were almost invisible in the dense clouds of steam rising from their sweat-soaked bodies: their lurching gait, which could not now even be called a trot, was token enough of the obvious fact that they had reached the limits of exhaustion. Mallory glanced at Andrea, who nodded and said: 'I agree. We'd make faster time on foot now.'

'I must be getting old,' Mallory said, and for a moment he sounded that way. 'I'm not thinking very well tonight, am I?'

'I do not understand.'

'Ponies. Neufeld and his men will have fresh ponies from the stables. We should have killed them – or at least driven them away.'

'Age is not the same thing as lack of sleep. It never occurred to me, either. A man cannot think of everything, my Keith.' Andrea reined in his pony and was about to swing down when something on the slope below caught his attention. He pointed ahead.

A minute later they drew up alongside a very narrow-gauge railway line, of a type common in Central Yugoslavia. At this level the snow had petered out and the track, they could see, was over-grown and rusty, but for all that, apparently in fair enough mechanical condition: undoubtedly, it was the same track that had caught their eye when they had paused to examine the green waters of the Neretva dam on the way back from Major Broz-nik's camp that morning. But what simultaneously caught and held the attention of both Mallory and Miller was not the track itself, but a little siding leading on to the track – and a diminutive wood-burning locomotive that stood on the siding. The locomotive was practically a solid block of rust and looked as if it hadn't moved from its present position since the beginning of the war: in all probability, it hadn't.

Mallory produced a large-scale map from his tunic and flashed a torch on it. He said: 'No doubt of it, this is the track we saw this morning. It goes down along the Neretva for at least five miles before bearing off to the south.' He paused and went on thoughtfully: 'I wonder if we could get that thing moving.'

'What?' Miller looked at him in horror. 'It'll fall to pieces if you touch it – it's only the rust that's holding the damn thing together. And that gradient there!' He peered in dismay down the slope. 'What do you think our terminal velocity is going to be when we hit one of those monster pine trees a few miles down the track?'

'The ponies are finished,' Mallory said mildly, 'and you know how much you love walking.'

Miller looked at the locomotive with loathing. 'There must be some other way.'

'Shh!' Andrea cocked his head. 'They're coming. I can hear them coming.'

'Get the chocks away from those front wheels,' Miller shouted. He ran forward and after several violent and well-directed kicks which clearly took into no account the future state of his toes, succeeded in freeing the triangular block which was attached to the front of the locomotive by a chain: Reynolds, no less energetically, did the same for the other chock.

All of them, even Maria and Petar helping, flung all their weight against the rear of the locómotive. The locomotive remained where it was. They tried again, despairingly: the wheels refused to budge even a fraction of an inch. Groves said, with an odd mixture of urgency and diffidence: 'Sir, on a gradient like this, it would have been left with its brakes on.'

'Oh my God!' Mallory said in chagrin. 'Andrea. Quickly. Release the brake-lever.'

Andrea swung himself on to the footplate. He said complainingly: 'There are a dozen damned levers up here.'

'Well, open the dozen damned levers, then.' Mallory glanced anxiously back up the track. Maybe Andrea had heard something, maybe not: there was certainly no one in sight yet. But he knew that Neufeld and Droshny, who must have been released from the block-house only minutes after they had left there themselves and who knew those woods and paths better than they did, must be very close indeed by this time.

There was a considerable amount of metallic screeching and swearing coming from the cab and after perhaps half a minute Andrea said: 'That's the lot.'

'Shove,' Mallory ordered.

They shoved, heels jammed in the sleepers and backs to the locomotive, and this time the locomotive moved off so easily, albeit with a tortured squealing of rusted wheels, that most of those pushing were caught wholly by surprise and fell on their backs on the track. Moments later they were on their feet and running after the locomotive which was already perceptibly beginning to increase speed. Andrea reached down from the cab, swung Maria and Petar aboard in turn, then lent a helping hand to the others. The last, Groves, was reaching for the footplate whe he suddenly braked, swung round, ran back to the ponies, unhitched the climbing ropes, flung them over his shoulder and chased after the locomotive again. Mallory reached down and helped him on to the footplate.

'It's not my day,' Mallory said sadly. 'Evening rather. First, I forgot about Baer's duplicate keys. Then about the ponies. Then the brakes. Now the ropes. I wonder what I'll forget about next?'

'Perhaps about Neufeld and Droshny.' Reynolds's voice was carefully without expression.

'What about Neufeld and Droshny?'

Reynolds pointed back up the railway track with the barrel of his Schmeisser. 'Permission to fire, sir.'

Mallory swung round. Neufeld, Droshny and an indeterminate number of other pony-mounted soldiers had just appeared around a bend in the track and were hardly more than a hundred yards away.

'Permission to fire,' Mallory agreed. 'The rest of you get down.' He unslung and brought up his own Schmeisser just as Reynolds squeezed the trigger of his. For perhaps five seconds the closed metallic confines of the tiny cabin reverberated deafeningly to the crash of the two machine-pistols, then, at a nudge from Mallory, the two men stopped firing. There was no target left to fire at. Neufeld and his men had loosed off a few preliminary shots but immediately realized that the wildly swaying saddles of their ponies made an impossibly unsteady firing position as compared to the cab of the locomotive and had pulled their ponies off into the woods on either side of the track. But not all of them had pulled off in time: two men lay motionless and face down in the snow while their ponies still galloped down the track in the wake of the locomotive.

Miller rose, glanced worldlessly at the scene behind, then tapped Mallory on the arm. 'A small point occurs to me, sir. How do we stop this thing.' He gazed apprehensively through the cab window. 'Must be doing sixty already.'

'Well, we're doing at least twenty,' Mallory said agreeably. 'But fast enough to out-distance those ponies. Ask Andrea. He released the brake.'

'He released a dozen levers,' Miller corrected. 'Any one could have been the brake.'

'Well, you're not going to sit around, doing nothing, are you?' Mallory asked reasonably. 'Find out how to stop the damn thing.'

Miller looked at him coldly and set about trying to find out how to stop the damn thing. Mallory turned as Reynolds touched him on the arm. 'Well?'

Reynolds had an arm round Maria to steady her on the now swaying platform. He whispered: 'They're going to get us, sir. They're going to get us for sure. Why don't we stop and leave those two, sir? Give them a chance to escape into the woods?'

'Thanks for the thought. But don't be mad. With us they have a chance – a small one to be sure, but a chance. Stay behind and they'll be butchered.'

The locomotive was no longer doing the twenty miles per

hour Mallory had mentioned and if it hadn't approached the figure that Miller had so fearfully mentioned it was certainly going quickly enough to make it rattle and sway to what appeared to be the very limits of its stability. By this time the last of the trees to the right of the track had petered out, the darkened waters of the Neretva dam were clearly visible to the west and the railway track was now running very close indeed to the edge of what appeared to be a dangerously steep precipice. Mallory looked back into the cab. With the exception of Andrea, everyone now wore expressions of considerable apprehension on their faces. Mallory said: 'Found out how to stop this damn thing yet?'

'Easy.' Andrea indicated a lever. 'This handle here.'

'Okay, brakeman. I want to have a look.'

To the evident relief of most of the passengers in the cab, Andrea leaned back on the brake-lever. There was an eldritch screeching that set teeth on edge, clouds of sparks flew up past the sides of the cab as some wheels or other locked solid in the lines, then the locomotive eased slowly to a halt, both the intensity of sound from the squealing brakes and the number of sparks diminishing as it did so. Andrea, duty done, leaned out of the side of the cab with all the bored aplomb of the crack loco engineer: one had the feeling that all he really wanted in life that moment was a piece of oily waste and a whistle-cord to pull.

Mallory and Miller climbed down and ran to the edge of the cliff, less than twenty yards away. At least Mallory did. Miller made a much more cautious approach, inching forward the last few feet on hands and knees. He hitched one cautious eye over the edge of the precipice, screwed both eyes shut, looked away and just as cautiously inched his way back from the edge of the cliff: Miller claimed that he couldn't even stand on the bottom step of a ladder without succumbing to the overwhelming compulsion to throw himself into the abyss.

Mallory gazed down thoughtfully into the depths. They were, he saw, directly over the top of the dam wall, which, in the strangely shadowed half-light cast by the moon, seemed almost impossibly far below in the dizzying depths. The broad top of the dam wall was brightly lit by floodlights and patrolled by at least half a dozen German soldiers, jackbooted and helmeted. Beyond the damn, on the lower side, the ladder Maria had spoken of was invisible, but the frail-looking swing bridge, still menaced by the massive bulk of the boulder on the scree on the left bank, and farther down, the white water indicating what might or might not have been a possible – or passable – ford were plainly in sight. Mallory, momentarily abstracted in thought, gazed at the scene below for several moments, recalled that the pursuit must be again coming uncomfortably close and hurriedly made his way back to the locomotive. He said to Andrea: 'About a mile and a half, I should think. No more.' He turned to Maria. 'You know there's a ford – or what seems to be a ford – some way below the dam. Is there a way down?'

'For a mountain goat.'

'Don't insult him,' Miller said reprovingly.

'I don't understand.'

'Ignore him,' Mallory said. 'Just tell us when we get there.'

Some five or six miles below the Neretva dam General Zimmermann paced up and down the fringe of the pine forest bordering the meadow to the south of the bridge at Neretva. Beside him paced a colonel, one of his divisional commanders. To the south of them could just dimly be discerned the shapes of hundreds of men and scores of tanks and other vehicles, vehicles with all their protective camouflage now removed, each tank and vehicle surrounded by its coterie of attendants making last-minute and probably wholly unnecessary adjustments. The time for hiding was over. The waiting was coming to an end. Zimmermann glanced at his watch.

'Twelve-thirty. The first infantry battalions start moving across in fifteen minutes, and spread out along the north bank. The tanks at two o'clock.'

'Yes, sir.' The details had been arranged many hours ago, but somehow one always found it necessary to repeat the instructions and the acknowledgments. The colonel gazed to the north. 'I sometimes wonder if there's *anybody* at all across there.'

'It's not the north I'm worrying about,' Zimmermann said sombrely. 'Its the west.'

'The Allies? You – you think their air armadas will come soon? It's still in your bones, Herr General?'

'Still in my bones. It's coming soon. For me, for you, for all of us.' He shivered, then forced a smile. 'Some ill-mannered lout has just walked over my grave.'

─── 10 ───

SATURDAY

0040–0120

'We're coming up to it now,' Maria said. Blonde hair streaming in the passing wind, she peered out again through the cab window of the clanking, swaying locomotive, withdrew her head and turned to Mallory. 'About three hundred metres.'

Mallory glanced at Andrea. 'You heard, brakeman?'

'I heard.' Andrea leaned hard on the brake-lever. The result was as before, a banshee shrieking of locked wheels on the rusty lines and a pyrotechnical display of sparks. The locomotive came to a juddering halt as Andrea looked out his cab window and observed a V-shaped gap in the edge of the cliff directly opposite where they had come to a stop. 'Within the yard, I should say?'

'Within the yard,' Mallory agreed. 'If you're unemployed after the war, there should always be a place for you in a shunter's yard.' He swung down to the side of the track, lent a helping hand to Maria and Petar, waited until Miller, Reynolds and Groves had jumped down, then said impatiently to Andrea: 'Well, hurry up, then.'

'Coming,' Andrea said peaceably. He pushed the handbrake all the way off, jumped down, and gave the locomotive a shove: the ancient vehicle at once moved off, gathering speed as it went. 'You never know,' Andrea said wistfully. 'It might hit somebody somewhere.'

They ran towards the cut in the edge of the cliff, a cut which obviously represented the beginning of some prehistoric landslide down to the bed of the Neretva, a maelstrom of white water far below, the boiling rapids resulting from scores of huge boulders which had slipped from this landslide in that distant aeon. By some exercise of the imagination, that scar in the side of the cliff-face might just perhaps have been called a gully, but it was in fact an almost perpendicular drop of scree and shale and small boulders, all of it treacherous and unstable to a frightening degree, the whole dangerous sweep broken only by a small ledge of jutting rock about half-way down. Miller took one brief glance at this terrifying prospect, stepped hurriedly back from the edge of the cliff and looked at Mallory in a silently dismayed incredulity.

'I'm afraid so,' Mallory said.

'But this is terrible. Even when I climbed the south cliff in Navarone—'

'You didn't climb the south cliff in Navarone,' Mallory said unkindly. 'Andrea and I pulled you up at the end of a rope.'

'Did you? I forget. But this – this is a climber's nightmare.'

'So we don't have to climb it. Just lower ourselves down. You'll be all right – as long as you don't start rolling.'

'I'll be all right as long as I don't start rolling,' Miller repeated mechanically. He watched Mallory join two ropes together and pass them around the bole of a stunted pine. 'How about Petar and Maria?'

'Petar doesn't have to see to make this descent. All he has to do is to lower himself on this rope – and Petar is as strong as a horse. Somebody will be down there before him to guide his feet on to the ledge. Andrea will look after the young lady here. Now hurry. Neufeld and his men will be up with us any minute here – and if they catch up on this cliff-face, well that's that. Andrea, off you go with Maria.'

Immediately, Andrea and the girl swung over the edge of the gully and began to lower themselves swiftly down the rope. Groves watched them, hesitated, then moved towards Mallory.

'I'll go last, sir, and take the rope with me.'

Miller took his arm and led him some feet away. He said, kindly: 'Generous, son, generous, but it's just not on. Not as long as Dusty Miller's life depends on it. In a situation like this, I must explain, all our lives depend upon the anchorman. The Captain, I am informed, is the best anchor-man in the world.'

'He's what?'

'It's one of the non-coincidences why he was chosen to lead this mission. Bosnia is known to have rocks and cliffs and mountains all over it. Mallory was climbing the Himalayas, laddie, before you were climbing out of your cot. Even you are not too young to have heard of him.'

'*Keith* Mallory? The New Zealander?'

'Indeed. Used to chase sheep around, I gather. Come on, your turn.'

The first five made it safely. Even the last but one, Miller, made the descent to the ledge without incident, principally by employing his favourite mountain-climbing technique of keeping his eyes closed all the time. Then Mallory came last, coiling the rope with him as he came, moving quickly and surely and hardly ever seeming to look where he put his feet but at the same time not as much as disturbing the slightest pebble or piece of shale. Groves observed the descent with a look of almost awed disbelief in his eyes.

Mallory peered over the edge of the ledge. Because of a slight bend in the gorge above, there was a sharp cut-off in the moonlight just below where they stood so that while the phosphorescent whiteness of the rapids was in clear moonlight, the lower part of the slope beneath their feet was in deep shadow. Even as he watched, the moon was obscured by a shadow, and all the dimly-seen detail in the slope below vanished. Mallory knew that they could never afford to wait until the moon reappeared, for Neufeld and his men could well have arrived by then. Mallory belayed a rope round an outcrop of rock and said to Andrea and Maria: 'This one's really dangerous. Watch for loose boulders.'

Andrea and Maria took well over a minute to make their invisible descent, a double tug on the rope announcing their safe arrival at the bottom. On the way down they had started several small avalanches, but Mallory had no fears that the next man down would trigger off a fall of rock that would injure or even kill Andrea and Maria; Andrea had lived too long and too dangerously to die in so useless and so foolish a fashion – and he would undoubtedly warn the next man down of the same danger. For the tenth time Mallory glanced up towards the top of the slope they had just descended but if Neufeld, Droshny and his men had just arrived they were keeping very quiet about it and being most circumspect indeed: it was not a difficult conclusion to arrive at that, after the events of the past few hours, circumspection would be the last thing in their minds.

The moon broke through again as Mallory finally made his descent. He cursed the exposure it might offer if any of the enemy suddenly appeared on the cliff-top, even although he knew that Andrea would be guarding against precisely that danger; on the other hand it afforded him the opportunity of descending at twice the speed he could have made in the earlier darkness. The watchers below watched tensely as Mallory, without any benefit of rope, made his perilous descent: but he never even looked like making one mistake. He descended safely to the boulder-strewn shore and gazed out over the rapids.

He said to no one in particular: 'You know what's going to happen if they arrive at the top and find us half-way across here and the moon shining down on us?' The ensuing silence left no doubt but they all knew what was going to happen. 'Now is all the time. Reynolds, you think you can make it?' Reynolds nodded. 'Then leave your gun.'

Mallory knotted a bowline round Reynold's waist, taking the strain, if one were to arise, with Andrea and Groves. Reynolds launched himself bodily into the rapids, heading for the first of the rounded boulders which offered so treacherous a hold in that seething foam. Twice he was knocked off his feet, twice he regained them, reached the rock, but immediately beyond it was washed away off balance and swept down-river. The men on the bank hauled him ashore again, coughing and spluttering and fighting mad. Without a word to or look at anybody Reynolds again hurled himself into the rapids, and this time so determined was the fury of his assault that he succeeded in reaching the far bank without once being knocked off his feet.

He dragged himself on to the stony beach, lay there for some moments recovering from his exhaustion, then rose, crossed to a stunted pine at the base of the cliff rising on the other side, undid the rope round his waist and belayed it securely round the bole of the tree. Mallory, on his side, took two turns round a large rock and gestured to Andrea and the girl.

Mallory glanced upwards again to the top of the gully. There were still no signs of the enemy. Even so, Mallory felt that they could afford to wait no longer, that they had already pushed their luck too far. Andrea and Maria were barely half-way across when he told Groves to give Petar a hand across the rapids. He hoped to God the rope would hold, but hold it did for Andrea and Maria made it safely to the far bank. No sooner had they grounded than Mallory sent Miller on his way, carrying a pile of automatic arms over his left shoulder.

Groves and Petar also made the crossing without incident. Mallory himself had to wait until Miller reached the far bank, for he knew the chances of his being carried away were high and if he were, then Miller too would be precipitated into the water and their guns rendered useless.

Mallory waited until he saw Andrea give Miller a hand into the shallow water on the far bank and waited no longer. He unwound the rope from the rock he had been using as a belay, fastened a bowline round his own waist and plunged into the water. He was swept away at exactly the same point where Reynolds had been on his first attempt and was finally dragged

ashore by his friends on the far bank with a fair amount of the
waters of the Neretva in his stomach but otherwise unharmed.

'Any injuries, any cracked bones or skulls?' Mallory asked. He
himself felt as if he had been over Niagara in a barrel. 'No?
Fine.' He looked at Miller. 'You stay here with me. Andrea, take
the others up round the first corner there and wait for us.'

'Me?' Andrea objected mildly. He nodded towards the gully.
'We've got friends that might be coming down there at any
moment.'

Mallory took him some little way aside. 'We also have friends,'
he said quietly, 'who might just possibly be coming down-river
from the dam garrison.' He nodded at the two sergeants, Petar
and Maria. 'What would happen to them if they ran into an
Alpenkorps patrol, do you think?'

'I'll wait for you round the corner.'

Andrea and the four others made their slow way up-river, slipping and stumbling over the wetly slimy rocks and boulders.
Mallory and Miller withdrew into the protection and concealment of two large boulders and stared upwards.

Several minutes passed. The moon still shone and the top of
the gully was still innocent of any sign of the enemy. Miller said
uneasily: 'What do you think has gone wrong? They're taking a
damned long time about turning up.'

'No, I think that it's just that they are taking a damned long
time in turning back.'

'Turning back?'

'They don't *know* where we've gone.' Mallory pulled out his
map, examined it with a carefully hooded pencil-torch. 'About
three-quarters of a mile down the railway track, there's a sharp
turn to the left. In all probability the locomotive would have
left the track there. Last time Neufeld and Droshny saw us we
were aboard that locomotive and the logical thing for them to
have done would have been to follow the track till they came to
where we had abandoned the locomotive, expectitng to find us
somewhere in the vicinity. When they found the crashed engine,
they would know at once what would have happened – but that
would have given them another mile and a half to ride – and
half of that uphill on tired ponies.'

'That must be it. I wish to God,' Miller went on grumblingly,
'that they'd hurry up.'

'What is this?' Mallory queried. 'Dusty Miller yearning for
action?'

'No, I'm not,' Miller said definitely. He glanced at his watch. 'But time is getting very short.'

'Time,' Mallory agreed soberly, 'is getting terribly short,' And then they came. Miller, glancing upward, saw a faint metallic glint in the moonlight as a head peered cautiously over the edge of the gully. He touched Mallory on the arm.

'I see him, Mallory murmured. Together both men reached inside their tunics, pulled out their Lugers and removed their waterproof coverings. The helmeted head gradually resolved itself into a figure standing fully silhouetted in the moonlight against the sharply etched skyline. He began what was obviously meant to be a cautious descent, then suddenly flung up both arms and fell backwards and outwards. If he cried out, from where Mallory and Miller were the cry could not have been heard above the rushing of the waters. He struck the ledge halfway down, bounced off and outwards for a quite incredible distance, then landed spread-eagled on the stony river bank below, pulling down a small avalanche behind him.

Miller was grimly philosophical. 'Well, you said it was dangerous.'

Another figure appeared over the lip of the precipice to make the second attempt at a descent, and was followed in short order by several more men. Then, for the space of a few minutes, the moon went behind a cloud, while Mallory and Miller stared across the river until their eyes ached, anxiously and vainly trying to pierce the impenetrable darkness that shrouded the slope on the far side.

The leading climber, when the moon did break through, was just below the ledge, cautiously negotiating the lower slope. Mallory took careful aim with his Luger, the climber stiffened convulsively, toppled backwards and fell to his death. The following figure, clearly oblivious of the fate of his companion, began the descent of the lower slope. Both Mallory and Miller sighted their Lugers but just then the moon was suddenly obscured again and they had to lower their guns. When the moon again reappeared, four men had already reached the safety of the opposite bank, two of whom, linked together by a rope, were just beginning to venture the crossing of the ford.

Mallory and Miller waited until they had safely completed two thirds of the crossing of the ford. They formed a close and easy target and at that range it was impossible that Mallory and Miller should miss, nor did they. There was a momentary reddening of the white waters of the rapids, as much imagined as seen, then, still lashed together they were swept away down the gorge. So furiously were their bodies tumbled over and over by the rushing waters, so often did cartwheeling arms and legs break surface, that they might well have given the appearance of men who, though without hope, were still desperately struggling for their lives. In any event, the two men left standing on the far bank clearly did not regard the accident as being significant of anything amiss in any sinister way. They stood and watched the vanishing bodies of their companions in perplexity, still unaware of what was happening. A matter of two or three seconds later and they would never have been aware of anything else again but once more a wisp of errant dark cloud covered the moon and they still had a little time, a very little time, to live. Mallory and Miller lowered their guns.

Mallory glanced at his watch and said irritably: 'Why the hell don't they start firing? It's five past one.'

'Why don't who start firing?' Miller asked cautiously.

'You heard. You were there. I asked Vis to ask Vukalovic to give us sound cover at one. Up by the Zenica Gap there, less than a mile away. Well, we can't wait any longer. It'll take—' He broke off and listened to the sudden outburst of rifle fire, startingly loud even at that comparatively close distance, and smiled. 'Well, what's five minutes here or there. Come on. I have the feeling that Andrea must be getting a little anxious about us.'

Andrea was. He emerged silently from the shadows as they rounded the first bend in the river. He said reproachfully: 'Where have you two been? You had me worried stiff.'

'I'll explain in an hour's time – if we're all still around in an hour's time,' Mallory amended grimly. 'Our friends the bandits are two minutes behind. I think they'll be coming in force – although they've lost four already – six including the two Reynolds got from the locomotive. You stop at the next bend up-river and hold them off. You'll have to do it by yourself. Think you can manage?'

'This is no time for joking,' Andrea said with dignity. 'And then?'

'Groves and Reynolds and Petar and his sister come with us up-river. Reynolds and Groves as nearly as possible to the dam, Petar and Maria wherever they can find some suitable shelter, possibly in the vicinity of the swing bridge – as long as they're well clear of that damned great boulder perched above it.'

'Swing bridge, sir?' Reynolds asked. 'A boulder?'

'I saw it when we got off the locomotive to reconnoitre.'

You saw it. Andrea didn't.'

'I mentioned it to him,' Mallory went on impatiently. He ignored the disbelief in the sergeant's face and turned to Andrea. 'Dusty and I can't wait any longer. Use your Schmeisser to stop them.' He pointed north-westwards towards the Zenica Gap, where the rattle of musketry was now almost continuous. 'With all that racket going on, they'll never know the difference.'

Andrea nodded, settled himself comfortably behind a pair of large boulders and slid the barrel of his Schmeisser into the V between them. The remainder of the party moved upstream, scrambling awkwardly around and over the slippery boulders and rocks that covered the right-hand bank of the Neretva, until they came to a rudimentary path that had been cleared among the stones. This they followed for perhaps a hundred yards, till they came to a slight bend in the gorge. By mutual consent and without any order being given, all six stopped and gazed upwards.

The towering breath-taking ramparts of the Neretva dam wall had suddenly come into full view. Above the dam on either side precipitous walls of rock soared up into the night sky, at first quite vertical then both leaning out in an immense overhang which seemed to make them almost touch at the top, although this, Mallory knew from the observation he had made from above, was an optical illusion. On top of the dam wall itself the guard-houses and radio huts were clearly visible, as were the pigmy shapes of several patrolling German soldiers. From the top of the eastern side of the dam, where the huts were situated, an iron ladder – Mallory knew it was painted green, but in the half-shadow cast by the dam wall it looked black – fastened by iron supports to the bare rock face, zig-zagged downwards to the foot of the gorge, close by where foaming white jets of water boiled from the outlet pipes at the base of the dam wall. Mallory trid to estimate how many steps there would be in that ladder. Two hundred, perhaps two hundred and fifty, and once you started to climb or descend you just had to keep on going, for nowhere was there any platform or backrest to afford even the means for a temporary respite. Nor did the ladder at any point afford the slightest scrap of cover from watchers on the bridge. As an assault route, Mallory mused, it was scarcely the one he would have chosen: he could not conceive of a more hazardous one.

About half-way between where they stood and the foot of the ladder on the other side, a swing bridge spanned the boiling waters of the gorge. There was little about its ancient, rickety and warped appearance to inspire any confidence: and what little confidence there might have been could hardly have survived the presence of an enormous boulder, directly above the eastern edge of the bridge, which seemed in imminent danger of breaking loose from its obviously insecure footing in the deep scar in the cliff-side.

Reynolds assimilated all of the scene before him, then turned to Mallory. He said quietly: 'We've been very patient, sir.'

'You've been very patient, Sergeant – and I'm grateful. You know, of course, that there is a Yugoslav division trapped in the Zenica Cage – that's just behind the mountains to our left, here. You know, too, that the Germans are going to launch two armoured divisions across the Neretva bridge at two a.m. this morning and that if once they do get across – and normally there would be nothing to stop them – the Yugoslavs, armed with only their pop-guns and with hardly any ammunition left, would be cut to pieces. You know the only way to stop them is to destroy the Neretva bridge? You know that this counter-espionage and rescue mission was only a cover for the real thing?'

Reynolds said bitterly: 'I know that – now.' He pointed down the gorge. 'And I also know that the bridge lies that way.'

'And so it does. I also know that even if we could approach it – which would be quite impossible – we couldn't blow that bridge up with a truckload of explosives; steel bridges anchored in reinforced concrete take a great deal of destroying.' He turned and looked at the dam. 'So we do it another way. See that dam wall there – there's thirty million tons of water behind it – enough to carry away the Sydney bridge, far less the one over the Neretva.'

Groves said in a low voice: 'You're crazy,' and then, as an afterthought, sir.'

'Don't we know it? But we're going to blow up that dam all the same. Dusty and I.'

'But – but all the explosives we have are a few hand-grenades,' Reynolds said, almost desperately. 'And in that dam wall there must be ten- to twenty-feet thicknesses of reinforced concrete. Blow it up? How?'

Mallory shook his head. 'Sorry.'

'Why, you close-mouthed—'

'Be quiet! Dammit, man, will you never, *never* learn. Even up to the very last minute you could be caught and made to tell – and then what would happen to Vukalovic's division trapped in the Zenica Cage? What you don't know, you can't tell.'

'But you know.' Reynolds's voice was thick with resentment. 'You and Dusty and Andrea – Colonel Stavros – *you* know. Groves and I knew all along that you knew, and *you* could be made to talk.'

Mallory said with considerable restraint: 'Get Andrea to talk? Perhaps you might – if you threatened to take away his cigars. Sure, Dusty and I could talk – but *someone* had to know.'

Groves said in the tone of a man reluctantly accepting the inevitable: 'How do you get behind that dam wall – you can't blow it from the front, can you?'

'Not with the means at present available to us,' Mallory agreed. 'We get behind it. We climb up there.' Mallory pointed to the precipitous gorge wall on the other side.

'We climb up there, eh?' Miller asked conversationally. He looked stunned.

'Up the ladder. But not all the way. Three-quarters of the way up the ladder we leave it and climb vertically up the cliff-face till we're about forty feet above the top of the dam wall, just where the cliff begins to overhang there. From there, there's a ledge – well, more of a crack, really—'

'A crack!' Miller said hoarsely. He was horror-stricken.

'A crack. It stretches about a hundred and fifty feet clear across the top of the dam wall at an ascending angle of maybe twenty degrees. We go that way.'

Reynolds looked at Mallory in an almost dazed incredulity. 'It's madness!'

'Madness!' Miller echoed.

'I wouldn't do it from choice,' Mallory admitted. 'Nevertheless, it's the only way in.'

'But you're bound to be seen, Reynolds protested.

'Not bound to be.' Mallory dug into his rucksack and produced from it a black rubber frogman's suit, while Miller reluctantly did the same from his. As both men started to pull their suits on, Mallory continued: 'We'll be like black flies against a black wall.'

'He hopes,' Miller muttered.

'Then with any luck we expect them to be looking the other way when the RAF start in with the fireworks. And if we do seem in any danger of discovery – well, that's where you and Groves come in. Captain Jensen was right – as things have turned out, we couldn't have done this without you.'

'Compliments?' Groves said to Reynolds. 'Compliments from the Captain? I've a feeling there's something nasty on the way.'

'There is,' Mallory admitted. He had his suit and hood in position now and was fixing into his belt some pitons and a hammer he had extracted from his rucksack. 'If we're in trouble, you two create a diversion.'

'What kind of diversion?' Reynolds asked suspiciously.

'From somewhere near the foot of the dam you start firing up at the guards atop the dam wall.'

'But – but we'll be completely exposed.' Groves gazed across at the rocky scree which composed the left bank at the base of the dam and at the foot of the ladder. 'There's not an ounce of cover. What kind of chance will we have?'

Mallory secured his rucksack and hitched a long coil of rope over his shoulder. 'A very poor one, I'm afraid.' He looked at his luminous watch. 'But then, for the next forty-five minutes you and Groves are expendable. Dusty and I are not.'

'Just like that?' Reynolds said flatly. 'Expendable.'

'Just like that.'

'Want to change places?' Miller said hopefully. There was no reply for Mallory was already on his way. Miller, with a last apprehensive look at the towering rampart of rock above, gave a last hitch to his rucksack and followed. Reynolds made to move off, but Groves caught him by the arm and signed to Maria to go ahead with Petar. He said to her: 'We'll wait a bit and bring up the rear. Just to be sure.'

'What is it?' Reynolds asked in a low voice.

'This. Our Captain Mallory admitted that he has already made four mistakes tonight. I think he's making a fifth now.'

'I'm not with you.'

'He's putting all our eggs in one basket and he's overlooked certain things. For instance, asking the two of us to stand by at the base of the dam wall. If we have to start a diversion, one burst of machine-gun fire from the top of the dam wall will get us both in seconds. One man can create as successful a diversion as two— and where's the point in the two of us getting killed? Besides, with one of us left alive, there's always the chance that something can be done to protect Maria and her brother. I'll go to the foot of the dam while you—'

'Why should you be the one to go? Why not—'

'Wait, I haven't finished yet. I also think Mallory's very optimistic if he thinks that Andrea can hold off that lot coming up the gorge. There must be at least twenty of them and they're not out for an evening's fun and games. They're out to kill us. So what happens if they do overwhelm Andrea and come up to the swing bridge and find Maria and Petar there while we are busy being sitting targets at the base of the dam wall? They'll knock them both off before you can bat an eyelid.'

'Or maybe not knock them off,' Reynolds muttered. 'What if Neufeld were to be killed before they reached the swing bridge? What if Droshny were the man in charge – Maria and Petar might take some time in dying.'

'So you'll stay near the bridge and keep our backs covered? With Maria and Petar in shelter somewhere near?'

'You're right, I'm sure you're right. But I don't like it,' Reynolds said uneasily. 'He gave us his orders and he's not a man who likes having his orders disobeyed.

'He'll never know – even if he ever comes back, which I very much doubt, he'll never know. *And* he's started to make mistakes.'

'Not this kind of mistake.' Reynolds was still more than vaguely uneasy.

'Am I right or not?' Groves demanded.

'I don't think it's going to matter a great deal at the end of the day,' Reynolds said wearily. 'Okay, let's do it your way.'

The two sergeants hurried off after Maria and Petar.

Andrea listened to the scrapings of heavy boots on stones, the very occasional metallic chink of a gun striking against a rock, and waited, stretched out flat on his stomach, the barrel of his Schmeisser rock-steady in the cleft between the boulders. The sounds heralding the stealthy approach up the river bank were not more than forty yards away when Andrea raised himself slightly, squinted down the barrel and squeezed the trigger.

The reply was immediate. At once three or four guns, all of them, Andrea realized, machine-pistols, opened up. Andrea stopped firing, ignored the bullets whistling above his head and ricocheting from the boulders on either side of him, carefully lined up on one of the flashes issuing from a machine-pistol and fired a one-second burst. The man behind the machine-pistol straightened convulsively, his up-flung right arm sending his gun spinning, then slowly toppled sideways in the Neretva and was carried away in the whitely swirling waters. Andrea fired again and a second man twisted round and fell heavily among the rocks. There came a suddenly barked order and the firing down-river ceased.

There were eight men in the down-river group and now one

863

of them detached himself from the shelter of a boulder and crawled towards the second man who had been hit: as he moved, Droshny's face revealed his usual wolfish grin, but it was clear that he was feeling very far from smiling. He bent over the huddled figure in the stones, and turned him on his back: it was Neufeld, with blood streaming down from a gash in the side of the head. Droshny straightened, his face vicious in anger, and turned round as one of his Cetniks touched his arm.

'Is he dead?'

'Not quite. Concussed and badly. He'll be unconscious for hours, maybe days. I don't know, only a doctor can tell.' Droshny beckoned to two other men. 'You three – get him across the ford and up to safety. Two stay with him, the other come back. And for God's sake tell the others to hurry up and get here.'

His face still contorted with anger and for the moment oblivious of all danger, Droshny leapt to his feet and fired a long continuous burst upstream, a burst which apparently left Andrea completely unmoved, for he remained motionless where he was, resting peacefully with his back to his protective boulder, watching with mild interest but apparent unconcern as richochets and splintered fragments of rock flew off in all directions.

The sound of the firing carried clearly to the ears of the guards patrolling the top of the dam. Such was the bedlam of small-arms fire all around and such were the tricks played on the ears by the baffling variety of echoes that reverberated up and down the gorge and over the surface of the dam itself, that it was quite impossible precisely to locate the source of the recent outbursts of machine-pistol fire: what was significant, however, was that it *had* been machine-gun fire and up to that moment the sounds of musketry had consisted exclusively of rifle fire. And it *had* seemed to emanate from the south, from the gorge below the dam. One of the guards on the dam went worriedly to the captain in charge, spoke briefly, then walked quickly across to one of the small huts on the raised concrete platform at the eastern end of the dam wall. The hut, which had no front, only a rolled-up canvas protection, held a large radio transceiver manned by a corporal.

'Captain's orders,' the sergeant said. 'Get through to the bridge at Neretva. Pass a message to General Zimmermann that we – the captain, that is – is worried. Tell him that there's a great deal of small-arms fire all around us and that some of it seems to be coming from down-river.'

The sergeant waited impatiently while the operator put the

call through and even more patiently as the ear-phones crackled two minutes later and the operator started writing down the message. He took the completed message from the operator and handed it to the captain, who read it out aloud.

'General Zimmermann says, "There is no cause at all for anxiety, the noise is being made by our Yugoslav friends up by the Zenica Gap who are whistling in the dark because they are momentarily expecting an all-out assault by units of the 11th Army Corps. And it will be a great deal noisier later on when the RAF starts dropping bombs in all the wrong places. But they won't be dropping them near you, so don't worry." ' The captain lowered the paper. 'That's good enough for me. If the General says we are not to worry, then that's good enough for me. You know the General's reputation, sergeant?'

'I know his reputation, sir.' Some distance away and from some unidentifiable direction, came several more bursts of machine-pistol fire. The sergeant stirred unhappily.

'You are still troubled by something?' the captain asked.

'Yes, sir. I know the general's reputation, of course, and trust him implicitly.' He paused then went on worriedly: 'I could have sworn that that last burst of machine-pistol fire came from down the gorge there.'

'You're becoming just an old woman, sergeant,' the captain said kindly, 'and you must report to our divisional surgeon soon. Your ears need examining.'

The sergeant, in fact, was not becoming an old woman and his hearing was in considerably better shape than that of the officer who had reproached him. The current burst of machine-pistol firing was, as he'd thought, coming from the gorge, where Droshny and his men, now doubled in numbers, were moving forward, singly or in pairs, but never more than two at a time, in a series of sharp but very short rushes, firing as they went. Their firing, necessarily wildly inaccurate as they stumbled and slipped on the treacherous going underfoot, elicited no response from Andrea, possibly because he felt himself in no great danger, probably because he was conserving his ammunition. The latter supposition seemed the more likely as Andrea had slung his Schmeisser and was now examining with interest a stick grenade which he had just withdrawn from his belt.

Farther up-river, Sergeant Reynolds, standing at the eastern edge of the rickety wooden bridge which spanned the narrowest part of the gorge where the turbulent, racing, foaming waters beneath would have offered no hope of life at all to any person so unfortunate as to fall in there, looked unhappily down the gorge towards the source of the machine-pistol firing and wondered for the tenth time whether he should take a chance, recross the bridge and go to Andrea's aid: even in the light of his vastly revised estimate of Andrea, it seemed impossible, as Groves had said, that one man could for long hold off twenty others bent on vengeance. On the other hand, he had promised Groves to remain there to look after Petar and Maria. There came another burst of firing from down-river. Reynolds made his mind up. He would offer his gun to Maria to afford herself and Petar what protection it might, and leave them for as little time as might be necessary to give Andrea what help he required.

He turned to speak to her, but Maria and Petar were no longer there. Reynolds looked wildly around, his first reaction was that they had both fallen into the rapids, a reaction that he at once dismissed as ridiculous. Instinctively he gazed up the bank towards the base of the dam, and, even although the moon was then obscured by a large bank of cloud, he saw them at once, making their way towards the foot of the iron ladder where Groves was standing. For a brief moment he puzzled why they should have moved upstream without permission, then remembered that neither he nor Groves had, in fact, remembered to give them instructions to remain by the bridge. Not to worry, he thought, Groves will soon send them back down to the bridge again and when they arrived he would tell them of his decision to return to Andrea's aid. He felt vaguely relieved at the prospect, not because he entertained fears of what might possibly happen to him when he rejoined Andrea and faced up to Droshny and his men but because it postponed, if even only briefly, the necessity of implementing a decision which could be only marginally justifiable in the first place.

Groves, who had been gazing up the seemingly endless series of zig-zags of that green iron ladder so precariously, it seemed, attached to that vertical cliff-face, swung round at the soft grate of approaching footsteps on the shale and stared at Maria and Petar, walking as always, hand in hand. He said angrily: 'What in God's name are you people doing here? You've no right to be here – can't you see, the guards have only to look down and you'll be killed? Go on. Go back and rejoin Sergeant Reynolds at the bridge. Now!'

Maria said softly: 'You are kind to worry, Sergeant Groves. But we don't want to go. We want to stay here.'

'And what in hell's name good can you do by staying here?'

Groves asked roughly. He paused, then went on, almost kindly:
'I know who you are now, Maria. I know what you've done, how
good you are at your own job. But this is not your job. Please.'

'No.' She shook her head. 'And I *can* fire a gun.'

'You haven't got one to fire. And Petar here, what right have
you to speak for him. Does he know where he is?'

Maria spoke rapidly to her brother in incomprehensible
Serbo-Croat: he responded by making his customary odd sounds
in his throat. When he had finished, Maria turned to Groves.

'He says he knows he is going to die tonight. He has what you
people call the second sight and he says there is no future beyond tonight. He says he is tired of running. He says he will wait
here till the time comes.'

'Of all the stubborn, thick-headed—'

'Please, Sergeant Groves.' The voice, though still low, was
touched by a new note of asperity. 'His mind is made up, and
you can never change it.'

Groves nodded in acceptance. He said: 'Perhaps I can change
yours.'

'I do not understand.'

'Petar cannot help us anyway, no blind man could. But you
can. If you would.'

'Tell me.'

'Andrea is holding off a mixed force of at least twenty Cetniks
and German troops.' Groves smiled wryly. 'I have recent reason
to believe that Andrea probably has no equal anywhere as a
guerilla fighter, but one man cannot hold off twenty for ever.
When he goes, then there is only Reynolds left to guard the
bridge – and if he does, then Droshny and his men will be
through in time to warn the guards, almost certainly in time to
save the dam, certainly in time to send a radio message through
to General Zimmermann to pull his tanks back on to high
ground. I think, Maria, that Reynolds may require your help.
Certainly, you can be of no help here – but if you stand by Reynolds you *could* make all the difference between success and
failure. And you did say you can fire a gun.'

'And as *you* pointed out, I haven't got a gun.'

'That was then. You have now.' Groves unslung his Schmeisser and handed it to her along with some spare ammunition.'

'But—' Maria accepted gun and ammunition reluctantly. 'But
now *you* haven't a gun.'

'Oh yes I have.' Groves produced his silenced Luger from his tunic. 'This is all I want tonight. *I* can't afford to make any noise tonight, not so close to the dam as this.'

'But I *can't* leave my brother.'

'Oh, I think you can. In fact, you're going to. No one on earth can help your brother any more. Not now. Please hurry.'

'Very well.' She moved off a few reluctant paces, stopped, turned and said: 'I suppose you think you're very clever, Sergeant Groves?'

'I don't know what you're talking about,' Groves said woodenly. She looked at him steadily for a few moments, then turned and made her way down-river. Groves smiled to himself in the near-darkness.

The smile vanished in the instant of time that it took for the gorge to be suddenly flooded with bright moonlight as a black, sharply-edged cloud moved away from the face of the moon. Groves called softly, urgently to Maria: 'Face down on the rocks and keep still,' saw her at once do what he ordered, then looked up the green ladder, his face registering the strain and anxiety in his mind.

About three-quarters of the way up the ladder, Mallory and Miller, bathed in the brilliant moonlight, clung to the top of one of the angled sections as immobile as if they had been carved from the rock itself. Their unmoving eyes, set in equally unmoving faces, were obviously fixed on – or transfixed by – the same point in space.

That point was a scant fifty feet away, above and to their left, where two obviously very jumpy guards were leaning anxiously over the parapet at the top of the dam: they were gazing into the middle distance, down the gorge, towards the location of what seemed to be the sound of firing. They had only to move their eyes downwards and discovery for Groves and Maria was certain: they had only to shift their gaze to the left and discovery for Mallory and Miller would have been equally certain. And death for all inevitable.

I I

SATURDAY

0120–0135

Like Mallory and Miller, Groves, too, had caught sight of the two German sentries leaning out over the parapet at the top of the dam and staring anxiously down the gorge. As a situation for conveying a feeling of complete nakedness, exposure and vulnerability, it would, Groves felt, take a lot of beating. And if he felt like that now, how must Mallory and Miller, clinging to the ladder and less than a stone's throw from the guards, be feeling? Both men, Groves knew, carried silenced Lugers, but their Lugers were inside their tunics and their tunics encased in their zipped-up frogmen's suits, making them quite inaccessible. At least, making them quite inaccessible without, clinging as they were to the ladder, performing a variety of contortionist movements to get at them – and it was certain that the least untoward movement would have been immediately spotted by the two guards. How it was that they hadn't already been seen, even without movement, was incomprehensible to Groves: in that bright moonlight, which cast as much light on the dam and in the gorge as one would have expected on any reasonably dull afternoon, any normal peripheral vision should have picked them all up immediately. And it was unlikely that any front-line troops of the Wehrmacht had less than standard peripheral vision. Groves could only conclude that the intentness of the guards' gaze did not necessarily mean that they were looking intently: it could have been that all their being was at that moment concentrated on their hearing, straining to locate the source of the desultory machine-pistol fire down the gorge. With infinite caution Groves eased his Luger from his tunic and lined it up. At that distance, even allowing for the high muzzle-velocity of the gun, he reckoned his chances of getting either of the guards to be so remote as to be hardly worth considering: but at least, as a gesture it was better than nothing.

Groves was right on two counts. The two sentries on the parapet, far from being reassured by General Zimmermann's encouraging reassurance, were in fact concntrating all their being on listening to the down-river bursts of machine-pistol fire, which were becoming all the more noticeable, not only because they seemed—as they were—to be coming closer, but also because the ammunition of the Partisan defenders of the Zenica Gap was running low and their fire was becoming more sporadic. Groves had been right, too, about the fact that neither Mallory nor Miller had made any attempt to get at their Lugers. For the first few seconds, Mallory, like Groves, had felt sure that any such move would be bound to attract immediate attention, but, almost at once and long before the idea had occurred to Groves, Mallory had realized that the men were in such a trance-like state of listening that a hand could almost have passed before their faces without their being aware of it. And now, Mallory was certain, there would be no need to do anything at all because, from his elevation, he could see something that was quite invisible to Groves from his position at the foot of the dam: another dark band of cloud was almost about to pass across the face of the moon.

Within seconds, a black shadow flitting across the waters of the Neretva dam turned the colour from dark green to the deepest indigo, moved rapidly across the top of the dam wall, blotted out the ladder and the two men clinging to it, then engulfed the gorge in darkness. Groves sighed in soundless relief and lowered his Luger. Maria rose and made her way down-river towards the bridge. Petar moved his unseeing gaze around in the sightless manner of the blind. And, up above, Mallory and Miller at once began to climb again.

Mallory now abandoned the ladder at the top of one of its zigs and struck vertically up the cliff-face. The rock-face, providentially, was not completely smooth, but such hand- and foot-holds as it afforded were few and small and awkwardly situated, making for a climb that was as arduous as it was technically difficult: normally, had he been using the hammer and pitons that were stuck in his belt, Mallory would have regarded it as a climb of no more than moderate difficulty: but the use of pitons was quite out of the question. Mallory was directly opposite the top of the dam wall and no more than 35 feet from the nearest guard: one tiny chink of hammer on metal could not fail to register on the hearing of the most inattentive listener: and, as Mallory had just observed, inattentive listening was the last accusation that could have been levelled against the sentries on the dam. So Mallory had to content himself with the use of his natural talents and the vast experience gathered over many years of rock-climbing and continue the climb as he was doing, sweating profusely inside the hermetic rubber suit, while Miller, now some forty feet below, peered upwards with such tense anxiety on his face that he was momentarily oblivious of his own precarious perch on top of one of the slanted ladders, a predicament which would normally have sent him into a case of mild hysterics.

Andrea, too, was at that moment peering at something about fifty feet away, but it would have required a hyperactive imagination to detect any signs of anxiety in that dark and rugged face. Andrea, as the guards on the dam had so recently been doing, was listening rather than looking. From his point of view all he could see was a dark and shapeless jumble of wetly glistening boulders with the Neretva rushing whitely alongside. There was no sign of life down there, but that only meant that Droshny, Neufeld and his men, having learnt their lessons the hard way – for Andrea could not know at this time that Neufeld had been wounded – were inching their way forward on elbows and knees, not once moving out from one safe cover until they had located another.

' A minute passed, then Andrea heard the inevitable: a barely discernible 'click,' as two pieces of stone knocked together. It came, Andrea estimated, from about thirty feet away. He nodded as if in satisfaction, armed the grenade, waited two seconds, then gently lobbed it downstream, dropping flat behind his protective boulder as he did so. There was the typically flat crack of a grenade explosion, accompanied by a briefly white flash of light in which two soldiers could be seen being flung bodily sideways.

The sound of the explosion came clearly to Mallory's ear. He remained still, allowing only his head to turn slowly till he was looking down on top of the dam wall, now almost twenty feet beneath him. The same two guards who had been previously listening so intently stopped their patrol a second time, gazed down the gorge again, looked at each other uneasily, shrugged uncertainly, then resumed their patrol. Mallory resumed his climb.

He was making better time now. The former negligible finger and toe holds had given way, occasionally, to small fissures in the rock into which he was able to insert the odd piton to give him a great deal more leverage than would have otherwise been possible. When next he stopped climbing and looked upwards he was no more than six feet below the longitudinal crack he had been looking for – and, as he had said to Miller earlier, it *was* no more than a crack. Mallory made to begin again, then paused, his head cocked towards the sky.

Just barely audible at first above the roaring of the waters of the Neretva and the sporadic small-arms fire from the direction of the Zenica Gap, but swelling in power with the passing of every second, could be heard a low and distant thunder, a sound unmistakable to all who had ever heard it during the war, a sound that heralded the approach of squadrons, of a fleet of heavy bombers. Mallory listened to the rapidly approaching clamour of scores of aero engines and smiled to himself.

Many men smiled to themselves that night when they heard the approach from the west of those squadrons of Lancasters. Miller, still perched on his ladder and still exercising all his available will-power not to look down, managed to smile to himself, as did Groves at the foot of the ladder and Reynolds by the bridge. On the right bank of the Neretva, Andrea smiled to himself, reckoned that the roar of those fast-approaching engines would make an excellent cover for any untoward sound and picked another grenade from his belt. Outside a soup tent high up in the biting cold of the Ivenici plateau, Colonel Vis and Captain Vlanovich smiled their delight at each other and solemnly shook hands. Behind the southern redoubts of the Zenica Cage, General Vukalovic and his three senior officers, Colonel Janzy, Colonel Lazlo and Major Stephan, for once removed the glasses through which they had been so long peering at the Neretva bridge and the menacing woods beyond and smiled their incredulous relief at one another. And, most strangely of all, already seated in his command truck just inside the woods to the south of the Neretva bridge, General Zimmermann smiled perhaps the most broadly of all.

Mallory resumed his climb, moving even more quickly now, reached the longitudinal crack, worked his way up above it, pressed a piton into a convenient crack in the rock, withdrew his hammer from his belt and prepared to wait. Even now, he was not much more than forty feet above the dam wall, and the piton that Mallory now wanted to anchor would require not one blow but a dozen of them, and powerful ones at that: the idea that, even above the approaching thunder of the Lancasters' engines, the metallic hammering would go unremarked was preposterous. The sound of the heavy aero engines was now deepening by the moment.

Mallory glanced down directly beneath him. Miller was gazing upward, tapping his wristwatch as best a man can when he has both arms wrapped round the same rung of a ladder, and making urgent gestures. Mallory, in turn, shook his head and made a downward restraining motion with his free hand. Miller shook his own head in resignation.

The Lancasters were on top of them now. The leader arrowed in diagonally across the dam, lifted slightly as it came to the high mountains on the other side and then the earth shook and ripples of dark waters shivered their erratic way across the surface of the Neretva dam before the first explosion reached their ears, as the first stick of 1000-pound bombs crashed squarely into the Zenica Gap. From then on the sound of the explosions of the bombs raining down on the Gap were so close together as to be almost continuous: what little time-lapse there was between some of the explosions was bridged by the constantly rumbling echoes that rumbled through the mountains and valleys of central Bosnia.

Mallory had no longer any need to worry about sound any more, he doubted he could even have heard himself speak, for most of those bombs were landing in a concentrated area less than a mile from where he clung to the side of the cliff, their explosions making an almost constant white glare that showed clearly above the mountains to the west. He hammered home his piton, belayed a rope around it, and dropped the rope to Miller, who immediately seized it and began to climb: he looked, Mallory thought, uncommonly like one of the early Christian martyrs. Miller was no mountaineer, but, no mistake, he knew how to climb a rope: in a remarkably short time he was up beside Mallory, feet firmly wedged into the longitudinal crack, both hands gripping tightly to the piton.

'Think you can hang on that piton?' Mallory asked. He almost had to shout to make himself heard above the still undiminished thunder of the falling bombs.

'Just try to prise me away.'

'I won't,' Mallory grinned.

He coiled up the rope which Miller had used for his ascent, hitched it over his shoulder and started to move quickly along the longitudinal crack. 'I'll take this across the top of the dam, belay it to another piton. Then you can join me. Right?'

Miller looked down into the depths and shuddered. 'If you think I'm going to stay here, you must be mad.'

Mallory grinned again and moved away.

To the south of the Neretva bridge, General Zimmermann, with an aide by his side, was still listening to the sounds of the aerial assault on the Zenica Gap. He glanced at his watch.

'Now,' he said. 'First-line assault troops into position.'

At once heavily armed infantry, bent almost double to keep

themselves below parapet level, began to move quickly across the Neretva bridge: once on the other side, they spread out east and west along the northern bank of the river, concealed from the Partisans by the ridge of high ground abutting on the river bank. Or they thought they were concealed: in point of fact a Partisan scout, equipped with night-glasses and field telephone, lay prone in a suicidally positioned slit-trench less than a hundred yards from the bridge itself, sending back a constant series of reports to Vukalovic.

Zimmermann glanced up at the sky and said to his aide: 'Hold them. The moon's coming through again.' Again he looked at his watch. 'Start the tank engines in twenty minutes.'

'They've stopped coming across the bridge, then?' Vukalovic said.

'Yes, sir.' It was the voice of his advance scout. 'I think it's because the moon is about to break through in a minute or two.'

'I think so too,' Vukalovic said. He added grimly: 'And I suggest you start working your way back before it does break through or it will be the last chance you'll ever have.'

Andrea, too, was regarding the night sky with interest. His gradual retreat had now taken him into a particularly unsatisfactory defensive position, practically bereft of all cover: a very unhealthy situation to be caught in, he reflected, when the moon came out from behind the clouds. He paused for a thoughtful moment, then armed another grenade and lobbed it in the direction of a cluster of dimly seen boulders about fifty feet away. He did not wait to see what effect it had, he was already scrambling his way up-river before the grenade exploded. The one certain effect it did have was to galvanize Droshny and his men into immediate and furious retaliation, at least half a dozen machine-pistols loosing off almost simultaneous bursts at the position Andrea had so recently and prudently vacated. One bullet plucked at the sleeve of his tunic, but that was as near as anything came. He reached another cluster of boulders without incident and took up a fresh defensive position behind them: when the moon did break through it would be Droshny and his men who would be faced with the unpalatable prospect of crossing that open stretch of ground.

Reynolds, crouched by the swing bridge with Maria now by his side, heard the flat crack of the exploding grenade and guessed that Andrea was now no more than a hundred yards downstream on the far bank. And like so many people at that precise instant, Reynolds, too, was gazing up at what could be seen of the sky through the narrow north-west gap between the precipitous walls of the gorge.

Reynolds had intended going to Andrea's aid as soon as Groves had sent Petar and Maria back to him, but three factors had inhibited him from taking immediate action. In the first place, Groves had been unsuccessful in sending back Petar: secondly, the frequent bursts of machine-pistol firing down the gorge, coming steadily closer, were indication enough that Andrea was making a very orderly retreat and was still in fine fighting fettle: and thirdly, even if Droshny and his men did get Andrea, Reynolds knew that by taking up position behind the boulder directly above the bridge, he could deny Droshny and his men the crossing of the bridge for an indefinite period.

But the sight of the large expanse of starlit sky coming up behind the dark clouds over the moon made Reynolds forget the tactically sound and cold-blooded reasons for remaining where he was. It was not in Reynolds's nature to regard any other man as an expendable pawn and he suspected strongly that when he was presented with a sufficiently long period of moonlight Droshny would use it to make the final rush that would overwhelm Andrea. He touched Maria on the shoulder.

'Even the Colonel Stavroses of this world need a hand at times. Stay here. We shouldn't be long.' He turned and ran across the swaying swing bridge.

Damn it, Mallory thought bitterly, damn it, damn it and damn it all. Why couldn't there have been heavy dark cloud covering the entire sky? Why couldn't it have been raining? Or snowing? Why hadn't they chosen a moonless night for this operation? But he was, he knew, only kicking against the pricks. No one had had any choice, for tonight was the only time there was. But still, that damnable moon.

Mallory looked to the north, where the northern wind, driving banded cloud across the moon, was leaving behind it a large expanse of starlit sky. Soon the entire dam and gorge would be bathed in moonlight for a considerable period: Mallory thought wryly that he could have wished himself to be in a happier position for that period.

By this time, he had traversed about half the length of the longitudinal crack. He glanced to his left and reckoned he had still between thirty and forty feet to go before he was well clear of the dam wall and above the waters of the dam itself. He glanced to his right and saw, not to his surprise, that Miller was still where he had left him, clinging to the piton with both hands as if it were his dearest friend on earth, which at that moment it probably was. He glanced downwards: he was directly above the dam wall now, some fifty feet above it, forty feet above the roof of the guardhouse. He looked at the sky again: a minute, no more, and the moon would be clear. What was it that he had said to Reynolds that afternoon? Yes, that was it. For now is all the time there may be. He was beginning to wish he hadn't said that. He was a New Zealander, but only a second-generation New Zealander: all his forebears were Scots and everyone knew how the Scots indulged in those heathenish practices of second sight and peering into the future. Mallory briefly indulged in the mental equivalent of a shoulder shrug and continued on his traverse.

At the foot of the iron ladder, Groves, to whom Mallory was now no more than half-seen, half-imagined dark shape against a black cliff-face, realized that Mallory was soon going to move out of his line of sight altogether, and when that happened he would be in no position to give Mallory any covering fire at all. He touched Petar on the shoulder and with the pressure of his hand indicated that she should sit down at the foot of the ladder. Petar looked at him sightlessly, uncomprehendingly, then suddenly appeared to gather what was expected of him, for he nodded obediently and sat down. Groves thrust his silenced Luger deep inside his tunic and began to climb.

A mile to the west, the Lancasters were still pounding the Zenica Gap. Bomb after bomb crashed down with surprising accuracy into that tiny target area, blasting down trees, throwing great eruptions of earth and stones into the air, starting all over the area scores of small fires which had already incinerated nearly all the German plywood tanks. Seven miles to the south, Zimmermann still listened with interest and still with satisfaction to the continuing bombardment to the north. He turned to the aide seated beside him in the command car.

'You will have to admit that we must give the Royal Air Force full marks for industry, if for nothing else. I hope our troops are well clear of the area?'

'There's not a German soldier within two miles of the Zenica Gap, Herr General.'

'Excellent, excellent.' Zimmermann appeared to have forgotten about his earlier forebodings. 'Well, fifteen minutes. The moon will soon be through, so we'll hold our infantry. The next wave of troops can go across with the tanks.'

Reynolds, making his way down the right bank of the Neretva towards the sound of firing, now very close indeed, suddenly became very still indeed. Most men react the same way when they feel the barrel of a gun grinding into the side of their necks. Very cautiously, so as not to excite any nervous trigger-fingers, Reynolds turned both eyes and head slightly to the right and realized with a profound sense of relief that this was one instance where he need have no concern about jittery nerves.

'You had your orders,' Andrea said mildly. 'What are you doing here?'

'I – I thought you might need some help.' Reynolds rubbed the side of his neck. 'Mind you, I could have been wrong.'

'Come on. It's time we got back and crossed the bridge.' For good measure and in very quick succession, Andrea spun another couple of grenades down-river, then made off quickly up the river bank, closely followed by Reynolds.

The moon broke through. For the second time that night, Mallory became absolutely still, his toes jammed into the longitudinal crack, his hands round the piton which he had thirty seconds earlier driven into the rock and to which he had secured the rope. Less than ten feet from him Miller, who with the aid of the rope had already safely made the first part of the traverse, froze into similar immobility. Both men stared down on to the top of the dam wall.

There were six guards visible, two at the farther or western end, two at the middle and the remaining two almost directly below Mallory and Miller. How many more there might have been inside the guard-house neither Mallory nor Miller had any means of knowing. All they could know for certain was that their exposed vulnerability was complete, their position desperate.

Three-quarters of the way up the iron ladder, Groves, too, became very still. From where he was, he could see Mallory, Miller and the two guards very clearly indeed. He knew with a sudden conviction that this time there would be no escape, they could never be so lucky again. Mallory, Miller, Petar or himself – who would be the first to be spotted? On balance, he thought he himself was the most likely candidate. Slowly, he wrapped his left arm round the ladder, pushed his right hand inside his tunic, withdrew his Luger and laid the barrel along his left forearm.

The two guards on the eastern end of the dam wall were restless, apprehensive, full of nameless fears. As before, they both leaned out over the parapet and stared down the valley. They can't help but see me, Groves thought, they're *bound* to see me, good God, I'm almost directly in their line of sight. Discovery must be immediate.

It was, but not for Groves. Some strange instinct made one of the guards glance upwards and to his left and his mouth fell open at the astonishing spectacle of two .men in rubber suits clinging like limpets to the sheer face of the cliff. It took him several interminable seconds before he could recover himself sufficiently to reach out blindly and grab his companion by the arm. His companion followed the other guard's line of sight, then his jaw, too, dropped in an almost comical fashion. Then, at precisely the same moment, both men broke free from their thrall-like spell and swung their guns, one a Schmeisser, the other a pistol, upwards to line up on the two men pinned helplessly to the cliff-face.

Groves steadied his Luger against both his left arm and the side of the ladder, sighted unhurriedly along the barrel and squeezed the trigger. The guard with the Schmeisser dropped the weapon,. swayed briefly on his feet and started to fall outwards. Almost three seconds passed before the other guard, startled and momentarily quite uncomprehending, reached out to grab his companion, but he was far too late, he never even succeeded in touching him. The dead man, moving in an almost grotesquely slow-motion fashion, toppled wearily over the edge of the parapet and tumbled head over heels into the depths of the gorge beneath.

The guard with the pistol leaned far out over the parapet, staring in horror after his falling comrade. It was quite obvious that he was momentarily at a total loss to understand what had happened, for he had heard no sound of a shot. But realization came within the second as a piece of concrete chipped away inches from his left elbow and a spent bullet ricocheted its whistling way into the night sky. The guard's eyes lifted and widened in shock, but this time the shock had no inhibiting effect on the speed of his reactions. More in blind hope than in any real expectation of success, he loosed off two quick snap-shots and bared his teeth in satisfaction as he heard Groves cry out and saw the right hand, the forefinger still holding the Luger by the trigger-guard, reach up to clutch the shattered left shoulder.

Groves's face was dazed and twisted with pain, the eyes already clouded by the agony of the wound, but those responsible for making Groves a commando sergeant had not picked him out with a pin, and Groves was not quite finished yet. He brought his Luger down again. There was something terribly wrong with his vision now, he dimly realized, he thought he had a vague impression that the guard on the parapet was leaning far out, pistol held in both hands to make sure of his killing shot, but he couldn't be sure. Twice Groves squeezed the trigger of his Luger and then he closed his eyes, for the pain was gone and he suddenly felt very sleepy.

The guard by the parapet pitched forward. He reached out desperately to grab the coaming of the parapet, but to pull himself back to safety he had to swing his legs up to retain his balance and he found he could no longer control his legs, which slid helplessly over the edge of the parapet. His body followed his legs almost of its own volition, for the last vestiges of strength remain for only a few seconds with a man through whose lungs two Luger bullets have just passed. For a moment of time his clawed hands hooked despairingly on to the edge of the parapet and then his fingers opened.

Groves seemed unconscious now, his head lolling on his chest, the left-hand sleeve and left-hand side of his uniform already saturated with blood from the terrible wound in his shoulder. Were it not for the fact that his right arm was jammed between a rung of the ladder and the cliff-face behind it, he must certainly have fallen. Slowly, the fingers of his right hand opened and the Luger fell from his hand.

Seated at the foot of the ladder, Petar started as the Luger struck the shale less than a foot from where he was sitting. He looked up instinctively, then rose, made sure that the inevitable guitar was firmly secured across his back, reached out for the ladder and started climbing.

Mallory and Miller started down, watching the blind singer climb up towards the wounded and obviously unconscious Groves. After a few moments, as if by telepathetic signal, Mallorwy glanced across at Miller who caught his eyes almost at once. Miller's face was strained, almost haggard. He freed one hand momentarily from the rope and made an almost desperate gesture in the direction of the wounded sergeant. Mallory shook his head.

Miller said hoarsely: 'Expendable, huh?'

'Expendable.'

Both men looked down again. Petar was now not more than

ten feet below Groves, and Groves, though Mallory and Miller could not see this, had his eyes closed and his right arm was beginning to slip through the gap between the rung and the rock. Gradually, his right arm began to slip more quickly, until his elbow was free, and then his arm came free altogether and slowly, so very slowly, he began to topple outwards from the wall. But Petar got to him first, standing on the step beneath Groves and reaching out an arm to encircle him and press him back against the ladder. Petar had him and for the moment Petar could hold him. But that was all he could do.

The moon passed behind a cloud.

Miller covered the last ten feet separating him from Mallory. He looked at Mallory and said: 'They're both going to go, you know that?'

'I know that.' Mallory sounded even more tired than he looked. 'Come on. Another thirty feet and we should be in position.' Mallory, leaving Miller where he was, continued his traverse along the crack. He was moving very quickly now, taking risks that no sane cragsman would ever have contemplated, but he had no option now, for time was running out. Within a minute he had reached a spot where he judged that he had gone far enough, hammered home a piton and securely belayed the rope to it.

He signalled to Miller to come and join him. Miller began the last stage of the traverse, and as he was on his way across, Mallory unhitched another rope from his shoulders, a sixty-foot length of climbers' rope, knotted at fifteen-inch intervals. One end of this he fastened to the same piton as held the rope that Miller was using for making his traverse: the other end he let fall down the cliff-side. Miller came up and Mallory touched him on the shoulder and pointed downwards.

The dark waters of the Neretva dam were directly beneath them.

12

SATURDAY

0135–0200

Andrea and Reynolds lay crouched among the boulders at the western end of the elderly swing bridge over the gorge. Andrea looked across the length of the bridge, his gaze travelling up the steep gully behind it till it came to rest on the huge boulder perched precariously at the angle where the steep slope met the vertical cliff-face behind it. Andrea rubbed a bristly chin, nodded thoughtfully and turned to Reynolds.

'You cross first. I'll give you covering fire. You do the same for me when you get to the other side. Don't stop, don't look round. Now.'

Reynolds made for the bridge in a crouching run, his footsteps seeming to him abnormally loud as he reached the rotting planking of the bridge itself. The palms of his hands gliding lightly over the hand ropes on either side he continued without check or diminution of speed, obeying Andrea's instructions not to risk a quick backward glance, and feeling a very strange sensation between his shoulder-blades. To his mild astonishment he reached the far bank without a shot being fired, headed for the concealment and shelter offered by a large boulder a little way up the bank, was startled momentarily to see Maria hiding behind the same boulder, then whirled round and unslung his Schmeisser.

On the far bank there was no sign of Andrea. For a brief moment Reynolds experienced a quick stab of anger, thinking Andrea had used this ruse merely to get rid of him, then smiled to himself as he heard two flat explosive sounds some little way down the river on the far bank. Andrea, Reynolds remembered, had still had two grenades left and Andrea was not the man to let such handy things rust from disuse. Besides, Reynolds realized, it would provide Andrea with extra valuable seconds to make good his escape, which indeed it did for Andrea appeared on the far bank almost immediately and, like Reynolds, effected the crossing of the bridge entirely without incident. Reynolds called softly and Andrea joined them in the shelter of the boulder.

Reynolds said in a low voice: 'What's next?'

'First things first.' Andrea produced a cigar from a waterproof box, a match from another waterproof box, struck the match in his huge cupped hands and puffed in immense satisfaction. When he removed the cigar, Reynolds noticed that he held it with the glowing end safely concealed in the curved palm of his hand. 'What's next? I tell you what's next. Company coming to join us across the bridge, and coming very soon, too. They've taken crazy risks to try to get me – and paid for them – which shows they are pretty desperate. Crazy men don't hang about for

long. You and Maria here move fifty or sixty yards nearer the
dam and take cover there – and keep your guns on the far side
of the bridge.'

'You staying here?' Reynolds asked.

Andrea blew out a noxious cloud of cigar smoke. 'For the moment, yes.'

'Then I'm staying, too.'

'If you want to get killed, it's all right by me,' Andrea said
mildly. 'But this beautiful young lady here wouldn't look that
way any more with the top of her head blown off.'

Reynolds was startled by the crudeness of the words. He said
angrily: 'What the devil do you mean?'

'I mean this.' Andrea's voice was no longer mild. 'This
boulder gives you perfect concealment from the bridge. But
Droshny and his men can move thirty of forty yards farther up
the bank on their side. What concealment will you have then?'

'I never thought of that,' Reynolds said.

'There'll come a day when you say that once too often,' Andrea said sombrely, 'and then it will be too late to think of anything again.'

A minute later they were in position. Reynolds was hidden behind a huge boulder which afforded perfect concealment both
from the far side of the bridge and from the bank on the far side
up to the point where it petered out: it did not offer concealment from the dam. Reynolds looked to his left where Maria
was crouched farther in behind the rock. She smiled at him, and
Reynolds knew he had never seen a braver girl, for the hands
that held the Schmeisser were trembling. He moved out a little
and peered down-river, but there appeared to be no signs of
life whatsoever at the western edge of the bridge. The only
signs of life at all, indeed, were to be seen behind the huge
boulder up in the gully, where Andrea, completely screened
from anyone at or near the far side of the bridge, was industriously loosening the foundations of rubble and earth round the
base of the boulder.

Appearances, as always, were deceptive. Reynolds had judged
there to be no life at the western end of the bridge but there was,
in fact, life and quite a lot of it, although admittedly there was no
action. Concealed in the massive boulders about twenty feet
back from the bridge, Droshny, a Cetnik sergeant and perhaps
a dozen German soldiers and Cetniks lay in deep concealment
among the rocks.

Droshny had binoculars to his eyes. He examined the ground

in the neighbourhood of the far side of the swing bridge, then traversed to his left up beyond the boulder where Reynolds and Maria lay hidden until he reached the dam wall. He lifted the glasses, following the dimly-seen zig-zag outline of the iron ladder, checked, adjusted the focus as finely as possible, then started again. There could be no doubt: there were two men clinging to the ladder, about three-quarters of the way up towards the top of the dam.

'Good God in heaven!' Droshny lowered the binoculars, the gaunt craggy features registering an almost incredulous horror, and turned to the Cetnik sergeant by his side. 'Do you know what they mean to do?'

'The dam!' The thought had not occurred to the sergeant until that instant but the stricken expression on Droshny's face made the realization as immediate as it was inevitable. 'They're going to blow up the dam!' It did not occur to either man to wonder *how* Mallory could possibly blow up the dam: as other men had done before them, both Droshny and the sergeant were beginning to discover in Mallory and his *modus operandi* an extraordinary quality of inevitability that transformed remote possibilities into very likely probabilities.

'General Zimmermann!' Droshny's gravelly voice had become positively hoarse. 'He must be warned! If that dam bursts while his tanks and troops are crossing—'

'Warn him? Warn him? How in God's name can we warn him?'

'There's a radio up on the dam.'

The sergeant stared at him. He said: 'It might as well be on the moon. There'll be a rear-guard, they're bound to have left a rear-guard. Some of us are going to get killed crossing that bridge, Captain.'

'You think so?' Droshny glanced up sombrely at the dam. 'And just what do you think is going to happen to us all down here if *that* goes?'

Slowly, soundlessly and almost invisibly, Mallory and Miller swam northwards through the dark waters of the Neretva dam, away from the direction of the dam wall. Suddenly Miller, who was slightly in the lead, gave a low exclamation and stopped swimming.

'What's up?' Mallory asked.

'This is up.' With an effort Miller lifted a section of what appeared to be a heavy wire cable just clear of the water. 'Nobody mentioned this little lot.'

'Nobody did,' Mallory agreed. He reached under the water. 'And there's a steel mesh below.'

'An anti-torpedo net?'

'Just that.'

'Why?' Miller gestured to the north where, at a distance of less than two hundred yards, the dam made an abrupt right-angled turn between the towering cliff-faces. 'It's impossible for any torpedo bomber – any bomber – to get a run-in on the dam wall.'

'Someone should have told the Germans. They take no chances – and it makes things a damned sight more difficult for us.' He peered at his watch. 'We'd better start hurrying. We're late.'

They eased themselves over the wire and started swimming again, more quickly this time. Several minuts later, just after they had rounded the corner of the dam and lost sight of the dam wall, Mallory touched Miller on the shoulder. Both men trod water, turned and looked back in the direction from which they had come. To the south, not much more than two miles away, the night sky had suddenly blossomed into an incandescent and multi-coloured beauty as scores of parachute flares, red and green and white and orange, drifted slowly down towards the Neretva river.

'Very pretty, indeed,' Miller conceded. 'And what's all this in aid of?'

'It's in aid of us. Two reasons. First of all, it will take any person who looks at that – and *everyone* will look at it – at least ten minutes to recover his night-sight, which means that any odd going-ons in this part of the dam are all that less likely to be observed: and if everyone is going to be busy looking that way, then they can't be busy looking this way at the same time.'

'Very logical,' Miller approved. 'Our friend Captain Jensen doesn't miss out on very much, does he?'

'He has, as the saying goes, all his marbles about him.' Mallory turned again and gazed to the east, his head cocked the better to listen. He said: 'You have to hand it to them. Dead on target, dead on schedule. I hear him coming now.'

The Lancaster, no more than five hundred feet above the surface of the dam, came in from the east, its engine throttled back almost to stalling speed. It was still two hundred yards short of where Mallory and Miller were treading water when suddenly huge black silk parachutes bloomed beneath it: almost simultaneously, engine power was increased to maximum revolutions and the big bomber went into a steeply banking, climbing turn to avoid smashing into the mountains on the far side of the dam.

Miller gazed at the slowly descending black parachutes, turned, and looked at the brilliantly burning flares to the south. 'The skies,' he announced, 'are full of things tonight.'

He and Mallory began to swim in the direction of the falling parachutes.

Petar was near to exhaustion. For long minutes now he had been holding Groves's dead weight pinned against the iron ladder and his aching arms were beginning to quiver with the strain. His teeth were clenched hard, his face, down which rivulets of sweat poured, was twisted with the effort and the agony of it all. Plainly, Petar could not hold out much longer.

It was by the light of those flares that Reynolds, still crouched with Maria in hiding behind the big boulder, first saw the predicament of Petar and Groves. He turned to glance at Maria: one look at the stricken face was enough to tell Reynolds that she had seen it, too.

Reynolds said hoarsely: 'Stay here. I must go and help them.'

'No!' She caught his arm, clearly exerting all her will to keep herself under control: her eyes, as they had been when Reynolds had first seen her, had the look of a hunted animal about them. 'Please, Sergeant, no. You must stay here.'

Reynolds said desperately: 'Your brother—'

'There are more important things—'

'Not for you there aren't.' Reynolds made to rise, but she clung to his arm with surprising strength, so that he couldn't release himself without hurting her. He said, almost gently: 'Come on, lass, let me go.'

'No! If Droshny and his men get across—' She broke off as the last of the flares finally fizzled to extinction, casting the entire gorge into what was, by momentary contrast, an almost total darkness. Maria went on simply: 'You'll have to stay now, won't you?'

'I'll have to stay now.' Reynolds moved out from the shelter of the boulder and put his night-glasses to his eyes. The swing bridge, and as far as he could tell, the far bank seemed innocent of any sign of life. He traversed up the gully and could just make out the form of Andrea, his excavations finished, resting peacefully behind the big boulder. Again with a feeling of deep un-

ease, Reynolds trained his glasses on the bridge. He suddenly became very still. He removed the glasses, wiped the lenses very
carefully, rubbed his eyes and lifted the glasses again.

His night-sight, momentarily destroyed by the flares, was now
almost back to normal and there could be no doubt or any imagination about what he was seeing – seven or eight men, Droshny
in the lead, flat on their stomachs, were inching their way on
elbows, hands and knees across the wooden slats of the swing
bridge.

Reynolds lowered the glasses, stood upright, armed a grenade
and threw it as far as he could towards the bridge. It exploded
just as it landed, at least forty yards short of the bridge. That it
achieved nothing but a flat explosive bang and the harmless
scattering of some shale was of no account, for it had never been
intended to reach the bridge: it had been intended as a signal
for Andrea, and Andrea wasted no time.

He placed the soles of both feet against the boulder, braced
his back against the cliff-face and heaved. The boulder moved
the merest fraction of an inch. Andrea momentarily relaxed, allowing the boulder to roll back, then repeated the process: this
time the forward motion of the boulder was quite perceptible.
Andrea relaxed again, then pushed for the third time.

Down below on the bridge, Droshny and his men, uncertain
as to the exact significance of the exploding grenade, had frozen
into complete immobility. Only their eyes moved, darting almost desperately from side to side to locate the source of a danger
that lay so heavily in the air as to be almost palpable.

The boulder was distinctly rocking now. With every additional heave it received from Andrea, it was rocking an additional inch farther forward, an additional inch farther backwards. Andrea had slipped farther and farther down until now
he was almost horizontal on his back. He was gasping for breath
and sweat was streaming down his face. The boulder rolled back
almost as if it were going to fall upon him and crush him. Andrea took a deep breath, then convulsively straightened back
and legs in one last titanic heave. For a moment the boulder
teetered on the point of imbalance, reached the point of no return and fell away.

Droshny could most certainly have heard nothing and, in that
near darkness, it was certain as could be that he had seen nothing. It could only have been an instinctive awareness of impending death that made him glance upwards in sudden conviction
that this was where the danger lay. The huge boulder, just roll-

ing gently when Droshny's horror-stricken eyes first caught sight of it, almost at once began to bound in ever-increasing leaps, hurtling down the slope directly towards them, trailing a small avalanche behind it. Droshny screamed a warning. He and his men scrambled desperately to their feet, an instinctive reaction that was no more than a useless token gesture in the face of death, because, for most of them, it was already far too late and they had no place to go.

With one last great leap the hurtling boulder smashed straight into the centre of the bridge, shattering the flimsy woodwork and slicing the bridge in half. Two men who had been directly in the path of the boulder died instantaneously: five others were catapulted into the torrent below and swept away to almost equally immediate death. The two broken sections of the bridge, still secured to either bank by the suspension ropes, hung down into the rushing waters, their lowermost parts banging furiously against the boulder-strewn banks.

There must have been at least a dozen parachutes attached to the three dark cylindrical objects that now lay floating, though more than half submerged, in the equally dark waters of the Neretva dam. Mallory and Miller sliced those away with their knives, then joined the three cylinders in line astern, using short wire strops that had been provided for that precise purpose. Mallory examined the leading cylinder and gently eased back a lever set in the top. There was a subdued roar as compressed air violently aerated the water astern of the leading cylinder and sent it surging forward, tugging the other two cylinders behind it. Mallory closed the lever and nodded to the other two cylinders.

'These levers on the right-hand side control the flooding valves. Open that one till you just have negative buoyancy and no more. I'll do the same on this one.'

Miller cautiously turned a valve and nodded at the leading cylinder. 'What's that for?'

'Do *you* fancy towing a ton and a half of amatol as far as the dam wall? Propulsion unit of some kind. Looks like a sawn-off section of a twenty-one-inch torpedo tube to me. Compressed air, maybe at a pressure of five thousand pounds a square inch, passing through reduction gear. Should do the job all right.'

'Just so long as Miller doesn't have to do it.' Miller closed the valve on the cylinder. 'About that?'

'About that.' All three cylinders were now just barely submerged. Again Mallory eased back the compressed air lever on the leading cylinder. There was a throaty burble of sound, a sudden flurry of bubbles streaming out astern and then all three cylinders were under way, heading down towards the angled neck of the dam, both men clinging to and guiding the leading cylinder.

When the swing bridge had disintegrated under the impact of the boulder, seven men had died: but two still lived.

Droshny and his sergeant, furiously buffeted and badly bruised by the torrent of water, clung desperately to the broken end of the bridge. At first, they could do no more than hold on, but gradually, and after a most exhausting struggle, they managed to haul themselves clear of the rapids and hang there, arms and legs hooked round broken sections of what remained of the bridge, fighting for breath. Droshny made a signal to some unseen person or persons across the rapids, then pointed upwards in the direction from which the boulder had come.

Crouched among the boulders on the far side of the river, three Cetniks – the fortunate three who had not yet moved on to the bridge when the boulder had fallen – saw the signal and understood. About seventy feet above where Droshny – completely concealed from sight on that side by the high bank of the river – was still clinging grimly to what was left of the bridge, Andrea, now bereft of cover, had begun to make a precarious descent from his previous hiding-place. On the other side of the river, one of the three Cetniks took aim and fired.

Fortunately for Andrea, firing uphill in semi-darkness is a tricky business at the best of times. Bullets smashed into the cliff-face inches from Andrea's left shoulder, the whining ricochets leaving him almost miraculously unscathed. There would be a correction factor for the next burst, Andrea knew: he flung himself to one side, lost his balance and what little precarious purchase he had and slid and tumbled helplessly down the boulder-strewn slope. Bullets, many bullets, struck close by him on his way down, for the three Cetniks on the right bank, convinced now that Andrea was the only person left for them to deal with, had risen, advanced to the edge of the river and were concentrating all their fire on Andrea.

Again fortunately for Andrea, this period of concentration lasted for only a matter of a few seconds. Reynolds and Maria emerged from cover and ran down the bank, stopping momentarily to fire at the Cetniks across the river, who at once forgot all about Andrea to meet this new and unexpected threat. Just as they did so, Andrea, in the midst of a small avalanche, still fighting furiously but hopelessly to arrest his fall, struck the bank of the river with appalling force, struck the side of his head against a large stone and collapsed, his head and shoulders hanging out over the wild torrent below.

Reynolds flung himself flat on the shale of the river bank, forced himself to ignore the bullets striking to left and right of him and whining above him and took a slow and careful aim. He fired a long burst, a very long one, until the magazine of his Schmeisser was empty. All three Cetniks crumpled and died.

Reynolds rose. He was vaguely surprised to notice that his hands were shaking. He looked at Andrea, lying unconscious and dangerously near the side of the bank, took a couple of paces in his direction, then checked and turned as he heard a low moan behind him. Reynolds broke into a run.

Maria was half-sitting, half-lying on the stony bank. Both hands cradled her leg just above the right knee and the blood was welling between her fingers. Her face, normally pale enough, was ashen and drawn with shock and pain. Reynolds cursed bitterly but soundlessly, produced his knife and began to cut away the cloth around the wound. Gently, he pulled away the material covering the wound and smiled reassuringly at the girl: her lower lip was caught tightly between her teeth and she watched him steadily with eyes dimmed by pain and tears.

It was a nasty enough looking flesh wound, but, Reynolds knew, not dangerous. He reached for his medical pack, gave her a reassuring smile and then forgot all about his medical pack. The expression in Maria's eyes had given way to one of shock and fear and she was no longer looking at him.

Reynolds twisted round. Droshny had just hauled himself over the edge of the river bank, had risen to his feet and was now heading purposefully towards Andrea's prostrate body, with the obvious intention of heaving the unconscious man into the gorge.

Reynolds picked up his Schmeisser and pulled the trigger. There was an empty click – he'd forgotten the magazine had been emptied. He glanced around almost wildly in an attempt to locate Maria's gun, but there was no sign of it. He could wait no longer. Droshny was only a matter of feet from where Andrea lay. Reynolds picked up his knife and rushed along the bank. Droshny saw him coming and he saw too that Reynolds was armed with only a knife. He smiled as a wolf would smile, took one of his wickedly-curved knives from his belt and waited.

The two men approached closely and circled warily. Reynolds had never wielded a knife in anger in his life and so had no illusions at all as to his chances: hadn't Neufeld said that Droshny was the best man in the Balkans with a knife? He certainly looked it, Reynolds thought. His mouth felt very dry.

Thirty yards away Maria, dizzy and weak with pain and dragging her wounded leg, crawled towards the spot where she thought her gun had fallen when she had been hit. After what seemed a very long time, but what was probably no more than ten seconds, she found it half-hidden among rocks. Nauseated and faint from the pain of her wounded leg, she forced herself to sit up and brought the gun to her shoulder. Then she lowered it again.

In her present condition, she realized vaguely, it would have been impossible for her to hit Droshny without almost certainly hitting Reynolds at the same time: in fact, she might well have killed Reynolds while missing Droshny entirely. For both men were now locked chest to chest, each man's knife-hand – the right – clamped in the grip of the other's left.

The girl's dark eyes, which had so recently reflected pain and shock and fear, now held only one expression – despair. Like Reynolds, Maria knew of Droshny's reputation – but, unlike Reynolds, she had seen Droshny kill with that knife and knew too well how lethal a combination that man and that knife were. A wolf and a lamb, she thought, a wolf and a lamb. After he kills Reynolds – her mind was dulled now, her thoughts almost incoherent – after he kills Reynolds I shall kill him. But first, Reynolds would have to die, for there could be no help for it. And then the despair left the dark eyes to be replaced by an almost unthinkable hope for she knew with an intuitive certainly that with Andrea by one's side hope need never be abandoned.

Not that Andrea was as yet by anyone's side. He had forced himself up to his hands and knees and was gazing down uncomprehendingly at the rushing white waters below, shaking his leonine head from side to side in an attempt to clear it. And then, still shaking his head, he levered himself painfully to his feet and he wasn't shaking his head any more. In spite of her pain, Maria smiled.

Slowly, inexorably, the Cetnik giant twisted Reynolds's knife-hand away from himself while at the same time bringing the lancet point of his own knife nearer to Reynolds's throat. Reynolds's sweat-sheened face deflected his desperation, his total awareness of impending defeat and death. He cried out with pain as Droshny twisted his right wrist almost to breaking-point, forcing him to open his fingers and drop his knife. Droshny kneed him viciously at the same time, freeing his left hand to give Reynolds a violent shove that sent him staggering to crash on his back against the stones and lie there winded and gasping in agony.

Droshny smiled his smile of wolfish satisfaction. Even although he must have known that the need for haste was paramount he yet had to take time off to carry out the execution in a properly leisurely fashion, to savour to the full every moment of it, to prolong the exquisite joy he always felt at moments like these. Reluctantly, almost, he changed to a throwing grip on his knife and slowly raised it high. The smile was broader than ever, a smile that vanished in an instant of time as he felt a knife being plucked from his own belt. He whirled round. Andrea's face was a mask of stone.

Droshny smiled again. 'The gods have been kind to me.' His voice was low, almost reverent, his tone a caressing whisper. 'I have dreamed of this. It is better that you should die this way. This will teach you, my friend—'

Droshny, hoping to catch Andrea unprepared, broke off in mid-sentence and lunged forward with cat-like speed. The smile vanished again as he looked in almost comical disbelief at his right wrist locked in the vice-grip of Andrea's left hand.

Within seconds, the tableau was as it had been in the beginning of the earlier struggle, both knife-wrists locked in the opponent's left hands. The two men appeared to be absolutely immobile, Andrea with his face totally impassive, Droshny with his white teeth bared, but no longer in a smile. It was, instead, a vicious snarl compounded of hate and fury and baffled anger – for this time Droshny, to his evident consternation and disbelief, could make no impression whatsoever on his opponent. The impression, this time, was being made on him.

Maria, the pain in her leg in temporary abeyance, and a slowly recovering Reynolds stared in fascination as Andrea's left hand, in almost millimetric slow-motion, gradually twisted Droshny's right wrist so that the blade moved slowly away and the Cetnik's fingers began, almost imperceptibly at first, to open. Droshny, his face darkening in colour and the veins standing out on forehead and neck, summoned every last reserve of strength to his right hand: Andrea, rightly sensing that all of Droshny's power and will and concentration were centred exclusively upon breaking his crushing grip suddenly tore his own right hand free and brought his knife scything round and under and upwards with tremendous power: the knife went in under the breast-bone, burying itself to the hilt. For a moment or two the giant stood there, lips drawn far back over bared teeth smiling mindlessly in the rictus of death, then, as Andrea stepped away, leaving the knife still embedded, Droshny toppled slowly over the edge of the ravine. The Cetnik sergeant, still clinging to the shattered remains of the bridge, stared in uncomprehending horror as Droshny, the hilt of the knife easily distinguishable, fell head-first into the boiling rapids and was immediately lost to sight.

Reynolds rose painfully and shakily to his feet and smiled at Andrea. He said: 'Maybe I've been wrong about you all along. Thank you, Colonel Stavros.'

Andrea shrugged. 'Just returning a favour, my boy. Maybe I've been wrong about you, too.' He glanced at his watch. 'Two o'clock! *Two* o'clock! Where are the others?'

'God, I'd almost forgotten. Maria there is hurt. Groves and Petar are on the ladder. I'm not sure, but I think Groves is in a pretty bad way.'

'They may need help. Get to them quickly. I'll look after the girl.'

At the southern end of the Neretva bridge, General Zimmermann stood in his command car and watched the sweep-second hand of his watch come up to the top.

'Two o'clock,' Zimmermann said, his tone almost conversational. He brought his right hand down in a cutting gesture. A whistle shrilled and at once tank engines roared and treads clattered as the spearhead of Zimmermann's first armoured division began to cross the bridge at Neretva.

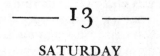

13

SATURDAY

0200–0215

'Maurer and Schmidt! Maurer and Schmidt!' The captain in charge of the guard on top of the Neretva dam wall came running from the guard-house, looked around almost wildly and grabbed his sergeant by the arm. 'For God's sake, where are

Maurer and Schmidt? No one seen them? No one? Get the searchlight.'

Petar, still holding the unconscious Groves pinned against the ladder, heard the sound of the words but did not understand them. Petar, with both arms round Groves, now had his forearm locked at an almost impossible angle between the stanchions and the rock-face behind. In this position, as long as his wrists or forearms didn't break, he could hold Groves almost indefinitely. But Petar's grey and sweat-covered face, the racked and twisted face, were mute testimony enough to the almost unendurable agony he was suffering.

Mallory and Miller also heard the urgently shouted commands, but, like Petar, were unable to understand what it was that was being shouted. It would be something. Mallory thought vaguely, that would bode no good for them, then put the thought from his mind: he had other and more urgently immediate matters to occupy his attention. They had reached the barrier of the torpedo net and he had the supporting cable in one hand, a knife in the other when Miller exclaimed and caught his arm.

'For God's sake, no!' The urgency in Miller's voice had Mallory looking at him in astonishment. 'Jesus, what do I use for brains. That's not a wire.'

'It's not—'

'It's an insulated power cable. Cant you see?'

Mallory peered closely. 'Now I can.'

'Two thousand volts, I'll bet.' Miller still sounded shaken. 'Electric chair power. We'd have been frizzled alive. *And* it would have triggered off an alarm bell.'

'Over the top with them,' Mallory said.

Struggling and pushing, heaving and pulling, for there was only a foot of clear water between the wire and the surface of the water, they managed to ease the compressed air cylinder over and had just succeeded in lifting the nose of the first of the amatol cylinders on to the wire, when, less than a hundred yards away, a six-inch searchlight came to light on the top of the dam wall, its beam momentarily horizontal, then dipping sharply to begin a traverse of the water close in to the side of the dam wall.

'That's all we bloody well need,' Mallory said bitterly. He pushed the nose of the amatol block back off the wire, but the wire strop securing it to the compressed air cylinder held it in such a position that it remained with its nose nine inches clear of the water. 'Leave it. Get under. Hang on to the net.'

Both men sank under the water as the sergeant atop the dam

wall continued his traverse with the searchlight. The beam passed over the nose of the first of the amatol cylinders, but a black-painted cylinder in dark waters makes a poor subject for identification and the sergeant failed to see it. The light moved on, finished its traverse of the water alongside the dam, then went out.

Mallory and Miller surfaced cautiously and looked swiftly around. For the moment, there was no other sign of immediate danger. Mallory studied the luminous hands of his watch. He said: 'Hurry! For God's sake, hurry! We're almost three minutes behind schedule.'

They hurried. Desperate now, they had the two amatol cylinders over the wire inside twenty seconds, opened the compressed air valve on the leading cylinder and were alongside the massive wall of the dam inside another twenty. At that moment, the clouds parted and the moon broke through again, silvering the dark waters of the dam. Mallory and Miller were now in a helplessly exposed position but there was nothing they could do about it and they knew it. Their time had run out and they had no option other than to secure and arm the amatol cylinders as quickly as ever possible. Whether they were discovered or not could still be all-important: but there was nothing they could do to prevent that discovery.

Miller said softly: 'Forty feet apart and forty feet down, the experts say. We'll be too late.'

'No. Not yet too late. The idea is to let the tanks across first then destroy the bridge before the petrol bowsers and the main infantry battalions cross.'

Atop the dam wall, the sergeant with the searchlight returned from the western end of the dam and reported to the captain.

'Nothing, sir. No sign of anyone.'

'Very good.' The captain nodded towards the gorge. 'Try that side. You may find something there.'

So the sergeant tried the other side and he did find something there, and almost immediately. Ten seconds after he had begun his traverse with the searchlight he picked up the figures of the unconscious Groves and the exhausted Petar and, only feet below them and climbing steadily, Sergeant Reynolds. All three were hopelessly trapped, quite powerless to do anything to defend themselves: Reynolds had no longer even his gun.

On the dam wall, a Wehrmacht soldier, levelling his machine-

pistol along the beam of the searchlight, glanced up in astonishment as the captain struck down the barrel of his gun.

'Fool!' The captain sounded savage. 'I want them alive. You
two, fetch ropes, get them up here for questioning. We *must* find
out what they have been up to.'

His words carried clearly to the two men in the water for, just
then, the last of the bombing ceased and the sound of the small-
arms fire died away. The contrast was almost too much to be
borne, the suddenly hushed silence strangely ominous, deathly,
almost, in its sinister foreboding.

'You heard?' Miller whispered.

'I heard.' More cloud, Mallory could see, thinner cloud but
still cloud, was about to pass across the face of the moon. 'Fix
these float suckers to the wall. I'll do the other charge.' He
turned and swam slowly away, towing the second amatol cylinder
behind him.

When the beam of the searchlight had reached down from the
top of the dam wall Andrea had been prepared for almost instant discovery, but the prior discovery of Groves, Reynolds and
Petar had saved Maria and himself, for the Germans seemed to
think that they had caught all there were to be caught and, instead of traversing the rest of the gorge with the searchlights,
had concentrated, instead, on bringing up to the top of the wall
the three men they had found trapped on the ladder. One man,
obviously unconscious – that would be Groves, Andrea thought
– was hauled up at the end of a rope: the other two, with one
man lending assistance to the other, had completed the journey
up the ladder by themselves. All this Andrea had seen while he
was bandaging Maria's injured leg, but he had said nothing of
it to her.

Andrea secured the bandage and smiled at her. 'Better?'

'Better.' She tried to smile her thanks but the smile wouldn't
come.'

'Fine. Time we were gone.' Andrea consulted his watch. 'If
we stay here any longer I have the feeling that we're going to get
very, very wet.'

He straightened to his feet and it was this sudden movement
that saved his life. The knife that had been intended for his
back passed cleanly through his upper left arm. For a moment,
almost as if uncomprehending, Andrea stared down at the tip
of the narrow blade emerging from his arm then, apparently
oblivious of the agony it must have cost him, turned slowly

round, the movement wrenching the hilt of the knife from the hand of the man who held it.

The Cetnik sergeant, the only other man to have survived with Droshny the destruction of the swing bridge, stared at Andrea as if he were petrified, possibly because he couldn't understand why he had failed to kill Andrea, more probably because he couldn't understand how a man could suffer such a wound in silence and, in silence, still be able to tear the knife from his grasp. Andrea had now no weapon left him nor did he require one. In what seemed an almost grotesque slow motion, Andrea lifted his right hand: but there was nothing slow-motion about the dreadful edge-handed chopping blow which caught the Cetnik sergeant on the base of the neck. The man was probably dead before he struck the ground.

Reynolds and Petar sat with their backs to the guard-hut at the eastern end of the dam. Beside them lay the still unconscious Groves, his breathing now stertorous, his face ashen and of a peculiar waxed texture. From overhead, fixed to the roof of the guard-house, a bright light shone down on them, while near by was a watchful guard with his carbine trained on them. The Wehrmacht captain of the guard stood above them, an almost awestruck expression on his face.

He said incredulously but in immaculate English: 'You hoped to blow up a dam this size with a few sticks of dynamite? You must be mad!'

'No one told us the dam was as big as this,' Reynolds said sullenly.

'No one told you – God in heaven, talk of mad dogs and Englishmen! And where is this dynamite?'

'The wooden bridge broke.' Reynolds's shoulders were slumped in abject defeat. 'We lost all the dynamite – and all our other friends.'

'I wouldn't have believed it, I just wouldn't have believed it.' The captain shook his head and turned away, then checked as Reynolds called him. 'What is it?'

'My friend here.' Reynolds indicated Groves. 'He is very ill, you can see that. He needs medical attention.'

'Later.' The captain turned to the soldier in the open transceiver cabin. 'What news from the south.'

'They have just started to cross the Neretva bridge, sir.'

The words carried clearly to Mallory, at that moment some distance apart from Miller. He had just finished securing his float to the wall and was on the point of rejoining Miller when he caught a flash of light out of the corner of his eye. Mallory remained still and glanced upward and to his right.

There was a guard on the dam wall above, leaning over the parapet as he moved along, flashing a torch downwards. Discovery, Mallory at once realized, was certain. One or both of the supporting floats were bound to be seen. Unhurriedly, and steadying himself against his float, Mallory unzipped the top of his rubber suit, reached under his tunic, brought out his Luger, unwrapped it from its waterproof cover and eased off the safety-catch.

The pool of light from the torch passed over the water, close into the side of the dam wall. Suddenly, the beam of the torch remained still. Clearly to be seen in the centre of the light was a small, torpedo-shaped object fastened to the dam wall by suckers and, just beside it, a rubber-suited man with a gun in his hand. And the gun – it had, the sentry automatically noticed, a silencer screwed to the end of the barrel – was pointed directly at him. The sentry opened his mouth to shout a warning but the warning never came for a red flower bloomed in the centre of his forehead, and he leaned forward tiredly, the upper half of his body over the edge of the parapet, his arms dangling downwards. The torch slipped from his lifeless hand and tumbled down into the water.

The impact of the torch on the water made a flat, almost cracking sound. In the now deep silence it was bound to be heard by those above, Mallory thought. He waited tensely, the Luger ready in his hand, but after twenty seconds had passed and nothing happened Mallory decided he could wait no longer. He glanced at Miller, who had clearly heard the sound, for he was staring at Mallory, and at the gun in Mallory's hand with a puzzled frown on his face. Mallory pointed up towards the dead guard hanging over the parapet. Miller's face cleared and he nodded his understanding. The moon went behind a cloud.

Andrea, the sleeve of his left arm soaked in blood, more than half carried the hobbling Maria across the shale and through the rocks: she could hardly put her right foot beneath her. Arrived at the foot of the ladder, both of them stared upwards at the forbidding climb, at the seemingly endless zig-zags of the iron ladder reaching up into the night. With a crippled girl and his own damaged arm, Andrea thought, the prospects were poor indeed. And God only knew when the wall of the dam was due to go up. He looked at his watch. If everything was on schedule, it was due to go now: Andrea hoped to God that Mallory, with his passion for punctuality, had for once fallen behind schedule. The girl looked at him and understood.

'Leave me,' she said. 'Please leave me.'

'Out of the question,' Andrea said firmly. 'Maria would never forgive me.'

'Maria?'

'Not you.' Andrea lifted her on to his back and wound her arms round his neck. 'My wife. I think I'm going to be terrified of her.' He reached out for the ladder and started to climb.

The better to see how the final preparations for the attack were developing, General Zimmermann had ordered his command car out on to the Neretva bridge itself and now had it parked exactly in the middle, pulled close in to the right-hand side. Within feet of him clanked and clattered and roared a seemingly endless column of tanks and self-propelled guns and trucks laden with assault troops: as soon as they reached the northern end of the bridge, tanks and guns and trucks fanned out east and west along the banks of the river, to take temporary cover behind the steep escarpment ahead before launching the final concerted attack.

From time to time, Zimmermann raised his binoculars and scanned the skies to the west. A dozen times he imagined he heard the distant thunder of approaching air armadas, a dozen times he deceived himself. Time and again he told himself he was a fool, a prey to useless and fearful imaginings wholly unbecoming to a general in the Wehrmacht: but still this deep feeling of unease persisted, still he kept examining the skies to the west. It never once occured to him, for there was no reason why it should, that he was looking in the wrong direction.

Less than half a mile to the north, General Vukalovic lowered his binoculars and turned to Colonel Janzy.

'That's it, then,' Vukalovic sounded weary and inexpressibly sad. 'They're across – or almost all across. Five more minutes. Then we counter-attack.'

'Then we counter-attack,' Janzy said tonelessly. 'We'll lose a thousand men in fifteen minutes.'

'We asked for the impossible,' Vukalovic said. 'We pay for our mistakes.'

Mallory, a long trailing lanyard in his hand, rejoined Miller. He said: 'Fixed?'

'Fixed.' Miller had a lanyard in his own hand. 'We pull those leads to the hydrostatic chemical fuses and take off?'

'Three minutes. You know what happens to us if we're still in the water after three minutes?'

'Don't even talk about it,' Miller begged. He suddenly cocked his head and glanced quickly at Mallory. Mallory, too, had heard it, the sound of running footsteps up above. He nodded at Miller. Both men sank beneath the surface of the water.

The captain of the guard, because of inclination, a certain rotundity of figure and very proper ideas as to how an officer of the Wehrmacht should conduct himself, was not normally given to running. He had, in fact, been walking, quickly and nervously, along the top of the dam wall when he caught sight of one of his guards leaning over the parapet in what he could only consider an unsoldierly and slovenly fashion. It then occurred to him that a man leaning over a parapet would normally use his hands and arms to brace himself and he could not see the guard's hands and arms. He remembered the missing Maurer and Schmidt and broke into a run.

The guard did not seem to hear him coming. The captain caught him roughly by the shoulder, then stood back aghast as the dead man slid back off the parapet and collapsed at his feet, face upwards: the place where his forehead had been was not a pretty sight. Seized by a momentary paralysis, the captain stared for long seconds at the dead man, then, by a conscious effort of will, drew out both his torch and pistol, snapped on the beam of the one and released the safety-catch of the other and risked a very quick glance over the dam parapet.

There was nothing to be seen. Rather, there was nobody to be seen, no sign of the enemy who must have killed his guard within the past minute or so. But there *was* something to be seen, additional evidence, as if he ever needed such evidence, that the enemy had been there: a torpedo-shaped object – no, *two* torpedo-shaped objects – clamped to the wall of the dam just at water level. Uncomprehendingly at first, the captain stared at those, then the significance of their presence there struck him with the violence, almost, of a physical blow. He straightened and started running towards the eastern end of the dam, shouting 'Radio! Radio!' at the top of his voice.

Mallory and Miller surfaced. The shouts – they were almost

screams – of the running captain of the guard – carried clear over the now silent waters of the dam. Mallory swore.

'Damn and damn and damn again!' His voice was almost vicious in his chagrin and frustration. 'He can give Zimmermann seven, maybe eight minutes warning. Time to pull the bulk of his tanks on to the high ground.'

'So now?'

'So now we pull those lanyards and get the hell out of here.'

The captain, racing along the wall, was now less than thirty yards from the radio hut and where Petar and Reynolds sat with their backs to the guard-house.

'General Zimmermann!' he shouted. 'Get through. Tell him to pull his tanks to the high ground. Those damned English have mined the dam!'

'Ah, well.' Petar's voice was almost a sigh. 'All good things come to an end.'

Reynolds stared at him, his face masked in astonishment. Automatically, involuntarily, his hand reached out to take the dark glasses Petar was passing him, automatically his eyes followed Petar's hand moving away again and then, in a state of almost hypnotic trance, he watched the thumb of that hand press a catch in the side of the guitar. The back of the instrument fell open to reveal inside the trigger, magazine and gleamingly-oiled mechanism of a sub-machine-gun.

Petar's forefinger closed over the trigger. The sub-machine-gun, its first shell shattering the end of the guitar, stuttered and leapt in Petar's hands. The dark eyes were narrowed, watchful and cool. And Petar had his priorities right.

The soldier guarding the three prisoners doubled over and died, almost cut in half by the first blast of shells. Two seconds later the corporal guard by the radio hut, while still desperately trying to unsling his Schmeisser, went the same way. The captain of the guard, still running, fired his pistol repeatedly at Petar, but Petar still had his priorities right. He ignored the captain, ignored a bullet which struck his right shoulder, and emptied the remainder of the magazine into the radio transceiver, then toppled sideways to the ground, the smashed guitar falling from his nerveless hands, blood pouring from his shoulder and a wound on his head.

The captain replaced his still smoking revolver in his pocket and stared down at the unconscious Petar. There was no anger in the captain's face now, just a peculiar sadness, the dull acceptance of ultimate defeat. His eyes moved and caught Reynolds's: in a moment of rare understanding both men shook their heads in a strange and mutual wonder.

Mallory and Miller, climbing the knotted rope, were almost opposite the top of the dam wall when the last echoes of the firing drifted away across the waters of the dam. Mallory glanced down at Miller, who shrugged as best a man can shrug when hanging on to a rope and shook his head wordlessly. Both men resumed their climb, moving even more quickly than before.

Andrea, too, had heard the shots, but had no idea what their significance might be. At that moment, he did not particularly care. His left upper arm felt as if it were burning in a fierce bright flame, his sweat-covered face reflected his pain and near-exhaustion. He was not yet, he knew, half-way up the ladder. He paused briefly, aware that the girl's grip around his neck was slipping, eased her carefully in towards the ladder, wrapped his left arm round her waist and continued his painfully slow and dogged climb. He wasn't seeing very well now and he thought vaguely that it must be because of the loss of blood. Oddly enough, his left arm was beginning to become numb and the pain was centring more and more on his right shoulder which all the time took the strain of their combined weights.

'Leave me!' Maria said again. 'For God's sake, leave me. You can save yourself.'

Andrea gave her a smile or what he thought was a smile and said kindly: 'You don't know what you're saying. Besides, Maria would murder me.'

'Leave me! Leave me!' She struggled and exclaimed in pain as Andrea tightened his grip. 'You're hurting me.'

'Then stop struggling,' Andrea said equably. He continued his pain-racked, slow-motion climb.

Mallory and Miller reached the longitudinal crack running across the top of the dam wall and edged swiftly along crack and rope until they were directly above the arc lights on the eaves of the guard-house some fifty feet below: the brilliant illumination from those lights made it very clear indeed just what had happened. The unconscious Groves and Petar, the two dead German guards, the smashed radio transceiver and, above all, the sub-machine-gun still lying in the shattered casing of the guitar told a tale that could not be misread. Mallory moved another ten feet along the crack and peered down again: Andrea, with the girl doing her best to help by pulling on the rungs of the ladder, was now almost two-thirds of the way up, but making dreadfully slow progress of it: they'll never make it in time, Mallory thought, it is impossible that they will ever make it in time. It comes to us all: but that it should come to the indestructible Andrea pushed fatalistic acceptance beyond its limits. Such a thing was inconceivable: and the inconceivable was about to happen now.

Mallory rejoined Miller. Quickly he unhitched a rope – the knotted rope he and Miller had used to descend to the Neretva dam – secured it to the rope running above the longitudinal crack and lowered it until it touched softly on the roof of the guardhouse. He took the Luger in his hand and was about to start sliding down when the dam blew up.

The twin explosions occurred within two seconds of each other: the detonation of 3000 pounds of high explosive should normally have produced a titanic outburst of sound, but because of the depth at which they took place, the explosions were curiously muffled, felt, almost, rather than heard. Two great columns of water soared up high above the top of the dam wall, but for what seemed an eternity of time but certainly was not more than four or five seconds, nothing appeared to happen. Then, very, very slowly, reluctantly, almost, the entire central section of the dam wall, at least eighty feet in width and right down to its base, toppled outwards into the gorge: the entire section seemed to be all still in one piece.

Andrea stopped climbing. He had heard no sound, but he felt the shuddering vibration of the ladder and he knew what had happened, what was coming. He wrapped both arms around Maria and the stanchions, pressed her close to the ladder and looked over her head. Two vertical cracks made their slow appearance on the outside of the dam wall, then the entire wall fell slowly towards them, almost as if it were hinged on its base, and then was abruptly lost to sight as countless millions of gallons of greenish-dark water came boiling through the shattered dam wall. The sound of the crash of a thousand tons of masonry falling into the gorge below should have been heard miles away: but Andrea could hear nothing above the roaring of the escaping waters. He had time only to notice that the dam wall had vanished and now there was only this mighty green torrent, curiously smooth and calm in its initial stages, then pouring down to strike the gorge beneath in a seething white maelstrom of foam before the awesome torrent was upon them. In a second of time Andrea released one hand, turned the girl's terrified face and buried it against his chest for he knew that if she should impossibly live, then that battering-ram of water, carrying with it sand and pebbles and God only knew what else, would tear the delicate skin from her face and leave her forever scarred. He ducked his own head against the fury of the coming onslaught and locked his hands together behind the ladder.

The impact of the waters drove the breath from his gasping body. Buried in this great falling crushing wall of green, Andrea fought for his life and that of the girl. The strain upon him, battered and already bruising badly from the hammer-blows of this hurtling cascade of water which seemed so venomously bent upon his instant destruction, was, even without the cruel handicap of his badly injured arm, quite fantastic. His arms, it felt, were momentarily about to be torn from their sockets, it would have been the easiest thing in the world to unclasp his hands and let kindly oblivion take the place of the agony that seemed to be tearing limbs and muscles asunder. But Andrea did not let go and Andrea did not break. Other things broke. Several of the ladder supports were torn away from the wall and it seemed that both ladder and climbers must be inevitably swept away. The ladder twisted, buckled and leaned far out from the wall so that Andrea was now as much lying beneath the ladder as hanging on to it: but still Andrea did not let go, still some remaining supports held. Then very gradually, after what seemed to the dazed Andrea an interminable period of time, the dam level dropped, the force of the water weakened, not much but just perceptibly, and Andrea started to climb again. Half a dozen times, as he changed hands on the rungs, his grip loosened and he was almost torn away: half a dozen times his teeth bared in the agony of effort, the great hands clamped tight and he impossibly retained his grip. After almost a minute of this titanic struggle he finally won clear of the worst of the waters and could breathe again. He looked at the girl in his arms. The blonde hair was plastered over her ashen cheeks, the incongruously dark eyelashes closed. The ravine seemed almost full to the top of its precipitously-sided walls with this whitely boiling torrent of water sweeping everything before it, its roar, as it thundered down the gorge with a speed faster than that of an express train, a continued series of explosions, an insane and banshee shrieking of sound.

Almost thirty seconds elapsed from the time of the blowing up of the dam until Mallory could bring himself to move again.

He did not know why he should have been held in thrall for so long. He told himself, rationalizing, that it was because of the hypnotic spectacle of the dramatic fall in the level of the dam coupled with the sight of that great gorge filled almost to the top with those whitely seething waters: but, without admitting it to himself, he knew it was more than that, he knew he could not accept the realization that Andrea and Maria had been swept to their deaths, for Mallory did not know that at that instant Andrea, completely spent and no longer knowing what he was doing, was vainly trying to negotiate the last few steps of the ladder to the top of the dam. Mallory seized the rope and slid down down recklessly, ignoring or not feeling the burning of the skin on the palms of his hands, his irrationally filled with murder – irrationally, because it was he who had triggered the explosion that had taken Andrea to his death.

And then, as his feet touched the roof of the guard-house, he saw the ghost – the ghosts, rather – as the heads of Andrea and a clearly unconscious Maria appeared at the top of the ladder. Andrea, Mallory noticed, did not seem to be able to go any farther. He had a hand on the top rung, and was making convulsive, jerking movements, but making no progress at all. Andrea, Mallory knew, was finished.

Mallory was not the only one who had seen Andrea and the girl. The captain of the guard and one of his men were staring in stupefaction over the awesome scene of destruction but a second guard had whirled round, caught sight of Andrea's head and brought up his machine-pistol. Mallory, still clinging to the rope, had no time to bring his Luger to bear and release the safety-catch and Andrea should have assuredly died then: but Reynolds had already catapulted himself forward in a desperate dive and brought down the gun in the precise instant that the guard opened fire. Reynolds died instantaneously. The guard died two seconds later. Mallory lined up the still smoking barrel of his Luger on the captain and the guard.

'Drop those guns,' he said.

They dropped their guns. Mallory and Miller swung down from the guard-house roof, and while Miller covered the Germans with his guns, Mallory ran quickly across to the ladder, reached down a hand and helped the unconscious girl and the swaying Andrea to safety. He looked at Andrea's exhausted, blood-flecked face, at the flayed skin on his hands, at the left sleeve saturated in blood and said severely: 'And where the hell have you been?'

'Where have I been?' Andrea asked vaguely. 'I don't know.'
He stood rocking on his feet, barely conscious, rubbed a hand
across his eyes and tried to smile. 'I think I must have stopped
to admire the view.'

General Zimmermann was still in his command car and his
car was still parked in the right centre of the bridge at Neretva.
Zimmermann had again his binoculars to his eyes, but for the
first time he was gazing neither to the west nor to the north.
He was gazing instead to the east, up-river towards the mouth
of the Neretva gorge. After a little time he turned to his aide,
his face at first uneasy, then the uneasiness giving way to apprehension, then the apprehension to something very like fear.

'You hear it?' he asked.

'I hear it, Herr General.'

'And feel it?'

'And I feel it.'

'What in the name of God almighty can it be?' Zimmermann
demanded. He listened as a great and steadily increasing roar
filled all the air around them. 'That's not thunder. It's far too
loud for thunder. And too continuous. And that wind – that
wind coming out of the gorge there.' He could now hardly hear
himself speak above the almost deafening roar of sound coming
from the east. 'It's the dam! The dam at Neretva! They've
blown the dam! Get out of here!' he screamed at the driver.
'For God's sake get out of here!'

The command car jerked and moved forward, but it was too
late for General Zimmermann, just as it was too late for his
massed echelons of tanks and thousands of assault troops concealed on the banks of the Neretva by the low escarpment to the
north of them and waiting to launch the devastating attack that
was to annihilate the seven thousand fanatically stubborn defenders of the Zenica Gap. A mighty wall of white water, eighty
feet high, carrying with it the irresistible pressure of millions of
tons of water and sweeping before it a gigantic battering ram of
boulders and trees, burst out of the mouth of the gorge.

Mercifully for most of the men in Zimmermann's armoured
corps, the realization of impending death and death itself were
only moments apart. The Neretva bridge, and all the vehicles
on it, including Zimmermann's command car, were swept away
to instant destruction. The giant torrent overspread both banks
of the river to a depth of almost twenty feet, sweeping before its
all-consuming path tanks, guns, armoured vehicles, thousands

of troops and all that stood in its way: when the great flood finally subsided, there was not one blade of grass left growing along the banks of the Neretva. Perhaps a hundred or two of combat troops on both sides of the river succeeded in climbing in terror to higher ground and the most temporary of safety for they too would not have long to live, but for ninety-five per cent of Zimmermann's two armoured divisions destruction was as appallingly sudden as it was terrifyingly complete. In sixty seconds, no more, it was all over. The German armoured corps was totally destroyed. But still that mighty wall of water continued to boil forth from the mouth of the gorge.

'I pray God that I shall never see the like again.' General Vukalovic lowered his glasses and turned to Colonel Janzy, his face registering neither jubilation nor satisfaction, only an awe-struck wonder mingled with a deep compassion. 'Men should not die like that, even our enemies should not die like that.' He was silent for a few moments, then stirred. 'I think a hundred or two of their infantry escaped to safety on this side, Colonel. You will take care of them?'

'I'll take care of them,' Janzy said sombrely. 'This is a night for prisoners, not killing, for there won't be any fight. It's as well, General. For the first time in my life I'm not looking forward to a fight.'

'I'll leave you then.' Vukalovic clapped Janzy's shoulder and smiled, a very tired smile. 'I have an appointment. At the Neretva dam – or what's left of it.'

'With a certain Captain Mallory?'

'With Captain Mallory. We leave for Italy tonight. You know, Colonel, we could have been wrong about that man.'

'I never doubted him,' Janzy said firmly.

Vukalovic smiled and turned away.

Captain Neufeld, his head swathed in a blood-stained bandage and supported by two of his men, stood shakily at the top of the gully leading down to the ford in the Neretva and stared down, his face masked in shocked horror and an almost total disbelief, at the whitely boiling maelstrom, its seething surface no more than twenty feet below where he stood, of what had once been the Neretva gorge. He shook his head very, very slowly in unspeakable weariness and final acceptance of defeat, then turned to the soldier on his left, a youngster who looked as stupefied as he, Neufeld, felt.

'Take the two best ponies,' Neufeld said. 'Ride to the nearest Wehrmacht command post north of the Zenica Gap. Tell them that General Zimmermann's armoured divisions have been wiped out – we don't *know*, but they must have been. Tell them the valley of Neretva is a valley of death and that there is no one left to defend it. Tell them the Allies can send in their airborne divisions tomorrow and that there won't be a single shot fired. Tell them to notify Berlin immediately. You understand, Lindemann?'

'I understand, sir.' From the expression on Lindemann's face, Neufeld thought that Lindemann had understood very little of what he had said to him: but Neufeld felt infinitely tired and he did not feel like repeating his instructions. Lindemann mounted a pony, snatched the reins of another and spurred his pony up alongside the railway track.

Neufeld said, almost to himself: 'There's not all that hurry, boy.'

'Herr Hauptmann?' The other soldier was looking at him strangely.

'It's too late now,' Neufeld said.

Mallory gazed down the still foaming gorge, turned and gazed at the Neretva dam whose level had already dropped by at least fifty feet, then turned to look at the men and the girl behind him. He felt weary beyond all words.

Andrea, battered and bruised and bleeding, his left arm now roughly bandaged, was demonstrating once again his quite remarkable powers of recuperation: to look at him it would have been impossible to guess that, only ten minutes ago, he had been swaying on the edge of total collapse. He held Maria cradled in his arms: she was coming to, but very, very slowly. Miller finished dressing the head wound of a now sitting Petar who, though wounded in shoulder and head, seemed more than likely to survive, crossed to Groves and stooped over him. After a moment or two he straightened and stared down at the young sergeant.

'Dead? Mallory asked.

'Dead.'

'Dead.' Andrea smiled, a smile full of sorrow. 'Dead – and you and I are alive. Because this young lad is dead.'

'He was expendable,' Miller said.

'And young Reynolds.' Andrea was inexpressively tired. 'He was expendable too. What was it you said to him this afternoon, my Keith – for now is all the time there may be? And that was all the time there was. For young Reynolds. He saved my life tonight – twice. He saved Maria's. He saved Petar's. But he wasn't clever enough to save his own. *We* are the clever ones, the old ones, the wise ones, the knowing ones. And the old ones are alive and the young ones are dead. And so it always is. We mocked them, laughed at them, distrusted them, marvelled at their youth and stupidity and ignorance.' In a curiously tender gesture he smoothed Maria's wet blonde hair back from her face and she smiled at him. 'And in the end they were better men than we were . . .'

'Maybe they were at that,' Mallory said. He looked at Petar sadly and shook his head in wonder. 'And to think that all three of them are dead, Reynolds dead, Groves dead, Saunders dead, and not one of them ever knew that you were the head of British espionage in the Balkans.'

'Ignorant to the end.' Miller drew the back of his sleeve angrily across his eyes. 'Some people never learn. Some people just never learn.'

EPILOGUE

Once again Captain Jensen and the British lieutenant-general were back in the Operations Room in Termoli, but now they were no longer pacing up and down. The days of pacing were over. True, they still looked very tired, their faces probably fractionally more deeply lined than they had been a few days previously: but the faces were no longer haggard, the eyes no longer clouded with anxiety, and, had they been walking instead of sitting deep in comfortable armchairs, it was just conceivable that they might have had a new spring to their steps. Both men had glasses in their hands, large glasses.

Jensen sipped his whisky and said, smiling: 'I thought a general's place was at the head of his troops?'

'Not in these days, Captain,' the General said firmly. 'In 1944 the wise general leads from behind his troops – about twenty miles behind. Besides, the armoured divisions are going so quickly I couldn't possibly hope to catch up with them.'

'They're moving as fast as that?'

'Not quite as fast as the German and Austrian divisions that pulled out of the Gustav Line last night and are now racing for the Yugoslav border. But they're coming along pretty well.' The General permitted himself a large gulp of his drink and a smile of considerable satisfaction. 'Deception complete, breakthrough complete. On the whole, your men have done a pretty fair job.'

Both men turned in their chairs as a respectful rat-a-tat of knuckles preceded the opening of the heavy leather doors. Mallory entered, followed by Vukalovic, Andrea and Miller. All four were unshaven, all of them looked as if they hadn't slept for a week. Andrea carried his arm in a sling.

Jensen rose, drained his glass, set it on a table, looked at Mallory dispassionately and said: 'Cut it a bit bloody fine, didn't you?'

Mallory, Andrea and Miller exchanged expressionless looks. There was a fairly long silence, then Mallory said: Some things take longer than others.'

Petar and Maria were lying side by side, hands clasped, in two regulation army beds in the Termoli military hospital when Jensen entered, followed by Mallory, Miller and Andrea.

'Excellent reports about both of you, I'm glad to hear,' Jensen said briskly. 'Just brought some – ah – friends to say goodbye.'

'What sort of hospital is this, then?' Miller asked severely. 'How about the high army moral tone, hey? Don't they have separate quarters for men and women?'

'They've been married for almost two years,' Mallory said mildly. 'Did I forget to tell you?'

'Of course you didn't forget,' Miller said disgustedly. 'It just slipped your mind.'

'Speaking of marriage—' Andrea cleared his throat and tried another tack. 'Captain Jensen may recall that back in Navarone—'

'Yes, yes.' Jensen held up a hand. 'Quite so. Quite. Quite. But I thought perhaps – well, the fact of the matter is – well, it so happens that another little job, just a tiny little job really, has come up and I thought that seeing you were here anyway . . .'

Andrea stared at Jensen. His face was horror-stricken.